THE SHARK MUTINY

ALSO BY PATRICK ROBINSON

One Hundred Days
(with Admiral Sir John "Sandy" Woodward)

True Blue

Nimitz Class

Kilo Class

H.M.S. Unseen

U.S.S. Seawolf

PATRICK
ROBINSON

HarperCollins*Publishers*

HarperCollins books may be purchased for educational, business, or sales promotional use. For information, please write: Special Markets Department, HarperCollins Publishers Inc., 10 East 53rd Street, New York, NY 10022.

FIRST EDITION

Designed by Ruth Lee

All maps by Justin Spain

Library of Congress Cataloging-in-Publication Data

Robinson, Patrick.
    The shark mutiny / by Patrick Robinson.—1st ed.
        p. cm.
    ISBN 0-06-019631-9 (acid-free paper)
    1. Submarine warfare—Fiction. 2. Petroleum industry and trade—Fiction. 3. Taiwan—Fiction. 4. China—Fiction. I. Title.

PR6068.O1959 S53 2001
823'.914—dc21

                                                      2001016850

01 02 03 04 05 ❖/RRD 10 9 8 7 6 5 4 3 2 1

This book is respectfully dedicated to everyone who opposes the reduction of U.S. Naval budgets, especially those politicians willing to reverse the process.

CAST OF PRINCIPAL CHARACTERS

Senior Command

The President of the United States (Commander-in-Chief U.S.
    Armed Forces)
Vice Admiral Arnold Morgan (National Security Adviser)
Robert MacPherson (Defense Secretary)
Harcourt Travis (Secretary of State)
General Tim Scannell (Chairman of the Joint Chiefs)

U.S. Navy Senior Command

Admiral Alan Dixon (Chief of Naval Operations)
Admiral Dick Greening (Commander-in-Chief Pacific Fleet
    [CINCPACFLT])
Rear Admiral Freddie Curran (Commander Submarines Pacific
    Fleet [COMSUBPAC])

Rear Admiral John Bergstrom (Commander Special War Command [SPECWARCOM])

USS *Shark*

Commander Donald K. Reid (Commanding Officer)

Lt. Commander Dan Headley (Executive Officer)

Lt. Commander Jack Cressend (Combat Systems Officer)

Lt. Commander Josh Gandy (Sonar Officer)

Master Chief Petty Officer Drew Fisher (Chief of Boat)

Lt. Shawn Pearson (Navigation Officer)

Lt. Matt Singer (Officer of the Deck)

Lt. Dave Mills (ASDV helmsman)

Lt. Matt Longo (ASDV navigator)

U.S. Navy SEALs

Commander Rick Hunter (Team Leader, Assault Team Two)

Commander Russell "Rusty" Bennett (Overall Commander, Assault Team One)

Lt. Commander Ray Schaeffer (Team Leader, Assault Team One)

Lt. Dan Conway (Second in Command, Assault Team One)

Lt. John Nathan (High Explosive Chief, Assault Team One)

Chief Petty Officer Rob Cafiero (Base Camp Chief, Assault Team One)

Petty Officer Ryan Combs (machine gunner, Assault Team One)

Combat SEAL Charlie Mitchell (Electrics, Assault Team One)

Lt. Dallas MacPherson (Second in Command and Explosives Chief, Assault Team Two)

Lt. Bobby Allensworth (personal bodyguard to Commander Hunter)

Chief Petty Officer Mike Hook (explosives assistant to Lt. MacPherson)

Petty Officer Catfish Jones (combat assistant to Lt. Allensworth)

SEAL Riff "Rattlesnake" Davies (machine gunner, Assault
    Team Two)
SEAL Buster Townsend (Assault Team Two)

National Security Agency, Fort Meade

Admiral David Borden (Acting Director)
Lt. Jimmy Ramshawe (Security Ops Officer)

The Court-Martial

President: Captain Cale "Boomer" Dunning
Judge Advocate General: Captain Sam Scott
Judge Advocate/Observer: Captain Art Brennan
Trial Counselor: Lt. Commander David "Locker" Jones
Defense Counselor: Lt. Commander Al Surprenant

Chinese High Command

Admiral Zhang Yushu (Senior Vice Chairman Peoples'
    Liberation Army/Navy Council)
Admiral Zu Jicai (Commander-in-Chief, Navy)

Civilian Oil Tanker Masters

Commodore Don McGhee (*Global Bronco*)
Captain Tex Packard (*Galveston Star*)

Fiancées

Kathy O'Brien (Admiral Morgan)
Jane Peacock (Lt. Ramshawe)

THE SHARK MUTINY

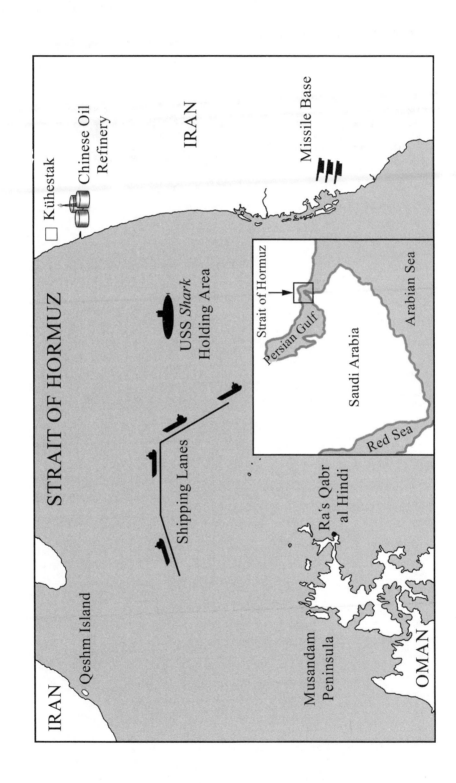

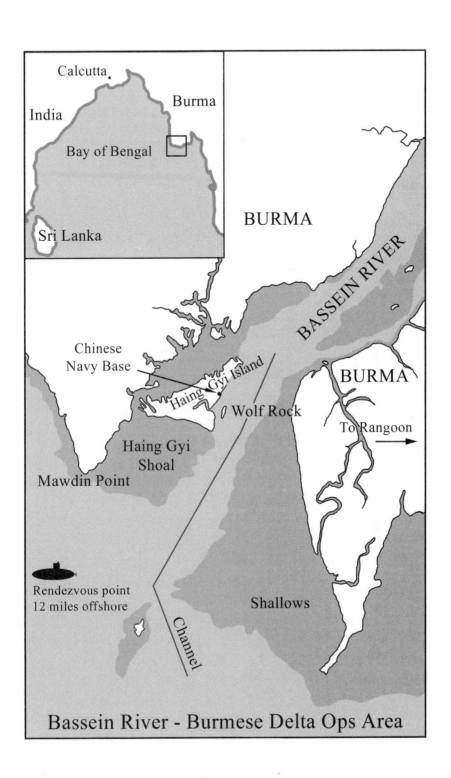

Calcutta

India

Burma

Bay of Bengal

Sri Lanka

BURMA

BASSEIN RIVER

Chinese
Navy Base

Haing Gyi Island

BURMA

Wolf Rock

Haing Gyi
Shoal

To Rangoon

Mawdin Point

Rendezvous point
12 miles offshore

Channel

Shallows

Bassein River - Burmese Delta Ops Area

PROLOGUE

Summer 1987.
Hunter Valley Thoroughbred Farms.
Lexington, Kentucky.

I T WAS PRETTY damn hot for baseball. Only a light breeze ruffled the sweltering bluegrass paddocks in this big thoroughbred breeding farm along the old Ironworks Pike, out near the village of Paris. And young Dan Headley couldn't hit Rick Hunter's fastball to save his life.

"Easy, Ricky . . . take something off it . . . I can't hit that. . . ." But again and again the baseball came screaming in, low and away, and slammed into the base of the red barn wall behind the hitter. And the tall 16-year-old pitcher kept howling with laughter as his best buddy swung and missed yet again.

"You gotta concentrate, Danny."

"On what?"

"The baseball, stupid."

"How can I, when I can't even see it? Nobody could see it."

"Pete Rose coulda seen it," said Rick solemnly, referring to the former Cincinnati Reds legend.

"Pete Rose coulda seen a howitzer shell."

"Okay, one more?"

"Nah. I'm all done. Let's go back and get some lemonade. I'm sweating like a bull."

Rick Hunter pulled off his glove, stuck the ball into the pocket of his jeans, and tied the sleeves of his warm-up jacket around his waist. He jumped over the post-and-rail fence into a wide paddock containing a half dozen mares and foals. Dan Headley followed him, swinging the Louisville Slugger bat, looking over at the foals, at the Kentucky-bred baby racehorses, the best of whom may one day hear the thunder of the crowds at Belmont Park, Royal Ascot, Saratoga and Longchamp. Perhaps even Churchill Downs.

"Still beats the hell outta me why you don't just stay here and get rich," said Dan. "Raisin' the ye'rlings, sellin' 'em for fortunes, just like yer daddy.... Jeez, Rick. You got it all made for you, right here."

"Danny, we been havin' this particular conversation for the biggest part of three years. And my answer ain't varied none. I just ain't interested. 'Sides, in my judgment, this bull market for thoroughbreds ain't here forever."

"Well, it's been here for more'n ten years. Ain't showing no sign of flagging."

"It'll collapse, ole buddy. Bull markets always do in the end. And right then there's gonna be a whole lot of penniless ole hard-boots around here ... guys who thought their good luck was some kinda birthright."

"Yeah, but that ain't why you plan to leave. You're leavin' because it bores you ... even with all that money swilling around. But why the hell you want to be an officer in the U.S. Navy instead of riding around here like some goddamned czar ... master of the Hunter Valley, right here in the thoroughbred breeding capital of the world ... well, like I said. Sure beats the hell outta me."

"Well, you're planning to leave with me, right?"

"Sure I am, Ricky. But, Christ, my daddy's just the stud groom here. Your ole man owns the whole place. And you don't even have any brothers and sisters. It's all gonna be yours. All two thousand acres of it. And all them goddamned blue-chip broodmares."

"Come on, Danny. You understand the horse-breeding business better'n I do. You could make a real go of it yourself, if you wanted. Your daddy's got a coupla mares of his own. Everyone has to start somewhere."

"Ricky, I couldn't save enough money for a place like this in a thousand years. I'd just end up another stud groom. Anyone could see why I'd rather be Captain Dan Headley, commanding officer of a U.S. Navy battle cruiser, than Danny Headley, stallion man at the Hunter Valley."

"Raisin' horses bores you too, don't it?" said Rick, grinning, in the sure knowledge that he had a soul mate.

"Some. But I just don't have the advantages."

"Wouldn't change nothin' in my opinion. You just want adventure . . . I guess like me. Fast horses take too long to raise. We just ain't got the time, right?"

Dan grinned. He was much shorter than the towering Rick Hunter, and he had to walk about half a stride faster to lay up with his lifelong friend. They moved steadily across the magnificent grassland, walking on a slight uphill gradient, watching the foals edging toward them, eager, curious, the mares moving at a much slower pace behind.

"Who's that chestnut filly by? . . ."

"Which one, Danny? The one in front with the white star?"

"Yeah. She's gonna have a backside like a barmaid when she grows up."

"Guess she could have a motor. She's by Secretariat, out of a halfway decent daughter of Nashua."

"That's real local, right? Nashua next door, and the Big Horse is just up the road."

Kentucky horsemen always referred to the 1973 Triple Crown

winner as the Big Horse, despite his unspectacular performance in the stud.

"Dad owns the mare, swears to God Secretariat's gonna be a great sire of broodmares. We'll be keeping that filly for sure."

"How about that little bay colt over there, the one who keeps pushing the others around? . . ."

"He's by Northern Dancer. Typical, kinda boisterous and small. He'll go to the sales, probably end up in Ireland with Mr. O'Brien. Unless the Arabs outbid everyone. Then he'll end up in Newmarket, which ain't quite so good."

"Guess the dark gray is by the Rajah, right?"

"That's him. He's by our own Red Rajah. Bart Hunter's pride and joy. That stallion is one mean sonofabitch. But my daddy loves him, and your daddy copes with him. Bobby Headley, best stallion man in the bluegrass. That's my old man's verdict."

"Well, I been around the Rajah for five years, and I ain't seen nothin' mean about him."

"I have. Trust me. He just don't like strangers, Dan. But he acts like an old dog when your daddy's with him."

They walked on, to the fence, climbed it and came around into the main yard, walked right into Bobby Headley, hurrying down to the feed house. He was a slim, hard-eyed Kentucky horseman of medium height, not as handsome as his dark-haired 16-year-old son, and he had a deep resonant voice that seemed out of place in a man so lacking in bulk.

"Hey, boys, how you doin'?" he said, looking at the baseball bat. "Still gettin' that fastball past 'im, eh, Ricky?"

"Yessir. But it ain't easy. Lose your concentration, and that Danny can really hurt you."

Bobby Headley chuckled. "Hey, Dan, do me a favor, willya? Run along to Rajah's box and pick up my brushes. I left 'em right inside the door."

"Sure. Rick, will I see you back at the house?"

"In five, right?"

Dan Headley jogged along to the three big stallion boxes at the far end of the yard, unclipped the lock on the eight-year-old Red

Rajah's door, and slipped inside, muttering softly, "Hey, Rajah, ole boy . . . how you bin? They still treatin' you good?"

The big stallion, just a tad under 17 hands, and almost milk white now with the advancing years, did not have a head collar on and he was not tethered on a long shank to the sturdy iron ring on the wall. This was a bit unusual for a stallion of his hot-blooded breeding. The powerful ex–California Stakes winner was a grandson of the fiery Red God, out of a fast daughter of the notorious English sire Supreme Sovereign.

To a professional horseman this was an example of breeding made in hell, a recipe for a truly dangerous stallion. Supreme Sovereign was so unpredictable, so lethal to any human being, they kept a high-powered fire hose in his box, in case of an emergency.

Red Rajah himself had several times attacked people, but he'd been a high-class miler in his time, a good tough battler in a finish, and he was a highly commercial sire, standing for $40,000. In the last couple of years, Bobby Headley seemed to have him under control.

The Rajah gazed at young Dan Headley moving softly behind him. He betrayed no anger, but those who knew him would have noticed his ears set slightly back, and his eye flicking first forward, then back; far back, looking at Dan without moving his head.

The boy bent down to pick up the brushes, and as he straightened up, the stallion moved, imperceptibly. Dan, sensing a shift in the horse's mood, reacted like the lifelong horseman he was, lifted up his right arm like a traffic cop, and murmured, "Whoa there, Rajah . . . good boy . . . easy, ole buddy."

Right then Red Rajah attacked, quite suddenly, with not a semblance of warning. He whipped his head around and slammed his teeth over Danny's biceps, biting like a crocodile, right through the muscle and splintering the big bone in the upper arm. And he didn't let go. He dragged the boy down, pulling him onto the straw, preparing for the killer-stallion's favorite trick, to kneel on his prey, like a camel or an elephant, crushing the rib cage. The thoroughbred breeding industry is apt to keep this kind of savagery very quiet.

Dan Headley screamed, with pain and terror. And his scream echoed into the yard. Rick Hunter was on his way down the walkway toward the main house when he heard it. No one else did. A thousand dreads about the true nature of the grandson of Red God flew through his mind.

Back in the barn, Danny screamed again. He was facing death. He knew that, and he kicked out at the stallion, but it was like kicking a pickup truck.

Rick Hunter was by now pounding across the grass quadrangle toward the boxes as he heard his friend's second scream. He dashed straight to the first box where Red Rajah lived. When he got there he searched instantly for a weapon, and saw the trusty Louisville Slugger against the wall. Grabbing it with his right hand, he whipped open the door and faced with horror the scene before him—Danny, blood pouring from his smashed right arm, trying to protect himself against the onslaught of the stallion looming over him, preparing to kneel.

Rick never hesitated, wound back the bat and slammed it into Red Rajah's ribs with a blow that would surely have killed a man. It did not, however, kill Red Rajah. The great white horse swung his head around, as if deciding which of the two boys to attack first. So Ricky hit him again, with all his force, crashing the bat into the ribs of the stallion, simultaneously yelling, "GET OUT, DANNY! FOR CHRIST'S SAKE GET OUT . . . SHUT THE DOOR BUT DON'T LOCK IT. . . ."

Dan Headley, half in shock, maddened by the pain, rolled and crawled out of the box. Still flat on the ground, he kicked the door shut. And 16-year-old Rick Hunter turned to face the raging horse again.

By now he was in the corner 15 feet from the door, watching the Rajah backing off a stride or two. Rick held the bat in both hands, not daring to swing in case he missed the head, and the horse came at his throat, or, much more likely, his testicles.

In a split second he got his answer. Red Rajah came straight at his face, mouth open. Rick shoved the bat straight out in front of him, still holding the handle with both hands. And the Rajah's teeth smashed down onto it, splintering it like matchwood.

Ouside Dan Headley had passed out from the pain.

And now Rick was on his own. Again the Rajah moved away a stride, his ears flat back, his white-rimmed eye still flicking back and forth. Rick's mind raced, back to a converstaion he had once had with an old local hardboot, who had told him, *There's only one way I know to stop a stallion who's bent on killing you.*

Rick Hunter dropped down onto all fours, knowing that if this ploy failed he might be as dead as Danny would have been if he hadn't arrived in time.

Rick flattened himself into the pose of the horse's most ancient and feared enemy, the lion. He tried to assume the crouched, threatening stance of a big cat preparing to pounce, trying to reawaken thousands of years of unconscious phobia in the psyche of the horse. He burrowed his boot into the straw, made a scratching noise on the concrete beneath, snarled deeply, staring hard into the horse's eyes.

Then he moved his head forward and let out a roar and then another, crawling one step nearer. Red Rajah stopped dead. Then he moved a half step backward, a slight tremor in both shoulder muscles. He backed up some more, dipping his head as if to protect his throat. It was an instinct, not a reaction.

Rick roared like a lion again, all the while trying to get the warm-up jacket from around his waist. The fight seemed to have gone right out of the Rajah, who was now standing stock-still. And he was not prepared when the six-foot-four-inch heir to Hunter Valley jumped up and dived at his head, ramming the jacket hard down over his eyes and face.

Red Rajah was in the pitch dark now, and no horse likes to move when he's unable to see anything. He just stood there, stock-still, trembling, blind now, with the jacket still over his head. And Rick carefully edged toward the door, eased it quietly open, and made his escape, slamming the lock shut as he went.

Outside, Dan was conscious again. Rick hit the alarm bell, and sat with his buddy until help arrived minutes later.

He, and both of their fathers, remained with Dan all night in Lexington Hospital, while two surgeons meticulously restitched the muscle, reset and pinned the shattered right arm.

And in the morning when Dan was in the recovery room, the patient finally came to, slowly focusing on the young lion from Hunter Valley. He shook his head in silent admiration of his friend's courage. And then he grinned, and said, "Jesus, Ricky. You just saved my life. I told you we'd be better off in a warship."

"You're right there, ole buddy," said Rick. "Screw this race-horse crap. You can get killed out here. I'd rather be under fire. You think Annapolis is ready for us?"

January 23, 2007.
The White House. Washington, D.C.

ADMIRAL ARNOLD MORGAN was alone in his office contemplating the two major issues in his life at this particular lunchtime. The first was his decision to stay on as the National Security Adviser to the President for one more year, against all of his better judgment.

The second was a Wagnerian-sized roast beef sandwich, fortified with heavy mayonnaise and mustard into a feast he would never have dared to order had his secretary and wife-to-be, the gorgeous Kathy O'Brien, been anywhere near the precincts of 1400 Pennsylvania Avenue. Happily she was out until 4 P.M.

The Admiral grinned cheerfully. He saw the sandwich as a richly deserved gastronomic reward for having succumbed to weeks of being badgered, harassed, coaxed and ultimately persuaded to remain in this office by some of the most powerful figures in American politics and the military.

His decision to hang in there had been wrung out of him, after nine weeks of soul-searching. The decision to hit a roast beef sandwich *el grando*, before Ms. O'Brien came sashaying back into the office, had been made with much less anguish. Nine weeks' less.

The Admiral, 61 years old now, was still, miraculously, in robust health, and not more than 8 pounds heavier than he had been as a nuclear submarine commander 27 years previously. Immaculately tailored, wearing a maroon-and-gold Hermès tie Kathy had given him for Christmas, he tucked a large white linen napkin into his shirt collar and bit luxuriously into his sandwich.

Through the window he could see it was snowing like hell. The President was, shrewdly, visiting Southern California where the temperature was a sunlit 78 degrees, and right here in the West Wing of the White House there was absolutely nothing happening of any interest whatsoever to the most feared and respected military strategist on the planet Earth.

"I still have no idea what the hell I'm doing here," he muttered to himself. "The goddamned world's gone quiet, temporarily. And I'm sitting here like a goddamned lapdog waiting for our esteemed but flakey leader to drag himself out of some fucking Beverly Hills swimming pool."

Flakey. A complete flake. The words had been used about the President, over and over at that final meeting at the home of Admiral Scott Dunsmore, the wise and deceptively wealthy former Chairman of the Joint Chiefs. Arnold Morgan could not understand what the fuss was about. Plenty of other NSAs had resigned, but, apparently, he was not permitted that basic human right.

Christ, everyone had been there. And no one had even informed him. He'd walked, stone-cold, into a room containing not only General Scannell, Chairman of the Joint Chiefs, but *two* former chairmen, plus the Chief of Naval Operations, and the Commandant of the United States Marines. The Defense Secretary was there, two senior members of the Senate Armed Services

Committee, including the vastly experienced Senator Ted Kennedy, whose unwavering patriotism and endless concern for his country make him always a natural leader among such men. Altogether there were four current members of the National Security Council in attendance.

Their joint mission was simple: to persuade Admiral Morgan to withdraw his resignation, and to remain in office until the Republican President's second term was over. A few weeks previously, at the conclusion of a particularly dangerous and covert Naval operation in China, the President had demonstrated such shocking self-interest and lack of judgment that he could no longer be trusted to act in the strict interests of the USA.

The world was presently a volatile place, and no one needed to remind Admiral Morgan of that. But the man in the Oval Office was prone to appoint "yes-men" to influential positions, and now in the final two years of his presidency he tended to think only of himself and his image and popularity.

Without Admiral Morgan's granite wall of reality and judgment in the crucible of international military affairs, the men in Admiral Dunsmore's house that day were greatly concerned that a terrible and costly mistake might occur.

Looking back, Arnold Morgan could not remember precisely who had put into words the hitherto unspoken observation that the President was a "goddamned flake, and getting worse." But he remembered a lot of nodding and no laughter. And he remembered their host, Admiral Dunsmore, turning to his old friend, the Senator from Massachussetts, and saying, "The trouble is he's interested in military matters. And we cannot trust him. Talk to Arnold, Teddy. You'll say it better than anyone else."

He had, too. And at the conclusion of a short but moving few words from the silver-tongued sage of Hyannisport, Admiral Morgan had nodded, and said, curtly, "My resigation is withdrawn."

And now he was "back at the factory." And he was ruminating on the general calm that had existed in the world's known trouble spots for the past month. The Middle East was for the moment serene. Terrorists in general seemed still to be on their Christmas break. India and Pakistan had temporarily ceased to threaten each other. And China, the Big Tiger, had been very quiet since last fall. Indeed, according to the satellite photographs, they were not even conducting fleet exercises near Taiwan, which made for a change. As for their new *Xia III*, there was no sign of the submarine leaving its jetty in Shanghai.

The only halfway-interesting piece of intelligence to come Admiral Morgan's way since Christmas was a report put together by the CIA's Russian desk. According to one of their field operators in Moscow, the Rosvoorouzhenie factory on the outskirts of the city was suddenly making large quantities of moored mines. This was regarded as unusual since Rosvoorouzhenie's known expertise was in the production of seabed mines, the MDM series, particularly the lethal one-and-three-quarter-ton, ship-killing MDM-6, which can be laid through the torpedo tubes of a submarine.

Rosvoorouzhenie was now, apparently, making a lot of updated, custom-made PLT-3 mines, moored one-tonners, which can be laid either through torpedo tubes, or from surface ships. The CIA had no information about where the mines were going, if anywhere, but their man had been certain this was a very unusual development. Most Russian-made mines these days were strictly for export.

Admiral Morgan growled to himself, *Now who the hell wants a damn large shipment of moored PLT-3s, eh?* He chewed on the roast beef and pondered silently. He did not much like it. *If the goddamned penniless Russians are building several hundred expensive mines, someone's ordered 'em. And if someone's ordered 'em, they plan to lay 'em, right? Otherwise they wouldn't have ordered 'em.*

Where? That's what we wanna know. Who's planning a nice little surprise minefield?

He finished his sandwich, sipped his coffee and frowned. When Kathy came back, he'd have her call Langley and make sure he was kept up to speed on Russian mine production. And if the overheads picked up any large mine shipments leaving any Russian seaports, he wanted to know about that. Immediately.

Just don't want some fucking despot in a turban getting overly ambitious, right? The Admiral glared at the portrait of General MacArthur that hung in his office. *Gotta watch 'em, Douglas. Right? Watch 'em, at all times.*

0900 (local). January 23, 2007
Renmin Dahuitang, the Great Hall of the People.
Tiananmen Square, Beijing.

The largest government building in the world, home of the National People's Congress, was locked, barred and bolted this Tuesday morning. All 561,800 square feet of it. Business was canceled. The public was banned. And there were more armed military guards patrolling the snow-covered western side of the square than anyone had seen since the 1989 Massacre of the Students.

Inside, there were more guards, patrolling the endless corridors. Sixteen of them stood motionless, with shouldered arms, in a square surrounding the only elevator that travels down to the brightly lit underground Operations Room, designated by the late Mao Zedong to be used only in the event of foreign attack on mainland China. The room was massively constructed in heavy cast-concrete. It was white painted, almost bare walled and functional, situated deep below the 5,000-seat banqueting hall.

Aside from the heavily armed members of the People's Liberation Army, there were fewer than a dozen people being gently warmed by the Great Hall's vast central heating system, designed to keep at bay the freezing outside temperatures that occasionally grip the Chinese capital at this time of year.

Today there were brutal north winds, right out of the high plateaux of the Inner Mongolian plains, and they were presently refrigerating this entire part of northern China. Snow coated the yellow roofs of the Forbidden City, out beyond the northeastern corner of the Great Hall. Sudden squalls hurled white drifts against the vermilion walls.

The Stream of Golden Water was frozen rock-solid beneath the five bridges in front of the towering Meridian Gate, the spectacular entrance once reserved for the Emperor alone. Tiananmen Square itself was under an immense blanket of white. The total absence of thousands of government workers gave the heart of Beijing a look of abandonment. It was windswept, quiet, deserted, like a great stadium after the games were over.

Inside the Ops Room there was an atmosphere of high tension. Standing at the far end of the room, next to a 10-foot-wide illuminated computer screen, was the formidable figure of Admiral Zhang Yushu, recently resigned from his position as Commander-in-Chief of the People's Liberation Army/Navy, and now installed, by the Paramount Ruler himself, as the senior of the four Vice Chairmen of the all-powerful PLAN Council.

Eight weeks previously, Admiral Zhang had leapfrogged clean over the other three highly experienced members, and now occupied a position of such authority he answered only to the State President, the General Secretary of the Communist Party and the Chairman of the Military Affairs Commission—and that was all the same person. The Paramount Ruler had once occupied these three Highest Offices of State, and there were those who thought it was just a matter of time before Admiral Zhang himself rose to such eminence. The Paramount Ruler would hear no word against him.

And now the Admiral addressed his audience for the first time, speaking carefully, welcoming them all to the most secretive meeting ever assembled in the 48-year history of the Great Hall— a gathering so clandestine they'd shut down the entire government for the day to avoid eavesdroppers.

Admiral Zhang's three elderly colleagues on the Military Council, all ex-Army commanders, were in attendance. The new Commander-in-Chief of the Navy, Admiral Zu Jicai, was there, seated next to Admiral Yibo Yunsheng, the new Commander of China's massive Northern Fleet. The Navy's powerful Political Commissar, Vice Admiral Yang Zhenying, had arrived the previous night from Shanghai in company with the Chief of the Naval Staff, Vice Admiral Sang Ye.

The most influential of the Chinese Navy's Deputy Commanders-in-Chief, Admiral Zhi-Heng Tan, was seated next to Zhang himself at the head of the broad mahogany table. Behind them was a single four-foot-high framed print of Mao Zedong, the great revolutionary whose only wish was for a supreme China to stand alone against the imperial West. The print was a replica of the giant portrait of Mao that gazes with chilling indifference across the square from the Tiananmen Gate. Today, it served to remind the Chinese High Command in this brightly lit room precisely who they really were.

The other three men in the room were Iranian: the most senior a black-robed, bearded Ayatollah, whose name was not announced. The two Naval officers accompanying the holy man were Rear Admiral Hossein Shafii, Head of Tactical Headquarters, Bandar Abbas; and Rear Admiral Mohammed Badr, the Iranian Navy's Commander-in-Chief Submarines.

Admiral Zhang, who stood six feet tall, was by far the biggest and the most heavily built of the Chinese. But he spoke softly, in an uncharacteristic purr, a smile of friendship upon his wide impassive face. The language was English, which all three Iranians spoke fluently. The words were translated back into Chinese by Vice Admiral Yang who had, in his youth, studied for four years at UCLA.

"Gentlemen," said Admiral Zhang Yushu, "as you are all well aware, the new Sino-Iranian pipeline from the great oil fields of Kazakhstan will come on stream within a few weeks. Thousands of barrels will flow daily, from out of Russia, right across your great country, south to the new Chinese refinery on the shores of the Hormuz Strait.

"This, gentlemen, should herald a new dawn for all of us, a dawn of vast profits for Iran, and thank God, an end to China's endless reliance on the West, in the matter of fuel oil. The alliance of the past ten years between our two superb nations was, indeed, made in heaven."

Admiral Zhang paused, and opened his arms wide. And he walked around to the right side of the huge table and stood beaming at the men from the desert. The Ayatollah himself stood first and took both of the Admiral's hands in his own, wishing everyone the everlasting peace of Allah. Then the two Admirals from Bandar Abbas stood up and embraced the legendary Chinese Navy commander.

Zhang walked back to his position at the head of the table, and glanced briefly at his notes. He allowed a flicker of a frown to cross his face, but then he smiled again, and continued: "I have no need to remind anyone of the enormous cost of building this one-thousand-mile pipeline, and the construction of the refinery. It ran, of course, into billions of U.S. dollars.

"However, as of this moment, there is but one dark cloud on our horizon . . . and that is the extraordinarily low cost of a barrel of oil on the world market. Last night it was down to thirteen dollars and falling toward a ten-year low. The Arab nations cannot be controlled because of their reliance on American protection and commerce. Which leaves us to sell at a half, or even a third of our oil's true value. Now, Iran is earning twenty percent of every barrel to reach the new refinery, and at present that's under three dollars. It will thus cost your country millions and millions in unearned revenue every month.

"Gentlemen, I ask you. What is the solution? And I must remind you, this is a PLOT . . . a diabolical Western PLOT . . . to devalue our great economies . . . to allow them to dominate us, as they have always tried to do."

Admiral Zhang's voice had risen during this delivery. But now it fell very softly again to the calm, gentle tones of his welcome. "We have the solution, my friends. It is a solution we have discussed before, and I believe it is a solution that will find much favor with both of our governments."

The Ayatollah looked genuinely perplexed. And he looked up quizzically.

Admiral Zhang smiled back, and without further ceremony, he said flatly, "I am proposing we lay a minefield deep in the historic, national waters of the Islamic State of Iran. Right across the Strait of Hormuz."

Admiral Badr looked up sharply and said immediately, "My friend, Yushu, you have become a tried and trusted confidant of my nation. But I feel I must remind you we have considered many times a blockade of the Strait of Hormuz. But we have been frustrated for the same three reasons every time—one, the far side of the strait belongs to Oman, a country that is totally influenced by the American puppets in London.

"Two, we could never lay down a minefield quickly enough without being seen by the American satellites, which would surely bring down upon us the wrath of the Pentagon.

"And three, well, ultimately the Americans would clear it and paint us as lawless outcasts, enemies to the peaceful trading nations of the world. No good could come of it, not from our point of view."

Admiral Zhang nodded, and asked for the forbearance of the meeting. "Mohammed," he said, "all of your reasons are correct. But now times have changed. The stakes are much higher. You and I have different oil both to sell and to use. We also have an unbreakable joint interest, our own oil routes from the strait to the Far East. And you, Mohammed, have the entire backing of the People's Liberation Army/Navy.

"Together we could most certainly lay down a minefield, using both submarines and surface ships. And we could achieve it so swiftly, no one would have the slightest idea who had done what."

"But they would find out, surely?"

"They would not find out. Though they might guess. And they would not be in time. Because one day a big Western tanker is going to hit one of the mines and blow up, and for the next year oil prices will go through the roof, except for ours. Which will of course cost us just the same—almost nothing. But that which we sell will be worth a fortune, while the world's tankers back up on both sides of the minefield, all of them afraid to go through. For a while, we'll very nearly own the world market for fuel oil."

Admiral Badr smiled and shook his head. "It's a bold plan,

Yushu. I'll give you that. And I suppose it just might work. But my country, and my Navy, have been on the wrong end of the fury of the Pentagon before. And it is not a place we want to go again."

"So has mine, Mohammed. But they are not invincible. And in the end they are a Godless society interested only in money. They will raise heaven and hell to free up the tanker routes to the gulf, but I think they will see it as a business problem, not cause for armed conflict. And besides they will not want an all-out shooting war in the gulf because that will just compound the oil problems and send prices even higher, and the sacred New York Stock Exchange even lower."

"But, Yushu, if they suspect China is behind it, they may become very angry indeed."

"True, Mohammed. True. But not sufficiently angry to want a war with us. That would send their precious stock market into free fall.

"No, my friends. The Americans will clear the minefield. Open up the tanker routes again, and send in heavy U.S. Naval muscle to make sure they stay cleared. By then we will have made vast sums of money, China and Iran. And, hopefully, many new friends, and customers, who will perhaps prefer to do business with us in future.

"One little minefield, Mohammed. Twenty miles wide. And we open a gateway to a glittering future together."

Same day. Headquarters, National Security Agency. Fort Meade, Maryland.

Lieutenant Jimmy Ramshawe downloaded his computer screen for the umpteenth time that afternoon. As SOO (Security Ops Officer), his tasks included designating printouts to selected officers all over the ultrasecret labyrinth of the U.S. military Intelligence complex; a place so highly classified the walls had built-in copper shields to prevent any electronic eavesdropping.

The Lieutenant had been routinely bored by the entire procedure since lunchtime, sifting through screeds of messages, reports and signals from United States surveillance networks all over the world. But these two latest documents just in from the CIA's Russian desk caught and held his attention:

> Unusual activity in Rosvoorouzhenie mine production factory outside central Moscow. Three heavy transit military vehicles sighted leaving the plant, fully laden. Sighted again at Sheremetyevo II Airport, Moscow, two hours later. Then again leaving the airport 1400 EST, empty. Destination unkown.

From the precise same source another signal came in 94 minutes later at 1534 EST. Langley had so far offered no comment. Just the bald fact: "Russian Antonov 124 took off Moscow 2300, believed heading due east. Aircrew only, plus heavy cargo. AN-124 took 3,000 meters to liftoff. CIA field officer traces no flight plan. Inquiries continue."

To Jimmy Ramshawe this was food and drink—a complex, slightly sinister problem that wanted studying, if not solving. He knew the gigantic Antonov freighter—known as the *Ruslan*, after a mythological Russian giant—could carry a colossal 120 tons of freight 35,000 feet above the earth's surface. He had a good imagination and did not need to utilize much of it before he could visualize 120 big sea mines hurtling through the stratosphere at 550 knots, bound for some distant ocean where they could be primed to inconvenience U.S. Navy fleets.

At the age of 28, Jimmy had been selected by the Navy to serve in the Intelligence service. A tall dark-haired young officer, he possessed an acutely analytical mind. He was a lateral thinker, an observer of convolutions, complications and intricacies. As a commanding officer he would have developed into a living nightmare. No team in any warship would ever have provided him with *quite* sufficient data to make a major decision.

But he had a superb intelligence, the highest IQ in his class at

Annapolis, and his superiors spotted him a long way out. Lt. Ramshawe was born for Intelligence work at the highest level. And while his young fellow officers went forward, following their stars as future commanding officers of surface or subsurface warships, the lanky, athletic Jimmy was sent into the electronic hothouse of America's most sensitive, heavily guarded Intelligence agency, where, to quote the admissions Admiral, "There would be ample outlet for his outstanding talents."

He was an unusual member of Fort Meade's staff for the simple reason that he looked and sounded like an Australian. The son of a Sydney diplomat, he had been born in Washington D.C., while his father served a five-year tour of duty as Military Attaché at the grandiose Australian embassy on Massachusetts Avenue. They'd returned to New South Wales for just two years before Admiral Ramshawe accepted a position on the board of the Australian airline Qantas, working permanently in New York.

Young Jimmy, with his U.S. passport, went to school in Connecticut, starred for three years as a baseball pitcher who sounded as if he should have been playing cricket. And then followed his father into a career in Dark Blue. American Dark Blue, that is. He'd been in the U.S. Navy now for 10 years, but a couple of weeks earlier he had still brought a smile to the lugubrious face of the NSA's Director, Admiral George Morris, by announcing, "G'day, sir. . . . I picked up that stuff you wanted . . . gimme two hours . . . she'll be right."

Ramshawe was always going to *sound* like Banjo Patterson and other members of Australian folklore, but he was American through and through, and Admiral Morris valued him highly, as highly as he valued his longtime friendship with Ramshawe Senior, the retired Aussie Diplomat/Admiral.

The trouble was, right now, Admiral Morris had just been admitted to the Bethesda Naval Hospital with suspected lung cancer, and the deputy director, Rear Admiral David Borden, was a more remote, formal figure, who was not instantly receptive to young Lt. Ramshawe's observations. And that might prove difficult for both of them—the acting director because he might miss something, for Jimmy because he might not be listened to.

He stared at the two signals in front of him, and attacked the problem as he always did: going instantly for the obvious worse-case scenario. That is, *some foreign nutcase has just bought several hundred sea mines from the bloody Russians with a view to laying the bastards somewhere they want to keep private.*

Lt. Ramshawe frowned. It seemed unlikely the Russians were using the mines themselves. They had nowhere to mine, and these days they rarely manufactured Naval hardware unless it was for export.

So who the hell did they make 'em for? Jimmy Ramshawe ran the checks swiftly through his mind. *One of those crazy bastards in the gulf . . . Gadaffi? The Ayatollahs? The Iraqis? No reason really for any of them, but the Iranians had threatened a mine-field more than once. But then the AN-124 would have been running south, not east. Or else the mines would have been transported by road. China? No. They'd make their own . . . I think. North Korea? Maybe. But they make their own.*

Lieutenant Ramshawe deemed the puzzle worthy of careful consideration. And he gathered up the two signals, muttering to himself, "I don't think we better fuck this up, because if ships start blowing up, somewhere in the Far East or wherever, we're likely to get the blame. 'Specially if an American ship was lost . . . bloody oath there'd be trouble then."

He stood up from his screen, pushed his floppy dark hair off his forehead and walked resolutely out of the ops area down to the Director's office. He was still reading the signals when he arrived in the hallowed area once occupied by Arnold Morgan himself. And he walked through absentmindedly, still reading, tapped on the door, pushed it open and walked in, as he always did.

"G'day, Admiral," he said. "Coupla things here I think we want to take a sharp look at."

David Borden looked up, an expression of surprise on his face.

"Lieutenant," he said. "I wonder if you could bring yourself to give me the elementary courtesy of knocking before you enter my office?"

"Sir? I thought I just did."

"And then perhaps *waiting* to be invited in?"

"Sir? This isn't a bloody social call. I have urgent stuff in my hand which I think you should know about right away."

"Lieutenant Ramshawe, there are certain matters of etiquette still observed here in the U.S. Navy, though I imagine they have long been dispensed with in your own country."

"Sir, this is my country."

"Of course. But your accent sounds like no other U.S. officer I ever met."

"Well, I can't help that. But since we're wasting time, and I don't want to get off on the wrong foot now that you're in the big chair, I'll get back outside and we'll start over, right?"

Before Admiral Borden could answer, Jimmy Ramshawe had walked out and closed the door behind him. Then he knocked on it, and the Director, feeling slightly absurd, called, "Come in, Lieutenant."

"Christ, I'm glad we got that over with," said Jimmy, turning on his Aussie-philosophical, lopsided grin. "Anyway, g'day, Admiral. Got something here I think we should take a look at."

He handed the two signals over, and David Borden glanced down at them.

"I don't see anything urgent here," he said. "First of all, we do not even know the mines were on board the Russian aircraft. If they were, we don't have the slightest idea where they might be going . . . and wherever that may be, it's going to take a long time for anyone to unload them, transport them, and then start laying them in the ocean. At which point our satellites will pick them up. I shouldn't waste any more time on it if I were you."

"Now, hold hard, sir. We got possibly several hundred brand-new sea mines almost certainly packed into the hold of the biggest freight aircraft on earth, now heading due east toward China, maybe India, maybe Pakistan, Korea, Indonesia? Brand-new mines specifically ordered and manufactured? And you don't think we want to trace the bloody jokers who own them, right away?"

"No, Lieutenant. I think we'll find out in good time without wasting any of our valuable resources, and in particular, your energies."

"Well, I suppose if you say so, sir. But that's a lot of high explosives, and . . . well, I mean some bugger wants it for something pretty definite. I think Admiral Morris would want it investigated . . . maybe alert the Big Man in the White House."

"Lieutenant, Admiral Morris is no longer in command of this agency. And from now on, I trust you'll respect my judgment. Forget the mines. They'll come to the surface in good time."

"Just hope they don't bring a pile of bloody wreckage with 'em, that's all."

Lt. Ramshawe nodded, curtly, turned on his heel and left, muttering to himself an old Australian phrase, "Right mongrel bastard he's turned out to be."

Evening, same day. Ops Room.
Great Hall of the People.

The big computer screen had been switched off now. The Iranian delegation was heading northeast out along Jichang Lu toward Beijing International Airport. And Admiral Zhang was talking with Zu Jicai. Everyone else had gone. The two great Naval friends and colleagues sat alone, sipping tea, which Yushu had coerced a guard to produce, in the absence of any staff whatsoever in the Great Hall. It tasted, he thought, like a leftover thermos from Mao's Long March of 1935.

"I am still slightly mystified, Yushu. Do you really think there is enough advantage in this for us to become involved in a worldwide oil catastrophe?"

"Ah, Jicai. You are ever the tactician, ever the strategist.

Always the battle commander. You see things very clearly, the immediate crunch, the immediate aftermath."

"Well, don't you?"

"I used to, when I was C-in-C of the Navy. But I must be political now, and I have changed my perspectives. I am trying to look at a wider picture."

"I think, my Yushu, you will face a very wide picture indeed if an American tanker should collide with one of those Russian mines in the Strait of Hormuz."

Admiral Zhang smiled, sipped his tea, grimaced and said softly, "Do you think they accepted my plan? Do you think Hossein will call back with the agreement of his government?"

"I am quite sure they accepted it. You can be very persuasive toward people who want to be convinced."

"That's part of my strategy, Jicai. I know that deep in the soul of every Iranian military officer there beats the heart of a revolutionary. Oh yes, they would like to make colossal sums of money from a world oil crisis. But what they really want is to strike a violently disruptive blow against the Great Satan, particularly one with the potential to cause widespread chaos in the everyday lives of ordinary Americans."

"I am afraid you read them accurately, Yushu. And I am afraid your plan will take place. The minefield will be laid. But I am very afraid of the consequences. The Americans are likely to turn up in the gulf with guns blazing. Possibly against our own warships, and we are not really a match for them. . . ."

"There you go again, my good Jicai. The immediate crunch. The immediate aftermath. Soon I will ask you to raise your sights. But not quite yet . . . not until we are given an affirmative answer by the Iranians. Then all will be revealed to you."

"I look forward to that immensely, Yushu . . . but we have been in this room for almost twelve hours now. I think we should go and find some dinner together."

The two men traveled up in the elevator to the central floor of the Great Hall, and an eight-man military escort took them to the main doors, beyond which lay the dark, freezing Tiananmen

Square. A long black Mercedes, its engine running, awaited them, and the guard escort remained in formation until its tires had creaked out across the fresh, uncluttered snow, bearing its two high commanders north. North along the west side of the square, toward the Forbidden City, the old guardian of the Dragon Throne, and still, in the eyes of most Westerners, the symbol of the might of Communist China.

The great portrait of the unforgotten Mao Zedong, staring out, somehow shy, and cold, may not have formed a secret smile through the falling snow, as the Admirals' Mercedes swept past Tiananmen Gate. But it should have. Mao, above all other men, would have loved Zhang Yushu's as yet unspoken plan.

2100 (local). Same day.
NSA. Fort Meade, Maryland.

Admiral Borden had gone home. A new shift of U.S. surveillance operators was working through the night. Only one member of the day staff was still on duty: Lt. Jimmy Ramshawe was in his office, still working, behind closed doors, poring over maps of Asia, pulling up charts on his computer, trying to ascertain where the giant Antonov-124, with its lethal cargo of ship-killing high explosives, could be headed, and where, more importantly, it would have to refuel.

Those four big D-18Ts have gotta guzzle up more than ten tons of fuel per hour—which gives it a range of two thousand six hundred miles maximum. The bastard's gotta stop somewhere. And it's gotta stop soon.

Jimmy's thoughts were clear and accurate. He thought the aircraft would have to land around five hours after takeoff. Twice he checked with the CIA's Russian desk at Langley, but there was nothing new. Three times he checked with MENA, Fort Meade's Middle East North Africa desk, and they knew nothing either.

Lieutenant Ramshawe, however, had a stubborn streak the size of Queensland, and he had resolved to sit right there until someone told him precisely where the world's biggest cargo aircraft had landed.

The hour 2200 came and went. Then 2230. And right after that the phone rang, secure line from Langley. No one was telling him where it had landed. But the news was definite. The Antonov had just taken off from a guarded airfield ouside the remote central Kazakhstan city of Zhezkazgan. The interesting part was the name of the airfield, Baykonur—top-secret home base of the Russian space program. The CIA had always had a man in there.

"Very nice and quiet, old mate," muttered Jimmy Ramshawe thoughtfully to the air traffic controller 7,000 miles away in central Asia. "Very nice indeed."

Then he pulled up his computer maps again, and tried once more to assess the destination of the 120 sea mines. He checked the routes southeast to India, and gazed at the great high-peaked mass of the Himalayas, but in the end there was only one conclusion: The mines were on their way to China.

"And since the bastards only work underwater," he murmured, "a mighty intellect like mine would conclude they might be going all the way to the ocean, possibly Shanghai, or maybe one of the Chinese Naval bases in the south."

Either way, he decided, the Antonov would certainly have to be refueled again. But that would probably happen at a remote Chinese military base in the western part of the country.

In which case, I'm going home to bed, he thought. *But twelve hours from now, a little before midday tomorrow here, I'm looking for a report that it's landed on the shores of the China Sea— probably near a Naval base.*

Still, there's no point getting excited since the new bloke I work for wouldn't give a kangaroo's bollocks for my opinions. And he walked, somewhat disconsolately, through the huge main room, the dimly lit National Security Operations Center (NSOC), heading home.

Thus Lt. Jimmy Ramshawe, like his boss, was sound asleep when the Antonov touched down to refuel on northwest China's remote and forbidden airstrip—the one on the edge of the pitiless

Taklamakan Desert, at Lop Nor, home of China's nuclear weapons research and testing facility.

The Taklamakan is China's largest desert, 1,200 miles long, uninhabited for vast areas. Its name means "the desert one enters, but never leaves." The Antonov, being Russian, completely ignored that, and one hour after landing, took off again with full tanks, heading southeast for another 1,700 miles to the headquarters of Admiral Zu's Southern Fleet.

Seven weeks later. March 13, 2007. Southern Fleet Headquarters. Zhanjiang, Province of Guangdong.

The dock lights along the jetties did their best to illuminate the gloomy late evening. But rain from the west swept across the sprawling Naval base under low cloud and cold, drifting mist. Out on Jetty Five a black Navy staff car, its engine running, headlights on, windshield wipers fighting the downpour, was parked in the shadows.

Its two occupants, Admirals Zhang and Zu, were watching the departure of, probably, the first Chinese blue-water fleet to depart these shores for a foreign mission beyond home waters since the treasure-ship voyages of the eunuch Admiral Zheng He in the first half of the fifteenth century.

Back then, the seven epic voyages of Admiral Zheng, across the Indian Ocean, to the Persian Gulf and the coast of Africa, were acclaimed as the highest achievements of the greatest Navy the world had ever seen. And it was a great Navy. At its zenith there were 3,500 ships, 2,700 of them warships, based in a network of major Navy bases and dockyards along China's eastern coast.

Admiral Zheng took more than 100 ships and almost 30,000 men to the east coast of Africa, to Kenya, to Arabia, way up into the Red Sea, right into the gulf, through the Strait of Hormuz, anchoring and trading their silks and porcelain for advanced Arab medicines, and the Egyptians' preservative, myrrh. Pearls, gold and jade were taken on board from Siam en route home.

Admiral Zheng's own flagship was a massive 400-foot-long nine-master, almost five times the size of Christopher Columbus's *Santa Maria*, 60 years later. The Chinese Navy's great explorer beat Vasco da Gama to the coast of East Africa by 80 years, and it was just as well they did not arrive at the same time because the massive warships of Admiral Zheng would surely have obliterated the "tiny," 85-foot-long Portuguese caravels that struggled around the Cape of Good Hope.

Whatever possessed the Ming Dynasty Emperor to willfully eliminate his mighty fleet a few years later can only be guessed at: China's endless suspicion of foreigners, all foreigners? Its view of itself, and its ancient feelings of superiority? Perhaps its own melancholic sense of isolation?

It is possible that the death of the immortal Admiral Zheng He, halfway across the Indian Ocean during the final homeward voyage in 1433, may have left a gap in the high command of the Chinese Navy that was just too large to fill.

But perhaps the ultimate truth of the amazing decision to ban entirely overseas Naval adventures may be found in the words of the young Ming Emperor Zhu Zhanji, who presided over many of Zheng's momentous journeys.

"I do not," he once said, "care for foreign things."

He was not of course referring to sweet crude oil from the vast fields of Kazakhstan. And now, fast-forward in the long winter of 2007, Admiral Zhang Yushu could not afford to ignore foreign things. And he was about to reverse almost 580 years of Chinese Naval policy: policy from which that huge nation had not departed. Not until World War I were the giant battle fleets of the Ming Emperors matched, either in size or relative firepower, by any of the world's great powers.

Zhang Yushu stared through the windshield of the Navy car, watching them cast off the lines of the 1,700-ton guided-missile frigate *Shantou*, a warship that would have been dwarfed by Zheng He's *Pure Harmony*.

"She's going, Jicai. And it's a historic moment in the long records of our sea power. . . . Just think of it . . . that little Type 053 Jianghu frigate is steaming off in the wake of our ancestors of five hundred years ago. The same old sea-lanes, from the most glorious days of our history . . . just like the Silk Road. They're going back as the main power in the Persian Gulf, in a sense to conquer the trading world all over again."

"I'm not sure the Americans would be appeciative of your phrasing, Yushu. They think they have rights to the gulf and its waters anytime they see fit."

"Ah, yes. So they might. But remember we were there as welcome guests and trading partners with the Arabs half a millennium ago, and longer. Remember, too, in recent years Chinese porcelain from the Ming Dynasty has been discovered along the shores of Hormuz. We have long historic roots in that area, and the Persians want us back to help them in the struggle against the West. . . . Oh yes, Jicai. We belong in those ancient waters of our forefathers."

"And we're taking a lot of high explosives to prove it. Eh, Yushu?"

Shantou eased out into the main channel, the driving rain gleaming on her big surface-to-surface guided-missile launchers. Her six twin 37-millimeter gun houses stood stark against the shore lights. Her five-tubed fixed antisubmarine mortar launchers could still be seen through the rain squalls.

What could not be seen, however, were the principal weapons of her forthcoming voyage, the 60 Russian-made sea mines, secluded under heavy tarpaulin from the prying eye of the American satellite that had passed overhead two hours previously.

Out on the pitch-black horizon, there waited *Shantou*'s two Shanghai-built sister ships, *Kangding* and *Zigong*. They were in company with the first of China's new $400 million Russian destroyers, the 8,000-ton, 500-foot-long Sovremenny Class, *Hangzhou*, with its supersonic guided missile, the Raduga SS-N-22 Sunburn.

But the *Hangzhou* was not there to engage in surface-to-surface warfare. Her mission was strictly clandestine. She would lead her three frigates on the 6,000-mile journey to Hormuz, essentially to carry 40 more mines, but also because in the event of a confrontation she was best equipped to fight the little fleet out of trouble—though she would be no match for a determined U.S. commanding officer in a big cruiser.

Their voyage would take them down the South China Sea, up through the Malacca Strait into the Bay of Bengal, where they would immediately rendezvous with the 37,000-ton Chinese tanker *Nancang*, operating out of their new Navy base on Haing Gyi Island, at the mouth of Burma's Bassein River, across the wide, flat, rice-growing delta, west of Rangoon.

Haing Gyi Island had occupied many a sleepless night for the American President's National Security Adviser, Admiral Morgan, who was suspicious of Chinese motives at the best of times. The creation of a big Chinese fueling base, and Naval dockyard in Burmese national home waters, sent a shiver right through him. Particularly since the Chinese had constructed a railroad from Kunming, the 2,000-year-old capital of Yunnan Province, straight across the Burmese border to the railhead city of Lashio, from where heavy military hardware could easily join the rest of the $1.4 billion worth of weaponry China had already shipped into Burma.

Back on the rainswept dock at Zhanjiang, Admiral Zhang pulled his greatcoat around him and stepped out to watch the *Shantou* heading out toward the black shape of the harbor wall, and beyond to the South China Sea.

"Don't you get a thrill from this, Jicai? Just seeing our great modern Blue Water Navy moving into action on this dark night, bound for a major foreign adventure, the first for more than five hundred years?"

"I suppose so, Yushu. I'll let you know more when we discover how seriously infuriated the Americans are by the exercise."

But even the wise and experienced Jicai looked quizzical at the non sequitur that served as a reply from his lifelong friend.

"A mere diversion, my Jicai. The merest diversion."

1200 (local). March 13.
The White House. Washington, D.C.

"Now where the hell are they going?" demanded Admiral Morgan, staring at the grainy, poor-quality satellite photographs taken through the rain clouds above the Chinese coast. "Looks like three frigates and a Sovremenny destroyer, going south. What the hell for? And how far? And who the hell's going to refuel 'em? Answer that."

"I'm afraid I'm not really qualified to do that," said Kathy O'Brien sweetly.

"Well . . . er . . . you ought to be. Ought to be general knowledge for anyone in Washington. . . ."

"Oh . . . I hadn't realized."

"How far do you think they're going, then?"

"How could I possibly know?"

"I know you don't know. I'm just asking for guidance. Is that too much?"

"Well for all I know, they're just going on a picnic," she replied.

"Well, I wouldn't care about that . . . nice basket of chop suey in the pouring rain on the South China Sea. But that may not be what's happening. What I'm interested in is whether they are going on a long voyage, maybe to visit their friends in Iran. And if they are, those frigates are gonna get refueled from that damned new base of theirs on that frigging Burmese island."

"Which Burmese island?"

"Haing Gyi Island, their first serious Navy base of operations outside of China—EVER," the Admiral thundered. "Right now we're returning to the goddamned fifteenth century, when their fleets dominated the Indian Ocean and the Persian Gulf.

"And another thing," he yelled. "What the hell happened to all those sea mines from Russia . . . the ones we saw getting unloaded at Zhanjiang? Where the hell are they? And why isn't anyone keeping me up to speed on this? Where the hell's George Morris?"

"As you well know, my darling, he has cancer of his right lung."

"Serves him right for smoking so much," grunted the Admiral, puffing away on his cigar. "Where is he right now?"

"He's undergoing intensive chemotherapy, as you also well know. Since that awful treatment has been making him extremely ill, I imagine he's asleep."

"Well, have someone wake him up."

"Honey, please," said the best-looking redhead in Washington with a sigh.

Two weeks later. March 27.
Fort Meade, Maryland.

Lieutenant Ramshawe was sifting methodically through a pile of satellite photographs. He had singled out a dozen shots, and he was trying to fit them together into a montage, trying to see if the three submarines were actually forming some kind of a small convoy, out there in the Arabian Sea.

He had a couple of VLCCs (giant tankers, Very Large Crude Carriers) in focus to help him, and the conclusion he reached was the submarines were all together, moving on the calm blue surface about a mile apart, heading north. More important, they were Russian Kilo-Class boats, the deadly little diesel-electric attack submarines, currently being exported by the old Soviet Navy to anyone with a big enough checkbook to buy them, especially the Chinese, the Indians and the Iranians.

Lieutenant Ramshawe was in the process of identifying the nationality of these particular ships. And now he was more or less certain. He had located all three of Iran's Kilos, one in Bandar Abbas, two in their submarine base at Chah Behar, outside the gulf on the north shore of the Gulf of Oman.

So far as he could tell, the Indians had no submarines at sea, which meant, almost certainly, the three Kilos were Chinese and they were headed directly to Chah Behar.

This was mildly unusual but not earth-shattering. Chinese warships were no longer rare in the Indian Ocean and the Arabian

Sea. They were occasional visitors to the Gulf of Hormuz, and just today there were new satellite pictures of a four-ship Chinese flotilla, including their big Sovremenny destroyer, heading across the Bay of Bengal toward the southern headland of the Indian continent.

"Wouldn't be that surprised if the whole bloody lot of 'em were going up to Hormuz," pondered Jimmy. "What with that new refinery and Christ knows what else up there."

Lieutenant Ramshawe was thoughtful. The four surface ships had been steaming very publicly all the way from the South China Sea. "No worries," he muttered. But the Kilos had been much more secretive. No one had spotted them since they had left their base, since they'd mostly been deep, only snorkeling for short periods. But here they were now, large as life, making their way up to their close friends on the southernmost Iranian coast.

"That's seven Chinese vessels, possibly going in the same bloody direction to the same bloody place," murmured the Lieutenant, reaching for the latest edition of *Jane's Fighting Ships*, the bible of the world's navies.

Now let me have a look here . . . right . . . Jianghu frigates . . . they can hold sixty sea mines apiece . . . and that destroyer has rails for forty more . . . now . . . how about the Kilos. . . . What's it say here? They can carry twenty-four torpedoes or twenty-four mines . . . not both. So if those little bastards were carrying mines, that'd be seventy-two, plus the two hundred twenty in the surface ships . . . that's close to three hundred. . . . My oath, you could cause a lot of trouble with that little lot.

The Lieutenant knew he was just trying to connect two separate mysteries. The first: What the bloody hell happened to all those sea mines that ended up in Zhanjiang? Second: What the hell are all these bloody Chinese warships doing in the Indian and Arabian Seas?

He had of course not the slightest shred of evidence there was one single solitary mine on board any of the ships. Certainly nothing that showed on the satellite photos, except for the big covers.

But still, he considered it his duty to alert his immediate superior, Admiral Borden, as to the possibility, even if it did mean rejection. So he drafted a short memorandum and sent it in.

Fifteen minutes later he was summoned to the Acting Director's office, knocked firmly on the door and waited to be instructed to enter.

"Lieutenant, I appreciate your diligence in these matters, but I heard earlier this morning from Langley the Iranians are staging some kind of a forty-eight-hour military hooley with the Chinese Navy down there in Bandar Abbas. Bands, parades, red carpets, dinners, speeches, television, the whole nine yards. Apparently the surface ships are scheduled to arrive there next Monday.

"So I'm very afraid your theory of a large traveling minefield is out. Thank you for your efforts, though . . . but do remember, I did warn you to forget about it . . . If someone's laying a minefield, we'll see them . . . all in good time. That's all."

"Sir," said Lt. Ramshawe, making his exit, muttering, "Supercilious prick. Serve him right if the bloody hooley was just a cover-up and the whole U.S. tanker fleet was blown up."

2015. Tuesday, April 3.
Navy Base. Bandar Abbas.

The festivities were over for the evening. The last of the Iranian public were driving home out of the dockyard and the great arc lights that had floodlit the magnificent parade were finally switched off. The huge fluttering national standards of the Islamic State of Iran and the People's Republic of China had been lowered.

A 60-strong guard of honor from the People's Liberation Army, resplendent in their olive green dress uniforms, hard flat-top caps with the wide red band, were retiring back to their quarters in the *Hangzhou.* The lines of electric bulbs that had floodlit the masts and upper works of both nations' warships were methodically being extinguished.

But as yet, no air of calm had settled over the fleet. They were

running down the flags, but turbines were humming, senior officers were on the bridge, lines were being cast off. It was a curious
time to arrange a night exercise after such an exhausting day of
preparation and celebration. But that, ostensibly, was precisely
what was happening.

The three Chinese frigates were already moving, slowly, line
astern, led by *Shantou*, out through the Naval basin into the main
channel, now dredged to a low-tide depth of 33 feet. Thirty minutes later, China's 6,000-ton Sovremenny-class destroyer, the
largest ship ever to enter this harbor, was escorted out by two 90-
foot harbor tugs, the *Arvand* and the *Hangam*.

Astern of the destroyer, a 900-ton twin-shafted Iranian Navy
Corvette, the *Bayandor*, almost 40 years old, originally built in
Texas, followed, still flying the green, white and red national flag
despite the late hour of the evening. Her sister ship, *Naghdi*, also
armed with modern Bofors and Oerlikon guns, awaited the flotilla
one mile southeast of the harbor, ready to guide them around the
long shallow outer reaches of the shelving Bostanu East Bank.

Their 65-mile journey would take them past the great sand-
swept island of Qeshm and on into the deeper waters of the Hormuz Strait. Forty miles farther on, east of the jutting Omani
headland of Ra's Qabr al Hindi, they would make their rendezvous, at 26.19N 56.40E. Admiral Mohammed Badr himself
was on the bridge of the *Hangzhou*, accompanying the Chinese
Commanding Officer, Colonel Weidong Gao (Chinese Navy COs
are all three-star Colonels).

Under clear skies they pushed on southeast through light
swells and a warm 20-knot breeze out of the west. Finally at
56.40E Colonel Weidong ordered a course change to one-eight-
zero, and running over sandy depths of around 300 feet they
headed due south for the final six miles.

Gradually the little flotilla reduced speed until the sonar room
of the big destroyer picked up the unmissable signal of the Chinese Kilos, patrolling silently at periscope depth in the pitch-dark
waters off the jagged coast of Oman.

The plan had been finely honed several weeks before. The

Kilos would take the southerly six miles of the designated area where the water was now 360 feet deep. Each of the three submarines would make a course of zero-nine-eight starting from the deep trough off Ra's Qabr al Hindi. They would thus move easterly a half mile apart, launching out of their torpedo tubes a one-ton Russian-made PLT-3 contact sea mine every 500 yards—the ones made at the Rosvoorouzhenie factory in Moscow: the same ones that had so vexed young Jimmy Ramshawe on their top-secret journey all the way across Asia to the South China Sea.

At the conclusion of these three death-trapped parallel lines, six miles long, the minefield would make a 10-degree swing north, and then run for 24 miles dead straight, all the way across the Strait of Hormuz to the inshore waters of the Iranian coastline, at a point 29 miles due south of the new Sino-Iranian refinery outside the little town of Kuhestak.

And right now the three Chinese mine-laying frigates were moving into position. *Shantou*, *Kangding* and *Zigong*, a half mile apart, heading east-nor'east, slowly in the darkess, the soft thrum of their big diesel engines interrupted only by the splash, every 500 yards, as they sowed their treacherous seed in a barrier across the world's most important oil sea-lanes.

The 60 mines on board each frigate would last for 17 miles. The final coastal area would be handled by the destroyer, and they would designate a sizable three-mile gap through which Chinese and Iranian tankers could pass, principally because they would be the only tankers informed of the position of the safe passage.

Meanwhile the newly laid mines sat at the bottom of the ocean secure on their anchors, awaiting the moment when they would be activated electronically, released on their wires to rise up toward the surface and then hang there in the water, 12 feet below the waves, until an unsuspecting tanker man came barreling along and slammed it out of the way, obliterating his ship in the process.

It was a two-and-a-half-hour journey back to Bandar Abbas and the surface convoy set off at 0400, leaving the Kilos to make their own way back to Chah Behar, running at periscope depth (PD). There was time to spare because the big U.S. satellite did not pass overhead until 0800.

The frigates and their 6,000-ton bodyguard docked in Bandar Abbas at 0630, when the next stage of Admiral Zhang's plan went into operation. The *Hangzhou* was immediately reloaded with 40 PLT-3 contact mines, plainly visible, as her original cargo had been the previous evening. When "Big Bird" took her photographs a few minutes after 0800, the fully laden Chinese destroyer would look precisely the same as she had on the last daylight satellite pass, just before the grand parade yesterday evening.

The signal back to Zhanjiang was as agreed, in the event of a successful mission: *DRAGONFLY*.

1130 (local). Tuesday, April 3.
Fort Meade, Maryland.

There is an irritating eight-and-a-half-hour time difference between the East Coast of America and Iran. This is caused by a time zone that runs bang through the middle of the country near Tehran. Instead of one half of the nation being four hours in front of GMT, and the other half only three, they compromised and put the whole place three and a half hours ahead of London, which is of course five in front of New York.

Thus satellite pictures taken at 1930 (Iran) were shot at 1100 (Fort Meade) the same day. And this particular set of pictures of Bandar Abbas Dockyard landed on Lt. Ramshawe's desk just as he arrived a half hour early for work.

Before him, in sharp focus, was the major event Admiral Borden had mentioned. Jimmy could see civilian cars parked in the dockyard with the joint Sino-Iranian fleet lit up brightly in the gathering darkness for the public to see. He guessed he would receive new pictures, intermittently, throughout the day, showing more or less what was happening in Iran's Navy Headquarters.

Still allowing the issue of the Russian mines to burn away at the back of his brain, Lt. Ramshawe searched the decks of the Chinese frigates, under a powerful glass, to see if there was a sign of them. But there was none. Not so the destroyer. All 40 of the mines she carried could now be seen on her rails, though they had plainly been covered during her journey from China.

A new set of pictures arrived midafternoon that actually caught the little fleet on the move. It was very dark in the gulf now, and the photographs were not of the same quality. But this hardly mattered. What did matter was the sight of three Chinese frigates, one destroyer and two Iranian Corvettes heading off on a mission in the middle of the night.

For all he knew, they were off to attack Iraq or Oman, "or some other godforsaken place," and Jimmy Ramshawe hit the button to the Director's office, from where he was given his usual short shrift.

"I wouldn't worry about it, Lieutenant, if I were you . . . they're probably going to conduct a night exercise together . . . not unusual at one of these international junkets between two navies. . . ."

"Yessir. But I can see a full load of mines on the destroyer. . . ."

"I expect they'll still be there in the morning, Lieutenant. That's all."

Jimmy Ramshawe put the phone down slowly. And the same question he had asked himself a thousand times popped into his mind: *Why had the Chinese plainly ordered an extremely expensive consignment of specialist contact mines from Russia if they weren't planning to lay out a bloody minefield somewhere?*

He also considered it a slice of blind luck that the Andropov freighter had been spotted taking off from Moscow, and then again at secretive Baykonur. No one ever traced its second refueling stop, and in Lt. Ramshawe's opinion it was entirely possible there had been a second trans-Asian flight of the giant aircraft. That would have brought the total mines carried to 240, sufficient to fill all four surface ships with their combined quota of 220. He had not given the three Kilos much thought since they had not been seen for a few days. But he could not get those mines out of his mind.

It was all very well Admiral Borden saying it was best to forget the whole thing until something more definite emerged, but, streuth! What if those crazy bastards were out there right now planting a minefield in the middle of the strait? What then?

Lieutenant Ramshawe wandered off in search of a cup of coffee, reasoning to himself that if the satellite pass was made at 0800 over Bandar Abbas, which he knew for certain, then he might see some good pictures of the ships back in harbor sometime after midnight Fort Meade time

Anyway, he was going nowhere until he had seen those pictures. And he knew this was a state of affairs guaranteed not to thrill his girlfriend, the dark-haired Jane Peacock, daughter of the Australian ambassador to Washington. The Peacocks and the Ramshawes were lifelong friends, and it was widely assumed that Jimmy and Jane would ultimately marry.

Right now he looked forward to telephoning Jane even less than he dreaded calling his boss. *The pair of them could probably run a contest to see who could give me the hardest bloody time.*

He was right, too. "Jimmy, for crying out loud, why this sudden interest in an Arab Navy?"

"They're not Arabs," he corrected her. "They're Persian. That's different."

"I don't care if they're bloody Martians!" she yelled. "We were supposed to have supper with Julie in Georgetown, and you're hopeless. . . . I'm not going by myself."

"Janie, listen. I believe this is really important. Like maybe a life-and-death matter."

"Well, there must be more important people than you to deal with it."

"There isn't anyone more important than me who even believes it, never mind wants to deal with it."

"Well, leave it alone, then, until someone instructs you to do something."

"I can't, Janie. I have to stay. But I'll pick you up early tomorrow and we'll have breakfast before you go to your class—I'm free till eleven-thirty, same time you have to be in Georgetown."

"Okay," she grumbled. "Nine at the embassy . . . but you're still a bloody nightmare. . . . Even your own mother thinks that."

Jimmy chuckled. He adored his beautiful, clever fiancée, and he hated letting her down. But in his own mind, he alone stood between world order and possible world chaos. *Well, something like that. I just don't trust the bastards. That's all.*

The night passed slowly. And he spent the hours before midnight reading a book about international terrorism, a fundamentally depressing read, citing samples of inordinate stupidity by the Intelligence services of various Western governments.

Jesus, a whole lot of this crap could have been avoided if people were just that little bit sharper. . . . Even at the business end of the Intelligence game there are still people more intent on protecting their own jobs, rather than concentrating on getting it right, at all costs.

Jimmy Ramshawe was still young enough to own those ideals. Just. But he would not want to work too long for a conservative cynic like David Borden, whose pension beckoned, and who preferred to pass the buck than start a high-profile scare over nothing.

Midnight came and went. It was a half hour since the morning satellite shots had been taken again, high above the harbor of Bandar Abbas.

Nothing arrived until 0040. And the young Lieutenant shuffled the new photos from the National Reconnaissance Office, searching for a shot of the Chinese destroyer. And here it was . . . fully laden with its mines, just as it had been before the midnight naval exercises in the gulf. The frigates too were back at their Iranian jetties, the tarpaulins that covered their cargo still in place.

There were also the standard daily shots of Chah Behar, and they showed empty spaces where the three Chinese Kilos had been last Saturday night. "Christ knows where they are," muttered Jimmy.

And he picked up his jacket and made his way out of the office, walking through the main doors of the building and across to the dimly lit parking lot where two Marine guards saluted him.

He climbed into the driver's seat and drove to the main gates, showed his pass to the duty guards and gunned his 10-year-old black Jaguar out to the exit road and on down to the Washington-Baltimore Parkway. It was a fast ride at this time of night, and he let the speedometer hover around 75 as he cruised down to the Beltway for the 10-mile run to Exit 33, Connecticut Avenue, which would take him straight into the center of the capital.

He made a right at Dupont Circle, skirted the campus of George Washington University, and ran on down to the Watergate complex where his parents had owned an apartment for the better part of 30 years. Naturally they rarely, if ever, used it, since they lived mostly in New York. Which was excellent news for Jimmy, who thus had a millionaire's residence for free.

He drove into his underground parking space and turned off the engine. It was almost 2 A.M., and he was almost too tired to get out of the car. But he still wished Jane could have been there waiting for him. And he thought again of how much easier life had been when Admiral George Morris had been in charge at the NSA.

The thing about George was, he was damned confident, and he had the ear of the Big Man in the White House. No one was closer to Arnold Morgan than George, and the two of them always consulted. Admiral Morris was thus a fabulous guy to work for. He always listened. He always weighed all the eventualities, and all the possibilities. Never tried to second-guess his staff. He worked on the theory that if one of his chosen men thought something should be investigated, then that was probably correct. Not like this bloody Boredom character.

Jimmy sat there in the driver's seat for a moment, pondering his dreary task tomorrow when he had to talk to Admiral Borden and admit the Chinese destroyer was still fully laden with her sea mines, as she had been the previous night.

He could hear the world-weary old bastard right now: "Well, Lieutenant, what a great surprise that must be to you . . . but don't say I didn't warn you. . . ."

"Just as long as he doesn't tempt me to tell him another unlikely truth," muttered Jimmy to himself. "That the bloody morning mines might be different ones from those we saw last night. He'll say that's bollocks. Probably paranoid bollocks. But it isn't. Because that's what I'd do myself if I wanted to lay a mine-field in the Strait of Hormuz."

He climbed out of the car and locked it. Wandering over to the elevator, still muttering, ". . . replace the mines on deck before the zero-eight-hundred satellite pass, right? Put the stupid Americans off the trail."

ON SATURDAY MORNING, APRIL 7, at first light, the Chinese warships sailed, apparently, for home. At least two of them did, the *Hangzhou* and the *Shantou*. The other two stayed right where they were at the jetties in Bandar Abbas harbor. Three hours later, shortly before 0950 (local time), the three Chinese Kilos pushed out of Chah Behar into the Hormuz Strait and made their way south toward the Arabian Sea.

The U.S. satellites picked up the entire scenario on bright sunlit waters, and back in Fort Meade, Lieutenant Ramshawe wrote a short memorandum to the NSA's Acting Director, detailing the ship movements.

Two days later a report came in from the Middle Eastern desk at Langley that Iran was moving heavy Sunburn missiles, plus launchers, plus antiaircraft artillery, to a point along their southeastern coast on the Gulf of Oman.

Langley's man did not know precisely where the hardware was headed, but Fort Meade made a slight adjustment in the satellite's photographic direction, and from way up in the stratosphere the massive U.S. camera snapped off two shots of the big

Sunburns being maneuvered into position facing out to sea, 29 miles south of the coastal town of Kuhestak.

Lieutenant Ramshawe marked up his wide chart, 26.23N 57.05E. He automatically glanced across to see the nearest point of land, but there really was nothing. If the missiles were fired westerly at 90 degrees to the coast, they would head straight out to sea. A slightly more southerly course would aim them at the northern headland of the Iranians' friends, the Omanis.

That headland, the outermost point of the barren Musadam Peninsula, scarcely had a town or a village on it. The only name marked on Jimmy Ramshawe's chart, way out on the jutting eastern coast, was Ra's Qabr al Hindi.

"Christ," he muttered. "What kind of a bloody name's that? Imagine coming from there, and traveling to the States . . . *er, Place of residence, sir? Ra's Qabr al Hindi.* Jeez, they'd probably lock you up on principle . . . heh heh heh!"

In any event, the Lieutenant drafted a report confirming they now had a firm position for the Iranian missiles. And then he returned to his consistent preoccupation, the two remaining Chinese warships in Bandar Abbas, the *Kangding* and the *Zigong*. The photographs that had just arrived showed both ships now flying Iran's national flag.

And Jimmy Ramshawe stared at them for a long time. *What if they had laid a secret minefield somewhere out there last week . . . What if the two frigates had been left behind in readiness to go out and activate the mines?*

He knew that such a theory would be ridiculed by Admiral Borden, who had of course ridiculed his every thought about the mines. And thus far had been proved right. Nonetheless, Lieutenant Ramshawe elected to go and see his leader, and present his worst fears.

The veteran Admiral smiled, with a jaded, indulgent air.

"James," he said. "May I call you James?"

"Jimmy, sir, actually. No one's ever called me James. I'd think you were talking to someone else."

The Admiral blinked at the Australian forthrightness, which always caught him off guard.

"Right, Jimmy. Now listen to me. . . . Do you know why the two frigates are now flying the flag of Iran?"

"Not really, sir. But it could be some kind of a Chinese cover-up, while they're getting ready either to lay mines or activate them."

"No, Jimmy," he said with heavy emphasis. "That is not the reason. They are flying the Iranian flag because Iran has just bought the two Chinese frigates. That was the objective of the big dockyard junket. It was a Chinese sales tour. . . . You don't think they'd come all that way for nothing, do you? . . . Not the Chinese. They like money a lot more than they like anything else.

"It was a goodwill sales visit. No doubt in my mind. They conducted a fleet exercise together, exchanged information, and at the conclusion of the festivities, Iran agreed to purchase the two ships. The first two guided-missile frigates they've ever owned."

"Well, sir, if that's your opinion . . . I'll have to agree."

"Do you have a different opnion?"

"Well, sir. I have been wondering about the mines. And I'm still not sure the Chinese haven't made some kind of a devious move with a view to laying them."

"Ah, that's your prerogative as an Intelligence officer, Jimmy. But it's been your prerogative for weeks, months, and nothing has happened, as I told you it wouldn't."

"Righto, boss. I'll buy that. Maybe they did just want to store up some Russian mines for some future mission. Anyway, if you're right, they just paid for them, with the frigate money. Good on 'em, right?"

The Admiral smiled. "You're learning, Jimmy. In this business, it's very easy to spend your life chasing your tail . . . seeing spooks, plots and schemes around every corner. Just stay focused, and a keep a weather eye out for the really big stuff, when you've got real evidence. That's all."

The young Lieutenant left, returning to his office, and gazing once more at his wide, marked chart of the Strait of Hormuz. He stared at it for several minutes, and muttered to himself, "I just wonder what's sitting down there on the seabed, right offshore of those new missile placements."

Two weeks later. April 24.
China's Southern Fleet HQ. Zhanjiang.

Admiral Zu Jicai, now C-in-C of the entire Navy, was back in his old office, and he opened up the secure line to Beijing, waiting quietly for Zhang Yushu to come to the phone.

When the great man finally spoke on the line from the Chinese capital, the conversation was unusually brief for two such old friends.

"Nothing on any foreign networks re DRAGONFLY."

"No suspicion anywhere?"

"None. Shall I activate the field in the next two days?"

"Affirmative."

"Good-bye, sir."

"Good-bye, Jicai."

Three days later. April 27.
The Strait of Hormuz.

Hardly a ripple disturbed the flat blue calm of the southern waters of the strait. It was one of those sultry Arabian mornings, in which the livid heat of the desert sun makes life on land almost unbearable, and life on board any ship not a whole lot better.

Six miles northeast of the Musandam Peninsula, the waters were almost oily to look at, as the tide began to turn inward from the Arabian Sea. There was no ocean swell, no little eddying cats' paws on the surface, no movement in the hot, still air.

But ripples were on the way. Giant ripples, from the big white bow wave of the 80,000-ton black-hulled gas carrier *Global*

Bronco, making a stately 18 knots, southeasterly through the water. The 900-foot carrier was laden down with 135,000 cubic meters of liquefied natural gas, frozen to *minus* 160 degrees centigrade. In more comprehensive stats, that's 3,645,000 cubic feet, or, a 100-foot-high building, 200 feet long by 200 feet wide. Which is a lot of frozen gas, and it forms, by general consensus, the most potentially lethal cargo on all the world's oceans.

Unlike crude oil, which does not instantly combust, liquid natural gas is hugely volatile, compressed as it is 600 times from normal gas. Tanker corporations are near-paranoid about safety regulations for its transporation around the world. Layer upon layer of fail-safe backup systems are built into every LNG carrier. They are not the biggest tankers on the ocean, but then, neither is the nuclear-headed torpedo the biggest bomb. In any event, the worldwide industry of transporting liquid gas has never once suffered a fire, never mind an explosion.

Up on the bridge, almost 100 feet above the water, the obsessively careful Commodore Don McGhee stared out over the four bronze-colored holding domes, which each rose 60 feet above the scarlet-painted deck. The bow of the *Global Bronco* was nearly 300 yards in front of him, and the veteran Master from the southeast Texas gulf port of Houston had a view straight down the massive gantry that ran as a steel catwalk clean across the top of each dome, all the way down to the foredeck.

Right now the ship was making its way well outside the Omani inshore traffic zone, with the local Navy's firing practice area 10 miles astern. Ahead of them was the narrowest part of the Hormuz Strait, and in this clear weather they would see plainly the Omani headlands of Jazirat Musandam, and two miles farther south, Ra's Qabr al Hindi. They were too far away to catch a glimpse on the horizon of the glowering shores of Iran on the eastern side of the crescent-shaped 30-mile-wide seaway.

Commodore McGhee was in conference with Chief Engineer Andre Waugh. And up ahead of them they could still see a Liberian-registered British tanker, a 300,000-ton VLCC bound for the North Atlantic. They had been catching her slowly all the way down from the new gas-loading terminal off Qatar, right around the Emirates peninsula, past Abu Dhabi and Dubai, and now they were less than 50 miles from the open waters of the Arabian Sea. All tanker captains were glad to get out of the gulf, and McGhee was no exception.

There was always a menace about patrolling Iranian warships, a menace compounded in the past few months by yet another Iranian militant threat to lay a minefield directly off its coast at the choke point of the entrance.

Both tanker officers knew there had been for several weeks a worldwide unease about China's warships currently moored in the Ayatollah's Navy base at Bandar Abbas. And they knew also of the tensions caused by the opening of the brand-new Sino-Iranian refinery at the end of the Chinese-built pipeline, which ran 1,000 miles, out of the Kazakhstan oil fields, across Turkmenistan, and clean through the sweltering Iranian Plateaux to the coast. Everyone in the Western oil business knew this pipeline gave China something close to a "lock" on the second-largest easy-access oil deposits on earth.

One more threat by Iran's increasingly noisy anti-West politicians to bottle up the entrance to the gulf would probably send the Pentagon into a collective dance of death. It was all politics, threat and counterthreat, but to men like Commodore McGhee, masters of the big crude-oil and gas carriers working the north end of the Arabian Sea, those politics had an edge of grim reality.

"This darned place always gives me the creeps," he said. "I'll just be glad to make the open ocean."

"I know what you mean," replied Chief Andre Waugh. "So do the British by the look of it . . . that's a Royal Navy helicopter up ahead, checking that big tanker out of the area. Right now they're checking every British ship in and out of the gulf. Guess they don't like the political situation, right?"

No ships in the entire history of navigation have been more political than the big tankers, upon whose safe passage half the world depends in order to keep moving. The fate and prosperity of nations literally hang in the balance as these great leviathans carry the principal source of world energy from where it is to where it is needed.

Commodore McGhee, a tanker man for thirty years, had never once entered Iranian waters, always keeping well over on the Omani side. Back home in Texas, in the Houston control room, on the thirty-second floor of the Travis Street headquarters of Texas Global Ships, Inc., Robert J. Heseltine III, the president, had issued specific instructions: Stay well clear of the Ayatollahs and their Navy. Don McGhee did not need reminding.

Texas Global ran six ships, but *Global Bronco* was the only LNG carrier. Heseltine was right proud of his Texan roots, and he had named the other five ships *Global Star*, *Global Rose*, *Global Brand*, *Global Steer* and *Global Range*. They were all 300,000-ton VLCCs, which normally plied among the Gulf of Iran, southern Africa, the northeast tanker ports of the USA, and Europe.

Bronco usually worked in the east, steaming between the gas-rich gulf ports of Qatar and Abu Dhabi, and Tokyo Bay, where Japanese Electric unloads millions of cubic meters of natural gas every week. This particular voyage, however, was shorter—just as far as the southern Taiwan port of Yung-An. The massive liquid-gas cargo would be used almost exclusively for electric power generation.

Robert J. Heseltine III had not laid eyes on one of his ships for three years, and probably wouldn't for another three years. Giant tankers cost $100,000 a day to operate and they have to keep working, roaming the world picking up cargo and unloading it. There never was a reason for any of the ships to return to home base in Texas, and both crew and supplies were ferried out to them, by commercial airlines, and then by helicopter, while the great energy ships kept right on moving, thousands of miles from home. No merchantmen since the days of sail, indeed since the clipper ships, had ever undertaken such vast and endless transworld journeys.

Commodore McGhee was now traveling a couple of knots faster than the VLCC up ahead, and he positioned himself accordingly, preparing to run past, a half mile off the tanker's port beam, a couple of hours from now.

The sun beat down on the scarlet deck as the *Global Bronco* crossed the 26.20-degree line of latitude right on 56.38 north. They were eight miles off Ra's Qabr al Hindi, and the captain could just make out the headland through his glasses. He ordered a steward to bring him up a cup of coffee, and a ham-and-cheese sandwich, and the 80,000-tonner ran on due south for another mile.

It was 12.10 P.M. precisely, in glaring sunshine on a still-calm sea, when the *Global Bronco* nudged into Admiral Zhang Yushu's Russian PLT-3 contact mine. The one-ton steel container of compressed high explosives, riding high on its anchor line, detonated with savage force. The massive forward inertia of the ship carried her on for just a few yards before the echoing underwater blast blew a huge hole in her hull, starboard side of the keel, right behind the bow.

All the for'ard plates along the starboard side buckled back with a tearing of metal showering a hailstorm of sparks inside the hull. The for'ard liquid gas tank, reinforced aluminum, held, then ruptured, and nearly 20,000 tons of one of the world's most volatile liquid gasses, its content bolstered by both methane and propane, began to flood out of its refrigerated environment. It hit an atmosphere almost 200 degrees centigrade warmer, and it flashed instantly into vaporized gas, exploding with a near-deafening *WHOOOOOOOSSSSH!* Consider the sound made by a cupful of gasoline on a bonfire just before you toss a lighted match into it—and then multiply that sound by around 40 million. That's loud.

The destruction to the entire front section of the ship was staggering. The liquid gas was, after all, just a highly compressed version of regular gas, and everyone has seen photographs of houses being obliterated by occasional explosions from this stuff. The sheer volume of LNG contained in the vast holding tanks of the *Global Bronco* caused a monumental blast, and the blast from Tank Four somehow smashed a hole in Tank Three, and seconds later the 20,000 tons of liquid fuel in there also blew.

The great ship shuddered. Flames leaped a hundred feet into the sky. Against all odds, Tanks Two and One held. But thousands of tons of fuel from the for'ard tanks poured through the fractured hull plates on the smashed starboard side of the ship, below the waterline, and into the waters of the Hormuz Strait, rising rapidly to the surface.

Commodore McGhee and his Chief Engineer were still on the bridge, almost in shock at what they had seen erupt 250 yards in front of them. Heat from the for'ard inferno was already melting the metal. They could see the white-hot bow end of the high gantry sagging like strips of putty. But the still-powerful forward motion of the *Bronco* was allowing her to leave a wide, unexploded slipstream lake of liquid gas in the water, which was evaporating at a diabolical rate, rising up off the water.

Don McGhee realized the danger. The gas, decompressed, and now in contact with the atmosphere, would evaporate over a relatively short period of time. But the danger of ignition was tantamout. Miraculously the great diesel engines were still running, and the Captain ordered, "ALL STOP!"

The bow of the ship was now dipping deep and the fires were reducing. The glowing-hot foredeck sent clouds of steam into the air as the waters of the strait washed over. But the gas continued to gush into the ocean, 20 feet below the surface. Don McGhee did not think his strongly compartmentalized ship would go down, and he did think the fires would reduce as the bow went lower. It was the unseen gas cloud he knew was rising rapidly up off the surface that worried him. Both he and Andre Waugh could smell it, light and carbonized on the air.

Members of the crew were racing toward the bridge, terrified, uncertain what to do. Astonishingly, no one had been for'ard at the time the ship hit, and no one was hurt. The problem was how to get off. There was no chance of jumping over the side into the toxic lake of liquid gas, and Commodore McGhee knew it would be lethal for a helicopter to try to reach them, since a tiny spark from the engine could ignite the gas cloud into a mountainous pillar of fire that would climb thousands of feet into the air, the heat almost certainly vaporizing the ship and the final two 20,000-ton tanks of liquid gas.

The roar of the for'ard fire way down the deck was like a 50-foot-high gas cooker, blasting out blue flame, too loud, too intimidating, to allow any question of trying to control it. Commodore McGhee ordered: *"ABANDON SHIP! MAN THE LIFEBOATS PORT SIDE."*

The crew charged off the bridge. The radio operator shouted, *"I'll transmit a MAYDAY! before we go."* The rest of them made for the three big orange Zodiacs moored on their davits along the deck rails. And then Commodore McGhee saw it—the Royal Navy's helicopter clattering toward them, low over the surface, totally unaware of the gas cloud rising up along the *Bronco's* aft starboard side and stern.

The tanker's master ordered his radio operator to open up the VHF on 16 and stop the chopper's advance at all costs. Then he opened the door to the viewing catwalk, a white-walkway jutting over the main deck. And he raced out onto it, jumping up and down, waving his arms, yelling to the pilot at the top of his lungs in futile desperation . . . *"STOP . . . FOR GOD'S SAKE STOP . . . PLEASE STOP . . . TURN AROUND . . ."*

Inside the helicopter both the pilot and his navigator saw the Captain's frenzied signal. The Navigator just had time to say, "Take a turn to the left here . . . this guy's waving us off. . . . I'll try the radio. . . ."

But it was too late. The Royal Navy's Sea King Mk 4, making just over 60 knots, flew bang into the middle of the rising gas-cloud, which ignited like a nuclear bomb, causing a gigantic blow-torch to rear up from off the surface of the water, roaring a black, scarlet and blue tower of fire 5,000 feet into the air.

The Navy helicopter was incinerated instantly. The *Global Bronco* and her crew perished in a split second, when the entire after end of the ship was enveloped by the searing near-2,000-degree-centigrade petrochemical blaze. Two minutes later there was just a blistered, white-hot steel-and-aluminum hulk, sizzling in the water, where once the mighty tanker had been. And the flames on board were dying. There was *nothing* left to burn, not even a coat of paint, not even an electric wire.

By some fluke of science and nature, Tank Two had held, but the aluminum of Tank One had melted and 20,000 more tons of liquid gas exploded in another deafening fireball. And the gas in the bottom third of the tank just poured out into the water, feeding the gas inferno, fueling the 200-yard-wide column of raging fire, which fought its way higher and higher as the liquid fuel flashed off into the atmosphere. Furiously hot now, sucking in oxygen and nitrogen like a tornado, it rose up thousands of feet into the clear skies. It was as if Satan himself were attempting to communicate with God.

0800. Friday, April 27.
Office of Admiral Arnold Morgan. The White House.
Washington, D.C.

Arnold Morgan was watching CNN news with rapt concentration. The destruction of a big U.S.-owned tanker, with no survivors, deep in the Gulf of Hormuz, was the lead item. Despite being six miles from Oman, and at least 40 from Bandar Abbas, the *Global Bronco* had very quickly become public property. Right now CNN was showing graphic pictures of the burning hulk, and its accompanying column of fire. The reporter was mentioning the overall problem, that Tank Two might suddenly blow, and for that reason no one was taking the risk of going closer.

Because the ship was well over on the Omani side of the strait, news-gathering operations were being conducted with a friendly nation, and most broadcasters and media organizations had offices and satellite facilities in nearby Dubai. Two clattering helicopters were already prowling the shore, trying to take pictures, but unable to fly in close.

The Omani Navy had two 1,450-ton guided-missile Corvettes circling the area, warning ships off, and CNN had close-up pictures of these two British-built bodyguards. There were also two Chinese-built guided-missile frigates, flying the flag of Iran, within 10 miles of the disaster.

The dimension of the story outshone the limited coverage possible at this time. And the 24-hour news station was already offline, reporting, wrongly, the *Global Bronco* was still burning. It wasn't the tanker on fire. It was the released gas in the water.

They interviewed a Royal Navy Lieutenant Commander serving with a patrol out of Dubai, who speculated it might be necessary to bang a torpedo right into the hull, starboard of Tank Two, in order to blow up the remaining liquid gas. Either that or shell the giant on-deck holding dome. "It cannot," he said, "just be left out there, ultimately to sink and take its twenty-thousand-ton cargo with it."

Arnold Morgan sipped his black coffee, and listened, nodding slowly, and pondering. "Now who the hell are Texas Global Ships. And what do they have to say for themselves? Come on, guys. Get some reporters on this . . . gimme the only information worth having. . . . What do the owners think of the destruction of their ship . . . accident? I suppose so. But if so, how? I don't think there's ever been a major explosion and fire on one of those gas ships . . . except for one in Tokyo Bay nearly twenty years ago."

He switched off the channel, and walked over to his desk. "I wish I knew a little more about gas carriers," he said. "They must have the best possible safety systems . . . *hmmmmm* . . . I suppose there's no chance the goddamned towelheads whacked it with a torpedo, or the Iranians planted a minefield out in the exit lanes from the gulf. No. I guess not. There seems to be no suggestion of that. Still I better get Fort Meade onto it. I'd just like to know a little more about the *Global Bronco*."

"*KATHY!*" he yelled, scorning as ever the delicate little green telephone on his desk, which would have connected him to anyone in the world, including the lady right outside the door, the spectacular redhead Kathy O'Brien, who for three years had refused to marry him until he retired.

The wide wooden door opened, and she came in, shaking her head, saying she understood he would rather have a ship's tannoy system so he could bellow at everyone at the same time, but this was the twenty-first century and normal telephones were becoming quite acceptable, and would he ever consider using one. "Darling rude pig," she added.

"Could I have a little more coffee?" he asked, smiling. "And then I've got a little task for you."

"I'm not here to do little tasks," she replied. "Don't you have any big ones?"

The Big Man chuckled, all five feet eight and a half inches of him. He ignored her request, and asked if she had been watching the news.

"No, but I heard on the radio about the tanker that just blew up in the gulf. Soon as they mentioned it, I guessed it would be right up there on the priority list."

"Well, Kathy, it's a volatile area, and we always have to guard against lunatic action by the locals. . . . Anyway, the ship was owned by an outfit called Texas Global Ships. I want you to locate them, and get their president on the line."

"You have an address?"

"No. But try Information in the Houston-Galveston area. It's bound to be down there in the gulf oil ports . . . you'll find it."

Five minutes later, she returned to tell the Admiral that she'd found it, but had spoken only to a security guard since the place was not yet open.

"What's the name of the president?"

"Robert J. Heseltine III."

"Call the guard back, and tell him to have the boss call the White House, right away. Give him the main switchboard number and have him put through here immediately."

Kathy retreated, full of optimism. She knew the galvanizing effect a call from the White House can have on any American, and she was right about the guard.

"Yes, ma'am," he said. "Right away."

Three minutes and fifteen seconds later, she answered her phone and a deep Texan voice said, "Morning. This is Bob Heseltine."

She switched him through to the Admiral, who commiserated briefly about the ship, and then asked him, "Bob, do you have any reason to think the *Global Bronco* might have run into some form of Naval hardware down there . . . a mine or a torpedo or something?"

"Well, every tanker man worries about the strait, but it's always been safe on the Omani side . . . We didn't hardly get a warning from the ship . . . apparently, according to the Royal Navy, our operator just had time to call '*MAYDAY!*' twice, before the line went dead."

"So whatever happened happened pretty damned quickly," replied the Admiral.

"Yessir. I do believe so."

"Any idea what might have caused the explosion?"

"Not really, Admiral. We do have some kind of an eyewitness report from a Liberian-registered crude-oil tanker about two miles ahead of the *Bronco*. Just said the for'ard holding dome definitely blew first. Then they saw the one next to it go up as well."

"I guess that would confirm the possibility of a mine . . . all ships hit them bow first. A torpedo would have been much more likely to come in amidships."

"Yessir. But I really don't think we ran into a minefield. On the other hand, it's hard for me to think of one reason why the almost-brand-new gas-holding tank, way up for'ard, two hundred yards away from hot machinery, or even people, should suddenly have ruptured and exploded."

"That's really my main question, Bob. How could it have ruptured, then blown up?"

"No reason I can think of, sir. 'Cept sabotage. But I can't imagine anyone wanting to blow up the ship they were in. Suicide sabotage's pretty rare."

Arnold Morgan persisted. "What causes natural gas to ignite?"

"Well, it's gotta be a flame or a spark of some kind. It's the gas, flashing off from the liquid that burns. Beats the hell out of me, a) how that gas started to leak, and b) what blew it."

"Well, keep your ear to the ground, willya, Bob? Anything shakes loose, lemme know right away. Just call the number here, and they'll find me."

"Glad to, sir. Nice talking to you." The last words were some-what lost because the Admiral had already rung off. Bob Hesel-tine was not yet aware of the National Security Adviser's habit of never saying "good-bye" to anyone, just banging down the phone. He even did it to the President. These days, especially to the President.

"KATHY!" he yelled. *"GET FORT MEADE ON THE LINE."*

Admiral David Borden jumped to it, front and center, as he prepared to take his first call from the Big Man.

"Admiral?"

"'Morning, David. Got that job under tight control?"

"Trying to, sir."

"Good. Start off by telling me all you know about that tanker just went sky-high in Hormuz."

"Well, sir. I only just received a preliminary report."

"You did? Well it's zero-eight-four-five now, and the tanker blew at right after zero-three-three-zero. What are you using for comms, satellites or pigeons?"

Admiral Borden gulped. "Sir, I only just got here."

"You mean you're not only operating some kind of Dark Ages communication system, you're also late for work."

It had been awhile since anyone had addressed David Borden in quite such a manner, but he knew Arnold Morgan's fearsome rep-utation. He also knew that his bite was a lot worse than his bark. And this conversation was headed south, in a significant way.

"Sir, will you give me a half hour to get right on this?"

"Yes. But please remember the following: Anytime there's an explosion as big as this one right in the middle of the Strait of Hormuz, or indeed anywhere near the Strait of Hormuz, you bet-ter get on it real quick. Right here we have a major incident involving a U.S. freighter being destroyed, forty miles from Ban-dar Abbas. We got goddamned Iranian missile ships circling her. We may have a fucking minefield out there.

"Admiral Borden, I don't actually give a flying fuck what you've been doing. I don't care if you have to turn up in your office in a goddamned nightshirt and jockstrap at three A.M. But when something goes off bang anywhere near the Ayatollahs, I want Fort Meade on it like a starving wolf chasing a pork chop. Do you hear me, Admiral?"

"Absolutely, sir."

"Then get your ass in gear, sailor. And get your best men moving. And don't bother chasing the ship owner. I dealt with him while you were still eating your fucking cornflakes." CRASH. Down phone.

Admiral Borden was visibly shaken, as many an occupant of Fort Meade had been before him. He actually debated putting in a written complaint to the President about the "unforgivably disrespectful" manner in which he had been treated by the National Security Adviser.

He went as far as to call his old friend in the White House, Harcourt Travis, the Secretary of State, who laughed and told him, "That would be, I am afraid, a suicide note. Arnold Morgan would probably have both you and the President out of here in an hour. Arnie's the Big Man on Campus right now. Don't even think of taking him on."

Admiral Borden retreated, but in his mind he was planning to play this whole incident right down, which he believed would exact him a quiet, dignified revenge: that of military intellect over a blowhard.

As plans went, that one was dead moderate. If David Borden did but know it, career-threatening moderate.

At that moment there was a knock on the Director's door. He called to enter, and was not especially pleased to see the frowning face of Lieutenant Ramshawe.

"Morning, sir. I got in here soon as I could when I heard about the tanker, but it didn't get on the news till 0500 so I guess I was a bit late. Anyhow, my conclusions are that we really do need to examine the possibility of a Chinese-backed Iranian minefield right out there in the strait."

"But I believe the tanker exploded off the coast of Oman, miles and miles from Iranian waters."

"I know that, sir. But there's still got to be a suspicion. We know the Chinese ordered a ton of mines from Moscow, and we know they could easily have brought them to Iran. We also know they were groping about in the strait with four warships, and possibly three submarines, all mine layers, at least one night, and possibly more. We simply cannot dismiss the issue."

"The Omanis appear to have done so. There's not a word from them to cast any suspicion on the Iranians whatsoever."

"That's because they don't know their ass from their elbow."

"Very possibly. Nonetheless in the absence of one shred of proof, one floating mine, one whisper of skulduggery from any of our people in Beijing or Tehran . . . Jimmy, I cannot instigate anything without being in possession of at least some evidence."

"But I have some evidence. First of all, the bloody mines, maybe several hundred, were delivered under top-secret circumstances, and have essentially disappeared. Then we had a fairly large flotilla of ships sail from Chinese bases, direct to Iran. Then we have these night exercises, during which they could easily have laid a minefield out there in the strait.

"Then we have a very strange situation. You know, and I know, you can lay a minefield and not activate it electronically till you're good and ready. Now, the Chinks bugger off toward the Bay of Bengal, leaving behind two mine layers, the frigates *Kangding* and *Zigong*. And what are the first ships to be seen after the bang? Those two frigates, out there in the strait, flying the Iranian flag. In my view they were out there activating just *some* of the mines.

"But here's what's really important. . . . Remember a couple of weeks ago we picked up pictures of the Iranian missiles being established way down the coast, twenty-nine miles south of Kuhestak? . . . Well, I marked the point hard on my big chart of Hormuz. The *Global Bronco* went up in a near-dead-straight line from there, about twenty-four miles west sou'west."

"Jimmy, you can make a dead straight line from any one point to any other. You need three to show evidence of a straight line."

"Well, sir, at least the proximity of the missiles must be significant."

"Not necessarily so, Jimmy. I am afraid that all the *'evidence'* is very circumstantial. By which I mean we know nothing. The mines China ordered may well still be in Zhanjiang. Their trip to Iran may easily have been to sell the two frigates. *Global Bronco* was carrying eighty thousand tons of the world's most volatile petrochemical. Anything could have set it off. I would be sympathetic if you could locate for me one indisputable fact. Leave it for now, Jimmy. Until we get hard evidence."

The Lieutenant stood up, and he looked Admiral Borden square in the eye. "I just have a damned weird feeling that when the next evidence turns up, we're not gonna love it."

Admiral Borden shook his head, and called back Arnold Morgan. "Sir," he said, "I simply do not have one single piece of Intelligence that points to anything but a bad accident on that tanker, which caused it to explode."

"I do not doubt that, Admiral. The issue is whether you should be raising heaven and hell to find some."

"Sir, sometimes there is simply nothing to find."

"The fact that you can't find it does not mean it doesn't exist." Arnold Morgan was beginning to dislike the Acting Director at Fort Meade, and that was bad news for the Acting Director. But Admiral Morgan was receiving a distinct impression that David Borden did not *want* to find anything.

"If I were you, David, I would be damned careful about taking a negative view, because if you delay us, put us behind the eight ball, I shall be forced to HAVE YOUR ASS, RIGHT?" Click. Down phone.

"KATHY!"

The door opened once again. And Ms. O'Brien entered, smiling sweetly. Too sweetly. "Would it make you any happier, my darling," she said, "if I went out and bought a ship's Klaxon so I could signal back to you? I expect people would get used to it . . . *'KAAAAA-THEEEEE! . . . BAHAA . . . BAHAAA. . . .'* Two blasts for positive, one for negative, three for panic. . . ."

The Admiral burst into laughter, despite his rising irritation at the attitude of David Borden.

"Kathy, upon whom the sun rises and sets for me, I wanna let you into a deep and, thus far, unspoken secret. Right here I suspect I'm dealing with a total asshole in the chair of the good George Morris at the NSA."

"Oh, how very depressing."

"Possibly more than you know. Book us a table at the restaurant in Georgetown tonight, will you? Between you, and Monsieur Pierre, and my old friend Billy Beycheville, perhaps you can raise my spirits."

"Why, sir . . . ," she replied, putting on a southern accent even more firmly than her own far-lost Alabama drawl, "ah sure would be deeply honored to bring y'all raaht back into the world of good cheer and fahn manners."

Arnold watched her strut out, shook his head, smiling, and turned CNN back on.

Meanwhile, back at his desk in Fort Meade, Jimmy Ramshawe, surrounded by ocean charts, was glaring at the one that mapped the Bassein River on the Bengal Bay coast of Burma, or, as it is now known, Myanmar.

"Crazy bastards," he muttered. "Like changing the bloody name of Australia to Michelob."

He picked up the telephone and called the embassy, trying to catch Jane before she left for Georgetown. He just made it.

"Just a quick question," he said. "Can I meet you at home tonight instead of in the bar?"

"You mean my home?"

"Right."

"Okay. What time?"

"Six. I got a little project you might want to help me with."

"No worries. I'll be waiting."

The day passed without further drama, or knowledge as to what happened to the *Global Bronco*. The great tower of fire alongside the ship raged on into the heavens until the evaporating gas had burned off, and when it finally died it left the starboard side of the *Bronco* shimmering white hot. The huge tanker was wallowing in the water, bow down, the waves now washing right up to the still-intact Tank Two, which sat full of liquid gas, poised between the devil of the melting aft quarter of the ship and the ripped-metal destruction in the deep blue sea up for'ard.

CNN, and the rest of the media, could eleborate no further. Bob Heseltine had called Admiral Morgan to inform him that Texas Global was sending its own investigators immediately to Dubai. He also mentioned he had been in conference with his technical advisers all day and no one could come up with one single reason how the for'ard tank could posibly have exploded, short of being blown apart by a mine or a torpedo.

When Arnold replaced the receiver, he was so thoughtful, so concerned, he had actually found time to say good-bye to the helpful Texan on the wire from Travis Street, Houston.

Lieutenant Ramshawe spent the day studying satellite photographs and charts of the strait. He also talked to the CIA's Middle East desk, searching for any clue as to whether Iran might have decided to lock the rest of the world out of the almost-landlocked sea they regarded, historically, as their own.

Satellite photographs showed the two Chinese warships, *Hangzhou* and *Shantou*, now moored alongside, in China's new Burmese Naval dockyard on Haing Gyi Island, which sits north of a wide six-mile shoal, surrounded almost entirely by sea marshes, but with a short easterly coastline facing a surprisingly deep trench with varying low-water depths of well over 40 feet.

In a massive building program in recent years, China had converted a stretch of this two-mile coastline into a concrete haven for its warships far from home. The island was strategically perfect, on the eastern coast of the Bay of Bengal, at the mouth of the 12-mile-wide estuary of the Bassein River. It was equipped with long jetties and standard shipyard equipment, cranes, loading facilities, refueling pumps, 16 big concrete holding tanks, and sprawling lines of ships stores. It was the first fully equipped overseas Naval base China had possessed for more than 500 years, 7,500 sea miles from Shanghai.

Jimmy Ramshawe did not like it. The two Chinese warships, even in a long-range satellite photograph, looked a lot too comfortable at the Burmese jetties, just around the coast from a foreign ocean. "Like someone parking a couple of Iraqi frigates outside the Opera House by Sydney Harbor Bridge," he muttered. "Seriously out of place . . . I just wish I bloody knew what the Orientals were at—maybe I'll get my last name changed to Rickshawe and get in there as a spy and find out."

Tickled by his own groan-inspiring humor, the Lieutenant made out a brief report, detailing the information that the Chinese frigate and destroyer were now refueling for the journey home. He made a note that the three Kilos were not in residence in Burma and presumed they had taken a more southerly route to avoid the Malacca Strait, through which they would have been forced to travel on the surface. "It looks rather as if they do not wish to be seen," he wrote. "For reasons unspecified." For good measure he added the words "as yet."

He then returned to his big chart of the Hormuz Strait, published by the U.S. Navy and likely to be extremely accurate. He took a long ruler and drew a line from the new Iranian missile position at 26.23N 57.05E. The line was precisely 14 inches long. The chart's scale was one inch: 125,000. So he divided 125,000 by 36 to give him yards, then that number by 1,760 to give him miles. The calculator told him that on this chart one inch equaled 1.97 miles. Which meant the tanker had exploded in 360 feet of water, 27.58 miles from the missiles, right along his straight line at 26.18N 56.38E.

He noted that from the point of the explosion the water stayed very deep west toward the Omani coast. Heading east it began to shelve up steadily all the way back along his line, growing a regular 30 or 40 feet shallower every few miles. Absentmindedly he muttered to himself, "If there really is a minefield out there, I'd say they used those Kilos to lay 'em in the deep water over on the Omani side and the surface ships where it gets shallower. . . . I wonder."

His shift ended officially at 1600, but he'd been in the office since before 0600, and he was still there at 1700, wrestling with his decision. It was a drastic step, he knew, and may very easily cost him his career. But he was going for it.

Jimmy Ramshawe folded up his chart and took it with him when left his desk. A minute later he was aiming the Jaguar toward the highway that would take him to the Australian Embassy on Massachusetts Avenue. The traffic was "the usual bloody awful," and he drove in through the gates just before 6 P.M. Jane Peacock and her mother were chatting in the parking lot, and they killed a few minutes discussing the spectacular spring weather, blossoms and associated flora, before Jane and Jimmy headed back into the embassy, to the ambassador's private quarters.

She ordered tea, and then sat down next to him on a large sofa and told him to spill the beans. "Come on, Jimmy, what's happening?"

"Well, it's like this. . . . I am planning to speak to the President's National Security Adviser, Admiral Arnold Morgan."

"You don't have to tell me his bloody name, sweetness. Everyone knows his name."

"Yeah, but everyone isn't about to call him on his private line."

"You have that number?"

"No, actually, I don't."

"Well, how're you going to get it?"

"You're going to get it for me."

"ME?"

"Right. The thing is this. . . . I'm going over the heads of all my superiors, including the Acting Director. If anyone finds out, I'm probably dead in the Navy."

"Wow! What would you do?"

"Well, I was thinking of changing my name to Rickshawe and becoming a Chinese spy."

Jane laughed, which pleased him. He'd thought it was a good joke earlier, but there was nothing like testing it on a live audience.

"Jimmy, may I ask why you are doing this, and how you expect me to find a number that is probably private to the President of the United States."

"No it's not that private. The switchboard here could get it, on behalf of the ambassador. At least they'd get patched through by the main White House operator."

"You want me to use Dad's name?"

"No. I'll talk. But I want to make the call from here, and then verify it, by having them call back on your dad's private line, which will be on record at the White House. They have a direct line to all major Washington ambassadors. That way I'll get patched through to the Admiral."

"Well . . . I suppose so. Doesn't seem much harm. And if there is, the only one in trouble is going to be you. You better have something pretty important to say—that bloody Admiral's supposed to be a tiger."

"Yeah, I know. My dad knew him a bit when he was in the Navy."

"Anyway, you picked a good night. Both my parents are going out."

"I know that, too. You told me. Dinner at the British Embassy, right?"

"Yup. They'll both be gone by seven o'clock."

"That's good. I want to call around eight. Because that way I'll know he's settled wherever he's going to be. Hopefully at home. I don't want to have to go through this rigmarole twice, or even three times. And that's what'll happen if I make the call while he's in transit somewhere."

"Can I know what you want him for?"

"Not really. But since I can't make the call without you, certainly not from my office, I have to tell you. Janie, I think the Chinese and the Iranians, between 'em, have put some kind of a minefield across the Strait of Hormuz. That tanker blew up this morning . . . no accident. And I think there might bloody easily be more."

"Jesus. I read about that . . . but why doesn't Fort Meade get onto it?"

"Because Admiral Borden, the Acting Director, doesn't believe it. Doesn't want to do anything until he has some proof."

"Well, why do you think Admiral Morgan will be any more interested than Admiral Borden?"

"I don't have a reason. Just a gut feeling, that's all."

"Pretty expensive gut feeling, if you're wrong and he goes to Borden and tells him he's got some kind of a nutter on his staff."

"Yeah. I know. What a ripper. But I don't think he will. . . ."

"Anyway, let's go and watch the news in Dad's study, see if they've blown any more ships . . . then you can get started on blowing your entire career. . . . Want some more tea?"

The 90 minutes passed quickly, Ambassador John Peacock came in for a brief chat, then went off to meet his wife. At eight o'clock sharp, Lt. Ramshawe went and sat behind the big desk in the study, picked up the blue phone and dialed the main number of the White House.

Jimmy, his Aussie accent undimished, said, "Good evening. I'm calling from the office of the Australian ambassador, and he would like to speak immediately to Admiral Arnold Morgan . . . You probably want to verify this call, so get back to me right away would you?"

"Yessir, we'll check the private number for the Australian ambassador and come right back."

Thirty seconds later, the phone rang . . . *"Ambassador Peacock's office?"*

"Correct."

"Sir, I'm afraid the National Security Adviser is not in right now. . . . If it's urgent, we can locate him."

"Please do."

"Hold a moment. . . ."

Three full minutes went by, mostly taken up by Le Bec Fin's maître d', Pierre, asking the White House to wait while he connected a telephone to the private booth occupied by Admiral Morgan and Kathy. He'd done this a few times before, and he placed it right next to the bottle of 1995 Château Beycheville, which was "breathing," as yet untouched, in the middle of the table.

Arnold Morgan thanked him, and picked up the phone. "Morgan . . . Speak." His telephone manner never varied, but Kathy still giggled.

"Just a moment, sir . . . connecting you to the Australian ambassador. . . . "

"Sir, is that Admiral Morgan?"

"In person, Ambassador Peacock. And I guess this is pretty important? I'm just sitting down to dinner."

"Sir, this is not actually Ambassador Peacock. My name is Lieutenant Jimmy Ramshawe, and I work in surveillance at Fort Meade, and I'm calling you under what you might think are somewhat dishonest circumstances."

Arnold Morgan's eyes opened wide in surprise. "Fraud phone call from an Aussie, right before a little dish of grilled prawns . . . Jesus, what's the place coming to?"

"But, sir, it is important."

"I guess it must be. You've gone to a lot of trouble to interrupt my goddamned dinner. What did you say your name was . . . Jimmy Ramshawe?"

"Yessir. Surveillance."

"Okay, Jimmy. Shoot. And hurry . . . Wait a minute. . . . *(aside)* Kathy, tell Pierre to put the prawns on hold for five minutes, and lemme have a glass of that Bordeaux . . . I have a feeling I'm gonna need it. . . . Go, Jimmy."

"I don't know, sir, how well up-to-date you are on the *Global Bronco* situation?"

"Well, I haven't spoken to the tanker's owner for at least four hours."

"Sorry, sir . . . Anyway, I was the operator who tracked, or tried to track, all those sea mines China bought from Moscow three months ago."

Arnold Morgan's antennae flew up like lightning rods. But he stayed calm. . . . "Aha."

"Well, sir, they transported them under terrific secrecy . . . then we had that little convoy of surface ships, three frigates and a Sovremenny destroyer make a special journey all the way from the South China Sea to Iran. Then I picked up three Chinese Kilo-

Class submarines making their way north up the Arabian Sea; they ended up in Chah Behar. All seven of the ships, as you know, have mine-laying capacity.

"Then we had night exercises with the Iranians. We picked up very little, but they were out there all night off the Omani coast. Then we picked up a missile movement, Sunburn S-As on the southeast coast. And suddenly, a couple of weeks later, a damn great tanker explodes, twenty-seven miles in a straight line from those missile launchers. And what's the first thing we see? Two of those Chinese frigates, now flying the Iranian flag, just five miles from the explosion, forty miles from their jetties in Bandar Abbas."

Admiral Morgan was listening.

"Sir, I think they may have been out there activating the mines, and it is my opinion that there may be a serious minefield out there, maybe running from the Omani coast, place called Ra's Qabr al Hindi, right across to Iran. And I think we ought to find out."

"Jimmy, I assume you have reported all this to Admiral Borden?"

"Of course, sir. But he doesn't want to know. Keeps asking for evidence. Well, I don't have any bloody evidence, but I've got enough clues to warrant a damned careful look."

Arnold Morgan thought carefully, and then he said, "I suppose you've considered the consequences of a phone call like this. Bypassing the regular channels of command?"

"Yessir."

"But you decided to take the risk anyway?"

"Yessir."

"Now, I'm going to be very formal with you. Lieutenant Ramshawe, it is entirely out of order for you to have taken this action. You must return to Fort Meade and place the entire matter with Admiral Borden. It is essential you use our regular channels of information. Neither the Navy nor the Intelligence services can afford this kind of undisciplined and unorthodox method of operation. Kindly see that it does not happen again." At which point he put down the phone.

"Kathy," he said, "that was rather an interesting phone call. It confirmed what I have unfortunately suspected . . . that the man sitting in George Morris's chair is a total asshole."

Back in the Australian Embassy, Jimmy Ramshawe was perplexed. "He listened carefully to all I had to say," he told Jane. "Then he gave me a right choking off for not going through Admiral Borden . . . Jesus, I was only calling him because I *could not* go through Admiral Borden."

"Well, I'm sure he understood that," said Jane. "Even I understood that, and I only heard one half of the conversation."

"Right. But it still puts me in a no-win situation. If Admiral Morgan believed me, he'll probably call and report me to the Director, and use the information to give him a right bollocking. If he didn't believe me, he'll probably call anyway and recommend I be removed from any position of trust. The ole bastard never even gave me a chance to ask him to keep it confidential."

"Jimmy, Arnold Morgan did not get where he is by being stupid. I'm sure he plugged right into the situation and will very likely be grateful for the call, may even act on it. He'll appreciate what you did, and I don't think he'll betray you."

"Christ, I hope you're right. . . . Come on, let's get out of here."

Jimmy and Jane did not dine as well as Arnold Morgan and Kathy, nor in such opulent surroundings as Le Bec Fin. But they were not far away in a bar in Georgetown, eating a couple of cheeseburgers and drinking Budweiser instead of grilled prawns, veal marsala and Château Beycheville.

The Lieutenant was on duty at 0600, so he dropped Jane off at home sometime before midnight and headed back to the Watergate, a distance of less than two miles. Inside the apartment he kicked off his shoes, put the kettle on, checked his messages (none) and switched on the television, CNN automatically, muttering to himself, "Just better make sure no one's declared war."

No one had. The news, he thought, was unfathomably dreary,

lightweight . . . health care, second-rate pop star getting divorced, famine in Africa, all-star third baseman dying of drugs. *Blah-blah-blah*, grumbled Jimmy to himself. *These guys ought to be called The Four Newsmen of the Apocalypse, Conquest, Slaughter, Famine and Death. Especially Death, on his pale horse. That's all they bloody think about.*

But then he stopped dead in his tracks as he headed back to the kitchen, half listening to some other late report from the newscaster:

"Reports are coming in of a major oil spill in the Gulf of Iran. A giant crude-oil tanker is currently listing off the coast of Oman, with an apparently damaged bow section. According to Dubai shipping sources, oil is pouring out of her for'ard tanks."

"HOLY SHIT!" The Lieutenant charged right back into the living room, but the item was over. They were back on the President's forthcoming visit to India. Jimmy picked up the phone, dialed Fort Meade, spoke immediately to Lt. Ray Carpenter. . . . *"You got anything on a tanker leaking oil in the gulf?"*

"Come on, Jimmy. What do you think this is? Greenpeace? Nothing right now."

Despite himself, Lt. Ramshawe laughed. Then he called CNN news headquarters in Atlanta and asked if they had an accurate fix on where the tanker was. He announced himself as a director of Texas Gas Transport, told them he was afraid it might be one of his ships. In return he'd keep them posted if it was.

The CNN foreign desk was not much help but said he was more than welcome to call their man in Dubai, since it was already almost nine o'clock the following morning in the Middle East.

He thanked them profusely, dialed the number in Dubai and spoke to the reporter, David Alidai.

"Sorry, pal. I'm dealing with the Omani Navy's public affairs office. The only person in there's called Hassam, but he doesn't know much. I think he's been told to shut up until they assess the damage to the environment. But if you guys own the ship, he might be a bit more forthcoming. I'll give you his number. . . . Good luck."

Jimmy hit the dial buttons to Oman, and was put through to the aforementioned Hassam.

"I'm sorry. I cannot tell you anything. We know very little ourselves."

"Listen, Hassam, this may be our ship. We had a VLCC right in that area. . . . I'm just asking for a position. . . . Surely you can provide us with that. . . . Please try, otherwise I'll have to speak to the Admiral."

Jimmy had no idea what Admiral he was going to speak to, and Hassam could not have cared less, kept him waiting on the line for five minutes. Then he came back and said, Mr. Haig, the damaged ship is positioned at latitude 26.19 north, 56.49 east. She's in 250 feet of water."

"Hassam, I'm grateful. But I don't think that's us. It's a bit too far south. Do you know if there are any other ships in the area?"

"Well, we have two Qahir Corvettes out there trying to keep order. The strait is very busy. All tankers are being brought to a halt right now. . . . I believe there are two Iranian frigates out there also, but I can tell you no more."

Jimmy hung up and sprinted out of the apartment, willing the elevator to take him instantly down to the parking lot. He unlocked the Jaguar and retrieved the chart that he had left in the leather side pocket. He relocked and sprinted back to the elevator, which had not yet resumed its upward journey. ·

Inside the apartment he spread the chart on the dining table, scrabbled around for a ruler and measured. The stricken VLCC in the Hormuz Strait was only nine inches from the missile site, a fraction less than 18 miles. It was six inches from the *Global Bronco*, just less than 12 miles.

And it was pretty much on the line that joined the Iranian missile site and the spot where the *Bronco* had exploded yesterday.

"Jesus, Mary and Joseph," breathed Jimmy. "The bastards have mined the strait. And it's dollars to doughnuts the VLCC hit one of 'em with its bow."

He reached into his pocket and found the scrap of paper with the White House phone number. He checked his watch and saw it was 12.45 A.M. "Well, I didn't manage to get fired five hours ago, but I'm damn sure certain I'm going to pull it off now."

And he dialed the main switchboard of the White House. When they answered, he said, "This is Lieutenant Jimmy Ramshawe, Chief Surveillance Officer Middle and Far East, National Security Agency, Fort Meade. I need to speak to Admiral Arnold Morgan on a matter of extreme urgency. He WILL take the call. Please make it and then patch me through."

For the second time that evening, the White House interrupted the fearsome Security Chief. He and Kathy were home, sipping a glass of their favorite Sauternes, a sweet, silky 1995 dessert wine from the Gironde, before going to bed, when the phone rang.

"Sir, this is the White House main switchboard. We have a Lieutenant Jimmy Ramshawe on the line, who would like to be connected to you."

Admiral Morgan raised his eyes heavenward. But he took the call. "Jimmy," he rasped. "This better be awfully important."

"It is, sir. There's a second big tanker crippled in the Hormuz Strait. I just heard a flash on CNN. But I called Dubai, then the Omani Navy, and I got a position on the ship. It's eighteen miles from the missile site I mentioned, and it's twelve miles from the *Global Bronco*. More important, it's on a *dead-straight line* linking the two ships and the missiles. The odds against that have gotta be a zillion to one. They've mined it, sir. Of that I am now very sure."

Arnold Morgan hissed his breath inward. His thoughts raged through his mind. "Jimmy, where are you?"

"I'm in my apartment, sir. The Watergate."

"You are? Hell, I used to know an Australian Admiral who lived in there. You any relation?"

"My father, sir. Naval attaché here a few years back."

"Jesus. This is getting worse and worse. Your dad and I had a few times together. Lives in New York now, right? With Qantas?"

"That's him, sir."

"Okay. Now listen. I want you to meet me in my office in the White House in twenty minutes. I'm leaving right now. I'll have an escort for you at the West Executive Avenue entrance. You know where that is?"

"Yessir."

"And, Jimmy, speak to no one. Not a sentence. Not a phone call. This is very important. Believe me."

"Yessir."

"And, Jimmy, make sure you bring your working chart with you."

"Yessir."

Arnold Morgan stood up and walked to the top of the basement stairs in Kathy's large Chevy Chase home. He yelled instructions to his Secret Service detail, organizing Lt. Ramshawe's escort at the White House. He kissed Kathy good night, pulled on his coat and headed outside where his car and two agents were waiting.

"Straight to the factory, sir?"

"You gottit."

It was almost 1 A.M. when the black White House staff car came barreling over the Taft Avenue Bridge, driving swiftly down Connecticut Avenue. It was raining now, and the city was quiet. They crossed Dupont Circle and made their way to Seventeenth Street, swinging into West Executive Avenue from where they could see a Jaguar already being waved through to the West Wing.

Admiral Morgan met Lt. Ramshawe right outside the door, while four duty agents attended to his visitor's pass and parked his car.

The Admiral stuck out his hand, smiled, and said, "Hello, Lieutenant. Arnold Morgan."

Jimmy Ramshawe had met a few major men in his life, but this was different. The Admiral exuded power. He was all of seven inches shorter than Jimmy but his gaze was dead straight, his eyes bright blue and his grip strong. The Admiral's dark gray suit had been tailored somewhere in heaven, and his black lace-up shoes were gleaming. The perfectly knotted tie was that of the Naval Academy, Annapolis, a place and experience that Arnold

Morgan had never forgotten, and never would. He made Jimmy Ramshawe feel like a little boy.

And in response to the Admiral's curt but warm greeting, he just managed, "Sir." He'd used up all his daring and bravado for one night, making two unauthorized calls on the private line to the right-hand man of the President of the United States.

"Follow me," said the Admiral, to anyone who might be listening, which included the two Secret Service agents who were with him at all times, four White House agents, and Jimmy. And, line astern, they set off in the wake of the Admiral, who never walked; he kind of pounded along the carpet, chin out, shoulders back, dead upright. If a regular wall had suddenly appeared in front of him, he would have crashed right through it, like a Disney cartoon, leaving just the outline of his silhouette. He conducted the business of the United States of America along very similar lines.

At the big wooden door to his office he came to a halt, and his commands were sharp. . . . "Get me a competent secretary to sit in Mrs. O'Brien's chair right now. Tell someone to bring us coffee. . . . You hungry, Jimmy?"

"Yessir."

"Chicken sandwiches for the Lieutenant . . . and make sure someone's attending to my phone exclusively at all times . . . Aside from that, my regular agents take up positions right here . . . and have the hot line to the President on high alert . . . I may have to speak to him in a major hurry."

Everyone nodded. Admiral Morgan glared; turning to one of his regular agents, he barked, "No bullshit, right, Bobby?"

Bobby snapped to attention. "No bullshit. Sir, nossir."

It was a well-practiced routine, and everyone laughed.

"Okay, gentlemen, that's it. Lieutenant, let's get to work . . . and tell 'em to hurry up with the coffee in case we both fall asleep."

Inside the office, Jimmy spread his chart out on the Admiral's big desk. Arnold Morgan stared hard as the key spots were pointed out to him . . . the missiles, the *Global Bronco*, the stricken VLCC, currently pumping oil into the strait.

"Okay, Lieutenant, first things first. I want to know what the master of that ship actually saw. I guess if they slammed into a mine . . . What was it, a contact PLT-3 from Russia?"

"That was what the Chinese ordered, sir. So I'm assuming that."

"So'm I. Well, they make a pretty big bang in the water. The Captain must have heard something."

"I agree, sir. But the guy I spoke to in the Omani public affairs office was giving nothing away. It took me all my time to get him to tell me where the ship was."

"Well, if that's the case, I may have to kick a little ass. Hard. Do we know the name or the nationality of the ship?"

"Nossir."

"Okay. Well, the news guys will have that very soon. Meantime I'm gonna get the Royal Navy in London to do our work. The Brits are well in with the Omanis, have been for years. Just about every warship they own is British."

He picked up the telephone and ordered the new secretary, "Get me Admiral Sir Richard Birley on the line in Northwood, England. The numbers are in my big blue book, top right-hand drawer. . . . He'll be at home, right near the base. He's head of the Royal Navy's submarine service."

Less than two minutes later, the Admiral's old friend from London was on the line. The two men exchanged greetings, and the English submarine chief instantly agreed to have someone call the Omanis and find out precisely what was going on, who owned the ship and what the Captain had to say.

"I'll be back inside the hour, Arnie. . . . By the way, may I ask why you're treating this so urgently?"

"Not right now you can't."

"Well, you always have to wonder in those waters, *hmmmm*?"

"You always have to wonder√talk to you later, Dick."

The Admiral turned back to Jimmy Ramshawe, and he said quietly, "Lieutenant, I want you to listen very carefully. Only two people in this country believe the Iranians and the Chinese may have put a minefield across the strait. That's you and I.

"We may be wrong. But I think not. Your straight line on that chart is just too much of a coincidence. And I would not be that shocked if another ship blew before we're much older.

"But this is what I want you to understand: If this turns out to be true, we're going to be sitting on a colossal world oil crisis. The gulf will have to be shut down while we sweep and clear it, which is going to take weeks. Oil prices will go through the roof. The entire global economy could go berserk. Japan could come to a complete halt. A gallon of gas could go to six bucks right here in the U.S. . . . and what I'm trying to do right here is avoid a national panic, if that is at all possible."

"Yessir."

The chicken sandwiches arrived, a large plateful. Jimmy Ramshawe attacked them, and the Admiral had one himself while they waited for the English Admiral to call back.

He was on the line before 0200. "Arnold, the ship is Greek, Liberian registered. Only two years old. It's huge, three hundred thousand tons deadweight. Loaded with Saudi crude. The Captain and the crew are still on board. The ship is not sinking but it's ten degrees bow down, and it's currently belching seventy thousand cubic meters of oil from its for'ard tank."

"Any word from the Captain?"

"Yes, he made a statement to the Omani coast guard. Says there was a massive explosion, for no reason, way up at the bow. It completely ruptured one of the five holding tanks."

"Was she double hulled, Dick?"

"Oh, yes. Very heavily built in the Daewoo Shipyard, South Korea. Compartmentalized, too, throughout the hull. She'd be just about unsinkable . . . I expect you know, but she's only twelve miles away from the *Global Bronco*, which blew up yesterday."

"Yeah. We do know that. And right now I'd have to say that this, Sir Richard, ole buddy, is not good."

"This, Admiral Arnie, old chap, is becoming deeply unattractive."

April 28. The White House.
Washington, D.C.

WITH LIEUTENANT RAMSHAWE on his way home now, sworn to total silence, Admiral Morgan stood alone in his office at 0230. It was a situation not entirely unfamiliar to him, even on a Saturday morning. He yelled through the door for someone to bring him some fresh HOT coffee, and debated whether or not to call the President.

"Maybe not," he muttered. "It won't do any good. And as soon as the President knows, everyone knows. I think we need a little more time before the crap really hits the fan."

The first thing to do was to get a couple of minesweepers into the strait and take a closer look. Jimmy Ramshawe was to spend the morning screening all satellite pictures to check whether any tankers were making a successful through-passage. Arnold Morgan suspected any big fuel-oil carriers that did make it through would be either Chinese or Iranian. And that their cargo would either be direct from the refinery just east of Bandar Abbas, or from the new Chinese refinery farther down the coast. But Lieutenant Ramshawe would find that out.

The problem was minesweepers, the little specialist warships that locate the mines by towing a sweep wire through the water until it hits and cuts the mine's cable. The USA had some extremely effective sonar mine hunters in the Avenger Class, but they were mostly based along the Texas coast, and made only 13 knots. "Damn things would take forever to get there," the Admiral grumbled.

He pondered the Brits, wondering about the Royal Navy's excellent Hunt Class minesweepers. But again, the same problem . . . *slow, and half a world away from Hormuz.* No. He had to get someone much nearer, which meant, essentially, the Indians. . . . *What the hell time is it in Bombay?*

The question was rhetorical. Arnold Morgan knew more or less what time it was *everywhere.* And right now in the great Indian city of Bombay it was somewhere around midday. He picked up the telephone and asked his night-duty secretary, whom he'd never even seen, to connect him immediately to the Indian Embassy in Washington.

When the duty officer answered, the Admiral said simply, "This is Arnold Morgan, National Security Adviser to the President of the United States. I'm in the White House. Take down the following phone number, and have the Naval Attaché call me in the next four minutes. . . . Thanks. And hurry up." Click.

Three minutes and 22 seconds later, the telephone rang on his private line.

"This is Vice Admiral Prenjit Lal speaking. I believe you wanted me?"

"Hey, thanks for calling. I do appreciate it's the middle of the night, but my request is easy. I would like Admiral Kumar, your Chief of Naval Staff, to call the White House immediately and ask for me. I guess he's in Bombay?"

"Yes, Admiral. Today he is. I'll contact him right away."

"Stress that it's extremely urgent, will you?"

"The hour of the night tells me of the urgency, Admiral. I'll do it personally and immediately."

It took eight minutes. Admiral Kumar came on the line, insisting that he would be honored to provide any assistance he could to India's very great friends in the White House.

Arnold Morgan, however, knew this was only half true. What the mannered and apparently pliable Indian officer had not said was "Just so long as it will not damage our relations with our neighbors or allies, and so long as the U.S. would assist with whatever the cost might be." Unspoken hurdles.

Admiral Morgan elected to lay out the facts as swiftly and brutally as he could. He pulled no punches. And he went very carefully over the iron-clad fact of Jimmy Ramshawe's Straight Line. And he ended his little speech by saying: "I'm afraid all of the world's oil consumers are in this together. But yours is the nation with the most easily accessible minesweepers. . . . Admiral Kumar, you will have the full backing of the USA. I'll have two destroyers there to meet you, and you may assume all costs will be met by the big oil consumers, the U.S., the U.K., Japan, France, Germany, everyone.

"I'm sure you can appreciate the urgency . . . we simply cannot just sit here and wait for another tanker to blow up . . . we have to get in there, check it out and if necessary sweep a safe channel . . . and your Pondicherry Class minesweepers are the nearest."

"Admiral Morgan," replied the Indian Navy Chief, "I am indeed grateful for your call and your trust. If the Iranian Gulf was closed for even three weeks, my country would be in the most terrible trouble . . . aside from the regular petrol supplies, almost all of our propane gas for cooking comes from there. My country could come to a complete halt.

"Obviously we had noted the two tanker accidents. But no one had any idea it might be a concerted plot by the Iranians and the damnable Chinese. You may assume we will sail six of the Pondicherrys in the next twenty-four hours. You think we should take a tanker?"

"Yes I do. And escorts. Admiral Kumar, we do not yet know

precisely what we are dealing with here. But I can assure you of massive U.S. protection once your ships arrive at the strait. . . . One squeak out of the Chinese or the Iranians, and we'll put 'em on the bottom of the ocean. That's a promise."

"Excellent, Admiral. My attaché in Washington will be in contact in a few hours to give you times of sailing, an ETA, and further details of our escort. It's one thousand miles to the strait from Bombay, but the Pondicherrys make sixteen knots. We'll aim to sail at first light tomorrow morning, which should put us in the strait before dark on Tuesday."

"Thank you, Admiral Kumar. We look forward to working with you. I just wish the circumstances were less serious."

Arnold Morgan replaced the telephone, checked his watch at 0320 and opened up his private line to the Pentagon. He told the duty officer in the Navy Department to get the CNO on the line right away.

Sixty seconds later, Admiral Alan Dixon, former Commander-in-Chief of the Atlantic Fleet, betrayed no sign that he had been called in the small hours of the morning. The new Chief of Naval Operations said crisply, "'Morning, sir. Sorry if I kept you waiting."

"Not a bit, Alan. But what I have to say is rather long and complicated. Can you come to the White House right away? Where are you, in the Yard?"

"Yessir. Give me thirty."

"See you then. West Executive Avenue entrance."

The minutes ticked by slowly for the National Security Adviser. He debated the rather appealing possibility of waking "that stuffed shirt, Borden," but decided there was nothing to gain from such a malicious act. So he waited. Sipped his coffee, thought of Kathy. And waited.

At 0348 sharp, Admiral Dixon was escorted into the office, and for the second time that night, to a second slightly incredulous Navy chief, Admiral Morgan went over the whole scenario in the Strait of Hormuz.

Alan Dixon, a veteran destroyer CO from the Gulf War, nodded gravely. "I guess two sinkings in much the same place are beyond the bounds of likely coincidence, almost impossible we could be mistaken—I haven't heard the theory before. . . . I suppose that's your day's work, eh?"

"Not so, Alan. One of the brighter sparks on George Morris's staff. I'd like to support it, though."

"An interesting bit of deduction. And to tell the truth, sir, the Pentagon had not yet received a position on the second tanker when I left the office."

"No. Neither had anyone else. This young Lieutenant bamboozled his way into the public affairs office of the Omani Navy and pried it out of them."

"Good job! Love to hear it. Anyway, sir, what now?"

"Well, the Indian Navy is going to work with us sweeping the strait. We obviously have to start a major mine-clearance operation ASAP. I hope on Tuesday evening. They'll have a half dozen of those Russian-built Pondicherrys working, with an escort of their own. But I want to get a couple of our destroyers in there, and a CVBG as soon as we can."

Admiral Dixon pulled out a personal notebook, which detailed all of the five currently operational U.S. Carrier Battle Groups. The 55 ships that surrounded the huge carriers were just a little too much to commit to memory. And the highly methodical Boston-born Alan Dixon never went anywhere without that little notebook.

"Okay, sir," he said. "We're pretty well placed. The *Constellation* Group's stationed up at the north end of the Gulf off Iraq. We got *John C. Stennis* with nine guided-missile ships and two nuclear boats exercising in the Arabian Sea, probably a day and a half from the strait.

"*Harry S. Truman*'s battle ready at Diego Garcia. She's got a full complement of escorts, one cruiser, two destroyers, six frigates, two nuclear submarines, an LA and a Sturgeon, plus a complete Under Way Replenishment Group. *John F. Kennedy* has a full operational group just about ready to leave from Pearl at any time, certainly in the next three days.

"Back in San Diego the *Ronald Reagan*'s almost finished a

major overhaul. Her Group can be ready inside two months, if we need it."

"That's great, Alan. I guess we ought to have one right in the southern approaches to the strait and one inside the gulf, spread across the exit, with a lotta muscle concentrated south of Bandar Abbas. There's been a couple of pretty heavy Chinese destroyers prowling around there these past few weeks. Once the Indian minesweepers get in there, we'll get the President to issue a private warning to the Iranians . . . any ship attempting any kind of interference will be sunk. By us. No bullshit. Right?"

"Right, sir. Meantime I'll order the *Constellation* Group to proceed south toward Bandar, and the *Stennis* to close the strait. We'll put the *Harry Truman* on twenty-four hours battle notice to sail north from DG. It's getting pretty damned hot out there right now, and it's hard to keep guys out there on station for more than a couple of months without sending 'em all crazy.

"If I order the *Kennedy* to leave Pearl in the next couple of days, she can go straight to DG. That'll give us a four-group *roulement*, keeping two of them comfortably on station all the time. We can keep that up for a year if we have to."

"Good. How's the *Kennedy* doing. Christ, Alan, she's damn near forty years old."

"No problem, sir. She had that complete complex overhaul in 1995, made her just about brand-new. There's nothing wrong with her. No, sir. Old number sixty-seven, a little smaller than the Nimitz-Class boats, but she still holds nearly six thousand tons of aviation fuel. Seen a lot of service. She's like Senator Ted—indestructible. And just as bloody-minded when she feels like it."

Admiral Morgan chuckled. The language of the Navy. He still loved it. Still felt pride swell in his chest when the big U.S. ships prepared to flex their muscles. He'd felt it during his first nuclear submarine command more than 20 years ago, and the feeling had never diminished. Arnold Morgan's soul was essentially held together with dark blue cord, and gold braid.

Monday morning. April 30.
Officers' Mess. U.S. Naval Base.
Diego Garcia, Indian Ocean.

Lieutenant Commander Dan Headley was just one tour of duty short of promotion to Commander in the U.S. Navy's Pacific Submarine Fleet. At age 35, he was very proud of that. Right now he was generally regarded as one of the best submarine Executive Officers in the entire Navy. Experienced, a lifelong submariner, weapons and sonar expert, he had just flown to Diego Garcia to take up the number-two spot on the aging Sturgeon-Class nuclear boat, USS *Shark*.

This was one of the Navy's underwater warhorses, probably on her last tour of duty, since she had been due for decommission in 2005. *Shark* was the newest of the Navy's four Sturgeon attack submarines, and probably the best. The 5,000-tonner could make 30 knots through the water dived, she carried 23 weapons, Harpoon and Tomahawk missiles, plus torpedoes. On her deck, forward of the sail, there were two twin dry-deck shelters designed for the transport of a deep-submergence rescue vehicle (DSRV), an Advanced Swimmer Delivery Vehicle (ASDV) or a dry garage for three, even four, high-powered outboard inflatables.

Shark was quiet, extensively fitted with acoustic tiles, with anechoic coatings. She had the capacity to fire nuclear-warhead weapons, and she was capable of operating under the ice, though Dan Headley doubted that would be needed on her next journey.

He had been at the base for only three hours when word began to spread that there was something happening up in the Strait of Hormuz. Everyone knew the CVBGs of USS *Constitution* and *John C. Stennis* were already in the area. The issue was, how soon would the massive 100,000-ton Nimitz-Class *Harry Truman* and her consorts head north to join them in the narrow waters that guard Arabia's landlocked Sea of Oil?

No one knew that, but senior officers considered it more likely to be hours than days. It was 2,600 miles up to Bandar Abbas, and the *Truman* Group could steam at 30 knots, making 700 miles a day. If they cleared DG by first light tomorrow (Tuesday), they'd be in the area before dark on Friday afternoon.

Lieutenant Commander Headley had a lot of people to meet in the next 24 hours, and from each of them he had a minor secret to conceal. SUBPAC was not really happy with the veteran Commander Donald Reid, *Shark*'s commanding officer, and they had specifically appointed Dan Headley to assist him in every way possible.

As far as Dan was concerned it was just a wink and a nudge, because no one would tell him what, if anything, was wrong with Commander Reid, only that he was, well, "kinda eccentric." No one actually said "weird." But he'd been in the submarine service a lot of years and according to observers had shown "very occasional signs of stress."

In the modern Navy these matters are taken extremely seriously, unlike in the past when any sign of weakness or wavering was put down immediately as "shell shock" or "cowardice." In was not unusual for the offender to be cashiered, or, for the latter transgression, in the Royal Navy on one occasion, shot.

Dan Headley was looking forward to meeting the boss with rather mixed anticipations. But before he met anyone he had a letter to write, so he parked himself in a corner of the mess with a cup of coffee, and, following the habit of a lifetime, addressed the envelope before he wrote the letter: *Commander Rick Hunter, U.S. Navy Pacific Command, Coronado, California 92118.*

Dear Rick,

Just a short note to congratulate you on your promotion. Well deserved, I'm sure, even in that crazy outfit that employs you. All those years ago, when we set off together for Annapolis, I always thought we'd both end up commanding U.S. warships—rather than just me (I hope!), while you roll around in the mud with a dagger between your teeth and a pocketful of explosives.

Anyway I'm here in Diego Garcia waiting to take up my new position as XO on USS Shark. *My last, I'm told, before they make me up to Commander. Sometime in the next 24 hours we're due to sail north, to guess where? Anyway, by the time you read this the Kentucky Derby will be over. Hey, what a blast if White Rajah wins it. I guess your dad will forever regret selling him as a yearling, and my dad will forever keep reminding him that he told him not to! Still, victory would be sweet, since Bart still owns the dam, and two full sisters. That would be a real lock on a major American classic family—make you guys even richer.*

Funny, isn't it, to look back at that wicked old bastard Red Rajah, and think he might be the grandsire of a Derby winner, rather than an automatic selection for a lead role in Natural Born Killers. *Jeez, every time I think about him, my arm hurts!*

I have to go now, meet my new crew, hope to catch a glimpse of you, certainly at Christmas, if not before.

Best always and love to Bart,
Danny

He folded the letter and sealed the envelope. Then he walked out to the front desk and asked the security guard to mail it. It was only a short walk over to the submarine jetties where the *Shark* awaited him.

Same morning. Monday, April 30. Southern Fleet HQ. Zhanjiang.

"Yushu, you are very disappointed. I can see that."

"Well, Jicai, you would have thought the Western press would have been much more alert to the consequences of two shattered oil tankers within a few miles of each other in the middle of the Strait of Hormuz."

"Yes, I agree. But the time difference made it awkward."

"How?"

"Well, the *Washington Post* ran a piece on Saturday morning covering the big fire in the liquid-gas tanker. So did several other American newspapers, but no pictures. I suppose the cameras were just too far away. But when the second tanker was damaged, it was too late for their editions. And it was a much smaller story . . . just an oil spill in the gulf."

"You've studied the media more than I, Jicai. Has anyone made a connection?"

Only the Sunday edition of the *Dallas Morning News* in Texas. They have an interview with the owner of the *Global Bronco*, and right underneath it, they run a story about the oil spill. But they're not making a major point about the closeness of the two 'accidents.' "

"Then, my Jicai, we will quickly have to persuade them otherwise."

"Oh, I don't think that will prove too much of a problem . . . we are extremely well organized."

0900 (local). Same morning.
Washington, D.C.

Arnold Morgan had just issued a severe roasting to the Acting Director of the National Security Agency. And Admiral David Borden, frankly afraid now for his future, had gone straight to the office of Lt. Ramshawe, full of quasi-indignation that he had not been kept up to speed on the Hormuz investigation.

Jimmy Ramshawe debated the possibility of telling his boss to knock before he barged in, but decided against it. Nonetheless he detected that the Acting Director had been on the wrong end of the Big Man's wrath, and that was not a great place to be.

"It is essential you keep me up to date," he told the Lieutenant. "I am the person who must answer to Admiral Morgan, and it is most inconvenient when he knows more than I do."

Again Lt. Ramshawe exercised discretion, resisting the overpowering temptation to tell Borden that everyone knew more than he did.

Instead he said simply, "Sir, I was under the impression that you wanted the whole subject ignored until there was hard evidence. That's what you told me."

"Correct. But when the second tanker was damaged, surely you knew I must be informed of your investigation, the fact that the ships were so close."

"Sir, I wrote up my report and handed it to your duty officer on Saturday morning. I came in especially."

"Well, it did not reach me. Which put me at a tremendous disadvantage, because Arnold Morgan had worked it out precisely as you did."

The Ramshawe discretion vanished. "Sir, it is beyond my imagination that anyone could work it out any other way. The bloody towelheads and the Chinks have mined the bloody strait. I've been telling you that for a month. We even know where the bastards got the mines. I've also been telling you *that* for weeks. And if you still want my advice, I'm also telling you there's more to come on this."

Admiral Borden retreated, saying as he left, "Just make sure I'm kept up to speed on this. It is essential that I'm on precisely the same knowledge level as Admiral Morgan."

David Borden shut the door noisily, missing Jimmy Ramshawe's "That'll be the bloody day."

More importantly he had forgotten to ask what further developments there were, even though he could see the pile of satellite photographs on the young surveillance officer's desk.

Big mistake. Jimmy Ramshawe had pictures of four tankers, three Iranian, one Chinese, making passage out of the gulf on the Iran side of Hormuz. They had all crossed the line of the minefield, exiting through an area less than three miles wide, four and a half miles offshore at the nearest point.

"That's it," he murmured. "They're still transporting Iranian crude, and Chinese refined oil from Kazakhstan, right through that gap, while the rest of the world sits and waits for clearance from the Omanis to continue on. And they're not going to get it. The strait is going to become a giant tanker park, while the Ayatollahs and the Chinese get rich."

He picked up the secure telephone and dialed the main White House switchboard, from where he was put straight through to Admiral Morgan, as instructed. "It's between fifty-six-fifty-six and fifty-six-fifty-nine-east, sir," he said. "Four ships so far, three Iran, one China."

"Thanks, Jimmy. Go tell your boss, while I tell mine."

The afternoon newspapers came up, and still no one was making any kind of speculation that something was drastically wrong in the Strait of Hormuz. Arnold Morgan paced his office, wracking his brains, waiting for the inevitable. Jimmy Ramshawe stayed at his desk long after his shift was over, staring at the satellite photographs, occasionally talking to the CIA's Middle Eastern desk at Langley. But there was nothing. Just the shattering coincidence of two ships damaged in the same stretch of water in the strait.

The President had listened to Admiral Morgan's suspicions with equanimity. The relationship between the two men was at a very low point. Eight months previously Arnold Morgan had threatened to quit, and to take the President with him. Everyone knew he could have done so. The grotesque scandal and cover-up over the incident last year in the South China Sea were like a loaded revolver at the Chief Executive's head. John Clarke would sit out his final months in the Oval Office, courtesy of his National Security Adviser.

And he was not a man to relish this. Thus he treated any warning from his supposed right-hand man with suspicion and a negative turn of mind. He had been receptive to the idea of moving heavy Naval muscle up into the strait, because he recognized the lethal consequences of being wrong. He stated curtly that such matters were what the Admiral was paid to do, and to proceed as he thought fit.

He later sent a memorandum to Admiral Morgan outlining the gist of their conversation, and absolving himself of any blame whatsoever if this thing blew up in everyone's face, with the entire Navy on the move at huge expense, for nothing.

Arnold Morgan screwed up the memo and tossed it, dismissing its contents as the ramblings of a disarranged mind, if not those of a "total asshole."

1900 (local). April 30.
The Strait of Hormuz.

The American-owned crude carrier *Galveston Star* was, without question, the biggest VLCC currently operating in the Gulf. She had a deadweight of 420,000 tons, and her six cargo tanks were fully laden with 450,000 cubic meters of oil, loaded from the man-made steel island at Mina al Ahmadi off the Kuwaiti coast. She was bound for the Gulf of Mexico, and making 20 knots, just about due east now, through Hormuz.

Her comms room had picked up the warning from the Omani Navy that temporary restrictions were in operation and that there was no clear seaway out to the Arabian Sea at this time. The restricted area ran in a line from Ra's Qabr al Hindi on the northern Omani coast right across to the Iranian shore more than 30 miles away at position 25.23N, 57.05E. No explanation was offered, save for the fact that a LNG carrier had burned out three days ago, and a damaged VLCC was still leaking oil a dozen miles farther east.

Captain Tex Packard was unimpressed. His tanker took almost four miles to come to a halt traveling at this speed. He was late, after a pump problem at al Ahmadi where he had spent almost 34 hours loading, instead of the scheduled 21. And it was hotter than hell. All he wanted to do was "drive this baby the fuck out of this godawful place and get home to the Gulf Coast of the USA," where, incidentally, it was also hotter than hell.

Captain Tex was not just a dyed-in-the-wool, lifelong tanker man. He was a copper-bottomed purist, even among the men who drive these technological atrocities along the world's oceans. His ship was almost a quarter of a mile long, and he knew every inch of her.

He was a great blond-haired bull of a man from the Panhandle plains of northwest Texas, where, he constantly reminded his shipmates, a man could still make a living on the back of a horse, riding the vast cattle ranches. Why, his own family had been doing so for generations, and he was the very first of the Packard cowboys to leave those wide-open spaces for a different kind of wilderness.

At the age of 47, Captain Tex still spoke fondly of the Panhandle city of Lubbock, where he had attended Texas Tech University in the hometown of the legendary rocker Buddy Holly. In fact Buddy had died the year before Tex was born, but the big sea captain spoke of him as if they had been fast friends "back home in Lubbock."

And there were still sweltering evenings in the Iranian Gulf when the distant cries of the mullahs summoning the faithful on the echoing loudspeakers above the mosques mingled out on the calm water with the unmistakable sounds of "Peggy Sue," "Maybe Baby," and "Oh Boy!" drifting out from the bridge of the gigantic *Galveston Star.*

First thing Captain Tex did when he welcomed a new crew was to make sure they could join in the chorus of "Peggy Sue," and to make equally certain the cook knew precisely how to make the fabled Texas dish of chicken-fried steak (CFS). He showed them how to pulverize the beef to within an inch of its life with a kitchen mallet, then hand-dip it in egg batter, double-dredged in seasoned flour, before dropping it into searing-hot oil in an iron skillet.

"That's CFS, boy," he would rumble in his deep baritone drawl. "Cook that raht, and you'll get a place on the highest honor role in mah home state. Ain't but a few cooks can git it just raht, and I want you to *join* that golden group, hear me?"

There was, however, nothing of the buffoon about Tex Packard. He was a superb navigator, and supremely confident in his own unique ability to handle his city-sized vessel, probably the biggest ship there had ever been, and just about indestructible, with her double hull and watertight compartments. As he frequently reminded his crew, "Fifty years ago the British and French landed an army at Suez with nothing else to do 'cept keep the crude-oil carriers moving."

He knew the history of the world of tankers, understood that normal life, for millions and millions of people, rested entirely on the free and unimpeded passage of these monster ships.

It was thus a surprise to no one when Captain Tex Packard told his Chief Engineer, his Cargo Officer and his Chief Officer he had no intention of stopping for the goddamned Omani Navy, whatever their problem was. "Christ, you could lose their entire country in West Texas. . . . We'll keep steering zero-nine-zero, and make our southerly turn when we're just out of Oman's national water, but not far enough into the Iranian side. Right then we're going straight through. Next stop, the Texas Gulf Coast, and no more bullshit.

"Hold this easterly course," he ordered. "And maintain speed."

The Chief Engineer, Jeb Duross, from south Louisiana, said routinely, "This course is gonna take us clear across the incoming tanker lanes. We'd better keep a good watch and a lot of radar."

"According to the Omanis, 'most every ship's stopped, waiting for clearance," replied the Captain. "So I don't guess we're gonna get a whole lot of tonnage coming across our bows. Anyway, we'll pick 'em up miles away. No problem."

The *Galveston Star* plowed forward. Twenty knots was a good speed for a VLCC, but she was already late, and at this time Captain Packard was prepared to sacrifice fuel for speed. His ship had a range of over 12,000 miles, and up on the bridge, 100 feet above the surface of the water, Buddy Holly was about to rock the high command of the tanker down toward the Iranian end of Jimmy Ramshawe's Straight Line.

By now there were several "paints" on the radar, showing tankers making some kind of a holding pattern inside the gulf in the northeastern national waters of Oman. The far side of the tanker lanes, incoming, seemed more or less deserted. There was a depth of 180 feet below the keel, and, in clear seas on longitude 56.44E, Captain Packard made a southeasterly turn, selecting a course that would take him five miles north of the stricken Greek tanker, before he turned due south and went for the Line.

Of course, only Admiral Morgan and Lt. Ramshawe were certain of the existence of the regular three-line minefield, the PLT-3-moored sea mines every 500 yards. The laying of mines in the dark is an inexact science, but in general terms, this meant there was a mine in the path of any ship separated by a maximum distance of around 170 yards.

It also meant that if a ship slid by the first one, missing it by, say, 10 yards to starboard, the next one would come up 160 yards to port, and the next two after that 340 yards to port, and 170 to starboard. It was thus possible to miss them altogether, as many ships had. But it was still the maddest game of Russian roulette ever invented, especially for this particular tanker. The giant *Galveston Star* was 75 yards wide.

Three miles short of the first line, Captain Packard received a formal warning from one of the Omani Navy Corvettes that it was dangerous to proceed. No one was yet admitting there may be a minefield, and the warning thus had no teeth so far as big Tex Packard was concerned. "Screw 'em," he confirmed. "We're outta here."

Up ahead the seas were clear. At least they were on the surface, and the *Galveston Star* came barreling down the strait in a freshly developed high wind off the Arabian desert, an early harbinger of the evolving southwest monsoon.

This part of the gulf was a wind-convergence zone, where, in the late spring, the northeasters out of the central Chinese desert, which prevail all winter, gave way to the southwesters from Africa. This year they were early. And strong gusty breezes can catch the massive hull of a VLCC and cause a significant leeway.

The *Galveston Star* was thus sliding infinitessimally east as she stood fair down the strait, plowing through the short surface waves, having completed her long gentle turn toward the south.

In fact, she missed the first of Admiral Zhang's mines by at least 150 yards to starboard. But the good news on Line One was almost certainly going to put her bows awfully close to the PLT-3 moored on Line Two.

On she ran for another 600 yards, still drifting very slightly east, closing the gap between her own course and the murderous one-ton, steel-encased hunk of TNT that bobbed on its wire mooring 12 feet below the surface.

The massive bows of the *Galveston Star* actually missed it completely, and the wash of the widening hull pushed the mine away on its wire. However, it swung back inward, hard and fast, crashing into the port side of the hull, 300 feet from the point of the bow.

At four minutes past 8 P.M. it detonated with awesome force, blowing the plates apart, right through both layers of the hull, blasting a massive hole in Cargo Tank Four. And Buddy Holly was still singing as the onrushing crude oil blew up in a raging fireball above the ocean.

"Stars appear and shadows a-falling . . . you can hear my heart a-calling. . . . Oh boy!"

Tex Packard could not believe his eyes. And the 420,000-tonner shuddered in its death throes as her colossal weight began to tear the entire hull apart. It was the biggest shipwreck in history, and it was only four miles from the Greek tanker that had been pouring out oil since Saturday. The *Galveston Star* was wallowing bang on Jimmy Ramshawe's Straight Line, 12 miles off the coast of Iran.

Captain Packard knew a career-blowing decision when he saw one. And he'd just made it.

"What are you going to do, sir?" asked Jeb Duross, anxiety written all over his face

"Probably buy a cattle ranch," replied Big Tex, thoughtfully.

"Actually, I meant right now."

"Send out a *MAYDAY!* Radio Oman and Dubai, see if we can salvage any of the cargo, which I doubt. At least not yet, till we can get a couple of big ships out here to start pumping. Meanwhile we just gotta watch the fires. Crude sometimes doesn't burn, but ours is doing just that, and once it gets started, it's likely to go on for a long time."

"Looks like the fire's inside the ship, and that might be real dangerous," said Jeb.

"Sure might. She gets much hotter, we'll have to abandon. Sure hate to leave her, but this stuff can really burn gets hot enough. I'm not planning to be the hero, least not the dead hero. . . . Have the lifeboats ready, Jeb, and have someone turn off the music, willya? . . . Just don't want Buddy singing in a death ship. 'Sides I wanna get mah CDs home to Texas . . . Buddy wouldn't wanna be singing to no towelheads."

All mah life I been a-waiting . . . tonight there'll be no hesi-tatin' . . . Oh boy!

Midday (local). Fort Meade, Maryland.

Lieutenant Ramshawe had his small office television turned on several minutes early for CNN's 12 o'clock bulletin, and when he heard the lead item there was no longer any doubt in his or anyone else's mind.

"We are receiving reports that one of the biggest oil tankers in the world, the four-hundred-twenty-thousand-ton Galveston Star *out of the Texas Gulf port of Houston, is currently on fire and breaking up in the Strait of Hormuz at the entrance to the Persian Gulf.*

"The cause of the accident is at present unknown, but the Captain and his crew are believed to be preparing to abandon her. Fires are reported raging over one hundred feet into the skies.

"This is the third major shipping accident in the strait in the past four days, following the inferno of the liquid-gas car-rier Global Bronco *of Houston, on Friday, and the explosion in the Greek crude carrier* Olympus 2004 *on Saturday."*

The newscaster ended the report by stating the U.S. Navy would be issuing a statement later in the afternoon, but as yet there was no suggestion that any nation had elected to place sea mines in the strait to endanger world oil-shipping routes.

Right at that moment Jimmy's phone rang, and he heard the gruff and distinct tones of Admiral Morgan. "Okay, Jimmy, I guess that does it. Go keep your boss up to speed, but keep me personally alerted to any information you get off the overheads."

The phone went down before Lt. Ramshawe could even answer. And before he could gather his wits, his other phone went, and Jane was on the line, telling him how clever he was, and would he be able to have dinner tonight with her, and her parents, at the embassy.

"You seen the television?" he asked her.

"Darned right I did. I was watching it with my dad. He said immediately the Iranians had mined the area, just as they'd been threatening to do.

"I told him that was my considered opinion, too. Told him I'd suspected something like that since the *Bronco* went up last Friday. . . . He gave me a real old-fashioned look."

"I should think he did. But he doesn't know about the phone call, does he—the one from his private line?"

"No. At least he hasn't said anything. Anyway, are you coming tonight? He's got some Aussie sailors coming, yachtsmen, America's Cup guys. Might be fun."

"Yup. I'll be there. 'Bout seven."

1300. Same day. The Oval Office.

Admiral Morgan recounted the events in the gulf swiftly and with no elaboration.

The President sat impassively, and asked curtly, "Your recommendations?"

"Sir, I have already ordered the *Constellation* CVBG south from the Iraqi coast, and the *John C. Stennis* Group is closing the strait immediately from the Arabian Sea. Our third Group in the area, the *Harry S. Truman*'s, should clear Diego Garcia by tomorrow morning and head north. I've arranged for the Indian Navy to begin a hunt-and-sweep operation with their Pondicherrys as soon as they can get there. Right now they're on their way from Bombay, probably be in Hormuz waters by tomorrow morning our time. . . . I had them leave on Sunday."

"Do you think there could be full-scale hostilities, Admiral? I don't want to get drawn into an unpopular war with Iran. Dead American sailors don't play well politically."

"Sir, this is probably the height of our national interest. Do you have any idea what might happen if the gulf had to be closed off for a month?"

"I cannot say I have given it deep thought, Admiral. But I am much more concerned about sitting in this chair being universally blamed for death, destruction and burned Americans. Because that's what happens when you start flexing the muscles of big warships."

"If we don't start flexing them, sir, the entire world oil supply could go right up the chute. And if the lights went out in the USA, you'd get yourself a very special place in history. Especially if you had refused to act in the Persian Gulf in the face of hostility and threats from Iran and their buddies in Beijing."

"As usual, Admiral, you have my best interests at heart." There was an edge of sarcasm in the President's voice.

"Perhaps not, sir. But I always have the best interests of this nation at heart."

"Then proceed as you think fit, Admiral. You always do, anyway. . . . Just let me know if I need to make a speech, will you? And perhaps Harcourt should make some kind of diplomatic overtures to the Chinese and the Iranians?"

"Two reasons not to, sir. One, it will alert the entire world to a crisis we may be able to strangle at birth. Two, they'll just deny everything anyway, and probably be very amused at our concern. 'Specially if they've done it, which I already know they have."

Arnold Morgan did not wait for a reply. He just turned on his heel and left, muttering to himself, "What a lightweight. What a goddamned lightweight. In five years he's gone from being a damned good president to a self-serving wimp."

By late afternoon every evening newspaper in the country was speculating about the possibility of a minefield in the Strait of Hormuz. The longtime threat of the Ayatollahs was uppermost in the mind of every defense correspondent in every corner of the media.

Television networks waited with scarcely contained excitement for the statement from the U.S. Navy. But when it came it was stark and noncommittal, precisely the way Arnold Morgan had instructed.

The CNO had declined a press conference and issued his written statement, deliberately late, at 21.30, through the main wire services, carefully avoiding anything that would suggest panic to either the Chinese or the Iranians.

It read: "*The United States Navy has noted the three tanker incidents in the Strait of Hormuz during the last four days. In particular we noted that two of them burned, and one suffered an apparent explosion that released large quantities of oil into the sea. In addition, we noted that all three incidents occurred in a narrow seaway between the countries of Oman and Iran.*

"*We have been in contact with our major allies in the area and have agreed to support them in their efforts to ascertain the causes of these incidents, and to discover whether there might be a link between them.*

"*However, it is too early to arrive at any conclusions. We expect at least one of our aircraft carriers and her escorts to arrive on station in the strait in the next 24 hours. Another U.S. CVBG is currently steaming toward the strait from the Arabian Sea.*

"*In company with several other industrial nations, we are extremely concerned to ensure the continued free passage of the world's fuel tankers through the strait both into, and out of, the Gulf of Iran.*

"*We have assured our allies of our continued assistance, should it become necessary to rectify any wrongdoing by any nation in these peaceful trading waters upon which so many countries depend.*"

It was signed, *"Admiral Alan Dixon, Chief of United States Naval Operations."*

It was good, but not good enough. Four East Coast tabloid dailies were already setting headlines like: MINEFIELD TERROR IN THE GULF . . . TANKERS BLOWN UP IN GULF MINEFIELD. IRAN'S MINES BLAST U.S. TANKERS.

All through the evening the television networks developed their stories, bringing in experts to discourse on the dangers in that part of the Middle East; recounting Iranian threats over the years; debating the possible involvement of China; discussing the consequences of an oil blockade.

By midnight, the President had called an emergency cabinet meeting in President Reagan's old Situation Room in the West Wing. And there the major brains in the Administration attempted to walk the tightrope between being prepared militarily and creating mass panic at the gas pumps.

Arnold Morgan, whose voice would be heard the loudest, since he had been effectively on the case since Friday, was, uncharacteristically, urging caution. He wanted the CVBG in the strait to protect and assist the Indian Navy's minesweepers. However, he saw no real advantage in making overt threats to either the Iranian or Chinese navies, save to make them absolutely aware that if any of their warships attempted to interfere, they would be sunk forthwith by U.S. Naval firepower.

As far as the National Security Adviser was concerned, the U.S. Navy had the matter well in hand. And with the strait now well and truly off-limits to all world shipping, there seemed little point in looking for trouble until the Indians' Pondicherrys had begun work clearing the mines. In order to clear a three-mile-wide safe passage on the Omani side, Admiral Morgan estimated they might have to sweep 40 of them, which might take several days beginning Tuesday night (local time).

Minesweeping was a thoroughly dangerous business, and it had to be conducted and executed with extreme care. The President wanted to know how it was done, and Arnold Morgan suggested that Admiral Dixon enlighten everyone.

"Sir," said the CNO, "when you locate the mine, it's going to be ten or twelve feet below the surface, attached by its cable to a mooring on the floor of the ocean. Basically it's buoyant, and it's trying to float up to the surface, but is held down by its own cable.

"Well, you sweep them by towing cutting cables from the minesweeper, pulled down to the right depth and out from the side by an otter board. When the sweeper's cable snags a mine's mooring line, it keeps moving until both cable and line are taut. Then the cutter severs the line, allowing the mine to float to the surface. There it can be detonated by small-arms fire from a safe distance. They're easy when they're on the surface, but of course impossible when you can't see them. However many times you've done it, you're always astounded by the size of the explosion."

"Hey, that's pretty neat," said the President.

"And pretty time-consuming," replied the Admiral.

"How many sweepers are the Indians bringing?"

"Six," replied Admiral Morgan. "That'll help speed things up."

"Cost?" asked the Secretary of Defense, Bob MacPherson, predictably.

"I told the Indian Navy Chief that we would arrange for all affected nations to share the costs. Between us, the U.K., the Japanese, Germans, France and some of the Middle East exporters, it'll come out as peanuts."

"No problem," said MacPherson.

"Look, Arnold," said the President, using his adviser's first name for the first time in months, "I know you want to play this down right now. But I'm not sure we shouldn't go straight into Beijing and demand to know if they have played any part in this whatsoever."

"Sir, they will simply deny any knowledge, whatever we say . . . and that brings me to a very serious point."

"It does?"

"Yessir. From our observations it looks very much as if the mines were transported to Iran in Chinese warships. And now we have a situation where, for the next couple of weeks, the Iranians are going to get pretty rich. And to an extent so are the Chinese.

They seem to have a way through the minefield, in Iranian national waters, and the price of oil futures is probably going to forty dollars a barrel for West Texas Intermediate on NYMEX and the same for Brent Crude on the London market.

"However, I completely fail to see what the Chinese are doing. How could it possibly be worth it?"

"Maybe they just want to show us they can be real world players in the oil game with their new Kazakhstan pipeline," offered Harcourt Travis.

"Maybe," replied Arnold Morgan. "But that's a hell of a dangerous card to play for such a slim moral victory. Christ, for all they know, we might get seriously pissed off with 'em. It just doesn't make any sense to me."

"Well, Admiral, perhaps the political minds at the table can offer something that may have escaped you?"

"Beats me, sir," said Harcourt.

"All I know is this," said the National Security Adviser. "The Chinese are very devious, very patient and utterly insincere when it suits them. What they are not is very stupid. And, so far, everything in the Strait of Hormuz is plain stupid. What the hell are they doing getting mixed up in something like this?"

"I guess they have their reasons," said the President. "But even more worrisome is what the hell are the Iranians playing at? I know they believe the gulf of Iran is, by its very name, theirs by rights, and that the West has no real business in there at all. But they also know that if they attempt a blockade of the gulf, we'll dismantle it, and probably them with it. They're not stupid, so what are they doing?"

"Six weeks ago, I could not have answered that question, sir," said Arnold Morgan. "But things are coming to light. And again we are seeing a new rise in Muslim fundamentalism. Again the balance of political opinion is swaying against the West, and every damn time that happens you get a new militant resurgence in Iran. All those pictures we got from Tehran a month ago . . . the street riots . . . the new calls for elections. They were all shouting for the same thing—total separation from the West, the right to their own oil, the right to make the gulf private . . . the enduring vision of Islamic world domination.

"It's a phase, but it's a problem. Meanwhile, the present blockade of the Iranian Gulf is a giant-sized PITA . . . pain-in-the-ass, that is. We gotta get it cleared or we're looking at world economic chaos."

Tuesday morning. May 1.
PLAN HQ. Beijing.

Admiral Zhang Yushu had just walked into his new office, where his Navy C-in-C, Admiral Zu Jicai, was already waiting.

"And what do the satellites tell us today?" he asked.

"Excellent news all around, Yushu. Two American CVBGs are closing the strait. The *Harry Truman* is plainly preparing to leave Diego Garcia today, and the U.S. carrier *John F. Kennedy* is under way, heading west out of Pearl Harbor."

"That leaves just the *Ronald Reagan* Group still in San Diego, correct?"

"Yessir, and all the signs are that she is accelerating her overhaul, planning to leave in the next few weeks. There is truly the most thunderous commotion in the United States—every newspaper, every television network. They're becoming hysterical about this threat to their national interest in the Strait of Hormuz."

"Perhaps we should offer to sell them some very fine Russian oil, direct from our refinery in Iran . . . very cheap . . . fifty dollars a barrel . . . ha ha ha!"

"Yushu, you are a hard man. Although I admit the prospect has great appeal, I would counsel silence. Say nothing. Do nothing. See nothing."

"Meanwhile, to more important matters, Jicai. Are these military estimates accurate? We still have sea-lift capacity for only twelve thousand troops? And two hundred fifty main battle tanks?"

"Yessir. But the turnaround time for our amphibians will be short."

"Are the ships on their way back from the Indian Ocean?"

"Yessir."

"Excellent. That's the three guided-missile frigates, plus two Kilos?

"Correct. They're all on their way home, sir. And as you know, the destroyer is making its way back toward Bandar Abbas, just as a warning to the USA . . . that we don't want them to attack our friends in Iran, under any circumstances."

"Ah, but it's a mission well achieved. Eh, my Jicai?"

"In the ancient tradition of the great Admiral Zheng He, sir. Just as you always dreamed."

"And such a dream, my Jicai. Remember the words we all learned, the words written by the immortal Admiral five hundred years ago . . . *And we have set eyes on Barbarian regions far away . . . while our sails, loftily unfurled like clouds, day and night, continued their course as rapidly as a star, traversing those savage waves. . . .*"

Zhang paused for just a moment. And then he said quietly, "That's our tradition . . . and it's only been dormant. Not dead. We will rise to rule those seas again."

0955 (local). Tuesday, May 1.
The International Petroleum Exchange.
London, England.

No day in the entire 26-year history of Europe's principal oil futures trading floor had ever been awaited with more dread, trepidation and alarm. Here in the shadow of the Tower of London, bounded by streets with echoing names like Thomas More, hard by the waters of historic St. Katherine's Dock, the industrial world's fate hung in the balance.

Five hours before New York's NYMEX oil trading gets under way on Wall Street, the London Exchange opens for business, setting the world's pricing benchmark for the day, maybe the month. The commodity is Brent Crude Futures, and the price per barrel of North Sea oil is the one upon which the major international traders and investors are prepared to speculate.

If the traders think there's likely to be a glut of oil in the foreseeable future, the price may go below $15, trading narrowly, varying by just a few cents either way. Any sign of a shortage, and the price may rise to around $30. A serious shortage can cause this swerving, volatile market to lose all sense of caution. When Iraq invaded Kuwait back in 1990, everyone thought the roof had caved in, and on one lunatic day at the International Petroleum Exchange (IPE), Brent Crude hit $70 a barrel.

Today the atmosphere was fraught. Captain Tex Packard's ship was still on fire in the strait, and in London nervous representatives of the big oil producers, refiners, shippers, distributors and marketers mingled with other major users. Brokers representing the power generators, airlines, truck fleet operators, chemical companies and even supermarkets were on tenterhooks. The world's most eminent money men from houses like Morgan Stanley were massed along with everyone else on the packed hexagonal-shaped trading floor, with its tiered pits, video surveillance and colossal security.

The previous night, Brent Crude had closed at $28 a barrel, up three bucks. And West Texas Intermediate in New York was tagged at a few cents below. Today cell phones were running up massive bills connecting the U.S. traders with London, long before the opening bell at NYMEX. What mattered right now was the opening bell in London, and the traders, wearing their identifying colored jackets, red, yellow, green or blue, thronged above the pits as the clock ticked on to 10 o'clock.

Bang on time it rang, signaling the floor was open for business, trading at first in natural-gas futures, the prices for which would explode before this day was done.

One minute went by, and then the clock hit 10:02 and the second opening bell rang sharp and loud, for the initial trades of Brent Crude Futures, the world pricing benchmark; at which point, on this day, the entire system of international oil commodity trading went berserk.

Pandemonium broke out as buyers yelled "PLUS TWO . . . PLUS TWO!" But these weren't cents, as in the regular cries of *"BRENT PLUS TWO!"* These were whole dollars. Thirty, then $32, then $35, then $40. Bedrock prices for a barrel of oil had jumped 33 percent in nine minutes.

"Mother of God!" breathed the broker for Shell. And the trader for a New York Bank roared "PLUS FIVE . . . PLUS FIVE FOR 500,000 . . . ." Which pegged the price of Brent Crude Futures at an astounding $45 a barrel.

Dealers left behind in the stampede for the best prices surged forward as a rumor swept the pits that the price was going to $70. Brokers for the big finance houses huddled together, uncertain whether to chase the price up further, or whether to wait for the retreat some thought might not come. At least not on this day.

Snatches of conversation fired the desperate atmosphere. Yelling, classless British voices from London, interspersed with louder American tones. . . . *"Jesus H. Christ! This can't last . . . Bullshit it can't . . . they've just closed the fucking Gulf of Iran. . . . It's only three ships, for chrissakes! It doesn't matter a flying fuck if it's only one . . . right here we're talking fucking minefields! That's one step from global war . . . the U.S. Navy's moving THREE aircraft carriers into the strait . . . you think this market's fake? Forget it. There might be no more oil out of the gulf for six months."*

Five minutes later the price hit $50 when a Rotterdam trader bid on a precious cargo of Shell crude currently on its way to Scandinavia. For a brief four minutes the price hung and then faltered at around $50. Then a rumor swept the floor that a major fleet of minesweepers from the Indian Navy was under escort moving up the Arabian Sea to the strait.

The price of Brent Crude Futures hit $55 in 42 seconds. And by now it was impossible to hear anything above the thunder of the pits as the traders piled in, bellowing bids for any available crude oil already free of the confines of the Gulf of Iran. On a normal trading day, 50 million barrels changes hands in this room. In today's uproar, almost 30 million were traded in the first 45 minutes. There was only one thing worse than paying through the nose for oil, and that was not having any.

"PLUS TWO . . . PLUS FOUR . . . PLUS WHATEVER IT TAKES."

By 11 o'clock that morning the price of world fuel oil had doubled. By the close of trade it stood at $72. Up over 150 percent. No one in the International Petroleum Exchange had ever seen anything like it. In New York, West Texas Intermediate had *opened* at $60 a barrel. Gas oil futures had gone through the roof, and Natural Gas futures, thanks to the exploded *Global Bronco*, were even higher.

1630 (local). Tuesday, May 1.
The White House.

Admiral Morgan stared at the pile of data before him. The minesweepers were in action in Hormuz, and there was no doubt the field was composed entirely of Russian-made PLT-3s. So far as the Indian commanding officers were concerned, they were looking at three lines, less than half a mile apart. Inshore on the Omani side, they were in deep water, and it looked as though the same three lines stretched clean across the strait to the Iranians' Sunburn missile site. Lieutenant Ramshawe had thus far been correct in all of his assumptions.

But now the tasks facing Fort Meade were different. Question One was Where is China now deploying the warships? The Kilos appeared to have disappeared from the face of the earth, but the two frigates that had been flying the national flag of Iran had been picked up by the overheads traveling toward China's Burmese base in the Bassein River. The *Shantou* had already left there and was making her way toward the Malacca Strait. But of China's big Sovremenny destroyer there was no sign.

Quite frankly, the Chinese completely baffled the President's National Security Adviser. For a start, he had no idea what they hoped to achieve by providing the hardware for the Ayatollahs to mine the Strait of Hormuz. Nonetheless they had plainly done it, and the Western world along with Japan and Taiwan, and to an extent South Korea, was presently in deep trouble. The world would run out of oil in a matter of weeks if the Gulf of Iran was not opened up very quickly.

The Chinese obviously thought they were immune to this chaos, and in Arnold Morgan's opinion they must be taught a very sharp lesson. It might be possible to tweak and irritate the United States, but when you start tampering with the national interest of the world's one superpower, you might very well end up in deadly serious trouble. Nonetheless Admiral Morgan was determined not to overreact until he could ascertain what the men in Beijing were doing.

Not so the President. He went into a complete dither as world oil prices went into some kind of meltdown, or rather a meltup. Constantly on the line to his Energy Secretary, Jack Smith, he kept asking, over and over, "But what's this going to mean for the average American at the gas pump?"

As early as midafternoon, answers were coming in fast and furious. And they were all the same. Up, up, and up again, as the big gas-station chains found themselves paying fortunes for every barrel of crude oil on either side of the Atlantic. West Texas Intermediate looked set to close even higher than Brent Crude Futures. And still Big Tex Packard's mighty tanker blazed alone out in the strait, lighting up the waters. When the gusting wind swung back around to the northeast, it sent a gigantic black oil cloud into the night skies above Arabia.

In a week when gas prices could very easily hit three dollars a gallon at the pump, or even three-fifty, President Clarke faced rampaging inflation on a scale that would send the Federal Reserve into shock. Every commodity and product in the USA was going to suffer because of drastic increases in transport costs. Taxis, buses, diesel freight trains, interstate trucks, airlines, especially airlines, anything that moved was going to be hit.

And that was not the worst of it. President Clarke had a vision of the ultimate national uproar. The United States starting to run out of oil, with no time to tap its own deep reserves. High gas prices were one thing. No gas at any price was entirely another. If the country ground to a halt, his name would surely be remembered as one of the most ineffective Presidents in the entire history of the nation. And what the hell was his oh-so-brilliant National Security Adviser doing about it? As far as he could see, a big fat zero.

He picked up his phone and asked a secretary to have Admiral Morgan report to him instantly. Two minutes later, Arnold came growling in through the open door to the Oval Office.

"You wanted me, sir?"

"Admiral, what the hell are we doing about this standoff in the gulf?"

"Sir, we got a minefield across the Strait of Hormuz, as I explained. The gulf is now shut. The Iranians are saying nothing, admitting nothing and they sure as hell aren't about to clear it. Neither are their buddies in Beijing.

"That means we have to clear the minefield ourselves, and the Indian Navy, working on our behalf, began that process several hours ago. They have six minesweepers, under our protection, locating and exploding the mines. But it's slow, and there's a lot of them. I understand they have attended to three so far, and my guess is forty still to go, in order to secure safe passage for essentially defenseless tankers. There's already an environmental nightmare of spilled oil in the strait."

"Well, what are we doing about the goddamned Iranians? That's your area, Arnold."

"Sir, you want me to declare war on 'em? Or at least advise you to do so?"

"I don't know, Arnold." The President's voice was rising. "I just know this could be a major national crisis. And we seem powerless."

"Well, we're not that, sir. However, I do not want to make any kind of extravagant move until we clear the mines, quietly, and with as little rancor as possible. A hot war raging around the minesweepers would clearly be absurd. However, when the field is cleared, I'll be happy to station a lot of muscle in the strait and warn both Iran and China that one false move means we'll sink 'em."

"Well, why not issue that warning right now?"

"I just did, sir. Three hours ago."

"You told 'em we'd sink them?"

"Sir, I just sent a joint communiqué to Tehran and Beijing informing them of our anger at their conduct, and our intention to eliminate any warship from any nation that tries to interfere with the removal of the sea mines."

"And what about the future, Arnold? The future. That's what my job is all about. What about the damned future? How do we know the Chinese might not mastermind this kind of stunt again?"

"Sir, as you know, they have a very large petrochemical and oil refinery on the southern Iranian coast. And it's tapped right into the heart of the oil fields of Kazakhstan. I was proposing to recommend its elimination."

"It's WHAT?"

"*Destruction*, sir. A better word altogether. I agree."

"You mean bomb it?"

"Sir. Please? Let's not be crude, like the oil."

"Well, what are you saying?"

"I'm proposing an insertion of Special Forces, to put that refinery out of action forever."

"You mean the SEALs?"

"Yessir."

"Can we get them in? And out again?"

"Sure we can. We can do anything."

"But surely everyone will know it's us?"

"Same as we know who mined the gulf. But no one's saying anything, at least not in a confrontational way. We make no accusations, at least not publicly. They make no admissions. We just do what we do."

"But surely the goddamned Chinese would go bananas if we blew up their refinery?"

"Nossir. They'd feel like going bananas. But they'd get a very quiet message from us . . . *You guys want to start fucking around with America's oil supplies? We'll show you how to REALLY fuck around.*"

"Arnold, your brutality occasionally takes my breath away. But I like it. Makes me feel safe in this big chair."

"My job, sir, is to make every American feel safe, no matter how big or small his or her chair may be."

"Should I now conclude this strategy meeting?"

"Mr. President, this is not strategy. This is direct action. Clear the strait. Protect the sweepers. And then guard the strait with all the menace we can. By that I mean four CVBGs on station between the area inside the gulf, and our base on Diego Garcia. Any foreign warship moves in that area without our express permission, that warship's history."

"Arnold, please go ahead as you think fit."

"That's not quite all, sir."

"It's not? What else? You planning to conquer Russia or something?"

"No, sir. But I am distressed by China's plain and obvious Naval expansion. It's no secret they want a blue-water navy for the first time in more than five hundred years. And it's no secret they are expanding at a rapid and apparently sustainable rate. In the past few years they've created a new submarine fleet. They've bought two aircraft carriers, three Russian destroyers and a ton of hardware from the old Soviet missile outfits. They're reaching out, sir. And we really don't like it."

"We don't?"

"Sir, we are staring a major problem bang in the face. China is on the move. They have cozied up to us for a lot of years. And they'll go on doing so for as long as it suits them. But when they feel they're good and ready to challenge us, to dominate the East and to swing the balance of power their way . . . that's when you'll see the real face of China. Trust me."

"Well, what do you plan to do about that?"

"I plan to stop that global expansion dead in its tracks. I want that damned great Navy of theirs back in the China Seas."

"But how do we do that without starting a shooting war?"

"Sir, how do we keep our own global presence? How do we keep our own Navy roaming the world's oceans making sure no one steps out of line? Right here the world enjoys *Pax Americana*. Just as it once enjoyed *Pax Romana*. That was peace on the terms of the Romans. Now it's peace on the terms of the Americans.

"And we do it by ensuring we have a succession of U.S. bases all over the place . . . in the Pacific Ocean, the Indian Ocean, in the Japanese Islands, with our buddies from London in the Atlantic. That's the only way. A chain of supplies and allies. That's what China does not have. Yet. Except for one place. Burma."

"You mean that new base of theirs in the swamps west of Rangoon?"

"That's the one, sir. The one on the island in the Bassein River. It's huge. Massive facilities for servicing and refueling warships of all sizes, including submarines. The Chinese once dominated the entire Indian Ocean and my instinct is they want to do so again, because that would give 'em control of the main eastbound oil route through the Malacca Strait. Right now that narrow, shallow freeway, with its goddamned granite bottom, is just too far from China to allow them any influence over its tanker traffic."

"Well, how do you propose to discourage them from using their new Burmese base?"

Arnold Morgan smiled. "Not too hasty right now, sir. We got bigger problems. But if you've got any shares in China's Naval operation on Haing Gyi Island in the Bassein River . . . sell."

020330MAY07. USS *Shark*. The Indian Ocean.
Speed 30. Depth 400.

B Y THE START of the final half hour of the midnight watch, Lt. Commander Headley was already mobile, moving quietly through the 30-year-old, 5,000-ton nuclear boat, a half hour before he was due to take over the control room from Commander Reid.

He had already been down to the main propulsion room where Lt. Commander Paul Flynn was watching a very minor seal leak on the main shaft. Right now the pumps were operating efficiently and dealing with the incoming fine spray with relative ease.

"Damn thing wouldn't want to get any worse, though," said the dark-haired engineering officer from south Boston. "Still, the rest of the stuff's looking good—reactor's smooth, shaft's steady. At twenty-nine knots she feels like she's cruisin'. No problems, sir."

Dan Headley made his way up to the Navigation Officer's corner of the ops room. He had only just met young Lt. Shawn Pearson, but he knew he had been rescued with the crew of *Seawolf* when that massive nuclear attack boat had been lost the previous year in the South China Sea.

"Hi, Shawn," he said, leaning on the big table and staring down at the chart. "What are we? 'Bout seven hundred nor'nor-west of DG?"

"Accurate, sir. Accurate. I like that in an XO . . . gives me confidence. . . . I just sent for coffee. Want some, sir?"

The Lieutenant Commander had immediately liked Shawn Pearson because he was sharp, amusing and never lacked respect for more senior officers. Whatever his part had been in the *Seawolf* debacle, he had been highly decorated for it—an honor Dan Headley assumed must have been well deserved.

"Good idea, Lieutenant," he said. "Keep me awake for the next four hours."

"Right now I have us five degrees north of the equator, on line of longitude six-five-zero-zero. As a matter of fact, we're running fast beneath about a zillion square miles of absolutely nothing. Maybe five hundred miles west of the Maldives, still way short of the most southerly latitude of the Indian Continent . . . but we're gettin' there, sir."

"Any ships around?"

"No, sir. Just our immediate escort, the frigate *Vandegrift*. She's steaming about three miles off our starboard beam, sir, same course . . . three-five-two. We're just about five miles off the carrier's port bow, and she's got a destroyer off each beam—*Mason* to port, *Howard* to starboard."

"How about *Cheyenne*?"

"She's way off the carrier's starboard bow, maybe four miles east of us. Same depth."

Dan Headley sipped his coffee. "Mind if I take this with me?" he asked companionably.

"Not at all, sir. It'll keep you sharp, while I'm sleeping gently."

"Well, remember you've still got fifteen to go. So long, Lieu-tenant . . . don't get us lost now."

"Nossir. I am right on top of this."

And as he wandered toward the control room, Dan Headley

thought again of the reality of the situation—this huge jet-black steel tube, forging north through the Indian Ocean, hundreds of feet below the surface, in complete secret, a lethal weapon of war, terminally deadly to any opponent. The *esprit de corps* in an attack submarine was like no other feeling in any other ship. He felt that he and Shawn Pearson were somehow friends for life, after an acquaintance of just a few hours.

U.S. Navy submarines do that. They fling people together, causing them to see only the best points in one another.

Dan Headley was proud to serve on this old ship, and so far he had been impressed with every one of his crew. He especially liked the Chief of the Boat, a big blond former center fielder from the University of Georgia, Drew Fisher. The Master Chief Petty Officer had dropped out of college to try his luck at professional baseball, but failed to make it through a chronic ankle injury.

He had ended up with no university degree, no money, and no career, in or out of sports. "Sir, I didn't even have a bat," he had told Dan Headley. "So I just joined the Navy, and kept right on going."

Drew had risen steadily up through the ranks, and in Lt. Commander Headley's opinion was not finished yet. It was widely rumored that the former Georgia Bulldogs left-hander was on the verge of accepting a commission, and that a full command might not be that far away.

Drew was only 36 years old, and in addition to his onerous duties on board, he had pushed himself through course after course, gaining qualifications in navigation, weapons, hydrology, electronics, marine engineering. Right now he was working on combat systems and spent a lot of time with Lt. Commander Jack Cressend from New Orleans, *Shark*'s CS Officer.

In fact the two men were together outside the control room directly up ahead of Dan, and both men greeted him cheerfully. The Master Chief, like Dan, was early for his watch and had already ascertained that *Shark*'s new XO was some kind of an expert on thoroughbred horses. Right now, in the small hours of the morning, running hard above the towering underwater mountains of the Mid-Indian Ridge, he wanted to know precisely which colt was going to win the Kentucky Derby at Churchill Downs this Saturday.

Four hours ago Dan Headley had been noncommittal on the big field, four of which in his opinion held live chances. This was not good enough for Drew, who wanted heavy inside information in fine detail, so he asked the *Shark*'s second-in-command again.

"Come on, sir. Give me your real, true selection."

"Well, Drew. My daddy raised one of the runners from a foal, big gray colt named White Rajah, trained in New York for Mr. Phipps."

"Can he run?"

"Course he can run. Otherwise he wouldn't be entered for the Derby, would he?"

"What did he win?"

"Three races as a two-year-old. Got beat by a nose in the Hopeful at Saratoga. But he improved over the winter. They sent him down to South Carolina for a spell, then he came out and damned nearly won the Florida Derby off a bad draw."

"That his last race?"

"Hell, no. He came back to New York, won the Wood Memorial over nine furlongs. That's the best Derby trial in my view: been won by some of the greats, Count Fleet, Assault, Native Dancer, Nashua, Bold Ruler, Damascus, Seattle Slew. The real big guns of the horse game. Christ, Secretariat got beat in it before his Triple Crown."

"Jeez, sir. You really know that horse stuff, right?"

"Guess so. It's in my blood. My family been raisin' racers out in the bluegrass for about five generations."

"Ah, but you still ain't told me one bit of real sensitive information about White Rajah."

"Oh, that's easy," replied Lt. Commander Headley. "His granddaddy damned near bit my right arm off when I was a kid. Vicious sonofabitch."

"Seriously? Jeez, I didn't know thoroughbred horses were savage."

"This particular bloodline is very difficult. Got a lot of temperament in there."

"Then why do people breed to it?"

"Because the suckers can run, that's why. And a lot of 'em can *really* run. Like the Rajah."

"Well that settles it. I'm bettin' him."

"You think they got an OTB in the Arabian Sea?"

"Hell, I forgot about that. . . . Do you think I could borrow the satellite link to San Diego?"

"Oh, sure. We're heading for the front line, in the middle of a world oil crisis, and our overhead link is somehow out of action because the Chief of the Boat is trying to back White Rajah in the Kentucky Derby."

"Shit, it's a cruel world, sir."

"Crueler if he wins, Chief . . . and you're not on."

All three men laughed. There was no doubt. Lieutenant Commander Headley was already extremely well liked, and now he strolled into the control room, wished the commanding officer "Good morning," and added, "Ready to take over whenever you say, sir."

Commander Reid looked at his watch. "Seven more minutes, XO. I like to serve a full four hours."

"Fine, sir. I'll be right here. No change in the satellite contact, sir? Zero six hundred as scheduled?"

"As scheduled, XO. That's the way I like it."

Dan Headley continued to familiarize himself with the control room, which was smaller than he was used to. His last tour had been, fortuitously, on the USS *Kentucky*, one of the huge Ohio-Class Trident strategic missile submarines. And he had been under the impression he might be awarded a full command on one of those 19,000-ton nuclear giants. But, quite suddenly, he had been posted to the USS *Shark*, on positively her final tour of duty, to assist Commander Reid, on his last tour of duty. Dan assumed this was because of the rising unrest in the Iranian Gulf area, and there was plainly some concern about the mental steadfastness of the veteran CO.

Thus far Dan had found Commander Reid to be reserved, polite, a little rigid in his thoughts for a submarine commander. And punctilious in the extreme. But he could work with that. So long as they did not come under serious pressure.

At 0400 precisely, Commander Reid handed over the control room. "You have the ship, XO," he said formally.

"Aye, sir. I have the ship."

Lt. Commander Headley checked *Shark*'s speed, course and position. He checked with comms the 0600 satellite contact, and ordered, "Maintain speed twenty-nine, depth four hundred. Course three-five-two." Then he picked up his telephone and checked in with the propulsion engineer.

The leak on the shaft was no worse. The pumps still were coping easily and the big Westinghouse PWR was running sweetly. The sonar room was quiet. Lieutenant Commander Josh Gandy reported no new contacts of any kind, not that this was likely at such speed.

All through the night, they ran north toward the Arabian Sea, until dawn began to break over the eastern waters, way off their starboard beam. Lieutenant Commander Headley ordered them to periscope depth and accessed the satellite. There was no change in their orders . . . *Proceed to the eastern waters of the Strait of Hormuz in company with the aircraft carrier* Harry S. Truman. *Then replace on station the* John C. Stennis *Group when it clears the area and runs back south to Diego Garcia.*

Both Lt. Commander Josh Gandy and Master Chief Fisher were with the XO when he checked the orders.

"Sorry, Chief," Dan muttered. "Nothing from OTB. Guess the Rajah's gonna run without your money to handicap him."

That was the last joke of the watch, and the rest of it passed slowly, as did the next two days. By 0400 on Friday morning, May 4, the *Shark* was almost at the gateway to the Gulf of Oman, which leads to the narrow waters of Hormuz. They had crossed the 24-degree northern line of latitude and were currently running 100 feet below the surface with another 250 feet of water under the keel. It would be light in a couple of hours, and, presumably, with the gulf closed, except for Iranian ships and very occasionally Chinese, the seas would be empty, with an inbound queue of empty tankers way over to the west.

1730 (local time). Thursday, May 3. Fort Meade, Maryland.

The first night pictures from the overheads that passed over the Arabian Sea, and southern Iran, arrived on Lt. Ramshawe's desk from late on the previous afternoon. Unsurprisingly they were packed with information, starting with a myriad of shots showing the Indian Navy's Pondicherrys still working across the line of the minefield. They were making slow progress, just five knots with long GKT-2 contact sweeps, still with their 5,600-ton landing ship *Magar*, which was acting as "mother ship" to all six of them.

An Indian Navy tanker was also in attendance, plus two 6,700-ton Delhi-Class guided-missile destroyers, built in Bombay, and sent on by Admiral Kumar to guard his precious Pondicherrys. Warships from the *Constellation* Carrier Battle Group were in the area, patrolling somewhat menacingly along the line of the minefield inside the strait.

Out on the outside edge of the line, U.S. frigates rotated patrols, under orders from the carrier *John C. Stennis*, which was calling the shots from 10 miles astern of the picket line. No six ships were ever more thoroughly guarded than those six Pondicherrys, and they swept the line assiduously, trying to free up an area three to five miles wide to open up the seaway on the Omani side to the world's oil tankers.

And every few hours, the waters of the strait erupted to a shuddering explosion, as they located, cut and blew one of the PLT-3 Russian-built mines. More than 11,000 miles away, Lieutenant Ramshawe studied the strange unfolding scene, making detailed notes, writing up his reports, blowing up photographs, extracting details, laying it all out for the thoroughly discredited

Admiral Borden, who now had a great deal in common with Commander Tex Packard, careerwise.

He put copies on the network to the Pentagon, attention CNO. Other copies were made for electronic transfer to Pacific Fleet Command in San Diego, from where they were scanned via satellite to Pearl Harbor and then Diego Garcia. By private, secure telephone, Jimmy Ramshawe kept Arnold Morgan up to speed on every possible development. So far, to the satisfaction of both men, the Iranians had not dared send so much as a secondhand felucca into the waters beyond Bandar Abbas.

It was 1830 when two grainy, poor-quality satellite pictures of the inshore waters of southeastern Iran suddenly caught the eagle eye of Jimmy Ramshawe, because there, like a ghost ship in the fog, was the unmistakable outline of some kind of warship.

He reached for his glass and peered at the image. He could see a little more, but not enough. The ship was running north toward the coast of Iran in 300 feet of water. According to the grid, the ship had just crossed 25.10N and was thus 60-odd miles short of the minefield Line. The lines of latitude suggested it was moving slowly, just seven miles in the half hour between the two images. Jimmy hit a button, summoning a staff member from the developing room, and requesting an immediate blowup of the top left-hand corner of the first green-tinted night photograph.

When it came back, 12 minutes later, the quality was not better, just bigger, and again Lt. Ramshawe peered through his magnifying glass. He could tell from the for'ard and aft guns the scale of the ship, which he calculated was in excess of 7,000 tons. If it was that big, it was a destroyer, and if it was a destroyer, the range of countries that might own it was relatively small. It wasn't American because he knew precisely where all the U.S. destroyers were in the area. It wasn't British, and it certainly wasn't Russian. The Iranians did not own a destroyer, nor did the Egyptians, nor the Omanis. The Indians had two working in the area, and five more Russian-built Rajput Class were all accounted for.

Could it possibly be the Chinese Sovremenny, the mine-laying *Hangzhou*, now returning for whatever reason to Bandar Abbas?

Jimmy Ramshawe looked again, pulled up the Sovremenny pattern on his computer. The helicopter was in the right position for a start. He could see that. It was parked way forward, and higher than the aft deck, right above the ASW mortars. He could also make out the distinctive gap between the fire control front dome (F-Band) and the air-search radar top plate.

"If I'm not very much mistaken," muttered Jimmy, "the bloody Chinks are back, and the bloody *Hangzhou* is creeping up the coast toward the gap in the minefield . . . I wonder what the hell their game is?"

He checked the pattern over and over. The quad launchers for the Sunburn missiles, the two aft-mounted Gadfly surface-to-air launchers. All in the right places. This was her, no doubt about that, the most capable warship in China's new Blue-Water Fleet, *Hangzhou*, built brand-new in the cold Baltic, North Yard, Saint Petersburg. And here she was again, in much warmer waters, returning to the scene of her plain and obvious mine-laying crimes.

Lieutenant Jimmy Ramshawe did not like it. This was a heavily armed warship that would make a fair match for anyone. He could not see the point of talking to Admiral Borden, who would probably remind him of her right to be in Iran's waters, if that was okay with Iran.

But it was not okay with Jimmy Ramshawe. *Bloody oath, it wasn't.* And he picked up the secure line to Admiral Morgan in the White House.

"How sure are you, Lieutenant?"

"Certain, sir. This is the *Hangzhou*, and no bloody error. Looks like she's headed back to Bandar Abbas."

Arnold Morgan was, for a change, hesitant. He had already ensured that the U.S. Navy had issued a formal warning to all countries not to interfere with the minesweeping, but he had not been prepared for the sudden arrival of the most important warship in the Chinese Navy, the one that had helped lay the mines in the first place.

"When do we get new pictures, Jimmy?" he asked.

"Probably in three hours, sir."

"God knows where she'll be by then. She's fast, and she's dangerous. Leave it with me. And don't forget to get a decent report in to your boss."

The President's National Security Adviser was concerned. And he paced his office, pondering the intent of the Commanding Officer of the *Hangzhou*. If she was there merely as an observer, the United States might have to put up with that. But she was so big and powerful, she would simply have to be warned off while the Pondicherrys were working.

Arnold Morgan knew the two Admirals commanding the *Constellation* and *John C. Stennis* Groups would be flying off their decks F-14 Tomcats, and the FA-18E Super Hornets. That's what they did on patrol. That's what they were there for, to intimidate any enemy. And these supersonic strike fighters found no difficulty in doing that.

The Admiral had not yet asked for details, but he was certain the Tomcats would be making their presence felt. What the Navy did not need was a large Chinese warship prowling around in those waters with its massive antiaircraft capability—the two aft-mounted SA-N-7 Gadfly SAMs. Not to mention its two twin 130mm guns, and its four 30mm/65 AK 630 guns—the ones that fire a withering 3,000 rounds a minute.

No. The U.S. Navy and its fliers could not put up with that. Particularly since the *Hangzhou* also sported two twin heavyweight 533mm torpedo tubes, right below the fire-control radars for the Gadfly missiles. She was also equipped with a strong antisubmarine capability, two 6-barrel RNU 1,000 ASW mortars. Her principal surface-to-surface weapon was the SS-N-22 Sunburn (Moskit 3M-80E), a supersonic Raduga, fired from port/starboard quad launchers. Range: 60 nautical miles, at Mach 2.5.

She was a formidable ship, no doubt about that. And Arnold Morgan guessed she had been detailed to escort the original mine-laying Chinese frigates, and possibly even the Kilos, out of harm's way. He also guessed, correctly, that she had been refueled from a tanker out of the Bassein River, which he found, frankly, infuriating.

"And now, where the hell's she going?" he growled to the empty room. "It had better be far away from any of our current operations. I don't expect the Indians will be too pleased to see her, either."

The question was, What to do? "I guess we can't just sink the biggest ship in the Chinese Navy without risking a world-class uproar, which will send gasoline prices even higher," he pondered. "But she has to leave the area. That's for sure. Before someone gets trigger-happy."

He picked up his secure line to Admiral Dixon and outlined the problem.

"Sir, I do agree. She cannot be allowed to remain in our area of operations. I have warned the Chinese, and everyone else to that effect. I think we have to take the view that the Chinese and the Iranians, in the absence of any denials, are plainly in breach of every world peace convention in mining the strait. I propose to issue one more formal warning, directly to Beijing. Either they get that destroyer out of the area, or we'll do it for them."

"You saying sink it, Alan?"

"Nossir. I'm saying cripple it. With minumum loss of life."

"Using?"

"A submarine, sir. Stick one of those MK 48s right into her stern. Blow the shaft, steering and propulsion all in one hit. Probably take out her missile launchers too with a couple of shells. Then let their friends from Iran come out and tow her in. That way we hold on to world opinion, with very few casualties, and a well-deserved warning to China to stay the hell out of the strait."

"What if she returns fire?"

"Sink her, sir. Instantly."

"Good call, Alan. Let's go."

040500MAY07. USS *Shark*. 24.40N 50.55E.
Speed 25. Depth 100. Course 352.

Lieutenant Commander Dan Headley, his early watch just one hour old, called for a transcript of the new orders just in from the carrier. "Hard copy twice, Jack," he called down to comms. "One for the CO."

Five minutes later he read the instructions, to the USS *Shark*, ordering them to locate and track a Sovremenny-Class destroyer, probably flying the flag of the People's Liberation Army/Navy. It had been picked up by the overheads moving slowly up the southernmost coast of Iran, course approximately two-seven-zero. According to Fort Meade, right now at 0530 it should be somewhere to their nor'noreast, maybe 27 miles up ahead.

Shark's sonar room had already located a ship right in that area, and the ESM had reported an occasionally transmitting Russian radar. The flag was correct. She was going slowly. The Sturgeon-Class American submarine would catch her inside 90 minutes. Their orders were simply to get in contact with the destroyer, track her silently and await further instructions.

Lieutenant Commander Headley ordered flank speed, course three-six-zero, which should put him in the correct position sometime before 0700. He had someone awaken the CO to apprise him of the situation and was mildly surprised when Commander Reid did not show up in the control room anytime in the next 45 minutes. "Guess he trusts me," thought the XO. "Even though he has known me for only five days."

In any event they rushed on north, remaining just below periscope depth, leaving a wake on the surface, which no one was around to see. At 0640, Lt. Commander Headley slowed down to come to PD and took an all-around look at the surface picture. Sure enough, out on the horizon, right on their one o'clock, was a large warship. Dan Headley had already memorized the profile of the Sovremenny, and this was her, large as life, steaming on six miles off the coast of Iran, as if she owned the place. The engine lines on the 8,000-ton double-shafted destroyer matched the GTZA-674 turbines on the computer model.

He went back below the surface, dictated a signal to the flag and had it transmitted, announcing he was in contact and was proposing to track the destroyer two miles astern pending further orders.

Dan ordered a course change . . . *"Come right seven degrees . . . down all masts."* At which point a frisson of excitement ran through the submarine, as it always does when any potential quarry is sighted, even in exercises. Now, with the most danger-ous warship in the Chinese Navy in their sights, USS *Shark* came unmistakably to life.

At 0700 the Commander came into the control room. He talked to his XO for a few minutes, bringing himself into the pic-ture. But he did not assume command. Rather he left "to find some breakfast," and asked Dan to let him know if anything important occurred.

By now they were running line astern to the destroyer, four miles behind. But the Chinese ship was moving faster now, still heading northwest along the Iranian coast. As far as Dan could tell she was not transmitting and did not even have her sonars switched on, which the Kentucky-born officer thought was "kinda eccentric." *Given she's just mined the Strait of Hormuz and the business half of the planet Earth is seriously pissed off with the ship and all who are sailing on her.*

Nonetheless, the *Hangzhou* ran on at a steady 20-knot speed, which again Dan Headley thought was ridiculous. By varying her rate of knots between say four and 25, it would have been much more difficult for a submarine to track her. Alternatively, at her quiet, low speed, she might have actually heard the submarine, charging along astern, trying to catch up, making a noise like a freight train. *Beats the shit out of me where they train these guys. Some Chinese laundry, I guess.*

And so the *Shark* slipped into a classic sprint-and-drift pursuit, running as deep as she dared in the 50-fathom waters along the coastline for fifteen minutes, then coming up for another visual setup, to update the operations plot for the Fire Controller, just in case they should be ordered into action. Naturally, every time they came up they lost speed, "drifting" quietly forward at five knots, losing ground all the time.

Six miles short of the minefield, the *Hangzhou* made a course change, swinging more westerly, as if to run along the line of the minefield. It was light now, and Lt. Commander Headley immediately accessed the flag to inform them of the change in direction.

Admiral Bert Harman, in the group ops room high in the island of the *Harry S. Truman*, was uncertain, although his orders were clear. He instructed his comms room to alert the destroyer she was straying into a prohibited area where U.S. warships were supervising a mine-clearing operation. She was to be warned in no uncertain terms to leave forthwith, to resume her course to Bandar Abbas and to remain in harbor right there until further notice.

But the Chinese Commanding Officer had been instructed to observe proceedings, and to bow to no threats from the U.S. Navy or any other Navy. The CO, Colonel Yang Xi, thought this might have been perfectly feasible from a desk in Beijing, but out here it looked very different. He could see U.S. Navy ships out on the horizon, steaming along the line of the minefield, in which he'd just seen a sizable explosion.

He decided to ignore the warning, since he considered the Americans were unlikely to open fire. Rather he would slow down and go in closer for two more miles. He was now in international waters, and he could take his time with his turn. Meanwhile he would place his surface-to-surface Sunburn missiles on full alert.

The carrier ops room observed the Chinese CO make no attempt to obey their warning. Admiral Harman picked up his orders and read them carefully. . . . *"Should any warship of any nation insist in straying into our prohibited area, you will order the tracking submarine to disable her, not sink her but put her out of commission."*

There was nothing ambiguous about that, and the *Hangzhou* was a hugely dangerous enemy to both U.S. ships and aircraft. Admiral Harman thus sent his signal to USS *Shark*, instructing the submarine to disable the Chinese warship should she fail to turn around.

Lieutenant Commander Headley read the signal, and ordered

the conn to take a long left-hand swing at flank speed in order to come up on the port side of the Chinese warship. He planned to fire one torpedo, well aft of her beam from range two thousand yards. This meant, essentially, that the MK 48 would strike the stern and cripple the propulsiom of the ship leaving her helpless in the water until assistance arrived.

He sent an immediate message to the Captain, who arrived in the control room at 0745. He seemed agitated, uncomfortable with the decisions, not at all eager to open fire on a major Chinese warship. He questioned the intelligence of the orders, wondering if they might not have been changed. If there had been some mistake.

Lieutenant Commander Headley brought *Shark* to PD once again and requested the CO take a look for himself. "The Chinese CO has ignored our warnings, no doubt about that," said the XO. "And these orders make our duty clear. We are to cripple it, put it out of action with minimum loss of life."

"Yes, I understand that," said Commander Reid, declining the periscope. "But the *Hangzhou* is not doing anyone any harm right now, maybe just taking a look." He repeated, absentmindedly, "Maybe just taking a look."

"These orders don't tell us to speculate, sir," replied Dan. "They tell us to hit the destroyer hard when we are told to do so. And this piece of paper right here says right now."

The Captain of USS *Shark* looked unenthusiastic. "It doesn't say how long we give it to turn around," he said. "I think we might check that with the flag, XO."

"As you wish, sir. But I would prefer you do it, because in my view these orders are specific. The Chinese ship has been warned, it has not turned around, and I have a piece of paper here ordering us to open fire."

"This is your watch, XO. I would like the writer to record my unease and my wish for a second opinion on the orders. But if you are certain as to the orders, you have my permission to proceed as you see fit."

"Thank you, sir. . . . *Now . . . torpedo room–XO, prepare tubes one and two . . . MK 48s. . . .*"

Lieutenant Commander Headley turned to Master Chief Drew Fisher, who had materialized at his side. "Check that out, Chief, will you? I'm only preparing a second tube in case of malfunction. I intend to fire just one."

"Aye, sir."

Inside the sonar room, the operators could still hear the steady beat of the *Hangzhou's* propellers, rising and falling in the ocean swell, making the same soft *chuff-chuff-chuff* sound in the water, now less than 2,000 yards away, dead ahead.

Dan Headley grabbed for the periscope handles at knee level as the "eyes" of the submarine rose up out of the deck of the control room. He scanned the ocean, called out bearing, then range . . . "*Zero-seven-zero . . . twenty-one thirty yards . . . down all masts . . . make your depth one hundred.*"

Seconds passed, and then the sonar room operator called it. . . . "*XO–sonar . . . track three four . . . bearing zero-six-zero . . . range two thousand.*"

Down in the torpedo room, both tubes were loaded, and the guidance officer was in direct contact with Lt. Commander Headley, speaking quietly into his slim-line microphone.

Dan Headley ordered the Officer of the Deck, Lt. Matt Singer, to take the conn. . . . "*Hold your speed at three knots.*"

The sonar team checked the approach, calling out the details softly to the XO. The rest of the ship was stone silent as they crept forward, preparing to fire the shot that would most certainly be heard in the Great Hall of the People.

Lieutenant Commander Headley took another fast look at the screen. Then he ordered, "*STAND BY ONE . . . stand by to fire by sonar. . . .*"

"*Bearing zero-six-zero . . . range two thousand yards . . . computer set.*"

"*SHOOT!*" snapped Dan Headley.

And everyone felt the faint shudder as the big MK 48 swept out into the ocean, making a beeline toward the Chinese destroyer.

"Weapon under guidance, sir."

At 40 knots, the torpedo would run for less than two minutes before hitting the utterly unprepared Sovremenny-Class destroyer. And it hit in the precise spot Dan Headley had specified, bang on the stern.

It slammed into the long, low aft section and detonated, blowing the main shaft into three pieces, the propeller into the deep water and the rudder into a split and twisted mess of steel. The *Hangzhou* could no longer maneuver, couldn't steer, couldn't move. As the pall of smoke began to clear away from her stern area, she looked more or less normal, but in truth she was powerless.

Her crew could hear the ship's tannoy blaring instructions, and the medical teams were already making their way aft to tend the wounded, but by the standards of torpedoed warships there was relatively little bloodshed.

The communications room was still intact, and the ops room was unharmed. In fury, Colonel Yang Xi was thrashing around looking for a target at which to lash back. But he could see nothing short range for well over two miles. He had missiles, shells and torpedoes, but nothing close at which to aim any of them specifically. Nor could he see what had hit his ship, if indeed anything. For all he knew, it was just an explosion. But he knew that was stretching the realms of coincidence.

Three minutes after the impact, he received yet another signal from the American carrier, again ordering him out of the area, but offering to request assistance from the Iranians if the destroyer's comms were down.

The Colonel did not answer. Neither did he consider it prudent to open fire with his missiles, because if he did the Americans would surely sink him. In his present situation he was the epitome of a sitting duck. Instead he relayed a signal to the Iranian Naval Command at Bandar Abbas requesting assistance.

Meanwhile Lt. Commander Headley turned USS *Shark* around and returned to his position on station 20 miles off the port bow of the *Harry S. Truman.*

0100. Friday, May 4.
The White House.

Admiral Morgan sat alone in his office in the West Wing. He had promised Kathy he would be home by 11 P.M., but that was before the *Shark* had planted a torpedo in the stern of the *Hangzhou*. He had been on the line to the CNO almost every moment since.

Right now the *John F. Kennedy* Battle Group was five days out of Pearl Harbor and making a swing to the south from her normal route up to the coast of Taiwan. Admiral Dixon had ordered her straight to Diego Garcia.

The increased tension in the Hormuz area had also caused the CNO to tell the Atlantic Commander-in-Chief to move the sixth operational U.S. CVBG, that of the *Theodore Roosevelt*, out of the Mediterranean and on to the Indian Ocean.

Like Admiral Morgan, he had no idea what the Chinese were up to, and he had a bad feeling about that new Chinese base on the Bassein River. Within a few days they would have four carrier groups conducting a *roulement* between Diego Garcia and the Hormuz Strait, with the *Roosevelt* free to roam the Indian Ocean, with her consorts, anywhere it looked as though the Chinese might cause more trouble.

As far as Arnold Morgan was concerned, he had seen enough. Always completely mistrustful of the men from the Orient, he now believed their true colors were being shown. They had cold-bloodedly caused a massive world oil crisis, they had caused scenes of chaos in the Gulf of Iran and right now no one dared to bring a big tanker across Jimmy Ramshawe's line, which defined the essential contour of the minefield.

The oil market frenzy had abated slightly thanks to soothing words from the American President that free-and-clear passage through the Strait of Hormuz would soon be resumed. But Americans were paying three dollars and fifty cents a gallon at the pumps, and Texaco, along with three other U.S.-based corporations, was threatening to put the price up to four dollars next week.

The President was at his wit's end, demanding the strait be reopened immediately, apparently unable to grasp the consequences of another tanker being blown up, and the global uproar that would surely follow if the USA had declared the route safe to resume trade.

The weekend passed more or less uneventfully. White Rajah was made the hot favorite, before losing by a half length at Churchill Downs after closing on the winner all the way down the stretch. But at 0530 (local time) on Monday morning, May 7, at the northern end of the Malacca Strait, an even more unexpected event happened. A 300,000-ton, virtually empty Japanese-registered crude carrier literally blew itself to pieces: went up in a colossal fireball right off the northern headland of Sumatra, within a few miles of the open ocean.

Like Hormuz, this is a very busy oil route, the seagoing highway to the Far East, the route of almost every tanker coming out of the Gulf of Iran, or even from the oil fields of Africa—straight across the Indian Ocean toward the Nicobar Islands, then through the Great Channel into the Malacca Strait, which divides Sumatra and the Malayan Peninsula.

The strait is close to 600 miles long, and the tankers use it for their outward and inward journeys. Almost 100 percent of all the fuel oil and gas requirements in the Far East are carried on the big tankers through that narrowing seaway, the shortcut to the South China Sea.

It saves over a thousand wasteful miles, for without the strait, ships would have to travel right around the outside of the old East Indies.

Arnold Morgan heard the news with an undisguised groan as he and Kathy sat down to dinner on Sunday night, 12 time zones back. "This," he grated, "is getting goddamned serious."

No word of complaint had been heard from the Chinese since their destroyer was damaged. Nor, of course, had there been any word of admission for their part in mining Hormuz in the first place.

Ms. O'Brien had actually heard the report on the news while Arnold was grilling some pork chops on the grill. They had been out all day, sailing along the Potomac on a friend's yacht, and for some reason there had been only drinks and potato chips on board. The President's National Security Adviser rarely, if ever, touched alcohol during the day, and both he and Kathy had concluded the voyage, cold after the sun went down, and hungry *in extremis*, as the Admiral put it.

They declined going to a restaurant with the other guests and sped home in Arnold's staff car. With heavy sweaters on, and glasses of wine from the Loire Valley, they had fired up the grill and were just moving into Arnold's favorite part of the day, when Kathy reported the demise of the giant VLCC.

"Now how the hell did that happen?" he asked Kathy's Labrador, Freddie, who made no reply but continued to look, with eyes like lasers, at the pork chops.

Kathy returned with the wine bottle but little information. "They just said the tanker was unladen," she said. "No information was available about how the accident happened. They did draw a parallel with the ships that blew up in Hormuz last week, and the newscaster mentioned that there seemed to be a jinx on the shipping of heavy crude oil these days."

"Yeah," he muttered. "A jinx wearing a goddamned lampshade on its head and eating its dinner with a couple of painted sticks."

Kathy laughed. No one had ever made her laugh like Arnold Morgan, especially when he was being sardonic. She threw her arms around him, and kissed him softly and slowly. No one that agonizingly beautiful had ever kissed Arnold Morgan. Certainly not like that.

"If it wasn't for about a billion tons of shipping blazing away in the Far East threatening to cause an end to civilization as we know it," he said, "I could get very involved with that kissing business."

"Well, you should think about it more often," she said. "Get a kind of rotation system going . . . you know, save the world . . . make love to Kathy . . . save the world . . . kiss Kathy for a few hours . . . then save the world again. If necessary. Meantime, I'll take you just as you are."

"Thank you," he said, grinning. "How about . . . eat the chops . . . make love to Kathy . . . drink the Meursault . . . kiss Kathy?"

"I'll buy that," she said. "But how about saving the world?"

"Screw the world," he said, putting his arm around her. "Can't the goddamned world see when I'm too busy?"

The Admiral removed the chops from the grill with a pair of long silver tongs. One of them broke, and the meaty part fell to the flagstone patio. Freddie dove at it as if he had not been fed during this century, and retreated sneakily into the bushes.

"Has that greedy little character got any Chinese blood?" he asked.

Kathy giggled, took the plate of chops from the Admiral and told him, "Sure he has. Freddie, honored grandson of the Dalai Lama."

"That's Tibet, dingbat," he said.

"Same thing, if you ask the People's Republic," she said.

It took only a few more moments for them to turn off the new gas grill and move inside to where the Admiral had lit a log fire in the study. This was a rather grand house, and Kathy had been awarded it, amicably, by her husband in the divorce settlement. He had been a fairly rich man, and his pride and joy had been his book-lined study, which was situated through a beamed arch from the dining room. Kathy assumed he had another such setup in his new house in Normandy, France, where he now lived with his French wife.

A studious diplomat, with a family grain business in the Midwest, he was always described by Kathy as kind, and lovely, totally preoccupied with the problems of the world and "about as much fun as a tree." He had been much older than she, as Arnold was. But the laughter she shared with Arnold, his willingness always to talk to her and the sheer joy of their being together made up for any age differential. They were as devoted as it was possible to be. And one day she would marry him. When he retired.

Meanwhile, she served the pork chops, salad and the french loaf, sat down and asked him, "How do big ships burn, when there's nothing in them? What's to burn? The newscaster said it was returning unladen to the gulf."

"Well, I didn't really hear it, but that sounds right. You see, those big tankers never really get rid of that crude oil when they unload at the terminal. I'm not sure what's left, but in a vast holding tank, there's probably several inches still slopping around after the pumps are turned off.

"Now then, it's not the actual crude oil, which is like a black sludge, that burns. It's the gases rising up from it. So you can very easily have a situation where a fully loaded tanker is a lot less inflammable than an empty one. Because the holding tanks in the empty one are full of gases, and those babies will go up real fast.

"It's the same with gasoline. If you could somehow plunge a lighted match into the gasoline without igniting the gases that are evaporating, the liquid would put the flame out, like water. You probably won't remember, but twenty-five years ago when the Brits fought the Argentinians for the Falkland Islands, a bomb came right into a ship—actually I think it came in low, and traveled right through and out the other side.

"Anyway, it started a minor fire, but hit a big diesel-gas tank on the way through and tons of ice-cold fuel cascaded out and extinguished the fire. That's how it works. And that's what caused the explosion in this latest tanker. The gases going up with a major bang."

"Thank you, sir. Nicely explained. What do you think caused it?"

"I'm afraid to think about that right now. But I know one thing: It's not another minefield. Both Singapore and Sumatra get rich on the pilotage fees through the Malacca. They're high and getting higher. Last thing they want is a blockade. The Chinese would get no help from them. That means we're looking for something else. But not tonight. We're having a quiet dinner . . . then I'm not going to save the world, and we'll go to bed quietly together.

"Tomorrow will be different. I'll be in the office early. So will you. And Admiral Borden wants to fasten his goddamned safety belt."

"I'm just beginning to feel a teeny bit sorry for the poor Admiral."

"Well, don't be. He's a negative guy. Which is bad in Intelligence. In Fort Meade, you gotta stay right on top of the game. Also Borden's obviously been very awkward with the excellent Lieutenant Ramshawe. I don't like that. Young men that sharp ought to be encouraged—not made to feel frustrated, so they have to phone the goddamned White House in order to get someone to pay attention."

"Well, you were pretty short with him when he did make the call."

"Kathy, there are formalities of command in the United States Navy, and they have to be observed at all times. And quite often they soothe troubled waters, even soften the truth. What they never do, howevever, is *hide* the truth. Jimmy Ramshawe knew that when he called. He probably knew I'd be kinda dismissive. But he also knew I'd hear him. That's why he called. He never had to tell me his boss was being pigheaded stupid. He didn't have to. He knew I'd get it. And he was right . . . more goddamned right than even he knew at that point."

"I guess it was pretty impressive how he got onto the Chinese involvement?"

"Sure was. He was a couple of jumps ahead of me, and we were running on the same track. I'm not real used to that."

"Do you feel a little resentful . . . someone that young?"

"Hell, no. I was pleased. Saved me a lot of thinking time. That boy just laid it right out . . . almost."

"What d'you mean, 'almost'?"

The Admiral leaned back in his chair, and took a deep sip of

Meursault. "Kathy," he said, "there's something real strange about this whole damned thing. Lemme ask you a question. What's the first thing any halfway decent detective wants to know about a murder?"

"Whodunit?"

The Admiral chuckled, leaned over, took her hand and told her he loved her. Then he stopped smiling and said, "Motive, Mrs. O'Brien. Motive. Why was this crime committed?"

"Okay, Sherlock, go for it."

"Kathy, I cannot go for it. Because I cannot for the life of me see one motive the Chinese may have had for getting heavily involved in a blocklade of the Gulf of Iran. I have wracked my brains, and every time we make a big move to protect the mine clearance, I get a damned funny feeling about the entire scenario."

"You do?"

"Well, we got a Navy that has to protect the Indians' ships. But right now we got battle groups standing by to relieve battle groups. We've even got battle groups coming out of the Med in order to get into the Arabian Sea.

"Kathy, do you know how many ships that is—in the five U.S. battle groups?"

"What are they, a dozen each? So I guess around sixty?"

"Kathy, that's enough Naval hardware to conquer the world about three times over. That's more U.S. warships grouped together than there've been since World War Two. So what the hell's going on? There's no hostile threat. The mines that blew three tankers are essentially passive, just sitting there in the water, and the Pondicherrys are quite steadily getting rid of them.

"Neither China, nor Iran, has opened fire on anyone. Christ, we just banged a hole in China's most important destroyer and they never even fired back, never even protested.

"I just got an awkward feeling I might be missing the big picture right here. Seems to me we got too much Naval hardware in one place. And I know that's because we've also got a President whose only real concern is the price of gasoline at the American pumps.

"And I'm wondering if we're overreacting to the oil threat to civilization. Could someone be very seriously yanking our chain?"

1700. Monday, May 7.
Headquarters, Eastern Fleet.
Ningbo, Zhejiang Province.

The streets were always crowded at this time in the ancient harbor town that lies 120 miles due south of Shanghai across the great Bay of Hangzhou. Ningbo traces its roots back to the Tang Dynasty, through more than a thousand years of trading, and every day in the early evening a commercial stampede seems to break out, as if the entire population was racing, to sail before the tide.

Throngs surged across the old Xinjiang Bridge in the main port area. Traders bought and sold all along the old central throughway of Zhongshan Lu. And yet, it was a curious place to see a senior Naval Officer, in uniform, hurrying through one of the oldest parts of town, along Changchun Lu.

Nonetheless, moving swiftly between the merchant houses along the crowded sidewalks was the tall, lean, still-upright figure of the Commander-in-Chief of the Peoples's Liberation Navy, Admiral Zu Jicai. He was no stranger to this city. He had been born here more than 60 years ago, and his Naval career had begun in the dockyards of Zhejiang Province and ultimately, before he was thirty years old, in Shanghai.

Following him closely among the shoppers were four uniformed Navy guards, with sidearms. Even for a mission as unorthodox as this, Admiral Zu was not permitted to travel so far from the dockyard without protection.

He reached a building on the left-hand side of the street, and paused briefly to confer with his guards, instructing them to wait outside, and to have a staff car ready in 45 minutes.

Then he walked up the steps, and entered through one of the wide, folded wooden screen doors of the Tianyige, the oldest private library in all of China, dating back to the sixteenth century, at the height of Ningbo's prosperity during the Ming Dynasty. A member of the family bowed formally to him, and the Admiral returned the courtesy, before he was led through the book-filled, paneled main room into a smaller inner sanctum, dimly lit and plainly designed for thought and as a home for reference books.

There was one single table in the room, and it stood beneath a deep, paneled, beamed ceiling, divided into wide squares, each one decorated with intricate inlays of light wood and ivory, each one of an entirely different pattern. Seated at the table, in the shadows beneath this great mosaic of ancient Chinese art, was the powerful figure of Admiral Zhang Yushu, senior Vice Chairman of the PLAN's Council.

"Ah, Yushu, you found my childhood hideaway," said Admiral Zu.

"Hello, Jicai. You were right. One of the most secretive rooms in China. We can talk here. But we must be swift and careful . . . and so, quickly, what can you tell me about the destroyer? . . ."

"Very little. The Americans warned her away from the area of the minefield, which she ignored, as agreed. And then one of the American ships opened fire and essentially crippled her. Blew both shafts, both props and rudder. There was no way of returning fire, and in any event she could not really see her assailant. Which makes me think they may have hit her from a submarine."

"Yes. Precisely. But the loss amounts to very little. Are the Iranians towing her in?"

"Yessir."

"And the tanker at the end of the Malacca Strait?"

"Our Kilo hit it with a torpedo and vanished. Apparently it was a good choice. Nice and big, and nice and empty."

"Excellent. Have the Americans panicked?"

"I'm not certain, sir. But they just diverted yet another CVBG toward the Indian Ocean. It's on its way through Suez now."

"And the carrier *JFK*?"

"Plainly on its way to Diego Garcia, taking a southerly route—

a long way south from its normal route up to the Japanese Islands and Taiwan."

"Which leaves them where?"

"With FIVE carrier battle groups either in, or heading for, the Indian Ocean, Diego Garcia or Hormuz."

"And the *Ronald Reagan* Group? Still in San Diego?"

"Yessir and nonoperational for a good two months yet. My guess is they'll call the *JFK* back for Taiwan."

"Then we'll have to deal with her, I suppose. But I don't think that will be beyond us. Not with our Kilos."

"Nossir."

It was a very Chinese relationship. Formal to a degree when the subject involved the Navy's business, Commander-in-Chief to the biggest chief. But when the conversation slipped from report to discussion and opinion, it instantly lapsed into the kind and understanding conversation of two lifelong and beloved friends.

"And now, Jicai, do we see any improvement in our amphibians' capacity?"

"Not really, sir. I think we have to accept eleven thousand."

"And are we ready?"

"Nossir. But we are preparing every day."

"Where do you see our critical paths?"

"Certainly the Kilos, sir. We will have them routinely overhauled and ready. Most other ships are on standby. Airborne troops I understand are training with some success but with more to learn. The infantry commanders have forgotten nothing. Tanks are ready. In the air, I fear, it will be costly."

"Do we have a date?"

"I'm looking at ten days, sir."

"A feint to the outer island first?"

"Absolutely, sir."

"Are you confident, my friend?"

"With great reservations, sir."

"That's good, my Jicai. All commanders must be a little bit afraid."

And with that Admiral Zu walked to the door of the little room, and he called softly to his friend, a member of the twentieth generation of the family to own this library.

And moments later, the librarian returned and handed each of his guests a small porcelain cup, containing sweet, heavy Shaoxing red wine, served warm.

"A toast, Jicai," said Admiral Zhang. "To the immortal memory of the ruler of all the seas, Admiral Zheng He."

1100 (local). Monday, May 7.
The White House.

Arnold Morgan wanted answers. And he wasn't getting any. At least not from Admiral David Borden. The Acting Director of the NSA was unable to grasp how urgently the Big Man in the White House wanted to know who had hit the tanker in the Malacca, and with what.

Admiral Borden actually said, "Sir, we do not I believe have any proof the tanker was hit at all." Which was tantamount to telling Evander Holyfield that nobody had just bitten a hole in his ear.

And Admiral Morgan was furious. He banged down the phone, just as news came in that Brent Crude had gone to $78 a barrel in London, on rumors of a worldwide strike by the masters of the big tankers. Right now America was looking at $5 for a gallon of gasoline at the pumps. Worse yet, if things did not shake loose very quickly, there could be shutdowns at some of the nation's major electricity generators, which ran on fuel oil, or natural gas.

"*KATHY!!*"

She came in through the open door, closing it hastily in case someone else heard the anger of the President's top military adviser.

"Get George Morris on the phone right now."

"Arnold, he had surgery early this morning. You know that. He must be asleep."

"Well, wake him up."

"Don't be ridiculous. We can't wake him up. He's very sick."

"He'll be a whole lot sicker if the goddamned lights go out and his iron lung shuts down."

"Arnold, they do not use iron lungs in modern surgery anymore."

"Try not to bore me with this high-tech crap. Electricity is the lifeblood of all hospitals, including George's. Okay . . . okay . . . don't wake him up till later, but tell him to get into Fort Meade tomorrow and kick that asshole Borden out of his office."

"Arnold, I guess you could arrange to bomb Shanghai, but you cannot instruct the head of surgery at the Naval Hospital in Bethesda to discharge probably his most important patient."

"Kathy, forget all that I've just said. But please ensure I speak to George the moment he regains his senses. Because this clown in Fort Meade is unlikely ever to regain his."

"Yessir. Meanwhile, anything I can do right now?"

"Yes. Get that good boy, Jimmy Ramshawe, on my private secure line. And hop to it—don't tell me he's asleep or anything."

"Of course I may murder you one day, my darling," she said, stalking out of the room, head high, trying not to laugh.

National Security Agency.
Fort Meade, Maryland.

Lieutenant Ramshawe's phone rang angrily, reflecting precisely the general demeanor of the caller.

"Hello, sir. Yup, this is Jimmy . . . Sir, I've been on it since I got here at three this morning. You want my opinion?

"I think the Chinese fired a torpedo into that tanker from one of those Kilo-Class submarines."

"What makes you think so?"

"Sir, I've had full coverage of those coastal waters, all the way down from the Rangoon Delta to the northern headland of Sumatra, right down from the Nicobar islands. And I'm here to tell you there's not been a warship in sight in those waters all through the weekend, and then suddenly . . . BAM! Another tanker goes up at six-thirty local time. And where does it go up? I have it at six-ten-north, ninety-four-fifty-east. That's six miles southeast of Point Pygmalion, the southern headland of Great Nicobar.

"It's also six hundred miles south of the Chinese Navy base in the Bassein River—I'd say less than three days running for a Kilo moving at twelve knots through waters without a serious Naval presence. At least nothing that's looking for them. They don't even have to be careful.

"Anyway, sir. That's not all."

"Go on."

"Sir, I got two satellite shots right here showing a Russian-built Kilo on the surface, heading right for the Mergui Archipelago . . . that's right off the Burmese coast. . . ."

"I know where the hell the goddamned Merguis are, for Christ's sake. . . . Keep going. . . ."

"Yessir."

Arnold Morgan smiled to himself.

"She's about one hundred eighty miles from the burning tanker, and that's fifteen hours from the hit. So she could have done it, but they don't seem to care too much who knows."

"Very strange, Jimmy. What do you make of it?"

"Not a great deal, sir. I can't see the point of it, except to cause chaos. All I know is, this does not look like casual maritime vandalism."

"Keep thinking, Jimmy. Write your reports, and keep me right in the game."

Ten minutes later, Admiral Morgan was standing in the Oval Office informing the President of the United States that the Chinese had, without question, been responsible for yet another tanker explosion, the fourth. And as far as he could tell, there was no reasonable motive for harming any of them. Except to cause a massive hike in world oil prices, which would damn nearly bankrupt Japan and knock the hell out of the USA's burgeoning economy.

"As for Europe, with their North Sea Oil beginning to run out, sitting there with virtually no resources except a lot of damned expensive people, and welfare programs big enough to stop the Earth on its axis, well, hell, God know what's going to happen to them without Arab oil."

"Arnold, I have to make a move. I have to do something. I cannot let this all go unremarked on by the United States. Do we have the gulf under control?"

"It's under control but not yet safe. We got enough forces in there to conquer anything up to World War Three, including the sun, the moon and the planet of the fucking apes."

The President laughed, but his concern overrode any humor there may have been in his mood. "Arnold," he said, "we gotta show a major presence. We gotta frighten everyone to death, show 'em we mean what we say."

"Sir, we could show 'em we mean what we say with one CVBG. Christ, they carry eighty fighter aircraft and right now we don't have a damn thing to shoot at. And we've got *five carriers* either in or on their way in. If the oil starts flowing again, those warships could almost suck the place dry."

"Arnold, there has to be something very odd about this Sino-Iranian pact. I just cannot tell what they're up to. I only know we cannot drop our guard."

"Maybe. But I have a feeling there's a goddamned hidden agenda right here that we are not tuned in to. There simply is no obvious motive for this action by the Chinese. But I do still think there is one thing we must do: lock 'em right out of the Indian Ocean."

"You mean what we discussed before?"

"Yessir. We've gotta get rid of that oil refinery they just built. And then get rid of that Navy base on the Bassein River. Send the little bastards home, right back to the South China Sea."

"Arnold, I think to do that, we will need the support of at least one ally, and I don't know where that might come from."

"Jesus, that's an easy one. We don't even need to frown over that."

"We don't?"

"Nossir. The Indian Navy would give their eyeteeth to get China out of the Bay of Bengal and all points west of there. Remember that old animosity is as ingrained as that between Iraq and Iran. The Indians do not want the Chinese Navy prowling around in their backyard. . . . Remember, too, India is very nearly bigger than China in terms of population, and richer. I have thought for years they should be our best friends in the East."

"*Hmmmmm.* You think they'll support us kicking some Chinese ass?"

"Basically I think we tell no one what we're about to do, except to tip off Admiral Kumar about our approximate plans. He's gonna love it. So's his Prime Minister."

"You still favor the actions of your favorite troops, the cutthroats of the Navy SEALs using their world-famous techniques of solving all problems with high explosives."

"Those are my methods of choice, sir. Mainly because no one quite knows what's happened. And yet they can't fail to know it must have been us."

"Well, Arnold, since I've been in this chair, I've allowed you to unleash these guys on several targets, and I'm obliged to say they always bring home the bacon, some of it nicely fried."

"This time it's gonna be stir-fried. I'm sick to death of this Chinese crap."

"Okay, Arnold, do your duty as you see it. Send 'em in, the silent destroyers."

"That's the way, sir. Maximum effect, minimum blame. We'll give 'em seventy-eight bucks a barrel. Crazy pricks."

He turned away from the Chief Executive and walked slowly out of the Oval Office. And his thoughts cascaded in on him, as his rich imagination took him into the hot, dark recesses of the sprawling refinery on the Strait of Hormuz.

And he thought of the guys, coming in hard and silent, out of the sea, moving across the sand, watching for armed sentries. And in his mind he felt their fear, and their strength, and their patriotism.

And he walked right by Kathy O'Brien's desk without stopping, snapping out briskly just one command as he opened his office door:

"Get me Admiral John Bergstrom on the line. SPECWARCOM, Coronado Beach. Secure line. Encrypted. We're talking Black Ops, Kathy. Usual procedures."

1330. Monday, May 7.
The White House.

ADMIRAL MORGAN'S CALL to SPECWARCOM was essentially a request to Admiral John Bergstrom to put two teams of Navy SEALs on 24-hour notice in Coronado, prepared to embark immediately for Diego Garcia. That conversation took less than four minutes.

"Just one thing. . . . Degree of danger?"

"High. But your guys probably won't work up a sweat."

The next call was likely to be more complex, since even Arnold Morgan could not take the United States to war all on his own. He asked his sole serving noncommissioned officer, Kathy O'Brien, to secure President Reagan's old Situation Room on the lower floor of the West Wing.

Then he ordered her to summon the Secretary of State, the Defense Secretary, the Energy Secretary, the Chief of Naval Ops and the Chairman of the Joint Chiefs to a meeting, top priority, classified, 90 minutes from then. He excluded the President, since he already had verbal Oval Office clearance to mount whatever military operation he saw fit. He assumed this particular President would deny all knowledge if the operation went wrong, which it had better not.

It was 1500 when General Tim Scannell came hurrying through the big wooden doors flanked by two saluting U.S. Marine guards. The door was closed firmly behind him, and he walked to his place at the head of the big table, at Admiral Morgan's right hand. "I'm sorry to hold you up, gentlemen," he said politely. "It's just that we've got more going on in the Middle East than we've had since Saddam got above himself seventeen years ago. We've got more ships out there, too."

To the left of the Chairman of the Joint Chiefs sat the Secretary of State, the steel-haired veteran diplomat Harcourt Travis, and the Energy Secretary, Jack Smith, probably the best CEO General Motors ever had. Opposite them were the recently appointed CNO, Admiral Alan Dixon, former Commander-in-Chief Atlantic Fleet, and the Defense Secretary, Robert MacPherson.

And because the meeting was convened and chaired by Admiral Morgan himself, the seating of the military men always placed them in some kind of ascendancy. *Civilians have their place, of course, but when you need to get stuff assessed and then acted upon, in a serious hurry, the military leave 'em standing.* The Admiral's view on that subject was both uncompromising and generally accepted, since he was unlikely to change his mind.

"Gentlemen," he growled, frowning deeply, "right here we got a major shit fight on our hands."

Jack Smith, attending his first effective war cabinet, smiled at the Admiral's poetically worded appreciation of the situation, and added formally, "There're reports of four-dollars-a-gallon gasoline in the Midwest."

"Jesus Christ," said Admiral Morgan.

He shook his head, and muttered, "If we're not damned careful, this could get right out of hand."

He then called the meeting to order and proceeded to outline the standoff in the gulf, and approximately what he proposed they should do about it.

"You all know roughly what's happened. The Iranians and the Chinese between them have constructed a deep, we *think* three-line, minefield, clean across the Strait of Hormuz, distance of about twenty miles. So far three tankers have been hit and burned. We have the Indian Navy in there sweeping the field, trying to open up a seven-mile-wide freeway for the world's tankers to start entering and leaving the gulf. But it's slow and somewhat perilous.

"Right now we have five U.S. CVBGs either deep in the area or on their way. That's essentially to protect the Indians, and make those seas safe again for the continued orderly conduct of the world's oil and gas trade. By now, most of that's routine and under control. However, in the early hours of this morning there was a development that I did not like. An unladen Japanese-registered tanker suddenly blew up at the north end of the Malacca Strait. I have reason to believe it was hit by a torpedo from a Chinese Kilo-Class submarine.

"I further believe that Kilo was refueled at the new Chinese Navy Base in Burma on the Bassein River Delta. I further believe it's on its way back there right now. But that's just a sideshow.

"The real problem is China. Her intentions. The depth of her involvement in the mining of the strait, and her ambitions in the Arabian Sea, the gulf area, the Indian Ocean and in particular the Bay of Bengal. . . ."

He paused, and no one spoke. "Gentlemen," he said, "I am quite certain that if we do not chase China out of those oceans, we will live to regret it. Remember, they have been passive in terms of sea power for more than five hundred years, just running a coastal Navy to protect their own shores.

"But not anymore. They're plainly in an expanionist mode, acquiring submarines, destroyers and a couple of aircraft carriers from the Russians. They're building a new ICBM submarine platform, and they are pushing westward. That new oil refinery of theirs south of Bandar Abbas gives them an excuse to send protective warships into the Arabian Sea. And that new base in Burma has given them a home port from which they could essentially control the oil routes through the Malacca Strait. That's all the oil routes to the west and north Pacific."

Admiral Morgan paused again. And then he growled, "Gentlemen, these guys are not just stepping lightly on our toes. They're running us over with a fleet of fucking rickshaws, and I'm not having it."

Jack Smith and General Scannell both smiled, and Harcourt Travis laughed out loud. "Arnold," he said, "you have such a way with words. You really should have considered the diplomatic service."

Everyone in the room knew the suave Secretary of State was not entirely enamored of the President's crusty National Security Adviser. And, some thought, the diplomat's calm, thoughtful intellect was a very good foil for the irascible ex–nuclear submarine commander. But the Admiral's mind was invariably superior, and he had won almost every one of their exchanges down through the years, even if he did occasionally sound like a Master sergeant in an ugly mood.

"Hey, Harcourt, old buddy. Glad to hear you're still sharp, because right now I want you to give me an assessment. If you wanted to chase the Chinese out of the Indian and Arabian Seas, what action would you consider taking?"

"You mean as an American?"

"Christ, no. As an Ethiopian."

This was too much for both Jack Smith and General Scannell, who both burst out laughing. Bob MacPherson and Admiral Dixon tried to restrain themselves. And even Harcourt permitted himself a deep chuckle—restrained, of course.

"You see, Harcourt," Arnold Morgan said, smiling, "that's the trouble with you Foreign Service guys . . . you're always looking for the extra half sentence, to give yourselves an extra few seconds to think . . . it's just a habit. . . . Yes, Harcourt, as an American. You got it the first time."

"Well, first of all, I'd go and pray at the tomb of my former

Emperor Haile Selassie, the Lion of Judah. Then I guess I'd come right back and advise you to blow the bastards right out of the water. Is that sufficiently primitive?"

"Harcourt," replied the Admiral, unsmiling, his bright blue eyes narrowing dangerously, "I like it."

At which point everyone laughed some more, but it was edged with nervousness, like telling a joke before an oncoming disaster. The Navy are good at that. In World War II no U.S. ship was ever blasted by bombs or torpedoes without one of the survivors observing, "Guess you shouldn't have joined if you can't take a joke."

The Admiral quickly regained his stride. "I'm talking politically. . . . You know our problems—the Iranian Naval base at Bandar Abbas, the new Iranian refinery, right there next to the warships, the Sino-Iranian refinery, effectively owned by the Chinese, just along the coast, and the new Chinese Naval Base and refueling docks on the Bassein River. All four of those installations represent a giant pain in the ass, not just for us, but for all nations that require oil and gas. . . ."

Harcourt Travis nodded, an air of caution written right across his face. "Arnold," he said, "I do not think we could just cold-bloodedly take out the Iranian base at Bandar Abbas. However covertly we moved, everyone would know it was us, and I think it would be construed as a blatant act of war. However, I think we would hold on to world opinion if we hit any warship we judged to be a threat to the free passage of shipping through the gulf."

"Uh-huh. And how about the Iranian refinery?"

"Bad idea. If the situation in the gulf turned really ugly, we might just need the oil out of that refinery. We might even need to seize it. Let's not destroy it, however pissed off we might be at the Ayatollahs."

"And the new Chinese refinery?"

"That's different. Because that refinery gives the People's Liberation Army-Navy a reason to be operational at the western end of the Indian Ocean and the Arabian Sea. I'm not saying we go in and blast the place to smithereens, probably starting World War

Three. But if that refinery was to . . . er . . . become disfunctional after some kind of . . . er . . . problem, well, I guess a lot of people would be pretty relieved."

"And the base on the Bassein River?"

"That," said Harcourt, flatly, "has gotta go."

"Any drift on the state of mind of the Burmese government? Or Myanmar, or whatever the hell they call it?"

"Well, you know it's a military junta, Arnie. It's in power regardless of the results of democratic elections. And recently they appear to have become much less friendly toward the Chinese. But the Big Dragon sits right against their back door, and the Big Dragon has built roads and even railroads right through the country to the port cities on the Bay of Bengal. The Chinese have armed the Burmese military, sold them God knows how much hardware on long lines of credit. I'm afraid the Burmese are in too deep to get out. We'll get no help from them. You want to get rid of that Chinese base, you're on your own. But you'd have some cheerleaders in India."

"They still pissed off about the tracking station on Great Cocos Island?"

"Very, very pissed off. The Chinese installed it with extreme cunning and furtiveness. Then they put an airstrip in there. Now they can pry deep behind India's eastern coastline. Myanmar says the Seventy-fifth AF Radar Squadron is theirs, but everyone knows it's Chinese. They probe straight across the Bay of Bengal and record all takeoffs from Calcutta Airport and any military airport along the coast. The Indians call them the Chinese Checkers."

Bob MacPherson, another veteran of this Republican administration, interjected here in support of the Secretary of State. "There's more trouble in that region than even we realize. The Chinese have spy ships all over the Bay of Bengal, and that's thanks largely to their base on Haing Gyi Island. It would be a hell of a lot more difficult for them if it wasn't there."

"Trouble is," said Harcourt, "that Burmese coastline is so damned strategic. The Cocos Islands are only just in Burmese waters, right on the Cocos Channel, the main seaway for *every* merchant ship bound for eastern Indian ports and Bangladesh.

"Immediately to the south, around ten miles, we have the northernmost island of the Indian archipelago . . . you know, the Andamans and the Nicobars, stretching five hundred miles to the south toward the Malacca Strait. No one in the area feels safe, with Chinese warships constantly on patrol there."

"I'll tell you something else," added Jack Smith. "On average there are three hundred ships passing through the Bay of Bengal every day. A lot of them are tankers to and from the east. There're some new economic projections which suggest that in the next twenty years, fifty percent of all world trade will center on the Pacific-Asian countries. God knows how many more ships that will mean."

"And China sees itself as the great controller of those seaways," said Bob MacPherson. "But the elimination of the base on the Bassein River would set them back a quarter of a century."

"So what are our priorities?" asked Admiral Morgan.

"I think we make it plain to the Chinese that we will sink any of their warships in the clearance zone in the Strait of Hormuz. We then quietly mastermind a problem in their refinery in Iran, and cause it essentially . . . er . . . not to work. That gets them out of the western waters of the Arabian Sea and the Indian Ocean. The oil issue is irrelevant because it's from Kazakhstan and the Chinese are going to get it anyway, probably via a pipeline into their western territories, and on to Shanghai."

"Christ," said Admiral Morgan. "That's, what, five thousand miles or something? They can't do that."

"With respect, Honorable National Adviser," said Harcourt in his best Cantonese accent. "They built a very long, very high wall. They'll probably manage to dig a fucking hole."

Arnold Morgan chuckled. But he was very preoccupied. "And our next priority?" he asked.

"I think you know the answer to that. Let's chase them out of the Bassein River. Somewhat secretly. And probably earn the thanks of many millions of people."

Admiral Morgan sat thoughtfully. He and Harcourt Travis had been through a few run-ins, but, despite everything, he liked the Secretary of State. And he liked him for one overriding reason . . . *smooth sonofabitch really knows his stuff . . . he's a scholar, a realist and a cynic. A guy you can count on for important opinions."*

"Harcourt," he said. "I thank you. I thank all of you. Civilians may consider the meeting concluded. CNO, Tim, I'd like a half hour more to discuss tactics." He stood and shook hands with the departing chiefs of Foreign Policy, Defense and Energy.

"I scarcely need to remind you of the hugely classified nature of the matters we have discussed," he added. "There is no one who needs to know, save ourselves."

Then he walked to the end of the room where Kathy had pinned up a large chart of the Strait of Hormuz, showing the coastline all the way from Bandar Abbas to the desert town of Kuhestak, way over on the long, near-barren eastern shore, forty-eight miles south of the Iranian Navy HQ.

"Come up here and take a look at this," he said. "You see this place right here, Kuhestak? The Chinese refinery is situated right here, two miles along the coast to the south. It's big. There's a massive pipeline system running in here, all the way from the oil fields in Khazakhstan, one thousand miles, right across the heart of Iran.

"This precious Iranian seaport is soon going to give China its energy from the heart of the second-largest oil producer on earth. Because it can run tankers in here of virtually unlimited size, and then drive out straight across the Indian Ocean, through the Malacca Strait and into the South China Sea.

"In my view, that's basically what the trouble is all about. That is precisely why China wants this growing military presence in the region . . . and precisely why we cannot allow it.

"You just heard the assessments of Harcourt and Bob. Now I want you to tell me how a dozen SEALs can take out that refinery. I say a dozen because the water's shallow and well patrolled. We're going to need an SDV, I'm certain of that. And we only have one in the area—the one stowed on the deck of the good old *Shark*. The good news is it does not take a whole lot of high explosives to blow up an oil refinery. Sonsabitches are apt to blow themselves up if you give 'em a head start."

"Guess you're referring to the Big Bang in Texas City back in 1947, eh?" said General Scannell. "I had an uncle lived somewhere out near Galveston. He told me when I was just a kid you coulda heard that explosion from one hundred fifty miles away."

"I was about three years old at the time, and we didn't live that far from the disaster," said Arnold. "I remember my daddy told me the ship that blew it exploded with such force its one-and-a-half ton anchor was flung two miles and embedded itself ten feet into the ground at the Pan American refinery."

The recollection of the Texas City disaster reminded all three men of the enormous problems involved in taking out a major refinery, with its attendant sites of sprawling petrochemical plants; just about every square foot of such industrial time bombs is filled with highly volatile, flammable materials, including vast pressurized storage tanks for natural gas. And the new Chinese installation at Kuhestak had all that, and more.

Hundreds were killed, thousands injured in Texas City, buildings all over town were blasted beyond recognition. And the devastation was not restricted to the waterfront, or to the refining towers and storage areas. It just about ripped the entire town apart. A radio announcer simply yelled, "Texas City just blew up!" The mushroom cloud rose 2,000 feet into the air. Massive, white-hot steel parts from the French merchant ship SS *Grandcamp* were hurled into the holding tanks hundreds of yards away, setting off secondary explosions, which in turn caused immense damage.

The burning *Grandcamp* with its heavy cargo of ammonium nitrate fertilizer was responsible for what remains the worst industrial catastrophe in U.S. history. At the time, so soon after World War II, there were few modern safety precautions in place. And of course there was none of the grim voyeurism of late-twentieth-century television, with its voracious, insatiable appetite for agony, heartbreak and disaster, which it finds so helpful in its endless, somewhat childlike, quest for drama and action.

Texas City 1947 remains a milestone in U.S. industrial calamity. And Admiral Arnold Morgan, a native-born Texan himself, had no wish to involve civilian casualties in the little Iranian town of Kuhestak, even though he gave not one jot for the lives of the Chinese technicians at the refinery. . . . *You guys wanna fuck around with the free passage of world oil and gas . . . guess you should have thought about that real deeply before ordering those mines from Moscow.*

In any event, the Chinese refinery had to go. The remaining questions were how quickly and how to get the SEALs out before the whole shooting match went up in smoke and took our guys with it.

Meanwhile, Admiral Dixon stared at the little numbers on the chart, checking out the water depth, turning over in his mind the equation . . . Shark *can't operate in depths of less than one hundred fifty feet . . . How near can she go before the guys have to leave in the little electric SDV, running until she touches the sand, and then unloading the SEALs to swim in the rest of the way?*

"What d'ya think, Admiral?" Arnold Morgan was stepping aside to allow the CNO some space.

"*Shark's* gonna need passageway through the minefield . . . then she's got a twenty-mile submerged run nor'nor'east up to this point right here . . . 'bout twelve miles off the Iranian coast. . . . She'll be in at least one hundred eighty feet of water all the way there, say 26.36N, right on 56.49E."

"That's precisely where I had the rendezvous point, Alan. . . . Great minds, right?"

"Realistic minds, at least, sir . . . *Shark* wouldn't want to move inshore any farther. She starts leaving a wake—that's asking for trouble. Iran's got a few fast attack craft with ASW mortars. We wanna stay real silent."

"How many guys does the SDV hold?"

"Well, the old ones carried only ten. That's the one on *Mendel Rivers* . . . crew of two and eight SEALs. This new one holds fourteen, so we got twelve active SEAL demolition guys. We're just lucky the SDV is on the deck of *Shark*, otherwise we'd be all over the damned place. Still, I guess we're due for a bit of luck. Haven't had much for a while, and I gotta real gut feeling about getting Beijing out of Arabia."

"You and me. What d'you say, General?"

Tim Scannell looked thoughtful. "I was just thinking: Something goes wrong, say the submarine gets hit and crippled, any thoughts on backup? You need a carrier in the area to frighten everyone away, or you want me to order up some fighter aircraft we can deploy out of Oman, with the Brits' help?"

"Good call, General. Anything hits our submarine, I mean a surface ship, we vaporize it, right?"

"Yessir, Arnie. But how about an Iranian or Chinese Kilo-Class submarine in the area? Both nations have 'em, and as you know they're little bastards under the water."

Admiral Dixon responded immediately: "I'll order a coupla LA-Class nuclear boats to ride shotgun on *Shark* while she goes in. They'll pick up a Kilo if it's close enough."

"And then?" Arnold Morgan looked quizzical.

"If it's under the surface, we sink it. No questions asked."

"Thank you, CNO. That's my language you're talking, right there. You can only fuck around with these towelheads and Orientals for just so long, right?"

"Right, sir."

"No bullshit," added Admiral Morgan, by way of emphasis.

"Matter of fact, sir," said Alan Dixon, "I'd say our biggest worry is getting the guys in, once they leave the SDV. . . . You see, the twenty-meter depth line is all of five miles offshore . . . the ten-meter line's only about a half mile farther in . . . then they got a coupla miles in about four feet of water on flat sand. . . . Terrain's fine, but there is a risk of detection . . . and it's a long way back to deep water and safety."

"A long way for you and me, Alan. But not these guys . . . they'll slide through those warm shallows like a shoal of Florida bonefish—fast, sleek, unpredictable and likely to fight like hell."

Arnold Morgan made a curving forward motion with the palm of his left hand. . . . "*Death to the Chinese oilers, right?*"

"Actually, I'm more worried about pursuit than anything else, Arnie, especially if they keep a fleet of helicopters at the refinery."

"Alan, if that place goes up the way I think it will, there's not going to be anything even resembling pursuit. Bergstrom has the charts, and his top instructors will be involved in the planning. I expect Commander Rick Hunter will lead the squad, but I'm not sure if he'll go into Iran or Burma. Not both."

"You have real faith in those SEALs, don't you?"

"Yes. If they can't do it, it can't be done. And I know that a group of the most highly trained demolition killers on this planet can blow up a goddamned oil refinery. Gimme a book o'matches, and I'll blow the fucker up myself."

Both Alan Dixon and Tim Scannell laughed at the President's top military adviser: always just the right combination of steel and intellect, respect and contempt, fortitude and laughter. Arnold Morgan really was anyone's idea of the perfect keeper of America's front line.

Both the Admiral and General now stood back and watched as Morgan once more stepped up to the chart, this time holding a grainy black-and-white photograph in his left hand while making a tiny drawing on the chart, a small pencil line five miles offshore right on the 20-meter depth line.

"See that?" he said. "That's the loading dock. Just completed construction. That's where the big Chinese VLCCs will be landing. The pipeline's already in, but we have no evidence of trade yet. Pity the sonofabitch is so far from shore, otherwise we could just hit some combustible merchant ship and give 'em Texas City Two. But, as the proprietors of the refinery might put it, *no can do*. So we'll just have to slam the fucker, bang in the middle of the plant. Then maybe take out the loading dock on the way back, if there're ships at it."

"Okay, sir. Sounds good, if a bit tricky. You wanna talk some about the Bassein River hit?"

"Not now, Tim. I'm judging that to be a lot more complicated.

We'll have John Bergstrom in before we finalize. And possibly a couple of his commanders—maybe forty-eight hours. Wednesday morning."

He saw the two service chiefs out, and then walked slowly back to the chart of the Strait of Hormuz. And he muttered to himself, "They must know that goddamned refinery is vulnerable. They must know there will be some form of retribution if the U.S. finds out they helped lay that minefield. Or maybe they figure we'll never find out for certain. . . ."

He paused for a full minute. And then he muttered, "Nah, they're just not that stupid. They must *know* we'll find out. . . ."

And if that's the case, he pondered, *there's only one question left: What in the name of Christ are they up to?*

072200MAY07.
Flight Deck, USS *Constellation*. Strait of Hormuz.
26.30N 56.50E. Speed 30. Course 225.

She was turned along the southwesterly run of the minefield now, the U.S. Navy's beloved forty-year-old *"Connie,"* plowing forward into the hot wind of this sweltering Arabian night. Right now she was about five miles north of the field, and the area seemed quiet as the Indian Pondicherrys moved steadily about their hazardous business, cutting the mines free and then blowing them on the surface.

But still the howling F-14D Tomcats, curtesy of U.S. fighter wing VF 2—the fabled Bounty Hunters—gunned their aircraft off *Connie*'s 1,000-foot-long flight deck, up and into the black skies that now blanketed the most lethal stretch of ocean in the entire world.

Each pilot wore on his right sleeve the Bounty Hunters' triangular emblem, the yellow delta-winged fighter-bomber on red-white-and-blue stripes. Most of them also sported the jaunty gunslinger patch, the cowboy tomcat leaning on a big *D*, with the new stitched lettering, *Anytime, Pal.*

And they flew right out on the edge of the envelope, banking in hard over the Iranian coastline and then back out to sea. This really was *Anytime, Pal*, because right now the U.S. Navy meant business, and everyone knew it. One squeak out of an Iranian antiaircraft battery, one illumination, one suggestion, and that battery would be obliterated by a phalanx of missiles with an accuracy record of around 100 percent.

Navy pilots are used to being accused of "U.S. bullying." But they were not bullies tonight, while the whole world awaited the reopening of the gulf to oil tankers.

Tonight the Navy fliers were the fearless White Knights of the Skies, the way they mostly saw themselves anyhow. And they hurled their Tomcats through the high darkness of Islam, the single most threatening airborne cavalry ever assembled, on a mission to shut down the menace of a known aggressor. *Anytime, Pal.* The patches said it all.

Back on *Connie*'s flight deck in the controlled chaos of a hectic night's flying the 22-ton Tomcats were slamming down in batches, because the carrier has to keep making ground downwind, altering course, between landings and takeoffs. Swarms of flight-deck personnel surrounded each aircraft as it thundered in, a team ever ready to rush forward and ram the Sidewinder safety pins into the pylon firing mechanisms. The hot swirling air, stinking of JP-4, burned rubber, searing hot metal and salt water, assaulted everyone's senses as the air boss snapped out commands through the 88,000-ton ship's tannoy system. This was *Connie*'s last tour of duty.

Out on the stern, oblivious to the earsplitting shriek of the incoming jets, the duty arresting gear officer, a lieutenant junior grade, sweating in his big fluorescent yellow jacket, was in contact with the hydraulic operators one deck below. The wires were ready to withstand the 75,000-pound force of the Tomcat hitting the deck at 160 knots, the pilot's hand still hard on the throttle just in case the hook missed.

The 28-year-old Lieutenant, Bobby Myers from Ohio, could

feel his voice rising now as he snapped down commands to the hydraulic men . . . *"Stand by for Tomcat one-zero-seven . . . two minutes."*

He looked back over the stern, 90 feet above the water, straining to catch the lights of the fighter-bomber. He knew the pilot personally, and, as it did every single time, his chest began to tighten, and his heart was racing. Nothing ever dismisses the nerve-twisting tension that grips the arresting gear officer when a fighter-bomber is on its final flight path. Every arresting gear officer who ever lived, that is.

Bobby had him now, five miles out, and he checked the wires again, checked on his radio phone that the huge hydraulic piston was ready to take the strain in the forthcoming controlled collision between deck and plane.

"GROOVE!" he shouted into the phone, the code word for *"She's close, STAND BY!"*

Two miles out now, bucking along in the warm erratic air currents of the gulf, the Tomcat pilot fought to hold her steady, watching the landing lights, always watching the balls of light, an iron grip on the stick. He could see the carrier's stern rise slightly on the swell, and the precision required for the high-speed landing would be measured in inches rather than feet. Every pilot knows he is a split second from death during every carrier landing he makes. One in five Navy pilots dies in the first nine years of his service.

Seconds later Bobby Myers snapped, *"SHORT"*—the critical command for everyone to stand right back away from the machinery.

And now Bobby saw the Tomcat right above, screaming in.

"RAMP!" he bellowed, and every single eye on the flight deck was lasered in on the hook stretched out behind. The blast from the jets shimmered in the night air. The ear-shattering din of the jet engines made speech impossible. One mistake now and it would not be just the pilot who died. A pileup on the flight deck could spark a jet-fuel fire that could put the entire ship out of action.

And hundreds of battle-hardened flight-deck technicians, already swarming forward, silently breathed *Thank God*, as the hook swung, and then grabbed the wire, hauling the Tomcat to a standstill. Just as they would all breathe *Thank God* again, one minute from now, as they coaxed yet another F-14D out of the sky to safety, refueled her and prepared her to go again.

So it is, out with the frontline steel fist of the U.S. Navy, where men face danger every minute, where they operate in harm's way every single day, always under orders, always working for the cause. Their rewards are modest, at least financially. But in a sense they have the biggest paychecks of all: not written out on some bank transfer. Written out on their own hearts.

And meanwhile 200 million citizens back home grouse and moan about the rising price of gasoline.

"Tomcat one-zero-six . . . one minute . . . STAND BY!"

080600MAY07. USS *John F. Kennedy.* ## 10.00S 137E. Speed 30. Course 270.

The 88,000-ton carrier was halfway between Pearl Harbor and Diego Garcia, steaming at flank speed through the Arafura Sea south of the Indonesian archipelago, heading for the near-bottomless waters above the Java Trench. They were well through the narrows of the Torres Strait, there was almost no wind off Australia's Northern Territory and it was hotter than hell. *Big John*'s 280,000-horsepower Westinghouse turbines were working. The giant four-shafter was fully laden with more than 40 fighter-attack F-14A Tomcats, F/A-18C Hornets and a dozen more radar-spotter aircraft, prowlers and ASW squadrons.

The flight wing patches worn by the aviators bore the names of legendary U.S. Navy outfits: the *Black Aces;* old Fighting 14; the *Top Hatters;* and VFA-87, the *Golden Warriors*. There might not yet be a full-scale war raging in the Gulf of Iran, but you'd never have known it watching *Big John*, armed to the teeth, driving forward on the second half of her 10,000-mile mission to Jimmy Ramshawe's minefield.

And now 5,000 miles of the Indian Ocean stretched before them. They would be the fifth U.S. CVBG to arrive on station, almost certainly to move north from Diego Garcia immediately, up to the gulf to relieve the *Constellation* Group.

On the bridge of the carrier, Rear Admiral Daylan Holt was studying the plot of his group, one cruiser, two destroyers, five frigates, two nuclear submarines and a fleet tanker. At this speed they were burning up fuel, fast. But his orders were clear: *Make all speed to DG and stand by for gulf patrol.*

That was one way to send someone on a 10,000-mile journey across the world. But Admiral Holt was prepared, even though it was difficult to get a handle on how serious things really were in the Strait of Hormuz.

He sipped black coffee in company with his Combat Systems Officer, Lt. Commander Chris Russ, as the sun began to rise blood red out of the ocean over the stern of the massive warship. There was an air of apprehension throughout the carrier, had been since they had cleared Pearl a week ago. The pilots were predicatably gung-ho. A bit too gung-ho. And now, for the first time, Lt. Commander Russ posed the question to the Admiral.

"Do you think we might actually have to fight this, sir? I mean, a proper hot war?"

"I think it's possible but unlikely, Chris. Look at our perceived enemies—Iran, who put down the minefield, and China, who made it possible. Well, for a start, Iran's not going to fire a shot in anger. They know we could ice their entire country in about twenty minutes. They have not fired yet, and in my opinion will not fire at all."

"How about the Chinese?"

"They might attack if the action were in the South China Sea where they have their main fleet and we have many, many fewer ships. But they won't attack in the gulf. They're too far from home, and anyway they know we'd wipe out their ships in about twenty minutes."

"That's a kinda busy twenty minutes, sir," replied the Lieutenant Commander, grinning.

"That's a lot better than a kinda dead twenty minutes," replied the Admiral, not grinning.

0600. Tuesday, May 8.
HQ SPECWARCOM. Coronado Beach.
San Diego, California.

Commander Russell Bennett, one of the most highly decorated U.S. Navy SEALs ever to serve in the squadron, was relishing his new job as the senior instructor for combat-ready men.

The ex–Maine lobsterman, lionized in Coronado for his daredevil role as forward commander in a sensational attack on a Chinese jail last year, was back home on the beach, running through the cold surf, driving his men ever onward, before the sun had fought its way above the cliffs.

They'd been out there since 0430 now and some of the newer guys, fresh out of their BUDs course, were finding it tough going. Rusty's methods were brutal in the extreme. He parked six Zodiacs a half mile offshore and ordered all 50 of the men into the surf to swim out and get on board. Then he had them drive forward with their paddles, beach the big rubber landing craft, turn it around, and then fight it back out through the crashing breakers, again using paddles only.

One half mile later they all jumped back into the freezing water wearing only swimming shorts and fought their way back to the beach, leaving only the six boat drivers behind. Tired, freezing, still in the dark, the men were then ordered to run four more miles back along the beach to a point where the Zodiacs were again waiting a half mile offshore.

They'd done the exercise twice now, and all they heard was

Commander Bennett's voice urging them onward: *"Keep going, son. I'm probably saving your life."* They were precisely the same words Rusty's own instructors had yelled at him 15 years before. More important, they had been prophetically correct, which was, essentially, why the hickory-tough Rusty Bennett was still breathing, after an operational career that had six times seen him square up and stare down the Grim Reaper. The carrot-haired ex–SEAL combat team leader was just a bit too tough to die. And today he was making sure that also applied to the men he was now training. Every last one of them.

Three times in the past 15 minutes, young SEALs had fallen flat down in the sand, too cold, too exhausted to care. And each time Rusty Bennett had stood above each man and roared abuse, swearing to God he'd blow his head off if he didn't *GET UP AND MOVE FORWARD.*

Two of the men were almost unconscious. One of them was sobbing. But all three of them reached down again, and found more, and then got up and moved forward in a combination of agony and defiance. At the end of the exercise, Commander Bennett took each of them aside and told him quietly, "That's what it's all about, hanging in there when you have nothing left. That's a great job you did right there. I'm proud of you."

Back in the SEALs' headquarters, Commander Bennett was summoned to the office of the SEAL Chief, Admiral John Bergstrom.

"'Morning, Rusty," he said. "How do they look?"

"Good, sir. Very good. Six of the veterans are already excellent leaders, and some of the new guys have terrific potential. We got great swimmers, good radio technicians, demolition guys and marksmen. Plus a few obvious hard men."

"Can we get two teams of twelve out of the group for a couple of critical missions?"

"I'm sure we can, sir. I really like what I'm seeing from them. But I wouldn't mind knowing roughly where we're going."

"Well, you and I are leaving for Washington shortly after midnight for a final briefing. We'll be there all day. I guess we'll know then."

"Are we seeing the Big Man, sir?"

"In person."

"Jesus. Are you sure I'm ready for this?"

"You're ready. Just as long as you remember his bark's bad, but his bite's worse. . . . Just kidding. The Admiral loves SEALs. Thinks we're the most important guys in the U.S. armed services. Anyway it's pretty obvious where we're going, isn't it?"

"I'm afraid so, sir. Middle East. But I just wonder what we're supposed to be doing."

"Probably not public relations. If Arnold Morgan wants us, he wants something either flattened or just plain obliterated. Trust me."

"Hell. I hope it's not the big Iranian Naval yard down on the gulf. It's swarming with military personnel."

"Of course, you're an expert, eh, Rusty?"

"Yessir. A very fair description. Damn place gives me the creeps."

"If I had to guess, I would say it's certainly not Bandar Abbas the Admiral wants to talk about."

"Why not, sir? He said to have two teams of twelve on twenty-four hours battle notice. That's two targets. Separate. Even Arnold Morgan could not possibly think twelve SEALs could take out an entire Naval base, with several thousand men on duty."

"We might have a shot if we went at night!" said Rusty, grinning. "But I agree. He's got something more passive in mind."

John Bergstrom walked across the room to a large-scale electronic chart of the ocean along Iran's southeastern coast. He stood staring at it as if checking reference points. And then he muttered, almost inaudibly, "*What about that damn Chinese refinery?*"

"Sorry, sir. I didn't quite get that?"

"Oh nothing, Rusty. Just a thought. Let's wait until tomorrow. See you right here tonight zero-zero-thirty. Civilian suit. We're meeting Commander Hunter at the White House."

"Aye, sir."

0859. Wednesday, May 9.
The White House Lawn.

Admiral Morgan turned his head sideways to the wind and stared into the skies to the southeast, searching like an air traffic controller for the big Navy helicopter bringing John Bergstrom and Rusty Bennett in from Andrews Air Base.

He checked his watch, one minute before touchdown, and no sign yet of the U.S. Marines' Super Cobra clattering across the eastern bank of the Potomac.

"If I could *see* the sonofabitch right now, they'd still be a minute late," he muttered. "Standing out here on the grass like some fucking rose pruner. Goddamned disorganized sailors. Where the hell are they?"

He had to wait only two more minutes. And then he spotted the Marine guided-missile gunship, with its brand-new four-bladed rotor, bearing down on the White House. The pilot swung over the building, banked the helicopter to its port side and dropped gently down onto the landing pad.

Seconds later the loadmaster had opened the passenger door and the U.S. Navy's Emperor SEAL, Admiral John Bergstrom, stepped down into a bright spring morning in the capital. Behind him, dressed in a dark gray suit, with gleaming black shoes, came the powerful figure of Commander Bennett. He wore a white shirt with a dark blue tie. His principal distinguishing feature was pinned on his left lapel, the combat SEAL's gleaming golden trident. Rusty Bennett's colleagues swear he pinned it on his pajamas each night without fail.

Arnold Morgan walked toward them with a welcoming smile. "Hello, John," he said. "Good to see you again." And he shook the hand of the Commander-in-Chief of SPECWARCOM. And then he turned to the junior officer, who was hanging back in the presence of a legend, and he just said solemnly, "Come and take me by the hand, Commander Bennett. This is a moment to which I have looked forward for a long time."

Rusty walked forward and said quietly, "Admiral Morgan, it's my pleasure to meet you."

And as their hands clasped, the Admiral found his imagination roaming out of control. Before him stood a clean-cut well-presented Naval officer, but in his mind Arnold Morgan saw a warrior, face blackened, machine gun cocked, leading his men out of the water, up the beach, face-to-face with unimaginable danger. He saw in Rusty's deep blue eyes the icy glance of a born leader, a veteran of three brutal SEAL missions, a tiger among men, and he shook his head and said, "Commander, I don't often get a chance to shake the hand of a real hero. I just want you to know I regard it as a great privilege."

Rusty nodded, and said without emphasis, "Thank you, sir. Thank you very much indeed." And in the background he could see the White House, the very citadel of American power, and he wished with all his heart that his widowed father, Jeb Bennett, the Maine lobersterman from Mount Desert, could have seen him right now. Just for a few seconds.

They walked companionably toward the main door to the West Wing, and the agents handed both SEALs special passes before they set off down the corridor to Admiral Morgan's lair. Kathy O'Brien greeted them as they arrived and informed the Admiral that Alan Dixon and General Scannell were waiting inside. She had just received a signal from the base at Quantico that Commander Hunter was in the area and that his helicopter would put down on the White House pad in five minutes, direct from the SEALs' east coast h.q. at Little Creek, Virginia, home of Teams Two, Four and Eight.

Inside the office the introductions were made, principally for the benefit of Rusty. The rest of the officers knew one another. Kathy ordered coffee for everyone but returned almost immediately to announce the arrival of Commander Rick Hunter, the SEAL team leader who had operated under deep cover in a murderous attack on Russian Naval hardware in the late Joe Stalin's northern canals; and who had been in overall command of the attack on the Chinese jail the previous year.

He walked through the door, a tall, hard-muscled warrior, standing 6 feet 4 inches tall and tipping the scales at a zero-body-fat 220 pounds. He was dressed like Rusty in a dark gray suit, with a white shirt and highly polished shoes. Like Rusty, he wore the gleaming golden trident of the combat SEAL on his left lapel.

Admiral Morgan vacated the big chair behind his desk and walked across the room to meet the battle-hardened SEAL leader from the Bluegrass State. He told him, as he had told Rusty, that it was an honor finally to talk to him.

"Sir," said Rick Hunter, "I had no idea you had even heard of me."

"Rick," said Arnold Morgan, "for me to refer to you as one of the finest combat commanders our Special Forces ever had would be to damn with faint praise. I know who you are, and I know what you have done. Please go over and sit in my chair, behind my desk, and allow me to bring you a cup of probably disgusting coffee. It's the best I can do."

Everyone laughed. And the big SEAL went and sat in the Admiral's chair.

"If you only knew, Commander, how many hours I've sat right there, wondering about you, and your missions, and whether you could possibly succeed . . . Well, you ought to feel right at home, right there. That's my Rick Hunter worry-myself-to-death seat."

Admiral Morgan poured coffee for everyone, then directed their attention to the electronic chart he had pulled up on a big screen at the end of the room. It showed the southeast coast of Iran and it was highlighted by three dotted lines, close together, joining the Omani coastal town of Ra's Qabr al Hindi to a point 20 miles east on the Iranian shore. It stretched like a wall across the strait.

"That the minefield, Arnie?" asked Admiral Bergstrom.

"That's it. And we should have a pretty-good-size seaway through it in a few more days. The Indian sweepers have done well. We're looking for a cleared gateway of three or four miles."

"Tankers start moving this week?"

"We're not that clear."

"Okay, boss," said the SEAL chief. "Lay it on me. What do we hit?"

"Up here, John. Twenty-nine miles to the north. See where it says *Kuhestak*? The new Chinese oil and petrochemical refinery is right there, two miles south of that little town. It's huge."

"You want it put out of action?"

"Uh-uh. I want it vaporized."

"Jesus," said Rick Hunter.

"What's the water depth inshore?" asked Rusty Bennett.

"Damn shallow," replied Admiral Morgan. "We got about five miles under nine feet, the last two miles are under four."

"Can we get a submarine in close?"

"Probably seventeen miles, then an ASDV into the shallows. The last five miles you have to swim, walk or wallow. Water's warm. No military presence that we know of. A deserted coastline."

Commander Hunter nodded. "We got the new ASDV, the one that holds fourteen guys?"

"You have. It's on board *Shark* right now. Two-man crew, twelve SEALs."

"Range?"

"Sixteen hours at six knots."

"Will it wait, using zero power? Or come back for the guys later?"

"It'll wait."

Commander Hunter nodded again. He turned to Admiral Bergstrom. "Am I going in, sir?"

"Not this time. You're leading Mission Two. That's two weeks later. If you agree. You've served your time on active duty, as you well know. I'm not ordering you in. But I'd be grateful if you'd answer in the affirmative."

"But I don't know the nature of the attack."

"It's on a Chinese Naval base in the Bassein River in Burma," interjected Arnold Morgan. "It's going to be dangerous, but highly organized. Failure is unthinkable."

"Well, sir, I'm not too bad at wiping out Chinese military."

"You're also the best team leader the SEALs have had since Vietnam, according to John. Except of course for the now-retired Rusty, here. Quite honestly, Commander, I'd be real unhappy with anyone else in charge."

"Will it be my last active mission, sir?"

"It will. And it will guarantee you make Admiral in the shortest possible time. Admiral Dixon, here, will give you that personal guarantee . . . Ask him, John."

"Commander Hunter, will you accept command of Mission Two, the forthcoming attack on the Chinese base in the Bassein River?"

No hesitation. "Affirmative, sir."

The three Admirals nodded curtly in the time-honored Naval code of recognizing a big decision, well made. And then they turned back to the screen, where John Bergstrom was pointing at the course *Shark* would steer up to the ops area. Arnold Morgan had already coded in the rendezvous point at 26.36N 56.49E, where the submarine would wait in 180 feet of water, 17 miles southwest of the Chinese refinery.

By now Commander Bennett was assiduously taking notes. Two big blue, yellow-and-white charts had been provided for him and John Bergstrom to take back to Coronado. Rusty had drawn in the lines of the minefield and was now marking water depths.

"That's a darned long way in those shallows," he said. "Is there any radar down there?"

"Not that we can see. Certainly no Chinese radar. We detect no military presence whatsoever by the Chinese. Nearest radar is down by the missile sites at the end of the minefield. That's around thirty miles away. If the guys are kicking in along the surface, even in three feet, there's no way they'd get picked up."

"It's the last coupla miles I'm concerned about," said Rusty. "Water's just about ankle deep, then a kinda swamp area, then flat rough sandy terrain. No cover."

"SEALs can move across that in under twelve minutes," replied Admiral Morgan. "It's gotta be ten thousand to one against a towelhead with a radar screen picking anyone up thirty miles away while the guys are going in."

"It wasn't that I was so much worried about, sir."

"Sorry, Commander. How do you mean?"

"My guys can get in," said Rusty. "I'm more worried about getting them out."

"Okay, Commander. I have given this thought," said Admiral Morgan. "Let's take a worst case. The refinery blows before your guys are clear. Let's say you did not hit the control tower hard enough, and the nonmilitary guards hit the buttons to their Iranian Navy buddies at Bandar Abbas. That's nearly fifty miles away. Too far for a patrol boat. Their only shot at catching you is helicopters, and by the time they've saddled a couple of them up, that's twenty minutes. Flight time at one hundred seventy knots is, say, fifteen minutes. By which time you've had thirty-five minutes to get into deepish water. It's pitch-dark, and they gotta find you.

"Right out there I got two guided-missile frigates. Your guys have radios. Those fucking choppers get too close, I'm gonna have them blown right outta the sky and blame the goddamned refinery explosion. Matter of fact, I might blow 'em right out of the sky on takeoff. Fucking towelheads."

"How about they happen to have a helicopter or two down by the minefield missile sites?"

"Anything moves into the sky anywhere near that minefield, it's toast," growled the Admiral. "Remember, right now the U.S. of A is in sole Naval control of the gulf, the Strait of Hormuz and the Northern Arabian Sea. No one moves there unless we say so. *NO ONE.*"

"Thank you, sir," said Commander Bennett.

"Anytime, Commander. Glad to be of help." Arnold Morgan smiled, thinly. He was loving this. Talking to real fighting men. Guys who knew something. Proper people.

He gazed at the SEAL, a veteran of more dangerous situations than most people could even imagine. Rusty stood there, still looking at the chart, still writing in his notebook, his bearing upright, his dark moustache perfectly trimmed, his gaze steady.

Arnold Morgan could have talked to him for a week. And at this moment he suddenly asked the SEAL from the coast of

Maine, "Commander, may I ask you a question? A rather personal question?"

"Of course, sir."

"When you hit the island in the South China Sea, at the head of your team last year, were you ever afraid?"

"Yessir."

"Did your fear subside once you got into action?"

"Nossir. I was afraid all the time."

"Did any of your men realize that?"

"Nossir."

"Were they afraid?"

"Yessir."

"Did anyone give in to his worst fears?"

"Nossir."

"How do you know?"

"Because they all wear the trident, sir. We don't give in to anything."

Arnold Morgan just nodded and said, "Of course."

It was plain that the Admiral was quite moved by the short conversation, and John Bergstrom stepped in and said, "Rusty, you will be going on the mission, I believe? Not into combat, but you are going to be there?"

"Yessir. I was unclear before what it entailed. I would like overall command, until they go in. Then I'll hand over to the Team Leader. I'll go with them in the submarine as far as the rendezvous point. That way I'll be close if something should . . . well . . . happen. Something . . . er . . . unexpected, I mean. I'd like your permission for that, sir."

"You have it, Commander."

Admiral Morgan said now that he considered that the insertion of the SEALs, plus the getaway, was clear to everyone and that it was time to take a look at the refinery itself. He clicked off the electronic chart and replaced it with an excellent color transparency, 30 inches by 24, taken by satellite of China's vast new petrochemical plant on the Iranian coast.

He told them it had cost close to $2 billion to build and would generate product worth more than $10 million a day. It refined petrol, kerosene, jet fuel, heavy fuel oil, liquefied petroleum gas, tar and sulphur. After just a couple of months operational, it was refining 250,000 barrels a day.

"You guys hit this hard, there's gonna be a lot of very, very angry Chinamen running around. It's a big place with a lot of pipes and towers and valves. However, it's no good just blowing holes in things. Busted pipes and bent towers can be shut off and repaired, with little lasting harm done. And that's not our objective. We intend to blow this place sky-high, and right here I'm looking for ignition, right? Pure combustion."

"No bullshit," said Admiral Dixon, in an undisguised parody of Arnold Morgan's favorite phrase.

"Precisely, CNO," confirmed the National Security Chief. "No bullshit."

He walked back to his desk, picked up his 36-inch-long steel ruler and came back to the screen. "Right," he said. "I'm going to stand off to the side here so you can all see the area I'm referring to. That way Rusty, here, can use a yellow marker on one of these prints I had done."

"Okay, now I'm assuming you are not all experts on refining, and I'm going to explain what you are looking for. By the way, twenty-four hours ago I knew none of this, but I do now because I had Jack Smith come down and explain it to me.

"I have had notes on this prepared for everyone to take back and study, but I do want to go over it. For a start, we should be clear: a refinery converts crude oil—in this case from Kazakhstan—into a whole range of products. The crude is really just a combination of hydrocarbons that are separated inside the refinery into various groups, or fractions. It's actually called 'separation, conversion and chemical treatment.' The stuff basically gets distilled, but it's complicated because some fractions vaporize, or boil, at very different temperatures—gasoline at seventy-five Fahrenheit, some heavy fuel oils at six hundred Fahrenheit. They also condense at different temperatures.

"What happens is the crude gets pumped via pipes, through a

furnace, which heats it to maybe seven hundred twenty-five Fahrenheit. The resulting mixture of gas and liquids then passes into a vertical steel cylinder, called a fractioning tower, or a bubbling tower.

"This little bastard is what we're after. Because inside that tower we got a lot of shit happening—the heavy fuels condense in the lower section, light fractions like gasoline and kerosene condense in the middle and upper sections. The liquids, all highly inflammable, are collected in trays and drawn by pipes along the sides of the tower. Some fractions never even cool enough to condense, and these get passed out through the top of the tower into a vapor recovery unit.

"Right here I'm talking high-test incendiary. One of these towers goes up because of a bomb stuck on its lower casing, can you imagine? It blows the heavy fuel oil into a blizzard of fire that hits gasoline, kerosene and then liquefied gas in the vapor unit. That tower, as far as you're concerned, is potentially one of the world's biggest fireworks."

He rapped the screen with his ruler. . . . "See this group here at the north end? There're ten towers . . . as far as I can see, the biggest maybe a hundred feet high. . . . We wanna bomb this one . . . this one . . . and this one, out here on the right by these holding tanks. According to Jack, they're full of gasoline. I'd say if the towers blow, they'll take the storage tanks with 'em. They might even take the entire local landscape, so I'd prefer you guys to be well clear before you detonate."

He paused for effect. But no one spoke. So he pressed on. "This tall building here," said Admiral Morgan, "is the control center. It is essential that you hit this. And hit it hard. Because in there they can turn off the flow of oil through literally miles of pipeline. We don't want that. We want that stuff flowing in, feeding the fire, keeping it raging.

"And finally we come to this group of holding tanks. Jack says this is where they store thousands of tons of deep-frozen liquefied natural gas. Looks like there're around thirty of them, and they are strategically well placed from our point of view. They are nowhere near the towers, and far from the control center, so we're not wasting any of our explosive assets. You can see from this picture the tanks are huge, maybe fifty feet high and forty feet in diameter. I'd guess if we hit five of them, that'd send the rest of them up. It would also give us a triangle of fire and explosions, the towers, the control center and the holding tanks, which will certainly take out this middle storage area that lies between them."

He looked at his audience and noticed that he still had their attention. "Gentlemen," he said, "out here on the northwest of the plant you can see yet another large grouping of tanks. Jack thinks this is the chemical area, maybe a lot of ammonium nitrate for fertilizer. I realize that you are going to be shorthanded, only twelve of you can go in . . . but if you found yourselves with some spare time, with a little spare explosives, you could do a lot of damage out there with the stuff that once blew up Texas City."

"Arnold," interrupted Admiral Bergstrom, "were you proposing to nail down the entire plan here for us to go away and . . . er . . . well, refine?"

"Absolutely not, John. I'm done. I just wanted us to be singing from the same hymnbook for the seaward insertion and getaway. And for the extent of the mission, the amount of TNT required and the main targets you must attack. The number of SEALs going in is dictated by the size of the ASDV. The rest is up to you, how and when you break through this high wire fence to get in, how you deal with possible alarms and guards. I'll have any and all information from Fort Meade fed into Coronado at all times during the next few days. And the Navy will be ordered to supply *anything* requested by either Commander Hunter or Commander Bennett during the missions. By that I mean, of course, heavy backup firepower. Whatever it takes."

"Okay, Arnold. Now, how about the Bassein River? Mission Two?"

"I'm in the process of taking some heavy-duty advice on that, John. But I have prepared charts for you and Rick to take back to California. I've also got a few godawful black-and-white pictures of the place, but NRO are working on some better, clearer stuff, which I'll get to you.

"This whole operation is strictly Navy. That's why Alan Dixon is taking overall command of it personally. Especially during this extremely classified stage. He and I will be in constant communication, but I'd prefer that you two work directly together. Depending on the advice we get, we may have to change tactics. I just don't want to get into anything that might be obsolete next Thursday."

"Understood, sir."

By 1145 the meeting was over. The three SEALs declined lunch and left to board their helicopter immediately: White House lawn to Andrews Air Base—Andrews direct to San Diego. Military aircraft. As Admiral Morgan would have phrased it, "No bullshit."

1000 (local). Thursday, May 10.
Headquarters, Eastern Fleet.
Ningbo, Zhejiang Province.

Admiral Zhang was puzzled. Here was the United States with the biggest concentration of Naval power assembled since the war with Iraq seventeen years ago, and they had made absolutely no communication with either of the nations that laid down the minefield in the first place.

"You think they may not know who the culprits were?" he asked the C-in-C, Admiral Zu Jicai.

"They know," he replied. "They saw our warships down there. Indeed, they just crippled our leading destroyer. At least I think they did. No proof, of course."

"Well, if that's the case we have a rather strange silent war going on, wouldn't you say? Two of the most powerful nations, plus the guardians of the old Persian Gulf, grappling in some three-way sumo headlock without one word being spoken by the protagonists."

"And, unhappily, no referee," said Admiral Zu.

"It's bizarre. The Americans have uttered no formal protest about the minefield. But they have moved a staggering lineup of Naval power into the area, and it's standing there like that ridiculous ape they all admire so much. . . . What's his name? Hong Kong? . . . No, Emperor Kong . . . King Kong, that's him . . . fists flailing, but no one to strike."

Admiral Zu chuckled. "The trouble with the Americans is they always have a hidden agenda. We cannot drop our guard. And we don't want our warships anywhere near them."

"You think they have an agenda for striking back at us? We have, after all, been responsible for the total destruction of four extremely expensive oil tankers."

"It's hard to know, Jicai. I don't think they would come after us and attack one of our cities, or even a Naval base. So what's left?"

"Well, we do have a very large oil refinery in Iran."

"Oh, yes. But the Americans won't attack that. They revere money too much, and oil is currently the world's most precious commodity. They might one day try to buy shares in it, but they wouldn't destroy it. That would just turn them into reckless cowboys like Saddam Hussein, ignoring the ecology of the region, not to mention a lot of civilian deaths."

"Nonetheless, Yushu, I think we should strengthen the guard at the refinery, perhaps borrow some of those attack dogs the Navy has at Bandar Abbas."

"It certainly could not be harmful, Jicai. And I agree with you. We ought not to underestimate the innate viciousness of those men in the Pentagon."

"Even if, for the moment, their actual agenda remains hidden, Yushu."

"As indeed does ours, my Jicai."

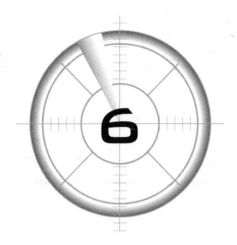

101200MAY07. USS *John F. Kennedy*. 10.40S 146E.

ON THE FACE of it, *Big John* was not making much progress. The giant carrier was back in warm waters 200 miles off the Australian state of Queensland, having passed once more through the narrows of the Torres Strait. There was still no wind, they were still running at flank speed and it was still hotter than hell. The only difference from one week ago was they were heading east, rather than west. *Big John* had been diverted.

No one had given a reason. There was just a terse signal from the Third Fleet HQ in San Diego to come about and head right back the way they had come. Forget Diego Garcia. Make instead for the Pacific, steer east of New Guinea and head on north, taking up station off the east coast of Taiwan.

There was a widespread suspicion on board that China must as usual have been growling around too close to the independent island in which the USA had such a major investment, and for which she was pledged to fight, very nearly, to the death.

However, the truth was more mundane. The Nimitz-Class carrier *Ronald Reagan*, just out of major overhaul in the San Diego yards, was simply judged to be in need of a considerably longer workup period than one week.

And with *Constellation*, *Truman*, *Stennis* and *Roosevelt* all in the Hormuz area, it was decided the *Reagan* ought to take the proper time to get into front-line shape, and that the *JFK* could perfectly easily swing around and make the Taiwan patrol, leaving the other four CVBGs to take care of the oil problems at the gateway to the gulf.

Those four battle groups packed enough of a punch to deal with any problem in the entire history of the planet. The mere presence of *Constellation* and *Truman* had frightened away the Iranians, the Chinese and anyone else wandering around trying to make a buck.

Which still left *Big John* thundering along toward the Coral Sea, with everyone sweating themselves half to death, wondering what the hell the Chinese had done, and what indeed the hell they had done to deserve making this lunatic circular route south of Indonesia, in seas that were of no interest to anyone.

0800. Thursday, May 10.
U.S. Navy Base, Coronado.

Even in the shadowy, unlit inner sanctum of SPECWARCOM, this was as secret as it gets. Deep in one of Coronado's underground ops rooms, behind locked doors and armed guards, twenty-four handpicked Navy SEALs were undergoing a two-day briefing by three of the toughest men who ever wore combat boots: Admiral John Bergstrom, Commander Rick Hunter and Commander Rusty Bennett.

The task before them was relatively compact by SEAL standards—the destruction of two foreign installations, one of them loosely guarded. But the overall intent of the operation was Herculean . . . to drive the Republic of China out of the Gulf of Iran, the Strait of Hormuz, the Arabian Sea, the Indian Ocean and, in particular, the Bay of Bengal. In that precise order.

Twenty-four members of America's most elite, ruthless Special Forces, against the collective will and determination of 1.3 billion Chinese citizens, and their 300,000-strong Navy. The odds, by any standards, were not in any way promising. For the Chinese, that is.

In fact there was a total of 28 battle-ready SEALs in the ops room, counting four "spares" should anyone be injured. Commander Hunter himself was one of the main group, and would personally lead in his team of 12 on Mission Two.

Right now Commander Bennett was going over the initial insertion of troops, the final four or five miles that Assault Team One would swim/wade, en route to the sprawling Chinese refinery on the shores of Hormuz. Before him was the chart of the shallow waters all along the beaches.

"Well, guys," he said, in the SEALs' usual informal method of command, "you can all see these depths . . . if you're lucky, the ASDV will get in, to within four miles, but this damn chart is obviously not reliable . . . if the submarine can make it right in here to the ten-meter line, that's about the best you can hope for . . . that'll be a three-mile swim in warm water not more than nine feet deep.

"Then it looks like you may have to wade the last mile. But the good news is there is no formal military surveillance. We've swept and surveyed it thoroughly and found nothing. The nearest foreign military is thirty miles away. Also you have tremendous cover right offshore, a U.S. Navy presence that for the past couple of weeks has plainly frightened everyone else to death."

Rusty paused and asked for questions. There were none. And now he flicked off the chart of the seaward approaches and zoomed in on the Chinese refinery. "Right here I want you to start taking notes," he said. "Each of you will be provided with a clear ten-by-eight print of the objective you see on the screen. And obviously you will make your approach from the west, through this marshy area, up the beach and across these sand dunes. You'll see from the satellite shots, there is cover in here, within four hundred yards of the perimeter fence, and that's important.

"Because we want you to make two separate entries. First night, you'll reach the perimeter fence at around midnight. I want you to cut it cleanly on three sides, a gap big enough for two men at a time to go through. I want a team of four, each armed with ordnance, to go to work right away on this near group of storage tanks."

He pointed at what looked like a cluster of 28 giant white tin cans, 30 feet high, 60 feet in diameter. "I want you to place the explosives at the base of three of these," he said. "They're made of cast concrete, with steel casing on the outside. Each one is full of just-refined pretroleum—see this pipeline? . . . You can follow it due west and then pick it up out near the new offshore loading bay. It's gotta be gasoline, which, as you know, burns up pretty good.

"This is not a time-consuming task. I'm talking twenty minutes' work, maximum, from the time you get in through the wire. Of course, if you should be caught or attacked, the entire mission is canceled."

Rusty paused again, took a long swig of iced water, and proceeded. "Three more of you will take care of cutting the wire on the outer fence, and then folding and clipping it back into position at the conclusion of the first night ops. That team will also be responsible for observing and avoiding guard patrols. For obvious reasons we do not want to be detected, because our main assault will be on the following night. . . . Questions?"

"How many bombs do we carry in, sir?"

"Six for the holding tanks, three for each of the two groups. Three for the towers, which could be overkill since I suspect one would blow the hell out of ten square miles of oil pipelines. And three more for the control center, two ground level, one higher up if possible. If there's time you'll need another couple for the petrochemical area, but I realize there may not be. That's a total of fourteen—one each for most of you. However, three mines go in through the wire the first night, eleven the second.

"I know that's a lot to do, with your own personal weapons, plus the Draegers, the attack boards and the detonation kit, but it's not that bad, except for the long wade-in through the shallows."

"Are we taking in any heavy weapons, in case we get into real trouble?"

"No. Nothing real big. If anything unexpected happens, you're one radio shout from help. We'll have helicopters ready to take off from *Constellation* at one minute's notice, get you the hell outta there."

"How about the goddamned Iranians get helos up if we're detected?"

"Anything takes off from any Iranian military or Navy base, we take it out instantly. As far as I'm concerned, your safety is not an issue. You're protected by the heaviest front-line muscle we have. . . . Danny, it's secrecy we're interested in. Just don't get detected."

"Okay, sir," replied Lt. Dan Conway, another decorated veteran of the South China Sea operation last year. "Softly softly, catchee Chinese monkey."

"Never mind Chinese monkey, sir. How about Chinese woofer—attack dogs? If they've got Dobermans or shepherds, we'd have to shoot them or they'll try to tear us to pieces . . . we'd be into a goddamned uproar at best."

"Right now we've seen no evidence of any guard dogs in the refinery. In fact, we've not even located formal guard patrols. Langley tells us there are no guard dogs. However, I agree we should consider the matter, because one damned dog going berserk and barking like hell could wreck the secrecy of the operation. Which would not be fatal, because our main objective is destruction. But we would very much like to get in, and out, unseen and unknown."

"If we shoot any dogs, they gotta know we're in there, right?"

"Correct. But we might find a way to silence a couple of Dobermans without killing them, if we were unlucky enough to run into a couple on the first night. Second night doesn't matter so much, since I don't plan any survivors."

The intricate details of the SEAL attacks wore on through the whole of that Thursday, and, after dinner, into the night. They reconvened on Friday morning, and concluded late in the afternoon, each man now fully acquainted with his task and how to carry it out to the letter. No one ever suggested it was going to be easy.

0930. Saturday, May 12.
200 miles west of San Diego.
30,000 feet altitude.

The huge U.S. Navy Galaxy, which carried the SEAL assault teams, was making 400 knots above the Pacific, bound for Pearl Harbor, Hawaii. After a short refueling stop there and the unloading of several tons of marine spares, the remainder of the 13,000-mile journey to America's Indian Ocean base at Diego Garcia would be nonstop.

The SEALs sat together in the rear of the aircraft, their personal gear stowed in packing cases with the rest of the combat equipment they would haul into the Chinese oil refinery. Each man had carefully packed his flexible, custom-made neoprene wet suit. His big SEAL flippers, for extra speed, were also custom-made. On the instep of each one was the lifetime identification number awarded to him after passing the BUD/S course.

All of them had packed two modern scuba-diver's masks, the bright Day-Glo colors for amateurs carefully obscured by jet-black water-resistant tape. The attack boards, which the lead swimmers would use on the swim-in, had been carefully stowed. To a marauding SEAL, this piece of equipment represents almost certain life or death.

The leader holds it with both hands out in front of him, his eyes constantly flicking between compass and small clock, neither of which betrays even a glint. No SEAL ever goes into the water wearing a watch, for fear a shaft of light off its bright metal casing might reflect back and alert a sentry or a harbor-wall lookout.

Thus the leader goes forward, kicking with his big flippers, counting between each forward thrust—KICK-TWO-THREE-FOUR-FIVE . . . KICK-TWO-THREE-FOUR-FIVE. Five-second intervals, 10 feet of distance covered every time, 100 feet in 50 seconds, 1,000 feet in a little over eight minutes, 1,000 yards in 25 minutes, a mile in 45 minutes, three miles in two and a quarter hours.

It was plainly critical that they get the ASDV as close inshore as possible. A two-hour-plus swim, even at a quiet steady pace, even by the iron men from Coronado, is a strength-sapping exercise, and they would need high-energy food, water and a half-hour rest before moving in to their target.

There were a dozen SEALs among the group with combat experience. Several of these men had made a swim-in before. They all knew the feeling of tiredness in the water. But they all knew they could dig deep and overcome that. The new ground for all of them would be the last mile, when it was too shallow to swim, possibly too tiring to wade fast carrying a lot of gear, including the flippers.

The twelve-man assault team for the attack on the refinery was essentially one and a half SEAL squads, from Group One, Coronado, the numbers being governed by the number of men who could fit into the ASDV. They would be led by the near-legendary combat SEAL Lt. Commander Ray Schaeffer, from the seaport of Marblehead, Massachusetts. Ray had taken part in two of the most lethal peacetime SEAL missions ever mounted, a submarine attack deep in the interior of northern Russia and the harrowing assault on the Chinese jail the previous year, for which he had been highly decorated.

In SEAL tradition, he was not required to accept another order to go into combat. But there was no need for any order. Lieutenant Commander Schaeffer not only volunteered; he insisted, and his old boss Rick Hunter was delighted to have him aboard. The attack on the refinery would be Ray's first, and last, overall field command, before he returned to the East Coast as a senior BUD/S instructor at Little Creek, Virginia.

Ray was eminently qualified for this command. Aside from his experience both under fire and undercover, he was a superb navigator and an expert seaman and yachtsman. He was the son of a sea captain and former platoon middleweight boxing champion.

He was not as big as Rick Hunter, nor as brute-force strong. But then neither was anyone else. But Ray Schaeffer was an ice-cold operator, ruthless with a knife, deadly with any firearm and, under attack, a trained, merciless killer. His men would follow him into hell.

His 2 I/C would be Lt. Dan Conway, from Connecticut, who had performed with highest distinction in the attack on the Chinese jail. He was thirty now, a tall dark-haired demolition expert from the submarine base town of New London. He'd finished in first place after the BUD/S "Hell Week," the murderous SEAL indoctrination that breaks one in two of the applicants.

A superb athlete, Dan had very nearly gone for a career in professional baseball, but Annapolis beat out Fenway Park for his services, and the ex–college all-star catcher had never looked back. Everyone knew he was destined for high office in the Navy SEALs, and his promotion to Lt. Commander after this mission in the Hormuz Strait was a foregone conclusion.

One other Lieutenant would be included in the first group, the 28-year-old Virginian John Nathan, serving on his first combat mission. John, the son of a prosperous Richmond travel agent, had elected to become a SEAL specialist in high explosives and their various detonators. He was thus in overall charge of the eleven limpet mines, now stowed in the hold of the giant Navy freighter. Six of them, with specially aimed charges, would be attached to the massive holding tanks in the gasoline and petrochemical areas— another three to the bases of the 100-foot-high steel bubble towers that separated the crude. All eleven were fitted with backpack straps for the swim-in, and large magnets to grip the target surface.

John Nathan had sat in on the meeting with Admiral Bergstrom and Commanders Bennett and Hunter while they discussed tactics to take out the Control Center. At first the Admiral had toyed with a plan to hit the center with Mk 138 satchel bombs: just hurl them through the windows and run like hell for the fence, right at the last minute, leaving the Chinese to deal with the chaos for a couple of hours before the main charges went off and, hopefully, blew the place to pieces. The destruction of the Control Center would, of course, render it nearly impossible to turn off the valves and isolators that regulated the flow of crude oil through the main pipelines.

But Rusty was skeptical of this strategy. The SEAL leader from Maine thought the explosion in the Control Center would cause the Chinese instantly to summon assistance from the Iranian base at Bandar Abbas to conduct a thorough search of the entire refinery. It would be, said Rusty, a search that would surely reveal the limpet mines on the tanks and towers. "They'd only need to find one," he said, "and they'd go through the place, searching every square inch until they found the rest."

In his opinion, that would be "kinda silly."

No, the Control Center would have to go off bang with all the other stuff, using a delayed charge of a couple of hours to give the SEALs time to get clear, out into the deep water. John Nathan recommended the plastic explosive C4, which looks like modeling clay and can be made into any shape. It works off an M-60 time fuse lighter, which burns through regular green plastic cord loaded with gunpowder at around one foot per 40 seconds. John preferred this fuse because it's a spring-loaded pin like a shotgun, no matches, no bright light, and extremely quiet, just a dull thud. Also there was a new timing device that could delay it several hours, and in John Nathan's experience it was just about 100 percent reliable.

Final details for the second SEAL mission, to the Bassein Delta, were not yet finalized, but all the necessary fuses, plastic explosives, mines and detonators were loaded into the Galaxy for storage at Diego Garcia. There was enough C4 alone in the hold to "blow up half the world," according to John Nathan, who carried with him the complete list of ordnance throughout the long flight.

"Something combustible hits this baby," he said, in his deep Virginian drawl, "guess we'd wobble the goddamned rings of Saturn."

Nathan had started off his Navy career as a navigation officer in a frigate, and still liked to pontificate about astrology, the universe and the solar system. The heavyset, fair-haired southerner answered to the nickname of Clouds, which everyone thought was hysterical, given its obvious proximity to his present field of expertise, with a progression to the word *mushroom*.

Sitting right next to Clouds, on the rear bench, was another southerner, Petty Officer Ryan Combs, from North Carolina. He was a tall, athletic outdoorsman, expert with a hunting gun and a fishing rod. Ryan was only 26, but he was a tremendous swimmer and as good with a machine gun as anyone on the Coronado Base. He could handle the 500-rounds-a-minute M-60E4 single-handedly, and he would carry it under the wire into the Chinese refinery. Commander Bennett had personally requested his appointment to the SEAL combat mission on the shores of Iran. It would be Ryan's first.

Rusty had also requested personally the big, beefy Pennsylvanian Rob Cafiero, the platoon's heavyweight boxing champion, who was as big and almost as strong as Commander Hunter himself. Rob was a mild-mannered giant, with dark, close-cut hair and not an ounce of fat on his 220-pound frame. At 32 he had made Chief Petty Officer, but Rob was ambitious and was studying to take a commission as soon as possible. Like Lt. Nathan, he was an expert in high explosives, but his best field of expertise was unarmed combat. He was a veteran of the conflict in the mountains of Kosovo.

These were the five key players in the 12-man assault force that would slide into the warm shallows along the coast of Iran fewer than five days from then.

111600MAY07. USS *Shark* with *Harry S. Truman* CVBG. South of the Hormuz minefield.

Lieutenant Commander Dan Headley could not make up his mind whether he was being trivial or not. The new orders had arrived that Friday night, while he and the CO had been together in the control room. Dan had read them out to the Commander, whose comment had been, at best, vague.

The orders specified a critical new mission, the insertion of a SEAL team, a precision task that always heightens tension on a submarine. But Commander Reid had merely said, "I really must take my shoes off." And then had proceeded to do so.

Lieutenant Commander Headley had thus found himself for the first time in his life next to a commanding officer who was standing in the control room in his socks.

It wasn't much. But it was new. And Dan Headley did not really do new. He was a devotee of the tried-and-tested ways of the United States Navy. He liked and expected his fellow officers to act in a predictable, cautious, but determined way: though sometimes with an added dash of daring, the way most senior warship officers are trained to view an often hostile world.

He particularly liked his commanding officer to react in a calculated manner. *I really must take my shoes off.*

"Jesus Christ," muttered Dan.

The trouble was, he could not get it out of his mind, though he knew it to be insignificant. The CO had swiftly returned to normal, even suggested they have a private talk about the insertion later in the afternoon. But he had left without really acknowledging the seriousness of the forthcoming Black Op the following Tuesday night.

Dan Headley found it curiously disconcerting. And now, as the submarine cruised slowly at periscope depth, 20 miles off the port bow of the *Harry S. Truman*, he made his way down to the confined privacy of the Commander's personal cabin and tapped on the door.

"Come in, XO," called the CO. "I've got us some coffee. Let me pour you a cup."

"Thank you, sir," said Dan, heading for the second chair at the little desk, and noticing for the first time a small framed print hung on the wall, a portrait really, just a head and shoulders of someone who was obviously an eighteenth-century nobleman.

While the CO splashed the hot, black coffee into their mugs, Dan Headley leaned over and took a closer look at the little portrait. The gentleman wore a tricorne hat, with a sash across his chest. Beneath the picture were the words *L'Amiral, le Comte de Villeneuve.*

Dan found that unusual, and he said cheerfully, "Nice little picture, sir. But why a French admiral?"

"Oh, you noticed that? It belonged to my grandmother. She was French, you know . . . my mother's mother. Lived in a little town called Grasse in the south of France, up in the hills behind Cannes . . . I went there a coupla times as a kid. Pretty part of the world."

"Yessir. I was in Nice once, just along the coast. It was crowded, but kinda warm and cheerful . . . my dad and I went together, trying to buy a racehorse . . . little provincial meet down there in the spring. . . ."

"I didn't know that was horse-racing country."

"It's not really, sir. But they have a meeting down there before the weather gets warm farther north in Paris. We went especially to buy back a mare we'd sold as a yearling. She'd won about four races, one at Longchamp."

"Long way to go to buy a horse."

"Yessir. But she was from a family that'd been real fast back in Kentucky. My daddy's the senior stud groom on a very big farm out there, and the owner just wanted her back as a broodmare."

"Did you get her?"

"Yeah, we got her. Probably paid too much, what with the shipping and all. But when Mr. Bart Hunter—that's my daddy's boss—wants a mare, he'll usually pay the price."

"Was she worth it?"

"Not really. She never bred a stakes horse. But one of her daughters was very good, produced a couple of hotshot milers in New York. Then her next foal, by a top stallion called Storm Cat, fetched $3 million at the Keeneland sales. He couldn't run worth a damn, but I guess that sale probably quadrupled ole Bart's money in the end."

"I find that very interesting, Dan. The way the talent of a fine family just keeps coming back, sometimes skipping a generation, but still hanging in there, ready to surface."

"That's the way it's always been in the horse-breeding business, sir."

"And it's not a whole lot different with people, if I'm any judge," replied Commander Reid.

"I'm not sure that's altogether politically correct, sir . . . breeding people's a tricky subject—aren't we all supposed to be born equal?"

"Believe that, XO, and you'll believe anything."

"You got any hotshot ancestors yourself, sir?"

"Well, we never really delved into it, but I certainly have some deep connections with the French Navy. Very deep."

"Not Admiral Villeneuve?"

"*Non.*" Commander Reed paused, almost theatrically raising his head. "We have a connection to the man who effectively won the American Revolution, Comte François-Joseph de Grasse, victor of the Battle of the Chesapeake."

Commander Reid dipped his head, as if in deference to the memory of the French Admiral who had held off the British fleet at the mouth of Chesapeake Bay on September 5, 1781.

"Hey, that's really something, sir," said Dan. "Was your grandma named de Grasse?"

"Oh no, the family of François-Joseph merely adopted that title, and named themselves after the town."

"Good idea, eh, sir? We get those SEALs in, and then out of Iran, I might do the same. How about Lieutenant Commander Dan of Lexington?"

Commander Reid never even cracked a smile. Le Comte de Grasse was plainly a man about whom he did not make jokes.

And this Friday afternoon was plainly a time when he did not make plans. The two men finished their coffee more or less in silence, and the CO suggested a more formal planning meeting at 1100 the next day.

The new XO left with two unimportant, but nagging, questions in his mind. One, what was this "*NON*" crap all about? And, two, what the hell was the CO of a U.S. attack submarine doing with a picture of the ludicrous Admiral Villeneuve on the wall? This was a man who had narrowly escaped the annihilation of the French fleet at the Battle of the Nile, and then commanded the new fleet at the absolute catastrophe of the Battle of Trafalgar, where he was taken prisoner, escorted to England and six months later committed suicide.

Dan Headley walked back to the control room confirming to himself that he was a loyal XO, resolved to support his immediate boss under any and all circumstances. But in his deepest, most private, thoughts it occurred to him that *this Reid weirdo might be a half-dozen cannonballs short of a broadside.*

0400. Monday, May 14.
U.S. Navy Base. Diego Garcia.
Indian Ocean.

The Galaxy freighter came thundering onto the runway in the small hours of the morning, 34 hours after having left the North Island Air Base in San Diego. Most of the men had slept during the second half of the journey, from Pearl Harbor, but they were all tired, in need of a stretch; and the stifling heat of the island, only 400 miles south of the equator, took them by surprise.

Unlike most arriving passengers after a trans-Pacific journey, the SEALs had to supervise their own cargo. Crates that were accompanying them on the next leg of their journey, up to the flight deck of the *Harry S. Truman*, 2,600 miles to the north, had to be carefully separated for reloading, while the rest of the explosives, which would ultimately be used at the far eastern end of the Indian Ocean, were taken on fork-lift loaders to the main storage area.

Lieutenant John Nathan and Commander Hunter took care of this task, and Rusty Bennett checked off the matériel being reloaded into a much smaller aircraft for that afternoon's flight up to the carrier.

They were escorted to specially prepared quarters, 15 small rooms set aside for the men who were going to work in Iran, 14 more for those who were waiting in Diego Garcia for their orders to embark for the Bassein River.

The SEALs hung around for only a half hour, during which time they demolished ham, cheese and chicken sandwiches and several gallons of sweet decaffeinated coffee. By 0600 they were all asleep, and would remain so until 1300, when they would eat a major lunch of New York sirloin steak, eggs and spinach, as much protein as they could pile in, before boarding the aircraft for the northern Arabian Sea.

That journey was of almost seven hours' duration, and the Navy pilot put down on the *Truman*'s deck in a light subtropical sou'wester just before 2200 on that same Monday night.

The carrier was busy that evening, and the howling Tomcats were coming in, in clusters every two minutes. The Admiral had ordered a separate crew to disembark the Special Forces fast and then move their gear down to the hangar for storage, before it would be ferried with the SEALs by helicopter to USS *Shark*, which would be waiting a half mile off their port beam at 1600 the next day, Tuesday, May 15.

Their ranks were thinned out now. Commander Bennett and Lt. Commander Ray Schaeffer supervised the opening of the crates and removing of the personal kit each SEAL would require before the short 30-mile submarine run up to the rendezvous point. Lieutenant John Nathan took care of the separate interior boxes that contained the weapons, breathing apparatus and attack boards, before carefully marking the containers of high explosives that would take down the Chinese oil refinery.

Forty minutes later, the three officers joined their colleagues in a corner of the huge ship's dining room for what carrier men call MIDRATS (midwatch rations). Tonight they ate specially pre-pared Spanish omelettes, french fries and salad, and they all ate together, no separation of officers and men. SEALs always ignore this distinction, particularly on the eve of a truly lethal operation, such as this one might very well become.

They retired to bed soon after midnight, but for most of them it was a fitful night. The first four hours of sleep were easy because of general tiredness after the endless journey. But by 0400 the SEALs were awake, each man wondering what the next 24 hours would hold for him. The younger first-mission SEALs would not sleep again this night, and even the veteran Lt. Commander Ray Schaeffer was anxious. He climbed out of bed and walked around his room, flexing his muscles, as if taking comfort from his enormous strength. But the mission weighed heavily upon him, and he could not take his mind off the warm shallows through which he must lead his men in the darkness of the following night.

Commander Bennett was sharing a bigger cabin with Lt. John Nathan, and the younger man was unable to sleep. Three times he stood up and walked over to the door, finally pulling on a sweater, waking Rusty and leaving to find a cup of coffee. Fortunately a big carrier never sleeps, and the dining room was full, mostly of Navy fliers. By some bush telegraph they seemed to know that the broad-shouldered young stranger in the corner nursing coffee in a plastic cup was one of the SEALs going in later that day.

None of them were strangers to fear and daring, but there is a certain aura surrounding a combat SEAL on the brink of a mission, and no one approached him. No one, that is, until a cheerful 24-year-old pilot from Florida, still in his flying jacket, showed up. He collected a tall glass of ice-cold milk and walked straight over to Lt. Nathan's table, stuck out his hand and announced, "Hey, how you doin'? I'm Steve Ghutzman."

The SEAL explosives chief looked up and nodded. He shook hands and said, "Hi, Clouds Nathan."

He felt awkward, sitting there in the middle of the night with this robust stranger, but in truth he was glad of the company. Steve swiftly regaled him with details of the hot, gusting southwest wind out there. "You don't wanna take your eye off the ball tonight, I'm telling you. The air's like a goddamned switchback coming in . . . it wouldn't be no trouble to slam one of them Tomcats bang into the ass of this fucking airfield. Gotta stay right on top of it, yessir."

Steve was unable to distinguish the rank and station of his new companion, and he was talking fast, in the slightly high-adrenaline way Navy pilots do after a tense landing on a flight deck. But he was a nice guy, born a mile from the runway at the Navy air base in Pensacola, a flier all his career, just like his father before him.

He inhaled the milk, got up to get another glass and brought back another cup of coffee for his new buddy. Winding down a little, he asked finally, "What's that first name of yours? I didn't quite catch it."

"Oh it's just a nickname. The guys all call me Clouds because I'm interested in astronomy. I used to be a navigator. I got kinda used to it."

"Hey, that's cool. Clouds . . . I love it. You just arrived? Didn't see you around before."

"Yeah, I'm pretty new. Got in a while before midnight. And we'll be gone by fifteen hundred."

Steve Ghutzman hesitated. Then he dropped his lower jaw in mock astonishment. "H-O-L-E-E-E SHIT!" he said. "You're one of 'em, right?"

"Guess so," said Lt. Nathan, smiling. "Guess I'm one of 'em."

The pilot knew better than to ask details of a classified SEAL mission, but like most of the 6,000-strong crew of the gigantic Nimitz-Class carrier, he knew there was a SEAL team on board for less than 24 hours, and that they were going into Iran later that day. He knew nothing of the mission, the objective or when they were due to return—just that they were "going in," God help them.

Throughout every corner of the U.S. Navy the SEALs were regarded as men apart. *And, Jesus Christ, I'm sitting here with one of 'em, right now.* Steve Ghutzman was hugely impressed, and he did not know quite what to say. This was a condition to which he was utterly unused, and he just muttered, "You having a little trouble sleeping tonight?"

The SEAL nodded. "Some," he said. "This is my first mission. Guess it's on my mind."

"You been in the platoon awhile?"

"Oh, yeah. Five years now. And I've done a lot of training . . . but you always think of this day . . . the day you're going in. And for me that's today . . . right now . . . and I can't sleep worth a damn."

Steve nodded. "They tell you a lot about it before you go?"

"Everything there is to know. I've never even been to the Middle East, but I know what I'm headed for. I know every hill, and every rock. I know how warm the water is and where to be careful. But it doesn't stop you from thinking about it. Can't get it off your mind, really."

"You think it takes courage, or is it just the training."

"Well, I guess it's mostly the training. But in my case it's gonna take courage. I don't really know about the others."

"Shit, Clouds, you scared?"

"Damn right, I'm scared. Wouldn't you be?"

"Damn straight I would. But you guys are the best. What do they say, one SEAL, five enemy, that's fair odds, right?"

"Seven."

Steve laughed. "Hey, you guys are indestructible."

"Not quite. We bleed. And we hurt like everyone else. We're just a bit tougher to get at."

Steve Ghutzman drained his glass. "I gotta go. I'm back up there at zero-eight-hundred." He stood up, stuck out his hand and said, "Hey, it was good to talk to you, buddy. Good luck tonight, wherever the hell you're going."

"Thanks, Steve. We're staying the hell out of Hell, that's for sure."

1500. Tuesday, May 15.
The Flight Deck. USS *Harry S. Truman.*

For the short run out to USS *Shark*, the 15-strong SEAL team embarked in one of the last of the Navy's old warhorses, the HH-46D support/assault Sea Knight helicopter. The explosives and other gear had been airlifted in a cargo net four hours previously, and now Rusty Bennett stood at the loading door and saw each of his men aboard.

They all wore just light pants and olive green T-shirts. They carried their heavy-duty welder's gloves for the hot-rope drop to the deck of the submarine. It was too hot for them to wear wet suits, and an area had been set aside in the submarine for them to change and prepare for the swim-in during the final hour of the journey up through the partially cleared minefield.

There were, as ever, the flight-deck crews on the takeoff area as the two rotors on the big white U.S. Marines Sea Knight roared into life. The SEALs had already blackened their faces with waterproof greasepaint, and were just about unrecognizable.

Among the crowd was Steve Ghutzman, and he just yelled a solitary, *"GO, CLOUDS, BABY!"* And his voice rang out in the general serious hush that surrounded this departure. But big Lt. Nathan heard him, and he half raised his right hand in response, smiling to himself at his new 20-minute friendship with the Navy Tomcat pilot. For all he knew, he might need Steve's fighter-attack aircraft not too long from now. The Navy had mounted rescue attacks for missions a lot less dangerous than this one.

They flew low, out over the calm blue water, toward the waiting submarine. It took less than 15 minutes, and as the Sea Knight hovered above the deck, they all saw the thick rope unravel downward to a point in front of the sail, right behind the long deck shelter on the right, where the miniature submarine awaited them. One by one the SEALs grabbed the rope and dropped fast, away from the aircraft, sliding down 30 feet, before gripping hard with the big rough leather gloves, their brakes, and coming in to land gently on the casing of the *Shark.*

Lieutenant Commander Schaeffer led the way, followed by Lt. Dan Conway, then Lt. Nathan, then Petty Officer Combs, then the big Chief Petty Officer Rob Cafiero. The next seven combat rookies came sliding in right behind them, with Commander Rusty Bennett bringing up the rear.

They were greeted by the Officer of the Deck, Lt. Matt Singer, who hustled them quickly through the door at the base of the sail, and on down the ladder. The hatches were slammed shut and clipped behind them, and Commander Reid ordered *Shark* to periscope depth heading north.

"Steer course three-six-zero . . . make your speed one-five for fifteen miles, then stand by for course change to zero-seven-zero."

They all felt the submarine's gentle turn to due north, settling on a course that would allow them to cleave right through the middle of the now-three-mile-wide "gateway" through the mine-field, and then on up the strait until she turned in toward the shore of Iran.

Lieutenant Commander Dan Headley led them down to a more-or-less empty area in which they could prepare for the mission. He fell into conversation with Rusty Bennett, and mentioned he had a good friend in the squadron . . . "Guy named Rick Hunter . . . Commander Hunter now, I believe. He and I grew up together."

"Hey, you gotta be from Kentucky, right?" said Commander Bennett. "Rick's a real good friend of mine. Just left him, matter of fact, down at DG."

"That right? I didn't know he was anywhere near here."

"Oh, just Rick and about seven-eighths of the entire United States Navy," Rusty replied with a chuckle. "I'm telling you, someone in the Pentagon's awful jumpy about whatever the hell's going on in the gulf."

"Guess so. All we know is what everyone else knows. The Iranians somehow mined the Strait of Hormuz and shut down most of the world's oil supply."

"Big minefield, I understand. That's gotta be a major worry."

"It ought to be," replied Dan Headley, smiling. " 'Specially for you. We're just about in the middle of it right now."

"Shit," said Rusty. "I knew I shouldn't have come. Your CO any good?"

"I don't really know him well enough to say. But I don't think he's hit anything recently."

"God forbid he starts now."

Both officers laughed. And *Shark*'s XO asked what Rusty's men needed between now and the 1900 ETD.

"They had lunch, steak and eggs, at fourteen hundred," said the SEAL Commander. "Maybe you could fix a few sandwiches, slices of pizza or something. Just in case anyone's hungry. But I don't think many of them will be. They'll need a lot of cold water, though. They got a two-hour journey in the ASDV, then a long swim . . . don't want them to get dehydrated."

"Okay. I'll get that organized. By the way, you're not going yourself, are you, sir?" The XO paid due deference to Rusty's higher rank.

"Not this time. But I'm gonna help your boys get the ASDV moving, if you think I could help. I've done it a few times in my life. And this is a very big vehicle."

"I'm sure my crew would appreciate that, sir. The damn things are always difficult. And this one's the biggest we've ever had."

"Anyhow, right now I want to talk to the guys while they're getting ready—so we'll catch up in a little while."

"Good enough, sir. My watch starts in a few minutes. I'll be in the control room, you need to find me."

By now the twelve combat SEALs were sorting out their gear. Each man had his own custom-made wet suit and numbered flippers. Each of them had a Draeger oxygen supply, the special SEAL air bottle that leaves no telltale bubbles on the surface. Each man would carry a knife and Heckler and Koch's superb light submachine gun, the MP-5, a close-quarters weapon, best inside 25 yards, but perfect for an assault on a nonmilitary establishment. Only Petty Officer Ryan Combs would carry in a bigger weapon, the lethal M-60E4 machine gun. They would carry in, between them, 14 ammunition belts, each containing 100 rounds. Ryan himself would carry the gun, plus two belts, to give him a total weight of 40 pounds to carry. The gun would be used only in a dire emergency if they had to fight their way out of the refinery.

Ryan would also carry on his back a limpet mine, which he could manage just fine. It was the walk through the shallows that was so worrying. The Draeger is just about weightless in the water, but it weighs 30 pounds in the air, and that gave Ryan Combs very nearly 100 pounds in weight to haul to the beach, which would probably prove too much after a quarter of a mile.

Rusty Bennett had ordered big Rob Cafiero to step up and share the load of the gun and ammunition if Ryan could not cope. All the SEALs were heavily laden, a bomb or mine for 11 of them. Two for three of them. The fusing wire and detonation devices would be carried by John Nathan. Between them, the SEALs would also haul camouflaged groundsheets, two shovels, wire-cutters, clips, plus night binoculars, the lightest possible radio for emergency only, water, high-protein bars and medical supplies. The return journey would be one hell of a lot easier.

In Rusty's final briefing back on the carrier, they had debated making a request for the crewman of the ASDV, not the driver, to accompany them in, strictly as a beast of burden, until they reached dry land. But that ASDV was priceless, the only one of its kind, and the CO of the *Shark* probably would wish to take no chances, leaving it in the hands of just one operator.

However, if push came to shove, Rusty would insist, and no CO wants to go against the express wishes of a SEAL commander on the edge of a dangerous mission, probably on orders directly from the White House.

And so they prepared for their final talk together. Spread out before them were the chart and the map. As they pulled on their wet suits in a temperature deliberately turned right down to 50 degrees Fahrenheit, they listened to Rusty, who was saying that the ASDV driver would take the vehicle in as far as possible, until the keel touched the sand.

"Right then we'll move into the dry hatch, one at a time; as soon as it floods, each man will drop straight through. The man with the attack board goes first, then his partner drops through and they move immediately, swimming east, bearing zero-nine-zero, until the water gets too shallow to swim comfortably. The six two-man teams rendezvous in the shallows.

They should be around five minutes apart. After that, you know what to do."

For forty minutes more the SEALs made their final preparations, and at 1750 they began to embark the ASDV, dragging in the gear, each man slipping expertly up through the hatch, finding his allotted seat and placing his equipment in the tight overhead space. The loading took all of half an hour as the SEALs struggled to find a reasonably comfortable position for the two-hour ride inshore in this sturdy 65-foot-long electric submarine.

Down in the control room Lt. Commander Headley had the ship, assisted by the Sonar Officer, Lt. Commander Josh Gandy, and the Navigator, Lt. Shawn Pearson.

"Right now I have us at our destination, sir. That's 26.36N 56.49E on the GPS."

"Okay, Lieutenant. Depth?"

"I was just coming to that, sir. We've still got plenty of water. I'm showing ninety feet below the keel, and we're sixty-five feet below the surface right now. You wanna save the battery on the ASDV, I'm certain we could run in maybe another three miles. This chart's kinda pessimistic about depth."

"You agree with that, sonar?"

"Yessir. I'm showing total depth right here of just over two hundred feet, and Shawn's chart gives one hundred seventy. We could certainly go on."

"*Okay . . . conn–XO. Make your speed eight, steer zero-four-five . . . depth six five . . . call out fathometer reading every five feet.*"

"Aye, sir. We just saved the ASDV a half hour's battery each way."

"Good call, Navigator."

At which point Commander Reid entered the control room, looking less than thrilled at the way the submarine was being run.

"Did you just countermand my orders, XO?"

"I adjusted our rendezvous point by three miles northeast, sir, because of clear and obvious discrepancies in the chart. We're still in deep water, and we can save the battery on the ASDV."

"The battery on the ASDV is not your concern, Lieutenant Commander. What is your concern is a set of orders, issued to us, by the flag, and signed by me as your Commanding Officer. I do not permit leeway in orders such as those."

"As you wish, sir." Dan Headley looked bewildered. But he replied with a calm demeanor.

"XO, turn the ship around and return to 26.36N 56.49E. The rendezvous issued by the flag."

"Sir, with respect, could we not let the guys out right here, a couple of miles nearer their objective?"

"I think you heard me, Lieutenant Commander. Turn this ship around immediately and return to our correct position. I have no desire to take my ship any nearer to the shores of Iran than is absolutely necessary."

And with that he turned on his heel and walked out of the control room, leaving all three of the ship's operational officers speechless.

Shawn Pearson spoke first. "Now that, gentlemen," he said, "was rather interesting."

"If you meant that the way I think you meant it, I do not want to hear any more," replied the XO, somewhat severely.

Lieutenant Commander Gandy just shook his head.

And they all felt the slight lurch as USS *Shark* made an underwater U-turn and began to transport Rusty Bennett's SEALs away from their target area.

Nonetheless, within 20 minutes they were back on station at 26.36N 56.49E, facing the right way, 17 miles southeast of the Chinese refinery, and the underwater deck crew was wrestling the ASDV out of the flooded shelter and clear of the big submarine's casing.

Rusty Bennett proved an enormous help to the four-man team, and they shoved the miniature submarine out in near-record time. It was on its way before they blew out the dry-deck shelter, and up in the bow Lt. Brian Sager was conning the little ship in, on instruments only, assisted by his navigator.

Behind them the SEALs were dry but cramped, and they traveled mostly in silence. The journey was made at six knots all the way, and Brian Sager kept on going well beyond their estimated point of departure at 26.45N 56.57E. He pushed on for another mile and a half, just below the surface, until they gently brushed the soft, sandy bottom, less than three miles from the beach. The sonar on the ASDV had picked up no vessel within 10 miles.

It was exactly 1900 and growing dark when Lt. Commander Ray Schaeffer, wearing his wet suit, hood up, goggles and flippers on, Draeger connected, attack board in his left hand, slid down into the dry compartment, ready for the flooding. Three minutes later he dropped through the hatch into the warm waters of the Strait of Hormuz.

Ray stared at the compass, breathed steadily and was grateful that his limpet mine, Draeger and weapons seemed to weigh nothing. He tried not to think of the abrupt difference there would be when they hit the shallows.

Moments later, one rookie combat SEAL, Charlie to his colleagues, knifed downward through the water next to him. Breathing carefully, he placed his right hand on Ray's wide shoulder. The Lieutenant Commander from Marblehead swung around until the attack board compass told him EAST, and then the two SEALs kicked toward the oil refinery owned by the Republic of China.

The extra distance covered by Lt. Sager meant the swimmers would essentially run aground inside of two miles. And the two lead SEALs kicked and breathed steadily, swimming about nine feet below the surface, covering 10 feet each time they snapped their flippers. After 30 minutes Ray estimated they had covered 1,200 yards, two-thirds of a mile, and right then nothing was hurting.

Behind them on Attack Board Two came Lt. Dan Conway, guiding another rookie; Clouds Nathan swam powerfully five minutes back; then Rob Cafiero, then two rookies, both ace swimmers. Last of all swam the tall Petty Officer from North Carolina, Ryan Combs, both hands on his attack board, leading his rookie, who dragged the machine gun in a special waterproof container, which made it nearly weightless.

The entire operation would have been a thousand percent easier if they had been able to row inshore in a couple of big eight-man inflatables. But senior management at SPECWARCOM had dismissed that as a possibility out of hand . . . *one alert Iranian patrol boat moving through its own waters four miles offshore could, legally, have blown the U.S. Navy SEALs to pieces.*

As Admiral Bergstrom had mentioned at the time, "Guess I'd rather have a dozen tired SEALs wallowing around in the surf than twelve dead ones floating faceup in the fucking Strait of Hormuz."

Ray Schaeffer had sat in on that meeting, and he smiled to himself as he thought of the diabolical difference between planning in an air-conditioned room in Coronado and making a swim like this thousands and thousands of miles from home.

Ray kicked and counted, kicked and counted, keeping his eye on the compass, staying on zero-nine-zero. They'd been going for an hour and a half now, and by Ray's reckoning that spelled 3,600 yards covered, which was two miles, give or take the length of a submarine. There was a rising moon now, and phosphorescence in the water. He thought he could make out the ocean bottom right below, but he was unsure and he did not want to waste energy, or his precious air, in finding out.

Also he was asking serious questions of his granite-hard body, and there were nagging pains high up in both thighs. His calves and ankles were mercifully fine; that was where the pain usually hit on a long swim. And there had been times when it had hurt like hell.

The kid behind him was only twenty-one years old, and there was no way Ray was going to betray tiredness, so he gritted his teeth, dug ever deeper and forced himself forward, ignoring the lactic acid now flooding into his joints and muscles, making every yard an ordeal.

Seventeen minutes after the two-mile mark, Ray felt his board sliding through sand. Instinctively he straightened up and was surprised to find himself standing up to his chest in about four feet of water, still holding the attack board. Charlie bobbed up right beside him and they both shut down their Draegers, reclining back in the water, resting their aching limbs.

They took their mouthpieces out and stored the air lines neatly. "You all right, sir?" asked Charlie.

"No problem, kid," replied the Lieutenant Commander. "Let's take five, then walk forward slowly for another five and wait for Dan to show up."

"Sounds good. . . . Can you see anything up ahead, sir?"

"I thought I could just then, a dark shoreline directly in front, maybe a half mile. But the moon's gone behind that cloud, and I can't see a fucking thing now."

By now the lead SEALs had removed their flippers. They were walking slowly forward, and they were quickly in less than three feet of water. The Draegers were beginning to weigh heavily; so were the mines. They were comfortable with the rest of their gear.

About 100 yards back, Dan Conway and his teammate broke the surface, and began to walk forward. By the time they caught up with Ray and Charlie, Clouds was in, then the rookies, only two minutes behind. Big Rob Cafiero and his rookie were in next, but they had to wait 10 minutes for Petty Officer Combs, who was of course carrying the M-60 machine gun, which might save all their lives in an emergency.

Ray Schaeffer aimed them all east, and they set off on the stretch they had all been dreading, wading, now in 18 inches of water through the long shallows, each man hauling 80 pounds plus. After 100 yards it was like walking through glue. No one complained but it was a muscle-throbbing exercise, and there was no efficient way to do it, except to keep pushing forward, lifting their feet just enough to take the real "tug" out of the water.

However, it was pleasantly warm, there was no surf to speak of and up ahead they could see the shore. And that was the good news. This walk could have been a mile and a half. As things looked, it would be only a little more than 1,000 yards. Ray ordered them to fan out and draw their weapons, which made a long line of black-hooded figures 30 yards apart. When they reached the beach, assuming it was deserted, they would close in to Lt. Commander Schaeffer's central position to check the GPS. The numbers they were looking for were 26.47N 57.01E.

The last 100 yards were easily the worst, and they struggled through a kind of kelp field, knee-deep and clinging. But eventually they walked up onto a completely empty beach of coarse sand and occasional rocks. There was not a light, and certainly not a person, to be seen. The numbers on the GPS were right on, which explained a lot. Nothing on this particular stretch of wasteland had been picked up after a hundred satellite passes carefully logged and studied at the top-secret National Reconnaissance Office in Washington. The even more beady-eyed operators at Fort Meade had found nothing either. One mile dead ahead, across slightly hilly terrain, was the sprawling Chinese crude-oil refinery.

It was 2130, and Lt. Commander Schaeffer ordered the SEALs off the beach and into the rougher ground behind. With exquisite timing the moon came out again, and they could more or less see where they were headed without using night goggles. Up ahead they would be approaching the southwestern corner of the refinery, and somewhere before that they would make the rendezvous point, dumping most of their gear.

Four SEALs only would enter the refinery that night. Two more would cut and fold back the wire, and Petty Officer Combs would ride shotgun over the operation with the big gun, and also join the wire cutters as lookouts. No one knew what to expect in the way of guards, or even lights. They knew only that Ray Schaeffer, Dan Conway and Clouds Nathan were going through the wire perimeter fence, assisted by Charlie, to lay down the piledriver explosives contained in the limpet mines, which they would attach to the inside-facing walls on the big gasoline holding tanks.

Chief Petty Officer Rob Cafiero would take charge of the base camp, when they found it, unloading groundsheets, setting up the radio, posting sentries, preparing the mass of explosives for the main assault the following night. But it took another hour before they found a three-corner outcrop of warm rocks, five feet above the ground at its highest point. It provided protection from the north and from the seaward side. The SEALs used the wire cutters to cut scrub and cover the camouflage nets. It had to be 1,000 to 1 against anyone stumbling across their "hide," and from the sea it was totally invisible.

They all removed their wet suits and wore only light camouflage combat trousers and jackets. They pulled on their desert boots, and the warriors going in that night increased the grease-paint on their faces and tied their matching green-and-brown "drive on" rags around their heads, in the style popularized chiefly by Willie Nelson.

They ate a couple of protein bars and drank water. Then shortly after 2300, Lt. Commander Ray Schaeffer led Assault Team One forward, a total of seven SEALs, carrying the three limpet mines and all the detonation equipment required to take out the group of holding tanks hard against the fence in the southwest corner of the refinery. No explosions until the next day, but a lot of the ground-work completed, with, hopefully, a thorough knowledge of the defense system the Chinese operated in their new refinery.

"Don't expect us back before zero-four hundred, Rob. We wanna take a very careful recon of this place. And it will take time." Lieutenant Commander Schaeffer's words were almost inaudible, and a light breeze from the ocean scarcely ruffled the poor, rough, brown grass that grew sporadically on this warm moonlike landscape.

They drew their weapons and marched forward, moving softly over the ground. Up ahead there was a glow in the sky, and they all knew what that was. The main surprise as they pushed east away from the ocean was the amount of light there was both inside and around the refinery.

Within 10 minutes they had a clear view of the western perimeter, which Ray Schaeffer knew was two miles long. They could see a line of lights, set high on steel pylons every 200 yards. But they were aimed into the refinery and cast almost no light on the dark wasteland around the outer edge. That was good and bad, because it made their approach easy. But one of the lights was throwing a lot of illumination right into the group of storage tanks toward which they were headed.

They lay flat on the ground, staring at the fence 20 yards in front of them.

"Christ," said Clouds, "it's gonna be like the stage of the New York City Ballet in there."

"Great," muttered Dan Conway. "We'll probably get a round of applause"

"Shut up, commedians," whispered Lt. Commander Schaeffer. "That light second from the end has gotta go. Guess we could shoot it, but I'd rather cut it."

"That would sharpen up the guards if they found the cut," said Dan.

"Yeah, it might," replied Ray. "But I've been looking down the line of lights. There's one every two hundred yards, but I'm only counting fifteen, not seventeen. That means there're a couple out already. Those bulbs go all the time, I'd say, and one more isn't going to put the place on red alert. These guys are civilians. They'll probably send a couple of electricians out, maybe tomorrow, to replace the bulbs. So we want to make a cut they won't notice."

"Okay, sir," said Charlie. "I'll do it. I'll slice down six inches and pull the inside stuff out. One little cut puts the bulb out. Then I'll fold it back inside the rubber casing. They might not notice it at all."

"Don't worry," said Ray Schaeffer. "I have a little roll of electrician's tape in my pocket, and we can thank Rusty for that. He told me before we left Coronado, we would almost certainly have to take out a couple of lights, and a little roll of black tape does a lot to cover your tracks."

"Beautiful," said Clouds. "Pity about the applause, though."

They moved in toward the fence, staying low, crawling across the ground on elbows and knees, the time-honored approach of the killer SEAL. Dan Conway and Charlie went to the base of the light pylon, and the two rookies began to cut a hole in the chain-link fence. There was no sign of guards, no sign of life in this remote part of the refinery in the small hours of the morning. The only sound was the snap of the wire cutters as they carved a doorway through the fence.

At 0017 the big light went out, plunging the storage tanks into darkness. The SEALs lay silently, waiting for a Chinese patrol to show up. But none did, and at 0035, they pulled back the wire and Ray Schaeffer, with Clouds Nathan, wriggled through, followed by Lt. Conway and Charlie. Clouds had the detonator, fuses, time clock and cord, plus one of the shovels. The other three carried the big limpet mines on their backs, and they raced for the cover of the storage tanks, three lines of 10, all owned by the China National Petroleum Corporation (CNPC). All now in deep shadow.

It did not look far on the aerial photographs they had been studying for several days, and they all knew the precise route to take. But it was a long 50 yards over flat ground, and they were glad to know that Ryan Combs was right inside the fence with his trigger finger on the machine gun.

Once in among the tanks they worked fast. They made for the middle one in line five, and the two outer ones in line six, which formed a triangle right in the center of the group. Clouds removed the mines from their straps, and clamped the magnets onto the lower inside-facing surfaces of the three tanks. He wired up the detonators and ran cord from each one to a central point at the western edge of the untargeted middle tank in line six. Right there he wired up the clock, which would dictate the time of the explosion of all three mines.

Then he took the shovel and buried the det cord in the soft sand. When he arrived back at the clock, he wrapped it in a plastic bag and buried that, too, without setting it. That would take about one minute on the way out the following night, if their luck held. Right then they were "outta here," and they flew for the fence, unnoticed by anyone, and made their way back through the wire.

It took another 10 minutes to clip the fence back into shape, and the SEALs retreated into the rough ground 20 yards back, from where they would watch whatever movement there was inside the refinery.

It was long, boring wait. The only sign of life was almost a mile away inside the control center. Occasionally they caught a glimpse through the binoculars of a door opening, and once they saw some kind of a jeep move from the control block up toward the main refining towers, but it was too far to see if anyone got out or in. By 0330 Lt. Commander Schaeffer concluded that the refinery was just about devoid of any security whatsoever, and he declared the recon was at an end. By this time the following night they'd be on their way out to the submarine. God willing.

They arrived back at base camp at 0400, reported on the distinct lack of armed guards, at least in that remote part of the refinery, and drank a lot of water. Lieutenant Commander Schaeffer and his men would sleep first, and Chief Petty Officer Cafiero organized the sentries.

They were all awake by 0800, and they spent the day lying low, under the camouflage, eating very occasionally one of the high-protein bars and studying endlessly the layout of the refinery's interior.

That night there were three targets: the towers, the control center and the middle group of storage tanks. If there was time, Lt. Dan Conway and Clouds Nathan would also attempt to insert high explosives into the more remote petrochemical compound, but that would be touch and go. It was almost 800 yards from the towers along a well-lit road.

Ray Schaeffer had divided the SEAL squad into three teams of four, one led by himself, one by Lieutenant Conway and one by CPO Rob Cafiero. Lieutenant Nathan would join Ray in the critical attack on the giant separating towers, Dan Conway and Charlie would take the central storage area, while Rob Cafiero and Ryan Combs would place the high explosives on the walls of the control center. Two young SEALS would accompany each team, acting as guards, lookouts and radio operators, should there be a need to communicate. Each time clock would be set to detonate at 0300.

They would all go under the wire together at 2300, and the watchword of the operation was *stealth*. At least for the first hour it was. Thereafter the SEALs would feel free to fight their way out and down to the beach using whatever means were necessary. Ryan Combs would bring two belts of ammunition and the M60-E4 machine gun with him.

They dug and buried all their surplus gear, including ground-sheets. They left the wet suits, flippers, Draegers and attack boards under the camouflage nets. Because of the 12-man limit on the team, they did not have the luxury of leaving anyone in charge, and at 2230 they all set off toward the refinery. It was warm and windless, with no moon. High clouds drifted in from the sea, and they marched in silence, in three lines of four, through the desolate area behind the beach toward the refinery.

The first thing Ray Schaeffer noticed was that the light they had deactivated the previous night was still deactivated. The second thing he noticed was a jeep moving swiftly along the outer perimeter along the narrow blacktop track they had crossed to get to and from the storage tanks.

The vehicle did not stop or slow down in this remote corner of the plant, but there were four people in it, and they were carrying weapons, a direct result of an instruction from the Chinese Navy, received 48 hours previously. The guards were in fact military personnel from the People's Liberation Army and they had been in residence for two months, although they had not found it necessary to mount any form of patrol. The area was, face it, deserted.

The SEALs flattened themselves into the ground as the jeep drove past, but then they moved quickly to the fence and the clips were removed to open their own personal gateway. Once inside, they placed three clips back on the wire to hold it, more or less in place, to attract no attention.

At this point they again checked their synchronized black pocket watches and the time clocks, which would be adjusted as the charges were put in place. Then they fanned out into three groups. They would meet again 90 minutes from then, at 0030, in the dark deserted area of the towers.

The first team on station was Dan Conway's. He and Charlie led the two rookies deep in the shadow of the hot crude-oil pipes, which cleaved a gantry right down the middle of the refinery. They moved slowly, creeping quietly along, directly beneath the great three-foot-diameter pipes. They provided excellent cover all the way to the central storage area. The four SEALs waited for 15 minutes until they were certain they were alone, then they bolted across the flat well-lit ground to the left and dived into the shadow of the first tank, remaining motionless on the sand for 10 minutes, heads down, but knives drawn.

Meanwhile Lt. Commander Schaeffer and his 2 I/C, Lt. Clouds Nathan, had made it to the tower area. They had crossed two sets of railroad tracks, well to the right of the central pipeline system, and were now crouched in the dark on the south side of a giant holding tank. The towers looked massive, but there were three very close together in the center of the separating plant, and these were the targets.

The problem was four Chinese technicians who had plainly arrived in a parked jeep, testing what looked like a large valve halfway up the biggest tower. "Oh, Jesus," said Ray, "if they're not outta here in thirty minutes, we'll go and place the two mines out in the petrochemical area, and then come back. We can't risk being seen, not yet, not until the stuff's in place."

They waited. So did the technicians. And finally Ray whistled up both of the other teams on the little radio, and announced he was going to the distant chemical area, and would use two of the mines. Dan Conway was instructed to get among the towers as soon as possible with the two extra mines his team was carrying.

They carried out their regular mine placing on the tanks, in precisely the swift, efficient way Clouds had worked the previous night. The time was precisely 2345, and they set the time clock for three hours and fifteen minutes.

Then they rushed back across the open ground into the shadow of the pipeline, and began working their way up to the tower area. Meanwhile, Ray and Clouds were jogging along the eastern perimeter fence, right in the shadow, directly under the lights, headed for the wide area of the plant owned by SINOPEC (China National Petrochemical Corporation).

When they arrived, the place was not only silent; there were also huge dark areas to the west of the tanks, and they worked right in there, shoveling a shallow six-inch trench in which to lay the det cord. By the time they'd finished, it was 0015, and Ray set the clock for two hours and 45 minutes. Then he buried it lightly in a plastic bag.

By the time SEAL Team One was out of the chemical area, Rob Cafiero and Ryan Combs were making steady progress around the control center. They had placed one mighty charge of plastic C4 explosives hard on the wall below the main downstairs window, and they had seen four white-coated technicians enter the building and four come out.

Both SEALs could also see there was a basement in the building, and realized this was the place to set a major C4 charge because it would surely bring the entire construction down, wrecking all the control systems, and allowing the hot crude to keep on flooding through the pipes, feeding the fires, just as it had in Texas City, 60 years previously.

And now they were ready. The center was plainly being staffed by the minimum number of people, and Ryan Combs told the two rookies to take the machine gun and cover them while he and Rob went through the front door, which had been unused for at least 25 minutes.

They raced across the yard, Rob carrying the explosives, detonator and plastic, Ryan now with a silenced, even lighter, machine gun, the regular MP-5, right behind him. They pushed open the door and moved into the hallway. Right in front of them was a down staircase, and they took the steps four at a time, swinging hard left at the bottom, and going to work under the stairs setting the plastic bomb for a timed detonation.

It was just 2350, and they set the clock for three hours and 10 minutes. They swung back out of the stairwell at exactly 2351, just as two Chinese staff members came out of a lower-floor operations room. The four men stared at each other in total disbelief, and the two refinery workers, confronted with two armed green-and-brown-faced monsters, turned to run back into their room.

One of them shouted one word in Chinese before Ryan Combs cut them both down in cold blood with a burst from his MP-5.

Instantly the two SEALs dragged the bodies back under the stairs, before there was too much blood to clean up. They made sure the two victims would not be easily seen, and then they bolted back up to the main hall, opened the front door and raced back to the shadows where the two rookies waited.

"Everything okay, sir?"

"Except for a couple of Chinamen."

"Christ, did they see you?"

"Not for long."

Right then the radio light flickered, and Ray Schaeffer was on the wire informing them of the new meeting point at the first tower at 0100. He was also on the line to Dan and Charlie checking their progress. And shortly after midnight the SEAL team leader knew that all their objectives had been achieved, with the exception of the giant towers.

By 0030, Rob and Ryan had placed their third and final plastic bomb right under a nest of incoming electric wires, and the Chief Petty Officer considered that this wrapped up the entire operation very tidily. He set the clock for two hours and 30 minutes, and, safe in the knowledge that this particular control center was not going to control anything after 0300, he led his men back toward the main pipeline for the shadowy 500-yard journey toward the refining towers.

When they arrived there, they found a scene of silent consternation. The Chinese were still there, still up on the tower, still working. At least two of them were. The others had gone.

"There's no way we can place the mines on that metal without those guys seeing us," said Ray Schaeffer. "The risk is too great. We'll have to shoot 'em. And that's not easy either."

"Well, they don't have a phone up there. How about a diversion, something to get 'em down? How about we set fire to their jeep? That'll do it."

"Yeah, and it'll bring a lot of other guys out here as well. Fire in a refinery is a goddamned nightmare."

"You don't say."

And then the SEALs received what looked like a piece of luck. Both the Chinese technicians began to climb down the ladder from the refining tower.

"How about that? They're going."

And so they were. They stepped into their jeep and drove off, leaving the entire area to the three teams of U.S. Navy SEALs, who instantly split up and clamped the magnetic mines onto the designated towers and primed the fuses.

Lieutenant Nathan raced between them, playing out the det cord, splicing it into place and then running it out for the three strands to meet at a central point in the shadows of the number-two tower. Behind him two SEALs carefully buried the cord in the sand, and Clouds checked his watch. It was 0150, and he set the timer for one hour and 10 minutes. It was time to leave.

For the SEALs, that is. Not a two-man patrol of Chinese guards hanging on to the leashes of two huge, brown-and-black, straining Doberman pinschers. They were just arriving. And they had been especially briefed, directly from Shanghai, to be on the lookout for U.S. Special Forces inside the refinery. And alert they were. They came around to the edge of the main tower and were confronted with eight big men, two of them with shovels, four of them with MP-5 machine guns, and all of them with hideously camouflaged green-and-brown faces.

At the moment of sighting, there were 40 yards between the forces of China and the U.S. SEALs. The guards reacted strictly in unison, unleashing the dogs at the touch of a button, and both blowing whistles loudly. Dan Conway reacted first, as the lead dog leaped at the throat of Lt. Nathan. He raised his unsilenced MP-5 and almost blew its head off.

The second dog swerved toward Lt. Commander Schaeffer, and Dan Conway almost cut it in half with a short burst into its neck. By now the guards had their hands on their own weapons, but like the dogs they were too late, and Ryan Combs aimed a withering round of fire from the M-60E4 straight at them. Both died instantly, but the whistles had done their job, and all 12 of the SEALs could hear the roar of a jeep heading from the main pipeline straight toward them.

"COVER!" roared Lt. Commander Schaeffer. *"GET RIGHT DOWN . . . IN THE DARK . . . RYAN, LET 'EM GET OUT AND THEN LET 'EM HAVE IT."*

The light was poor, but they all saw the lights of the jeep as it came screaming into the clearing between the towers. And they saw the two new guards jump out. Ryan Combs opened up again with the machine gun, and as the guards went down, Ray Schaeffer and Charlie charged forward.

But they did not see a third guard in the back seat who swung his Kalashnikov on them, and shot Ray Schaeffer through the head at point-blank range. His second burst caught Charlie high on the right-hand side of his chest, and both SEALs fell to the ground together.

Again Ryan Combs opened fire, and instantly took out the third guard, leaving just the jeep running noisily, with one dying SEAL on the ground, and another unconscious beside him. There were also five dead Chinese.

Lieutenant Conway took command, ordering the rookie SEALs to get the two wounded men into the jeep. He jumped into the driver's seat himself and told the rest of them to get in or on, anywhere, but to hold tight while he drove for the southwestern perimeter.

Somehow they all hung on, as the ex–Connecticut baseball catcher gunned the jeep forward, slamming it over the railroad tracks, swerving through the sand, going for the dark pylon, second from the end.

Fifty yards from the fence, he rammed on the brakes, and Clouds Nathan scrambled out and bolted into the holding tanks to their right, where he swiftly set the timing clock on the previous night's mines for 61 minutes. At this time an eerie siren went off loudly in the control center, just as Clouds came charging around the corner and reboarded the jeep.

"TIME?" yelled Lt. Conway. *"WHAT THE HELL'S THE TIME?"*

It was just about 0200. The action had taken less than five minutes, and their team leader was down. Dan Conway rammed the jeep right up against the fence, and two more SEALs opened up their private doorway. They piled out and dragged the two wounded men through the gap in the fence. Then the Lieutenant reversed the jeep right against the gap, jumped out and crawled under it to safety on the other side of the wire. Before they left, he tossed their one grenade into the vehicle and blew it to smithereens, covering the gap in the wire with red-hot metal and burning fuel.

And then they set off on their longest journey, carrying their leader and the rookie Charlie between them. They no longer had the mines and the explosives. But their burden was heavy, pursuit was inevitable and their chances of survival were not much better than 60-40.

They reached base camp, administering morphine to the badly wounded Charlie and desperately trying to stop the blood seeping from Lt. Commander Schaeffer's shattered skull.

But they all knew it was hopeless. Ray was breathing very erratically, and he died in the arms of Lt. Dan Conway, who was unable to stop the tears cascading down his camouflaged face.

The task of carrying the body back out through the ocean was plainly Herculean—and might even result in their capture, if the Chinese had a further squadron of guards. But the SEALs would not leave him. They changed into their wet suits, and big Rob Cafiero hoisted the Lieutenant Commander over his shoulders and began walking steadily to the beach.

Clouds Nathan and Dan Conway carried Charlie, who was losing blood at a serious rate. They were unable to stop the flow, but they got him into a wet suit and just kept going forward.

At the beach, they regrouped. They had no option but to drag the body of Ray Schaeffer into the water and tow it out to the submarine. The time was 0240, and they had to move, and they had to get their big flippers on, and it took too long because of the mild trauma, despite their training in dealing with death.

But they made it to the shallows and Dan Conway led the way, pulling Ray behind them, much lighter now as the water grew deeper.

Twenty minutes later they were in about four feet, a half mile offshore, and they stopped to look back and witness whatever damage they had wrought. For a few moments nothing happened, then an unbelievable explosion ripped into the night air as the big refining towers went up, every last one of them, sending a bright orange-and-purple sheet of flame into the heavens.

Seconds later the ocean seemed to shake as 60 massive gasoline storage tanks blew up like an atomic bomb. They heard the distant rumble as the control center exploded in a crashing, rolling fireball of flame and falling masonry, and the sky seemed to light up as the oil fire took hold, thousands of barrels of prime crude from Kazakhstan thundering into the inferno, fueling a fire that would burn for six days.

They could feel the heat out there in the water, almost two miles away.

"Jesus Christ," said Ryan Combs. "Whatever they wanted, I guess we've done it."

"But it wasn't damn well worth it, was it?" said Dan Conway.

"Steady, Dan," said Rob. "I don't think Ray would have wanted you to say that."

The new team leader just nodded. And the two SEALs turned out to sea, to the west, where the ASDV awaited them. And they kept swimming just below the surface, towing the still and silent body of Lt. Commander Schaeffer between them.

160500MAY07. USS *Shark*.
26.36N 56.49E. Gulf of Hormuz.
Speed 3. Racetrack pattern. PD.

THE MESSAGE FROM the communication room was not very clear.

"XO–comms. We're getting something on VHF. But it's kinda shaky. I'd say about twelve miles away, from the ASDV. I guess they've surfaced and may be using a hand-held aerial. But they keep breaking up. We're still trying. Whatever it is, doesn't sound good."

"Comms–XO. You're not dealing with a *MAYDAY*, are you?"

"Nossir. But they're in some kind of trouble . . . wait a minute, sir . . . there's something right now . . . oh, Jesus, they've lost a man, sir . . . wait a minute . . . I'll be right back . . . stay on the line, sir."

Lieutenant Commander Dan Headley could hear the background noise in comms. . . . *"Say again . . . over. . . . Say again . . . over. . . ."*

He heard *Shark*'s radio operator repeat twice . . . *"You're say-ing 'dead,' right? D for Delta? Right? . . . Please say again . . . over. . . ."*

Three minutes later, the comms chief was back on the line. "As far as I can make out, sir, Lieutenant Commander Ray Schaef-fer has been killed, and one of the rookie SEALs, Charlie Mitchell, is very badly wounded . . . they're afraid he might die . . . and they're asking if we can get the ship in any closer . . . you know, of course, the ASDV makes only six knots flat out . . ."

By now Commander Rusty Bennett had materialized in the control room, and Dan Headley repeated to him the bad news.

No one heard the mission commander mutter, "Oh, no. Not Ray." He just said formally, "Are they sure it's Ray?"

Dan Headley added, "They were broadcasting from the ASDV. It wasn't very clear, but I'm afraid we better prepare for the worst."

"Did they say how badly Charlie Mitchell was hurt?"

"Badly. They're afraid he might die if he doesn't get attention soonest. They want us to bring the ship in to meet them. And I'm happy to do so, but you know what happened with the CO last time. He nearly had a heart attack when I changed the orders in even a minor way."

"Where is he now?"

"I guess asleep."

"Do we wake him?"

"No. Fuck him. Let's go get the guys out."

"Okay. Down all masts. Conn–XO . . . make your speed twenty knots . . . steer zero-three-four . . . fathometer, report the depth. . . . Navigator–XO . . . report to me immediately."

The submarine surged forward, and everyone who was awake heard the distinct change in the rhythm of the ship. Lieutenant Pearson came hustling through the doorway, holding a chart. "Right here, sir," he said. "We're in two hundred feet of water, and we can go at least six miles on this course without even thinking about it."

"Thanks, Shawn. . . . " But he was cut off from further communication by the sudden appearance in the control room of Captain Reid, wearing his pajama trousers, shoes, socks and a Navy sweater.

"XO, might I ask where precisely you are taking this ship when our orders are perfectly clear to remain on station?"

"Sir, right now we are on a rescue mission. The ASDV just radioed in. The SEAL team leader, Lt. Commander Schaeffer, has been killed, and another of the twelve is badly wounded. They called to request we come in and meet them. They are afraid the second SEAL might also die. We're going in six miles to a probable depth of one hundred fifty feet. If I have to, we'll continue on the surface until we find them."

"Lieutenant Commander Headley, you do of course realize that your orders are directly countermanding both mine and those of the flag?"

"Sir. There are ample provisions in Navy regulations to provide for emergency actions in order to save life. Especially one of our own."

"XO. DO NOT REMIND ME OF THE NAVY'S REGULATIONS. I KNOW A GREAT DEAL ABOUT THEM. AND THE ONE I SUGGEST YOU CONSIDER IS THE ONE THAT GIVES THE COMMANDING OFFICER ABSOLUTE POWER ON HIS OWN SHIP."

"I am well acquainted with that one, sir."

"Then, for the second time in as many days, I am ordering you to turn this ship around and return to our correct waiting position at 26.36N 56.49E."

"Sir," interrupted Commander Bennett, "as you are well aware, I outrank Lieutenant Commander Headley and it was at my request he agreed to go on a rescue mission, possibly to save the life of one of my most valuable men."

"Then I must remind you, sir, that you have no rights whatsoever on this ship. And I will not have this interference. What exactly is this? Some kind of damned conspiracy? Well, you've picked the wrong man to make a fool of ... waiting until I'm asleep and then flagrantly disobeying my orders."

"Sir, may I just—" But Rusty was cut off in midsentence.

"N-O-O-O. YOU MAY NOT. TWENTY-SIX THIRTY-SIX NORTH, SIR. FIFTY-SIX FORTY-NINE EAST, SIR. THAT'S OUR CORRECT POSITION. AND THAT'S WHERE WE'RE GOING. YOU CANNOT RUN A NAVY FOR A GUY WHO'S PROBABLY CUT HIS GODDAMNED FINGER . . . RETURN TO OUR DESIG-NATED POSITION. AND THAT'S AN ORDER, XO!"

Midnight. Wednesday, May 16.
Office of the National Security Adviser.
The White House. Washington, D.C.

Admiral Morgan had been alone for two hours, since Admiral Dixon had returned to the Pentagon. Both men knew the SEAL team had gone into Iran and that the attack on the refinery was scheduled for the small hours of Thursday morning, an eight-and-a-half-hour time difference from Washington.

Both men knew it had already happened from several different sources: the satellites, the CIA, the embassy in Tehran, the Brits via Oman on the other side of the strait and a very sketchy item on CNN. The flight-deck crew and almost everyone else on board USS *Constellation* had seen the fireball from 20 miles offshore. The U.S. Navy knew comprehensibly, from Diego Garcia to Pearl Harbor, from Coronado to Norfolk, Virginia, that a 12-man team of SEALs had just destroyed the world's biggest and newest Middle Eastern oil refinery.

What no one knew was the fate of the SEALs, and Admiral Morgan paced his office awaiting some news. In his mind he guessed they'd be back in the *Shark* by around 0800 their time.

As far as he could tell, that was a half hour ago, and so far he'd heard *NOTHING. What the hell's going on?* That was Admiral Morgan's question. He'd kept Kathy on duty, watching her e-mail screen, sitting by the phone, ever ready to bring in the message that everyone was safe. It was a curious trait in his character, since he was now, at least according to his job description, a political adviser. But he was not a political adviser in the place that counted. In his heart, he was still a Navy commanding officer. And that did not permit him to leave the bridge until he knew absolutely that the men were home unscathed.

So why is no one telling me they're safe? Maybe they aren't safe? And if not, why not? Again, *what the hell's going on?*

"KATHY!"

The door opened, and Ms. O'Brien came through it, still quite incredibly glamorous despite the late hour. "I do wish you wouldn't yell like that," she said. "It's so . . . so . . . well, uncool."

"Who the hell else would hear me in this goddamned graveyard?" he rasped.

"Only everyone."

"Like who? You think they could hear me in the Oval Office, if the President's still working?"

"My darling, they could hear you in the Rose Garden."

"Oh, of course. I forgot we got that midnight pruning crew in there, snipping away until breakfast."

"Arnold, I am merely suggesting that it might be unnecessary for you to sound like a drill sergeant, in the White House, in the middle of the night. And, by the way, sarcasm does not become you."

"Yes it does. It becomes me better than anyone I ever met. And anyhow, where the hell're my SEALs? Answer that, Miss Decibels 2007."

Before she could answer, with something suitably pithy, the phone rang at her desk outside the main office. Secure line. She walked quickly out through the doorway, and instantly put the call through to the Admiral.

"Yup. Morgan. Speak."

"Arnie, it's Alan Dixon. Good news and bad news, I am afraid. The SEALs wiped out the refinery, but only ten of them got back."

"Are they inside the *Shark* right now?"

"They are. But they lost the team leader, Lieutenant Commander Ray Schaeffer. And they lost one of the new guys, young Charlie Mitchell."

Admiral Morgan was stone silent for at least a half minute while he composed himself. "They didn't die in the fire, did they?"

"No. There was some kind of battle inside the refinery. The Chinese had a military guard patrol, which we were just not expecting. With attack dogs. The guys were cornered, but they took out all five guards and both dogs, blew up their jeep and then the entire oil plant. Apparently the guards managed to get a couple of bursts out of their old Kalashnikovs. Hit Ray and Charlie at less than twenty feet, point-blank range. They never had a chance."

"They didn't leave our guys behind, did they? Not in that god-forsaken country?"

"No. They did not. They brought the body of Ray Schaeffer out. At the time Charlie Mitchell was still alive, but he died in the ASDV about fifteen minutes before they got back to the submarine. It was a long journey at only six knots, and they couldn't save him."

"Thanks, Alan. Let's talk in the morning."

"Good night, sir."

Arnold stood up from his desk, and he walked to the window. He stared out into the darkness, and before him he saw the half-lit refinery, and he imagined the SEALs, out there alone, trapped in a firefight, and he imagined the gallantry of the young Americans, the terror, the air alive with bullets, Lt. Commander Schaeffer, the leader, charging forward trying to save his men. *Ray Schaeffer. Goddamnit. He went into Russia for me. He went into China for me. And he's gone into Iran for me. And now he's dead.*

Admiral Morgan heard Kathy return to the office. But he just stood with his back to her, staring out into the pitch-black of the White House garden, because he could not bear for her to see him this upset.

"I've ordered us some coffee," she said. "How many did they lose?"

"Two."

"I guessed from your voice it was bad."

And she saw him wipe the moisture from his eyes with his shirtsleeve before he turned to face her. And she noticed his voice was tight when he said, "Please make sure that both Admiral Dixon and I attend the funeral in Marblehead for Lieutenant Commander Ray Schaeffer."

"What about the President?"

"I don't think so. He wouldn't understand."

"He'd understand the death of a Navy officer, wouldn't he?"

"Possibly. But he'd never understand the courage. The duty. The honor. The mind of such a man."

"Well, I'm sure the people of Marblehead would like to see the Lieutenant Commander given the honor of the President attending his funeral," replied Kathy. "Couldn't you explain it to him?"

"That, I am afraid, would be like trying to teach a pig to speak. You would succeed only in irritating the pig. . . . I'm afraid the simple truth of a military officer prepared to lay down his life for his country will forever remain a mystery to men like President Clarke. Because they do not do it for money. It's not for glory either. Most of them find it impossible even to talk about it. And it's not for power. It's for something else. Something very private, to people like Lieutenant Commander Schaeffer. And believe me, there aren't many of them. And I guess you can see how upset it makes me when we lose one."

"Yes. Yes I can. I've never seen you like this before."

"Guess not many people have. They think of me as some kind of civilian SEAL in a gray suit . . . but inside I'm like everyone else. So are the SEALs. They get scared, they feel pain, and they bleed from their wounds. Sometimes I guess I bleed for them."

"Yes, my darling. Don't you."

The coffee arrived, and Kathy poured it. The Admiral sat at his desk saying nothing. But suddenly he stood up, and told her, "I'm not paid to sit around worrying about yesterday. I'm paid to start figuring out tomorrow . . . in my game, you gotta keep going forward or the bastards will trample you to death."

He came and put his arms around her, but she could still see the sorrow in his face, as he privately mourned the dead SEALs. And she did not think it possible that anyone had ever loved anyone more than she loved Arnold Morgan.

0900. Thursday, May 17.
Southern Fleet Command HQ.
Zhanjiang, South China.

News of the total destruction of the Chinese refinery hit Beijing at around 0800 local time. By 0900 the world's media had put something together on the lines of "yet *another* diabolical oil fire in the Strait of Hormuz—this time a massive refinery." The world's oil markets were about to go collectively berserk for the second time in a month.

Admiral Zhang believed, correctly as it happened, that the price per barrel might go right back to $85, off its weeklong low of $65, when the major trading market in Tokyo opened.

Surprisingly he remained calm. "Well, Jicai," he said to his friend, "I suppose we might have expected something like this."

"You mean you believe someone did this to us, that it was not just an accident in a big refinery?"

"Jicai, the Pentagon just blew up China's most important oil refinery in revenge for the minefield we helped to create in the Strait of Hormuz."

"You mean they bombed it, or hit it with a guided missile? Surely not—they would not dare instigate such an act of war so publicly."

"Jicai, it is entirely possible that no one will ever know what happened to our installation in the Strait of Hormuz. It is also possible that the world's media will never even consider that such an act could have been perpetrated by the oh-so-high-and-mighty United States. But I shall always know differently."

"Do the media sense there may be something sinister? Are they linking the other fires?"

"Not so far. But of course they are not tuned in to our involvement in the minefield yet. Though I am quite certain the American military knows. That's why they just blew the refinery."

"Do we hit back?"

"We cannot. There's nothing for us to hit in the immediate area of the refinery. Anyway, it would not be in our interest to do so. The Americans would then start to destroy our entire Navy, and I am afraid we could not stop them. I'm rather of the opinion that our days in the Arabian Sea and the Gulf of Iran are over. For the moment, anyway. The Americans are in charge there now."

"This is so unlike you, Yushu. So accepting of such terrible events."

"Well, I did remind you I was half expecting something of this kind to happen. And now I should remind you, the essence of all war throughout our long history has been attrition. We can affford losses, both physically and emotionally. The rule is that we never take our eye off the main objective. And that grows ever nearer. We must let the oil fires burn, and later this morning we will have our own light in the sky."

Admirals Zu Jicai and Zhang Yushu were now joined by the recently appointed Commander-in-Chief of the Southern Fleet, Vice Admiral Yang Linzhong, a short, stocky ex–frigate captain from Canton.

"Gentlemen," he said, entering his own office, and bowing his head. "I have just been visiting our sonics laboratory, and they are ready to demonstrate for you their work over the past six months. I think you will be impressed."

The two senior Admirals in the entire Chinese armed forces rose, and followed Yang out to a waiting Navy staff car, which drove them immediately a distance of less than a mile to the domain of Lt. Commander Guangjin Chen, the PLAN's Mr. Underwater, their great mastermind of deep-sea listening countermeasures.

His rank of Lt. Commander was honorary. Mr. Guangjin was essentially a scientist, more at home in a white laboratory coat than a naval uniform. In fact no one had ever seen him in a uniform, even though it was rumored he was the highest-paid officer in the Chinese Navy, below the rank of rear admiral.

His kingdom was underwater, in the strange, eerie caverns of the oceans. He marched to the orders of the tides, he listened to the evidence of the echoes and he acted on the lingering ping of the sonic pulses. Much of his work had been in the field of decoys, disguising, hiding the beat of the engines of the warships, seeking always to confuse and deceive the enemy.

What very few people knew, however, was that Guangjin Chen had masterminded a private project of such brilliant deception it almost took Admiral Zhang's breath away. He had heard about it only a year ago while he was still Commander-in-Chief of the Navy. And he had heard about it just by chance. And great was his fury when he found out that Mr. Guangjin had offered the idea to the Navy for development 10 years previously, four years before he even joined the Senior Service. Guangjin had been turned down flat, probably because he was just a civilian.

In any event, Admiral Zhang knew brilliance when he heard it, even if it might not work. And last August he had summoned Mr. Guangjin to his home for dinner, and there he conducted an interrogation, to the great glee of the scientist.

Like all scientists, the lean and earnest Guangjin adored talking about his work, especially a project he had believed to be long dead. And he shyly admitted to the great Chinese Admiral that he had continued working on the project, just at his home, these past several years.

And the night proved to be magical. They had sat outside Admiral Zhang's beautiful summer house on the island of Gulangyu, just across the Lujiang Channel from the South China seaport and Navy base of Xiamen.

The air was warm, a light southwest wind drifting across the great estuary of the Nine Dragon River, and Guangjin in company with the Zhangs sipped fragrant tea out on the stone patio beneath the curved red roof. The scientist was on his feet answering questions and pointing with a cane at the stone squares upon which he walked.

"But where's the carrier now?"

"Right here, sir. In this stone square."

"But where's our Kilo?"

"Right here, sir, in the middle of this paler stone square."

"Is it transmitting?"

"Nossir. Not yet."

"Well, when will it?"

"When I tell it to do so."

"But how will you know when?"

"I'll be watching all the time."

"But how?"

"Via the satellites, sir. It's very easy to track a large ship in the open ocean. You can hardly miss it."

"How long is the transmission?"

"Oh, just a few seconds. Long enough to be heard."

"Then what?"

"Well, if the U.S. Admiral has a modicum of sense, he'll bear away and make a more northerly course."

"I suppose he will."

"And he'll keep going until I frighten him again."

The Admiral remembered just shaking his head in amazement, and he had said, "Chen, I am deeply impressed. And I want you to continue your work on this as a priority. Move it to a secure area in your working block, and perfect it. Essentially you will answer only to Admiral Zu, or myself. I regard it as our personal mission, and I'm going to code-name it right away, in memory of this evening. From now on, it's Operation Paving Stone."

Admiral Zhang would never forget the conversation. It had been on his mind for months. This very brilliant person, who had joined the Navy strictly as a sonics expert, was on to something. And now he was going to find out just how big, and whether it would work.

The three Admirals climbed out of the staff car, and two guards escorted them into an inner office of this highly classified laboratory. And there before them stood Lt. Commander

Guangjin, who bowed politely, never having quite mastered the traditional Navy salute.

"Welcome, gentlemen," he said, "to my humble quarters." He'd never quite come to grips with the normal greeting of "sir" from a two-and-a-half to an admiral. But great scholarship has a dignity of its own, and no one noticed.

"Yushu," he said, with an earth-shattering lack of formality to the highest-ranking Admiral in the world's biggest nation, it is especially nice to see you again—and I think you will be very pleased with me."

Admiral Zhang smiled and patted his prodigy on the shoulder. The project belonged of course to the scientist, but Zhang had made it possible, and if it worked, history would judge them both kindly.

Mr. Guangjin walked to the rear of his long, bright work area and led the way into a darkened room, lit only by the backlighting of the computer screens, in almost every respect a replica of a warship's ops room.

He paused before a screen upon which there was an illuminated grid. "That's it, Yushu, just as we planned it. Operation Paving Stone, eh? Ha-ha, and now, as you know, we have two test sites ready for us. We have a towed-array frigate way up in the north in the Yellow Sea, and another in the Pacific, six hundred miles off our southern coast. Both ships have in the last hour thrown the device over the side, and are ten miles distant.

"The device is at present passive . . . and now I am going to activate the one in the Yellow Sea. You, Yushu, will speak personally to the sonar room in the frigate."

He handed a telephone to the senior Admiral, who spoke into it. "This is Admiral Zhang. Will you please inform me what is happening?"

"This is Lieutenant Chunming, sir. Right now we have nothing on the screen. Just the usual waterfall. Please stay on the line."

And now, Guangjin moved to the control keyboard that was set before the grid-screen. "Activating now," he said pressing the keys.

The room was silent, as the electronic pulses flashed to one of two Chinese satellites. And then Admiral Zhang heard down the phone, "Lieutenant Chunming, sir. I'm getting something . . . and it's engine lines . . . transient contact . . . just seven seconds . . . but I'm certain it's a submarine . . . making a turn . . . one moment, sir, the computer's trying to match the lines . . . it's coming up, sir, this is a Russian-built Kilo-Class diesel-electric. No doubt. The pattern fits precisely."

The Admiral replaced the telephone. And he turned to the scientist and held out his hand. "Remarkable," he said. "Quite, quite remarkable."

"And now we shall try the second one, way out in the Pacific. Please hold this telephone, and I will attempt to activate . . ."

Four minutes later, an almost ecstatic Zhang Yushu heard another sonar officer in a distant Chinese frigate say to him, "Here it comes, sir. Right here we've caught a transient on a Russian-built Kilo-Class submarine."

201300MAY07.
USS *John F. Kennedy.*
20N 125E. Speed 20. Course 315.

Big John was steaming over 3,000 fathoms of water. All flying had been canceled for two days because of a severe storm, and the personnel of the Black Aces, Top Hatters and Golden Warriors were bored by the inactivity. Nonetheless the forecast was good, the storm had abated and the carrier was currently in the Philippine Sea, 180 miles northeast of Cape Engano. That put her 270 miles southeast of the Taiwan coast, but just 150 miles short of her ops area.

These were the usual patrol waters of the U.S. Navy, the world's policeman, protecting the rights of the citizens of the nation of Taiwan. The area was a triangle, its shortest side 90 miles long facing the central eastern coastline of the island, around 50 miles off the beaches. The other two sides were each 150 miles long, joining at a point close to the 125-degree line of longitude. Most of the water inside that triangle was 15,000 feet deep.

And the *JFK* was steaming straight toward it, high, wide and handsome, no secrets, no subtlety, no intent to deceive. Just one thunderous iron fist, the same one that had warned Red China for half a century: *Stay out of our buddies' backyard.*

And now, here they came again, pushing through the long Pacific swells, cleaving through 30-foot waves, 88,000 tons of steel-clad power, daring anyone to raise an objection. The new emblem patch of the Tomcat pilots uttered a thousand words in just two. *Anytime, Pal.*

Five hundred and seventy miles away, on a bright computer screen in the Southern Fleet HQ in Zhanjiang, there was a replica of the op area of the *JFK*. It showed a line 100 miles long, 50 miles off the eastern seaboard of Taiwain, and it fell back 150 miles into an oblong rather than a triangle. Essentially it represented the guesswork of a dozen ex–Chinese warship commanders, and it was not a bad guess at that. The *JFK* triangle fitted very neatly into Guangjin's "box," and the positional accuracy of the 100-mile line opposite the Taiwan beaches was nearly uncanny.

It was, of course, the result of years of study of U.S. Navy patrols, and all around the Chinese version of *JFK*'s op area was a 600-mile-long line in the shape of a sloped roof on its side, representing Admiral Zhang Yushu's assessment of the Americans' likely line of approach.

That was the line they were now watching for the carrier, and in precisely three hours from now, Big John would breach that line at 20.41N 124.18E. And the Chinese Navy satellites would relentlessly track her wherever she went.

Back in Zhanjiang, Lt. Commander Guangjin made another adjustment to his screen, and right over his U.S. op-area chart, there was now a much bigger square, 240 miles long north to south, 240 miles wide west to east. It was divided into grid squares numbered 1 to 6, and A to F. At almost every corner of each of the 36 squares there was a black circle. And every one of those circles of course had a number, A-5 or C-4, just like any map reference. The U.S. ops area, into which the *JFK* was headed, was bang in the middle of this computerized grid.

Big John steamed on, now making just 12 knots since Admiral Daylan Holt had cleared the flight wings to begin operations at 1500. And the deck once more came alive to the howl of the jets and the surge of the deck crews, as the fighter-bombers screamed into the bright skies above the deep Pacific Ocean.

The course of the carrier now became erratic, certainly on the distant Chinese chart in Zhanjiang, because the *JFK* had to keep changing course to east-southeast, into the wind, for the landings and takeoffs. But her basic northern track up to the ops area remained steady.

She crossed Admiral Zhang's outer line of approach at 1900. And the busy flying evening wore on in the great waterborne fortress of *Big John.* The Admiral's ops room was receiving no reports of foreign warships anywhere in the area. Nothing from either of the two nuclear submarines riding shotgun out there off his port and starboard bows. Not a thing from the S-3B Viking ASW aircraft ranging out in front, dropping sonobuoys into the water, seeking any foreign submarine that might be lurking in these deep waters.

Behind this fast, powerful, deep-field ASW screen the rest of CV-67's Battle Group, two destroyers and five frigates, moved safely through seas that had been "swept" by possibly the world's sharpest ears.

At the current low speed, with a lot of course adjustments, Big John and her men were about eight hours short of their op area. Though Lt. Commander Guangjin did not need them to be in it, just heading up that way. And at 2200 he activated, via the satellites, the Chinese decoy station B-5.

Floating in the water, identifiable only by its ultrathin aerial wire, B-5 was just about invisible at 50 feet. It made one short, sharp transmission from approximately 100 miles northwest of the carrier, and three of the sonobuoys dropped by the Viking picked it up instantly at range 15 miles and under.

Lieutenant (jg) Brian Wright had the signals on the aircraft screen instantly, and he assessed a rough position of a patrolling submarine at 21.20N 122.21E. The engine lines fed into the Viking's onboard computer and moments later Brian Wright was contemplating the presence of a possible Russian-built Kilo-Class diesel-electric, in the water 100 miles from Big John. He guessed the submarine had just made a "dynamic start" of her engines, probably to charge her batteries. Everyone connected, in any way, with a big carrier is wary of a diesel-electric underwater boat because of its stealth at low speed.

And Lt. Wright punched in his signal to the Admiral's ops room "... *Dynamic start possible Kilo Class position 21.20N 122.21E. Transient contact ... attempting to localize.*"

The Viking, heading north, banked back hard to the east in search of the "intruder," sweeping the sea with radar, looking for a submarine that did not exist. It was just a brilliantly invented transmitter with a slim aerial wire jutting three feet out of the water, almost invisible by day, totally invisible by night. It was being activated at will by Lt. Commander Guangjin Chen 600 miles away in Zhanjiang: activated to transmit the uniquely chilling engine lines of the Kilo-Class Type 636.

Admiral Daylan Holt received the signal from comms at 2220 and instantly ordered a course change.

"*Come right as soon as you can to zero-three-zero ... cancel all flying.*"

The *JFK* quickly retrieved two more fighter aircraft and then slewed slowly around in the water, settling thirty degrees east of north. It took the ship a full 15 minutes to make those maneuvers, and five minutes later, the Viking picked up a new transmission from one of the sonobuoys.

Again it was transient. To the sonar operator thundering through the dark skies above the Pacific it looked like a dynamic stop. He could see just a little curl at the base of the tiny bright "paint" near the bottom of his screen. It looked no nearer than the first contact, and he recorded it in essentially the same spot, suggesting in his signal to the flag that it was almost certainly the same contact they had located 20 minutes previously.

And there the minor drama seemed to end. Nothing more was heard from anyone. Flying continued unabated, Big John continued her zigzagging course for the landings and takeoffs and another 45 miles of water slipped beneath her keel.

But out over that pitch-black water, at 0145 in the morning, another Viking picked up another transient contact off two sonobuoys. And again they judged it to be a Kilo, but no one was certain whether or not it was the same one, because its position was roughly 50 miles northeast of the last one. Which meant it must have been making over 10 knots: unlikely because the American sonar would have picked it up.

For the second time that night a big U.S. Navy Viking banked around again to the east and again never caught a glimmer of anything. At least, not for a half hour, when a different buoy picked up what appeared to be a dynamic start. Neither of the two U.S. submarines, both deploying towed arrays, picked up anything. And the signal from the Viking to the flag was similar to the others ... *"Transient contact. Kilo-Class 636. Possibly same as Datum One. Rough position 21.53N 122.45E. Attempting to localize. Prosecuting."*

Guangjin Chen's C-4 was proving as elusive as B-5. And now both of these devilish decoys, being instructed from the satellites, remained silent. And the entire U.S. Navy could have set off in pursuit and they would have found precisely nothing.

Nonetheless Admiral Holt was obliged to move his carrier farther east from his northern course, because a Kilo is simply too dangerous a ship to risk going close to, and anyway, easy to sidestep.

And once more the ocean world beyond Taiwan's east coast went more or less silent. *Big John* steamed on approximately toward her ops area, but her present course would carry her right past the triangle, past the point to the east, unless she could turn in. But that seemed very doubtful at present, since there appeared to be at least one and possibly two Chinese submarines somewhere off her port beam, patrolling where *Big John* wanted to be. And the U.S. submarines were picking up nothing on the towed arrays.

Then, at 0545, the patrolling Viking tracker picked up the signal again, and this time it was appreciably closer to the carrier. In fact, it was still C-4 transmitting but the *JFK* was only 75 miles from the decoy now, instead of 100.

Admiral Holt did not like it. And he edged east again away from his op area. He simply could not go in there, if there should be one or more Chinese Kilos awaiting him. Particularly since everyone in the Navy now knew the SEALs had just banged out a $10 billion Sino investment down in the Strait of Hormuz.

The Admiral pressed on North for another 30 miles, and at 0804 on Monday morning, May 21, Guangjin Chen hit the computer buttoms to activate C-3. A new field of U.S. sonobuoys picked up the transmission immediately, and the patrolling Viking's signal to the flag caused major consternation. They assessed that this was an entirely different Kilo, and it was waiting bang in the center of CV-67's op area.

Admiral Holt had the distinct feeling he was being pushed around by the Chinese Navy, and he was beginning to sense a feeling of rising frustration. Right now he had only one option, to make a swing right around the northeast end of the triangle and try to move in sometime in the next few days when the Kilos had tired of this game of cat and mouse. Nonetheless he could not take any risks, and he ordered a course change to the northeast, with his submarines moving out to his west, and the Viking pilots scanning the ocean with ever more vigilance.

For a long time there was nothing, and then just before midday the Viking picked up a new contact, and again it was a Kilo. It could have been the same one they heard at 0804, but it may very well have been a different one. The Chinese only own four Kilos, and privately Admiral Holt thought there were probably two of them out there. However, at 1200 (local), that was not quite the point. What mattered was that the Viking operator put the transmission only 56 miles off *Big John*'s port beam, and that was not good. Worse yet, it was continued, but not localized, by either of the SSNs.

In Admiral Holt's opinion, this was becoming quite serious. There was, it seemed, at least one Chinese Kilo possibly as close as 50 miles from the carrier, and it seemed to be extremely elusive. Which was a shuddering thought for a U.S. admiral accustomed to controlling the ocean, on, above and below the surface for 200 miles in any direction wherever he roamed.

No admiral commanding a carrier battle group wants to go anywhere within 300 miles of a foreign, unfriendly, land-based air force, and he certainly wants no part of a marauding submarine. The Chinese ploy to have two Kilos on permanent patrol in the Taiwan Strait is based on the simple assumption that no U.S. admiral would steer a carrier down the Taiwan Strait if this were so. Neither would he.

And now, the steel-haired Daylan Holt, a Texan from Mesquite on the western edge of Dallas, was face-to-face with a brand-new kind of hardball international politics out on the northern edge of his own ops area. Of course he could sink the Kilo if he could catch it below the surface . . . IF he could find it.

But at that point, no one could find it, or even them, if there were two, despite having flooded the probability areas with radar, ESM and active and passive sonar from his submarines, aircraft and towed-array frigates. And it was beginning to look as though the *JFK* would have to continue northeast into the deep water at the southern end of the lonely Sakishima Islands, where Japan finally peters out into the Pacific. This is a very remote corner of the ocean, 300 miles southwest of the American base at Okinawa. The Sakishimas stand 120 miles west of Taiwan, 60 miles from the op area of *Big John*. Admiral Holt had an uneasy feeling he was being herded away from his objective by the demonic, near-silent Chinese submarines.

And the Chinese not only tracked the Americans all the way, at 1400 they activated E-1, some 80 miles north of the carrier, undetected by the outriding nuclear submarine. The Viking picked it up and signaled the flag. Admiral Holt briefly changed course, and as he did so, Guangjin activated D-2. Just a transient, seven-second transmission, which had the effect of pushing the carrier toward the waters south of the tiny island chain, to Ishigaki, where the water was deep, and which, by a grand design hatched in distant Zhanjiang, lay neatly in two outer squares of Lt. Commander Guangjin's grid.

Admiral Holt was forced to turn north again, and he reasoned that the Kilo force, however many, was now to his left and right, but falling astern. If they wanted to get at his carrier, they'd have to transit northwest through the massive ASW barrier he'd set up. The decoy Kilo-buoys were indeed on either side of him, but the wily Zhang had stationed two real Kilos just 30 miles ahead of the CVBG. And he'd done it seven days ago.

And now they were almost stationary, transmitting nothing, preparing to launch a copybook attack on the U.S. carrier, identical to that of Commander Ben Adnam when he destroyed the Nimitz-Class carrier USS *Thomas Jefferson* in the Arabian Sea five years previously.

They had chased and pursued nothing. They had just waited, silently, for the prime moment to fire, when Lt. Commander Guangjin's ingenious invention had done its work. Unlike Ben Adnam they had not needed to assess the wind and the carrier's time of approach. The very occasional transmissions from the floating electronic buoys had "herded" Big John into the appointed place like so many sheepdogs.

The Chinese submarines were in there, in 600 feet of water, the Kilo-Class hulls 366 and 367, jet-black 3,000-ton diesel-electrics built in Russia's Admiralty Yard at Saint Petersburg. They were each armed with 18 TEST 71/96 wire-guided passive-active torpedoes, homing at 40 knots to 15 kilometers. But the

Chinese COs would fire their two torpedoes, with their 205kg nonnuclear warheads, from a lot closer than that.

But Admiral Zhang was not out to create world havoc and mass destruction. He just sought, quietly, to cripple the great U.S. warship, despite all the difficulties that would involve.

And at 2100 that Monday evening, his underwater commanders drew a bead on *Big John*.

Same time (0800 local, Monday).
The White House.

Everything about the *goddamned Chinese* baffled Arnold Morgan. He had no idea why they would have wanted to infuriate the entire Western world, not to mention much of the Eastern world, by assisting the *goddamned towelheads* in mining the Strait of Hormuz.

Maybe just for money. Maybe they really thought they could make a huge financial killing by selling their oil from Khazakhstan at the massive world prices that would follow the blockade of the Gulf of Iran.

Maybe. But maybe not. It made some sense to the President's National Security Adviser. But not enough. Well, the USA had slammed back hard, as China must have known they might. And no one had complained to anyone. Certainly the USA knew there was no point remonstrating with the Chinese over the minefield, because they would say nothing. Equally the Chinese had said nothing to anyone about the destruction of the oil refinery.

Admiral Morgan knew he was not going to receive any answers to anything. Which was why he had summarily requested the presence of the Chinese ambassador to Washington, the urbane Ling Guofeng. Arnold might not be getting any answers, but he was about to deliver one or two truths.

Kathy O'Brien politely ushered the ambassador into the main office at 0815. The two men knew each other, of course, but it was always a cool relationship. The Admiral had passed one or two withering broadsides across the bow of the Chinese ship of state in the past few years, and Ling Guofeng had frequently been obliged to keep his head well down.

In another life, they might actually have been friends. Both of them knew more about the world than was good for anyone. And both of them knew implicitly where their loyalties were. Arnold Morgan, a natural aggressor, was constantly issuing warnings, making threats and, occasionally, carrying them out. The veteran Ambassador Ling, in his role as China's chief appeaser in Washington, was thus obliged to absorb a substantial amount of grief from the Admiral. But the diplomat from Shanghai knew how to roll with the punches.

"Good morning, Admiral," he said, bowing. "What a very kind invitation. It's been too long."

Arnold Morgan raised his eyes heavenward . . . *Too long! Never mind the blown-up tankers, never mind the minefield, the world oil crisis, Japan almost going bankrupt because of it. Never mind that the blasted refinery's still spouting flames one hundred feet into the air. . . . Will someone ever save me from this Oriental bullshit? . . . "Too long," he says. Jesus Christ.*

"Ambassador, the pleasure is, as always, mine," replied the Admiral. "Please sit down. I have ordered a pot of Lapsang Suchong, your favorite China tea, I believe—at least your favorite in this country."

"Now that is very kind of you, and I hope it will smooth our way during our discussions."

And Arnold slyly congratulated himself on Kathy's call to Ling's secretary on Friday afternoon to establish the subtleties of the ambassador's tastes. He had no recollection that Kathy had made the call without even asking him.

Anyway, the tea was delivered and poured by a polite and attentive waiter, and Arnold Morgan stepped up to the plate.

"Ambassador, there is much that cannot be said at this discussion—much, possibly, that never will be said. I have asked you here because I believe that you and I understand each other."

"I think and hope that we do," replied Ling in his impeccable English accent.

"Well, let me begin by saying that we are very well aware of China's complicity in the placing of the minefield in the Strait of Hormuz."

"Oh, really?" replied Ling. "I have not been so informed."

"And I guess, if I wanted to, I could inform you myself of the origin of the mines, the date they left Moscow, the times of the refueling stops for the Andropov freighter that delivered them, and the date the PLAN assisted the Iranians in laying the fields."

Ambassador Ling said nothing, betrayed nothing, not a flicker of understanding—the precise way all great ambassadors are supposed to operate under this kind of pressure in a foreign capital.

"But there is no need for me to do so, since we both understand the . . . er . . . rather heated game we are playing. But I would like to mention the fire that is still raging in the strait at the Chinese refinery. That, ambassador, represents the collective wrath of the entire industrial world. So I would warn you about the danger of writing it off as an accident and blithely rebuilding it."

"Am I hearing *an admission* that the United States of America actually attacked and destroyed the ten-billion-dollar Chinese refinery in the strait?"

"No more than I am hearing *an admission* that China purchased hundreds of sea mines at vast expense from Moscow, and then tried to shut down the principal power supply of every oil-consuming country in the world. Damn nearly all of them, that is."

Ambassador Ling said nothing.

And Admiral Morgan continued: "And so, my good friend, Guofeng, I would like to conclude with this piece of advice for you and your government. In our opinion, and in the opinion of all our allies, you have committed a crime of vast proportions in the Strait of Hormuz. And it is a crime that must not be repeated. It is therefore my rather sad duty to advise you"—and here his voice rose to its familiar growling quality—*"to stay the fuck out of the Middle East oil routes."*

"And if we should insist on our right to trade in any international waters?"

"You would find no objection from us, because your ships are welcome to visit us at any time. But if you continue to put Chinese warships anywhere near the north reaches of the Arabian Sea, inside the Strait of Hormuz or indeed in the Gulf of Iran, we shall have no hesitation if it comes to sinking them. Your nation has committed a terrible crime, for reasons best known to your masters in Beijing. But the rest of the world will not permit you the leeway to repeat that crime. Ling, old buddy, your Navy is on its way right back to the South China Sea."

"I shall indeed report your views to my government. But do I have your permission to inform them that the United States willfully destroyed the Chinese refinery?"

"No, Ambassador. You do not. You may tell them that the elimination of the refinery was in your opinion an act of retribution against your government for crimes committed by China in the strait. You may also say that the U.S. government was not unsupportive of the action against the Chinese oil. But as to who perpetrated the destruction, that may never be known. But if I had to guess, I'd say you should look to some of those Arabs who are currently unable to sell their oil because it's all trapped in the gulf."

"Yes, of course," replied the ambassador. "How foolish of me not to have identified the culprit at once."

"Well, for the time being, that would appear to be all. But heed what I say, Ambassador. Because I would not want things to become any more tense between us. And you guys have done quite sufficient damage for one month."

"And, quite frankly, Admiral, so, might I say, have you."

Same time (21.45 local).
Off the island of Ishigaki.

Hardly moving through the water, both Kilos waited silently, 10 miles apart, in the path of the carrier's approach from the southeast. The *JFK* was clearly identifiable by her noise signature, and at 2215 the westerly Kilo assessed that the Americans would pass within 3,000 yards.

The Chinese prepared to fire, while the easterly Kilo decided to wait, just in case an attack by her consort should cause *Big John* to swerve her way. It is almost impossible to coordinate a torpedo attack by two submarines. Only one would open fire, since charging in at high speed would simply give the game away.

The westerly Kilo's two torpedoes would come in from the carrier's stern arcs on predictions from the last-known bearing. The big TEST weapons would be launched quietly at 30 knots, staying passive all the way, which at least gave them a chance of avoiding a full, frontal smash into the hull. The Chinese wanted only the shafts, and there would be nothing *Big John* could do. There would be no time.

2150. "Stand by one . . ."

"Last bearing check."

"SHOOT!"

The Chinese torpedo came powering out of the tube, hesitated for a split second, then whined away into the dark waters.

"*Weapon under guidance . . .*" Kilo 636 was right on top of her game.

"*Arm the weapon.*"

"*Weapon armed, sir.*"

Ninety seconds go by. "*Weapon now one thousand yards from target, sir.*"

"*Weapon has passive contact.*"

"*Release to auto-home passive.*"

Moments later, Kilo 636 loosed off a second torpedo, which, like its colleague, was now streaking through the water toward the lights on the stern end of the carrier's flight deck. It was a classic submarine attack, conducted with ruthless professional-ism in a manner that would tolerate no comeback. There simply was no time.

Inside the ops room of the carrier, the sonar men picked up the torpedoes. At least they picked up one of them.

"Admiral—sonar. TORPEDO! TORPEDO! TORPEDO! . . . bearing Green one-nine-eight—Torpedo HE tight-aft . . . REAL CLOSE, SIR. REAL CLOSE . . ."

"Real close" now meant no more than 500 yards. Which put the lead torpedo 30 seconds from impact somewhere on the stern of the carrier. Firing back was out of the question. An 88,000-ton carrier is simply not built for close combat of this type.

Someone yelled: *"DECOYS!"* But that was about two minutes too late. The Combat Systems Officer alerted all ships that the flag was under attack. But before he could even utter the words "Chinese submarine," the first TEST 71/96 smashed into the port outer propeller, blowing it off and buckling two of the four shafts.

Moments later, the second torpedo, undetected, slammed into the port inner propeller and blew up with staggering force, caus-ing distortion to the starboard inner as well. *Big John*, even if she was still floating, was not going anywhere for a while.

The *JFK* was well compartmentalized, and she would not sink. But with her massive shafts damaged, she was no longer capable of operating aircraft. The great leviathan began to list slightly. Damage-control teams were right at work on the flood-ing. Engineers stared in horror at the extent of the harm done to the shafts.

The Admiral, still wondering where the next torpedo would come from, recalled the LA-Class submarines from deep water out to the southwest, bringing in one destroyer and a frigate for a close ASW hunt near the carrier.

The signal being sent to Pearl Harbor was as shocking to the communications room as the Japanese attack had been to the Naval staff 66 years previously:

"212155MAY07. Position 24.20N 124.02E. To CINCPACFLT

from U.S. carrier John F. Kennedy. *Hit by two torpedoes, passive homing unknown origin. Two explosions in shaft area. Three shafts out of action. One shaft remains serviceable. Max speed available 10 knots. Fixed-wing flying not feasible in less than 25-knot headwind. Initial assessment damage severity: requires early docking."*

Same time (0800 local).
Office of the CNO.
The Pentagon.

Admiral Alan Dixon was aghast. But the signal from CINC-PACFLT Headquarters left no room for doubt. The Republic of China had unquestionably fired two torpedoes at a U.S. carrier, 125 miles off the east coast of Taiwan. Worse yet, they'd both hit, and the carrier had been powerless to stop them, and, so far, take any form of retaliatory action. Further attacks had to be expected but had not yet materialized.

Admiral Dixon decided that if the Chinese could torpedo the ship, they could also bomb it, and he ordered the immediate evacuation of all aircraft currently stationed on the carrier. Whatever crew could be spared and moved to Okinawa should go, too. All other manpower surplus to the essential running of the crippled ship should be removed to the *JFK*'s accompanying destroyers and frigates.

And now he hit the secure line to Admiral Morgan and broke the news to the incredulous, but thoughtful, National Security Adviser. "The thing is, Arnie, I am going to get the carrier back to Pearl—might have to tow her. Sounds too big for Okinawa. Anyway, she's effectively out of action."

"Yes. That's a big ship to try to fix, so far from a major U.S. base," replied Admiral Morgan. "Anyhow, I guess you better get over here . . . bring all the information you have and we'll try to decide what the hell to do."

Same time (2300 local).
Southern Fleet HQ.
Zhanjiang.

"Well, Jicai, very satisfactory," purred Zhang Yushu. "That's all of them, I believe. The *Roosevelt*, the *Truman*, the *Constellation*, and the *John C. Stennis* all so very busy seven thousand miles away in the Strait of Hormuz. The *Ronald Reagan* stranded nearly nine thousand miles away in San Diego. The *John F. Kennedy* out of action. Which leaves us entirely free to conduct some local business of our own."

And at 2200 on the clear, moonlit evening of Tuesday, May 22, 2007, deploying the most massive display of military power since the UN's 1991 advance on Saddam Hussein, the People's Republic of China attacked Taiwan.

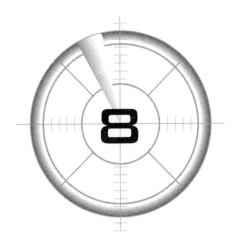

I T WAS TOO quick even for STRONG NET, the brand-new multibillion-dollar air defense early-warning network. Taiwan's Hawk surface-to-air missiles remained in their launchers as the Chinese onslaught came in. And there was not a bleep out of the new ultrasensitive Tien Kung medium-to-long-range system based on the old U.S. Patriot, and deployed around Taipei.

Everything about the attack from the mainland was utterly unexpected. Even the target was essentially way out in right field. But in the small hours of May 22, China was undeniably bombarding, presumably with a view to capture, the picturesque archipelago of the Penghu Islands, which sit 60 miles off Taiwan's eastern shores.

Of course, the Penghus are not entirely picturesque. Taiwan maintains a 17,000-strong offshore island command army on Penghu. There is an airport, and outside the city of Makung a big Navy base, home of the 154th Fast Attack Squadron.

Now, at these midocean marks, China was literally hurling

short-range ballistic missiles (SRBMs), launched into the night from the opposite shore from bases in Fujian and Jiangxi Provinces. And high above the Taiwan Strait an armada of China's newly built B-6/BADGER long-range bomber aircraft, laden with land-attack cruise missiles (LACMs), was preparing to strike the Penghu Naval Base.

It was six minutes before Taiwan could respond, by which time the Makung shipyard was ablaze, with two 3,000-ton Knox-Class guided-missile frigates, the *Chin Yang* and the *Ning Yang*, burning ferociously alongside the jetties.

Taiwan launched her opening batteries of Tien Kung missiles from the west coast of the main island, straight at the incoming BADGERs and downed nine of them in 15 minutes. But they could not prevent the first wave of SRBMs from screaming into the outskirts of Makung, almost demolishing the entire Hsintien Road to the north of the base, in the process reducing both the Martyrs' Shrine and the Confucian temple to rubble.

The precision bombardment hit the airfield, blitzed the telephone company at the north end of the main Chungching Road and the main downtown post office.

Within 10 more minutes Taiwan had a squadron of U.S.-built F-16 fighters in the air howling out of the night in pursuit of the BADGERs, which were no match for them, and the U.S.-supplied deadly accurate Sidewinder missile blew eight more of them out of the sky.

Below the opening air battle, a big flotilla of Chinese warships was moving in on the Penghus, led by the second of their Russian-built Sovremenny destroyers, in company with four Jangwei-Class guided-missile frigates and six of the smaller heavily gunned Jianghu Class, which had been conducting regular fleet exercises in the strait for the past five days.

Shortly after midnight they opened fire with a long-range shelling assault on the tiny islands of Paisha and Hsi, obliterating the three-mile-long bridge that joins them. They slammed two missiles into Hsi's spectacular Qing Dynasty Hsitai Fort from which, on a clear day, you can see the mountains of both Taiwan *and* China. Then they turned southwest and battered the islands of Wang'an, Huching and Tongpan.

The Taiwan High Command in Taipei was forced to the opinion that China was in the process of capturing all 64 of the Penghu Islands, with their historic 147 temples, mostly dedicated to Matsu, the goddess of the sea, who would always protect the islanders but who was not having that much effect right now.

The Penghus have been for centuries permanent home mostly to fishermen and farmers. Walls of coral, built to protect large crops of peanuts, sweet potatoes and sorghum, form a unique landscape. The endless beaches and blue waters have made the Penghus one of the great tourist attractions in the East.

However, at this precise moment the beautiful Lintou Beach, on the seaward side of Makung, resembled Dunkirk, 1940, more than anywhere else. Batteries of China's CSS-X7 missiles—a new version of the Russian-designed M-11 with a 500-kilogram warhead—were detonating everywhere. Oceanfront bars and restaurants were flattened, huge spouts of salt water and sand blasted over the city.

In Taipei, the President, in conference with the Premier and his military Chiefs of Staff, ordered an immediate defense of the islands, "before the Chinese attempt a landing."

Lieutenant General Chi-Chiang Gan, Commander-in-Chief of the Army, ordered 25,000 troops from all military bases on the northeast coast to head south by road and rail. At 0200, the government commandeered every fast train on the electrified west coast line, particularly the Ziqiang and Zuguang expresses. The General ordered an airlift of 20,000 troops from the Taipei area to the big southern Navy base at Kaohsiung.

Admiral Feng-Shiang Hu, Commander-in-Chief of the Navy, ordered the 66th Marine Division based in Kaohsiung to embark and sail immediately to reinforce the island garrison at Makung. He put three Newport-Class troop landing ships and a 9,000-ton Cabildo-Class LSD on four hours battle notice. The *Cheng Hai* docks down three small Japanese-built LSUs, each capable of carrying 300 men right into the beaches.

In the small hours of the morning, the Taiwan High Command desperately signaled the U.S. Seventh Fleet HQ requesting immediate military assistance, informing the United States that Taiwan was under attack from the forces of mainland China. Admiral Feng-Shiang personally told Admiral Dick Greening, Commander-in-Chief Pacific Fleet (CINCPACFLT) in Pearl Harbor, that he feared for his country's existence, that right now an air battle was raging over the Taiwan Strait, and that his pilots were winning it. But on the sea, China had a major flotilla of warships both bombarding and preparing to land on the strategically important Penghu Islands, which everyone knew China had *always* wanted to own.

"We badly need a carrier battle group, anything to get them away." Admiral Feng-Shiang was almost pleading. But there was nothing CINCPACFLT could do. Nothing anyone could do. The United States did not have a CVBG available except in the Middle East, which was nearly two weeks away from the Taiwan Strait. And anyway, it could scarcely be spared.

Powerless in Pearl Harbor, the Admiral knew now why *Big John* had been hit in such a brutal and unexplained manner. "Holy shit," breathed Admiral Greening. "The bastards are gonna take Taiwan. And as far as I can see there's not a damn thing we can do about it—we don't even have the hardware to attack China."

He promised to get right back to the distraught Taiwanese Admiral, but right now he had to call Washington and inform Alan Dixon about precisely what was happening.

They patched him through to the White House, where the CNO was with Arnold Morgan. Kathy put the secure call on the conference line, and both Washington-based Admirals listened aghast as Admiral Greening informed them that China had militarily invaded Taiwan. At the conclusion of the call, Admiral Dixon requested 30 minutes to thoroughly appreciate the situation.

But Arnold Morgan stood up, and there was a strange smile on his face. He shook his head, over and over, and kept saying, "Those little bastards . . . those cunning little pricks."

Finally he turned back to the CNO, and he said, "Alan, old buddy, did you ever hear the term 'checkmate'?"

"Guess so."

"Good. Because we're in it."

Every piece of information he had absorbed in the past several months, every twist and turn of the plot in the Gulf of Hormuz, sprang now, miraculously, into place. Right back to that moment when Lt. Ramshawe had called him in the restaurant. Arnold Morgan could remember the young Lieutenant's words verbatim: "*It is my opinion that there may be a serious minefield out there, maybe running from the Omani coast, place called Ra's Qabr al Hindi, right across to Iran. And I think we ought to find out.*"

The Admiral was talking aloud now. "Jimmy was right. And he ought to be promoted for brilliance. Borden is going to be relieved of command at Fort Meade. George Morris is gonna get better in the next twenty minutes or he's fired too, so are all his fucking doctors. And I'm about to admit I've been outwitted by the goddamned Chinese pricks. They never wanted to screw up the oil, never gave a flying fuck about the oil, they just wanted to tie us up, at least tie up the carriers, thousands of miles from the South China Sea.

"I guess we threw 'em a curve when we diverted the *JFK* back to Taiwan. So by some damn clever means they crippled her. *And then there were none.* . . . Hours later they attack Taiwan, *knowing* beyond any doubt there is nothing on earth we can do about it, save for starting World War Three with nuclear missiles. And even Taiwan ain't worth that."

"Holy shit," breathed Alan Dixon. "You mean there's nothing we could do to save her?"

"There's plenty we could do. But not in time. Taiwan will fall inside two weeks. That's how long it would take the *Truman* Group or the *Roosevelt* Group to get there. The fight would be all over before they could get out of the Indian Ocean."

"But so far they've only taken a few shots at the Penghu Islands."

"Alan, that news is gonna be so out of date by tomorrow morning it'll make the Washington Monument look like Stonehenge."

Admiral Morgan checked his watch. It was already 1700 hours—0600 hours the following morning over the Penghu Islands, where, suddenly, the rumble of battle grew steadily more faint, and the surviving Chinese bombers swung back toward the mainland. The flotilla of warships ceased their bombardment but closed rapidly, effecting a complete blockade of the islands. Anyone wanting to get in would have to fight the Chinese Navy.

With half the armed forces of Taiwan already well on their way south, Admiral Zhang, who had assumed command of the entire operation, moved to Phase Two. And as the sun rose bloodred out of the Pacific Ocean, he unleashed the massive missile bombardment of the west coast of Taiwan he had been planning for six months.

It started in the north with Chiang Kai-shek International Airport, the powerful SRBMs blasting craters in the runways, but surprisingly taking out only the air-traffic control tower. The regular passenger terminals were not targeted.

Zhang's ballistic missiles slammed into the road system, blasting huge chunks out of the coastal highway. They hit the town of Chungli, where the main south-running freeway crosses Route 1. They obliterated that junction and took out 400 yards of the railroad track.

They blew apart a freeway road bridge west of Hainchu. They hit the Mingte Dam, west of Miaoli, and three times more they knocked serious hunks out of the south-running roads, freeways and railroads before they reached the majestic bridges that span the estuary of the Choshui River.

And there, with a withering salvo of missiles, the Chinese took out all four of them, blasting steel and masonry into the water, stopping Route 17 in its tracks, ending the long winding path of Route 19, splitting asunder the great north-south freeway, and closing down the south-running railroad.

The entire transportation system that crosses the pancake-flat, rice-growing plains of west-central Taiwan was in ruins. And that was before the Chinese missiles reached the southwestern city of Tainan, Taiwan's provincial capital for more than 200 years until 1885.

Zhang's missiles completely destroyed every runway on the airport. They hammered Routes 17 and 19 north of the river and blasted yet again the main highway south. There were three massive separate hits on the most important road-freight artery in the country as it swept west of the city toward the port of Kaohsiung, 30 miles farther south.

At that point it was just about impossible to move troops or anything else back to the north. Admiral Zhang's brilliant feint to the Penghu Islands had drawn half the Taiwanese army 235 miles away from his main objective, Taipei.

And the Chinese warlord had not even begun. Again he launched his remaining 120 B-6/BADGER aircraft, and they headed out over the coast in three great waves of 40, again loaded with the new land-attack cruise missiles. This time their targets were strictly military, Taiwan's air-defense installations, Air Force runways and Naval bases, places the PLAN had been watching and checking for years.

The BADGERs were accompanied by Air Force fighters, the Q-5B Fantan and more bombers, the newer JH-7s and the SU-30MKKs. Air-superiority aircraft, J-10 and J-11 Flankers, flew sortie after sortie, trying to protect the bomber force and downing several Taiwanese fighter aircraft in a sustained attempt to gain air superiority over the strait.

The opening attacks hit the brand-new, but untried, Modified Air Defense System (MADS), with its super-PATRIOT antiballistic missiles, which had been installed all around the capital. They slammed the airfields of the new Indigenous Defense Fighter aircraft in Taoyuan County and farther south in Yunlin. All along the flat west coastal plain they took out the Tien Kung air-defense systems. They hit the high slopes of the central mountains where the Taiwanese military had major west-facing air-command and -control centers, built especially to deal with a massive incoming attack from the mainland, as this most certainly was.

For years Chinese agents had reported to Beijing every detail of the key Taiwanese logistic centers and the military Intelligence headquarters (C-41). And now the land-attack missiles, launched from the air, were aimed at every one of them, backed up by the huge short-range ballistic missiles that were still thundering into the sky every few minutes from their launchers 100 miles across the strait in Fujian and Jangxi Provinces.

Brave little Taiwan shuddered under the withering onslaught of the Dragon from across the water. But they conceded nothing. Hour after hour, their pilots had fought those F-16s into the sky, attacking the incoming missile bombers. And by midday it was apparent that China had made an error of judgment in not locating Taiwan's mobile short-range air-defense systems, CHAPARRAL, STINGER/AVENGER and ANTELOPE.

CHAPARRAL consists of four modified AIM-9C Sidewinders mounted on tracked vehicles; the STINGER/AVENGER SAMS is a pedestal-mounted system with two pods, each one containing four STINGER missiles, mounted on the back of a High Mobility Multi-Purpose Wheeled Vehicle (HMMWV). ANTELOPE, developed and perfected at Taiwan's Chung Sang Institute of Science and Technology, fires from an HMMWV four Tien Chien-1 missiles with a 14-mile range. A deadly low-flying intercepter, it has an outstanding target acquisition system.

The Taiwanese moved these three systems along their west coastline to lethal effect, launching their missiles doggedly and accurately, from anywhere they found cover. They fired from the rice fields, from behind barns, woods and coral walls. They fired from any of the foothills of the coastal mountains they could reach. And by midafternoon they had devastated the Chinese fleet of BADGER bombers. Of the 120 that came in from the mainland, fewer than 70 made it back.

But they had only stopped the aircraft, not the missiles, and by nightfall Taiwan's entire transportation system in the west was wrecked. The communications systems, both civilian and military, were nonoperational. And their permanent air-defense systems were essentially destroyed. There was nothing left of the much-vaunted SKYGUARD installations. The AIM-7M/SPARROW antiaircraft missiles had scarcely left the ground.

In the entire history of aerial combat, the monstrous struggle for supremacy above the Taiwan Strait was right up there with the battle of Britain, except that both Admiral Zhang and Taiwan's Air Force C-in-C, General Ke-Chiang Wong, had it all over H. Goering and Adolf.

By nightfall on May 23, China had achieved the destruction of many of its objectives, but somehow Taiwan had fought them off. In addition to the battering of the BADGER fleet, China had lost 10 Fantans, plus 12 more bombers and nine Flankers.

The Taiwanese had lost a total of 43 combat aircraft, which meant, in a sense, they were somehow winning the air battle. But China had 2,200 fully operational fighter and bomber aircraft, while Taiwan had a total of only 400 combat aircraft. As in every war in its long history, China was perfectly prepared to suffer massive attrition in pursuit of her goals, safe in the knowledge that ultimately she had more of everything, especially people, and these days, aircraft and ships.

The fact was, at this rate of killing, China could go on losing this air battle twice as long as Taiwan could go on winning it. The absence of the always-expected heavy U.S. air support was a death blow to the island, which suddenly found itself fighting for its life.

And the situation at sea was, if anything, worse. The Chinese Navy comprised 275,000 personnel, with more than 50 destroyers and frigates, 60 diesel-electric and six nuclear submarines, nearly 50 landing ships, plus several hundred auxiliaries and smaller patrol vessels.

Taiwan had an excellent Navy of 22 destroyers, 22 frigates, 50 fast-attack craft, but only 10 submarines. Their 40 landing ships were plainly not required in a conflict with China.

Unsurprisingly first blood on the water went to China. In the middle of the afternoon a PLA Naval Aviation long-range maritime patrol aircraft, a Y-8X Cub, flying down the center of the strait, picked up the small flotilla carrying the first wave of Taiwanese Marines going in to reinforce the Penghus.

The Cub signaled back to Southern Fleet HQ, and two hours later, two Chinese Kilos moved in and made a fierce underwater attack upon Taiwan's warships. They slammed a torpedo into each of the Newport-Class LSTs and hit the *Cheng Hui* with two more, leaving the big LSD on fire and listing with more than 400 casualties on board.

And with every hour, more and more Chinese warships arrived on station around the Taiwan coast, securing their sea-lanes, plainly preparing to protect the Chinese landing force, which everyone now knew was inevitable.

0730 (local). Wednesday, May 23.
The White House. Washington, D.C.

The atmosphere in the Oval Office was subdued. Indeed an air of melancholy hung over the entire capital, as America's friends, colleagues and partners on the other side of the world fought for survival.

The President was worried, mainly that he might somehow be blamed, and he was beginning to see himself as some kind of Nero figure, fiddling around in Washington while Taiwan burned.

"There must be something we can do," he kept saying. And Bob MacPherson, the Defense Secretary, kept telling him that as far as he could see there was nothing. The Secretary of State, Harcourt Travis, thought the less said to anyone, the better, although he knew the USA was bound to defend Taiwan under the Taiwan Relations Act, Public Law 96-8.

Arnold Morgan paced the room, wracking his brains for a solution, concentrated now on trying to spell out the situation for the President. And he knew it would be difficult, because this President these days saw the world only in terms of himself, and his reputation at the end of his second term.

Finally, he was prepared, and he said, "Sir, as I have already explained, the Chinese have pulled off a stupendous act of deception, forcing us to put eighty percent of our available sea power into a false, but dangerous, situation in the Strait of Hormuz. In the process they have sunk three VLCCs and caused the death of several seamen, most of them American, inside the Gulf of Iran. They have further hit and sunk a Japanese tanker north of the Malacca Strait and plainly torpedoed a U.S. aircraft carrier in the Pacific. They are now moving ahead and conquering Taiwan, the *only* objective they have ever been interested in."

He paused to allow this catalog of Chinese transgressions to be fully appreciated. And then he continued, "In return, we have smashed their oil production in the gulf area. And I have warned their ambassador that we see no purpose in Chinese warships entering the area of the northern Arabian Sea in the future. Should they ignore this warning, they understand we will not hesitate to hit and sink any and all Chinese ships anywhere near the oil sea-lanes of the Middle East. They have done quite sufficient damage to the world oil market already, and the international community simply will not put up with their presence in the area any longer. The Chinese understand that. I think."

"Arnold, I kinda know all that," said the President. "I want you to deal with Taiwan."

"Very well, sir. But you'll forgive my reminding you that all these matters are very closely connected."

"I'll forgive you. Taiwan."

"Okay," said Admiral Morgan, declining to mention what he actually thought about the conversation—*Some cheek, this fucking ignoramus trying to keep ME on track.*

But he rose above it, more or less effortlessly, and continued on: "Sir, this attack on Taiwan has been very carefully planned. And we thus find ourselves watching a rather ungainly giant swatting and whacking his way to victory. But he is well prepared, he's in his own waters, he doesn't give a damn about the attrition of ships, aircraft or people and he wants the prize of Taiwan more than any Chinaman has ever wanted anything.

"We cannot intervene, mainly because we don't have anything to intervene with. And even if we did, I'd be inclined to advise against. Because we would find ourselves in a very serious sea battle, and the upshot might be that we could lose three or four major ships, and a couple of thousand American crewmen. They on the other hand might lose twenty ships and ten thousand crewmen. The difference being that they wouldn't care a fuck, and would just go on fighting. We, on the other hand, could not put up with that.

"We'd have riot conditions at home, you'd be swept from office along with the rest of us and we'd all be accused of deliberately starting a new Vietnam on account of some goddamned no-account Chinese island, which is about a mile and a half from Shanghai anyway. That's how the public and the press would react.

"It's all very well our patrolling the waters, as we've been doing for years, and frightening everyone to death whenever we had to. But it's quite another to be prepared to go to war, to send our young men to fight and die, thousands of miles from home. Sir, if we took this country into armed conflict with China over a bunch of fucking pottery makers in this goddamned island right off their coast, you could wind up with another civil war in this country, and I'm not joking."

"But we always were able to drive the Chinese off before. . . ."

"Yeah, but they were only goofing around then. This is entirely different. This is a nation on a war footing, perfectly happy to fight and die for their belief that Taiwan is a part of China, an offshore province that needs to be brought back into the motherland. On the other hand, we are really prepared only to posture over Taiwan. No president of the USA is going into a real shooting war with China over their goddamned island.

"We'd fight 'em over Middle Eastern oil, if we had to, because that's in our national interest and the public would understand that. But they would not understand American sailors being blown to pieces over the territorial claim of one Chinaman over another."

"I guess you can understand the Chinese wanting this offshore island back," said the President. "Same as they wanted Hong Kong, which was even farther inside their own backyard. I just never understand this obsession. Never understand what they really want."

"What they *really* want, sir," replied Admiral Morgan, "is the National Palace Museum of Taipei."

"The museum?"

"Correct. Because it contains the most priceless collection of Chinese art and history. It is without question the greatest museum in the world, the greatest museum there has ever been."

"Is that right?"

"That, sir, is right."

"Well I thought the Chinese regime hated culture. Didn't Chairman Mao and his wife try to destroy every vestige of their country's culture, burning books, destroying university libraries and all that?"

"They sure did. And that was a big part of it. The entire heart of China, every ancient book, manuscript, tapestry, sculpture, painting, porcelain, silver, jade, gold, whatever, dating right back to the ancient Shang Kingdom, thousands of years ago, was contained in one collection. About ten thousand cases of it. Held for five hundred years in the Forbidden City in Beijing."

"Well, how did it get to Taiwan?"

"Basically Chiang Kai-shek took it."

"Christ! All of it?"

"Nearly. It was just about the last major act he undertook before he and the Kuomintang were exiled to Formosa. He just felt that Mr. and Mrs. Mao might destroy the entire thing, so he packed it all up and somehow shipped fourteen trainloads of Chinese tradition across the water to his new home."

"Did anyone care? I mean back on the mainland?"

"Not for a while. But then Formosa had its name changed to Taiwan, and its capital, Taipei, became a world financial power. So Chiang Kai-shek decided to build this fabulous museum in a park to the north of the city . . . kinda showcase to display this colossal record of the cultural history of China."

"Don't tell me, Arnie. Right then the Chinks wanted it all back?"

"That's right. The museum opened sometime in the mid-sixties, and the Chinese Communists almost immediately started to lay claim to the entire collection, ranting on about the cultural tapestry of China being displayed in this offshore island that somehow claimed to have nothing to do with the mainland."

"And what did Chiang Kai-shek say to the that?"

"Plenty, sir. He said plenty. He told them that in his view they were nothing more than a murderous communist rabble who would probably have burned the history of China and never given it another thought. He told them he, Chiang, was the rightful ruler of China, that Taiwan was the rightful cradle of the Chinese nation, and that one day he and his armies would return and reclaim the mainland, and he'd see 'em all in hell before he'd submit to their barbarism."

"And the collection of Chinese history?"

"That was even easier to deal with. Old Chiang Kai-shek told 'em to go fuck themselves."

"And the stuff's been there in the museum ever since?"

"Right. They even called it the National Palace Museum, after the original in the Forbidden City."

"And did the stuff survive all this turmoil?"

"By some miracle, not one piece was ever broken. Which, in the opinion of the Taiwanese people, proves that the collection is precisely where it's supposed to be. And they do have the unanswerable argument that Mao and his wife would most certainly have destroyed it."

"And what does the modern Chinese regime have to say about that?"

"Nothing. Except to stamp their feet and shout, *WANT TREASURES BACK! WANT TREASURES BACK!*"

Everyone in the room chuckled. They would have laughed out loud if the situation had not been *quite* so serious.

"Jeez. There must be literally thousands of pieces," said Bob MacPherson.

"I think there're more than seven hundred thousand," said Admiral Morgan. "I went to see it once a few years back. But they can only display fifteen thousand pieces at a time. They rotate every three months. So if you lived in Taiwan and went there four times in a year, you'd still only see sixty thousand pieces, which is less than ten percent of the collection. It'd take twelve years to see everything."

"But where do they keep all the stuff that's not on display?"

"No one really knows," Arnold continued. "But it's supposed to be hidden in some vast network of vaults in the mountains behind the museum. They say it's all connected by tunnels."

"You'd think with all that stuff they could do some kind of a deal, wouldn't you? Display half of it in Beijing or something." The President slipped automatically into the politician's instinct for compromise.

"The Chinese mind-set does not work like that," said Arnold. "Mainland China wants this irritating little rebel island to hand over the culture of China, which, they say, Chiang Kai-shek stole from the people."

"And the Taiwanese are still telling 'em to go fuck themselves?"

"Exactly," said Admiral Morgan. "And before we're a lot older, I'd say there's going to be a ferocious battle over that museum. And you can bet the Taiwanese have put in some very thorough security systems. Even if Taiwan falls, as it plainly must, there's no guarantee that collection will not be wiped out. The Taiwanese may even use it as a bargaining card."

"You mean, 'If we can't have it, nobody's having it'?"

"Possibly. But more likely, 'We have the power to destroy it, at the touch of button . . . if you go and guarantee to leave us alone forever, you can take it with you. Failing that, no one shall have it.'"

"Meanwhile, gentlemen, what are we going to do about the situation militarily? I ask this in the full knowledge that my National Security Adviser has already spelled out the plain and obvious truths of the matter. There's no possibility that the United States of America is going to all-out war with China over Taiwan. The most we would ever have done would have been to place a lot of very heavy muscle in the area and dare anyone to take us on.

"Today, however, that is not an option. China is, as Arnie has said, already on a war footing, prepared to fight and die for her cause, which she is already doing. We're not going near the place."

"And how do we answer Taiwan's cry for help?" asked Harcourt Travis.

"We offer to negotiate for them," said the President. "We threaten to make China into a pariah in world trade. We threaten to withdraw all trade with anyone who trades with China. We rescind their most-favored-nation status. We ban their exports. Call in their debts. All that and more. But we're not trading missiles, shells and bullets with 'em."

"Nor torpedoes," said Arnold Morgan.

"You mean, really, we just sit back and let the battle play out?" asked Bob MacPherson.

"'Fraid so," said Arnold Morgan. "But I am working on a plan to make them pay a very high price for what they have done. And I think we can confine their future activites to the China seas."

"Sounds like a particularly ambitious plan," said Harcourt Travis, "since we're dealing with a nation that has just stood the world on its head, and apparently has no qualms about wrecking economies and then going to war."

"It is an ambitious plan," said Admiral Morgan. "And it's a plan that I like a lot for two reasons. First of all, because it involves a large amount of dynamite, and second of all because it will create a multitude of hugely pissed off Chinamen."

"I like it, too," said the President. "Don't know what it is, but I like it."

The meeting continued for the rest of the morning, and still made no headway with regard to military discouragement of China. It was agreed the State Department would send the most strongly worded communiqué to the Beijing government "deploring in the extreme the vicious military action undertaken this week by China against their peace-loving neighbors, an independent state now recognized by the United Nations."

Harcourt Travis pointed out that no civilized single country had undertaken any such unprovoked action in the past quarter of a century, save for Serbia, and earlier Argentina against the Falkland Islands. In Harcourt's opinion the Chinese would do well to take note of the fate that befell the leaders of these countries, and would be advised to *cease and desist* in this totally unwarranted bullying of a small island neighbor.

He did not anticipate a reply, nor did he get one.

Travis had been reluctant to put American threats of any kind into writing, and that afternoon Admiral Morgan had the Chinese ambassador brought in to answer some hard, searching questions. But the ambassador merely stalled and said that China was simply answering a request from the Taiwan government "to stabilize the situation in their country, with a view to normalizing relations with the mainland, which would be in everyone's interest."

Arnold Morgan, who by now had pictures of the burning Naval base in the Penghu Islands, produced them and asked if that was China's way of "stabilizing the situation."

Somewhat uncharacteristically, Ling Guofeng produced two pictures from his own briefcase and offered them to Arnold, who stared in amazement at the 500-foot-high inferno that was still blazing from the oil refinery in the Strait of Hormuz.

"And might I assume this is your way also?" asked the ambassador.

"You may assume anything that makes you happy," growled Admiral Morgan. "And I'll accept, if you like, that persons unknown blew up a few barrels of your oil. But that's a whole hell of lot different from going to war with another, much smaller country, killing the civilian population, hitting them with bombs, cruise missiles and your entire Navy. That's not even comparable. And I want you to express to your government our horror at your actions and to warn them in the strongest possible terms that there will be consequences, which none of you will much enjoy. That's all."

Ambassador Ling considered himself lucky not to have been expelled from the United States forthwith, and he wished the National Security Adviser good-bye and hurried from the West Wing of the White House.

All week long such meetings would take place as the USA argued, cajoled and threatened the Republic of China in any way it could. It recruited support from every one of its allies, from Britain, France, Germany, Russia, Canada, Australia and Japan. Canceled China's most-favored-nation status, banned imports from China, and had its allies do the same.

Meanwhile, on the seas beneath the endless air battles, the Chinese Navy continued to deploy its warships, running them down from the Northern Fleet to form a silent blockade of the great port of Keelung, home of Taiwan's Third Naval District and the northern patrol squadron. The Taiwan Air Force, its airfields and runways severely damaged, half its pilots now dead or missing, spent the nights licking its wounds, repairing airstrips and fueling fighter aircraft ready to face the Dragon again tomorrow.

And all the while, the Chinese warships moved into control positions, dominating the strait, establishing safe lines of communication and supply. Overhead, to the north of the island, Special Forces were packed into aircraft dropping behind Taiwan's beaches to the west of Keelung, the remote area chosen by Admiral Zhang and his senior commanders for the opening beachhead of the conflict.

This Chinese strategic planning had taken many months to finalize, but ultimately the tactics had evolved almost of their own accord. The vast majority of the Taiwanese people live on the coastal plains on the western side of the island, principally in the north around Taipei, and in the major population centers in the south around Tainan and Kaohsiung.

Inland, the country is mountainous and forbidding, and the east coast is guarded by towering cliffs rising up from the sea. Any attempt to attack from the east would have been absurd, and the prospect of serious operations in the mountains would have been daunting to any invader. And China's objectives were clear: to bring about the total surrender of the island without having to fight for every inch of territory or for the outlying islands.

Plainly the objective had to be secured in the shortest possible time, at any cost, to avoid unnecessary collateral damage. The

Chinese military had no wish to destroy what they wanted before they even laid hands on it. There was also a determination to avoid excessive casualties on both sides, and an unspoken need to avoid damaging China's world political standing any more than was absolutely necessary.

Nonetheless, they had to get troops in there, and all through the week they landed Special Forces under the cover of darkness by parachute and from the sea. They were delivered by submarine, small merchant vessels, and fishing boats, dropped into the shallows along Taiwan's 1,000 miles of coastline on suitably lonely beaches—made even more lonely by the near-total destruction of the island's military communications systems.

Shortly before midnight on Saturday, May 26, the land attack began. An armada of massive transport aircraft protected by squadrons of jet fighters began roaring over the Taiwain Strait, slightly north of the island itself.

An entire divison of China's 15th Airborne Army rumbled eastward, packed into recently acquired Russian-built IL-76MD/CANDIDs, specially configured for airborne operations. Flying right astern of them, low over the ocean, was a fleet of Y-8X/CUB transporters, likewise packed with troops, the entire fleet under the control of their Airborne Command, a gray-painted A-501 Mainstay.

Taiwan's air defenses were all but useless now, and the massed ground forces of the Army, which had been swept to the south in the false panic over the Penghu Islands, was now unable to get back because of the wrecked roads, bridges and railroads. Which effectively allowed China's first landing force to hit the beaches from out of the night, unchallenged. One by one, the huge low-flying aircraft climbed to an altitude of 1,000 fect and disgorged their live loads into two separate dropping zones seven miles apart, two miles behind the glorious white sands of Chinsan Beach.

This spectacular tourist area is situated 13 miles west of Keelung on the north coast of Taipei County. And tonight hundreds and hundreds of paratroopers came thumping into the soft sand behind the wide shoreline, several miles from the nearest urban districts.

By 0230 there were 3,000 to 4,000 on each landing beach, and the Chinese commanders were rallying the Division quickly and efficiently, ordering the airborne troops to move off as soon as they were formed, heading inland away from the sea, forward of the landing area, for almost a mile.

And here the Chinese began to dig in, establishing, well forward of the beachhead, two crescent-shaped screens, which would become the first line of defense Taiwanese troops would encounter should they attempt to attack the forthcoming amphibious force from the mainland.

Taiwan's problem right now was communication. The military systems were in such bad shape it was nearly impossible to transmit a message, never mind a detailed conversation or report. Certainly there were small units stationed near Taipei that were aware of air activity out on the northern region. And they may even have assumed there were troop drops being made. But they had no forces in contact, no Intelligence, no way of knowing what the invasion force was doing, certainly no way of assessing whether a beach landing was in any way imminent.

Meanwhile the Chinese were thundering forward with their two steel defense perimeters, one astride the road from Taipei, just north of Yangmingshan, the other astride the main approaches to the beach landing areas from Keelung—clean across the road from Feitsuiwan.

They strived in pouring rain all through that Sunday, digging trenches, preparing ammunition, setting up machine guns. The ground mission of China's 15th Airborne Division was to stop a Taiwanese counterattack at any and all cost. And they had to be ready to protect the landing craft of the big Chinese Marine Division when it hit the beaches, complete with its own armor, artillery and air defenses, early on Monday morning, May 28.

And ready they were. While the main forces had been digging in, a small Chinese marine force, similarly trained to the U.S. Navy SEALs or Britain's Special Boat Squadron, had checked out and cleared the landing area, marking the lanes, staking out their own positions to supply local machine-gun cover while they guided the landing craft in.

By 0300, three hours before the sun would clear the distant horizon, the sea was suddenly alive with the unmistakable signs of invasion, tiny black landing craft, packed with armed troops streaming in toward the shallows. And as the sky brightened and long, pink fingers began to form among the predawn rain clouds, the sound of the ramps echoed along the shoreline. Big, clanging ramps, manhandled by shouting troops. And down those ramps came the big tracked vehicles, engines howling, as they drove down the steep gradients and splashed into the surf, driving forward, looking for their lane lines on the beach.

Out beyond the waves in the calmer waters a half mile offshore there was a kind of controlled chaos, as ships maneuvered into position, the hydraulic docks opening up to allow more and more of the landing craft to break cover from the LCDs. This was D-Day Normandy on only a slightly smaller scale, and if any Taiwanese units were watching, they were watching the opening round of an unwinnable fight.

Six hours later, everyone who was going ashore had gone ashore. And the ships were turned back across the strait to reload with thousands and thousands more troops, and this time they would be joined by dozens of civilian ships, all making their way to the northern beachhead out on the Chinsan sands.

Rarely had a capital city the size of Taipei experienced such mass confusion. Its three million inhabitants—and three million more in the surrounding district—knew, of course, their island was under attack from the Republic of China. But the Chinese had thus far gone to extraordinary lengths to avoid harming even one building in the great northern metropolis. They had attacked, exclusively, military installations and military communications, with the exception of the international airport, which they completely disabled but left the passenger terminals untouched.

Thus for the people of Taiwan there was television news bringing hourly reports of the continuing air battles over the central waters of the strait. There were reports of the destruction of the Navy base in the Penghu Islands. And there were further reports of the Taiwanese Navy preparing to defend the shores against a mass invasion from the sea. But nothing was being reported from the beachhead, and there were no signs of bombs, rockets, shells or missiles. The city seemed normal, save for the tension and fear. But there were no sounds of war. It was as if China had decided to shut down the military effectiveness of Taiwan, but possibly nothing further.

Thus Taipei itself continued to function. Shops opened as usual, schools and universities remained active, traffic was its usual hideous mess, but buses ran and people went to work. Hotels stayed open and thousands of tourists trapped in the city booked in for extra weeks. It was impossible to leave Taipei, but equally impossible to travel to Taipei. The major long-distance freeways were virtually deserted, the railroad station was dead, the airport was dead, the runways wrecked. And a curious, uneasy calm enveloped the capital, even though, on the surface, there was the appearance of normality.

The United States had informed the government it would begin an evacuation of its citizens caught in the entanglement of the Chinese invasion, but it quickly became apparent that there was nowhere in the north of the island where a U.S. passenger aircraft could land. And, of course, there were no proper foreign embassies in Taipei, because of the problems of upsetting mainland China. There were just the "pseudo-embassies" where diplomats operated under the cover of the American Institute on the Hsinhyi Road, the British Trade and Cultural Office on the Jenai Road, the France-Asia Trade Association on the Tunhua Road, none of which had any serious clout with anyone.

And so, as the first waves of Chinese troops splashed ashore 17 miles to the northeast, Taipei continued to function, both citizens and visitors alike, with no option but to await the inevitable arrival of the conquering hordes from the mainland. There was no escape, and life moved precariously forward for all of them.

Five days later, on Saturday morning, June 2, the National

Palace Museum was busier than usual. It was somewhere interesting to go for the new prisoners of the city, and the tourists
buses were full, wending their way across the Keelung River, up
through the northern suburbs to the Waishunghsi neighborhood
at the foot of the Yangming Mountains.

The museum is probably the most imposing building on Taiwan. It is set in elaborate parkland, with tree-lined gardens. The
sweeping, extravagant approach leads to a massive flight of wide
stone steps, like those at the Capitol building in Washington.

At the top of this giant stairway stands an unmistakable Chinese palace, built in traditional style with white walls and green
tiled roofs. Curiously there is never much sign of security in the
outer grounds, save for the occasional uniformed guard, and
today there was absolutely nothing. The military garrison two
miles down the road was almost deserted since three-quarters of
its entire force had been swept south along with most of the
northern Taiwanese Army.

By 1.30 P.M. there was a line of six buses creeping up to the dis-
embarking area. Five of them carried a normal passenger load of
men, women and children, husbands, wives, schoolteachers and
tour guides. The sixth bus, a regular number 213, fourth in the
line, was transporting only men, 50 of them, each dressed in light
civilian clothes. Forty-two of the seats were occupied by bored-
looking men reading newspapers. But the eight passengers in the
rear of the bus were sitting on ammunition cases in front of the
back bench seat, upon which rested the big machine guns and
boxes of hand grenades that might very well be required in the
next 20 minutes, depending on the level of resistance.

The bus driver, a lean, hard-eyed Chinese agent, had spent all
morning rounding up his passengers, collecting them from a
series of safe houses in the Sungshan District, where they had
been lying low since the first parachute drops of the Special
Forces five days previously.

These were the elite of the Chinese Army, supremely trained
Oriental SAS men, and now they were poised to strike, each man
armed only with a concealed machine pistol or a folding subma-

chine gun, as bus number 213 crept slowly up to the base of the wide stairway to the palace.

It stopped, leaving its engine running, and the doors slid swiftly open. Forty-two men stepped slowly out into the rain, gathering in groups of six, separating on various levels of the steps. Slowly, without urgency, they made their way to the top and walked through the huge doors into a somewhat grim, drab and unspectacular interior main hall, in almost shocking contrast to the grandeur of the exterior. On either side of the hall was a towering wing, filled with spectacular treasures, and the groups of Special Forces, unsuspected, unrecognized, moved up to the ticket office and paid their entrance fee of $80 new Taiwan dollars, which is around U.S. $2.50.

In their original groups of six, they dispersed among the crowds into various great rooms, to the left and to the right, and to the upper floor. No one made a move, until the final group moved up to the counter and requested six tickets, handing over a NT $500 bill. On it was painted a tiny machine gun, and the young Lieutenant who offered it told the cashier, "Right now, Lee, GO!"

Lee, who had been in place on behalf of the PLAN Intelligence Service for the past five years, swung out of his booth and walked swiftly across the hall to the information desk and disappeared into a door marked EMERGENCY EXIT ONLY.

Still no one betrayed anything. Until, two minutes later, every light in the building went out. Great pictures were no longer illuminated, the glass cases full of treasure went suddenly dull beneath the limited natural light still filtering in through the windows of this dull June day. The National Palace was without electric power, and deep beneath the stone-and-marble floors Major Chiang Lee flew along the underground corridor, a flashlight in his left hand and a hand grenade in his right. He reached the giant automatic generator with just 25 seconds left before it kicked in, and he ripped out the pin and hurled the grenade straight at the big 600-gallon gas tank to the right of the main machinery.

He dove back around the corner of the massively reinforced concrete walls and flung himself to the ground. Four seconds later the thunderous explosion and contained fire ensured that not only was the National Museum without power; it was also going to stay precisely that way for the foreseeable future.

Every secure door both inside the museum itself, inside the labyrinth of underground tunnels and inside the echoing vaults that held the treasures of five thousand years was suddenly useless. If they were open, they would stay open. If they were closed, they would open up easily enough without the power locking devices. Major Chiang Lee, after hundreds of hours of study, a million deceptions and the patience of a Buddha, had done his work.

And now he moved back through the dark passage toward the area where the elevator from the main floor emerged. In the fire-control doorway, right opposite, he retrieved his Kalashnikov machine gun. And he walked back up the emergency stairs into the wide foyer where there were now scenes of some disquiet, though nothing resembling panic. The building had been constructed to such a heavy-duty standard, the rumble of the explosion, 100 yards away deep below ground, had scarcely been detected.

Major Lee fired a short burst from his machine gun, into the information desk, by way of attracting attention. Then he blasted a volley at the six high-security cameras, which he knew would operate for several hours on emergency batteries. Then he ordered everyone to stand back against the walls. He seemed a small, insignificant-looking figure to be issuing such a command, but suddenly he was joined by two groups of six men all leveling smaller, but just as deadly, weapons.

The Taiwanese guards, indoctrinated for years as to the Jihad seriousness of their responsibilities, immediately moved as a trained unit of four men, racing into position behind two huge stone pillars, and opening fire at the aggressors in the lobby. But they were not in time. At the first sign of movement, Admiral Zhang's commandos hit the ground, returning fire toward the pillars. No one hit anyone, but right behind the museum guards there was a team of six Chinese Special Forces, now with their weapons drawn, and, firing from the rear, they cut down the security men in five seconds flat.

And now nine uniformed guards from the upper floors, pistols drawn, raced down the wide interior stairs. And this was like the Saint Valentine's Day massacre. Women screamed as the Chinese Special Forces, crouching beneath the benches along the walls, opened up with a sustained burst of fire that left no survivors—just nine bodies sprawled on the wide staircase, blood trickling down the gray stone steps.

Up on the overlooking balcony, a further troop of museum guards had seen the appalling situation and retreated into the main exhibition rooms, slamming shut the massive wooden doors and locking them by hand with their six-inch-long master keys. They used mobile phones, desperately trying to raise the military in the nearby garrison. The Taipei Police were on the line swiftly and assured them of assistance within 10 minutes. Down in the tunnels the underground guards, and those who protected the doors into the vaults, gathered in the dark, 23 of them, heavily armed and massively confused.

By now there were several dozen tourists trying to open the outside doors, and Major Chiang Lee and his men began to herd the crowd inside the foyer toward the main entrance, which was guarded by Special Forces. Each visitor to the museum was searched. All mobile phones were confiscated. The double doors were opened just a couple of feet, and each visitor was dispatched out into the crowd with instructions to leave the area immediately.

By now it was obvious the National Palace Museum had been captured, at least temporarily, by a small squadron of Chinese Special Forces. Lines of tourists returned to the waiting buses, and the eight men remaining in number 213 were now outside their bus brandishing Kalashnikovs and ordering the drivers away.

Inside the main foyer another gun battle broke out when guards from the tunnels broke through the emergency exit and began shouting orders to the crowd. Unaware of the gravity of the situation, they never had a prayer when the Special Forces gunned them down at close quarters. Six of them died instantly, the rest retreated back down to the dark tunnels, which was going to pose a substantial problem for the Chinese.

Ricocheting bullets had already injured four American tourists, one of them a very young boy, age around eight. The four-man medical unit that was integrated into the attacking force was attending the wounded, using their own supplies, and as they worked, the large crowd was slowly exiting the building and moving down to the buses.

At this point, the Chinese moved to secure the museum. Two bigger machine guns, plus ammunition, were brought up to the foyer from the waiting buses. All outside doors were locked by hand, and a dozen sentries were posted. The remaining 28 attackers split into three groups of six, and one of 10, the main assault force that would storm the exhibition rooms where there were still armed security guards.

They hit the one on the upper left first, blasting the door open with machine-gun fire and then spraying the room with 50 rounds, calling for total surrender. A stray bullet shattered a glass case and smacked straight through an early-seventeenth-century Qing Dynasty helmet used by a long-dead emperor for reviewing troops. The bullet cracked open the head of one of the three decorative dragons, split a large ruby in half and probably did about a million dollars worth of damage.

But the helmet survived, and it fared better than a black pottery wine jar, fashioned in the shape of a silk-worm cocoon, and dating back to around 300 B.C. This shattered on impact with another Kalashnikov bullet, and joined the remnants of a priceless foot-high, jade Kuei tablet from the early Shang Kingdom, more than 1,000 years before Christ.

A line of bullet holes also decorated the upper reaches of one of China's most valuable paintings, *A Literary Gathering*, a massive work exquisitely done in ink on silk for the Emperor Hui-tsung of the eleventh-century northern Sung Dynasty. It still hung, high on the east wall, and might ultimately be restored.

The four cowering guards plainly realized that if the Chinese

Special Forces were prepared to inflict millions of dollars' worth of damage on the contents of these rooms, their own lives were not worth four cents. And they came forward, unarmed with their hands high, and as they did so they heard the thunder of the second machine gun as it obliterated the lock on the door that guarded the room across the wide stone corridor on the upper right.

Again the Chinese Special Forces came in low and hard, the machine gun ripping bullets into the room, from a floor-level position. The two central glass cases were blown apart, glass from the tallest one flying everywhere. But the principal casualty was a large carved ivory Dragon Boat from the Qing Dynasty, again early seventeenth century, perfectly created, right down to the eight oars, the 16 pennants, and the deck canopy, all set in a gold-painted lacquer box. The Russian-made bullets hit it broadside on, reducing it to shards of split white ivory: a destruction of history sufficient to reduce any curator of any museum to unashamed tears.

Two paintings, set high on the west wall, above a colossal stone table, also were raked with machine-gun fire. The large one to the left was priceless, a sixteenth-century work by one of the four masters of the Ming Dynasty, Ch'iu Ying. Entitled *Late Return from Spring Outing*, it was a world-acclaimed picture, ink and color on silk, executed by one of the greatest artists of the Emperor's Imperial Painting Academy. The bullets had ripped right across it in two lines, and it would never be restored.

The slightly smaller picture to the left, however, was in ruins, and its demise would be mourned by art historians for years to come. It was a rare and magnificent work by Chao Kan, the tenth-century painter from Nanking, and its title evokes the elegant quality of the landscape: *Early Snow on the River*. It was a masterpiece by a great master who had trained at the Academy of Art of the southern T'ang court. He had used just ink and light color on silk, outlawing any trace of worldliness, as his fisherman worked the icy river, with a small band of travelers wending their way wearily along the windswept bank. Twenty million modern greenbacks would not have bought one half of it.

Two of the security guards, sheltering under the stone table, were hit and killed; the others begged for mercy and were permitted to surrender. And they trooped outside to join their colleagues with their faces to the wall, hands high above their heads, under the scrutiny of the Chinese raiders.

Room by room, the Special Forces took the museum, the staff was taken prisoner, the last tourists ejected from the building and the machine guns placed strategically on front and rear balconies.

At 1445, the sound of helicopters could be heard, out over the surrounding park. The Special Forces commander, in conference with Major Chiang Lee, knew they must be Taiwanese reinforcements, because the signal had not yet been sent back to the beachhead at Chinsan that the museum was secure.

Instantly they ordered all prisoners out onto the steps with instructions to clear the area, and they radioed Bus 213 to open fire at will on the incoming helicopters. Crammed with special police and the remnants of the Army still in the area, the choppers came clattering in over the trees, and immediately flew into a hail of bullets, from the high front balcony and the area to the rear of the bus.

The lead aircraft took the brunt of the heavy fire from the balcony and suddenly exploded, veering over almost in a full somersault and crashing, rotor first, bang into the green tiled roof. The second helicopter was hit from below and its main engine stopped dead, which caused it to drop like a stone from 100 feet, obliterating itself on the stone forecourt and then exploding, killing 15 tourists and injuring 39 others.

The third one banked left across the trees and flew swiftly back to the nearby Army garrison. Meanwhile Major Chiang Lee sent in the signal to the beachhead that the National Palace Museum was safely in Chinese hands for the moment, save for the underground tunnels and vaults, which still contained resisting security forces of an unknown number.

Twenty minutes later, the first of two waves of Chinese airborne battalions came in over the park, the big helicopters and transporters containing two antiaircraft detachments equipped with QW-1 SAMs. This new modified missile with its 35-pound warhead is equipped with a lethal IR homing device accurate to three miles.

The incoming battalion was also equipped with portable antitank weapons and light mortars, and the troops began to jump out into the park, swarming out of the aircraft onto the wet, green grass below, and forming an instant steel ring around the museum. They tied up with the commandos on the Special Forces that had originally taken the museum, and swiftly moved their missile defenses into position.

The museum was not yet completely secure from attack. But it would need a formidable modern force to break through right now. Taiwan had no chance of recapturing the palace, and only a remote shot at destroying it from the air at this point, because its air force was tragically weak and its missile defenses just about spent.

But the treasure trove of the Chinese centuries was firmly under the control of Beijing for the very first time since Chiang Kai-shek's 14 trains, bearing the very soul of his vast country, had rumbled down to the east coast ferries, almost 60 years previously.

0900. Wednesday, May 30.
The White House. Washington, D.C.

NEWS OF CHINA'S tightening stranglehold on the island of Taiwan was emerging with leaden slowness. Beijing, unsurprisingly, was releasing nothing. And there had been no time for any of the Western media's Far Eastern correspondents even to reach Taipei before the iron grip of the Chinese military took hold of the region.

Add to this the complete rupture of all Taiwanese military communications, and the West was left with no sources, no information and no prospects of obtaining any. The only news emerging from the island was the occasional sly and undercover dispatch from the pseudo-embassies, and they had access to very few hard facts. The air battles, which had now been fought over several days, had taken place more than 60 miles from mainland news reporters, out of sight, out of earshot, basically out of reach.

And on this Wednesday morning, the mood in the West Wing of

the White House was very somber. The hard men of the United States armed forces, Admiral Arnold Morgan, Defense Secretary Bob MacPherson, the Chief of Naval Operations, Admiral Alan Dixon, and the Chairman of the Joint Chiefs, General Tim Scannell, had been proved powerless to fight two enemies in two separate theaters. They were tied up in the Strait of Hormuz, guarding the world's main oil routes, and China was effectively left to do whatever it liked.

News was trickling in of a very large Chinese force landing on Chinsan Beach. It was already moving southeast to the port of Keelung. It had taken three days to muster, and the Chinese airborne troops had accepted very heavy casualties as the depleted but still determined Taiwanese forces constantly attacked them on the ground.

Nonetheless, the tide of warriors sweeping across the strait from the mainland, by both air and sea, was just too great, too engulfing for the Taiwanese to stop. Tens of thousands of Chinese troops made the beaches from the vast flotilla of civilian boats, merchant freighters and naval ships. This was a mission that had all of China behind it. And all the efforts of the remaining battalions of Taiwan's northern army proved unable to break through the "screen" of Chinese marines who fought doggedly to protect their beachhead from attack.

And now they were on the move, and Admiral Dixon considered they would swiftly attempt to capture the port of Keelung. Early reports, telephoned in secret from the pseudo-embassies, had the Chinese growling along the road, marching behind tanks and armored vehicles. But the Admiral offered a ray of hope here, because there was a major Taiwanese defensive force in this area. It had been formed six years previously with the express purpose of holding off a Chinese attack on Keelung, and the invaders would have to fight for every inch of ground in the port city.

It would perhaps come down to attrition, like most of China's wars. And then there could be only one winner. In Arnold Morgan's opinion, the Taiwanese would be suing for peace within 10 days.

This was Black Wednesday, no doubt. And at 0915 a White House agent entered the office of the National Security Chief to inform all four men that the Navy helicopter taking them to Andrews Air Base was on the lawn.

From there they were flying up to Cape Cod, landing at the sprawling Otis Air Force Base, and then heading on by Navy helicopter to Marblehead, Massachusetts, 20 miles up the north shore from Boston, for the funeral of Lt. Commander Ray Schaeffer. Admiral Morgan himself had insisted that the SEAL Team Leader be awarded, posthumously, the highest possible decoration in the United States Armed Forces, the Medal of Honor. As a SEAL, Ray Schaeffer's award was for many, many services rendered to his country. It would be awarded with no public announcement whatsoever.

Three thousand miles away in California, the funeral of U.S. Navy SEAL Charlie Mitchell was also taking place, and it would be attended by Admiral John Bergstrom and the Pacific Fleet C-in-C, Admiral Dick Greening. CINCPACFLT had personally recommended that the rookie combat SEAL quietly be awarded the Navy Cross.

In Marblehead, there was an air of terrible sadness. The Schaeffer family had lived there for generations, and Ray's wife, Wendy, with their two little boys, Ray, Jr., age nine, and Bobby, six, was returning to live in the old family house down by the water, where Ray's widowed father now lived alone.

The church was packed, with crowds lining the narrow street outside, and General Scannell read a moving eulogy, regretting that the Lieutenant Commander's area of operations was classified to such a degree that no one would ever know precisely where he had served, and with what "unfathomable courage" he had carried out his duties. "I hope," he concluded, "that his Medal of Honor, and the presence here of the senior military figures in America, will offer some testament to the regard in which he was held in the United States Navy."

Eight Naval officers carried the casket bearing the fallen SEAL to his last resting place, and the church bell tolled out over the little seaport as they lowered the body of Ray Schaeffer into the ground.

Admiral Arnold Morgan read the final prayer, offering the sentiment that "ordinary people, like ourselves, may sometimes find it difficult to understand what drives a man like Lieutenant Commander Schaeffer forward, to comprehend that selfless gallantry which is bestowed upon so few. I don't suppose Ray would have been able to explain much, either. And so we will just have to accept that God granted him an inner light, and we now wish him farewell, sure in the knowledge that light will guide him home. Amen."

At the graveside Wendy Schaeffer was erect and brave with her arm around Ray, Jr. But little Bobby wept uncontrollably for his lost father and Admiral Dixon knelt down to comfort him.

The only good news throughout the day was the formation of a Schaeffer family trust, which was begun with a $100,000 personal donation from the former Chairman of the Joint Chiefs and Boston banking heir, Admiral Scott Dunsmore.

The rest was a catalog of sorrow and remembrance, and the four military chiefs from Washington took their leave as soon as the burial was over. They were back at the White House by 1630, and it quickly became clear that the flight had done nothing to lessen their fury toward the Republic of China.

Back in his office, Admiral Morgan yelled, formally, for Kathy to order them some fresh coffee, with cookies, and answered his telephone as it tinkled.

"Faggot phones," he muttered, snatching it up and growling, "Morgan. Speak. And I am busy. So make it quick."

Kathy's dulcet voice murmured, "Outside desk to home base. Message received about the coffee and cookies. And I have one incoming signal, O rudest of pigs . . . Admiral George Morris is ready for duty tomorrow."

"Beautiful," replied the Admiral, and turning to Tim Scannell, without breaking stride, he snapped, "Fire Borden. Get him the hell out of there. George is coming back." And then, as if doubting the possibility that his thin, pastel green phone would be man enough to transmit a message, he replaced it and yelled through the door, "KATHY! Make sure that coffee's HOT!"

General Scannell told the Admiral he would indeed arrange to have Admiral Borden transferred to somewhere more amenable with his talents.

"Christ, Tim," he rasped. "Don't do that. We can't have someone of his seniority driving the harbor launch."

The General grinned. "I'll take care of it," he said. "But to return to our subject, you really do intend us to move forward and either destroy or disable that Chinese Navy base in Burma, and then warn them out of the area?"

"In one, Tim, old buddy. That's our plan."

"Timing?"

"I think right now. Give the little bastards something to think about while they're strangling Taiwan."

"Is John Bergstrom up to speed on this, Arnie?"

"As far as he can be. He has the charts, but no decent satellite pictures. And he knows we're moving on it. He has a SEAL team in place in Diego Garcia. And we got the right SSN available with the biggest ASDV we have. Same one we used to get the guys into the refinery."

"So this meeting now constitutes the finalization of the attack?"

"Guess so, Alan. We have to start somewhere. So let's get into it—let's hit these commie bastards hard . . . one for the Schaeffer, right?"

"One for the Schaeffer it is, Arnie." General Scannell was not smiling.

Admiral Morgan pulled up a big computerized chart on a wide screen at the end of his office. . . . "Come on over here, guys," he said, striding forward. "Let's take a good look at the position."

The chart showed the vast delta area between the port of Rangoon and the coastal mouth of the Bassein River, 125 miles to the west. This is the fabulous rice bowl of Burma, interlaced by rivers, streams, canals and tributaries, which irrigate millions of acres of farmland. Through here the mighty 1,350-mile-long

Irrawaddy River (today it's Ayeyarwady) splits and meanders to the ocean, packed with freshwater fish and monsoon waters that originated hundreds of miles to the north toward the Indian and Chinese borders.

It is a sprawling, wet tidal basin, with great promontories of land jutting out between the estuaries of nine rivers, all of which flow into the hot, steamy corner of the Bay of Bengal known as the Gulf of Martaban. The agricultural produce from here feeds much of the nation and much of China, too. The endless paddy fields are interrupted by mango swamps and the occasional monsoon forest, but this land is F-L-A-T.

Admiral Morgan frowned and pointed his ruler at the far left section of the chart. "This last wide stretch of water right here," he said, "is the Bassein River Delta. It's the widest of the south-flowing waters in this area, and you'll see that this island, the long triangle, here, on the left-hand side of the estuary, is called Haing Gyi. You will also notice that the goddamned place sits in about six inches of water, which is a pretty fucking crazy area to build a Navy base on, even if you happen to be a Chinese prick."

General Scannell came very close to blowing his coffee clean down his nose, so unexpected was Arnold's swift turn of phrase. But he moved in closer, and observed the wide area of green swamp that stretched all the way along the northern shoreline of Haing Gyi, almost joining it to the Arakan Peninsula.

"Well, we ain't going in that way," he said, unnecessarily. "And what about this light blue area that stretches right across the southern approach?"

"Oh, it's much better in there," said the Admiral, sardonically. "There is a maximum of nine feet shelving to about nine inches . . . and on the face of it, gentlemen, we have to assume the Chinese are nuts."

But his face relaxed, and he continued, "But nuts they ain't. This is a very strategic corner of the ocean. As we have discussed before, warships from here have the capability of controlling the Malacca Strait. And if I pull up this chart a bit, get us in closer, you'll see what the little bastards are up to. . . ."

"Right here, in this central stretch of the island's east coast, we got water.... See? More than forty feet right up to the shore ... and it stretches out here into what looks like a natural, but narrow, channel, all the way up from the mouth of the estuary, mimimum depth forty feet, maximum fifty-five feet.

"However, if you follow it down here ... about four miles, the whole damn place goes shallow again ... so if you're trying to get in from the ocean, you got a ten-mile stretch with only twenty feet of water. Which you'd think would be impossible. Right here we got a deepish water throughway into deepish water jetties. But you cannot get a big ship in there.

"But, I know they can ... because I happen to have located, on a very poor photograph, a Chinese Kilo-Class submarine, right in there, moored alongside. And that little bastard draws thirty-five feet on the surface, and they didn't carry the sucker in, did they?"

"Probably not," replied Admiral Dixon with mock seriousness.

"What they've done is dredged a channel, which does not appear on any Navy charts," said Admiral Morgan. "And what's more, it isn't going to appear on any Naval charts, because they're not about to allow anyone in there. There's been a major building program by the Chinese on that eastern shore, and they have a very neat little situation—a fully equipped Naval dockyard, right in an area where there are very few other facilities for overhauling a ship or even refueling. And they got it all to themselves, and they're going to be an even bigger pain in the ass than usual if we do not, gentlemen, get 'em the fuck out of there ASAP."

"What do they use for power?" asked the CNO.

"I'm not absolutely certain, but Lieutenant Ramshawe's on the case. And I appreciate the question. That island is in a remote place, and it's difficult to see what they are using. But the area is well lit and plainly operational. It's possible they are using the reactor of a nuclear submarine, but we can't find it. And the water is not deep enough for it to hide. Ramshawe thinks they have a major power plant, but we can't yet tell the source. Anyway, when we do, I think we should destroy it. . . . Gentlemen, we have to get them outta there."

"Do you think China has a major single objective in all of this, Arnie?" Bob MacPherson looked pensive.

"I think it's pure expansion, Bob. For so many years they've restricted themselves to their own area of the world, which ought to be big enough for anyone. But they increasingly see themselves as powerful global players. They are envious of us, and see themselves as our equals. They covet our influence, our allies and, above all, our muscle.

"But what they really covet is the world's oil supplies. Because as China gets rich, it's going to require more and more fuel. And most of that fuel is in the Middle East and south central Asia. Of course there's a ton of it in Siberia, but that means negotiating with Russia, which is not about to trade away one of its very few natural resources.

"Which brings us back to the Malacca Strait, the single great throughway of all oil to the Far East. If we allow China to dominate the Malacca, we give them the power to force some tankers right around Indonesia, and that's going to cost the Japanese a vast amount of money. All their fuel costs will rocket upward, natural gas, propane, jet fuel and gasoline.

"And the key to China's domination of that strait is their new base in Burma. Without it, they're damn near helpless, because they simply live too far away. And, gentlemen, right now we have world opinion on our side. We can force them right out of the Bassein River Delta, and no one would support any of their claims of U.S. bullying. That's what we're going to do."

"Anyway, who's to know what happened if the SEALs pull it off?" asked the CNO.

"China will know, because we'll fucking tell 'em. But they have made the mistake of striking the first blow against the West with that minefield in Hormuz. And then literally conquering Taiwan. Everyone knows they deserve whatever the hell's coming to them. And my guess is that if we hit Haing Gyi, the ole Chinks are going to go real quiet for several years."

"Meanwhile how the hell do we get in there to hit it?" asked

Bob MacPherson. "And since we're going to tell them what we've done, what's wrong with just bombing the sonofabitches?"

"The USA does not bomb people, without a drastic and just reason," replied Admiral Morgan. "However we may justify an attack on China's Indian Ocean east base, it is no more than a power play—the superpower bangs the pretender into his rightful place. Second place.

"But it's so much better that the guy with the busted nose is the only one aware of who's whacked him. That way it goes quiet. Some accident, on some remote island, in the Bay of Bengal. That's the way to run the world these days. Keep it quiet, keep it tight, but make it count."

"Well, you were right about the refinery in Hormuz," said Admiral Dixon. "We've heard nothing from China by way of complaint."

"That's because they know," said Admiral Morgan. "They know and they understand. And quite honestly, I don't think they care. Their objective was Taiwan, and they were prepared to pay the price for it. I doubt they'll ever bother to rebuild that refinery. But in the next several months you're gonna see the start of a trans-Sino pipeline, all the way from Kazakhstan to their eastern seaboard. It's the Chinese way. They'll build the world's longest ditch, containing the world's longest pipe, just the way they built the world's longest brick wall, and the world's greatest dam at Three Gorges. They have the labor, and they're not afraid to use it. A lot of it, one suspects, slave labor."

"Meanwhile," said Admiral Dixon, "how the hell are we going to get the guys into Haing Gyi, and what are they going to do when they get there?"

"First question, how to get in." Admiral Morgan moved closer to the chart, zooming back a little to show the water depths out in the bay.

"And that's a problem," he said. "You can all see the fifty-meter line out here, fifteen miles from the central seaway into the estuary. I'm not completely crazy about this chart, but they have the fifty-meter line well defined. It follows the coastline very accurately, all the way down from the narrow border with Bangladesh. Anywhere you look it's showing depths of around one hundred sixty-five feet to the left and one hundred twenty feet to the right. So we gotta assume it's more or less correct. So our submarine is going to have to make a rendezvous point somewhere right there on that line, where she can still hide in one hundred fifty feet of water.

"But that's up to the SEALs and to *Shark*'s CO. More important is the insertion of the troops. And I've given it a lot of thought, because that ASDV is so damned slow. And fifteen miles is a long way at only six knots, and that only gets us into the mouth of the estuary. It's another ten up to the deeper water off Haing Gyi. That's a total running time of more than four hours, and it leaves us with the ASDV in a pretty vulnerable spot.

"My conclusion, therefore, is that we bring the guys into the estuary, which will take two and a half hours, and then creep up the new channel as far as Rocky Point, right here on the southeastern headland of the island, and let 'em swim in. We then have the ASDV return to the *Shark*."

"Leaving the guys alone in there?"

"For a short while. Because I think we have to get 'em out with fast, rigid inflatables. The possibility of pursuit by the Chinese is high, and they may have fast patrol boats out searching. If they locate the ASDV crawling through the mud, in a channel less than forty feet deep, with nowhere to maneuver right or left, we could be light one boatload of very precious guys. And that would not be good."

"You mean we set up a rendezvous point somewhere right along the island beaches?" asked General Scannell. "Then get 'em out fast, running all the way back to the submarine at high speed on the surface?"

"No alternative. ASDV in, for maximum stealth, when we're not expected. Top speed run out, when the Chinese Navy is searching around in the dark, but may not catch us. Those fast inflatables make twenty-five knots. The guys will obviously get a good start . . . maybe fifteen minutes . . . and that way they have a real shot no one's gonna locate 'em."

"Okay, Arnie. Sounds good, so long as they don't get caught in the base. We got a contingency to rescue if the crap hits the fan while they're still working?"

"No, Alan. No I'm afraid we don't."

"Nothing?"

"How can we? We wouldn't know if they were in trouble. The only thing we can do is have an accurate rendezvous point on the island, with fast boats waiting to evacuate. The ASDV cannot fight, and the submarine is too far away."

"Jesus, that's a tough call for the guys. Who's in charge?" asked Tim Scannell.

"Commander Rick Hunter."

"That makes me feel better. But it's still tough. I hate to send the guys in with no backup."

"So do I. But they will be armed to the teeth, and very thoroughly prepared. Chinese guards wouldn't have a prayer against them if push came to shove."

"They didn't have one against Ray Schaeffer, either," replied Admiral Dixon. "But shit happens."

The four men were thoughtful for a few moments. And as they each contemplated the horror of discovery while the SEALs were ashore, plying their devastating craft, the door swung open and the beautiful Kathy O'Brien came in bearing a brown envelope addressed personally to Admiral Arnold Morgan, delivered by hand from Fort Meade to the White House.

"Just a moment," said the Admiral. "This might be just what we need. If it is, it should have been here two hours ago. But if Borden's taken my advice, the newest observations are gonna be real thorough."

And thorough they were. Fort Meade had apparently solved the mystery of the power source of the sprawling Naval complex on Haing Gyi Island.

Report on Haing Gyi Island Power Source

Comprehensive overheads have revealed no external power sources or supplies to Haing Gyi Base. This includes possibilities of the use of a generating ship or nuclear power plant.

Power supplies for operation of the base facilities all appear to emanate from a single large building in the center of the base.

Detailed examination of the foundation area of this building, in particular its size and scope beyond the building itself, suggests a possible geothermal source of power. This is confirmed as entirely consistent with local geophysical characteristics, supported by the known existence of mud volcanoes within 15 miles of the Haing Gyi facility.

An attachment is a full engineering statement of how geothermal energy is tapped. It indicates its vulnerability, and opportunities for disruption/accident.

Arnold Morgan mumbled about another cup of coffee, and asked his three colleagues to "hold everything" while he skipped through the notes on geothermal power. Bob MacPherson poured, and Arnold yelled *"KATHY!"* once again, and asked the goddess of the West Wing to have three copies made of the photograph of Haing Gyi.

Three minutes later, the Admiral looked up, complained that his coffee was half cold and told his guests that the principal mission of the SEAL attack on the Chinese base would be to destroy a power station, and with it the entire electronic network that runs from it. There would also be some other Naval hardware that had to go, but basically they were knocking out a major power supply, which would shut down the base entirely.

The four color photocopies arrived and were duly studied by Admiral Dixon, General Scannell and Bob MacPherson. Admiral Morgan pointed out the building in the center and asked if anyone knew how a geothermal power station worked. And no one did.

"Well, what you're always looking at is an area where heavy rainfall has filtered through the earth's surface for millions of years. And right here we have such an area. It's sandy in a lot of places, and it gets a lot of sudden, fierce rain from the monsoons in a very flat basin, where it can hang around and filter through.

"And right here we have an area with volcanic activity, where the earth's plates can pry apart, shifting way below the surface, forming giant, hollow caverns thousands of feet deep. Now in these caverns we get huge underground lakes, and the bottoms of those lakes are so deep the water becomes colossally hot from the earth's core.

"If you drill down in the exact right place, you hit one of these lakes, and the compressed, boiling water flashes off into steam. If you let it, it will blast three thousand feet into the air, in a clean, clear white plume of steam. The Nevada Desert is the big steam-well area in the USA. Some of 'em light half of San Diego and occasionally Las Vegas."

He paused to let everyone absorb what he was saying. "Right," he added. "Got that? Now look at the picture. See that building? Well, here's how it got there. The Chinese geologists located the steam lake and capped the drill hole. Then they dug deep and poured a solid concrete foundation, probably fifty yards by fifty yards by fifty yards deep.

"Clean down the middle of this, they sank their main shaft into the vast cavern that contains the lake. They capped it with a massive valve at the top, right on the concrete, and then they built their power-generating station all around it, right on that big concrete cube. They installed the electric turbines to run on steam power, and when they completed their electronic grid for the whole dockyard, they opened the valve.

"The steam surged straight up the shaft in the middle of the fifty-yard cube, into the system, and began to rotate the turbines. The clever little Chinks thus had virtually free, endless electric power for years to come. It sounds complicated, but it's not really. It's just a kinda upside-down dam with the force coming upward from the earth, rather than downward from released water. One thing about electric turbines: The only thing you have to do is turn 'em."

"And our guys have somehow to get in there and blow it up?" said the General.

"I think that would do very nicely," replied the Admiral. "Because that would shut down the base indefinitely."

"Is John Bergstrom on side?" asked the CNO.

"He is. Right now they're consulting their main demolition guys, and I have to get this stuff to Coronado right away. Then two of the main SEAL explosives officers will leave immediately for Diego Garcia to brief Commander Hunter and his team."

"Do we have any handle on how well this place is guarded?"

"Fort Meade's been watching it carefully for some weeks now. And there is some security. But not overwhelming. Haing Gyi is in such a strange, inaccessible place. It's literally surrounded by Burma, whom the Chinese have been financing. It looks to me as if they have not even considered the possibility of an attack on the base.

"But of course it is a military installation. And there will be patrol boats, and guard patrols on the jetties. But we have not found any sign of patrols in the interior of the base. Just some activity close to the visiting ships. The trick is to get in there nice and quiet. Then cause absolute havoc, and get out while everyone's trying to find out what's going on. It nearly always works. Surprise. You can't beat surprise."

"Meanwhile, where's the SEAL team?"

"They're all in Diego Garcia, waiting. The refinery team are all there too, waiting to fly back to Coronado. They made it back from Hormuz in one of the carriers. The *Shark*'s in there too, waiting to embark the SEALs for the coast of Burma."

All four men took a break from the charts to watch the CNN evening news, and the lead item was more or less what Admiral Morgan had expected. The Chinese were fighting fiercely for the port of Keelung, and according to the news had swiftly secured the actual dockyard area with a team of Special Forces, which had overpowered the mainly civilian security guards. Most of this information had leaked out through merchant ships' radios via Hong Kong.

But the rest of the picture was very blurred. The Chinese had breached the wire fences and now controlled the container docking areas, but the surrounding town was still very much Taiwanese. The local garrison was well equipped and was backed up by continuing air strikes from a remote strip in Hsinchu County. The Chinese assault force thus found itself badly bogged down, sustaining heavy casualties out on the Yehliu Road, four miles from the town.

The Taiwanese had somehow managed to conserve eight of their most modern ground-attack aircraft. Armed with cluster bombs and cannon, the Taiwanese pilots came in groups of four, from the south, constantly harassing the great mass of Chinese troops, tracked vehicles and artillery moving ponderously toward Keelung.

CNN had found access to satellite photographs that showed a mass of fire out along the western approaches to the seaport. And, in some ways, the Chinese were in a very difficult position. They had a Special Force in control of the port area, but it could not hold out forever, and right now the advancing army from Chinsan was at a standstill. The Taiwanese had found the range with a battery of cruise missiles, which were currently smashing up the entire road system from the west. They had 40 M-48X medium tanks on that side of the town, arranged defensively, and the Chinese commanders knew beyond doubt they were in a serious fight for this seaport, and they were not winning it.

The problem was they had to win it. Otherwise this local war might drag on for weeks. The Chinese needed heavy reinforcements. They needed possibly 300,000 men on the island of Taiwan in order to secure it. And they could not land that many without capturing a major container port and bringing in major transport ships that could land men in the thousands. They needed the jetties, they needed the docking facilities. They needed Keelung.

And out on the Yehliu Road things were going from bad to worse. The Chinese army was having constant problems with its surface-to-air missiles, and after 16 hours of sustained attack from Taiwan's brave fighter pilots they had hit only one, and had themselves sustained hundreds of casualties. It was impossible to evacuate them all back to the beachhead, and their hospital capacity on the long sands was negligible. The fact was, China had to take Keelung, not just to provide proper inbound port for her massed armies, but to give her a proper mechanized base for supplies of both food and ammunition, treatment of the wounded and communications. Right now they had no base on the island of Taiwan.

Admiral Morgan stared at the screen, trying to read between the lines. He was a military officer attempting to picture the scene in his mind. As were General Scannell and Admiral Dixon.

And it was the CNO who spoke first. "They don't get ahold of that goddamned seaport in the next two days, they could find themselves in serious trouble," he muttered.

"Think they might switch the attack altogether, maybe go south to Kaohsiung?" asked Bob MacPherson. "That's as big as Keelung."

"I wouldn't have thought so," replied Admiral Dixon. "According to our information, the bulk of the Taiwanese Army is trapped in the south, can't get back north. But that army is probably in pretty good shape, mainly because they're kinda stranded, with nothing to fight. By the look of this, the Chinese are determined to win the battle in the north, and right now they're in some trouble."

"They are that," interjected Arnold Morgan. "They got a foothold in the container port, and another in the museum, which is what this war is at least partially about. But they have to consolidate, and that does not seem to be happening."

"You know what their real problem is?" said General Scannell thoughtfully. "They are bound and determinded *not* to knock down Taipei. And you take that option away from an invading army, you cut its balls right off. You render them unable to use the ultimate force. If they rolled up their sleeves and began a bombardment of the capital city, flattening major buildings, destroying the downtown area, Taiwan would surrender inside of an hour. It's not like the London blitz, or Berlin. It's different. More like a civil war.

"And, faced with imminent death, or normal life under an ultimately benevolent ruler on the mainland, there's only one answer
for Taiwan. And until China gets prepared to slam Taipei, she's
gonna be fighting a half-assed conflict, against a very proud
enemy. And that's gonna cost them a lot of guys."

"Not that they care about that," said Arnold Morgan. "But I'm
with you. They have to *take* Taiwan by force of arms . . . with an
army occupying it mile by mile. Until Taiwan formally surrenders."

"And the longer they take to get their asses in gear at
Keelung," said the CNO, "the worse it's gonna get. In my opinion,
they'd be better off knocking down Keelung to save Taipei."

"They might at that," added General Scannell. "But one thing's
for sure: They can't stay long as they are now."

The second item on the news was just as serious. The conflict
in Taiwan had again sent the world oil markets into a complete
frenzy. The prospect of a war, into which the United States
might be drawn, always does. And here was the CNN newscaster reporting another chronic rise in the price per barrel.
Brent crude was up $10, back to $64, having subsided from its
peak of $72 as the Pondicherrys did their work in the Strait of
Hormuz.

But Americans in the Midwest were paying four dollars a gallon at the pumps. And Texaco was intimating this could go to five
in the weeks ahead, while the world's VLCCs struggled to replen-
ish supplies. Now the latest "spin" being placed on the news of
China's war with Taiwan was frightening the markets all over
again.

What if the Chinese somehow seized control of the Malacca
Strait? What would happen to Japan if the price of their fuel doubled again? They were still the world's second-largest economy,
and they needed fuel for everything. What price would they pay
to survive? And where would this put the West?

Essentially this was a newsroom's dream, free rein to terrify
the populace, ratchet up the ratings and look wise. There were
frowns, set beneath perfectly coiffed hairstyles and -pieces.
There were expressions of deep concern and superior learning

from men who had zero firsthand experience of politics, the military or the world's financial markets. Save as onlookers.

"The question is, Where is this all going to end?" asked one of the network anchormen. "And what is the U.S. government planning to do about it? That's what's concerning every American here tonight." He said it as if he had just plumbed the very depths of Socrates.

"What a total asshole," observed Arnold Morgan.

Nonetheless the oil crisis remained exactly that. And the situation in Taiwan was out of control. Admiral Morgan knew only one thing—the United States had to get China out of the Bay of Bengal. The U.S. Navy had to lead the way in freeing up the oil routes both to the east and to the west.

He stood up and walked over to the window, staring out into the darkness. And he mused to himself in the silence of his profound intellect: *Whichever way you look at it, the financial fate of the modern industrial world right now lies in the hands of a dozen U.S. Navy SEALs, and may God go with 'em.*

1100. Saturday, June 2.
U.S. Navy Base. Diego Garcia.

Commander Donald Reid had temporarily handed over the wardroom in the recently arrived USS *Shark* to his XO, Lt. Commander Dan Headley, and the Team Leader of SEAL Assault Team reunited somewhat surprisingly in this remote U.S. outpost in the Indian Ocean, had not yet progressed to their principal business.

Far from the steamy Bassein River Delta, their talk centered on a cool, sunlit afternoon in Maryland, two weeks previously, on Saturday, May 20, when a big gray colt named White Rajah had won the Preakness Stakes, by four lengths, over nine and a half furlongs, the second leg of the American Triple Crown.

White Rajah, bred in Kentucky by Rick Hunter's father, Bart, raised from a foal under the supervision of Dan's father, Bobby, thus joined the immortals who had thundered to victory in the

134-year-old classic: Man O'War won this, so did his son War Admiral. Then there were Whirlaway, Assault, Count Fleet, Citation and Native Dancer. Bold Ruler and his peerless son Secretariat, the greatest of all twentieth-century stallions, Northern Dancer, the Triple Crown winners Affirmed and Seattle Slew. They all won in Maryland.

White Rajah would retire to stud with a book value approaching $8 million. Breeders would line up to send mares to him at $50,000 each. And according to Rick there was a chance he would begin his new career at Hunter Valley Farms, the land of his forefathers, the land of his vicious grandpa, Red Rajah, who had once nearly bitten off the young Dan Headley's arm.

"Been in touch with your dad?" asked the XO.

"Oh, sure. We fixed up some kind of a computer hookup right here a few days ago. I watched the race on one of the screens."

"Hey, Ricky, that must have been really exciting."

"Sure was. Even though I knew the colt had won. Christ! You should have seen him . . . heading into the last turn at Laurel Park . . . you know how damn tight it is . . . and it was a big field . . . bunched right up . . . the Rajah stuck in the middle . . .

"But they fanned out like always on that track, and there he was . . . two on his inside, three on his outside . . . holding his place . . . waiting for the split. Jorge hit him once, and he dug in . . . deep in the stretch he hit the front and at the eighth pole he was clear . . . drew right off . . . beat 'em by four lengths. No bullshit."

"Fantastic, Ricky. Just fantastic. How 'bout the Belmont Stakes? They gonna let him take his chance in New York next week?"

"Dad says not. None of that family went twelve furlongs, and they think he only just saw it out at Churchill Downs. They don't want to get him beat over a distance too far for him. I think they'll put him away for the Travers at Saratoga, and if he wins take a shot at the Breeders' Cup Classic. But they're not gonna run him a yard over ten."

"Yeah. Sounds right. The family really throws milers. But how come the owners don't want to keep him and send him to stand at Claiborne?"

"Well, Dad's put in a big offer, and of course he knows the bloodline. They been raising those big fiery bastards for years at Hunter Valley. I think the Rajah's trainer thinks he'd be better among people who knew him as a foal. Guys who're aware of the family's tricky temperament. If he comes to Hunter Valley, the owners will probably hang on to four shares."

"Guess so. And I guess my own daddy's gonna end up in charge of him."

"No doubt of that. And that's gonna be real good news for you . . . if we get him, Bart's giving your dad a breeding right to him. He told me."

"One pop?"

"Hell no. Every year. First classic winner we've bred since 1980, and your dad gets to share the wealth. The Rajah hits in the breeding shed, your retirement is buttoned up safe."

"Shit, Ricky. We gonna end up drinking cold beers in the bluegrass, singing the music, and raising the yearlings."

"Nah . . . not us. We got bigger things to do. That's an ole man's game. You and me gonna run the goddamned United States Navy."

"Well if we are, we better get this next sonofabitch right or we might both end up dead. 'Specially you." Dan Headley looked pensive.

He stood up and asked the steward for more coffee. "Have you looked at this mess?" he asked the SEAL boss. "According to the chart, there's no way in except on a fucking Jet Ski."

Rick Hunter chuckled. He'd spent a lot of his life chuckling with, or at, the son of his father's right-hand man. When they were kids, Danny had always been the funnier one of the inseparable pair, and when they were old enough to sustain an interest in girls, it had usually been Danny who had attracted them most. Until they realized the potential of one day becoming the chatelaine of Hunter Valley Farms.

"Seriously, Dan, I can't see how we can make it in there on the surface . . . straight up the middle of the channel. They'll surely have a patrol boat. And there's not enough water to bring even the ASDV in submerged."

"I got a few notes right here, Ricky. Apparently there's an unmarked channel in there, maybe forty feet deep, enough water to get a diesel-electric submarine into the jetties."

"You mean right in the center of the tidal stream? Jesus, that's only about as wide as the home stretch at Laurel Park."

"Guess so."

"I don't need a submarine. Be better off on White Rajah. He knows how to stay straight."

"Well, at least you're not gonna be driving. Last time you and I tried to stay straight in the middle of the night you hit a telephone pole with your dad's truck and knocked out half the lights in Bourbon County."

"Yeah," said Rick. "But I was only eighteen years old."

"Nonetheless, old buddy, your legend lives on. No one's achieved anything like that with that particular pole since Arthur Hancock hit it in the middle of the night back in the 1960s."

"Keep pretty good company, don't I? The great Arthur Hancock and the future Admiral Rick Hunter. You want someone to put your lights out, you can't do a whole lot better than us."

"Well, I hope someone's put 'em all out when you get into this Bassein River. You get caught, Chinese sailors slice off balls of aging Kentucky hardboot. First gelded SEAL reporting for duty, yessir."

"Shut up, Dan, for Christ's sake. You're making me nervous."

"Okay. No more jokee. Let's have another look at that chart. Now, see this mark here, this is where your boss, Admiral Bergstrom, suggests we make the rendezvous point. We got one hundred sixty feet of water, and we can put *Shark* under the surface with room to spare. That's 16.00N 94.01E, about twelve miles off the Burmese coast west sou'west of Cape Negrais.

"We launch the ASDV right there and steer one-two-zero straight into the mouth of the delta. It's all of sixteen miles, and it's going to take two and a half hours. That's where it gets tricky, because you have to find the damn channel. We know it's there, because we know they got a submarine in there. But we do not know where the hell it is, and right here we got a real issue.

"And a big question: Does it run north or south of this little island here . . . what's it called? Thamihla Kyun. There's a little deep water to the south, maybe sixty feet plus. But your men in Coronado think they dredged straight across this narrow shoal. It's easier to drag silt out of the shallows. Your guys think the channel's right in there. . . . see? Right here . . . by this fifty-foot trench northwest of Thamihla."

Commander Hunter stared at the chart. "Okay, but what if they're wrong? We'll just plow the ASDV straight into the bottom, and we might never get it out. How are we supposed to do this?"

"Very, very slowly, my lad. Using your sonar, sounding the bottom, carefully checking the surface picture whenever you dare. See this mark here? That's a red can, flashing light every two seconds . . . I want you to take a visual on the periscope . . . the guys think you'll pick up the main entry channel, right here . . . less than a mile east of the can. And that's where you alter course. Speed three knots, steer three-five-zero for two thousand meters and change course at 15.53N 94.16E. At this point you are going to be in patrolled waters, and you're gonna be awful careful, hear me?"

"Yessir, Danny. Jeez, you really know this submarine crap, right? I can see why your boss handed the insertion over to you."

"Nearly. I had to ask him. I just didn't want you going in there briefed by anyone except me. Kinda surprising how easily he agreed, though."

"Guess he recognizes a young master."

"Guess so. Just keep paying attention to what I'm telling you. We got another hour before lunch. Then the first formal briefing of your guys starts at fifteen hundred hours. I'm sitting in on it, so don't fuck it up. Don't want to have to keep correcting you. So listen."

"How 'bout you listen for a minute, shithead?"

Dan chuckled at the sobriquet, an ageless boyhood term of endearment. But Rick Hunter continued seriously, "What happens if we do bump the bottom and we can't find the goddamned channel? What then?"

"Look, I realize you've been rolling around in the dirt strangling guards, killing terrorists and blowing things up all your life. But what I'm going to show you requires careful thought . . . now look here . . . this deep trench is very important because it's a haven for a small submarine, moving through waters that are plainly too shallow to allow it free passage.

"You want to get a channel into this main lane, which your guys have marked here; you want first to get into the trench where you don't have to dredge. Got it?"

"Got it."

"Right. Now there are two ways into the trench. The long way, across here, maybe two and a half miles, dredging all the way, in water only fifteen feet deep. That'll take months. Or, alternatively, you could take this three-mile detour, west of the island, in deeper water, and that way you only need to cut a channel three hundred yards long max, and you're in the trench. What do you think?"

"I'll take the three hundred yards cut, any time, any day."

"And that's what our oceanographers think the Chinese Navy will have done. Therefore your driver will take the ASDV around through the deeper water, and we think he'll find the hole straight into the trench. When the water settles at, say, fifty feet, you guys go to PD and you'll see the flashing light about a mile up in front. At which point you're headed straight for the channel, and that'll take you right in to where you wanna be."

"What happens if some bastard's coming the other way down this narrow ditch?"

"Edge hard to starboard. Drop down to the bottom and sit in the mud, act like a recently drowned pig. Whatever it is will go right by. If you hear anything, just lie very quietly on the bottom. Gently."

"You keep saying 'quiet' and 'gentle.' You suggesting I'm some kind of a gorrila, young Danny?"

"Not really, but you're the leader and you got a lot more in common with a gorilla than a sea wraith."

"Well, anyway. I'm not driving."

"Thank Christ. But what I was going to mention was the utter unlikelihood of your meeting another ship. I mean right now the latest satellite picture shows only two warships in there, plus a submarine, with two or three patrol boats running around some of the time.

"We have no pictures of any boats running around after midnight at any time. Personally I think you will find the channel easily, and you will make your landing with no trouble. After that, you're in charge. But my guys will get you out, Rick. On that you can trust me. That's a promise."

"Who's driving the ASDV?"

"The best man in the Navy. He's a specialist. You might even know him. He's Lieutenant Mills, and he can maneuver that little ship anywhere. He's calm, expert and very instinctive about danger. Better yet, he's done it before. And you could not be in safer hands. He'll get you in, and if there's trouble, he won't get caught. You can't ask for more than that."

"Yes I can."

"What?"

"Just for you and me to be sipping a coupla cold beers on my daddy's side porch, listening to the music, watching the mares and foals moving across the paddocks in the evening. Instead of raising hell in some Chinese dockyard."

"Yeah, doesn't that sound great right now? Guess it's because we're right around the corner from real danger. But it's too late now to think of our own world. It's too late. We're in someone else's world, big time. And we gotta make it happen."

Two hours later, Commander Rick Hunter stood before the team that would shortly embark for the eastern end of the Indian Ocean. They had taken over a brightly lit, concrete-walled ops room, with a five-foot-wide computer screen placed at the side of a long trestle table.

The eleven SEALs who would accompany the Commander into Burmese waters were seated casually along the other side of the table with notepads and pens. Each man was issued a map of the delta of the Bassein River, plus various views, shot from the satellites, of the Chinese base itself. Everyone had a blowup of the geothermal power station that sat almost in the center of the dockyard complex.

And behind the SEALs sat the additional, but critical, personnel: The CO, Lt. Commander Dan Headley, who would take the USS *Shark* in and supervise their escape; Lt. David Mills who would drive the ASDV inshore; Lt. Matt Longo from Cincinnati, the ASDV navigator; and Commander Rusty Bennett, who would not join the mission but whose guidance would be greatly appreciated.

Behind them, the steel door was shut and locked. Two Naval guards remained on duty immediately outside, with four more patrolling the area beyond the main door to the otherwise-deserted building. No one, including the C-in-C of the Fleet, was permitted to enter. Even to exit the ops room, each SEAL needed to have his notepad personally signed by the Team Leader.

No one was permitted a phone call. There was absolutely no further contact with the outside world. Nor would there be until they were back in the USS *Shark* at the conclusion of the mission. They were scheduled to sail at 2200 that night, Saturday, June 2.

Commander Hunter immediately introduced his second-in-command, 28-year-old Lt. Dallas MacPherson, a wide-shouldered southerner from South Carolina who had started life at The Citadel, the state's near-legendary miltary academy, but had switched after only a couple of semesters to the Naval Academy at Annapolis.

He rose rapidly in dark blue, making Lieutenant in double-quick time, and serving as a gunner and missile officer in an Air-leigh-Burke destroyer before the age of 25. This was good, but not good enough for the restless Dallas, who suddenly, to the surprise of his colleagues, requested a transfer to the US Navy SEALs.

He crashed through the BUD/S course, finishing in third place, complaining he'd probably "been stitched up"—most SEALs are happy to pass through in the first 30. And throughout his short, but meteroic, career people had been more or less divided on whether he would end up in Admiral Bergstrom's chair, or in a box with a posthumous Medal of Honor. He was tough as hell, brave as a lion and smarter than almost everyone. But there was a daredevil in his soul, and that might either save the lives of an entire squadron or, alternately, get them into terminal trouble.

Commander Hunter was in no doubt. Lieutenant MacPherson was reputed to be the most brilliant young explosives expert on the base, a progressive Naval scientist on the subject of demolition in all its forms. Rick Hunter would take Lt. MacPherson any day, on the strength of his swiftness of thought. When he appointed him, he had said, "Dallas, where we're going, the only thing that's gonna keep us alive is brains. Keep using 'em, and we'll make it out."

In fact, Lt. MacPherson's father was a distant cousin of the veteran Secretary of Defense, Robert MacPherson. And when news of this had seeped through various wardrooms, one senior commanding officer had remarked playfully, "Well, young Dallas, you can't beat a few family connections in the military to ensure you advance your career."

"Sure can't, sir," replied the twenty-two-year-old Midshipman. "I taught that Bob MacPherson damn near everything he knows."

And now, right here in the most secretive room in the most remote American Naval base, Dallas was about to undertake an awesome responsibility, not only to accept command of the entire force, should anything befall the leader, but to ensure personally the total destruction of the geothermal power station on the island of Haing Gyi.

Rick Hunter introduced him carefully, as a young officer in whom he had the utmost confidence, and from whom they must take orders unquestioningly while working in the Chinese electricity-generating plant.

He then introduced his personal bodyguard, Lt. Bobby Allensworth, with whom he had served on another highly classified mission the previous year. He provided no background, certainly not the information that young Bobby had fought his way out of a life of petty crime in south-central Los Angeles and obtained his commission in the U.S. Marine Corps. He said merely that Lt. Allensworth would be personally responsible for the safety of the force, particularly if they had to fight their way in, though he hoped this would not be necessary.

Chief Petty Officer Mike Hook, also from Kentucky, a medium-sized supreme athlete and swimmer, was included as the number-two explosives expert on the team. He would be personal assistant to Lt. MacPherson during the time setting of the charges and the guardian of the special bomb they would carry in—the one Dallas said would split the steam shaft asunder, releasing a massive geothermal force, which might very well blow up the entire base.

"How far in the clear do we want to be when that happens?" asked someone.

Before Commander Hunter could reply "One hour," Lt. MacPherson remarked he thought back in Coronado would be just perfect.

That was the deceptive side of Lt. MacPherson's character. He sometimes sounded merely flippant, but the truth was he was always a few strides in front. He knew "one hour" was correct, but he'd gone past that and was instinctively trying to defuse the tension, trying to reduce the fear factor, the prospect of the unknown. Some officers think this approach has no value whatsoever. But you still have to be extremely able to do it. And Commander Hunter laughed anyway.

Only Lt. MacPherson understood the perfect timing required to send that armor-piercing, steel-cased bomb thousands of feet down the main steam shaft, to blast the giant well-head valve apart and release the seismic energy from the core of the earth.

"Gentlemen," said the Commander, "details of the in-base mission will be clarified during the three-day journey to the Bay of Bengal. Right now I am intending to show you precisely where we are going, how we land, where we get off and the main drive of our objective."

Briefly he introduced other key members of the team: two

SEALs who had also served under his command the previous year in the South China Sea, Riff "Rattlesnake" Davies and Buster Townsend, the radio operator. Both were from St. James's Parish down in Louisiana's Mississippi Delta. Both had served in surface warships.

He also brought forward the toughest man in the squad, Petty Officer Catfish Jones, an ex–deepwater fisherman from the coast of North Carolina. Catfish, 29, was a combat veteran of the Kosovo campaign. He had a 19-inch neck, and forearms of blue-twisted steel. Bobby Allensworth had instructed him in unarmed combat. And these two represented the front line of the Assault Team's heavy muscle if they came face-to-face with the Chinese inside the Navy base.

For his opening remarks, Commander Hunter played down the danger of the mission. "We are going into a lightly defended Chinese Naval base," he said. "It's a relatively new facility, and we've had it under observation for several weeks. Our Intelligence conclusion is that the owners do not anticipate a serious attack from anyone. Which should give us a reasonable chance of accomplishing our mission. Which is, incidentally, to take it off the face of the earth as quickly as possible."

At this point a ripple of disquiet could easily be sensed in the room. And the Commander elected to clear up the question that was on everyone's mind: Why are we doing this?

"As most of you know, we are in the middle of a world oil crisis, caused principally by the Chinese. In the judgment of our colleagues in National Security, China has further plans for disruption at the other end of the Indian Ocean. But she can only instigate this disruption by maintaining a major Navy base in the area.

"This one, at the mouth of the Bassein River, is the sole means by which China can have a catastrophic effect on the free and peaceful flow of the world's oil. Our instructions come direct from the White House. We are to take that Naval base out, on behalf of the government of the United States of America.

"The successful achievement of our objective will not only

send the Chinese right back to their home waters, where they belong. It will also deservedly earn the gratitude of every person in the industrialized world. Although they will not know, of course, to whom they are grateful. But we'll know. And that's what matters."

Everyone in the room nodded approval. And Commander Hunter told them that for the purpose of this initial briefing he wished to demonstrate to the entire group precisely where they were going, and how they were going to find their way in, in the pitch dark.

"Okay," he said, "look at your own charts, and follow my bigger electronic one as we go." He used a long ruler and pointed it at the rendezvous point where the *Shark* would arrive with the entire mission on board.

"Right here," he said pointing precisely, "we get into the ASDV, in about one hundred sixty feet of water. We then take this route, down toward this little island here . . . and according to our experts we take this route, to this slightly deeper water right here. We believe this flashing light on the red can, marked here, will guide us into a newly dredged channel. Then we pick up the main throughway up to the island of Haing Gyi, where the base is.

"You'll see right here on your chart, we adjust our course to zero-two-zero and run on up here in the main channel, as far as the next light—right here . . . it flashes every two seconds. We'll pick that out probably a mile before we get there. And though we have not absolutely finalized our landing spot, we are leaning toward this area here . . . Rocky Point.

"It's a headland with deep water in front, right up to the beach. Maybe fifteen feet. We can swim in there, and it's far enough away from the base to carry no sentries. About one and a quarter miles. We have to walk that, with our equipment, but there're no hills, no swamps, and just a tidal river to cross. We'll take a look when we get there. This looks like a bridge, and if it's quiet we'll use it."

"We coming out the same way, sir?"

"Absolutely not. Because there's no way we can make our

business look like some geothermal accident. The Chinese are going to know it's us very early on. The ASDV's too slow, and it'll need to turn around as soon as it drops us. So they're bringing in rigid inflatables to get us out fast. The water's very flat this time of the year. We'll be back in the submarine in fifty minutes."

"How many buildings are we planning to hit?"

"Probably three, but the big one's the power plant. That's our mission critical. We slam that, the base is useless. There are also a couple of Chinese warships in there. We'll take a crack at both of them if we can. Just a couple of stickies."

"Any idea of the strength of the guard, sir?"

"Well, our guys have counted only about eight men patrolling at any one time. Four on the main jetties, and four back here a little, where this destroyer seems to be farther inshore. That probably means if we arrive there at around zero-one-hundred, there'll be eight guards we may have to eliminate before we enter the power plant. If we're quiet we may not see any more for two or three hours, by which time I hope we'll be on our way out.

"If we do have to fight again, we may have to eliminate eight more. But I am not sure that will be necessary."

"How about knocking down the guardhouse with everyone in it, maybe at midnight when they probably change over?"

"We thought about that. But it's awfully noisy. And we're not quite sure where the Chinese keep reinforcements. But we don't want a bunch of Chink helicopters chasing around all over the goddamned place. Especially as one of 'em might locate and kill us. Generally speaking, we think stealth is the best way to accomplish our objectives."

"Okay, sir. No problem."

"Final refinements will be made throughout our journey, via the satellites. We got a lot of guys working on this, and things will develop before we reach the coast of Burma. Broadly speaking, we think the element of surprise will be decisive in our favor."

"How about the getaway, sir? Can we board the inflatables

*up close to the base . . . like we don't want to end up running
through a fucking paddy field for about ten miles pursued by the
goddamned coolies, right?"*

"Dallas, no we don't. Neither do we want to look as if we're
running boat trips round the fucking harbor in the middle of the
night. We'll have that organized in another day or so. My own
view is we take the edge of the swamp in the south."

*"But that's a hell of a distance, sir. Do we have any chance of
immediate help if we come under fire, or if we are seriously
pursued?"*

"No, Dallas. I am afraid we do not."

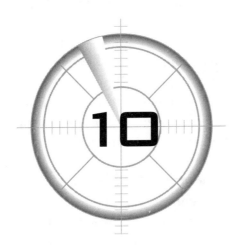

0900. Monday, June 4.
Northern Taiwan.

THE BATTLE FOR Keelung had now lasted for five days, and despite heavy casualties, the Chinese began inexorably to win it. They kept coming forward, landing thousands more men on Chinsan Beach, and calling in more and more air sorties from the mainland. But they left more than 3,000 dead along the Yehliu Road, before they finally forced their way into the inner suburbs of the seaport.

Street by street, block by block, yard by yard they fought their way toward the docks. The Taiwanese defended with their courage high, and they were never really defeated. Merely engulfed.

And then, as the Chinese Army prepared for the one push that would drive them into the vast container port area, the Taiwanese pulled off a master stroke. A team of their Special Forces crossed the railroad out along the Chungshan-1 Road, swam in to the harbor and severed the mooring lines of two massive container ships, just as the tide was turning.

Thirty minutes later, with these two gigantic ships slewed beam-on across the entrance to the docking areas, the Taiwanese scuttled them both with high explosives, partially blocking the main route both into and out of the harbor. It would take the Chinese Navy three more days to drag the wreckage clear and make a free passageway for their big troopships.

Scuttling the containers caused a momentous commotion on the docks, and it allowed the Taiwanese Army to escape cross-country, dropping back to Taipei, leaving the invaders from the mainland victorious but in something less than good order.

For a start, Keelung was a shambles both in the harbor and in the streets. There were debris and rubble everywhere. No one knew how to get anywhere. In addition, there were several isolated pockets of local resistance, and the Chinese were desperately trying to avoid killing civilians.

This was a serious hindrance, since the civilians were well supplied with grenades, rifles and machine guns. And they fought furiously, night and day, to eliminate the invading army using ancient tactics of snipers and booby traps against unsuspecting troops.

Not in living memory had the Chinese armed forces been so extended, engaged in highly complex combined operations. This was an adventure the like of which they had had absolutely no previous experience in modern times. Much of their equipment lacked any form of sophistication, and there were glaring shortcomings in their military processes and procedures.

And it all began to take its toll. There were Chinese commanders who began to believe the only way to capture Taiwan was to knock it down. And everyone knew China's top Special Forces units were trapped in the museum, without supplies. Their helicopter squadrons had been savagely depleted both over the ocean and in the air above northern Taiwan. Attempts to air-drop food into the museum grounds had been met with vicious rocket, shell and missile fire from regrouping Taiwanese antiaircraft battalions.

General administration of those who had been in battle was very poor. No one was being fed on a regular basis, personal equipment was often inadequate and almost all the logistics systems had fallen apart. Lines of combat resupply were crashing. Ammunition, fuel, lubricants, rations and water simply could not be brought in fast enough to keep up with the thousands of troops on the ground.

There was of course scope for the Chinese forces to requisition water and fuel supplies from local sources, even to scavenge food supplies, but this was a hostile area. Everyone was a sworn enemy, and it took a huge amount of time and effort just to stay alive and moving. Failure to bring forward munitions for armor, artillery, air defense and attack helicopters took another heavy toll.

Chinese progress was thus becoming fearfully slow, and the morale of the ground troops was beginning to suffer. By midday on this June morning the High Command, now meeting in Beijing, was being informed that the Taiwanese Army was again moving north, throwing pontoons across the rivers, heading back to defend their beloved Taipei. This was too much even to contemplate, another ferocious fight through city blocks, having to fight around every corner, not knowing what lay ahead, around any corner.

Admiral Zhang Yushu knew about warfare in all its facets, but specialized street combat in a foreign capital, against a reinforced enemy, was too much even for him. But, wily old warrior that he was, he came up with the only solution there was: He decided their best strategy was to stretch the limits of the remaining Taiwanese resources, and at 1300 on that Monday afternoon, he ordered the Chinese Navy to open up another front in the south, with immediate effect.

More particularly, he ordered a Naval bombardment of the northern beaches of Taiwan's banana-belt city of Tainan, followed by a second full-scale amphibious assault at Luerhmen. In Zhang's opinion, this would surely stop the headlong rush north of the Taiwanese Army.

And Luerhmen had precisely the correct historic credentials to attract a strategist of Zhang's abilities, with his curious mixture of grim reality and flights of *folie de grandeur*.

Luerhmen, a beachfront suburb of Tainan, was where the great Koxinga had landed 400 war junks, containing the 35,000-strong Ming Dynasty Army, and hurled the ruling Dutch out of their Tainan stronghold in 1661.

As far as Zhang was concerned, the ruling Taiwanese were at least as alien as the Dutch, and the vibes about the old provincial capital were all good. And he turned the full might of his Navy against the southwestern city, sending in his second Sovremenny destroyer with three frigates, to soften up the area for the forthcoming landing the next day.

His principal mistake was miscalculating the strength of the Taiwanese Air Force at the Naval air base outside Kaohsiung. They still had 19 F-16As and they had repaired the long-range radar facility on the outskirts of the base. At first light on the morning of Tuesday, June 5, they picked up China's Sovremenny, cruising six miles off Tainan, making a racetrack pattern in a light-quartering sea.

Admiral Feng-Shiang Hu, C-in-C of the Taiwanese Navy, was on duty himself, pacing the ops room, still determined to fight off the marauders from across the strait. He instantly dispatched a flight of five of his F-16s, the ferocious little single-seaters, converted now to carry a 500-pound bomb under each wing instead of their usual Sidewinder missiles.

They took off overland at 0620, swung out south of the island and made a long right-hand loop over the strait, coming in from out of the west, 50 miles off the Taiwan coast at 600 knots, wave-top height, in a formation of three, and then two, dead astern. The 8,000-ton Sovremenny destroyer was silhouetted against the rose-colored eastern sky, and her ops room acquired at 0628. The missile director's fingers flew over the keyboard, sending up four SA-N-7 Gadfly weapons into the launchers.

But the CO of the Sovremenny was devoid of real-time battle experience, and he spoke swiftly to his accompanying frigate, which had also picked up the incoming Taiwanese fighter-bombers. They conferred briefly, and the destroyer captain ordered his ship to make a hard turn to port in order to reduce his radar echo signature to the incoming bombers. In a grotesque, elementary error he offered them the knife edge of his narrow bow, instead of the broad beam of his ship.

Temporarily the radar control operator lost the F-16s altogether when they ducked down below the radar, but at 27 miles they "popped up" again, and the Sovremenny instantly acquired, the operator calling, his voice rising:

"... Track one-zero-four-eight ... incoming six hundred knots ... bearing two-seven-zero ... range twenty-five ..."

Higher now above the waves, the Taiwanese pilots heard the Sovremenny's radar locking on, squealing on their radar warning receivers, but they pressed on grimly toward the Sovremenny. Streaking in over the water, making 10 miles a minute, a mile every six seconds, the three leaders aimed their aircraft straight at the huge Chinese warship.

They spotted it eight miles out and lined themselves up only just in time. Then they unleashed all six of their bombs in a dead line at the bow of the ship, the one nonvariant, the one computer calulation that could not significantly change.

The machines were fighting the engagement, but it was men who were directing it. The Chinese missile director, in the same split second, launched the Gadflies, which blasted into the air even as the bombs flashed across the waves propelled by the colossal speed of the aircraft.

The F-16s tried to bank away, but the one on the left took the missile head-on and blew up in a fireball. The center bomber was also hit right behind the wing and exploded as it made its turn, both pilots dying instantly.

The third and fourth missiles both missed, and now the bombs were screaming in, bouncing like flat pebbles hurled across the water. The first one smacked into the waves and leaped high over the destroyer's bow. Had it been the beam, it might have cleared the ship and gone right by, but it was not the beam. It was the bow, and the bomb slammed off the water, shrieked over the foredeck and smashed straight through the bridge windows and down deep into the hull before it exploded.

The next bomb came in a fraction of a second later, again clearing the bow in a high arc and down through the middle of the superstructure, wrecking the ops room, the communications room and every missile-control system on board. The third bomb cannoned into the water, 30 yards off the bow, and slammed into the hull, just aft, crashed through the plates on an upward trajectory and removed a large slice of the foredeck of the ship.

But it was bomb four that did the real damage, albeit entirely accidentally. This one, dropped from beneath the wing of the escaping F-16 out on the right, crashed into a rising wave 100 yards in front of the Sovremenny, deflected left, and rose high, 150 feet into the air. It screamed down into the aft area behind the main superstructure, its descent so steep it slammed straight through the deck, into the engine room, and detonated with a shattering blast, close enough to the keel to blow the bottom out of the ship.

The Sovremenny, listing sharply to port, capsized within three minutes, and, 10 minutes later, sank with all hands to the bottom of the strait.

The two Taiwanese backup bombers, running in four miles astern, were not acquired by the stricken Sovremenny, and they raced past the already burning warship and banked hard left, straight to the frigate that was supposed to be riding shotgun for the bigger ship, but had made no move to fire her missiles.

The ops room of the frigate, distracted by the carnage on the destroyer, finally launched her shorter-range missiles. But it was too late. One malfunctioned, and the other blasted off way after the F-16s had launched their four weapons and turned away.

Nonetheless the CO was well trained, and he offered the incoming bombs the beam of his ship, as indeed the destroyer should have done. The first one flew harmlessly overhead; the second one flew almost harmlessly but smashed the mast and radar equipment as it came through. The third one came in low, crashed through the hull and went straight out the other side, demolishing almost the entire central deck area.

The fourth bomb detonated in the water before it reached the ship, and miraculously no one was killed, though two sailors were wounded, mostly by bomb splinters. Equally miraculously, the frigate was still floating; crippled, largely useless, but still floating. Generally speaking, Admiral Feng-Shiang considered it a very good hour's work by the Taiwan Navy fliers, since it was not yet time for breakfast. But one of the downed pilots was his nephew, age only 20, and it was 15 minutes before he could bring himself to face his senior commanders.

Admiral Zhang was furious. The sheer numbers of the bombs that had hit his Russian-built ship meant that plainly there had been a monumental mistake. And Zhang Yushu had been in the Navy sufficiently long to believe the most common mistake by Naval commanders in all of modern warfare: the realization that any bomb, hurled forward at low level by an aircraft making over 600 knots, hardly *drops* at all. It is flung forward with enormous force, and when it finally catches a wave, it slows right down, then ricochets upward, maybe 80 feet, and onward. Still on line, but high.

In Zhang's view, to stay alive in the path of this ship killer, you should offer your beam, which will afford a fair chance of the lethal bouncing bomb whizzing over the top, since the deck is only about 50 feet wide. Offer your bow, especially on a ship as large as the Sovremenny, and you present a target the entire length of the ship, 500 feet from bow to stern, 10 times more surface area than its width: a 1,000 percent greater chance of being hit and sunk.

Admiral Zhang knew the overriding temptation to turn bow-on, presenting a target so narrow it must be safer. But he remained convinced of his theory, since the incoming bomb's line trajectory is pinpoint accurate to about three inches. Zhang's Law on Bombing said, the only issue is the *length* of the target, not the width.

And now his commanding officer had paid for his error not only with his life, but also with the lives of his ship's company. Not to mention the $500 million ship itself.

"What a complete and utter . . . ," ranted the Admiral, employing a Chinese colloquialism normally heard on the lower decks of his ships, rather than in the offices of the military's highest command in Beijing.

He simply could not believe the price he was paying for the rebel island of Taiwan. He could not believe the manpower, the death rate, the number of lost ships, the near-destruction of dozens of his aircraft. And now the great destroyer.

Zhang Yushu was going to end this war. And he was going to end it fast. *If this goes on, the damned U.S. Navy will get here, and then there'll be all hell to pay. I cannot allow this to go on. We have to move, and move big.*

Meanwhile, the airborne troops were piling out of the transporters high above the drop zone, three miles northwest of Tainan airport, and the Taiwanese Army was awaiting them on the ground, raking the landing fields with a steel wall of ordnance. All attacking armies, down the centuries, have sustained far greater losses than the defensive forces. But this was getting right out of hand. It took a succession of air strikes, sustained for more than two hours, finally to clear the Taiwanese Army out of the area.

Wind speed for the airborne landings was around 15 knots, and there were heavy Chinese casualties because wounded men were being blown off course from the central area. The commander on the ground had set up his "hospital section" way upwind, and several troops became involved in bringing the wounded in for emergency treatment. Eventually they would be transported on for evacuation, to the airport, which was of course China's immediate objective.

The opening assault force was late reaching the airport. It was broad daylight now, and due to a total failure of communications—as usual, Taiwan's weakest link—the Chinese, by some miracle, achieved an element of surprise. They stormed the perimeter fence and swarmed onto the runways, capturing entire sections of the complex.

They moved 2,000 troops into the roads surrounding the airport, securing the area. They dug in and established their portable low-level air-defense weapons, principally the QW-1 surface-to-air missile. They blasted their way into the control tower and occupied it. They also secured the fuel farm, and commandeered a vast supply of gasoline and jet aviation fuel. They seized every airport vehicle and sent a task force back to the drop zone to evacuate the wounded paratroopers.

By midday Tainan Airport was in Chinese hands, their first major airhead on the island. Within a half hour, massive troop reinforcements and equipment began to fly in. Almost two complete divisions were on the ground by 1400, and they were accompanied by 30 attack helicopters, checked, refueled and armed, ready for the assault, first on Tainan, and then on to the great Taiwanese port of Kaohsiung.

By this time, a division of Marines was attempting to land on the beaches at Luerhmen, and scores of landing craft, protected by warships from China's East Sea Fleet, were driving forward into the shallows, only to be met by a strong, well-disciplined force of Taiwanese militia.

Again the Chinese commanders on the landing beach had little option but to fight, and the two forces met on the main road at Tucheng. The early advantage went to the home troops, and they mowed down the invaders, firing at will from rural positions more in tune with guerrilla warfare than a formal confrontation of twenty-first-century armies.

With hundreds more troops pouring onto the beaches, the Chinese began to crash forward in a major breakout early in the afternoon. They left more than 500 dead on the field, but the remnants of the Taiwanese militia, bombarded now by Chinese mortars and howitzers, were forced to retreat, and the newly landed

Marines kept moving up, marching on toward the airport to join the massed divisions of the Army, which would surely now capture the southern part of the island.

Meanwhile, back in Beijing, Admiral Zhang Yushu stared in dismay at the reports coming in from the front. He could see there had been a long delay in the attack on the airport; he could read the reports of more heavy casualties, and what seemed like carnage both in the drop zone and on the Luerhmen beaches. He weighed all this against the crushing loss of the Sovremenny. And, with fury in his heart, he ordered a total abandonment of the new beachhead at Tainan and instructed his commanders to maximize the airhead at Tainan airport. He also demanded to know the precise position around the city of Taipei.

And from here, things almost went into slow motion. Again, on the outskirts of Tainan, the Taiwanese fought heroically. China's huge army was stopped dead, just as it had been on the outskirts of Keelung. And again there was bitter fighting, block by block, street by street, as houses, shops and industrial buildings were systematically cleared. But there was a huge price to pay, both in manpower and a colossal expenditure of ammunition

Simultaneously, in the north, the Chinese Army had reached the outskirts of Taipei, and they too ran into a fight that would drain their limited resources. Casualties were appalling. The Chinese lost more than 1,000 men in the first two hours.

The Chinese commander on the ground was in satellite contact with Beijing, and Admiral Zhang himself decided that if he had to knock down Taipei in order to subdue the island, then so be it. He ordered his senior battle commanders to take drastic measures, whatever it took to reduce the level of casualties. As things stood, the invading Chinese would need to capture and control the National Taiwan University Hospital in Taipei, and certainly the Chengkung University Hospital in Tainan.

And so China began to send in an armada of Z-9W Dauphin attack helicopters, heavily armed with antitank missiles. These 140-knot monsters cruise at 15,000 feet, and with the airhead established at Tainan Airport, and the main airport outside Taipei now under Chinese control, they were free to clatter over the strait, land and refuel and await deployment.

That happened late in the afternoon. The Dauphins took off and swooped into the western approaches to Taipei. They came in low over the Tamsiu River, through sporadic antiaircraft fire, and slammed four missiles straight through the granite outer wall of the Presidential Building on the corner of the Paoching Road. They hit the Armed Forces Cultural Center, almost blew apart the Tower Record Building and for good measure banged a missile into the great Chiang Kai-shek Memorial Hall. That killed eight people but failed to put a dent in the giant white statue of the departed father of the Taiwanese nation.

This was the first attack on the city, and members of Taiwan's ruling party were petrified, because from where they stood among the crushed masonry and collapsing ceilings in the Presidential Building, it seemed as if China had reluctantly decided to knock down the entire capital.

And things seemed even worse far to the south in Tainan, where again, the Chinese Navy's Dauphin choppers came in hard and sudden, firing their big missiles at will. They slammed the biggest religious temple in east Asia, the Shengmu, flattened the police station, blew up the Department of Motor Vehicles. Knocked down an outside wall of the biggest department store in the city.

And right behind this apparently indiscriminate air attack, the Chinese sent in their hard-trained Marine and airborne forces. In both cities, they moved forward tactically, behind the air attack. The remainder of the Taiwanese forces began to melt away, some throwing down their weapons. Civilians fled the central areas by the thousands, women and children picking their way through the rubble, accompanied by local soldiers who had discarded their uniform jackets.

The Chinese Army kept coming, but there was a subtle change taking place. The massed soldiers and Marines of Admiral Zhang's military had no stomach for killing civilians, especially Chinese civilians, which the Taiwanese still plainly were. And the commanders on the ground knew it. The Army marched on to the entrance to the Presidential Building near the Peace Park, and blew open the locked main doors with three hand grenades. The guards fled, and six minutes later the President of Taiwan, in company with eight of his senior ministers, sued for peace.

They came out with their hands high, and were greeted with immense respect by their conquerors. The leaders of both sides went formally to the high cabinet room, and the national televison station was summoned to hear their government command the Army, Navy and Air Force of Taiwan to lay down their arms and surrender.

Communication lines were immediately opened up to Beijing, and Admiral Zhang, with his senior commanders, announced they would land at Chiang Kai-shek Airport at 1030 the following morning, to agree to the terms of surrender.

Thus, shortly before 6 P.M. on the afternoon of Tuesday, June 5, 2007, the independent Republic of China, known internationally as Taiwan, returned to the rule of the "other China," the Peoples' Republic, the communist successors to Chairman Mao Zedong. It was the ultimate horror, the endless dread of the peace-loving, profit-worshiping populace of the defiant little island across the strait. And thanks to the guile of the smiling Admiral Zhang Yushu, Taiwan's mighty friends in Washington had been powerless to raise a finger to save them.

Which left Admiral Morgan in his dressing gown, sitting in the book-lined study in Kathy's house in Maryland at 6 A.M., watching the news, sipping black coffee, with buckshot, in a mood that hovered somewhere between disbelief and rank poison.

"Just so long as they don't think for one moment they're going to get away with this," he growled. "They got the island. Needless to say they got the museum, which was why they went to war in the first place. And there's not a damn thing we can do about any of it, short of going to war ourselves. But there's a lot of ways to skin a cat, and we're gonna make those little bastards regret the day they decided to fuck around with Uncle Sam."

"Sorry, darling, lay that on me again, will you?" Kathy O'Brien had slipped into the study bearing orange juice and hot croissants with preserves.

The Admiral's eyes were still glued to the screen, but he was hungry, having been there, on and off, all night. He said nothing but reached out absentmindedly for one of the croissants, and he let out a yell, it was so hot.

"Jesus Christ!" he cried, adopting one of his favorite mock-wounded expressions. "What the hell is that? A pastry grenade?"

Kathy was wearing a dark green silk robe, and she laughed as ever at the speed with which Arnold Morgan could coin original material.

He turned toward her, smiling in appreciation of the woman he loved. "I shouldn't think this burn's worse than second degree," he said pompously, shaking both his head and his right hand. "I shall require ice, cold water, towels and the home number of my lawyer. You did keep your insurance premiums up? I do hope so."

"You should of course have been on the stage rather than wasting your time trying to eliminate Red China," said Kathy, expertly cleaving the croissant sideways with a serrated knife and spreading it with butter and strawberry jam. "Here, take this," she added, offering the plate.

"Well, why the hell didn't the damn thing burn you?" he demanded.

"Probably because I didn't clamp my hand around the hottest part on top," she replied. "Heat tends to rise, you know."

Arnold then firmly informed her that as the former master of a large nuclear reactor on a U.S. Navy attack submarine, he was acquainted with the rudiments of physics, even if he had temporarily forgotten the heat-retentive properties of the common croissant.

She poured him some cold orange juice, and advised him to take the greatest care with the glass since he would probably get frostbite. But Arnold was no longer listening.

"Jesus, Kathy, will you look at that?"

She turned to the screen where the giant U.S. aircraft carrier

John F. Kennedy could be seen listing slightly to starboard and moving slowly through the water.

"The accident on board the *JFK* happened two weeks ago in Japanese waters," the newscaster reported. "These dramatic pictures show her making under ten knots, limping toward the U.S. base at Okinawa. They were taken by our associate station in the western Pacific region, and according to our sources they caught the *JFK* forty-seven miles south of the American base.

"The U.S. Navy has denied our request to put a camera team on board for the final miles of the journey, and they have denied us all requests for an interview to explain precisely what happened. Last night the Navy was showing no signs of any intention to clear up the mystery of what happened out there west of the Ishigaki Islands on the night of May twenty-second."

Admiral Morgan ate his croissant thoughtfully. Like the Navy, he was of course keenly aware of what had happened. Two Chinese torpedoes, fired from one single Kilo-Class submarine, had crippled the 88,000-tonner. Which made her the fifth Battle Group leader to become unavailable for the protection of Taiwan. Counting the *Ronald Reagan* Group, still in San Diego, *Big John* was actually the sixth.

"Maybe it was for the best," offered Kathy. "Maybe Taiwan is ultimately better off as a part of mainland China. And maybe the carrier would have been drawn into a real shooting war if she'd been in her regular patrol area. And there might have been God knows how many dead, and we could have been sucked right into a long conflict."

"Wrong," replied Arnold, uncharmingly.

"What do you mean, 'wrong'? You're not always right about absolutely everything."

"Wrong again," replied Arnold, even more uncharmingly.

Kathy poured them both some more coffee and awaited the short, bludgeoning lecture she knew was on its way.

"Katherine," he said, "a mighty navy, with nuclear weapons and a strike force of devastating guided missiles, has nothing to do with inflicting defeat and destruction upon another nation. It has to do with prevention. An all-powerful nation like ourselves has one useful purpose, and that's to frighten the life out of anyone who might step out of line.

"That's why this world is mostly at peace. By that I mean there has been no global conflict for years and years. It's *Pax Americana*, as I have often explained. Peace on our terms. If the *JFK* had been on patrol, with its full air force operational at the north end of the Taiwan Strait, China would not have attacked. They would not have dared, because we have the capacity to eliminate their ships, their aircraft, their Army, their military bases, their Naval bases, their goddamned cities, if you like, anytime we feel like it.

"They attacked Taiwan because we were not there to scare 'em off. As we know, to our cost, they made damn sure we were not there. But it would not have happened if we had been."

"Well, I suppose not. But I still have never understood why the carrier was so far out of its operational area, and how the Chinese were somehow lying in wait. I know that's what you think. But I don't really get it. It was almost as if they *lured* the *JFK* into that bay. That's what the media should be trying to find out."

"The media are probably going to find out that the carrier was hit. But I agree, it's a real puzzle why the carrier was so far out of its area. I look forward to reading Admiral Holt's preliminary report next week. So do a lot of other people."

061600JUN07. USS *Shark*. Bay of Bengal.
15.53N 93.35E.
Speed 15. Depth 100. Course 084.

The aging black hull of the 5,000-ton Sturgeon-Class submarine moved slowly through the warm blue depths of the eastern Indian Ocean. She was just about at the end of her 2,000-mile journey from Diego Garcia, and she moved to the northeast, about 30 miles short of the great shelving Juanita Shoal, where the ocean floor suddenly rises up from 3,000 feet to 120 feet, to form a massive, almost sheer, underwater mountain wall of rock, shale and sand.

Lieutenant Pearson, watching the chart, in constant communication with sonar officer Lt. Commander Josh Gandy, would order *Shark* well south of that particular hazard, while they made their way east to the rendezvous point at 16.00N, 94.01E, twelve miles off the coast of Burma.

Lieutenant Commander Headley, now in sole control of the insertion of the SEALs, deliberately ordered their speed cut to 12 knots, which would put them on station at the RV point at 1800, approximately two hours before dark.

For the past four days they had steamed steadily, submerged all the way through the near-bottomless waters that surround the southern shores of the Indian subcontinent. It had been the busiest underwater journey Dan Headley could ever remember, with frequent satellite communications, while Fort Meade and the Pentagon battled for information about the Chinese base on Haing Gyi Island.

Lieutenant Shawn Pearson, like many navigators, was an excellent draftsman, and he provided immeasurable assistance to the SEAL commander, making detailed scale drawings of China's newest Naval complex. By the third day, they had it pretty well nailed down. They had located a tough-looking chain-link fence that guarded the southern border of the dockyard. They also had located a guardhouse on the southern perimeter.

But as far as they could see, the fence ended abruptly at some dense woodland that protected the northwestern perimeter of the dockyard from the most treacherous-looking marshland area where the Letpan Stream splits and forms two wide channels. Each one runs straight through the swamp and out into the unnavigable Haing Gyi Shoal, which provides only four feet of water in some places at low tide.

The new satellite pictures being beamed into the submarine were grainy and of very moderate quality, but Lt. Pearson's sharp pencil drew hard, accurate lines through the chart of the swamp. And *Shark* was just about at her halfway point on her journey from Diego Garcia when Commander Rick Hunter had seen for the first time an excellent way out for his team.

"We bolt through these woods at the back of the dockyard," he'd told them, "until we reach the swamp, right here. According to Shawn's map, that gives us a run of thirteen hundred yards, at which point we're only a hundred yards from this deep tidal stream, and that's where the guys are gonna be with the inflatables."

"Christ, sir," said Catfish. "You sure there's enough water in there to get the boats running?"

"Shawn says yes," replied the Commander. "According to his chart there're one-point-three meters of water at dead low tide. For the truly ignorant that's about four feet, and the boats draw less than a foot when they're running."

"They draw more than that when they're stationary," said Catfish. "Those big engines drop down around two feet, more as she starts to come bow up."

"Catfish, baby," said Rick. "There are guys in this submarine who can make those inflatables talk. They raise the engines, skid 'em along the surface, and then slowly drop 'em down, and whip 'em up on the stump, no sweat. Don't worry about it. Those boats will get us out. I've just never been sure where to bring 'em in. But I am now."

"Aye, sir," said Catfish. "And I agree it's a damn good spot, right around the back of the island. It's got to be deserted. Shawn says he can't find even a track from the pictures."

"It's probably full of fucking cobras, and creepy crawlies and Christ knows what else," said Rattlesnake Davies.

"Well, thank God you're gonna be with us," said Buster Townsend. "You can do your jungle thing, blow the heads off a few pythons and stuff."

"Seriously, guys. We're in good shape for a run through country like that," said Rick. "We'll be in our wet suits and black trainers. We'll have our gloves on, carrying just flippers clipped to our belts. We'll have no heavy baggage, because the explosives will be gone and we'll leave the Draegers behind. They weigh thirty pounds, and we don't need 'em if we're going back on the surface. Speed's everything. And we'll have our knives, machine guns and ammunition. Soon as we're done, we'll pull up our hoods and get going."

"You worried about that one hundred yards of green marked swamp before the channel, sir?"

"Hell, no. It's tidal there so there'll be thick grass and probably rushes; we'll run straight through it, but the guys in the boats are going to be less than one hundred yards away, and they'll have ropes to help us if we need 'em. Plus, of course, the spare Draegers we brought in case we have to go over the side. We'll get there. Don't worry."

"When's high tide?" asked Dallas MacPherson.

"Right here on your chart," said Shawn. "I've marked it zero-three-three-zero. The water should still be rising when you get to the water's edge. That's if your timing stays the same. You make your shore landing before midnight, after the warship operation. Then you have a three-hour shore mission, and a half hour to reach the embarkation point at zero-three-three-zero. That's correct, isn't it?"

"If there's a real chance of that fucking steam well going up," said Dallas, "I'm likely to break the Burmese all-comers record down to that swamp. I'll probably be there at about zero-three-zero-one."

All the SEAL meetings were like this, informal but completely relevant in every aspect. Each man was free to offer any opinion, or ask any question. Then, when the mission was under way, every man knew not only what he was going to do; he knew precisely what everyone else was going to do as well.

Commander Reid had allocated a section of the submarine for the SEAL team to meet and it turned into a kind of locker room, a place where the leader lectured the guys, pored over the charts, discussed the mission, perfected the split-second timing that would spell success or failure.

For the first two days of the journey from Diego Garcia, the problems were academic, but as the voyage wore on, there was a strange, underlying tension right below the surface. Everyone could feel it, particularly Lt. Commander Dan Headley and his old buddy Commander Rick Hunter.

And everyone knew it all traced back to the night of May 16, out in the Strait of Hormuz when *Shark*'s commanding officer had refused permission for the ship to move in toward the ASDV and evacuate the SEAL team, with their dead leader and dying explosives expert. And then Charlie Mitchell had died before he could receive help, and every single member of the big group from Coronado believed that Commander Reid had personally signed the young SEAL's death warrant. Commander Rusty Bennett, mission chief of the team that went into Iran, was extremely angry and felt that the entire tragic incident should be taken to the highest possible authority.

He and Commander Hunter had spent much time on it when Assault Team One finally returned to DG. And Lt. Commander Headley was more worried than either of them, because he had made the decision to save the SEALs at all cost and been overruled by his own CO. Dan Headley was unused to being overruled. Indeed he had been informed that this appointment as Executive Officer on the Sturgeon-class ship was because of an unspoken concern about the mind-set of the Captain.

Both the SEAL leaders and the XO felt they could not count on the CO to make the right decision if the combat troops came under serious threat. It was always possible that a fast unorthodox rescue might be required, and no one believed they would receive the correct degree of support from the Captain.

Reid had delegated all details of the insertion to Lieutenant Commander Headley, cautioning him only about hazarding the submarine. Any deviation from the strict, agreed orders of position and timing would almost certainly be met by a rigid adherence to the rules by the CO. The XO had seen it, and he was extremely concerned. Rick Hunter, briefed by Rusty Bennett before he left by air for Coronado, was making a conscious effort not to let it play on his mind.

"Danny," he said, "I'm trying to get my mind straight. I'm trying to lead these guys in to accomplish an unbelievably difficult objective. I cannot allow the possible conduct of this nutcase CO to occupy my thoughts. It'll get in the way of the real stuff. I just haven't the time."

But then, two nights previously, an incident had taken place that had truly unnerved Dan Headley, and the only colleague he had confided in was Rick Hunter.

It had started a half hour before the Captain's normal appearance in the control room around 2000. He had asked the XO to come to his office/cabin to confirm their ETA at the rendezvous point off Burma. Entering the room, Dan had been quite startled to find it lit by just a single candle, in a holder on the table.

"Hello, sir," he had said cheerfully. "Bit dark in here, isn't it?"

The Captain's reply had been, in Dan's view, pretty weird. "XO," he had said, "sometimes I feel the need for some spiritual guidance. And I am usually able to find it in communication with a fellow traveler."

Dan Headley had looked quizzical. But the CO had not wanted to elaborate, and the number-two officer on USS *Shark* did not feel like pressing the matter further. He returned to the control room and gathered up his partially completed plans for the insertion, and decided to take them down for Commander Reid to peruse for a few minutes before moving up for his watch.

But when he arrived outside the CO's room, the door had been slightly open, and he could not help but hear the voice of the ship's boss talking inside to someone. But the stilted quality of the language was most unusual.

"Gregory, I am trying to reach you again. I feel you very close but someone stands between us . . . I think an American officer . . . please tell him to go, Gregory. Then we can communicate as we did before . . . Captain Li Chin . . . I believe we must talk before I am forced to follow you . . . wheverever that may lead . . ."

Dan Headley did not know who was in the room with Commander Reid, and he was not absolutely certain of the words he had heard. He was pretty sure about Gregory, but there was no

Gregory aboard *Shark* as far as he knew, and if there had been, he would have been called Greg. Forget Gregory.

Still, maybe he was just on the line to someone. God knows who. But *Captain Li Chin*. What the hell was all that about? *Li Chin*, thought Dan Headley. *That's a fucking Chinaman!* For a brief moment he actually wondered if the CO of *Shark* was some kind of a spy, maybe in touch with an agent. But then he thought, *Steady, Dan, he can't be a spy. He's been a career Naval officer for thirty years, commanding nuclear submarines for ten. He's an oddball, no doubt about that. But he can't be a spy.*

At this point, he doubted whether he had heard the conversation correctly. He was dead sure of the Gregory name, but the more he pondered, the more he doubted the part about Captain Li Chin. Nonetheless, he had not felt much like making an embarrassing entry carrying the plans for the SEAL insertion, and he had tiptoed quietly away, back up to the control room. And there he had sat thoughtfully for at least 15 minutes, running over the conversation he had heard, and carefully committing it to his notebook, in the manner of a lifelong Naval officer, as if ensuring an accurate entry in the ship's log.

Lieutenant Commander Headley doubted his ability to solve all of the puzzle. But he was determined to take a look around that cabin of Reid's, and he waited until the CO came into the control room. After formally handing over the ship to the OOD, he said, "Oh, sir. Those insertion plans. I just had a couple of details to fill in . . . you're busy now, but I'll put 'em on the table in your cabin if you like . . . then you can take a look when you have a bit of time."

"Thank you, XO. That will be fine."

Dan Headley headed once more down to the CO's room, and pushed open the door. The desk light was already on, and the little portrait of Admiral Pierre de Villeneuve stared out across the small room. Dan put the plans on the desk and kept a ballpoint pen in his hand in case he was disturbed. There was a small bookshelf to the left of the Captain's chair, and Dan leaned over to inspect the half dozen volumes it contained.

There was a travelogue about the south of France, a biography of de Villeneuve, and an account of the Battle of the Chesapeake. A book called *The Stress of Battle and Trauma* stood next to the *Oxford Companion to Ships and the Sea.* There was also something called *Edgar Cayce on Reincarnation,* by Noel Langley. Dan picked this one up and glanced at the blank sheets inside the jacket. In pencil there were the following words: *Another life, another battle, so many mistakes in* Bucentaure. *I must never repeat them now that I have another chance. June 1980. DKR.*

Dan Headley frowned. He could not risk hanging around for long. Quickly he skipped through the pages of the volume on reincarnation, and then pulled out the Oxford companion. On instinct he flicked through alphabetically to page 883, which gave an account of de Villeneuve's highest/lowest moment: Trafalgar. And he ran his finger over the the French Fleet's line of battle . . . *here it is* . . . "Bucentaure, *the flagship* . . . *struck its colors*" . . . *Fuck me! This crazy prick I work for thinks he's the reincarnation of de Villeneuve, one of the worst battle commanders in Naval history.*

Dan Headley put the books back. He still had no clues to the identity of the mysterious Chinese Captain Li Chin. Nor indeed to "Gregory." He glanced down to the writing pad on Commander Reid's desk and could see only a small sketch of a submarine. Beside it was the name Lt. Commander Schaeffer. And through the name were two hard diagonal lines forming a cross, as if to eliminate the name of the late SEAL Team Leader.

Dan shook his head, and left, in a hurry. *Do I give a shit who he thinks he is? Does it matter? A lot of people believe in reincarnation, right? I just don't know how seriously people take this stuff. And it would be a lot better if he thought he was General MacArthur, or Admiral Nimitz, even Admiral Nelson. But de Villeneuve? Jesus. He's even got his picture on the wall, and the guy was a catastrophe. Do we have a real problem here?*

The XO made his way up to the wardroom, poured himself some coffee and sat alone in a corner seat, thinking. *What do I really know about the CO? Have I actually seen him make decisions of really momentously bad judgment?*

Dan thought some more, and decided that he had twice seen him make decisions that went absolutely by the book. Rigid. Unswerving adherence to the rules and regulations. The kind of adherence submarine commanders consistently ignored. The nature of the underwater beast means you have to be flexible. And everyone knew it. Holding hard to the rule book was okay on a peacetime surface ship. But it was often not okay on a combat submarine.

Do we have a problem here? Yes. I think we do. Because Commander Reid twice deliberately made an operation LESS successful when we plainly needed to make a change in our orders. He caused unnecessary battery-running time in the ASDV for the insertion into Iran. And he may have cost us the life of one of Rusty Bennett's best combat SEALs. He certainly refused to save that life. Two decisions. Two mistakes. Both important. We got a problem.

Lieutenant Commander Headley had no member of the crew in whom he could confide. It was simply unthinkable for a senior U.S. Navy executive officer to mention to a colleague, who must, by definition, be of a lower rank, that he, the Exec, considered their commanding officer had lost his marbles.

He also thought it was not anything he could bother Ricky with, since the SEAL commander was trying to prepare his team for the big push into the Chinese Navy base. *Oh, by the way, the officer in overall command of your only escape route is probably insane.* "Holy shit," breathed Dan Headley.

He contemplated the prospect of dinner. But he wasn't hungry, and he walked back to the area of the wardroom aft of the dining room table, where they kept a small library for officers and in fact for anyone of the crew who requested a book on a particular subject. *Shark*, like most U.S. Navy submarines, was a literary democracy.

Dan had no idea what he was looking for. What writings might shed light on a commanding officer who once, certainly in 1980, had believed he was the reincarnation of someone else? And anyway, did it matter? Dan himself had once read that General George Patton had believed himself to have been a major-league warrior in another life. And wasn't there some story that the General claimed to have known the precise spot where Caesar had pitched his tent when he arrived in Langes, France, to assume his first command?

Maybe it's not that bad, he thought. *Not that bad at all. However, I wouldn't give a shit if Reid thought he was Alexander the Great, or even Napoleon, but DE VILLENEUVE! I mean, Christ, that's beyond belief for a Navy officer.*

I used to be the the the world's worst battle commander, and from now on, I'm playing it dead safe, right by the book. And that's what I think we've got right here. Except this fucking nutter might be in cahoots with the Chinese.

The XO scanned the bookshelves until he reached the section on psychology, a complicated subject for men who command warships, and an increasing concern in the modern Navy. He stopped at a volume entitled *Post Traumatic Stress Disorder.*

"I suppose it's possible this character has adopted the kind of symptoms he believes de Villeneuve may have developed after Admiral Nelson took out twenty of his Fleet at Trafalgar. The most decisive sea battle ever fought. Maybe Commander Reid feels he is supposed to suffer the French Admiral's pain for him." *Steady, Headley, you're getting crazier than he is.*

He opened the book and paused at one of the earliest sections of the textbook formula—*The Effects of Having Survived a Frightening Traumatic Event.* The subhead read, "Armed Combat, Shell Shock, Battle Fatigue." It was fully 20 seconds before he realized the block of type had been pointed up with a yellow highlighting pen.

The next part was not highlighted, but it contained such lines as, "Reliving the painful memories, images and emotions, i.e., intense fear, horror, helplessness, as if it were happening. Recurring nightmares. Trying to erase the memories. Intense emotional stress in the face of events, present, future or even imagined, which may resemble any part of the traumatic event."

"Sudden emotional outbursts," the author wrote, "anger, fear or panic, may occur, for no apparent reason, as the person tries to avoid thinking or talking about the trauma that haunts him."

What exactly is this? some kind of damned conspiracy? Well, you've picked the wrong man to make a fool of . . . waiting until I'm asleep and then flagrantly disobeying my orders.

These were the words of Commander Reid, uttered in temper, without logic, without concern, and without reason. Dan Headley pictured that scene in the control room last month, as the SEALs tried to fight their way back from their mission.

Was it actually possible that their own CO, as he addressed them, was hearing not just the quiet hum of *Shark*'s turbines as she made her turn in the silence of the dark waters of the gulf? Was he actually hearing the crash and thunder of British cannon, as Nelson and Collingwood came in quite slowly, in a light quartering wind, hammering both the French and Spanish Fleets to a standstill? Two hundred years ago, the morning of October 21, 1805? Was that actually possible?

Lieutenant Commander Headley shook his head, skimmed the rest of the chapter, but every few moments phrases jumped right out at him—*avoiding responsibility, isolation, symptoms increasing with age, guilt feelings for the deaths of others.* "And through it all," the author wrote, "the person may still appear a strong and capable leader. Only those who serve closely with such a man can see the sudden moments of utterly illogical behavior, so often anger, or an obdurate adherence to the rule book, all to camouflage self-doubt." And for good measure, the author added that, in his view, real-life trauma was no different from imagined trauma in the mind of such a personality.

Dan Headley liked it less now than he had 10 minutes ago. There was a final section on military officers who believed themselves to have been commanders in past centuries. But it was not written in a sinister way. Indeed the author believed the association with long past greatness may have given certain men inspiration, even knowledge, into the conduct of a battle.

But Dan noted that the author did not go into any detail of a commanding officer who thought he had been a catastrophic, world-renowned failure in a past life, had committed suicide, and, in his own handwriting, believed he now had a chance to make amends by eliminating mistakes.

One thing he knew for absolute certain: He needed Rick Hunter, and he needed him right now. And he did not even finish his coffee. Dan stood up and set off down to the SEALs' locker room in search of his oldest friend. He knew the Commander was pretty good with the minds of fractious racehorses, and he hoped he could make the species jump, straight into the unbalanced psyche of a certain human being.

He located him at a good time. It was almost 2100, and the SEAL boss had been briefing his team for hours, poring over the new pictures of the Chinese base. When Dan Headley had come wandering into the conference area, aft of the control room, he had stood up and said, "Okay, guys. That's it. Go get food and rest. Lieutenant Commander Headley and I are about to solve the problem of the Belmont Stakes. Which horse stays one and a half miles? That's the key. Because most modern racehorses won't last out twelve furlongs in a horse box, never mind running. We come to any definitive conclusions, I'll let you know who to bet."

"No mistakes now, sir. We don't want any screwups, right?" called Lt. MacPherson.

Commander Hunter and the XO thus returned quietly to the wardroom, and asked the steward to bring them some dinner . . . "Coupla steaks, green vegatables and salad," said the SEAL.

"You eating them both?" asked Dan. "Or may I have one?"

"For your information, I no longer have the appetite I had at eighteen," replied Rick. "'Specially when I'm confined to this ship. No fresh air, no exercise, no physical activity except the communal set of weights we're all using to try to stay more or less ready to hit the Chinese."

"Okay, Ricky. But I came to find you on a matter of great concern."

"You did? What?"

"Well, I am assuming that you know the details of the altercation that took place in the control room of this ship when Rusty Bennett and I tried to take her inshore to save the badly wounded SEAL?"

"Doesn't everyone know the details? Even the staff in Diego Garcia have no other subject to discuss."

"They're probably correct, too. Because I think we have a major concern here."

"You mean he might make another foul-up like that?"

"I mean, I think it's inevitable he *will* make another foul-up like that."

"Why?"

"Because I think that right here we are dealing with a dangerously flawed personality."

"You do?"

"Yes. I do. That's why I need to talk with you." And for the next 20 minutes the XO shared with the SEAL team leader the evidence he had found that Commander Reid believed he was the reincarnation of the French Admiral Pierre de Villeneuve.

"Well, everyone in the Navy knows about Trafalgar and the disastrous command of the French Fleet, Dan. We all learned it at Annapolis. "Wasn't he some kind of a coward? . . . I forget the details."

"Ricky, this guy was terrified of Admiral Nelson. He spent most of 1805 trying to get away from him. Napoleon had him under threat of suspension if he didn't get his act together. Right before the battle, he ducked back into the port of Cadiz, trying to hide. And when he finally came out, he literally froze with fear.

"Nelson and Collingwood split the French line right near the flag. And the French ships took terrible broadsides from the Royal Navy. Admiral Nelson fell at 1315, and never really saw his sensational victory. De Villeneuve was merely taken prisoner after his ship surrendered."

Commander Rick Hunter nodded quietly. "And you mean our CO actually thinks he is de Villeneuve?"

"Yup. That's what he believes. I just showed you my note of what he wrote in the book . . . *So many mistakes in* Bucentaure ... *I must never repeat them now that I have another chance ...*"

"Well, maybe he won't," replied Rick Hunter.

"Shithead, you're not hearing me. I am saying that in his mind this guy is suffering from the trauma of what happened out there off the coast of Portugal in 1805. He believes he is responsible. The stress of the battle is in his mind, and he is exhibiting classic symptoms of that kind of behavior. I've just been reading about it. Trust me, it fits."

"Okay. It fits. But he doesn't do it all the time, does he?"

"Course not. They never do. Just sometimes, when events seem to be getting too big, or out of hand, or there is clear-and-present danger. Or everyone is watching him, willing him to make a major decision. That's when this kind of stress-damaged character can't cope. Because in his mind he hears again the thunder of a past war, and he is consumed with self-pity, and it gives him a feeling of superiority because he knows no one else is going through what he's going through. No one else understands the tragedy of a great Naval commander, which is why he feels free to shout and lay down the law in that self-righteous way.

"That's where it all came from, Rick. The words are like cast concrete in my mind ... *But, sir, we're just trying to conduct a mission of mercy for our own injured people.* And what did he reply? *What exactly is this? some kind of damned conspiracy ... well, you've picked the wrong man to make a fool of ...*"

"*Hmmmmm,*" said Rick Hunter. "And where we're going, he may have to make a few more major decisions before we're all a lot older."

"And that's not all."

Rick Hunter looked at his old friend, questioningly. And Dan told him of the conversation he had overheard in Commander Reid's cabin. He read over to him, verbatim, what he had written down about Gregory and Captain Li Chin.

"That makes no sense, does it?" asked the SEAL.

"Not to us, maybe, but it might for the CO."

"What are those names again? Gregory and Captain Li Chin?"

"Yup. That's exactly what I heard, or thought I heard."

"And you don't think there was anyone in there with him?"

"No. I do not. It's just that I never heard of anyone with either of those two names."

"Well. Let's try to piece them together. Say it all at once. How about Captain Gregory Leechin?"

"That's not right. He said LYchin."

"Okay. But you cannot be called Gregory Li Chin. Because that's a very American name, coupled with a Chinese one. And that would be very unusual. Gregory is a long name, and it sounds very definite. It's not like Ronnie or Tommy. You sometimes get Chinese people called that. I think you heard Gregory right, but I think you might have Li Chin wrong."

"I might have. But the CO did call him captain. I'm not wrong about that."

"Well, maybe he was talking to a guy who had trouble with the truth. Maybe he was Liar-chin...."

"You know, Ricky, that sounds really familiar to me. Liarchin. Do we know someone called Liarchin? Captain Gregory Liarchin. Someone maybe famous. Liarchin. That's got a real ring to it."

"You're right. Who the hell was Captain Liarchin?"

"Dunno. But it sure does sound familiar. How about Gregory...how about Gri-Gory like eastern European...how about Captain Gri-GORY Liarchin?"

"Tell you what . . . we need to hit the ship's library, conduct a quick search through recent Navy records . . . there's a good reference section."

"Someone down there will do it for us, I guess. I don't want the CO to see us down there."

"Haven't you got a buddy who'll do it quietly?"

"Yeah. The Navigator, Shawn Pearson, will get it done. I'm outta here, back in five minutes and don't eat my fucking steak."

The XO was back in a few minutes. "Shawn's going to have a look himself. I told him to fool with the spelling . . . Grigory Liarchin, or with a y, like Lyachin. Something foreign, right?"

"You got it. There's your steak, which, you will doubtless note, I did not eat."

The two officers settled into their dinner, trying not to speak too much about the submarine's CO. Occasionally a new officer came through the door, but no one stayed more than a few minutes. There must have been urgent vibes being given off by the XO and the SEAL Chief, because no one seemed interested in engaging them in conversation.

It was 25 minutes before Lt. Shawn Pearson came in bearing a sheet of paper. He handed it to Lt. Commander Dan Headley, who read the following four lines of type:

"*Captain Grigory Lyachin, commanding officer of Russia's 14,000-ton nuclear submarine* Kursk, *which sank with all hands in the Barents Sea, 60 miles north of Severomorsk, on Monday, August 14, 2000.*"

Dan Headley whistled softly through his teeth. "Jesus Christ," he breathed. And he silently handed the sheet of paper to Commander Hunter.

"I knew that name was familiar."

"Sure was. But do you realize what this means, Rick? Our CO thought he was talking to Captain Grigory Lyachin. He thought he was in communication with a guy who's been dead for almost seven years. I'm telling you. He was chatting away as we are now."

"If I'm reading this correctly, Danny, it's a lot worse than that."

"How do you mean?"

"What do Admiral de Villeneuve and Captain Lyachin have in common? They both presided over major Naval catastrophes. And that's what our CO identifies with. He thinks he *is* de Villeneuve, and he thinks he has something in common with the Russian submariner. I imagine he's been trying to talk with him for years."

"The way he was speaking, they're old buddies."

"Yeah," said Rick. "In his dreams."

"Well, do you think this has sinister connotations for us, and the people who work under his command?"

"Normally, I'd say, maybe not. A lot of people are spiritualists, trying to get in touch with people 'on the other side.' Doesn't make 'em necessarily crazy. And certainly not dangerous. I mean, there're institutes of learning for spiritualists all over the place. A lot of very clever people think there can be communication between the living and the dead. And who the hell are we to say there's not?"

"I know. But it's not just any old dead we're dealing with right here. We're dealing with a couple of guys who have suffered traumatic catastrophe. And my immediate boss, who is about to be charged with the execution of one of the most dangerous Special Forces insert-and-rescue missions ever mounted, *thinks* he's one of them, and wants to have a chat with the other.

"It's as if your bank manager thinks he jumped out of a high-rise window eighty years ago, in the crash of twenty-nine. And now he's desperate to get in touch with another suicidal bankrupt bank president before he invests all your money."

"Well, Danny, you always did have a way with words. But this time I don't like 'em much. But hell, what can we do? We can't just lay it on him. He'd have us both court-martialed for causing riot and unrest in the ship."

"I'd sure as hell rather that than have *him* court-martialed for causing everyone's death in the face of the enemy."

"I know. And you think this problem he has manifests itself when there's some form of pressure being exerted on him?"

"No doubt in my mind. I've seen it twice." And now Lt. Commander Headley spoke very slowly, very deliberately. "This, Ricky, is a guy I guarantee will fold up completely, if something goes wrong, or if we had to throw the rule book overboard and play a very bad situation by ear—you know, if we really had to wing it. Which is always possible in missions like this one coming up."

Those had been, virtually, the last words the two men had spoken on the distressing subject, because there really was nothing more for them to say. And they were both trained to say nothing about Naval operations unless it was absolutelty necessary. They finished their dinner in near silence.

That entire private investigation of the CO by the XO and the

338 ★ PATRICK ROBINSON

SEAL boss had taken place two nights previously, on Monday, June 4. And since then they had both tried to cast it to the back of their minds.

And now it was Wednesday, June 0, and the guys were going in, that night, in less than two hours. USS *Shark* came nosing up to her rendezvous point, with her cargo of SEALs making final preparations for the launch of the ASDV.

Commander Hunter had everyone ready. They were sitting in shorts and T-shirts only, but their faces were blackened with waterproof combat cream. The atmosphere was tight, as they checked over their wet suits and flippers, personal weapons and underwater breathing equipment. And they all listened to the monologue of Lt. Dallas MacPherson, as he checked the explosives list against the hardware.

He seemed to be wisecracking his way through it, as always. "One velly big bang right here, blow off many Chinese borrocks." But Dallas wasn't joking. He was coping—coping with the pressure the best way he could, steadying his nerves, fighting down the icy fear they all felt as they prepared to board the ASDV.

Every now and then, one of the younger SEALs reached out and just touched the shoulder of the man next to him, maybe ruffled his hair, punched him lightly on the arm.

It was a technique Commander Hunter had taught them— *Don't go quiet. Don't let it wash over you, or you'll get overwhelmed before you start. Stay in close communication with each other. Remember: In this outfit, we don't SEND anyone anywhere. We all go together.*

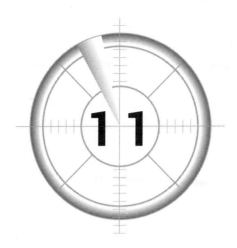

11

061830JUN07. USS *Shark*. Bay of Bengal.
16.00N 94.01E. Speed 2. Racetrack pattern. PD.

THIS WAS COMMANDER Rick Hunter's final briefing of his team. They had already gone over and over the details, infinitesimally, back and forth, every measurement, every millisecond of time, every piece of equipment, how much it weighed, where it would be stored in the ASDV, who would carry it in. They knew the point where they would breach the outer fence. It was too high to climb with the stuff. They would have to cut it.

They knew the precise yardage along the fence to the guardhouse, the precise distance, to the inch, up to the power station. They knew the timing of the guard changes, the location of the lights. They knew there was the likelihood of a bright moon; they knew the terrain, its firmness, its chances of being muddy. They knew the doors they must go through. And they knew the precise location of the massive main shaft down to the geothermal core. They also knew there was a probability of having to kill to survive.

And now the SEAL team leader was painting with a much broader brush. Each man had a small Navy chart in front of him, and a small, detailed scale map of the Chinese Naval complex. And each man was marking up both sheets, strictly as they applied to him, and the part he would play in the attack.

Each man had already completed his last will and testament, and a short letter home to either his wife or parents, in case he did not survive. All 12 of the wills were secured in one of the submarine's safes.

Rick Hunter stood before his team, and he looked much the way they did, but bigger—face blackened, wearing his wet suit, and black running shoes. A larger-scale Navy chart of the area was pinned to a board behind him and he was pointing with a ruler at the critical points of the mission, talking the SEALs through the timing ... "Okay, we leave here at seventeen hundred, proceeding to this point on your chart right off Thamihla island. That's a distance of fifteen miles, and it's going to take us two and a half hours. From there we expect to find the deepwater channel right here, and we head on up to this can with the flashing light, okay? We then move up here for four more miles to this buoy with the flasher, right at the start of the natural deepwater channel leading right into the base ... we'll see it easily. Now that's all clear, right?"

The SEALs all nodded in the affirmative, and Rick carried on. "At this point right here, a half mile off the jetties, we exit the ASDV, Catfish, Mike, Buster and myself. We carry in four sticky limpets and place them on the underside of the hulls of the two Chinese warships that are moored alongside ... there's a six-thousand-ton Luhai-Class destroyer right here in the photograph.

"It's five hundred feet long and fifty-four feet wide, twin shafts and a lot of guided missiles, and torpedoes. Right next to it is a much smaller ship, a two-thousand-ton Jangwei II frigate, only three hundred sixty feet long. But it's fast and it carries a lot of antisubmarine mortars. Gentlemen, I assure you it's in our best interests to get rid of it very thoroughly. Both these ships carry helicopters, and it would be nice to somehow have them tip into the harbor."

"Sir, I forgot to clarify. Are you guys getting back in the ASDV to go to our next stop? Or do we just meet up there?"

"No, we're getting back in. The insert wants to be in a much more lonely place, and it's too far back down the channel. We're hitchin' a ride."

Commander Hunter then confirmed the landing site, a point less than one mile south of the jetties, behind a half-mile-long navigational hazard marked on the chart as Wolf Rock. "We'll all get out right there, about five hundred yards offshore; one hundred fifty of those yards are marked as a marshy area with a lot of vegetation. We'll walk through there, and when we hit the beach we're gonna be only a half mile from the dockyard fence. It's gonna be dark, desolate and without military guards. The first place we meet people will be the guardhouse, and there're only two people in it—one engineer and one Navy patrol guard. That's all. You know what to do."

From that point on, Commander Hunter talked quickly through the well-documented plan. Everyone knew it by heart. This was just a brief refresher before departure, one final look at the campaign map. One final look, perhaps, into the face of death. They were frightened, as Special Forces must always be a little frightened. But no one flinched.

At 1855 the SEALs began to embark the ASDV, climbing up through *Shark*'s dry hatch, into the minisubmarine itself, which rested in one of the round, twin deck shelters up on the casing. Right now it was dry in there, and as each SEAL entered the tiny electric underwater craft, he checked the precise location of the gear he would personally carry in.

Lieutenant Dave Mills was already at the controls, seated next to his sonar operator/navigator, Lt. Matt Longo, upon whose brain would fall the task of locating the secret Chinese channel into the harbor. And one by one the SEALs moved into position, the five rookies from Coronado, then the veteran combat SEALs Catfish,

Bobby, Rattlesnake, Buster, and Chief Petty Officer Mike Hook, followed by Lt. MacPherson who slipped expertly up through the gap, and took his place next to Bobby Allensworth.

Last of all came Commander Rick Hunter, who was talking to Dan Headley in the small area below the dry hatch.

"Guess this is it, ole buddy," said the huge SEAL leader. "Don't forget your promise. You're gonna get us out of there no matter what."

"We'll get you out. The boats are coming in to RV Two one hour before you need them. They'll be transmitting every thirty seconds as from zero-two-four-five. Two single beeps right on your frequency . . . Good luck, Ricky . . . it's gonna be fine . . . but for Christ's sake, be careful."

They shook hands, formally, unsmiling; nodded curtly one to the other, and then parted. Lieutenant Commander Headley going back to the control room. The SEAL chief climbing up into the little submarine.

Immediately the hatches were closed tight and clipped. And Rick Hunter's team all heard the sudden rush of water as the departure crew outside flooded down the shelter. They could hear the metallic thuds in the water beyond the hull as the ASDV came free of its steel lines. Six hefty frogmen began to heave it forward on its tracks, away from the mother ship. They waited for 10 minutes, riding free in the water, for the deck shelter to close, and for the outside crew to rejoin the *Shark*.

Then they saw Lt. Mills switch on the electric motor, and the ASDV swung right, onto its course one-two-zero, creeping now at its maximum speed of six knots toward the tiny Burmese island of Thamihla, and the deep-water channel they hoped to God they would find. Because if they did not find it, they knew they would have to postpone, until someone did find it, because these orders came from On High. Really High. And most of the SEALs preferred to get this thing done right now.

Inside the ASDV it was dry, but as they traveled it grew colder. There was no heat in this vehicle, but the SEALs were warm in their superbly insulated Navy wet suits. They could talk if they wished, but water magnifies all sound, and SEALs are trained to say nothing unnecessary on a combat mission. Thus there was hardly a word spoken for the first two hours. Not since Lt. MacPherson had mentioned, as they flooded down the shelter, that he usually charged a lot of money for his "world-famous imitation of a fucking goldfish."

All journeys in an ASDV seem to take forever. They travel blind, instruments only, and the passengers can see nothing. The submarine is dark, except for the light cast from the orange-colored screens on the control panels, and that left each of these highly trained assault troops with nothing to do except think about their tasks on this night.

Sometimes it was possible to see a couple of particular friends, like Bobby and Mike Hook, catch each other's eye, and perhaps smile. But it signified only that they were aware of the other's thoughts, and the colossal dangers they were facing, and the possibility that one of them, or perhaps even both, might not make it back. SEALs only think such private thoughts. They never say them.

And so the little submarine pressed on forward, 40 feet below the surface all the way. After two hours and 15 minutes they slid up to PD, and Dave Mills sent up the mast. Seven seconds later they went back down to 25 feet, and Matt Longo said quietly, "We're getting into the area, guys. I got us at fifteen fifty-one north and ninety-four fifteen east on GPS. Right now I'm searching for the channel."

All the SEALs knew now precisely where they were. Hours of study had committed that chart indelibly to their memories. They were in only 36 feet of water, but they were headed for a shoal over which there were only 15 feet in some places, which would put them damn close either to the surface or on the bottom.

Everyone, involuntarily, held their breath as Lt. Mills eased the ASDV along the southern edge of the shoal. They could hear the tiny click of the sounder, testing the seabed.

Lieutenant Longo's monologue never stopped. . . . *"We got twelve feet below the keel . . . make that ten . . . steady at ten . . . looks like we got it first time. We need a course of zero-eight-zero."*

Lieutenant Mills: *"Zero-eight-zero it is."*

Longo: *"Sir, this must be the channel. Suggest we speed up a touch . . . sounding still steady at ten."*

Five minutes and 300 yards later the ASDV was in 50 feet of water, right in the trench northwest of Thamihla. The Chinese had dredged precisely where the engineers in Coronado had said they would. And Dave Mills again brought the ASDV to periscope depth. Right in front of him the mast slid upward, and he peered through the viewfinder, ranging right, from dead ahead to zero-four-zero. There it was, about a mile off their starboard bow, the light flashing every two seconds on the red can they had imagined so often on the chart.

Slight course change at 15.53N 94.16E on the GPS . . . come to zero-four-zero through the dredged channel . . . but we're in patrolled waters . . . advise visual every three minutes.

"That Longo. Clever little prick, right?" Lieutenant MacPherson whispered it just loudly enough for the Navigator not to hear.

"Shut up, Dallas," hissed Rick Hunter. "I'd like to see you doing what he's doing."

"Me? Sir, you must be joking. How many times do I need to tell you? I can do it all."

"As a navigator you'd probably hit it all."

There was lot of stifled laughter, which defused some of the tension but not all of it. And the ASDV crept forward through the dark narrow channel, its only "eyes" an occasional look through the periscope. It took them another 40 minutes to move all the way to the north end of the dredged channel, and right at the entrance to the natural deep water they spotted a patrol boat through the periscope.

And it was coming straight toward them, the unmistakable Hainan Type 037 fast-attack patrol boat, heavily gunned, with a phalanx of ASW mortars. This ship is the coastal warhorse of the Chinese Navy. They have a hundred of them, divided among their three fleets. Lieutenant Longo spotted it way up ahead, with its distinctive low freeboard, making 30 knots through the water, with a big white wake astern, almost as if it had nothing to do with the Chinese Naval dockyard off to the west.

Lieutenant Mills whipped down the periscope and took the ASDV as deep as she would go, cutting her speed, and steering left toward the edge of the Haing Gyi Shoal, trying to put a mile of the Bassein Delta between the U.S. SEALs and the oncoming Chinese patrol.

She was not transmitting, but Lt. Mills was taking no chances. He cut the engines and allowed the submarine to drift down and settle on the sandy bottom. And everyone heard the Hainan go charging past.

"You know what I think?" whispered Matt Longo. "I think she was Burmese, coming straight down the estuary from their Naval base up at the city of Bassein, several miles upstream from here. She looked too settled on her course, and she was going too fast, to have just exited the dockyard. And she sure as hell didn't look like a patrol boat snooping around the deep waters beyond the Chinese jetties. She was in a real hurry."

Lieutenant Mills started the engine and engaged the shaft. The ASDV moved immediately forward, bumping off the soft bottom, heading northeast again. Another three miles, and they'd be right off the jetties. Thirty minutes from right now, the SEALs' four hit men would be on their way.

They moved on slowly, transmitting on the fathometer occasionally. At 2250 Lt. Mills slid quietly up to PD for a visual, and there, 500 yards off their port beam, he could see the lights along the jetties. He could also see the shape of one small frigate moored dead astern of a large destroyer.

"Okay, guys," whispered Longo, "we're a bit too close. Get out right here. We're still in the fifty-foot channel. Targets are five hundred yards to our west. Steer course two-eight-five and you'll come in right against the hulls."

Rick Hunter came forward to take a visual on the targets. And Lt. Mills decided they could exit on the surface, since there was not a single sound of any ship, radar or even a remote sonar. The dockyard was silent, unsuspecting, as everyone had expected. And of course the little ASDV is dead flat along its upper casing. There is no sail and it's invisible from 500 yards in dark water, just a jet-black steel tube in the night.

The Lieutenant, already at periscope depth, lowered the mast, quickly pumped out some more ballast. The ASDV rose another five feet, just breaking the calm harbor surface with about one foot of freeboard, and stopped in the water. Lieutenant Mills opened the deck hatch and Catfish Jones, mask on, flippers on, hood up, Draeger connected, a heavy limpet mine harnessed to his back, attack board under his arm, heaved himself up and over, rolling silently into the water without as much as a ripple.

Buster Townsend, similarly equipped, minus the attack board, was next. Then Chief Petty Officer Mike Hook, and finally Commander Hunter. The SEALs sorted themselves out, treading water, heads above the surface, waiting for their adrenaline to die down. Adrenaline eats oxygen. And the wait was frustrating. They were already running at least 20 minutes late. The detonator clocks would be set for 0345 instead of the planned 0330.

Commander Hunter would lead the way, with Mike Hook on his left shoulder. Catfish Jones, his attack board set on course two-eight-five, would swim in right behind them, with Buster's right hand on his left shoulder. They would not use their arms or hands for the swim, just their legs, kicking the oversized special SEAL flippers every five seconds, covering 120 feet per minute. It would take them around 13 minutes to reach the Chinese warships.

It was 2307 when Rick Hunter, facing east, finally held his attack board out in front of him with both hands. And then the big farm boy from central Kentucky drove himself forward, kicking hard and counting for distance. He was a human torpedo, scheduled to inflict about a billion dollars worth of damage on the People's Liberation Navy. And Commander Hunter could kick like one of his dad's stallions. Battleships have left their jetties with less power.

The four SEALs drove forward, the three younger men settling in to their leader's now-easy pace ... kick ... one ...

two . . . three . . . four . . . kick and glide all the way in. After eight minutes, the Commander came to the surface for his last look through the mask. Their course was accurate, and he paddled quietly back down to their regular depth, 14 feet below the surface. They were exactly on schedule, heading for the twin propellers of the destroyer, almost underneath the bow of the frigate.

Five minutes later, they were there, right under the shafts, in the shadow of the stern, and Rick signaled them to wait while he went deep to check the distance the keel floated above the harbor floor. As he suspected, it was only about three feet. This meant he and Buster would swim from the stern to the halfway point of the 500-foot-long ship, just about two minutes at 12 kicks every 60 seconds. Then Buster would swim right under the keel and place his mine exactly opposite Rick's. The subsquent detonation would hopefully break the back of the Chinese destroyer.

Catfish and Mike had only 60 yards to swim, which translated into 18 kicks, each taking them 10 feet, at which point they too would be just about halfway along the hull. Then Mike Hook would swim right under the keel and place his charge. Swimming under a hull is a nerve-wracking business when it's tight, as this most certainly was. But they were on a rising tide, which was lifting the ship higher, and that's a lot less stressful than a falling one.

Rick Hunter rejoined the other three, about eight feet now below the surface. They could hear the hum of the big generators inside the destroyer. Rick and Catfish clipped their attack boards on their belts and then they separated into two pairs, diving down into the dark, kicking their big flippers, driving along the steel hull of one of Zhang Yushu's most prized warships.

Rick Hunter counted carefully. On the twenty-fourth kick he stopped, confident now he was right under the section of the destroyer where all the guided missiles and torpedoes were stored. Right here he could see the lights of the ship reflected in the water, but both SEALs knew it would be pitch-black when they reached the keel.

Rick felt the surface of the hull as he went, and it was very rough, covered with barnacles and small sea growth. None of this was good news unless you happened to be a naturalist: the magnetic clamps of the mine were never going to grip this. Buster would realize the same thing when he reached the other side.

Within a few seconds both SEALs were standing on the sandy bottom in water black as oil. They could feel the rough surface, and they unclipped the harnesses that held the limpet mines on their backs. Rick saw Buster turn and swim underneath the keel, feeling his way in the dark. And he himself again ran his hand against the metal of the ship.

He uncovered his magnetic clamp and screwed it into the mine with its five pounds of explosives. He tried it on the hull, but it would not grip. So he drew his kaybar fighting knife and, holding the blade with two hands, he scraped a section clean on the hull. Again he tried the clamp, and this time he felt it pull, then lightly thud home. He could see the small dial of the timer glowing lightly, showing its 24-hour setting. Rick checked its timing again against that of the clock on his attack board. Then he set it for 0345. Then he ducked under the keel and showed the exact time to Buster, who was just finishing scraping with his kaybar knife.

Thus synchronized to the split second, they made the fix to the hull of the ship, took a compass reading and kicked straight back down course one-zero-five, straight back to where the ASDV awaited them. Fifty yards in front were Catfish Jones and Mike Hook, whose swim down the hull of the frigate had been much shorter, and whose hull had been much cleaner.

They picked up the intermittent homing beeps from Matt Longo's fathometer, and kicked in toward the hull of the minisub. Only when Commander Hunter signaled with four knocks on the hull, that all four of them had made it back, did Lt. Mills return to the deserted surface of the water, and one by one they clambered up and into the dry compartment. They were all breathing heavily as they unhooked their Draegers, pulled off their mask and sat down. Again the hatch was shut and clipped, and Lt. Mills took her 20 feet down once more, right in the now-desolate main channel.

"Okay, guys?" asked Rick Hunter.

"No problems for us," replied Catfish. "What took you two so long?"

"Much longer swim down the hull, and when we got there it was coated with barnacles. You know what little bastards they are to clean off. We couldn't get the magnets to pull until we'd scraped a section. But it's fine. All set for 0345."

"Same," said Catfish. "Damn creepy down there under the hull, though. Wouldn't wanna do it every night, I'll tell you that."

Lieutenant Mills ran back down the channel, steering course two-zero-zero from the 16-degree line of latitude on the GPS. They ran for just less than 20 minutes at six knots, then they all felt the ASDV make a turn to starboard, slowing down while Lt. Longo scanned the water for Wolf Rock. He found it just to their north, and then he guided Lt. Mills in until the submarine was 150 yards off its southernmost point. They took a visual, and Matt could see its shape jutting out of the water.

"Okay, guys," he said, "this is where we say 'so long.' Your landing place is dead ahead. Steer three-two-zero, for no more than 350 yards. Right there you'll be in the marshes, north of that river, so you won't have to cross it. You just got a short walk in from there."

Rick began to distribute big plastic cups of cold water. "I'm suggesting you drink one of these before we go. Because we're probably going to get hot, and we have no time to get our suits off. Just don't want anyone getting dehydrated, because it makes you feel lousy."

The SEALs drank, pulled up their hoods, loaded up with six satchel bombs, plus medical supplies, radio and one shovel. They took the greatest care loading up two of the rookies with two 50-foot rolls of "det cord," the hugely volatile detonator link that burns at the rate of *five miles per second*, and is beloved by all SEALs.

Then they slung their personal weapons on their backs, the Heckler and Koch light submachine guns packed in waterproof cases. And they lifted out the bigger M-60 machine gun, which would be used only in a dire emergency, if they had to fight their way out. But their most precious cargo was two heavy armor-piercing bombs, about three feet long in special waterproof carrying cases. These had been especially adapted by Naval ordnance in San Diego. They would not explode in contact with other explosives: they would only explode with heavy impact on the point of the nose cone. And heavy impact they were going to get.

Inside the ASDV, Draegers were connected and tested, masks pulled down, flippers fitted on and several belts of ammunition in waterproof sheaths were split among the SEALs not using attack boards. The vicious-looking kaybars were adjusted in combat belts, ready for easy access.

At 0016 they began to exit the submarine, one by one, each man rolling out of the deck hatch and into the still, calm waters of the Bassein Delta. There was a pale moon rising to the east casting low, ghostly shadows on the water. And there was no sign of life save the increasing number of black-hooded heads above the surface, each man breathing in the fresh night air deeply, treading water and waiting for the adrenaline to die down.

It was 0026 when Dallas MacPherson, manhandling the big machine gun with Bobby Allensworth, slithered down the hull and essentially fell into the water, the heavy gun now made much lighter by the special air pockets inside its waterproof cover.

Rick Hunter dived to their swim depth of 10 feet, adjusted his attack board and kicked forward on the short swim into the marshes. Ten minutes later all ten of them grounded into long marsh grass growing out of firm sand. Rick stood first and listened, pulling back his hood and shoving his mask into a holster on his belt.

They had already decided to hide the Draegers. They were too heavy to carry, and they walked on together to the beach, found a wooded area beyond the sand and dug out a hole to bury them. In an emergency they could run back and find them, if they needed to escape. If not, no one would ever find them. They covered them over with grass, then wet sand, and dumped the shovel under thick undergrowth.

The six men with the light attack boards clipped them onto one another's backs; the bombs were similarly carried. The SEALs drew their weapons, Rattlesnake Davies held the wire cutters, and Rick Hunter checked the compass and decided on a tight group in single file walking carefully through the light grasses 100 yards inshore from the beach.

The landscape was uninhabited as far as they and the satellite could tell. The first sign of life they would encounter would be in the guardhouse right on the south perimeter wire. And so they went forward, moving steadily across the ground, their start point no more than 1,200 yards from the fence. Their watchword was *stealth*. There was no mileage in causing an uproar, nothing to be gained from a gunfight, except almost certain death. The SEALs had no immediate backup, no hope of immediate rescue. The Chinese guards in the dockyard had access to at least three helicopter gunships, plus almost a thousand armed Navy personnel—not to mention the entire Burmese Navy base upriver with even more access to fast patrol gunboats.

It was imperative that no one see them and live more than three seconds. It was the opinion of the Coronado brains that the guardhouse would contain a bank of television screens, closed-circuit from all over the base. That way one man could watch over the entire complex, positioned down on the main perimeter fence that guarded the base from the outside world—one guard with access to a panic button that would summon heavy reinforcements immediately. The only colleague he would require through the night would be an engineer ready to attend to any problems in the electric generation plant, the refueling areas or anywhere else in the high-tech areas of the Naval yards.

The SEALs' plan was almost primitive in its lack of subtlety, but everyone thought it would work. The one thing they must not do was cause a panic in the guardroom, which would cause the guard to hit the appropriate button. And they walked on, each man certain in his own mind of the sequence of their actions in the next 10 minutes.

At 0110 they picked up the lights inside the fence, and it was plain they were not designed as a security aid, but rather to light a blacktop interior path along which a jeep carried the guard-house personnel. The lights were dim and focused on the ground, not the fence. The SEALs could see only one light along the fence, not high, about 100 yards from the guardhouse itself.

It was thus dark as they made their approach, and they had no need to hit the ground and snake their way forward on elbows and knees until they were as close as 50 yards.

They reached the fence in good order, and Rattlesnake began to cut a hole in the wire in a dark area 40 feet from the little building. It took just a few minutes, and Buster Townsend folded it back away from his buddy's hands as the thick strands were severed. The hole was five feet wide by the time Dallas MacPherson and Bobby Allensworth hauled the big gun through, followed moments later by the entire team with all their equipment. Thus the Chinese guard and engineer, watching the television inside the brightly lit room, were in fact sitting 40 feet from one of the most lethal platoons of fighting men in the world.

The only man not through the wire was Chief Petty Officer Mike Hook, and no one could see him crouched outside the fence in deep grass carefully aiming a silenced M-14 rifle, the only one they carried, at the light nearest the guardhouse on the wire. At 0130, right on time, the veteran SEAL pulled the trigger and shot the bulb out the first time, missing the metal cover. There was not a sound. But inside the guardhouse a tiny light flickered, confirming that a bulb had gone out somewhere along the south fence. Instinctively the young guard stood up and walked to the screen door, opened it, stepped through and looked along the fence, noticing immediately that the light they could see through the window was no longer there.

In Cantonese he called, "We have a light blown, Tommy—we may as well replace it now. The television program is awful." At which point the engineer also walked out into the night, carrying a white box and a tall stepladder. It was obvious that the cheap Korean bulbs blew out on a regular basis, even without Mike Hook's valuable assistance.

And now both men were outside in the dark, the guardhouse unmanned. And right then the SEALs pounced. Rick Hunter took the guard from behind, breaking his neck with a tremendous blow from the butt of his machine gun. The man fell dead without a murmur, mainly because the SEAL leader had a massive hand clamped across his mouth as he died.

The engineer never even saw it, because Bobby Allensworth slammed a blow into his throat at the same time as Rattlesnake rammed his kaybar into the man's heart. Two down, the guardhouse in SEAL control. Not a sound as they fell. It was 0136.

Rick and Dallas raced into the guardhouse and stared at the screens. From there it looked as though the place was deserted. There was no sign of a human figure on the top line of three screens. On the second line there was also no sign of life. The trouble was the lettering under the screens was in Chinese, and the two SEALs were unable to read which television recorded which area.

They stayed watching for a few moments, and then suddenly there was life on screen six in the lower line, four men walking across a room, dressed in engineering overalls. In the background there was a tall construction, which seemed to have a large wheel on top, but the quality was not good enough for an accurate assessment. In Rick's opinion it was almost certainly the interior of the electric power station.

No surprises. They had guessed there would be little night security, in a remote Chinese base in the middle of a Burmese river, literally hundreds of miles from *any* known enemy, like India. And thousands of miles from *the* known enemy, the USA.

Commander Hunter's one problem so far was the possible discovery of the bodies. There would almost certainly be a watch change at 0400, but by that time the SEALs would be, hopefully, long gone, and the base would be, hopefully, nonoperational. Nonetheless there was a chance that a patrol might call at the little guardhouse sometime before 0400. Finding it deserted was one thing. Finding two plainly murdered occupants was quite another.

Rick's instinct was to disable the televisions so that no one else could look at them, but he did not dare for fear the disconnection could trigger an alarm that would send more engineers down to the guardhouse. It was the lesser of two evils, but he elected to leave them operational, counting on no one else seeing the pictures before the 0400 guard change.

Rick watched the bodies being dragged out through the hole in the wire and hidden in the long grasses through which they had just walked, at least 50 yards away from the fence. They clipped the wire back into place. If a patrol did show up, it would be confronted with a mystery, but not with unmistakable evidence of an attack on the base.

It was 0150 when they began their advance on the Chinese dockyard. The 12 black-clad figures walked steadily toward the lights of the main complex, a distance of 200 yards. According to Rick's map, there were five main buildings—the power station, the main control and communications room, a large accommodation block, a long warehouse facing the surface ship jetties and an ordnance store right next to it.

Beyond here was the wide sea inlet where the Chinese had constructed jetties for their patrol boats, and farther in, two large dry docks, the type that flood down and sink to allow ships to navigate in and then wait for the docks to pump out the ballast and rise again to the surface.

Opposite the patrol boat landings were the submarine jetties, but according to Coronado's latest Intelligence, there was no underwater boat in residence. And then, even farther along the shore, was the fuel farm, containing 12 massive holding tanks, an area 200 yards long by 150, containing a million gallons of diesel. Between the fuel farm and the refueling jetties there was a main fuel-control block, a sizable three-story building 240 feet long. With that out of action, and possibly a bad fire among the holding tanks, the base would be totally diminished as a possible operations center. That fuel-control block was the farthest building from the SEALs' point of entry. It was also their first target.

And Rick Hunter led his men on a 300-yard diagonal route

across the rough ground between the outer fence and the accommodation block, deep in the interior of the base. It was all surprisingly badly lit, for which each of the SEALs was grateful, particularly the two rookies bringing up the rear, carrying the big machine gun and ammunition belts that Lt. Allensworth would handle in an emergency. A big weight like that always makes assault troops feel vulnerable, slow and less mobile than everyone else. And the two rookies, carrying the machine gun between them, preferred the dark to the light.

The Commander led them carefully, and they made no sound as they crossed the uncut, uneven grass. They saw no one, and even as they passed the rear of the accommodation block there was no discernible light in any window. Rick was trusting his map now, because the base was unknown territory, and the map was telling him that at the end of the accommodation block they would make a right-hand turn and see in front of them a floating pontoon dock, with a gantry crossing the sea inlet, right behind the innermost dry dock.

The gantry was better lit than any other area, and Rick decided that if they were going to be seen, and caught, it was going to be as a team right in the middle of that illuminated bridge. He thus decided to regroup on the pontoon and send each man over the bridge one at a time, nice and slowly, attracting no attention. He sent Dallas MacPherson over first, and the young Lieutenant did as he was ordered, strolling nonchalantly over the metal bridge as if he owned the place.

One by one they made the crossing, until 11 men were over. Then Rick Hunter picked up the big machine gun on his own and walked it over the gantry to join the others. And right then the pace stepped up about 200 percent. There were almost no lights on this side, just a low four-foot steel-railed fence to protect the fuel farm.

Rattlesnake and Buster cleared it together, racing through the holding tanks and planting a powerful, high-explosive Mk-138 satchel bomb against each of the two central ones. They joined them with det cord and wired it into the detonator, setting the timer for 0345. Then they jumped the eastern fence and worked on two more bombs, carried in and left in position on the outer back wall of the control center by Rick and Bobby. Each satchel held 10 blocks of explosives. There was enough TNT against that wall to knock down Yankee Stadium, and Rattlesnake thought privately, *I just hope to Christ no one finds it before H-Hour, 0345.*

Meanwhile Dallas and Mike Hook were edging around the control block searching for a main electricity inlet or outlet. The other team, Rick Hunter and Bobby Allensworth, was searching for the main fuel lines, which they never found. Dallas and Mike, however, were lucky. They opened up a big manhole in the ground and found a labyrinth of heavy-duty cable, coated with plastic, in brown, red and blue. Dallas said to wind six turns of det cord around the central point and set the timer on the detonator for 0345.

"Okay, guys, we're done on this side of the inlet," whispered Rick Hunter. "Let's round up the lookouts and head right back over that creepy little bridge." Twenty minutes later they were back in the shadow of the accommodation block, their loads lightened considerably.

It was 0225. And there were two targets left, the control and communications block, which represented about 5 percent of their problem, and the power station, which was the other 95 percent. The control block was important because, without it, the Chinese would be unable to contact the outside world. But the power plant represented a fighting chance of obliterating the entire Naval base.

With incredible stealth, the SEAL team moved way back into the rough ground over which they had walked from the guardhouse. And now they could see the silhouette of the station, and as Dallas MacPherson oberved, "It looks a whole hell of a lot bigger right here than it did on the photograph."

And Dallas was right. The building loomed high, maybe five stories up. On its southern side it was 90 feet long, and it was plainly bigger than that on the western and eastern walls. The only door they could see was set into the wall on the west side, right-hand corner looking in. There was a high outside metal staircase running up the east wall, probably for use as an emergency exit.

A high chimney jutted out of the roof, probably to release surplus steam.

To the right of the station, as the SEALs lay watching, was the control and communications block, situated centrally between the station and the dockside warehouse. They would deal with that first, because it was relatively simple, the mere placing of two bombs strategically.

The planners in Coronado had discussed the possibility of getting a couple of guys on the roof and winding a few coils of det cord around the entire bloom of rooftop aerials, but decided, in the end, against it: too hard to climb it without special gear, and the SEALs were already fully loaded; too much chance of being detected, even stranded up there if things went awry below; too little advantage gained, since there was soon to be no electricity whatsoever throughout the base. Or whatever was left of it.

This time the bombs would be placed by Buster and Rattlesnake, both experts in such matters. Mike Hook, carrying the big gun for covering fire, accompanied them across the ground assisted by one of the rookies. They set themselves in position covering the main door of the building and the short southern wall. They could also cover the blacktop perimeter road.

The two SEALs from Louisiana moved like lightning to the building, and their luck held. At the rear of the structure there was a short flight of concrete steps going down to a semibasement, and remarkably, the door was open. Buster and Rattlesnake crept in and placed their two satchel bombs right by the main boiler. They spliced in the wires, set the detonator for 0345 and moved briskly out of the area, shutting the door carefully behind them. And still no one disturbed their lethal tasks. It was exactly 0245. And they were now running a half hour late, not 20 minutes.

But no one could deny that the Fates had been with them. The base, though occupied by a large number of military personnel, was, like all bases, quasi-civilian in character. One of the two duty guards had been an engineer/electrician. All the men on duty in the power station were civilians, and there was no duty guard whatsoever in there. They had seen no patrols along the docks either, presumably on the basis that no one was espected to attack a Chinese guided-missile warship with several hundred trained Navy staff on board.

And now, late or not, the SEAL team was moving forward to its main objective, taking no chances, moving on elbows and knees through the rough grass. The plan had been perfectly memorized by each one of them. Commander Hunter would enter the station, backed by Lt. Allensworth, Catfish Jones, Mike Hook, Dallas MacPherson and two rookies. They would take in with them the two steel armor-piercing bombs and four sizable hunks of C-4 plastic explosive. Plus a couple of hammers, jammed in the rookies' belts.

In Commander Hunter's opinion they would have to fight to take control of the power station, probably killing everyone who stood in their way. They knew from the television screens in the guardhouse that there were at least four, and possibly more, engineers on duty, but as it was a civilian installation that would probably be all. The problem with an assault like this was that anyone who got in the way had to die. There was no question of stunning, or disabling or even drugging with chloroform. What if the victim suddenly awakened and sounded an alarm. The stakes were too high for such a risk. Any risk, for that matter.

Outside the power station, 20 yards into the rough ground, Buster and Rattlesnake would man the big machine gun, covering the door and the approach road. The rookies would be deployed as lookouts on the near corners of the building. At 0255 the seven-man SEAL assault force set off toward the raised door of the geothermal generating plant. It was pitch-dark, the moon having vanished behind low rain clouds, and there was just one dim bare bulb lighting the eight steps up to the doorway.

The SEAL leader opened it carefully, but did not enter. No one moved, and certainly no one came to find out who had opened the door. One by one the team slipped into the building, weapons poised to cut down any opposition. If it was just one man or two, they would use knives. Any more, they would simply take them down with submachine-gun fire: noisy, and slightly risky, but the only option. They shut the steel door hard behind them, trying to contain any noise they might make inside the reinforced walls of the building.

They knew what they were looking for. The engineers at Coronado had sketched it for them several times over—one massive shaft with a giant cast-iron valve on top, the kind of heavy-duty machinery that might feasibly be holding back a volcano, powered by the core of the earth.

The room they now stood in was pure concrete, with a square exit into a room in which the noise was all-embracing. They could see huge turbines, with 10-foot-high wheels, spinning at a steady speed, plainly generating the electricity. The Coronado guys had said they should immediately look for a kind of mezzanine floor below, because the steam power was upwardly powerful. It would surge up the shaft and then find itself guided by the valve system, just below the turbines.

What Rick Hunter sought was steps, downward steps, and the seven men fanned out walking through the turbine room, hesitating as they came out from behind the giant machines, treating the room as if they were clearing a block in a conquered city.

They moved stealthily, their MP-5s held out in front, trying to listen, trying to catch any additional sound above the hum of the machines. Up ahead they could see another opening in the thick, cast-concrete walls. And right in the center of that gap was a wide flight of stone steps, 10 of them, leading down, Rick thought, to the main geothermal shaft.

So far the place seemed deserted. But no one imagined it could be, with millions of dollars of machinery working ceaselessly, apparently unsupervised. There had to be a team of guys in charge somwhere. But where were they? That's what Commander Hunter wanted to find out.

And the answer was not long in coming. Right at the bottom of the steps leading to the main shaft, three Chinese engineers suddenly appeared. In absolute shock, they stared up at the black-faced hooded giants who towered above them on the upper steps, armed with submachine guns. No one knew quite what to do, certainly not the engineers. One of them helplessly raised his hands, another called out loudly, a third shouted something in Chinese. And then Bobby Allensworth stepped in front of Commander Hunter and hit the trigger, firing from the hip, four short bursts. No one was as fast as Lt. Allensworth. In another life he'd have been at the OK Corral.

Bullets from his MP-5 slammed into three men, each of whom took at least three shots, either to the head, throat or heart. It was a whip-crack reaction from a trained professional killer. And no sooner had the bodies slumped to the ground when a fourth man came running around the corner, stopped dead in his tracks, then stopped dead in his life as the MP-5 held by Rick Hunter's bodyguard spat a single round into his heart.

Even the SEALs were shaken at the speed at which it had happened. Commander Hunter turned to Bobby, whose prime task it was to protect the SEAL leader, and he just nodded, confident the noise from the turbines had suppressed any possibility of the shots being heard outside.

Lieutenant Allensworth said, "Sorry I had to do that, sir. But I was afraid one of them might have had a buttom or an emergency bleeper. Just didn't wanna give 'em no time. No time. Nossir."

"Thanks, Bobby. There was no alternative. I agree. Come on, let's get after that main shaft."

And still their luck appeared to hold, and they located the shaft two minutes later at exactly 0310, at which precise time the telephone was ringing forlornly in the guardhouse out on the fence.

Lieutenant Bo Peng, an engineer in the moored destroyer, was trying to call his brother Cheng who was on duty on the perimeter. He usually called him when they were both on the midnight watch, and they sometimes shared tea in the ship's wardroom when the watch was over. Lieutenant Bo could not for the life of him understand why Cheng was not replying, or alternately, why the answer-and-automatic-relay machine was not connected. It was a golden rule among the guards, and Bo was baffled by the silence out on the boundary guardhouse.

He was a persistent and ambitious young man of 24, and he called the duty officer of the base, reporting that there was no reply to the telephone in the guardhouse. And why was that? There was not even a way to leave a message, and that was disgraceful in a military complex.

The duty officer was not altogether crazy about Bo's tone, but he was also wary that a warship officer with a serious complaint about the shore personnel would be listened to. In a few minutes he could be on the line to the destroyer's CO, a chore he was not prepared to deal with.

So he answered crisply. "I'm sorry about that, Lieutenant. I have no idea what could be wrong, but I'll play it by the book, and send a full night guard-patrol down there, right away.

Three minutes later, a complement of six Naval guards, all armed with Russian Kalashnikovs, was piling out of the accommodation block and boarding a waiting jeep. It was the first time they had ever been summoned to do anything after dark, and they almost went the wrong way.

Rattlesnake and Buster watched them leave, burning rubber outside the building and then making a U-turn, heading wrongly for the dry-dock inlet. At the end of the first throughway between the buildings, they swung right, down between the power station and the main workshops. They shot through the gap between the warehouses and the ordnance store, and then made a corrective right turn along the jetties. Lieutenant Bo, high above on the upper deck of the warship, watched them go roaring down the blacktop toward the guardhouse.

And there, of course, they discovered that the place was strangely empty. No duty guard. No duty night engineer. All six men jumped out and began to look around outside, spending several minutes calling out for the missing men. However, the patrol leader, Lt. Rufeng Li, went back into the little outpost's control room and took a look at the television screens.

And at that precise moment in the power station, Rick Hunter, noticing a scanning camera in the corner of the steam-entry room, took it out with a volley of bullets at 25-foot range. Lieutenant Rufeng was thus watching the screens when one of them just blanked right out. It did not even fizz, or show interference. It just blacked into nothing.

The Lieutenant, however, did not suspect something drastic was happening. He just thought instantly that the two missing men were working wherever that screen had failed. And he took a close look at the wording below, which told him the camera was located on the upper southwest corner of the main shaft room in the power station.

He walked outside and summoned his patrol. He took his time, and lit a cigarette and told them laconically that he had solved the mystery: the two missing men had gone to attend to some kind of machine failure in the power station, and while it was irregular to leave the guardhouse unmanned, the problem may have been quite serious. They had obviously gone to deal with it together. After all, no guard had ever been called to deal with a prowler of any kind since the base had opened six months ago. He, Lt. Rufeng, understood those kinds of priorities, which was only to be expected.

He held his cigarette in his front teeth, an affectation just learned from a tobacco commercial on the Internet. He smiled languidly. It was a smile that said, "Don't worry, gentlemen. The reason I have achieved a position so superior to your own is my natural penchant for using the little gray cells rather than running around in a frenzy." At this particular moment, Lt. Rufeng, in his own mind, was the Hercule Poirot of the Orient.

It was 0325, and Rick and his team were working furiously in the shaft room, trying to shut off the lower valve, the one three thousand feet down, right above the boiling steam lake. They had located a control board and made the switches, three big ones, which Rick and Dallas believed had shut down all three valves.

The main one, located on the huge pipe where the steam divides off into the separate turbine feeds, was certainly closed.

The turbines were already slowing. Any second now the reserve diesel generators would kick in, and it would not be long before the failure of the power plant was noticed.

The massive control valve at the head of the shaft, located at floor level in the lowest room, was also closed. But the SEALs could not read the most important one of all, constructed in cast concrete, high in the roof of the lake, the first line of defense, if for any reason the steam had to be halted. However, the switches were all three in the same position, and they could do no more. In any event, they now opened up the top two valves and let the remaining steam escape.

Lieutenant MacPherson observed that if they were wrong about the switches, they'd probably blow up most of East Asia, including themselves. "And wouldn't that be a blast?" he added. Dallas always found time for irony even when he was working flat-out. It was impossible not to like him.

Right now Lt. MacPherson was sweating like a Burmese panda. He had just blown out two sections of pipe right below the center and upper valves, and there was steam leaking, but it was not pressurized.

The bottom valve, right over the underground cavern, was plainly shut. The opening of the top two for several minutes had allowed the pressured steam to rise up through the system and then die out.

It was hot, but not diabolically so. Dallas and Mike Hook were feverishly trying to fix the first bomb inside the fractured shaft, winding it tight with det cord right below the center valve.

There were only 17 minutes left to tie up the second bomb through the hole in the shaft below the higher valve, directly above. That, too, had to be secured with det cord. Then, when the first detonater popped the cord, the lower bomb would scream down the shaft, arrowing through the remaining steam and slamming into the bottom valve with terrific force. It just might split the entire main shaft asunder.

Thirty seconds later the second det cord would pop, and a large hunk of white semtex explosive would blow the cast-iron upper valve to pieces. And this would release the second bomb to drop down the shaft, gaining speed for three thousand feet, then exploding somewhere in the rubble at the shaft base, or even in the waters of the underground lake itself; maybe even in the *floor* of the lake, slightly north of Hell, presumably.

Dallas thought if that happened it might actually cause a brand-spanking-new volcano to erupt from the core of the earth. "I always told my daddy I intended to leave a mark on this earth, but I bet he never thought I was gonna change its goddamned shape!"

Even without the wit and imagination of Lt. D. MacPherson, this was a drastically complex and dangerous set of linked explosions, and no one knew what on earth the result would be.

But whatever happened, the colossal forces of the steam, sufficient, it is always said, to blow a four-ton rock 400 feet into the air, would now be unleashed to roar furiously into its only escape route, straight up the remains of the shaft. It would most definitely blast off the roof of the power station, and probably rupture the entire foundation of the structure. The milk white superheated plume of steam, thundering into the sky, from the floor of the generating plant, would probably reach 3,000 feet.

It would take weeks to cap it, especially if the concrete foundation was split, and even this would take special equipment unlikely to be available within 1,000 miles. But the main issue was, from the U.S. Navy's point of view, that the Chinese base in the eastern waters of the Bay of Bengal should become history.

Meanwhile, Dallas MacPherson, assisted by Mike Hook and Catfish Jones, was manhandling the second bomb up to the huge upper valve, the one that had to be obliterated. It was 0330, and they had the bomb well secure on its moorings. They eased it through the gap and made it fast, hanging in the shaft, swinging in the spooky plumes of white steam still drifting up from below.

Dallas wound in the last of the det cord, wrapping it around the spokes of the red wheel on top of the valve. Then they placed the C-4 plastic explosives in three places on the cast-iron casing of the valve itself. Just below them Rick checked his watch, it was 0334. They had to get out of there before the base started to explode. And they didn't dare to set the timers in the power plant for anything less than a half hour from the moment they began to head for the marshes where the boats were waiting.

The leader's mind raced. *Say 40 minutes from now . . . gives us ten minutes to get clear of the building . . . then a half hour to get clear of the island . . . is that enough? Don't wanna get killed by flying masonry . . . I'm gonna make it forty minutes from now. Just hope to hell it's not too much time for the Chinks to discover the plot.*

"Set that clock for zero-four-one-five, Dallas," he said. "That's thirty minutes after the ships, the fuel and the buildings blow. There's gonna be a lot of chaos. Hopefully the blast from the control and comms building, plus the ships, will blow the ordnance store as well. But we have to get outta here in one piece. And we're not committing suicide. My daddy wouldn't like it. Nossir."

At this exact time, 0334, the night-patrol jeep was running back down the blacktop from the guardhouse. When it arrived at the point where the road swerved right along to the jetties, the driver swerved left and headed directly for the power station, driving across the rough ground.

Rattlesnake Davies, lying in the grass with the machine gun, nudged Buster, and they turned around and saw the lights of the jeep coming toward them—not directly, but approximately.

"Jesus Christ, have they seen us?" he whispered.

"No. But I hate the coincidence," replied Buster. "What do we do?"

"Nothing. Keep our heads down. I think they'll go by. First sign they ain't goin' by, we take 'em out with the ole MP-5s, all of them, however many."

By now the Chinese jeep was almost on them, still making a straight line, at a narrow angle toward the southern wall of the power station. If it did not stop, it would pass 25 feet in front of them.

Buster and Rattlesnake, now gripping their small submachine guns, followed the vehicle with their eyes, every sense alert. If it stopped, there were going to be six dead Chinese guards, no question about that, because they would not see the prostrate SEALs until it was much, much too late. But Buster and Rattlesnake both knew the real problem would come after that, after the base rippled into life at the sound of gunfire. Ten minutes later it would ripple into death at the sound of high explosives. It was 0335.

And events were moving rapidly. Rick Hunter and his team were moving swiftly back through the power station toward the exit room through which they had arrived. And, to their horror, Rattlesnake and Buster were watching the Chinese patrol's jeep pull up right outside that door.

There was no sense of urgency, but it was obvious they were going in. The SEALs' rookie lookouts were flying across the grass back to the rendezvous point. They hit the ground together right next to Buster. "Jesus Christ," said one of them, "the bastards are going in. They'll be behind the guys . . . oh, shit . . . Buster . . . they'll fucking kill 'em."

By now the guards were climbing out of the jeep, and Rattlesnake Davies, without a word, wriggled left to the standard M-60 machine gun they had set up in the grass. Buster had already laid the 100-round ammunition belt in the clip. And it was aimed right at the power station door. Lieutenant Rufeng and his deputy were on the steps, the other four right behind them. Each one carried his Kalashnikov. And without a word Rattlesnake Davies, the SEAL from the Louisiana bayous, opened fire with the M-60.

The range was only 70 feet, and the fatal 7.62-NATO rounds tore a path straight at the steps, killing the man now opening the door, and virtually taking Lt. Rufeng's head off. The other four guards, stunned at the explosion of blood running down the steel door in the dim light of the bare bulb, wheeled around, trying to see where the gunfire was coming from. They tried to raise their Kalashnikovs, but they were facing Rattlesnake Davies directly now, and that was a very poor strategy. He blew all four of them away; the force of those big shells, almost four inches long, slamming into them, actually knocked them sideways into the jeep, one of them hurtling backwards over the hood, his uniform riddled with bullet holes.

It was 0336 in the morning, the darkest time, and the sound of the SEALs' machine gun, rattling away in the night, had echoed around the base. A light went on in the accommodation block, someone came to the window of the communications room. Up on the foredeck of the Chinese destroyer, two seamen on their watch looked up in surprise. It was gunfire. Unmistakable machine-gun fire. And it was only 160 yards away. Both of them raced aft toward the near-deserted comms room below the aerials.

At which point, 175 yards away, Commander Hunter opened the door to exit the power station and nearly fell over the blood-soaked bodies of Lt. Rufeng and his colleague.

The thick, reinforced walls of the turbine room had spared them the anxiety of listening to Rattlesnake take out the entire Chinese night patrol, but Rick was amazed by what he saw. He jumped over the two bodies, followed by Catfish, Bobby and Dallas, grabbed the rail and jumped the steps in two bounds. In front of him was the jeep, three more bodies lying around it, and one lying on it.

"What in the name of Christ? . . ." he muttered, just as Rattlesnake, Buster and the three rookies came charging in from the rough ground, Buster saying too loudly, "We had no choice . . . let's GO-GO-GO . . . down to the marsh . . . do we take the jeep . . . ?"

"Hell NO!" said Rick. "It's too easy to follow. We're better off in the dark, running on our own. Get my fucking attack board off my back, will you? We need the compass. . . . Okay . . . let's go, that way . . . make a diagonal back to the fence at the jungle end . . . *GO NOW! ALL OF YOU! FOR FUCK'S SAKE, RUN!*"

And with that, the SEAL leader grabbed the M-60 from Rattlesnake and one of the rookies and tucked it under his arm, checking the belt to see what was left—about 36 rounds. He was the only one of them strong enough to handle it comfortably alone.

"DALLAS! Quick. Blow that fucking jeep up, willya? It's faster than us and they may follow. Catfish's got the grenades."

But Catfish was off and running. Dallas, who had once considered an athletic career at 200 meters—an ambition abandoned only when he failed to make the 1992 U.S. Olympic team at the age of 14—could still run like hell, and he caught Petty Officer Jones in short order. He ripped the pin out of the grenade, and hurled it back at the jeep. Six second later, with the SEALs in full flight heading for the woods, it exploded in a fireball.

And it attracted the attention instantly of all four half-dressed but fully armed guards running out of the accommodation block. The light from the jeep illuminated the 11 black-hooded figures pounding across the rough ground making a southwest course toward the trees. And the frightened but disorganized Chinese instinctively opened fire. They were shooting almost blindly into the dark, in high but flickering light from the gasoline flames. But a bullet caught Buster to the right of his shoulder blade, paralyzing his arm, and knocking him flying to the ground.

The Chinese saw the SEAL go down, but they did not see Commander Hunter rumbling along 30 yards behind his men with the M-60 poised. Rick stopped, steadied the weapon, then opened fire at the four running Chinese, cutting them down, dead in their tracks in a bloody scream of anger and fear. Then he turned the machine gun onto the accommodation block itself and blew out all the side windows, in an attempt to discourage anyone else from giving chase.

Meanwhile Dallas and one of the rookies had the wounded Buster on his feet with both arms around their necks. But the pain in his right side was agonizing and he screamed as they tried to carry him to the trees. Rick Hunter finally caught up with them, ordered everyone to stop for 20 seconds, and then he injected a shot of morphine right into the stricken SEAL's right shoulder.

"Let's go . . . ," he said. "Fast as we can . . . Buster . . . that shoulder's gonna ease in a few minutes, old buddy. Don't worry about it . . ."

Buster Townsend, blood pouring down his back, nodded and smiled. "Thanks, guys," he said.

And so they struggled on, plunging into the woods, glad of the dark, glad of the cover.

Behind them they had left abject chaos. The fact was that the Chinese Navy was fully aware the base was under attack. They had no idea, yet, of the scale of the attack. Nor indeed who was mounting it. They knew only that there appeared to be a gang of madmen running around murdering people.

The air was alive with the transmissions of cell phones as the comms rooms in the two warships talked both to each other and to the main control center of the base. The Commanding Officer of the Jangwei frigate was fastest into his stride. He hit the buttons to the destroyer suggesting they get helicopters into the air, with lights and pilots with night goggles. It was plainly essential to locate the killers as soon as possible.

The CO of the destroyer reacted equally quickly. Both of his helicopters were in a ground-crew service area, way over beyond the fuel farm. It was a workshop complex, with fuel pumps. But the choppers rarely used it, and the U.S. satellite trackers had scarcely bothered with it. The Captain knew they were there, and he moved fast to alert his air crew.

And this was just as well, because it was 0344 when the destroyer's CO was on the phone, and his ship was just about 23 seconds away from being blown sky-high. And so was the frigate directly astern of him.

0345. Thursday, June 7.
Haing Gyi Island, Burma.

ON AN ACADEMIC level, it was the limpet mine of Commander Rick Hunter, expertly clamped flat among the barnacles on the port side of the Luhai destroyer's keel, that exploded first. Buster Townsend's mine exploded two and a half seconds later. The viciously tailored "shaped" charges magnified the power of the detonation fivefold, and the limpets blew two gaping holes, one on either side of the keel, the blast slicing through the steel hull of the 6,000-ton warship.

Generally speaking this was all bad news for the People's Liberation Army/Navy, but not quite as severe as it would become four seconds later when the Luhai's torpedo magazine went up with a thunderous explosion, killing half of the ship's company.

Any onlooker might have been dumbfounded at the scale of the explosion, stunned by the flames and billowing jet-black smoke. But it would nonetheless have been difficult to focus attention strictly on the destroyer, because eight seconds after the torpedoes blew, the 2,000-ton Jangwei II frigate, moored dead astern, did a passable imitation of Hiroshima 1945, when the limpet mines fixed by Petty Officer Catfish Jones and Chief Mike Hook detonated with massive force right under the guided-missile magazines.

The little Jangwei, only 360 feet long, a ship that punched a lot harder than its size, paid the penalty for that and literally blew itself to pieces. The entire complement of guided missiles, the SSM 6 YJ-1 Eagle Strikes, the CSS-N-4 Sardines, the 1-HQ-7 Crotales, all contributed to the crushing explosion, and the docks shuddered, lit up with two towering fires that could be seen 10 miles away.

Only six men would survive in the frigate, only 50 out of 250 in the destroyer. Automatic fire alarms began to howl throughout the base, but they were drowned out by the colossal explosion in the fuel farm as one million gallons of diesel and jet fuel detonated into a raging furnace, courtesy of the Louisiana SEALs Rattlesnake Davies and the now-wounded Buster Townsend. Their carefully timed Mk-138 satchel bombs had blown apart a total of five holding tanks, and within moments the other seven had formed a gasoline inferno.

The roar from the fire almost, but not quite, drowned out the noise of the two other bombs blasting apart the fuel control center. In the middle of all this the coils of det cord, wrapped around the main electricity cables by Dallas MacPherson and Mike Hook, exploded with sufficient force to blow the manhole cover 60 feet into the air and permanently wreck the electronic fuel-control system.

And way over on the other side of the inlet, an unbelievable blast right by the main boiler in the basement of the control-and-communications center paid further tribute to the smooth black skills of Buster and Rattlesnake. The explosion literally caused the entire building to cave in, crushing all of its five occupants to death.

Residents of the base, at least those not gunned down in their tracks by the marauding U.S. Navy SEALs, believed they were witnessing the end of the world. Any other explanation seemed utterly inadequate. And the whole spectacularly awful scenario had erupted in under two minutes; out of nowhere. There was zero evidence of an attack either from the air or the sea. The place just seemed to be blasting itself to pieces.

Meanwhile, struggling through the woods on the north side of the base, the SEALs were still 1,200 yards from the edge of the marsh. Buster was losing blood, and he was still in pain despite the morphine. Rick Hunter ordered them to stop while he examined the wound, and to his dismay he discovered the bullet was still lodged in the flesh on the right side of Buster's upper back, and he was losing blood fast.

He took Dallas MacPherson aside and told him to bring out the rest of the medical kit. Between them they had sticky and plain bandages, plus disinfected swabs for just this kind of wound, plus more disinfectant. But they had no groundsheets and they had to kneel Buster down, and he kept losing consciousness, and Rattlesnake held his head and splintered shoulder. Dallas held the tiny pinpoint light beam they had brought, and Rick Hunter gritted his teeth, and using a large pair of tweezers, designed for this particular task, gripped and pulled the bullet out.

Blood cascaded from the wound and Dallas tried to stop it with a strip he tore from his own shirt. Rick used a gauze pad soaked in strong disinfectant to clean it. And for the first time, Buster Townsend screamed, and Rattlesnake Davies, one of the toughest men ever to wear the trident, broke down and wept at the agony of his lifelong friend.

Rick Hunter kept going. He used another gauze pad and pressed it on the wound. Dallas fixed it tight with a roll of bandage that he wound around Buster's chest, then stuck it down firm with the sticky tape. They stuck another length of this around Buster's upper arm, taping it tight to his side. Then Rick Hunter injected him with more morphine, and the SEAL climbed back to his feet, and Rattlesnake just said, "I'm taking him."

He put Buster's good arm over his shoulder and held his wrist, and with his own arm around the wounded man's waist, they pushed forward, walking as well as they could through the undergrowth of the Burmese forest.

"I'm glad we did that," said Rick. "We've stopped the blood, stopped the infection, and it isn't going to get worse before we reach a doctor."

Moments later Mike Hook's radio, tuned to the frequency, picked up the bleep-bleep-bleep of the homing device in the inflatables, now parked somewhere down by the Letpan Stream. "Got 'em, sir. They're waiting."

"Good job, Mike . . . we just gotta stay on this course," said Rick. "It's due west and right now the attack board compass has us headed two-seven-zero. We're right on the money—gonna pop right out of these woods on the left-hand fork of the stream, right where Shawn drew the spot."

"You want a couple of us to make a bolt for it?" asked Lt. MacPherson. "Just to let the boat drivers know we're on our way—tell 'em we got a problem?"

"Good call. Why don't you, Mike and one of the rookies take that other little radio and get down there. Bobby'll handle the transmitter. And use your compass—you know they say it's impossible to walk through trees in a straight line?"

"Okay, boss. See you in about fifteen minutes."

070400JUN07. USS *Shark*. Bay of Bengal.
16.00N 94.01E. Speed 3. Racetrack course. PD.

The watch changed at 0400, and Lt. Commander Dan Headley still had the ship. No sign yet of Commander Reid, who had remained distant throughout the SEAL operation at Haing Gyi. Dan Headley knew he was not coming, at least not formally, to take over the watch. Although he thought the CO might show up casually a little later. He had just seemed extremely relieved when the XO had requested that he handle *Shark* during the Special Forces operation.

At that moment Lt. Pearson came into the control room and said the CO wished to see him in his room immediately.

"Any clue why, Shawn?"

"None, sir. He just stuck his head out of the door when I was passing and said to tell you."

"Okay . . . Officer of the Deck, you have the ship."

"I have the ship, sir," replied Lt. Matt Singer.

Dan Headley made his way down to Commander Reid's room, and was surprised to find the CO unshaven and looking fraught, which he considered was several degrees worse than worried.

"Hello, sir," he said. "What's up?"

"We have a very serious problem," replied the boss of USS *Shark*.

"We do?"

"We certainly do. And before I elaborate, I want you to understand that I am talking about a subject on which I am something of an expert."

"Of course, sir."

"Mercury, XO, is just coming into retrograde."

Dan Headley had rarely, probably never, been quite that bewildered.

"No shit?" he said, lamely.

Commander Reid glared at his second-in-command. "Do you, XO, have any idea how serious that can be? ANY IDEA WHATSO-EVER?"

"Who, me?"

"Plainly, Lieutenant Commander, I am addressing you."

"Well, sir. I'm not quite sure what you mean."

"MERCURY, XO! One of the greatest planets of the universe, will be in retrograde by dawn. MOVING BACKWARD. CAN YOU UNDERSTAND THE SIGNIFICANCE OF THAT, XO?"

Commander Reid's voice was rising. And so were Lt. Commander Headley's antennae.

"Astrology is what we are discussing, Mr. Headley. Astrology. The ancient study of cycles—created originally by the Chaldeans

376 ☆ PATRICK ROBINSON

of Babylonia three thousand years before Christ. Babylon, XO, Iraq in the modern world."

"Oh, Saddam's mob. Guess I hadn't figured them as students of the universe."

"Maybe not, maybe not. But I am a student of the universe. And I must tell you that when the planet Mercury begins to turn in an apparent backward motion, things can become extremely difficult. It's one of the ancient laws of the zodiac."

"Sir, look, I am sure this is all very fascinating, but I've got twelve brave men trying to get out of a Chinese Naval base under the most terrible circumstances. Could we go into retrograde some other time?"

"XO. ARE YOU ACCUSING ME OF IRRELEVANCE? THERE IS NOTHING MORE RELEVANT THAN MERCURY IN RETRO- GRADE. I'M TALKING OF MATTERS AS OLD AS TIME, FOR GOD'S SAKE!"

"Sir, I'm talking about high explosives, the destruction of a major Chinese Navy installation. I'm talking about life and death."

"And what could be more significant to that matter of life and death than the slow reverse motion of a mighty planet, stilled briefly in the heavens? MERCURY IN RETROGRADE, SIR! WE ARE ABOUT TO BE BOMBARDED BY THE TIMELESS, MAD- DENING EFFECTS OF THE PLANET THAT CONTROLS US!" And his voioce rose even higher. *"CAN YOU UNDERSTAND THAT, XO?"*

Dan Headley was at a loss. But at that moment the phone rang. The CO grabbed it and handed it over immediately. "Sir"—Lt. Singer's voice was almost as urgent as Commander Reid's—"can you come back? The SEALs have a problem. Buster Townsend has been badly wounded. They're being hunted down by helicop- ters, sir. It's bad. Please come back up here."

Dan Headley's heart missed at least two beats, maybe three. "Sir, excuse me. We have a problem."

"PROBLEM? PROBLEM? OF COURSE WE HAVE A PROB- LEM! WE'RE IN RETROGRADE. AND WHICH PLANET IN THE

GREAT SCHEME OF THE UNIVERSE DO YOU THINK CON-
TROLS ALL TRANSPORTATION AND COMMUNICATION
ISSUES? . . . "

"Me? I'm not really sure about that, sir. But I gotta go." And
with that Dan Headley charged out of the door, and long after he
had turned the corner for the companionway, he heard the CO
shout, "MERCURY, SIR, MERCURY! AND WHERE THE HELL
DO YOU THINK IT WAS ON AUGUST 14, 2000? ANSWER THAT,
DAMN YOU."

Dan heard that, all right. It was the day the *Kursk* hit the bottom of the Barents Sea. *We got a problem okay. But it's not some
hunk of fucking rock flying backwards around outer space. It's
sitting right back there in that little room—Reid in Retrograde
is a lot more like it.*

Inside the control room, there was an atmosphere of extreme
concern. Lieutenant Singer was on the line to comms. The satellite signal just in from the driver of the lead inflatable was brief
and forbidding.

It read: *"070410JUN07. 16.00N 94.19E—SEAL team delayed
in escape from Haing Gyi. Townsend walking wounded. PLAN
has helos up searching shoreline to Letpan Stream. Nine SF
trapped in high woods unable to reach boats. Attempting new RV
downstream. Inflatables not located. Chinese base history.
Hunter."*

Master Chief Drew Fisher had the conn, and Lt. Commander
Headley read the signal carefully. Lt. Singer handed him one of the
10-inch-wide scale maps on which Lt. Pearson had drawn in the
details of the triangular island, and they assessed the situation.

There was a distance of 1,000 yards downstream of the rendezvous point along the edge of the marsh. Right there the map
showed a wide inlet of water running right into the shore.
Shawn's map showed trees almost 40 feet high all the way. There
was no doubt Rick would make his way along there and make a
rush for the boats. Since the helos had plainly not yet located the
inflatables, there was obviously high grass cover in the marsh.

The problem was probably the inlet—everyone would have to break cover in there, and then attempt to charge out through the shallows across the Haing Gyi Shoal. Three miles.

"Mother of God," whispered Lt. Singer. "They haven't got a prayer on the open water."

"You mean the helos?"

"Yessir."

"Actually, they have two chances, Lieutenant. To break cover in secret, unseen by the helos. Or to shoot the fuckers down. They have three standard M-60s, right? One already in each boat, one with the team."

"You need to be a bit lucky to down a helo with one of those, sir. But I know it's been done plenty of times, and they do have six belts of ammunition in each boat."

"Where would you rather be, Lieutenant? On the ground with the guys holding the ammunition belts, or in a helo being machine-gunned by Commander Hunter?"

"On the ground with the Commander, sir. No question. . . . But what are we going to do?"

"Tell comms to get a signal in. Tell the boat driver to let us know the moment they're under way. We're going in to get 'em."

"Christ, sir. There're only about thirty-five feet of water this side of the big shoal."

"I don't actually give a fuck if there're only two feet. We're not leaving them."

"I'm afraid that decision will be made by me." And all three men in the control room turned to see Commander Reid standing there, very calmly, in marked contrast to his demeanor of just a few moments ago.

"Debrief me, XO. I need to appreciate the precise situation if you are planning to endanger the lives of my entire crew, and indeed of USS *Shark* itself."

Lieutenant Commander Headley walked over to him, and his tone was icy. "This is the map of the island, sir. The X there marks where the boats came in to embark the SEALs. This mark is where we anticipate the team will move, in order to embark farther downstream. There are PLAN helos up, but they have not yet discovered either the boats or Commander Hunter's team."

"I assume they will attempt to cross this wide shoal at high speed?"

"I agree, sir. And I'm proposing we come in on the surface and meet them. If we have to, I'll take the helos out with Stingers."

"Not on my watch, you won't, XO. How dare you decide in my ship virtually to declare war on China? In the open sea, firing publicly on Chinese aircraft quite properly defending their own base. No, sir. For that, you will need not only my permission, but that of the flag, and probably CINCPACFLT. Do you have any idea of the consequences of what you are proposing?"

Dan Headley stared him hard in the eyes. There was total silence in the control room. Commander Reid shook his head and turned away, walking out through the door.

Lieutenant Commander Headley did not acknowledge what had been said. He just turned back to Lt. Singer and ordered, "Please carry out my last order, Matt. Get that signal in to the boat drivers. We must know immediately when they leave."

"But what about the CO, sir? He plainly doesn't think we should go in."

"No," replied Dan. "He doesn't. Now get that signal away, and tell comms to stand by for the reply."

The Boat Chief, MCPO Drew Fisher, looked at the XO, and said quietly, "We're going in to get 'em, right, sir?"

"Do you want to leave Rick and the guys to die out there, Drew?"

"Nossir. No. I do not."

0414. Haing Gyi Island.

It was just beginning to rain now, and Commander Hunter with his eight SEALs were struggling through the thick tropical forest. They'd made their course adjustment in radio contact with Lt. MacPherson, who was now helping to drag the big inflatables along the shore in about two feet of water, too shallow to paddle, under a canopy of insect-ridden grasses.

"Jesus," he said, "I'm supposed to be a combat SEAL, not Humphrey fucking Bogart." And he was right. It was like a scene from *The African Queen*. All they needed was Katharine Hepburn manning the machine gun.

However, the deadly nature of this night was brought into all of its terrible reality by the clattering of the helicopters overhead, searching, searching for the murderers who had infiltrated their base and very nearly destroyed it.

Back under the trees Rick could hear them coming in low, circling the area. But right now all nine of the SEALs had but one thing on their mind. It was just 0415 and the armor-piercing bomb should be on its way. They would not hear the blast, one mile away and 3,000 feet below the surface of the earth. But they should hear something in the next couple of minutes.

Rick told them to keep moving, and the sense of anticipation grew more intense with every stride they took. Then they did hear it . . . a dull, muffled rumble, more like a distant earthquake.

And then there was nothing. But quite suddenly in the weird silence of the night, an explosion shook the island to its foundations. A colossal crash, erupting out over the forest, as the roof of the power station was blasted a hundred feet into the air, followed by a shattering white light that lit up the area.

A giant bright plume of incineratingly hot steam, 50 feet across, gushed skyward. Higher and higher above the island, burning into the rain clouds, 1,000 feet, 2,000 feet, roaring like the oil flame on an old-fashioned boiler. A million old-fashioned boilers.

The noise was an unearthly, unnatural, uncontrollable sound, gushing out of the very core of the earth. Up through the trees Rick Hunter and his men could see the dead-straight, ivory-white tower, like an endless skyscraper reaching up into the stratosphere, into the heavens, for all they knew.

Aside from the fact that it most certainly signaled the end of China's Naval base in Burma, the howling tower of steam did the

SEALs one other colossal favor. It totally distracted the three PLAN helicopters, two Russian-built ASW Helix-As and a single Helix-B assault craft carrying its full complement of UV-57 rockets. All three of them had been a mere 500 feet away from the power station when it blew, and they swerved instinctively away from the white inferno as it slammed the roof into the sky, showering the local airspace with bricks, concrete, dust and metal beams.

With everything on fire down below, it was difficult for them to land. Also there was no electric power, anywhere. There was no one to consult with. The pilots did not even know if there was anyone left alive. All three of them had managed to get airborne as a result of the last-second message from the late CO of the destroyer, but they had done so at huge risk, flying out and away from the fire in the fuel farm, and then picking up a new signal from the emergency transmitter in the accommodation block.

The officer had delivered the message under immense stress. He was badly wounded and his signal was more like a MAYDAY than an order. He just had time to tell the lead pilot the direction the murderers were headed—down to the marsh, before the radio went dead. As it happened, there were six officers still in the accommodation block, and they were trying to transmit to the helos. There was no one else at this stage to transmit to.

The big red-and-white Helix choppers were all very capable; two of them had the weapons to destroy a submerged submarine, and the other had rockets to outrange the U.S. Stingers. But they were very exposed, and very noisy. With their twin high rotors and four-corner landing wheels, they looked like a cruising flight of pterodactyls.

And now the pilots brought them in to land, out on that rough ground, 200 yards from the stream. And all nine of the occupants, pilots, navigators and gunners, ran for the accommodation block to receive whatever orders there might still be.

And that left the SEALs, for the moment, unthreatened. Commander Hunter told them to keep going. He told them to carry

Buster somehow between them, and Rattlesnake and his rookie assistant made a chair with their linked hands. Buster was able to sit in it, and he could lean back into the powerful arms and chest of Catfish Jones. Once they found a regular stride they were able to move fast, with Buster's weight distributed between them. Much faster than if he had had to walk himself.

They pressed on beneath the trees, struggling forward, dreading the sound of the returning helos. But none came, and Rick led them on down to the inlet, watching the compass, trying to keep on course two-five-five, more southerly than their previous route. And the sound of the roaring steam provided them with an inspiration, a feeling of self-congratulation. They had done what they came to do, and to a Navy SEAL that represents the meaning of life.

At 0440, they noticed the reeds and grasses petering out, and there was a new urgency in the bleeper, sounding out from the inflatable boats. Rick knew they must be close, and then he saw the water, gleaming in a kind of aerial phosphorescence from the snow-white steam towering over the entire island. It was a wide, shallow inlet, probably 50 yards across, and down the inlet, possibly 100 yards away, they could see five black figures trying to drag the boats nearer.

Rick Hunter snapped sharply into the radio receiver, *"DAL-LAS. RIGHT HERE . . . over."*

"Okay, sir," the reply came back. "It's just too shallow. We can't get the boats nearer, even empty . . . I'm coming back to the shore now . . . hold everything . . . over."

One minute later, Lt. MacPherson, followed by Mike Hook, came splashing through the shallows. "Sir," he said, "how about that? What about that steam? Way to go, right!"

"Way to go, kid. What now?"

"The bottom of this creek's firm. Let's get Buster inboard. The guys are hiding the boats under that grass. It's a beautiful over-hang—choppers never even saw them. C'mon, Rattles . . . okay, Buster, ole buddy, let's go home."

And now the full team stepped into the water and began to

move on down to the boats, Rick now carrying the M-60, all the others holding the MP-5s, one rookie with the second belt of ammunition. Their hoods were up now, wet-suit trousers folded and clipped over the tight rubber shoes, custom-made to fit the flippers. With no Draegers, bombs, explosives or hardware, it was easy going.

Except that out there above the trees there could suddenly be heard the sound of the helos returning, the pilots now firmly briefed as to the direction the fleeing murderers had taken. *They have to be down along the shore of that stream. Look for boats . . . and look for men in black combat suits.*

All three of the helos had their square rear doors open, and inside each one a gunner crouched behind a machine gun twice the size of the M-60, aiming it out through the gap. Up front, the navigator, wearing night goggles, sat beside the pilot, calling back target instructions.

This was big trouble. The SEALs were close to the boats, but there was no protection in there. And walking down the bright water of the inlet they were at their most vulnerable point of the entire mission.

"Get into the shore, and hit the deck right now." Rick Hunter was not joking. And he was not in time, either. The lead helicopter came battering in over the treetops. It was heading west out over the water when the rear navigator spotted movement in the shallows. He snapped out an order to the pilot to bank left, and hover at 100 feet. Then he told the gunner where he had seen movement, and he opened fire, raking the shoreline with a fusillade of bullets, ripping into the grass, making vicious lines in the water.

The first burst hit the last man into the reeds, and Catfish Jones took the full volley in his back and head. He fell dead into the shallows, still trying to hold on to Buster Townsend. Rattlesnake Davies, now left carrying Buster all on his own, saw Catfish hit the water, saw the bullets lashing all around him, and still went back to try to drag him to safety.

By some miracle the bullets missed Rattlesnake, and even

though he knew Catfish was surely dead, he would not let go, and he dragged the former North Carolina fisherman out of the firing line, and he kept saying over and over, "C'mon, Catfish, buddy, we'll be all right. I know we'll be all right . . . just keep comin' buddy . . . we're gonna be fine."

When at last he was under cover, he turned Petty Officer Jones over so the others could not see the terrible effects of the bullets, especially not the gaping hole in the back of his head.

Rick Hunter knew what had happened instantly. And he told them all, "We just have to keep still. Remember that machine gunner has no idea whether he hit anyone or not. Heads down, don't move. And say a prayer for Catfish. He was a great and brave man. But we have to go forward and save ourselves."

"Sir, we're not leaving him, are we, sir? " Rattlesnake Davies was beside himself. "I can't leave him, sir. I can't leave him."

"Don't be fucking stupid, Rattles. Of course we're not fucking leaving him." The Commander knew exactly how to talk to people who were on the verge of losing their grip.

"Jesus, sir. How the hell are we going to get outta here?" asked Lt. MacPherson.

"By using our brains, staying quiet, holding our nerve, hiding when we have to and hitting back hard when we get a chance."

"What worries me most is the daylight coming," said Dallas. "It's headed for zero-five-hundred, and I'm guessing it's gonna be light by six-thirty—we got ninety minutes max to make the open water."

"And it ain't gonna be all that great when we do, unless we can get some help. I'm counting on my buddy Danny for that."

And now they could hear the three helos making a long circle out over the Haing Gyi Shoal, and their clatter died out to the east, which signified they were coming right back in roughly six minutes from now. Commander Hunter rallied his team. They got Buster to his feet and walking, and two of the rookies dragged the body of Catfish Jones out into the water, faceup, and began to pull him through the shallows toward the inflatables, now only 50 yards away.

It was slower than anyone wanted, but the skies seemed clear and the fresh water running down toward the ocean was cleaning the wounds of the dead SEAL who had destroyed the Chinese frigate.

They reached the boats safely, placed the body in one and stretched Buster out comfortably in the other. The two Navy boat drivers, Seamen Ward and Franks, helped load the rest of the men inboard. Rattlesnake was in with Buster, plus Rick Hunter and the two rookies who had served with them outside the power plant. Lieutenant MacPherson was in the other boat.

Two more rookies went into the second craft, where Mike Hook was already sorting out the gear and organizing the M-60. Everyone was still in the cover of the overhanging grass, but the weight had put the boats on the bottom. Commander Hunter and Lt. Allensworth went back in the water, and the skies were clear. It was still dark and the team leader decided they should at least be floating ready for the moment when they would make a run for it, straight down the widening river and across the shoal.

"The grass is just as good to hide in down there another fifty yards as it is up here," he said. "And there're probably five feet of water. Bobby and me'll drag us down there. I'll pull, he'll shove. I don't like boats aground in a foot of water."

Rick Hunter siezed the painter of the lead boat and heaved. Astern Bobby Allensworth pushed with all his strength, and the boat moved. Rick heaved some more, and the boat slid off the mud with water under its keel.

"One at a time. We'll take 'em separately," he said. "Use the paddles to stay as far into the grass as you can." And Commander Hunter began to haul the boat along, with Bobby at his side, preventing it from drifting out into the bright stream.

They'd gone 25 yards when the helos came back, and the sound of the steam roaring out of the power plant deadened the sound of the engines. Bobby Allensworth saw them before he heard them, and he yelled at Rick to shove the boat inshore and then hit the water.

The SEAL commander turned, saw the helos about a half mile

off, racing into the inlet where they had opened fire before. The pilot banked right, losing height as he came in over the trees. The navigator thought he spotted something in the water, and he ordered the gunner to open up along the bank again.

Once more the bullets from the big Russian-made machine gun ripped into the left bank, and he kept firing all the way down its length. The two SEALs dived facedown into the water, and the the first helicopter overflew them. But the second one didn't. Rick Hunter and Bobby surfaced without knowing it was there and the second machine-gunner, wearing night goggles, spotted them, and rained fire down on them.

The chopper was so low it could hardly miss, and with heart-breaking courage the SEAL from the Los Angeles ghetto flung himself onto his Commander's back and took eleven bullets that jolted his entire body, obliterating his spine, neck and head. He died instantly, still clinging to Rick's back. Still the devoted bodyguard.

Rick Hunter forced himself up out of the mud, safe but wet. "Shit, Bobby," he said. "You trying to drown us both?"

And then he saw Bobby Allensworth, lying in the water, faceup, blood streaming down his face where two bullets had almost gone right through. And Rick just had time to lift him up and into the boat, before he broke away, momentarily burying his head in the blank rubber side of the hull. No one had ever seen Rick Hunter that close to breaking before.

Lieutenant MacPherson saw what had happened and now he too went over the side, manhandling the craft into the deeper water. "Those fucking little creeps," he said. "But at least we know where we stand. We gotta float and we gotta fight. Get those fucking M-60s ready right now, and start the engine."

They drove along to Commander Hunter, while Chief Mike Hook laid out the ammunition belts for the M-60s. And none too soon. All three Chinese helicopters were making a long turn, plainly to return to the inlet.

"Sir, I'm sorry," said Dallas. "Really sorry. But I got the machine gun ready in our boat. You all set here? Get under the grass again. We'll let 'em have it as they come in, sustained fire on the leader, right? Everything we got, to down one of 'em. Discourage the others, right?"

"Right, Dallas. Let's go."

But the Chinese pilots were not certain they had done any damage at all so far. And they fanned out, with just the leader flying back down the bloodstained little waterway. He came in low, and as he did so the SEALs opened fire with everything they had from the little boats behind the grasses. Dallas blew 30 rounds straight into the rear door of the chopper killing the gunner and, somehow, the navigator.

Mike Hook blasted away at the engines, set topside left and right below the rotors. And Commander Hunter, firing with a venom he had never experienced before, emptied an entire belt of 100 rounds into the cockpit area of the rocket-firing Helix-B. It might have been the engine, it might have been the bullets smashing through the side windows, it might have been anything. But whatever it was, the helicopter was suddenly belching flames, and it spun right over and slammed into the water at 130 miles an hour.

"Fuck me," said one of the rookies.

At which point they could all see the lights of the two remaining Helix choppers wheeling around to the north, running up the narrow island where the downstream channel parts, before slowly turning east, back toward the blazing Naval base.

Both pilots were confused. They had just seen 33 percent of their attack force destroyed. The ships upon which they normally served were gone. There was no fuel. No electricity. Hundreds were dead. The entire base was engulfed in fire. At the epicenter of the inferno was a roaring white phenomenon, directly from Hell. They had no one, formally, to whom they must report, and they had just seen, firsthand, the firepower of their adversaries. No two Chinese warriors had ever had so little stomach for the fight. And they headed once more for that rough ground opposite the power station, to land once more and inform the remaining group of officers what had befallen them.

The SEALs, of course, did not know all this. But Commander Hunter again rallied his battered team.

"Guys, we have to break out of here sometime . . . it might as well be now. . . . How many ammunition belts do we have?"

Seaman Ward, a tough-looking Irishman from Cleveland, said, "We brought six. You guys had one left, which you used, sir. So we got four unused, and half of two others."

"Okay, divide 'em up. We'll take one gun in the lead boat, which I'll handle. Lieutenant MacPherson and Chief Mike Hook will operate the other two. Get the paddles and shove out. Soon as the water's deep enough, drop the engines and go. Someone fire up the radio, and I'll get the signal into the satellite."

The two boats paddled out through the shallows and into the wide channel. It was definitely getting light now, not sufficiently to see Shawn Pearson's map clearly, but the tiny point of the flashlight showed three feet of water. They dropped their engines at 0520, and under deserted skies, still lit up to the east by the burning Naval base, they accelerated the engines mildly, making eight knots, course two-six-zero, straight for the uncertain waters of the Haing Gyi Shoal.

0528. USS *Shark*. 16.00N 94.01E.
Speed 3. Racetrack course. PD.

Lieutenant Commander Headley read the new signal with absolute horror:

"070520JUN07. 16.00N 94.18E. Under heavy fire from pursuing helos. Lt. Allensworth, Petty Officer Jones both killed. Inflatables undamaged. Headed for Haing Gyi Shoal course two-three-zero flank speed. Downed one Helix. We have ammo, and still three M-60s. Request Shark assistance. Difficult for us in open waters. Hunter."

The CO was again not in the control room. And Dan Headley now summoned the senior executives in the submarine. Master Chief Drew Fisher was already in there, and the Officer of the Deck, Lt. Matt Singer, had the conn. Lieutenant Pearson came in, accompanied by the Combat Systems Officer, Lt. Commander

Jack Cressend. The Sonar Officer, Lt. Commander Josh Gandy, came in last.

"Gentlemen, I am going to read out to you two signals we have received in the last two hours from the SEAL team we inserted last night into Burma."

From their faces, it was not difficult to discern the personal pain each man felt from the death of the two SEALs and the wounding of another.

"As you can see from the signal, they are essentially making a run for it," said the XO. "A high-speed run back to this ship. They have around eighteen miles to travel, which puts them in open waters for around forty-five to fifty minutes.

"The Helix will make 130 knots, no sweat. He could get here in about eight minutes. Which makes the SEAL team sitting ducks. Those damn Russian choppers, either the ASWs or the assault versions, carry a lot of hardware. And they plainly have heavy machine guns. The guys might shoot one of 'em down, but they might not. The odds have to favor the helos. Which means that Rick and the rest of the guys will all be dead sometime in the next hour."

Dan Headley paused, and he could see the unease written on their faces. "It is my view," he said, "that we comply with their request and head on in to save them. As you know, we're just about on the fifty-meter line and we have about eighty feet below the keel. We can probably move in at fifteen knots PD for four miles, but we can make twenty-plus on the surface, so I'm proposing we surface right now and go straight for it. There is no serious Chinese Naval presence left in the area, thanks to them. But we may have to take the Helix out with Stingers; the sooner we get the inflatables under Stinger cover the better chance they'll have.

"Gentlemen, I am proposing we make all speed inshore to rescue them. Is anyone not in favor of that action?"

Lieutenant Pearson and Lt. Commanders Cressend and Gandy said, almost in unison, "In favor, sir."

Chief Fisher said, "Why are you asking, sir? Sure we're in favor. We have the gear to save 'em. Jesus Christ, let's GO."

"Officer of the Deck, steer course one-one-zero, stand by to surface . . ." There was no mistaking the firm edge to his voice.

"Aye, sir . . ." said Lieutenant Singer, with equal emphasis. Like the XO, and like Chief Fisher, he understood that this was tantamount to a total confrontation. He had, after all, heard their Commanding Officer insist that such a decision was going to be made only by him. Commander Reid had also left little doubt that his decision was likely to be negative. His own words had betrayed his own worst fears . . . *"Do you have any idea of the consequences of what you are proposing?"*

USS *Shark* nonetheless surged forward, shoving her blunt nose through the water at 22 knots on the surface of the Bay of Bengal.

"Depth twenty fathoms, still fifty feet below the keel, course steady one-one-zero . . . making twenty-two knots."

The submarine had been virtually stationary for 12 hours, and the sudden dramatic change in speed was obvious to everyone. But to the XO, Lt. Singer and Chief Fisher there was something far more dramatic waiting in the wings. And there was not long to wait.

Commander Reid came through the door with a face like an ocean storm. But he spoke quietly. "Lieutenant Commander Headley," he said, "where, precisely, do you think you are taking my ship entirely without my permission? And, I suspect, entirely contrary to opinions I have already expressed?"

"Sir, I am taking the ship inshore on a rescue mission to save a team of United States Navy SEALs from what I consider to be imminent death. I am certain this course of action is approved by every man serving on this ship, including, I hope, yourself."

"Well, your certainty is misplaced. I wonder if you would be kind enough to inform me why you believe death to be imminent?"

"Because they are being pursued, sir, by two Russian-built Helix helicopters. And they are in open boats, inflatables, on the open sea, protected only by three M-60 light machine guns, which will probably be no match for the weapons against them."

"Are the Helix aircraft ASWs?"

"I believe one of them must be, sir. They came from the two warships moored in the base. So I doubt there would be more than one Type-B assault craft. There were almost certainly two Type-A ASWs, which means there's at least one left. The guys downed one of the three."

"I see. And how do you propose to continue this mission of mercy. On the surface?"

"Yessir."

"I see." Commander Reid's tone was cold. "Now I want to get this straight. You are proposing to take *my ship, on the surface* into the direct path of an oncoming Russian-built helicopter, which may be carrying rockets that outrange us? IS THAT COR-RECT, LIEUTENANT COMMANDER?"

"Yessir."

"Have you gone mad, XO?"

"I do not believe so, sir."

"Then explain yourself, sir. And while you are about it, con-sider, if you will, the conversation you and I had less than two hours ago."

And now Commander Reid's eyes were moving back and forth across the control room. His head was turning only slightly, and his stare was upon all three of those present.

"*RETROGRADE! RETROGRADE, XO!* The great planet Mer-cury is in retreat. I have tried to explain this to you, and I trust you have relayed my concerns to the crew? WELL, HAVE YOU?"

"Nossir."

"*WHY NOT, DAMN YOU! DO YOU THINK THERE IS SOME-THING MORE IMPORTANT?*"

"I am not really qualified to offer an opinion on that, sir."

"*NO, XO. NO, YOU ARE NOT.* Because you are an ignorant man. Like all these others. You know nothing of the cycles of the universe. You know only minor details. Details of your own insignificant life and those immediately around you. You know nothing, XO. Nothing."

"As you wish, sir."

"I have tried to be patient with the terrible depths of your ignorance, Lieutenant Commander. I have tried to explain that Mercury rules so much of our lives, particularly those of serving Naval officers. Because of the planet's supreme involvement with transportation and communications.

"It is apparent to me, as it must be apparent to you, that the forces of the planet are already at work. If you happened to have been Chinese, working at the Naval base, you would have faced catastrophe probably unprecedented in your lifetime. And what has been destroyed? Ships, fueling facilities and communications. The essence of any Naval base. The targets of the great planet.

"And as for our own operation: Plainly the SEAL mission has gone drastically wrong. The journey they are now on may be their last. *AND YOU, XO, ARE TRYING TO TAKE MY SHIP INTO THE PATH OF A HELICOPTER ARMED WITH ROCKETS THAT CAN PIERCE OUR PRESSURE HULL? RIGHT NOW, WITH MERCURY IN RETROGRADE? NOSSIR. NO YOU WILL NOT.*"

"Not everyone believes in astrology, sir."

"No, of course not. But many great men believe in it. Who was the greatest U.S. President in recent years, the man who rebuilt the Navy?"

"President Reagan, sir."

"Exactly so. He and his wife believed. They understood the cycles of the universe. They took expert consultation, as many great men before them have done. And now, XO, turn this ship around. And return to our official rendezvous point, 16.00N 94.01E.

"AND WHILE YOU ARE CARRYING OUT MY ORDERS, REMEMBER THE OLDEST RULE OF THE NUCLEAR SUBMARINE COMMANDER . . . NEVER . . . NEVER, EVER . . . TAKE YOUR SHIP TO THE SURFACE IN THE FACE OF THE ENEMY. TURN IT AROUND, LIEUTENANT COMMANDER."

Dan Headley replied slowly and carefully. "I am afraid I cannot do that, sir," he said.

"Lieutenant Commander, I am going to pretend, for the moment, I never heard that. And I say again, Turn this ship around, RIGHT NOW!"

"I think you heard me, sir. I am afraid I cannot do that. Under any circumstances whatsoever . . . *Conn–XO, continue course one-one-zero at flank . . . same course, same speed.*"

"Lieutenant Commander Headley, you are forcing me to conclude that you are conducting a one-man mutiny on this ship. And I now formally place you under ship's arrest, and I command you to leave the control room."

"I am afraid that will not be happening, sir." And with that, Dan Headley summoned again the senior executives of the ship back to the control room. And one by one they entered, the Lieutenant Commanders, Jack Cressend and Josh Gandy, and the Navigation Officer, Lt. Shawn Pearson. Master Chief Fisher and the Officer of the Deck, Lt. Matt Singer, were already there.

"I have consulted with the ship's senior execs already, sir," said Dan Headley. "And it is the opinion of each man that it is our duty to save the platoon of SEALs if that is possible. We are a warship, and we're certainly equipped to deal with a couple of aging Chinese Navy helos.

"The SEALs have just acted with the utmost bravery, successfully carrying out the orders of, I understand, the President of the United States, the National Security Adviser, and the Chief of Naval Operations. Only if I receive direct orders from one or all of those three men will I cease and desist in my efforts to save our colleagues."

Commander Reid swelled into what looked like the opening moments of a towering rage. "XO!!" he bellowed, "do you have any idea what it would be like if one of those helicopters hit and sank us—could you imagine us being like the Russians in the *Kursk*, trapped on the floor of the ocean, suffocating to death. CAN YOU IMAGINE THAT, XO?"

"Perhaps not as well as you can, sir."

"If you only knew, Lieutenant Commander. If you only knew, as I know, the terror of such moments."

And now Dan Headley, surrounded by his fellow officers, stared straight back at the Commanding Officer, and he spoke kindly. "Sir, it is my opinion that you have not been feeling terri-

bly well recently. You have been under strain, and I think everyone would prefer you to grab some sleep, while we take care of
this rescue. As you know, we are moving toward the SEALs as
fast as we can go, and I am afraid nothing is going to stop that.
The crew will not leave the SEALs to die, and that is the end of it."

Commander Reid once more bristled with fury. *"THE ONLY
THING AT AN END RIGHT NOW IS YOUR CAREER, XO. AND
THE CAREERS OF ANYONE WHO WISHES TO SUPPORT YOU
IN THIS LUNATIC ADVENTURE."*

"I don't think so, sir. But perhaps you would now leave the
area, because we are about to become very busy. . . . Lieutenant
Pearson . . . if the guys were in the shoal waters at zero-five-
three-five, making twenty-five knots . . . where are they now?
How far from us? . . ."

But before Shawn Pearson could run those calculations, Com-
mander Reid exploded: "I WILL NOT HAVE THIS DEFIANCE . . .
I AM THE COMMANDING OFFICER OF THIS SHIP, AND I
WILL NOT HAVE HER TAKEN DELIBERATELY INTO A FATAL
CONFRONTATION. . . . NOW STEP ASIDE, OFFICER OF THE
DECK . . . I'M TAKING THE CONN. . . . XO, YOU WILL ALSO
STEP ASIDE WHILE I ISSUE NEW, CORRECT ORDERS TO THE
PLANESMAN. I WANT THIS SHIP TURNED AND RUNNING
BELOW THE SURFACE IMMEDIATELY."

No one spoke. No one moved. And *Shark* kept running forward, fast, on the surface, toward the SEALs.

Lieutenant Pearson broke the ice. "Sir, I do not think they
could have reached the shoal before zero-five-four-zero. The
approach from the channel through the marshes is very shallow,
medium speed at best. But they could have rushed across the
shoal. There're always three or four feet there, even at low tide in
the worst parts. Four miles would have taken them probably
twelve minutes, so they should be right off Mawdin Point, running fast, west, at zero-five-five-two . . . right now I have zero-five-
five-zero . . . two minutes from now there should be eight miles
between us . . . closing at forty-seven knots. Probably see 'em
from the bridge in around ten minutes."

Lieutenant Pearson spoke as if the CO were not even in the control room, never mind in control of the ship.

And the XO turned once more back to Commander Reid, and said quietly, "I'm putting you on the sick list, sir. I think that would be best for everyone."

"XO, you are doing no such thing. I am taking command of this ship and I am turning around, and going below the surface, where I intend to remain. If the SEAL team arrives being pursued by the Helix helicopters, I will remain below the surface. Because, XO, unlike yourself and others in this room, I am governed by Navy regulations. Nuclear submarines do not travel on the surface in the face of the enemy. NOW STEP ASIDE."

Lieutenant Commander Headley did not move. He simply said, "Under Section one-zero-eight-eight of United States Navy Regulations I am relieving you of further duty. Since you have refused my offer of placement on the sick list, I am placing you under arrest. I am next in the succession to command. I am plainly unable to refer the matter to a common superior, and I am confident that your prejudicial actions are not caused by instructions unknown to me . . ."

Commander Reid raised his arms in exasperation, holding them high and slightly to the front, like a Catholic priest before communion. "MY 'PREJUDICIAL ACTIONS'! How dare you, XO. This entire episode has been caused by your childhood friendship with Commander Hunter. We all know you and the SEALs have been buddy-buddy ever since we arrived in Diego Garcia. And this has come down to loyalty. Your loyalty to those damn brutes in the rubber inflatables, against my loyalty to the one hundred seven officers and men on this nuclear submarine. YOU ARE A DAMNED CHARLATAN, Lieutenant Commander. And you may have fooled some of the crew. But you have not damned well fooled me. SO STEP ASIDE."

"COMMANDER REID. YOU ARE UNDER ARREST." Dan Headley was not speaking kindly anymore. "Chief Fisher, go and round up six seamen and escort the former Commanding Officer to his room, where he will be confined until further notice. . . .

"NOW, Officer of the Deck, continue at the conn and continue this course with all speed . . . Lieutenant Commander Gandy, have comms try to contact the little boats . . . Lieutenant Commander Cressend, have Stinger missiles brought up, ready to be fired from the sail . . . Lieutenant Pearson, report to the bridge . . . I'll be there in a few minutes. . . . That's all."

Every man so addressed replied with a sharp "Aye, sir." And then Lt. Commander Headley turned back to Commander Reid. "I would very much like to think you are just undergoing psychological problems, which may have been with you for a long time. However, the only alternative view available to me is that you are nothing short of a damned coward."

"Those are the remarks of an insolent and very misguided officer," replied the ex-CO. "I have the lives of the one hundred seven officers and men on this ship very much on my mind. And I am aware that in order to save your friend Hunter, you are quite prepared to sacrifice the lives of every one of us."

"I suppose it would never occur to a man like you that we can fight and win this thing, down the Chinese helicopters flying out of their burned-out base. And then save the lives of perhaps ten of the bravest men ever to have operated on behalf of our country. I don't suppose it would have occurred either to that French creep you so admire, or think you once were, or whatever crackpot thoughts go on in your mind."

"You'll damned well pay for this, Headley. I'll have you court-martialed the moment we return to an American port."

"You may try; of course that's your prerogative. I'd be surprised if you didn't have a few questions to answer yourself, about the death of yet another SEAL you flatly refused to help. Charlie Mitchell was his name, and I can tell you now, Commander Bennett is not pleased."

At that point, Master Chief Fisher arrived with a group of seamen. "Take him below, Drew," ordered the XO. "Lock him in his quarters until further notice. If he resists, carry him. Just get him out of my sight."

"And what am I supposed to do shut up in there until you feel inclined to release me?"

"I neither know nor care. Why don't you ask your dead friend Captain Grigory Lyachin. He'd probably help. I wouldn't bother to contact Villeneuve. He'd probably tell you to commit suicide, as he did."

Commander Reid departed under escort, hissing venomously, "You out-and-out bastard, Headley."

0554. Bay of Bengal.
Off Mawdin Point,
West Coast of Burma.

The two fast inflatables, throttles wide open, raced across the flat sea. Out to the east, the skies were colored rose-pink, but the sun had not yet risen out of the endless rice fields of the delta. No sun, no sign of the helicopters returning.

They made a course change, heading now roughly west nor'west, two-nine-zero, directly toward USS *Shark*. If the submarine remained at the rendezvous point, they had a run of 15 miles and perhaps 40 minutes. But everyone hoped against all hope that *Shark* was on her way in to try to save them. One of the rookies was balancing, standing up in the inflatable, holding an aerial way above his head, while Lt. MacPherson attempted to raise the submarine's comms room on the VHF radio. So far they were receiving nothing.

They raced on for another mile, and then the lookout in the rear boat spotted them—the two Chinese Helix-A choppers battering their way across Burma's western headland, slowly, making a search along the shore, under strict instructions now from the gathering of surviving officers at Haing Gyi to hunt down and destroy the criminals who had blown up the base.

Instantly, Commander Rick Hunter shouted, "Man both the M-60s . . . don't waste your ammunition by firing too soon . . . they'll probably come in right on our six o'clock and then bank away . . . all three of us go for the cockpits first . . . then, Dallas, go for the rear doors . . . try to take out the gunners . . . Mike, you again go for the engines . . . I'll keep banging away at the pilots. FIRE on my command."

Moments later, the Chinese pilots spotted the little boats, almost two miles away now, holding a steady course, separated by a distance of only 30 yards. Commander Hunter then ordered the boats to split up, "Just make sure neither helo can fire at both boats at the same time."

Thirty seconds later the Helix-As were on them, coming in low, dead astern. *"FIRE!!"* yelled Rick Hunter, and the SEALs opened up, but it was very difficult in the bucking inflatables. They drove them away, neither helicopter managing to get a clean burst of fire at the boats.

But now they came around again, and the leader banked right, giving his gunner a clear shot, and he raked the water and then the inflatable with bullets, ripping four large tears in the rubberized hull, and hitting Commander Hunter in his upper thigh and one of the rookies in the chest. A blistering fusillade of bullets from Dallas and Mike Hook drove the other one away, but neither chopper was damaged, and with blood pouring from his wound, Rick Hunter swung his machine gun around and turned to face them again.

But now the two pilots flew back to the east. One of their machine gunners was badly wounded, and they needed to caucus. That gave the SEALs three more minutes to restore order. Buster Townsend, using his good arm, tried to get a tourniquet around Commander Hunter's thigh but it was not very successful, and the blood kept flowing.

And then they saw it, the black hull of USS *Shark* barreling in over the horizon, a huge bow wave flooding blue water aft down the hull, splitting at the sail, and cascading off port and starboard.

Commander Hunter, gritting his teeth, shouted, *"Steer straight for the submarine. GO-GO-GO!"*

There was about a mile distance between them now, and they

were closing at 47 knots. That represented only a little over a minute's running time. Too long. The Helix-As were heading back toward them, and they had the hang of it now. They came in low at an angle, the machine gunners now firing at will.

Rick and Dallas both went for the rear door, and again they hit one of the gunners, but the Chinese fired four lethal bursts, and again they hit the lead boat, which was now shipping water. A vicious line of bullets ripped through the little craft, hitting Buster Townsend three times in the chest, and killing him instantly as he tried to bandage the Commander. One of the rookies was also killed, and Rattlesnake Davies took a bullet in his upper right arm.

The SEALs could not possibly survive such an onslaught. And now both helos were on their way back again. Dallas and Mike Hook were still trying to clip in a new ammunition belt, and Rick Hunter, his hands sticky with blood, tackled them alone, blasting away at the cockpits. But this time the lead helo changed tactics, kept going forward and then swung hard to port, right across the bow of the sinking inflatable. Big mistake. Because it flew right into the range of one of *Shark*'s missile men, waiting patiently on the deck behind the twin dry-dock shelters, the only one not up on the sail.

He aimed the five-foot tube straight at the helo, hit the buttons the infrared homing, heat-seeking Stinger needed, and then fired it dead straight at 600 yards range. It blasted out of the tube, almost knocking the operator flat, adjusted its flight, and then streaked in at Mach-2 straight at the Helix.

It slammed into the starboard engine and blew the entire aircraft to shreds. The second Helix banked around, determined to loose off a depth bomb against the hull of the submarine. But he was not in time. The missile men up on the sail had two more Stingers in the air before it could adjust height and course, and the astounded SEALs watched both engines explode in one single raging fireball, right below the rotors, before it joined its cohort, crashing into the waves right off *Shark*'s port-side bow.

And now more boats were being launched off the deck to pick

up the SEALs who were in the water and the crew of the second inflatable, which was still floating by some miracle, since its entire starboard side had been split open by the bullets.

Rick Hunter and Rattlesnake were hauled out first, and assisted up on deck. Stretchers were produced immediately for both the wounded SEALs. Body bags were brought up for Catfish, Bobby, Buster and the young SEAL Sam Liefer. And they hauled Mike Hook, Dallas MacPherson, the two drivers and the four rookies back aboard.

Commander Hunter was drifting in and out of consciousness now, and they strapped him into the stretcher while they lowered it through the hatch on its way to the medical room, where the Navy doctor and his assistants awaited him.

Lieutenant Commander Dan Headley was also down there to meet his old buddy, but Rick was very weak and needed a blood transfusion. Buster's tourniquet may have saved his life, because a bullet had hit within millimeters of the femoral artery, the one that almost always causes matadors to die, if the horn of the bull happens to rake through their thigh.

He was awake for just a few seconds under the lights of the medical center when he saw Dan standing next to him.

"I can't believe this. . . . I thought the game was up," said Rick.

"You didn't think I'd leave you to die, did you? You didn't leave me."

"Hey, thanks, shithead," muttered the SEAL Commander, as they wheeled him into the emergency area.

And Now Lt. Commander Headley was alone with the consequences of his actions. He returned to the control room and ordered *Shark* back into deep water. Then he found a quiet corner to draft a signal back to San Diego, and it took him longer than he had spent saving the SEALs.

In the end it read: *"To: COMSUBPACFLT. 070700JUN. Am 16.00N 94.01E. At 0540 this morning under Section 1088 Naval Regulations, I took command of the ship, and placed Commander Reid under arrest on grounds of psychological instability. Commander Reid refused request for assistance from U.S. Navy SEAL assault team operational in Bassein Delta. All senior executives in agreement with my actions. USS* Shark *subsequently carried out rescue. Four SEALs killed in action before we arrived to save remaining eight men, including badly wounded Commander Hunter. Two Chinese Helix helicopters destroyed with missiles. Submarine undamaged. Request immediate orders to return either Diego Garcia or San Diego. Signed: Lt. Commander D. Headley, CO USS* Shark.*"*

Dan put the signal on the satellite a little after 0700. He then appointed an official second-in-command, the Combat Systems Officer, Lt. Commander Jack Cressend. Then he retired to sleep until 0900, having been awake for almost 24 hours. To sleep, perhaps to come to terms with the word *mutiny,* and to await his fate.

It was 1430 in Pearl Harbor when the communication from Lt. Commander Dan Headley landed on the desk of Rear Admiral Freddie Curran, Commander Submarines Pacific Fleet. In fact, it did not actually land; it just fell right out of the sky with a resounding thud, like a time bomb. Not in living memory had there been a mutiny in a United States warship on the high seas.

Rear Admiral Curran just stared at it for a few moments, and tried to decide whether to have *Shark* routed back to Diego Garcia to rejoin the *Harry S. Truman* Carrier Battle Group. Or to order the submarine to make all speed home to its base in San Diego, a distance of more than 12,000 miles—three weeks' running time.

As far as Admiral Curran was concerned, most of the U.S. Navy was already in the area of the Indian Ocean and the Arabian Sea, so it was scarcely imperative to get USS *Shark* back on station. And right now he was holding not so much a hot potato as an incandescent potato, and that three-week cushion would give everyone time to decide a reasonable course of action.

It was clear from the signal that *Shark*'s XO had acted with the highest possible motives, and there was no doubt that the veteran

Commander Reid was something of an oddball. *But Christ!* thought Admiral Curran. *Mutiny is mutiny, and it took place in a United States warship on the high seas.* And he hit the secure direct line to the Pearl Harbor office of CINCPACFLT, Admiral Dick Greening, and read him the signal.

The Commander-in-Chief of the Pacific Fleet gulped. Twice. "Mother of God," he said. "Mutiny?"

"Well observed, sir. I'd come to a similar conclusion myself."

"I assume you've ordered the submarine back to San Diego."

"I was about to do so. And I will have done it in, say, fifteen minutes."

"Okay."

Admiral Curran's signal was carefully worded . . . *"Lieutenant Commander Headley. Received your signal 1430. Return USS* Shark *San Diego immediately. Admiral Curran. COMSUBPAC."*

Dan Headley read it minutes later. "Wonder if they'll give me a job at Hunter Valley?" he pondered. "Because if the Navy court-martials me for mutiny, it's all over in dark blue. This is probably my first and last command. Kinda unusual end to an otherwise exemplary career."

Meantime the surgeon operated on Rick Hunter's ripped thigh. The bullet had mercifully not damaged the femoral, but it had wreaked havoc with all the other blood vessels. And the doctor stitched carefully for three hours, after a major blood transfusion for the mighty SEAL leader.

It was several hours before Rick could sit up in his bed and make any sense. During the late afternoon he listened to Dan Headley's account of the mutiny in the privacy of the sick bay.

At 1800 he decided to send in his own short satellite signal to Coronado. It read: *"SEAL mission on Haing Gyi Island accomplished. Naval base plus two PLAN warships destroyed. Four of our platoon killed, including Lt. Allensworth, Petty Officer Jones and Buster Townsend. We also lost combat SEAL Sam Liefer. Both Riff Davies and myself were wounded. We would all have died but for the actions of Lt. Commander Dan Headley. Signed: Commander Rick Hunter, on board USS* Shark."

That signal went straight in to SPECWARCOM and arrived on the desk of Admiral John Bergstrom in the small hours of the morning. Its result was to put the Navy of the United States of America into one of the biggest quandaries it had ever experienced: whether to court-martial for mutiny a man who was not only an outstanding commander but also a plain and obvious hero.

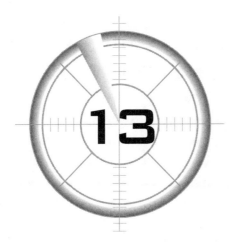

LIEUTENANT COMMANDER HEADLEY had offered Commander Reid every courtesy, including the freedom to send in his own signal to CINCPACFLT in Pearl. It went, of course, directly to Admiral Dick Greening and portrayed the actions taken by *Shark*'s XO as nothing short of "making a mutiny."

It stated: *"My command was removed by my own Executive Officer in the most shocking and totally unjustifiable manner. The XO was tacitly supported by other senior officers in the crew, but not verbally. They merely failed to object to this plain and dangerous breach of Navy regulations. I am thus drawn to the opinion that Lt. Commander Headley stands guilty of making a mutiny, and ought, by rights, to be court-martialed forthwith. Signed: Commander D. K. Reid, Commanding Officer, USS* Shark."

"That," pondered the Commander-in-Chief, "is not the message of a man looking for peace." And in that moment he understood that battle lines were about to be drawn, despite the obvious danger that press and public opinion might consolidate behind the hero who had saved the embattled SEALs, and against

406 ★ PATRICK ROBINSON

the right and proper Commanding Officer of the nuclear submarine.

And so, as USS *Shark* made her way home across the wide Pacific Ocean, the High Command of the United States Navy was forced to acknowledge the probability of a court-martial: a court-martial that could very well split opinion in half, both in the service and in the entire nation, if the press managed to grasp its significance.

Admiral Greening viewed the situation with such seriousness, he consulted immediately with the Pacific Submarine Chief, Admiral Freddie Curran. And the two men left Hawaii that evening for Washington, to consult with the CNO, and then with the Chairman of the Joint Chiefs, before taking the matter inevitably to the White House.

There was nothing on record in the annals of the U.S. Navy that showed a court-martial for mutiny, and the CNO, Admiral Alan Dixon, was especially anxious for that situation not to change, certainly not on his watch. Because mutinies, although rare, possess a special glory of their own. The leader inevitably presents himself as a Samaritan, saving his ship from disaster. Worse yet, he is frequently believed. Even in fiction, the most famous case being *The Caine Mutiny*, Captain Queeg was widely accepted as some kind of obvious nutcase.

Admiral Dixon greeted Admiral Greening with grave concern. Essentially this should have been the province of the Submarine Fleet Commander, Admiral Curran, but it was likely to be bigger than all three of them. And one hour later, only one fact was obvious: To get rid of the spectacle of putting a Navy hero on trial for his life and career, it would be necessary to stop Commander Reid from pressing charges.

Even then, a Navy Board of Inquiry might very well recommend a court-martial. In fact, they would almost certainly recommend that in any instance of mutiny on the high seas, the offending officer must, by the very nature of his crime, face the most searching examination by his peers.

That, of course, was all very fine, since Navy Boards of Inquiry can be carried out in the strict privacy of the service. But there are certain crimes, transgressions and errors that, if committed by a senior officer, must be examined. And certain findings must, by their very seriousness, be continued into a court-martial.

The U.S. Navy is not as stringent as the Royal Navy in these matters, but they both operate out of a near-identical rule book. And whereas the Americans are often content with a Board of Inquiry, and a stern letter of censure to the officer concerned, the Royal Navy is much more inclined to court-martial, on principle, *any officer* who manages to lose, or even mislay, his ship. And that applies to a departmental chief who is considered to have created a major foul-up.

Practically the only exception to those rules occurred in the Battle for the Falkland Islands in 1982, when Prime Minister Margaret Thatcher made it subtly clear she wanted no tarnish upon the shining glory of victory.

Admiral Alan Dixon was extremely worried. They must, he knew, convene a Board of Inquiry, just as soon as *Shark* reached San Diego. And although it might be possible to lean on its members not to recommend court-martial, that was a risky course of action. Members of official Navy boards are apt to consider themselves sacrosanct in all their deliberations, and they would be fully capable of recommmending a court-martial, and making their decision public.

Meanwhile he and the two Admirals from Pearl Harbor were obliged to inform the Chairman of the Joint Chiefs that they stood on the verge of a public relations nightmare, and that they faced a terrible quandary: Do we charge and court-martial Lt. Commander Dan Headley for "mutiny in a U.S. warship on the high seas"? More important, What the hell can we do to stop it?

At 0900 the following morning they all stood in the office of the CJC, General Tim Scannell, and deliberated the problem . . . to court-martial the hero of the Bay of Bengal, the fearless Naval Lieutenant Commander who drove into the face of the enemy, destroyed that enemy and rescued one of the finest U.S. Navy SEALs assault teams ever to serve the American people.

"Jesus Christ," said General Scannell. "The Big Man, over yonder, is not going to love this."

Nor did he. The three Admirals and the General carefully explained the ramifications to Arnold Morgan, and the President's National Security Adviser told them the whole scenario was a "complete goddamned horror story." And his reason was, characteristically, one that they themselves had not considered.

"Gentlemen," he said, "I may not yet be ready to inform the People's Republic of China about our actions, neither in the Strait of Hormuz, nor in the Bassein River Delta. I intend to let them know when I'm good and ready, but that may not be quite yet. Now, the trouble with a court-martial, such as the one you are considering, is that it will promote, for one reason or another, *outrage*.

"Outrage, on the one hand, in support of the case of an American hero, recognized by the SEALs as the savior of their mission. Then there will be another kind of outrage, by the traditionalists, on behalf of the Commanding Officer, *outrage* that any half-assed little two-and-a-half can suddenly seize command and control of a U.S. Navy nuclear submarine just because he doesn't damned well agree with something.

"Either way, whichever way a court-martial jumps, you're gonna get *outrage*. And you know what outrage does? It makes people talk. Animatedly and indiscreetly. In short, gentlemen, it blows gaffs, hard and fast. It causes people to vent their outrage to media assholes and other third-class citizens. And it causes that which we want to remain secret, for the greater good, suddenly to become very public.

"Media assholes, who know close to nothing in any depth about any subject, cannot tell the difference between what they believe is an exciting and dramatic story and blowing a major secret straight to the pain-in-the-ass Chinese, in flagrant disregard for the stability of world peace and world markets. That's what being a media asshole is. They have to take an examination in advanced ignorance and intermediate crassness before they're allowed to join.

"But, and you can mark my words on this, not one of them will put in a check call to the military—*Is this okay to use? Or might it put us in a compromising position with the Chinese?*

"No, gentlemen, that is not what they will do. They will instead seize upon the outrage of someone involved in this court-martial and blab it all over the earth, to the possible damage of the USA. And not one of them will give a damn about the consequences. Children, gentlemen. Always remember, they are essentially children. Which is why we gotta try to head off this court-martial."

Admiral Morgan's military visitors nodded in agreement. Alan Dixon was extremely worried. "It's just the procedures, Arnie," he said. "And you know them better than I do. Right here, we have a wounded, hurt and dangerous commanding officer. He's been humiliated in front of his friends, in front of his peers and in front of his family. There is nothing else in his mind except clearing his name. On the other hand, we have a plainly gallant and probably brilliant XO who, for whatever reason, believed his own CO was prepared to let the SEAL team die. So he seized the ship, arrested the CO and carried out his own program perfectly, destroyed the enemy and saved the SEALs."

"Well said, CNO," replied the NSA. "That states it just like it is. And I realize there is no way we can avoid a formal Navy Board of Inquiry. Just to establish the facts. It's the events after that which may burn out of control. Because to exonerate Headley, they gotta write the CO off as some kind of nut. And they will not do that unless they are certain, to a man, that the guy is deranged."

"And that's not going to happen," said Admiral Freddie Curran. "Commander Reid is going to show up at the inquiry, all scrubbed up in his number-ones, and give his evidence in tones of calm, but surprised, incredulity. They might make him look a bit eccentric, but no group of veteran officers serving on a Naval board is going to write off a fellow officer, of thirty years standing, ten of them commanding a nuclear submarine. *There, but for the grace of God, go I.*"

"Then our only chance," said Admiral Morgan, "is to get with

Commander Reid, as soon as he arrives back in the USA, and try to persuade him to admit he was not feeling well, and that he handed over command of the *Shark* voluntarily to his XO, who performed heroically."

"That is correct, Admiral," replied the CNO. "But there's not a snowball's chance in Hell of his agreeing to that. I can nearly guarantee we'll find a man bent on revenge, determined to punish the men who overthrew him in his own ship."

"Yes. I am afraid you are right," replied Admiral Morgan. "But we have to try. Because in the end, if Commander Reid wants that XO court-martialed, the Navy will have absolutely no option but to court-martial him."

"And at that moment, we will be holding the flimsiest of redoubts against a massively hostile press and public. And I, for one, am not looking forward to it," said Admiral Dixon.

"Do you think we could try the national security tack, the highly classified nature of the entire mission?"

"That's probably our best shot, sir," replied Admiral Dixon. "And certainly the one we should try first—and of course we do have the argument that events proved Lt. Commander Headley correct. He achieved his objectives."

"It's a powerful, but not necessarily winning, argument," said Admiral Morgan, thoughtfully. "Though an old friend of mine, Iain MacLean—he's an ex–Royal Navy flag officer, submarines—once told me it was the best way to convince everyone of the merits of the case."

"They'd never had a tougher one than this, though?" asked Admiral Curran.

"Tougher," replied the National Security Adviser. "They went to war over such a quandary."

"They did?"

"Sure they did. The Falklands War. Iain MacLean was there."

"I don't quite follow, sir."

"Well, when the Argentinians invaded in the spring of 1982, they put a force of about fifteen thousand on the islands. And that put the old Brits in a bit of a spot. They had this group of goddamned rocks, containing about eighteen hundred of their citizens, in the middle of the South Atlantic, eight thousand miles from home. They'd sold their carriers, there was no air cover for any assault force to land, the Falklands were now fortified by a well-equipped army, protected by a land-based air force.

"Unsurprisingly, the military advice was absolutely negative. The Royal Air Force said forget it, the Army said no air cover, no go. The United States wrote the whole thing off as impossible. In fact everyone said it was impossible for the Brits to travel that far and win the islands back.

"Except for one man, and he happened to be the First Sea Lord, Admiral Sir Henry Leach, another old friend of mine. He said it could be done. He knew the carriers were sold, but not yet gone, and he convinced Margaret Thatcher the Navy could do it.

"As most of you know, it was a goddamned shaky exercise. The Brits lost seven warships, more than two hundred fifty men, and they fought like fucking tigers to pull it off. But they damn near lost it, and if they had lost it, one man would have taken the blame for probably Britain's most humiliating defeat: Henry Leach.

"However, they did not lose it. They won it, thanks almost exclusively to Admiral Sandy Woodward and the parachute regiment. Without them, they *would* have lost it. Trust me. And the notion of taking an unforgivable risk, which you could say Henry Leach did, is never mentioned. Why? Because he was proved RIGHT."

"Guess we could do with a few more like him around here," said Admiral Greening. "Guys with the courage of their convictions, guys prepared to operate with no thoughts whatsoever for their own self-interest."

"Guys like Dan Headley," said Arnold Morgan, softly.

Two weeks later.
Friday, June 24. San Diego.

Admiral John Bergstrom paced the inner sanctum of the offices of SPECWARCOM. Before him sat the silent figures of the professional heads of America's Pacific Strike Force, Admirals Freddie Curran and Dick Greening.

"You realize that my ultimate successor in this chair, Commander Rick Hunter, is quite prepared to put his entire career on the line and resign his commission over this, do you not?"

"Of course we do, John," replied Dick Greening. "I am just trying to ask you if you feel just as strongly. Will you also resign if Dan Headley is court-martialed and found guilty?"

"Right now it is not necessary for the United States Navy to know whether I will resign. However, you should bear in mind that I have not yet decided not to."

"John, I know how bad you all feel about this," said Admiral Greening. "But I am afraid you have to inform the appropriate authorities if you intend to announce your retirement, if the Navy board recommends the court-martial of Lieutenant Commander Headley."

"Listen, you guys," said Admiral Bergstrom, slipping into the easy informality this particular High Command had always enjoyed. "We've all known each other for a lot of years, and I think we all know the pros and cons of this case.

"But I am here to tell you I have never known such intense feelings of betrayal by the SEALs. It is common knowledge that this nutcase captain of yours refused to help the guys coming out of Iran. Indeed, he left one of my men to die. And he would have left all my men to die coming out of the Bassein Delta. You guys somehow appointed a fucking psychopath to take my SEALs in and out of an area of operations. Twice. And there's no way we're gonna sit still for that.

"Anyway, my position here would be untenable if you decided to jail Lieutenant Commander Headley for making a mutiny. I'd never be taken seriously again. Not by the Special Forces. I would *have* to resign, because I'd be a standing joke—the SEAL chief who sent the guys in, put 'em in the hands of a rule-book shit, who everyone knew was fucking crazy. Do you have any idea what that would do to the morale of this place?

"Guys, somehow you have to stop this bullshit; you have to award Dan Headley a high decoration, and somehow get this fuckwit Reid the hell out of the United States Navy. Quietly, if possible."

Admiral Greening nodded in agreement. "If it were that damned simple, we wouldn't be sitting in this room, John," he said. "But it isn't. These things develop a life of their own. We have, right here, a ten-year veteran of a nuclear submarine command who was arrested on the high seas by his own XO and fellow officers, relieved of command of his own ship, locked up and told to shut up, while his orders were flagrantly contravened. Those actions plainly give the right to be heard, at least. The right to request a full Naval Board of Inquiry. The right to defend himself in front of his peers."

"Okay, okay, I get it," replied the SEAL boss. "But let me ask one question: In this specific case, who was right, Headley or Reid? And I mean both morally and in terms of war-fighting expertise? And even gallantry, concern for others? Headley or Reid?"

"Headley. Plainly. Headley was right," replied Admiral Greening. "But I'm afraid that's irrelevant. Being right gets you off the hook, as long as no one cares to push the case. But here we have an antagonist, who has been wronged in his own eyes and does not give a flying fuck whether Headley was right or not.

"We have a CO, who is brandishing the goddamned official book of rules, and saying loudly, *I'm the injured party*, and it says so, right here between these sacred covers. . . . Well, Admiral Bergstrom, right here we got a problem. A real, live problem. And we gotta deal with it. And if you don't like it, Johnny, baby, I'm afraid that's show business."

Admiral Bergstrom chuckled. "You want me to get a couple of guys to take him out, nice and quiet?"

It was of course only a joke, a black, macabre joke. But the sheer simplicity of the solution was not lost on the two visiting Admirals, and neither of them laughed.

Admiral Freddie Curran just said, "Precisely the kind of solution one would expect from the SEALs . . . What's that motto of theirs? . . . Oh, yes . . . *'There are very few of the world's problems that cannot be solved with high explosives.'* Isn't that it?"

"Guess so, and it's mostly right." The SEAL Chief looked grim now, because the consequences of this impending Board of Inquiry were beginning to look so far-reaching, they were out there beyond the horizon.

"When do you want to initiate the inquiry?"

"Oh, right away, John. Here in San Diego, as soon as *Shark* arrives back. She's due Tuesday night. We'll aim for Thursday. Most of the men are entitled leave, so we'll get under way while they are all right here at the base."

"Will it take long?"

"I'm not sure. If the board is in any way compliant they'll agree to make a firm decision, one way or another, as soon as they have ascertained the facts. They are not sitting in judgment on the case. They are just being asked to establish the simple truth, and most of that's not in dispute:

"One. Was there a mutiny on board the submarine?

"Two. Was Commander Reid relieved of his command and placed under arrest?

"Three. Who was responsible?

"Four. Did that officer have the support of the senior officers?

"Five. Why? What had the CO done wrong?"

"Dick, we're talking real basics then, at this stage?"

"Absolutely. And those basics should be established very quickly. Which will allow the board to arrive at one of two conclusions: A) There was a mutiny, and the ringleader MUST be court- martialed under Navy regulations. B) There was no mutiny, the CO was under psychological stress and Lieutenant Commander Headley was well within his rights to assume command of the ship under Navy Regulation one-zero-eight-eight."

"Yeah," said Admiral Bergstrom, "but B requires the CO to *agree* he was under stress, and that Headley was correct to take over."

"Afraid so," said Admiral Greening. "And my forecast is that he will do no such thing. We will talk to Commander Reid at the highest level. Admiral Dixon will have him into the Pentagon, maybe even to Admiral Morgan's office in the White House. They'll pressure him, but I cannot see him agreeing to accept the most complete humiliation any CO can suffer. Just can't see it."

"Well, I've got another curve for you," replied Admiral Bergstrom. "Tonight, at approximately twenty-one hundred, Commander Rusty Bennett is arriving back here from Diego Garcia, and he has a major problem with your Captain Reid, leaving that young combat SEAL to die out there in the gulf. To my certain knowledge he is filing a formal complaint about the conduct of *Shark*'s CO during the time the guys were trying to get out of Iran.

"He's alleging that the seas were clear of any potential foreign warships, and the skies were clear of foreign fighter aircraft. And he's alleging cowardice of the very worst kind against your Captain Reid. I've seen the preliminary, and it ain't pretty reading. Rusty, you know, was in the submarine at the time."

"I think that may be rather helpful," said Admiral Curran. "Even Captain Reid may not relish the idea of appearing at a court-martial and having to listen to two counts of cowardice against him, by two different officers, from two different but connected areas of operations."

"The problem there is Commander Reid's degree of wackiness," replied Admiral Greening. "Let's face it—not to go beyond this room at this moment—he must be a wacko. You don't get guys like this hitherto outstanding XO Dan Headley and two proven SEAL combat Commanders, Hunter and Bennett, *all* thinking he's a complete jerk, along with a lot of other senior submarine officers, unless there's something the matter with him.

"And it's been my experience that the more of a wacko a guy is, the more he's likely to adopt a firm, unyielding defensive position. If he were normal, he might say, '*Okay, I'll back down, you guys save my career, I'll go for a little psychological help and I'll leave the Navy with honor, and a full pension. No courts-martial, no trouble.*'

"Unhappily, that is not the way of the greater-crested common wacko. He is apt to see the world from a very narrow perspective. His own. The psychologists call it Loss of Insight. It means that you can no longer grasp the views of anyone else.

"How many major murderers appear sorry? Full of regret? Very few. They try to justify their actions. Remember Son of Sam, in New York. Wasn't his fault, was it? There was a voice telling him to get out there and start killing. And what about that fucking dingbat they had in England, the Yorkshire Ripper who murdered all those women? He was just cleaning up the streets, right? He wasn't sorry, despite battering innocent women, students, to death. He went to jail mystified that society had turned against him. Pleaded not guilty, I think.

"Plainly, I'm not saying Commander Reid is a criminal. But I'd bet he's a wacko. And wackos never make life easy. They defend. To the death."

Tuesday evening, June 26.
San Diego Navy Base.

The journey back from the Indian Ocean had been fraught with tension. *Shark*'s original CO being confined to his cabin was a constant reminder to the entire crew that they were steaming back into big trouble. In the beginning, a lot of the younger crew, anxious to see wives and girlfriends, wished to hell that Commander Reid could be reinstated in order to free them up to go home as soon as they docked.

They anticipated a very formal welcome, which might even see certain popular and trusted members of the crew placed under arrest. Everyone knew they had been to some degree a party to a mutiny. However, the presence of the wounded SEALs on board was a vivid reminder of the supreme heroism of the *Shark*'s XO and his fellow officers.

Everyone was in awe of Commander Hunter and "his guys," and rumors of their success and bravery swept through the submarine. The four body bags stored in the torpedo room were also a chilling reminder of the SEALs' desperate battle for the Chinese base, and by the time the submarine approached California's coastal waters, opinion was hardening. Opinion that they, the *Sharks*, were a part of this great and selfless campaign, and more and more of them began to stand four-square behind the Exec who had saved the Special Forces.

It was 2030 when USS *Shark* came in sight of the coast. She was making 20 knots through a warm evening, on a calm surface, which rose with the long Pacific swells but offered no discernible chop. On the bridge stood Lt. Commander Dan Headley, the Navigation Officer, Lt. Shawn Pearson, and the Officer of the Deck, Lt. Matt Singer. Directly below them in the control room, Lt. Commander Jack Cressend had the ship, with Master Chief Drew Fisher at the conn.

They rounded Point Loma, heading up into the narrow channel that leads both to the U.S. Naval stronghold of San Diego and to the headquarters of SPECWARCOM. Above them, to their port side, on the heights, was the Fort Rosecrans National Cemetery, where Buster Townsend and Bobby Allensworth would both be laid to rest this week. The bodies of Catfish Jones and his colleague were being flown to their home states.

Shark slowed as she reached the narrows. She stood fair up the channel leaving the North Island Naval Air Station to starboard. Then she made her hard right turn toward the towering stilts of the Coronado Bridge, and into the sheltered waters of San Diego Bay.

Lieutenant Commander Headley brought her alongside at 2120, and the mooring lines were attached. On the dock stood the resolute figure of Commander Rusty Bennett, in company with Admiral Bergstrom. The Pacific submarine boss, Admiral Freddie Curran, was also there. And there were eight Naval guards on duty, along with a throng of wives, girlfriends and colleagues from the base.

As *Shark* was made fast and the men began to file out onto the deck, there was a spontaneous burst of cheering from the crowd. The figure of Lt. Commander Dan Headley stood motionless, unsmiling, on the bridge, watching the scene below as families looked forward to being reunited after months and months apart.

It did not seem that much different from any other submarine homecoming in San Diego. But it was different. No ship had ever returned here after a mutiny on the high seas. And there were certain protocols that had to be observed. Plainly Commander Reid would be escorted immediately to the offices of the Submarine Fleet HQ in San Diego, and, probably separately, Lt. Commander Headley would also be required to attend a debriefing.

Admiral Curran had made it quite clear that no one was to be arrested. There was not to be a semblance of authoritarian action, just a formal welcome, and a routine conference among senior officers. The less anyone knew about the events in the Bay of Bengal, the better. Meanwhile, the two conflicting signals sent from a distant ocean by *Shark*'s Captain and XO were not much short of nuclear meltdown in Admiral Greening's private filing system.

Commander Reid was the first officer to leave the ship, and he was greeted by Admiral Curran. The two men left immediately in a staff car for the central office complex. Thirty minutes later, Lt. Commander Headley, in company with the limping Commander Rick Hunter, crossed from the submarine to the shore, where Commander Rusty Bennett and Admiral Bergstrom awaited them. They shook hands and separated, the two SEALs boarding a staff car with the Admiral, Dan Headley boarding another car alone with a staff driver.

Curiously, there was little for the XO to say. His defense of his actions would be unwavering, scarcely varying from the short signal he had already sent. The problem was Commander Reid. Could he be persuaded to agree he was not in a proper frame of mind to conduct the SEAL rescue and that he had willingly handed over command of the ship to his number two?

Within a half hour, the answer to that was obvious. No. And

with Admirals Greening and Curran, *Shark*'s former CO boarded a military jet for Washington at first light on Monday morning, June 27.

They arrived at the Pentagon from Andrews Air Base at 1500, and were escorted immediately to the office of the CNO, Admiral Alan Dixon. And there, for the next four hours, the head of the United States Navy, the head of the Pacific Fleet, and the head of the Pacific Submarine Fleet attempted to persuade Commander Donald Reid that there was nothing to be gained from the court-martial of his XO, save the worst publicity the Navy would ever suffer.

The Commander did not agree. He felt there was something else to be gained: the salvaging of his own personal reputation. And he was damned if he was going to condone in any way the actions of a group of mutineers who had seized his ship and contravened his perfectly reasonable orders not to put a nuclear submarine in the path of anti-submarine-warfare Chinese helicopters with long-range capacity.

Nothing that any of the Admirals said made even the slightest impression on him. Commander Reid knew his rights, he knew the regulations of the United States Navy and he was going to play those rights by the book, the way he had always conducted his career.

"I intend, CNO," he said, "to stand before the Navy Board of Inquiry and to tell the absolute truth about the events that took place in the Bay of Bengal. And I shall demand the court-martial of the ringleader of the mutineers. With respect, sir, you must know I am entitled to that."

"You may be so entitled," said Admiral Dixon wearily, "but we are asking you to reconsider, in the interests of the greater good of the United States Navy, and its image before the public."

"Then your request, with the greatest respect, is declined," he replied firmly. And then Commander Reid shook his head and spoke almost in a mutter, as if speaking only to himself: *"This is not my fault, not my fault at all . . . I told him over and over the planet was in retrograde. . . . If he had just had the sense to listen to me . . ."*

"I'm sorry, Commander," said the CNO. "I didn't quite catch that."

"Oh, nothing, sir. Nothing at all. I was just thinking and wishing things could be different. But I'm afraid they cannot."

All three of the Admirals realized there was no point in pursuing this. Reid's mind was made up. And nobody was going to change it for him.

Commander Reid had no grasp whatsoever of the evidence that would be given on behalf of Lt. Commander Headley, and he had no interest in it. He knew only one thing: He had wished to play it safe, to keep his submarine out of harm's way, and he had been thwarted by the reckless actions of some damned two-and-a-half, who had never commanded a warship in his life.

On the flight back to San Diego, Donald Reid sat separately and silently, all the way, several seats behind the two Admirals. In contrast, they had much to talk about, because they were both struggling to find a way out of this particular mess. But there was no way out. Not unless Reid reconsidered his position.

And judging by his demeanor in the office of the CNO, *Shark's* former CO had a very private agenda of his own, an agenda that would not easily be intruded upon.

"He's a strange kind of a guy, don't you think?" said Admiral Curran, quietly. "He has that confidence some people have. As if they could never be wrong. By the way, what did you make of that last stuff he was muttering? I couldn't really hear it."

"No. I couldn't either," replied Dick Greening. "But I seemed to catch the word *retrograde*. Tell the truth, I'm not really sure what the word means."

"It means going backwards, doesn't it?"

"Beats the hell outta me. But if it does mean that, he must have been referring to our conversation. That sure as hell was going backwards."

Eight days later.
0900. Wednesday, July 4.
San Diego Naval Base.

America's national summer holiday was still in beach-bound progress on this bright sunlit California morning. The temperature was a near-perfect 78 degrees, and a light southwester off the Pacific promised to keep the sun worshipers relatively cool before the fireworks in the evening.

In the shaded gloom of the big office he always used in San Diego, Admiral Dick Greening felt almost sick with worry. He had before him a memorandum, signed by Captain Stewart Goodwin, who was presiding over the Board of Inquiry.

It read: *"After three days hearing evidence in the USS Shark case, it is clear there was indeed a mutiny on board the submarine while on patrol in the Bay of Bengal. The facts are not in dispute. There was great sympathy for Lt. Commander Headley, whose actions were courageous in the extreme. However, Commander Reid is demanding the court-martial of his Executive Officer for making a mutiny on the high seas. And Naval regulations permit a Commanding Officer to make such a demand.*

"With reluctance I, and my fellow members of the board, believe there is a prima facie case for a court-martial, and we are sending our findings to the Trial Service Office. The Judge Advocate General will then decide whether Lt. Commander Headley should indeed stand trial."

Admiral Greening stood up and walked across the office to a wide computer screen on the wall, and he punched up the numbers 16.00N 94.01E. And there before him was the exact stretch of ocean where this terrible drama had been played out. He could see the island of Haing Gyi, the swamp, the little creek running through it. He could see the Haing Gyi Shoal marked clearly, the shallow water across which the fleeing SEALs had raced in their fast but tiny outboards. He could see the low marshy headland of Mawdin Point, and in his mind he pictured the scene.

The Chinese helicopters mercilessly machine-gunning the Americans as they tried to get away. Catfish Jones dead, Bobby Allensworth dead, Buster Townsend badly wounded, Rick Hunter pouring blood, still firing, all of them helpless sitting targets in the open boats. He imagined the terror. Imagined the courage. And then he imagined the sudden appearance of the *Shark*, lambasting the choppers with their Stingers, saving the eight survivors of this awesome SEAL mission.

And now they want me to approve the court-martial of the man who commanded the submarine?

"Jesus Christ," said the Pacific Fleet Commander. And it was as well there was no one in the room to see him so upset, as he stared at the screen, hearing again in his mind the staccato rattle of the murderous Chinese guns.

1500 (local). Same day.
Office of the National Security Adviser.
The White House. Washington, D.C.

Admiral Morgan was displeased in the extreme. "Alan," he said, "there's gotta be some way we can stop this. You want me to get the President to intervene?"

"I don't know," replied Admiral Dixon. "The trouble with the damned Navy is that certain things are just like presidential elections—ain't nothing anyone can do to stop 'em. They just happen."

"Tell me about it. How about a presidential pardon for Lieutenant Commander Headley? The man in the Oval Office, as Commander-in-Chief, has to be able to do at least that."

"Well, I guess he could. Somehow. But that's not really the issue, is it, Arnie, old buddy? The press will want to know if the Navy has gone off its trolley, court-martialing such a man as Dan Headley. As you pointed out, it's the very act of court-martial that is going to bring this whole thing right out into the open, where we don't want it to be."

"Who's the Judge Advocate General in this case?"

"Veteran surface-ship commander, former lawyer, Sam Scott from Oregon. About as rigid a man as you could find. He'll play this case right by the book. He'll look at the recommendations of the board, check his goddamned law books and then decide that Lieutenant Commander Headley should stand trial as charged."

"Could we reason with him?"

"No chance. He'll just ask, What happens if the CO resigns and goes public, in a book, which will inevitably detail what he thinks is a cover-up."

"Well, I guess it would be."

"Sure would."

"Well, what can we do?"

"We can put in a massive effort to help Dan Headley beat the rap."

"But that'll mean we have to prove Reid is insane."

"Correct. And then the media will jump all over us for putting in charge of submarines men who ought rightly to be in an institution for the seriously nerve-wracked."

"Damned if we do. Damned if we don't."

"This case was always thus, Arnie. Either we talked Reid into a complete capitulation, which we couldn't, or we were going to find ourselves in the deepest possible shit. Where we now are."

"Yeah. But it's not quite over."

"Enlighten me, NSA."

"We owe it to this Lieutenant Commander Headley to help him prove his boss was both nuts and a fucking coward. And the press can go fuck 'emselves."

"Yessir."

0900. Wednesday, July 18.
Office of CINCPACFLT.
Pearl Harbor.

The Judge Advocate General's decision took two more weeks to arrive. And now it lay smoldering on the sunlit desk of Admiral

Dick Greening, just as it lay smoldering on the desk of Admiral Alan Dixon in faraway Washington, D.C.:

After careful consideration of the evidence and observations of the Naval Board of Inquiry which examined the events on board USS Shark *in the Bay of Bengal, I have decided there is a prima facie case for the court-martial of the Executive Officer, Lt. Commander D. Headley. He will thus stand trial for Making a Mutiny on the High Seas on the morning of June 7, 2007, on which date he did relieve his commanding officer, Commander D. K. Reid, of his duties, under Section 1088 of Navy Regulations.*

On the basis of the depositions before me, I have recommended that Commander Reid undergo psychological examination by three doctors, including but not limited to one civilian practitioner.

My findings have been referred to the Trial Service Office, for selection of trial counsel and defense counsel. I have recommended a senior judge advocate shall attend the proceedings, which will be heard in the trial Service Courtroom at the San Diego Navy Base on a date to be arranged. Signed: Captain Sam Scott, Judge Advocate General.

It was not unexpected, but the reality of the situation suddenly loomed before the Pacific Fleet Commander. This was it, the court-martial of a U.S. Navy hero, whose actions were witnessed not only by a crew of 107 completely supportive, very talkative seamen on board a fighting nuclear submarine, but also by eight highly regarded members of the U.S. Navy's Special Forces, all of whom owed their lives to the actions of Lt. Commander Headley.

Their story was already well on its way around the SEAL bastions of neighboring Coronado and Little Creek in Virginia. Offhand it was difficult for Admiral Greening to think of any member of the service who would not know at least a vague version of this melodrama by nightfall.

As Commander of the Pacific Fleet, he was required to "sign off" on the court-martial, as indeed was the CNO in the Pentagon. And Dick Greening was going to hate doing that. But he had no choice.

Admiral Greening picked up the phone to Admiral Dixon, who was already on the line to Arnold Morgan. It was merely a matter of waiting for the press to get hold of the details, from any one of the hundreds of Navy men, and women, who now knew all about it. But the media would not be looking, and it might take them a while. Though they'd sure as hell make up for their lateness when they did find out.

Admiral Morgan's wishes were very clear: Lt. Commander Headley and his lawyer were to be given every assistance in their case to prove that Commander Reid was in no fit state to run the SEAL escape and rescue from the Burmese island. It was the only way out of a scandal that would surely engulf not only the senior service, but also, possibly, the administration itself.

In fact it took five days, and even then only half of the story was published. On its front page, the *San Diego Telegraph* ran a double-column item, toward the top of columns four and five, under the two-deck headline *MYSTERY OF NAVY SEAL RESCUE OFF BURMA*.

To the connoisseur of such matters, it was plain the writer knew more than he dared print. But the newspaper printed enough:

The United States Navy last night refused to comment on a report that a U.S. Navy SEAL assault team, out of Coronado, came under direct attack from Chinese helicopters while escaping from a mission on a Burmese island.

It is believed that at least two of the SEALs were killed and that others may have been wounded. There were no details available as to the nature of the mission, and a Navy spokesman would only say, "All Special Forces operations are highly classified, and this one is no different."

Five weeks ago reports from Rangoon stated that a new Chi-

nese Navy base on the island of Haing Gyi in the delta of the Bassein River, western Burma, had been badly damaged by a massive explosion inside a geothermal electricity generation plant.

The Navy spokesman would neither confirm nor deny that the SEAL team had been involved in this destruction.

Further reports suggest there was an American nuclear submarine in the area of the Bassein Delta on or around June 7. There was no information available as to the identity of the ship, but an insider told the Telegraph *last night that the Sturgeon-Class nuclear boat USS* Shark, *under the command of Commander Donald K. Reid, was operational in the Bay of Bengal at the time.*

Last night Commander Reid could not be reached. His Executive Officer, Lt. Commander Dan Headley, would not comment on any part he may have played in the rescue of the surviving SEALs.

He would only say, "Throughout Shark's *recent Middle East patrol, I carried out my duties as a U.S. Naval officer to the best of my abilities."*

Accompanying the story was a single-column picture of Commander Reid, under which was the caption "Unreachable." There was also a picture of Lt. Commander Dan Headley, beneath which was the caption, "I carried out my duties."

The story was just signed *Geoff Levy, staff writer.* But he had plainly been briefed about the entire scenario, either by a member of the submarine's crew or by a San Diego resident SEAL. However, young Geoff had been unable to obtain any official confirmation, and he wrote only what he thought was more or less safe, given the fact that he was trespassing in a top-secret military area.

The Navy's high command, in Pearl Harbor, San Diego and Washington, glowered at the report as the e-mails were downloaded from computers all over the fleet and its executive offices. The media's high command, almost shrieking with glee, set about pinning the story down. But they made little headway, because essentially reporters needed to be in San Diego where most of the crew and SEALs were stationed.

And once more Geoff Levy's source delivered and on Wednesday night, July 25, the *San Diego Telegraph* went to bed with end-of-the-world-size type stacked in two decks, clear across the top of its front page: *NAVY COURT-MARTIALS SUBMARINE EXECUTIVE OFFICER FOR MUTINY ON THE HIGH SEAS.* Beneath the headline was the subhead "Heroic U.S. Officer Who Saved the SEALS Is Accused."

Someone had not only blabbed. Someone had blabbed in spades; leaked the court-martial recommendation from Captain Sam Scott, and suddenly Geoff Levy was a media star. And Admiral Arnold Morgan held his head in his hands as the young San Diego journalist said on national television, "I've been on the Navy beat for my newspaper for three years now, and I have never known such outrage. There are a lot of very furious guys in the U.S. Navy right now. Most of 'em think Dan Headley should be given the Medal of Honor."

"Holy shit," groaned the CNO.

By midday on July 26, the fertilizer was clogging the bilge pumps. The Navy Department in Washington was under siege from the media. The San Diego base switchboard was jammed by phone calls from newspapers and television. All lines to the command office of the SEALs in both Coronado and Virginia were occupied by journalists, researchers and columnists.

And the questions were all the same . . . What really happened out there in the Bay of Bengal? . . . And why is the hero of the operation being court-martialed by his own Navy? . . . Where is Lt. Commander Headley? . . . Can we speak with him? . . . If not, why not? . . . Do the SEALs agree Lt. Commander Headley should be court-martialed? . . . What has he actually done to deserve this?

Photographers were camped in groups at the main gates to the base. They were massed outside the Pentagon, outside the base at Coronado and at Little Creek, Virginia. By late afternoon, infu-

riated by the lack of cooperation of the U.S. Navy, they swung
their attention to the White House, demanding a statement either
from the National Security Adviser, the Defense Secretary or the
Commander-in-Chief himself, the President of the United States.

In the opinion of both Arnold Morgan and Admiral Alan Dixon,
there was absolutely nothing to be gained by saying one word to
any of them. "No comment" would send them into a frenzy. "We
are unable to confirm anything at this time" would drive them
mad. "All matters such as these are highly classified, and in the
interests of national security we will say nothing." That last one
would have been a red cape to a fighting bull.

What national security? Are you saying the SEALs attacked
that Burmese island? How many of them died? Why are members
of the crew saying Lt. Commander Headley rescued the survivors? What's he done wrong? If he mutinied, why did he
mutiny? Did the CO blow it or something?

To hold a press conference, or even to issue a press statement,
would be to open the floodgates. Better to let them get on with it,
block all calls at the switchboard, or the automatic answering
machines, and let the cards fall where they may.

Where they fell was all over the place. In the following three
days, right up until the last editions of the Sunday tabloids were
on the presses, it was as if no other story in the entire country
mattered. The inaccessibility of the Navy bases and the personnel involved seemed only to fan the forest fire of leaked knowledge. There was even a posse of photographers outside the
locked wrought-iron gates of Bart Hunter's farm in Lexington,
Kentucky, trying to catch a glimpse of the SEAL leader's father.
Local journalists even managed to interview Bobby Headley,
Dan's father, when he mistakenly answered the telephone late
one evening.

But the Navy said nothing. And the media slowly pieced it all
together in various forms. The general scenario put forth was that
the SEALs had attacked the Chinese base in some kind of retribution for China's capture of the Island of Taiwan. They had been
caught and attacked on the way out, and there had been an alter-

cation between the Commanding Officer of USS *Shark* and his Executive Officer.

The CO had been overruled by the XO, supported by the majority of the officers on board, and *Shark* went in to save the SEALs. This mission was accomplished, and now the Navy was charging the Lieutenant Commander who masterminded the rescue with mutiny. It was obvious to everyone that almost every officer and enlisted man in the U.S. Navy was up in arms about this. And almost every commentator in the entire country, newspaper, radio or television, was of the opinion that the Navy, the government and presumably the President, the C-in-C of all the armed forces, had, collectively, gone mad.

The *New York Times*, with a searing inside "exclusive," revealed that the entire high command of America's most elite troops, the Navy SEALs, had threatened to resign en masse if the court-martial proceedings were not called off.

All this was achieved without one single identified source inside the U.S. military. It was as Admiral Morgan had forecast, *the outrage.* That's what binds people together, a shared grievance, a communal anger. And there sure was profound anger at this ensuing court-martial of Lt. Commander Dan Headley.

Nonetheless, media or no media, the legal wheels turned relentlessly inside the Navy's Trial Service Office. The trial Counselor was duly appointed, Lt. Commander David "Locker" Jones, a 46-year-old lawyer from Vermont, who had attended the Naval Academy but left the service for the law after three years in a surface ship. Ten years later he returned after a messy divorce involving a client's wife. For the past four years he had been an extremely able Naval lawyer, much admired throughout the legal department both on the West Coast and in Washington.

David Jones was a broad-shouldered ex-athlete of medium height and thinning fair hair. He wore the nickname "Locker" with good humor; *Davy Jones's locker* being, of course, seamen's slang for the bottom of the ocean, the final resting place for sunken ships, articles thrown overboard or burials at sea. And Locker Jones was renowned not so much for his thoroughness as for his grasp of the very finest points of law, an ability to cut a swath through evidence and make it irrelevent, a knack for nailing the one salient fact that could make a case swing one way or the other. Lieutenant Commander Headley could hardly have been dealt a more deadly opponent.

The Judge Advocate, who would sit in on the case, ensuring that the significant points of law were followed, was the veteran Atlantic destroyer commander Captain Art Brennan. He was a tall gray-haired former lawyer from Rhode Island, again a man who had joined, left and then rejoined the Navy. He was a traditionalist with a wry sense of humor, and a surprisingly irreverent way of looking at the world. On the face of it, you would put the 54-year-old Captain Brennan in the corner of the wronged CO. But those who knew him better suspected he would keep a careful watch on the rights of Lt. Commander Dan Headley.

The defense counsel was a matter for agreement between the Trial Service Office and the accused officer. And they chose easily the best man available to them—the sardonic, dark-haired Lieutenant Commander Al Surprenant, whose career, thanks to a wealthy father, had gone: Choate School, Harvard Law School, excellent degree, boredom with law, United States Navy, commission, rapid promotion, missile director battle cruiser Gulf War, U.S. Navy lawyer, Norfolk, then San Diego after he married a Hollywood actress.

Lieutenant Commander Surprenant was generally regarded as the one man in the U.S. Navy who could nail Commander Reid, and bring in a "not guilty" verdict for Dan Headley. He would prove thorough in his preparation, single-minded about the innocence of his client and brutal in his treatment of the CO, whom he knew beyond any doubt had left one man to die and had been about to leave another eight to the same fate.

The date of the court-martial was set for Monday, August 13. It would be the first such trial for mutiny in a U.S. Navy warship, ever. It would take place deep inside the San Diego base, in the Trial Service courtroom, which was much like a civilian courtroom, except for the fact that it was all on one level, no raised dais for the men who would sit in judgment on the submarine's XO.

The panel would consist of five men, three Lieutenant Commanders and one Lieutenant, all serving under the President, an ex–submarine CO, Captain Cale "Boomer" Dunning. This particular officer would bring strong combat experience to the deliberations of his team, and, to those who knew him, a genuine appreciation of the split-second flexibility required in the command of a nuclear ship on a classified mission.

By anyone's standards, the U.S. Navy was giving Lt. Commander Headley every possible chance of a sympathetic hearing— perhaps more in their own interests than in those of the hero of the Bay of Bengal.

Meanwhile, the media continued to worry the life out of the story. They had no official information, but they were getting a ton of unofficial leaks. It seemed that with each new breakthrough, each new snippet of possible truth, there was a counterattack. One television network came up with an entire career study of Commander Reid, citing his exemplary record. No sooner had this aired than a newspaper came blasting out onto the streets with the story that he had allegedly left a combat SEAL to die.

It went on day after day . . . WAS THE HORSEMAN FROM KENTUCKY A RECKLESS GAMBLER? DID THE LIEUTENANT COMMANDER OWE THE SEAL CHIEF MONEY? HAD COMMANDER REID LOST HIS NERVE? WAS THERE A FISTFIGHT IN SHARK'S CONTROL ROOM? IS THE U.S. NAVY OUT OF CONTROL?

Day after day, the media bore into the events that surrounded the mutiny. But still the Navy would reveal nothing. Not even the date of the court-martial. And the press seethed with indignation, not because of a potential miscarriage of justice but because this story about the wronged hero had captured the imagination of the American public, and the press were unable to get a serious grip on the facts. Nor would they ever.

The day of the court-martial dawned bright and warm. Shades

in the white-painted courtroom were down, and the air-conditioning was humming. The long, curved mahogany table at which the panel would sit formed a shallow well in the room. And the deadly serious nature of the case was highlighted by twin flags of the United States of America, set immediately behind the five oak captain's armchairs.

Between the flags, hung at an angle, was a ceremonial Naval sword, which would be used especially at this court-martial, reviving an old tradition. Its gold-plated brass hilt was set around a white fishskin-covered grip. The backpiece was surmounted by an eagle-head pommel. The 31-and-a-half-inch steel blade was encased in a hand-stitched black rawhide scabbard, with brass fittings.

Before the verdict was announced, it would be removed from the wall, unsheathed from its scabbard and placed upon the table. If the verdict was to be guilty, the sharp end would point directly at the accused officer. If he was to be judged innocent, it would be pointed away from him, toward the wall.

Aside from the five-man panel that would sit in judgment, there would be the two opposing lawyers, plus the observing Judge Advocate. Also permitted to sit in on the trial were the SEAL Commander-in-Chief, Admiral John Bergstrom, plus the Pacific Submarine Fleet Commander, Admiral Freddie Curran. There would be two regular court stenographers, officially recording the proceedings. Two armed Navy guards would be on duty at all times, with two more outside the door. Witnesses would be called into the courtroom but would not be permitted to remain after their evidence had been presented. No outsiders, public or media, would be permitted within a mile of the place.

At 0900 sharp, Lt. Commander Headley arrived with his defense counsel. They took their seats at the table set up for the accused man and began poring over the trial papers. In the following 30 minutes the witnesses arrived and were seated in a large anteroom along the corridor. Two Naval lawyers plus two guards were detailed to ensure that there was no discussion about the case, no possibility of corroboration between interested parties.

At 0930 the three Lieutenant Commanders, plus the much younger Lieutenant, walked into the courtroom from a private door behind the long table and took their seats. Captain Dunning, like his colleagues, in full uniform, arrived three minutes later, carrying a large leather binder, and sat in the center chair.

He wished everyone a formal "good morning" but wasted no further time. "Gentlemen," he said, "please proceed with the case against Lieutenant Commander Headley, charged this thirteenth day of August with making a mutiny on the high seas, while serving in the nuclear submarine USS *Shark* on the morning of June seventh, in the Bay of Bengal. . . . Lieutenant Commander Jones . . . perhaps you would outline the case for the benefit of the court."

The prosecuting counselor rose from his seat, a look of obvious concern upon his wide, frank face. He hesitated for a few moments, and then said, firmly, "Sir, it gives me no great pleasure to prosecute this charge, because I do not believe any of the parties acted in any way through self-interest. On the one hand we have a dedicated, experienced commanding officer concerned with the safety of both his ship and his men. And on the other we have an equally dedicated Lieutenant Commander desperate to save a team of U.S. Special Forces that was under attack.

"The facts are not in dispute. The Navy SEALs transmitted a cry for help, citing their Chinese attackers in hot pursuit with helicopters and heavy machine guns. Commander Reid's view was that the helicopters were almost certainly ASW aircraft, and at least one of them would be armed with rockets, and that to bring USS *Shark* to the surface was tantamount to suicide, because of the threat both to the submarine and the crew. It was, in a sense, one of the oldest quandaries any CO can face—will I sacrifice a very small number of men, in this case eight, in order to protect one hundred ten men, plus a very expensive nuclear ship?

"Gentlemen, Lieutenant Commander Headley thought not. He thought he could save the SEALs, and he rallied the senior officers to his cause. Despite the protests, indeed the orders, of his Commanding Officer, he seized control of the ship. He arrested the CO under Section one-zero-eight-eight of Navy Regulations and had him marched off under escort to his cabin, where he was incarcerated. And then the XO went in and successfully saved the SEALs under the most gallant circumstances.

"But I submit we are not here to assess gallantry; we are here to assess right and wrong. And I quote now the regulation that governs the actions of Lieutenant Commander Headley on that most fateful morning.

"Naval Regulations, one-zero-eight-eight. The Relief of a Commanding Officer by a Subordinate:

1. It is conceivable that most unusual and extraordinary circumstanmces may arise in which the relief from duty of a commanding officer by a subordinate becomes necessary, either by placing the CO under arrest, or on the sick list. Such action shall never be taken without the approval of the Commandant of the Marine Corps or the Chief of Naval Personnel, as appropriate. Or the senior officer present, except when reference to such higher authority is undoubtedly impracticable, because of the delay involved, or for other clearly obvious reasons.

2. In order that a subordinate officer acting upon his or her own initiative may be vindicated for relieving a commanding officer from duty, the situation must be obvious and clear, and must admit of the single conclusion that the retention of command by such commanding officer will seriously and irretrievably prejucice the public interest."

Lieutenant Commander Jones paused, and then continued, "The Section is quite detailed but I mention the salient points, that the subordinate officer so acting must obviously be unable to refer the matter to a common superior, and must be certain that the prejudicial actions of the CO are not caused by instructions unknown to him. He plainly must have given the matter much careful consideration, and—this is important—*have made such exhaustive investigation of all the circumstances as may be practicable.*

"The final paragraph in this area is one with which I take the gravest issue: *that the officer must be thoroughly convinced that the conclusion to relieve the CO is one that a reasonable, prudent and experienced officer would regard as a necessary consequence from the facts thus determined to exist.*

"I intend to convict Lieutenant Commander Headley on the words of that last paragraph, and I call Commander Reid as the first witness for the prosecution."

The doors to the court were opened, and the former CO of USS *Shark* walked into the room. He was immaculately dressed in uniform and made his way to the witness chair, which had been placed on the left-hand side in order that witnesses could address both the panel and the examining lawyers.

The Judge Advocate rose and walked across to ensure that the oath was taken correctly. With his hand on the Bible, Commander Donald Reid calmly swore to tell the truth.

After the briefest of identification procedures, Locker Jones went straight to work.

"And on the morning of June seventh, were you startled to find your ship was moving fast at periscope depth in flagrant defiance of your most recent orders?"

"I was."

"And where were you at the time?"

"I was in my cabin. The XO had the ship."

"And what action did you take?"

"I returned to the control room immediately, and I ordered Lieutenant Commander Headley to turn the submarine around and to return to our rendezvous point, the place defined in our orders, sixteen degrees north, ninety-four-zero-one east."

"And did he carry out your orders?"

"No. He did not. He refused."

"For what reason?"

"He said he was on a mission of mercy to save the very small team of Navy SEALs—only eight of them, I believe."

"And how did he propose to do this?"

"He said he was taking the submarine on the surface at flank speed in order to effect a rescue."

"And were you able to approve this?"

"Certainly not. No commander of a nuclear submarine takes his ship to the surface in the face of the enemy. It's one of the oldest rules in the book. No one does it."

"And were you aware of the enemy?"

"Well, I knew they were Chinese. And I knew they were helicopters. Two, we were told."

"And what did you deduce from this?"

"I assessed that they would be helicopters from the two ships we knew were in the Haing Gyi dockyard, a frigate and a destroyer. The chances were very high that at least one of them, probably both, would have an ASW capability, plus, probably, rockets that would both outrange us and pierce our pressure hull. We are not really built to fight on the surface, you know." The court was listening to the refined voice of reason.

"No, of course not, Commander," replied the prosecuter. "Absolutely not. I am sure everyone in the room appreciates that. But I continue: And did you communicate your assessment of the situation to your Executive Officer?"

"I sure did. I pointed out to him that there were almost one hundred ten officers and men on board my ship. We had a brave and experienced crew, a first-class crew. And I pointed out that to take the ship straight into the range of air-to-surface missiles, on the surface, on the open ocean, was contrary to everything I had ever known, been taught or believed in the U.S. Navy.

"Quite frankly, it was a risk I could not possibly take. Nor I suspect would anyone else in my shoes. Also I did not believe the U.S. Navy would be greatly thanked for putting a smashed nuclear reactor in the middle of the Bay of Bengal to pollute it for the next forty years. I had much to consider. And I did not believe the lives of the SEALs, just eight of them, warranted the potential destruction of USS *Shark* and her crew."

"Thank you, Commander. No more questions."

The court was amazed at the brevity of Locker Jones's examination, amazed that he had not extracted chapter and verse the circumstances of the arrest of the CO. Instead he had concentrated on one precious factor—the course of action the Captain of the submarine had proposed, and was it sufficiently crazy to have him placed under arrest and relieved of command?

It was a vintage ploy by the prosecuting counsel, a method of avoiding endless testimony and confusing contradictions. He had presented his star witness in a lean, pared-down light: the order he had given, and the reasons for it. Was it the order of a madman? Not so far, of that everyone in the room was very certain.

And now the frowning figure of the defense counsel, Lieutenant Commander Surprenant, climbed to his feet to begin his cross-examination. And he was perhaps more aware than anyone of the brilliance of the strategy of Locker Jones.

"Commander Reid," he began, "I want to ask your indulgence right here, because the reasons for Lieutenant Commander Headley's actions date back for several weeks, and I am sure you will not object to answering my questions while we establish them in this courtroom."

Commander Reid shook his head, as if to say, "No problem," but his counsel was instantly on his feet, snapping, "Objection."

Captain Dunning stared quizzically at the prosecuter, who said, "Sir, the CO is not on trial. He is here to give his reasons for his orders on that particular morning, in those particular circumstances. I am at a loss to understand why defense counsel wants to delve into the past. Lieutenant Commander Headley, under Section one-zero-eight-eight of Navy Regulations, must demonstrate that his CO issued an order that could not possibly be obeyed, without being prejudicial to the public interest."

Captain Dunning looked doubtfully at Al Surprenant, who responded quietly, "Sir, it is possible that a pattern of behavior by a single individual may become so unnerving for those who serve under him that an action to relieve command becomes neccessary. Not just from the immediate orders, but from that pattern of unreliability. With respect, I intend to proceed along those lines."

"*Overruled.*"

Lieutenant Commander Surprenant now took his time. He shuffled his file papers, and then looked up and inquired, "Commander Reid, may I ask if you recall the events of May sixteenth in the early morning, just before first light?"

"Well, I certainly know we were waiting at our rendezvous point for the Special Forces team to return from a mission."

"Who had the ship?"

"Lieutenant Commander Headley. Our orders were clear. It was a highly classified operation, and we were detailed to remain at our RV in the Gulf of Iran while the ASDV returned with the team on board."

"And were you ever informed of a problem during their escape from plainly hostile shores?"

"No I was not."

"I believe you were not in the control room?"

"That is correct. My XO had overall responsibility for the return of the SEAL team."

"And what caused you to return to the control room?"

"The submarine began to move forward in complete contradiction to our orders, which had been issued by the flag. Our RV point was in hard copy."

"And when you did return, what did you learn?"

"Well, there had been some kind of an attack on the team, inshore, and they were on their way back, bringing with them an apparently wounded man."

"They were also bringing back the body of their leader, Lieutenant Commander Ray Schaeffer, I believe?"

"So I was informed."

"So. The leader had been killed, and another SEAL was badly

wounded, and they were desperately trying to get away, trying to get back to safety after achieving their objective?"

"So I believe."

"And did Lieutenant Commander Headley inform you that it was perfectly safe under clear skies, and on empty seas, to go in six miles, fast, toward the ASDV and get them back on board with all speed?"

"He was already headed inshore when I reached the control room."

"And when you learned they had a top combat SEAL on board, dying, next to his already dead Leader, I believe you issued an order for USS *Shark* to turn around and return to the rendezvous point, leaving this heroic blood-soaked American Special Forces unit essentially to get on with it as best they could?"

"Well, I was certain about my orders: to remain on station until they arrived back."

"When Lieutenant Commander Headley informed you of the seriousness of the situation, that a man was dying, I believe you uttered the phrase 'You can't run a Navy for a guy who's probably cut his goddamned finger'?"

"I do not recall that."

"And so you turned around and went back to the RV?"

"Yes."

And do you recall a strong protest from the SEAL mission controller, Commander Rusty Bennett, almost begging you to go inshore and save his man?"

"No. I do not recall that."

"Do you recall the condition of the wounded SEAL when they finally arrived back?"

"You know perfectly well that I do."

"What was that condition?"

"Do you really have to persist in this unhelpful manner?"

"WHAT WAS THAT CONDITION, COMMANDER?"

"The SEAL was dead."

"Thank you. And is it your opinion that he might have been saved if you'd gotten him aboard a half hour earlier?"

"I have no idea. I'm not a doctor."

"And how long had he been dead before your crew got him back aboard?"

""I believe fifteen minutes."

"Thank you. And would it surprise you to learn that from that moment on, both your crew and the SEAL assault teams regarded you as a heartless, somewhat remote figure who cared nothing about any of them."

"OBJECTION! Counsel is harassing the witness, asking a question to which he could not possibly know the answer."

"Sustained. Strike that last question from the record."

But Al Surprenant smiled the quiet smile of a man who had said precisely what he wanted to say. And he rephrased it, good-naturedly . . . "Commander, would it suprise you to know that a lot of your crew did not agree in any way with your decision to let the man die?"

"OBJECTION! Commander Reid did not decide to let the man die. He simply followed the orders of the flag. Counsel continues to harass the witness."

"Sustained. Strike the question."

"Very well," replied Al Surprenant. "In the light of everything, let me ask you this: Thirty-six hours previously, do you recall refusing to go inshore for a few extra miles, thus saving the battery of the ASDV when the navigator had informed you there was plenty of water depth."

"No. I do not recall that."

"Would you feel happier if I read it directly to you from the ship's log?"

"OBJECTION. Counsel is treating the witness as if he were on trial, attempting to humiliate him before the court, and now he wants to produce evidence against him we have not even seen."

"Sustained. But leave the record." Boomer Dunning was a picture of calmness in increasingly stormy waters.

"Commander Reid," continued the defense counsel, "would

you say you were a man who followed orders to the letter, allowing no leeway, and no room for flexibility."

"No I would not. I'm as flexible as the next man. But not when it comes to the safety of my ship."

"Would you say you were as flexible as, say, Admiral Pierre de Villeneuve?"

Locker Jones shook his head, and held his hands apart in mock outrage. Captain Dunning stared at the former CO, awaiting an answer. And when it came, there was a frisson of unease in the room.

"Damn you, Headley," he hissed, almost under his breath.

And now Lieutenant Commander Surprenant was on him. "Damn who, sir? Damn who? I did not quite catch that."

Commander Reid's face was beginning to redden, and he was starting to look angry. He made no reply.

And again Al Surprenant came in. "I asked if you were as flexible as Admiral de Villeneuve. Please answer me. I know you are well acquainted with each other."

Locker Jones had never even heard of the French Admiral, or if he had, he'd clean forgotten it. But it was hard to object because he could not tell if there was venom behind the innocence of the question.

Still Commander Reid said nothing. And the president stepped in, requesting defense counsel to clarify the question for the benefit of the panel and indeed the prosecutor.

"Sir," said Al Surprenant, "Admiral de Villeneuve was the commander of the French Fleet at the Battle of Trafalgar. He presided over probably the biggest disaster in a sea battle in history. He lost twenty ships, was captured by the British and soon afterward committed suicide. There is a picture of him on the wall of Commander Reid's cabin, which is unorthodox for a U.S. Navy commanding officer, at best."

"I see," said Captain Dunning. "Well, I suppose it may be relevant. Please proceed."

"Thank you," said the counselor, and, turning back to Commander Reid, said flatly, "Is it not a fact that you believe you WERE Admiral de Villeneuve in a previous life?"

"Millions of people believe in reincarnation," replied the Commander.

"And so they may," said Lieutenant Commander Surprenant. "But that scarcely answers my question, does it? Shall we try again? Do you believe you WERE Admiral de Villeneuve in a previous life?"

"Well, even General Patton believed he had been a great warrior in a previous incarnation."

"So he may have. But would you be willing to give my question yet another try? Do you believe, Commander Reid, that you actually WERE Admiral de Villeneuve in a previous life? That's a yes, or a no."

"Well, we do share some deep French roots."

Captain Dunning interrupted. "Commander Reid, please answer the question. Yes or no."

"No," replied *Shark*'s former CO. I do not believe I actually *was* Admiral de Villeneuve."

"Thank you, Commander," said defense counsel. "And now, if I may, I should like to read something to you—'*Another life, another battle, so many mistakes in* Bucentaure. *I must never repeat them now that I have another chance. June 1980. DKR.*' Do you recognize those words, Commander."

"Well, vaguely, yes I do."

"Who wrote them?"

"I did."

"Where did you write them?"

"In a book, I believe."

"A book about reincarnation, wasn't it?"

"Maybe."

"Commander, perhaps you would care to tell the panel whose ship the *Bucentaure* was?"

"It was Admiral de Villeneuve's flagship."

"In your own words, Commander: '...*so many mistakes in* Bucentaure. *I must never repeat them now that I have another* chance.' Sir, you believe you are the reincarnation of one of the worst Naval commanders in history, correct?"

Locker Jones had had enough. He leaped to his feet and almost shouted, "*OBJECTION!* This quotation, written more than twenty-five years ago, was plainly pilfered from the private quarters of the Commanding Officer of USS *Shark*, unlawfully and digracefully. It cannot be admissable evidence in any court of law in the free world."

Captain Dunning nodded. But he said, "This is not a civilian court of law, where lawyers are trained to find loopholes to free guilty people. This is a United States Navy court-martial, and we have no other objective except to find the truth. We are assessing the guilt or innocence of men who are trained to take charge of ships worth four hundred million dollars. Everything is relevant in this regard."

"But my client is not on trial, sir," protested Lt. Commander Jones.

"I know he's not," replied Boomer. "Objection overruled."

Al Surprenant continued. "Commander, do you think it might be unnerving for a crew to discover that their leader believed he was a navy disaster area in a previous life?"

"I cannot say what they might feel."

"But do you think they *might* quite properly be concerned?"

"*OBJECTION. The question's been asked and answered.*"

"*Sustained.*"

"Commander," asked the counselor, "are you a spiritualist?"

"In some ways."

"Does that mean you have merely inherited the spirit of Pierre de Villeneuve, or do you believe you have been in contact with people from . . . er . . . the other side, I believe is the phrase?"

"Like many millions of others, I may have."

"Commander, have you spoken lately with Captain Grigory Lyachin?"

Donald Reid remained silent.

"Someone enlighten me," interjected Boomer Dunning. "Who's Grigory Lyachin?"

"He's that Russian commanding officer who died with his crew in the *Kursk* submarine, Barents Sea, seven years ago," said Al Surprenant.

"Commander Reid, would it surprise you to know that certain senior members of your crew heard you talking to him by candle-light in your cabin?"

"DAMN THIS. DAMN YOU ALL! I'M NOT ON TRIAL HERE." The ex-CO of *Shark* was standing now, shouting back at the defense lawyer, all semblance of self-control slipping away.

Lieutenant Commander Jones was also on his feet. "Sir, I really must object most strenuously to this line of questioning. Defense is attempting to paint this veteran commander of many years standing as an oddball, which is patently unfair."

"Your word, not mine," interrupted Al Surprenant. "Thoughtful of you."

"SILENCE!" snapped Captain Dunning. "Please be seated, and listen carefully. "If I consider the questioning of a witness to be irrelevant or unfair, I shall make my views known. If you object to anything, please say so, and I will make a judgment. But I will not tolerate banter.

"And, for the record, I do think it is extremely important to know that Commander Reid has some unusual views. I was once in a ship where the Captain was known to pray extensively on a nightly basis, and it damned near caused a mutiny. Ships are like that. Little things can mean a great deal, especially concerning a CO.

"This evidence about Commander Reid matters. And I am afraid he is going to have to put up with it. He was, after all, instrumental in bringing this court-martial, and my sympathies are not with him in these instances. Please proceed, Lieutenant Commander."

"Thank you, sir," said Al Surprenant, humbly. "Commander Reid, have you ever tried to contact Grigory Lyachin in a spiritual way? Perhaps to seek counsel or guidance from a man who has paid the ultimate price for carelessness?"

"It was never his fault. Any more than it was de Villeneuve's. They were both let down by others."

"Then you have been in contact?"

"In a sense."

"Thank you. And now I would like to return to more immediate concerns. As you know, Lieutenant Commander Headley, by the morning of June seventh, had much on his mind. His CO, a spiritualist who associated himself closely with two massive Naval disasters, had twice made decisions apparently detrimental to a SEAL operation—we have established that. He was dealing with a man who played rigidly by the book, presumably to avoid making the same foul-ups he had committed at Trafalgar."

This was too much for Captain Dunning. "Counselor," he snapped, "kindly desist from this soliloquy. You are not asking questions. You are merely ridiculing the witness. Ask, or sit down."

"Of course, sir," said Lieutenant Commander Surprenant courteously. "Commander, would you be surprised to learn that Lieutenant Commander Headley *knew* you would refuse flatly to help the SEALs. Because of your beliefs and your record?"

"Yes, it would."

"You will later hear that he did indeed know. It was the predictability that caused the mutiny—that they all knew you would leave the SEALs to die. I have no more questions."

"Commander Reid, you are excused. But please do not leave the building." Captain Dunning wrote carefully in his book.

And then Lt. Commander Jones called his second witness, *Shark*'s Combat Systems Officer, Lt. Commander Jack Cressend, who testified very briefly that he had indeed been asked by Lt. Commander Headley to take part in an act of defiance toward the Commanding Officer, in order to save the SEALs.

At the conclusion of his evidence, a short account of how they did not turn the ship around but proceeded inshore to meet Commander Hunter and his men, Al Surprenant had just one question.

"Lieutenant Commander," he said, "if you could live June the seventh over, would you still support the XO in his determination to save the SEALs?"

"Absolutely, sir. I would. No doubt in my mind."

At this point, Lt. Commander Jones announced that he had no more witnesses—but would confine his cross-examination to those appearing on behalf of the accused.

Immediately, Al Surprenant called Commander Rick Hunter, who walked into the courtroom and swore to tell the truth before being seated.

After identification, the SEAL Commander admitted under oath that he had the gravest worries about the possible conduct of Commander Reid under pressure. He and Lt. Commander Headley knew each other well, and had discussed the "unreliable" nature of the CO, even before the mission began.

"When you first transmitted your distress call to *Shark*, while your men were fighting and dying in the open boats, did you think help would come?"

"Not if Commander Reid had his way. I knew it would not come."

"Did you think you had a chance to survive?"

"Only if Dan Headley took over the ship, in a big hurry."

"But for Lieutenant Commander Headley's actions, would you and your men have been killed."

"Yessir."

"Do you think he deserves to be court-martialed?"

"Nossir."

"Why not?"

"Because he's just about the best officer I ever met. And he saved all of our lives."

"Do you intend to make any protest whatsoever if Lieutenant Commander Headley is found guilty of mutiny?"

"Nossir. But I shall resign my commission immediately."

"After a working lifetime in the Navy? And the very real prospect of becoming C-in-C of SPECWARCOM?"

"Yessir. I could never feel the same about the service if they convicted Dan Headley."

"Thank you, Commander."

Locker Jones arose. "You stated that you and Lieutenant Commander Headley knew each other well. That was not quite the whole truth, was it?"

"Sir?"

"You and Dan Headley are boyhood friends, correct? Best friends, correct? You went to school together, correct? Your father employs his father, correct?"

"All correct, sir. I am privileged to have him and his father as my friends."

"Is it not probable that you would never hear a word against Dan Headley, from anyone?"

"Very probable. Because he does not do things to cause people to utter words against him."

"He has now, Commander."

"But not by people who really know him, sir."

"And you think you know him well enough to say he could not be guilty of the crime of with which he is charged?"

"I know him a lot better than you do."

Locker Jones had had enough sparring with the towering wounded hero of the Burma operation. "No more questions," he said.

Al Surprenant next called the SEAL Commander Rusty Bennett, who confirmed the counselor's earlier contention that he had tried to remonstrate with Commander Reid about his decision not to move the ship forward in the Gulf of Iran mission to assist the wounded SEAL.

"And do you recall his precise words, Commander Bennett?"

"Some of them. I told him the rescue was at my request to go in and save the life of one of my most valued men. He then reminded me that I had no rights whatsoever on his ship. Told me he would not have this interference. Then he said, '*What exactly is this? Some kind of damned conspiracy? Well you've picked the wrong man to make a fool of. . . .*' Then he said we had waited until he was asleep and then flagrantly disobeyed his orders."

"And what did you think of this outburst?"

"Seemed very strange. You know, like paranoia. . . ."

"*OBJECTION! The witness has no idea about the meaning of such a medical term . . .*"

"*Sustained.*"

"How about *nuts*?" offered the SEAL from the coast of Maine.

"Better," said Captain Dunning.

"*OBJECTION! The Commander has no right to be making wild statements about insanity.*"

"I'll take the word of an experienced Navy SEAL commanding officer that in his opinion someone seemed nuts," replied Captain Dunning. "*Overruled.*"

"And now, Commander," said Al Surprenant, "let me ask you the same question I asked Commander Hunter. Do you hold a strong view about the possible conviction of Lieutenant Commander Headley."

"Yessir. I shall resign my commission if they find him guilty of mutiny."

"Reason?"

"Same as Commander Hunter's. Dan Headley saved the SEALs' lives."

"No more questions."

Locker Jones had none either, and the SEAL team leader left the room, clearing the way for Al Surprenant to bring in a succession of minor witnesses, Lt. Commander Josh Gandy, Master Chief Drew Fisher, Lt. Matt Singer, all offering unerring support for the XO. He brought in two more SEALs, the wounded Rattlesnake Davies and Lt. Dallas MacPherson, who both offered the opinion that they would have been killed but for the appearance on the scene of USS *Shark*.

He then called, in fairly quick succession, the three psychiatrists who had independently examined Commander Reid. One of them was definite: There was nothing wrong with Commander Reid, and on that he could not be shaken.

The other two were not so sure. Neither would say he was crazy, but they both agreed he held some very strange views, for a U.S. Navy commander.

Al Surprenant questioned and badgered, overstepped the bounds of polite interrogation and then dived back behind them against a barrage of *"OBJECTIONS"* from the prosecutor. Once he nearly had an admission that Commander Reid was just too strange, too bound up in his perceived French antecedents, to be trusted with a modern nuclear submarine.

But a belief in reincarnation, and indeed spiritualism, simply did not constitute "crazy." Surprenant proved eccentricity, and he proved a profound instability. He *almost* proved a long-held emotional cowardice on the part of the CO. But he did not obtain an admission that Commander Reid was so unbalanced as to have been relieved of command on that particular morning.

It was immediately after the lunch break when the defense finally called the accused Executive Officer to the witness chair to testify under oath in his own defense. And before he did so, counsel requested permission to "read just two or three lines from Section Three of Navy Regulation one-zero-eight-eight, which the prosecution apparently deemed irrelevant."

And he then stated, very simply, *"Intelligent, fearless initiative is an important trait of military character. It is not the purpose of these regulations to discourage its employment in cases of this nature."*

Lieutenant Commander Headley sat motionless in the witness chair as the short but powerful words were read out to the court. He saw Captain Dunning nod, and he continued to sit bolt upright, immaculate in his uniform, as he began to answer his counsel's questions, firmly and without hesitation.

"And when it came right down to it, why do you think Commander Reid refused to help the SEALs?"

"Two reasons, sir. One, he did not want to be associated with another disaster, like he had in another life. Two, he kept yelling that the planet Mercury was in retrograde."

"He what?"

"He told me that the mighty planet that controls us was stilled in the heavens and that by dawn it would be in retrograde—going backwards, that is."

"Did you have any comment?"

"I believe I just said, 'No shit?' I found it a bit bewildering, given the urgency of our situation."

"Did this conversation take place in front of anyone?"

"Nossir. This started in his cabin. But then it continued back in the control room in front of everyone after the SEALs had transmitted their call for help."

"Did you go back to the control room, leaving the CO in his cabin?"

"Yessir. I was in charge of the rescue operation, and I immediately ordered the submarine inshore to get the guys out."

"You knew they were under attack, from Chinese helicopters?"

"Yessir."

"And how did you assess the danger?"

"I planned to down the helos with our Stinger missiles from range eight hundred yards, handheld right off the bridge. They're very accurate."

"And what about the danger to your own ship?"

"Negligible, in my view. I thought the Chinese might have a couple of missiles. But there was a morning mist, and I thought they'd be preoccupied with the guys who were battering them with the M-60 machine guns. If they carried ASW mortars or depth bombs I knew they'd be largely useless if we were on the surface with Stingers. I thought we were in there with a good shot at success."

"You were not afraid the *Shark* might be sunk?"

"Sir, *Shark* is a U.S. Navy fighting ship. We had eight valued colleagues being wiped out by Chinese gunships. Of course we went in to save them. That's what we're for. This is the Navy, not the Cub Scouts. And yes, I was afraid. But not too afraid to try."

"And what happened when the CO arrived in the control room?"

"I told him precisely what we were doing. And he objected, as I knew he would."

"How did you know?"

"Because Commander Reid is nothing short of a goddamned coward. And he's plainly crazy."

Finally uttered, the words hung like the sword of Damocles over the courtroom. *"OBJECTION!"* shouted Locker Jones, springing to his feet.

"Overruled," snapped back Captain Dunning. "That is the heart of this case. The accused XO has been asked his opinion. And he has given it."

"Was he afraid the ship might be hit and everyone killed?" asked Al Surprenant.

"Of course. And he thought because Mercury was in retrograde, that might happen."

"Did he say so?"

"He shouted out, sir—*'RETROGRADE! RETROGRADE! The great planet Mercury is in retreat.'* He called me an ignorant man for not knowing what was happening in the zodiac, in front of everyone. He said my life was insignificant, that I knew nothing. That all of our lives, particularly in the areas of transportation and communication, were ruled by Mercury. And now the darn thing was kinda spinning backwards."

"And then?"

"He told me there was no way he was going to allow his submarine to continue on the surface, in the path of an ASW helicopter, not while the planet was in retrograde."

"Lieutenant Commander, is the direction in which the distant planet Mercury spins a normal consideration in the United States Navy when making combat decisions?"

"Nossir."

"Ever?"

"Not in my experience, sir. It was a new one on me."

"And then what happened?"

"He ordered me to turn the ship around, and to proceed in a direction away from the SEALs."

"And did you do so?"

"Nossir. I told him I could not do that. Would not do that. And he told me I was making a one-man mutiny."

"And did you change your mind and retreat, like Mercury?"

"Nossir. I did not."

"You proceeded with the rescue?"

"I did. I told the CO I had the support of the entire command of the ship. That I would not leave the guys to be killed. I offered him the sick-list option as laid down in the regulations. But he declined."

"And then?"

"I ordered the conn to hold our course on the surface. And I ordered the missiles to be brought up from below."

"And then, you and the crew carried out the rescue. And were you on the bridge, in the line of fire, as it were?"

"Yessir. I was."

"And did you direct the firing of the missiles."

"Yessir. I fired one myself, hit and blew up the second Chinese helicopter."

Lieutenant Commander Al Surprenant just shook his head and blurted out, *"My God! And now they want to court-martial you?"*

"Yessir."

"No further questions."

The silence in the courtroom was devastating as defense counsel finally sat down. And there was a slight air of resignation in the body language of Locker Jones as he stood up to cross-examine.

"Lieutenant Commander, the court has heard of your lifelong friendship with Commander Hunter. Would it be true to say you would have done anything to save him, including the making of a mutiny aboard your ship?"

"Yessir, it would. I would also have done anything to save any of the others . . . and, if I may, sir?"

"Please continue."

"Sir, you may question me for a thousand years. But I'm going to save you a lot of trouble. I did not hesitate to remove the CO and to proceed with the rescue myself. And if I could live it over again, a thousand times, I'd still do it. I hope I make myself clear, counselor."

"Perfectly clear. In fact you are the perfect mutineer. No further questions. I rest the case for the prosecution."

There was no summing up by either the court president or the lawyers, as there would have been in a civilian case. And Captain Dunning rose and led his panel out. Lieutenant Commander Headley and his attorney also left the room, in company with Admiral Bergstrom and Admiral Curran.

Their wait would not be long. In the room behind the main court, Boomer Dunning called his team swiftly to order.

"I'll take the view of the Lieutenant first, since I do not wish him to be influenced by the opinions of those who outrank him. . . . Lieutenant?"

"Not guilty, sir. Reid is plainly crazy. In my view *he* should be court-martialed, for cowardice in the face of the enemy."

Boomer nodded. "Lieutenant Commander?"

"Guilty. If the CO says no, the risk is too great, that's an end to it. The CO stands or falls by that decision, and no one's charged him with anything."

Captain Dunning turned to the second Lieutenant Commander. "And your verdict?"

"Guilty. Headley, for all of his good intentions, had no right to seize the ship. Certainly no right to have his CO arrested."

"And you?" replied the Captain, turning to the last of his four assistants.

"Not guilty. I think the XO was right to assume command. There were grave doubts about the suitability of Commander Reid to make sound judgments."

"Excellent. But may I just clarify that none of you is interested in a possible change of mind? Anyone want to go over the issue? Or discuss it further."

No one did. Minds were made up at 2–2. Captain Dunning would decide Lt. Commander Headley's fate.

"Very well, gentlemen. In a few minutes, we will return to the courtroom and I will make my casting vote, plus a short summation for the court, in order that they understand our verdict."

He sat at a table and wrote carefully on the pages of the large writing tablet inside the leather folder. Then he stood up, and beckoned his four colleagues to follow him. They walked through the door, and Captain Dunning removed the sword from the wall and placed it upon the table. "Ask them to come in," he ordered.

Lieutenant Commander Headley entered last and stared at the sword almost in disbelief as he took his seat at the defense counsel table.

"I should tell you the votes are divided two to two in this case, and I now have the duty to pass the casting vote, and with it the judgment of the court," said the ex–submarine Captain.

"And I should begin by stating that Lieutenant Commander Headley's opinions about Mercury in retrograde or any of the other foibles displayed by Commander Reid are not the bedrocks of the case. And we are not here to stand in judgment on them either.

"We are here, very simply, to decide whether Commander Reid issued an order in the early hours of that June morning that was so wrong, indeed so crazy, that he had to be arrested and relieved of the command of his ship under Section one-zero-eight-eight.

"And what was that order? He said he would not leave his nuclear submarine on the surface, and risk the lives of his one hundred seven–member crew, and the ship, in order to save eight men. Was that wrong? Possibly, in the light of events. Was it crazy? No. It wasn't crazy. Was there a suggestion of cowardice? Again, possibly. No more.

"But was it sufficiently outlandish for him to be relieved of command of his ship, arrested and incarcerated in his cabin while his number two took over?

"The answer is plain. NO. ABSOLUTELY NOT.

"The defendant is guilty as charged. Guilty of making a mutiny on the high seas. But the court does not recommend he be jailed, as would be expected in such a case. But rather that he be dismissed from the service immediately, under the severest censure. The court further recommends that Commander Reid never again hold the position of Commanding Officer on a U.S. Navy submarine involving Special Forces. That's all, save to remind everyone in this room of the following:

"If you permit every lieutenant commander to seize control of a warship because he does not agree with his CO, you no longer have a Navy. You have a rabble, in a very dangerous ship. My verdict was reached strictly for the greater good of the United States Navy. It was the only verdict to reach. And it always has been, ever since the morning of June seventh."

And long after the principals of the Navy's first court-martial for mutiny had departed, Dan Headley still stood helplessly at the defense counsel's desk, still staring at the long mahogany table. Still staring at the cruel steel blade of the gilded sword, which was pointed at him alone.

EPILOGUE

RICK HUNTER AND Dan Headley returned home to the bluegrass together. Old Bart Hunter said it was about time, and promptly retired, leaving the entire operation of the sprawling Hunter Valley Thoroughbred Farms to his son.

Rick thus moved from U.S. Navy SEAL Commander to president of a multimillion-dollar Kentucky corporation in the space of a week. His first action was to deed a 10 percent shareholding of the land, mares and stallions to the ownership of Dan Headley.

Within one more week the headed writing paper of Hunter Valley contained the words *Directors, Richard Hunter (President), Dan Headley (Vice President, Thoroughbred Operations), Bart Hunter (consultant), Robert Headley (Stallions).*

Bart was surprised, but agreeable. "Took me and my daddy fifty years to build this place," he said. "Took you about ten minutes to start dismantling it, giving it away to our good neighbors."

"It only took Danny ten minutes to save my life," replied Rick. "Guess it's called quality time, right?"

"Well, I'm glad he did. Whatever you think's fair, boy. That's the way to run a business."

"And a life," said his son.

Rusty Bennett also resigned from the Navy and returned to the coast of Maine, where he took over the operation of his father's two lobster boats, working out of the little island of Frenchborough, home of his mother's ancestors for 150 years. Six months later he married the prettiest girl on the island, 12 years his junior.

Commander Donald Reid was never heard from again, resigning his commission and moving his wife and family to France, to a small town house in Grasse.

Admiral John Bergstrom was seething at the loss of two of his top commanders, and it took Admiral Morgan five weeks to persuade him not to resign. Admiral George Morris recovered and returned to Fort Meade. His newly promoted personal assistant was Lt. Commander James Ramshawe.

The Chinese ambassador to Washington, His Excellency Ling Guofeng, ran into the most thunderously hard time from Arnold Morgan. The U.S. National Security chief, forced to admit U.S. involvement in the destruction of the Naval base at Haing Gyi, made it crystal clear that the United States would tolerate no further Chinese expansion into the Indian Ocean and its confines.

He told him the United States could, and would, make their actions on the Burmese coast look like kids' stuff if the Beijing government ever again elected to tamper with the free passage of the industrial world's oil supply.

The Admiral actually stood up and lectured him. He told him that Beijing now understood what happened when the American superpower was riled. "Just you remember, Ling, behave yourselves. No more adventuring in foreign waters. Because if you do, we'll hammer you again.

"Okay. Okay. I guess you don't care. You got Taiwan, which is what it was all about in the first place. The price you pay is to know that's as far offshore as you guys are going. At least, it is as long as I sit in this chair. As for your most-favored-nation status, you can forget all about that."

The ambassador stood up to leave. He nodded curtly and headed for the door. And as he opened it, Arnold Morgan said quietly, "*Pax Americana*, Ling. And don't forget it."

"I'm sorry. I don't quite understand?" replied the ambassador.

"Go figure," grunted the Admiral, rudely.

ACKNOWLEDGMENTS

AS USUAL, I have a list of serving officers who have no desire whatever to be formally acknowledged as my advisers. The subject is always too secretive, too classified in its nature, and my sources too senior for identification.

Do I want to be named in one of YOUR books? Are you kidding! And yet they help me every year, ensuring that I am able to tell my story, handing me advice and detail, which they believe will give the public a greater appreciation of the armed heroes of the United States military.

Mostly my land attacks are planned with the help of former Special Forces officers. My insights into the diabolically secretive Intelligence world of Fort Meade are provided by a couple of former spies who seek only to highlight the sheer professionalism of the place.

However, at sea, my principal adviser, as always, is Admiral Sir John "Sandy" Woodward, the Task Force Commander of the Royal Navy fleet that won the Battle for the Falkland Islands in 1982.

On, and under, the surface, Admiral Sandy plots and plans with me to help bring readers right into the control room of the submarine. Without him, I could not bring reality to the subject of underwater warfare.

I did not trouble him with the final details of the court-martial, but rather relied on legal sources in the U.S. Navy, who again did not wish to be named.

They joined a whole range of new advisers who wished to protect their anonymity: the oil tanker captains who expressed their opinions on their highly combustible cargo; the oil company executives who tried to guess what they would have done in the face of crisis; the Aeroflot exec who told me all about the Andropov, not knowing the purpose for which it was being used!

One of my rare identifiable sources, however, is the excellent geopolitical writer, traveler and scholar Charles Stewart Goodwin of Cape Cod, who provided research on the ancient Chinese fleets and the contents of the National Palace Museum in Taipei. He knows how grateful I am. His own writings on global politics provide for me an unfailing guide.

For insights and expertise on the subject of reincarnation and post-traumatic stress, I have to thank Dr. Barbara Lane of Virginia, whose own book, *Echoes from the Battlefield: Past Lives from the Civil War*, is probably the best of its kind. Dr. Lane's wide knowledge of both these subjects, plus a certain surefootedness in planetary matters, provided research of the highest order. In matters of battle stress, her own views dovetailed almost precisely with those of Admiral Woodward.

I thank also my friend Chris Choi Man Tat, whose suave and courteous manner running Kite's, Dublin's best Chinese restaurant, quite conceals the fact that he was once bosun on a gigantic crude-oil tanker plying between the Gulf and the Far East. His insights on the great ships were constantly helpful.

Finally I thank my friend Olivia Oakes, who thought she was coming for a quiet weekend with my family and ended up reading this manuscript for almost fifteen hours, checking spelling and punctuation. For any errors in this regard I intend, unfairly, to blame her.

The Shark Mutiny is a work of fiction. Every character in it is a product of my imagination only, though there may be certain college baseball players who recognize their names but not their lives, nor any other connection with reality.

—Patrick Robinson

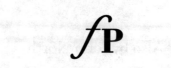

Also by John North

The Measure of the Universe
Richard of Wallingford
Horoscopes and History
Chaucer's Universe
Stars, Minds and Fate
The Universal Frame
The Norton History of Astronomy and Cosmology

STONEHENGE

A New Interpretation
of Prehistoric Man
and the Cosmos

JOHN NORTH

THE FREE PRESS
New York London Toronto Sydney Singapore

The Free Press
A Division of Simon & Schuster Inc.
1230 Avenue of the Americas
New York, NY 10020

Published by arrangement with HarperCollins*Publishers*

THE FREE PRESS and colophon are trademarks
of Simon & Schuster Inc.

Manufactured in the United States of America

10 9 8 7 6 5 4 3 2 1

Library of Congress Cataloging-in-Publication Data is available.

ISBN 0–684–84512–1

TO
MARION

CONTENTS

LIST OF FIGURES

LIST OF PLATES

GLOSSARY

acronycal rising The last visible rising (in the course of the year) of a star at evening twilight. See Appendix 4.

alignment An arrangement in which three or more objects (strictly points on objects) are in a straight line. The word is often used of prehistoric rows of stones, but is here almost always used where one of the points is a rising or setting star, or a point on the Sun or Moon, on the horizon.

altitude Angle above a level plane, sometimes called *elevation*.

anthropomorphic In human form (to be interpreted generously). Neolithic slabs, often a metre or so across, are often carved in low relief with a face and other human characteristics. Archaeologists, however, cannot always agree on what these characteristics were meant to be.

architrave The main beam that rests on the plate (abacus) topping the capital of a column, as in Greek temple architecture.

ard A primitive plough with a ploughshare of stone or hard wood, and no mouldboard to turn the soil (and so create a furrow).

azimuth A direction in the horizontal plane, usually specified in degrees or as a compass bearing. Any clearly understood conventions for the starting point and direction of increase are acceptable, but star azimuths are commonly measured from north, increasing in a clockwise (eastwards) direction. East is then equivalent to an azimuth of 90°, south 180°, west 270°, and north 0°.

barrow A mound, deliberately erected out of earth and other materials (such as chalk, stone, or wood, depending on time and region), and having a conscious architectural structure. Usually, but not always, built for burial purposes. Long barrows, often but not always chambered, are typical of the Neolithic period, and round barrows of the Bronze Age and later. For various forms of round barrow, see Plate 2.

BC and bc (dates before the Christian era) are distinguished to indicate between ordinary calendar dates and uncorrected dates arrived at from radiocarbon methods. See Appendix 1.

beaker Drinking vessel with the profile of its side S-shaped profile, and often decorated with impressions made by a chord, bone or other tool. The general style seems to have arrived in Britain from the Rhine area in the mid third millennium BC. Many variations of shape are distinguished. **Bell beakers** look like an inverted bell or cloche hat. They carried incised decoration in horizontal bands round the body and seem to have begun as a regional variant (lower

Rhine delta) of Corded Ware beakers. Like the latter they were often placed in single male burials, with weapons.

Belgae A population taking its name from Caesar's references to a group in Gaul occupying lands to the north of the Seine and Marne. (Certain of their tribes, he said, settled in Britain.) Archaeologists apply the name to earlier cultures in the same general area.

bell barrow See **barrow**.

Beltane A Celtic feast, in celebration of the beginning of summer, but at a time of year roughly corresponding to our beginning of May. Approximately mid-way between vernal **equinox** and summer **solstice**. The festival was associated with fire.

bluestone A name given to some of the stones at Stonehenge, on account of their colour. They are in fact of several rock types (rhyolites, dolerite, volcanic, and some sandstones).

berm The level area usually left between a ditch and its adjacent bank or mound.

Bronze Age The period during which copper and its alloys were first used in significant quantities. The dating of the period depends on the place and culture. For Britain, various definitions have been offered, such as 2500–1800 BC for the early bronze age, 1800–1300 BC for the middle, and up to 700 BC for the later period.

cairn A mound of stones, often erected as a covering for a tomb. A form of barrow.

capstone Stone forming the roof of a burial chamber.

causewayed enclosure Any area enclosed by a system of rings of ditches and banks through which an entrance passage has been left.

Celts A name used by ancient writers of a population group occupying much of Europe and now distinguished by a common language (dialects of which are still found in Brittany, Wales, Ireland and Scotland) and artistic tradition (characteristic is the Swiss La Tène style). Celtic culture seems to derive from a Bronze Age urnfield culture of the upper Danube region of the mid second millennium BC. They might have arrived in Britain by the eighth century BC.

chamber passage The entrance passage in a chamber tomb.

chamber tomb Any tomb with a chamber, usually of stone, and usually with the evident intention of adding successive interments over long periods of time. The word is not usually applied to tombs with only a **cist** or coffin within them. In the Severn–Cotswold type (Neolithic period) the mortuary chamber was covered by a long barrow in the form of a mound of earth or stones. The chamber was often at the high end of the barrow. When the chamber was reached from the side, there was often a false doorway (**false portal**) at the high

end, with horn-like protrusions to the barrow creating a **forecourt** (in some cases paved) in which ritual involving fire took place. Cairns with burial chambers are common in Ireland, northern Britain, and Brittany, but not in southern Britain (but there are some in the Scilly Isles, Cornwall and Anglesey).

Charon See **obol**.

cinerary urn An urn in which the ashes of the dead are placed after cremation.

circle A loose description of a roughly circular arrangement of standing stones or posts, whether or not surrounded by a ditch and/or bank. The word is often used by those at pains to prove that prehistoric people were unable to draw circles.

cist box, usually applied to a box of stone slabs used for burial purposes.

combe or **coomb** A hollow or valley, especially on the flank of a hill, dry during most of the year.

conjunction An alignment of two celestial bodies (say the Sun and Moon) and the observer, so that the two appear to be together in the sky; or, more generally, appear to be at the same ecliptic longitude. (The latter qualification is added since objects on separate paths may pass close, but not strictly meet.)

constellation A conspicuous grouping or pattern of bright stars, named on the basis of things the shape seems to resemble, or on the basis of an important star in the group. The Greek astronomer Ptolemy named 48 constellations, many traceable to earlier Mesopotamia. Astronomers now accept 88, strictly defined with reference to convenient boundaries (so that all the sky is covered) rather than shapes.

cosmical settings The first visible setting (in the course of the year) of a star or planet at dawn. See Appendix 4.

cove Three or possibly more upright stones, often in a U-shaped arrangement at the centre of a stone circle or henge.

cremation The burning of the dead.

cromlech A stone slab supported on blocks (a Welsh word for a **dolmen**). The word has occasionally been used for the circle formed by blocks of stone surrounding a barrow (in the form of a peristyle), and past writers have applied it even to Stonehenge and Avebury.

cropmark An evident variation in crop colour, usually visible only from the air, caused for example by variations in soil chemistry, water distribution, or very local weather patterns.

culmination The highest point reached by any heavenly body (Sun, Moon, star, planet, etc.) in the course of the daily rotation when it crosses the meridian.

culture A homogeneous grouping of material effects (tools, weapons, ornaments, pottery, burial paraphernalia, houses, and so forth) and physical and mental habits. In prehistory the latter is almost always inferred from the former.

cup and ring decoration A form of incised or pecked design found on stones, which may be parts of a monument or outlying crops of rock that have never been deliberately moved. The 'cup' is a hollow of say 5 cm diameter, and it is surrounded by incised rings, spirals, or other intricate shapes.

cursus Literally a course, as for a race, but applied now by archaeologists to a type of monument where a strip of land is enclosed between long parallel banks and adjoining ditches to the inside or outside of them. Long barrows may be built into cursus. (The plural of this Latin word is also *cursus*, but some treat the word as English and use the plural *cursusses*.) See Chapter 3.

declination The angle between a star (or of a point of the Sun or Moon, or other heavenly body) and the celestial equator. This coordinate is paired with right ascension. See Appendix 2 for more details.

disc barrow See **barrow**.

divination Foretelling the future by some sort of hidden, magical or supernatural means.

dolerite A basic igneous rock, resembling basalt, but coarser grained.

dolmen A Welsh, Cornish and Breton term (due allowance being made for spelling) for a stone table, in prehistory usually comprising upright unhewn stones supporting a large and relatively flat stone. The whole was usually originally covered with stones or earth and functioned as a burial chamber.

druid A priest of the Celtic people who spread across northern Europe and into the British Isles a few centuries BC. Archaeological artefacts excepted, most of what is known about them and their religion comes from classical Greek and Latin authors.

drystone (walling) Stone built up without mortar.

dyke or **dike** A ditch (occasionally to conduct water) or an embankment to keep water off land. The ambiguity stems from the fact that the two usually go together, for obvious reasons.

ecliptic The (mean) apparent path of the Sun through the stars, covered in the course of a year. The constellations through which the ecliptic passes define the traditional **zodiac**, but most of the familiar constellations in that band are of Middle Eastern origin, and are probably not prehistoric.

equator (celestial) The great circle in the heavens midway between the celestial poles. Poles and equator are determined by the Earth's rotation, and the terrestrial equator is in the same plane as the celestial. See also **equinox**.

equinoctial See **equinox**.

equinox Loosely speaking, the time of year (spring or vernal equinox, autumnal equinox) when day and night are of equal length. These are the times when the Sun is on (or nearly on) the celestial equator, which is therefore sometimes called the equinoctial.

extinction altitude The altitude of a star below which it is invisible. This depends on various factors such as the brightness (magnitude) of the star and atmospheric conditions.

false portal See **chamber tomb**.

fiducial Regarded as a fixed basis of comparison (said of a line, point, or other marker).

flint A hard stone, usually steely grey or brown in colour, found in pebbles or nodules within a white incrustation. A relatively pure native form of silica, if suitably struck (knapped) it flakes so as to form (or leave) a sharp cutting instrument. Used for arrowheads, blades, scrapers, adzes, etc.

forecourt See **chamber tomb**.

gallery grave A chambered tomb in which the entrance passage, running into the burial chamber, is hardly (or not at all) distinguishable from it. There may be side chambers (as in the Severn–Cotswold type).

glaciation An Ice Age, the condition of being covered with an ice sheet or glaciers.

gnomon An upright (for example a stone or post, or later of finely contrived metal) from whose shadow time is estimated. Hence gnomonics, the science of calculating sun-dials.

gnomonics See **gnomon**.

grooved ware See **Rinyo–Clacton**.

heliacal rising/setting The rising of a star or group of stars just before sunrise, or the setting of the same just after sunset. See Appendix 4.

henge Circular banked enclosure with internal or external ditch and often one or more internal rings of timbers or stones. (This generic term is used in different ways by different writers, but ultimately derives by analogy with the name of Stonehenge.)

hillfort Hilltop defended by walls of stone, banks of earth, palisades of timber, ditches, or a mixture of these. Whether Neolithic causewayed camps had a defensive function is a moot point, but hillforts are usually taken to have been a late Bronze Age development, and most known examples date from the Iron Age.

hippodrome A course or circuit for horse-races or chariot-races.

Iron Age The period from say 700 BC onwards (the date varying from region to region) when iron had become the chief metal used for tools and weapons. (Bronze and flint continued in use, however.)

kerb Piled up stones forming a retaining wall around a mound. Kerbs may be internal or external and visible.

kist See **cist**.

leptolith Literally a slender stone. The word is used of slender flint cutting tools.

ley The name given by A. Watkins (around 1921) and his followers to certain alignments of natural and man-made objects that many of them believe follow the lines of certain unspecified kinds of force or energy emanating from the terrain. Their leys typically take in prehistoric, medieval, and even much more recent sites. An interest in leys was revived with the UFO craze in the 1960s.

libation The pouring out of wine or other liquid, whether or not conceived as a drink, in honour of a god or ancestor.

limb (of the Sun or Moon) The edge of the apparent disc of the Sun or Moon.

lintel A horizontal stone or timber, placed across the top of two uprights, as in a door frame.

long barrow See **barrow**

lozenge A rhomb, a geometrical figure in the shape of the 'diamonds' on playing cards.

lynchet A terrace cut into the slope of a (usually chalk) down, intended for cultivation.

magnetic flux A measure of the magnetism crossing a surface. More precisely: the surface integral of the product of the permeability of the medium and the magnetic field intensity perpendicular to the surface.

magnetometer An instrument for measuring the strength and direction of a magnetic field, in archaeology usually the Earth's.

magnitude (of a star) A measure of the brightness of a star or planet. The Greek astronomer Hipparchus (second century BC) grouped stars on a scale from first (brightest) to sixth magnitude (barely detectable). It was eventually realized that the physiology of the eye is such that each step corresponds to a roughly similar brightness ratio. In 1856 N. R. Pogson established a standard scheme in which a difference of 5 in magnitude corresponds to a brightness ratio of 100 to 1. A difference of 1 in magnitude then corresponds to a brightness ratio of 2.512 to 1. The only magnitudes relevant to this book are magnitudes apparent to the eye. (Other definitions relate to the intrinsic luminosities of stars and to the type of radiation received by the detector.)

marl A soil comprising a mixture of clay and lime.

megalith A large stone (by implication, one that is thought to have had a monumental use). (From Greek *mega*, large, and *lithos*, stone.)

Megalithic Yard (MY) A unit of length (0.829 m or 2.72 ft) that was used, according to Alexander Thom, in the construction of stone rings and other megalithic monuments.

menhir A single standing stone of appreciable height (a Breton word, said to be from *men*, stone, and *hir*, long). The word occurs in many Breton place names, but seems to have entered archaeology only in the eighteenth century.

meridian The plane containing the northernmost and southernmost points of the horizon, the north celestail pole, and the zenith overhead; or that part of the great circle on the celestial sphere through the last three points. (From the Latin *meridies*, midday, when the Sun crosses the meridian.) The word is also used of the terrestrial counterpart of this, namely a line of longitude on the Earth, as in 'the meridian of Greenwich'. See **culmination**.

Mesolithic The period between the end of the last Ice Age (say 8000 BC) and the introduction of farming and pottery making (in Britain around 4500 BC).

Metonic cycle The cycle of 19 years or 235 months (these being approximately equal) that brings the Moon back in step with the Sun, so that new and full moons repeat on the same dates. From Meton, a Greek astronomer of the fifth century BC.)

mica A mineral (often aluminium silicate) occurring as small glinting flakes in granite and other rocks.

micaceous Containing **mica**.

microlith A very small stone tool, in some instances meant as part of a larger tool (for example as a blade fitted in a haft).

midden In general use now a dunghill, but in archaeological use a rubbish dump, often containing bones, shells, and charcoal.

Minoan The name applied by Sir Arthur Evans to the Bronze Age civilization of Crete (3000 to 1000 BC, divided by him into three periods, Early, Middle and Late).

mortise A cavity cut into wood or stone into which fits the end (or some part) of another piece of wood or stone (this being called a tenon) so forming a joint. The Stonehenge lintels had mortises into which fitted tenons at the tops of the uprights. This was obviously copied from earlier practice with timbers.

Mortlake ware A characteristic form of late Neolithic pottery with thick rims and heavy decoration. See **Peterborough ware**.

mortuary house A house of the dead, in some cases of stone and in others of wood, wattle and daub, as in houses of the living. Used for the deposit of the corpse, and occasionally offerings, at the time of burial. The starting point of many burial mounds.

Mycenaean A mainland Greek civilization that developed in the late Bronze Age, which in its early period (sixteenth century BC or before) was strongly influenced by the **Minoan** civilization. Named after the place Mycenae, although the term is applied more extensively.

Neolithic The period (literally 'New Stone [Age]') in which agriculture was first practised, pottery was made, and fine tools mainly in stone, all of these things being eventually the subject of trade. Typical monuments of the period were the long barrows and causewayed enclosures. The period in southern Britain can be conventionally taken as lasting from about 4500 BC to about 2800 BC.

node A point where two great circles on the celestial sphere intersect (see Appendix 2). Two great circles of much importance are the apparent paths of the Sun and Moon through the stars, and the lunar nodes (where they cross) are of especial interest since eclipses take place when the Sun and Moon are at or near them. The lunar nodes are not fixed but moved slowly round the sky in a sense counter to the Moon's monthly motion, completing the circuit in about 18.6 years.

obol or obolus A silver (or later bronze) coin of ancient Greece, which was often placed in the mouths of the dead as a fee for the ferryman **Charon**, who conveyed the shades of the dead across the rivers of the lower world. The tradition was taken over by the Romans.

oolite A form of limestone, in which the calcium carbonate adopts a granulated form around grains of sand. Usually fossil-bearing.

Ordnance Datum (OD) The level with reference to which ground levels (heights and depths) are quoted in the Ordnance Survey.

orthostat An upright stone.

Palaeolithic The period (literally 'Old Stone [Age]') of human existence when stone tools first played an important technological part in human evolution. There are many definitions, but the Palaeolithic period is often conventionally taken to have lasted to the end of the last Ice Age, about 10,000 years ago, and to have begun around 700,000 years ago. Britain was occupied intermittently during certain warmer periods of this long stretch of time, which is usually divided into Lower (say to 200,000 years ago), Middle (up to between 40,000 and 30,000 years ago) and Upper Palaeolithic (continuing to about 10,000 years ago).

passage grave General term for a tomb in which a long stone passage leads into a burial chamber, the whole being then covered with a mound of stone or earth.

paving Usually flat stone slabs covering the ground.

post pipe The space in the ground left after the decay of a post, or its filling. Its precise size and constitution depends on local circumstance (outside pressure, the treatment of the original post, surrounding soil, and so on).

Peterborough ware Pottery of a style associated with the second half of the third millennium BC in southern Britain (as far north as Yorkshire). Typical is the heavily ornamented necked bowl, at first with a rounded base, later in a flat-based form. The ornament is often added with a twisted cord impression. S. Piggott recognized three distinctive styles: Ebbsfleet, Mortlake and Fengate.

precession (of the equinoxes) The slow drift of the equinoctial points (see **equinox**) round the sky (the apparent sphere of stars). The effect is that the measured ecliptic longitudes of the stars increase by about 1.5° per century, but it also means that what stars are visible, and where precisely they rise and set over the horizon, change with time—and change substantially over millennia.

quern A device in which grain is ground, usually comprising two discs of stone, the lower one hollowed and fixed, the upper rotated or moved from side to side by hand.

radiocarbon A radioactive isotope of the element carbon, used as an indicator of the time that has passed since the death of a specimen of organic matter (wood, bone, antler, etc.). See Appendix 1.

reave A land boundary.

resistivity A measure of relative electrical resistance, in archaeology usually that of the soil. (The term is usually defined as the resistance measured across a specimen of certain standard dimensions.) Variations in resistivity may indicate past soil disturbance (ditches, post holes, etc.) or the existence of buried material (stones, the remains of posts, etc.).

revetment A retaining wall, usually of stone, timber or turf, supporting a rampart or mound, or even the side of a ditch.

rhomb or **rhombus** A parallelogram with four equal sides. A lozenge-shaped plane figure.

rhyton A vessel from which **libations** are poured. (From the Greek.)

Rinyo–Clacton ware A major pottery style of the late Neolithic, with typically linear patterns and a more homogeneous form than that of **Peterborough ware**. It tends to have a bucket shape with thick walls and a flat base, and to be poorly fired. Known throughout Britain (found at Rinyo in Orkney and Clacton in Essex, of course), it is rare in Ireland. S. Piggott used the name to replace the more descriptive **grooved ware**, which carries no implication of a single material culture responsible for it, but which some regard as too narrowly defined.

sabbath Originally the seventh day of the week, a day of religious rest as enjoined on the Jews of Israel; more generally, any comparable periodic day of rest.

sarsen A form of micaceous sandstone (see **mica**), as used for the larger stones at Stonehenge. The word was perhaps peculiar to the Wiltshire region.

scaling posts The name given here to the timber posts, traces of which are often found under the high end of a long barrow. They are not symmetrically placed, and it is here argued that they provided a guide to the astronomical architecture of the barrow.

shard or **sherd** A fragment of broken pottery.

solstice The times of year at which the Sun is at its maximum northerly or southerly declination. The days are then at their longest and shortest respectively. These times are traditionally called midsummer and midwinter, although astronomers, among others, define the *beginnings* of summer and winter in terms of them. They occur now around 21 June and 21 December, but it makes little sense to ask for equivalent Neolithic dates, when there was no comparable calendar. At the winter solstice, the Sun's noon **altitude** is at its lowest, and at the summer solstice it is highest.

standstill (lunar) A maximum or minimum of the lunar declination. (Compare the solar solstices.) This is only in the mathematical sense of there being a zero rate of change, and does not imply that there will be no greater or lesser values attained. See Appendix 2 for a fuller account of the Moon's complex motions.

stele A standing stone or slab of modest size (say less than a metre, and often less than 30 cm) with one face only sculpted in low relief. An Anglicized Greek word. (Pronounced like the English word *steel*.)

tenon See **mortise**.

terminal The end of a monument (in this book usually a **cursus**) on the assumption that it was regarded as such by its builders and has been correctly identified.

theodolite A portable surveying instrument, usually now mounted on a tripod and fitted with a telescope, with graduated circular scales with which angles of **azimuth** and **altitude** can be accurately measured.

transept A side compartment in a passage tomb, often doubled to form a plan in the form of a cross, or even quadrupled.

trapezium A plane quadrilateral (a closed figure with four straight sides) that is not a parallelogram. Some use the word in a more special sense, adding the condition that just one pair of opposite sides be parallel.

treehenge The name given here to a **henge** with mainly timber components (uprights, lintels, etc.).

trilithon Three stones, in the form of two uprights and a lintel across the top.

trixylon Two massive timber uprights with a timber lintel across the top (by analogy with **trilithon**).

tropical year The time taken by the Earth to travel once round the Sun, from **equinox** to equinox. Alternatively, from the point of view of an observer on the Earth, the time apparently taken by the Sun to pass once round the sphere of stars, from equinox to equinox. This is the common year, of about 365.242 days.

tumulus A term used loosely for any artificial mound, called into use especially when the precise nature of the mound is unknown.

twilight The periods after sunset and before sunrise when the sky is partially illuminated through the scattering of sunlight. Various definitions are offered (*civil, nautical, astronomical*) according to the degree of darkening thought to be significant.

urnfield A field of pottery urns used for burial by cremation. (Also used of the culture in which this form of burial was practised.)

vallum A wall or rampart of earth, sods, or stones, possibly palisaded.

weald or **wold** A wooded tract of country. (The Weald is a name used especially of an area formerly wooded between the North and South Downs of Kent, Surrey and Sussex.)

wedge tomb A very long megalithic tomb, with the covering sloping down towards the end furthest from the entrance. A common Neolithic Irish form.

Windmill Hill culture The name given to a culture typified by the Neolithic culture responsible for the causewayed enclosure at Windmill Hill, near Avebury.

wristguard A plate of wood, stone or metal attached to the inner side of the wrist (of the hand with which an archer holds the bow), to protect the wrist from the bowstring.

zenith The point of the sky directly above the observer. The point to which the string of a plumb line may be regarded as directed. (More precise definitions are strictly necessary if the non-spherical form of the Earth is to be taken into account.)

zodiac The band of sky now associated with twelve constellations through which the Sun seems to pass in its annual path. See **ecliptic**.

PREFACE

To the Greeks, the primary sense of *cosmos* was that of order, harmony, and proportion. When the word was applied to the universe as a whole it was to insist that those properties—appropriate to a well regulated state, a finely decorated vase, a formally beautiful building—belonged to the universe too. Aetius tells us that Pythagoras was the first to use the word in this sense, and Stonehenge had stood for two millennia by his time. Today, as it presumably did then, Stonehenge impresses the onlooker more for its engineering than for its cosmic qualities, but it too was in a very real sense a cosmos, a geometrically ordered monument aligned on the universe of stars, Sun and Moon, and an embodiment of the spiritual forces they represented to most of mankind.

Such a claim is easier to make than to justify. It is not easy to catch at the mind of a people who lived more than four thousand years ago, and who left no written history, but the aim of this book is to do just that. Except indirectly, its concern is not with the realities of daily life, not with social structures, habitation, subsistence, or sheer survival, but rather with types of Neolithic monument that speak for the qualities of mind of the people responsible. We may have no texts, but the relatively large scale on which so many Neolithic monuments were built, combined with the modest way in which they merged into the landscape, have together ensured that time has not quite managed to obliterate them or all of their meaning. The monuments in question might not have compared in appearance with the polished glories of Egypt and Greece, but they have hidden qualities, and when those are found, the fact that they were concealed makes them all the more surprising.

What was the motivation of those who invested so much care and energy in them? The view to be defended here is that, as well as being religious, that motivation was in a strong sense astronomical, and that in this respect, few cultures of the time can compare with it. Such a claim is neither new nor precise. What is new here is the detail with which probable observing procedures are worked out, and connected with others detectible from at least as early as the fifth millennium BC. Stonehenge is like no other monument in the world, but there are many respects in which it is mistaken to regard it as unique. To understand it we must fit it into its context, both in time and space. In time, it can be shown to have continued in a venerable tradition. In space, its context is the remarkable landscape in which it stands. The number of prehistoric

monuments within two kilometres of the site is to be counted not in tens but in hundreds. What is less widely recognized is that the astronomical properties of Stonehenge, as of so many earlier Neolithic monuments, were also heavily dependent on that landscape. But not entirely. Their design depended also on the state of the heavens.

It will not of course be suggested that the monument on Salisbury Plain was an astronomical observatory, at least in the current meaning of that word. The stones were not erected as a means to *investigating* the heavens in a detached and abstract way. The aim was not to discover the patterns of behaviour of the Sun, Moon or stars but to *embody* those patterns, already known in broad outline, in a religious architecture. There are signs that such ritualized architecture had been practised in the Wessex neighbourhood and elsewhere for well over a thousand years before the first phases of building at Stonehenge. While that monument in stone surpassed all before it, in architectural subtlety as well as in grandeur, to appreciate even this point one must know something of the earthen and timber structures that went before it and consequently about half of the book is concerned with that earlier material.

The book was prompted by a certain symmetry I noticed in 1979 in some published plans of excavations made on the site of a Bronze Age burial mound at Harenermolen in the northern Netherlands. (The monument in question is discussed and illustrated in Chapter 7 below.) When built, that mound had been surrounded by rings of wooden posts that had of course rotted away millennia before the excavation performed by A. E. van Giffen in the 1920s. As at many other comparable sites, he and others have been able to chart the traces of the original posts with considerable accuracy, through the discoloration of the sandy soil. It soon became clear that when such rings of posts were erected they were placed with reference to the rising and setting of the Sun and Moon at critical times and seasons. A similar claim has often been made for many of the stone circles, but the positioning of the timber posts seemed to offer more reliable evidence as to precisely *how* the Sun and Moon had been observed.

Using the key astronomical ideas that emerged in this way, it was natural enough to try to apply them to the much earlier Aubrey holes at Stonehenge, and to timber monuments at Woodhenge, Mount Pleasant, and elsewhere. Doing so led me in turn to consider the potential astronomical implications of the much earlier English long barrows, tombs roughly similar in form to others in various regions of Neolithic northern Europe. Many of them seemed to indicate that the stars, rather than the Sun and Moon, were for their builders the prime focus of religious attention. Needless to say, the order of the book is

more or less the reverse of that of my search, and begins with the long barrows. The path to Stonehenge is well trodden, although usually more direct.

The direction of the argument as presented here might disturb the casual archaeological reader, with eye trained to find the nub of the argument by looking for histograms and comparable statistical tools of evaluation. They could have added little of value, and they are certainly not the only valid way of assessing an argument. Like most archaeological reconstructions of the past, mine follows a perfectly conventional method. It puts forward a series of hypotheses about past human actions, and it tries to determine which of them best survive attempts to refute them in the light of the evidence. The evidence in question concerns not only the excavation but what is humanly possible and humanly probable. Those last two factors are all too often left out of the equation, but they play an important part in the initial search for alternative hypotheses. A rigorous search for alternatives is often far more important than a blinkered analysis of only one. To take a simple example: the existence of large temples as evidence for the organization of society into chiefdoms (the positive argument for the fact that large numbers of people can be controlled efficiently in chiefdoms is irrelevant for the moment) is worthless if one cannot rule out all the engineering possibilities for building such temples with small groups of people. And to take an astronomical example: a typical histogram of notable celestial events to which a monument seems to point is worthless if only one observing position and only one technique are considered, and viable alternatives are ignored. Open-mindedness as to alternatives is a much harder lesson to learn than statistics.

How this general method will work out in practice may be illustrated in regard to the long barrows, the subject of a long chapter in which the pattern might easily be overlooked. At an early stage the hypothesis is made that the very brightest stars were observed rising and setting over the barrows, and this according to a series of very simple but precise rules, at which the barrow architecture seems to hint. Making that assumption, the barrows can be reasonably precisely dated, even without evidence of a scientifically high quality. These dates fit well with radiocarbon dates (which are occasionally used to help select alternatives, but not to refine them after the initial stage). A single instance is not compelling, but statistically the argument is strengthened by the fact that this can be done in several independent ways at a single barrow, and the dates usually then hang together well. (The evidence for this is evaluated in passing, for example, at pp. 45, 52-3, 79-80, but more especially at pp. 131-5.) What is more, the case is strengthened when it is found that the same procedure gives acceptable results at all the barrows examined; and that the same fundamental principles can be readily extended to other monuments,

such as chalk figures and causewayed enclosures. A thousand instances might give the reader more satisfaction than a dozen, depending on the mentality of the reader, but the evidence from even a few is compelling. And there are other respects in which this is so.

I am referring here to the way some hypotheses have of leading up to unsuspected situations. In the case of the long barrows, for example, it comes as a surprise to find that, accepting our starting point, it turns out that there were strong preferences for certain simple gradients—for example, one in five and one in ten—in the angles of observation set by the barrows. These gradients conform with the known architecture of the barrows, also often in unexpected ways, and the same simple gradients even turn up on critical ridges of the landscape on which later monuments were placed. There are other unexpected shared elements to be found in monumental design, and a fair-minded reader will admit that they are at least as objective as many other archaeological constructs—for instance, the common social structures held to be discernible on the basis of monumental building techniques in widely separated cultures. (Perhaps they are even more so, since those of the first sort were quite unexpected while those of the second often owe as much to Max Weber and Émile Durkheim as to mounds of earth.) Just as unexpected is another finding of ours, namely that the long barrows fall into regions in which they are aligned on the landscape in groups of three or more. This cannot be explained by chance, and it is therefore of enormous value to our general thesis that the very stars that seem to have been the focus of attention at the long barrows were evidently used to align the barrows on the landscape over great distances (pp. 164-78). Of course it may be that there is a better archaeological explanation than mine for those extraordinary alignments of barrows—ley lines of cultural stress, perhaps—but I doubt it.

There have been numerous attempts to interpret the Stonehenge monument in astronomical terms, and what has been said of tacit presuppositions in archaeology was never truer than there. One of the greatest of omissions has been to ignore potential observing techniques almost totally, and to imagine that an observer stood in some position that was only roughly defined, 'near such and such a stone'. Rules of a much more exact kind are offered here. Of course they may be wrong, but since assuming them leads to a much more precise fit with astronomical data than those offered previously, the rules of evidence require us to accept them until something better is suggested. Some of the earlier astronomical interpretations of Stonehenge, dating from the seventeenth century, are sketched in Chapter 7. Archaeologists as a whole remain quite properly sceptical about most of them—in fact they are usually prepared to accept only the approximate alignment of the Heel Stone on sunrise

at the summer solstice. They have had good reason to resist the astronomical hypothesis, in view of the fact that hardly a single really precise line of sight has hitherto been found, but they have not been sceptical enough, for even that old favourite, the line to the Sun at summer solstice, is a very sorry specimen that has been quite misunderstood. Stonehenge was indeed built to an astronomical design, or rather succession of designs, but all of them were much more ingenious than has previously been recognized. (The real test of honest druids hereafter will be their readiness to face the elements on Salisbury Plain in midwinter. Since Stonehenge is now seriously outdated, the most honest of all will learn the necessary techniques from the pages that follow, and build another temple far away from it.)

The true astronomical arrangement of the stones would have been appreciated sooner had there not been an almost universal preoccupation with plans of the monument, that is, with charts in only two dimensions. To understand the acumen of its builders one must study its three-dimensional form—a hard lesson that we are taught by the long barrows and timber circles. Another obstacle to progress has been an obsession with the idea that sightings from prehistoric stone circles were usually made towards points on distant horizons. The horizon is all-important, of course, but the people of the Neolithic and Bronze Ages will prove to have been in the habit of creating artificial horizons, just as surely as astronomers and surveyors today use something of the sort in their levels and theodolites, albeit for quite different reasons. Such reference planes were created long before the time of Stonehenge—in the first place, no doubt, to remove the irregularities of a tree-covered horizon. They were incorporated into the Stonehenge monument in several different ways, and the alignments of the stones there will be properly understood only if they are systematically taken into account.

Addressed as it is to a general rather than a professional audience, this book includes only the barest details of the underlying calculations, but those who wish to repeat them should be able to do so—with the help, if needed, of the appendices. There is not a single result in it that might not be made more precise after closer study and field work, but there is a law of diminishing returns in these matters and I believe that the main drift of the argument will survive such improvement. The analysis of prehistoric astronomical alignments demands accurate data, and the Stonehenge archaeological record is not in the best of shape. I have drawn heavily on the field work of archaeologists who are likely to feel uneasy at the use to which their work is being put. They inhabit an earth-bound world that makes them uncomfortable with lines of geometrical straightness, and it is not surprising that they have often omitted to record precisely the information needed here. The real cause for surprise is that they

have so often recorded what was needed, and my debt to their recording is almost total. Many will be horrified at my defence of Alexander Thom's Megalithic Yard (0.829 m), and even more so by its occasional use in plans. By this I do not mean to prejudge the question of whether it was in use, but merely to simplify the task of judging whether it might have been so. Of one historical truth one may be quite certain, when adding a scale to one's plan: the metre was not in use in the Neolithic period.

The interpretations offered here do not lend themselves to exactness, and it is all too easy to quote results to a nonsensical degree of accuracy that might suggest otherwise. There are writers who publish declinations and directions that by implication are accurate to a thousandth of a degree, but who have not even taken astronomical altitude into account, although it would have displaced their findings by angles of the order of a degree, twice the diameter of the Sun. There have been archaeologists who have considered that they have done their duty by the points of the compass if they have marked them on their plans to within five or six degrees. Those who repeat the threadbare story of Mrs Maud Cunnington, who is said to have made some of her measurements with an umbrella, should compare her azimuths with their own. A good umbrella is far better fitted to the accurate measurement of length than is a pocket compass to the accurate measurement of direction.

The many different sorts of monument to be considered were first and foremost religious centres, or at least focal points of religion, built by people in whose spiritual lives the stars, Sun, and Moon played an important role, perhaps even a central role. There are limits to what an insight into past observational practice can reveal about prehistoric religion, its symbolism and ritual, but one should not be unduly apologetic about its genuinely scientific nature. The activities reconstructed here were rule-directed, scientific in a very real sense, and their implications for human history, intellectual and practical, are anything but trivial. Here, for instance, we can dimly perceive the beginnings of mathematical astronomy, the oldest of the exact sciences, not to mention the roots of a geometry of proportion—which was destined to have an important place in ancient Greek philosophy and science. As a window into the beliefs of the past, this all surely deserves at least as much attention as a showcase of flint scrapers.

*   *   *

My debts are numerous. I was very fortunate to have Bill Swainson cast an editor's eagle eye over my script. To the late A. G. Drachmann I owe the idea of self-denial in the matter of footnotes. I have weakened only occasion-

ally—but then at some length—when adding asides that might have stood in the way of the main argument. Appendices and Bibliography are included at the end. (Those unaware of the distinction between dates BC and bc, for example, might consult Appendix 1. A few readers might want the basic astronomy in Appendix 2.) I should never have turned in the direction of Stonehenge in the first place without the encouragement of Francis Maddison thirty years ago, and his broad view of archaeology has certainly coloured my own. Richard North passed a critical eye over my Scandinavian asides. Above all I owe a debt to an entire profession that is not really mine, and especially to Tjalling Waterbolk for his expert comment, on the continental material in particular. The book's dedication, however, can only be to my wife Marion for her unstinting support. And to her patience, not even Chaucer's Clerk could have done justice.

J. D. N.
July 1996

A few typographical corrections to the first printing have been made here, together with some minor adjustments to the star maps of Figs. 4 and 210. That the corrections called for were not more numerous I owe largely to the care of my editor Toby Mundy. My indebtedness to him has accumulated steadily since he first took the book in hand.

J. D. N.
November 1996

ACKNOWLEDGEMENTS

Permission to reproduce line drawings has been kindly given by the following, who retain copyright:

For Fig. 7 (p. 30), The Society of Antiquaries of London; for Figs. 10 and 11 (pp. 39–40), Executors of the estate of R. J. C. Atkinson, and Antiquity Publications Ltd; for Fig. 25 (p. 74) and Fig. 49 (p. 122), English Heritage; for Fig. 113 (p. 293) and Fig. 114 (p. 299), the Department of Archaeology (Biologisch Archaeologisch Instituut), University of Groningen. Full references to sources will be found in the Bibliography.

CHRONOLOGY

Years BC	General	Britain	Stonehenge
6500	Farming in Balkans	*... Mesolithic ...*	
	Britain separated from Continent		
6000	Mediterranean farming villages		
	Central European farming has reached the Low Countries with Bandkeramik pottery		
5000	Gold and copper artefacts in the Balkans		
	First megalithic tombs in Western Europe		
4500	Copper ore mined and smelted in Eastern Europe		
	Copper objects traded as status possessions	*Early Neolithic...*	
	Round-bottomed pottery in Britain		
	Carnac (Brittany)	Fussell's Lodge Wayland's Smithy I	
4000	Flint more systematically mined and worked	Sweet Track (Somerset) Lambourn, Horslip Dorset Cursus begun Skendleby, Radley, Uffington	
	First stone circles	West Kennet, Wayland's Smithy II, Wilmington	
3500	Simple plough (ard) in Northern Europe	*Middle Neolithic...* Hazleton N, Windmill Hill	
	Newgrange (Ireland)	Hambledon Hill, Nutbane	Lesser & Greater Cursus
		Beckhampton Road, Coombe Bissett	

Years BC	General	Britain	Stonehenge
	Writing in Mesopotamia	South Street Skara Brae	Ditch, post holes
3000	First Egyptian hieroglyphics		Aubrey Holes
	Corded Ware pottery in Northern Europe	Arminghall	Q- and R-rings
		Later Neolithic... Sanctuary begun	
	Beaker wares in Britain, first copper artefacts		Trilithons
	First Egyptian pyramid (stepped pyramid of Zoser)	Avebury stone circles	Sarsen ring
2500	Great Pyramid of Khufu (Giza); Royal graves at Ur	Mount Pleasant	
	and city states in Northern Mesopotamia	Durrington Walls	
	First Old World Empire (Southern Mesopotamia, Sargon)	Woodhenge, Kennet Avenue begun	Bluestone circle
		Early Bronze Age...	Bluestone horseshoe
2000	States founded in Minoan Crete	Climate deteriorates	
	Approx. end of Beaker manufacture		
			Z-holes
1700		*Middle Bronze Age...*	Y-holes
	Linear A script		

1

INTRODUCTION

... the Discovery whereof I doe here attempt (for want of written Record)
to work-out and restore after a kind of Algebraical method, by comparing
those that I have seen one with another; and reducing them to a kind of
Aequation: so (being but an ill Orator my selfe) to make the Stones give
Evidence for themselves.

John Aubrey, *Monumenta Britannica,*
ed. J. Fowles and R. Legg (1980), p. 32

The People

MOST of the achievements recorded in this book were those of people
who lived between three and six thousand years ago—a relatively short
period by comparison with the quarter of a million years that Britain has been
inhabited. During that long earlier period, following the arrival of the first
hunters in these northern latitudes, there had been gradual but massive
fluctuations in climate, and long glacial periods during which it would have
been necessary to retreat southwards. Much of what is known about the general
pattern of existence of early peoples derives from evidence as to their diet, for
example from middens, and hunters are in this regard by their very lifestyle
elusive. The few hunter-gatherers who were cave dwellers—and especially
those from temperate regions in the same period—tell us that there were other
dimensions to their lives than subsistence alone, for they have left us carved
and modelled figurines in stone and clay, including those notorious 'Venuses'
who look as though they were meant as wives for Michelin man. Even from a
time as early as the Leptolithic period (say 35,000 to 10,000 BC) there have
been found in France not only many specialized tools and weapons, but
spectacular cave art. Among surviving artefacts are bones scratched in ways
suggesting that some sort of *counting* was taking place, and on the basis of the
grouping of incisions into sets of around thirty, claims have been made that
some of the counting was of the days of the Moon.

It is from the Leptolithic period that the first clear indication of ritualized burial in Britain has been found, that of the 'Red Lady' (or was it a young man?) found in a cave at Paviland on the Gower Peninsula in Wales. The body had been covered in red ochre—presumably to give it a semblance of life in death—and had been dressed in ornaments of ivory and shell. Radiocarbon dating puts this at well over twenty thousand years ago, when there was still a land bridge to the continent of Europe.[1] Both shells and ochre have been found with similar Middle Palaeolithic burials in France and southeastern Europe, and indeed red ochre was to be used in the same way throughout Europe for many millennia thereafter.

The last of the long periods of glaciation lasted for about sixty thousand years, and drew to a close about eleven thousand years ago, even though there are signs of intelligent activity with stone implements from an earlier date. As the climate changed, and temperatures rose to levels more or less those of the present, northern Europe was drastically affected. Much is known of the environment of the time from the evidence of pollen and molluscs. The most striking changes were to the forests. First birch and pine made a recovery, and then hazel, elm, oak and lime moved into the older forests, with ash and alder following later. The population began to expand again after hunting and collecting methods were adapted to the new flora and fauna. Habits did not develop in the same way in all northern centres, but speaking generally, man tried to live near to large stretches of water at least in winter and early spring. Britain was linked to the continent by land until about 8000 BC. It is to this (Mesolithic) period that the first known human activity in the immediate neighbourhood of Stonehenge belongs. A series of pits was dug then a few hundred metres to the north of the stones, and they appear to have held massive upright posts of pine, for reasons that are entirely a matter for speculation.

As the forests developed, deer, elk, ox and boar moved northwards into them, and were hunted for food, but also for clothing, weapons, and implements that could be made from antler and horn. Long afterwards, ditches at places like Stonehenge were still being dug with antler picks. There are signs that the hunting way of life in Britain was giving way to farming by 4400 BC or thereabouts. It was long supposed that this change was a consequence of immigration by an alien people, but the matter is likely to have been more complicated. Hunter-gatherers had actually been opting for a relatively settled

---

1   The date found for the burial was 16,510±340 BC. For an introduction to the subject of radiocarbon dating see Appendix 1.

existence long before this new phase, a fact that would have made them more receptive to farming techniques than if they had been nomadic. It has even been claimed that they had previously indulged in a form of agriculture, namely the cultivation of the hazel for its nuts, but this is unproven. They had by this time certainly developed simple but efficient stone tools—unpolished axes and adzes, for example—and had proved themselves capable of sculpting animal figures and of decorating antler and bone tools, but the farming economy, which typically involved the cultivation of grain and the raising of such animals as sheep, cattle, swine, and goats, had much earlier beginnings, and those far away from Britain. Radiocarbon dating methods have pushed back the origins of settled agricultural communities in southwest Asia to well before 8000 BC, and similar communities may be as old in southeast Asia. Farming soon spread into the Mediterranean: it was practised in Thessaly, Crete and Cyprus even before the development of pottery there. It also made its way westwards along the Mediterranean coast, and again the domestication of sheep and goat evidently preceded pottery-making. By the sixth millennium BC, farming villages where pottery was made were present over the entire Aegean area, from whence farming made its way into the Balkan peninsula and the Hungarian plain, mostly following river valleys. The most important phase in the spread of farming to northern latitudes, however, took place early in the fifth millennium, when it moved northwards from the Hungarian plain, westwards along the Mediterranean coast, and in all directions along the Atlantic and Baltic coasts, where the population had become relatively stable. Finally it was carried inland to other parts of Europe by small groups, in particular lake-dwellers.

The main movement northwards is associated with a characteristic type of pottery, decorated with linear patterns, and usually known by its German name, *Bandkeramik*. The explosion of the Bandkeramik culture from the general area of the Hungarian plain is also characterized by its remarkable settlements, each with ten or twenty long wooden buildings, dwellings five or six metres wide and roughly eight times as long, with a roof supported by three rows of posts. A typical house was divided into three sections: the living quarters were in the middle, there was a granary at one end, and at the other there was a section of uncertain purpose that might have been a house temple for cult purposes. There is no clear evidence for animal stalls. In each village, one of the buildings was usually notably larger than the rest. As this culture spread westwards and northwards it finally made contact at length with settled communities along the Mediterranean and Atlantic coasts of western Europe, including Britain and Ireland. These coastal communities already had a certain

cultural homogeneity, and the new farming habits did not exclude the old but supplemented them. Baltic peoples, for example, now learned how to grow grain and raise cattle, but they did so on a limited scale and continued to fish, to collect shellfish, and to hunt along the coast and inland as they had done before. Their contacts with the distant Danubian tradition are nevertheless evident from their pottery, from copper imports, and the style of their long houses.

By what route farming eventually reached southern Britain is not entirely clear. On one view it arrived through a migration of peoples from perhaps two or three directions, in particular from western France and from the northern and southern Netherlands. It has been suggested that some immigrant groups might have settled in Britain and coexisted for centuries alongside the older hunting population, the two merging only by slow degrees. Another hypothesis, at least as plausible as the first, is based on the fact that early dates for food production have been found from along the Irish Sea, in the neighbourhood of important centres of polished stone axe production that later sent their wares at least as far afield as Wessex. It is possible, therefore, that agriculture was brought to Britain by an Irish Sea population that had learned of it and acquired stock and skill through coastal contacts. Whatever the answer, by 4000 BC farming was established to some degree in places across the length and breadth of Britain and Ireland. Although the population was then still very small, it was growing steadily. There were of course important differences between forms of agriculture developed in different centres, differences that depended on history and environment, but there are such strong affinities between Britain and the continent of Europe from this time onwards that whether or not we are to believe in the migration of peoples in appreciable numbers it is impossible to doubt a continuing interchange of ideas.

The narrower focus of these pages is southern Britain, roughly south of a line from the Wash to the Bristol Channel, and the Neolithic 'Windmill Hill' culture and its successors down to the Bronze Age. (That culture takes its name from a hilltop site near Winterbourne Monkton and Avebury in Wiltshire, where it was first given archaeological recognition as a characteristic form.) (See Fig. 3.) The people concerned seem to have had a liking for chalk downlands, which were then covered in a dense forest, largely of oak and elm. The claiming of land from forest has been traced though the analysis of pollens that show, for instance, a decline in the numbers of elms and the corresponding advance of small light-seeking flora. It is possible that land clearance was at first only for animal fodder. The soil at least was light, and easy to cultivate with simple tools, such as those fashioned from antlers—it has even been

suggested that deer were at times actually farmed for their antlers. The chalk also had the merit of yielding seams of flintstone, much used for cutting-tools. The farming communities of the region certainly left their mark on the land.

They left other marks on the landscape, in the form of ditches, enclosures of various sorts, defensive earthworks, tombs of various sorts, stone circles, carvings on stone, and so forth—but stones, earthworks, flints, antler picks, pots, even bronze and golden ornaments, are only the husks of human existence. Had these people left behind them even a rudimentary literature, we should no doubt think of them in a very different way. The intelligence and intensity of feeling that is evident from so many of their tangible remains, together with what is known of other non-literate cultures, makes it virtually certain that they had a rich and imaginative oral tradition, even though there is clearly no hope of our ever recovering it.

One of the theses of this book is that various astronomically guided rituals were in use by the time of the very earliest farming communities in Britain. This does not mean that such rituals necessarily followed the same routes as agricultural practices, or that either remained constant over long periods of time. There was a slow evolution in both, with many local variations in tradition. Problems of diffusion of influence are among the most difficult to solve, and once again, a movement of ideas does not necessarily mean a significant movement of populations. While it would be unwise to hazard many general conclusions on astronomical grounds alone, the evidence from this quarter is that the exchange of ideas between adjacent peoples was much greater than is usually recognized.

Alignments and Orientations

The overall aim of this book is to discover certain patterns of intellectual and religious behaviour through a study of archaeological remains that seem to have been deliberately directed in some way towards phenomena in the heavens. Much use will be made of a handful of words and ideas that are certainly not a part of everyday discourse but that are, even so, essentially simple. One of these, the notion of an astronomical *alignment*, is easily explained by reference first to the stars and then to the Sun and Moon (see also Glossary).

Each day, from a given place, if I can see an identifiable star rising, it will always seem to rise over the same point on the distant horizon. (This will be on its eastern half. It will culminate due south of the pole for anyone living in the northern hemisphere. And in view of the context, this qualification need not be repeated.) If it can be seen setting, the star will similarly always

seem to set over a fixed point on the western horizon. If the star is sufficiently important to me, I might choose to remind myself of those points of rising and setting, perhaps by such irregularities as hill-tops or isolated trees; or I might choose to mark the *directions* in which they lie by setting up pairs of posts or other markers relatively near at hand. I should not have to revise the alignments of such markers materially during my lifetime, unless I wanted extreme accuracy of a sort that need not be considered here. (The word 'alignment' will usually be used here to refer to two or more terrestrial objects lined up on a celestial object, and not exclusively to sets of three or more terrestrial objects in line, which is an unnecessarily narrow archaeological usage.)

I might choose to direct my buildings—say the main axis of my church—in the same way. Reversing the order of discussion, however, is a hazardous undertaking: the fact that the orientation of someone else's church happens to produce an alignment with an astronomically interesting event does not necessarily imply that the orientation was deliberate. Deciding between deliberate and accidental alignments is one of the central problems of this book.

Just as with the stars, I may notice the Sun rising at a recognizable place on the horizon, but in this case, as the days go by, that place will seem to change. In midsummer, the Sun in the eastern half of the sky will rise over its most northerly point of the horizon. It will attain its most northerly point of setting

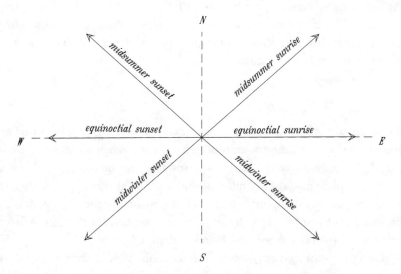

FIG. 1.   The directions of the rising and setting Sun at Stonehenge, around 2000 BC, at the times of summer and winter solstice. The directions for the equinoxes are also marked, but are barely distinguishable from the (broken) east–west line. In all cases it is supposed that the upper limb of the Sun (first or last glint of the Sun) is seen on the distant natural horizon.

on the horizon's western half at the same season. I could mark these directions as I did those of the rising and setting star; and as the year progressed and the days shortened, I should notice that those distant points of the Sun's rising and setting move southwards, and that in midwinter they reach to their furthest points south. Again I could mark those southern extremes in one way or another. The markers (both near at hand, or one near and one distant) would then be aligned on four critical phenomena, namely midsummer and midwinter risings and settings of the Sun.

Approximately halfway between the directions of sunrise at precise midsummer and midwinter (that is, at the solstices), is the true direction of east; and true west is similarly more or less mid-way between the extreme directions of setting. The actual sizes of the angles depend on various factors, and in particular on the geographical place (or more precisely the geographical latitude) and on the irregularities of the actual horizon. In Fig. 1 the angles are drawn for Stonehenge at a nominal date of 2000 BC. The angles are not precisely divided into equal parts by the east–west line, for reasons explained more fully in Appendix 2.

As early as Neanderthal man—say thirty or forty millennia ago—there were burials aligned accurately east–west, which suggests that some or other celestial body was in the thoughts of those responsible for organizing the rituals of death. A grave excavated at L'Anse Amour, in Labrador, incorporated what were evidently ritual fires arranged to the north and south of the body, which was laid in an east–west direction. The east–west and north–south lines seem to have been key directions in the placement of later burials in many parts of the globe, but—religion apart—how is this tendency to be interpreted? East and west are the directions of the rising and setting Sun at the equinoxes, but they are not easily established, and the positions of the fires might rather be thought to suggest that in the Labrador case the critical directions were north and south, the line having perhaps been decided by the Sun's midday position. A body with head to the north might have been regarded as lying towards the pole, the region where stars do not move. Granted more sophistication, east and west might have been regarded as midway between the Sun's extremes of rising and of setting. Alternatively, the four cardinal points of the compass might have been settled not by reference to the Sun but to the daily rotation of the stars: a star culminates (reaches its highest point) on the meridian, just as does the Sun, and the meridian also bisects the directions of a star's rising and setting. Culminations are not easy to settle precisely, since the altitude of the Sun or star is changing least rapidly then; but this does not mean that culmination was not uppermost in the thoughts of those who chose these

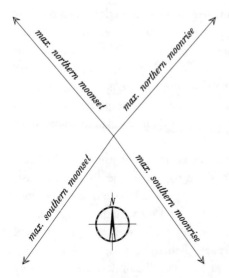

FIG. 2.   The absolute extreme directions of the rising and setting Moon at Stonehenge, around 2000 BC, assuming that the Moon is fully visible, and just touching the natural horizon.

directions for burials. Then again, at various periods of history certain bright stars have risen and set due east and west, so that alignment might have been on them. Skeleton directions that have so often been interpreted in solar terms can all too easily be reinterpreted in numerous ways, without our presupposing any particularly sophisticated techniques of observation. Which of these alternatives should one favour?

The evidence, based not on skeleton positions (which are often dubious) but on the forms of tombs and other structures, is that all of these ways of considering the cardinal points of the horizon, east and west, north and south, are likely to have been familiar in late Neolithic Europe. It is all too easy to become hypnotized by the idea of observation of the Sun and to forget the stars, but there is strong evidence from the period before the first phase of Stonehenge that observation of the stars was then important, perhaps even more important. In some early cultures from which written records survive—in Egypt, for instance—the direction of north was significant, and was found from observations of the stars circling the pole, or of a particular star near the pole at that time. (This was not the star that now serves us as the Pole Star, which in the remote past was well removed from its present position.)

The directions of the Moon's places of rising on the eastern horizon and setting on the western also change with time, but the pattern of change is much more complicated than in the case of the Sun. The details are put aside for the time being (they are treated more fully in Chapter V and in some detail in Appendix 2), but again there are four absolute extremes of direction, just as with the Sun. The angle separating the northern and southern extremes of the Moon's rising and setting is greater than in the case of the Sun. The angles in question, which depend as before on several factors, actually fluctuate in the course of time in a way that at first seems erratic. Alexander Thom and others have suggested, however, that the pattern of change lent itself to an analysis of

quite extraordinary penetration by the people of the Bronze Age, or even earlier. For the time being, Fig. 2 will suffice to give an idea of the *absolute extremes* of lunar direction at the latitude of Stonehenge.

The earliest written astronomical records—notably the Egyptian, Babylonian, and Greek—reveal a preoccupation with risings and settings and periods of visibility generally. They show a concern with what was to be observed at the horizon, and with intervals of time between special events in the heavens, and their recurrences. This is not to say that there was necessarily a concern with directions towards points of rising and setting, for there are other ways of using horizon observations. Consider, however, a passage from a Mesopotamian astronomical text compiled early in the first millennium BC and known as MUL·APIN:

> The Sun which rose towards the north with the head of the Lion turns and keeps moving down towards the south at a rate of 40 NINDA per day. The days become shorter, the nights longer. . . . The Sun which rose towards the south with the head of the Great One then turns and keeps coming up towards the north at a rate of 40 NINDA per day. The days become longer, the nights become shorter . . .

The MUL·APIN text is famous for its catalogue of stars and planets. Although distant in time and place from the Neolithic monuments of northern Europe, the quoted passage provides written testimony to observations of a sort that could well have been made there at a much earlier date. The shifting of the *Sun's* place of rising over the horizon was in Mesopotamia related to the rising of *stars*, or to *constellations*, distinguished in turn as staging posts along the monthly path of the Moon round the sky. The people concerned worshipped the Sun in various ways, and took the entrance to the land of the dead to be where the Sun descends over the horizon. Many of the writings from which such beliefs are known, in particular the Gilgamesh epic, are much earlier than MUL·APIN, and even antedate the main structures at Stonehenge.

There appear to be no preferred alignments among the numerous Babylonian and Assyrian tombs excavated. In contrast, the alignments of Egyptian pyramids were settled accurately and deliberately, typically towards the four cardinal points of the compass. The interred ruler faced east, while his dependents faced west to the entrance to the kingdom of the dead. Confronted by such utterly different practices among two peoples who simply happen to have left written testimony of their attitudes to celestial affairs, it is on the whole wise to start with a clean sheet, and to base northern practices on northern archaeological remains. Whether there is an element in common to all of these peoples, in the form of a shared psychology, driving them all to

found their religions on their common experience of the heavens, is highly questionable. There are certainly a surprising number of patterns of behaviour that many of them have in common, but they are beyond the scope of this book.

What if it should be possible to produce evidence that many prehistoric monuments were deliberately directed towards the rising and setting of Sun or Moon or star? Why devote so many pages to such a trite conclusion? There are some who will consider that the *ways* in which this was done were remarkable enough to be put on record, but others will naturally hope to draw conclusions as to motivation, whether religious or of some other kind. Does it not follow that the celestial bodies must have been objects of *worship?* Historians of religion who have come to this conclusion have rarely used orientations as evidence for it. On the other hand, many of those who have written about the alignment of monuments have taken for granted the idea that the motivation came primarily from the need to provide farmers with a *calendar* for the seasons. The religionists have interpreted isolated symbols found in the religious contexts of birth and death as self-evidently lunar or solar. They have claimed that worship of the Moon would have long preceded worship of the Sun, on the grounds that the tides and the menstrual cycle in women would have pointed to obvious links between the Moon, the weather, and fertility. The calendarists have argued from a supposed practical need, one that they find in evidence in early Greek texts relating the chief points of the agricultural year to events in the heavens. Both lines of discussion have rested far too heavily on intuition. There are a few tentative pointers to Neolithic and Bronze Age religious beliefs to be found from Stonehenge and its surroundings, but they belong to the end of the book, not the beginning.

FIG. 3(a) (Left) Britain and Ireland, showing (as small circles) the main henges as known at present. The rectangle covers the Stonehenge region as drawn in Fig. 3(b).

FIG. 3(B) (Below) Some of the principal prehistoric monuments of southern Britain, discussed in the following chapters. The rectangular grid (at intervals of 100 km) is that of the Ordnance Survey, and will provide a frame for more detailed maps of the Stonehenge and other regions in later chapters. Small squares mark modern towns.

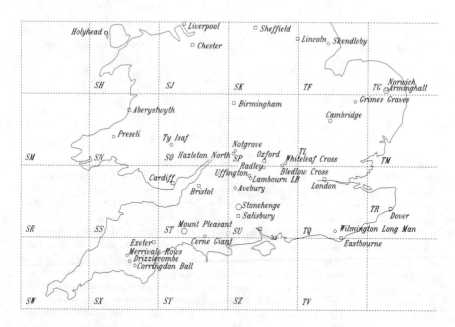

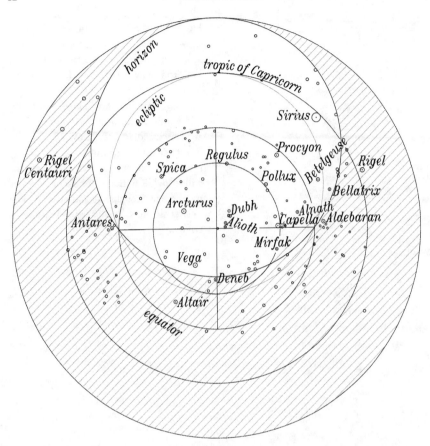

FIG. 4   A star map for the year 3000 BC, here meant only to introduce the names of the brightest stars then visible from Wessex and mentioned in later chapters. The constellation names will be found in a similar figure in Appendix 2. It should be appreciated that star positions change with time, and that no single map can do justice to them over a period of a century, let alone two or three millennia. Other relevant astronomical matters will be introduced as needed, and the following points are added only for those interested in the type of representation adopted in the figure, which might be used to make rough estimates of visibility. It may be thought of as a movable diagram, in which the stars are moving and the shaded area is fixed. The aperture in the latter, bounded by the horizon circle, represents the visible region of the sky. Circles on the star sphere (such as the equator and tropics of Cancer and Capricorn) all appear as circles on this map, since it is in a projection known as *stereographic*. Stars are shown graded in size according to their brightness (thus Sirius is much the brightest star in the sky). Stars shown covered by the shading may move into view as the heavens rotate clockwise about the central point, representing the north celestial pole. Whether the stars will then actually be visible will depend on whether the Sun is visible or not. Star maps follow various conventions. Stars can be shown as they are seen looking out from the centre of the star sphere or as they would be seen from the outside of the sphere, looking inwards. The second convention, which is that used on a star globe, is the one adopted here. Had the figure been on a larger scale, scales of degrees could have been added, for instance the equator and the horizon (azimuths). The former graduations would have been uniform, but the latter not. (They would have crowded together more in the lower part of the figure.) The two points in which the tropic of Cancer (the smallest of the concentric circles) crosses the horizon represent the most northerly rising and setting points of the Sun. The most southerly points of its rising and setting are where the horizon meets the tropic of Capricorn (also concentric). The tips of the central cross are in the directions of the four points of the compass, north (below), east (left), west (right) and south (above).

2

THE LONG BARROWS

Neolithic Chamber Tombs—an Introduction

IN all of those ancient cultures from which written records survive, worship of the dead seems to have been bound up not only with religion, but with law and custom generally. The dead are typically considered as guardians, upholding order within family and tribe. Farming in particular encourages an appeal to the power of deceased ancestors, for there is no more conspicuous object of inheritance in need of defence than land. Farming communities not only depend on the landscape but help to redesign it. In northern Europe, for example, they created large enclosures, roughly circular in form, by throwing up banks of earth and stone taken from the surrounding area. In the course of doing this they usually created well-defined ditches which are likely to have had a purpose going beyond the mere supply of material for the bank. Some of the enclosures might have had a simple farming purpose, and others must have functioned as gathering points of some sort, since they show evidence of communal feasting. Evidence will be presented later that like so many of the smaller ditched enclosures that surrounded tombs and acted as focal points for religious ritual, the large enclosures also had a ritual function.

Tomb and landscape together preserve what is known about Neolithic and Bronze Age ceremonials of death. Building materials were usually determined by what was locally available, earthen tombs predominating where stone was in short supply, but existing simultaneously with dolmens elsewhere. ('Dolmen' is a Breton, Welsh and old Cornish word for 'stone table', and was originally used with an eye to the slabs of stone that had become visible when the covering material, usually earth, had disappeared. The word is widely used now for any stone monument, covered or not, containing a chamber created from upright stones capped with a roofing slab.) Some had an entrance passage, but almost all were originally covered with a cairn of stones or a mound of earth, or a combination of the two. If the dolmen was once a tomb, then it is usually called a *chamber tomb*, even where the chamber was only of timber.

Where the soil acidity is low, skeletons will survive, and since undisturbed dolmens in such regions seem invariably to contain skeletons, equating dolmens generally with chamber tombs is not likely to be seriously misleading. Not all *mounds* were used as tombs, even when resembling others that clearly did, and even tombs served other purposes than burial alone. Several tombs have been found surrounded by thousands of shards of pots that had originally been placed on the tomb, a witness to some or other ritual of offerings continuing long after the primary interment. Similar collections of shards deposited over very long periods of time are found at many Neolithic sites throughout Europe.

There are two broad categories of chamber tomb: a *passage grave* is one in which it is easy to distinguish between the burial chamber and a passage leading into it, while a *gallery grave* is one where there is no clear distinction, but where the chamber-passage, usually slab-lined, is long—a substantial fraction of the length of the tomb as a whole.

Although there are large patches of territory without them, chamber tombs abound in a region of Europe and north Africa lying to the west of a line running roughly from south-central Sweden to Poland and across Europe to Tunis, taking in Sardinia and Corsica. There are also chamber tombs to the northeast of the Black Sea (the Caucasus), to its southwest (north of Istanbul), in Malta, the heel of Italy, and Palestine. Early in the twentieth century, surveys were made across Europe of modern human skull-formations, and it is a curious fact that the remains of chamber tombs generally are concentrated in much the same regions as those where the modern populations with longest skulls were then found to be living (dolichocephalic, those with highest cephalic index). The skulls those tombs yield up are similarly dolichocephalic.

Chamber tombs are found in a multitude of forms and sizes, and some date from at least as early as the fifth millennium BC. Tombs built with dry-stone walling—that is, using relatively small stones—seem to have given the lead to the builders of megalithic tombs, tombs with very large component stones. In the Iberian Peninsula and Brittany, and in Britain, the two techniques went on being used side by side, even under a single covering.

Many of the earliest of the chamber tombs had a long, tapered, trapezoidal form, almost always with the burial section lying across the broad end, which was also the higher end. (Various Wessex examples will be illustrated later in the present chapter. The word *trapezoidal* here indicates a four-sided figure with two sides parallel and two not so.) In Poland the taper may come almost to a point, while in Denmark and Britain the plan is often a long and narrow rectangle. The traditional English name used loosely for such tombs, without

regard to their internal structure, is *long barrow*. It is possible that some rectangular tombs were of constant height rather than wedge-shaped, but until firm evidence is offered for this idea it is best ignored. In Britain—for example at Wayland's Smithy, on the Ridgeway near the well-known White Horse at Uffington—as well as in northeastern Europe, there are long asymmetrical barrows that were quite obviously made deliberately so. That the lie of the barrows' sides was not random, or a product of incompetence, will soon be evident from aspects of their *internal* structure.

While regional fashions do assert themselves, several properties of the tombs clearly rule out the idea that they were developed in the various centres entirely independently. The problem of the spread of tomb design across Europe is a difficult one. The homeland of farming and cattle-breeding seems to have been in Asia Minor, from whence it worked its way into the Mediterranean and Europe. The spread of European languages, however, followed different routes. The historical Indo-European languages are thought to have radiated from the Balkan–Carpathian region, around the fifth and fourth millennia BC. The spread of the Neolithic peoples responsible for the long tombs, one that took place over millennia rather than centuries, seems to have radiated from Anatolia or the Balkans. As an archaeological measure of cultural movement, pottery styles link the later English long barrows with the tombs of the Funnel Beaker Culture of Northern Europe, but long barrows had been built by earlier Neolithic groups, who had also come from the continent. There are those who believe that the (Belgian) Michelsberg culture is a part of the Funnel Beaker Culture, and that it was a group of Michelsberg people that crossed to Britain and influenced the earlier Neolithic Windmill Hill culture there, with its characteristically simple 'baggy' pottery.

Many centuries after the immigration that had brought funnel-shaped beakers, a new immigrant people introduced beakers of bell shape—the 'Bell Beaker people'. They favoured round rather than long barrows. The Bell Beaker expansion was an important agent of cultural change in western Europe during the earlier Bronze Age, say from 2500 to 1800 BC. It is impossible to do justice to it in a brief space, but its movements were evidently largely sea-borne, with influences passing from the Low Countries down the Rhine, and to Britain and Brittany, thence to the Atlantic rim of France and Spain, as well as into the western Mediterranean.

The Funnel Beaker Culture—also known as 'TRB' from its German name, *Trichterbecherkultur*—covered at one period or another most of the area from the Low Countries in the west to central and southern Poland in the east, and from southern Scandinavia down to Bohemia and Moravia in the south. No doubt

the great rivers of Europe, not forgetting the Elbe, helped with the dispersion of its influences. Most sea navigation would have been chiefly coastal, with crossings to Britain kept as short as possible, and presumably made in skin-covered boats capable of carrying at most two or three tonnes.

There are other traces of contact between the distant peoples of the Danube area and those of the north and west. The styles of fortification and enclosure they had in common are hard to overlook, if only because they are on such a massive scale. Use was made of rings of concentric ditches broken at intervals by what have been described as 'causeways'—a potentially misleading name, in view of the fact that while some 'causeways' were several metres wide, others were only a few centimetres across. Causewayed enclosures are typically found on promontories, with the ground falling away—in Denmark often to water or bog—on two or three sides. Links between some of these structures and the long barrows will be proposed in Chapter 3.

Quite apart from similarities of form, and cultural traces of those responsible for them, it will soon emerge that there are very specific astronomical parallels between the long barrows of Northern Europe and Britain. While this reinforces the idea of a continental source for custom and ritual in Britain, it seems quite possible that a number of island practices developed independently, and then passed back to the continent. Megalithic tomb styles as such do not seem to be traceable to the cradle of the TRB culture, but their relatively rapid spread becomes a little less mysterious if we are prepared to suppose that there were established and continuing cultural links over great distances between different groups. If only by hearsay, these groups could have known much about each other—much more than we know about them, for instance. In short, the essential movements need not have been of whole peoples, but of *ideas*, carried in all probability by a few individuals. It has often been said that the outward forms of northern and western graves agreed far more closely than the grave goods in them, and the rituals to which they point. The astronomical principles they embody, simple as they might appear to us, must have represented a great mystery to many of the prehistoric community, so yet again the movement of a few experts might be of greater significance in the cultural transmission than the movement of whole peoples.

The densely populated long barrows of the earliest Neolithic Windmill Hill culture in Wessex have been intensively studied. There are less numerous groups in other regions, such as Sussex and Kent, the Hampshire Uplands, the Chilterns and East Anglia, the Lincolnshire Wolds, Yorkshire, Wales, Western Scotland, and Ireland. The British long barrows, like their Northern European counterparts, are usually a few tens of metres in length, although an unusual

bank barrow running across the ditched camp at Maiden Castle in Dorset, and later surrounded by an Iron Age fort, is as long as 540 m. More than half of all British earthen long barrows are between 30 and 60 m long, and outside the Sussex area few groups of small barrows are without at least one long example. The Stonehenge district is well populated with earthen long barrows, some of the properties of which are summarized in Fig. 5.

Long barrows in Northern Europe frequently occur in tight clusters, and conventional wisdom is that this was not so in Britain—although this is largely a question of definition. Colin Renfrew has claimed, on the basis of the distribution of around 120 long barrows in Wessex, that the region was divided into five territories, each with its group of long barrows and a so-called 'causewayed enclosure'. The prime example of such a site, but perhaps not the oldest, is at Windmill Hill itself.

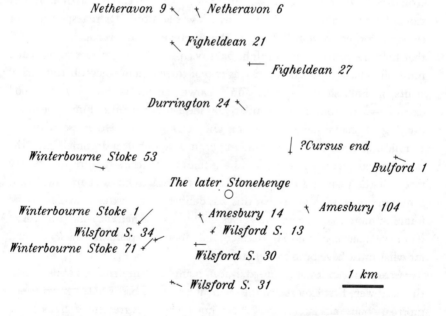

FIG. 5. Earth-covered long barrows, all well within an hour's walk of Stonehenge. The crosses mark the barrows, the directions of the lines represent the approximate directions of the barrows (with the cross always the lower end) and the lengths of the lines are proportional to the estimated lengths of the barrows (but they are not to the scale of the map). The average length is about 40 m. The circle marks the main surviving circle of stones at Stonehenge, to the same scale as the barrow-lines. The naming of barrows might seem odd, if it is not realized that they are conventionally numbered within parishes. There are more than fifty long barrows on Salisbury Plain as a whole.

The deep ditches that flanked the long barrows and provided the soil for the covering-mound were in some cases three metres or more deep, and occasionally ran in a U-shape round one end of the barrow. In some instances they formed a virtually complete perimeter. They were often shallower, say the height of a man, and they play an important part in our story, for it will be argued that significant observations of the sky could have been made by people standing at suitable points in these ditches.

In Britain, as well as on the continent, the grave mound often covered a wooden mortuary house. The forms of some of these will be discussed in the following sections. The evidence has often been taken to point to structures in the shape of a ridge-tent, with very heavy end-posts supporting the ridge-pole, on which inclined and close-packed rafters rested. This 'tent' interpretation has been offered for structures found in Denmark, Poland, and Germany, and in all of these centres examples have been found of *burning* in the timber structure. The first structure was in some cases first covered with a layer of stones (in Britain often flints), over which was laid turf. Those responsible for excavating them have remarked on the excellence of the verticals in the pits that held the posts—which might have been seven or eight metres high and must often have weighed as much as two or three tonnes apiece. Excavators of shafts on English sites—Normanton Down (Grinsell's no. 330) is a good example—have commented similarly on the evident use of a plumb line in the digging of shafts and the dressing and setting of stones. These marks of technical competence are of some importance to our later argument that the posts helped to create a network of sight lines within the structure, for the very fact that the plan of a mortuary house at the heart of a long barrow lacked symmetry must then mean that this was deliberate. That the same plan can be found in more than one barrow serves only to strengthen the conclusion. And if our explanation of it is to be rejected, then another explanation must be found for what must have been a deliberate act.

Customs seem to have varied, but in many cases in Britain it appears that the dead were first exposed to the elements, and the bones only moved to the mortuary house at a later stage. (This is not a customary reading of the evidence in northeastern Europe, although barrows there may contain several interments.) In some cases at least, the covering mound of the earthen barrow proper was added only after the house had stood for many months, or even years. The sheer weight of the soil or stone or chalk rubble covering the mortuary house could then cause its collapse, as was the case at Fussell's Lodge (Clarendon Park, barrow 4a), 12 km southeast of Stonehenge—where the house was an oak structure, about six metres long and a little over a metre wide. In this particular

case the house contained the remains of more than fifty men, women and children. It was certainly well established before the end of the fifth millennium BC.

Apart from human remains, several long barrows have been found to contain the skulls of oxen as well as their hooves. This has been thought to hint at the hanging of hides (with horns and hooves still attached) as cult objects. Evidence for such a cult from the Bronze Age has been found in the form of wooden horns at the corners of a rectangular wooden temple-like structure at Bargeroosterveld, in Drenthe (the Netherlands). These are important pieces of evidence as to religious practice, and might be connected with astronomically guided ritual, the cult of the bull linking with the celestial bull, Taurus. What seems to be an example of this, requiring a new interpretation of the Uffington 'White Horse', will be given in Chapter 4.

Of the many hundreds of long barrows recorded in Britain, a large proportion seem to have been used to house multiple burials—typically five or six, but occasionally twenty or thirty or more. It has been argued that such long barrows indicate an egalitarian society. This presupposes what is not at all certain, that long barrows represent the norm rather than the exceptional means of burial; that they are for the family unit, and not shared, as religious centres might have been shared among a much more extensive group; and that bodies were placed in them close to the time of death. Variations in grandeur, complexity, and grave goods, seem to indicate variations in wealth and political power. A little light is thrown on this question by two facts taken in conjunction. First, there is the sheer magnitude of the enterprise of building a long barrow: this required, say, between 5,000 and 15,000 man-hours. Second, as time progressed, the number of burials in each long barrow seems to have fallen drastically, often to one or two. The great investment of time and labour has therefore been often seen as a symptom of a steady growth of political or religious hierarchies, the barrows having been set aside for the burial of highly favoured personages. The social function of the tombs might of course have been much the same, whatever the number of burials, large or small.

It does not follow that the religious meaning remained constant. In places as far apart as Ile Carn in Brittany and Corrimony in the northeast of Scotland, individuals were selected for burial alone in a vast tomb. On what social or religious grounds this favoured treatment was meted out is a difficult ethnographical problem, but it is one that should not be addressed without reference to barrows that were used for no burial at all. Horslip, Beckhampton Road, and South Street, for example, all in Wiltshire, have left no evidence that they were ever used for burial. If barrows generally are to be understood as adjuncts

of a religion of the stars, capable of religious meaning even in the absence of burials, all arguments for the distribution of social power based on the number of burials will need to be reviewed. What if, for example, in the gradual reduction in the number of burials at certain places and times, we are seeing no more than a slow transition from a religion based mainly on ancestor-worship to one at a higher level of abstraction, based, for instance, on a more sophisticated and extensive mythology of the heavens? Selection for burial might in this case have been made on spiritual grounds, and might in principle have had no implications for a decline in the breadth of the power base. Spirituality might as well have resided in an epileptic, an innocent chosen by lot, a captive, a priest, or a prince. A barrow without burials could mean simply further progression along the same spiritual road. The whole question of a possible religion of the heavens is one that cannot be easily evaded.

Orientation of the Body

There are well over five hundred known long barrows in continental Northern Europe, of which more than a hundred have been investigated professionally. Relatively few have been adequately charted for our present purposes. Rough statistical analyses have occasionally been made that divide the compass into eight or sixteen sectors and take counts of general orientations of the tombs. Across Europe, orientations have seemed to show a definite tendency to cluster around certain preferred directions, and the same tendency has often been remarked in Britain. Such coincidences tell us virtually nothing of value, however, if the aim was everywhere to be astronomically precise, since the most probable astronomical orientations—whether involving Sun, Moon, or star—depend heavily on factors that are ignored in such simple accounts, notably geographical latitude, irregularities in the height of the local horizon, and even the form of the monument itself. Poor statistics make a poor guide. The only acceptable approach is through a comprehensive set of detailed analyses of individual cases—a programme far beyond the scope of this book. A few important examples will be touched on in the remaining parts of this chapter: they conform closely to a few simple principles, and it would be very surprising to find that others failed to do likewise. But first to a related theme, a favourite object of archaeological comment, namely the orientation of the body within the tomb.

There seem to have been many local variations in burial rites. In the Wessex long barrows the bones were generally placed in the tomb in a disarticulated state, sorted by type, presumably following exposure of the body elsewhere.

Where a skeleton in a chamber tomb is found in a recognizable direction, however, it is often with the head to the west or to the east—occasionally both are found in the same tomb. Opinions differ as to whether these variations indicate differences of age or sex. In a study of the positions of very many skeletons in tombs in Bohemia and Moravia, W. Schlosser and J. Cierny found some interesting patterns. It seems that the culture responsible for linear pottery (in the centuries around 5000 BC) had a very strong preference for placing the head roughly to the east; that among the 'corded ware' peoples (around 2200 BC), west and east were favoured in roughly similar numbers, with a slight preference for west; but that the Bell Beaker peoples favoured placing the head to the north or south (in the ratio now of about two to one), with a small subgroup roughly northeast or southwest, and a few roughly southeast. Three thousand years later, many Germanic groups were still putting the feet of the corpse to the north. In an English Saxon cemetery at Fairford, for example, this habit was found to be almost universal. J. Grimm, writing on German mythology in 1854, drew attention to something that appeared to point back from the Middle Ages to an ancient pagan tradition of worshipping towards the north. Thus in some stories of Reinard the Fox, the wolf did just that, while the fox adopted the Christian convention, facing east.

It has to be said that in the Bell Beaker class of burials the bodies were no longer laid out full length, but in a contracted posture, with the knees drawn up in the manner of an embryo, and that for this reason, a precise direction of the body simply cannot be specified. Nevertheless, some rough statistics from the Wessex round barrows belonging to the Bell Beaker culture fit well with the continental evidence. In a count of 55 instances made by William Long in 1876, on the basis of previous reports, in 35 cases (in other words, more than six out of every ten) the head was said to have been to the north. Six had heads placed to the northeast, and five to the east. All eight points of the compass with the exception of south were mentioned in one report or another, but the three named were the most common. (West and southeast accounted for three each, northwest for two and southwest for one.)

Rough and ready as these data are, it does seem that customs in the orientation of the body of the deceased are almost as characteristic as pottery types, although possibly not as subtle. They were obviously 'astronomical' in some degree, but how are they to be interpreted? Some of the problems to be expected have already been mentioned. Death has some plain analogues in the heavens. It seems natural to represent death by the western half of the horizon, the place of the dying Sun for peoples in the northern hemisphere, and this is borne out by many later religious rituals known from direct textual evidence

or report. (The eastern half of the horizon tends to represent life or birth.) In those Neolithic practices in which a near north—south line was preferred, the body might have been lain with head turned to *face* an appropriate easterly or westerly direction. Why east or west? Was it the *general* phenomenon of rising and setting of heavenly bodies that counted? (It was obviously not a precise arrangement, if the Sun was involved at any other season than the equinoxes.) It will shortly be noted in connection with tomb architecture that an approximate north—south line was associated with the behaviour of the star Deneb, in which case that more obvious explanation counts for nothing. Granting for the sake of argument that this was so, how should one interpret the intentions of those who laid out a body east—west? Might the relatives of the deceased have looked across the body, perhaps, towards Deneb? Or did they look over the length of the body towards Aldebaran, the brightest star in the constellation of Taurus, which happened to rise near east and set near west? There is evidence from some much later societies that the feet are placed towards the land of the dead, but this of course is often related to the daily passage of the Sun.

Is the argument helped out by the orientation of the tomb itself, as for example in certain passage graves that restrict a line of sight? At Gavr'inis in Brittany, for instance, and Newgrange in Ireland, where there are chamber tombs dated to within a century or two of 3500 BC, the main corridors were clearly directed towards midwinter sunrise, in the sense that they opened towards it and were illuminated by it. (There might also be lunar directions implicit in both.) And if we settle on a solar ceremony at the laying out of the body, there remains the question of the timing of events. Was the body preserved until the Sun was in the right position, say setting at one of the solstices? Or was the Sun's direction preserved, marked out as something appropriately sacred, say at the time of one of the solstices, and used for burial even if the Sun was not rising or setting in that direction at the time of the burial? Another possibility is that in some cases there was human sacrifice, a death that was contrived rather than natural, at precisely the appropriate season.

There is some evidence from modern anthropology as to comparable burial customs, but it is not coherent. All told, it is virtually impossible to place a reliable 'astronomical' interpretation on even comprehensive statistics as to the directions of burials, if they are merely to the four cardinal points of the compass. Even so, there is a conclusion to be drawn that is far from trivial. Whether or not the ritual interpretation can be discovered, there is no doubt that burial was in these cases *an activity governed by rules relating to celestial*

phenomena, for only by reference to the heavens can the cardinal points be found. To progress further it is necessary to look to the tombs in which the bodies were placed.

Inconstant Stars

Long barrows were built in Britain from perhaps the middle of the fifth millennium BC to the early third, and as time progressed, several changes of style and custom took place. To hint at a change in custom one must first be quite sure that there was a consciousness of the need to act in a particular way. That there were architectural rules of some sort is strongly suggested by the fact that in a large proportion of the examples surveyed, the higher and wider end of trapezoidal structures heads (roughly) *east*. This might not be thought a very profound principle, but it was true of the long mounds of the Linear Pottery culture in Northern Europe, and it is reminiscent of the characteristic habit of that same culture in Bohemia and Moravia, where the body was so often placed with the head to the east. This encourages a search for more precise rules.

Those who have recorded the directions of unexcavated long barrows have usually been content with rough approximations, referring, say, to only eight or sixteen points of the compass. The original structures have almost always been largely destroyed, modified by rabbits and badgers, or ploughed out of existence—usually by the farmer, but occasionally in the course of military exercises with tanks. (Unfortunately here, the better the barrow the greater the challenge.) The line of the major axis of a barrow is often as much as we can expect, and this seldom to better than a degree or two, unless we are convinced that it was deliberately aimed at some distant point. One should not be satisfied with the axis alone, for the principal lines of sight will be shown to have often differed from that line.

A direction without reference to the location is worthless. The midwinter Sun at Stonehenge rises about 40° south of east; at Newgrange, the angle is nearly 44°. Such directions vary with geographical latitude and the altitude of the horizon, but they also vary with the century. All such data are needed. The first two items of information can usually be taken from the Ordnance Survey. For structural details, an archaeological survey is needed. It is worth bearing in mind that whatever the quality of the original, a third-hand copy might be in error by as much as 20°. One much-copied plan—by one of archaeology's most expert draftsmen—displaces the West Kennet long barrow by 15°.

An approximate date for construction calls for independent archaeological

evidence. The orientation of a monument might provide a date, but only in conjunction with an opinion as to precisely what the prehistoric practices of orientation were. The vicissitudes of star positions are at the root of one method of astronomical dating. What are often called the 'fixed' stars are anything but fixed. They move among themselves by very small amounts (their so-called 'proper motions'), and these can often be ignored, although it is dangerous to do so when very long time-spans are concerned. Less subtle is another slow change in the apparent positions of all of them, making them seem to drift very slowly round what can be thought of as the celestial sphere (the sphere on which they seem to be carried round the sky with the daily motion). The movement of the stars round the sphere follows a path parallel to the Sun's yearly path, but it takes them roughly seventy years to cover a single degree. (The Sun's yearly path through the background of stars is called the 'ecliptic'.) The change may be slow, but in spans of time of the order of four or five thousand years, the shift in star and constellation positions, amounting to about a sixth of the way round the sky, is highly significant.

The drift in question is actually a consequence of the instability of the Earth, which in relation to the Sun provides the frame of reference against which star positions are measured. Just as the longitudes of places on the Earth are measured from the Greenwich meridian, so star longitudes are measured from a point on the celestial equator (a great circle on the celestial sphere directly above the Earth's equator). By convention, this is the point where the Sun, moving along the ecliptic, crosses the equator in spring, one of the two 'equinoctial points'. What was earlier described as a drift in star positions, amounting to a slow increase in their 'celestial longitudes', is really a drift of the zero point from which their positions are measured. The drift is for this reason now called the 'precession of the equinoxes'.

The increasing longitude of a star changes its apparent (angular) distance from the north pole of the sky, and in turn affects the point on the horizon over which it rises and sets. To take just one example: the Pleiades rose 10° south of east at Stonehenge in the early forty-second century BC, but twelve centuries later they rose due east.

This brings us back to a serious problem, hinted at previously. How are we to know whether an orientation indicates a concern with the Sun rather than with a star? East–west directions in long barrows, for example, are relatively uncommon but not unknown. Like alignments that seem to be to the rising and setting Sun at the solstices (midsummer and midwinter), they might well have been directed to a particular star. The change in the direction of sunrise and sunset at the solstices is very slow—say a fifth of a degree of the

horizon in a thousand years. Over the same period of time, the point of rising of the Pleiades would have moved by twelve degrees. Continuity of custom is less obvious with the stars than when the Sun was involved. Prehistoric peoples might have aligned all their barrows on the rising or setting of a particular star or group of stars and have done so with great deliberation and precision at different periods of history, and yet have left us with a scattered set of compass directions, in short, with an impression of carelessness and imprecision. Fortunately there is a way of cutting through this problem, for it will soon emerge that the custom was to align long barrows on two or more stars simultaneously, and to consider mostly very bright stars. This greatly reduces the number of ways of interpreting individual cases, and from a study of well excavated examples a coherent picture gradually emerges, as clear in its way as that of the later monuments with their more stable solar orientations.

In brief, it turns out that the Wessex long barrows were mostly stellar, while the later circular monuments were solar and lunar. The later long barrows already show signs of change. There are two different criteria here—alignment

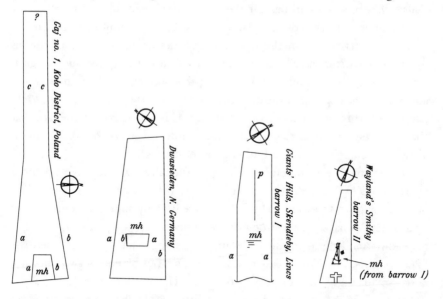

FIG. 6.   Four different examples of taper in long barrows, one from Poland, one from northern Germany, one from Lincolnshire, and one from Wessex. All have left interesting traces of mortuary houses (*mh*), the sides of all of which are approximately parallel to the sides of barrows erected later on the same site, or perpendicular to them. Note the letters (*a*, *b*) marking these highly significant properties. The scales and orientations of the different barrows are approximately correct, with Wayland's Smithy, the smallest, about 55 m long. The outlines of barrow/mortuary house were formed by either timber posts (*t*) or stones (*s*). From left to right, the materials were: *s/t, s/s, t/t, s/s*. A mortuary house at Wayland's Smithy, hinted at in the figure but redrawn in Fig. 19 was of timber.

and illumination. Matters were sometimes so arranged that at one of the Sun's extremes it could illuminate the end of a long gallery in the tomb, through a suitable entrance slot. Even this will prove to have followed a similar arrangement with stars, from an earlier period.

First Thoughts on the Taper of Long Barrows

While some of the longer and earlier examples of earthen long barrows were parallel-sided, or nearly so, and just possibly of constant height over their length, most were tapered in height and width. (An idea of the plans of some of the different styles may be had from Fig. 6. The rationale of their three-dimensional forms is the subject of this chapter, and the differences are too subtle to be readily illustrated at this stage, but Fig. 53 should give an idea of what taper in height and breadth entails.) It is doubtful whether the property of taper originally had any astronomical purpose, since it is found in many early post-built houses throughout Europe, but the precision with which those houses were built—for instance in the alignment of their side walls—is usually greatly inferior to that of most large tombs. Precision might have signified respect, a wish to give something perfect to the dead, but there are good reasons for thinking that it served also to direct the eye towards significant risings or settings over the horizon. Even supposing that the trapezoidal form was first adopted for the housing of the dead by analogy with the housing of the living, support for this other explanation is strong. It is buttressed by the fact that time and again, on an astronomical reading, different sites seem to indicate an allegiance to a relatively small number of select bright stars.

Accepting the astronomical idea provisionally, two or three potential explanations of the taper in plan offer themselves. (Taper in height will turn out to be another question.) The first of these is easily appreciated in terms of what seems to have been a strong desire to find lines that point to the rising of an important star in one direction and the setting of another in precisely the opposite direction. This is easier said than done, but by taking two lines at a fairly small angle, it can always be done. Using those two lines as the orientations of the sides of a barrow, the assumption that stars were viewed along the barrow's sides provides one possible explanation of taper.

It is not difficult to imagine others. As illustrated in Fig. 1 (Chapter 1), the direction of the rising midsummer Sun at an arbitrary place on the Earth's surface is usually near to, but not precisely the same as, the reversed direction of the setting midwinter Sun. Since the (angular) height of the horizon helps to determine the directions of rising or setting over it, if there were hills of

different heights in the two directions, the angle between the lines might be several degrees. This difference might have been built into a long barrow in various ways. The broad (interment) end of the barrow might have been made to point to midsummer sunrise, and another part, say a side or axis at the other end, to midwinter sunset. (There is an instance fitting this description in the Winterbourne Stoke group in Wiltshire.) On level parts of Salisbury Plain the difference between the ideal directions would have been only about 3°, so that there an edifice with only a 3° taper could have served both directions at once. It would be wrong to place much emphasis on a solar explanation at this stage, however. It is certainly not relevant to the early history of the taper of long barrows, the alignments of which will prove to have been primarily stellar.

At first sight it might seem that a single building alignment—say that of a central ridge along it—cannot cater for two opposed solar extremes—for both midsummer rising and midwinter setting, for example. This is where taper in height might have come into play. Something like the technique to be explained in broad outline here might have been applied at the Skendleby 2 (Lincolnshire) long barrow and more certainly at Stonehenge itself. The directions in which the first glint of the rising Sun and the last of the setting Sun are seen depend appreciably on the altitude of the horizon. By directing a tomb to horizons of different altitudes, or alternatively, by creating an artificially elevated horizon out of the tomb itself, the directions of rising and setting can be adjusted, and under certain circumstances brought into exact opposition. (The Skendleby case is illustrated in Fig. 40 in a later part of this chapter.)

This last possibility puts paid to a claim that has been made on many occasions, that the minor variations in the directions of chambered tombs and long barrows show that their builders were very casual about directions, and were happy enough if they could get them roughly right. Our hypothesis is capable of explaining why the chamber-tombs in an otherwise apparently coherent group are almost, but not at all precisely, parallel—say with a scatter of 4 or 5°. The differences in direction, which might in some cases have been the results of variations in the height of the distant land-horizon, might in others be the result of taper in height, that is, of differences in the slopes of monuments that were themselves used to set artificial horizons close at hand.

Apart from the rectangular and trapezoidal forms of long barrow, which are found often in an area stretching from Jutland (Denmark) to Western Pomerania, there is the near-triangular form already mentioned, not unlike the trapezoidal: it is a long isosceles triangle with very slightly concave sides, higher at the wide end. This is the form at the site of one of the best collections

of well-excavated long barrows in Europe, the Sarnowo group in Kujavia (Poland). There are nine in all, ranging in length from 30 m to 83 m, and judging by a radiocarbon measurement, their dates are probably all within a few centuries of 4500 BC. They are all on spurs of land, with the wide ends always in the northeast quarter, and facing down gently sloping ground.

The Sarnowo barrows are in a parlous state, and it is at present difficult to assess more than their general orientations. (Even this is a dangerous undertaking, since two modern surveys display compass directions which may differ by as much as 14° on a single monument.) Nevertheless, there seems to be much the same pattern in the directions of the barrows as is to be found in a selection of four or five of their English counterparts. Three are conceivably aligned on the following stars: Aldebaran or the Hyades (nos. 2, 4, and 5); the Pleiades (no. 6); two perhaps simultaneously on Bellatrix and Regulus (nos. 1 and 9); one simultaneously on Deneb and Rigel (no. 7); and one on Sirius (no. 3). Only one (no. 8) seems to be aligned on the Sun—and even there it is possible that Orion's belt is somehow indicated. All of these are possibilities within the approximate period 4500 to 4100 BC. The uncertainties are chiefly inherent in the disordered state of the remains, and archaeological plans that cannot provide exact orientations. Perhaps at some future date the Sarnowo stellar orientations will be studied more thoroughly. Perhaps other stars were observed across the mounds, as at the Wessex barrows. Whether or not the long barrows reflect back on earlier European practice, they are vital to an understanding of later stone and timber circles relating to Stonehenge. They are also intimately related to the Avenue that leads up to Stonehenge and to the strip known as the Cursus, to the north of both.

The Orientation of Long Barrows

There are more than sixty long barrows on Salisbury Plain, and many hundreds elsewhere in Britain and Ireland. They tend to be on high ground with open views of the surrounding country in two or three directions. In Britain, Ireland, and on the continent, there was a mild preference for a near east–west orientation, a fact already the subject of comment as long ago as William Stukeley's *Abury, a Temple of the Druids* (1743). While crude statistical surveys of the orientations of large numbers of chambered tombs will obliterate most of their essential differences, there are a few simple rules of this sort that are easily appreciated, if not easily interpreted. As a purely descriptive measure, the key direction may be regarded as that from the narrow end to the broad.

(One might have said 'looking out from the entrance' were it not that many barrows had blind entrances.)

Taking the chief regions of Britain and Ireland with remains of such tombs, there are definite tendencies that are more or less duplicated in places of similar geographical latitude. Cairns in Orkney are like those in Shetland, in that in both places most cairns tend to look southeast. Those who built the earlier passage graves of Brittany had also favoured this direction. Coming down to the northeast of the Scottish mainland, the tombs of Caithness resemble those of Ross and Cromarty, in that most look very roughly east. The nearby Clava cairns, on the other hand, look southwest, a quality they share with tombs of an outwardly different pattern in Ireland, the 'wedge tombs' that are especially numerous in the southwest of the country. (This last name derives from the fact that the burial chamber is trapezoidal in shape, although it is usually given a round cairn as cover, so hiding a certain similarity with the overall wedge shape of many English long barrows.) Surviving megalithic tombs in Ireland number about twelve hundred, and more than a quarter of these, mostly in the northern third of the country, have a small court at the entrance. Such 'court tombs', especially common in the Atlantic coastal regions of Mayo, Sligo and Donegal, often look northeast; and in this, if not in their shape, they resemble the long barrows of the Clyde region, across the water in Scotland. The passage graves of the Boyne valley on the eastern coast of Ireland tend to look east and southeast, as do the long barrows of the Cotswold–Severn area in England.

Such broad rules as these are subject to many exceptions, but they confirm the principle that custom changed appreciably with place and time. This is hardly surprising, bearing in mind that the time-span of the groups mentioned here covers more than two millennia. Contrary to a common belief, these tendencies tell us absolutely nothing about orientation towards the Sun. After studying several individual examples more closely it will become clear that interpreting rough proclivities of the sort outlined above is a dangerous business. Even without doing so, the dangers of summarizing motives of the architects of the long barrows too hastily can be seen from the fact that, in England as a whole, there are at least ninety long barrows along a roughly north–south line; and yet in no single region was the number great enough to have merited mention in the brief list of tendencies just given.

Fussell's Lodge

Many chambered tombs from the fifth millennium BC still survive in eastern France. Relatively few barrows in Ireland and Britain have been assigned such

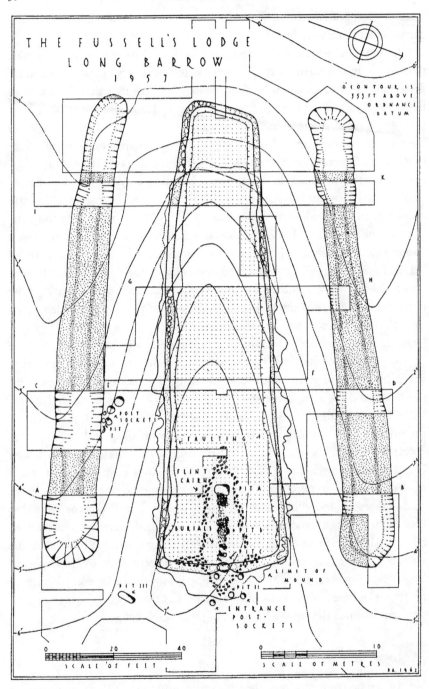

FIG. 7. A general plan of the Fussell's Lodge long barrow, drawn by P. J. Ashbee.

an early date, but among them there is the mortuary house from the Fussell's Lodge tomb—which radiocarbon dating puts in the calendar (corrected) range 4250–3950 BC. This barrow, roughly 12 km from Stonehenge and 5 km from Salisbury, has been well excavated (1957) and described by Paul Ashbee. When it was first erected, Salisbury Plain was heavily wooded and is unlikely to have had more than a few dozen families living on it. The tomb was an earthen long barrow, raised after a period of time over a mortuary house of still greater interest. This first structure, of wood, was at an early stage apparently covered with turf, and then with crushed chalk. Later a cairn of flints covered the burial area. This cairn stage might have followed the collapse of the timbers of the mortuary house, or might indeed have precipitated the collapse—in either case probably within a few decades of the foundation structure. The flint cairn had wings anticipating the later façade (see Fig. 7). The mortuary house was used as a place for the systematic deposition of the bones of the dead—skulls in one place and long bones in another. Many bones were missing altogether. The

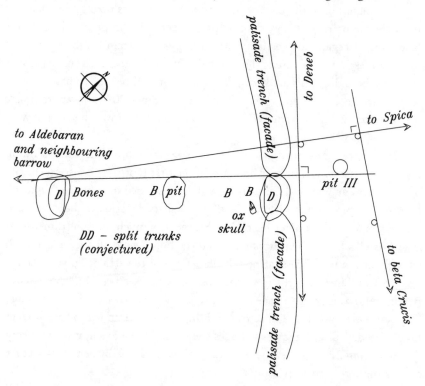

FIG. 8. The letters *B* show where the collections of bones were found. The central pit might originally have been used for a central support to a massive beam—or double beam—spanning the two main uprights. Note that the palisade trench interferes with the socket for one of these, showing that it is a later and independent structure.

bodies had presumably been exposed to the elements, or buried and disinterred after decomposition. Despite the small population, building the mortuary house—barrow apart—would have required a high degree of social organization. It was bounded at east and west by two colossal oak trunks or split trunks, each—depending on length—weighing in the region of 2 to 10 tonnes, assuming a green state. When the time came to erect an earthen long barrow on the site, its mound was enclosed within a retaining wall of nearly two hundred timber posts, a palisade bedded in a deep trench. The old mortuary house was at the eastern end of this enclosure, the whole lying roughly east–northeast. Into this frame were packed many hundreds of tonnes of chalk that had come from the ditches flanking its long sides, chalk that had been dug out with antler picks. Ashbee estimated that if men worked ten hours a day at the task of infilling, it would have taken no less than 487 man-days. Whatever the precise dimensions of the mound—and here a somewhat smaller mound than his will be preferred—it was certainly no light undertaking.

The planning of the barrow must have been no less taxing, for there can be little doubt that it was done with reference to the peculiarities of the landscape in regard to the risings and settings of certain bright stars. Even more interesting is the case of the original mortuary house. At a cursory glance the posts bounding this are badly skewed, but it will be seen to have pointed within two or three degrees of 22° north of east. Since 20° is the approximate mean direction of the splayed sides of the later barrow, this is not very surprising.

To progress any further, we must make reference to certain striking resemblances between its plan and that of the first mortuary house on the site of the barrow at Wayland's Smithy. As will be described shortly, the Wayland's barrow had split trunks with the flat of the D-shaped section to the inside, and the trunks were of diameter 1.2 m. The pits were of much the same dimensions as at Fussell's Lodge. The areas on which the bones were placed were at both sites about a metre across, although the length of the area at Fussell's Lodge was greater. Lines of sight from the posts of what has been interpreted as a porch would have skimmed the two sides of the western trunk at Fussell's Lodge had it also been about 1.2 m across, and the other is presumed to have been of much the same size. The stacked bones were found to lie in a neat line not very different from 22° to the east–west line. This can reasonably be taken as a first approximation to the direction of the axis.

Now it so happens that another long barrow, today virtually obliterated, was on the skyline at a distance of 1.85 km and in a direction just 21.7° south of west, as seen from the Fussell's Lodge barrow. The sighting of one barrow

from another will later prove to be so common that this line must be treated as important, and doubly so when we discover that it indicates the setting of the star Aldebaran over the neighbouring barrow at about the right period of prehistory. (As for the precise date, some of the deciding factors must first be explained.) Working from this assumption, we are no longer, therefore, entirely dependent on the edifice itself in establishing at least this property of its orientation. The observed altitude of the barrow (not the star) would have been about 1.32°, depending on the height and position of the observer. This raises an important point: the quoted altitude is based on the assumption that the observer is standing at ground level. A study of the relatively extensive and important collection of human remains from the Fussell's Lodge barrow, by D. R. Brothwell and M. L. Blake, led to the conclusion that the average adult male stood 170 cm (5 ft 7 in) and the average adult female 157.5 cm (5 ft 2 in).

At a given date, any star has a particular position on the celestial sphere, that is, can be assigned a given set of sky coordinates comparable to latitude and longitude on the Earth's surface. There are two particularly useful reference planes comparable to that of the Earth's equator: one is the celestial equator above it, and the other is the ecliptic (see Chapter 1 for a simple account, and Appendix 2 for more detail). Taking the equatorial system for the time being, *declination* is the coordinate corresponding to terrestrial latitude. If its value is known, then using methods outlined in Appendix 2 one can say exactly where on the horizon the star would have been seen rising and setting at any date in the past from any given place—and conversely, what was the date at which it rose or set in such and such a position. A star of declination in the neighbour-hood of −12.67° can be said categorically to have been seen setting over the now defunct barrow, but only if the star was visible down to the horizon. Aldebaran had this declination in 4365 BC, but for reasons to be explained, the star would not have been seen as low as the true (natural) horizon.

Whenever a distant natural horizon enters into the calculation it is necessary to take possible tree cover into account, since a star descending into even distant trees leaves one unable to decide precisely when it disappears. In the present example the horizon was topped by a barrow, however, so that tree cover can there be ignored. (Trees seen against the sky do not necessarily modify the effective horizon altitude when the Sun and Moon are being observed. If the trees are not in leaf, as at winter solstice and spring equinox, and the horizon is defined by a fairly sharp ridge, the Sun and Moon are often easily visible through the trees down to ground level.)

In the reverse direction of the axis at Fussell's Lodge, 21.7° north of east, the ground above and below the tomb slopes at about 3° to the horizontal, this being effectively also the altitude of the eastern horizon. The ground is near at hand, and was no doubt cleared of trees. It is no accident that the slope of the final earthen barrow, according to a plausible reconstruction, was also of about 3°. One may see relatively faint stars at such an altitude. Over the barrow to the west, however, where the horizon altitude is lower, few stars are bright enough to be visible at the horizon proper. This difference needs to be explained.

How low in the sky one may detect a star depends on weather conditions, of course, but even under the most favourable conditions there is a limit to what is possible that depends on the star's brightness. Astronomers classify the luminosity of stars by their so-called *magnitude*. The brighter the star, the smaller the magnitude. Sirius, the brightest star in the sky, has now a magnitude of −1.46. Only one other star then visible from Britain, Arcturus, has (and had) a markedly negative visual magnitude. Our concern here will be with only the brightest stars, of which about 45 have magnitudes less than 2, although not all of those are visible from northern latitudes.

Typical minimum altitudes for viewing the very brightest stars under favourable viewing conditions from the downs of southern England, are these: Aldebaran 2.00°, alpha Crucis 2.42°, Altair 2.01°, Antares 2.32°, Arcturus 1.43°, beta Centauri 1.86°, beta Crucis 2.35°, Betelgeuse 2.06°, Capella 1.48°, Deneb 2.35°, Pollux 2.24°, Procyon 1.71°, Regulus 2.44°, Rigel 1.53°, Rigel Centauri 1.58°, Sirius 0.74°, Spica 2.12°, Vega 1.48°. The cluster of stars known as the Pleiades is a difficult case, but it was probably rarely seen below 4°, with 4.4° more typical.

These 'extinction angles' are for specific viewing conditions, and the accuracy with which they are quoted here is rather excessive, although useful for purposes of comparison. Actual values are as uncertain as the weather itself. Climatic conditions were not identical to those of modern times, and even local air currents may affect the issue. Fortunately it will soon be discovered that in very many cases precise values are unimportant—that is, when the height of the actual (natural or artificial) horizon is appreciably greater than the extinction angle.

To return to Fussell's Lodge. Since Aldebaran might have been seen only down to about 2°, it is necessary to review the earlier statement of what was seen over the neighbouring barrow. The declination, recalculated for this slightly higher altitude, turns out to be −12.07° and the corresponding date 4245 BC. The shift of more than a century from such a seemingly insignificant

change of altitude draws attention to the importance of working with precise data.

If we are to believe that the star Aldebaran was observed setting along the axis of the mortuary house, how would it have been sighted? It is wise to consider the possibility that a distinction has to be drawn between an initial act of design and later acts of ritual observation. At the foundation of the mortuary house, however, the alignment would have been the same on both occasions: just as the designer had done, so others would have been able to look in the direction defined by the two massive vertical posts, each presumed to have been a split trunk (by analogy with Wayland's Smithy, where the post holes are also ovals). The fact that the large posts define a line to Aldebaran's setting raises an interesting possibility. The skull of a domestic ox was found by the eastern post, and it seems likely that this star—which in historical times was regarded as the eye of the bull—had already acquired an association with the bull, although not necessarily quite the same one.

The alignment on the setting Aldebaran will be acceptable only if the date is confirmed by independent evidence. To decide on what might have been seen in the eastern direction, at the altitude set by the natural horizon (very close to 3.0°), one must again decide on a precise azimuth. There is of course no barrow in this case, and simply reversing the line to the first barrow yields nothing of real interest, but from the very similar structure at Wayland's Smithy there is reason to think that the line grazing two of the posts of what has usually been regarded as an 'entrance porch' will be significant.

For reasons to be explained shortly in connection with that other monument, the posts will be referred to as 'scaling posts'. Taking the four relevant post holes at Fussell's Lodge (see Fig. 8), and making estimates of post diameters on the basis of later evidence and of the lines of bones, the azimuth appears to be about 61.8° from north (with an error unlikely to be much more than half a degree). The star Spica rose at an altitude of 3° in this direction when its declination was 19.51°, a declination it had in approximately 4250 BC. The agreement in date is remarkable, but one should not make too much of it, in view of the various uncertainties.

The scaling posts fairly certainly served a similar function, defining lines to the rising and setting of other stars, both over natural ground and over certain artificial horizons. For the time being only the first sort of alignment will be considered. Unfortunately, even here there are two possible arrangements. It will be found repeatedly hereafter that viewing was apparently at right-angles to certain lines in the barrows and their associated ditches. Briefly, the question is whether, in looking across such a line, the line is defined by a

part of the barrow's structure on the near or the far side of the barrow from the point of view of the standing observer—or in this case, on the near or far side of the quadrangle of scaling posts. This often makes a difference of a few centuries to a derived date, although occasionally it rules out a solution completely. For some barrows, making the right choice will prove to be of fundamental importance, but for the moment all plausible results will be quoted.

As shown on Fig. 8, there are two more alignments to be found yielding dates in rough agreement with the others. With estimated dates in parentheses they are: to the rising of beta Crucis (4220 BC) and to the rising of beta Centauri (4220 BC). (The posts nearer to the monuments are very close to aligning on the setting of Deneb to the north and the rising of Rigel to the south, but if this was the intention, the line does not seem to have been as accurately engineered as the others.) It is here assumed that the observer was standing on level ground.

A few brief remarks are in order here, in view of the coherence of these results. The posts were only two metres apart, and various assumptions have been made as to their sizes and positions in their sockets. The line to the rising of Rigel (grazing the sides of the two posts in a way to be discussed in connection with Wayland's Smithy) was over a nearby natural horizon of about 4.6°, assuming no tree cover. Whether or not there was forest cover, the Deneb alignment is poor, but there is much evidence from elsewhere of the enormous importance of this star. It is assumed that nearby trees were removed in Deneb's direction. (The hill over which Deneb set was destined to become the site of a sizeable Iron Age monument, Figsbury Ring.) Dropping Deneb from the process of averaging dates from the six stars, an astronomical date can be quoted for the mortuary house of 4235 BC (rounding to fives). The probable error here is anything up to a century either way. With Aldebaran (4250 BC) more confidence is in order, since the neighbouring barrow is a far more accurate marker than nearby posts; and yet the Aldebaran date might just possibly relate to activity on the same site before the mortuary house was built. The radiocarbon range for charcoal from one of the D-post pits, perhaps relating only to a clearing operation, was 3230–3150 bc, which when corrected produces a range of calendar years from 4250 to 3950 BC. The agreement is not perfect, but respectable.

There are one or two conclusions to be drawn from these findings. The first concerns the purpose of the various structures. When the mortuary house was covered with a cairn, that might have obliterated some of its earlier sighting-line properties, although trunks would have had a longer lifetime than smaller timber. Some of its astronomical properties, however, as yet to be described,

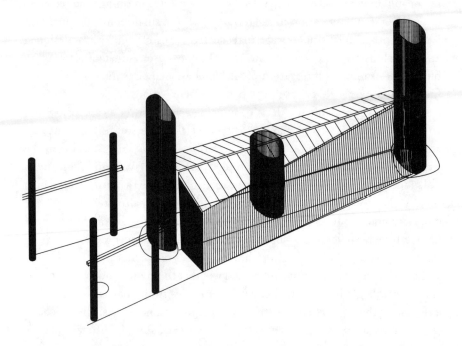

FIG. 9.   The Fussell's Lodge long barrow, viewed from the north. An outline of its probable appearance at the time of its foundation. The shading is added to suggest the lie of the walls and roof.

almost certainly remained to it. These probably—but not necessarily—involved observation across the cairn from short ditches, small versions at the eastern ends of the later (much enlarged and deepened) ditches that flanked the great barrow.

The mortuary house was no doubt a self-sufficient edifice with a wider spiritual function than this name for it might suggest. The argument that it was a religious focus is supported by what can be said of the *visibility* of the various stars. There are stars that are so close to the north pole of the sky as never to rise or set. Whether or not they are visible depends only on cloud cover and whether the Sun is up or not. The visibility of stars like Aldebaran, Spica and beta Crucis that do rise and set is obviously limited twice over, restricted as it is by the horizon and the need for the Sun to be below the horizon. It emerges that there was no season at which *all* the phenomena of rising and setting mentioned in conjunction with the Fussell's Lodge mortuary house could have been seen. The conclusion is that it was erected, and its site carefully chosen, on the basis of knowledge about risings and settings acquired over a

reasonably long period of time, indeed with long-term meaning, and recorded in wood or stone in relation to the terrain. This is a small point, but it makes it unlikely that any astronomical ritual enacted at Fussell's Lodge was designed around celestial events appropriate to only one season—that of a founding burial, for example. Observation of the stars at such sites must have been a fundamental rather than a purely ephemeral affair.[1]

It is not yet possible to offer a convincing argument for a conclusion that will be reached at a later stage, to the effect that the scaling posts had an architectural function in establishing directions that would be needed in the later building. For this the more complete evidence of Wayland's Smithy is called for. It is conceivable that those posts also supported a platform on which the dead were exposed, before the larger bones were finally brought into the mortuary house; but on the whole this seems unlikely, for the platform would neither have been very substantial nor well fitted to the purpose.

One can only guess at many of the finer details of the mortuary house, such as the height of the massive uprights, and whether they bore another split trunk of comparable girth as a lintel between them. This might have made for a less leaky house than otherwise, but the sheer weight and rarity of such a splendid trunk makes the idea improbable, as does the fact of slightly different depths at the two ends—suggesting posts of somewhat different heights. Fig. 9 is offered here as a mere outline of the arrangement at the time of foundation, and in it no attempt is made to indicate supporting timbers, apart from a short intermediate trunk that could have been interposed to take most of the weight of the roof. (It is placed in Ashbee's 'pit B', which is 60 cm deep and 50 cm across. The fill was found to contain burnt bones, and the area was covered with bones, but not from the earliest date.) Access to the interior was probably from the eastern side of the southern D-post. The form suggested for the roof will be justified in a later section.

---

1   Beta Crucis and beta Centauri—which will be often encountered again—made no great impression on classical mythology, since by classical times they had moved far into the southern sky as a consequence of the precession of the equinoxes (see Chapter 1). Spica has for us a mythological character inappropriate to this early period of prehistory. In the constellation of the Virgin, in classical antiquity it was then the ear of wheat in the Virgin's hand. The constellation in question was at a very early age linked with harvest, but the time of harvest varies between very wide limits, according to latitude and climate, so that the association can only be properly discussed in relation to particular cultures. The tenth brightest star in the Wessex sky, at the end of the fifth millennium it would first have been seen rising in deep winter, say a month after the solstice, so that here the harvest association is best forgotten.

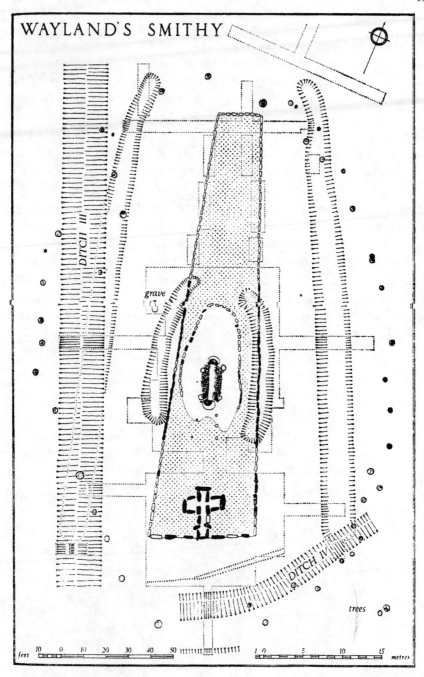

FIG. 10. A general plan of the long barrow at Wayland's Smithy (after R. J. C. Atkinson). This shows both phases of the tomb, and later field ditches superimposed on them.

Wayland's Smithy

The chambered long barrow at Wayland's Smithy was extensively restored in the 1960s. It is trapezoidal, and despite its asymmetry shows great regularity in its geometrical design (see Fig. 10). An earlier mortuary house found during its excavation closely resembled in overall style the mortuary house at Fussell's Lodge, and the two, taken together, provide valuable information as to astronomical practice. They offer a challenge, too, because although they are so similar in form, their orientations are radically different.

It is hard to think of a more famous long barrow than that at Wayland's Smithy. Here lived an invisible smith, who would shoe travellers' horses at a groat apiece: the owner would leave horse and coin at the spot, and return to find the horse shod. Francis Wise printed the traditional story in 1738, and it has been retold often since then, perhaps the best known versions being those in Walter Scott's *Kenilworth* and *Tom Brown's Schooldays* by Thomas Hughes, who was born nearby. The name of Wayland, always a craftsman of some sort, is not uncommon in Germanic mythology. The oldest literary reference to him is in the Anglo-Saxon poem *Deor*, but there is a reference to Wayland's Smithy in a charter of king Eadred, dated 955, while the Franks Casket in the British

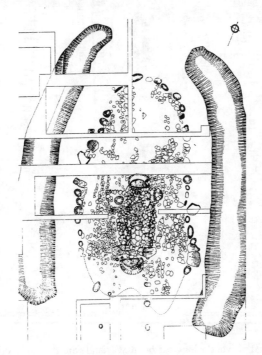

FIG. 11.   The central area of Wayland's Smithy, phase I.

Museum, from the early eighth century, depicts the same character. In later Berkshire stories, Wayland the Smith was not always so well-disposed, as the imp Flibbertigibbett discovered. When hit on the head by a large sarsen[2] stone, thrown at him by the smith, the imp went away snivelling—as a proof of which the sarsen stone is still to be seen at Snivelling Corner, 2.5 km to the northwest. (It has to be added that Wayland's abilities were as nothing compared with those of a British Parliament that in 1974 managed to throw the entire monument from Berkshire into Oxfordshire—an unfortunate act, bearing in mind the archaeological habit of listing monuments by parish and county.) Stones of this kind are typical of the downs to the northwest of Marlborough, and the barrow that has somehow become associated with the name of Wayland can be regarded as the easternmost of the group of stone-chambered long barrows on the Marlborough Downs, although it is relatively isolated from monuments of the same period. In style, it fits most comfortably into the Cotswold–Severn class of chambered tombs, but again only as an outlying example.

At Fussell's Lodge, in looking along the line of the barrow in either direction, one looks upwards to the distant horizons. At Wayland's Smithy, which is almost on the highest ridge of the downs, the surrounding terrain lies below, except to the east. Along the prehistoric track known as the Ridgeway, which passes close by, lies Uffington Castle, 2 km to the east. This is a natural plateau with the remains of an Iron Age hillfort. Adjacent to it is the Uffington White Horse, a figure large enough to be visible from many miles distance, when not hidden by the downs that enfold it. Formed out of chalk exposed where the turf has been cut away, it is of indeterminate age. It was once supposed to be Saxon work, and is now said to be of the late Iron Age, but in a later chapter it will be suggested that the White Horse has Neolithic origins. Whatever the answer, the neighbourhood of Uffington has long been a very special place.

The barrow at Wayland's Smithy was newly excavated in 1962–3 by Richard Atkinson and Stuart Piggott, who confirmed earlier suspicions that it had been constructed in at least two phases. The first structure (at the centre of Fig. 10) had contained a wooden mortuary house lying between two extremely sturdy end-posts made out of split tree trunks, each 1.2 m across the

---

2 'Sarsen' is a word used of the largest stones at Stonehenge. Whether or not it derives from 'Saracen', or from the name of Sarsden, a place once renowned for its stone, it has been applied at least since the seventeenth century to boulders of sandstone deposited over the chalk downs, especially in Wiltshire. The uprights of the circle and avenue at Avebury are sarsens.

dividing diameter. The turf had been stripped from the ground before a pavement of sarsens was laid on the chalk. The skeletal remains of at least fourteen persons were found on the pavement. A bank of timbers, which Atkinson took to have rested against a mortised ridge pole, and sarsen stones to both sides of their bases, had formed the walls. The central tomb was at some stage covered by an oval mound outlined by sarsen slabs up to a metre tall, but these were not set into the ground. That particular mound was a cairn of small sarsen boulders at its base, topped with chalk rubble taken from ditches to the east and west. The oval structure, which even with its ditches fits into an area of only 15 by 20 m, was later covered completely by the final tomb, and is no longer visible.

One curious fact about the skeletal remains in the older tomb is that many of the smaller bones were missing, particularly hands, feet, kneecaps, and lower jaws. The absence of jaws is intriguing, in view of the fact that in some cultures with a literature testifying to their beliefs—the Egyptian, for example—the jaw-bone was preserved separately, and was supposed to have the spirit of the dead person attached to it. It is often missing from Irish barrows, and near the south entrance to the circle at Avebury a fragment of skull was found in the topmost layer of rubble, together with no fewer than five mandibles. A similar collection was found at the Sanctuary, not far from Avebury, and such examples could be multiplied. Perhaps the mandible was associated with the voice of the dead.

Just as at Fussell's Lodge, there are posts at Wayland's Smithy arranged in a quadrangle at one end of the first mortuary house—here the southern end. One pair of posts is nearly parallel to the eastern kerb of the later structure, which was about 22.3° west of north. The ditches are not straight, but the average angles of reasonably straight sections are about 19.5 and 20.5° west of north. Putting a median line through the central tomb by eye, it lies at about 21° west of north, but judging by what was found at Fussell's Lodge, the lines grazing the D-posts are probably what mattered. The directions of their flat faces are about 22° north of east. The fact that these are almost at right angles to the line of posts mentioned earlier, and to the later east wall, makes us suspect that—even for the first structure—we should be paying special attention to angles in the neighbourhood of 22°. A very straight Iron Age ditch (ditch 400 on the plan of the whole, see Fig. 10) was in a direction 22.4° west of north. Even more significant: the virtually straight section of the Ridgeway between the tomb and Uffington Castle lies at an average of 21.5° north of east, that is, nearly at right angles to the directions under discussion. (For a map of the area see Fig. 80 in Chapter 4.)

In his report of the excavation of 1962–3, Atkinson pointed out that after the massive tree-trunks had rotted and collapsed, many small boulders from the surface of the mound fell into the void created. This suggested to him—in view of their large diameters—that the timbers may have projected far above the top of the mound, and that 'perhaps carved or painted, they may have formed a landmark visible for miles around'. Were they, perhaps, together with some celestial object, observed from a point on the Ridgeway, say from the dip in the path, 800 m east of the tomb, or even from the shoulder of Whitehorse Hill? It is extremely probable that such sightings took place.

The visitor to Wayland's Smithy today sees only the later barrow on the site, a trapezoidal mound nearly 55 m long and tapering from about 14 m wide at its southern end to under 6 m at its northern. The ditches that originally flanked it, as much as 4.5 m wide in places, and of graded depths (of roughly human proportions), are today completely filled and invisible. The southern façade originally had six large sarsen stones, the highest rising to a height of about 3 m on either side of the entrance to the burial chamber. (The arrangement roughly resembled that of timber façades known from earlier barrows.) Two stones are now missing. The eastern long side will here be taken as having been at 22.3° west of north, with the façade precisely at right angles to it and the western long side at 13.7° west of north.

Earlier excavators of Wayland's Smithy reported a much disturbed interior, with the disordered bones of perhaps eight skeletons, including that of a child. The chamber was in the form of a cross, the main corridor being 1.8 m high at the crossing, and 1.35 m in the transepts. Before the second barrow was built, the ground had been cleared by fire, and a specimen of charcoal from a tree branch or small trunk yielded a radiocarbon reading corresponding to a calendar date in the probable range 3800–3440 BC. The degree of silting was thought to point to an interval of perhaps not more than fifty years between the two barrows; but this was to assume that the ditches were not regularly cleaned, and much of the evidence of this book will be that this was very probably—indeed religiously—done. Bearing in mind the strong similarity of the first mortuary house at Fussell's Lodge and its Wayland's Smithy equivalent, these dates imply that the overall architectural style might have been preserved for four centuries or more.

After the Iron Age ditch was dug, perhaps even before, it seems that the area between it and the barrow came under the plough. During the Romano-British period the ditch was re-cut, and a fourth ditch was cut to the southeast of the barrow. What is particularly interesting is the fact that the angle of that third ditch is almost identical to those incorporated into the older structure.

Why this persistent orientation, not to say precision, and why was the line of the Ridgeway displaced by exactly a right angle from it?

The near-northern line is towards the setting of Deneb in the fourth millennium. No precise discussion of dates should ever begin with this star, however, since it has the property that its horizon positions change very slowly with the centuries. This fact, while it is annoying for anyone who wants to use a Deneb direction to establish a date, would have been an excellent reason for early peoples' fidelity towards it. To give an idea of just how constant was this star: its declination (angular distance) from the celestial equator in 4200 BC was almost exactly 37°, and this gradually reduced to 36.22° around 2800 BC before increasing again. (It reached 37° around 1400 BC, and had not quite reached 39° by 200 BC.) Its risings and settings, which depend on that declination, changed correspondingly little over this enormous period of time, and if any religious ritual required its observation at an early date, it would not be at all surprising to find that a similar ritual continued to be used, especially at a site like Wayland's Smithy, which lay close to centres of intense human activity for so long. It is no doubt for reasons relating to the behaviour of Deneb that the directions of the eastern edge of the second long barrow and the central line of the Iron Age ditch 400 differ by only about a tenth of a degree, while they might be two millennia apart in age. To reinforce the point: Deneb had almost exactly the same declination in 1600 BC as in 4000 BC, so that the direction of the star's setting was the same at both times. This does not mean that it had not changed in the intervening period; but even then it had changed little.[3]

---

3   As already explained, the star Deneb, which turns up repeatedly in the analysis of Neolithic monuments, had a commendable constancy in its places of rising and setting, which no doubt helped to keep it in favour. Deneb was the fourteenth brightest star in the Wessex sky, and so was notable for its own sake, but it would also have drawn attention to itself for its way of coming down to earth in the north, and rising again, often the same night, from a point not far away from the first—all this depending, of course, on geographical position and horizon altitude. Deneb, like Altair, has been associated with a bird from early historical times in near-eastern and European cultures. It is the brightest star in the constellation of the Swan (Cygnus), and the Arabic name 'Deneb' means 'tail of the hen'. Its constellation, Cygnus, is in the Milky Way. No brighter star rose and set nearer to the northern point of the horizon at these Wessex latitudes. There was surely a rich northern mythology centring on it, in view of this property. The northern star Arcturus was brighter—indeed the second brightest in the Wessex sky, where the brighter southern star Canopus was never seen—but it was circumpolar, and was permanently above a level horizon as seen from Britain.

Although any connection can at best be very remote, there was a Sabaean custom that lasted

There are other conspicuous lines, such as that of the façade, the flats of the split trunks, and the Ridgeway itself, that are at right angles to the Deneb line. From the dip in the Ridgeway, and looking along it and up over the barrow, at 21.55° south of west, Aldebaran could have been seen setting around 4200 BC, when its declination was −11.83°. Alternatively, the setting Betelgeuse could have been seen along the same line four centuries later (3780 BC), and for the moment there is no way of deciding between these alternatives. There is a 'disused pit' marked on the Ordnance Survey actually on the Ridgeway, close to the optimum point for viewing either of the two stars, and it would be interesting to know whether the pit is of prehistoric origin, or whether its position is merely fortuitous. (The monument was constructed in a place cleared of woodland and sarsens, and the finds of pottery and stone implements on the site have raised suspicions that there might have been a trading centre here.) From the shoulder of Whitehorse hill, the setting of Aldebaran would have been seen around 4300 BC. The rising of Altair in the reverse direction over the shoulder of Whitehorse hill (with or without tree cover, since the extinction angle is paramount) occurred at about the same period of history, and this might be an indication of the date of the track itself. Betelgeuse, at the later date, had no very bright star as its 'opposite'.

Turning to the posts at the southern end, which so closely resemble those at Fussell's Lodge, it emerges that—within the limitations of accuracy set by relatively close posts—looking southwards along the direction set by the western edges of the D-posts (16.8° east of south), alpha Crucis would have been seen rising, the optimum date being around 3940 BC, or 3890 BC if we take the other edges (making a direction 16.0° east of south). Two of the scaling posts align perfectly at 23.1° with the eastern edge of the northern D-post and the direction of Deneb's setting, around 4040 BC, but there are the usual large uncertainties in a Deneb date.

As for Aldebaran and Altair, which seem to be indicated by the Ridgeway, the southernmost pair of scaling posts is suited to the marking of Aldebaran's

---

to modern times—judging by a report in the London *Standard* of 19 October 1894—whereby their priest, during a September ritual, entered a temporary open rectangular tabernacle at the south, and paid homage to a certain star to the north. This 'pole star' was considered to be the paradise of the elect and the abode of the pious hereafter. A sheep and a dove were sacrificed to it, a cake smeared with the blood of the sacrifice was eaten, and a dove was released. The association of a bird with a northern star—perhaps misidentified by the writer—might well hint at the involvement of Deneb in this ritual at that time or some earlier period of history.

setting in one direction around 4144 BC,[4] and the rising of Altair in the other, around 4190 BC.[5] An azimuth of 21.0° north of east and south of west is assumed here, taking the posts to have been centrally seated in their holes.

This spread of dates is not very satisfactory. The posts are of course too close together to allow very accurate dating, but it is a fact that if we assume the post in the southeastern hole displaced to make the azimuth 19.5°, the two alignments bring the named stars more or less into agreement in time, with Aldebaran at 3984, Altair at 3970, and alpha Crucis (as before) at 3940 BC. While this may seem to be a very devious move on our part, there are arguments in its favour. First, it makes for consistency with yet other dates, that are to be derived in a different way from the first barrow, but only after an analysis of its successor. And second, as an examination of the excavator's drawing reveals, the hole in question is oval, unlike the others, and the required shift leaves the post well within the oval. In short, the first barrow can be provisionally placed at, say, within a century of 3965 BC.

In reporting on the excavation, Atkinson noted that the posts south of the main chamber must have predated it, since the northeastern post hole was covered by the sarsen slab leaning inwards at that point. This offers support

---

4   The manner in which certain stars appear to enter and leave barrows, if observed in the ways suggested here, might have helped to foster, if not to form, religious views relating star and soul. The phenomenon of setting, when the star itself dies, has often been associated with death and with killing. Aldebaran was bright—the ninth brightest in the sky—and was to become mythologically important. Whether or not the connection with the Pleiades is an illusion, the same cluster of six or seven stars will be met again. They are not at all as conspicuous as Aldebaran, but no star cluster is better known. The Pleiades are almost invariably figured somewhere or other in the historical constellation of Taurus. Not only do they often share in much of the bull symbolism of Aldebaran but they too play an important part in the mythology of many early literate cultures.

5   In seeking stars capable of carrying the spirit of the deceased upwards to the heavens, Altair is an obvious historical candidate. The brightest star in the constellation of the Eagle (Aquila), it has been linked with birds of one sort or another since early times in Middle Eastern and Mediterranean cultures. On a Mesopotamian stone of about 1200 BC, the constellation is called Eagle, or Living Eye. Altair has been given an important place in star lore. It was used to divide up the sky into quarters, and it is coupled with the Pleiades in the chorus lines of a work ascribed to Euripides: 'The Pleiades show themselves in the east / The Eagle soars in the summit of heaven.' Having said as much, there is a great danger in taking calendar traditions of this sort at their face value, as was seen in connection with Spica. A mythology based on suggestive constellation shapes, such as the shapes of the bull's head and Orion, seems more likely to have survived from very early times than one based on first and last visibilities, which depend on the Sun and the placing of stars with respect to the equator and equinox.

for our view that what we are calling 'scaling posts' were destined to be discarded after they had been used to ensure a correctly aligned mortuary house, and were not for use after its completion. Fussell's Lodge offers comparable evidence.

There is more to be said about potential sightings over the first mortuary house, but the way to discovering them is through an examination of the later barrow. The neat trapezoidal form of this will provide evidence that risings and settings were observed by people standing in the ditches flanking it, and will lead on to a realization that the first structure had very probably already been used in the same way. Parts of the ditches will prove to have been for continuing ritual use, and other parts to have been of use only at the design stage, like the scaling posts.

Wayland's Smithy II

It will be seen from Fig. 13 that the ridge line of the old mortuary house at Wayland's Smithy was in one direction more or less the line of the eastern wall of the new grave chamber, while in the other direction it passed through one vertex of the trapezoid. Apart from a very slight shift in orientation, there was an evident awareness at the new barrow of the traditions by which the old was planned. The precise form of the new barrow, however, is something about which we are not yet in a good position to speculate. On the face of things, the line linking the two structures could not have been the line of a ridge running all of its length, since that would have made the surface slope too steeply at its northwest corner. Reasons will be given for thinking that the ridge was displaced very slightly from the perfect line to the northwest vertex.

Judging by the higher end, the angle of view from the ditches could hardly have been less than eight degrees to the horizontal and is unlikely to have exceeded 15°. Taking this as starting point, consider then which important stars could have been seen from the two ditches, on the assumptions (1) that viewing was at right angles to the long edges of the barrow, whether the near or the far side, and (2) that viewing from opposed positions in the two ditches set the same altitude for viewing.

What seems to have been a constant concern for creating features at right angles to the ditches at many long barrows—for instance here and at Fussell's Lodge, but in quite a different way there—offers superficial support for (1), while (2) is underwritten by the near-symmetry of the flanking ditches of most long barrows, especially of their inner edges. Accepting these principles provisionally, potential lines of sight of a typical pair of observers are shown in

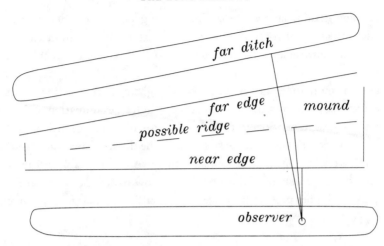

FIG. 12.　　It is wise to keep an open mind over the question of whether viewing was at right angles to the far edge (or far ditch) of the barrow, or to the near edge (or ditch). There seems to be no evidence that a right angle was taken with an intermediate ridge.

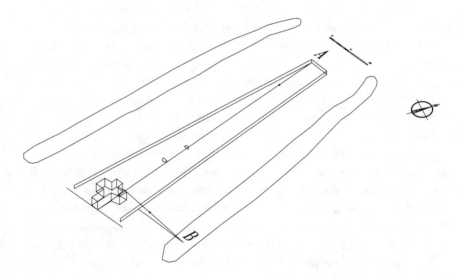

FIG. 13.　　The long barrow, Wayland's Smithy II. Observations were made by people standing in the ditches, for example at B, using the barrow as an artificial horizon. The barrow set horizons of identical altitudes to observers in opposite ditches, but the directions (azimuths) were not the reverse of one another. Another potential observer stands on level ground at A and looks up the ridge of the barrow. The dimensions given to the chamber are only approximate, and are for the *outer* surfaces of the stones.

Fig. 12. The assumption in the case illustrated is that the perpendiculars are to the *near* sides of the barrow. The lines are chosen to pass over the northeast corner of the new sarsen chamber, which it will be recalled lies on the line through the old *D*-posts. This point would have been at the same distance from both observers. Assuming that the section across the barrow was reasonably symmetrical at its high end, we have all that we need.

Since the joint principles (1) and (2) will be invoked on many other occasions, a defence of their great naturalness may be offered here. It is easy to believe that a perfect arrangement was regarded as one in which *the rising of one star exactly opposes the setting of another.* There would have been times when this was found over open ground, but if the horizon was to be set by a barrow, then the simplest and most appealing arrangement would surely have been a *parallel-sided barrow* in ridge-tent form, with the observers *square on to it and at the same distances.* Granted that the observers are at the same level and equally distant from the ridge, the two stars would have had equal altitudes. (There is no suggestion that the person observing them was necessarily conscious of viewing at right angles to any particular feature, or that the altitude of view was a significant angle—although evidence will be gradually accumulated that the latter might have been the case.) The stars would almost invariably have failed to cooperate in this ideal scheme, however. While not all of these conditions could in general have been met, the barrow could nevertheless always have been built with (a) the direction of one star perpendicular to the ridge, the same ridge being used for the other star, observed obliquely now (that is, not at right angles to the ridge) from exactly the same distance. Alternatively, the two observers could still have looked along lines perpendicular to the ridge, and yet view at different altitudes, either by (b) standing at different distances from the ridge, or (c) varying the levels of the ground on which they stand. Judging by the structural features of barrows, options (b) and (c) seem to have been generally disliked. There are exceptions to this rule, but even a cursory survey of styles of ditching round long barrows shows that if viewing was indeed from them, then there was a preference for symmetry of viewing position—in distance and in level. Even when a barrow runs along a contour on steep ground, so that one side is appreciably higher than another (it will later be seen that this was so at Giant's Hills, Skendleby, Lincolnshire), this ambition was evidently aimed at and achieved in ingenious fashion, by stepping the ditch edge.

It appears that oblique viewing was usually preferred to (b) and (c); but that having sacrificed directly opposed viewing, their architects managed to preserve viewing at right angles to a new ridge, or at least across a new edge.

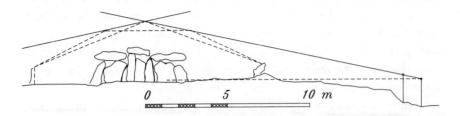

FIG. 14.   Lines of sight (altitude 11.7°) from the eastern ditch over the crossing in the burial chamber at Wayland's Smithy. The vertical lines in the ditch (terminating in points corresponding to the observer's eye) represent two possible viewing positions that share the same line of sight. The broken lines are suggested limits to the cross-section of the mound at this place. The stones fronting the mound (not shown here) would all have fitted under the sight-lines, and in the case of three out of the four surviving stones, the fit would have been rather precise. Only one (at extreme left) would have failed to fit under the three-part broken line.

Our double principle ((1) and (2) together) is in fact an extremely natural way of preserving monumental symmetry; and if, on a plan, ditch symmetry seems to be absent, then that is likely to be because one or both of the ditches is parallel to an edge that is not obvious. The directions of ditches offer important clues as to the directions (azimuths) of viewing, but here there is a difficult decision to be made—one to which allusion was made in an earlier section. Is viewing to be at right angles to the local ditch or to that on the other side of the mound?

The most natural solution at first sight is one that puts the right angle near at hand. At the Beckhampton Road long barrow—which will be placed in the thirty-fourth century BC—it was seemingly there the *far* edge that counted. The scaling posts at Fussell's Lodge and Wayland's Smithy are ambiguous, but the placing of the ditches in relation to the latter will turn out to fit better with the idea of viewing at right angles to near edges. All told, we are left with little choice in the matter: every example must be worked out for both possibilities, and the solution preferred that is more consistent, internally and with radiocarbon dates.

All possible angles of view are considered until a pair of declinations is found that were simultaneously held by two bright stars at some likely period of prehistory. This is done on both assumptions concerning the right angle, whether it is with the near or far side. There are two qualifying objects that seem most likely to have been observed across the barrow at Wayland's Smithy, namely the Pleiades (setting) and Spica (rising). (The position of the Pleiades

will always be taken as that of the brightest star in the cluster, Alcyone, then of magnitude 2.86.)

First for a near-side perpendicular: for viewing at an altitude of 11.7°, a pair of simultaneously valid declinations is derived. The Pleiades (at azimuth 247.7°) would have had declination −4.14°, and Spica (azimuth 76.3°) declination 17.47°. These values are appropriate to dates in the neighbourhood of 3670 BC. The altitude of 11.7° is close to a gradient of 1 in 5. Whether the true ridge was visible from the ditch depends on the precise shape of the barrow. If viewing was from mid-ditch, the distance to the ridge (17.4 m) would imply a maximum height for the barrow of about 3.6 m, again depending on the form of the cross-section. This is the height above the observer's eye, but judging from the only relevant ditch section available to us, the eye must have been very near to ground level (see Fig. 14). The height of the top of the stone covering of the chamber is approximately 2 m, which is well below the required maximum.

If this solution is to be accepted, with more than a metre's depth of soil above the stone capping, then at least it fits with the greatest problem in viewing the Pleiades—their high extinction angle (about 4.4°). The mound, on this hypothesis, would have set an appreciably higher angle of view.

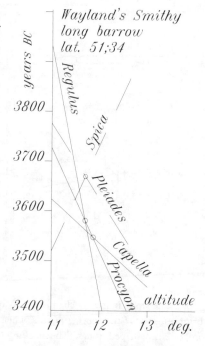

Repeating the calculation for a set of azimuths perpendicular to the far edges, other dates are obtained, in one case with very different implications for the *form* of the barrow. The stars are the same (Spica and the Pleiades), the date 3710 BC, but the angle of view is only 5.35°. The lines of sight would in this case not have been high enough to clear the chamber, and so this is rejected, but another two solutions present themselves on this second hypothesis. Both are for the thirty-sixth century. One pairs the settings of Procyon

FIG. 15.   Three potential solutions (marked by small circles) for the viewing of stars across the Wayland's Smithy long mound. Continuous lines are for viewing at right angles to the far edge of the barrow, broken lines for the near edge.

and Regulus (around 3581 BC, altitude 11.70°), the other the settings of Procyon and Capella (around 3549 BC, altitude 11.85°). These various solutions are shown graphically in Fig. 15.

Which of the three viable solutions are we to favour? All the dates derived fit comfortably into the range found from the radiocarbon dating of a branch or small trunk that the excavators linked with the operation of clearing vegetation from around the previous barrow by fire (2820±130 bc, or 3620±180 BC). This is an ill-starred situation, and other evidence must be brought to bear on it.

Procyon and Capella are both brighter than Spica, and they and Regulus are much brighter than the Pleiades. If one inclines to the Spica–Pleiades

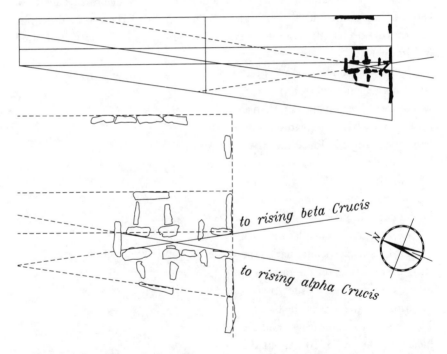

FIG. 16. The stone mortuary chamber of Wayland's Smithy II, showing how rays from the brightest stars of the Southern Cross, when rising, fell diagonally across the chamber, grazing carefully shaped stones. (The blocking stone at the entrance, used to seal the tomb, is omitted. The places of missing stones are not indicated, but should be obvious.) The faces of the large stones at the ends of the transepts are likewise carefully placed so as to parallel the sides of the mound, and so would have aligned on alpha Crucis and Deneb before the mound covered them. If the arrangement indicated is not an illusion, then it is plain that religious conceptions were more important than astronomical observations. The upper plan covers the entire mound, and shows how beautifully the geometry of the chamber is related to that of the mound. The details hardly need to be spelled out.

combination, it must be for other reasons. Independent dating from other possible alignments might offer us a way.

The tomb begs to be considered as an artificial horizon for a view of the southern sky over the length of the barrow. The slope of the barrow was evidently small: judging by its dimensions, known and inferred, the angle set by it to an observer standing at ground level was a little under 2.36°, depending on its form. The massive central stones at the southern end would have been hidden to an observer at the north. Now it so happens that during the period in question the only reasonably bright star in anything approaching the required direction was the rising alpha Crucis, which has an extinction angle close to this figure. The star could have been seen over the chamber by an observer standing at the northeast corner along a line exactly parallel to the western long side. This was very precisely true around 3750 BC, assuming an extinction angle of 2.42°. (It has to be remembered that estimates of extinction angles are not absolute. To give an idea of potential uncertainties: bringing the angle down to 2.1° would in the present case advance the year by a century.) Alternatively, an observer standing at the northwest corner would have seen the same star rising at the same altitude, as if it were coming out of the large sarsen stone at the southwest corner. (This stone is unfortunately now missing, but was probably higher than the corresponding stone on the other side.)

There are interesting resemblances between old and new chambers: the *internal* measurements of the stone chamber were such as to bring in the ray from the rising alpha Crucis to the northeast corner of the chamber at this time. (With an estimated azimuth of 167.8° and an extinction angle of 2.35°, a year of 3640 BC is obtained.) There is, however, a new and quite unexpected alignment with the other main diagonal of the chamber, this time on the rising of beta Crucis.[6] As in the other case the line is uncertain—they are estimates for standing observers rather than prone skeletons—but an azimuth of 150.1°

---

6 Alpha Crucis was encountered along a substantially different line in the analysis of the first phase. Alpha Crucis is nominally, if not in fact, the brightest star in the Southern Cross (the Latin name of the constellation is simply *Crux*). Its magnitude was at this period 1.33, as against 1.25 for beta Crucis. The star was regarded by early Mediterranean writers as being in the foot of the Centaur. By late antiquity it was already low or invisible even at Mediterranean latitudes, and for this reason no common name for it entered the languages of later Europe before exploration of the southern hemisphere made it familiar, under its present name. To the simple reasoning of the people of Wayland's Smithy I, it would have been Deneb's 'opposite' in two respects. When considering Deneb's significance, we hazarded a guess that it was connected with the fact that no brighter star rose and set nearer to the northernmost point on the horizon. In the same way, *no brighter star than alpha Crucis rose and set closer to the southernmost point* until, that is to say, it finally ceased to rise at Wayland's Smithy at all, in the 28th century BC.

and an extinction angle of 2.42° suggests a period around 3680 BC. The west ditch is just long enough to accommodate that same alignment over the crossing point in mid-chamber (see Fig. 16).

In sum, taking these additional dates into consideration inclines us to take the Spica–Pleiades combination, with its earlier date (3670 BC) and its more intuitively acceptable style of viewing at right-angles to near edges. Doing so, moreover, brings us to the middle of the radiocarbon range. All the dating is subject to error. For the time being, all too little is known of the ditch floor, but one thing at least seems probable, albeit based on only two sections: the floor falls gradually towards the north, as the ditch is pulled in to the tail of the barrow. This is surely how the angle of view was preserved, while lowering the height of the barrow. (Note that the principle of viewing at equal altitudes was generally implemented by having *opposed sections* at

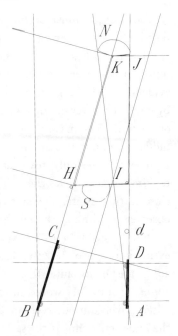

FIG. 17.   The central area of the next figure.

equal levels. It does not require level ditches, although they were indeed usually level.) When the ditch is completely excavated, the barrow's form will be better known, but even now one can say—on the basis of ditch sections at the transept and at mid-mound—that the barrow was falling over this stretch at a gradient of about 4.3°. This gradient would have brought it down almost perfectly to ground level at its very tail, but perhaps the gradient was levelled out towards that end, so that the tail retained some height.

This analysis has an important consequence for the sequence of building. For those who reject an astronomical interpretation, it makes little difference whether the mound preceded or followed the chamber. The precise astronomical alignment of the stones of the chamber, however, makes it seem certain that they were set up first, rather as the scaling posts for the older barrow had been.

Some people have seen the massive sarsens flanking the entrance to the surviving barrow as male to the right and female to the left. Alpha Crucis has a natural partner, beta Crucis, then slightly brighter, and to be seen on the side

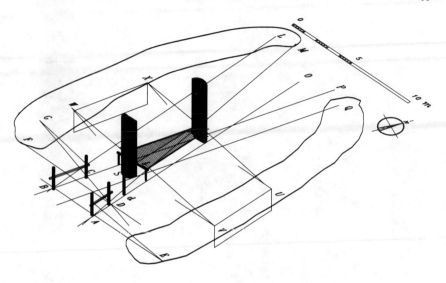

FIG. 18.   A general view of the planning of the mortuary house and its ditches at Wayland's Smithy. For lettering, see the previous figure, and for a detail, see the next figure.

of the 'male' stones flanking the entrance. (One might equally say that it illuminated the 'female' side of the interior, and it would take a Jungian psychologist to decide on the more probable interpretation.) The two stars might well therefore have been regarded as male and female. Was gamma Crucis (magnitude 1.63) their child? The fourth star making up our cross is relatively feeble—but a second child, perhaps?[7]

---

7   Procyon takes its name from the Greek, meaning 'rising before the dog (star)', that is, before Sirius. This was true in the fourth millennium. The two are not particularly close. The Milky Way passes neatly between them. Opinions differed as to whose dogs they were, but the claims of nearby Orion are as good as any.

Only Sirius and Arcturus were brighter in the Wessex sky than Capella, the 'she-goat' in our constellation Auriga, the Wagoner. The constellation is nondescript in shape, but its brightness makes the star easily distinguishable, halfway between Orion and the pole. Some northern cultures have associated it with a ploughman.

Regulus, a diminutive form of the Latin *Rex* (king), has been associated with kinghood since at least early Babylonian times. It was the eighteenth brightest star in the Wessex sky, the brightest in the constellation we know as Leo, and has in fact often been called by names equivalent to 'Lion's Heart'.

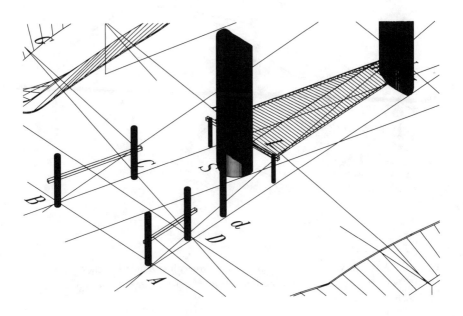

FIG. 19.   A detail of the previous figure, showing the shape of the shallow pitched roof of the earliest mortuary house at Wayland's Smithy. No attempt is made to show constructional details. Hatching is added simply to make the pitch (and the ridge) more evident.

Frame and Form at Wayland's Smithy I

What has now emerged about potential uses of the later barrow at Wayland's Smithy reflects back in an important way on the earlier phase of activity on the site. All the evidence of scale rules out the idea that observation of risings and settings of stars *across* the earlier structure was done by people standing at ground level, which would have required a higher central edifice than the later barrow. But what if Spica and the Pleiades were observed from the ditches, as it seems likely that they were with the second barrow?

An artificial barrier of wood or chalk or stone over the mortuary house would then have provided the horizon. Only two or three of the edges defined by what is known of the monument are acceptable for the purposes of observing the two stars, on the hypothesis that viewing was at right angles to the edges. They are the lines labelled *KB* and *JA* (or parallels to them) in Fig. 18, and

they set azimuths (measured from north) of 73.2°, towards the rising of Spica, and 246.9°, towards the setting of the Pleiades, at an altitude and period as yet undetermined.

Note that whereas the second direction represents a shift of less than a degree from what was set by the later monument, the other direction differs from its later equivalent by three degrees. This alone should lead one to expect an appreciable time interval between the two monuments.

Applying exactly the same argument to the first phase of the barrow as that applied earlier to the second, perfectly consistent results are obtained only around the year 3940 BC. The two stars—the only bright stars with the property of being seen as stipulated over the right spread of centuries, would both have been observed at an altitude of 10.4°, when the Pleiades' (Alcyone's) declination was −5.59° and Spica's was 18.58°.

Since Procyon, Capella and Regulus offered alternatives with the later mound, it is worth mentioning here that the dates they yield, whether on the assumption of viewing at right angles to near or far edges, are either much too early or too late (4555, 3490, 3415 BC).

However implausible it may seem to claim that we can make such a precise statement (overlooking small uncertainties in the azimuths) about a monument that has left hardly more than two-dimensional traces of its existence, there is much circumstantial evidence for our conclusion, as will appear in the course of the following suggested reconstruction of the procedures adopted by its builders:

The holes were prepared for the split trunks N and S, and N was erected. Scaling posts were set up at D and A, aligned with the eastern edge of N on the star Deneb. (Post d was also used along the same line, but for mechanical reasons and not geometrical, so that here it will be passed over in silence.) The opposition of Aldebaran's setting and Altair's rising was well known at the site, as was the fact that their directions over a natural horizon were almost perfectly at right angles to the Deneb line. Post B was set up to provide the requisite Aldebaran–Altair line. Some fine trimming in the position of A was needed, hence the oval hole. Post C was next placed so that it yielded a right-angle DCB, needed for the 'viewing at right angles' rationale of the monument. Once the lines of the artificial horizons had been so defined by the scaling posts AD and BC, the experimental part of the operation began. Beams were tied across those posts (see Fig. 18), the first of them perhaps to d too, and carefully adjusted in level and height (always kept equal) so that the rising of Spica and the setting of the Pleiades was always viewed across them at right angles. This

was easily arranged: they simply used the uprights, C with D and A with B, to define the direction in conjunction with the appropriate beam. But viewing now had to be precisely done from a definite height, ground level, and the ditches were dug accordingly. Viewing was later going to be by people standing more or less in the ranges UV and XW of the ditches. The UV area was dug first, and the ditch extended to a point (E) suitable for observing the Pleiades. There was to be no wasted effort: digging was to be done as far as was needed, and no further. The same was true for a point G in the western ditch. (But later the ditch was extended to F so that an overland sighting of Spica was possible.) Care was needed to ensure that E and G were at precisely the same distances from their respective beams. At last the requisite height of the beams was found (it was about 1.09 m *above eye level*), and the roof of the mortuary house could be erected.

This was in the first place a wooden structure, and its being pitched would have aided the run-off of water, although it was only at a shallow angle of $10°$ or so. The perfect pitch for observing the stars was $10.4°$. It was the two edges that were really crucial, and these were defined by marks cut into the split trunk N and by the short posts flanking S. These short and puny posts did not bear any load: they were levelling posts, each hammered into the chalk until level with the edge of the corresponding beam. The nearby sarsens bore the weight of the roof ridge.

By an unhappy circumstance—heavy sarsens in the ditch-fill—the inner ditch sections were not always excavated to the bottom, and never where they are of greatest interest to us. However, the inner ditch gives every sign of having been a normal viewing ditch, flat-bottomed and within a few centimetres of 1.65 m below the thin chalk soil (rendsina) under the cairn. (The estimated heights of eight adult males in the tomb yield an average of 1.70 m, and the average eye-level of the tallest three would have been about 1.65 m.) This has important implications for the astronomical argument. Clearly the remnants of the later cairn must allow for the idea that the viewing angle did not greatly differ from $10.4°$. This they do, but the two sarsens at the southern D-post—which on our reconstruction supported the roof of the earlier wooden chamber—if set upright in the (known) stone holes from which they came, set a more reliable criterion. Each would have been almost exactly 1.05 m above the floor. The viewing angle requires the ridge at this point to be a minimum of about 1.20 m, and for more comfortable viewing 1.30 m, so that there is ample leeway for a (probably solid) roof of 15 or even 20 cm thickness. Trunks of this diameter could have provided a frame for the roof, bringing it up to the

right height. The need for waterproofing might be thought to argue for a covering of turf or even compacted chalk, but solid trunks, split, trimmed to shape, and calked in some way would have been better.

The shallow ridge of the roof runs from K to I. What might easily have been taken as a sign of incompetence on the part of the builders, who might have been thought simply incapable of positioning one massive trunk precisely opposite another, is now on the contrary seen as testimony to genius of a high order. The trapezium outline of the horizon-roof is very much the same as the shape of the later long barrow, and no doubt its pitches were much the same. Furthermore, there is an exact analogy between the placing of the stone mortuary house within it, to the side of the central line, and the mortuary house under the roof between the split trunks (compare Figs. 13 and 19). In other words, the great barrow at Wayland's Smithy was very probably a replica of that original roof, in all but the fine details of the angles, which the precession of the stars had altered.

The observing ditches were dug so that the ranges XW and UV were equidistant from the roof edges, just as G and E had been from their beams. Each range had space for six or seven people standing side by side. (Could they have been three men and three women, like the sarsens fronting the barrow?) Each person probably had a place-marker, say a ridge cut in the chalk. Note that the chalk at X was dug so as just to accommodate a viewing position, but with little more expenditure of energy than was necessary. Later extensions to the ditch took it up to other viewing positions L, M, and Q—and again took it no further than was necessary—from which the stars under discussion here could have been seen in different ways. Which stars they were will be appreciated without further comment, if Fig. 18 is examined for parallels to the lines of sight already discussed.

Fussell's Lodge Revisited

In possession of our several new principles, it is possible to re-examine the first chamber at Fussell's Lodge, here previously dated at around 4235 BC on the basis of individual stars—Aldebaran, Spica, beta Crucis, and beta Centauri. The broad principles embodied in the use of scaling posts, whose positions are at Fussell's Lodge known fairly accurately, are now taken to be the same as at Wayland's Smithy; and these provide a pair of directions, across which it will be supposed that viewing was at right angles. Examining them for stars at low altitudes, no qualifying pair emerges at all, but as the altitude is increased it

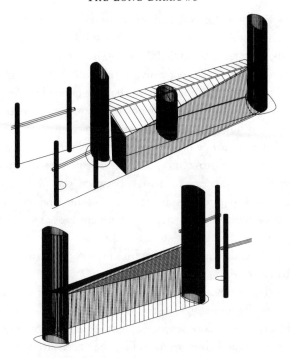

FIG. 20.   Two possible forms of roof for the Fussell's Lodge mortuary house, seen from different viewpoints. The first form, anticipating the shape of the barrow, is favoured here.

becomes clear that the setting Arcturus to the north[8] and the rising Betelgeuse or Bellatrix to the south[9] are possible candidates.

Although they are similar, the mortuary houses at the two sites differ in ways reflected in the final forms of their associated barrows. First, it seems that

8   Arcturus is in the constellation Boötes. Some derive that constellation name from the Greek *Bous*, Ox, while others take it from another Greek word, meaning the shout of a driver to his oxen, or of the hunter in pursuit of the Bear. The name of the star Arcturus has figured in literature at least since the time of the Greek poet Hesiod—in other words, for more than twenty-seven centuries. (It is on the basis of an astronomical statement by Hesiod about Arcturus, in his *Works and Days*, that the poet is now generally placed in the eighth century BC.)

9   Early allegiance at Fussell's Lodge to the brilliant Arcturus and Betelgeuse—variable in brightness, but around eleventh brightest in the sky—is not surprising, although the stars'

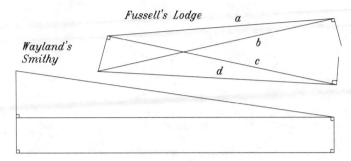

FIG. 21.   Potential right angles in the (highly stylized) forms of the barrows at Fussell's Lodge and Wayland's Smithy, drawn to approximately the same scale.

one of the right angles within the quadrangle of scaling posts is exactly as before, but that the other is not. It seems to have been drawn to the *axis*, and perhaps relates to a post in Ashbee's 'Pit III' at the centre of the four. Second, the Fussell's Lodge example is not itself plainly associated with a pair of viewing ditches and there was certainly none for use with the scaling posts. As for the way they functioned, much the same procedure could have been followed as at Wayland's[10].

Again it is necessary to consider viewing at right angles to near (qualified as explained) and far edges. In both cases the stars would have been the same. At an altitude of no less than 20.4° a perfect fit for the first alternative is produced, with Arcturus at declination 54.89° and Betelgeuse at −14.36°. The required year is 4240 BC.

---

readiness to collaborate across the centuries is another question. In the space of half a century, Betelgeuse had moved away, and in any case required a higher barrow; but its partner Bellatrix was available for service and was evidently accepted. Betelgeuse is Aldebaran's nearest first-magnitude neighbour. If the human figure the Greeks knew as Orion is imagined to be facing us, the star is seen as his right shoulder or arm. Betelgeuse was at the time actually only the second brightest star in the constellation, being second to Rigel (the left foot). Bellatrix was the third brightest star in Orion, and corresponds to his left shoulder or arm.

10   If later viewing was to be done from the ditches and not by observers at ground level, the method would have yielded viewing altitudes that needed to be transferred to the mortuary house by a 'drawing' of parallels (in terms of beams), so dropping the roof level by the height of the architect. Those capable of accurately constructing trapezia of 50 m and more in chalk would not have had any difficulty here, and in any case, trimming of the roof to produce the desired result would have constituted a final stage.

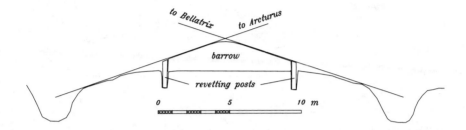

FIG. 22.   A cross-section of the ditches at Fussell's Lodge (P. Ashbee's section *CD*), roughly
15 m from the wide end and 25 m from the narrow. Note that the revetting posts have one
third showing and two-thirds buried—a sound constructional principle.

Again it is necessary to consider viewing at right angles to near (qualified
as explained) and far edges. In both cases the stars would have been the same.
At an altitude of no less than 20.4° a perfect fit for the first alternative is
produced, with Arcturus at declination 54.89° and Betelgeuse at –14.36°. The
required year is 4240 BC—complementing in an unexpected but very welcome
way the date (for the foundation barrow) previously obtained by averaging over
individual (and different) stars, that is to say, 4235 BC.

Taking the second alternative, the altitude increases to 23.64° and the year
is 4180 BC. In all cases small errors in the fundamental directions can alter
appreciably the dates derived. (An idea of how sensitive the method is to error
in the directions of key edges will be given briefly in a later section.) This
alternative fits marginally more comfortably with the radiocarbon dates for
material from the *D*-post pit (4250–3950 BC), but the first is to be preferred
if Wayland's style is to be followed. Far more important than those dates,
however, is the fact that procedures derived from a study of Wayland's Smithy
can explain this monument equally well.

Was there a viewing ditch for the mortuary house? The palisade trench for
the later barrow would not have served, for it would have been much too
cramped, but short sections of the ditches known from the final barrow would
have served very well. These ditches were relatively cavernous in the necessary
region, reaching a depth of about 3.6 m below the base of the mortuary house.
This great depth, slightly more than twice human height, might at first seem

to be an insuperable objection to the idea that viewing was from them, but in fact the ground chalk is cut away, especially on the inside edge. The excavator, P. Ashbee, interpreted this as a weathering ramp, and no doubt some weathering has taken place—although presumably fairly uniformly. The angle of this ramp, however, is suspiciously close to what we require it to be, and not only in one section but in all seven places where Ashbee's profiles allow us to measure it. To both sides of the house, an adult observer of normal height standing at the *back* of the true floor of the ditches—almost symmetrically now—would have been perfectly placed to look along a line barely skimming the ground at between 16° and 19°. The angles are not easy to measure accurately, but rejecting Ashbee's section *K* (which lacks the flatness of the chamfer of the others, but certainly produces something in excess of 14°), the other six range from 16° to 19° and average at about 17.5°. This might not seem particularly close to 20.4°, but that is hardly surprising, for in its present form it does not belong to the mortuary house phase at all. It is a figure germane to the *final* barrow phase, and as we shall see shortly this figure is within a degree of what is predicted—again very welcome evidence in favour of the general principles being proposed.

The implied height of the ridge of the mortuary house is 2.45 m, almost identical to the height of the final barrow at this point, as estimated by Ashbee—although the loaf shape he favoured for the final barrow does not fit with the ideas being put forward here. Accepting the idea of two distinct phases, with the cairn an intermediary, building around the old house was just as rooted in tradition as at Wayland's Smithy. Again, the form derived for the roof of the old mortuary house very probably resembled the flared form of the later barrow, for which there is the evidence of the palisade trench. It is conceivable, however, that the roof had a simpler form into which the gradients for the two different directions were nevertheless worked. The two alternatives are illustrated in Fig. 20. The fact that the pit between the split trunks is somewhat east of centre seems to favour the flared alternative, for if the pit was meant for another short trunk supporting the roof, it would have been appropriate to place it at the centre of gravity of the roof. It is in fact placed precisely where one would judge the centre of gravity of the flared, barrow-shaped, roof to have been.

At Wayland's, we worked back from the later to the earlier. At Fussell's Lodge, we now know something of the local tradition, and also the directions of the bounding lines of the barrow across which viewing at right angles would have been planned. The outline of the later structure has been corrupted to some extent through the collapse of parts of the palisade trench, but averaging

across sizeable lengths, the lines of sight seem to have been at 16.2° west of north and 23.3° east of south. From those data, using the same sort of argument as before, the conclusion is drawn that the date of the barrow was around 4180 BC and that viewing was at an altitude of 18.1°. The same star, Arcturus, was observed setting, but now the rising Bellatrix rather than Betelgeuse seems to have been observed. (The stars now observed were at declinations 54.63° and −17.83° respectively.) Even if viewing was at right angles to far edges, the same stars produce the only acceptable solution, with the altitude 20.23° and the year 4082 BC.

The lower angle seems preferable, as already explained. Other options might be thought relevant, for it does seem that the Fussell's Lodge barrow has certain right angles deliberately built into it. (Fig. 21 shows three, and the Wayland's barrow is added, to scale, as a reminder of the arrangement there.) If, instead of viewing across lines *a* and *d*, lines *b* and *c* were taken, the (equal) altitudes of the same stars Arcturus and Bellatrix would have been about 16.0° and the year approximately 4140 BC. If planning was based on *b* and *d*, then the angle was 17.1° and the year 3960 BC. The differences are not as great as one might have imagined, and simplicity favours the original choice.

In appearance, with viewing at such relatively steep viewing angles (see Fig. 22), the barrow must have resembled an upturned boat. It is conceivable that there was chalk *outside* the revetting posts of the barrow, so that only the tops of them were visible. In this case, the whole thing would at first have taken on the appearance of an isolated giant white wave in the landscape. If duly trimmed as the stars changed their declinations, and regularly scoured to prevent vegetation settling on it, this form could have been kept for decades. The revetting posts would have rotted, perhaps within a century, but the downward wash of the cover might have been repaired even for several centuries. Of course it could be that alignment on stars was merely a foundation activity, regarded as done once and for all, and that the stars were not observed over the barrows thereafter, or were observed for only a few years. Perhaps, in time, closer attention to ditches will produce the much-needed evidence—the burning of lamps on the walls, the tread of feet on the floor and on sloping platforms, provision for drainage inside and on the lip, scouring tools on the ditch bottom with unexpectedly late radiocarbon dates, and so forth.

It has been shown by experiment that weathering of the surroundings of a ditch can cause it to fill in five or ten years, and it has usually been taken for granted that the ditches of a long barrow filled up quickly in this way, soon after its completion, since it has been assumed that the only purpose of the

ditches was to provide raw material for the barrows. If the barrows were used as suggested here, however, and not merely in a foundation activity, then they would have been regularly cleared of rubble, baled out, and possibly even recut from time to time, to accommodate changing star positions. They might even have been given penthouse roofs to keep them dry, and so have weathered much more slowly than if they had been exposed. This last is a purely speculative remark, in the absence of any remains; but such roofs would have been as nothing by comparison with those often postulated for circles like the Sanctuary and Woodhenge, which would make them into prehistoric equivalents of St Paul's Cathedral. And needless to say, the bigger the roof postulated, the more surprising that no traces of its fallen timbers have been found.

Lambourn

A radiocarbon date for the long barrow on the Lambourn Downs, 4 km north of Lambourn, provides it with a venerable status that has not had much influence on its preservation. Corrected in the usual way, the date falls in the calendar range 4200 ± 200 BC. Part of the long barrow not in woodland has been badly ploughed down, and part in woodland has been interpenetrated by tree roots. It was excavated in a peremptory way by Martin Atkins in the 1850s and rediscovered by Leslie Grinsell in 1935. It was so ruthlessly ploughed that a rescue excavation was mounted in 1964 by John Wymer, who found that very little remained of the exposed mound.

Grinsell described it in outline, and following his plan its central axis seems to have been about $74.7°$ east of north, which is probably true to better than a degree. Wymer's plan is more detailed, and shows that the ditches were tolerably straight, and had mid-ditch azimuths (corrected for $4.0°$ compass error) of about $76.2°$ (south side) and $73.2°$ (north side). The average corresponds exactly to the figure obtained from Grinsell's plan. It differs only slightly from that of the Fussell's Lodge barrow, but so, of course, do the geographical latitudes and horizon profiles at the two places, and the conclusions to be drawn from the two are very different.

Scattered sarsen boulders are still to be found at the eastern end of the barrow, deriving from a chamber there, and at the exposed western end many of the boulders still lying at the edge of the field are what were removed by the farmer, through deep-ploughing. The modern partial excavation of the head of the mound, within the wood, revealed that sarsen boulders in the mortuary area followed a well-defined line (azimuth about $72°$). The Lambourn barrow was perhaps a two-stage structure, like those at Wayland's Smithy and

Fussell's Lodge, containing a primary wooden-framed tomb that was covered over by the present barrow at a later stage.

Atkins, who tells us that a farmer had already dug into it before him, and that 'human remains and a quantity of black earth' were found, also unearthed other skeletons. One was lacking its skull—as a result, he thought, of the farmer's enthusiasm. More recently, Wymer found a crouched burial in a rough sarsen stone cist, together with seashells, but this was not a primary burial. It is unfortunate that the character of the first structure is unknown, and that we are left with only the decrepit remains of the outer barrow as a guide.

The slope of the badly worn mound when Grinsell charted its profile in 1936 was about 2.3° upwards to the east, and an estimate of the barrow's maximum height to be made shortly suggests that it might originally have been about 3.0°. The critical land horizon (eastwards) is 2.02° and had there been trees on the horizon 10 m tall, the angle would have risen to 2.32°. (Corresponding western altitudes are 1.54° and 1.97°.) It looks very much as though, just as at Fussell's Lodge, the slope of the barrow was made to mask the distant horizon, as would be explained if the viewing of a rising star to the east was along its spine by a person standing in the natural hollow at its western end. This appears to have been a ditch, judging from old aerial photographs, and Grinsell took it to be such, like those he knew from Dorset barrows, but Wymer did not detect any such ditch.

Accepting an azimuth of 72° for the line of the barrow's sarsen core, the rising of the star Altair would have been seen at the stated altitude around the year 3960 BC—a very tentative date, of course.

The barrow was certainly tapered, like that at Fussell's Lodge, and judging by the ditches the taper amounted to only about three degrees. Observation towards the west was also in principle possible, using the natural horizon. Another way of looking at a star on the western horizon would have been to use the gentle incline up to the tomb entrance from the place of the present road (there is no path in that position now). A person of average height would have seen the foreground (land, track) coincide with the far horizon—assuming trees of more or less 10 m. The high end of the tomb, at 2.6 m above the surrounding ground or thereabouts, would have made a third (intermediate) horizon for the ray to skim, rather as at Wayland's Smithy, which is less than 5 km away. The artificial altitude would in this case have been 2.0°, which is the extinction angle for the most likely star in that direction, the setting star Aldebaran. There is little point in setting down what are no more than directed guesses, based on a very superficial survey, but a line of sight of azimuth 250.5° would have been needed for the fortieth century BC, not far from the reverse of

the supposed direction to Altair's rising. Both of these alignments might have been embodied in a set of scaling posts, as at the head of the barrows at Fussell's Lodge and Wayland's Smithy.

Another possible observation along the barrow to the west could have been in connection with the setting of the Pleiades at the same period, as at Wayland's Smithy. Not enough detail is known of the Lambourn structure to speculate on a precise alignment. Another long barrow over which the setting of the Pleiades might have been observed is at Nutbane, in north Hampshire, 20 km or so from Stonehenge, a barrow that is perhaps five centuries younger.

The use of the Lambourn barrow as an artificial horizon for crosswise viewing admits of two distinct solutions. One of these involves the setting Arcturus to the north together with the rising Bellatrix to the south. The estimated date (4272 BC) fits well with the corrected radiocarbon date of 4200±200 BC, and yet reluctantly the solution must be rejected. It requires viewing in both directions at an angle of approximately 19.0° to the horizontal, a figure that implies a mound 4.7 m high, seemingly much more massive than the ditches could have provided.

The alternative solution, which is tentatively accepted, is that the setting of Vega was observed to the north and the rising of Sirius to the south, around the year 3970 BC, both stars being viewed at an altitude of 11.0°.[11] The implied maximum barrow height (2.6 m) fits very well with what is known of the ditch sizes and their potential for providing material for the mound. The derived date is probably not in error by more than a century. The dates obtained for Altair and Aldebaran along the barrow's length are compatible with it, but why then does it not square with the radiocarbon date?

---

11 Like so many stars, Sirius has many rich literary associations, although many of them stem from its use in marking the seasons in classical Antiquity, and are—at least in their details—entirely inappropriate to northern latitudes and the Neolithic period. Since the first morning visibility of Sirius (Sothis) after a period during which the star rose unseen in daylight (its so-called heliacal rising) was close to the summer solstice and the time of inundation of the Nile, the Egyptians based their calendar on the event. There is written evidence for their having done so as early as the mid third millennium BC, somewhat earlier than the main phases of the stone monuments at Stonehenge. The near coincidence of solstice and heliacal rising is quite inappropriate to northern latitudes at the same approximate period—when the discrepancy was two or three weeks. (For more details on the subject of heliacal risings, see Appendix 4.)

The great brilliance of Sirius gave it another set of associations in literature—as a guardian of the horizon, or as a dog, for example, a companion to the human figure now known as Orion. The star will be met with not infrequently in the analysis of long barrow alignments, but it is hardly possible even to conjecture as to its mythical associations.

The latter was based on a patch of burnt wood from the floor of the tail end of the south ditch. It could have originated with timber from an old mortuary house, or from posts that had been removed from an old structure by burning—broadly speaking, the bigger the post the older the timber. As one of the long barrows at Skendleby will later demonstrate, a set of more than a dozen radiocarbon dates from a single site may span two millennia, and any one of them in isolation might have given an entirely false impression. In a sentence: the Lambourn barrow we (barely) know is perhaps not as old as is generally supposed.

Although the Lambourn barrow is now in a relatively isolated spot, there was considerable later prehistoric activity nearby. It is unlikely to have been by chance that, almost in line with it, and half a kilometre to the east, is a disc barrow. Mostly to the southeast of it, and within a circle of radius under a kilometre, there are remains of at least thirty round barrows of various types of the early and middle Bronze Age. A dozen of these lie together in a group with the collective name of 'Seven Barrows' (the English having always found barrows difficult to count), and six of them lie virtually in a line that passes directly over the long barrow, while another four lie roughly on another line, parallel to the first. The former and better alignment is about 40° north of west (or south of east), but this depends on how one selects the barrows, for the line is not perfect. It seems obvious that these much later tombs were aligned on the setting of the Sun over the long barrow at the summer solstice—a direction which changed very slightly with historical period. (The calculation depends on the horizon altitude, which in turn depends on the line chosen.)

It is hard for us now to comprehend how such a simple mound as the Lambourn long barrow could have kept its reputation as a place of great sanctity for perhaps two thousand years after it was first erected. Having accepted the idea, however, we seem to catch a glimpse of one reason for shifting allegiance away from the stars to the Sun in these matters of alignments: the directions of the Sun's risings and settings are more or less constant over very long periods of time. For most of the stars this is not true, even though Deneb, as we have already seen, had a certain constancy in its behaviour.

Horslip (Windmill Hill)

One of the most valuable of modern reports on long barrow excavations is that in which Paul Ashbee, I. F. Smith, and J. G. Evans describe respectively excavations that took place between 1959 and 1967 at Horslip, Beckhampton Road, and South Street, all in or near Avebury. The Horslip barrow lies a kilometre due south of Windmill Hill, and so is often called after that

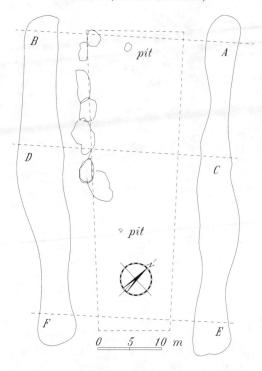

FIG. 23.   Plan of the Horslip long barrow. Details of most of the inner area had been removed by ploughing. The letters indicate Paul Ashbee's ditch sections. The broken-line trapezium represents no more than a directed guess at the outline of the limits of the barrow. The line of pits at the north western end might represent viewing positions for an earlier mortuary house on the site.

enclosure—which in turn has given its name to a whole culture. Selected radiocarbon dates for the three barrows produce the ranges 4000±160, 3550±185, and 3300±100 BC in calendar years (3240±150, 2750±135, 2517±90 bc). There is no unambiguous evidence that any of these barrows was built in more than a single phase, although Horslip probably was; and none has produced evidence that it was used for burials at all in the earliest phase, a discovery that has caused much surprise. All three barrows have been ploughed down considerably in recent centuries, but even so, the second and third retained extremely valuable clues as to the astronomical and architectural procedures followed by those who built them.

The Horslip barrow was originally perhaps of trapezoidal form, since the ditches that flank it are slightly splayed (Fig. 23). In 1743 William Stukeley described it as being 'of large bulk, length, and height', but ploughing after his time virtually removed all surface features. Its orientation was roughly 45°

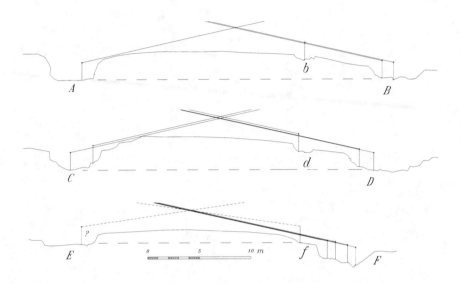

FIG. 24.   Sections of the ditches at the Horslip long barrow, with labels following those
of Fig. 23. The lines of sight are arrived at entirely on astronomical grounds. The verticals
represent the height of the eye of a male observer of average height. The broken horizontals
show the excellent levelling of observing positions, which ditches purely for quarrying
purposes would not have had. The maximum height of the barrow can be judged easily
enough from the suggested lines of sight, and is not indicated. The broken lines of sight
are what might have been used had the ditches changed direction here, for example with
a lower barrow. Note that observers' heights may still be equal.

south of east, and in this direction the ground falls away. The southeastern end
is the higher in relation to the surrounding ground, but the overall slope of the
ridge of the barrow when it was erected was very probably between four and
five degrees upwards in the opposite direction, that is, to the northwest.
Observation in this direction seems unlikely, for want of bright stars, but
looking the other way, over the natural horizon, the rising of Sirius might
have been seen. The line is not securely known, and trees might have been
a factor, but all plausible directions indicate a date within a couple of
centuries of 4000 BC.

    The orientation of the barrow can be estimated from the average direction
of the inner edges of the ditches (135.0° for the northeastern and 140.8° for
the southwestern), or from an interesting pair of pits (134.5° through their
centres) that might well have been related to the line of the ridge itself, or

perhaps to that of an earlier mortuary house on the site, as at Wayland's Smithy. The pit near the northwest was roughly a metre square and three quarters of a metre deep; the other, about a third of the way up the ridge from the southeastern end, was circular in section and had dimensions about a third as great as the first. Other pits in a rough line following the southwestern edge are also represented in two cross-sections of the ditches, illustrated in Fig. 24.

Even from a single ditch, there are possibilities of multiple viewing positions. It is conceivable that the pits (here at *b* and *d*) are meant to add more, but the spread of a reasonably stable mound, of a height to be suggested shortly, makes it more probable that they are vestiges of an earlier phase in the history of the barrow, perhaps relating to the two pits on the axis. The ditches are interesting for their equalization of the lower levels, the places which on our basic assumption offer the ideal positions for viewing. Section *E* appears to be an aberration, failing to conform to our principles, and yet in the *EF* section there is a ledge providing viewing from the very same level. A change of ditch and barrow directions here could well have changed the requirements for viewing heights, to fit a later date, but still, it seems, the possibility of viewing at equal angles is being retained. The height of the spine of the barrow above the old ground level was perhaps around 3 m. The evidence for this comes from the astronomical possibilities offered by the lines of the ditches.

Applying yet again the principle of viewing at equal altitudes, at right angles to barrow and ditch edges, near or far, there is only one likely star to the north, namely the rising Deneb, but to south there is a choice of two, Aldebaran and Betelgeuse. The setting of Betelgeuse seems preferable, since it produces dates fully consistent with the radiocarbon date—which came from a piece of horn of red deer from a ditch fill. Taking the option of right angles to near edges, the date is 3809 BC (altitude 16.21°), while far edges give 3940 BC (altitude 12.26°). Coupling Aldebaran and Deneb, the angles would have been little changed, but the date would have moved earlier by three and a half centuries. Out of these four options, 3940 BC seems most acceptable. (The latitude is 51° 25' 58". Azimuths are taken as 50.8° and 224.7° (near) or 44.7° and 230.8° (far). The favoured declinations are: Deneb 36.76° and Betelgeuse −12.69°.)

In the case of the Horslip barrow, there is an odd piece of evidence supporting our preference. There is no chamfered inner edge to the ditch to suggest a viewing altitude, but if one tries to superimpose lines of sight on the ditch sections (as in Fig. 24) the *floors* of the ditches turn out to be better suited to the lower angle of view (12.3° rather than 16.2°), in the sense that they can accommodate more usable viewing positions. The sizes of the excavated ditches therefore give a rough idea of the height of the barrow, twice over, since they

also provided the materials for it. They are quite consistent with the implied
height of around 3 m above eye level.

The finer points of barrow construction, as illustrated by Fussell's Lodge
and Wayland's Smithy, are at Horslip completely beyond recall. As already
suggested, there was very probably an alignment down the line of the barrow's
axis on the setting of Sirius over natural ground (the declination being around
−26.2°). This in itself would have been notable enough, in combination with
the alignments on Deneb and Betelgeuse, but in the thirty-ninth century BC
the Horslip site had another very remarkable property: the natural horizons
there are not equal, but are such that the direction of the rising of Sirius was
then at right angles to that of its setting. (Without tree cover the extinction
angle was operative to the southeast but the altitude to the southwest was
1.26°.) In view of the Neolithic preoccupation with right-angled viewing, this
would have endowed the site with exceptional importance, even though the
right-angle property was relatively short-lived, and within a century or so was
to be lost. But was it matched by another, which persisted?

It will be shown later in this chapter that the planet Venus, the brightest
of the planets, might just have been seen when she was at her southern limit
of setting, along the same direction as Sirius. The planet would have had this
property already in the fifth millennium, and would have kept it long after it
ceased to hold for Sirius. While it is a property to which one is led by
considering the barrow, it is really one that belongs to the *site*. There are later
qualifications to be made, in regard to a fundamental difference between Venus'
extremes of rising and setting, but assuming that the property was discovered
at the time to apply to Sirius and to one or more of the four extremes of Venus
(risings, settings, north or south), there would have been ample reason for
building a barrow along one of the key directions. It is just conceivable that
this property influenced the choice of a site for the Windmill Hill settlement
in the first place.

West Kennet and its Star Chambers

Today almost as well known as Wayland's Smithy, the chambered long barrow
on a ridge of the chalk downs to the south of the hamlet of West Kennet in
Wiltshire is even grander in scale. Just over a hundred metres in length, and
tapering from about 24 m at its eastern façade to 12 m at the western end, it
is (with that at nearby East Kennet) the largest in the region, and among the
largest in the country. Its sheer size has enabled it to survive a number of crude
onslaughts. One of these was by a certain Dr R. Toope of Marlborough, who

in 1685 raided it for bones, for their supposed pharmaceutical properties. John Aubrey gave a vague account of the tomb at about the same time. It is in a letter to him from Toope that we learn of the doctor's attitude to prehistory, and of how already in 1678, alerted to the large quantities of bones in the area around the Sanctuary nearby, he had acquired 'many bushels' with which he had made 'a noble medicine' that relieved many of his distressed neighbours. (One might doubt whether those particular bones, lying near the surface and closely packed in the open field, skull to skull, were prehistoric at all, although Toope did insist that their feet were all directed to the Sanctuary.)

William Stukeley made valuable drawings of the West Kennet long barrow, and described it, in 1723–4. 'It stands east and west', he wrote, 'pointing to the dragon's head on Overton-hill.' (This is the hill on which stood the Sanctuary, now known to have comprised a succession of concentric rings of timber posts, before they were replaced by rings of stones.) The long barrow was partially excavated in 1859 by John Thurnam, who reported that farmers had cut a wagon-road through it, and had raided it for flints and chalk rubble. The definitive excavations were done in 1955–6 by Stuart Piggott and Richard Atkinson, like those later at Wayland's Smithy.

The West Kennet barrow has much to tell us about the evolution of a single long barrow, but it shows, too, that it is a mistake to consider that changes in ditch direction necessarily imply additions to an old barrow at a later time, as is often supposed. It will be discovered that it was probably built in two distinct phases, a century or so apart, but that there is a change in direction *within* the first barrow. Quite apart from its intrinsic interest, this long barrow has an importance deriving from the fact that it is in the neighbourhood of an extraordinary complex of prehistoric remains. Silbury Hill, the largest man-made mound of prehistoric Europe, is less than a kilometre away (NNW), and less than 5 km in the same direction is Windmill Hill. Roughly 1.3 km east of the barrow lies the site known as the Sanctuary, and from there the Kennet Avenue of stones stretched, initially roughly westwards, then turning closer to north and heading for the southern entrance to the stone circle at Avebury. (The Avenue will be discussed again in Chapter 5.) Avebury, by far the largest of all British stone circles, is only a little over 2 km to the north of the West Kennet barrow. The almost equally large long barrow at East Kennet is just under 1.5 km to the southeast. On most days, all of these places are to be seen from the West Kennet barrow.

The barrow is flanked by ditches, running alongside it for all of its length. Its orientation was said by Stuart Piggott, in his report of the excavations, to be 265° 20'—that is to say, a person looking at the façade would be facing

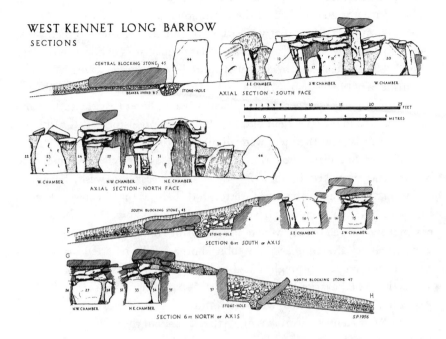

FIG. 25.   Sections of the West Kennet long barrow, as drawn by Stuart Piggott.

4° 40' south of west. To define an axis, however, one must be able to identify the intentions of the builders, and this figure presumably rests on the assumption that the stones of the central passage were set symmetrically about an axis that agrees with the spine of the mound. Another interpretation, to be offered shortly, substitutes a figure of 267.0°.

The mound had a central core in the form of a long cairn of sarsen boulders, rising to about 2 m in the excavated section. This core was in turn overlaid with chalk rubble from the ditches, and at the higher end this virtually doubled the height. A kerb round the barrow, resembling that at Wayland's Smithy, was robbed of its stones long ago, and consequently a much less accurate picture is available of the outline of the tomb. As for the difficulty of assessing the orientations of the sides, their sheer length makes this a little easier, compensating to some extent for the loss of the kerbstones. The northern ditch apparently changes direction so that it is in at least four sections, while the southern ditch is in at least two. The bounding edge of the mound seems to follow those changes closely (Fig. 26). Viewing across the barrow, it will be shown that section *A* was paired with *B*, but not with *C*, which is a linking

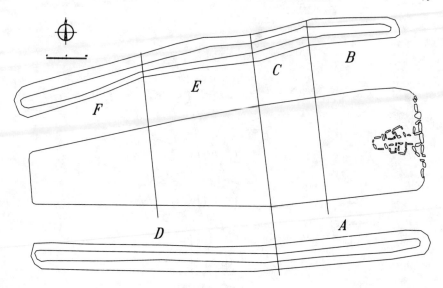

FIG. 26. Outline plan of the West Kennet long barrow and ditches, showing the deliberate changes of direction, resulting in four sections to the north but only two to the south. (The inset scale at upper left is 10 m long.)

section only, while *D* was matched with both *E* and *F*, but at times a century apart.

The most obvious stone structures, now largely restored, are at the eastern end, built out of massive local sarsen stones and dry-stone walling of oolite slabs. The sarsens were brought up the hill perhaps 2 km or more from the southeast, and the smaller stones from a distance of 10 km or more. The chambers form a 'cross of Lorraine'. They are arranged around a roofed passage running for more than 8 m down the spine of the barrow: a burial chamber

FIG. 27. The five chambers at the eastern end of the West Kennet barrow, with surviving blocking stones in position.

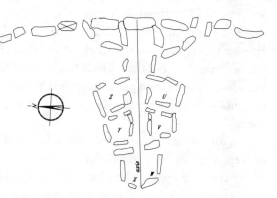

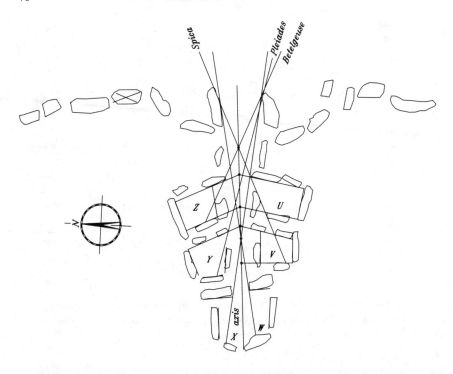

FIG. 28.   The West Kennet chambers with blocking stones removed, showing potential lines of sight, limited by the edges and faces of stones. The other lines added to the figure (see also Fig. 29), show the great care that went into the planning, and justify the position given to the axis.

opens off it at its end, lengthening it to 12 m, while two others open off at each side. The passage is as high in places as 2.3 m. It is entered from a crescent-shaped forecourt formed out of large but rather irregular uprights, and a false front closes off the forecourt, making the façade seem more or less flat. There are two stones flanking the entrance, immediately behind the large blocking stone in the middle of the façade. They should not be dismissed as merely helping to seal the entrance, for they have another important function. As will be seen from Fig. 28 (from which blocking stones are removed), they help to limit lines of sight from particular points within the five chambers. These lines of sight—of which more shortly—seem to have been directed to five significant stars.

As for the number of burials, the solicitous Dr Toope missed the bones of at least forty-six individuals, for he—and even Thurnam—found only the chamber at the western end. The others were closed with blocking stones. As at other Neolithic sites, the skeletons were often incomplete. Some have held

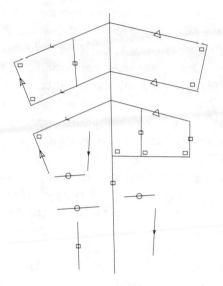

FIG. 29.   The surprisingly systematic construction lines, abstracted from the previous figure, defined by the faces of stones. Close parallels and perpendiculars are indicated by similar marks. On this basis it is easy to make conjectures concerning slight changes of plan, forced on the builders by their materials, terrestrial and celestial. Note that four stones are almost perfectly in line with the axis, whilst five stones (including the three marked with a circle) are parallel to ditch sections.

that this implies a systematic removal of certain bones—especially skulls and long bones—but on this point opinion is divided. The adult men seem to have been between 1.57 and 1.73 or even 1.80 m in height, the women from 1.49 to 1.64 m. The characteristically round skulls of the Beaker peoples are not represented, although their pottery is found among what are presumed to have been later ritual offerings. They were perhaps well represented in Dr Toope's medicine, since the western chamber was the most readily accessible.

In time, the chambers were filled to the roof with chalk rubble, stone and earth. Numerous bone objects and flints were found in the modern excavation, as well as pottery that included early Windmill Hill ware, Peterborough ware, grooved ware (Rinyo–Clacton), and Beaker types. This pottery shows that the tomb was in use for perhaps more than a thousand years, and deposits of Romano-British ware show that some sort of interest in it continued for well over three millennia. (Much material from the tomb is displayed in the Devizes Museum.) Long after the tomb ceased to be used for burial, it must have continued to function as a focal point for religious practice—much as do the

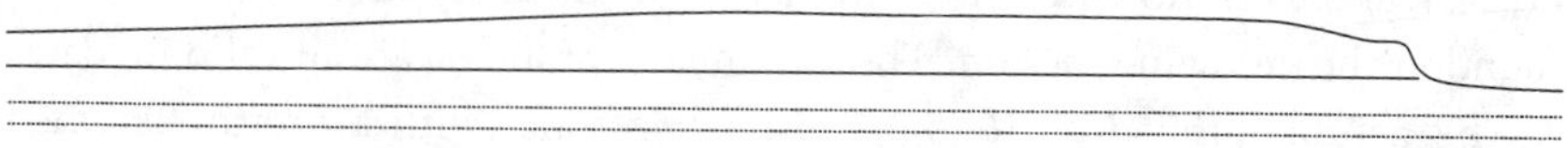

FIG. 30.   Suggested profile of the original West Kennet long barrow, looking across it from the south. The barrow might have been of constant height over even more of its length. The ground rises very slowly to the west and falls to the east. The two lowest lines are conjectural levels of the observer's eye and the ditch floor.

cathedrals of the Christian era quite regardless of the fact that they too are the sites of burials. If it is hard to envisage such loyal devotion to a low ridge of earth and stone, that is only because we are ignorant of the systems of belief preserved by those who revered it. At what stage the enormous blocking stone 3.7 m high was placed across the façade it is impossible to say, but this must have come last, if the lines of sight of which we have spoken were precisely that, and not theoretically drawn rays, falling on the sightless dead. The massive stone sealed off the tomb's contents, but even then did not mark an end to its ritual function.

The barrow tapers off towards its western end and loses height in relation to ground level, but the ground rises gradually to the west. The profile of the barrow is now degraded, but in its prime was probably not very different from that shown in Fig. 30. Its present contours suggest that there was originally a well-defined ridge. This is borne out by Thurnam's statement: 'Dr Took, as they call him, has miserably defaced South Long Barrow by digging half the length of it. It was most neatly smoothed up to a sharp ridge.' One assumes that there is intended irony in the substitution of 'Took' for 'Toope'.

The rays capable of entering the five chambers do so in much the same way as the pair of rays (from the stars in the Southern Cross) at Wayland's Smithy, being limited to a greater or lesser degree by the uprights. Those passing to the southern and northern parts of the central chamber (W and X, Fig. 28) have slightly more latitude than the others, but if it is assumed that at least two stones must always be involved in fixing the direction, even they are tightly governed. Most of the key uprights are carefully worked, and in this respect alone can be distinguished from the rest. In all cases a normal adult male could just have stood upright to see the rising star appropriate to the chamber, and there is no question of this being an imagined possibility only for the deceased lying on the ground. The horizon over which all these stars rose is therefore here assumed to be the natural horizon, so that extinction angles hold good.

It seems that the axis was not directed to any star, but that at least three and possibly four of the chambers were, and no doubt consciously. There is some uncertainty in the precise original positions of the stones, which are critical, and the following brief statement is made solely with a view to a date found in the following section. The alignments proposed are all valid for dates in the neighbourhood of 3625 BC, for *rising* stars (with azimuth, assumed extinction altitude, declination and year in parentheses): Spica, in chambers U and V (63.7°, 2.1°, 17.53°, 3630); the Pleiades in chamber Y (101.8°, 4.4°, −3.99°, 3640); and Betelgeuse in chamber Z (109.9°, 2.0°, −10.85°, 3610). It

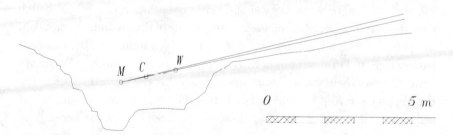

FIG. 31. Section of the northern ditch of the West Kennet Long Barrow near the end of the section marked *B* in Fig. 26. An adult male (eye at *M*) of average stature would have stood in the ditch bottom to see the brief appearance of Sirius over the tomb. A woman or shorter person (eye at *W*) or even a child (eye at *C*) could in principle have seen the same phenomenon. Of the two rays marked, the upper is at 13.5° to the horizontal, and the lower at 12.5°.

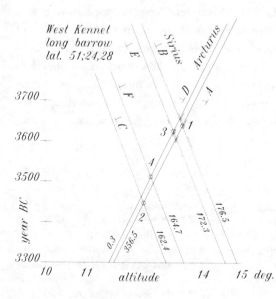

FIG. 32. Years at which the two stars Sirius and Arcturus could have been seen at right angles to the various sections (*A* to *F*) of the West Kennet barrow, plotted against altitude. The years corresponding to equal altitude viewing in opposite directions are marked with circles. Azimuths from north are marked on the graphs. The broken lines in the neighbourhood of points 1 and 3 represent shifts in azimuth of half a degree.

is conceivable that beta Tauri[12] was to be seen at W and Antares[13] at X in the western chamber.

It is assumed here that the star Spica entered chambers U and V, although once the chambers were surrounded by the rubble of the mound, the ray could not pass into V at all. At the time of foundation it might have been allowed free passage, and in entertaining this possibility one is reminded of Wayland's Smithy, where there was a strong presumption that the vertical stones of the chamber were set up astronomically before the building of the mound was begun around it, and without any hope of astronomical use thereafter. (The capping stones were presumably—but not necessarily—dragged up some sort of inclined plane, but even this need not have been the mound itself.) Surely the same is true at West Kennet. Several of the stones there are notable for their relatively flat faces, and the very fact that there are so many good parallel lines in the plan of the chamber might be thought to hint at alignment on common stars. In fact three stones (chambers U and V) seem to align on the setting alpha Centauri, three stones (chamber W and the western chamber) on the setting Procyon, and three (chambers Z and Y) on the setting Deneb. All this holds good for dates within two centuries of 3600 BC; and there are potential alignments too on Spica, Bellatrix, and Antares. The greatest problem here is that it is impossible to quote azimuths without an inordinate number of qualifications: the stones are at most a couple of metres across, they have been moved slightly in their long history, and in some cases their hidden sides were possibly those used in aligning them. Uncertainties of two or three degrees (even of one degree, taking averages) leave too much room for doubt over specifics. That the plan of the chamber has a definite geometrical rationale can

---

12 The star beta Tauri is not as bright as those introduced previously, but it was one of the two dozen brightest stars in the sky, and the second brightest in our constellation of the Bull. In what was to become conventional, it was the star at the tip of the Bull's northern horn. As in the case of Aldebaran, one can only conjecture that it had an association with bulls, for the builders of the tomb. In plan, the stone parts of the barrow certainly have a rough resemblance to a bull's head—with the horns of the domesticated short-horn, rather than the lofty horns of its ancestors usually depicted on the bull in the sky. Whether or not this was accidental, it is hard to believe that building took place without a small-scale plan or model, of wood or stone. The tip of the southern horn is the much fainter star zeta Tauri (magnitude 3.0). This too could have been seen through the entrance, but not along one of the well-defined directions.

13 Antares is encountered here for the first time. There is much leeway in the placing of the relevant line of sight. Antares was the fourteenth brightest in the Wessex sky, the brightest in what for us is the constellation of the Scorpion.

hardly be denied, however; and we are certainly not short of independent evidence that Neolithic geometry and stellar astronomy were closely allied.

The West Kennet Ditches

There is good reason for assuming that viewing would have taken place across the West Kennet barrow, in accordance with the double principle of viewing at right angles to the barrow—here closely parallel to the line of the nearby ditch—at equal altitudes from *opposite* sides. Any lingering doubts as to the broad correctness of these ideas should fade as the pairing of the ditch-sections stipulated earlier is investigated. As before, in all cases an initial search is made for possible stars, within the limits set by the barrow's form and age. There can be little doubt that the star observed across sections A and D looking north was Arcturus, while looking south across any of the four northern sections, Sirius was most probably the main object of attention. (Rigel is a candidate that initially falls by the wayside, since it seems to provide dates between 3222 and 3057 BC. These dates are much too late, if the radiocarbon dates available are to be believed.) Here are the two brightest stars in the sky.

In discussing similar cases at an earlier stage, little was said about the errors involved in the method. At West Kennet the situation is precarious, for the only part of the ditch so far excavated is close to being in the worst of all possible places, that is, near the change of direction from B to C (Fig. 26). Putting everything aside for the time being except the directions of the ditch (and matching barrow edge), all of them involving averaging over sizeable lengths, our principles lead to the following results—quoted with pseudo-precision, without any regard for their qualities.

Viewing at right angles to *edges near at hand* (this will prove to be the likelier option):

(1) across sections A and B, viewing at 13.5° in 3638 BC

(2) across sections A and C, viewing at 12.5° in 3447 BC

(3) across sections D and E, viewing at 13.3° in 3624 BC

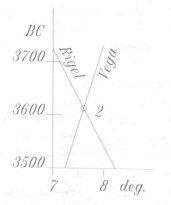

FIG. 33.   A supplement to Fig. 32, with the graphs for Rigel (across C) and Vega (across A), both observed by observers at ground level, but at the same period as Sirius and Arcturus from the ditches.

(4) across sections *D* and *F*, viewing at 12.7° in 3512 BC.

Viewing at right angles to *far edges*:

(5) across sections *A* and *B*, viewing at 13.4° in 3677 BC

(6) across sections *A* and *C*, viewing at 14.5° in 3395 BC

(7) across sections *D* and *E*, viewing at 13.8° in 3677 BC

(8) across sections *D* and *F*, viewing at 14.5° in 3514 BC.

In the case of West Kennet it appears that the two different starting points make only about forty years difference to the final results at the head of the barrow, and almost none at the tail. There is a slightly more material difference in the sizes of the derived viewing angles, however. Combining the very limited evidence of the one known ditch section with the height of the mound opposite it, an angle of about 11.9° is obtained for that point. Since some slight settlement and loss of the surface layer can be assumed, any angle between 12° and 14° must be considered acceptable. The height of the observer's eye is taken as 1.6 m, following the male skeleton sizes at the barrow itself. Even those of smaller stature could be accommodated, for as will be seen from Fig. 31, there was a viewing platform which could have been used by people of all heights above about 1.10 m—so perhaps even children were admitted to the ritual of observing the stars over the barrows. There is some later support for this intimation of democracy, in the ditches at Stonehenge, Woodhenge, Mount Pleasant, and elsewhere.

The later date is here preferred to the earlier. This preference is partly because the later dates fit better with the radiocarbon date (from three specimens of human bone from the barrow, giving a calendar range of 3575±215 BC), and partly it implies marginally smaller viewing angles and *a mound of reducing height in relation to the observer*.

The head of the barrow seems to be a few years later than the third section. This need not be real, for it must be accepted that our azimuths are subject to error. The results spelled out above are shown graphically in Fig. 32, and broken lines in the neighbourhood of the points representing (1) and (3) are added to show the errors to be expected corresponding to errors in azimuth of half a degree. Roughly speaking, a single error of this amount moves the date by four years. A less superficial analysis might one day therefore easily reverse the order of building these sections.

There are two small residual problems. The year under (2), is obviously entirely spurious, as therefore is the altitude too. It would be interesting to find from future excavation how the altitude was handled in this region. Perhaps levels were changed to preserve the visibility of one star, or to substitute another. One possibility is that section *C* of the ditch was simply

being made to change direction to link up with a section (E) that had already been—or was planned to be—cut with a different orientation from B 's. But why change direction at all? The answer had perhaps something to do with the wish to reduce the barrow's height, and with the lie of the natural ground making up the tail of the barrow. The last date quoted, however, would seem to indicate that an addition was made to the mound, over a century after the first mound. The only other likely explanation is that viewing angles were not being kept equal, or equal enough.

There is an interesting alternative explanation, that might be extended to preserve the integrity of the entire barrow. Before explaining it, one must consider the way in which the ditches would have been used to observe Arcturus and Sirius. These stars would both have been seen behaving in a very striking and memorable way. At Wessex latitudes Arcturus did not rise and set at all over a level horizon; but here, looking from the southern ditch over the barrow, the star would have dipped down to touch the tomb, seeming to rest there, and then have risen again about half an hour afterwards. Some four and a half hours after that, Sirius would have risen over the tomb, as seen from the northern ditch, and again in much the same time would have sunk back into it at a point not far away.

The two brightest stars were not alone in these comings and goings. Vega would have copied the behaviour of Arcturus very closely, descending into the tomb and rising again, although as seen from the ditch it would have lacked the finesse of Arcturus. In fact the optimum altitude for observing Vega during the period in question (around 3620 BC) would have been a low angle of 7.8°, if the star was to be viewed at right angles to section A, as Arcturus had been viewed. Vega's visitation would then have begun almost simultaneously with Sirius' re-emergence.

On what grounds can it be claimed that this additional item of very striking behaviour was in fact observed? Quite simply on the grounds that the angle 7.8° is close to what should be expected—if the mound height conforms to the altitudes found from the ditch—for *an observer standing at ground level* near the back edge of ditch A.

Having gone so far, did the people of West Kennet leave matters in such an unsymmetrical state? Could they not find a fourth star, in the southern sky, to complete this remarkable pattern? They undoubtedly did so, and the star was Rigel. Rigel, like Sirius, rises only a little way out of the tomb and then quickly falls back in again. On this occasion an altitude of about 7.5° is needed, and this is so similar to the angle from the ground looking north that we know exactly what we must do. We must consider the possibility that equal altitude

normal viewing took place from ground level across section *A* and the aberrant section *C*. The azimuths taken are 162.4° and 356.5°, and in the usual way an altitude and year are found—7.6° and 3610 BC—at which the arrangement would have been perfect (Fig. 33). It seems probable, therefore, that the ditches will eventually prove to have platforms at the back, at the same level, capable of yielding this common angle.

The anomalous date having been removed, we are now left with a series of dates. Rounding to tens they are (1) 3640, (2) 3610, (3) 3620, and (4) 3510 BC. There is no point in trying to eliminate the spread in the first three dates, in the absence of a more complete excavation. Those dates are so close that for want of better evidence we may take the date of the mound as their mean, 3620 BC. The fourth still seems to indicate a later phase.

The pattern of observing the stellar phenomena was therefore as follows: Arcturus from ditch *A*, Rigel[14] from behind ditch *C*, Sirius from ditch *B*, Vega[15] from behind ditch *A*. The seasonal limits during which these phenomena could have been seen vary from star to star, but all three could in principle have been seen on every clear night between roughly a fortnight before the autumnal equinox and a month before the winter solstice. The interval between the mid period of Arcturus' visit, and the mid period of Vega's visit the same night, was about six hours.

At this six-hour period, and in this way, the West Kennet people had evidently contrived a series of apparitions, involving four spectacularly well-chosen stars, of a character that might have been interpreted as somehow relating to the spirits of the dead. Only one star visible in Wessex was the equal of any of these four. (Capella was then Vega's equal—it is now less bright—and both were brighter than Rigel. Canopus, second only to Sirius, never rose at these latitudes, and was unknown.) It would be hard to imagine a simpler monumental design showing more intellectual brilliance than this.

There is, in conclusion, a remote possibility that Sirius might have played a part in the selection of the West Kennet site many centuries before the present

---

14 The star Rigel—designated beta Orionis, as though it was the second brightest in the constellation of Orion—is and was then much the brightest, although Betelgeuse is variable. Rigel was the fifth brightest star in the Wessex sky. Very few constellation figures are suggestive of the shapes seen in them by the creators of stellar myths, but the belted human figure of Orion, whether seen as hunter or warrior, seems to have been an exception. If he faces us, Rigel is the star at his left foot (on our right)—it is to the foot that the Arabic name Rigel refers.

15 Vega, third equal in brightness in the Wessex sky, was the brightest star in the constellation the Greeks knew as the Zither or Lyre. It has a pale sapphire brilliance. Its name has an Arabic origin, but the star is mentioned in early Greek and Babylonian sources.

long barrow was built. It is a strange property of the entrance to the barrow that, from it, two low hills to the south are more or less symmetrically arranged, one 37.3° west of south, the other 38.8° east of south. Although these angles are not equal, neither are the altitudes. (With five-metre trees, for instance, the altitudes would have been 1.8° and 1.2° respectively.) This fact compensates almost perfectly in the case of Sirius, so that if it rose precisely over one hill it set precisely over the other. Without trees, this would have been so around the year 4460 BC. Trees would have brought the date a decade or two later. The hills are not prominent, and the early date must seem very improbable, but the possibility is a very curious one. Even stranger is the fact that at exactly the *same* period it fits the star Rigel Centauri[16] (not to be confused with Rigel), which has the same declination as Sirius in the year 4450 BC. Whether or not this is a pure coincidence, it seems worth putting on record.

The same property fits the star beta Centauri in the forty-second century and Rigel in the thirty-fifth. The Rigel case could not explain the choice of site, although the other might.

The West Kennet Neighbourhood. Silbury Hill

The East Kennet barrow, the later of the two neighbours, is now tree-covered, and has not been excavated in recent times. Except in orientation, it seems to resemble its neighbour: it is only a metre or so longer, there are signs of a sarsen burial chamber, and there are traces of flanking ditches. The barrow as a whole looks as though it might have been aligned on the rising of Rigel. On the basis of its direction, about 145°, it might be tentatively placed not far in time from the West Kennet barrow. In view of the sophistication of the latter it would be foolish to draw any conclusion about a cult of Rigel. Such might have lasted here until the building of the artificial mound at nearby Silbury Hill, however,

---

16 The star Rigel Centauri or alpha Centauri will not often be found proposed here for any important alignment. It is one of the brightest in the sky (magnitude 0.00), although it was somewhat less bright in the fourth millennium than now (magnitude 0.19 in 3200 BC). It was then the seventh brightest fixed star visible from southern England, and of course the brightest in the constellation of the Centaur—the man-horse called Chiron in Greek mythology. The name 'Rigel Centauri' is as much a hybrid as 'Chiron': it is a mixture of Arabic and Latinized Greek, and means simply 'the Centaur's foot'. The 'Rigel' here is not to be confused with our other Rigel, the star that is accounted Orion's foot. The two are now very close in brightness, but then Orion's foot was the brighter. Alpha Centauri has not been visible from English latitudes during the last four thousand years, but in the fourth millennium BC it rose to a point well above the horizon.

FIG. 34.   The character of the internal structure of Silbury Hill.

for the star would have been visible from the top of that mound, rising over the East Kennet barrow in the late third millennium. Against this idea is the fact that the first stages of the construction of the hill had begun centuries before—but in the mid-fourth millennium, Sirius would have had the same property. There are too many imponderables about the height reached at various times for any specific claim to be made.

It seems likely that when two monuments were involved in a stellar alignment, the star was seen from the newer and over the older of the two. (The converse arrangement would have been perfectly possible, of course.) The principle seems to be illustrated at West Kennet. The Sanctuary, a succession of concentric circles, first of timber and later of stone, was to the east of the long barrow, across the valley of the river Kennet, and on its own small hill. (Its name was one used by local people, according to Stukeley.) Robbed of its stone in the eighteenth century, the site was rediscovered and excavated in 1930 by Maud Cunnington. As seen from the centre of that succession of circles, the West Kennet barrow would have been in a direction about 8.5° south of west, and at about 0.5° altitude, slightly less than that of the spur of the hill behind the barrow. Aldebaran could have been seen setting over the barrow when the star's declination was about −3.96° (taking its extinction angle of 2.0° as the deciding altitude). This was its value in approximately 2800 BC, a date compatible with other archaeological evidence relating to the early phases of the Sanctuary. There is a pair of post holes defining a diameter of the oldest structure (Sanctuary IA) in exactly the required line.

The most impressive of the monuments immediately surrounding the West Kennet barrow is Silbury Hill. Built on a spur of chalkland, its base is nearly 30 m below the level of the barrow, and yet the Hill rises 10 m or so higher. (Its top is currently about 3 m lower than the East Kennet barrow.) It is a cone, with steepest slope close to 30°—a gradient that was perhaps chosen deliberately for its 'one in two' property, one unit rise to two up the slope. Several exploratory tunnels have been dug into the hill, the latest of them by Richard Atkinson (1968–70), who suggested four phases in its construction. After the first two phases had been completed, the hill was still not particularly

remarkable for its height. It is probable that there was never any primary burial there. Certainly none has ever been found, although some have suspected that the shaft from an eighteenth-century excavation destroyed signs of one. The third phase required a change of plan, resulting in a stepped cone. The stepping can still be easily seen by the casual observer. The last phase was an extension of the main ditch to the west, presumed to be for chalk to fill in the steps. The overall construction involved moving well over 300,000 cubic metres of chalk—less than would have been needed had part of its base not been the end of the spur of the natural hill—and those responsible for the third phase especially knew much about soil mechanics, for they gave it great stability through a series of internal walls, built out of chalk blocks, the resulting cells being then filled with rubble (see Fig. 34).

What was the final purpose of this extraordinary structure? Since it is thought to have been four or five centuries in the making, one need not suppose that its purpose remained unchanged. Attempts have been made to find an astronomical explanation for it. In 1902 the American writer Moses B. Cotsworth, in his *Rational Almanack*, suggested that it carried a colossal gnomon to cast shadows on the world's largest sundial, marked out on the ground below. He was evidently influenced by the Rev. Edward Duke, who in 1846 had made it out to be the centre of a vast planetarium on which the planets were represented by 'temples' in the neighbourhood: Stonehenge was Saturn, Avebury was the Sun and Moon, and so on. One must be charitable to all enthusiasts, in the hope of being treated likewise. Sundials and planetaria are really no more exotic than the vision of one respected contemporary archaeologist, Marija Gimbutas, who sees the hill as 'a gigantic representation of the Pregnant [Earth Mother] Goddess in a seated position'.[17]

There is a range of Silbury radiocarbon dates running from 2725±110 down to 2145±95 bc. The extremes of this range correspond to 3630 and 2500 BC in calendar years. Building probably began a century or so after the West Kennet barrow, an undertaking by the same group of people.

From Silbury Hill, the West Kennet barrow is nearer and more prominent than that at East Kennet. The *place* where it stands is such that looking over the head of the future West Kennet barrow from a point at the centre of Silbury Hill, Rigel could have been seen rising in the thirty-ninth century. The place

---

17 One property of Silbury Hill that appears to have gone without previous comment is that, as viewed from the Sanctuary, it fills what would otherwise be a notch in the natural horizon in that direction—and it appears to come more or less up to the level of the flanking natural horizon (around 0.6°). Spica could have been seen setting at its extinction angle over Silbury Hill in approximately 2480 BC. Again, however, the fact may be of no significance.

of rising would gradually have moved to the forecourt area, and eventually off the scene completely, but at the date accepted here for the foundation of the present barrow, namely 3625 BC, beta Centauri rose precisely over the chamber as seen from the same point. An earlier long barrow near Windmill Hill (Horslip) is more or less on the same line, and the East Kennet barrow is near it too, so that many further possibilities are added to the list—for example, Rigel rose over the place of the future West Kennet chamber as seen from the Horslip barrow in 3710 BC. It might be thought that when barrows are not intimately related—for instance directed one towards another, as at Fussell's Lodge—such alignments are best ignored. That they are part of a conscious strategy covering a much wider territory, however, will be demonstrated in the following chapter. (Maps will also be found there and in Chapter 6 showing the principal long barrows and other prehistoric remains in the West Kennet region. See Figs. 69 and 101.)

Beckhampton Road. Stars and the Sun

The long barrow off Beckhampton Road lies less than 4 km west of that at West Kennet. As mentioned earlier, it is one of an important trio excavated between 1959 and 1967—in this case in 1964 under the direction of I. F. Smith. It was described by William Stukeley in 1743 as 'pyriform' (pear-shaped), and 'longish, but broad at one end'. It had been over 50 m long, and was originally flanked by splayed ditches, with its broad end roughly northeast. That end had been transformed when a round barrow was superimposed on it, millennia before nineteenth-century farmers levelled and ploughed the whole thing. In that same century it was dug into by archaeologists too. One of them, John Thurnam, recruited his labour from among his patients at the Wiltshire County Asylum in Devizes. Despite all of this activity, the ground beneath the barrow retained a few secrets of immense interest, to be recovered in the modern excavations.

Especially important were signs of the care with which directional properties had been assigned to the barrow. A row of stake holes was found to run along the axis, changing direction abruptly in a middle section, before returning to the original direction. Offset from this bent axis were traces of further straight rows of stake holes, making for at least twenty bays at the wider end. The staking out of some of the bays on the northern side, where the round barrow had been superimposed, and probably that of others at the narrower end, have been lost. Other rows of stake holes mark the edges of the mound, and those to the southeast side make an extremely well-defined line. Some rows

were pushed out of true by the weight of soil, although much care had obviously gone into establishing them in the first place. Generally speaking, stake holes had a depth of from 15 to 60 cm, and the stakes, of diameters up to about 8 cm, had been pointed, so they must have been hammered into the ground. Much the same procedures were followed at the South Street barrow.

In Fig. 35, the better-defined rows of stake holes have been indicated, that is, when they are of reasonable length and have clearly not suffered distortion through soil pressure. (To see the individual holes, the original report will have to be consulted.) The excavation brought to light even more valuable structural evidence than this, in the form of hollow casts representing rods and poles that had been used in various ways and had later rotted. Traces of poles were found to the side of each row. They had clearly been tied in some way to the uprights, certainly not to hold back the material of the mound, but surely to fix a straight line. The line was important because it was what settled the precise form of the barrow, and on the assumptions made here that form was intimately related to a line of sight. From signs of accidental spillage of material during the construction it was clear to the excavators that the bays, or opposite pairs of bays, were built one at a time.

Bays such as those at Beckhampton Road are reminiscent of others in barrows at Sarnowo (Poland), Skendleby (Lincolnshire), Ascott-under-Wychwood (Oxfordshire), and the neighbouring South Street barrow. Paul Ashbee has noted, furthermore, that various Cotswold long barrows dug into in the nineteenth century were found to be split axially and into bays with stones, and that stake holes might there have been missed. The Beckhampton Road barrow is an important guide to the meaning of these bays, and it is no exaggeration to describe them as an astronomical plan, analogous to the scaling posts of the barrows at Fussell's Lodge and Wayland's Smithy.

The stake holes constituting the bent axis of the barrow begin and end (*rr*) at two almost perfectly identical azimuths, paralleled at the northeastern end by the bounding rows *p* and *t*. The accuracy with which these are laid out is noteworthy: averaged over their lengths, the mean azimuth is 49.8°. It gives great satisfaction to find that the transverse lines of stake holes turn out to be perpendicular to one side or the other, for this is exactly what our principle of perpendicular viewing at equal altitudes leads us to expect. As explained earlier in this chapter, however, it is chastening to find that the *b*-rows are at right angles to features on the opposite edge of the mound, judging by row *q* to the distant side. There can be no doubt that viewing was along the lines of the *b*-rows from the southeastern ditch (sector *EG* at the very least), and that viewing was along the lines of rows *a* looking southeast from ditch sector *AB*

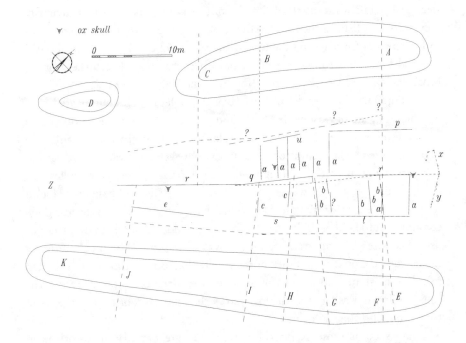

FIG. 35.   The overall structure of the Beckhampton Road long barrow, as indicated by the ditches, the approximate edges of the mound (coarse broken lines) and selected rows of stake holes (continuous lines within the mound). A few individual stake holes are marked at the northeast. These are joined by broken lines (*x* and *y*). Note the precision with which they cross on the axis, and note also the merest hint of a scaling-post construction near the letter *x*. Where transverse stake hole rows are close to parallel, they are labelled with the same letter: there are only three clear groups. Judging by consistency alone, the estimated edges of the ditch and the mound are plainly less reliable as astronomical indicators than the stake hole rows. The ditches are divided into sectors (see letters *A* to *K*) according to supposed astronomical function. Ox skulls were found at the points marked.

and perhaps *BC*. The mound edges seem to be perversely arranged, but they matter less than the ridges. The *a*-rows are well suited to row *r*, but not to row *q*, and the *b*-rows to row *q* (where they are not to be found) but not to row *r*.

Does this not fit uncomfortably with the principle of perpendicular viewing? Not at all. The axial rows cannot be taken as a simple ridge line. The supposed lines of sight would have been tangential to the mound below the ridge, unless the spine came to a sharp edge. Any axial ridge would not have been strictly seen, and would have been slightly flattened, if only by weathering, so that the effective ridge would have been double. The angle of view on this occasion was almost certainly about 15.3°. The reasoning follows the

principles laid down earlier. Starting from the azimuths of *a* and *b* (both derived with the help of longer rows *t* and *s* but not the less reliable edge of a turves line *e*), stars at equal altitudes are sought. Ditch depths are compatible with this idea, although further excavation of them would not come amiss. From azimuths 135.8° and 309.8° and a latitude of 51° 24' 28", it seems that the setting of Deneb was observed to the northwest and the rising of Bellatrix to the southeast. A strict application of previous principles, overlooking imperfections in their implementation, provides a common altitude 15.32° and a year of 3320 BC. There are many imponderables here, but the date is probably accurate to better than a century. (The altitude is finely tuned, since Deneb's declination changes so slowly, and no other bright star offers itself.) As for the date, it is perhaps not without significance that the mid-section of the barrow (row *q*) aligned accurately on the setting of Rigel around 3320 BC, over the *natural* horizon.

Stukeley's 'pyriform' barrow was so only because it had been deformed by the later addition of a round barrow to the wider end. It is clear that it originally had a trapezoidal form, and since the ditches extend so far to the southwest, we must suppose that the barrow ended in the neighbourhood of Z (Fig. 35). The directions of lines *x* and *y* were clearly those of a chevron-shaped façade. How this was used is less clear, but over natural ground, Pollux set in the direction of *x* (around 3360 BC) and beta Centauri rose in the direction of *y* in 3380 BC—or say a century earlier with a cover of seven-metre trees.[18]

The lines of *x* and *y* meet almost precisely on the *axis*, at a point well fitted, therefore, for a triple observation, if only there were something to be seen along this part of the main axis. There was indeed something to be seen: the last glint of the setting midwinter Sun (that is, at the solstice) was along this line. Precise dating is impossible, but taking the azimuth as 226.2° (it differs from that of the westernmost part of the axis by half a degree) and the altitude of the horizon set by a treeless valley floor as 2.3°, the direction is virtually perfect for the period in question. Viewing could have been along the ridge itself, given a platform on which to stand, but it would have been easier to look along the edges *p* and *t*. Long barrows may bend, but never, as far as can be seen, in such a way as to block views along their edges at the head of the barrow.

This is a highly significant finding—the first Wessex long barrow considered here that clearly incorporated an alignment on the Sun, although there must surely be many more, since six or seven centuries earlier a Lincolnshire

---

18 The star Pollux is the brighter of Gemini, the Twins—Castor and Pollux in Greek mythology. It was thirteenth in brightness in the Wessex sky.

long barrow (Skendleby 2) had done the same, and a square, overtly humble, but cleverly designed barrow at Grendon in Northamptonshire had done so too, say a century before South Street. (They will be discussed later in this chapter.) Sirius and important stars in Orion were within a degree of aligning, but not to the standards of accuracy found previously. The alignments of later circular monuments were almost invariably on the Sun and Moon, and it seems probable that the Beckhampton Road long barrow was colonized by the builders of the round barrow at its head precisely because it aligned on midwinter sunset.

Three ox skulls were found more or less in the line of the ridge, which again gave rise to speculation that the ox heads, perhaps with skins and hooves attached, had been set up on posts penetrating the back of the barrow. There is no sign of Aldebaran here, but as it happens there is an independent case to be made out for a switch of bull symbolism to midwinter sunset.

The main disadvantage of the scaling posts of the old structures at Wayland's Smithy and Fussell's Lodge was that they required a transference of levels, not very difficult when structures were of wood, but more so with earthen mounds. In some way or another, a horizon had to be built up until it produced the desired effect—but strictly in accordance with the requirements of right-angled viewing. There would have been only minor difficulties with the progressive shaping of the artificial horizon, as the bays were filled in, one by one, until at last rising and setting were seen in the required directions. The main intellectual problem was quite different: it was that of settling the directions. To reconstruct the method it is necessary to make a conjecture as to the starting point. There is a strong sense in which Beckhampton Road is a Rigel barrow. Rigel is the brightest of the stars concerned, and the alignment on it belongs to the site in the pre-barrow period. Assuming, then, that this was the star from which the builders began, here is a potential procedure:

> Some method or other is needed to establish the positions of a pair of ridge poles at equal heights and at right angles to the lines of view to opposed stars, northern and southern in this case. Once they were established, ditches could be marked out, if not extensively dug at this stage, with appropriate sections parallel to the ridge-poles. There was still a degree of freedom left to the architects, who would have tried to accommodate other stars in their length-wise barrow lines. The central portion of the line of stakes will be assumed to align on the setting of Rigel, and the other pair on Deneb and Bellatrix:
>
> (1) The stake holes XX were arranged to be in line with Rigel's setting.
> (2) Fences of stakes, to which poles were tied as cross-pieces, were set at right angles to that first line, and a viewing ditch cut parallel to it, for sighting on Bellatrix. Horizontal poles were raised along the ridge line until the star rises

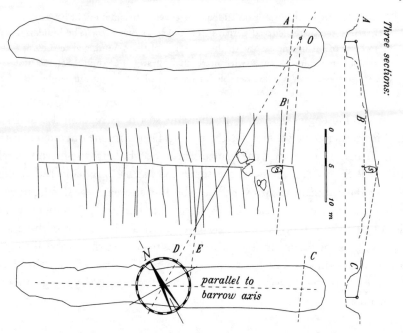

FIG. 36. The overall plan of the South Street barrow. The three most important sections are combined into one, for convenience, at the right. They correspond to the broken lines A, B, and C on the plan. Lines of sight to the eyes of observers in possible viewing positions, at approximately the correct calculated angle, are shown on those sections—which are, however, not perfectly chosen for our present purposes. The diagonal line of stakes (D) crosses the entire barrow. The larger sarsens are marked on the plan (notably S), in their present positions. On section B, however, sarsen S is placed upright, as it might at one time have stood, even before the barrow.

at that level and in the direction set by the transverse stakes. Hides could have been draped over them to give an obscuring horizon. The lengths of such poles would have been between 1.5 m and 3 m, and their weight offers no problem. Infilling of ditch material to make a solid horizon might have begun at this stage—in slices almost the reverse of an archaeological dig.

(3) A provisional ditch was started for viewing Deneb. (Approximate positions were of course known all along.) Another ridge-pole, at precisely the same level, was varied in its orientation until Deneb was seen to set precisely at right angles to it. Fences of stakes at right angles to the Deneb ridge-pole could then have been set up to confirm the arrangement, with viewing directions again made more easily visible by poles tied along them. This established perhaps all remaining directions.

(4) Ditches could next have been completed and the fences largely filled in. An arch of spaced parallel poles, like stringers in the body of an aircraft, could have been tied to the rows of stakes, to define the barrow's form, although the removal of the stakes from one section might have been thought necessary

before an adjacent section was added. The curve of the arch might have been
fixed by templates, curved perhaps like longbows, with tow. The builders'
job was to fill up the arch with the materials of the mound, and to dress it
smooth in a suitable way—with marl, chalk gravel, and turves. Section by
section the barrow was so assembled, its wedge-like shape guaranteed by the
lines of the ditches.

Assuming angles derived from the same sort of astronomical analysis as
used for earlier barrows, now for the setting Deneb in one direction and the
rising Bellatrix in the other, the resulting profile of the barrow conforms closely
with I. F. Smith's estimates of the shape the barrow originally had. Pollen
analysis showed that the barrow had been built in an area of grassland, but with
arable and wooded areas nearby. This barrow was not on high ground, and the
best of all possible motives for the relatively steep angles of view of those who
looked across the barrow from the ditches was to observe the stars well clear of
nearby trees—in this case 15 m trees further away than 75 m would have
presented no problem except in the line of the barrow—that lay along an arable
valley floor.

South Street

The last of the important trio of long barrows in this district is that off South
Street in the parish of Avebury. It was erected in an area of arable land that had
been cleared in the early fourth millennium BC. The surrounding country,
predominantly woodland, contained hawthorn, oak, birch, elm, alder, pine,
and other species, with all-pervasive hazel scrub invading the open pasture
from time to time. It will be shown that this barrow was always extremely
humble in outward appearance and material structure, and as an artificial
horizon set rather low altitudes, but that it was high enough for sight-lines to
clear nearby scrub and woodland. William Stukeley, in his book *Abury* (1743),
described it as 'broad and flat, as if sunk into the ground with age'; but broad
and flat it had always been. Humble though it appeared, it embodied a most
beautiful astronomical symmetry, and one that leaves us in no doubt that the
people of Wessex were still actively developing their art.

The barrow was excavated under the direction of J. G. Evans in 1966–7.
The road—South Street—runs across a corner of it, and the site has been much
ravaged by time, not to mention proximity to the village. There are two large
standing stones 120 m to the west of it, known as the Longstones, or Adam
and Eve, but these belong to a much later period, as will be shown in connection
with the Avebury avenues. Although there are no great quantities of stone in
any of the three Avebury barrows, here at South Street there are several large

and small sarsens at its principal end, and the larger stones were evidently set in place before the main construction, since all lines of stake holes curve round them where necessary. This barrow repeats in several respects the structure at Beckhampton Road, revealing a similarly straight row of stake holes defining an axis, and indeed more complete transverse rows than at that other barrow. The South Street barrow was divided by them into about 20 bays to each side of the axis. Again they were occasionally deformed in places by pressure of the mound, and again there were numerous traces of collapsed rods that had originally been fixed to them. There is a pair of ditches, uninterrupted in the South Street case, and splayed but not very markedly so. A simplified plan of the site as a whole is shown in Fig. 36, where rows of stake holes are represented by continuous lines (marking the axis and bays). Once again, those who dislike the element of approximation in all this may consult the original publication for the many hundreds of holes.

Applying the principle of viewing at equal altitudes, it is found that looking across the ditches, along the directions set by the bay-fences, Vega was observed rising in the northeast, and that Sirius was seen setting at an altitude of about 9° to the southwest. The date was in the neighbourhood of 3260 BC. A date seven centuries earlier, with Arcturus and Bellatrix, is rejected because it makes for an improbably high barrow, in fact over 5 m along the spine. The radiocarbon dates also speak against that solution.

This very general conclusion has to be qualified in several respects, since the large number of paired lines of stake holes means a large number of solutions, and not all are superficially in agreement. As Fig. 36 shows, these lines are by no means constant in direction, but it would of course be mistaken to take averages of azimuths, north and south. While—on our basic assumption—opposed altitudes are ideally *equal*, it need not be supposed that they were *constant* along the whole length of the ditches. Until the ditches are fully excavated we shall remain ignorant of the pattern of altitudes, but even now it can be said categorically that (1) the known ditches were almost perfectly equal in depth (in relation to the Ordnance Datum rather than surface levels) at the eastern end; and that (2) the ditch floor was somewhat lower there than in the neighbourhood of the point at which the compass rose is placed on Fig. 36. This second fact, that might at first sight seem to refute our basic principles, will on the contrary eventually serve to vindicate them.

From a naïve application of the principle of equal-altitude viewing, ten of the twenty pairs of stake hole rows are found to be usable to yield ten corresponding dates (and altitudes). The graphs giving a result for the *first bay* (actually based on the second pair of fences) are shown on the right-hand side

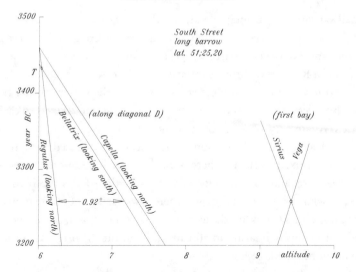

FIG. 37.   The dating of the South Street barrow. On the right, the graphs for the setting of Sirius as seen in line with the first bay from the north ditch and the rising of Vega as seen similarly from the south, meet opposite the year 3260 and altitude 9.42°. On the left is the evidence for the sighting of Regulus and Bellatrix along the line of the diagonal row of stake posts at about the same time, but now at altitudes differing by about 0.92°. On the case of Capella, see the text.

of Fig. 37. The date derived is 3260 BC and the altitude 9.42°. Until such time as further information on the ditches becomes available, this result will be the most reliable of the ten, since the corresponding observers are known to have stood at equal depths. Performing the same calculation for all ten of the straightest pairs of rows of stake holes, one finds a mean result of 3220 BC, but this is certainly less reliable than the first result, since it is known that not all corresponding points in the ditches further west are at exactly equal levels.

The date of 3260 BC, probably good to within half a century, fits well with two out of four radiocarbon dates obtained from the site. The four, briefly, are these: from oak under the mound (2810±130 bc, equivalent to 3535±165 BC); from an ox vertebra (2750±135 bc, 3495±150 BC); from a red deer antler, north ditch (2670±140 bc, 3360±260 BC); from another, second bay of the mound (2580±110 bc, 3190±150 BC).

Without a knowledge of precisely where the observer stood, it is impossible to give a precise height for the barrow at the eastern end, but it was very close indeed to the height of a man's eye above the carefully levelled ground on which the mound was erected (see sections at the right hand side of Fig. 36). This means that it was just possible to look over the barrow from its façade, for instance, in ways that might have been indulged in before the barrow was built.

The calculated height in question is so close to the length of the sarsen marked *S* on the figure that it is tempting to suppose that it originally stood upright. It needed no significant stone hole, since it would have been held up by the chalk of the mound. This was not the opinion of the excavator, J. G. Evans, however, who noted that the mound material gave no evidence of collapse. He noted too that the three largest had been prepared for the positions in which they were found by having a slice of stone removed. We might have been inclined to see in *S* not a sighting stone but a stone that was meant to remain only just covered by the mound. Oddly enough, although it is too low for the mound in its prone position, it could have served this very purpose at an earlier stage, when a still lower angle had to be set by the mound. (This lower angle will be discussed later.) Attrition of such carefully prepared mounds by rain, wind, and invading plants must have been a serious problem, and regular shaping must surely have taken place.

Other sarsens shown on our figure seem to have had a part to play in the planning of the diagonal *D*, and the spine as far as the third and fourth bays. The idiosyncratic line of stakes marked *E* in the diagram was very probably a simple alignment on the rising Deneb—but this explanation must be abandoned if the southern ditch eventually turns out not to be unusually shallow.

Had there been only the transverse rows and the ditches, South Street would have added nothing to what has already been discovered about long-barrow astronomical practice, but a most unusual aspect of this barrow lies precisely in that very straight row (*D*) of stake holes that ran diagonally across it. As emphasized by the placing of the compass rose in the figure, this line has a most beautiful symmetry with the axial line of stake holes, for the angle between them is almost perfectly bisected by a north–south line.

There are two possible explanations for this diagonal, one of them almost certainly correct, the other perhaps true of an earlier period of history. If, before the barrow was built, observations had been made at the same horizon altitudes along the two lines (axis and diagonal), both to the south or both to the north, then the symmetry implies that the same star would have been seen rising along one line and setting along the other. In the case of the South Street barrow, horizon altitudes were far from being equal in any pair of the four key directions, but this offers no problem, for the stars to be seen rising and setting in this way would have been seen at their extinction angles—Pollux to the north around 3600 BC or Bellatrix to the south around 3920 BC. In either case, therefore, one could have expected perfect symmetry with respect to the north–south line. As it happens, the Pollux date falls comfortably within the range of radiocarbon dates obtained from the piece of oak found under the

mound. This is surely not the date of the mound as it is now known, or of the diagonal row of stakes, but it is quite possible that the direction was embodied in some nearby material structure—say a pair of stones or another barrow. In fact at a distance of only 300 m the line runs along the southern edge of another long barrow (one of three parallel barrows northwest of the Beckhampton roundabout).

Whatever the truth of this explanation, why the diagonal line was incorporated into the barrow itself is of more immediate interest, and can be explained in a different way, not necessarily ruling out the first. It is difficult to give a precise argument for want of data from the ditches, but the rising of Regulus could have been observed along it to the northeast and the setting of Bellatrix to the southwest. Assuming that the line was regarded as very important, the entire mound could have been designed around it, with these new stars in mind. Perhaps somewhere else in the neighbourhood, or perhaps on this very site, these two stars were regularly observed along this line at equal altitudes (just over 6°) in the thirty-fifth century (point T on Fig. 37). Had this been done at South Street—and the radiocarbon dates tell us that this was not impossible—the mound would have been lower then, or the ditches shallower, or both; and then as the years passed, the direction no longer functioned as it had done, and it became necessary to look south at a higher angle than north *in order to keep the old direction*.

By 3260 BC the difference was about 0.92°. Had Capella and Bellatrix been taken as the pair of stars, it would have been found that there was never a time when they could be seen at equal altitudes along the diagonal. As the figure shows, they were much closer, however. The reason for opting for the larger separation is to be found in the ditches. It is not difficult to calculate that no matter what the height of the mound, within reason, the required difference in viewing angles would be provided if the observer looking north were standing about 33 cm higher than the observer looking south. The precise value depends on where in the ditches the observers stood, but on the evidence at present available it seems that there was probably a difference of levels somewhere between 25 and 40 cm. The required viewing altitudes for the year 3260 BC (see the figure) imply a barrow that would have been about 33 cm lower at the crossing point of the diagonal than at the barrow's eastern end. This is precisely a quarter of the way along its length of 36.8 m as judged by the bays—note that it comes after five out of twenty bays. If it sloped regularly, therefore, the barrow would have fallen from 1.66 m at its head to 33 cm in the last bay, measuring above the base so carefully prepared for it.

These proportions are unlikely to have happened by accident, and one

cannot help wondering whether the derived viewing altitude across the first bay, estimated at 9.42°, was not likewise deliberately chosen as a gradient of 1 in 6 (or 9.46°). There is much evidence from a later date for the use of such simple ratios. One can only make this assumption freely, on the other hand, if there was no other constraint, and there can be little doubt that there was one very important constraint accepted by the designers. The first four rows of stake holes on the northern side were almost certainly meant to be *exactly* at right angles to the axis—the average angle was around 89.8° even at the time of the excavation. This was surely the builders' second precondition—the first being *acceptance of the diagonal*. It is unlikely that they waited until the old Bellatrix line (the axis) was at a perfect right angle to a one-in-six Sirius line, before setting up the barrow. Had they done so, however, they would only have been playing yet another round in a science of barrow-symmetry and precise alignment that one suspects was becoming an end in itself.

Skendleby: Giants' Hills 1 and 2. Stars and Sun

While the focus of attention is Wessex practice, there are other important long barrows that are worth mentioning since they reveal so much in common with it. Two of these are at Giants' Hills, Skendleby, Lincolnshire. Both Skendleby barrows were constructed using the technique of fences of stake posts, now emphatically holding multiple horizontals (hurdling), and not only single fence-top poles. Each barrow was at some stage fronted by a façade of heavy timber posts, which in the earlier case were used to mark the extreme directions of the rising of the midwinter Sun and the setting of the midsummer Sun. Skendleby 2 long predated Beckhampton Road, and seems to have set its perpendiculars towards far edges, as did that barrow. At a later stage two other early instances will be added to our list of long barrows with solar alignments.

The two Skendleby barrows are near neighbours on the same hillside—they are only 250 m apart—and are among fifteen or so long barrows on the Lincolnshire Wolds. Skendleby 1 (latitude 53° 13' 05") was excavated under the direction of C. W. Phillips in 1934, and Skendleby 2 (latitude 53° 12' 40"), in what amounted to a rescue operation, under the direction of J. G. Evans and D. D. A. Simpson in 1975–6. It is likely that each went through at least two distinctive phases, which it will be convenient to distinguish as Skendleby 1A and 1B, and Skendleby 2A and 2B, and so forth.

Both were almost wholly surrounded by ditches, and those flanking the barrows seem at first sight to have been by no means at equal levels. Had this been wholly true it would have meant that our fundamental assumption was

inapplicable, and that our method would have needed to be applied, if at all, in a modified form. (To every observing altitude from one ditch there corresponds a unique ridge height and therefore a unique observing altitude from the other ditch. Given a complete ditch survey it would in principle be possible to extend the method to such cases, matching disparate observing levels.) In fact on closer examination it appears that a ledge was deliberately placed in the lower ditch to be at the level of the floor of the upper (see the left lower part of Fig. 38). This ledge was vital to the planning of the barrow: it was clearly cut to satisfy the general precept that observation must be at equal distances from the ridge, and from places at equal levels below it. As can be seen from the same figure, however, when the ditch was cut of necessity to a lower level, for materials, the possibility was retained of observing at precisely the same angle albeit from that lower level. At Skendleby 1 the same principle is to be seen in reverse (see the upper left of the same figure). Here the key positions for the planning of the ditch were in mid-ditch, but an additional place was provided on a wide inner ledge. Something similar was seen at the Horslip long barrow.

The excavation of Skendleby 1 was a model for its time—perhaps one day a return will be made to Phillips' attempt to draft ditch contours—and the monument yielded good geometrical detail. Fig. 39 abstracts what from our

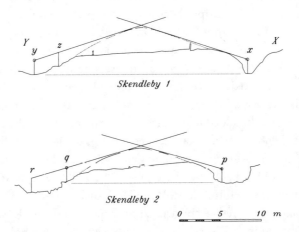

FIG. 38.   Important sections of the ditches at barrows 1 and 2 (in their final forms) at Giants' Hills, Skendleby. Both barrows run close to contours on hillsides, and the fall of the ground across the barrows is easily appreciated here. A rough idea of likely mound forms is given by the lines of sight, astronomically derived. The upper section corresponds to the line XY in Fig. 39 and the lower to a roughly similar place on the similar barrow Skendleby 2. Key viewing positions at the planning stage were x, y, p, and q. Note the optional viewing positions, z and r, to the left (south west) of the sections.

point of view is the most important information. The façade, in what was described by Phillips as a revetment trench, is at *R*. The posts in it had been split, and the flats of the semicircles set against the outer curve, to the northwest, suggestive of a wall intended to be a solid curtain. *H* was a large hole, *B* a platform for the burial, and *S* a line of stones, perpendicular to the axis of the barrow.

Skendleby 2 had been severely damaged by long ploughing, but the mapping of the barrow was done meticulously, and radiocarbon dating

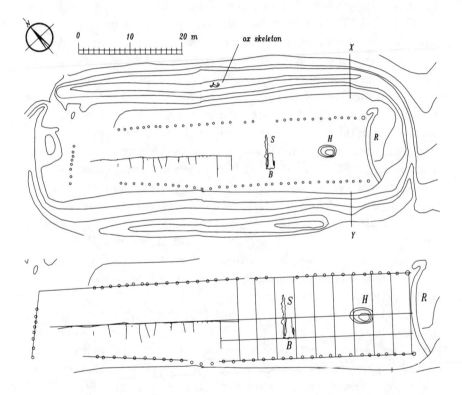

Fig. 39.   Outline of Skendleby 1 (upper figure). The contours are at 2 ft (about 60 cm) intervals, and although unnumbered, their change can be estimated with the help of Fig. 38, showing the section *XY*. The mound base (outer contour of hole *H*) is 236 ft above the Ordnance Datum. The positions of many of the revetting posts round the edge follow the conjectures of C. W. Phillips. The stake holes for the fencing of the bays, and collapsed poles, once tied to them, are at the northwest. The studied proportions of the southeastern end are intimated in the lower figure (drawn to a larger scale), where construction lines are conjectured. The width of one of our hypothetical bays is double the interval between revetting posts, that is, about 3 m.

produced no fewer than fourteen dates in all, covering a perplexing spread of time—almost two millennia. Its end-ditches were clearly meant for observation. There were actually two end-ditches at the northwest: the first had been filled in before a new one was cut about 10 m further from the façade. This might mean that the mound was at some stage lengthened—say from 60 m or less to 70 m. The former, as it happens, is the length of Skendleby 1. The deeper ditch to the front of the façade was well fitted to observation over the mound. The rough equality of the distances of observers, from side ditches to ridge, and from front ditch to façade, will eventually be used to confirm that there was at Skendleby 2 a set of *three* equal viewing angles.

These twin barrows provide us with an object lesson in the importance of precision, something that can be best illustrated by the fact that, while the barrows differ in direction by only a few degrees, and are of much the same form and dimensions, the star Deneb was much implicated in the design of one but not the other (Skendleby 2, but not Skendleby 1, which was begun several centuries later). There are some difficult problems here, not only internal, but of the relations between the two barrows. Even after two exemplary excavations, there is much simple but desirable surveying information that is lacking, and that might one day allow a more complete analysis.

The bowed form of the façade of Skendleby 1 seems to hint at a clever architectural device for holding back the soil of a mound. On these grounds it might be made the later of the two—and the astronomical arguments fall in with this idea. In both cases, a mere glance at the plans is enough to suggest that there are components of the barrows that are skewed with respect to the axes of the mounds. This should be enough to alert us to the presence of multiple celestial alignments.

Consider first Skendleby 2. The southern edge of the mound has been irretrievably lost, but long stretches of the northern edge are known in minute detail—for which the excavator's report must of course be consulted—and a perpendicular to the first and best sets an azimuth of 225.7°. An average for five transverse fences of stakes on the *south* side gives azimuth 45.8°. Together, these suggest that the principle of setting right angles to *far edges* is being observed here, as at South Street. The figure of 45.8° is doubly significant, as will be seen, for the observation of Deneb. This is the first crucial azimuth.

The façade sets a good line at right angles to a row of thin stakes (see Fig. 40, azimuth 133.8°) at its centre. It was likewise almost exactly perpendicular to four posts of intermediate size at the northeast side, which were no doubt an aid to setting out the façade, with properties to be explained. The direction of the façade is comparable with that of the front edge of the mound and that

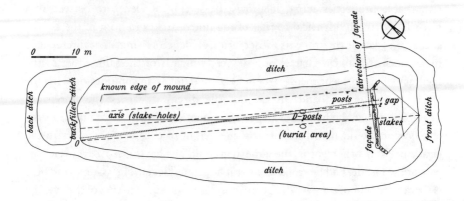

FIG. 40.   Outline of the Skendleby 2 long barrow. The coarse broken lines pick out some of the symmetries of the plan. Lines numbered 1 and 2, passing through the gap in the façade, are sight lines for solar observation in two directions. For further detail see Fig. 41.

of a transverse stake fence on the northern side, but again these will be kept in reserve. It will be assumed that viewing across an unspecified mound (not the last erected there) from the northern ditch was done at an azimuth of about 223.8°. This is the second crucial azimuth.

Combining it with the first, in the now standard way, one finds that the rising of Deneb could have been seen over the mound of Skendleby 2A to the northeast from the southwest ditch at altitude 13.96° around 4020 BC, together with the setting of Betelgeuse at the same date and altitude, looking from the other ditch to the southwest.

In this first phase of the monument, the ditches might well have differed somewhat from the later ditches, as is known from the excavation, but it must be said that the change cannot have been great, for what is known of them fits very well with the derived viewing angle. The ditch to the front, moreover, is everything that we could wish for. By a fortunate chance, the excavators took a section almost exactly where it is needed. The short row of stake holes in front of the façade (not to be confused with the long row along the axis) meets the front ditch at a very special point indeed (Fig. 41). Lines from this point to the extremes of the observation trench run due west and due north. (This is our oldest example of a more than tacit occurrence of precise cardinal points.) Not only this, but there are two steps cut into the chalk at this point (see the right-hand side of Fig. 42), and from the upper step, observation could have been made over the top of the façade at the very angle (nearly 14°) to be derived

from the assumption of cross-viewing from the side ditches. This angle has two remarkable properties. First, it allows the setting of Deneb to be seen in a direction virtually identical to that of the line of stakes in front of the façade, at the same date as the crosswise observation of Deneb's rising. (The discrepancy in azimuth is about a quarter of a degree, which is of the same order as the accuracy of our present measurements.) Second, taken in conjunction with the levels of the ground and distance of the ditch, it carries the important implication that the height of the eye of a man of normal stature making the observation would have been exactly the height of the operative posts in the façade itself. In other words, the same man could just have seen over the relevant part of the façade, had he stood against it at ground level. The assumption here is that the height of the eye (E, in the figure) is made equal to that of the average West Kennet male (nominally 1.66 m).

It is hard to avoid the feeling that the near-perpendicularity of the two Deneb directions was the result of an attempt to make them precisely so. Had they been so then each would have been precisely 45° from north, that is, yielding azimuths of 315° and 45°, rather than 314.2° and 45.8°. The discrepancy might have been adjusted by a slight difference in viewing altitudes. It is not likely to be entirely due to our own error in the azimuths, since the need to bring Betelgeuse to the same altitude was surely enough to thwart any ambition to produce a Deneb right angle. What is certainly of great interest is the similarity between the Skendleby 2A's use of perpendicular sighting lines to Deneb and the presence of perpendicular sighting lines to Sirius over the natural horizon at the Horslip long barrow. The date assigned above to that barrow was only three quarters of a century later than the date obtained here for Skendleby 2A.

The façade held thirty-one posts, and showed signs that at some stage posts had been removed by burning. This is of course one of the easiest ways of removing an old heavy post, but it should not be assumed that removal was once and for all. The façade functioned, if the present analysis is accepted, for many centuries, and might have been replaced many times. Traces of the posts of the façade show that they were by no means of constant girth, and some posts—especially towards the middle—were no doubt appreciably taller than others. How they were arranged it is impossible to say, but the excavation produced fragments of charcoal from small branches that the excavator inter-preted as possibly indicating a wattle and daub arrangement. This fits very well with the idea of a curtain of timber through a gap in which observation of the first glint of the rising midwinter Sun was seen, in a way that will be explained.

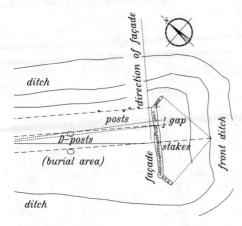

FIG. 41.   Plan of the area around the façade of the Skendleby 2 long barrow. An observer in the front ditch, looking over the façade in a direction originally marked with four stakes, saw the setting of Deneb. Note the north–south and east–west directions to the corners of the façade from the observer. An observer at the gap could observe the setting Sun at its midsummer extreme, along line 1. Line 2 is the sight-line towards the midwinter rising Sun from the ditch at the northwest (see Fig. 40).

The line of four posts meets the backfilled ditch at its very centre, and there are two equally spaced parallels to it that graze the holes for the large D-posts in the burial area and bring us to the corner of the (original) end-ditch. Over a natural treeless horizon, midwinter sunrise was at altitude 0.57° and azimuth 132.7°, and midsummer sunset at an altitude 1.44° and azimuth 311.6°. From a point near the northwest corner of the original back ditch (see Fig. 40), the Sun would have been observable at its midwinter extreme along the line marked 2 in the figure, grazing one of the burial split trunks and one side of the gap in the façade. The burial post would have covered the solar image as it rose, being about 10 per cent larger in angular diameter. The first glint of the Sun's image would thus have been trapped between two posts, almost (but not quite) in a manner that was to become classic over the following two millennia. Midsummer sunset was similarly observable by an observer looking along the line of sight marked 1. The posts flanking the gap in the façade were unusual, as it happens, in that they had flattened faces to the inside. It was easy to follow the rising Sun, by shifting one's own position slightly, opening and closing the slit at will. The angular width of the D-post was well matched to that of the Sun, as seen from the end-ditch, being about 10 per cent larger. From the façade, of course, the post was nearer and the margin much greater.

While we do not have a ditch section at the observer's position—a high priority for any future excavation—we do have one not far from the centre that offers support for the claim that the end ditch was used for solar observation. As shown in Fig. 42, a ledge there—had it been used for viewing—would have brought the observer's eye to the same level as the top of the posts over which the setting of Deneb was observed. Given no other obstacle, in other words, the observer can see perfectly well down to the natural horizon. This suggests

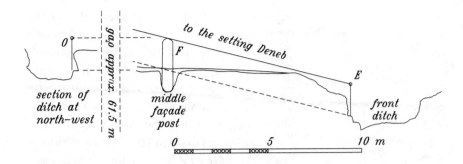

FIG. 42. The front ditch (right-hand side) and (original) rear ditch of the long barrow Skendleby 2A. The observer stands in the front ditch on the upper step in the chalk, with eye at *E*, and views the setting Deneb at altitude of nearly 14°. The same observer at ground level would just have been able to see over the posts at *F*. The lower step was cut for the later barrow (Skendleby 2B). At the left of the figure a section is reproduced probably resembling others from which midwinter observations of the Sun could have been made with Skendleby 2A (and possibly later). The observer's eye (*O*) is at this end evidently also on a level with the top of *F*. The places actually used no doubt offered a more comfortable place to stand than the one shown. At the optimal point for the natural horizon the observer stood virtually at the old ground level, but with eye at the same level as shown here.

solar viewing, since no star, not even Sirius, is visible down to that level (0.57° without trees). Observations would have been made by someone standing at the point described, but level with the step and at the inside edge of the ditch—in fact more or less at the old ground level.

This all leads to the suspicion that here are signs of the very first activity of this sort on the site. The old ditch at this end could have been cut only after the ditches for crosswise viewing of Deneb and Betelgeuse were added. If the unsymmetrical solar arrangement ever made it seem desirable to view the Sun from a more central place, this would have demanded a higher altitude, easily arranged by building up the relevant façade posts. (For viewing along any of the set of three parallels, for instance, they would have been 2.9 m above ground level at mid-façade.)

One cannot be certain that there was no tree cover on the horizons needed for solar observations of the sort described, but both horizons are set by land fairly close by. It was shown from an analysis of molluscs sampled during the excavation that the immediate neighbourhood of the barrow was grassland, and that the mixed deciduous woodland that had covered the area had been cleared not long before. There are good reasons for thinking that the site was chosen for its solar properties: to bring the sighting lines to the solstices as near

to parallels as possible, a higher altitude was needed towards midsummer setting than towards midwinter rising. The idea of perfectly reversible solstice alignments will be met with repeatedly elsewhere, but only at a much later date. Skendleby 2A is remarkable chiefly because it is such an early example of a carefully designed solar structure.

What of the implications of the *mound*, our Skendleby 2B? It should be plain enough that it brings alternative azimuths into the reckoning. The mound edges mentioned earlier provide much the same azimuth as the second crucial figure, and it seems that an effort was made to keep it, presumably not only for continuity's sake in some abstract sense but because of its implications for observation of the Sun (the change in which is so slow that we can here ignore it). This, however, does not explain the direction of the very well defined line of stake posts and larger rubble running down the spine of the barrow.

Viewing across this would have provided azimuth 228.9°, which replaces the previous 233.9°, in our conjectural reconstruction of observing practice. Each of the options may be combined with a direction (48.9°) perpendicular to the spine of the barrow and the other related lines. In view of the barrow's imperfections, it is unlikely that much more reliable data than this will ever emerge. Applying the usual method then yields a rather surprising result. The first option suggests viewing of the rising of Deneb and the setting of Aldebaran at an altitude of 15.76° around 3750 BC. The second option suggests viewing of the rising of Deneb and the setting of Betelgeuse at an altitude of 15.75° around 3730 BC. What is surprising is that the same mound could have been used to observe the setting of Aldebaran and Betelgeuse at more or less the *same* dates, as long as the directions of viewing were not too stringently set. (Aldebaran and Betelgeuse could have been seen setting across Skendleby 2A at points 5° apart in azimuth.) We have always assumed—for want of any sign of *permanent* direction markers—that observers after the initial architectural act had no precise means of knowing that the direction of view was strictly at right angles to any particular edge. It is for this very reason that a long barrow, used as explained, could have avoided becoming plainly outdated, in the minds of those who used it, for decades, even centuries. From the moment of foundation of a barrow, the stars were slowly shifting their places of rising and setting, but it would have been long before any but the expert realized the extent of the drift.

This is to assume that the barrow was used for ritual observation after its foundation, and that it was not just a question of 'building the stars into the monument' and then paying little attention to its properties. That the front ditch was still being used at Skendleby 2B to observe the setting Deneb, in

exactly the same way as before, seems very likely, and the evidence is beautifully simple. The upper step on the inside wall of the ditch (Fig. 42) is just 32 cm above the lower, and this is exactly what would have been needed to change the viewing angle from 14.00° to 15.75°, at the distances in question, assuming that the property was to be retained whereby the relevant façade post came to the height of the observer's eye. As for the character of what are here being referred to as steps, it is not to be supposed that they resemble those at St Paul's. They were rough-hewn. They do seem to have been worn with some use, although very frequent use would surely have worn them more. These things have not been properly studied, since ditches have usually been regarded only as quarries for mound building. Either observation was done relatively infrequently, say by a single person at selected seasons, or the step was protected, perhaps by a wooden platform that it was meant to support. The second seems in any case not unlikely, just as ladders allowing entry to ditches in general would have been almost essential.

Skendleby 2B, with its long mound, perhaps built in more stages than suggested here, was thus brought into existence to redress the changes of the centuries. Some centuries later, and perhaps because of dissatisfaction with yet further changes nearby, a completely new barrow was built along similar lines, namely Skendleby 1. Very briefly, starting from azimuths 36.3° and 218.6°, one may conclude that the rising of Vega was seen from the southern side and the setting of Bellatrix from the other, both at altitude 17.4° around 3120 BC. It has to be said that there is another possibility, and that around the year 3550 BC the rising of Vega could have been combined with the setting of Betelgeuse, at altitude 19.0°. Other things being equal, the (later) option with lower altitude seems more fitting to the known scale and architecture of the ditches. Perhaps the two phases were both known; and it might even be prudent to assume that there was a still earlier 'façade' phase, as at the barrow nearby—in which case the labels Skendleby 1A, 1B, and 1C ought to be reserved. The chief reason for favouring the year 3120 BC (with the usual uncertainties) is that Skendleby 1 has provided two radiocarbon dates, equivalent to 3125 ± 225 and 3000 ± 300 BC (2460 and 2370, each ± 150 bc). The first of these could hardly be closer to our figure, although it would be unwise to claim better than an accuracy of a century or so in our own dating.

It seems that there were three centuries between Skendleby 2A and 2B. In a third phase, or even in a tail appended to 2B, it might have been used with Deneb still, but with Bellatrix in place of Betelgeuse—at the mound head around 3420 BC, say. Deneb would eventually have become unusable there. It is just conceivable that in due course Skendleby 2 passed into yet other phases.

It would in this case have been built up slightly higher, making the viewing angles around 20°, and it could then have been used successively with Vega and Aldebaran (around 3310 and 3070 BC, in different ways) and Vega and Betelgeuse (around 3030 BC). On the whole it seems safer to put aside all these options, and to associate a highly specific structure only with a first probable use, that is, the use for which it seems to have been deliberately designed.

Did Skendleby 1 have any solar use? Its axis is less than 2° away from the required direction. There is an almost perfect alignment set by the revetting posts running from the northwest corner of the mound towards the right-hand (southwest) edge of the entire façade, but this part of the façade has been lost. The burial area might have been implicated in some alignment using the middle of the façade, but it is difficult to see how, and much less is on record concerning the fine structure of the façade here than at the other barrow.

Most of the fourteen radiocarbon dates associated with Skendleby 2 provide support for the gamut of astronomical dates offered here. The oldest, for a piece of façade charcoal, was equivalent to about 4250±100 BC (1965±80 bc). This was presumably large and very old timber, and is recognized as anachronistic. There followed three highly consistent specimens, of oak charcoal and antler, the oldest being 3910±120 BC (3155 bc), and so belonging to phase 2A. One item of charcoal from the north burial post pit (3790±150 BC), a solar observing post, shows this phase continuing in use. Another specimen from the same post was well over a century earlier—supporting the idea of post renewal. The mound and burials produced more, hovering around 3500 BC, all with similar ranges of uncertainty; and there were others still later. These dates, however, are less interesting by far than the simple fact that the Sun's turning points were being accurately observed at a Lincolnshire long barrow in all probability just before the beginning of the fourth millennium.

As a postscript to this section, it is worth putting on record a curious fact about the nearest stretch of the A1028 road, marked on the Ordnance Survey as a 'Roman Road'. A consistently straight tract of this is still in use, and covers nearly 4 km. The now disused part of the road continued in exactly the same direction for 7km more, taking it south to the village of Burgh le Marsh. The section still in use passes within 400 m of both Skendleby barrows, and its azimuth is 133.7°—differing therefore by only a fifth of a degree from the line of stake holes in front of the façade of Skendleby 2. This does not imply any immediate connection with the barrows, of course, but it does seem highly probable that the road embodies an alignment on the Sun, and that this was pre-Roman. The gradient is very slight (averaging 0.23° upwards in the direction 313.7°). The direction of the road never matched that of the extreme

of midwinter sunrise, but it did once perfectly match that of *sunset (last glint) at the summer solstice* in the Neolithic period. Using the figures quoted here implies a date in the neighbourhood of the twenty-second century BC, but there are slight uncertainties in the direction and altitude, and these are far more critical than in the case of dating by the stars. (The direction of midsummer sunrise changed by only two-fifths of a degree over the previous two millennia, for the stated altitude.) This is our first example of a trackway aligned on the Sun, but as will be shown in the following chapter, it was by no means an isolated instance.

The Radley Parallelogram

A barrow nearer to those of Wessex that seems to have shared some of the contrivances of Skendleby 2 has a most unusual shape, for its mound was in the form of a parallelogram, and not especially elongated. It was excavated at Barrow Hills, Radley, Oxfordshire, in a rescue operation led by Richard Bradley in 1984—as one of many prehistoric monuments on a site destined to be submerged under a housing estate on the northeastern edge of the town of Abingdon. Lying on a gravel terrace a little more than a kilometre north of the River Thames there, this site had seen Neolithic, Bronze Age, Romano-British and Anglo-Saxon settlement. (The tradition of refusing to treat the land as a museum is clearly an ancient one in Abingdon.) The nearby Abingdon ditched enclosure was separated from the barrow by a very shallow valley, and it is assumed that the two were set up at much the same time.

The long barrow is difficult to analyse not only because most of its surface detail has been lost but because it had ditches that were superimposed on it, in some places cutting through an older trench, assumed to have been a post trench. Fig. 43 shows the ditches in rough outline. It was suggested by Bradley that there were four phases:

(1) A fenced enclosure, the posts of which were later removed. Our outline figure hints at the existence of the narrow trench in which these were taken to have been placed. He thought that the grave might have belonged to this phase, or more probably to the next. It was very shallow and held two crouched burials of adult males laid along the axis of the site with heads at opposite ends of the grave and legs laid across one another.

(2) A three-sided ditch (surrounding the first trench to the north of points x and y on our figure) and large post holes E and F, the former seeming to have held a split trunk. (For the notation, see Fig. 46.)

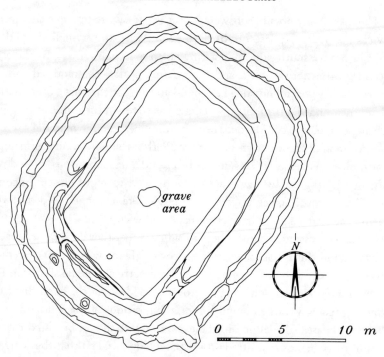

FIG. 43.   Outlines of the ditches surrounding the long barrow at Barrows Hills, Radley.

(3) The open end (below x and y, where a causeway was left) was closed with another length of ditch avoiding one of the large posts.

(4) The outer ditch was cut in a series of segments between 2m and 5 m long, with a causeway at the southernmost corner. There were deposits of pottery and flint scrapers near both causeways.

Stretches of the sides of the outermost ditch were clearly deliberately curved, in contrast to the inner ditches, which contain some quite passable straight lengths, for example on the ditch floor. Averaging over three of these in the short direction and four in the long, the plan can be provisionally taken to have been meant as a parallelogram with sides at azimuths 136.0° and 216.0°.

It is very unfortunate that all detail of the structure of the mound has been lost, but one thing is clear: the trench and inner ditches were intimately related in shape. The material thrown up from the trench would not have been enough to build a mound worthy of the name. Even the material from the inner ditches would not have created an artificial horizon to a person standing anywhere but in the ditch. This presents a difficult problem. Why did they cut into the trench at all?

There are many possible answers, but it is not easy to find one that carries conviction. The first phase might have begun with the *outer* ditch, perhaps starting from the south side, and looking north to Deneb's rising. By the usual procedures—possibly using E and F as scaling posts—the required angle of view would have been known. The mound area might then have been marked out and surrounded with short revetting posts to retain the soil. But the outer ditch alone (about 90 cu m) would not have provided enough material to create a revetted mound setting an angle of 12.3°. Perhaps labour was in short supply, or for some other reason it was decided to build a less ambitious mound. For the same viewing angle they would have needed to move closer. Since the mound was so much lower, the revetting posts were no longer needed, so that they and the trench would have been dispensed with.

A first impression of the ditches at Radley is that they are a rather chaotic patchwork, but this is not so. There are surprisingly many points of agreement between the excavation outline plan and a geometrical scheme shown in Fig. 44, tending to support—rather than prove—the idea that the outer ditch was planned in relation to the mound limits, the positions of the southern posts, and the grave area (ill-defined to the excavators). It should be noted that all circles in the scheme are centred on the parallelogram, and that the centre in all probability was originally at the head of the grave. The scheme otherwise speaks for itself. Only those with the experience of making geometrical constructions on the open landscape, with antler pick and ox-bone spade, have a perfect right to say that agreement could have been closer.

Another explanation of the discarded trench might be that an attempt was made to build a mound with high edge—say half a metre—from a shallow *inner* quarry ditch, but that quantities were misjudged, and the revetting, growing increasingly unstable, was abandoned in favour of a low mound. The inner ditch (about 75 cu m) would have provided just enough material for a 12° mound tapered to the ground, without posts (Fig. 45).

No matter what the explanation, it can make little difference to the astronomical geometry of the situation that has come down to us, which has interesting echoes of Skendlebury 2. There, matters were so arranged that Deneb could be seen rising across the barrow and setting down its axis. Here, at Radley, conversely, Deneb was to be seen rising along the length of the barrow (by the observer at C), and setting across the mound (by observers at points marked D, or between them). More details will be given shortly. At Radley, however, there was exactly the same doubling of function with respect to Bellatrix too: it would have been seen rising across the mound by observers

between points marked *A*, and setting along the barrow's length by an observer at *C*.

There is some latitude in the placing of observers in the inner ditches, since all that we require of them is that the lines of sight pass over points of maximum altitude of the mound. In fact each of the viewing positions marked on the figure has something more to recommend it, however insignificant it may seem (*B* was at mid-ditch to *E*, *B* was off centre at a point where the ditch was cut slightly deeper, and so on).

Ignoring for the time being the slight discrepancies between those ditch lines and azimuths that are exactly multiples of 45°, the following solution illustrates principles found from earlier barrows. Ensuring the same viewing altitude in the two directions would have guaranteed that Deneb—observed at *right angles* to a short edge and *parallel* to a short edge—was to be seen rising and setting. Neither here nor at Skendleby is viewing strictly along an axis. The same goes for Bellatrix with respect to the long sides. All four possibilities, however, would have held *simultaneously* only at one particular time in history.

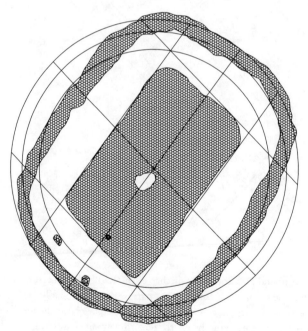

FIG. 44.   Potential geometrical construction lines for the entire original system of ditch and mound at Radley. Only the surviving ditch edges are shown. The short sides of the parallelogram in particular are based largely on the ditch structure and not only on its outline as drawn here.

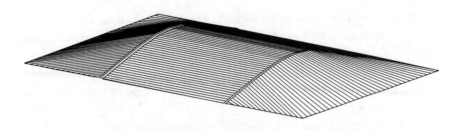

FIG. 45.   The probable overall shape of the Radley mound, in idealized form.

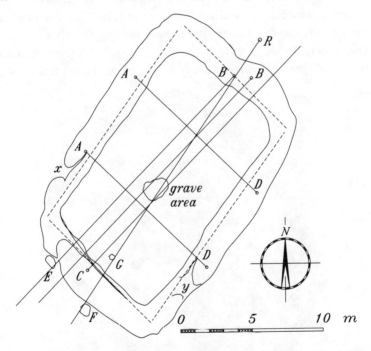

FIG. 46.   The mound area and inner ditches of the Radley long barrow, in the form of a parallelogram. The mound was limited by a narrow trench, probably before these ditches were cut. The broken lines show what is here taken to have been the ideal aimed at. The short sides are drawn here at exactly 45° to the cardinal points, differing only very slightly from what would be suggested by internal features of the ditches. The lines of sight are drawn parallel or perpendicular to the sides. Another ditch, omitted, but more or less surrounding what is shown here, was about 2 metres distant from it. Points A, B, C, D, and R are potential viewing positions for the stars Bellatrix, Deneb, and Rigel.

To find that time and the shared viewing altitude for the latitude of Barrows Hills (51;40,45°), our usual procedure is followed. Given the ideal as explained, the year turns out to be 3700 BC and the viewing altitude 12.3°.

The date is of course very sensitive to the chosen directions, and in all of them there are uncertainties attendant on the relatively small dimensions of the barrow. The measured azimuths quoted earlier produce a year of 3740 BC and a viewing altitude of 11.6°, with various qualifications that are hardly worth explaining. It would not be unreasonable to quote the date 3700 BC and to set the range of uncertainty as a century and a half either way. A reason will be given shortly for preferring a slightly later date.

The broad scheme explained here, with two pairs of perpendicular sight-lines to Deneb and Bellatrix, seems to be the only viable one. (Betelgeuse with Deneb offers the only other significant solution with any plausible lines of sight, but it is in the fifth millennium.) Lines along the axis, for observers in the ditches north and south, seem to offer no alternatives, and viewing at right-angles to ditches is in any case something we have found used often enough elsewhere. But why, under these circumstances, did they not simply build a *square* barrow, or at least a rectangular one? Why did they produce a skewed parallelogram?

The answer is that the *axis* had an importance of its own, for it was aligned on the setting of Rigel over the natural horizon. The barrow mound, following the altitudes derived here, would have been no more than 1.36 m above the eye of the ditch observers, and so no obstacle to an observer standing at ground level. As for the natural horizon, the town of Abingdon has long stood in the line of sight, but it seems likely that in Neolithic times the passage to the river in this direction would have been clear of trees, and that it is reasonable to take the extinction angle for Rigel. But what should that be? The site was not on high ground with good viewing conditions, but looked across the Thames valley. Using the norm for favourable viewing, the extinction angle would have been 1.53°. The derived declination in this case fits a year around 3600 BC. The extinction angle here could well be half a degree higher, however, which would bring the date a century later.

The Abingdon ditched ('causewayed') enclosure produced radiocarbon dates in the first half of the third millennium bc, quite consistent with all estimates made here, but why are these spread over a century and a half? The most probable error is in the azimuths, which are probably all a degree too high. On this assumption, all dates fall within three decades of 3700 BC. Whether or not this is so, it seems likely that the Radley barrow is half a century or more later than Skendleby 2. This is not certain, but what does seem certain

is that both made use of the same clever device for introducing the rising and setting of the same star.

What of parallels with Skendleby's alignments on the Sun? At Radley, there is no sign whatsoever of a solar alignment. The southern extreme of the Moon's setting might have been observed in the same direction as Rigel's, but this idea presupposes a level of sophistication for which we have no other evidence, and it must be abandoned. An isolated direction is no evidence at all. What is needed is evidence that other extremes were also observed, whether here or in the same general context, and this is lacking.

The Grendon Square Barrow

The last earthen long barrow to be considered here in detail was intermediate in date and place between the solar barrows at Skendleby and South Street. It was revealed in another rescue excavation, this time in the Nene Valley near Peterborough in the seasons 1974 and 1975. This 'short long barrow' at Grendon, Northamptonshire, has an importance out of all proportion to the quality of our knowledge of it, for it seems to signal a transition between two different astronomical traditions of barrow construction. At first it was thought to be a round barrow, like others on the same site (which also included an Iron Age farm), for it was enclosed within a double ring ditch. It was eventually found to enclose a square structure with a façade strongly reminiscent of Skendleby 1 (Skendleby 2 was excavated only in 1975–6), and the ring ditch was seen to be a later addition. In advance of gravel quarrying on the site—which had been discovered from aerial photography—the barrow was excavated, but not completely, and an 'overzealous removal of topsoil' meant the loss of much information as to the sequence of construction. But in this case the very geometry of the barrow comes to the rescue, and it is in some ways reminiscent of Radley's.

The 'long barrow' components of Grendon (strictly area C, barrow V) are shown in Fig. 47, while the surrounding ring ditches are added to Fig. 48. All signs of the mound have been lost, but there is one good and one passable line from the façade, and one excellent straight inner edge to the ditch. What is more, the curved ditch opposite the façade fits closely to two arcs of circles of different radii, and the resulting ensemble of construction lines has some remarkable geometrical properties, quite independently of any assumption we might choose to make about potential astronomical lines of sight. Briefly, the angles marked x in Fig. 47 radiate from the centre of the circle bounding the inner edge of the ditch and are all equal to 22.5° (a sixteenth of a circle), while

the angles marked *y* are at the centre for the outer edge, and are within half a degree of 60°. The quadrant made up of the four *x*-angles is not set to the cardinal points of the compass, but in any case these are not sight lines.

Looking for lines of sight one may begin by taking parallels to the façade. (Perpendiculars to edges, which differ only slightly, will be considered shortly.) The azimuths are 314.5° and 125.4° (each of course might be reversed) for crosswise viewing. These at first make for uncertainty as to which stars were involved. Looking northwest, there can be little doubt that the setting of Deneb was observed, but in the other direction one might choose between Aldebaran (beginning of the fourth millennium), Bellatrix (mid-third millennium) and Betelgeuse. Following the standard procedure, the rising of Betelgeuse is indicated, with the setting of Deneb, both around 3450 BC and at altitude 12.7°. This fits well with stylistic considerations, but it is ultimately the radiocarbon dates obtained from the site that confirm this preference.

Mature oak from the façade trench gave a date equivalent to only 2900±120 BC (2330±70 bc), but there is now good reason to expect the renewal of posts, so this is no embarrassment, when taken in conjunction with a date of 3490±140 BC (2750±130 bc) for a sample of mixed oak and blackthorn from the ditch. One of the post holes—that nearest the bottom corner of the figure—contained 'fairly mature oak' datable to 3690±140 BC (3000±80 bc), which it was thought might have come from old charcoal or be from a first use

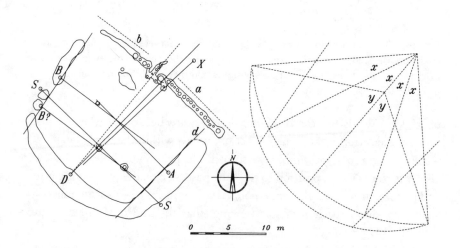

FIG. 47.   The Grendon square barrow. Potential lines of sight are added as continuous lines, and possible construction lines are shown as broken lines, some of them being placed—to avoid confusion—on the right-hand figure.

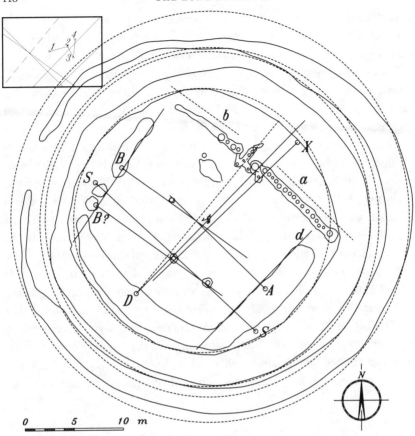

FIG. 48.   The two Grendon ring ditches surrounding the earlier square barrow. The broken circles are the suggested aims of those responsible for the ring ditches. Their centres are marked (near the upper crossing of lines of sight), and they are shown in the inset figure in more detail.

of the site. Whilst we can bring our date forward by a century, by assuming half a degree error in the Deneb direction, it falls within the stated range even without doing so, if old timber is assumed. The pair of post holes at the lower corner is so similar in position to the split posts at Skendleby 2—lying across and to one side of the sight-lines though the gap in the façade—and makes for such a consistent pattern of star viewing, that the mid thirty-fifth century seems highly probable.

The similarities do not end here, for despite their utterly different orientations—one is almost at right-angles to the other—the two barrows were clearly designed for observing Deneb twice over. The rising of Deneb would have been seen at Grendon by an observer in the ditch at D, looking over the

mound along a line parallel to the inner edge of the southeast ditch. The azimuth of this is taken to be 45.5°, so that it would have fitted perfectly with the angle assumed for cross-viewing. They are not perfectly at right angles, but only a degree removed, and if the error is ours, rather than theirs, then the date—as alluded to earlier—moves to about 3550 BC. Like Skendleby 2, therefore, Grendon was aligned twice over on Deneb and once on Betelgeuse; but now, four or five centuries on, the last alignment is not on the setting but the rising of Betelgeuse.

The other important similarity of function involves solar observation. To decide this question it is first necessary to make an estimate of the size of the mound. One cannot say exactly where were the preferred positions for crosswise viewing, but those marked A and D (for Deneb's setting and rising, respectively, parallel to the lines a and d on Fig. 47) and B (for Betelgeuse's rising, parallel to b) are the most likely, in view of the large post positions, and the lines crossing over the centre of the square seem the most significant of all. The proximity of the crossing point to the centres of the ring ditches adds credence to the idea that the mound was at its highest there. Even though there might originally have been a ridge, it would in any case have passed through this point. The height needed here, to set equal angles of 12.7° to observers in the three viewing positions, is about 1.9 m above eye-level. Perhaps the ditches were in fact 1.9 m deep at the appropriate places, so that by standing at ground level an observer could have seen the natural horizon over the mound from any position around it. If the eye of a normal male observer was at ground level—our previous findings fitted perfectly an assumption that the height of a man's eye was critical—then the mound would have been about 23 cm above his eye were he to have stood at ground level. It is not even necessary to make this assumption, however, to make a claim for solar viewing at the site: the southernmost pair of posts would have been usable in connection with the *natural* horizon, using the line (at azimuth 132.4°/312.4°) marked on the figure, in order to observe the rising midwinter Sun in one direction and the setting midsummer Sun in the other. This is so because at a conservative estimate the height of the mound here would have been no higher than about a metre, and it might have been less. (The placement of such a sight line with respect to the posts in the manner shown was to become standard, as will be discovered in Chapter 7.)

What is surprising here is the fact that, at a mere glance at the Grendon plan, midsummer sunrise or midwinter sunset would have been thought the likeliest candidates, either of them viewed along the axis of the barrow, just as at Skendleby 2 we found midwinter sunrise and midsummer sunset along its

axis. At Grendon, this method is impossible; but by taking a line *across* the barrow, it is clear that what was observed could have been exactly the same as at Skendleby 2, namely midwinter sunrise or midsummer sunset or both. (It is also possible that these phenomena were observed by looking along the façade in some way.)

The Grendon barrow is of greatest interest, not because it mirrors a much earlier style but because it seems to signal the approaching demise of the truly *long* barrow. This was not to occur for several centuries, but neither was the transition a sudden one. Beckhampton Road was built at least a century after Grendon, and was converted to a round barrow presumably more than a century after that. Long chambered tombs in stone were probably still being built in the third millennium. Grendon shows that it is unnecessary to postulate an invading culture, such as the 'Beaker People', to see how circular barrow-forms might have arisen quite naturally. Of course it is not being suggested that it was Grendon in particular that supplied Neolithic peoples with the idea that barrows might just as well be square, or round, as long—Radley, after all, had even greater economy of line than Grendon. It is rather that this barrow is symptomatic of changing Neolithic attitudes to barrow construction. It symbolizes too the great naturalness of three prominent features in those circular mounds that qualify as early ancestors of Stonehenge: (1) the circular ditch, which is no more than a rationalization of the encircling ditch of a shortened long barrow; (2) a low mound of height roughly equal to that of the human eye, within that ditch, and corresponding in some way to it; and (3) an assortment of posts within the mound area, at first arranged for crosswise viewing, and later supplemented by others in ever more perfect circles.

Hazleton North and Burn Ground—Cotswold–Severn Long Cairns

Whilst the chambered long barrows at Wayland's Smithy and West Kennet fit easily into the Wessex tradition, they also have affinities with the Neolithic stone long barrows (long cairns) of the Cotswolds, which might just as reasonably be considered their natural neighbours. (West Kennet is little more than 20 km from the string of known examples, and the isolated Wayland's Smithy is hardly further from several at the northern end of the string than it is from West Kennet.) The differences are chiefly in the material used, although—threatened by endless classifications of type—it is wise to add that there are many differences of design too. Where easily split stone was plentiful it was used for the mound, and if larger upright stones (orthostats) were not locally available, then they were imported, from appreciable distances, if need

be. Most barrows in the group were essentially roughly trapezoidal in plan, often with a Cupid's-Bow wall at the high end (usually referred to as 'horns'). Almost all seem originally to have been surrounded by a dry-stone revetment, a containing wall that even when excavated is usually found to be remarkable for its straightness along the sides. Changes of direction are much rarer than with earthen barrows, no doubt because good viewing positions are much harder to create along the length of the barrow, in a stony district. Like so many earthen barrows, there is a clearly identifiable spine, now usually of slabs of stone pitched together. Some of the stone barrows—perhaps all—have internal walls running across the width of the mound, dividing them into cells.

These internal walls are exactly analogous to the much flimsier lines of stakes found in so many earthen barrows, and clearly mark the stages of construction. The conjecture made earlier in this chapter, that the stakes were deliberately set in the directions of lines of sight, and at right angles to the neighbouring or far barrow edge, is harder to test with a dry-stone wall, but all the evidence suggests that the same principles were indeed applied, and nowhere is that evidence clearer than in the report—by Alan Saville and many collaborators—on excavations carried out in the period 1979–82 at Hazleton North, in Gloucestershire. The pattern of internal cells at Hazleton North, taken from that report, is shown in Fig. 49.

The long cairn in question is one of a pair, in a field known as Barrow Ground, 13 km east of Cheltenham and about 45 km west of Oxford. Many other long mounds are nearby, including Notgrove, Belas Knap, and Burn Ground (Hampnett). Hazleton North is on a bedrock of limestone, rising gently to the northwest. It is well placed for viewing over reasonably distant horizons in the southern half of the sky. It lies east–west and is fairly unusual in one respect, for its highest part was to the west—although it was once thought to be otherwise. In common with so many others in this, the finest English group of stone chambered tombs, it was being steadily destroyed by ploughing. The rescue excavation, for which several groups had been pressing hard, resulted in one of the most meticulous Neolithic surveys ever carried out. It revealed traces of human activity on the site before the mound (cairn) was erected. Tentatively grouped with this phase in the estimation of the excavators were a number of post holes and stake holes beneath the mound. Some of these follow the line of one of the transverse internal walls so closely (Figs. 50 and 51 below) that they were almost certainly aligned on the same astronomical event. Some of the posts involved were too substantial for merely staking out the mound, however, and their arrangement roughly resembles that of post holes bounding burial areas on the sites of earthen mounds. For want of more

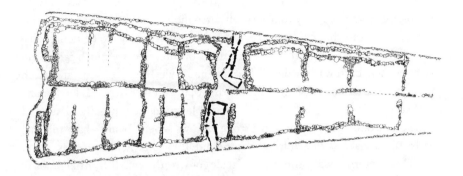

FIG. 49.   The general arrangement of the dry-stone walls that gave the Hazleton North cairn its form (after the much larger plan in the excavation report by Alan Saville). For the quarries, a scale, and a key to the lettering used in the text, see Fig. 52.

surface detail, they are not discussed further here, beyond the remark that if used for viewing over the natural horizon, the heavier posts might possibly have been aligned on the rising of alpha Crucis a little before 4000 BC. Early or late, the fact that they all come so close to the line separating cells U and S suggests that the mound was deliberately related to them.

The arguments offered for the West Kennet chamber's having been set up before the surrounding mound was begun might have been applied here, had the upright stones been more precisely tooled. As it is, one can only say that there are certain significant directions that they seem to define—for example, the longest side of the north chamber probably aligned on the rising Pleiades, and the spine on the setting Pleiades. If this is not an illusion, then once more it can be said that the alignments would not have been possible had a significant part of the mound preceded the uprights. One would naturally expect any viewing of stars across the finished mound to have taken place opposite them, if nowhere else; and in fact the quarry-ditches to north and south are best suited to such activity opposite the middle of the mound. Those quarries have never been extensively excavated, but their estimated outlines are as shown in Fig. 52. The floors of quarries, by the nature of things, are mostly very uneven, but since in the act of quarrying the builders reached down to marl at some points—especially in the central areas—they had at their disposal two flat areas from which to view. The inner area marked on the figure, namely the south quarry, the better excavated of the two, was extremely flat and level. As in the

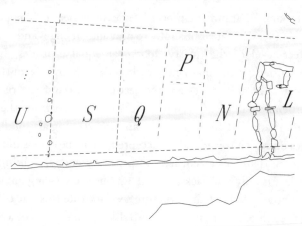

FIG. 50.   A detail of Fig. 52, showing the relation of the posts to the division between cells *U* and *S*.

case of chalk ditches, levels are virtually identical to both sides of the barrow. To the south, small 'islands' of stone were left in place that could have been used as steps. One of these, opposite the south chamber, would have brought the adult male observer's eye to the level of the base of the mound, but there is no way of knowing whether such a step was used—an unfortunate fact, for it would have allowed us to estimate the height of the finished mound. The excavator's discussion of heights was inconclusive. The favoured reconstruction suggested a maximum height of around 2.5 m, while analogies with other cairns seemed to hint at a somewhat higher figure. While our

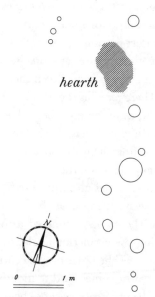

FIG. 51.   The stake holes and post holes under the Hazleton North cairn.

earthen barrows have shown us that analogy is an unreliable guide, the angle of view to be derived shortly (11.85°), taken together with the symmetrical viewing positions marked *Y* and *Z* on the figure, imply a height of about 2.9 m—or about 25 cm more than this if the eye had been precisely at the level of the mound base.

The astronomical argument proceeds exactly as before. The possibilities are considered of viewing at right angles to near and far edges and—as justified by the perfect level of the quarry floors—at equal altitudes. In the half millennium centred on the many radiocarbon dates known from the site, the only stars that offer themselves are the setting Vega and the rising Sirius. Viewing perpendicular to near edges, the date derived from the azimuths assumed (340.3° and 171.8°) is 3870 BC, and the viewing altitude 11.85°. (If the principles on which it is found are accepted, then the date is unlikely to be in error by more than half a century.) Surprisingly enough, taking far edges instead, the date is only put back to 3950 BC, but the viewing angle becomes 9.6°, and the known facts of the structure seem to rule this out conclusively. Once again, therefore, the orientation of cell divisions seems to be a misleading guide to viewing direction. In fact the pattern of these divisions is extremely interesting: at the head, perpendiculars are to the *axis*; in the middle, the business area, they are to *far* sides; and at the tail of the mound one of each sort, *near and far*, crossing the entire mound. This seems to suggest that if there was no perfect pairing of stars across, and perpendicular to, the line of the axis, then the mound was used as a 'precise' artificial horizon only across its middle region. In fact as far as can be seen there was no other reasonable option.

There remains the possibility that stars were observed along the line of the barrow, as found elsewhere. The barrow sloped upwards to the west, and on our estimate of heights (2.9 m over the chamber and 0.5 m at the tail, 32 m distant from it) it did so at an angle of about 4.3°. Although this working is very approximate, the figure is so close to the extinction angle of the Pleiades that it comes as no surprise to find that indeed the Pleiades cluster could have been seen setting over the mound by an observer at the lower end, looking along the spine (estimated azimuth 256°) in the thirty-ninth century BC. (Taking the extinction angle, the year comes out at 3870 BC, but the uncertainty is of the order of two centuries.) This finding fits the other evidence so well that it comes hard to modify it. The ideal arrangement would have been with the observer's eye at or below (depending on distance) the tail edge of the barrow. Our estimate of the mound's overall shape is shown in Fig. 53, for which the line of sight is the right-hand half of the white line along the ridge. In short, we should expect some sort of pit or quarry beyond the tail edge of the mound. None was found, although the excavation did not extend very far in this direction. Of course the Pleiades could still have been observed setting in this direction, but they would have vanished from view somewhat above the ridge, rather than descending into the mound. The Pleiades might have been

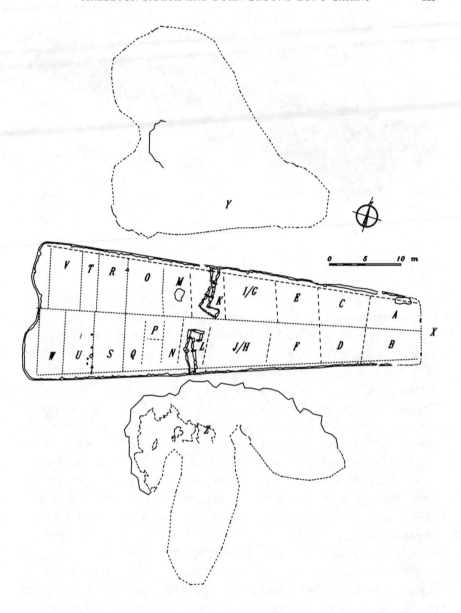

FIG. 52.   The proposed cell structure of the Hazleton North mound, with construction lines drawn at right angles to the south or north mound edges or to the axis.

observed ritually by a large number of people, in the course of setting over the natural horizon along the same direction.

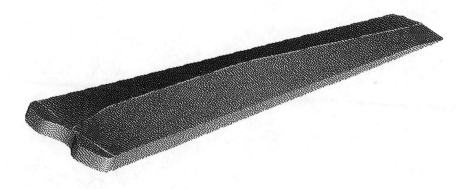

FIG. 53.   The probable overall shape of Hazleton North.

This example of a barrow of Cotswold–Severn construction is taken chiefly to show that a shared set of principles governed the design of mounds, whether they were of chalk or stone. One last brief visit to another long cairn of the same group may be made to show that Hazleton North is not an isolated case. Only 5 km to the southwest the remains of a much-damaged long cairn of similar overall shape were excavated as part of a rescue operation in 1940–41. The barrow was at Burn Ground, to the northeast of the village of Hampnett in Gloucestershire. About 30 m of its length remained at its head, and perhaps as much again had been lost from its tail. Its general orientation, and the shape of its tomb chamber, strongly resembled that of the West Kennet barrow, except that at Burn Ground the chamber faced to the west, and was entered from either side of the mound via a passage running right across the mound. The internal walls were ill-defined, but the fragmentary remains of the stone edging of the cairn were in excellent straight lengths, and provide an opportunity to work from an absolute minimum of data.

The orientations of the north and south sides—at the head of the mound, at least—are taken as 84.5° and 91.0° respectively. Our usual method then provides us initially with three solutions worth examining, the first-named star rising in the south and the second setting in the north:

(1) Sirius and Vega in 4270 BC at altitude 10.3°
(2) Sirius and Arcturus in 3530 BC at altitude 13.4°
(3) Rigel and Arcturus in 3020 BC at altitude 10.6°

There are no available radiocarbon dates now, but (1) is surely too early and (3) too late. Recommending (2) is the fact that it is just a century after our preferred date for West Kennet, and that it introduces the two brightest stars in the sky, as at West Kennet. The altitude is high, but not impossibly so. In his report of the excavation, W. F. Grimes showed that no great attention was being given to possible ditches or quarries. (Two strips at right angles to the mound, north and south, were probably not dug very deep.) If the original overall height was the same as at Hazleton North, and the eye was at ground level, then the observer was at Burn Ground between roughly 12 m and 16 m away from the axis—depending on the mound shape—and 7 m less, measuring from the edging stones. The higher the mound, the larger these figures.

An Assessment

Granted that the building of long barrows was guided by the behaviour of the stars, presumably held in esteem for religious reasons, many questions still remain unanswered. Some of these are technical. How, if at all, did their builders achieve such excellent levels at corresponding points in opposite ditches? Did they use water channels for this? Or long beams fitted with plumb lines, as in a type of builders' level used from ancient times to the present day? And what standard of perfection did they achieve? The question of quality of level seems never to have been asked by excavators, although the excellence of verticals has occasionally drawn comment. And what of the levelling of mound sites? Are the Neolithic plough marks under the South Street barrow not an indication of how seriously this task was taken, rather than a sign of earlier agriculture?

Other questions are essentially social. Where did it all begin, and did any of the manifest advances in technique stem from overseas? Without doubt, chambered tombs entirely of stone from fifth-millennium Brittany served similarly as artificial horizons, across which risings and settings of stars were observed. Their similarity to the Cotswold–Severn group of long barrows (cairns) is too great for the two to be independent, although both might simply have shared a third common source of inspiration. The problem of finding where observers stood in relation to stone cairns is more difficult than in the case of long barrows on chalk, for suitable quarries are not as easily manipulated as ditches in chalk; but the example of Hazleton North strongly suggests that future excavation will produce suitable viewing points, possibly confined to places opposite the side chambers. Once again, while the general principles are

likely to prove to have been imported from distant places, there is every expectation that many specific local variations will emerge.

And where did it end? In some ways it has never ended. Given that this Neolithic intellectual activity was inspired by religious motives, it was also surely becoming an end in itself. It should come as no surprise that barrows are found that contained no burials, and thus no other clear practical purpose. Here are some of the roots of astronomy as an intellectual discipline, but they are tenuous, and one should not omit to ask about the social mechanisms through which similarities of style were preserved across wide territorial areas and over long periods of time. The planning of such monuments was presumably done by an elite—but was it an itinerant elite? No doubt some of the most important principles were generally unknown and enigmatic. For example, that observations were made over these barrows at equal altitudes, and exactly at right angles to one line or another, does not imply a general awareness of the fact, even on the part of generations of people who might themselves have taken part in ritual at the monument. They did not look in a particular direction and wait for a star to rise or set along it. They knew the star and waited for it to rise or set. It was the designer who had ensured that when it did so it would be in the perfect direction. On the other hand, the labour required, even for a small mortuary house, was so great that society at large must have been dimly aware of some of the fundamental principles. In the first phases of activity at Fussell's Lodge and Wayland's Smithy, for instance, it is likely that the heavy wooden roof was regularly moved, for repair or replacement by another, even at a cairn stage—for it could have been lifted off by a score of men. Burning out old posts and replacing them, like keeping the mound and ditches in good order, would likewise have called for general cooperation when wood was an integral part of the monument. Some aspects of design would have been generally known and appreciated—for example the splitting of trunks for the sort of D-posts used at Fussell's Lodge, Wayland's Smithy, Skendleby, Nutbane, Wor Barrow, Radley, and so on. Splitting them was one thing, but positioning them correctly was another, and could only have been done under intelligent direction, by those with a rigorous training in basic principles. Was this a member of an itinerant elite, or did communities compete with one another in new ideas? Were there regional or tribal affiliations to particular stars? At all events, some awareness of what was going on must have been shared by the community, and again only a long comparative study will provide answers.

Yet other questions concern the frequency with which observations were made from the ditches. Were they associated only with the foundation of the barrow, and not made thereafter? For such activity to have gone on regularly

might seem bizarre to us—although, on a cold night, a ditch is no bad place to be—but that is in part because we do not share the beliefs that prompted it. Are there no signs of activity in the ditches, such as of fires or lamps? There is an almost universal acceptance of the idea that ditches were allowed to silt up immediately they were dug. Forgetting, for a moment, our own reasons for doubting this idea, where did the silting material come from? From the mound, which had cost so much in labour and time to build up with so much precision? If it washed down, would it not have been replaced? And if the ditches were truly an integral part of the barrow, as claimed here, then they would have long been kept clear in their own right.

The strong resemblances between one long barrow and another show that principles of a certain generality were involved in their design, but to reinforce the point that barrow design was truly scientific, it is necessary to consider also the *differences* between the monuments, the constructive element that makes barrows interestingly different. Wayland's might to modern eyes seem less satisfying in outline, less symmetrical about its axis; but to those bound to a principle of right-angled viewing, it was superior to the Fussell's Lodge barrow, to the extent that its designers managed to reduce the façade to a single line. The superficially greater symmetry at Fussell's Lodge, which was built into the site at the mortuary house stage, was easier to achieve. It was the Wayland's site that made a more elegant solution possible there—but finding that site was an act of some genius. The same genius was shown when the Horslip site was sought out, with its Sirius directions at a perfect right angle. The West Kennet site too had remarkable intrinsic properties, but there one finds a more constructive element in the brilliant achievement of a doubly symmetrical arrangement of descent and ascent of the very brightest stars. And then at Beckhampton Road there comes evidence at last for a Wessex alignment on the Sun—which may well be one of many, however, since the Sun is emphatically a focus of attention in the Skendleby 2 barrow, dating from before 4000 BC.

It should by now be clear that the impressionistic classification of long barrows with respect to summer and winter sunrise and sunset is more or less worthless, and that even a precise orientation alone can give a very poor indication of a long barrow's potential astronomical purpose. Without a rather exact knowledge of its internal structure, its ditches and terrain, one is virtually helpless. To examine a barrow superficially, the most to be hoped for is a star in line with its axis. To go no further is to miss entirely the possibilities of crosswise viewing that chiefly distinguish one barrow from another. It seems that Rigel, for example, might have risen in line with important long barrows

Brixton Deverill 2 and Bishops Cannings 91, and have set in line with Heytesbury 4. Or was it Sirius at an earlier date or Rigel Centauri at a later? Given better data on potential crosswise viewing, one is in a better position to decide.

The examples examined closely in this chapter have been found directed to bright stars, and there is little evidence that the Sun and Moon were then objects of the same sort of attention. There are chamber tombs elsewhere with a solar alignment, but they are relatively late—the oldest example previously investigated, Newgrange in Ireland, is a century or more younger than Beckhampton Road. They are a sign of changing interests, and yet with these and other new types of solar and lunar monument one still finds some of the old techniques in play.

The successful creation of internal elevations to make for symmetries of orientation—as in the case of cross-viewing, and viewing at right angles—will shortly be found to have been extended to the Sun and Moon in the circular monuments, of which Stonehenge is of course the supreme example. It is this kind of practice that allows us to say of northern European Neolithic people that at least as early as the fifth millennium they had turned the religious observation of the stars into a scientific activity. In AD 1068 Abul'l-Qāsim Ṣā'id ibn Aḥmad of Toledo, in his book *The Categories of Nations*, listed the eight elite nations that had cultivated the sciences: the Hindus, the Persians, the Chaldaeans, the Jews, the Greeks, the Romans, the Egyptians, and the Arabs. Had he been able to look back another four or five thousand years, he would have added another culture to his list.

A Postscript on Venus

By comparison with the staid progression in the positions of the fixed stars, the behaviour of the planets is erratic and the calculation of their risings and settings correspondingly burdensome. Perhaps it is for this reason that they have not been discussed more often in the context of monumental alignments. The fact is that Venus is known to have played a very important part in the astral religions of ancient Middle Eastern and Mediterranean peoples; and not surprisingly, since the planet is potentially much brighter than any 'fixed' star, even Sirius. Venus can even cast a shadow, under the right circumstances. Like the Moon, and unlike the fixed stars, it rises and sets on successive occasions at different points of the local horizon. Those wandering points offer a problem—but so they did with the Moon, and few who have studied the

question honestly now doubt that the Moon's risings and settings were the subject of careful observation.

The pattern of Venus' behaviour may be easily described in general terms. The Earth moves round the Sun once in a year—so that from the point of view of an observer on the Earth the Sun moves round the Earth once in a year. Venus too circles the Sun, in an orbit lying between ours and the Sun. Since Venus stays in a plane close to that of the Earth, the planet seems to us to stick more or less to the ecliptic, the Sun's apparent path through the stars. Because the orbits of our planets are not quite in the same plane, however, Venus wanders away from the ecliptic periodically. It does so in a highly systematic but complex way.

Consider the place of Venus in relation to the Sun. As the year goes by, the Sun moves nearer to, and further from, the north pole of the sky, so producing the seasons. Venus moves—but not in time with the Sun—a few degrees north and a few degrees south of the ecliptic. Consider the plane of the ecliptic, our reference plane containing the Sun and the Earth's orbit. The angle of tilt of Venus' orbit to it is more or less fixed, although the plane of the orbit itself swivels round with time. Suppose that Venus is at its greatest distance from the reference plane. A few moments thought will show that when Venus is then lying between us and the Sun, its angular distance from the reference plane will seem to be much greater than when it is lying on the far side of the Sun. In the distant position it will seem closest to the ecliptic—in other words, its ecliptic latitude will then be least. Its declination—the corresponding angle in the reference system based not on the ecliptic but on the Earth's equator—will follow suit. It is when Venus lies between us and the Sun that the planet has maximum declination, north or south, and so is capable of rising and setting at its extreme north and south positions on the local horizon.

So much for a general description of the pattern of Venus' behaviour, which is somewhat like the Moon's. When looking into the matter more closely, however, one finds complications of various sorts. First, when the planet lies roughly between us and the Sun, it is in the same situation as the new moon, presenting to our sight a crescent, rather than its potentially brilliant disc. (The crescent-form will not be appreciated by the untrained naked eye.) When too close to the direction of the Sun, though, the planet will not be visible at all, but lost in the Sun's rays. Another complication arises from the fact that Venus will be visible either before sunrise in the morning or after sunset in the evening, but not both, and this is still true when it is at its most northerly (or southerly) declination. Venus is never far from the Sun. If seen as a morning

star, the Sun will be up by the time it sets; and if seen as an evening star, the Sun will rise before it.

Suppose that the patterns of rising and setting of Venus on the horizon were noted in prehistory, and the extremes were recorded in some physical way—by posts, mounds, or whatever. This implies a much greater tenacity of purpose than with the 'fixed' stars, which hold to more or less the same positions for years on end. This fact and other subtleties apart, the Neolithic problem would not have been a very difficult one, but what of ours, that of analysing any suspected alignments on Venus? We can calculate the date when Venus reaches its most southerly declination, for instance, but that is not enough to give us a direction for a monument aligned on the most southerly rising of Venus, say, if the planet was an evening star on the date in question. In the period that interests us, the extremes of Venus were fortunately mostly observable in the evening, but the point of principle must always be borne in mind. It complicates the analysis, but we cannot remind ourselves too often that the necessary observations would have been essentially simple.

It is not possible to quote a simple single figure for either extreme of Venus' declination, north or south, but some very general rules are in order here. (A fuller account will be found in Appendix 5.) A working rule for the period 3600 to 2000 BC is that extremes of declination lie in the range $25.9° \pm 0.2°$, north or south of the ecliptic. Three cases to the north and three cases to the south might have been observed in a typical period of eight years. Extreme settings, with Venus an evening star, are very much more likely to have been observed than risings. At the geographical position of Avebury and Stone-henge, for example, those figures imply azimuths of orientation within, say, half a degree of 44° north of west and 44.5° south of west, using natural horizons. The separation of these is close to a right angle.

Looking back over our very limited survey of Wessex long barrows, there is scarcely any alignment that could have been interpreted in this way. The Horslip (Windmill Hill) barrow presented the most likely example. What was found there was interpreted as a splendid pair of directions at right angles, one to the setting of Sirius and one to its rising, when its declination was −26.2°. Did the Horslip people observe the extremes of Venus, which were close to this value? Three times every eight years it was visible over the same position; and for many scores of days in that period it was within a degree of the extreme. Granted systematic observation of a kind needed to appreciate the Sirius property, the observation of Venus at its southern extreme of setting could hardly have been avoided. That does not mean that the observation of Venus' complicated behaviour necessarily played a part in establishing the properties

of the site. On the whole it is better to assume that it did not. Observing the changing pattern of a planet's risings and settings is a much more complex activity than observing a star's relatively fixed behaviour. The only sure way of guaranteeing Venus's involvement would be to date an astronomically aligned monument securely, and then to show that there remained an alignment that could be explained with reference to no other star. The likelihood of being able to do this is very remote.

A Postscript on Chance

Those who reject the idea of alignments on stars must find explanations for a whole range of circumstances. How does it come about, for instance, that a barrow (and its mortuary house), so similar to others in plan, but lying on ground with an utterly different curvature and direction, manages to indicate the same pair of stars, and at dates broadly in agreement with radiocarbon evidence? Before leaving this chapter, in which stars have taken a clear precedence over the Sun and Moon in the matter of alignments, an attempt must be made to anticipate those critics who make such statements as that if one takes a long enough interval of time, some bright star or other is likely to rise or set along almost any line one cares to specify.

Such criticism cannot be answered unless it is more precise. Arbitrary decisions must be made, for instance, as to which stars can qualify as likely to have caught the observer's attention. Let us first take all stars that rise and set and are visible from southern Britain with a brightness no less than that of Betelgeuse (visual magnitude 0.9). There are nine (Arcturus and Vega are circumpolar in Wessex, that is, they do not rise and set). In descending order of brightness they are: Sirius, Capella, Rigel, alpha Centauri (also called Rigel Centauri), Procyon, beta Centauri, Aldebaran, Altair, and Betelgeuse. Add to these Deneb and the Pleiades, each for a special reason already explained. There is a subjective element in all this: to have gone to much fainter limits when searching for alignments, we might have been criticized for trying to weight the odds in our favour by increasing the number of potential hits. As for those who object to restricting the number of stars considered as likely to have attracted attention, the only plausible answers possible are in terms of psychology and history. Most of the stars mentioned here are known to have been assigned significant roles in later mythology, which is not a bad guide, but of course so were others.

Taking such a limited group of stars for test, and assuming the latitude of Stonehenge, there are two quite different types of problem worth investigating:

(1) What, if a given landscape is assumed, are the chances that a randomly chosen azimuth will align on a single star? (2) What, given two approximately opposed azimuths, are the chances that it will be possible to find a reasonable shared altitude at which stars can be seen along them? (The second alludes to the technique explained at length in this chapter.)

The first problem approximates to that which is usually addressed by modern writers on the statistics of the later stone circles. They ask whether there are so many astronomically significant alignments revealed in the course of a particular analysis of many stone circles, say covering a whole region, that they cannot be attributed to chance. This problem demands a subsidiary study of such questions as bias in the selection of features of the landscape, and of lines of sight generally. In some cases the statistical query is turned into a method for discovering plausible alignments: large numbers of lines are amassed (the selection problem remains), each line yielding up a particular declination, and the hope (and usually the reality) is that the declinations cluster around certain favoured values that are then taken to indicate authentic objects—stars, or lunar or solar extremes. That is only distantly related to the approach adopted here, where emphasis is put instead on producing a hypothesis, an explanation for individual architectural acts that have no other obvious explanation. It is here claimed that certain principles can be found (abstracted, conjectured) that explain how monuments that are superficially different can ultimately have the same astronomical purpose; and that one may be reasonably satisfied with those principles, even on the basis of only a handful of monuments. Still the principles must be capable of resisting attempts to refute them, and this is where statistics are useful. One way of refuting them would be to show that what they predict is not at all surprising, and that there is a high probability that some stellar alignment or other is bound to be produced in the way explained, or is so likely that the conjectured principles are too weak to be safely accepted. (They may still be true.) This is how (1) and (2) are to be understood here.

(1) Single Stars

Case (1) relates to alignments in a predetermined situation, such as a landscape or—at a stretch—a monument that leaves no room for imagination as to how it was used. To simplify matters, it will be supposed that all stars are seen at a fixed altitude, say two degrees. (No such simple convention can be realistic, but a more intricate one will scarcely affect the conclusion.) Consider then a reasonably long period, say from from 3500 to 3000 BC. What are the chances that one of the eleven stars named above would be indicated, rising or setting,

by an arbitrary line to the horizon in that period? To begin with Sirius: at the beginning of the 500-year period the star was rising at an azimuth of 132.2° from north, and at the end of the period it rose at 128.5°—an interval of 3.7°. The chances of aligning by accident on the rising of Sirius are then about 1 in 48.6 (180° divided by 3.7°). The arbitrary line has an equal chance of hitting the direction of Sirius' setting, and this reduces the odds against a random hit of either rising or setting to 1 in 24.3.

The shift in the azimuth of rising or setting over such a period of time as our 500 years varies from star to star. Data (corresponding to the −3.7° for Sirius) for the other ten stars on the list are: Capella −5.3°; Rigel −5.8°; alpha Centauri +8.1°; Procyon −2.9°; beta Centauri +6.3°; Betelgeuse −4.3°; Aldebaran −4.5°; Altair +2.8°; Deneb +0.6°; Pleiades −5.9°. It so happens that only the ranges quoted for the stars in Centaurus overlap, although those for Procyon, Aldebaran, and the Pleiades are all close to one another. Note that the chances of hitting Deneb with a random line are 1 in 150.

A crude impression of the inherent unlikeliness of hitting by chance at least one of the stars mentioned, for viewing over a given 'natural' horizon, may be had from simply adding the ranges (allowing for overlap) and proceeding as with a single star. Dropping the southerly stars in Centaurus, which distort the picture for obvious reasons, the ranges total 35.8°, making for a 1 in 2.5 chance of success (remembering rising and setting). On this argument, one needs only to add a few more stars to the list to guarantee an even chance of scoring a hit of one sort or another. This is not impressive, but combining alignments for approximately the same date can push up the odds considerably. (With a reasonable set of criteria, the odds against all our Fussell's Lodge alignments having occurred by chance turn out to be 880 to 1, at a conservative estimate.) Added to this, a strong allegiance to certain stars has been suspected, notably Deneb, Aldebaran, Sirius, Rigel—and the circumpolar Arcturus. The odds against finding a single pair by chance in the (shortened) list, in a period of say two centuries, are nearly 16 to 1 against. The odds against finding an independent pair twice are 244 to 1. And by taking multiple alignments, the odds increase very rapidly.

(2) Paired Stars at Equal Altitude

The second problem, requiring an estimate of the odds against pairing possibilities, is much more complicated. The proposed technique of taking two roughly opposed directions for lines of sight from barrow ditches cannot be tested in the same way as over the given natural landscape. It is here maintained that the angle of view was artificial, and by admitting that it could be between

wide limits, the chances of our finding a solution in at least one direction were obviously much increased. But in two?

To narrow down the problem, reasonable limits need to be established for the altitude set by a barrow, to a person looking across it. But is the problem to be addressed in the context of long barrows in general (where a range from, say, 4° to 16° might be in order) or for an individual barrow, where potential limits will be very much closer? And is the angle in azimuth between the two (roughly opposed) lines of sight to be taken as fixed (or at least within a narrow band of uncertainty) in relation to a known barrow, or as lying between generous limits that are capable of taking in all long barrows? And third, there is the analogous question as to dating. Is the spread of possible years to be related to a single barrow or to the 'age of the long barrow' in general, or perhaps to some sub-group?

It should now be clear that there are very many different types of initial assumption. A sceptic might argue thus, taking fairly wide limits for the ranges mentioned: 'I do not believe that long barrows were placed in relation to the stars. If I were to drop a typical long barrow on the landscape at random, the chances are eight in ten that I should be able to find a date within a plausible period of prehistory at which your roughly opposed lines of sight would align accurately on bright stars'. (In round numbers, the 'eight in ten' (0.8) is not unreasonable, taking the former list of eleven stars. The calculation cannot be given briefly.) Following this line of argument in a very crude way, and multiplying probabilities, the chances of finding solutions for two barrows would be 0.64, of finding three 0.51, of finding seven 0.21, and so on. One might reduce still further the chances that the claims against which the unbeliever is arguing are illusory—for instance, by appealing to multiple solutions for the same epoch (usually in close agreement with radiocarbon dating), especially solutions paired at right angles, and having relations with the surrounding landscape—but all this is unlikely to convince resolute sceptics, who are used to having figures in millions quoted against them.

So much for the 'generic barrow on the landscape'. A more reasonable approach is to take a single known long barrow, say Wayland's Smithy, and to ask about the likelihood of finding a solution by chance. It may be supposed, for example, that the long barrow is placed at random on the landscape, with appropriate closely limited characteristics. They might be something like these: opposed azimuths are splayed at an angle between 170° and 172°, and viewing over the mound could only have been at an altitude of less than 12° and more than 11°. What then are the chances of finding a precise solution involving bright stars in both directions between 4000 BC and 3000 BC?

To take this specimen case, even after adding five more bright stars (Pollux, Spica, Antares, Vega and Regulus) to the previous list, there are only three distinct solutions, each with two orientations (interchanging rising and setting), making six in all. Without giving the lengthy calculations, one can say that for the opening decades of the period, the barrow could be dropped into one of only six narrow sectors of the compass, each covering between about 1.4° and 3°. With time, those sectors drift somewhat, shifting by amounts varying from approximately 7° to 12°; and one pair eventually ceases to be useful but another takes its place. The details are not important, but it can be said that at a very generous estimate, the barrow could have been assigned an azimuth falling within sectors totalling 54° of the whole compass. In short, a randomly placed Wayland's Smithy has a three in twenty chance (0.15) of accommodating a pairing of bright stars in the way explained in the present chapter. This is generous, and on another count far too generous: the thousand years considered could have been narrowed down appreciably, greatly increasing the odds against finding a random solution. And even with odds of 0.15, to find seven solutions—if they happened to produce the same odds, which of course they would not—would mean odds of less than two in a million of finding the whole set of solutions by chance.

These figures could all be qualified endlessly, taking local circumstance into account. They are lacking in precision, but they show clearly enough that it is a fallacy to suppose that the methods advocated are bound to produce a whole range of easy solutions. The odds against consistently hitting a solution by chance are very great indeed, and the conclusion must be that astronomical activity at the long barrows is not an illusion.

3

CURSUS AND ENCLOSURE

The Great Earthen Monuments

THE EVIDENCE for the nature of Neolithic houses and settlement is surprisingly scanty, no doubt because many dwellings—at least in the milder climate of southern Britain—were without deep foundations. Even so, remains have been found from the fourth millennium, and even from the fifth, showing that some communities were capable of building substantial timber houses (50 sq m or more in area) with a pitched roof of thatch or turf. There the extended family lived, in some cases with a part of the building set aside for cattle, as in parts of Europe even today. The land would have been sparsely settled, with families in some districts perhaps two or three kilometres apart. The long barrows tell us something of the communities who built them—of their vitality, for instance. William Startin estimates about 7000 worker-hours for the building of an average long barrow, and even greater effort went into the building of enormous rings of banks and ditches. These enclosures, which at first sight were roughly circular, and often double or triple, could be in excess of 200 m across. The first great ditched enclosures seem to come from the later centuries of the long barrow period. At least fifty have been recorded from southern England, and they are known at least as far north as Staffordshire and Lincolnshire. Various suggestions have been made as to their purpose, such as that they were ritual centres, meeting places for trade or recreation, even cattle corrals. They were not well designed for defensive purposes. They might have had a mortuary function, perhaps for the initial exposure of the dead, as some have supposed. Not all of these alternatives are necessarily mutually exclusive.

Two other sorts of monument speak for a high degree of organization in Neolithic society. There is in Dorset a distinctive group of so-called *bank barrows*, which could be considered as a class of long barrows, except that they are very large, and some of them seem to change direction appreciably halfway. This is true of the largest yet recorded, a colossal mound, 546 m in length. It was constructed over the Neolithic enclosure at Maiden Castle (Winterbourne

St Martin) when that was already out of use, judging by the fact that its ditches had already three-quarters filled up with chalk.

The other type of large-scale monument is the *cursus*, of which—given a suitably broad definition—about fifty are known in southern England. A cursus may be several kilometres long, and may have required an investment ten or twenty times as great as was needed for a long barrow. Typically it has two roughly parallel banks, each adjacent to the ditch from which it was quarried, but no central mound worth speaking of. It is usually closed at one or both ends. Two or three of the most notable examples will be considered in this chapter, and then other linear monuments that might be related to them. Whatever their function, it will be shown that their orientations were decided by the places of rising and setting of bright stars and perhaps in some cases of the Sun. Like the long barrows, a cursus offered a means of directing the eye towards the appropriate part of the heavens—we recall the relationship between Wayland's Smithy and the Ridgeway, from an earlier period.

Windmill Hill and Barrow Rings

Of the type of monument known variously as 'causewayed enclosure', and 'causewayed camp', that at Windmill Hill near Avebury is undoubtedly the most famous, having given its name to a whole culture. The phrases describing them are mildly unsatisfactory: 'enclosure' is a modest enough term, although if taken to hint at the deliberate setting apart of a space, even this might impute more to its builders' intentions than is justified. To draw attention to the gaps in the surrounding ditches, however, is rather like describing a text as an assemblage of spaces, rather than of words. The potential social or religious functions of these places are a matter for speculation, but their design forces one to conclude that what mattered to their makers were the ditches and associated mounds. These enclosures are in the strictest sense nothing other than rings of (usually) single-ditched long barrows, and the simplest acceptable description of them might be 'barrow rings'. The beauty of their arrangement is that whereas only a handful of stars, usually no more than six, could have been viewed across the artificial horizons created by a long barrow, at a barrow ring any reasonable number of stars could in principle have been accommodated.

The claim being made here as to their purpose is easily defended in a general way without any calculation whatsoever. In their general pattern, the Windmill Hill rings (Fig. 54) are typical of the class under discussion. Those who have excavated these vast enclosures have often remarked on the fact that

their ditches are remarkably flat-bottomed, and have at least one good straight and near-vertical inner face. In the light of what was claimed in the last chapter, those faces are nothing other than fiducial edges, comparable with the inner edges of long barrow ditches. The ditches and banks are by no means good approximations to circles, even allowing for the fact that they are built up out of generally straight sections. Mounds tend to be on the insides of the ditches—not the natural way to place them in relation to a hill, if economy of effort is at a premium and the ditches are merely quarries. Building on a hillside is certainly the best way of achieving a high angle of view from a ditch with a minimum of effort. That enclosure-ditches were meant for viewing in the way described in the previous chapter is suggested, in the first place, by ten ditches in the middle ring (excluding three untypical fragments), for which the average depth measured by Keiller was 1.57 m. The outer ditches were appreciably deeper, for reasons to be explained, and the inner ditches much shallower (1.12m over seventeen sections) and more variable.

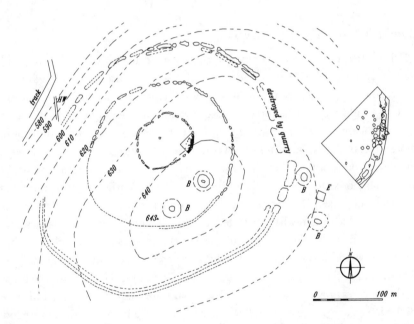

FIG. 54. The rings of ditches and mounds at Windmill Hill, near Avebury. The part of this monument excavated by A. Keiller lies to the east and northeast. The approximate lines of still-unexcavated ditches are shown in broken lines, as are a few of the remains of the banks to the northeast. *HW* is what Keiller described as a 'hollow way'. The broken circles marked *B* are Bronze Age round barrows. *E* is a linear-ditched enclosure. The inset box to the right shows a detail of the inner ring, with the numerous post holes excavated in and near the ditches to the east. The contours are heights in feet above Ordnance Datum.

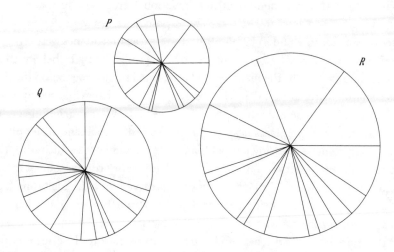

FIG. 55. The directions at right angles to straight sections of the ditches at Windmill Hill. *P*, *Q* and *R* are for the inner, middle and outer ring respectively, all looking outwards. In view of the uncertainties in interpreting the uneven lines of a much-damaged and largely unexcavated monument, these directions are all approximate, but their general resemblance to the pattern of (significant) barrow alignments over the landscape (Fig. 71, taking only the valid directions marked with small circles) will be fairly obvious.

The most telling qualitative argument, however, comes from the directions of the ditches. If lines are taken at right angles to them, the result is a fair approximation to the general pattern of lines towards the risings and settings of bright stars in the region, with relatively few lines to the north, and most to the east–west line and the directions south of it. This is shown in Fig. 55. Later in this chapter this pattern will be examined in more detail. (Compare Fig. 71.) One can see the pattern even at a glance, from the far fewer directions set by the sections to their southern sides. The same is often true elsewhere—for instance at the double-ringed monument known as Robin Hood's Ball, in the Stonehenge region (see Fig. 65).

H. G. O. Kendall excavated at the Windmill Hill site, beginning in 1922, but was at first aware only of the inner ditch. He was there with O. G. S. Crawford in January 1923 when they noticed the hollows of the other ditches, picked out by the slanting rays of the Sun. Soon afterwards, when it was threatened with the building of a radio transmitting station, his friend Alexander Keiller managed to buy part of the site, and his first serious excavations there took place between 1925 and 1929, beginning with aerial observations and photographs. Having eventually purchased the entire site, in 1937–8 Keiller re-excavated the ditches examined earlier. He died in 1955,

having bequeathed the monument to the National Trust, and further excavations were carried out in 1957–8. The exposed ditches were found to be deteriorating rapidly, and in 1959–60 all the re-excavated ditches were refilled. A report on the various excavations was finally published by Isobel Smith in 1965. Not unnaturally, the main focus of attention at that time was on the rich collection of material found in the ditches, much of it having clearly been thrown or placed there deliberately. There were querns for grinding grain, shards of pottery from places nearby and far afield, flint tools and antler picks. There were stone axes, many animal bones and human bones—including the complete skeletons of two young children. That fertility rites of some sort had taken place there was proved by various objects carved in chalk, including four phalli that have earned their anonymous sculptors much posthumous fame.

It is not surprising that Windmill Hill has left its mark on archaeology, but the contents of the ditches surely do not take us back to the origins of the monument. The tacit assumption has been, as always, that the ditches, having supplied the material for the banks, had done their duty and would have been allowed to silt up willy nilly. If they were used to view the heavens in anything more than a dedicatory rite, however, then they would surely have been kept clean and open, perhaps even beyond the point when they functioned as originally intended. A radiocarbon date obtained from a mixture of material from the ditches is therefore almost certainly misleading as to the origins of the three rings of ditches. (When calibrated it takes us only as far back as the range 3210±290 BC.) The mean date is three or four centuries later than those obtained from radiocarbon dates for roughly comparable monuments at Abingdon, Cherhill, Hambledon Hill, High Peak, Knap Hill, Orsett, and Rowden. Another hilltop specimen from Windmill Hill yielded a date which, when calibrated, covers the range 3730±215 BC. It will now be tentatively shown that the inner ditch could well have been as early as this, and that the outer and middle ditches were no later than the thirty-fifth century BC.

Tentatively, since the evidence is incomplete. It will be assumed with good reason that viewing was carefully planned to be at right angles to ditch edges, as at long barrows, so that a decrepit edge is a serious impediment to any analysis. Many directions are measurable to no better than two or three degrees. As in other cases where more than two directions of viewing at equal altitudes are involved, the measured directions can be taken two by two (but not opposed now), although doing so now yields a very large number of possibilities, most of them of very poor value. Since the longer lines are the most reliable, it is natural to start with the outer ditches, and then only with those that seem most dependable (90°, 122°, 138°, 157°, 276°). This is a challenging set of data,

for all must ideally be satisfiable with a single mound altitude and date. The solution need not be discussed in detail. The optimum altitude appears to be in the neighbourhood of 21.8°, at which the azimuths quoted yield solutions (in the order given) for the rising of Spica in 3450 BC, of Antares in 3520 BC, of Aldebaran in 3520 BC, of Bellatrix in 3510 BC, and the setting of Pollux in 3480 BC. (The latitude of the place is 51° 26' 25".) In view of the uncertainties in the directions, the consistency of the results, with a mean value of 3514 BC, is surprisingly good.

Any suspicions that the viewing angles are excessive are misplaced, for the three excavated ditches are of depths 2.43 m, 2.65 m, and 2.93 m., while their profiles all fit well with the suggested altitude of view. What is more, 21.8° is a very special angle, corresponding to a gradient of 2 in 5, just double the gradient we have begun to regard as having often been deliberately chosen in long barrow design. From the contour-lines in Fig. 54 it may be verified that the gradient of the *ground* near the outer ring of ditches on the northwest slope of Windmill Hill is almost exactly 1 in 5. It is unlikely to have been by chance that the vertical drop (for a given horizontal distance) arrived at by artifice was just double that over natural ground at the outer ditches to the northwest. But when one comes to analyse the middle ditch, the optimum solution is found to require almost exactly a viewing altitude of 11.3°, that is, a gradient of 1 in 5 once more.

We are not so fortunate with ditch azimuths where the shorter middle sections are concerned, but azimuths of 23°, 107°, 130°, and 275°, with the quoted altitude, correspond to the rising of Vega in 3520 BC, of Antares in 3420 BC, of Bellatrix in 3480 BC, and the setting of Altair in 3600 BC. The mean date is 3505 BC, but the uncertainties here and in the outer ring are so great that they cannot be put in order of date with any confidence.

The inner ring is by far the most enigmatic. Its ditches are of varying depths: four of them are of a depth that might easily have gone with a viewing altitude of the same magnitude as that at the middle ditch, while the other depths are between 60 cm and 1.34 m. The best approach seems to be first to concentrate on the three ditches of roughly 'standard' human depth. The one at the very north is kidney-shaped and was very probably for observing the rising and setting of a single star. Its shape makes it difficult to measure, but it might have been meant for the same star as the ditch to the northwest, which is here taken as facing azimuth 156°. The ditch east of the southernmost faces a direction of azimuth 346.5°. In short, there are here only two independent directions, but they come from comparable ditches and are usable with our standard method. They yield an altitude of 9.5° and a year of 3760 BC, on the

assumption that the three northern ditches are for the rising and setting of Sirius and the southern for the setting of Vega.

The uncertainties here are of the order of two centuries—even allowing for the fact that we might be working with much too low an altitude. Introducing other ditches into the reckoning it is hard to make any headway except with one of the very shallow ditches (the long one in the northeast, facing azimuth 225°). Assuming viewing at its extinction angle, Sirius's setting would have been observable around 3880 BC, with higher angles corresponding to later years (3580 for 2° altitude, for instance). This might therefore possibly point to the fourth way of observing Sirius from the site, now from the inner ring. The irregularity of these other ditches in depth, however, soon reduces these problems to sheer guesswork, and it would be wise not to go beyond claiming, very hesitantly, a date in the thirty-eighth century for the innermost area of Windmill Hill.

On balance, it seems probable that the two outer rings of ditches and banks were put up together, not many decades in time from 3500 BC. The crucial altitudes were evidently 2 in 5 and 1 in 5. The inner ring might have been assembled over a relatively long period of time, perhaps even as a pioneer work of combining ditches into ring-formation. The kink to the northwest and the assortment of depths certainly speaks for something less than perfection of technique. Were it not for the uncertainty of the solution offered here, it might have been argued that the viewing altitude mentioned (9.5°) was equivalent to a gradient of 1 in 6. Whether or not this last ratio is to be taken seriously, much more evidence will later emerge for the acceptance of comparable gradients, involving the ratios of small whole numbers.

It is not unlikely that some of the post holes found near the eastern ditch of the inner ring and elsewhere were used in a way comparable to that of the scaling posts at some of the earthen long barrows. Their plans have been published only in part, and in any case the incomplete state of the excavation makes it premature to consider them in detail. From the detail in Fig. 54, however—or better still from Isobel Smith's report—one should be able to spot three or more lines parallel to nearby ditch edges. To study the case properly, of course, post hole depths are needed. Generally speaking, Windmill Hill gives the distinct impression of a monument whose surface has been little more than scratched.

The Two Stonehenge Cursus and their Dorset Precursor

If the function of 'causewayed enclosures' has been prejudged by those who gave them this name, the same is even truer of monuments of cursus-type. They

ultimately take their name from the larger of two examples at Stonehenge. Seen from the air, the Greater Stonehenge Cursus is by far the most easily discerned of the many prehistoric monuments in the district. It runs for 2.74 km across the chalk downs, and lies about 700 m north of Stonehenge at its closest point, along an axis that is only a few degrees from an east–west line. The structure was first noted by William Stukeley in 1723, and what in his diary he referred to as a [h]ippodromeC255 became in his book *Stonehenge* (1740) a *cursus*. He was implicitly likening it to a Roman racecourse (*cursus*, plural the same), although of course he considered it a more ancient, British, equivalent,

> a most noble work, contriv'd to reach from the highest ground of two hills, extended the intermediate distance over a gentle valley: so that the whole *cursus* lies conveniently under the eye of the most numerous quantity of spectators. To render this more convenient for sight, it is projected on the side of rising ground, chiefly looking toward Stonehenge. A delightful prospect from the temple, when this vast plain was crowded with chariots, horsemen and foot, attending these solemnities, with innumerable multitudes!

An astronomical orientation for the Greater Stonehenge Cursus was suggested in 1906 by Sir Norman Lockyer, who decided that it was parallel to the stone avenues at Merrivale (Dartmoor). Since he believed that those were aligned on the rising of the Pleiades, he decided that the Cursus was 'like them, used as a processional road, a via sacra, to watch the rising of the Pleiades', and he deduced a date of 1950 BC. This much derided conclusion is unacceptable, but for good reason or bad, Lockyer's chronology was certainly better than the general archaeological consensus of the time. His assumption that a cursus was some sort of roadway has been less often criticized, but it is based on a number of assumptions that are far from self-evident.

A typical cursus is intimately related to long barrows in its neighbourhood. Across the eastern end of the Greater Cursus, for example, lies the long barrow Amesbury 42. Whether or not this long mound ever incorporated burials—opinions are divided—it is likely to have had a function similar to that of the mounds of long barrows. (The word 'barrow' originally meant any hill or mound, and there is no good reason for restricting its use to burial mounds.) Stukeley had thought it to be the dais of the judges of the races, an idea that at least had the merit of avoiding the assumption that all mounds were once tombs. The long barrows in the neighbourhood of any cursus may often prove to be a more important guide to its functioning than even the precise course of its defining banks.

There is a much smaller structure, the 'Lesser Cursus', to the northwest of its better-known neighbour. Sir Richard Colt Hoare drew attention to it in the

first volume of his *Ancient History of North and South Wiltshire* (1812). It is now almost completely ploughed out of existence, but it can be seen from the air, and is shown on the Ordnance Survey in a form rather more regular than it has in reality. Roughly 45 m wide and 380 m long, it is open at the eastern end and closed at the western, and is directed about 15° north of east.

The Greater Stonehenge Cursus has many affinities to another on the Cranborne Chase in Dorset. Since that seems to be appreciably older than either of those at Stonehenge, and is the largest and perhaps the most complex cursus of all, it will be given priority in a search for the principles underlying cursus construction. It is in some respects the largest of all prehistoric British monuments. Following a meandering course—but one that is made up of reasonably straight sections—it covers almost exactly 10 km in its track length. The widths of its sections are fairly uniform, at between roughly 80 m and 100 m. Richard Atkinson estimated that in its original state it involved moving some six and a half million cubic feet of earth (184,000 cubic metres), nearly twice as much as was shifted at Avebury, and two-thirds of the volume shifted at Silbury Hill. Much labour would have been required to do this and to clear trees and other vegetation—William Startin estimated a minimum of 450,000 worker-hours. (The Hambledon Hill complex might have involved twice as much work, but that was a multiple enterprise.) The Dorset monument covers a large area—more than three times that of the Greater Cursus at Stonehenge. Without maps charting its course, following it on the ground is now difficult and in parts impossible—and the older Ordnance Survey maps are in places misleading. Parts can be seen from the B3081 road at Bottlebush. The nearest villages are Gussage St Michael and Gussage St Andrew near the southern end, and Pentridge, adjacent to it at the northern end.

This particular cursus is important, for it seems to show how such a structure can evolve naturally out of the customs associated with the alignment of barrows. There are twelve long barrows in its immediate neighbourhood (within a kilometre of it), and at least thirty-two in what we shall later come to regard as its territory. Many of them are certainly related to it, and yet unfortunately very few of them have been fully excavated. This fact makes more than a modest analysis quite impossible. Its overall course is shown in Fig. 56, and an idea of the inclines—systematically exaggerated on the figure—can be obtained from Fig. 58. The southern end is on Thickthorn Down, adjacent to two long barrows (at A on the figure; there are many other, later, earthworks not shown on it). The end there is closed by a three-sided and roughly rectangular (-shaped) bank with external ditch. The bank is still preserved in places to a height of 1.2 m above the turf. It is likely that the custom was to

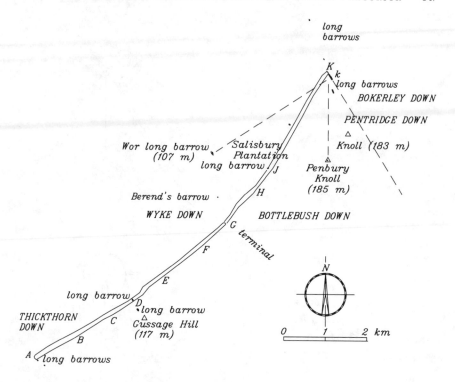

FIG. 56.   The Dorset Cursus and its surroundings. For keys to the long barrows, see Fig. 59 and 70.

look over it, perhaps standing at places marked in some way. The northern end, also adjacent to two barrows, was no doubt once similar, but has now lost much more of its height.

There are two conceivable ways of sighting stars in relation to a ditch—one along it, the other at right angles to it. One might imagine that a long shallow ditch, or a very deep ditch, was used in the first way, and that a ditch about as deep as a man is tall was more appropriate to the second. It is possible that there were sightings over a steep artificial horizon of stars that do not otherwise set, but there is not enough information available to allow an accurate estimate of what they were, and most attention will here be given to low-altitude alignments over long distances, of which there are a few that seem to fit into a coherent pattern. (One must of course also consider the possibility that the Sun and Moon, rather than the stars, were observed.) It has to be said that there is a danger here of being seduced by the long and fairly straight sections of the cursus into supposing that its overall plan was conceived at the outset of construction. As will soon be evident, it was more probably patched together

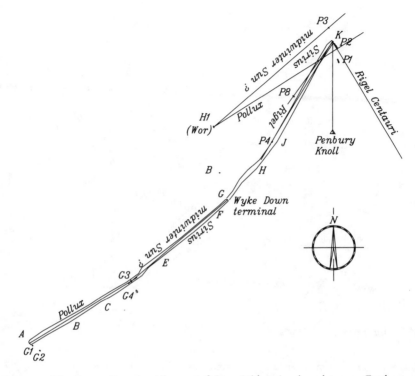

FIG. 57. The Dorset Cursus, with some of the neighbouring long barrows. For key, see Fig. 59. The alignments will be introduced at a later stage.

from elements that had their origins in simple alignments of long barrows on other long barrows. But first to a rough description of the composite entity.

At the southern (Thickthorn) end the low parallel banks are now often quite ploughed out of existence. They cross water meadows (B) until at nearly 3 km they reach, and pass to either side of, a third long barrow (D). This is on the highest point of its course across Gussage Down, and the barrow, which is visible from the starting point, could have made a horizon marker for viewing from both sides. Whether or not it was a true artificial horizon, down to which stars came, is something still to be decided. It should certainly not be regarded as a foresight, unless we have reason to think that it was visible, whether by the light of the Sun or Moon, or by fire. It is just over 50 m long, over 20 m wide, and even now stands about 3.5 m high. Its form could be described as a pear sliced down the middle, with its higher and wider end roughly southeast. In the neighbourhood of this enclosed barrow, but outside the monument on Gussage Hill, there are two other long barrows (the nearer of the two we shall

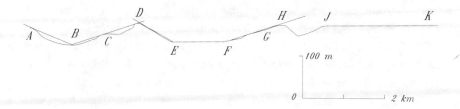

FIG. 58.   The changing levels along the Dorset Cursus. The vertical scale is exaggerated by a factor of ten in relation to the horizontal, and the profile *follows the cursus*, that is, it is not in a unique plane. Note how some potential sight-lines (assuming observers in the valleys) might have grazed the intervening ground between *B* and *D*, and between *F* and *H*.

mention again), and many later round barrows. This was a place of central importance, and in the later Bronze and Iron Ages there was an important settlement here that must have removed many traces of Neolithic activity.

The path of the cursus now follows a gentle curve for a limited stretch (about a kilometre), and Atkinson saw in this a sign that there had been a failure to match up exactly two sections coming from different directions. It continues in this way across a dry valley, and then up into what is now woodland (the Salisbury Plantation). On high ground—now among densely packed trees—the northwest bank actually incorporates another small, pear-shaped, long barrow (Pentridge V, at *J* on the figure, with high end to the north). It looks as though the cursus, the bank of which overlies the mound of the barrow, was aligned in some way on a pre-existing long barrow, but the line of the bank here is not exactly that of the barrow, so that we are probably dealing with the continuation of an earlier tradition, when the selected star rose or set at a different azimuth. (There are said to be traces of an earlier, shallow, ditch at the northern end of the cursus.)

The final, northern, sections of the Dorset Cursus are today difficult to detect. Having passed the village of Pentridge—where in hot dry weather parts are detectible from the colour of the grass—it ends with a suitably bracketed bank and ditch near Bokerley Ditch on Bokerley Down. There is a sudden change in direction of the cursus at the end (*K*). There are here, at the northern end, more long barrows. The nearest are Pentridge II *a* and *b*, which used to be regarded as two barrows built end to end. Fieldwork in the 1980s, and the study of aerial photographs taken before the modern plough had done its worst, showed that the nearer mound to the cursus was a complete barrow, with high end to the east, while the other mound seems to have been erected later (with

distinct ditches). Richard Bradley saw it as a tail added later than the terminal, since it would otherwise have been placed away from the burial end of the original barrow, but it is not at all clear that it needs to be treated as subsidiary to the first barrow, for it does not follow quite the same direction. The question of the relationship of the two to the terminal will be touched on later. There is some sort of relationship between the terminal at the southern (Thickthorn) end of the cursus and two quite separate barrows there. They have very approximately the same orientation as the end bank, aslant the direction of the side banks.

The three terminals (A, G, and K on Fig. 56) were built on a more massive scale than the banks. When in 1912 Herbert Toms drew a profile of those at the Bottlebush end, before they came under the plough, the depression of the ditches was about 30 cm and the banks within were about twice that in height. Each seemed to be about five or six metres across. Sections cut in 1982 and 1984 showed that the ditch was a clean-cut affair, steep-sided and flat-bottomed. Where it crossed level ground it had been 3m across at the top, 2 m across at the bottom, and perhaps 1.4 m deep. It seemed that the bank had been only 3 m wide at its base. To estimate how high it was, one must know whether it was revetted or not. If the chalk was simply dumped, it would have made a bank 1.7 m high and about 6 m wide. To have been only 3 m wide implies revetting: it could have been supported to 1.26 m and heaped above that to a total height of 2.12 m. (These estimates by Bradley all assume that the quarried chalk rested stable at an angle of 35°.) The centres of ditch and bank were about 8 m apart, which means that the viewing angle, on this second estimate, would have been around 13°, or somewhat less allowing for spillage, settlement and spread. It is hard to believe that viewing across the cursus, in long barrow fashion, could ever have been accurately arranged over more than short sections for very long, but the important point here is that cross-viewing could have been done, if at all, at much the same angles (altitudes) as were found, in the last chapter, at the long barrows.

This observation concerning the northern and southern terminals will be called upon later, and it will be tried out on specimen intermediate stretches.

The Probable Evolution of the Dorset Cursus

A series of conjectures will now be made as to the course of evolution of the main elements of the cursus. Its great length means that changes in geographical latitude have to be taken into account in our several calculations, a rare situation. (The latitude of the south end is 50° 54' 42" and of the north end

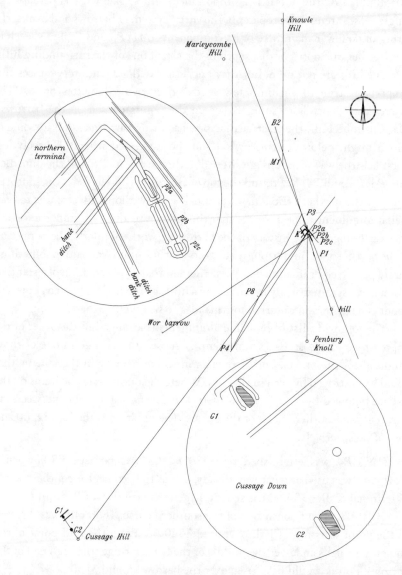

FIG. 59.   The principal alignments of *locations* at the northern end of the Dorset Cursus.
K is the Bokerley terminal. (See also the inset detail on the left (scaled up 10x), where
fragments of surrounding ditchwork are also shown, almost giving the appearance of
another terminal.) The chief long barrows in the neighbourhood, with the notation used
here and in Fig. 60, are Gussage St Michael I, II, III, IV (*G1* to *G4*), Pentridge I, IIa, b
and c, III, IV and VIII (*P1* to *P8*), and Handley I (better known as Wor Barrow). *M1*
(Martin I) and *B2* (Broadchalke II) are long barrows in Vernditch Chase, now wooded. The
three lines running north–south are drawn exactly so. Hilltops are the centres of the small
circles. The lower inset detail shows the barrows on Gussage Down (also scale 10x).

50°58' 20".) At the outset it is important to emphasize what is perhaps the single most interesting property of the entire system of barrows and banks: the siting of no fewer than three of its components (*M1*, *P3* and *P4*) puts each of them either due north or due south of the top of one of the surrounding hills.

The hills are not high, but they are clearly defined, and in two cases this property is true to within a few metres over two kilometres or so. (The discrepancy depends to some extent on the points chosen on the barrows.) Marleycombe Hill, the least satisfactory, has many earthworks on it, some of which might belong to this period and the suggested scheme. Scarcely less notable is the way locations are aligned in threes: *B2*, *K*, *P1*, and the unnamed hill; *P3*, *P8*, and *P4*; *K*, *P8*, and the top of Gussage Hill. Here *K* is the southern angle of the northern (Bokerley) terminal. Even without any attempt to date stellar alignments, one suspects that this point was of much importance at a very early stage of the history of the barrow network. Similarly, the perfection of the north–south lines strongly suggests that attention was paid to something dimly perceived or imagined at West Kennet, that is, observation of a star that rose and set symmetrically in relation to a hilltop. Too little is known at present about the barrows in question for this idea to be taken further.

The following list of probable alignments is arranged in the order of the approximate dates derived from them. A substantial change in one of those might affect the others, but there is an inner consistency in the scheme that could be destroyed by certain changes. Where the numbers of the items on the list are followed by *N* or *S*, this is merely to distinguish roughly between the northern and southern parts of the cursus. The notation is that of Fig. 60 and Fig. 59, respectively.

(1*N*) *P4* was established by 3880 BC (as was perhaps *P8*), when a viewpoint was used at what was already, or was to become, the southern angle of terminal *K*. In 3880 BC the setting Rigel was visible over *P4* from *K*.

(3*S*) *AB*, on the south side of the southern cursus (Fig. 60), was directed to the point of rising of Pollux around 3520 BC. From the mid-point of the end of the cursus and over the middle of the barrow ridge (the high end of the barrow), Pollux would have risen over the barrow around 3550 BC.

(4*N*) Around 3550 BC, *P3* was established with reference to *P4*, over which Rigel Centauri was setting. *P8* lay across this line.

(5*S*) The northern side *GF* of the southern half of the cursus aligns on the setting of Sirius around 3490 BC, the star being then seen over the barrow ridge at *D*.

(6*N*) Around 3400 BC, *P2a* was established with reference to the centre of the end ditch at *K* and possibly *M1* if it was in existence then (but see below),

but in such a position along this line that the setting Rigel was visible over *P8*. The date depends on the viewpoint and the part of *P8* chosen, covering a range of about twenty years as the observer's position changes from the northern end of the barrow to the southern.

(7N) If Wor Barrow was not previously in existence, it might have been set up in 3360 BC as a viewpoint for the rising of Pollux over the head of *P2a*, or its forecourt (the gap between it and *P2b*). The more southerly the viewpoint, the earlier the date. What seems more likely is that Wor Barrow already existed, and that *P2b* was erected so that the gap was fitted to the rising star (although the star was only at its extinction angle above the gap).

(8N) The setting Sirius was observable over Wor Barrow from *P3* around 3250 BC. This occasion might have been linked with the next, since a barrow could always be placed so as to satisfy two alignments, by locating the point where they cross.

(9N) The rising Rigel Centauri was observable from *M1* or *P3* or *K* over *P2b* and *P2c* (or from any of these over another to the south of it) around 3180 BC. There are circumstances in which the star would have been seen down almost exactly to the natural horizon.

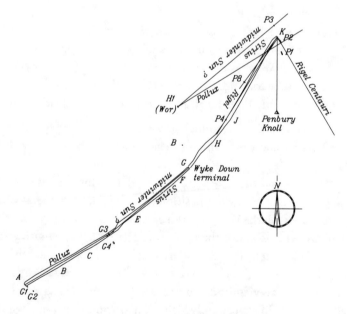

FIG. 60.   The principal astronomical alignments at the Dorset Cursus. For abbreviations, see Fig. 59. Berend's Barrow (*B*, to the north of Wyke Down terminal) is a conical mound reminiscent of Silbury Hill, but on a much smaller scale.

(10N) Around 3070 BC, the rising Rigel Centauri was visible at the natural horizon along the line *B2, P3, K, P1*, and over the top of the unnamed hill.

This collection of ten alignments, involving no fewer than twenty different structures or prominent places, is achieved *on the basis of only four stars,* including three out of the six brightest in the Dorset sky. But still it does not exhaust the possibilities. Alignments on the Sun will be considered shortly, but only after we have tried out our conjecture of the last section, that there was equal-altitude viewing around the end banks and across the now widely separated banks.

The levels at which observers would have stood in opposed ditches were not quite equal—it would have been remarkable had they been so, over a distance of 80 m—but this was not of the first importance, since the angles of view were set by two different mounds. The changing directions of the cursus present a great number of possibilities, in applying our standard method for seeking out stars that could have been observed at equal angles and at right angles to the line of the mounds. Unfortunately the various published plans of the cursus present an even greater variety of alternatives, and the gross uncertainties in the directions of the ditches, especially at the two extreme terminals (at *A* and *K*), leave us with many doubts that are only partially resolved by other evidence.

Here, listed without any assessment of their worth, are three possibilities. There are as yet no adequate surveys, and the errors might be a couple of centuries or more. What is of interest, even so, is the fact that our method throws up an altitude consistent with the side bank sizes discussed earlier, while suggesting appreciably higher altitudes for the north and south terminals:

(11S) At the southern terminal, at a viewing angle of about 15.5°, the rising of Bellatrix and the setting of Vega could have been observed; around 3680 BC.

(12N) At the northern terminal, created for this purpose around the important pre-existing viewing position (see (1N) above), and at a viewing angle of about 16.8°, the rising of Aldebaran and the setting of Deneb could have been observed, as well as the setting of Bellatrix looking southwest across the broad end of the terminal; around 3590 BC. It may be recalled that similar triple possibilities were found at long barrows. An unusually large proportion of long barrows in this vicinity are surrounded by a U-ditch, and when properly surveyed they will almost certainly yield similar triple-viewing possibilities.

(13S) Across the southern banks at the low point by the stream, at a viewing angle of about 11.1°, the rising of Sirius and the setting of Vega could have been observed; around 3050 BC. (It is a surprising fact that in the following

section an arrangement will be found giving the setting of Sirius with the rising of Vega, at an earlier date but a very similar altitude.)

In 1973, A. E. Penny and J. E. Wood argued for a number of potential astronomical alignments in and around the Dorset Cursus. All of them were solar or lunar, and for want of other guidance over dating, they assumed that there was an analogy with the Stonehenge Cursus, and that both belonged to the first half of the third millennium BC. Most of their results can be reworked for the fourth millennium.

Five of the seven lines of sight suggested by Penny and Wood pass through only one significant point of the cursus. Of the other two lines, one to the midwinter setting Sun has the observer at the Wyke Down terminal (G) and looking to one side of the barrow across the Gussage Down ridge (D). A second alignment is on a turning point in the Moon's motion (a lunar minimum), and has the observer at one corner of that ridge and looking to the Thickthorn terminal (A). In the first case the Sun sets to the left of the barrow on the ridge. In the second case, the true horizon is provided by a distant hill, and not by the terminal. Other sight lines pass from barrow to barrow (two) or from terminal or ridge to barrow (three). None of the seven lay directly along the lines of the banks of the cursus itself, although it may well be a mistake to suppose that the gleaming white of the chalk banks was ever meant as a precise guide to the eye.

Penny and Wood needed one solar and one lunar phenomenon in order to explain the lower half of the total cursus. Such phenomena can only be accepted as having *motivated* the digging of the cursus, however, if the stellar alignments offered above are dismissed completely. While it is difficult to dismiss lunar alignments absolutely, they will be neglected here on the grounds that there is as yet no clear supporting evidence for such alignments elsewhere at the early period of prehistory we are advocating. That there are deliberate *physical* alignments in this area cannot be doubted, but it is hard to believe that they were directed by design towards both the stars and the Moon. This is not impossible, but one should not overwork the idea that these Neolithic people 'just happened to notice' that their scheme fitted both stars and the Moon, especially when one is dealing with the far from obvious minor lunar stand-stills. On the other hand, it is hard to believe that certain facts did escape their notice, and in particular the fact that the points of rising and setting of Sirius over a certain period in the second half of the fourth millennium were near to the points of midwinter sunrise and sunset.

(If 'near' is defined as within a solar radius of the upper limb of the Sun—that is, within one solar radius of the part of the Sun most likely to have

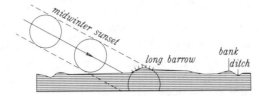

FIG. 61.   The path of the setting Sun as seen from the centre of the Wyke Down terminal, looking over the cursus long barrow on the ridge of Gussage Hill. This is drawn in what seems to be the most inherently probable arrangement, but it also happens to place the last glint exactly mid-way between the banks. It was so in the late fourth millennium. During the year, the Sun always set to the right (north) of the extreme position shown. The later the historical period, the further to the right was its extreme of setting, but not until 600 BC was the extreme at mid-barrow, for an observer in the middle of the Wyke Down terminal.

been observed—then the two were near between 3480 and 3350 BC. Two Sirius alignments have been found in this neighbourhood, that is, for 3490 and 3250 BC, but they are not strictly comparable, since the Sun can be seen down to the horizon, whereas Sirius is seen only down to its extinction angle.)

From our findings at a number of long barrows, we know that solar and stellar alignments could be mixed. The Beckhampton Road barrow, for example, combines a solar alignment in the thirty-fourth century with alignments on stars including Pollux. There can be no fundamental objection to adding the midwinter alignments to our list, duly moved into the fourth millennium. In fact it fits extremely well with the position of the long barrow (*G3*) on the ridge. Seen against the sky from the *midpoint* of the Wyke Down terminal (*G*), which is just low enough on the slope to allow the barrow to appear above the distant hills, the last glint of the setting midwinter Sun for a century or two around 3750 BC would have seemed to be at the very entrance to the barrow, or just above its higher end. (The form of the barrow is not known, so that it is impossible to be precise.) The path of the descending Sun is as shown in Fig. 61.

A certain amount of leeway is possible in the supposed arrangement. Moving the viewing position northwards implies an earlier date, and southwards a later; but doing either affects the dating very drastically. If for some reason one prefers the idea of sunset over mid-barrow, then an observer three-quarters of the way from the southern angle to the northern (at *G* still) will suffice, say for 3400 BC; but this is not at all as intuitively acceptable as the arrangement previously suggested, which puts midwinter sunset over the place of the dead, and the observer in midcursus.

The advantage of sunset observations over observations of the stars is that there are no problems in setting up the alignments over great distances. There is a fundamental difference between aligning the stars on the parts of a barrow near at hand, and working at distances of a kilometre or more. This is not quite the same as the problem discussed earlier, when we said that in any ritual, all the observers had to do was to follow the descent of a star that they recognized, and that the designer had taken care of the way in which it set, or rose. The white chalk of the cursus banks and ditches would have helped to fix the observer's gaze, especially by moonlight, although not without other help in total darkness. This, however, is the ritual observer's perspective. The architect of it all would have needed help, and would doubtless have made use of fire on the horizon—the same might, of course, have been used in ritual too. Traces of fire have been found inside the Grey Wethers stone circles on Dartmoor, as well as Fernworthy and Brisworthy there, at all of which places observations comparable to those on the Dorset Cursus were almost certainly made.

In sum, the cursus on the Cranborne Chase—which could easily have been the prototype for others of more regular form—is in many ways capable of misleading us. We recall how the Wyke Down terminal led to the idea that the southern part of the cursus was closed off and complete, and so was earlier than the northern half. The dates obtained here leave much to be desired, but they do suggest a much more complicated picture, with the banks and ditches not at all the centrepiece of a single grand plan for the region, but almost an afterthought. The traditional idea is based on the feeling that the transverse 'bracketing' ditches are meant to seal off what is, *de facto*, an enclosure. Some archaeologists have seen in this a sign that this type of structure was designed expressly to exclude outsiders. It seems, however, that the 'terminals' were in place before there was anything for them to terminate. The lines of the banks and ditches are not crooked by virtue of incompetent planning, but simply because they were added as a frame to pre-existing components. As a frame, astronomically speaking, they were inspired by long-barrow practice.

Another Bokerley Cursus?

Cutting across the Bokerley (northern) terminal of the Dorset Cursus there are traces of a ditch that in its oblique situation is reminiscent of a ditch cutting across the western end of the Greater Stonehenge Cursus. It would be a mistake to suppose that the two are analogous, though, for in the Dorset case the ditch seems to be part of the terminal of a much more extensive system heading roughly southwest (Fig. 62). It seems almost as though it was planned as a

cursus, but never finished. It will in fact be suggested that it was built in even more stages, beginning with a 'terminal'—again with nothing much to terminate—interlaced with the terminal to which all our attention has so far been given. This was followed, as it seems, centuries afterwards, with the long straight sections. And long after this, a very degenerate ditch system was added.

The part drawn in the figure is in straight sections, and is not to be confused with Bokerley Dyke, a much larger and later earthwork to the north, which follows a winding path that at one point almost touches it. (There is now a comprehensive survey of the Bokerley Dyke available, prepared by Collin Bowen for the Royal Commission on the Historical Monuments of England.) Our straight sections are romantically known—like many other entirely unconnected ditch-systems in England—as Grim's Dyke. (The ascription is of course irrelevant. Grim is potentially an Anglo-Saxon name, but is related to an alternative Scandinavian name for their god Woden. Ditches were often ascribed to gods or the devil in northern Europe. Compare Wansdyke, namely Woden's Ditch.) To the east of the section drawn here there is another, heading north of east in a very irregular path that soon approaches what was apparently an Iron Age settlement. This part is so different in character from the rest that one can only suppose it to have been a later extension, and Grim is welcome to it.

Consider first the double ditch and bank cutting across the Bokerley terminal of the main cursus. If indeed it is symmetrical, as it appears to be, then it can be treated in the same way as a long barrow, lending itself to

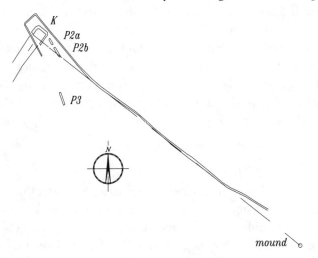

FIG. 62.   An unfinished cursus on Bokerley Down? If, as seems possible, this has a double ditch at its terminal (see Fig. 59), then it has affinities with the Greater Cursus at Stonehenge.

cross-viewing at equal altitudes. It has never been accurately surveyed, but the azimuths are about 24.7° and (its opposite) 204.7°. These lead us in the usual way to suppose that the rising of Vega and the setting of Sirius were viewed across the central bank, at an altitude of 11.3° around 3440 BC. This would put it a few decades before stage (6N) in the previous section. What is interesting about this fact is the close parallelism of the bank under discussion and the nearby barrows *P2a–c*, and it seems not at all improbable that they, when excavated, will reveal ditches that indicate a similar attachment to Sirius and Vega on the part of their builders. The same pair of stars—but with rising and setting roles reversed—was earlier indicated by a section of the southern cursus.

The main long section of the new system—we ignore a shorter section to the north—while it follows only a single line, nevertheless has two interesting properties. First, it suggests a viewing position at the southern end of the long barrow *P2b* or *P2c*. And second, it heads for a small mound on the shoulder of Blagdon Hill. Whether or not this mound is of comparable age is of no great importance as far as the altitude of view is concerned: this would have been in the neighbourhood of 1.4°, depending on the observer's place. An observer at *P2b/c* would have seen this horizon easily, given no tree cover. Even standing in a ditch to the northwest of *P2b/c*, an observer would have been able to see it over the old terminal bank had this been about 2 m or less in height. (If the observer stood at ground level, the limiting height would have been about 3.6 m.) *P2b/c* would then have been no obstacle unless well over 4 m, which is virtually impossible.

There are surprisingly few possibilities for viewing a star in the direction followed by the ditch (127.1°) at a plausible historical period. The rising of Sirius could have been observed around 2690 BC, or the rising of Rigel around 2120 BC. The former alternative seems the more likely of the two, since Sirius is the brightest star of all, and since it has been indicated so often before by monuments in the region. That the Sirius option is closer in time to the last date found for the other cursus must count for a little, although four centuries separate the two. One might modify the result by choosing a different position for observers. If they stood at the corner of the new terminal, a date of 2820 BC is implied, with the sight line passing over the ditch rather than grazing its bank. Ten-metre trees on the horizon would make the Sirius dates seventy years later. There seems to be no possibility of moving them much further back in time than this.

The Bokerley semi-cursus, like the main Dorset cursus, thus appears to be a composite object, created by the joining of elements over a very long period

of time. It has affinities with many other smaller linear earthworks in the neighbourhood, but relatively few have such straight sections. Before leaving it, one of the properties of the suggested long line of sight is worthy of note: it passes diagonally across open ground from one side of its 'terminal' to the other, before finally following the line of the ditch, which it then does for a considerable distance. This is roughly the pattern of the Rigel line on the main cursus, from K to $P4$. What is more, if the viewing position meant that the line had to cross a bank-horizon near at hand, then it did so more or less at right angles to its path. And this property is found at the cursus to be discussed next.

The Lesser Stonehenge Cursus

The Lesser Cursus, on the top of a very flat ridge less than a kilometre to the northwest of Stonehenge, seems small and simple by comparison with the Dorset network. About 45 m wide and 400 m long, it is open at the east and closed at the west, and crossed by a bank roughly halfway along its length (see Fig. 63). A similar bank crosses the Greater Cursus not far from its western end. The peripheral banks lie generally *inside* their ditch at the Lesser Cursus, just as in the Dorset case (but not at the Greater Cursus). It was levelled by

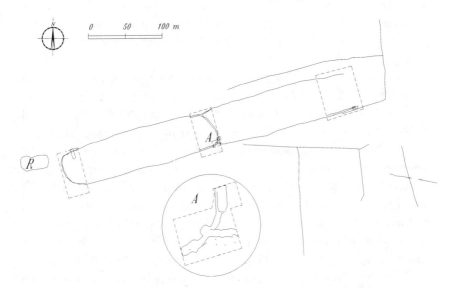

FIG. 63.   The Lesser Cursus to the north of Stonehenge. For its relation to the surroundings, see Fig. 65. The detail of the region A in the circle shows how an earlier ditch was crossed by a later. It also shows six stake holes.

ploughing in the mid-twentieth century, but seems also to have had a bank to the east of the tranverse ditch, which is what one would expect if viewing was mainly eastwards, as will turn out to be the case. (It might only have had this eastern bank in a second phase of building, if the western enclosure was built ahead of the rest. The original monument might have roughly resembled the simple Coombe Bissett parallelogram, to be discussed later in the present chapter.)

The lesson of the Dorset Cursus seems to be that one should not attach too much weight to the slight variations in the directions of the sides, unless they are in some way related to other features. The two long sides are not perfectly straight (Fig. 63), but there is no doubt that they were envisaged as following a constant direction, the same for both. Parts of the cursus (the areas shown in the broken rectangles in the figure) were excavated in 1983 by Julian Richards and others, showing by good fortune a particularly important region, at the southeast corner of the enclosed part, A in the figure. From this area it was clear that an earlier ditch system had been later supplemented by another, presumably following its course, but only over the western half. Stake holes were found in the neighbourhood of the junction, suggesting that *directions* were of some importance to the enterprise (see the detail in the figure). Some of the evidence most valuable to us comes from a magnetometer survey (done

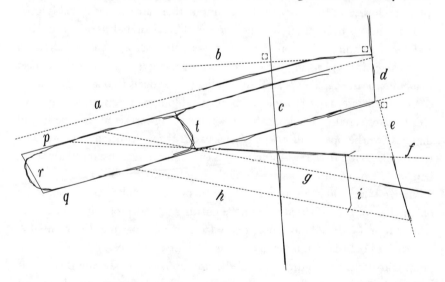

FIG. 64.   The geometrical plan of the Lesser Cursus (lines *p*, *q*, *r*, and *t*) and neighbouring features. All construction lines will be seen to follow the directions of the structural details (shown in the previous figure) very closely, with the exception of sides *r* and *t*, which are added in an arbitrary way. Right angles are indicated by small squares.

by the Ancient Monuments Laboratory) and from what was shown up by drought conditions during the excavation. Not only was the entire ditch then visible as a parchmark in the grass, but also a pattern of soilmarks following lines that confirm to what might have been suspected on independent grounds as to the directions of viewing from the monument. It may be imagined that viewing was in two modes, one over the banks as artificial horizons, the other over the natural horizon. Since the cursus is on the almost level top of a low eminence, the natural horizon is low and distant, so that the extinction angle of any star observed would have been the critical altitude.

According to the first carefully prepared archaeological map of the Stonehenge area, published in Sir Richard Colt Hoare's *Ancient Wiltshire* of 1810, there was formerly a long barrow adjacent to the western end, but this has been destroyed. (It might have overlapped with a modern covered reservoir, R in the figure.) Even before the 1983 excavation, it seemed likely that a line from the lost barrow towards the distant Bulford 1 barrow (of which we shall say more at a later stage) would have crossed the southern end of the transverse bank, that is, in the region of A. That the point A is a very special one is now shown much more convincingly by the fact that two of the soil marks (along lines f and g in Fig. 64) also converge on it.

The geometrical arrangement of the ditches and soilmarks is in fact not at all as random as at first appears. For example, there are three reasonably good approximations to right angles; the line a is closely parallel to sides p and q; b and f are symmetrical around the north–south line, and indeed align on Antares' setting and rising, respectively; f and g converge on A; d, e, and q meet in a point, as do b, d, and p; and b is parallel to diagonals to both halves of the cursus, the western one passing through an old long barrow 300 m away. This all indicates careful planning of some sort. Looking further afield, the second diagonal to the open half of the cursus passes through distant barrow Durrington 24, lying to the east; side p passes through the very distant (9 km) long barrow Milston 1; and f passes through long barrow Bulford 1. A barrow of unknown type, 300 m to the west of the cursus, is now obliterated, but it lay on the line of the northern side of the cursus and was probably deliberately related to it. (We shall have more to say later on these barrow alignments.)

As for potential alignments on stars, of course the most obvious starting point is to consider the directions of the sides in isolation. Taking the distant barrow (Milston 1) as a guide (azimuth 74.0°, which is certainly within half a degree of the mean direction of the sides), there is a potential alignment on the rising of the star Altair around 3420 BC. Increasing the azimuth by half a degree would move the date forward in time by about ninety years.

The sight lines through the other barrows fit extremely well with this date. While not indicated by soilmarks, a line at azimuth 65.1° over the head of Durrington 24 indicates the rising of Spica around 3420 BC.

The line already mentioned as passing over the barrow at the west (azimuth 265.1°) indicates the setting of Antares around 3420 BC. The line to Bulford 1 is at azimuth 94.3°, indicating the rising of Antares around 3490 BC.

Finally, the direction of *g*, and perhaps *h*: this does not seem to pass over any conspicuous distant point, but its azimuth (99.55°) points to the rising Pleiades around 3400 BC.

The overall consistency of these initial results is extremely surprising, in view of the minimal information we have been obliged to use. An average date of 3430 BC is consistent with two radiocarbon dates of 2600±120 bc and 2690±100 bc found at the site, and falls squarely within the period of the Dorset Cursus.

It remains to consider the possibility of cross-viewing at equal altitudes, as carried out at long barrows and—as suggested earlier—at the Dorset Cursus. Looking across the long banks at perfect right angles to their supposedly shared azimuth of 74.0°, the rising of Sirius and the setting of Arcturus could have been seen at an altitude of 13.7° around the year 3310 BC. At the lower angle of 9.0°, the rising of Rigel and the setting of Vega could have been seen around the year 3540 BC. The arrangement is reminiscent of both West Kennet and Hazleton North. These dates depend on directions to which we are obliged to approximate, for want of a survey of ditch directions—although, judging by other examples, they are unlikely to have been very different from those supposed. The question of the feasibility of relatively high-angled viewing is a more difficult one. The ditches excavated were found to be no more than 1.1 m deep, but they were not in the most suitable positions, and in any case little is known about the positions of the banks or their heights. Were there places with especially deep ditches and high banks? At present all one can say is that high-angled viewing is unproven, even unlikely.

If the bank was only about half a metre high, so that an observer could just comfortably see over it, then it is conceivable that places in the northwest ditch were marked as viewing positions for directions *f* and *g*, looking through a gap at *A*.

The Lesser Cursus was in itself presumably an entirely earthen structure, with the possible exception of stakes within the banks. There is a standing stone to the east, in direct line with its northern edge, 320 m from its open end. It is unlikely that it is there by chance, although whether it was deliberately placed in connection with an Altair alignment it is impossible to

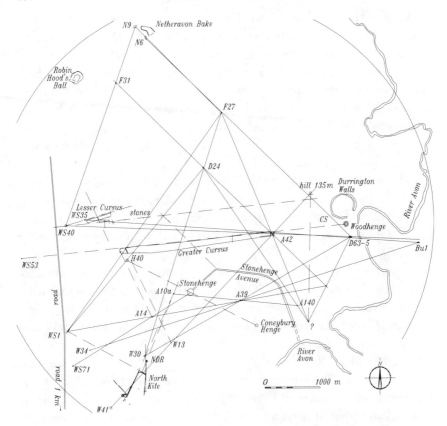

FIG. 65.   Alignments of the positions of long barrows in the Stonehenge region. Most of the barrows are numbered in the usual way by parishes, but using the following abbreviations: *Bu* – Bulford; *D* – Durrington; *F* – Figheldean; *N* – Netheravon; *W* – Wilsford South; and *WS* – Winterbourne Stoke. *CS* is a large sarsen stone, the Cuckoo Stone; *NDR* is the Normanton Down enclosure; *H40* is a colossal round ('bell') barrow, from a later period. (Colt Hoare's number. He called it 'the monarch of the plain'.) *A39* is a bowl barrow, but presumably on the site of an earlier monument of importance. Two sections of modern roads that follow ancient roads are shown in the west. The lower runs perfectly north–south; the upper is perfectly perpendicular to the cursus alignment.

say. There is an entire row of stones, starting in an eastward direction just to the south of this isolated example, but this row, for most of its length, runs parallel to the *Greater* Cursus, with which it is more likely to be linked.

Long Barrows, Territories and Totems

Before considering the Greater Cursus at Stonehenge it will be wise to consider its setting, for there is no doubt that parts of the cursus were related to the

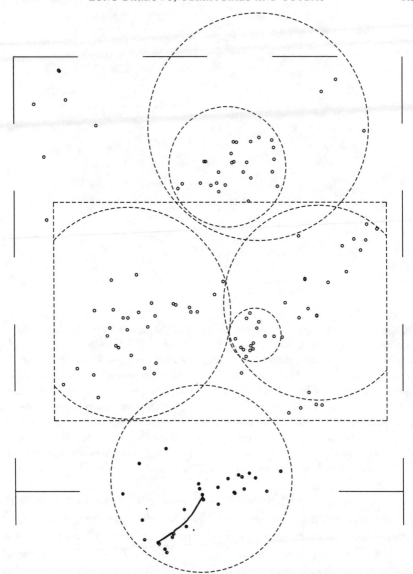

Fig. 66.   The distribution of long barrows in Wiltshire, based chiefly on L. V. Grinsell's list in the *Victoria County History*, vol. 1, part 1 (1957), together with some from Dorset and Hampshire to the south (Cranborne Chase). For the sake of visibility on this small plan, the centre of each barrow is marked by a circle of diameter corresponding to 400 m, that is, not at all to scale. The broken lines correspond to the regions distinguished in later figures. The radii of the circles in the Avebury region are 9 and 17 km, and that of the Cranborne Chase region 14 km. The large broken frame, enclosing all the Wiltshire barrows, follows lines of the National Grid. The lower left corner is ST 75/20 and the upper right is SU 35/85. The short lines are each of 10 grid units (10 km).

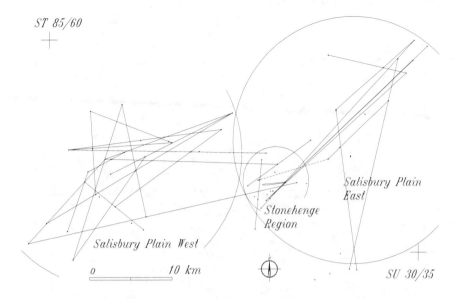

ST 85/60
+

Salisbury Plain
East

Stonehenge
Region

Salisbury Plain West

0   10 km

SU 30/35

FIG. 67.   The long barrows to the east and west of the Stonehenge region. Those to the
west show numerous internal alignments of threes, even some fours, with the appearance
of an independent system, although a few link up with the regions to the east. The outliers
to the northeast of Stonehenge show some dependence on that region, but those to the
southeast are only loosely connected. All barrows are represented as circles of 100 m
diameter, but alignments have been admitted only if they are able to cross three circles of
20 m diameter, each centred on the centre of a barrow. (The average barrow length is about
40 m.) The black spot is the Stonehenge circle, and the two cursus are added to help in
correlating with Fig. 65. The broken line from the Lesser Cursus shows its alignment on
Milston 1. The two crosses are National Grid references.

long barrows in its neighbourhood—something that can be proved with
nothing more than a map. Several examples have now been produced of
significant astronomical lines of sight that pass over distant barrows. In at least
one case (Milston 1, to which the Lesser Cursus was directed) it is doubtful
whether the remote barrow could have been made out, even in daylight. It
would be unfortunate if this were thought to cast doubt on the reality of the
alignment, and even more so if readers were to turn tail and run, at the thought
that this marks the beginning of a slippery ley-line slope, for the fact is that
long barrows were most emphatically arranged in lines of three or even four.
Alignments that have been claimed for only two barrows and a star might have
left the reader with much room for scepticism, but with the frequent and
undeniable alignments of long barrows in threes, astronomy can be kept out
of the initial discussion entirely. Concentrating here chiefly on the Stonehenge

region, but also on the Avebury region to the north and Cranborne Chase to the south, will in each case produce astonishing results. In all three places it is difficult to find a long barrow that is *not* in line with at least two others.

First to the Stonehenge region. Several mounds have been described as long barrows by one author and dismissed by another. Here a generous interpretation will be taken, one which can make little difference to the certainty of the conclusion. In Fig. 65, a circle of 4 km radius is drawn in such a way that it takes in all, or almost all, of the cluster of possibly twenty-three long barrows in the Stonehenge region. At first this cluster is selected in an impressionistic way, but it will eventually emerge that first impressions are reasonably reliable. A few broken lines are added to show interesting alignments of other sorts, or dubious cases. There are seventeen clear cases of lines of three or four long barrows, and it seems that there is not a single long barrow that is not on one of these lines. There are numerous ways of calculating the odds against this situation having arisen by chance. The result depends on the presuppositions made about the sizes, directions, the permitted proximity of barrow to line, the bounding area of the region, and so forth. At conservative estimates, the odds are many billions to one against these alignments having occurred by chance, and there is little point in our refining the statistical argument here.

Looking beyond the Stonehenge region to the west, one does not find that the pattern continues, but rather that a new pattern begins. In Fig. 66, all the long barrows of the county of Wiltshire as listed in the *Victoria County History* (1957) are drawn, to give an idea of their overall distribution. As it happens, the county boundary does not seriously split a major cluster of long barrows. The broken lines across the middle of the map correspond to the more detailed Fig. 67, in which three areas are distinguished, that around Stonehenge (illustrated in detail in Fig. 65) and the more extensive regions to the west and east of it. Immediately above and below the rectangle are the Avebury region and Cranborne Chase, to be considered in detail shortly.

No effort has been made to take barrow size, shape or orientation into account—had this been done we should certainly have been able to add further alignments of three or more barrows. The message that seems to be conveyed by the scheme, even so, is that the territory to the west was relatively autonomous, despite a few links with the Stonehenge region. (Note the almost perfect right angle in the middle of the southernmost linking line.) The outliers to the east, on the other hand, seem to look towards the Stonehenge region. And reflected in this geometrical and astronomical viewpoint we may surely see a social orientation on the part of the communities that built them, even social dependence.

The most remarkable fact of all is that no fewer than three new lines are found to converge on Amesbury 42, the barrow at the end of the Greater Cursus, so bringing the total of which we are aware to seven, and possibly eight. (The three lines can be identified as those converging on the Stonehenge region from the northeast.) At least nineteen mounds that have at some stage or another been deemed 'long barrows' are thus implicated in geometrical alignments taking in Amesbury 42, which therefore clearly makes a very special twentieth. In fact on geometrical grounds alone we can say that activity on its site—but of course not necessarily at the final mound—is likely to predate all, or almost all, of the nineteen barrows in question. Amesbury 42 has a good title to being the most important Neolithic centre on the whole of Salisbury Plain. The fact that the Stonehenge circle hardly enters the scheme shows that it was almost certainly never the site of a long barrow.

Judging by lines passing through it (at least four, involving seven or eight other long barrows), Amesbury 39 was also on an important site. This barrow lies adjacent to the modern road—running along the line of the alignment to A10a, as it happens—as it approaches Stonehenge Bottom. (The road forks there, the northern branch going off to Stonehenge itself.) It is ostensibly a bowl barrow, and a radiocarbon date from the burnt remains of a pyre or mortuary structure found in an excavation by Paul Ashbee in 1960 indicate a calendar date late in the third millennium. Since he found there many shards of earlier Neolithic pottery, Peterborough and Grooved ware, it is not improbable that the bowl barrow replaced some earlier monument.

There is at first sight an uncomfortable truth in the numerous geometrical alignments: it would often have been simply impossible to see from one end of the line to the other. (There is an obvious case at the upper right of Fig. 65. To give an idea of visibilities, heights of key points in metres above the Ordnance Datum are shown in Fig. 68, which corresponds to Fig. 65.) In reality this is a welcome obstacle. One cannot gainsay the alignment, but one might be tempted to explain it away merely in terms of a staking out of directions over the very long distances involved. That the accuracy encountered could have been maintained using only sighting posts—an accuracy of 10 or 20 m over 10 or 12 km—is simply not credible. There was a far easier way: in a simple alignment they simply sighted the same star from two points of the three. Where the middle barrow is the high point, say B in a series $A–B–C$, the star may be seen from B over C at its extinction angle. A perfectly straight line ABC will then be obtainable if, in looking towards B from A, the altitude of the slope is less than that extinction angle. (This assumes roughly the same period of history.) This 'low hills' condition holds almost always for the long

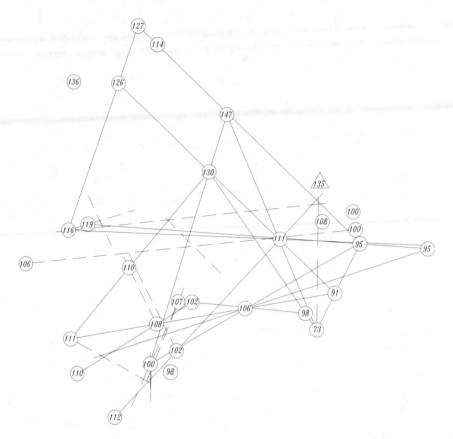

FIG. 68.   Heights in metres (above the Ordnance Datum) of long barrows and other key points in the Stonehenge region of Fig. 65.

barrows on Salisbury Plain. It is to this type of procedure that the alignments testify, not to some Neolithic road-building genius—although aligned road-ways there undoubtedly were, and if *B* was not visible from *A* then intermediate markers would have been needed. Speaking generally, the fact that there are several near-perfect parallel lines on our map, more than a kilometre apart, is not the result of Neolithic rope-and-rod surveying over great distances, but of careful star sightings. The nature of these will be considered shortly.

There is one property of our map that should not go unnoticed, a property that requires us to qualify the claim that there is little sign of 'civil' surveying here. At several places there are excellent approximations to right angles in alignments. That between the Greater Cursus and the road past Winterbourne Stoke 1 has already been mentioned. There is one at Amesbury 42 and a weaker

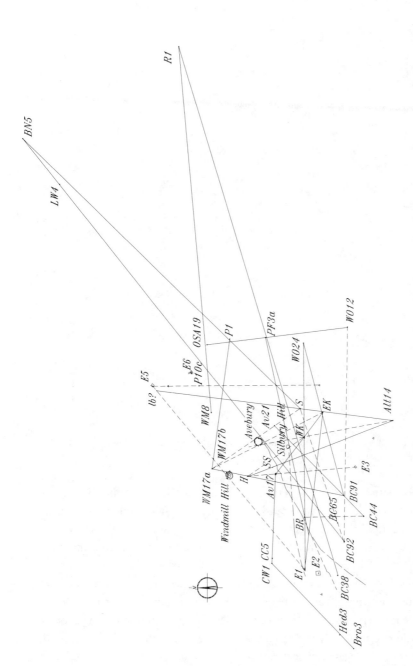

Fig. 69. Alignments of long barrows in the Avebury region. Abbreviations for parish names: *Alt* – Alton; *Av* – Avebury; *BC* – Bishops Cannings; *Bro* – Bromham; *BN* – Bishopstone North; *CC* – Calne/Cherhill; *CW* – Calne Without; *EK* – East Kennet; *Hed* – Heddington; *LW* – Liddington/Wanborough; *P* – Pitton & Farley; *R* – Ramsbury; *WM* – Winterbourne Monkton; *WO* – West Overton. Common names preferred previously here, with equivalents in parentheses: *BR* is the Beckhampton Road barrow (*BC76*), *H* the Horslip barrow (*Av 47*), *SS* the South Street barrow (*Av 68*), *WK* is the West Kennet barrow (*Av 22*). *Alt* 14 is better known as Adam's Grave. *E* is here used for linear enclosures generally.

example at Durrington 24. There are two more on Fig. 67, at lower left and upper right. There are three others on Fig. 69, below, one at East Kennet, one at the barrow north of Windmill Hill, and one near Ogbourne St Andrews 19. These are surely witness to the custom to be found repeatedly in long-barrow design, that is, the custom of seeking out lines of sight at right angles. The custom was in evidence, for example, in the arrangement of scaling posts, in the rows of stakes within earthen mounds, and in the geometry of the Lesser Cursus. Its reflection in the landscape is a direct consequence of this feature of long-barrow design, surprising only for the accuracy with which it was put into effect. Those of little faith who, looking at a crumbling ditch wall or a crooked row of stakes, are inclined to say that they do not speak for any sort of surveying precision, must face up to the fact that when some of the same lines were drawn across the landscape, from barrow to barrow, they gave surprisingly

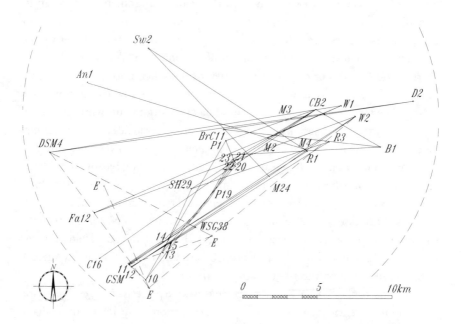

FIG. 70. Alignments of long barrows in the region of Cranborne Chase. Numbering follows that adopted by the *RCHM*. Abbreviations for parish names, mostly Dorset, but some in Hampshire and Wiltshire: *An* – Ansty; *BrC* – Broad Chalke; *C* – Chettle; *CB* – Coombe Bissett; *DSM* – Downhead St Mary; *F* – Farnham; *GSM* – Gussage St Michael; *M* – Martin; *P* – Pentridge; *R* – Rockbourne; *SH* – Sixpenny Handley; *Sw* – Swallowcliffe; *W* – Whitsbury; *WSG* – Wimborne St Giles. Unlabelled numbers are for Gussage St Michael and Pentridge. Apart from long barrows (not to scale), the Dorset Cursus and three rectangular Neolithic enclosures (*E*) are indicated to scale. Broken straight lines are alignments involving the enclosures.

good results. One cannot say exactly how good, without knowing the precise vertices of the perpendiculars. Those as drawn here, however, in the order mentioned, are 89.15°, 89.47°, 87.41°, 89.72°, 89.24°, 89.77°, 86.7°, and 88.51° (always taking the smaller angle on the line). And if our explanation is correct, then the fact that these angles are not perfect is only partly due to a weakness in surveying technique. It depends also on a failure to discover a perfect right angle between points of risings and settings of stars—an excusable failure, for the stars are not to be pushed around. That we can nevertheless find a mean of 88.75° with a standard deviation of 1.13°, over eight items of data (arbitrarily taking the component angle that is less than 90°), says much for the success with which the programme of searching for right angles was carried through.

To enter into a discussion of the classification of mounds would take us too far out of our way, but we can only hope that mound alignments will be given a small place in future discussions, for they are surely at least as objective as an impressionistic classification of monuments by outward shape, and they might even reveal something of the precursors of a monument. Amesbury 10a and Durrington 63–65, for example, were described rather ambiguously by Colt Hoare, and are now usually discarded from the long barrow list, not without reason. The former, however, enters into one good alignment, while the latter has no fewer than six lines through it, giving it an exceptional status that cannot be ignored. This is not to say that an alignment of itself proves the affinity of the monuments along it, for clearly an old and revered long barrow could have been a focal point for much later alignments. But when a barrow is the third member of several alignments, each of them with two undoubted long barrows on it, as is the case with Avebury 39, then it is unlikely to be a late arrival on the scene. On the other hand it is plain enough that old habits died hard: notice, for instance, the line through H40, Stonehenge, and the Coneybury henge, all of them presumably from the third millennium.

Turning to the Avebury region, much the same pattern emerges. There are now around twenty-eight long barrows, rather more than in the immediate Stonehenge region (represented by the smallest circle of Fig. 67). Fig. 69 shows them, as well as six enclosures and Silbury Hill, and the later Sanctuary and the Avebury circles. Again there is not a single long barrow that cannot be somehow accommodated by the scheme. Again there are outliers to the northeast, the outermost pair of which define (in relation to barrows in the central region) almost precisely the same two angles as those set by the outermost pair on the eastern part of Salisbury Plain. There are many other points of similarity that it would be tedious to list, but that should be evident

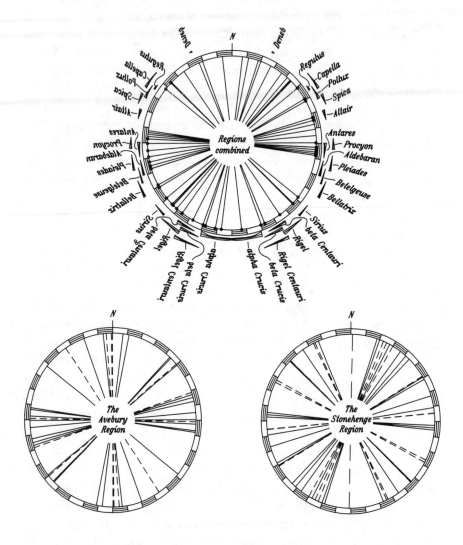

FIG. 71. The azimuths of lines connecting three or more long barrows in the Stonehenge and Avebury regions. The lower diagrams show the azimuths for the two regions separately, and they also include (as broken lines) the secondary information from the relevant map (Fig. 65 or 69). The upper diagram combines the main alignments, and round its edge arcs are drawn showing the limits of rising and setting (mirror printing) of bright stars at their extinction angles, that is, over a natural horizon up to those angles. (Arcturus and Vega do not rise and set in this way.) The limits indicated by the arcs are 4000 BC (the thick end of the wedge) and 3000 BC. Extrapolation a short distance either way is reasonably safe, except, for Deneb. Alpha Crucis had passed out of view before the end of the millennium.

from a comparison of Figs. 69 and 65. The most important will be considered next in relation to the astronomical meaning of the alignments.

The long barrows of the Cranborne Chase region are still more numerous. Fig. 70 shows 31, and no fewer than 30 alignments involving them. Again, not a single barrow fails to be included in the network. There are many irregular enclosures in the region, but three rectangular examples are marked on the figure since they have their own alignments, giving them on that account a sort of long-barrow status. The main alignments are even more tightly knit than in the two other regions, but the merest glance shows them to follow different preferences. One obvious tendency relates to the direction of the corresponding cursus: at Stonehenge, as in the Greater Cursus, there is a strong east–west preference in the alignments, while here we observe a bundle of four lines (and others closely parallel to them) that follow more or less the direction of the southern part of the Dorset Cursus. At Avebury there might have been links with the Beckhampton and Kennet avenues, a subject to be considered in a later chapter. In every case, however, whether of cursus or avenue, the long-barrow alignments undoubtedly had priority.

There are many ways of considering the alignments. They could be taken one by one in relation to the terrain and the available information—still usually scanty—concerning the long barrows at the nodes of the network. This would give a series of dated lines, and starting from a few simple principles it might even be possible to assign dates to the long barrows. One might expect lines of three barrows, for instance, to cover one old barrow and two later examples of roughly equal age. (If they were not of much the same age then the line would not have been produced by sighting on a single star.) Very often one finds that the ridge of a long barrow lies in the direction of the alignment. This strongly suggests a barrow that is not the oldest in the line. (Examples easily seen on Fig. 65 are Winterbourne Stoke 1, Durrington 24, and Durrington 63–5, but there are many others.) To illustrate another such principle with a concrete example: if a line for 3500 BC crosses a line for 3200 BC at barrow A, then one might expect A to be *at least* as old as 3500 BC. Continuing round the net, this type of argument should provide much information about the dating of the barrows. There are, however, at least two difficulties to be faced here.

First: the two later barrows need not have been set up at the same time. The alignment might have a different explanation. Purely for the sake of argument, suppose that (as was probably the case) the alignment *WS1–Cursus terminal–F27* preceded the simple alignment of two barrows only, *WS1* and *D24*. The first should perhaps be dated around 3640 BC and the second 3260 BC, both from an alignment on the setting Rigel. It would in principle have

been possible for *H40* to have been added to the second alignment at a much later stage, when it was found by observation that another star happened to set along the same line, for example over *D24* as seen from the other two, or over *WS1*. (Admittedly in neither case it is easy to see what the star could have been, but this is meant only to illustrate an available procedure.)

The second problem has as much to do with our own expectations as with historical events. There are strong reasons for supposing that on a local scale the barrow designers aimed to find a line of sight towards a rising star that, when reversed, was directed towards another star's setting. They were able to do this by the use of variations in the altitudes set by the landscape. Over long distances, this trick can rarely be expected to work. Occasionally it might be thought to do so. Consider the line *F31–D24–A42–unnamed* of Fig. 65. Looking one way along it, the setting of Capella could have been seen around 2890 BC, and the other way the rising of Rigel at the same date. This seems perfect—it would apply of course only to the youngest barrows on the line—until we ask whether the rising of Sirius might not have been intended, around 3730 BC. There are similar difficulties in many other cases—for instance with the parallel lines to the north of this—and the only really satisfactory way of solving the problem is to examine the barrows individually—which is of course at present out of the question. There are, even so, some general conclusions that can be be reached without going to these lengths.

For every line in the net it turns out to be possible to find at least one bright star, and occasionally two, for the fourth millennium. In many cases there is no bright star in the reverse direction, and in others, where there is such, it is at a very different date. To appreciate the possibilities without listing them individually and in detail, they are shown in the diagrams of Fig. 71. The radii represent azimuths taken from Figs. 65 and 69, for the Avebury and Stonehenge regions separately, and for both regions combined. These regions are closer in tradition than either is to the Cranborne Chase. In the separate diagrams, the broken lines represent alignments other than those between three or more long barrows, but they are omitted from the combined diagram. One alignment that is treated as a three-barrow affair, and is not given a broken line, is *WS1–Cursus terminal–F27*. Giving the terminal the honorary status of long barrow might be defended by analogy with the Lesser Cursus and the way both enter into alignments with barrows. (Note how the lines cross the end sections diagonally.)

The first thing to be noticed here is the strong tendency of the azimuths to cluster. More than that: in some cases two or three lines are so close that they cannot be distinguished at the scale of reproduction of this book. There is a

distinct tendency to favour directions close to east or west. Scarcely less surprising are the empty areas. Of course one should not forget that even if all lines represent alignments on stars, up to half of them might be redundant, that is, if lines were only for one-way use. This is not an entirely hopeless complication, as can be appreciated more easily from the upper (combined) diagram. Around its edge the names of stars are written that might have been seen rising or setting *at their extinction altitudes* in these regions between 4000 and 3000 BC precisely. It is accurate for the latitude of Stonehenge, but for other places it gives only an approximate indication, since the latitudes vary appreciably—but if used for Avebury the errors are not great.

A graph giving the azimuths at which stars of a known declination rise and set, assuming an extinction angle of 2° (a reasonable average value for bright stars) is included in Appendix 2, section 4. It might mislead appreciably with the very bright Sirius or the faint Pleiades.

From the figure we can see that the bundle of azimuths to the rising of Antares, if reversed, indicates no bright star, so that in that case there is no ambiguity. Small circles have been added to the lines to indicate plausible viewing directions, but only on the assumption that we remain in the fourth millennium. There was a distinct tendency to look to the south, but risings and settings are both well represented. Occasionally, viewing in both directions is possible (with Sirius and Capella, for instance), and then both ends of the line are marked, but the dates at which they hold good will usually differ, so that without independent evidence the testimony of an ambiguous single line is worthless. The rising of Sirius and Rigel, for example, offer alternative solutions to three almost perfectly parallel lines at Stonehenge, but they differ by almost a thousand years (3730 BC, 3730 BC, and 3820 BC for Sirius, 2750 BC, 2750 BC, and 2820 BC for Rigel). What might be thought surprising is the gap in the combined figure that suggests a lack of interest in the *rising* of the Pleiades, Aldebaran, Betelgeuse and Bellatrix; and yet their *settings* are all potentially represented. Regulus was apparently ignored as always, but the avoidance of Deneb is mildly surprising.

While, for the reasons explained, it would be premature to read off the ages of individual long barrows from the azimuths of the lines connecting them, the totality of derived dates can be legitimately regarded as characterizing the network as a whole. These dates—some of them no doubt redundant and a few mistaken—are quite consistent, if two or three fifth-millennium dates are ignored, and six or seven from the mid-third millennium. If this tells us anything, it is that the activities described here continued steadily over the fourth millennium. All the signs are that something like it

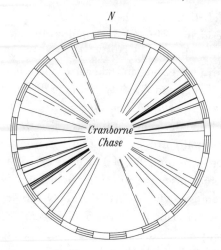

FIG. 72. The azimuths of lines connecting three or more long barrows in the Cranborne Chase region. There are thirty lines in all. Those that are difficult to distinguish in the neighbourhood of 60° are eight in number. The five alignments involving enclosures are shown by broken lines. All are near to conventional alignments.

continued through the age of round barrows. It would be hard to think of a more graphic illustration of continuity in this respect than the surviving view—easily seen from the road—of the long barrow Winterbourne Stoke 1 with a string of round barrows loosely following the direction of its axis towards the north east. (That axis lies precisely on the alignment *WS1–Cursus terminal–F27*, as mentioned earlier, and began in all probability as a Rigel line around 3640 BC, in conjunction with the western terminal of the Cursus.) Almost all of the barrows in this rich and varied group are very probably arranged for sighting Rigel, and the alignments of adjacent pairs may well in many cases provide the dates of building. The same is perhaps true of the string of four round barrows to the south of Amesbury 42, the so-called 'Old King Barrows'. They do not follow the axis of the long barrow, but are roughly parallel to the last part of the Stonehenge Avenue, which is another Rigel line, as will be seen shortly. There is yet another line to Rigel's setting—but of course for a different period of history—actually running through Amesbury 42 itself, namely the barrows alignment *A42–W13–W41*.

Finally, producing a chart of the alignments for the Cranborne Chase region strengthens the impression that here too was a distinct territory, with traditions that differed slightly from those to the north. Just as at Stonehenge each of the barrows Amesbury 42 and 39, and Figheldean 27 was a clear focus of attention, judging by the number of lines passing through, so on the Cranborne Chase Gussage St Michael 12 and 15 and Coombe Bissett 2 had an important status—or perhaps merely antiquity—with four, five, and six lines respectively. The thirty triple alignments between barrows cluster strongly, just as in the other regions, but they indicate different preferences. To some extent these have already been seen in the course of the analysis of narrower territorial band around the Dorset Cursus. Once again there are directions to Rigel, Sirius,

Rigel Centauri, Deneb, Aldebaran, and Bellatrix, but what is now very striking is the absence of lines flanking the meridian, and the dense bundle of lines to the rising of Pollux, and possibly Capella. This bundle follows the direction of the southern part of the cursus, as already pointed out, and taken in conjunction with the different preferences at Stonehenge and Avebury gives the distinct impression that *in different territories there were allegiances to different stars*.

This is surely the trace of a true cultural difference, at least as real as those between pottery types, axe-head forms and barrow shapes. Our notion of a totem comes of course from a very different culture, that of the natives of North America, where the use of hereditary emblems of the tribe is far from unique. It is impossible to do more than speculate as to whether in the case of Neolithic Wessex stars were used as totems, whether clans were named after them, or whether they were regarded as ancestrally related to the clan, even to the point of representing a guardian spirit to be worshipped. The evidence we do have is not inconsistent with such ideas.

The Greater Stonehenge Cursus

By examining the network of long barrows in the Stonehenge region four important ways were found relating to the Greater Cursus. Its northern side is on a line through *WS53*, which is at right angles to the road. (For all abbreviations, see the caption to Fig. 65.) The enclosure at its western terminal is crossed diagonally by *WS1–F27*, a potential Rigel line for 3640 BC. Most notably, the mound Amesbury 42 is crossed at its eastern extreme by eight alignments of barrows. One of those alignments starts at *F27* (which is therefore linked to the Cursus twice over); and *F27* might be datable as lying on another alignment (*N9–N6–F27*) directed to the rising Sirius around 3740 BC. And finally, many of the long barrows aligned with *A42* or the western terminal have their axes along or very close indeed to the appropriate line. (Examples are *A140*, *D24*, *F31*, *WS71*, *W13*, and *W34* to the barrow *A42*, and *A14*, *WS1*, and *WS53* to the western terminal.) While one should not simply identify the Greater Cursus with its terminals or Amesbury 42, all the indications are that in one form or another it was no latecomer to the Stonehenge scene. It would be a mistake, though, to imagine that these initial indications mean that it is older than the Lesser Stonehenge Cursus. This has often been regarded as a prototype for the larger version, and this assumption need not be disturbed to any serious extent.

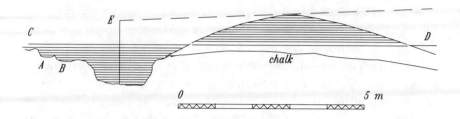

FIG. 73.   The chalk levels in a section of the southern bank, 225 m from the western end of the Greater Stonehenge Cursus (1983 sample excavation). Note the channels *A* and *B* parallel to the ditch. *CD* is an approximation to the level of topsoil before the cursus was created, and an entirely conjectural bank has been added, based on the assumption that all excavated material was used in it. The eye of an adult male observer would have been in the neighbourhood of *E*. The line of sight as drawn is 2.3°; the important point is that the altitude set by the bank might have been less but could not have been very much more than this.

The Greater Cursus runs for 2.74 km across the chalk downs in a roughly east–west direction, about 700 m north of Stonehenge at its closest point. At its western end it is more or less level, and from there it runs down the slope to a dry valley known as Stonehenge Bottom, rising again to the east. It is a strange fact that almost exactly half of it can be seen from the Stonehenge site, that is, the eastern half, and that it ended at that point in the east (short of Amesbury 42) beyond which the ground was no longer visible. Amesbury 42 is visible from the western end of the cursus, but it does not seem particularly well sited, for it is neither high nor flat. The cursus varies in overall width between about 100 m and 150 m—the second figure holding over most of its length. Apart from a few gaps, it was evidently completely surrounded by a bank and ditch that for most of the perimeter was only on the *inside*. Each of them today is about 6.5 m across by 0.5 m high (or deep). Both ends may actually be seen from Stonehenge, but that fact has no relevance to its origins.

The cursus comes to an end in the east about 40 m short of Amesbury 42. (Whether that is to be called a 'mound' or a 'barrow' is immaterial as long as the word 'barrow' is not thought to prejudge the question as to whether it had a burial function.) Mound or barrow, it is now in a sorry state: a bridle road runs along its length, one of its ditches is in a field under cultivation, and the other is in a modern plantation. As already seen, the Dorset Cursus had burial

mounds incorporated in it, but excavation in 1983 seemed to indicate that Amesbury 42 was not originally a tomb. It was found to have had ditches of considerable size, over 5 m wide at the surface and nearly 3 m deep. An earlier and smaller ditch was also located—complete with a fascinating pile of flint-knapper's debris—and the site will not be fully understood until more is known about that earlier phase, which may or may not have been connected with part or all of the adjacent cursus. Amesbury 42 seems to have more affinities with the *terminals* of the Dorset Cursus than with the transverse barrow there. Note how the southern side of the Greater Stonehenge Cursus seems to head for its midpoint, the point over which several of the barrow alignments pass. We shall eventually conclude, even so, that the mound was in place before the cursus.

A small excavation was carried out near the western end of the Greater Cursus in 1947 by J. F. S. Stone (southern ditch), another in 1959 by P. M. Christie (terminal and interior), and yet another in 1983 by Julian Richards (southern ditch and bank area). It seems that the ditch bottom in the last case was of the order of 80 cm deep and very flat (on section *B* in Fig. 74). Other excavated ditches are now typically 0.4 m deep and their banks are at most

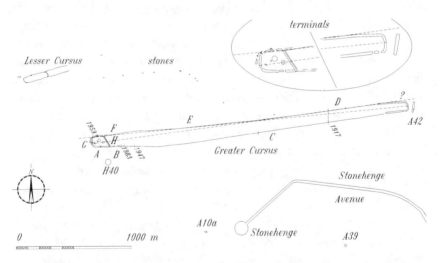

FIG. 74.   The Greater Cursus at Stonehenge. The places at which minor excavations have been made are marked with the appropriate year. For the relation of the monument to its surroundings, see Fig. 65. A rough indication of the bank structure at the two ends is based only on aerial photographs. The conjectured outlines of the ditches have not been shown. The transverse ditch has its bank to the east, and so was no doubt used to observe a rising star. There might just possibly have been another, approximating to a reflection of it, at the eastern end—perhaps for viewing the setting of the same star. Round barrows at the western end are from a later period.

about as high, each being 6 or 7 m across. The ditches at the western end were both wider (up to 2.75 m) and deeper still (0.75 to 2 m). For the bank structure see the figure.

For ditch-edge directions one must still for the most part rely on conjectures based on old aerial photographs, but such incomplete evidence as has been gleaned as to depths is this: that any cross-viewing done outside the terminal area—looking southwards from the northern ditch and northwards from the southern—would have been at a low angle, hardly more than the extinction angle of any bright star (2.3° is the value arrived at in the proposed reconstruction of Fig. 73). The greater depth of the ditches at the western end, however, and presumably at the eastern end too, means that there cross-viewing might have been at appreciably higher angles. This arrangement might prove to be typical

FIG. 75. One potential method of viewing, using a forked staff to achieve a standard eye level.

of all monuments of the cursus-type. As Christie noted, in connection with the disproportionate scale of the southern terminal of one of three such monuments at Rudston, in Humberside, when it was excavated by Canon W. Greenwell in the last century it was so massive that he thought it to have been a long barrow. He did in fact find human remains under it.

Much of the western end of the Greater Cursus was until recently under woodland (the Fargo Plantation). This end seems to have remained undamaged by ploughing until after 1810, when Colt Hoare described and mapped it. Military buildings during the First World War—later used as a pig-gery—played havoc with the western end. There are two round Bronze Age barrows (Amesbury 56 and Winterbourne Stoke 30) inside the cursus there, but they were set up much later, and are not relevant to the planning of it. Crossing the cursus nearby (and perhaps at the east too) there is a diagonal bank (H on Fig. 74), reminding us of that at the Lesser Cursus, and perhaps even of the northern end of the secondary cursus in Dorset. The direction of this bank at the Greater Cursus is not easy to establish from published plans, on which its azimuth (west of north) varies between extraordinary limits—from 9° at one extreme to 22° at the other. From aerial photographs it seems that it might be closer to 33°.

The Greater Cursus, unlike the main Dorset complex, is at more or less a constant latitude (averaging 51° 11' 06"). In each case the length of the structure makes it necessary to look closely at its contours. Here the gradients of the ground are in fact so slight that even viewing over the terminals from Stonehenge Bottom would have set angles (at most 0.27°) well below the extinction angle of any star. For the record: neither the eastern nor the western direction of the long sides could have been an accurate alignment on the Sun at the equinoxes. The southwestern section, marked A on Fig. 74, follows an almost perfect east–west line (average azimuth 89.9°) on a nearly level surface, with the ground falling away to east and west.

In sum, the possibilities that now present themselves are of (a) cross-viewing at moderately high altitudes at the terminals, at low altitudes along the intervening sections; (b) using the terminals or Amesbury 42 as distant foresights; and (c) viewing across the transverse ditch at a right angle, at low altitude. Despite the fact that some of our data are very poor, a surprisingly consistent picture emerges. It is presented here more or less in order of date, although this may well prove to be faulty:

From the middle of the pre-existing Amesbury 42 (or possibly from inside the eastern end-mound at its middle) a line of sight over some pre-existing mound in the region of F was taken towards the setting of Antares. This line of sight followed the course of ditch E, which was perhaps established at that time to pick out the line. (An azimuth of 265.3°, with the extinction angle of the star, suggests a date of 3420 BC.)

Cross-viewing northwards at low angle from the middle areas suggests nothing, but looking south from all middle ditches, the very brief appearance of alpha Crucis might have been observed. (Precise right-angles from the northern ditch were to be had for its rising at its extinction angle in the thirty-fourth century.)

Looking over the middle of the western mound (G) from the northern end of Amesbury 42, or some point inside an eastern terminal mound, assuming azimuth 263.6°, the setting of Antares was observable in 3250 BC. The line of sight follows a long section of the northern ditch (D).

Looking over the transverse mound, for example from the bottom corners of the western terminal or from its own ditch, but in all cases at right angles to it, the rising Pollux would have been seen at its extinction angle in 3240 BC. (This assumes an azimuth of 33°, which as already explained is our own very uncertain value.)

Cross-viewing at the eastern terminal (azimuth 353.1° for the setting

Arcturus and 185° for the setting Rigel) indicates 3240 BC with a viewing altitude of 11.4°.

Cross-viewing at the western terminal (azimuths 6.5° for the rising Arcturus and 172° for the rising Rigel) indicates 3230 BC with a viewing altitude of 11.5°.

Artificial phenomena of the last sort, so close to the meridian, provide us with a number of problems. Could accurately equal altitudes have been guaranteed? Would not a slight raising or lowering of the eye have shifted the time and direction of rising appreciably? Two facts speak in favour of the result, however: the dates are close to the others, and the viewing altitudes are yet again in the neighbourhood of 11.3°. This last finding leads us to suspect, once again, that a gradient of 1 in 5 was the aim. As for the possibility of viewing at the wrong angle and time, we can only repeat that it was presumably the *design* that mattered. We know nothing of observational technique, but viewing through the fork of a staff of standard length—precisely two 'megalithic yards', in fact—seems quite probable.

There is another question of timing that presents itself naturally here. Arcturus did not set over the low natural horizons at Stonehenge, but at the altitudes deduced here, it first set (as seen from the east) and then rose (as seen from the west) at times about eighty minutes apart. Rigel's rising (seen from the western end) and later setting (seen from the eastern end) were almost exactly an hour apart. These intervals were such as would have allowed a normal adult ample time to walk the length of the cursus—in fact to have done so three or four times at a brisk pace. Each of these intervals is appropriate to a particular star, and it might be thought that there is nothing particularly striking about them. It is interesting, however, to discover that the interval between the setting of Antares (seen from the east) and the rising of Pollux (seen from the west) was of the same order of magnitude—a little over seventy minutes. Such facts as these, rather than the overall form of the cursus, make one wonder whether some sort of processional ritual was associated with the Greater Cursus.

These various events could have been seen over long periods of the year, but the optimum seasons differed. Without going into fine detail, these were: mid-spring (Pollux/Antares), a month into autumn (Rigel), and late winter (Arcturus).

No precise conclusion as to dating can be drawn from all this, but the occurrence of four dates within a decade of 3240 BC should no doubt be interpreted as showing that the bulk of the Greater Cursus was built in a short

period of time—perhaps as little as a year or two—but only after prior activity had been taking place for at least two centuries, at what were to become its two ends. The date obtained for that activity (around 3420 BC) was almost exactly the date found for the Lesser Cursus. It is therefore of great interest that both monuments incorporated sight lines to the stars Antares, Rigel and Arcturus.

The greater antiquity of Amesbury 42, as indicated by the oldest of the eight barrow-alignments crossing it, is not challenged by anything brought to light in this section. It will be recalled that the line in question, the oldest of the eight, was to the star Rigel.

The disposition of the Greater Cursus prompts us to look briefly towards a later period in the history of the Stonehenge region. One interesting consequence of the scheme discovered here is the prominence it gives to the northern side of the cursus. An alignment involving this northern side was found earlier, with the long barrow Winterbourne Stoke 53 at one end and the Cuckoo Stone and the centre of Woodhenge at the other. Woodhenge is a much later monument and will be considered in more detail in Chapter 8. The Cuckoo Stone probably had no early connection with the cursus. It is a rough block of sarsen stone, about 2 m tall. (In the eighteenth century it was the Cuckold Stone. Some maps simply call it the Durrington Stone.) Looking in a westerly

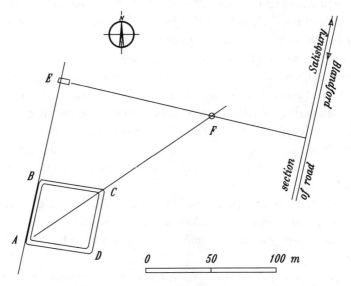

FIG. 76. The parallelogram on Coombe Bissett Down (latitude 51° 01' 20", O. S. ref. SU 104249). The precise directions of the sides are uncertain.

direction, given a clear line of sight, the stone would have reached more or less to the horizon as seen by a person standing at Woodhenge.

The 1947 excavation of the Greater Cursus produced a piece of sandstone originating in the distant Milford Haven area (at the southwest tip of Wales). It was found on the southern edge of the ditch, on the chalk bedrock, 30 cm below the present surface. J. F. S. Stone saw this as a link with the 'foreign' circles of the Stonehenge monument, the so-called 'bluestones', the smaller monoliths. Richard Atkinson drew the conclusion that the bluestones were transported from Wales in what he called period I (his rounded dates of 2800 BC to 2100 BC now need revision to, say, 3180 BC and 2170 BC respectively). He thought that they were brought to a site and for a purpose still unknown, and that they were re-used in Period II for an unfinished double circle. For two or three generations, the generally accepted view of their origin was broadly that of H. H. Thomas, put forward in 1921, that they were brought to Salisbury Plain by raft over sea and river and then over land for the last part of the journey on rollers. The pendulum of opinion has swung at least twice since then, a point that will be raised again in Chapter 9. As for their early presence in the area, it has long been known that there is a bluestone in the long barrow known as 'Bowls Barrow', but not until the 1960s and 1970s did it become plain that long barrows were very much older than the final placement of the Stonehenge bluestones. The greater part of the infill of the cursus ditch had certainly occurred by the time the bluestones were added to the nearby monument. There is also the evidence of chips of bluestone that speak for the *working* of the stone on the site of the Stonehenge Cursus, again an event long preceding the bluestone ring.

The Coombe Bissett Parallelogram

The parallelogram at Radley was essentially a long barrow, and there were no doubt many similar earthworks to be found elsewhere, but not everything with the same apparent outline is to be classified with it. One instance having closer affinities to a barrow ring or cursus than to a long barrow with a single mound is to be found on Coombe Bissett Down, about 6 km southwest of Salisbury. It has not been excavated, but there is an excellent aerial photograph made at the time of the discovery of the earthwork. (It was published in 1928 in the pioneering work *Wessex from the Air* by O. G. S. Crawford and Alexander Keiller.) The bare essentials of the ditch-work are shown in Fig. 76. A section of the modern road is drawn there for reference, but this particular stretch also happens to be nearly parallel to the sides *AB* and *CD* of the ditched and banked

parallelogram, and it will be shown at a later stage that this is no accident. The shared direction is much the same as that of the contours of the ground, which after rising very steeply from the roadside to a ridge, thereafter rises at only three or four degrees. There is a combe (dry valley) immediately to the north of the area, and this will prove to have important properties.

Barely discernible in Crawford's photograph is what was described as a mound (E in our figure), 'very green and mossy, 17 ft [5.23 m] wide and 40 ft [12.31 m] long'. There is also a round mound (F) said to be 16 ft [4.92 m] in diameter. While quoting the lengths of the sides (162 [49.85 m] and 171 ft [52.62 m]), Crawford did not give accurate directions for them. His photograph was taken at a slightly oblique angle, and so needs correction. While this is scarcely possible from internal evidence, the following phenomena were probably observed from the ditches, viewing at right angles to the sides and at azimuths that were perhaps all within a degree of the quoted figures:

(1) across *AD* at azimuth 6.2° Arcturus was seen rising
(2) across *AB* at azimuth 101.7° Procyon was seen rising

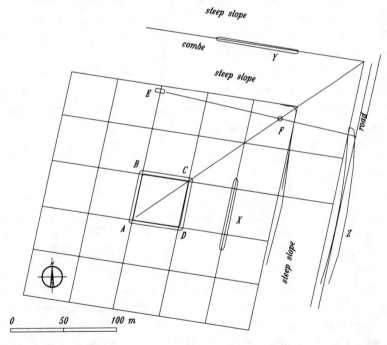

FIG. 77.   The probable plan of the parallelogram within the 'field' on Coombe Bissett Down. The outermost ditches *Y* and *Z* and the mound-like feature labelled *X* are mainly conjectural. The figure ignores some additional earthworks to the west of *E*, and lynchets across the entire field (in the direction of *X*, which may be an illusion created by one of them), that we assume to have been added later.

(3) across *BC* at azimuth 187.3° Rigel was seen setting
(4) across *CD* at azimuth 281.7° Spica was seen setting

These statements are of course made on the basis of our standard type of calculation, in which dates and altitudes are found that are consistent with equal-altitude viewing from opposite sides. Paired in this way, Procyon and Spica give 3315 BC, while Rigel and Arcturus give 3270 BC. In such cases as this, one may of course pair other sides than opposites in order to estimate a date—as in the more difficult case of Windmill Hill. Taking Arcturus with Procyon and Spica with Rigel would, as it happens, have given dates only a decade or so removed from those already quoted. The altitudes required by these combinations are all in the neighbourhood of 11.6°.

That four stars can be so placed at much the same period of history must be counted as yet another argument for this extension of the principles governing viewing across long barrows, rings of mounds, and cursus banks. The consistency of the picture can be further strengthened, if we suppose that an observer looked up the slope along what was to become the 'green and mossy' mound, that is in the direction *FE*. This line, be it noticed, is almost perfectly at right angles to the road. One can only guess at the altitude set by the mound, but if it matched the natural horizon, the setting of Altair would have been visible around the year 3320 BC. In precisely the reverse direction, looking in a manner that we cannot fully specify, but over open country now, the rising Aldebaran would have been visible at its extinction angle around 3300 BC.

What is very puzzling is the absence of any star along the line *ABE*. This would seem a very obvious arrangement for viewing a star rising out of the mound, but the declination derived (about 40°, depending on altitudes) indicates no bright star. The fact that six bright stars have already been found is not to be taken lightly, however, in view of the highly coherent dates they suggest. It is conceivable that a future survey might force substantial revision of them, but this pessimistic conclusion is muted by evidence that the structure is only a part of a much more extensive system, partly natural and partly artificial, and that when this is finally investigated we shall know much more about potential lines of sight. It seems probable that the modern road follows the approximate line of another ditch (*X* in Fig. 77), which it now mostly covers, and that this was a viewing position for an artificial horizon created by a bank of earth at the top of the steep slope between the road and the field containing the earthworks. At a rough estimate, the altitude set by this horizon was within a degree or two of the 11.6° calculated for the parallelogram. This would make excellent sense of the arrangement: looking up this mammoth

barrow-like slope—natural apart from its ridge—the setting of Spica would have been seen, exactly as over the bank *CD*.

Another possible ingredient of this system not remarked upon by Crawford is the hint of a ditch (*Y* in Fig. 77) running for some distance up the combe, and almost perfectly parallel to the other sides of the parallelogram. There is now no surviving artificial ridge to set the horizon, but there very probably was one originally, over which the rising of Rigel would have been observed, as over the bank *CB*. In fact in these respects, the gently sloping table at the top of the slopes mentioned—one may call it the 'field'—is simply the central parallelogram writ large. The dimensions of the parallelogram were indeed very probably meant to be exactly one fifth those of the larger area, as indicated in our only slightly conjectural figure.

There are still further possibilities, for there are steep and still very impressive slopes to the east of the road and to the north of the combe. It seems therefore that all types of observation that could be made from the central parallelogram could also have been made by looking in two directions from ditches *Y* and *Z*, assuming them to have been suitably symmetrical. For precisely the same results, the angles set by the natural ground would need to have been the same all round (approximately 11.6°). This is possible, but at present not certain. This type of two-directional viewing from a single ditch is something we have found in the context of cursus-type monuments—to which the Coombe Bissett structure is related in much the same way as the Radley barrow is related to a more traditional long barrow.

Whatever the results of any future excavation, at present it looks very much as though the division of the 'field' into five parts speaks for a favourite ratio: the viewing altitude was once again at a gradient in the neighbourhood of 1 in 5.

4

STARS IN CHALK

THE previous chapter was concerned with important ways in which the principles of long barrow construction were extended. There were yet other extensions of those principles before the fashion for long barrows waned. Avenues enclosed within earthen banks, or within rows of stones, would seem an obvious extension, but in fact another type of monument seems to have priority, and avenues will be put aside until the next chapter. Figures cut into the turf on exposed hillsides, especially on chalk downland, are rare, but they were probably once commonplace. They may seem a very far cry from the monuments discussed thus far, but they will prove to have been in a sense no more than an extension of the principles seen in action at the Windmill Hill rings of mounds. In short, those who created them were apparently seeking out natural hills that produced the same effects as artificial long barrows had done, albeit now on a much grander scale.

One of the commonest mistakes in analysing chalk figures is to pay attention only to their *form*, which is likely to have changed appreciably over the years. Many have suspected a celestial connection, but even they have only called on the historical mythology of the stars, without any thought for the reasons behind it. Many stars obtained their supposed characters, their reputations, only from the relations between their risings and settings and the seasons of the year. The precession of the equinoxes changes such relationships drastically, so that a millennium is more than enough to upset the basis of any astral myth. If that myth originated in Mediterranean latitudes, it is even less fitted to an interpretation of attitudes in northern lands. With the few remaining ancient chalk figures we must rest our case on the evidence of monument and landscape, and little else. Doing so, one can be reasonably sure that three or four of the examples surviving derive from prehistoric times, and that at least one is in some way a representation of stars observed over it. Our first example will be the White Horse at Uffington, which will be shown to

have marked—among other things—the rising of the constellation we know as Taurus. More precisely, taken together with the adjacent Dragon Hill, it marked the rising of Aldebaran and other stars in the head of the bull, and the stars in what later mythographers saw as its horns. One surprising consequence here is that Aldebaran seems not to have been marked by the eye of the bull, but rather by its penis.

The Uffington White Horse

As explained in connection with nearby Wayland's Smithy, Whitehorse Hill at Uffington in Berkshire is not only crossed by the Ridgeway but it has on its top an impressive Iron Age enclosure known as Uffington Castle. The White Horse itself is on a ridge tangential to this earthwork, to the northeast (see Fig. 80). It is a strange figure, cut into the turf of the chalk downs, and to untutored eyes is more a dachshund, or perhaps a dragon, than a horse. It has been said to have certain affinities to images on Belgic coins and metalwork of the Late Iron Age, but as in the case of man and the apes, one cannot rule out collateral descent. Minor changes have certainly occurred in historical times: its exposed chalk surface was for long scoured at seven-year intervals by the local inhabitants, most of whom were more interested in the social event than in history. It will here be assumed only that its overall situation and dimensions have remained more or less unchanged—and even its dimensions are not of the utmost importance. Finer points of detail are of no great consequence in the first instance, although of course there are limits to what can be sacrificed. The argument starts from two essential properties: the animal lies in a fairly well-defined direction just below the ridge, on the western side of it. Looking along the ridge from the plain below it serves as a perfect (but in shape entirely

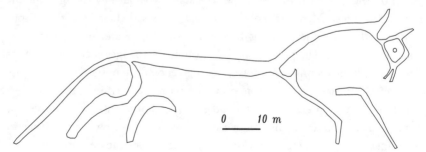

0   10 m

FIG. 78.   The White Horse as it was when Flinders Petrie measured it (against the hillside, not in plan) late in the nineteenth century. The ridge of the hillside on which it lies is just above its back, as shown here, and its head is at the higher end of the ridge, the profile of which is shown in Fig. 79.

unrecognizable) marker for the setting of Rigel. And it is to be seen—and seen upright—from the west, from which side it marks the rising of Taurus.

Even from the west it is not easy to make out its animal form. Had it been intended to position it for its pictorial value, rather than as a star marker, it would have been much better placed lower on the hillside. This is surely not a trivial point. Tolerably good views are to be had from three or four kilometres distance—along the Longcot to Fernham road, for instance—but closer at hand it is often concealed by folds in the downs. It can be well seen from a steep-sided valley with a fairly flat bottom known as the Manger, a natural coraal lying below it and to the northwest, and it is visible from beyond this and from various points off the roadside as one climbs the hill to the car park that has been built for visitors to this group of monuments (Fig. 80). Parts of this bow-shaped road give the impression that they might be the vestiges of a ditch and bank system. If so, this would have been a very fitting place for it, for the view from there over the White Horse had some remarkable properties in the fourth millennium. Finally, moving back, westwards from the road, one soon descends into dead ground from which the White Horse cannot be seen at all.

Various types of observation might have been made from near the relevant stretch of road (the bay *AB* in the figure), but with respect to the middle of the Horse.

Two stars in the constellation of Taurus are of interest here, namely Aldebaran (alpha Tauri) and gamma Tauri (one of the Hyades). These are the two brightest stars in the V-formation that in historical times has been seen as the head of the bull. When the V is setting, the head, with horns above it, is the right way up. When rising, this is not so, and in Wessex latitudes the V rises on its side, with gamma only slightly above alpha, and to the right of it. When the slope of the line joining the stars as they rise is calculated, it is found to be almost precisely the same as the slope of the ridge above the White Horse.

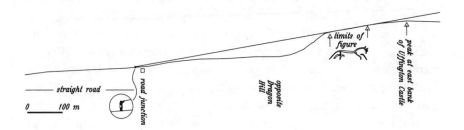

FIG. 79.   The profile of Whitehorse Hill.

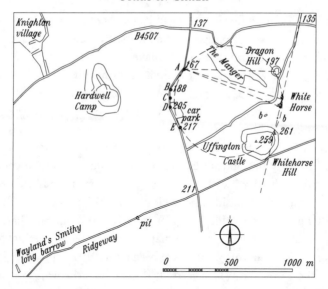

FIG. 80.   The setting of the White Horse in relation to other monuments at Uffington.
Wayland's Smithy long barrow is near the Ridgeway to the southwest. A few spot heights
have been added in metres above OD. Uffington Castle (at the highest point) and Hardwell
Camp are later earthworks. Uffington village is 3 km to the north of the 'Castle'. The main
road from Wantage (9 km) is the B4507. There are oval mounds at the two points marked
b. Excavated in 1857, one of them yielded 46 Roman skeletons. Dragon Hill is a natural
mound, now flat-toppped. Key observation points are at the road junction at the top right,
and at some or all of the places marked A to E.

No assumption needs to be made about the precise point of observation, for
this property is maintained fairly closely all along the gallery AB.

   To an observer in this area, two other stars in Taurus would have been seen
directly above the now flat-topped cone of Dragon Hill. This is a hill below
(and seen to the left of) the White Horse in Fig. 81, where the two stars are
shown. It now looks at first sight like a miniature Silbury Hill, but is not in
fact man-made, although its top seems to have been levelled by human agency.
A local tradition had it that St George slew the dragon on top of Dragon Hill,
but this of course has to be a post-Christian notion. From the point A at the
bottom of the gallery, the hill would have provided a perfect rising marker for
zeta Tauri (with beta Tauri above, as illustrated) had it been about 3 m higher
than it is now—not at all an implausible arrangement.

   If the chalk 'Horse' was planned for use *only* as explained, with only one
observation point in mind, then as time progressed it would have been found
necessary to move to a point higher up the slope. A fresh cutting would have
been made into the hill for a ledge on which to stand—bringing the eye

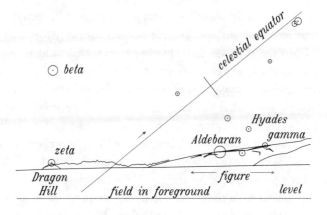

FIG. 81. The profile of the ridge with the White Horse, as it might have been seen from the lower part of the gallery *AB* in the late fourth millennium BC. Stars in the constellation of Taurus, including the four brightest, are marked with circles indicating their brightness. (They are of course point sources of light, at the centres of the circles in question.) The equator, with arrow above it, shows the general sense of the daily rotation of the stars as they rise. Note the near-perfect fit of the two stars in the recumbent bull's head (Aldebaran and gamma Tauri) to the slope of the White Horse; and the near-perfect vertical set by beta Tauri and zeta Tauri (traditionally the tips of the bull's horns), above Dragon Hill. This hill, now flat-topped and no longer visible against the skyline (note the tree-covered hill beyond), would have been visible if it was originally only 3m higher, and this is how it is drawn here. For reference, the equinoctial point is drawn on the equator for the year 3000 BC.

presumably not far above the ground level to the east. It need not be assumed that the chalk figure observed always had its present proportions, although the fact that most of the present figure can be seen from all points inclines one to believe that the animal's overall size has not changed much, but whether its eye has always had a special significance it is impossible to say. The eye certainly has a mound-like structure, but so too does the area at what we might take to be the testicles of the beast. If we take the eye to be the point over which gamma Tauri was seen, then Aldebaran (alpha Tauri) will have risen at the forward tip of the boomerang-like appendage that was presumably meant as the penis. To each point of the bank, a date can be assigned at which this phenomenon would have been visible: the stars would have risen as explained as seen from the bottom end of the gallery (*A* in Fig. 80) in 3230 BC, and from the top end (*B*) in 2220 BC, and one could so continue into the next bay, bringing us to *C* in 1740 BC. The gallery could in principle have been built up in this way as far as *E*, a position appropriate to the second century AD.

To be more specific and give a precise date, a precise viewpoint and a precise target are needed, and neither is strictly available to us. For example, if

Aldebaran rose over the tip of the boomerang as seen from B, then the date was 2220 BC. If it rose over the eye—which in later history Aldebaran came to symbolize—then the year was 2610 BC; but then the remarkable property of the simultaneous rising of gamma Tauri is lost.

The symmetrical arrangement of the curving road between A and E (Fig. 80) in relation to the chalk figure suggests that the entire 'bow' had some part to play, but how can one decide whether it was a viewing gallery built up over many centuries, or a feature cut at a single time? The latter option can easily be defended: allowing for uncertainties in viewing position, from C, Procyon would have been seen rising over the tip of the boomerang in 3320 BC; and from E, Altair would have risen over the same point also in 3320 BC. Taking a viewpoint a little further down the hill than A, this date can be matched there with the beautiful Taurus rising explained at the outset. And an argument will be given shortly for much the same date (3380 BC) based on a completely different analysis, for which the form of the chalk figure is irrelevant. (It would obviously be wrong to sweep aside its symbolic form, but its function as marker can be separated conceptually from it.)

The case for a gallery built up over time is not a weak one. To ensure that two points of the chalk figure, the eye and penis, retained the property of marking the rising points of two stars, it was necessary to choose observation points lying almost on a circle, as indeed the points A to E do. (See the broken circle in Fig. 80.) The truth of this statement follows from a well-known property of the circle: the angle subtended at the circumference of a circle by any chord is constant. The separation of the two stars in azimuth remains fairly constant over time. But a perfect circle will not be obtained, since altitudes shift slightly as one climbs the hill.) The need to satisfy the condition as regards angles would explain very well why the road takes its very peculiar course at this point, and does not head straight down the hill. And what has been said of the spacing of the two main stars in the head of our Taurus goes also for the space between them and the stars at the tips of its horns over Dragon Hill, since the near rim of that hill is close to the circle.

For the final stage in the argument that the White Horse was indeed a Neolithic star marker, it is necessary to consider the view it presents to an observer near the road junction at the upper right corner of Fig. 80. Looking *down* from the chalk figure, in the direction of the junction, it is a very striking fact that the road there (heading slightly east of north) is very straight and runs directly away from the lower end of the figure. The backbone of the figure is not in this line—in fact the angle between their directions is exaggerated by the perspec-

tive from above—but in any case, from below, only a white splash created by the central part of the body can be clearly seen. The profile of the hill in this direction is shown in Fig. 79, and this too is remarkable, for it will be seen that the chalk figure more or less fills the flat part of the ridge. Whether or not the ridge was flattened with a purpose, the line that skims it comes to earth very close to the road junction as shown. Of course it is quite impossible to make out the form of the figure from below in this case. With an altitude of about 9.7° for a standing observer at the present land level (a level slightly too high for prehistory), and an azimuth of about 192.3°, a declination of −27.85° is found, and this fits only Rigel in any plausible period of history. The year is around 3380 BC.

What was the function of the straight road? It is hard to believe that some forerunner of it was not connected with the alignment explained. At its northern end, from which the white splash of the chalk figure can still be made out—although this is not of much relevance to the use of the hill for observation—the derived declination would have been appropriate to a year around 3740 BC, which lies between the dates found for the two chief phases of Wayland's Smithy. The road might originally have gone on in a straight line even further northwards, to Sower Hill Farm perhaps, in which case we have a date in the neighbourhood of Wayland's Smithy I.

It looks very much as though the White Horse might have been arrived at in two stages: first as a marker of no significant shape, perhaps only as a simple white marker to draw attention to some mound or other, higher up Whitehorse Hill (see Fig. 80). Then, in the thirty-fourth century, the hill itself might have been shaved and further markers have been cut, whether or not they were as yet related to the bull that was seen to rise over it from the west. But what of the question of the *simultaneous* versus the *gradual* cutting of the sections of the gallery from which we have supposed viewing was done? In favour of the latter, it would help to explain the preservation of the chalk figure into Roman times. One of the oval mounds near its head was opened in 1857 and forty-six Roman skeletons were found in it, five of them with coins between their teeth, in what was Greek and Roman fashion, to pay Charon for their passage across the river Styx.

Is it really a bull? I once heard a local boy at Uffington Castle reading out the historical notice there to his grandfather, whose response was unanswerable: 'If you ask me, they're only guessing.' It is anyone's guess as to how the figure was changed in the centuries following the first two phases proposed here, but the changes were probably much smaller than we have any right to expect.

On the interpretation offered here, the White Horse at Uffington is the descendant of a marker for stars that constitute our Taurus; but it is more than a mere marker. Those stars were obviously seen as an animal at some stage. We see the compact V-shape in the constellation of Taurus as the head of the bull, but without its horns. The V could well in the past have been seen as having included horns; but since beta and zeta Tauri (the tips of the horns, as now conceived) stood over Dragon Hill at the moment of the head's rising, we do not have to insist on this point. Taurus is one of the few constellations on whose symbolism many different peoples have been able to agree. There are said to be records of Amazonian tribes who, quite independently of colonizing influence, saw a bull's head or jaw in the V of the Hyades. But a description of the White Horse as 'the oldest known prehistoric star-map' must be forestalled. Quite apart from its resemblance to George Washington's hatchet—which has had six new handles and three new blades—it might have worked as a symbol in at least two quite different ways. The chalk figure might have symbolized the stars, rather as a star map does; but one might imagine equally easily that both symbolized some third idea—with chalk and stars both serving as symbols of the bull, and also of what in turn the bull meant.

If the chalk figure was not radically redrawn in later times, and turned head to tail, then as an entity in itself the V of the stars would simply have announced the notion of 'bullhood'. Looked at in this way, the component stars would not have represented the parts of the bull. Aldebaran, for instance, would not have symbolized the eye, but the quality most revered in the bull. No matter which way we read the symbol, we have here yet another prehistoric fertility symbol.

Looking at the symbol in this most abstract way, one can see that the rising constellation might even have been interpreted differently from the setting constellation—as the awakening or living bull on the one hand and the sleeping, dying, or sacrificed bull on the other, perhaps. As for its historical priority, considered purely as a marker, it seems to be the oldest of the five chalk figures considered at length in this chapter. Considering it as a symbolic figure, and one that might have been cut into the hillside long after the marker was first inaugurated, the most we can say is that it is potentially the oldest.

The Wilmington Long Man and Neighbouring Barrows

Most of the hillside figures of England, of which the White Horse is one of the best known, are no more than two centuries old. There are two crosses in Buckinghamshire, one at Whiteleaf, near Princes Risborough, and one at

Bledlow, nearby, that are often mistakenly taken to be medieval, although they will later be shown to have Neolithic origins. Some ancient hill figures have been lost within the last few centuries: they include one on Shotover Hill, Oxford, a double figure on Plymouth Hoe, and perhaps one on the slopes of Wandlebury Camp, near Cambridge. The most notorious of all surviving examples is the Cerne Abbas Giant. It represents the constellation of Hercules, and those who have argued for a Romano-British origin were probably right, even though it seems to have perpetuated a practice with prehistoric origins. Hercules is an undistinguished constellation that probably entered the stock of astral mythology at a relatively late date. The one constellation that has seemed to be in human form to people of many different cultures is Orion. The Cerne Giant could not have marked Orion's rising in a reasonable way at any period of history, but there is at Wilmington in East Sussex a figure perfectly placed to mark Orion's movement across the ridge above it. The star that provides the key to an understanding of this phenomenon is Rigel, the star that was to be seen over the White Horse from the junction of the road to Uffington.

The Long Man of Wilmington has attracted speculations of so many different sorts that it would be tedious even to list them. It was not a drawing of Nebuchadnezzar, or of the Colossus of Rhodes, or of the statue of Zeus at Olympia, for it is older than all of them. It was not a polite copy of the obscene Cerne Giant, made by the monks of Wilmington—although they might have had a hand in preserving or modifying it. It is much older than the Cerne figure, which could even have been inspired by the Sussex icon, for it will soon be clear that both were used in very similar ways, albeit with different constellations.

The Long Man of Wilmington is an outline—no more—of a male human figure looking roughly northwards towards the village of Wilmington. He is formed by a trench in the turf on the north side of South Down ridge. Although past drawings have filled in some detail, they are not convincing, and neither are recent suggestions that turf depths indicate that the figure was once helmeted. The Long Man looks to modern eyes rather as though he is skiing, for in each hand he holds a vertical staff (Fig. 82). A drawing by Sir William Burrell made in 1766 represents the staves as a scythe and a rake, both shorter than now. It has often been said—for instance by Christopher Hawkes—that they might have been spears. Hawkes thought that the figure could have represented Woden, demilitarized with the coming of Christianity to Sussex. It has no doubt meant many different things to successive generations.

The figure was renovated by the Rev. W. de Ste Croix in 1874 and filled with yellow bricks and cement, to preserve it. The only perceptible detail reported by Sir Flinders Petrie, when he charted it nearly half a century later,

was in the face. He said that the eyes were marked by hollows and the nose and lips by raised mounds. These things are not evident today, and the mounds were probably turves added by the renovators. Certain hollows in the ground leave a casual observer with the suspicion that other detail has been lost, but it is doubtful whether there was ever anything quite comparable with the manhood of the Cerne Giant. It has been said that the left (western) foot once pointed west, rather than downwards, and that the legs were once more splayed than now, but the evidence of most early sketches and descriptions is best taken with a pinch of salt.

The figure of the Long Man might seem a naïve piece of work, but this is very far from the truth, as one may see by simply considering the frame formed by the staves: they are nearly equal in length (70.3 and 71.8 m, east and west), and are spaced at about half the common value (35.6 and at the top and 34.8 m at the bottom). The man is cut into the hollow of a natural coombe in the hillside, over which the ground was artificially flattened, or even given a slight convexity, cambered to counter the natural concavity of the combe. That it slopes down from its central axis to flanking parallel ditches out-

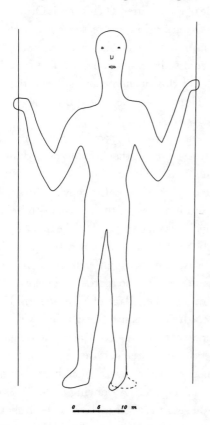

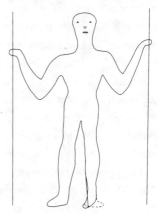

FIG. 82.   (Above) The 'Long Man', a chalk figure cut into the downs at Wilmington, East Sussex, drawn following Flinders Petrie's measurements—made against the ground rather than in plan. (Right) The shape of the foreshortened version visible from a point near the modern road, and with better human proportions.

side the staves will have helped to run water off the figure. The ground was carefully chosen: its incline is about 28.2°, and from the top of the hill to the feet very close to 30°—shades of Silbury Hill. Perhaps there was a deliberate attempt here to introduce geometrical harmony into the construction. The spacing of the staves, slightly closer at the bottom than at the top, tends to reduce the effect of foreshortening, when it is viewed from a distance. The perspective of the figure has been ingeniously handled: what is, when viewed from the air, a very tall and spindly man becomes, when seen from more than a few tens of metres, a well proportioned, even rather stocky, individual.

It is no simple matter to decide on the precise point from which the figure was meant to be viewed. In line with the *centre* of the Long Man, there are relatively few places on the present-day terrain that look like potential sighting points. The first of these is a ditch at the edge of the area containing the figure,

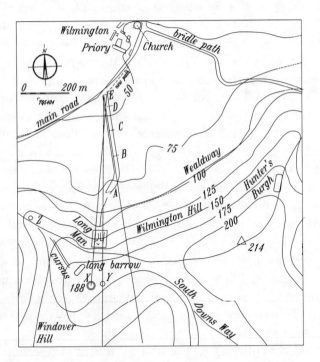

FIG. 83.   The surroundings of the Long Man. The village of Wilmington lies to the north of the Priory. Contours are in metres above OD. The curved part of the path running south to the Long Man is at two levels. Only a few of the many footpaths in the area are marked, most as single lines. The steep natural amphitheatre of Wilmington Hill is effectively bounded by the Wealdway at its foot and the ridge followed by the path through Hunter's Burgh (a long barrow) above. There are mounds of unknown character at X, Y, and Z, and perhaps others now destroyed through flint mining in the southern area.

separating it from a field under cultivation, near *A* on the map of Fig. 83. The path (*DCB*) approaching the figure from the minor road through Wilmington twice crosses the line of the eastern staff (at the ends of its curved section) and once crosses the line of the western staff. If continued, both of those lines meet with the old buildings of Wilmington Priory, less than 700 m to the north of the Long Man. The curved section of the footpath (south of *B*) is remarkable in one respect: it has something of the appearance of an old bank and ditch system. It is now much overgrown, and split into an upper and lower footpath. It does not appear to have ever been excavated archaeologically.

From the footpath one may look across to the east to a ridge on which is a well-preserved long barrow known as Hunter's Burgh. The entire region is—for Sussex—rich in Neolithic remains: there are at least eight long barrows within 10 km of the Long Man, all but Hunter's Burgh lying to the west. The finest long barrow of all is the nearest, near the top of Windover Hill above the Long Man, only 100 m away, In fact this, Windover Long Mound, is invisible from it, but is visible against the horizon as one walks down the footpath, and it finally disappears from view as the footpath ends. Here is one reason for thinking that the lie of the footpath might be important.

The Windover Hill long barrow is about 55 m long and 15 m wide, a mound of more or less uniform height and width, except at its ends, with seemingly parallel side-ditches. Its southern end is unusual: a circular plat-form-mound that might almost be thought a separate affair, were it not for the fact that the two parts are deliberately joined. There are numerous signs of prehistoric activity in its immediate neighbourhood, much of it later than the long barrow. The hilltop is pockmarked with flint mines; on the southern edge of the quarry there is a fine bowl-barrow; and to the southeast a small platform barrow.

The barrow itself has not yet been excavated. Its azimuth can be very tentatively put at about 226.5°. An axial observation over the platform-mound at the southern end, at the extinction angle, might have been of Sirius, setting of course, the declination being then –25.5°, and the approximate year within a century or so of 3800 BC.

The Windover Hill long barrow is of interest in part because there is something resembling the remains of a cursus running for more than 100 m at a steep gradient up to the southern end of it. It is not a very elegant one, for it tapers in an ungainly way, reducing in width from nearly 6 m at the bottom (northern) end to less than half that figure as it reaches the platform end of the mound. This very taper makes it probable that the feature was used in much the same way as those discussed in our last chapter. The track above the slope

containing the Long Man, and the long barrow itself, had probably long been in existence when it was decided to build this small cursus up an incline that was not very well fitted to it, one side being inevitably higher than the other. Directing such sides independently to the rising of the same star would have resulted in their having slightly different directions. Both were seemingly aligned on the rising of Sirius, just as the tomb had been directed towards the setting of that star. The azimuths and altitudes are not constant—the area has been much ravaged by time—but they average around 150.7° and 11.3° respectively. (In round numbers we can say that only half a degree difference in altitudes would force a divergence of more than a degree between the tracks.) Note that here yet again is a one-in-five gradient. The derived declination is about −22.9°, which is right for Sirius around 3100 BC, but the viewing position is a matter for speculation. In the absence of a thorough survey the uncertainty here is of the order of two or three centuries at least.

The Hunter's Burgh long barrow lies on an escarpment close to north–south. There is a horseshoe-shaped ditch at the southern end, running some way up the sides. It is about 58 m long, and 23 m wide at its higher (and wider) southern end, but its tear-drop form makes its intended alignment difficult to estimate. Here again it is rash to speculate on the functioning of an unexcavated barrow, but estimating its azimuth at about 193.6° it seems quite possible that to the north the rising of Vega was seen; and to the south, over the ridge, the setting of Rigel. The dates derived for Vega are so uncertain as not to be worth quoting. For Rigel, if the ridge set the altitude, 3690 BC would be a reasonable estimate. An artificial horizon above the true ridge horizon would bring the date later, perhaps by as much as three centuries. Errors in the azimuth of the barrow, however, are quite forgiving: an azimuth of 191°, for instance, only moves the date to 3760 BC.

The History of the Long Man and his Staves

The Windover cursus—if that is not too grand a name for it—is not without precedent in this region, for the staves held by the Long Man are in some respects of the same character. Perhaps this rudimentary two-staves cursus stood unembellished by a human figure for many centuries, but if so, the figure was surely added before the connection with the human constellation (our Orion) had been entirely forgotten. At all events it is the staves that point the way to an understanding of the functioning of the giant, whose human form merely confirms what is to be deduced without reference to him at all in the first instance.

Bearing in mind the alignment of the road directly towards the Uffington White Horse, the path running roughly south to the Long Man (starting at a gateway to the minor road from Wilmington to Litlington) is disappointingly oblique, so that the connection between the two is not immediately obvious. Nevertheless, there are points on it that demand attention. The line of the western staff meets the path not far from the main road, at a point that has some important properties. An observer looking along this line—which also passes over the Windover Hill barrow marked Y on the map of Fig. 83—could have seen Rigel on the western horizon around 3440 BC. Note that the path has an appreciable width, so that in this case, for instance, we are in some doubt as to whether to take the observer on the eastern side of the path at E (the gate) or the western side at D, or somewhere between.

There is a far more interesting possibility than this, however, for an observer at E (west side). This is illustrated in Fig. 84 (compare the map of Fig. 83). Looking over the mound Y—which cannot now be seen, and might not even have existed at the time—the line passes over the top of the eastern staff. This does not seem very auspicious in itself, but Rigel set, or rather was on the western horizon in this direction, around 3480 BC. (The altitude is 10.7°, the azimuth 182.5°.) There are several reasons for taking this possibility seriously. From the same place, looking along the line of the path—assumed to have been in better trim then than now—the other foot of Orion (kappa Orionis) would have been on the horizon to the east of the meridian, and this at exactly the same period of history. (The azimuth is taken as 172.9° and the altitude 12.4°.) In other words, the human constellation of Orion would have stood on the horizon. In fact the daily rotation of the stars, combined with the bow of the natural horizon set by the downs would have kept it more or less there for some time, providing one of the most pleasing of all the properties of this remarkable site. If we refuse to interpret 'being on the horizon' too severely then we can say that Orion would have seemed to walk along the ridge between Rigel's rising and final setting. The ridge is not perfectly regular—it was much more so in the past than now, for it has been mined for flints and excavated by archaeologists—but one wonders whether at some stage in prehistory there was not an attempt to trim it so as to make the effect more perfect. This was very probably done for the lip of the bay, a ridge marked RR in Fig. 84, the function of which has yet to be explained.

From the gate, Orion can no longer be seen striding across the horizon as he once did. One no longer has to look for Orion at an altitude of around 10 or 11°, but at about 30°. Doing so, the old effect can almost be seen not far from the foot of the figure. (Whereas Orion's right foot was formerly above the

ridge, now it is out of sight below.) Here we have one of the vital properties of the configuration of land and sky that explain how it could have come about that what made perfect sense in the fourth millennium BC continued to hold the attention of the people of the Sussex Downs for well over three thousand years, to the period of the Cerne Giant and beyond. To preserve the effect of the striding giant it was only necessary to move closer to the figure. But before such possibilities are considered, there is more to be said in defence of the configuration of the thirty-fifth century, over and above the fact that it brings both feet precisely to the ground simultaneously.

First, the near-vertical lines joining stars are remarkably similar to the appearance of the Long Man's staves, and the whole tilt of his head and body

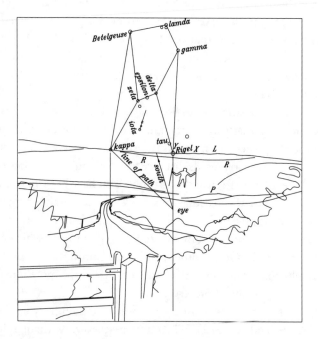

FIG. 84.   A reasonably accurate sketch of the present view of the Long Man from the gate to the road (E on the map of Fig. 83). The chief stars of Orion are added in the positions they would have occupied around 3480 BC—point sources of light, but here represented by circles, with the brighter stars drawn proportionately larger. A few dimmer stars are added to give the sense of the human form of the constellation and its resemblance to the Long Man. Compare the lie of the staves on land and sky. RR is the lip of the bay that acts as a horizon for an observer nearer the chalk figure. L is the Windover Hill long barrow, and X and Y mark the horizon positions of mounds shown on the map. P is a flat-topped platform to the side of the chalk figure, of unknown purpose. The line of the path marks kappa Orionis. Rigel is hardly off the meridian, but will remain visible, as the constellation seems to walk for a time down the ridge, with the daily rotation of the stars.

as seen from this point seems to mirror that of the stars. Even the downward-pointing (west) foot of the chalk figure seems to have a purpose, in the sense that Rigel is lower in the sky than kappa Orionis.

Second, it seemed highly probable that the sighting of Rigel was done in much the same way at Uffington, at a somewhat earlier date. Even more surprising is the fact that, looking to the east over the Hunter's Burgh long barrow from the same viewpoint, still at the same period, Aldebaran could have been seen rising out of the escarpment with the other stars of Taurus, exactly as they were to be seen over the White Horse at Uffington. (In the most probable arrangement, the azimuth was about 116° and the altitude 10.2°, giving a declination of −7.81°, which is right for about 3480 BC.) It is no accident that the line from E to the head of the long barrow is a tangent to the contours of the ground there, or that the barrow was placed on an escarpment with an average gradient of that old favourite 1 in 5, which happens to be almost perfect for the slope of the rising bull's head. Given a little help from the long barrow's profile, the slope was no doubt quite perfect, and was only lacking in its 'Dragon's Hill'.

We are now in a position to see how the key observation point was chosen. It must be supposed that the strange phenomenon of Orion's walk along the downs was well appreciated. In choosing a suitable observation point for this, there was little freedom as regards distance from the ridge, but some flexibility in azimuth. The Taurus effect to the left must also have been appreciated, and it would have been discovered that this was easier to obtain: many azimuths are possible if one is prepared to vary one's distance from the Hunter's Burgh ridge. It was therefore not too difficult to find a point from which *both* could be seen simultaneously. On the other hand, time ruined the combination, and it was no doubt the Orion effect that was considered the more remarkable of the two, and most worthy of preservation.

Just as at Uffington, the main argument rests only lightly on the form of the chalk figure, and it can be taken a stage further without reference to anything more than the staves. What if we take the cursus idea more seriously, and consider an observer at the very foot of each of them in turn? Looking along them up the hillside, a view of the sky will be limited now by the lip of the bay RR (Fig. 84), at an altitude in the neighbourhood of 30°. There can be little doubt that this was done, for Orion's right hand, the bright star Betelgeuse, was to be observed along both staves, first the eastern and a little later the western. It is impossible to be precise about the timing without knowing the exact form of the lip of the bay and the exact viewing positions, but as anyone who visits the site may verify, there are depressions in the ground

at the foot of each staff, and they would certainly repay excavation, if only to rule out the possibility of viewing ditches there. Observers standing at ground level might well have seen Betelegeuse hovering over the horizon around 3480 BC.

The Wilmington people chose the largest area they could find with something near to a thirty-degree angle, and trimmed the terrain to make it almost perfect. The flat-topped cone below and to our right as we face the figure (*P* in Fig. 84) also presents a 30° slope to the observer, just as that at Silbury, and indeed, as at the plainly Neolithic Priory Mount in the nearby Sussex town of Lewes. What was to be seen from *P* ? The rising Altair could have been seen from the flat top in 3480 BC, but there is so much latitude for the observer's position that the point should not be pressed.

To return to the path: why did it eventually veer to the right? In part, of course, to bring people to the foot of the Long Man—and it has already been shown why the path did not take a direct route. It has already been noted that as precession carried Rigel closer to the celestial equator, the observer would have needed a new observation point. There was no harm in keeping the same line of sight, for as happened at the long barrows, any ritual observance could have been continued without its conforming to every aspect of the designer's intentions. With the same line of sight, it would have been necessary to advance only 300 m in fifteen centuries, to keep Rigel's rising in view, a few metres in the life of a man. (It is assumed that Rigel's behaviour was much more important than that of the other foot; the two could not have been kept perfectly simultaneously on the ridge any more.) This would have been so up to the end of the straight section of the path. After the short bend, it settles for a time in a new line (approaching the present gate to the area containing the figure, maintained by the Sussex Archaeological Society). Someone looking directly along this line would have seen Rigel set, at a date around 1600 BC. Of course the earlier rising and ridgeway walk would still have been visible. This line too would soon have ceased to be useful. The people of Wilmington might have tried to increase the angle to the horizon by excavating the ground on which they stood. Perhaps it is significant that here the path is divided, one branch being appreciably lower than the other. But this ruse, if that is what it was, would not have achieved the desired effect for much more than a century.

As they closed up to the end of this stretch, sight of the Windover long barrow was lost (near the present gate to the field) and the direction of the path was changed yet again, now heading at azimuth 197°. The angles are right for the setting of Rigel around 1280 BC—assuming that this final section of the path is ancient, which might not be so. Beyond this point it would be idle to

speculate, beyond repeating that the bay can still function after a fashion, for observers close to the figure.

The first section of the path was almost certainly created at the outset—and the others perhaps also—so that their later value was coincidental. Whether they had a clear astronomical function at the beginning of this activity is hard to say. The two-level path might be a sign that they had just such a function. The bend seems to look towards Hunter's Burgh, but only at a much later date did any bright star rise in that direction.

No assumption has been made here concerning the date at which the human figure was cut, but a few weak conclusions may be drawn, even so. On stylistic grounds it is hard to believe that it dates from the fourth millennium—but what criteria can one use, when dealing with something that is in so many ways unique? It certainly fits into a tradition that belongs to that time. To deny this, and to accept the constellation association, one would have to claim that either the constellation was not originally seen as human, or that it simply did not get the full artistic treatment when the frame of staves was cut. The constellation was in either case important enough to demand the 'cursus' of staves; and when the figure was added to them, early or late, people still understood its function. I can only offer a half-hearted protest against this. The line of the Windover Hill long barrow seems to pass through the head of the Long Man, as though he was being represented as looking over it in the time-honoured fashion. Interpretation apart, if this was not a coincidence then those who cut the first figure evidently had the long barrow in their thoughts. (And there are still a few of whom the same can be said.)

The Bledlow and Whiteleaf Crosses

The crosses cut into the turf of the Chiltern hills at Bledlow and Whiteleaf in Buckinghamshire are in some ways the most remarkable of all English hill figures. Although they are just over 6 km apart, they are certainly related, not only in general form, but in the way they were used, and in the fact that the second can in principle be seen from the site of the first. (In practice, at present, intervening trees make this impossible.) As with all chalk figures, historians have usually worked backwards from recorded tradition, but again this can be of no real value here. The fact that the cross is the supreme Christian symbol has misled most of those who have speculated on the Chiltern crosses on the basis of their form. Other writers have taken great pains to deduce their origins from their measurements. Sir Flinders Petrie, in particular, was struck by the supposed equality between the length of the triangular base of the Whiteleaf

cross (Fig. 85) and the diameter of the main (sarsen) circle at Stonehenge. Both, he thought, were about 400 Etruscan feet across; and he drew the conclusion that they were of comparable antiquity. The Whiteleaf measurement, however, has been increased by perhaps as much as 40 m over the last two centuries, as a result of erosion and attempts at 'improvement', a fact that takes the wind out of the sails of such reasoning. We are very fortunate that the precise dimensions of neither cross matters greatly to the sorts of argument to be offered here, and no call whatsoever will be made on their symbolic nature.

Flinders Petrie began his career as a land surveyor. His father had been captivated by the pyramidology of John Taylor and Piazzi Smyth, and one of the son's many achievements in the eyes of his contemporaries was to demolish Smyth's theory of the pyramid-inch. His own 'Etruscan foot' is now in the same archive of forgotten standards.

From a drawing made by the Rev. Francis Wise in 1742, it seems that the cross was then less clearly the 'Latin cross' to be seen in the nineteenth century and today. It was rather like an inverted V with a crosspiece (see Fig. 85), and we shall soon be in a position to explain why it was given this shape. It happened in prehistoric times, but long after the cross was first cut.

The Whiteleaf Cross is very conspicuous: it looks out over the town of Princes Risborough and the Oxfordshire plain to the west, and so can be seen from great distances. The often-repeated story that it can be seen from a mound in the gardens of St John's College, Oxford, can be dismissed, for Shotover Hill—which once had its own hill figure—stands between them. That the Whiteleaf Cross is visible from Shotover itself is plausible: at 26 km and a slightly negative altitude of view, the entire cross and base would have looked about the size of a comma in this book, held at normal reading distance. Wise, who thought the crosses were Saxon, claimed to be able to make out Whiteleaf from Uffington White Horse, 56 km away. Under the very best atmospheric conditions this feat approaches what is possible for the human eye; but one cannot help wondering whether he first used a telescope and then his imagination.

From the site of the Bledlow Cross, the Whiteleaf Cross would have been very easily visible by day, as far as its size and angle of presentation are concerned. The line joining them, at a bearing of 60.45° from north (Bledlow to Whiteleaf), narrowly misses being obscured by the shoulder of Wain Hill, on which the Bledlow Cross is cut. Tree cover presents a different problem: today the Bledlow Cross is completely surrounded by trees. Even without trees it would have presented only its profile to an observer at Whiteleaf, and as a cross would have been utterly invisible from there. A fire would have been the

only way to guide the eye to the site—but in any case this is not an astronomically significant direction, as far as can be seen.

The two *crosses* have in common the fact that they are not greatly different in size (see Fig. 85). Both lie within about 300 m of the prehistoric Upper Icknield Way, parts of which are now in the so-called Ridgeway Path. They would have been visible from parts of it, although not in such a way as to have made them suitable aids to navigation, as is often suggested. It is hard to see why such aids should have been thought necessary to guide the traveller, when the track itself was there. Both crosses are in close proximity to Neolithic and Bronze Age barrows. There are two (or even three) only a stone's throw from the top of the Whiteleaf Cross, and we shall shortly find a link between the cross and one or perhaps two of them. It is provisionally assumed that these crosses are to be placed in the same category as the chalk figures at Uffington and Wilmington. The aim is to try to discover the points from which they would have been observed.

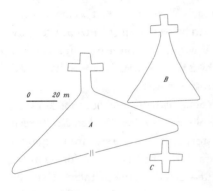

First the Whiteleaf Cross: the name is a corruption of 'Whitecliff', which very aptly describes the appearance of the massive triangular plinth, stripped of its turf and so steep as to discourage grass to take root. One very natural place of observation is a point in line with it on the Icknield Way. The best positions are no longer easy to find, since some modern houses stand in the way, but roughly in line with the stem of the cross there is a kink in the ancient track, which begins to curve very slightly for 80 m or so, convex to the east, and along this curve the remains of a bank and ditch system seem to be in evidence (Fig. 86). Looking from this region, an interesting fact becomes apparent: the angle of the part of the hill with the crossbar is such that it is seen almost edgeways on, more or less disappearing from view, reminding us of Uffington. In short, only the upright marks the place of the cross.

FIG. 85.   The Whiteleaf Cross according to Wise in 1742 (*B*) and Petrie in the 1920s (*A*) and the Bledlow Cross according to Petrie (*C*).

This ditch offers us a choice of viewing positions, and it is very difficult to choose between them in the first instance. The bay has a counterpart to the north, the relevance of which may be illusory, and neither faces into the cross. One might assume that they post-dated the ancient road, and that these

viewing positions were chosen for the convenience of the traveller. There is reason, though, for dismissing this idea, and for making the road come to them, rather than the reverse. The reason is that both bays, and the crossroads between them—another potential viewing position—were such that the angle of view set by the cross would in all three cases have been very close indeed to a gradient of 1 in 5. This gradient has revealed itself often enough in other Neolithic contexts for the idea to be accepted that it did not occur on this hilly landscape by accident. The cross itself is much degraded, but was conceivably cut so as to have arms five times as long as they are broad. The flat part, the cross proper, is at a gradient very close to two in five.

Despite this promising situation, the problem facing us is hardly soluble without further help. There is a whole range of viewing angles from which a choice can often be made only by seeking a consistent set of consequences. If the bay to the north is not illusory—it is in line with the upper edge of the cross's northwest plinth—then it suggests the rising of Aldebaran or Betelegeuse (or both) over the cross in the mid-fourth millennium. The southern bay is better defined: looking from its northern end over the brow of the hill above the cross, the rising of Spica would have been visible in the period around 3620 BC. (The azimuth is tentatively taken as 76.1°, the altitude 11.4°, and the declination of 17.52° is derived. It is assumed, perhaps wrongly, that the eye is near ground level.) From the other end of the ditch, the rising Capella would have been seen in the same way around 3650 BC (azimuth 67.8°, altitude 10.9°, declination 22.26°). There are numerous possible variations on this theme, in which no use is made of the middle stretch of the ditch. Allowing for uncertainty on that question, we should have to reject Spica but might choose to assign Capella to a date three centuries earlier. The reason for preferring the pair of stars, and the thirty-seventh century, must be sought elsewhere, in fact at Bledlow; but it has to be said that the evidence of Bledlow is also hard to interpret.

There is another surprise to be had, when one examines the view from the very foot of the 'white cliff' itself. This escarpment, now bared to the chalk, is very steep indeed, varying from say 25° to 45° in slope. (Fig. 87 shows three of its sections) From its foot, the shape of the cross cannot be made out at all, but old descriptions speak as though there was a bank and ditch below its base, where the road is now. I take it that this is the bank on the other side of the road, to the back of an observer who, while standing on the road, faces the cliff. To a person standing at the foot of that bank the chalk surface presents a horizon of almost precisely 30°.[1]

footnote overleaf

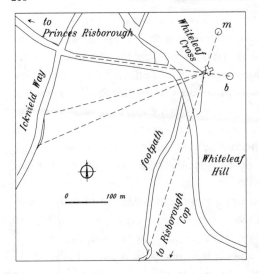

FIG. 86. The surroundings of the Whiteleaf Cross. The cross is on a steep (30°) slope, cut into which is a minor road from Monks Risborough. A Neolithic barrow at *b* and a mound at *m* (on which stood a windmill, but which was previously no doubt a barrow), subtend a right angle at the centre of the cross. Sighting lines (all towards the cross) are suggested by broken lines, those on its axis meeting the extremes of what is presumed to have been a prehistoric ditch. This bow in the Icknield Way has a partner to the north (not shown, and possibly irrelevant) where the way meets the northwest line of the cross's plinth.

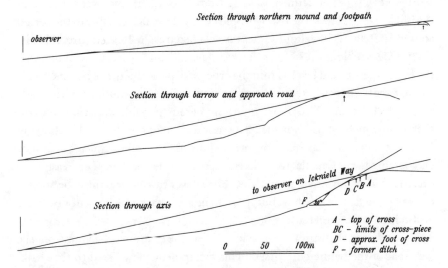

FIG. 87. The three important sections through the Whiteleaf Cross. The three viewing positions are chosen for their viewing potential, and it is all the more surprising to find that gradients very close to 1 in 15 and 1 in 5 (at least twice) were set by their choice—quite apart from the 30° incline from the ditch at the foot of the cross's 'plinth'.

---

1   Ridges in the chalk, cut chiefly by rain, are ignored here. My first measurement from a token 1.66 m eye height was within a single minute of arc of this. Changing position on the road alters the angle by only a few minutes, and all factors considered it is doubtful whether the original angle differed much from 30.25°.

This is in itself remarkable, bearing in mind the similar angle at Wilmington, Lewes, Silbury, and elsewhere, but here the arrangement points unequivocally to Deneb. Taking 30° to be the ideal altitude, this in conjunction with the azimuth of the stem of the cross (measured as 68.3°) provides an alignment on the rising of Deneb (the derived declination being 36.22°). The white chalk at Whiteleaf is thus one of the most perfect examples of surviving Neolithic 'artificial horizons'. What was artificial was not the hill but its selection. Observers looked at the sky up the steep incline along the axis of the cross—perhaps the groove that has since become very pronounced through erosion actually began as a deliberate cut. Close at hand they saw, and needed to see, nothing whatsoever of the cross's shape. From our point of view, as always, the problem with the star Deneb is that it is without much value for dating any structure.

The Icknield Way was a road following the western slopes of the Chilterns between the middle section of the Thames valley and East Anglia. Above the cross, as explained, there are the remains of an unusual kidney-shaped barrow standing on the crest above and to the east of the cross's centre. When this was excavated by Sir Lindsay Scott between 1935 and 1939, a wooden burial chamber was found in it. Part of a male skeleton was found there, and the rest was scattered over a forecourt on the eastern side. The remains of fifty-one freshly broken Neolithic pots (of Windmill Hill type) were found in the soil covering the chamber, evidence of a burial ceremony known from other sites. The pots—since the shards had sharp edges—were presumed to have been broken at the funeral feast, and scraped up with the material used to create the mound. They are taken to be evidence for the Neolithic date of the Icknield Way itself, but there is other evidence—long barrows near Dunstable and Royston, for example—to which we can now add our own.

The roughly eastern-facing nature of the barrow is of great interest, since that part of what is now the main road up the hill (Peters Lane) aligns on the lower part of the cross and the barrow, in a line about 10° south of east. From where the road crosses the Icknield Way, the top of the barrow would just have been seen above the chalk surface. (See the profile in Fig. 87. Trees now obscure the view.) The azimuth (100.5° from barrow to centre cross) and altitude (11.0° from the crossroads, but increasing appreciably as one advances up the slope) together suggest that a star of declination in the neighbourhood of 2.5° would have been seen rising over the barrow from this region. The first candidate is Procyon (3140 BC), but other possibilities are the Pleiades (2480 BC) and Aldebaran (1620 BC). There are yet others, and none can be ruled out, since the cross has evidently been a focus of local attention right up to modern times.

If our earlier dates are acceptable, then it would appear that the cross was used in only a simple line-ahead mode for many centuries, and then supplemented at least once.

In fact the same sort of thing seems to have happened twice. To the north of the excavated barrow, on the end of the ridge above the cross there is another mound. This has a grooved cross imposed on it. It has been held to be the base of an old windmill, but others have claimed it as a pond barrow. It could have been both. Down below, a section of an old path parallel to the Icknield Way, and eventually turning to join with it, aligns on this mound and the lower part of the cross, in a way very roughly symmetrical with the former barrow-alignment. The terrain is here much more difficult, for it slopes steeply across the direction of the path, which has had to be cut into the hillside. Once again, however, there is the phenomenon met at Uffington, Wilmington, and Whiteleaf, namely of an apparently pointless deviation from an otherwise straight or gently curved track following the natural contours of the hill. At a certain point the track turns sharply up the gradient before continuing, and at this new elevation the cross and mound would just have been visible, whereas previously they were out of sight (see Fig. 87 for the profile of the ground). When it continues, the track runs in a straight line with cross and mound, and holds the line for about 150 m. The area is overgrown, and sighting of the mound is now impossible, but observing from the extreme of the kink in the present track the mound's azimuth would have been 17.3°. Only 500 m behind the observer there is a very steep and prominent little hill (Risborough Cop, 200 m, gradient 1 in 3), and from its peak the azimuth of the mound is 17.5°. What is perhaps surprising is that the suggested observation point is *exactly* midway between the mound and the Cop. How such a point could ever have been determined except by chance over such hilly ground is hard to imagine. The symmetries of the situation speak strongly for this as the ideal place of observation. The extreme of the path is the only place from which a person of reasonable height could see both eminences.

But with what result? From the observation point on the path, Arcturus could have been seen as early as 1360 BC, depending on the precise viewing position; and from Risborough Cop to the mound, the same star (declination 37.0°) might have been seen rising in the twelfth century BC. There are yet later possibilities, and the only firm conclusion to be drawn is that the old art was not forgotten. There was at least one good reason for this: the star Deneb would have continued to rise over the cross up the 30° slope for centuries on end.

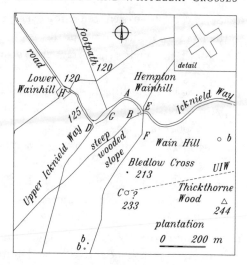

FIG. 88. The surroundings of the Bledlow Cross (Wainhill, Buckinghamshire). The cross is virtually due north of a mound that might be the remains of a long barrow (C), which seems to have been aligned on a straight section of the Icknield Way (off the map, see the direction *UIW* to the east). The central area is a complex network of paths that might prove to be remnants of a prehistoric ditch system. Points *A* to *F* are potential viewing positions, circles marked *b* are round barrows. Double and single lines (roads and path) merely indicate the present situation. Approximate spot heights are in metres.

What in its way is quite as interesting as the stars and dates finally selected are the implications of the two sets of transverse alignments for the peculiar *form* of the Whiteleaf Cross. In order to make a smooth white horizon out of the escarpment for sightings from the two new directions, it was necessary to splay open the base of what was presumably at first just a simple cross, like that at Bledlow. The general shape of the cross as recorded by Wise was just what was needed for the two new alignments. One must assume that later Victorian scouring was too ruthless by far, in its efforts to make the cross conform to the image of what a good Christian cross should be.

Travelling down the Icknield Way to the Bledlow Cross, this is found to reveal many similarities with that at Whiteleaf, although the stars involved were not the same. The cross is on a steep escarpment facing approximately northwest, above the hamlet of Lower Wainhill (in the parish of Bledlow-cum-Saunderton, and near Chinnor). It is difficult of access, in woodland in a nature reserve, but hidden from view by dense scrub—and so rather well protected. Here again, the cross would once have been visible from a fair distance, although the crosspiece would never have been clearly visible from observation-points close at hand, of which there are several. From some of these points

we find that the star Spica could have been seen rising over the ridge above the Whiteleaf Cross in the late fifth millennium, but this is presumably without significance, since the plinth that makes the distant cross visible was not then cut.

The great interest of the Wainhill (Bledlow) area is that there is a veritable network of ancient paths and roads below the cross which either radiate from it or which seem to have once had banks and ditches from which observers could have faced it. This speaks for a marker that was long in use, but it also very effectively hides the clues that are needed as to viewing position. There are far too many possibilities, such as the places A, B, D, E, F, G, and H on Fig. 88. Taking the profiles of the terrain through the centre of the cross and these various points, as illustrated in Fig. 89, there are no 30° tangents, to be sure, but there is something strongly reminiscent of profiles found often elsewhere. The limiting ray runs tangential to a flat and quite extensive tract of land—considerably more so than at Whiteleaf, for example. The sloping ground is not perfectly flat. If it were, the cross would of course not be seen at all in this way. It has been dug away in the lower part of the cross and is in any case very slightly concave in the immediate neighbourhood of it. It is hard to decide how much chalk has been removed by excessive scraping in later times. The cross's lower edge has seemingly been given a pronounced lip, but this perhaps represents only accumulated surface residues from an age that did not know the cross's function. The crosspiece is still more or less level (in depth and breadth), and would have completely disappeared from view when seen from the foot of the hill. This is reminiscent of Whiteleaf, where the disappearance of the cross-piece is not complete, but might once have been so when observed from key positions.

The overall view at Bledlow would never have been as dramatic as that finally obtained at Wilmington, but the two clearly began life presenting much the same appearance. There is even the faintest suspicion of the mound of a long barrow on the ridge above the cross at Bledlow, included tentatively as C on Fig. 88, to show its whereabouts. This would make for another point of similarity with the Wilmington and Whiteleaf figures. It has not been recorded, and might be an illusion. A cursory examination of the ground, now seriously overgrown, suggests a slight eminence at an azimuth of about 215°. If so, then it might have been aligned on Rigel around 3660 BC.

Few natural sites in the Chilterns were as well suited to the purposes of Neolithic astral religion as the inclined plane here on Wainhill, yet in interpreting it one is torn between two different stars—Sirius and Rigel—and consequently between two very different sets of dates, and even they can be

stated only very imprecisely. The problem is that of choosing viewpoints. The most promising point of departure is to consider the path followed by the road *DGAE*. Its central bow is symmetrical with respect to the north–south line through the cross. The curved path presents a natural gallery for observing the cross, reminiscent of that at Uffington. It might be argued that this is just another 'wave' in the generally serpentine course of the Icknield Way at this place. In fact, other such waves follow the contours of the hill, whereas this does not, but cuts across the contours and slopes uphill. The present path *EF* is another that looks as though it is the remains of a bank and ditch.

Making a guess as to the position of the observer, one can say that a sight line from *A* over the cross (and over *C* if it is not illusory) would catch the instantaneous flash of a star of declination −24.9° as it rose and immediately set. Making a similar guess as to the best position for viewing from *E*, the declination turns out to be −25.8°. In other words, if there were ever a tradition of walking along the arc *AE*, perhaps along a ditch, the star could be kept in view for the short period between its first appearance on the meridian and its

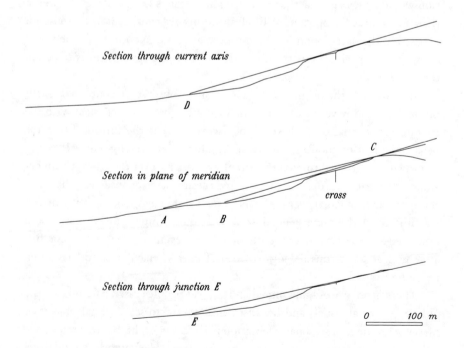

FIG. 89.   Three sections through the Bledlow Cross. Note the unusually long flat section of the slope. Letters correspond to those of Fig. 88.

true setting about an hour later. The star would have 'walked' along the horizon in a way reminiscent of Rigel's behaviour at Wilmington.

But was it Rigel, and did Orion stand above it? If so, we are in the period around 2820 BC. If it was Sirius that rose (when the casual observer would suppose that it should be setting) then the date was around 3620 BC. In each case, the uncertainties of position mean an uncertainty of two centuries either way.

For the viewing positions B, G, H, and some others, declinations in the range $-19°$ to $-22°$ emerge. They could belong to the same star at a later period, or by seeking out slightly different positions they could be Sirius dates corresponding to the Rigel dates quoted in the third millennium. Sirius (thirty-seventh to twenty-sixth centuries) and Rigel (twenty-eighth to twenty-first centuries) are the only two bright stars within the necessary ranges, in the four millennia ending with the Christian era.

Which alternative is to be favoured? The arc swept out by the star—whether Sirius or Rigel—in its walk along the ridge was certainly small, by comparison with the vast arc at Wilmington, but in character the observation would have been exactly the same. This perhaps favours Rigel. However, the dates found for Spica at Whiteleaf are highly consistent with those for Sirius, and the dates found for Wilmington are close to both. Since the *type* of activity at both places was the same, this should perhaps incline us to accept the earlier date.

If Sirius was the original aim, and if Sirius observance continued—as it probably would have done—after the fit ceased to be perfect, then with the passing of time it would have been discovered that the hillside fitted the behaviour of Orion and Rigel in the old way. In the intervening centuries, Sirius would have continued to hold the attention, passing over the cross at a higher and higher altitude. After Orion captured the attention of observers, thanks to the appearance of Rigel over the cross, it too would have gone on rising higher and higher in the same general way, and could quite plausibly have been described as appearing 'over the Bledlow Cross' even into the Roman era. But at Whiteleaf, for reasons already explained, Deneb's behaviour would have been much more stable.

There is no way of knowing when the local people ceased patching up the old astronomical rituals and began to treat these crosses as ritual objects or places of religious or seasonal celebration in their own right, but this must have happened. The urge to visit them at the appropriate season would have continued. Perhaps fires were lit above them in the earliest phases, in which case people would have gone on lighting them, long after their meaning had

been forgotten. There are plenty of examples of such behaviour, for instance in the fires lit at midsummer and midwinter (the solstices) by all northern peoples. Even after World War II, victory was celebrated on Whiteleaf Hill by the burning of brushwood that had been used to camouflage the cross. The need to scour them has perhaps been exaggerated. It is hard to imagine anything much taking root on the steep slopes at Whiteleaf, and Bledlow seems to be surviving a neglectful age remarkably well. Scouring might nevertheless have been one of the continuing rituals, whether or not it was needed for visibility.

There is no firm documentary evidence even of the existence of the two crosses before Francis Wise, unless one is to count the reference in a Saxon charter of AD 903 to a boundary mark in the neighbourhood, called 'Weland's stoc' ('Wayland's stick'), and said to be approached by a 'straet'. Perhaps this street was the Icknield Way. Clearly the writer did not consider the stick in question to be a Christian symbol, or he would not have given it to Wayland the Smith, the larger-than-life character of Saxon legend. Those who have quoted this Saxon reference have usually seen in it a phallic allusion, but we need not go any further down this particular street, for the charter is a mere eleven centuries old. When it was written, if we are not mistaken, the two Chiltern crosses were four times as old as that, and the religion by which they were inspired was neither Saxon nor Christian.

The Cerne Giant

The male figure of the Cerne Giant, with club in hand, is cut into the turf of a steep escarpment above the village of Cerne Abbas in Dorset. The outline of the icon is shown in Fig. 90, where Flinders Petrie's measurements are followed. Including the club, the figure of the Giant is 64.5 m high and 51 m wide. It has no doubt changed in some respects since it was first cut, whenever that may have been, but published illustrations of it are not a reliable guide. By investigating how different draughtsmen represented the Cerne Giant at different periods of history, Leslie Grinsell showed that while on paper the nineteenth century was one of high decorum, it was probably then that on the ground the navel was incorporated in the penis, increasing its length by 1.6 metres and making it an even greater local marvel. Grinsell conjectures that this might have been done to spite a local vicar who tried to put an end to the scouring of the Giant, lest it corrupt the morals of his flock.

The Giant's origins have mostly been discussed in terms of his form. Dorset local historians have been puzzled by the absence of specific references to him

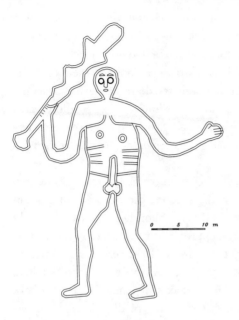

FIG. 90.   The outline of the Cerne Giant, following Flinders Petrie.

before the late seventeenth or early eighteenth centuries, and this in a well-documented parish. F. J. Harvey Darton thought it probable that it was cut in the mid seventeenth century—but his key reference might mean only that it was recut then. Giant Hill was in 1617 known as Trendle Hill, an allusion to a ring, circle, or wheel of some sort, and certainly not to a giant. Some, however, have tentatively linked it with late Iron Age earthworks close by. (There seems to be no obvious ring that would explain the 'Trendle'.)

In the thirteenth century, Walter of Coventry reported about Cerne that 'the god Helith' was cultivated there, and this remark might be an allusion to the Giant, since the name has the appearance of an Anglo-Saxon word for *man* viewed as *warrior* or *hero* (*hæleð*). Some have argued for a Roman origin. Stuart Piggott associated it even more narrowly with an attempt by the Emperor Commodus (AD 180–93) to revive a cult of Hercules, and spelled out possible links between the names 'Helith' and 'Hercules'. There are parallels in early astronomical illustration. The Giant's posture resembles that of Hercules in classical Roman and medieval *constellation images*, such as those illustrating an influential astronomical poem by Hyginus. The Romans chose to associate Hercules with the character the Greeks had called Engonasin, 'the kneeling man'. Hyginus, a native of Roman Spain who lived perhaps in the first century BC, used the Greek name. One early medieval illustration of the constellation is shown in Fig. 91. It does not much resemble a fertility emblem, but the overall similarity of Hercules figures to the Wilmington Giant cannot be denied, overlooking the fertility element—which was at least in part a fertility of late Dorset imagination. The Cerne Giant does not now carry a lion's skin on his left arm, as every good Roman Hercules should, but there have been claims to detect signs that he originally did so. This is not such a critical matter as many appear to believe, for in some early representations

the figure carries neither club nor skin. This is so on the stone star sphere known as the Farnese globe, for instance. That globe, now in Naples, was of the first or early second century AD, and was a Roman copy of a Greek original.

The constellation figure of Hercules found in most late medieval astronomical star catalogues is fundamentally different from that illustrated here. It is in mirror image, and so might not have given rise to the chalk figure as we have him. The mirroring in constellation pictures is not always strict: one may see only the back of the person in the alternative version, and when this is so it has nothing to do with the artist's essential modesty. It is a question of whether one imagines oneself to be looking at the star sphere from the inside or the outside. Since both types of image were called for, both versions of the drawn figure were to be found at all stages of history, from ancient times onwards. On the Farnese globe, for instance, Engonasin (or Hercules) quite naturally presents his back to us. At Cerne, on the other hand, the figure is as he would be seen by an observer looking at the stars in the sky.

There is much to be said about the representation of Hercules in early manuscripts, but it is not relevant here. One simple point should be heeded, though: the 'kneeling man' of early illustrations only gradually straightens his limbs with the passage of centuries. Naturally the rule is not absolute, but broadly speaking, the straighter the legs, the later the figure. This tendency speaks weakly against a Roman origin, and yet a Roman origin will be favoured here. At Cerne Abbas, as at Wilmington, it is vital to distinguish between the outward *form* of a figure that might have been cut and recut, and the *placement* of that figure and the general character of ritual associated with it. On both scores the Cerne image seems to belong to classical antiquity or later, rather than to prehistory.

Not only does it seem that the figure was a portrayal of Hercules—with or without the skin and one kneeling leg—but it was very well fitted to mark the rising of the constellation of Hercules over the slope into which it is cut. It is admittedly difficult to be precise on this point, since it is now much harder than in our Neolithic examples to decide on the point from which observations were made, and hence on the angles both of altitude and azimuth. The figure does, nevertheless, have a clear central axis with azimuth about 75°. The ground runs down to the banks of the river Cerne, which offers what seems to be the most natural point for the observer to stand, making for a horizon altitude of between 11° and 12°. If one assumes that the rising of the brightest star in the constellation of Hercules was crucial, then its declination had to be between about 18.7° and 18.0°, corresponding to the interval −20 BC to 200 AD.

leonif. iiii. fumma xvi

tellaf.viii. inorbem pofi

FIG. 91. A manuscript illustration of the classical figure representing the constellation of Hercules (after Madrid, Biblioteca Nacional, cod. 3307, f. 55r).

The Cerne Giant is on both scores unlikely, therefore, to be a monument of prehistory comparable with the Uffington White Horse and the Wilmington Long Man, although all three seem to share a character of astral symbolism. The Cerne Giant is worlds away from the stark simplicity of the Chiltern crosses. Many prehistoric hill figures must surely have been lost, but it is odd that the dates we have derived for the Sussex, Berkshire, and Buckinghamshire figures were so very close together. It is strange indeed that we know of little truly comparable in the long intervening period, although the older chalk figures might have been kept in use, century after century, in continuation of the old ways. This would explain well the use in Roman Britain of a constellation figure on the hillside. It is in this respect that the Cerne Giant is of value to our case, no matter what its precise age: it helps to support the argument that chalk figures were astral in meaning.

But the argument cannot be left here. If one is to suppose that there was backwards continuity of observance at chalk figures in southern Britain, then why not at the Cerne site, which saw much activity in the Iron Age, and perhaps even earlier in time? And in this case, is it not possible that there was previously some other marker there, of a simpler kind, that was abandoned merely because it could no longer be made to function as it should? The question is unanswerable, but the possibility remains. Among other things, there is the surprising fact that the gradient of the slope is once again around 1 in 5. Is this not a Neolithic signature? If so, all we need is a bright star with the necessary prehistoric declination. They are not as numerous as one might imagine, but Spica, as at Whiteleaf, would have done very well in the fourth millennium. After that, it would have been necessary to go for a star dimmer than those on our earlier list. The brightest in Hercules was very modest, with a magnitude of only 3.1, but it would have served its purpose well only in Roman Britain. Of the many interpretations offered of the Cerne Abbas Giant, Stuart Piggott's seems in the end, therefore, by far the most plausible—but on the understanding that it was an astral symbol, like the Uffington White Horse and the Wilmington Long Man, and not merely a picture cut in chalk for want of a better artistic medium.

SUN AND MOON

The Seasons—an Astronomical Sketch

I N the next chapter, reference will often be made to the places on the horizon over which the Sun and Moon rise and set in the course of their annual and monthly cycles. The subject has so far been touched on only briefly, and this is a suitable point at which to supplement the earlier account of the rising and setting of stars, but only in very general terms. More detail will be found in Appendix 2.

As already explained, the stars may be regarded as lying on a sphere, turning as a whole daily around the north and south poles of the sky (Fig. 92), with a 'celestial equator' midway between the poles. With a level horizon any star on that equator would rise due east and set due west. Actually the 'daily' rotation of the stars takes place in a few minutes less than one day. That the time is not exactly equal to a day is a consequence of the fact that our day is decided by the Sun, and the Sun moves against the stars at a rate of about one degree every day. (This should be obvious, since it moves round the 360° of the sky once every year of 365.25 days, or thereabouts. The sense of its annual movement is from S_1 to S_4 in the figure, whereas the *daily* rotation of the star sphere, Sun, and Moon is that of the arrows.) The Moon, moving once round the sky every month, moves against the background of stars more than twelve times as fast as the Sun, but in the same general direction. The apparent paths followed by the Sun and Moon through the stars are inclined to the celestial equator, but at different angles. In the Sun's case, the angle of its path (the 'obliquity of the ecliptic') changes, but very slowly indeed. (It is now about 23.5°, but in 2700 BC was very close to 24°.) The Moon's apparent path is inclined to the ecliptic at approximately 5.25°, but the angle changes some-what more rapidly. Important for many astronomical purposes—especialy for calculating eclipses—is the fact that the Moon's orbit slides around the ecliptic in time, and relatively rapidly: the two points in which it meets the ecliptic make a complete rotation in about 18.6 years.

The *summer solstice* is defined as the moment when the Sun is closest to the north pole (and so furthest from the celestial equator). At this time it rises at its furthest point north of east on the horizon, sets furthest north of west. Daylight, decided by the angle swept out by the Sun in its passage above the horizon (ignoring twilight), will be longest then. The *winter solstice* is defined as the moment when the Sun comes nearest to the south pole of the sky. It will rise and set furthest south of east and west respectively. The *equinoxes* (spring and autumn) are the moments in the year when the Sun crosses the equator. The celestial equator is for this reason often called the 'equinoctial'. At the equinoxes, daylight and night are more or less equal—hence the Latin root of the name.

Precisely how the Sun appears to move against the stars depends largely on its orbit in space with reference to our observing platform, the Earth. Its motion fluctuates somewhat in the course of the year, so that the year is not quite symmetrically divided by the solstices and equinoxes. The current lengths of the seasons are a poor guide to the past, but roughly speaking one may say that the interval from summer solstice to winter solstice, in the period

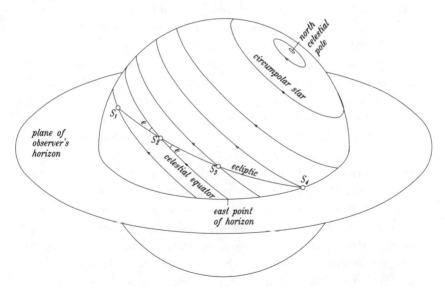

FIG. 92.   A short section of the ecliptic, the annual path of the Sun through the stars. The Sun moves in the direction S_1 to S_4. At S_2 it crosses the celestial equator (at the spring equinox), and rises at the east point of the horizon. In its daily rotation the Sun moves with the stars as a whole in the direction of the arrows along specimen arcs. The Moon's path (not drawn) is inclined to the Sun's at a little over 5°, but the points in which the paths meet slide round the ecliptic once every 18.6 years. The extremes of the points of rising and setting of the Sun and Moon are shown in the next figure.

of prehistory around 2000 BC, was about a week shorter than the remainder of the year. Considering the year to be split into two parts by the equinoxes, one can say that the difference would have been of the order of five days. In round numbers of days, the seasons would have been 94.25 (spring), 90.75 (summer), 88.5 (autumn), and 91.75 (winter).

Risings and Settings of the Sun and Moon

To calculate accurately the precise directions of rising and setting over the local horizon, the theory set out in Appendix 2 is needed. Here it will be enough to note some of the more important factors on which the directions depend:

(1) The *inclinations* of the appropriate path (the Sun's or the Moon's) to the equator. Both change slowly with time. The inclination of the Sun's path is known as the *obliquity of the ecliptic.*[1]

(2) The *altitude of the effective horizon* (its angular elevation as seen from the observing position).

(3) The *geographical latitude* of the observer.

(4) Whatever was taken as the *significant moment* of rising and setting. Was it the first or last glint of the disc of the Sun or Moon, or when the disc as a whole rested on the horizon? Or was the centre taken to be on the horizon? Or was it the position of furthest reach that counted? (See Appendix 2 for a fuller explanation of this idea.)

(5) *Atmospheric refraction.* When a ray of light from the Sun is first seen, the ray is being bent (refracted) by the layers of the Earth's atmosphere. When seen over a horizon at zero altitude, for example, the actual direction of the upper edge ('upper limb') of the Sun is about 35 minutes of arc below the true horizontal (the 'geometrical horizon'). One usually calculates from the Sun's centre. In the example, this will be about 16 minutes of arc below the limb, making it about 51 minutes of arc below the geometrical horizon in all. (By an odd dispensation of fate, the Sun and Moon are both about half a degree across as seen from the Earth.) Refraction depends to some extent on atmospheric conditions (temperature, pressure, humidity, etc.).

---

1   There is a fairly simple formula relating the obliquity of the ecliptic to the epoch (Appendix 2, equation (9)). As a useful rule of thumb one may work from these reasonably accurate reference values: 23° 50' was the value in 1150 BC, 23° 55' in 1900 BC, and 24° in 2700 BC. But the important point is that alignments are not of permanent value, even though they are much more enduring than in the case of the stars.

The angle between the extreme positions of solar rising and setting (at the solstices) changes only slowly over long periods of time. For the Moon, matters are much more complicated. The observed places of rising and setting naturally vary during a single cycle, that is, during a single month, and there are extremes for that month; but the extremes themselves vary from month to month. They lie between certain limits, however, generally now called 'major and minor standstills'. The limits are actually subject to certain subtle variations that will not be considered here (but see Appendix 2, section 5). A few specimen extremes of rising and setting are given in Fig. 93. For the time being it is enough to keep in mind the different characters of solar and lunar extremes, for they require somewhat different techniques of observation.

The major and minor lunar standstills are not as such directly related to either new or full moon—in fact they occur near certain first and third quarters. They repeat, more or less, in the cycle of 18.6 years. They would not have been easy to judge exactly, but the complicated pattern of risings and settings might have been appreciated through tenacious observation over long periods of time, and some of the possibilities are touched upon lightly in Chapter 10.[2]

Some Examples of Extremes of Rising and Setting

To give an idea of the effects of the different factors mentioned on the horizon positions of the rising and setting Sun and Moon, some examples may be given, based chiefly on the latitude of Stonehenge (51° 11'). When dealing with the Sun and Moon there are some advantages in measuring azimuths—that is, angles around the horizon—north (positive) and south (negative) from the east–west line, so that for instance northeast and northwest will then both be quoted as +45°, and southeast and southwest as −45°. This alternative to quoting azimuths clockwise from north gives a much better feel for the range

---

2   There would have been a difficulty for early observers, for two reasons in particular. First, only near full moon would it have been easy to make a judgement by night as to the Moon's precise place on the horizon, especially if observing first glint at rising. And second, the absolute extremes of the Moon's potential rising and setting will never actually be attained precisely. The rising point may be thought of as determined by the Moon's proximity to the north celestial pole. The graph of their separation is, as it were, a switchback riding upon the back of another switch-back (illustrated in Appendix 2). Only when the two cycles reach their maxima at the same moment is the absolute extreme rising position attainable; and the Moon must actually cross the horizon at that very moment, for the true standstill to be directly observable. Alexander Thom has argued that people of the Bronze Age devised interpolation schemes to remedy the fact that the true extremes are not strictly observable. It is possible that the full moons that came closest to major standstills were, at least in some instances, preferred to the true extremes themselves.

over which the rising (or setting) Sun or Moon swings, in the course of its cycle. Since there is no need to continually add and subtract 180°, it is easier then to avoid mistakes: apart from irregularities in the horizon, the azimuth of rising and setting should be the same. As for the convention by which some angles are being quoted here in degrees and minutes of arc, and others in decimal parts of a degree, this is a measure of the continuing grip of Babylonian astronomy on the modern world.

1. Latitude of Stonehenge, with horizon assumed level. Upper limb on horizon (first or last glint)

AZIMUTHS FOR SPECIMEN YEARS: 3500/2500/1500 BC

Midsummer (solstice) sunrise: +42.00°/+41.82°/+41.61°
Midsummer sunset: the same
Rising and setting at equinoxes: +1.05°/+1.05°/+1.05°
Midwinter (solstice) sunrise and sunset: −39.22°/−39.05°/−38.85°.

2. Latitude of Stonehenge, level horizon, Sun standing on horizon:

AZIMUTHS FOR YEAR 2500 BC

Midsummer sunrise and sunset: +40.93°
Rising and setting at equinoxes: +0.39°
Midwinter sunrise and sunset: −39.91°.

3. Latitude of Stonehenge, different elevations (horizon altitudes). Upper limb on horizon:

AZIMUTHS FOR YEAR 2500 BC. SPECIMEN ALTITUDES 0°/0.2°/1.0°

Midsummer (sunrise and sunset): +41.82°/+41.41°/+38.89°
Rising and setting at equinoxes: +1.05°/+0.75°/−0.40°
Midwinter sunrise and sunset: −39.05°/−39.44°/−40.95°.

4. Various latitudes, level horizon, first glint of Midsummer sunrise:

AZIMUTHS FOR YEAR: 2500 BC

lat. 51° 10': +41.80°   lat. 51° 30' :+42.19°
lat. 52° 30': +43.39°   lat. 53° 30': +44.69°
lat. 54° 30': +46.11°   lat. 55° 30': +47.66°
lat. 56° 30': +49.36°   lat. 57° 30' :+51.23°.

5. Azimuths of the rising and setting Moon at standstills, upper limb on level horizon, latitude of Stonehenge:

AZIMUTHS FOR SPECIMEN YEARS: 3500/2500/1500 BC

Maximum north, rising or setting: +51.22°/+51.02°/+50.78°
Maximum south, rising or setting: −51.05°/−50.85°/−50.62°

From these few results, we can see how drastic is the effect of a change in geographical latitude. Note the absence of perfect symmetry between the rising midsummer Sun and the rising midwinter Sun, with reference to the east–west line. And note once more that the upper and lower limbs of the Sun do not,

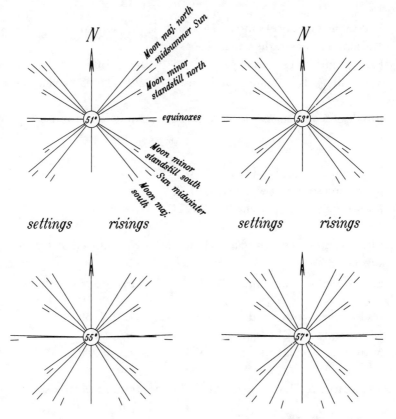

FIG. 93.   Extreme directions of the rising and setting of the upper limb of the Sun and Moon, for altitude zero at four specimen latitudes, 51° (south Wiltshire), 53° (northern Netherlands, the Wash, north Wales), 55° (southern Denmark, Newcastle, Londonderry) and 57° (northern Denmark, Aberdeen, southern tip of Skye). Each direction marked has a short line to the south of it, corresponding to the corresponding direction for an altitude of 2°. Risings and settings are symmetrically arranged with respect to the north–south line, since the horizon altitude is here assumed to be constant.

strictly speaking, rise due east at the equinox, although one may make the upper limb do so, by choosing a suitable geographical location or by creating an artificial horizon, in some such way as was encountered with the long barrows.

Remembering that the Sun's disc, like the Moon's, is about half a degree across, it will be seen that even in a thousand years the rising points of both luminaries move less than half of that diameter along the horizon. A change of quite a small horizon altitude, however, has a very marked effect: elevating the horizon by a quarter of a degree may move the rising point by a complete solar diameter, for instance. The importance of horizons is one of the lessons already learned in connection with the stars, in their risings and settings over the long barrows.

Switching attention from the case where the limb of the disc is just visible to that where the disk is just fully visible produces a shift in azimuth of the order of one solar or lunar diameter. If a monumental alignment fits the one case, therefore, it will certainly not fit the other.

6

AVENUE AND ROW

From Cursus to Avenue

MODERN writers have been hesitant to accept the old idea that monuments of the cursus type were chiefly meant for ritual procession, but
less so when considering the 'avenues' leading up to stone circles—for example
those at Stonehenge, Avebury (where stones of the 'Kennet Avenue' survive),
and Callanish on the Isle of Lewis. Some have seen cursus terminals as
processional limits, and yet it was found possible in Chapter 4 to make good
sense of them without that assumption. It is at the very least premature to
imagine that an alignment of earthen banks or stones, ending in a ring of stones,
must have that ring as its processional beginning or end.

The idea is often supposed to require no defence, even when the 'avenue'
may in one case be merely the space between a pair of *parallel banks of earth*, in
a second case a pair of *parallel rows of stones*, and in yet a third case a set of *multiple
rows of stones* that are arranged in a *fan-shape*. Treating them as a coherent group
implies belief in a common purpose—and if they have this, then it is surely
more profound than a possibility of walking from one spot to another. The
processional idea is perhaps to be favoured whenever an avenue leads to (or
from) water, as at Stonehenge, and at Stanton Drew, near Bath. Many of the
'avenues' of stones, however, are terminated by neither stone circles nor water,
but have blocking stones at their ends—in a way reminiscent of a cursus. Even
treating these different 'avenues' in a single chapter requires an apology at the
outset. There is every reason for thinking that the span of time between creating
the banked earthen avenues and the most famous stone rows of all, those in the
coastal area of Brittany, covered well over two millennia. During that long
period of time, many changes took place in religious practice, as evidenced by
burial custom and what are here taken to be associated astronomical observances. Whilst it is convenient to give an astronomical treatment of avenues
and rows in one place—for it does seem likely that most were aligned on
astronomical events in one way or another—to do so is to risk losing sight of

the fact that they may be intimately connected with primary monuments (rings, cairns, mounds, or whatever) that had very different purposes.

It is usually taken to be an essential part of the definition of an avenue that it should lead to or from some such monument. If one focuses attention on the property of interconnectedness—without prejudging the question of ritual procession—then it perhaps becomes possible to detect signs of a transition from cursus to avenue. There is a whole class of monuments that are of cursus type but intimately connected with circular monuments of one sort or another. These will be discussed in a cursory way here, simply to draw attention to a possible process of evolution.

Dorchester

About 2 km north of the Roman town of Dorchester-on-Thames in Oxford-shire, and the same distance east of Clifton Hampden, an archaeological site covering a wide span of prehistory has twice been subject to rescue excavation. This was done initially by Richard Atkinson and others, before part was wholly destroyed in the extraction of gravel; and later by Richard Chambers and others, prior to the construction of a Dorchester bypass. The site revealed the remains of a cursus. The northern end of this Dorchester Cursus is still unknown, but measuring from the southeastern terminus its known extent is at least 1.62 km. Its width along the known section is a fairly constant 64 m. Its line is directed to the saddle between two small low hills in Nuneham Park to the north, where one might expect some sort of structure, perhaps a barrow, to have been. Continuing in the same direction, downhill to the river Thames (skirting Nuneham Mansion), and crossing to the Radley bank of the river still on the same line, there is the site of a henge-type circular earthwork. The Dorchester cursus runs almost tangential to a similar large structure ('Big Rings'). The two circles, centre to centre, are on a line exactly parallel to the cursus (azimuth 309.4°).

The southwest ditch of the Dorchester cursus was actually interrupted at two other points to avoid circular structures, one being of three concentric ditches enclosing a *circle of pits* (site XI). We shall later come across evidence for the custom of sighting celestial objects over pits.

Even had there been very tall trees at Nuneham they would not have reached to the extinction angle of stars setting in line with the ditches. The most plausible solution in terms of a star seems to be the setting of Pollux around the year 2450 BC. As it happens, the line is close to that of the setting of the midsummer Sun, but not close enough. (It would have been a degree or two out of line, according to circumstances.)

The known terminus at Dorchester was closed off in much the same way

as those at Stonehenge and in Dorset. Not only was the terminal ditch interrupted by a central entrance at Dorchester, but two parallel ditches were driven obliquely across the end of the cursus through the terminal entrance. There is a similar diagonal in the cursus at Fornham All Saints, Suffolk; another at Springfield in Essex, but perhaps added only later; and yet another possible example is a curious cursus-like structure discovered from crop-marks at Northfield Farm, Long Wittenham, Oxfordshire. At the latter there is an associated henge-like monument, as well as ring-ditches and pits.

Springfield

There is a cursus that has been carefully investigated at Springfield, not far from the River Chelmer in Essex. It was some 40 m wide and 670 m long, and a pit surrounded by a semi-circular ditch abuts the southern ditch at 200 m from the eastern end. There are in the vicinity traces of various other monuments, including possibly an oval long barrow, and at the eastern terminal there has been a ring of posts (about 26 m diameter), possibly placed there at a late date in its history. In the neighbourhood of the Springfield ring there were many small pits containing burnt flints and cremations of cattle, sheep and pig. There is no firm evidence as to date. A find of Mortlake style pottery in a ditch inclined its excavators to place the cursus at the end of the third millennium or later. This is hard to reconcile with potential alignments on Spica, Pollux and alpha Centauri, which would suggest the thirty-fourth century BC, but a more careful analysis might indicate alternatives.

Brandyshop Bridge, Thornton Wood, and Fornham All Saints

At Brandyshop Bridge, Welshpool, on the flood plain of the River Severn, there was a cursus that ran tangentially to a structure of ring-ditches and pits, lying now on the *outside* of the cursus, and wider than it. This might have aligned on the setting of Rigel around 2700 BC.

At Thornton Wood, Ettington (near Stratford-upon-Avon) two magnificent concentric oval ditches were actually crossed diagonally by a cursus.

There was a circle at the very terminus of the Fornham All Saints Cursus, Suffolk, as can be seen in photographs of crop-marks, visible from the air. The circle is of about the same overall width as the cursus and touches it internally.

Pits and Posts

The relative ages of these paired linear and circular structures are unknown, but even if the rings came first, they might have been meant to function jointly with the lines. Much evidence will be shortly produced for the practice of

sighting across rings, and along tangents to rings. To have placed a cursus ditch in any such line would have been a very natural thing to do. There might even be traces of a shared technique of using posts for sighting, in the pits mentioned in connection with Dorchester, Springfield and Brandyshop Bridge. Holes were found in the floor of one of the circular ditches at Dorchester, and a similar discovery on the site of another cursus at North Stoke, also in Oxfordshire, was reported by Humphrey Case, this time with holes in the cursus ditch floors. Between 20 and 45 cm in diameter, and perhaps twice as deep as wide, they would have served well as postholes, and yet no traces of wood or decayed organic matter was found in them. They were spaced at an average of 90 cm, and offset from the centre-line of the ditch. There is some doubt as to whether they were produced by natural means. At the time, Atkinson and Case saw them as a sign of some ritual or magical practice connected with the digging of the ditch, and Atkinson wrote that they may have been 'true *bothroi*, dug as a means of communication with a nether world whose domain was to be disturbed by the excavation of the ditch, and through the medium of which some propitiatory or prophylactic offering could be made'. As Leslie Grinsell said later, a ritual pit is 'any pit found by archaeologists the meaning of which is not evident to them'.

Another possibility is that the pits were used to hold posts needed to align the ditch system accurately. As soon as the ditch system was complete, the posts would have been removed, as no longer needed. They might even have been moved from hole to hole, as work proceeded. They might have been used to bring into alignment places not in direct view of one another—such as the Dorchester and Radley circles. Another possibility is that they were for use in establishing a cursus where the horizon was tree-covered. To work towards a point on a normally accessible horizon it would not have been difficult to mark out the point of aim on the ground with much smaller timber, but in a wooded area it would have helped to break the horizon with posts of perhaps five or six metres near at hand. And these remarks do not, of course, apply only to the possibly illusory ditch-bottom holes. At the cursus at Lechlade in Gloucestershire, postholes occurred on the *inside* of the ditch, and in that at Scorton in Yorkshire postholes have been found *outside* the ditch.

The main North Stoke cursus changes direction at one end (the northern) and seems there to have been aligned on the rising of Deneb. Other possible alignments at the end of the fourth millennium or the early third would have been on alpha Centauri, Rigel and Sirius.

Avenue and Row

The short accounts of avenues and rows that follow will take for granted a number of points that will be presented in detail only at a later stage. The avenues and rows will provide advance warning of a growing interest in the precise movements of the Sun and Moon, something that seems to have begun in the fourth millennium, but to have become an obsession only by the end of the third. Many of the short (single) rows of stone, for example, seem to have been aligned on midwinter sunset, although most of them are probably much later still.

While the rows of large stones at Carnac (Brittany) have much in common with others in Scotland, more than 1000 km away, and while the northeast of Ireland also has numerous examples, and there are others in the English Lake District, they are relatively rare in southern England, except in the region of Dartmoor in the southwest. The pressure to re-use the stone from rows in southern England, where the population is densest, might be put forward as an explanation; and in places such as Kent and East Anglia, the lack of a supply of large stones might be part of the answer. However, in view of the fact that more than seven hundred rows have been recorded in Brittany, Britain and Ireland, while comparable traces of rows of wooden posts have been found radiating from round barrows in the Low Countries, where there is no stone to speak of, it does seem likely that there were also simply differences of taste and style at work.

Numbers are difficult to estimate—less so now that Aubrey Burl's gazetteer is available. It has to be said that archaeologists are capable of counting a single *pair* of stones as a 'row', in which case the total number of rows comes to over a thousand. The habit is not justifiable unless a third thing—astronomical or otherwise—can be introduced along the two-stone alignment, and it is often hard to see what this was, or is, meant to be.

There is no shortage of analogies of style between avenues and rows and other early monuments. The banks that limit the Stonehenge Avenue will be shown to be roughly comparable to those that limited the nearby Cursus long before it; but how do stones fit into the picture? Some very appealing analogies present themselves as possible explanations for stone avenues. Paired stones flanking an entrance to a stone circle, if multiplied, would produce a stone avenue, and some rings do have portals of four or more stones set in a rectangle. Even the stones of outmoded Neolithic chamber tombs might have prompted the same idea, although they were generally more closely packed and were often tooled flat. We shall shortly, however, come across a situation in which a stone circle might have been created out of terminal stones in a long succession of

stone rows. Finally, bearing in mind that the opposite sides of a cursus could be involved in astronomical alignments on *different* stars, there would be nothing mysterious about a transition in style from double to single rows, or to triple or higher numbers.

The Stonehenge Avenue

Since the Stonehenge Avenue is near to the Greater Cursus and resembles it in several ways, it will be considered first. The stone circles at Stonehenge are enclosed within a much larger circular ditch with an internal bank. The main entrance causeway passing through this is to the northeast, and is less than 11m wide. The causeway is much narrower than the so-called 'Avenue' that leads away from it in the general direction of the Greater Cursus, a structure defined by its own ditches and banks. Where the Avenue approaches the old

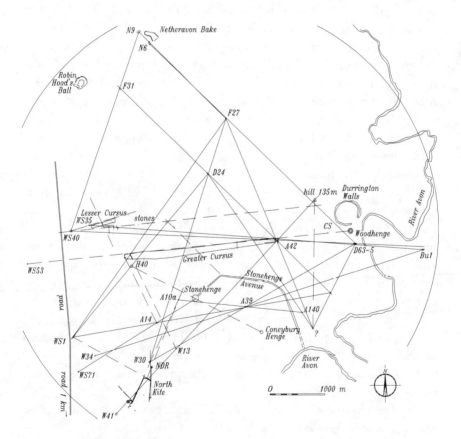

FIG. 94.   The area around the Stonehenge Greater Cursus (a repeat of an earlier figure).

circular bank around Stonehenge, that bank does not seem to have been appreciably lowered, and perhaps was not lowered at all. If the Stonehenge ditch was deliberately filled at this place to match the width of the Avenue and so provide a formal entrance, as is often supposed, then judging by its contours it was not done particularly well. The modern road cuts across the Stonehenge Avenue near its upper end, and the large Heel Stone, very near to the road, lies on it. It was in August 1721 that William Stukeley with his friend Roger Gale first noticed the Avenue running down from the entrance past the Heel Stone and down the hill 'where abouts the Sun rises when the days are longest'. On the lower side of the road, the Avenue can still be seen easily enough, falling away to the very shallow and usually dry valley, Stonehenge Bottom.

Only in recent times has its subsequent course been well charted, with the help of aerial photography. (The oldest aerial photographs of archaeological interest anywhere were actually taken from a military balloon over Stonehenge as long ago as 1906.) The excavator Colonel William Hawley noted in 1921 that RAF pilots from a nearby airfield said that they could trace the Avenue 'a long way across country'. In 1923, when examining old RAF negatives, O. G. S. Crawford found that he could see on them—with the advantage of hind-sight—the route of the ditches between the monument and the village of Amesbury. From Stonehenge Bottom the Stonehenge Avenue turns roughly eastwards for a distance comparable to the length of the first section, finally curving round and heading south to the bank of the River Avon at what is now West Amesbury.

Near the Heel Stone at the top of the first part of the Avenue, and partly under its northern bank, Hawley's excavations in the 1920s revealed a row of four post holes (now known as the A–holes). The fact is important, for it shows that the Avenue at this point was constructed later than either those posts or any other structure that can be reliably associated with them. The circular earthwork and the ring of holes within it—the Aubrey holes—apparently constituted the first of the main Stonehenge structures, and the Heel Stone and such posts as stood in the four post holes seem likely to have belonged to this early phase. (Some fragments of Windmill Hill pottery have been found associated with the erection of the Heel Stone.) In his book *Stonehenge*, Richard Atkinson argued that the principal section of the Avenue corresponds in date to the bluestone phase, his Stonehenge II, which is later than the ditch phase. His argument was as follows:

(1) The axis of the Avenue coincides with that of two of the stone circles (the double one of bluestones, that he called Stonehenge II, and the sarsens, his Stonehenge IIIa).

(2) Seven or eight metres of the eastern end of the circular ditch appear to have been filled in to match the entrance to the width of the Avenue. (This was first noted by William Hawley, but as pointed out already, if this was the purpose of the infilling it does not give an impression of good workmanship.)

(3) The clean chalk filling goes down about a metre, and this is the level at which the earliest chips of bluestone and fragments of Beaker pottery have been found. This suggests that the Avenue is contemporaneous with Stonehenge II (notably with the double bluestone circle).

In 1978, however, in an article in the journal *Nature*, Atkinson reported on a careful new survey he had made of the azimuths of the ditches (49° 52' 19" end to end for the northern side, and 49° 56' 05" for the southern, azimuths measured from north). Assuming a coherent Stonehenge II period of construction, he was surprised at the absence of geometrical symmetry. The axis of the Avenue, as newly estimated, missed his assumed centres—that of the sarsen circle by 1.46 m, that of the bluestones by 1.14 m, and that of the circle of Aubrey holes by 1.74 m, all to the northern side. By 1978 there were in addition two radiocarbon dates available, both from deer-antler picks found on the bottom of the two ditches of the Avenue close to Stonehenge (1728±68 bc, 1770±70 bc). The weighted mean of the two dates, when corrected, was given as 2165±80 bc. Atkinson believed that the date derived from the antler picks was consistent with the azimuth of the most notorious of all Stonehenge apparitions, apparent summer solstice sunrise (first glint) over the *natural* horizon as seen looking north-east from the centre. (He assumed the existence of trees on the skyline to a height of 10 m.) This is more or less true, but the type of argument is dangerous, unless supported by another for the place and method of observation. In addition, when one is dealing with the Sun, changing the height of a cover of dense trees by 5 m can shift the derived date by as much as a thousand years, playing havoc with azimuths that were quoted to seconds of arc. This standard interpretation will be much revised at a later stage.

Why should the median line of the Avenue pass through any of the centres mentioned above? Presumably there is here the tacit assumption that the Avenue should 'lead up to' one or other circle, in a strong geometrical sense. If avenues and circles are set up with reference to the heavens, then the terrain may change fundamental directions in quite short intervals of distance. And lest the cut-and-dried azimuth quoted above from the Atkinson survey obscure the fact, it ought to be added that the line of centres whose coordinates he listed follows a refined zigzag. Starting at the top, the section-azimuths measured from north are 50.07°, 50.78°, 48.52°, 49.05°, and so on—giving an appreciably different impression from that to be had from an end-to-end figure over

seventeen sections. In producing a weighted average of these, clearly the outcome will again depend on one's attitude to any sighting technique. Assuming that those responsible for it looked outwards from the circle, it will be the top figure that is counted most important. If they are assumed to have looked up the slope, it will be that at the bottom.

It would be folly to deny flatly that solar observations were of the general character suggested by Atkinson and others, that is, over trees and in the direction of the downward-sloping Avenue, but it will surely be admitted that observations of this sort are much less natural than observations up the slope. Ample reason has now been given for the use of artificial horizons that obviated the need to view over the ragged skyline of tree-covered ground. Are we to suppose that the technique was here forgotten, at this, the flagship of Wessex prehistoric sites? Looking up the slope presents problems too, although they certainly do not relate to the line of sight. There is a certain peculiarity in the terrain that makes the turning point of the Avenue a highly appropriate observation point, regardless of the precise direction of the ditched sides. A ray of light reaching the eye of a person of standard height who was standing at or somewhat beyond the turn, would have cleared the intervening terrain in a very satisfactory manner, and have grazed almost perfectly the area on which the stone monument stood, or was destined to stand (Fig. 95). Similar instances of such near-perfect grazing rays were encountered in Chapter 4, but with hills at much steeper slopes, at Uffington, Whiteleaf and Bledlow. The problem at Stonehenge is simply that there was neither Sun, Moon, nor bright star to be seen along the line at the period of history generally supposed to be correct.

There are many alternatives to be considered—and there would be fewer were it not for three facts: that earthen avenues leading up to stone circles are extremely rare (Arbor Low and Milfield being possibly the only other sizeable examples known), that their forms suggest an affinity to a typical cursus, and that there might once have been stones along the Stonehenge Avenue. Opinion on this last point is divided, and the debate goes back to the eighteenth century.

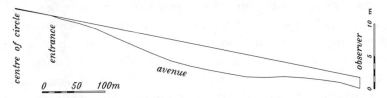

FIG. 95.   The profile of the ground along the axis of the first section of the Stonehenge Avenue. As shown by the scales, the vertical is exaggerated by a factor of 10, to emphasize the excellent fit of the grazing ray (at altitude 1.17°) through the central area of the Stonehenge monument.

William Stukeley was in no doubt that the stones had left 'manifest hollows', and that they had been removed after the advent of Christianity. He claimed to have been able to measure the 'very intervals of almost every stone', and it is hard to see any reason for doubting his claim, which implies a strong resemblance between the avenues at Stonehenge and Avebury. The wide range of possibilities open to consideration then include the following:

(1) The possibility that the approximate line that the Avenue follows was established before the date suggested by the antler picks—which might have been used either for renewal or extension; and that this part of the Avenue began life as a cursus-like entity in its own right. There are two distinct alternatives, one for a star and one for the Sun.

(a) The upward-sloping Avenue could have been directed towards the setting of Sirius in the late fourth millennium. Taking Atkinson's figures for the mean azimuths, this would have been precise around the year 3180 BC, assuming no mound at the top of the slope (altitude 1.17°, azimuth 229.9°). There is today no similarly well-defined physical line along the ground in continuation of the Avenue *behind* such an observer, but looking in precisely that direction over the Cursus banks from the point mentioned, Capella would have been seen rising around 3200 BC (extinction altitude, azimuth 49.9°).

(b) An early version of the upward-sloping Avenue could have been directed towards the last glint of the setting Sun at winter solstice, but only granted that it differed in direction by about a degree. The azimuth would have been 228.61° in 3200 BC and 228.80° in 2200 BC. (Increasing the altitude, for instance with a mound, makes matters worse.) Such an avenue can hardly have been ditched or it would have left evidence of its existence.

(2) The possibility that a person standing at the foot of the slope in either of the Avenue ditches could have seen Rigel set over the banks of the Stonehenge earthwork, assuming them to have been across each ditch-line. They would have just comfortably set an angle in excess of the extinction angle. Taking the extinction angle 1.53°, the date for azimuth 229.9° was 2470 BC. Assuming high portals at the entrance to the area encircled by the ditch, about the size of the so-called Slaughter Stone when it was upright, an altitude in the neighbourhood of 2° would have been set, bringing the date to 2380 BC.

(3) The possibility that there was some form of cross-viewing, at right angles to the ditches and banks, either cursus-style or in the manner that we shall later discover to have been in use at Avebury, with stone-lined avenues. The second seems highly probable, in view of many similarities to the Avebury alignments. There would in such cases be two plausible possibilities: Capella setting, at its extinction angle, around 2320 BC, and the setting of the Moon

(last glint over the natural horizon) at its extreme northern latitude. The precise dating of the latter is difficult, but the optimum altitude for the radiocarbon date (around 2165 BC) is 0.32°, which is close to the average over the natural landscape. Cross-viewing techniques with the Moon would have been helped by stones or wooden posts, in a way that will be described in general terms later.

This is all inevitably indecisive. The lunar option (cross-viewing) seems to be the best, the downhill line being perhaps regarded as the continuation of a solar line used in a completely different way—which will also be described in a later chapter. This solar line, however, was quite certainly in use in both directions at the date of the Rigel alternative. Are we to believe that, even though attention was chiefly fixed on a relatively stable solar alignment, those responsible failed to notice that it also served for Rigel?

There are various potential stellar alignments for the remaining sections of the Stonehenge Avenue, but most of them are impossible to reconcile with the meagre radiocarbon dates obtained there, the weighted average of which is equivalent to 1075±100 BC. Vega might well have been observed setting over the middle of the Avenue by anyone ascending the section coming up from the river, at an earlier historical period, and Deneb's setting is another possibility. Further speculation is pointless, since there is here a problem of uncertainty twice over, that is, in the horizon that was critical and in the poor present state of information as to the Avenue's direction in the neighbourhood of the river. Walking along the middle section of the Avenue from east to west, Aldebaran might have been seen setting (say five hours after Vega's setting), but again our data are very uncertain. Such settings would of course have been easier to observe than risings, since in both cases the view was up the gradient. As it happens, it will be suggested in Chapter 8 that Vega and Aldebaran were observed during the third millennium at the nearby Durrington Walls site, along 'avenues' of another sort, that is, corridors of posts.

The Stone Rows—Tracks across Dartmoor

There are on Dartmoor, in Devonshire, more than seventy rows of unworked stones of assorted sizes—rarely of much more than human height, and more often barely knee-high. Judging by their associations, some might be from the first half of the third millennium, and others from as late as the mid second. Many rows are simple, while others change direction several times, but all are made up of lengthy sections that were almost certainly intended to be straight. In nearly half the known examples there are two roughly parallel lines of stones, separated by no more than

a metre or two, while in a handful of cases there are triple lines. These Dartmoor rows have been given many names—including 'cursus' and 'avenue'.

At least some of the general principles that inspired the creation of monuments of the cursus type also explain the aim and purpose of the Dartmoor rows. It is generally agreed by those who have walked them that they do not give the impression that they were 'processional ways'. There is first the fact that so many of them are single; and even the double rows would not have been very congenial for a procession of more than a small number of people. It will be shown here, even so, that good sense can be made of some of them if they were indeed walked by night, but that few, if any, of the double or multiple rows are likely to have been designed as a corridor, or later regarded as one. A single row was 'track' enough.

It seems probable that in their original form all rows had some sort of special terminal at one or both ends. In some cases this was a particularly tall stone (menhir) in line with the rest, sometimes with its flat face set across the row. In many cases, however, the terminal was a round barrow or cairn, with or without an accompanying circle of stones. There are often burial mounds of various sorts in the immediate vicinity. A burial cairn will often be found to have a cist in the middle—a coffin of stone slabs in which the human remains were placed, often cremated. These cists were themselves set in strongly preferred directions, a fact that can fairly certainly be explained in terms of a rough alignment on the heavens. In view of their strong sepulchral connection one cannot help wondering whether the rows were not also meant for a *notional* procession, that is, either of the spirits of the dead or of the gods of the sky descending to the dead. Perhaps this was also one way of conceiving a typical cursus.[1]

Most of the Dartmoor stone rows are found in the southern half, and especially the southern and southwestern fringe, of the present-day moor. There is also a cluster in the northeast, often of doubles. Neolithic remains are not numerous there. There are stone circles, but they are modest in their proportions. It is a moot point whether a large immigrant population of 'Beaker peoples' adapted to their own ends many of the ideas of the native population, or whether it was merely a Beaker *culture*, a set of enticing new ideas, that spread

1 Of over a hundred known cists only a handful fail to be directed to the northwest/southeast quadrants. This in itself is very remarkable. It rules out, for instance, the idea that the cist was invariably directed to the Sun at rising or setting on the day of burial or death. One might imagine that a particular community would have favoured a given direction, but this is not the case. There are, nevertheless, favoured directions, perhaps the directions of the setting of certain bright northern stars. The great majority of known directions can be explained in terms of the settings of Arcturus, Capella, Castor and Pollux, and possibly Spica. The time of year might have determined the choice of star.

through the land without a particularly large immigration. One way or another, the characteristic Beaker pottery is more likely to be found associated with the smaller circles; and so, broadly speaking, small means late. Although the southwest of England—Somerset, Devon, and Cornwall—does possess some earlier, Neolithic, remains, the signs there are of a borrowing from the past, and the Dartmoor rows, like the many small stone circles there, seem to speak for the continuation of old ambitions in a new guise.

The Dartmoor communities were small, and constrained by a less friendly environment than that further east. Dartmoor is a bleak plateau of about 500 sq km in area, crested with granite masses that rise in places to over 600 m. The heights are interspersed with morasses, and the wild nature of the place contrasts with the wooded lowlands around it. In the early Bronze Age there was settlement in increasing numbers and a gradual clearing of woodland that had earlier covered the moor. There has as yet been little excavation of the row sites, but the implications of one by G. Eogan, and of an environmental study by I. G. Simmons, are that some of the rows might have been from the earlier Bronze Age, and that—in the earlier words of Lady Aileen Fox—they might be visualized 'occupying open swathes in an oak forest, rather than marching across open moor'. The presence of large tracts of forest at the crucial period is sometimes presented as an insuperable obstacle to an astronomical reading of the evidence; but it is nothing of the sort.

Dartmoor has what is perhaps the best-preserved prehistoric landscape in northern Europe, and few places in Britain can supply better evidence for domestic dwellings from this period. There are recorded traces of more than two thousand stone huts. This large number obviously has something to do with the habit of building in enduring granite, but also with the fact that the area was not densely settled in later times. It speaks for the esteem in which the rows were held, perhaps even for their sanctity, that those who built the numerous huts in enclosures (pounds) near some of the rows, even in later prehistory, did not rob the rows of stones for the purpose. The habit of appropriating the stones for other purposes is a relatively modern one.

In his classic work on Dartmoor, published posthumously in 1953, R. Hansford Worth described the stone rows in much detail, and took the opportunity of censuring those who saw in them alignments on the stars. His war cry has been echoed at regular intervals by many who understood the situation much less well than he. His book ends with an appendix which ought to be compulsory reading for all who suspect the existence of such alignments. It is an extract of an address he had given in 1906, criticizing the claims made by Sir Norman Lockyer, whose book on Stonehenge had recently appeared.

Lockyer had the misfortune to make a number of statements suggesting that he had neither visited the Dartmoor rows nor otherwise checked that one part of a row was visible from another, as he required it to be. He was taken to task for loading the odds in his own favour by accepting alignments on many different stars and on the Sun. Lockyer was justifiably criticized for his free and easy way of dismissing as mere footpaths those rows that failed to produce an alignment; and for allowing a very wide spread of dates, so as to be able to accommodate his preconceptions. Four or five centuries in the construction of a relatively simple monument may seem excessive, but an even longer period seems to be signalled by at least one of the complex monuments.

Lockyer's instincts were broadly correct. As many others have done since, Worth exaggerated the ease of finding suitable solutions: 'Granted the same wide range,' he claimed, 'you can obtain coincidences anywhere.' He added that he was prepared to prove that the rope walks of Devon and Cornwall all have astronomical significance, given Lockyer's loose criteria. This is amusing but it is wrong-headed, and no amount of poking fun at Lockyer's ideas of white-robed priests preparing the morning sacrifice can justify what was a very strong claim indeed by Worth, namely that the changes in direction of the longer Dartmoor rows cannot be explained in terms of the changing horizon altitude as the observer moves along them. Worth never proved his claim, and Lockyer never properly answered his criticism. A full answer would require a thorough examination of every known stone row, and this will not be attempted here, but it will be shown briefly how, in seven of the rows by which Worth set great store, and one other, plausibly complete solutions can be found that require neither many stars nor a wide spread of dates that cannot be defended.

First to be considered is the Corringdon Ball group, described by Worth as three rows, one single and two triple. There is also a separate example to be examined, not listed by him. It is included in the first place because there is nearby the only chambered long barrow on the whole of Dartmoor. One of the unexpected consequences of taking this first group is that it shows how mistaken was Worth's classification—which at first sight seems so eminently reasonable. Three rows in the Erme Valley are examined next, in the hope of finding there some sort of homogeneity. The first row, from Stall Moor to Green Hill, is the longest on Dartmoor. Brown Heath is a small row near to this. Butterdon Row in the same valley is another that by its length and variety represents more of a challenge than the simple rows. Finally Staldon Row in the Yealm Valley is considered because it begins and ends without terminals, whether of barrow or tall menhir, and yet is the most prominent of all in the

Dartmoor landscape. What follows is a summary account of the alignments found. The names adopted are R. H. Worth's.

The Corringdon Ball Group

In the Corringdon Ball Group, according to Worth, there is (A) a single row of small stones, now much robbed of them. It starts in the northeast with a cairn, and was over 154 m long. (B) is a triple row, near parallel to (A), and 63 m long. (C) is also triple, and near parallel, 67 m long. (B) and (C) do not terminate with cairns but both are said to have issued from a stone circle ('retaining circle'). Calculating the declinations of stars indicated by (eight) separate lines of stones as found on Worth's map, corrected for the direction of north, the average is −21.61°. The range of values suggests that the star under observation was Rigel setting and that the rows were set up over the approximate period 2210 to 2080 BC. (Here, and in the discussion that follows, the declinations on which the dates are based could be interpreted as indicating Sirius, but then they would be five or six centuries earlier, and on archaeological grounds dates so much earlier seem very improbable.)[2]

This is only the roughest of beginnings, but before taking matters further, two neighbouring potential 'Rigel' monuments will be considered briefly. First, the chambered long barrow nearby seems as though it might have been aligned on the rising of Rigel around 3500 BC. Second, in line with Worth's row (A), across the East Glaze Brook to the northeast of (A), there is another row evidently aligned on the setting of Rigel. (For some reason Worth did not list it.) Although looking along the row to the cairn at the northeast of it one is looking downhill, nevertheless it is possible to see the stones of (A) on the horizon ahead, and this was no doubt the direction intended. The building of this row, assuming an alignment on Rigel, was around 2060 BC.

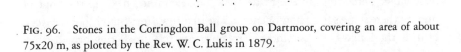

FIG. 96.   Stones in the Corringdon Ball group on Dartmoor, covering an area of about 75x20 m, as plotted by the Rev. W. C. Lukis in 1879.

---

2   Grid reference of the Group: SX 666612; latitude: 50;26,05°; range of azimuths of Worth's rows: 230.8° to 232.2°; mean altitude 1.84°. Worth's azimuths, which were probably established using some sort of averaging procedure taking all stones into account, are not used here.

The Corringdon Ball Group had been charted before Worth, by the Rev. William Collings Lukis in 1879. His accuracy can be checked in various ways, and is often better than Worth's. Lukis also included many more stones, and at a first glance they seem less well organized than those on Worth's plan, which was perhaps to some extent influenced unconsciously by his desire to solve the problem of sorting out the stones into single, double, and triple rows. Following Lukis's plan of a part of the system (Fig. 96), at least seventeen different (individual) rows emerge. There may have been one or two more. Taking the azimuths of these, which vary between 227.2° and 236.5°, and putting them in ascending order of size (which corresponds to their order in time, on the Rigel hypothesis), an extremely interesting result emerges. In fact since relative chronology is more or less a question of orientation on this hypothesis, very little calculation is called for, to appreciate the conclusion. (The derived dates are added for convenience, however.) The earliest row (2720 BC) radiates from the centre of a circular patch of ground about 5 m across over which Lukis found small stones scattered. This is not only the earliest, but it seems to be the only one with this character. There is a ring of stones to the northeast of most of the other rows, and row 2 (2630 BC) is roughly tangential to the ring, on its northwest side. Row 3 (2620 BC) passes roughly through its centre. Row 4 (2610 BC) and row 5 (2540 BC) are roughly tangential to the ring, but on its southeast side (and at slightly different angles).

The central row 3 terminates in a stone, not at the centre but at the end of a diameter. In all strictness, of course, there is no complete circle to which tangents can be drawn. In each case there is a stone marking the end of the alignment. Did those stones only later take on the shape of a ring, perhaps by moving some of the older terminators, or did stones in a pre-existing ring provide terminating stones for the rows, and indeed so determine the positions of the jumble of rows? The fact that three stones would determine the circle completely inclines one to take the second alternative, but on the other hand the arrangement of the stones does seem to suggest that the ring was laid out at least twice in the long history of the group (see Fig. 97, which shows all relevant terminating stones, and two suggested base circles). It is doubtful whether the ring was ever very complete. Certainly in Lukis' plan its south-western side is denuded; but that is exactly what one would expect, for it is a ring of terminators, and the observer stood to the northeast. (Row 5 is the only instance where the rule seems to have been broken.) At this early stage, say after row 4, one has a structure reminiscent of a cursus, with approximately parallel sides and a semicircular end. If nothing else, this serves to remind us

that a deviation from parallelism in the sides of a cursus should not be regarded as a mark of deficiency in the skill of its builders.

Row 6 (2520 BC) headed in a nondescript way for neither tangent nor centre. And then, with the entire area occupied by the rows decidedly cluttered—but it was to grow much worse—a new venture was begun. Another ring altogether was set up, perhaps by analogy with the circle that had been gradually forming. From that new circle a pair of rows radiated, first row 7 (2400 BC) and then row 8 (2340 BC). Then back to the old ring. Row 9 (2310 BC) is not far from being central; row 10 (2260 BC) is near a southeast tangent; row 11 (2260 BC) passes to the other side of centre. Rows 12 (2250 BC; there seems to be no perfect terminator for it), 13 (2220 BC), and 16 (1920 BC) are central; 14 (2190 BC) and 15 (2080 BC) are near together in the southeast, and finally row 17 (1700 BC) clears the circle entirely, also to its southeast. Note that the placing of rows is not altogether systematic. Although empty spaces on the landscape were gradually used up, the intervals of time were long in relation to human memory, and it is very improbable that there was any forward planning. Had the rows been more systematically arranged, there would have been more reason to doubt the analysis offered here.

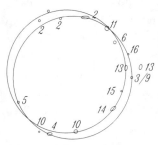

FIG. 97. The terminal stones for rows in the Corringdon Ball group, indicated here by row number. The numbering is by order of date, on the assumption of alignments on Rigel.

Had this set of rows been more ancient we might even have thought that it explained the origins of stone circles, as the accumulation of end-points of stone rows. It shows something almost as important, namely that circles were strongly associated at the time with the idea of a place from which, or to which, astronomical sightings were made. It is an interesting fact that whereas single rows are usually terminated by cairns, doubles and more complex arrangements tend to begin or end in stone circles.

No less important is the conclusion that the apparently double and triple rows are so by accident rather than by conception. Much has been made of the fact that 'double rows' do not always define a 'path' of constant width. It is, we are told, a sign of the casualness with which they were thrown together. On the contrary, this apparent weakness reveals a positive virtue, in the sense that it shows a refusal to be satisfied with a row that was no longer sound, the star's direction of rising or setting having changed with time. Regularity in the spacing of the stones is also no measure of architectural merit. Neither is the

1. *Left* West Kennet long barrow from the air. (*English Heritage Photographic Library*)

2. *Below* Barrows near Winterbourne Stoke crossroads, Wiltshire. Of the four largest near the centre, the two in line with the long barrow are of bell type, while the two above them are disc barrows. The three on the right, like that above the long barrow, are of bowl type. (*Photograph by G. W. G. Allen/ Ashmolean Museum, Oxford*)

3. *Right* Beaker of a continental style, from the north west chamber of the West Kennet long barrow. (*Devizes Museum, Wiltshire*)

4. *Below* Pots from the long barrow at Fussell's Lodge. (*Salisbury and South Wiltshire Museum*)

5. *Bottom* Arrowheads, flint axes and an adze, a polished flint knife, an antler mace- or mallet-flint, flint flakes and boar tusk blades. From a pit dug into the top of a round cairn at Ayton East Field, North Yorkshire. (*The Trustees of the British Museum*)

6. A neolithic wooden trackway of 1800 metres in length, crossing part of the Somerset Levels (c. 3806 BC) at Meare Heath, Somerset. (*Somerset Levels Project*)

7. A section of the massive ditch surrounding the Avebury circles, during the excavations by H. St. George Gray. (*English Heritage Photographic Library*)

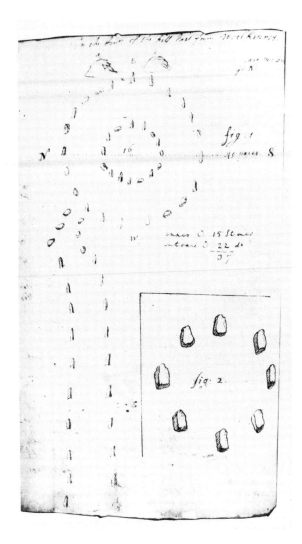

8. *Left* The Sanctuary end of the Kennet Avenue, no longer extant, as drawn by John Aubrey (for his *Monumenta Britannica*, vol. 1). East is at the top of the figure. The stone monument at this site was a successor to perhaps four earlier timber monuments, all of them double circles not unlike this. Note how, after the initial kink in the avenue, each row of stones follows a direction nearly tangential to one of the circles of stones. (*The Bodleian Library, Oxford: MS.Top.Gen.C.24–25, f.51*)

9. *Below* The final stretch of road leading into the Avebury enclosure, with Windmill Hill beyond. The midsummer sun sets precisely over the top of the hill as seen along a tangent to Avebury's north circle of stones. (*William Stukeley*, Abury, *1743*)

10. *Overleaf* Avebury from the air. Silbury Hill (upper right) and West Kennet long barrow (barely distinguishable) lie beyond. (*West Air Photography*)

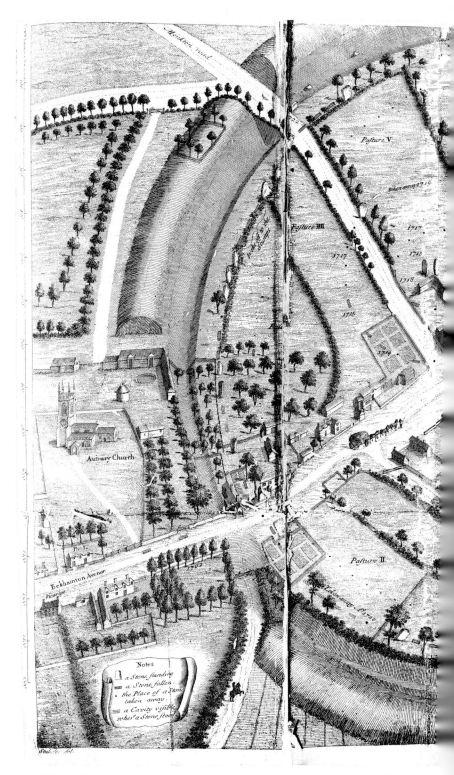

Labels visible within the image: Mendon road, Pasture V, taken away 1719, Pasture IIII, 1717, 1717, 1717, 1713, 1718, 1715, 1714, this ſtone is ſtanding, Aubury Church, Bekhampton Avenue, Vicarage, 1702, Pasture II, Taken away 1702, Stukeley del.

Notes
a Stone ſtanding
a Stone fallen
the Place of a Stone taken away
a Cavity viſible wher a Stone ſtood

11. William Stukeley's frontispiece to his book, a bird's eye view of Avebury: 'The Groundplot of the British Temple now in the town of Aubury, Wilts, Anno 1724.' (*William Stukeley*, Abury, *1743*)

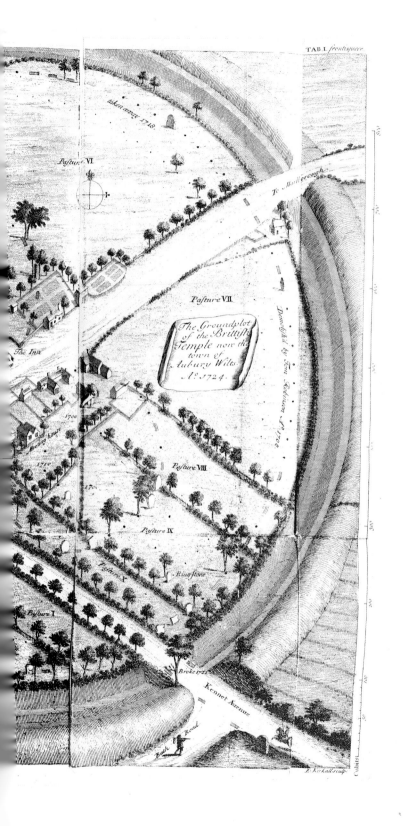

TAB. I *frontispiece*

taken away 1718.

Pasture VI

To Marlborough

Pasture VII

The Groundplot of the Brittish Temple now the town of Aubury Wilts. A⁰. 1724.

Demolish'd by Tom Robinson A⁰ 1700

The Inn

1700

Meeting house

1710

1700

Pasture VIII

Pasture IX

Pasture X

Ring stone

Pasture I

Broke 1722

Kennet Avenue

Bath Road

Cubits.

E. Kirkall sculp.

12. *Above left* Cylindrical stone 'mother goddess' (according to conventional terminlogy) from an unknown Millaran megalithic tomb in Estremadura, Spain (height 16.5cm). That it is a female form is suggested by other idols in which the pudenda are added. That the circles above the ribs are eyes, rather than breasts, is suggested, however, by the eyebrows, which are almost always indicated in some way. (*Archaeological Museum, Madrid/Photo. MAS*)

13. *Above right* The Bush Barrow lozenge. (*Devizes Museum, Wiltshire*)

15. *Above* The 'Folkton Drums', from North Yorkshire. The stylized eyes and eyebrows suggest a distant connection with such figures as those of plates 12, 16 and 17. The diameter of the largest drum is just under 15cm. (*The Trustees of the British Museum*)

16. *Left and below* Two of the many known pots from Los Millares, Spain, decorated with a pair of eyes on the outside in a way very obviously derived from the engraving of upright stones and small plaques (*see plates 12 and 17*). Often bowls have pairs of eyes inside them, and some have several – these being often described as suns. (*Photo. MAS*)

14. *Left* The Trundholm Horse, found in a bog in Trundholm, north-west Zealand, Denmark, and dating from around 1000 BC. Bronze, with parts covered in gold. The disc, with a complex spiral motif, is about 25cm across. (*National Museum, Copenhagen*)

17. Small plates of schist from Estremadura, Spain, scratched with designs (zigzags, eyes, arms and pudenda) reminiscent of those pecked on many standing stones in Britain and Western Europe. (*Photo. MAS*)

18. Looking northwards down the ridge from just above the eye of the White Horse at Uffington. The flat-topped Dragon Hill is straight ahead, and the aligned road is visible to the right. (*Mick Sharp*)

19. The central stone circle at Callanish, Lewis (Western Isles of Scotland). The monument overlooks Loch Roag. (*Mick Sharp*)

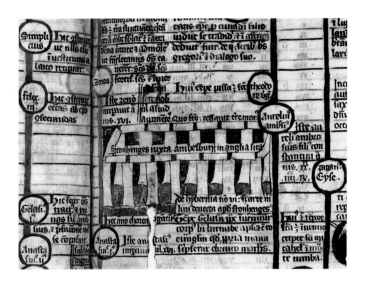

20. *Above* The earliest known drawing of Stonehenge, from a fourteenth-century manuscript now in Corpus Christi College, Cambridge. While the ring appears rectangular, this is no more than a typical disregard for true perspective. Above the near lintels are the words 'Stonehenges iuxta ambesbury in anglia sita' ('Stonehenges, near Amesbury in England'). (*The Master and Fellows of Corpus Christi College, Cambridge: CCC MS. 194, fol. 56v.–57r.*)

21. *Left* The giant Merlin building Stonehenge, from a fourteenth-century manuscript of French verse, now in the British Library. (*By permission of the British Library: Egerton 3028, fol. 30*)

length of the row. What matters is *direction*, in relation to *horizon altitude*. From the 'generally random nature of stone placing throughout', D. D. Emmett drew the conclusion that the rows were not precisely designed monuments, but 'structures built for an overall impression'. The initial 'overall impression' of the Corringdon Ball rows is one of chaos, of seemingly random lines; but it is one that can be reduced to a sequence of deliberate and intelligent acts. The rows are admittedly far from perfect in small detail, but the same might be said of the M1 motorway.

Emmett was also mistaken in suggesting that tree-cover would have stood in the way of astronomical alignment. Trees to the side are immaterial, and trees beyond the row that are below the actual horizon likewise. Even trees 20 m high will be out of sight if they are more than 573 m beyond a ridge viewed at 2° altitude. In the neighbourhood of habitation, this is not asking too much. The rows themselves, after all, are often very much longer.

The dates quoted here to decades are all probably within half a century of the truth. The pattern that emerges is of a beginning in the twenty-eighth century followed by dissatisfaction more or less every century or so, with the consequent building of a new row, until in the twenty-fourth century there began a period over which renewal was on average once every thirty years. Later the tempo of renewal slowed down again. There was evidently throughout a clear allegiance to a single star, Rigel, or perhaps to the whole constellation of Orion that stood above that bright foot-star.

Stall Moor to Green Hill

The row from Stall Moor to Green Hill surpasses all other Dartmoor rows in length (3.38 km) and in rise in height from end to end (100 m). It is even longer than the multiple rows near Carnac in Brittany. At the southern end is a barrow with stone circle (about 18 m across) and outside ditch. It passes along the right bank of the Erme, crosses it near Erme Pound, crosses another stream and mire (known as Redlake, after its bed of red pebbles), and finally climbs Green Hill, changing direction near the top. At least six different stretches can be distinguished, judging by directions, and one of these may be divided according to the horizon altitude. (Very short sections that seem to be of the nature of fillets are here ignored.) One of these sections (the second, working north) indicates Deneb, and might have been used as a connecting link long after the others were in place. *All the rest indicate the star Arcturus.* The only other contender is Vega, which was only marginally less bright, but to accept Vega would be to imply that the rows took twelve centuries to complete, rather than the three and a half suggested by Arcturus.

The first, third, fourth, and seventh (last) components, working north, are virtually but not quite precisely in the line of the meridian, and point to Arcturus' touching down on the horizon. Of the others, the fifth points to the setting of the star and the sixth to its rising. What is particularly satisfying is that the derived declinations of the star are in a tolerably uniform progression. They imply that the general sequence of construction began in the north, even though on every stretch the star was sighted from the south. There is nothing particularly odd about this. It might be said that the time span required according to our scheme, three and a half centuries, is unduly protracted, but this would not be a very cogent objection. The evidence offered below is that during those very centuries other rows were being set up; and Rome was not built in a day. The resulting sequence of declinations, with corresponding dates in parentheses, is as follows: 42.8° (2010 BC), 41.4° (1780 BC), 42.4° (1930 BC), 41.6° (1800 BC), 41.1° (1730 BC), 37.5° (Deneb), 40.7° (1660 BC).[3]

The Brown Heath Row

The Brown Heath Row is just across the Erme Valley from the 'Deneb' row in the long Stall Moor–Green Hill complex, but it is evidently older than anything in that system. It is adjacent to the Erme Pound prehistoric settlements, and judging by the direction of its single row (azimuth 9.1°, horizon altitude about 5.7°) was aligned on the rising of Arcturus when its declination was 45.04°, that is, around 2280 BC.

The Butterdon Row

The Butterdon Row is high above the left bank of the Erme, its south end near the top of Butterdon Hill starting with a barrow and retaining circle (10.5 m across). It is a single row, 1914 m long, with at least three distinct sections. The turning points are a cairn and a stone with a cross cut into it ('Hobajon's Cross'). It ends—much robbed of stone at the northern extreme—in a menhir, now fallen. The star indicated is undoubtedly Arcturus once more, in one case just touching down on the horizon, in the second and third cases setting. The declinations and dates are: 41.06° (1720 BC; Vega had the same declination at this time, so sighting it in the same line could hardly have been avoided), 40.22° (1580 BC), and 40.74° (1670 BC). The inherent probable error here is at least half a century, but would be much improved by an accurate survey. For

---

3   Grid references: SX 635644 to SX 647678; latitude at south end 50° 27' 48", at north end 50° 29' 36"; azimuths of successive principal stretches (with rounded effective horizon altitudes): 1.6° (1.5°), 23.9° (2.3°), 358.8° (2.0° and 2.2°), 354.7° (3.3°), 5.5° (2.4°) and 358.3° (3.5°).

present purposes it is enough to have confirmation of the habit of observing Arcturus in this district and at this time.[4]

The Staldon Row

The Staldon Row, which has large and well spaced stones, highly prominent in the landscape, turns out to be a joined pair of 'Arcturus' rows. It is only 800 m south of the Stall Moor–Green Hill complex. Visible against the skyline from many points in the Erme Valley, it caught Worth's imagination because of its appearance of 'a line of mounted men advancing towards the observer'. The declinations indicated are now 40.67° (northern component) and 40.72° (southern), both figures corresponding to dates around 1660 BC for both Arcturus and Vega. Arcturus seems the more probable, as the brighter of the two. The idea of Vega might be entertained, although on a previous occasion it was rejected to avoid an undue spread of dates. The great strength of the Arcturus case is the fact that the star seems to be so often indicated on Dartmoor.

The northern row at Staldon is for setting, and the southern for rising. This is not, perhaps, as one might have expected. There is an interval of only three-quarters of an hour or so between setting and rising. (Arcturus spends most of its time above the horizon, and setting would have been observed first, followed by rising, generally during the same night.) Assuming that both were seen on the same night, this implies that observers walked away from the star under observation, indeed, turned their back on it—unless they walked backwards. The value of this pair of rows is precisely that it seems to force on us the idea that a walk was a part of the ceremony or liturgy. Once the idea is accepted, it will be seen that the rows on Green Hill carry the same message, but that there the observers would have approached the star Arcturus as they waited for its reappearance. Why the difference? The answer lies in the terrain. Suitable places to achieve the desired effect are few and far between, and it is conceivable that people would not have strayed beyond the bounds of their own territory. (Andrew Fleming has argued that large prehistoric field systems and an elaborate network of land boundaries or 'reaves' are still to be detected on Dartmoor.)[5]

For present purposes there is little to be said for any further multiplication of examples. An essentially simple point has been made, one that flies in the face

---

4   Grid references: SX 656588 to SX 654607; latitude at south end 50° 24' 49"; azimuths of successive principal stretches (with rounded effective horizon altitudes): 0.0° (1.5°); 351.6° (1.5°); 342.7° (3.9°).

5   Grid. ref. SX 631622; latitude 50° 25' 40"; azimuths 354.9° (alt. 1.64°) and 5.5° (alt. 1.72°).

of conventional wisdom. Taking chiefly material that R. H. Worth thought important, it has been shown that the stone rows—structures adjacent to others that were concerned with the rituals of death—were aligned on the risings and settings of stars. Even the zigzagging of the Stall Moor–Green Hill row, whose vagaries, according to Worth, had 'broken the hearts of the astronomers', turns out to be explicable—in this case in terms of Deneb and (chiefly) Arcturus. Even the Corringdon Ball rows that caused Worth many sleepless nights, on his chart resembling a pile of ticktack sticks, are explicable, in terms of Rigel's setting. From the slight evidence presented here one might draw the conclusion that in the second millennium attention shifted away from Rigel to Arcturus. (The Fernworthy rows perhaps related to Arcturus, around 1550 BC.) But Rigel continued to be a focus of attention, and a more extensive study of the rows might have shown that other stars too were observed—Capella and Pollux, for example, at Drizzlecombe (1500 BC). The rows were simple and the custom of building them lasted more than a thousand years. Old rows were not destroyed to make new, and this fact alone is surely a measure of their local sanctity.

The Avenues near Avebury: Introduction

Avebury entered the English national consciousness in a small way in 1663. John Aubrey had come across this, the largest of all henge-type monuments, on a hunting expedition at Christmas 1648/9. Charles II—who had been impressed by Stonehenge when a fugitive after the Battle of Worcester—was introduced to the more northerly monument of the two in 1663 by his physician Walter Charleton and Lord Brouncker. They passed on Aubrey's opinion that 'it did as much excell Stoneheng, as a Cathedral does a Parish church'. It had been discussed at a meeting of the Royal Society earlier in 1663, when Charleton had deposited plans of the monument, and Aubrey was one of two men then asked to investigate it. The king later visited the place with a large retinue on his way to Bath, in the company of these scholars, and climbed to the top of Silbury Hill into the bargain.

This was all before the beginning of the most serious onslaughts on Avebury's stones by the local people, who before the end of the century were to use it as a quarry on a massive scale. The original number of large stones inside the banks was of the order of two hundred. Aubrey's plan notes about eighty stones. When William Stukeley visited and charted the place—he went there six times between 1719 and 1724—he saw about seventy, while now there are only fifty or so, some only fragments. The great complex of bank, ditch, and stone circles at Avebury was more impressive then than now, but

those who were to rob it of so many of its stones fortunately had no interest in destroying its vast peripheral bank and ditch, which is an important part of it.

Although the village of Avebury, built out of its stones and within this boundary, contrives to hide the scale of the ditch and bank, the magnitude of the enterprise is now best appreciated from the air. Looking south over it—in the general direction of the West Kennet long barrow and the village of West Kennet—it is possible to make out the partly restored Avenue of stones that once ran for a distance of nearly 2.5 km to the Sanctuary, on the southeast side of the village. Stukeley, who had spoken to a man who remembered a complete Kennet Avenue, developed the idea that there had been a second Avenue, running to Beckhampton to the west of the Avebury complex. He gave very specific details as to the stone holes and a few stones he had seen, and their course. (Aubrey did not record the Beckhampton Avenue.) He believed that the Kennet Avenue ran into a peripheral passage between the ditch and the outer stone circle of the Avebury enclosure. At one stage in his life he thought it belonged with the southernmost of the two circles of stones inside the outer ring; that the southern was a *solar* temple; and that the Beckhampton Avenue was more closely related to the northern stone circle, which he saw as a *lunar* temple. Stukeley later abandoned these ideas. After taking holy orders in 1729, he used Avebury to illustrate his belief in the evolution of the doctrine of the Trinity from primitive religious ideas. Oddly enough, Sir Fred Hoyle tried much the same exercise in relation to Stonehenge, nearly two and a half centuries later.

Sporadic modern excavation of the site began at the prompting of the British Association, and was done by Harold St George Gray between 1908 and 1922. His survey was thorough and he was the first in modern times to appreciate the vastness of the ditch round the henge, not to say the Neolithic beginnings of it all. Most later knowledge derives from the work of Alexander Keiller in the 1930s. He and Stuart Piggott excavated and restored much of the Kennet Avenue, re-erecting surviving stones and marking the positions of those known only from their stone holes. They were inclined to reject the idea that there had ever been a second avenue going as far to the west as two surviving stones ('the Longstones', or 'Adam and Eve'). This would have had to cross the River Kennet as it approached Beckhampton, which seemed to them improbable. They thought that the Longstones might be the remains of a stone circle that once had its own separate avenue. Reasons will be given for thinking that the Longstones were intimately related to Avebury; and Stukeley's numerous sketches of detail are so specific on the existence of fallen stones from an avenue in their neighbourhood that it seems perverse to doubt

that something of the same character as the Kennet Avenue ran westwards from Avebury.

Many of the stones of the Kennet Avenue weighed over ten tonnes, some much more. Our respect for those who set them in position is all the greater when we read of modern difficulties in merely setting fallen stones upright, using in some cases forty- and fifty-tonne railway jacks. Using what was considered to be prehistoric equipment—but with steel cables—a team of a dozen men working for Keiller were able to right a modest eight-tonne sarsen in five days. In the main monument and avenues together, there were more than six hundred stones, all of them needing to be dragged from their places of origin on the Marlborough Downs. They are now badly weathered, but they were once carefully dressed, again a time-consuming process.

The stones in the Avenue were paired by shape. Type A is a pillar, and type B a lozenge, the one higher than it is broad, the other rather like the sail of a Chinese junk. As in the façade at Wayland's Smithy, it is tempting to see in these shapes 'male' and 'female'. (Oddly enough, the Longstones at Beckhampton are sometimes called 'Adam' and 'Eve', but with the now conventional distinction of the sexes reversed.) Taking one side of the Avenue at a time, the stones alternate in shape, A, B, A, B, and so on, spaced on average at 24 m; and opposite each A there is a B. The Avenue's width was about 16 m.

The route of the Avenue seemed like a snake to Stukeley, who eventually wove the idea into his Trinitarian fantasy. Considering the panoramas he sketched, it is easy to see that the positioning of the avenues relative to local features (crossroads, hills, and so on) is accurate, but that the avenues tend to carry the landscape with them, rather than the other way about. His much-maligned figures are accurate in their way—but they are topologically accurate, schematic, not photographic. The point is well illustrated by one sketch in which he represents his entire surroundings on the surface of what looks like a bowl, with the complete circle of the horizon as its rim and all that he could see within it—a kind of super-fisheye-lens picture of the world around him.

The course of the Avenue is still often described as sinuous, but as Keiller and Piggott noted, it is made up of joined *straight* sections. This fact—which may be easily verified from their detailed plan, supplemented by Alexander Thom's—removes one of the standard arguments used in the past against the thesis that the Avenue was aligned on certain stars. Lockyer was first to take this possibility seriously: he decided that the Kennet Avenue had been established using alignments on alpha Centauri in the mid-fourth millennium, which is quite certainly mistaken. Since he wanted to link the Avenue with the southern ring of stones within the Avebury complex (just as he tried to

link the northern ring with the Beckhampton Avenue) he was driven to assume that Avebury's vast enclosing bank was a later addition. He was criticized by E. H. Goddard for misinterpreting Stukeley's notes on Avebury, but his arguments deserved better answers than they ever got.

There can be no doubt that the Avenue had a religious character, for those who built it. In one region the area around the stones was pitted with clay-lined hollows, pockets of flint chippings, broken flint arrowheads and knives, shards of broken pots, animal bones, charcoal from shrubs, and stones from many distant regions. Several of the stones had burials at the foot, and in one case the burial *preceded* the erection of the stone. Each of these burials was on the northeast side of the nearest stone. In view of their occurrence, the other deposits—which at first sight might have seemed to be no more than domestic refuse—are far more plausibly interpreted as part of a long tradition of burying broken things with the dead. Broken pots are commonplace, and in the Bronze and Iron Ages it is not unusual to find graves with knives and swords broken in some way. There have been attempts to date the Kennet Avenue burials on the basis of the styles of the associated pottery, with results lying between the twenty-sixth and twenty-first centuries. This range fits reasonably well with what may be deduced on the assumption that the stones were aligned on stars.

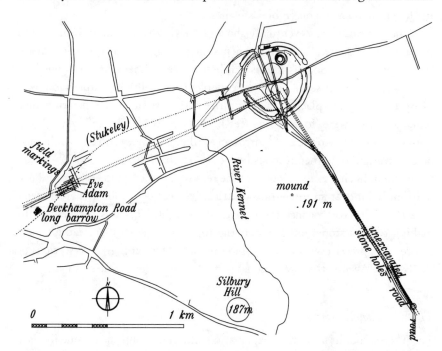

FIG. 98.   The Avebury circles and avenues, and their surroundings. The principal roads have been added, several of them loosely following the properties of the original monument.

The way in which the Kennet Avenue joined the stone circle of the Sanctuary, according to a plan drawn by John Aubrey in the late seventeenth century, is shown in Plate 8. Its estimated overall course—first downhill from the Sanctuary, running for a short distance nearly due west, then turning roughly northwest (310°), more or less along the line of the modern road over Overton Hill—is shown on the left of Fig. 99. The main part of the figure provides more detail of the surviving or excavated northern sections: after a further 900 m it turned through twenty degrees or so, bringing it closer to north in its main uphill approach to Avebury. (One of Aubrey's more stylized plans made a perfectly straight Kennet Avenue turn at right angles to the Sanctuary stretch, which ran respectively due north and due east; but he would not have wished to be judged as a map-maker.) There are occasional stones in the next 700 m, some still to be seen along the roadside; but then for the last 800 m, ending at the entrance to the Avebury enclosure, the stones of the Avenue are more numerous, and where they are absent their positions have been marked during the twentieth century by plinths over their stone holes. The Avebury bank and stones are not visible until the last descent, covering around 300 m. In its final approach to the entrance, say of 100 m, the Avenue makes a sharp turn almost to due north, in a way reminiscent of the kink in its direction as shown on Aubrey's plan.

The Sanctuary was eventually shown by its excavator Maud Cunnington to have seen a succession of monuments, beginning with concentric pairs of timber post circles. She distinguished three phases in them, or four if one is to count a replacement set of posts in new holes (Ia and Ib). The stones followed phase III, and were placed exactly on the periphery of the timber ring they replaced. They were 'four or five feet high' (1.2 to 1.5 m), and were finally removed in 1724—to the great sorrow of William Stukeley and the neighbours of the avaricious farmer responsible (one Green of Beckhampton). We are fortunate in having Aubrey's plan of the removed stones, more especially since it strongly hints at an intriguing practice that had been followed at so many sites that it is worth considering in its own right. This was the practice of making rows of stones either tangential to circles of stones, or head for their centre. The practice will be discussed only after examining those sections of the Kennet Avenue that are reasonably well known from modern surveys.

The West Kennet Avenue

The Thoms sought a metrical explanation and divided up the avenue into six straight sections with breaking points *between* stones. In this way they were

able to quote lengths of 45, 55, 60 and 50 'megalithic rods'. Here a different possibility will be considered, namely that successive stretches of the avenue were directed towards the horizon positions of stars. Viewing might also have been *across* the line of the avenue, towards the Moon. In either of these cases, precisely where the breaking points occur, whether between or at the stones, will be astronomically irrelevant.

Keiller and Piggott first numbered the stones of the Kennet Avenue individually, but in Isobel Smith's publication of Keiller's materials—followed by others since then—they are numbered by pairs, beginning at the Avebury entrance (Fig. 99). Pairs 7 to 37, sixty in all, are of greatest importance. Pairs 1 to 6 will be considered at a later stage, for they were certainly not poor relations of the rest.[6]

Eastern and western sides of the sections are invariably parallel to within a degree, and the azimuths range from 304.7° to 335°. It is tempting to quote the values in full, but to do so would be to draw attention away from the fact that there is an unsolved problem here. How could stars have been observed along the rows? In the case of most of the complex Dartmoor rows, each straight section points up to its own private horizon. In the Kennet Avenue, this is not so. Standing at the foot of section (7), the stones up to section (4) zigzag in their course up to the horizon. There is a flat-topped ridge in the neighbourhood of section (2), and since stones 13w and 13e are the tallest of all (a little under and over 4 m respectively), one would expect section (1) to have directed the view to the southeastern horizon, and (4)–(7) to the northwestern, the intervening sections being somewhat ambiguous. The breaking point, in other words, is in the neighbourhood of the elbow of the Avenue.

There are other surprising facts that repeat in such a way as to suggest that they are not pure coincidence. Standing at either of pair 28, south of section (5), the stones of that section are not blocked by the rest, but 28e is in line with the western row of section (4), and the line of sight passes over a burial at stone 22w. The ray from 18w to 37w passes over a burial at 25w. The ray from 18e to 37e passes over a burial near 29e. One would not normally have supposed that the ray from 18e to 37w was a suitable one, but it passes directly over the eastern row of section (4) as well as over burials at 22e and 29w. Since stone 18w has a burial by it, alignments of stones have now been related to all the burials found by Keiller and Piggott. Even the fact that the grave actually forms part of the stonehole of 25w, which so surprised them, might be

---

6   The avenue is here divided into straight sections as follows: (1) pairs 7 to 14, excluding 13, which is the beginning of the next section; (2) pairs 13, 14, 15, and 17; (3) pairs 16, 17, and 18; (4) pairs 18 to 22; (5) pairs 22 to 28; (6) pairs 28 to 32; (7) pairs 32 to 37.

explained in terms of the fact that the line from 18w to 37w passes almost over the centre of the stone 25w.

The rule of concentrating on a horizon stone seems to be the same for the northern section (1)—with which, by their general direction, sections (2) and (3) are associated. From pair 7, sighting was along the rows on pair 16; likewise from pair 13 on 17; and from 16 on 18. There are even more possibilities, if one introduces the anomalous stones that make the Avenue seem to coil like a snake heading for the entrance to the enclosure. From pair 4 the aim might perhaps have been at 17 and 18; and from 5 at 13 and 17. The ray from 17e to 6e is more or less parallel to section (1).

We are now in a position to ask whether these highly suggestive alignments of stones correspond to any coherent set of star positions. There are some difficulties with the changed levels of the ground, especially near the road, but looking south, all directions suggest declinations in the neighbourhood of what would be expected for Rigel or Sirius, and looking north a rather unhappy choice remains, between Deneb and Capella. There is also the possibility of the setting of Cassiopeia. This constellation has an easily recognizable W-form, but since it has no outstanding stars it will not be considered further—despite a temptation to remark on its resemblance to the zigzag motif of pottery and other artefacts.

For the first two sections it is difficult to quote an altitude, but if the first section is for the rising Sirius and the second for the rising Rigel, both of which seem reasonable, the natural horizon was close to the extinction angle, for which declinations of $-20.4°$ and $-21.3°$ are obtained, respectively. The corresponding dates are 2320 BC and 2120 BC, but the uncertainty here is not less than two centuries, and there is no strong reason to deny that the sections were contemporaneous.

The southern sections are more difficult to resolve. Deneb is close, but will not do unless observation was not done precisely. The extinction angle of Capella so closely matches the natural horizon over much of the avenue that it seems a very natural choice, but the declinations derived produce dates after 1830 BC, apart from allowances for error. This is where we need to remind ourselves that much is unknown about the more southerly avenue. Resistivity surveys (and see Fig. 101) suggest that the Kennet Avenue was at one time interrupted by a series of concentric circles (ditches?) reminiscent of a pattern found on Dartmoor. The Ordnance Survey of 1883 shows a stone that is now missing but that seems to have been at the centre of the rings. Joining their centre to the centre of the south circle inside the Avebury monument, the line

passes through stone 16w of the avenue. If this was a Capella line, it would correspond to 1750 BC (declination 32.73°).

There seems to be a consensus that the enclosure at least antedates the Avenue, and that the date of neither is earlier than the second half of the third millennium. The argument rests heavily on the discovery of packing material in stonehole 9w (Keiller and Piggott no. 57), which came from the geological stratum of Lower Chalk, reached only when the ditch was dug deep.

In discussing the West Kennet long barrow the conjecture was made that

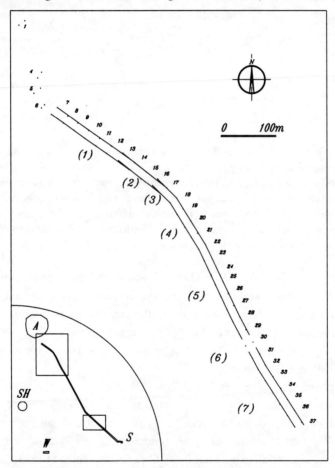

FIG. 99.   The northern sections of the Kennet Avenue, numbered in pairs as explained in the text. This is a detail of the area in the larger rectangular box of the plan at the lower left. The overall plan is drawn at one tenth the scale, partly by conjecture. (For more detail of the lower box see Fig. 100) S is the Sanctuary, SH is Silbury Hill, W is the West Kennet long barrow, and A is the Avebury stone circle.

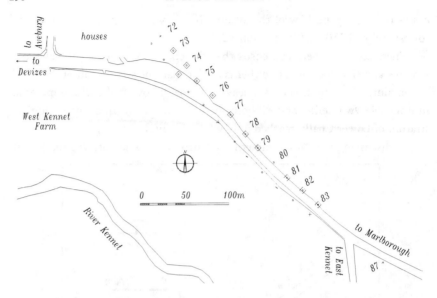

FIG. 100. Stones of the Kennet Avenue (1961) in the neighbourhood of West Kennet village, from positions given by Isobel Smith. Only two stones are standing, while stones 80w, 80e, 82w are fallen. (This notation will be used to distinguish between the eastern and western members of any pair.) The positions of eleven stones that were only estimated by her, on the basis of symmetry, have here been enclosed in small lozenges. Stones 72w, 75w, 78w are known from their excavated holes. The information available from this part of the avenue is obviously of no astronomical value.

the Sanctuary was placed so as to allow Aldebaran to be seen setting over that much older structure, and that if so, the date of foundation was perhaps 2800 BC. As an end to the Kennet Avenue, on the other hand, the rising of Rigel would have been seen over it at dates in the neighbourhood of 2315 BC (2235 BC assuming 15 m trees on the hilltop beyond). As explained, section (2) was for the rising of the same star.

The potential alignments of the Kennet Avenue on stars certainly do not exhaust the possibilities, for there are interesting alignments *across* it. This is a difficult matter to discuss in precise terms, since there is so much uncertainty in the relatively short lines of sight, but the avenue has some remarkable properties that should not go unnoticed. On or to the north of the ridge there are at least sixteen stones that can be paired so that they could be used for sighting more or less due east. (The mean direction is 0.9° north of east, with a standard deviation of 2.2°, using grazing lines of sight.) To the south of the ridge there are thirty-two stones providing sixteen lines very close to due north (mean 0.5° east of north, standard deviation 2.4°). These lines have nothing to do with the Moon as such, but lend support to the idea that the pairing of

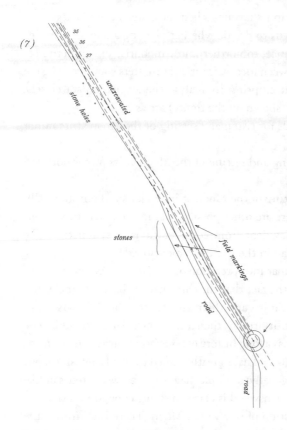

FIG. 101. Parts of the Kennet Avenue known chiefly through resistivity surveys of the ground to the south of stones 37. This is based on recordings published by P. J. Ucko and others (see the bibliography). It is not known whether the marks seen adjacent to the road are prehistoric, but they appear to be connected with the concentric circles with which a 'cove' of stones was once associated, as discussed below. The three broken lines join those circles to the centre of the southern circle within the Avebury monument. The centre line passes through stone 16w, on the ridge.

stones other than opposites was done in a carefully contrived, and astronomically meaningful, way.

Looking then for other significant cross-lines, at least five promising sets are produced, all shown on the figure. The problem is complicated, in view of the fact that the horizon changes in subtle ways from pair to pair; and the re-erection of the stones and the fact that some are missing only add to the uncertainty. There is no point in trying to present this as a case for even remotely precise working, without first making an intensive study of all the evidence, which would mean eliminating many of the preconceptions according to which stone positions have been estimated in the past. One cannot be certain of the technique of observation used, or indeed whether any was regularly used. Looking in either direction, only a few of the far stones would have appeared to clip the horizon for an observer standing at the present ground level. It is possible that the arrangement was only an ideal, justified by the fact that the Moon was 'built into the avenue', as it were.

Azimuths can at present be estimated to only two or three degrees in many cases, but if the idea of lunar observation is accepted—and the evidence of the

main Avebury monument is in its favour—then the different gradients of the terrain to east and west help us to decide whether viewing along a given line was to east or west (for instance, to northernmost moonrise or southernmost moonset). The difference between ideal azimuths, as matters stand, may be ten or more degrees. Without attempting to analyse the available data closely, potential alternatives (as also shown on the figure) are as follows.

Sections (5) and (6): diagonals for rising and setting of the Moon at its minor southern standstill.

Section (7): diagonals for rising and setting of the Moon at its minor northern standstill.

Section (1): diagonals for setting of the Moon at its major southern standstill.

Although not listed, there are other possibilities in the northern sections for major lunar standstills (evident from considerations of symmetry). The available data fit less well than in the five cases mentioned.

In further support of a lunar interpretation of the Kennet Avenue we have the shapes of the stones and the fact that they alternate as between 'male' and 'female'. If we follow Isobel Smith and the many others who have wished to associate the stones with fertility ritual, then a lunar association should come as no surprise, for the Moon has a long history of association with fertility. In any case, the alternation of shapes would have greatly helped to avoid confusing stone with stone, when looking diagonally: a simple diagonal is between stones of like shape, whereas a simple short transversal is between stones of opposite shape.

Finally, there is the question of star versus Moon. There is a limit to the number of constraints that can be imposed on geometrical constructions of the sort offered here. Could *all* of the alignments suggested have been deliberately built into a perfect system—as opposed to a system that just happened to be found to work after long experience of observation across a given terrain? For the sake of argument, consider the four stones in pairs 36 and 37, and let us speak as though the stones are represented by points. Looking up to the ridge, at a particular period, the long sides can first be established, regardless of the stones. One stone, say 36w, is then put on the line. The directions of minor northern moonrise and moonset will then settle the positions of 37e and 36e, the stones from and over which the Moon is observed; and from 37e we are likewise led to 37w. This all gives no guarantee, however, of that other claim we made, concerning the north–south direction of the other diagonal. What is more, it is quite impossible in general that it should do so. In fact out of the five directions (north–south, two Moon directions, and a star direction) we can achieve a perfect construction making use of only four of them. Even then there is another potential constraint on our construction that some would claim to

be patently obvious: the stones seem to be placed directly opposite one another, making the parallelograms *rectangles*.

Which two of these constraints is to be abandoned? One could reject one of the Moon diagonals, for example, but keep the other on the grounds that Avebury itself is replete with Moon alignments. One might also drop the star alignments—which were doomed not to endure for long. In real life, however,

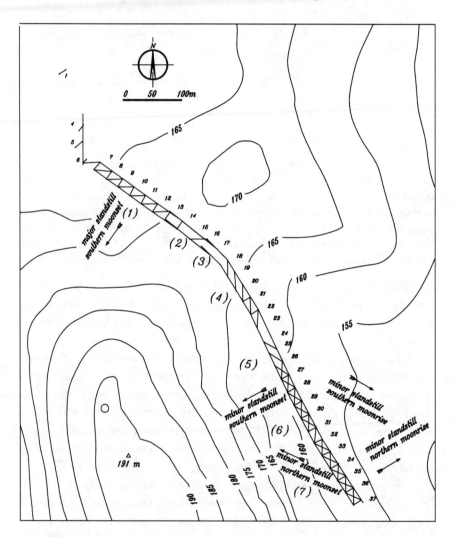

FIG. 102. The pattern of some of the potential lines of sight to lunar phenomena, seen *across* the Kennet Avenue. Contours to the west give a good idea of altitudes. Ground to the east rises to over 200m at a distance of rather more than a kilometre from the edge of the plan. The figure gives little idea of whether or not the stones break the horizon when seen from their opposite numbers. By and large they do not.

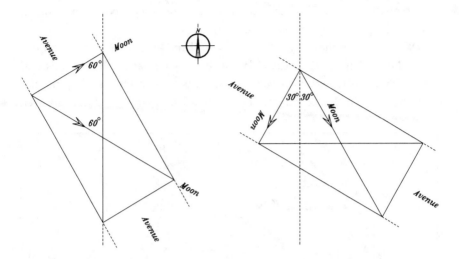

FIG. 103.   An idealization of the rectangular cells formed around lunar lines and lines
north–south (left-hand figure, applying to the Kennet Avenue south of the ridge, for minor
standstills) or lunar lines and lines east–west (right-hand figure, between the ridge and
Avebury, for major standstills). The ratio of the length of such an ideal cell to the width of
the avenue will be 1.732 to 1. These patterns fit well many of the longer cells in the avenue,
if the short side of the rectangle is taken to the insides of the stones. (Their spacing might
have been intended as 18 of Alexander Thom's Megalithic Yards (1 MY = 0.829 m).)

the situation was not as desperate as this purely geometrical account might
lead one to believe. In fact the Moon's behaviour would have allowed the people
of Avebury to preserve a very respectable avenue and *almost* keep to all of the
six constraints.

First to the star alignments. It could have been known that a bright star
was rising or setting at right angles to one of the eight favoured lunar lines at
that time. This must sound improbable, but then, if our reading of the stones
is correct, the builders did not quite manage to achieve perfection in this
respect, for they focused not on the stones of their own sections but on horizon
stones. Those who wish to drop the whole idea of star alignments, but keep
the Moon, may however do so at this stage.

The question of the claims of the rectangle versus those of the north–south
line are harder to settle, but assuming one of them, the other will follow to a
fairly good approximation, keeping both Moon diagonals. The reason is that
both Moon lines are by a fortunate chance at angles of roughly 60° to the
north–south line. In Fig. 103 an idealized figure is drawn as an approximation
to the reality of the near-rectangle created by the quadrangles of stones. Star
observations can then be assumed to have been made in any direction reasonably

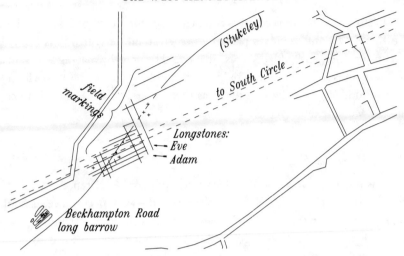

FIG. 104.   Marks shown up in a resistivity survey in Longstones field, and possibly relating
to the Beckhampton Avenue (based on recordings published by P. J. Ucko and others).
Potential stone holes are marked with a cross, and an approximation to the line of the avenue
as derived from Stukeley's drawings is added. The broken lines from Adam and Eve relate
to a different property: they head directly for the centre of the south circle at Avebury and
are at right angles to the common tangent to the north and south circles there. Note that
their courses are parallel to the linear markings found from the resistivity survey of the field.

close to the long sides. The play needed in the diagonals of the actual rectangle
will be of the order of one degree. The pattern fits well with many of the longer
cells in the avenue, but not with all, and there was obviously a strong element
of makeshift in the whole enterprise.

It is particularly satisfying to find the rectangle property preserved, since
it plainly continues—albeit weakly, since viewing altitudes are not now
equal—a tradition established for the architecture of the long barrows, two
millennia earlier.

It becomes doubly pleasing to find that a weaker version of much the same
account can be given of the avenue north of the ridge. The natural horizon is
there such as to bring the lunar line for setting (for the major standstill) to
within a degree of 30° of the north–south line. Unfortunately, the natural
horizon was not so kind with the sight line directed to extreme southern
moonrise, which was over five degrees in error. Juggling with stone sizes might
have served to hide the discrepancy even here, however. By making use of
diagonals tangential to stones it is certainly possible to produce a set of virtually
perfect east–west diagonals. The unattainable ideal figure, with stones represented by points, is included in Fig. 103. It can be made to fit the longer cells
in the avenue quite well.

In summary, if this account is accepted, then for all its modest appearance the Kennet Avenue involves principles of great subtlety. It differs from the Avebury monument, which shows what could be done by placing stones in an *artificial* landscape. Those who built the Kennet Avenue seem to have found a kind of hidden geometry, one that was the property of the *natural* landscape and the Moon taken together.

The Beckhampton Avenue

There is no reason to doubt Stukeley's testimony to the existence of an avenue to the west, meeting the Avebury monument at the western entrance, although Maud Cunnington thought it a figment of his imagination. When we are able to test his statements they are generally reliable, but an independent argument will be offered here for the avenue's existence, based on a remarkable symmetry with the Kennet Avenue. Stukeley was able to note the positions of about thirty stones, some in pairs, and he suggested that the spacing was the same as in the Kennet Avenue, both across and along the cells. The only stones surviving today that might have been a part of the Beckhampton Avenue are the Longstones, Adam and Eve, but many have questioned their status, even making them out to have been part of a separate circle. Stukeley himself sketched them in a way that showed that he imagined the western stone (Adam, the more massive) to be independent of the avenue (Fig. 109).

A resistivity survey of Longstones field, which should have covered 300 m of the avenue, was disappointing inasmuch as it showed very few signs of possible stone positions, and those signs were weak. Some of them seemed, however, to fit with a plausible rendering of Stukeley's interpretation of the avenue in this region, making Adam and Eve neighbours on the north side of the avenue (Fig. 104). This is in a way surprising, for reasons that may be noted without any suggestion that they should carry much weight. If it is supposed that Adam and Eve were on *opposite* sides of an avenue of the same width as the Kennet Avenue, then the line of the supposed section may be extended, and it will pass through the centre of the south circle at Avebury. In doing so, it turns out to be (a) very precisely at right angles to the common tangent to the south and north circles there, and (b) parallel to the markings in Longstones field. Even the roads in the area seem to pick up this alignment (see the earlier Fig. 98). If then, in total ignorance of all other testimony, one were to conjecture as to the line of an avenue that followed strictly the pattern of its Kennet twin, one would probably choose to take it on this line as far as, say, the river, and thence along a rough tangent to the north ditch, before joining with Avebury

High Street (where it peters out). Of course this sort of conjecture is not of comparable worth with the evidence of Stukeley's senses, but the directions stipulated are not so very different from his—about which in any case it is impossible to be altogether precise.

Whether or not we dismiss the idea of a different line for the Beckhampton Avenue, can we fit Adam, at least, into a cove of the sort Stukeley drew? One way might be to liken the 'cove' to whatever structure it was that produced circular patterns in the resistivity survey of the Kennet Avenue (see the lower right corner of Fig. 98). In fact in doing so, we find that Stukeley has been there, or almost there, before us. In the fourth chapter of his book *Abury* he recounts how, having seen 'longstone cove' and having measured its distance from Avebury as fifty stones (of the Beckhampton Avenue), he conjectured that there must have been another of the same sort on the Kennet Avenue. Measuring carefully, he found what he had anticipated: at the fiftieth stone there was an 'entire vacancy', and it was on an eminence where the road crossed the avenue. He later abandoned the idea of a Kennet cove, when it failed to fit in with his desire to have a double snake of avenues. The place he specified is not the same as that with the circular marks.

In our case we wish to use the argument in reverse, and this can be done very well. The key to the argument is in the distance from the centre of the small circle that seems to stands on, or to the side of, the Kennet Avenue—approximately 1648 m from the centre of Avebury's southern circle. This is 1988 of Thom's Megalithic Yards, near enough to 2000 (the discrepancy of only six parts in a thousand merits this description) for the interval to be at least worthy of further investigation. (The width of the avenue has already been put at 18 MY, and other examples will later emerge of long intervals in multiples of 50 MY.) Measuring then from Adam—the larger of the Longstones and a part of what Stukeley saw as the cove—along plausible routes for the Beckhampton Avenue, where does a line of the same length bring us? Not to the centre of either the northern or southern circles, but to the middle of circles to the northeast, known only from the recent resistivity survey. The route drawn in the earlier Fig. 98 as an estimate of Stukeley's avenue, assuming that the line to the circle's centre strikes northeast from the entrance in the Avebury banks, would in total length have been about 1656 m, or 1997.6 MY, even closer to 2000 than before. There is excellent reason, therefore, for supposing the two avenues to have existed in a broadly symmetrical form.

The form of the Kennet structure is difficult to make out, but it might have had several stones round the edge of a ditch, in a circle about 30 m across; and whether or not that structure existed, there seem to be the signs of three

or four stones in the middle. Perhaps it all resembled in character the circles found interrupting some of the Dartmoor rows. The last stone from this place was very probably the one now lost that was marked on the 1883 Ordnance Survey. In preparing his book *Monumenta Britannica*, John Aubrey made a sketch of a cove in the ploughed field near Kennet, 'Southward from Aubury', that he said was called the Devil's Coytes. (Were these 'coytes' by reputation the devil's quoits, or dice, or coats ?) This trio is a good candidate for the structure that interrupted the Kennet Avenue.

If the Beckhampton Avenue was linked to the northeast circles inside Avebury, its final course might have passed somehow through the north circle—although supposing its course to have been diverted would spoil the fit in length. If not, it seems on balance likely to have been the earlier avenue of the two. Its precise course is a matter only for speculation, but it is tempting to suppose that Stukeley was right, and that the cells of the avenue were of the same dimensions as those in its partner. The approximate direction of one long stretch (Stukeley's avenue, as interpreted from his work, of course) is at least open to conjecture, so that we can guess at the diagonals and transversals of the cells. They seem to offer no hope of any solar alignment, but the diagonal roughly to the northeast (40° to 44°?) might have been designed for the maximum northern declination of the (rising) Moon; and the line of the rows might have been towards the rising Spica in the late third millennium.

Stukeley's early characterization of the north Avebury circle as a Lunar Temple and the south circle as a Solar Temple had nothing to do with the avenues, but rather with an interpretation of stones within them. He silently dropped these names, but as in the case of the twin coves, there was a grain of truth in the idea, as will be shown in an examination of the internal arrangement of stones. But first we turn to a general principle of the alignment of stones, and one that is in evidence, for example, in Aubrey's drawing of the Kennet Avenue at its Sanctuary end.

The Principle of Tangent and Centre

That the avenue there had a final curl in its direction is supported to a minor extent by Maud Cunnington's excavation, which was carried out far enough from the Sanctuary's centre to reveal three short rows commencing in a roughly northwesterly direction. She followed them for a short way only (three, three, and two holes). The rows were probably from different periods, and whether the third continued any further is unknown. The main approaches of the two rows comprising Aubrey's avenue are different. The pseudo-three-dimension-

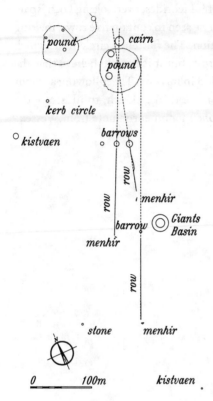

FIG. 105. The Drizzlecombe stone rows, after a plan by R. H. Worth. These are on ground sloping south to the river Plym. Since the scale is large, the rows are shown here as continuous lines. The three broken lines drawn through the rows pass through two centres (four if we count barrows) and are twice tangential to circles of some sort (and once to a small barrow). The row to the east is in some places double, and follows the rule of tangent and centre in relation to its own barrow. The labels are Worth's. 'Kistvaen' is an antiquated half-Welsh word for a small burial chamber of stone slabs. The 'pounds' are circular enclosures, earthworks containing 'hut circles' that have been habitations at some periods of history. Giant's Basin is a large cairn.

ality of his plan, and the fact that he measured by pacing, makes it impossible to be precise, but it does seem that one row heads towards the centre of the circle while the other heads as though it will end as a tangent to it. This is a situation found at various places on Dartmoor. It was seen at Corringdon Ball (Figs. 97 and 96), but there were so many rows on that site that it will not carry much conviction. A clearer example is in the triplet of rows at Drizzlecombe, illustrated here in Fig. 105.

Drizzlecombe

The line of the easternmost Drizzlecombe row is tangential to the pound and to a small round barrow. Each of the other two rows passes through the centre of the round barrow terminating it, then through the centre of the pound, and finally through the centre of the cairn in one case, tangential to the cairn in the other. The last pair of these lines possibly aligned on Pollux and Capella around 1510 BC, while the other was perhaps for Pollux from a much later period, or possibly for the northern extreme of the Moon's rising. While there are three different types of circular structure involved in all this, and none of them is a circle of stones as at Corringdon Ball, there are many other examples of all types on Dartmoor.

Callanish

A situation more difficult to analyse, but revealing a similar custom, is that of the beautiful monument of tall stand-

ing stones at Callanish on Lewis in the Outer Hebrides, overlooking Loch Roag. (For a plan see Fig. 106.) This system will be seen to contain five rows, making allowance for no subtle changes of direction. The flattened circle from which they radiate is at its widest only 13 m across, but it is hard to believe that the monument did not have a a great reputation in its time. The following account of its possible properties is meant as no more than a sketch, to illustrate the importance of centre and tangent in a stone monument remote from Wessex.

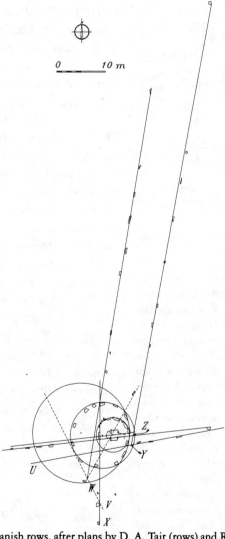

FIG. 106.   The Callanish rows, after plans by D. A. Tait (rows) and R. Curtis (centre). For more detail of the centre, see the next figure. M. R. and G. H. Ponting have shown that important lunar phenomena could have been seen from the north end of the avenue.

One possible geometrical construction of a minimal sort is added to the plan of Fig. 106. Alexander Thom gave a rather different set of circles, with extra filleting arcs, and others have followed suit with slight variations, producing a smooth curve of what he designated a 'flattened circle of type A'. The construction here is not meant to deny that possibility, but the stones are few and the present fit is good enough for our purposes. Of course any claim as to a custom involving centres and tangents will depend on the geometrical construction superimposed; but it will also depend on the acceptability of the astronomical sight lines proposed. At least with the three short rows there are several ways of interpreting the evidence. Thom was working from a plan made by Boyle Somerville in 1912, and put a line at 0.1° from north, but passing through S. Judging by more recent surveys, the accuracy actually achieved might have been even better than this (our line XV). As it happens, and as we shall see shortly, this is not a critical matter, but with the directions of the eastern and western rows, much hangs on the interpretation.

The stones have attracted considerable astronomical interest since Lockyer (1909) and Somerville (1912) decided that the two northern rows aligned on Capella, around 1720 and 1800 BC respectively. Somerville was first to appreciate the moonrise at lunar maximum. In a summary of careful work done at this and other Callanish sites over more than a decade, Margaret Ponting has shown that from the northern end of the long avenue three striking phenomena could have been seen, none of them visible from the central monument:

(1) The Moon at maximum southern declination could have been seen rising out of the Seaforth Hills, keeping very low on the horizon and skimming the stones of the east row, disappearing again into a distant outcrop of rocks, and then gleaming again at the base of the tallest stone (S). (The last possibility would however imply that the cairn was not piled up significantly around S.)

(2) The Moon at its maximum northern declination set, only to reappear again in a notch in the horizon. (This implies looking away from the central monument altogether.)

(3) The Sun near to winter solstice did much the same, setting and then flashing as it passed a notch on the southern horizon as seen from the north end of the avenue. This would have required use of a pair of stones, but the line passes well away from the central monument.

While obviously important, these possibilities make little use of the monument as such and do not illustrate the simple point being made here,

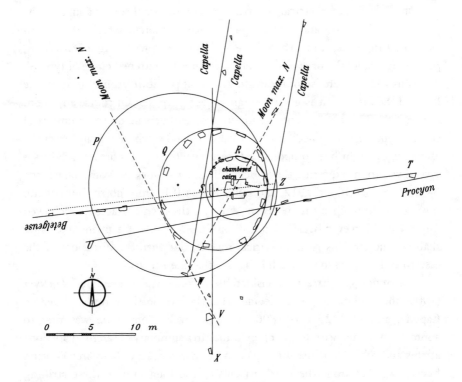

FIG. 107.   The central region of the circle and rows at Callanish. The three circles added
to the plan are conjectured limits for the arcs within which the main stones (P and Q) and
the cairn (R) seem to have been placed. Their three centres are marked with black spots,
the centres used for the original construction having no doubt been in line. (The largest
circle cannot be as well determined as the other two, but this is of little consequence.) It
seems likely that viewing of risings and settings was along lines on which targets are named,
in the directions in which the names are written. Potential sighting positions are Z or T,
V or W, V or X, W (twice more), Y, and U or Y. Three of the lines are roughly tangential
to conjectured circles, and three pass near to their centres. Other lines could be added—for
example from the sighting position X through the centre of the cairn, and thence through
the middle of the northern rows to Capella. This figure takes no account of solar lines.

which is that the rough rule of centre and tangent operated at Callanish as well
as in Wessex. The following scheme does so, offering three stars, a lunar extreme
(rising and setting), and perhaps a solar extreme (multiple views of rising and
setting). The stellar phenomena would have been visible close to 1800 BC and
the others for a period of several centuries. (The latitude is 58° 11' 48".)

(1) The long rows to the north, not quite parallel, are both (separately)
directed to Capella around 1800 BC, a possibility arising from the fact that

they point to parts of the horizon at different altitudes, higher than the extinction angle.[7]

(2) Looking over the cairn from Z (or from T) to the west, the setting Betelgeuse would have been seen around 1800 BC. The line is almost precisely parallel to the suggested line of centres. If the observer moved back to the end of the eastern row (T) the cairn might have provided an artificial horizon just about equal to the extinction angle.

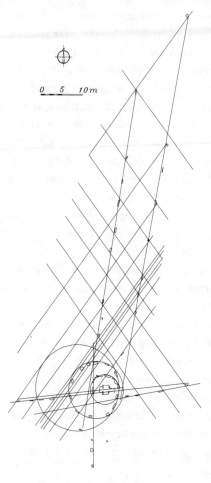

(3) Looking (eastwards) from Y (or U) along the eastern row, the rising Procyon would have been seen around 1790 BC. Again there might have been a stone to allow the observer to look across the cairn at the lower extinction angle of about 1.7°. Note how the line crosses the lower part of the cairn.

(4) Looking once again from W, once along a tangent to the grand ring Q and once over the centre of the cairn slightly to the right of the scarcely detectible peak of Beinn Mhór, the setting and rising directions of the Moon (last or first glint) at the maximum of its northern range might have been observed around 1800 BC. The original sight-lines are not now recoverable, since the stones have weathered and slipped, and since the precise observing position is unknown. The general character of the placing of the two sight-lines will later be recognized as quite typical of post and stone circles elsewhere. There are in fact sight-lines at

FIG. 108. Approximate lines of sight at Callanish for the first or last glint of the Sun at its midwinter extreme.

---

7 The additional line through the monument that runs almost due north is puzzling. When Capella was due north at the same date it was above the horizon (altitude of 1.0°, natural horizon about 0.95°), but this was half a degree below the star's extinction angle. Perhaps an attempt was being made to establish the direction of true north, say in the sense of the direction in which any circumpolar star reaches its lowest point.

Stonehenge strongly reminiscent of the setting line at Callanish—that is, tangential to the 'drum' formed by the uprights—and there are others at Avebury.

(5) There is another tangent to the main circle from the third stone along the east side of the avenue, at azimuth around 216.5°, which is approximately correct for the last glint of the Sun at its midwinter extreme, over the natural horizon in that direction. The line in question is more interesting for another reason: it is parallel to a number of diagonals between stones in the northern avenue, or between those and the western row. This fact draws attention to the corresponding lines to the rising of the midwinter Sun. Eighteen lines of one sort or the other are drawn on Fig. 108, not in positions that can be claimed as precise, but here strictly parallel and so only approximately correct for midwinter risings or settings. Regarded as sight-lines, most are, from the observer's point of view, trapped between two stones, and this undoubtedly constituted a standard observational technique. The approximate character of the lines drawn in the figure must be emphasized. To discuss these solar lines properly it would be necessary to consider each one separately—the precise horizon profile along it and the shapes of the two stones that determine it. The lines help to explain the spacing of the stones in the eastern and western rows. They suggest the positions of missing stones in the northern rows. And above all they draw attention to the possibility that as many as ten people might have observed midwinter risings and settings simultaneously.

Finally, note how the arrangement takes care of two stones (V, W, and that to the northeast) that at first sight seem to be misplaced. There is hardly a redundant stone on the site, it seems. It should not pass unnoticed that an astronomical interpretation of this monument explains qualitatively why there were two long rows running north and south but only short single rows to east and west. It is that the grazing phenomena, with Capella and the Moon staying close to the horizon, had no equivalent at this site to the east or west. Those who dislike the astronomical hypothesis should be prepared to offer a better explanation for the northern axis of the stones.[8]

---

8 Somerville proposed that viewing had been of the Moon at its furthest south as seen from the central region. Gerald Hawkins and Alexander Thom separately accepted this idea, while adding a number of solar and lunar alternatives. Hawkins later revised his opinion when he found that Mt Clisham, the horizon supposedly seen from the north of the northern rows looking south, was invisible from there. There have been other suggestions that need not be seriously discussed—for example those involving the equinoctial Sun. On the question of the possible line to true north, we have found comparable Wessex examples at a much earlier date, but they do not remove the mystery of how such accuracy was achieved, and Thom was probably right in his assumption that the method used was the method still in use—of bisecting the angle

Inside Avebury

The examples of tangent and centre given so far can now be supplemented from what is to be found inside Avebury itself. Inside the vast banks and ditches there, and the ring of approaching a hundred stones, there were at one time or another at least four lesser circles, perhaps all of stones—the north and south circles and the northeast concentric pair. Stukeley and others—prompted by an isolated stone and the example of the Sanctuary (Plate 8)—represented the two that survived almost up to his day as two pairs of concentric circles. Others, even recently, have followed suit, although most now doubt the existence of those inner rings.

Despite modern excavations, the northern end of the Kennet Avenue leaves much open to conjecture. As it approaches Avebury, it turns at first as though to be tangential to the crude curve of the southwest ditch, and then heads through the entrance, narrowing considerably as it does so. The line on the west side defined by stones 6w and 5w seems to have been tangential to *both*

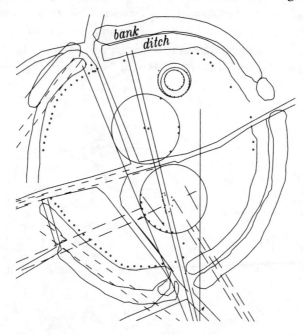

Fig. 109.   Relations between the north of the Kennet Avenue and the north and south circles at Avebury.

between the directions at which a circumpolar star reaches equal altitudes. We have already, after all, offered cases where a northern star was seen coming down to a level horizon and very soon afterwards rising again. This would have given a very good feel for the star's rise and fall with the daily rotation. Bisecting the angle between rising and setting would have been a very natural thing to do.

inner circles, south and north (circles Y and X on Fig. 109). Other stones (6e, 5e, and perhaps 4w) seem to head over a straight row of stones (known only from their holes) in Y and on to the centre of X. Some of the stones (6w, 5e, 4e) might possibly have been deliberately set in a line due north. These are at first sight trifling facts, but the shared tangent to the two circles was very probably aligned on the setting Deneb. The loss of stones from X makes deriving a Deneb date problematical, however.

After these uncertain beginnings, what is really astonishing about Avebury is how the employment of tangents and centres helped to mould the entire internal plan of the monument best known to us—that is, the north and south circles, the two rings to the northeast known only from marks on a resistivity survey, the placing of the four entrances, various stones (Figs. 110 and 111). Alexander Thom and his son Alexander Strang Thom surveyed the surviving stones and plinths and believed that they had discovered several very precise geometrical properties of the stone rings and avenue. Their essentially geometrical approach will not be followed here, however. First and foremost, the hand of the designer of Avebury was forced by rising and setting positions over which there was only limited control—and this control was through the adjustment of the heights of artificial horizons. Having begun with the observation of

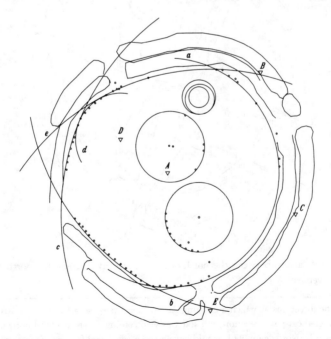

FIG. 110.   The main rings of large stones at Avebury, with some potential construction arcs. No stones survive from the northeast rings, for which see the next figure.

risings and settings, geometrical forms could then to some extent be added to the simple network of lines resulting. Any explanation of the complex geometry of Avebury must give an account of this sequence. The rectangles with diagonals at angles close to 60° in the Kennet Avenue, for instance, were primarily astronomical, with the geometrical ideal representing an ambition, but one that surely took second place when it could not be achieved.

Although not a counsel of perfection, in the following cursory account no distinction will be made between surviving stones and now empty stone holes. The shapes of the individual stones would have been an important factor had the scale of Avebury been less than it is—the main ring is vast, more than 400 m across, and the north and south circles about 100 m. The stones will be represented in our plans only by circles approximating to their size. The main point to be made—one concerning a predilection for centres and tangents—will prove not to be heavily dependent on this approximation.

The alignments found in the area within the Avebury banks will be listed in clockwise order from north, with brief comments. They involve three important structures that have not been mentioned previously:

The Cove is best known from sketches of it, first by Aubrey and later by Stukeley, when it still contained three colossal stones forming three sides of an open rectangular space, at the middle of the northern circle. The back stone was 4.9 m broad and 4.4 m high, the side stones slightly higher but narrower. The survivor is 4.9 m high and about half as broad; that which fell in 1713 was said to have been 'full seven yards long'. From Avebury practice generally, this would suggest a height of 4.6 m above ground, but the estimate was based on memory only, and it is not unlikely that this stone too was 4.9 m high. There is on one of Stukeley's sketches what could have been a fallen fourth stone, that would have made the cove an enclosed space, but it could just as well

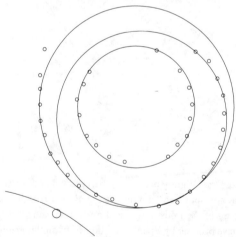

FIG. 111.   The estimated positions of whatever was responsible for the marks on the resistivity survey—presumably post holes or stone holes. See circles U, V, and W from the following figure. It would be possible to offer many different construction lines, especially for the outer set, but astronomically speaking this is not a critical matter.

have been a table, in the general sense of a level stone surface. Very approximately, the direction set by the surviving broad stone is 135°/315°.

The Obelisk had fallen by Stukeley's time, and was apparently a stone of circular section at its base, 2.67 m diameter there, and 6.4 m long. It stood very near to the centre of the south circle. Stone D appears to have been an isolated stone in the same circle, but it is what led Stukeley and others to

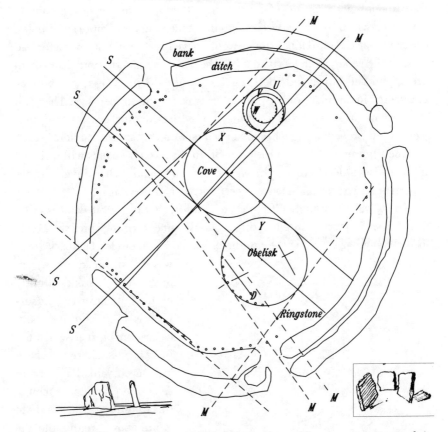

FIG. 112. The chief internal astronomical alignments set by the components of the Avebury circles. Those to the northern and southern extremes of the Moon's risings and settings end with M, those to the setting of the midsummer and midwinter Sun with S. The horizon is in all cases assumed to have been set by a bank masking the natural horizon. (The known dimensions of the bank make this possible.) The circles U, V, and W are known only from a resistivity survey (the work of P. J. Ucko and others). Alignments drawn as continuous lines (five cases) are fixed by tangents and centres only. Those drawn with broken lines involve tangents and individual stones. Two lines pass through entrances. Lines to the northwest (to midsummer sunset) pass over Windmill Hill. The sketch in the lower left corner is of the two remaining stones of the Cove, as seen from the southwest. The sketch at lower right is based on Aubrey's view of the Cove from the northeast, which he added as a detail to his own map.

suppose that there was here a circle within a circle, as at the Sanctuary.

The Ringstone (south of the south circle, see Fig. 112) still stood in 1724, but now only a stump remains. It was 'not of great bulk' but it had 'a hole wrought in it', wrote Stukeley in his book *Abury*, where he added that it was probably 'design'd to fasten the victim, in order for slaying it'. Some have thought that the hole was merely a depression, an irregularity in the stone, but since he spoke of tethering an animal, the stone was probably pierced right through. From excavation, it is known that the ringstone had been set on a plinth, possibly to adjust its level, or perhaps because the stone had a special status.

The main alignments found are solar or lunar.

(1) A line from the west entrance, tangential to X: major northern lunar standstill, first glint of rising Moon over the bank. The line is drawn parallel to the next, and has no independent value.

(2) A line roughly at right angles to the very flat southwest arc of the main ring, passing over the centre of X and then tangentially to W: the same phenomenon as in (1). Uncertainties as to the precise position and size of circle W are unimportant here, since there are ground marks at the point of tangency. How the line was related to the stones of the Cove, and where an observer would have stood, are problematical. Only from the neighbourhood of W would the bank have covered the natural horizon to the northeast. From a stone at the southwest of X the covestones would have broken the natural horizon (approx. $1.7°$, depending on position). An observer at the broad covestone might have seen a stone on the northeast side of X barely breaking the horizon, but only with the eye near to ground level could the same have been seen right across the circle, that is, from a stone at the southwest. This all strongly suggests that the right-hand (southeast) edge of the broad covestone was the main foresight. Agreement is good: azimuth about $42.7°$ from north. A similar line of sight, not drawn on Fig. 112, might have passed from the lower end of the flat southwest arc, past the Obelisk and over the 'island' bank.

(3) Two parallel lines of sight: one grazes the northern circle X and the Ringstone, the other the southern circle Y and the stone on the east side of the southern entrance. A soil mark extending from one of the stones of Y to the stone D is in a closely similar direction. These alignments are on the rising Moon at its major southern standstill, with azimuths near $144.4°$. The bank could have masked the southern horizon (approx. $1.2°$) for observers at similar distances to those mentioned under (2).

(4) A line grazing Y and the Ringstone could have been towards the setting Moon at major southern standstill (altitude $0.6°$, azimuth $217.1°$).

(5) Lines to the setting midwinter Sun: one is tangent to circle U and then passes through the gap in the Cove, grazing the broader stone; the other is tangential to U and X. The ground levels have been so modified here that it is difficult to estimate altitudes (1.2° and 0.9°?), but azimuths are around 228.5° and 229.0° respectively.

(6) Lines to the setting midsummer Sun: one is from the Obelisk (centre of Y) and then tangential to circle X ; the other is tangential to Y and then grazes the broad covestone (centre of X). The symmetry here is reminiscent of that under (3) and (5). These lines are especially interesting since they pass over the crown of Windmill Hill, presumably just masked by the bank. Note that the bank here is not much longer than was needed for its function as artificial horizon (approx. altitude 1.0°, azimuths 310.2°).

Stukeley's conjecture, that the inner circles were one for the Sun and one for the Moon, was not far from the mark. Both were involved in setting lunar and solar sight lines. How precisely the stones were used is something we shall appreciate better at a later stage. For the time being, it is enough that we are aware of the widespread custom of creating solar and lunar alignments with the help of tangent and centre. It seems that the custom might have been first developed for stellar use, in the context of rows, but that as interest shifted to the Sun and Moon, it was there applied even more assiduously.

Long Barrow, Cursus, Avenue and Row

Cursus, avenue and row have been chiefly presented here as means of directing the eye to the heavens. There is a clear case for saying that in this respect at least they are all extensions of long barrow architecture. The evolutionary succession as it has emerged here is in retrospect a very natural one. A long barrow presented artificial horizons for crosswise viewing from both sides of a single mound, and likewise for lengthwise viewing, which was directed over the burial chamber. A cursus provided artificial horizons for crosswise viewing over banks separated by an appreciable distance, while lengthwise viewing along the bank sections might also pass over a burial mound in line with one of the banks, or a mound athwart the line of a section of the bank. An avenue was designed to allow crosswise viewing, perhaps always with stones to guide the sight—although at Stonehenge this is not certain—but lengthwise view-ing was generally towards a circular rather than linear monument, with a strong preference for passing through a centre or at a tangent to that structure. And finally the rows of stones kept up the traditions of lengthwise viewing, with preferences for lines through centres or along tangents to circular structures,

but in many cases there was no longer any attempt to establish transverse lines of sight. All these monuments were artificial, but in a degree that increases with time. Superficially, long barrow and cursus were modifications of the chalk downs, of the very earth. The avenues and rows, with their stones, and the terminating monuments of stone, were more contrived additions to that landscape. All were a witness to human power, for it was an essential part of their design that they provided what the natural terrain could not, namely a perfect horizon. But all were directed in some way to reminders of death, and in this sense were religious symbols at an ever-increasing level of abstraction. Astronomical explanations do not rule out a religious purpose, of course. Cursus, avenue and row were all in some way closely associated with the trappings of burial. The Kennet Avenue shows us ways in which the settings of stars could be aligned on individual burials.

Did cursus, avenues or rows not function as processional routes, so extending cosmic symbolism into the realm of liturgy? If so, this general idea was not new, for the Ridgeway near Wayland's Smithy had been astronomically aligned long before, and its alignments linked with those of the grave itself. We have found reasons for thinking that the processional function might have been linked with the observational. There are many cases in which observing the rising and setting of the same stars over the long barrows would have been very naturally done—for example at West Kennet, where it was tempting to speculate that the star's entering and leaving the chamber symbolized successively death and rebirth, or perhaps the rising of the spirit of the ancestral dead after its descent to earth. Similar possibilities exist at avenues and rows. Some of the Dartmoor stone rows, for example, apparently incorporated alignments on the rising and setting of the same star, events that might both have been observed as part of a liturgy. The Dorset Cursus had earlier been aligned on rising stars as viewed from the southern end and on setting stars from the northern, and it too might have been used from the different directions on different sorts of occasion.

Many of those who in the past alluded to the *via sacra* idea seem to have had in mind something like the mass perambulations of the churches in historical times, a kind of Mardi Gras procession with a priesthood leading, votive offerings being carried, and so forth. If we are to insist that these various linear monuments were processional ways, it should not simply be because they have a road-like appearance, but because for a person to have observed both a rising and a setting, or more than one such event on the same night, a walk would in most cases have been necessary. With the smaller stone rows and cursus, the idea of a walk between the observation of two events offers no

difficulties. It would have taken at least an hour and a half to have walked the Dorset Cursus from end to end, and much longer had suitable stellar observance been introduced into the procession; but walking was not then an unfamiliar activity.

Walking need not necessarily have been through the middle of the structure, however. This might well have had the character of a sacred space, generally inaccessible, as so many modern commentators seem to wish it to be. (Those who see a cursus as a droveway or an enclosure for cattle must face up to the fact that they are very ill-suited to the purpose.) It is dangerous to assume that what we see as an 'avenue' is for walking on, just as it is dangerous to assume that a complete 'cursus' must of its nature be a closed area. The Lesser Cursus at Stonehenge is one of several that are not. It is a circular argument that proceeds from a comparison of the Greater Cursus with the Lesser Cursus to the conclusion that the latter was never completed. From the point of view of potential ritual stellar observance, closure is in principle entirely inessential.

There are still writers who are content to allude to the possibility of racing on the site of a cursus, or of holding funereal games there—as described by Homer, albeit some two or three thousand years after our structures were built. It is hard to see what evidence one could ever find in support of these ideas, but when we consider the matter at all we are forced to acknowledge one important truth: from the fact that a monument was laid out with reference to the heavens it does not of necessity follow that it was always used with that reference in mind. The rituals of foundation are not necessarily the rituals of use. To take a simple parallel with a later Christian practice: a parish church may have been aligned on the rising of the Sun on the day of its patron saint, but most worship in the church will reflect that fact in no way whatsoever.

The great variety of Neolithic linear structures could have been easily multiplied here, by looking to Scotland or Brittany, for instance. For some of these monuments Alexander Thom offered a highly sophisticated analysis in terms of a series of rules for perfecting lunar alignments. This possibility will be considered briefly at a later stage, in connection with Stonehenge.

The various linear structures discussed in this chapter and Chapter 3 appear to have been aligned at first on the stars alone, and later on stars, Sun and Moon. In other words, there seems to have been a slow evolution in astral religion. Different sorts of risings and settings would no doubt have had different religious meanings. In trying to infer those meanings, one should not forget the fundamental difference between the risings and settings of a particular star,

which are observable in a constant manner *daily* for long periods of the year, and the extreme positions of the Sun, which follow a *yearly* cycle. The pattern of the Moon's movements is of course still more complex. On the other hand, the slow precessional changes in the positions of the stars, although not likely to have made themselves felt in the lifetime of a single person, would eventually have played havoc with any stellar monument, whereas monuments to the Sun and Moon would have been much longer lasting. The changing direction of various linear monuments—for instance the Kennet Avenue and the multiple Dartmoor rows—has here been explained in part in terms of changes necessitated by precession. If accepted, the explanation has important implications: it means that these things were not simply used for a short time and then forgotten. Even a cursus that looks essentially simple, like some elegant razor-shell or boomerang, may turn out to be compounded from several revised alignments. In the Scorton Cursus there is evidence of the recutting of the ditches, and a change of ditch alignment by three degrees, at some time after the initial construction. This is precisely the sort of thing to be expected, if the ditch-directions are determined by the behaviour of the stars. Broadly speaking, however, the presence of circular elements in any monument tends to point to solar or lunar interests.

The general custom of building vast linear structures lasted for more than two millennia. Attention to the stars was not entirely superseded by later fashions for the Sun and Moon. Long after the period of the later Dartmoor rows, Grim's Dyke (or Grim's Ditch) shows how compulsive were the old traditions. This immense earthwork, running chiefly across Oxfordshire, Buckinghamshire and Hertfordshire, is generally thought to have formed a northern boundary to territory occupied by tribes of the Iron Age. It comprises a bank taller than a man ('rampart' would suggest a military purpose, which may or may not have been the case) and a V-shaped ditch, usually somewhat deeper than a man was tall. Occasionally the ditch had banks to both sides. This would have been a singularly bad defensive device. Its sections changed direction abruptly, sometimes at right angles. They were often long, occasionally of the order of a few km, but there have always been gaps of the same order of magnitude, so again the entire system—if a single system it was—would have been ill adapted to defence. The orientation of surviving sections calls for detailed study. A first impression is that some were aligned on Arcturus and Rigel, not far in time from the ninth century BC. This is not to say that their function was astronomico-religious. It might simply be that a boundary was

deemed to be in some way more 'correct' if it incorporated alignments on especially sacred stars.

There has been much allusion to Neolithic monuments as part of a 'ritual landscape'. R. H. Worth made much the same point long ago about the Dartmoor rows, but recent discussion has centred on the fact that in many religions, especially those in which many gods are worshipped, a multiplicity of sacred buildings is used. Since a cursus, for example, is invariably found as part of a complex of monuments, it is easy to suppose that the cursus is somehow explained by its role in the resulting 'sacred geography'. The approach is not inconsistent with ours, although in generally concentrating on monuments in isolation we have run fewer risks of error in relative chronology—Bronze Age monuments, for example, are obviously at best of only secondary relevance to the motivation of those responsible for their Neolithic antecedents. There is no simple succession of monument-types, with one disappearing before another comes on the scene. The Dorchester-on-Thames cursus, for instance, seems to overlie a henge ditch; conversely, at Thornborough one of three henges overlies the cursus. If nothing else, their proximity reveals the continuing sanctity of those places, for—as will be shown in the following chapter—the henges were just as surely aligned on the heavens as long barrow, cursus, avenue and row had been before them.

7

TREEHENGE AND AUBREY CIRCLE

Changes of Style

JUDGING by the numbers of datable artefacts that have been excavated, the farmers of the earlier Neolithic period prospered until some time around 3200 BC. For reasons that are not clear, their fortunes appear to have then gone into relative decline for three or four centuries. Various explanations have been offered for the change, for example plague, and the over-cultivation of land. Volcanic eruptions are known to have led to a worsening of the weather. When the tempo of activity appears to begin to rise again, many new styles are in evidence—in pottery, in burial rite and tomb design, and in the design of monuments generally. It seems likely that part of the reason is to be found in the coming of new peoples and new ideas to southern Britain from continental Europe.

The earliest drift of agriculture across Europe, from its centres of origin in the Middle East long before—say around ten thousand years ago—had been one of the chief determinants of genetic differences in Europe, but the Wessex population seems to have been fairly homogeneous by the end of the third millennium. Even a small number of immigrants could at a much earlier period have had a considerable impact, by introducing agricultural methods that would have enabled rapid increases in the population that had knowledge of them. Assuming intermarriage, great genetic differences between the native and the immigrant could in this way have been rapidly reduced by relatively small migrations. Pigmentation would have been one very obvious difference at the time: a lighter skin colour had long provided northern peoples with an evolutionary advantage in regions of low sunlight, enhancing as it does the production of vitamin D, a preventative of rickets. The gradations of pigmentation across Europe are known to follow quite closely the advancing prehistoric tide of the earliest agriculturalists. In the third millennium, however, other genetic differences are found in Britain that bring themselves more readily to archaeological notice, namely a stocky build, and a broad skull with

flattish hind part (occiput). The earliest Neolithic agricultural peoples of Britain—themselves obviously a racial mixture—were generally long-headed (dolichocephalic).

It is skeletons with the new physical characteristics that tend to be found with Beaker pottery in Britain and central Europe, although the type is not predominant in the Iberian peninsula, which some see as the homeland for the Bell Beaker culture. It is all too easy to look for simple formulas—if not as simple as the caricature 'long barrows, long skulls; round barrows, round skulls'—but the truth is obviously complex. Bell Beaker ceramics seem to have been evolving in Iberia long before they were known elsewhere, and they persisted there long after they were replaced elsewhere. The ceramics were elegant in form, resembling a bell—of the sort that is pinched at the waist, like a cloche-hat, with many hybrid varieties and novel decoration. They arrived on the European scene with great suddenness, say over a century or so on either side of 2500 BC, but the means of their arrival had seemingly been prepared long before. There were certain Iberian customs in the building of passage graves, for instance, that had earlier spread beyond the Pyrenees, even to Britain and Ireland, in such a way that it can be assumed that sea-routes were established from there long before the beginning of the third millennium.

The maritime groups responsible for carrying the Bell Beaker ceramic forms to Britain, assuming that it was such groups that settled, are said to have been not racially typical of the Beaker peoples of southern Spain and Portugal, but they did introduce Iberian pottery and much more besides. So many of the objects they seem to have introduced in Britain and elsewhere—copper daggers, arrowheads, archers' wristguards, dress fasteners and gold ornaments, for instance—are found associated with Bell Beakers in Iberia at an earlier date, that this has as good a claim as any place to have been at the centre of the 'Bell Beaker explosion'. It is likely that they had learned much about the working of copper and gold from other parts of Europe—the Balkans and Poland were both more important centres by the beginning of the fourth millennium—but this transfer of knowledge long preceded the sudden spread of Beaker influence. The eastern groups are thought to have introduced wheeled transport into northern Europe, and perhaps also the domesticated horse. The style of pottery characteristic of the Beaker culture is found in areas of Hungary, Germany, Poland, the Netherlands and Belgium. It is found in England, western Scotland, and parts of Ireland (north and southwest); in Brittany, the Rhone Valley and the Mediterranean coast of France into Catalonia; in pockets in Italy, Sicily, and Sardinia; and in the centre of the Iberian peninsula as well as on the western and Mediterranean coasts.

No matter what its origins, the natives of Wessex must have found many aspects of the new culture exciting. This was a time of rapid change in the astronomical design of monuments, but again, it is difficult to decide whether the new styles were introduced in their finished forms by Beaker people, or whether they represent a combination of local tradition with Beaker cult practice—for example paying now greater religious attention to the Sun. The history of the Grendon long barrow shows that a simplistic equation of 'Beaker' and 'circular' will not do, but earlier continental influences on circular design can hardly be doubted. The Iberian peninsula shows many signs of sophisticated tomb-building practice from the fourth millennium that might prove to have been linked to a cult of the Sun. One of the richest groups is at Los Millares (Almeria), near the joining of the rivers Andarax and Huechar. A typical Millaran decoration is a circle with rays that is usually now interpreted as a Sun. A pot with several such 'suns' inside it is shown in Plate 16. (It has to be said that there are arguments for making these out to be eyes rather than suns, however.) The Iberian tombs are frequently circular mounds containing circular chambers into which an entrance-passage leads. There is such a plain resemblance between these and chamber tombs in France, Britain and Ireland that it would be perverse to pretend that they all arose independently; but the to-ing and fro-ing of imitation is another matter, and influences on the design of later Wessex round barrows and circular henges could have come from many quarters. Circular chamber tombs in most of the centres mentioned were in the fourth millennium often enclosed within walls of larger stones, megaliths, primarily as a means of retaining the central mound of stones or earth, and it is conceivable that here we have the beginnings of the idea of a circle of megaliths without mound. A more likely explanation, however, is that the stones were substituted for timber posts, which were used in a way to be explained in the course of this chapter. In short, the characteristic Wessex combination of rings of posts or stone with banks and ditches may be found a simple astronomical explanation.

After roughly 2500 BC, not only did burial styles change in outward form, but they were used increasingly for the display of wealth and power. By the second millennium, the majority of known—which is to say generally notable—graves contain only a single burial, and the fact that ever richer grave goods were included in them points to an increasing differentiation of rank and power within the population. Judging by the weapons included with grave goods and the incidence of fortifications, the population as a whole had become more warlike, but again, there is no firm evidence that there was strife across the divide between native and immigrant, or that a Beaker culture established

an autocracy in Britain. External cultural influences were making themselves felt, but the pattern of existence was changing for other reasons. In Wessex agriculture, for instance, the farming of sheep was gradually yielding place to that of pigs: it has been suggested that the invasion of worked-out land by scrub and weeds, and particularly by bracken, favoured this substitution, since the pig thrives on, and so limits, the spreading roots of bracken. Cereals were perhaps eaten less, and meat—including much from hunting—was eaten more. The middle of the third millennium was evidently a time of rapid social change for a variety of reasons, with consequences that are mirrored in religious practice. For example, just as the Beaker people of Bohemia and Moravia favoured placing the dead in a north–south direction, so—as Sir Richard Colt Hoare, William Cunnington and John Thurnam all observed long ago—in the Beaker culture of Wessex the heads of the dead (or only of males, as they thought) were placed to the north. Bearing in mind the various marked preferences shown for the alignment of Dartmoor cists, there were doubtless socially complex rules of some sort in use in all of these places. To discover them would be to come a stage nearer to appreciating the astral element in the religion that dictated them.

The first inhabitants of Britain and Ireland with agricultural knowledge, living in the late fifth and the fourth millennia BC, had settled both highland and lowland areas, and what they had built depended on the materials at hand. The use of large stones in the passage graves of the later Neolithic period was natural enough in Ireland, the Orkneys, and the West of Scotland, but the Neolithic people of the southern chalk downlands, where stone is scarcer, were at first inclined to build their long barrows and related monuments mainly out of chalk. When the people of Wessex did eventually turn their attention to stone, it was not for its use as rubble in mound-building—here chalk had many advantages—but to create markers more permanent than timber. Megaliths of the sort found at Avebury and Stonehenge, stones that had to be dragged many miles, had a grandeur of their own—and here there was surely a strong element of keeping-up-with-the-Joneses.

Their ancestors had chosen the chalk downs in the first place most probably because the soil there was easily worked, and not because there was no forest cover. The present state of the downs is misleading: there were then thick oak forests everywhere. It goes without saying that all Neolithic peoples made much use of wood. Mention was made earlier of the extensive use of wood by the Bandkeramik peoples of Europe in the building of their long houses. There are signs that even in the fourth millennium BC steps were being taken to control tree growth (through pollarding, for instance), and that the people of

southern Britain were capable of ambitious and even subtle work in wood. The remains of a footpath of split planks of oak, ash and lime that stretched at least two kilometres, complete with rails and pegging (these mainly of ash and elder), have been found in swamp in the Somerset Levels. A short section of this, the so-called 'Sweet Track', now in the British Museum, has been dated very precisely by tree-ring dating to 3807/3806 BC. This is not unique. Another Neolithic causeway that crossed boggy moorland, this time about 3m wide and of logs, has been found at Nieuw-Dordrecht, southeast of Emmen in the northern Netherlands. Woodworking tools from the Bronze Age and Iron Age have also been found at many centres, and fragments of waterlogged wood found at Bargeroosterveld in Drenthe hint at the probable skills of those who used them. Although these fragments date from only 1200 BC or thereabouts, it has been shown that they were associated with a rectangular setting of posts that had lintels fixed to the uprights using mortise and tenon joints, and that the lintels terminated in wooden imitations of the horns of cattle. Tenons at the lower ends of the uprights had been fitted into mortises in planks on the ground.

For obvious reasons, relatively few items of wood have survived except in suitably damp conditions where they have resisted decay, but there is much later historical evidence that wood played an important part in the cultural and religious outlook of early European peoples. Although liable to decay, wood was no doubt revered for its various associations. The tree had life, and changed with the seasons. It provided shelter, and was the medium of the home and the temple. There is what might be taken as evidence for this reverence at Stonehenge, where by not too great a stretch of the imagination several of the stones (those numbered 2, 16, 52, perhaps 56 and also the Slaughter Stone) are tooled in what might be imitation of the bark of an oak (see Plate 29). Another, the fallen trilithon (59), has tooling across it reminiscent of that of a beech.

Henges of Timber

The jointing technique used for the lintels at Stonehenge indicates an indebtedness to the practice of carpenters. Wood was used in the construction of almost all of the monuments so far discussed, even though it would rarely have been outwardly prominent in the finished result. There was a whole class of monuments, however, that were themselves primarily wooden, and in this chapter and the next an attempt will be made to reconstruct their probable outward appearances and function. The fashion for the building of *timber* henge monuments, rings of timber posts surrounded by banks and ditches, was well

established some centuries before the earthen round barrows—which were likewise often surrounded by bank and ditch and at least one circle of posts. In the earlier discussion of Windmill Hill one possible evolutionary sequence was offered for monuments composed of rings of banks and ditches. While Windmill Hill did not systematically incorporate rings of posts, it did make use of several posts in one capacity or another. Posts could well have been used to help establish lines of sight, as they had been used for the scaling posts of long barrows at a much earlier date. There is no suggestion here that such an explanation must be paraded every time a post is found on a site, but if one is to accept the argument for the affinity of the elements of Windmill Hill to long barrows then posts are quite simply to be expected. And from thence could have come the idea of a ring of posts. If every short length of ditch was provided with its complement of one or more posts, the idea of a post ring would have arisen in a perfectly natural way. Something similar seems to have happened at certain decidedly *linear* monuments, not necessarily only those on a grand scale.

Rings of stones or posts are usually treated independently of round barrows, simply because they are assumed to have had different religious functions. That the design of the rings influenced in some small measure that of the barrows, however, surely follows from what will be demonstrated below: they shared an astronomical function. This presumably reflected a shared religious context. The situation reminds one of the 'long barrows': some had burials within them while others did not, but both could be used to provide a horizon across which the stars could be seen leaving and entering the mound.

The general description 'henge-monument' was formed from the name of Stonehenge, and is said to have been first used by Thomas Kendrick and Christopher Hawkes in 1932. This followed an earlier coining of 'Woodhenge' for the timber monument near Stonehenge, discovered from the air in 1925. The phrase was applied to stone rings such as those at Arbor Low (Derbyshire) and the Ring of Brodgar (or Brogar, Orkney Islands). They were roughly circular rings of uprights surrounded by a bank and ditch, broken by one or more entrances. In 1939 Stuart Piggott published an account of Dorset rings, and classified the henges by the number of entrances. Between one and three hundred are now known in Britain—the number depending on the definition chosen—the majority only from aerial photographs of crop marks, and there are many others on the continent. Richard Atkinson's definition (1951, published with his account of the Dorchester excavations) has been perhaps the most influential. He demanded that the ditch be *within* the bank; but he was prepared to admit a circle of pits or simply burials, in place of uprights of wood

or stone. The tendency is now to be less exclusive: sites with nothing known beyond a circular bank and ditch are occasionally treated as henges, but presumably only in the pious hope that something will one day turn up in the inner area.

For obvious reasons, definitions concentrate more on *structure*—which can often be seen or reconstructed—than on *function*, which is more problematical. They may have functioned at different levels—say for the worship of gods or ancestors or stars, for invoking help from any or all of these, or for the rituals of burial or sacrifice. The placing of the entrances and other features by which archaeologists classify them might have been dictated by any or by none of these alternatives, and intuitive assessments of evolution in structural style can be very misleading. There is, on the other hand, much to be said for the common assumption that the earthworks of ditch and bank surrounding 'causewayed enclosures' evolved in time into the smaller and neater versions around henges. We are now in a position to explain this evolution, but the implications of the very phrase 'causewayed enclosure' should not escape notice. A causeway is usually regarded as a means of access. The builders of the mounds and ditches between the causeways might just possibly have responded to this description in the way that Christopher Wren would have done on hearing St Paul's described as a 'windowed enclosure'.

Once the earliest type of ring (of the Windmill Hill variety) is understood as a ring of single-ditched long barrows, directed to the risings and settings of stars, then it is easy to understand how a shift of interest from the stars to the Sun or Moon led to more strictly circular ditch systems. The reason is that their rising and setting positions mark out nearly symmetrical arcs in their cycles. Even the old rule of observing at right angles to the ditch could still be applied, for with a circle this will allow observation in *all* possible directions, given the right observation point. Of course a marker or pair of markers, whether stones or posts, is now needed for that observation point. Two would have been preferable—one as foresight and one as backsight—and a similar number for each phenomenon observed. Looked at in this way, the henge, comprising ditch and bank and a handful of markers, seems an almost inescapable development. But it is in the details that the interest really lies, for many new techniques were to be added to the rich traditions of linear mound design, leading on in due course to the astronomical systems of historical times, known from written texts.

Half an hour's walk to the northeast of Stonehenge are the relics of a henge monument once thought to be no more than a very large disc barrow. That this

was a reasonable inference from its appearance can be judged by an old local name for it, 'the Dough Cover'. In 1925, however, Squadron Leader G. S. M. Insall, flying a Sopwith Snipe, observed circular patterns in a wheat-field then covering the site. Excavation by Maude Cunnington and her husband B. H. Cunnington between 1926 and 1928 revealed six roughly concentric (but oval) rings of holes that had once held wooden posts. (The Cunningtons also investigated five smaller circles to the south of Woodhenge). Those posts once covered an area larger than the largest ring of stones at neighbouring Stonehenge, although the enclosing bank and ditch were smaller. It is probable that the timber structure had decayed before the last phases of construction at Stonehenge, but the two will prove to have been intimately related in function, and presumably for a time were of comparable importance.

Woodhenge will be considered in detail in Chapter 8, together with a number of other large henges. The largest Woodhenge oval, with its longer axis 43 m across, was surrounded by a bank and ditches, of roughly twice that diameter. The oval with the largest posts was the third from the outside, and each of its sixteen posts was of considerable girth. Each had its own ramp to enable the post to be set in position, and perhaps replaced in the course of time. When the monument was named 'Woodhenge', after its famous neighbour, it was without any thought for potential analogues of the 'hanging' lintel-stones that provide the second component in the name of Stonehenge, but 'henge' proves to have been a well chosen word, for as will be seen when we eventually come to analyse the wooden structure, it almost certainly incorporated lintels.

In 1929, again from the air, Insall discovered traces of another structure that was later proved to have once sported a ring of massive posts—oak trunks more than three-quarters of a metre in diameter (as shown by Grahame Clark's excavation, 1935). This monument was at Arminghall, Norfolk, and radiocarbon dating suggests that it belongs to the end of the fourth millennium (2490±150 bc, 3150±300 BC). From Woodhenge Mrs Cunnington turned her attention to the Sanctuary south of Avebury (excavated 1930). It has already been noted that there was once a set of six (here circular rather than oval) rings of wooden posts on that site, not to mention the later stone rings.

Not far to the north of Woodhenge lies the Durrington Walls enclosure, the second or third largest known henge monument in Britain, judged by its earthwork. This is an untidy oval, outlined by a wide bank with a vast internal ditch—typically five or six metres deep. It is about half a kilometre across and contained two sites on which were placed successions of circular structures of timber posts, the meaning of which will be considered in Chapter 8. Geoffrey Wainwright directed a rescue excavation of this giant earthwork before a new

road was built across it in the 1960s. (It had been subject to exploratory cuttings in 1951–2.) It is indeed massive: he estimated that 900,000 man-hours would have been required to complete the project, a figure based on the excavation of 49,000 cubic metres of chalk with antler picks, baskets and ropes—more evidence, if any were needed, of the strong motivation of the society responsible. Not far in time from the date of its construction, say 2500 BC, a large circular timber structure was erected inside one of its two entrances, that at the southeast. This structure was about equal in diameter to the most obvious circle of stones at Stonehenge (the lintelled sarsen stones), and had concentric rings of oak posts. A similar but smaller circle of timber was built 145 m to the north of the first (centre to centre), approached from the south by an avenue, again of timber posts. There were perhaps three concentric rings in this case. The north and south rings now lie under the new A345 road, but other rings remain to be excavated at the Durrington site, which has all the appearance of the centre of a vigorous religious cult.

Each of the rings in the southern Durrington circle was built and then rebuilt to a modified plan. Extracting the old posts and substituting new ones can have been no easy task—one post hole was 2.2 m across and 2.9 m deep, implying a post weighing several tonnes. (Green oak would have weighed around 1070 kg/cu m, and well-seasoned oak roughly four-fifths as much.) In many cases ramps had been cut to ease the erection of some of the largest posts. The problem of substitution of posts in the avenue is of great interest, for when the posts of the linking avenue were replaced they were put in a different alignment. This might be seen as an example of carelessness, that is, as an indication that direction was not of great importance, but it might also hint at an attempt to *revise* an alignment on the horizon position of a particular star. It will later be suggested that this was so and that the star was Vega.

Wainwright followed with a series of excavations at what were ostensibly similar sites, at Marden (1969) and Mount Pleasant (1970–1). Marden in the Vale of Pewsey is only 15 km or so to the north of Durrington Walls, rather more than halfway to Avebury. Again he found traces of rings of timber posts there. Mount Pleasant, to the south, is more distant—near Dorchester (Dorset), and only about 8 km from the sea. There, too, post holes were found that suggested a structure of the Woodhenge type.

Two more recent discoveries of Dorset timber henges from the same period as that at Mount Pleasant deserve mention. One was an enclosure at Flagstones, only 200 m to the west of Mount Pleasant, the other a colossal timber circle at Greyhound Yard in the centre of the modern town of Dorchester. Carvings were found on the sides of the Flagstones ditch (around 2650 BC), the ditch

being of a type that was very probably astronomically inspired. A curved line of holes that had held twenty-one massive posts was uncovered at Greyhound Yard, each post about a metre in diameter and standing in a pit about 2.5 m deep. It is thought that the line of posts might have been part of a circle no less than 380 m in diameter, comprising some 600 oaks in all. There is evidence for a ditch and bank outside the ring.

There are many other sites where smaller henges of timber have left evidence of their existence, usually in the form of cropmarks visible in aerial photographs. Taken together, these 'treehenges'—as they might reasonably be called—seem to span most of the third millennium BC and some of the second. Although they and numerous circles of stones were evidently being erected simultaneously in Britain, yet for reasons already given, the wooden structures were very probably prototypes in many respects for their more permanent cousins, and for this reason they are considered first. There is much to be learned from them about Stonehenge. At the risk of upsetting our chronological sense, however, we shall begin with another, and much later, species of 'treehenge', one that is found in large numbers in the Netherlands, where stone has always been in short supply.

Round barrows are numerous there—perhaps as many as 2500 survive, and many hundreds have been excavated. They are frequently found to have had rings of posts associated with them: the first post circle monument in the country was found by J. H. Holwerda in 1908. Some of their many forms will first be considered, and the possibility that they embody astronomical orientations. This idea has often been considered in a very general way, but has almost as often been dismissed, for quite the wrong reasons. A suitable case to study first will be that of a very modest grave mound that once stood at Harenermolen, a village in the north of the country. The chief reason for studying such tombs as these is their simplicity, and the fact that from the peculiarity of the terrain the decayed rings of wooden posts could be very accurately charted. Many of the posts at Durrington Walls left similar clues as to their precise positions and sizes, in the form of 'post-pipes', but this is not a common situation in England, and Durrington Walls is anything but simple. Also in the Harenermolen case, two particularly well-defined circles of sandy soil—the ditch boundary—remained outlined in the terrain, throwing some light on the principles by which the tomb was laid out. Clearly, the fewer the geometrical constructions superimposed by a modern hand the better.

The Dutch barrow rings are not without near equivalents in England. Perhaps the first timber circle to be reasonably well recorded in any country was that around barrow 23 in the Callis (or Calais) Wold group in Humberside.

(This is about 20 km east of York, in the former East Riding of the county.) Excavated by J. R. Mortimer in 1865 and 1868, it was found to contain a central oval grave cut into a rock floor, with a crouched burial. Surrounding it were two circles of post holes numbering twenty-three (the inner, diameter 6.55 m) and twenty-four (the outer, diameter 8.53 m), with four additional posts outside these and perhaps six trapped between them. Some of the posts had survived in the mound at that time to a height of a metre or so. The barrow was surrounded by a berm and ditch. At Bleasdale in Lancashire, at the very end of the same century, Shadrach Jackson and Boyd Dawkins found another fine example, which was re-excavated by W. J. Varley in 1938. It was found that a post circle there had surrounded a low turf barrow, in the middle of which was a grave with two inverted collared urns containing cremations. The ring, of eleven oak posts that are marked today by concrete pillars, had been embedded in the mound itself, which was surrounded by a ditch and then a bank. A radiocarbon assay for one of the oak posts puts the probable date in the range 1900 to 1720 BC. The similarity with continental examples is obvious, but one unusual geometrical property distinguishes it from the rest. There was an outer ring of thirty-two posts with stakes between them, about 45.7 m in diameter and double the diameter of the bank round the barrow, which touched it internally at an entrance to the east. A double avenue led up to this.

Mortimer interpreted what he found at Callis Wold as the remains of a wattle-and-daub hut with a conical roof. Four external posts he saw as potential masts for guy-ropes. He published his excavation only in 1905, when timber circles from excavations in Denmark and Germany were being published.

The habit of seeing the remains of houses in these circles was at that time almost universal. Occasionally classical Greek influences were dominant. J. H. Holwerda, building a model for the Leiden Museum in 1909 to show the original form of another such timber structure, gave it a dome-shaped vault resembling Mycenean beehive tombs. As W. Glasbergen wryly observed, he needed iron nails to hold it together. The 'conical hut' interpretation—applied almost immediately on their discovery to Woodhenge and the Sanctuary—is still received wisdom in some quarters, and was lent much weight by Stuart Piggott in the late 1930s and after. Proving that it is mistaken, which it almost certainly is, will require a painstaking demonstration that there is a much simpler explanation, which calls on no engineering miracle.

There are some who wish to draw a distinction between large 'henge-like' structures and the more modest timber-enclosed barrows, but there are at least two examples of the latter in North Brabant, and others in England, that beg

to be interpreted as having carried lintels—compare them with the Stonehenge trilithons—since their posts occur mostly in pairs, with larger spaces between. (Lintelled pairs of wooden posts, with two uprights and a third timber across the top, are sometimes called *trixylons*.)

Barrow Rings in the Low Countries

In 1954, in a doctoral dissertation, W. Glasbergen presented an important and thorough study of a series of barrows in a district of North Brabant known as the Eight Beatitudes, to the southwest of Eindhoven, and near to the Belgian border. (The name, in Dutch 'Acht Zaligheden', is a play on words, eight villages having names ending with 'sel', making for eight 'selligheden'.) By coincidence, the geographical latitude is roughly that of the area between Avebury and Stonehenge. The numerous mounds in the district had often been dug into by farmers and shepherds, who occasionally put their finds back into the ground as an act of piety, and by nineteenth-century archaeologists, who did not. At various times the barrows have been raided for sand, flattened for ease of ploughing, and planted with trees. Archaeologists have been allowed to remove many of the trees—but not the tree planted atop one barrow to commemorate the birth of Queen Juliana in 1909. One barrow was dug into for an air-raid shelter, and many suffered from land reclamation and the ravages of the Second World War.

In seven campaigns between 1948 and 1951, thirty-four barrows and a ring-ditch urnfield were examined, mainly using the method of excavation by quadrants that had first been applied by A. E. van Giffen in 1916. About a quarter of the barrows excavated were found to belong to two or more periods, often widely separated, and often with changes in style that might indicate changes of ritual. The same has often been found in Britain, and proves at the very least that the sites long retained their essential sanctity. Supplementing the new findings with the numerous excavations by Van Giffen—and many more have been added since, without changing the picture materially—Glasbergen distinguished five important classes of rings of wooden posts, and some minor variants (Fig. 113). Radiocarbon dating has since shown the rings to have been mostly from the first seven or eight centuries of the second millennium, in other words, later than the first large henges in Britain.

Holwerda's idea of wooden domes was mistaken, but Van Giffen found that in the Netherlands generally in some early barrows the dead had been interred sitting or lying in a contracted position in a cavity of beehive shape, perhaps initially constructed of wattle. The sandy ground in which these are

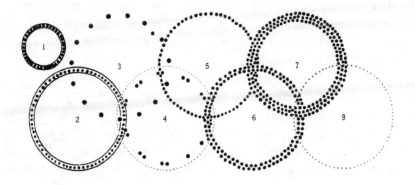

FIG. 113. W. Glasbergen's types of post rings, as found surrounding barrows. Even when he was writing, more than 200 such rings were known in the Netherlands alone, many of the simpler rings being slightly oval in form.

invariably found is easily worked. The cylindrical enclosure seems sometimes to have rested on a rectangular base (giving rise to the name 'hut grave'), sometimes a circular one with a ditch or ring of stakes, or both, around it. The grave goods—corded and herringbone beakers, flint axes and daggers—point to a Beaker culture in a late Neolithic period. In the Middle Bronze Age there was a veritable flourishing of styles and numbers of timber circles. Occasionally the posts were placed just inside the edge of the barrow, sometimes just at its edge, and in some cases both were surrounded by a bank, in a style common in Britain. Inhumation continued, with long trunk coffins placed in rectangular pits. From an early Bronze Age period, however, the body and coffin were often cremated, keeping a rectangular cavity, but gradually this custom gave way to cremation on a smaller scale, perhaps without a coffin, and with the final remains placed in a modest bowl-shaped cavity. The preference for cremation over inhumation seems to have been a regional question, and there are no easy rules. When in Brabant a switch from the first to the second was taking place, in Drenthe and its surroundings it seems almost as though the reverse was happening.

If the sense of orderly alignment of the immediate burial was being lost, what of the arrangement of the posts around the barrows? Even with a small number of posts it is difficult to analyse all potential alignments on the Sun, Moon and stars, and the posts were often very numerous. In the case of one German site there seem to have been well over three hundred posts, and there is a clear tendency for numbers to increase with time. The nine types illustrated in Fig. 113 are numbered in a roughly chronological sequence, although with

much overlapping. Types 1 and 2 are Neolithic, and although they must have influenced later developments to some extent, they differ somewhat in the manner in which they are set in the ground. An interpretation of the main style (style 3) will be offered shortly.

Circles of slender stakes might have had a very different function from circles of posts. Stake circles might have been quite trivial—meant, perhaps, to support wattle fencing to keep out animals during the early rituals of burial. If parallels with burial rites in historical times are in order, then this might be a sign that funeral rites lasted many days. (Ten is the number of days between the two high points of the rituals in the burial of a Bulgarian, as reported by Ibn Fadlân, and it is also the period needed for the construction of Beowulf's barrow, in Anglo-Saxon literature.) Several similar stake circles have been found in Britain, and Sir Cyril Fox argued that they were probably tied (probably with wattle), since although they were slender and under pressure from a certain weight of earth, they kept their parallelism. In the cases he discussed, the stake circles were quite regularly spaced and often multiple and concentric, and so perhaps had a temporary constructional value, say to get the form of the barrow and its post-structure right, in much the same way as was done at the earthen long barrows.[1]

When cremation occurred, the remains were placed in the grave while they were still smouldering, as is shown by the sintered sand at the grave's edge. The rectangular settings of stakes at the centres of post circles do not necessarily indicate a pyre, however, for in many cases there is no trace of any cremation associated with them. Small stakes in a rectangular arrangement presumably indicate a mortuary house—they were often removed before the barrow was erected. In some cases very substantial posts are set in the same way, and some of these seem to have reached to the top of the barrow, perhaps even above it,

---

1   Pits have been commonly found near the graves, and presumably had a ritual use. The occurrence of cremated bones in them has implications for the meaning of post holes, where similar deposits are found. As in many similar cases in Britain, the posts themselves were clearly regarded as having some special status. This suspicion is reinforced by a contrast between two nearby Bronze Age mounds in Gelderland. In the first of these, with a simple cremation, there is *no* peripheral construction but there are perhaps fifty secondary interments around the edge. In the second, an elaborately prepared grave of a child, complete with mortuary house and a post circle (Glasbergen type 5), there were no later interments whatsoever. Mounds and rings of posts were probably always the exception rather than the norm, and there are reasons for suspecting that common burials were not under mounds at all, but under the common heath. Posts and rings of posts were somehow bearers of a special meaning. Glasbergen mentions a historical example of the awe they inspired: a Roman writer (Amianus Marcellinus) says of the Alamanni (a German tribe) that they were afraid of fenced-in barrows.

as Fox showed was the case in a Welsh example (Sheeplays 293', Llantwit, Glamorgan). In some cases they are only a pair, one at the head and one at the foot of the burial. Even given a rectangle, they are set in the direction of the burial they surround. Several appear to have been aligned on the star Capella. All this is reminiscent of the much earlier practice at English long barrows (for example with the D-posts at Wayland's Smithy and elsewhere).

There are some avenues of post holes radiating from barrows with compound rings of posts. A good example at Zeijen (Drenthe) could also have been aligned on Capella. The usual interpretation, following Fox, is that such avenues show the direction to the local settlement, from which the funeral procession approached the grave. The idea is not necessarily inconsistent with alignment on a star: it is all a question of which came first, an arbitrary placing of the grave, which would have determined the line to the settlement, or the line to a star, which would have determined the direction of the grave. Settlement or not, there is some support for the astronomical alternative, since English barrows are often to be seen against the sky. Fox himself gave this custom a name that is still often used, 'false crest siting', without appreciating that there might be an astronomical reason for it.

The rectangular arrangement of substantial posts was envisaged by Van Giffen as the forerunner of temple cults of the dead. Here there are many historical examples seeming to continue the old ways. Pausanias (in the second century AD) tells of buildings of columns with roofs like that of a temple, placed over a grave mound by the Sicyonians. (Sicyon was near Corinth in Greece.) Glasbergen drew attention to burial customs in his own day in the province of Friesland, and more pointedly in Nordhorn, just over the German border from the province of Overijssel. There a trapezoidal mortuary house with a tent-like roof was placed over a grave for six weeks, being covered for the first eight days by a black pall that was afterwards given to the poor.

Most of the Dutch landscape is of course relatively flat, and although in most places there was forest near at hand, the habit of choosing somewhat elevated sites meant that the horizon as viewed was usually near-level. A few tendencies are worthy of note. The posts often pair off, north and south, reasonably accurately, although often only over one half of the ring, the western half or the eastern—of which more shortly. There was an odd number of posts in rather fewer than half of all easily counted cases, and the question then arises as to whether there was any system in the placing of the residual post.

There are at least two ways of judging which is the residual post. Where posts are paired off north and south, for example, there is often an isolated post remaining due west of centre. (When there is north–south pairing with an even

number, there are usually no posts due east and west, as there might well have been.) Symmetry around the east–west line is not the only kind, however. Another property of many of the rings—first remarked upon by Humphrey Case for an English example but worked out in more detail for Dutch post circles by Johan Gerritsen—is what might be called their 'radial alignment'. Expressed loosely, it is that however badly the post ring approximates to a circle, *the lines joining opposite posts all pass rather accurately through a single point.* This point is rarely at the precise centre of the ring. It was not usually within the area of the burial but rather immediately outside it.

For reasons that will become clear from pages 303–7 below, the rule is best reinterpreted in relation not to the lines joining post *centres* but to lines of sight *tangential* to the posts. (When checking a plan to see whether the rule applies, however, the difference between a common tangent to opposite posts and a line drawn through post-centres can usually be ignored, for reasons that should be obvious.) Sighting was presumably along a line trapped between opposite posts and passing over a slender stake. No trace of such a central stake is ever found, but it would have been very slender, and would have been removed after serving its purpose. Since the 'centre' of the rays is often found to lie to one side of the coffin or mortuary house, where traces of these remain, it seems likely that a stake was tied to, or propped against, one or the other of these.

With the rule of radial alignment in mind, the question of which was the residual post (when the total number was odd) can be asked again, and it need not yield the same answer as before. The question needs more attention than can be given to it here, but the following conclusions are tentatively offered: (1) Radial alignment is not universal. It is common when the number of posts is even but rarer when the number is odd. (2) When it is found with an odd number of posts, the residual post is often at the southwest, and is a post in line with which the setting midwinter Sun could have been observed—it is so at Harenermolen, for example. (3) Where no single 'false centre' can be found there is often a suspicion that *two* such centres were used. (4) The false centres do not appear to have been chosen with any deep geometrical principle in mind, for instance as points that would guarantee equal spacing of posts around an oval.

This all serves to give the impression that radial alignment was simply used as a means of introducing moderate but not exact uniformity into the spacing of posts around the circle. There are cases where the principle may be used today as an aid in estimating the positions of posts in damaged or unexcavated regions, and even (as H. T. Waterbolk has found) in detecting

mistakes in excavation plans, although since the rule was not universal it must obviously be applied with caution. What it can tell us about the technique of setting out the posts should not be exaggerated, however. It does not—as is sometimes claimed—argue against the astronomical orientation of the posts. On the contrary, it is quite consistent with the astronomical use not only of circular rings of posts but of many types of oval. where it still seems to have been applied. As an introduction to the astronomical technique, a specimen ring will be examined, one that can point us in the direction of deeper basic principles.

Harenermolen and the Counting of Holes

The barrow to be considered was that at Harenermolen, excavated in 1922 by A. E. van Giffen. Van Giffen pioneered three methods of barrow excavation, and in this case he used the so-called *sector method*, a time-consuming procedure, but one that allowed him to map the structure in fine detail, starting from four vertical sections. Inevitably, the barrow was destroyed in the course of the excavation. His influence in archaeology was considerable. Sir Cyril Fox, who adopted his methods, tells in his *Life and Death in the Bronze Age* of how during the Second World War he remonstrated with an officer of the Royal Netherlands Army who had set up a machine-gun post on a barrow at Six Wells, only to discover that the man was a student of Van Giffen's, who took the point. It could be added that the British army at the time was not above using the Dartmoor stone rows for target practice; and that, short of hills in the Netherlands for tank exercises, the Allies chose to use Bronze Age barrows instead. But then, they were not Fox's students.

The Harenermolen site lies at the northern end of a sandy glacial fold, the Hondsrug (Dog's Back), running south from the town of Groningen and through the province of Drenthe. It dates from a period when stones rather than timber posts were commonly used in British circles, but stone was scarce in the Drenthe neighbourhood. (There were some erratic boulders, the largest of which were incorporated in the many dolmens in the province.) From the present point of view, the most interesting parts of the barrow were its two roughly concentric rings of posts, the outer numbering eleven and the inner fifty-one. The inner posts were erected in a ditch that was then filled with soil. This simple method was typical of Beaker practice, but was not as sound, from a structural point of view, as the method of digging individual holes. Over this post ditch the barrow stood, extending about a metre and a half *outside* it. When

the wood and other organic materials decayed, a sandy loam of a different colour remained, giving its later interpreters a three-dimensional notion of how matters stood at the various stages of building, lasting many centuries. An astronomical analysis to be given below rests on measurements taken from Van Giffen's survey directly, but the best analysis of the evidence as a whole is that in a study by J. N. Lanting, who distinguished six Harenermolen periods. (Fig. 114 shows a general plan.)

In the *first period*, the mound was built up to about 90 cm in height, and in diameter approached 12 m. It had a shallow east–west grave chamber, and the silhouette of a skeleton (skull and legs only) was found in it, the head to the east, and facing south. The grave was surrounded by its ditch with the fifty-one posts, each of 15 to 20 cm diameter. This first structure is dated to between perhaps 2100 and 2000 BC, making it close in time to the high period of activity at Stonehenge and a few centuries after the period of the great henges of southern Britain.

In the *second period* at Harenermolen, from about 2000 to 1500 BC, there seems to have been no boundary structure, and indeed any remains of the first ring of posts were then evidently covered over.

The circle of eleven posts from a *third period* is of great interest. Lanting placed it in the Middle Bronze Age, say between 1500 and 1100 BC. Its builders seem to have had some sort of reference points before them still, for the centre of their own circle was only 20 cm or so distant from that of the first circle—even though the base ground was no longer clear.

The *fourth period* is archaeologically the richest, with various bronze artefacts left in its urns (of the Late Bronze Age), but neither it nor the later periods concern us.

In trying to make sense of the design that so many post rings (mostly circles) seem to share, to a greater or lesser degree, broadly three different approaches have been taken—arithmetical, geometrical, and astronomical—or a combination of them. (There are of course those who believe as a point of principle that it is wrong to attempt to find any rational scheme behind the creation of the rings, even circularity.) One of the attractions of the arithmetical approach is that it seems likely to offer quick returns, since counting seems a relatively simple matter. (It is deceptively simple. There is all too often a problem of deciding what is to be counted.) Can there have been some deep meaning in the numbers of posts in these barrow rings—in the fifty-one, for example? In view of the many different arrangements and numbers of posts in Dutch post rings, all culturally related, the idea must seem at first sight unlikely, and yet—especially in relation to potential calendars—it surfaces in

the literature of 'astro-archaeology' with great regularity. The outermost ring at Mount Pleasant (Site IV) had between fifty and fifty-four posts. These numbers are not far removed from fifty-six, the number of so-called Aubrey

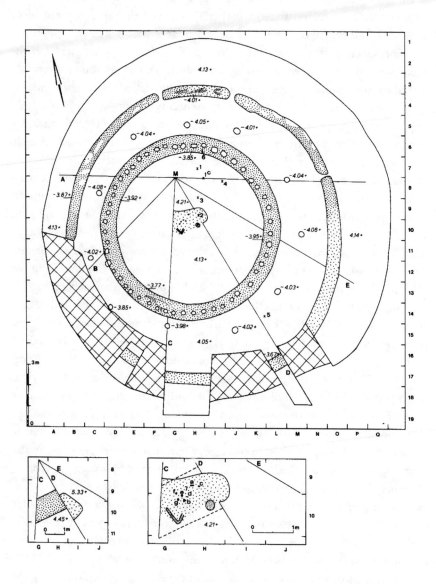

FIG. 114.   The Harenermolen barrow, drawn for J. N. Lanting by G. Delger from the excavation records of A. E. van Giffen. The lower details are for graves of periods 1 and 3. The grid is in metres and the straight lines radiating from *M* are the sections cut during the excavation.

holes round the perimeter of Stonehenge. Archaeological opinion is divided over whether the Aubrey holes ever held posts. Indicated now only by white markers, various unconvincing astronomical roles have been found for them, again mostly having to do with a calendar. To those who argue that they were only counters for calendar use, whether they ever held posts is presumably irrelevant, but that alas only makes the calendar hypothesis more resilient.

The techniques recommended by Sir Fred Hoyle and others for the prediction of eclipses by the use of the Aubrey holes are almost certainly mistaken, for reasons to be given shortly, but the idea of a simple calendar is more difficult to dismiss, because it is essentially so simple. Hoyle's eclipse hypothesis requires that the Aubrey holes were, among other things, day counters (for recording the Sun's movements), a marker being moved one hole every six and a half days. This could have been done by alternating 'weeks' of six days and seven, or by giving half-days (say day and night) their own identity, and counting off thirteen of them. A '364-day year' would result from 56 Aubrey holes (or posts)—not much more than a day short of the tropical year, and of course observations at the solstices might have put matters to rights at regular intervals. (Even that is easier said than done, however, since the precise time of the solstice is not easy to determine.) Stretching the evidence from the Harenermolen inner ring of Period 1, and supposing that a post hole is missing—there is a larger gap than normal to the southeast—one could again arrive at a total of 364 days, but now with the simpler rule of marking one new post every seven days. In the more likely event that there was no fifty-second post, a calendar rule of sorts would still not be difficult to devise. 'By counting (52 times 7, or 51 times 7, or whatever) you will be carried forward to a time when you should begin to observe the Sun daily with care, in expectation of the Sun's reaching an extreme direction in its rising and setting (at midsummer or midwinter solstice).' This rule is certainly not being canvassed here, but it is not completely implausible. In this case, whatever the number of days in the counting procedure adopted, it would have fallen short of a year. It becomes extremely hazardous, therefore, to claim to detect the belief held at the time as to the number of days in a year, or even that there was the concept of a solar year at all. It is perilously easy to devise rules for turning almost any collection of objects into a plausible calendar; but unfortunately, the fact that it is easy does not mean that it is wrong. Where is one to turn for help?

There is no unambiguous evidence that the year was divided into weeks of seven days at this early period, although any indication that the lunar month was quartered might reasonably be taken to point in that direction. A lunar quarter seems a natural enough span, and there is some slender early literary

evidence, but only from the Middle East. The early Babylonians had a sabbath every seventh day, for instance, and in the Babylonian Gilgamesh epic—which was committed to writing in the early second millennium, but probably existed in similar form some centuries earlier—its hero wept over his friend Enkidu for six days and seven nights before giving him up for burial, which again suggests the week as a measure of time. Lest it be thought that there is something inevitable about this division, note that although the Egyptians first divided the lunar month into quarters, they eventually settled on a month of three 'weeks' of ten days each.

Parallels with eastern and Greek astronomy known from literary sources are dangerous. There is no firm evidence that earlier people were able to handle fractions of days, with or without the use of recurrent cycles. A bronze calendar found in 1897, that had come from second-century Coligny in Gaul (about 60 km west of Geneva), provides evidence for a European culture moderately but not excessively skilled in such matters: for three years of a five-year cycle this calendar seems to accept thirty days to the lunar month. The rest is uncertain. When scholars make conjectures about the next two years, for which the bronze is incomplete, it is usually with a view to making the answer come right. Going further back into history, to the lunar calendar of Athens in the fifth century BC, this was inaccurate enough for Aristophanes to deride it, in his play *The Clouds*. In view of all this, we should beware attributing too much to the Bronze Age and earlier cultures without good reason.

A far more telling argument against the calendar hypothesis is the social fact that despite many standardized patterns of behaviour in Beaker cultures, there seems to have been no set standard as to the number of posts a monument should have. Among the many similar circles of timber posts found in Britain and northern Europe, there is scarcely a number between three and a hundred that could not be found represented in one place or another. There are many other shared principles of design. Had one or more calendar rules been invented and embodied in a post circle it would almost certainly have set a precedent that would have been followed elsewhere.

Calendars based on divisions of the year derived from *directions* are another matter entirely. Alexander Thom thought he had evidence from stone circles not only for the summer and winter solstices and spring and autumn equinoxes, but that the four parts of the year were further sub-divided to produce eight parts. Such a division is known to the Lapps, and an Old Norse and Icelandic method of dividing the horizon into eight sectors and of relating the time of year to the place of sunset, survived in Iceland even into the twentieth century. And at the risk of straying into the Middle East: that a division of the horizon

into eight is an extremely ancient one there is clear from the way the Sun-god Shamash in the Gilgamesh epic pins down the ogre Humbaba with eight winds, allowing Gilgamesh to decapitate him. It seems that the 'wind rose', a forerunner of our compass rose, has truly ancient precedents. But eights and sixteens are a far cry from some of the ingenious schemes involving counting that are currently in vogue for post and stone circles.

Harenermolen: Symmetries and the Spacings of Rings

In view of the deficiencies of the circles one should not be too zealous in quoting diameters, but at the end of its history the inner ring was approximately 8.5 m in diameter, and the outer (the later) about 10.6 m. The circumference of the outer is thus only slightly more than 40 of Thom's Megalithic Yards (40.17 MY as drawn in Fig. 114). Thom paid little attention to such Neolithic monuments as causeways, barrows, and chambered tombs, and most of his work concerned the period from roughly 2500 to 1500 BC. He maintained that certain favoured multiples of his unit (25, 50, and so on) were used for circumferences, with corresponding diameters taken to be whole numbers (8, 16, etc.; 4 and 12 are also found). He argued that the builders occasionally distorted circular monuments, to make the relationship perfect, and that this is at the root of the custom of creating oval rings. A different explanation will be offered here (in terms of adjusting altitudes set by lintels) but the two might not be incompatible.

Thom's unit of length, which has already turned up in the Avebury avenues and which is undoubtedly in evidence at Stonehenge, might also have been known on the continent. A measuring rod of hazel, found in an early Bronze Age burial mound at Borum Eshøj in East Jutland (Denmark), was close to it: it was slightly curved, and although only 78.6 cm long as against Thom's standard 82.9 cm, had shrunk somewhat in drying out. An oak rod found at a Danish Iron Age fortified settlement in Borre Fen was 135 cm long. It had a button at one end and was pointed at the other. That these were intended as measuring rods seems to be assured by the fact that *both* were divided into units close to one fifth of a Megalithic Yard. A now obsolete Spanish measure, the *vara*, was also very close in length to the latter, and many other old measures have been canvassed as preserving a similar prehistoric unit. The ease with which a standard of length may be preserved must clearly depend on the material with which it is replicated but also to a great extent on the stability of social circumstances: our own circumstances are admittedly very different from those of the second and third millennia BC, but it is perhaps worth

mentioning that the Tudor standard yard of five centuries ago differs from the modern Imperial yard by only four hundredths of an inch.

Without pressing for the idea that the Harenermolen builders were aiming at 40 MY in the circumference, there is another small item of evidence that might be relevant. For all its apparent irregularity, on examining it closely we find that the Harenermolen ditch followed two concentric circles surprisingly closely; and while their estimated separation will depend to some extent on the depth at which Van Giffen's survey was made, following that strictly a separation within a centimetre of 1 MY emerges. The geometrical centre of the ditch lies very precisely on the line joining the most easterly and westerly posts—in fact it was more or less at mid-thorax of the skeleton. If the inner circle of posts was set up at a period when such geometrical considerations weighed with its builders, then either a circumference of 32 MY or a diameter of 10 MY is plausible.

That the site was long in use does not mean that the wooden structures were long-lasting. Wooden piles, even of oak, that might have lasted a century or more in the Wiltshire chalk, would in the sand of the Hondsrug have lasted for no more than a few decades. When posts at such sites as Harenermolen rotted, it seems that renewal was done, if at all, in a set of newly dug holes, but still following the old broad principles of alignment. Allegiance to such principles at a single site, in some cases over several centuries, is something that cannot usually be detected in a single stone structure. It remains to be seen what those principles were.

Probable Styles of Observation Using Posts

If the way the Sun was observed is known, then it should in principle be possible to derive a date from the measured azimuth of rising or setting and the altitude. On the other hand, since the changes in azimuth with time are much slower than with most bright stars, that date—assuming the same accuracy in specifying the azimuths—will be much less precise, and rarely better than two or three centuries. Although few early surveys are accurate enough to allow even this, they do often point with a fair degree of probability to the method of observation that was used. In fact the method that seems intuitively the most obvious fits well with the Harenermolen situation, and seems to be repeatedly confirmed, even at much more complex and earlier British henges.

Using a pair of wooden posts at Harenermolen, the distant post would have been easily wide enough to hide the Sun or Moon completely, if used as a foresight. There are various plausible cases to consider, but all may be reduced

to the four illustrated in the lower part of Fig. 115. In the upper part of that figure, imagine that both cases illustrated (cases 4 and 1) are in the northeast quadrant. In case 1, the body observed (the Sun or Moon) at its extreme northern rising is imagined to be just able to emerge beyond the foresight, on the side furthest away from east. In case 4, it can reach no further than to the east of the far post. In both cases, there is a slit created between the posts. The observer, by shifting position slightly, can adjust the breadth of the slit at will. Cases 2 and 3 are not illustrated except in the lower part of the figure. The disc of the Sun or Moon is no longer trapped between foresight and backsight. By day the Sun may be unbearably bright, and by night the Moon will not be so easily locatable in relation to the posts. It is hard to believe that methods 2 or 3 were often used.

In the figure, the *upper* limb of the Sun or Moon is shown trapped between posts. Other possibilities are that the *side* limb of the disc is seen, or that the slit is filled with the full breadth of the disc, when the *lower* limb is just touching the horizon. Since latter-day astronomers tend to specify the Sun's position by its centre, this is sometimes assumed to be what was observed, and

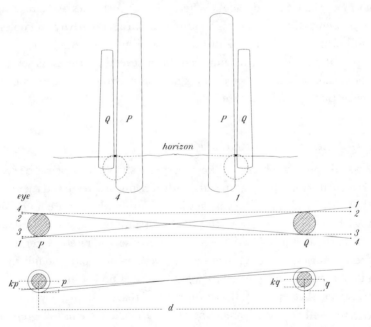

FIG. 115.   Different ways of using two upright posts to align on a part of the disc of the Sun or Moon. The upper of the two figures in plan shows four potential sight-lines, but the most practicable are 1 and 4, as shown in the upper part of the illustration. The lower plan figure shows how a tapering of the posts affects the azimuth of the line of sight, bringing it closer to the line of centres of the posts.

since it is taken to be a simple matter to note when the Sun or Moon rests on the horizon, this too is occasionally favoured. Neither is in fact easy to observe with the naked eye, and indeed it is difficult to imagine any human meaning in such arrangements at 'rising' or 'setting'. A more subtle phenomenon is the observation of what in Appendix 2 is called the 'position of furthest reach'. This differs little from the case in which the upper limb is on the horizon. In human terms, it was surely first or last glint that mattered, and that would have been seen to correspond to a beginning or an ending, to a birth or to a death of the Sun or Moon. Harenermolen and many other circles support this choice. Thom found some statistical evidence from stone circles that first or last glint on the one hand and the full disc standing on the horizon were both observed; but it does not plainly emerge from the examples examined here.

What has been said of the northeast quadrant applies, in all but the matter of the direction taken by the moving disc in the figure, to the other quadrants. To the southeast, for instance, 4 will represent the case where the Sun's or Moon's rising position (first glint) has barely managed to pass beyond the far post, while 1 might represent the case where the Sun's or Moon's rising position has just reached to the eastern side of the far post.

It is easy enough to test these methods: one only has to look along the sides of two well-separated posts to have a strong preference for methods involving a gap between sights. Not only is it easier to position one's eye, but as the disc rises or sets, one can continue watching it without being unduly dazzled. Moreover, the more one experiments, the more convinced one becomes that lintels capping the posts (as in the most famous cases of all, at Stonehenge) were used not only for architectural stability but to cut down glare, by hiding all but a small part of the Sun's or Moon's disc. An argument for lintels in barrow rings has already been given: Glasbergen's type 4 has posts in pairs. Lintels at Harenermolen would all have been less than 3.5 m long. Lintels or not, the custom must have been established at some stage in history of protecting the tops of posts from rain and consequent rot. The slab of stone (known as an abacus) capping a stone column in the simple Greek Doric style was probably descended from a device with just such a function in a wooden temple.

What of the shapes of the posts? None of the Harenermolen post holes for the outer circle shows any sign of having been flattened at a part of the perimeter, although this is to say nothing of the posts themselves. Some of the inner holes seem to be flattened along one or more sides, and this is found at many sites in the Low Countries and Britain, especially with large posts. With tree trunks, however, a part of the circumference is often naturally much flatter

than the rest, and one must not read too much into a post hole profile, even when there are post holes that were quite clearly trimmed foursquare. A careful study might reveal a tendency for surfaces to be flattened when they were to be used for lunar observation. What seems like a clear example for the Sun (at a site near Goirle) will be mentioned later. It is conceivable that some square holes were simply produced by a digging technique, but in the last case only the four most important solar posts are square.

In taking alignments from a plan showing post holes, there is the added complication that tree trunks are always *tapered*. With trapped lines of sight (cases 1 and 4 in Fig. 115), the effect is to rotate the line of sight towards the line of centres by an amount depending on the taper of the post. Each monument must be considered on its own merits, but the shift would rarely have exceeded a quarter of a degree. It is even conceivable that half of the slender posts were inserted with the narrow end down, to cancel the effect of taper, but matching angles actually derived to ideal directions of rising and setting do not support the idea at all plainly, and its rationale will perhaps be thought a trifle too ingenious. (An inverted taper is not unknown in later architecture. Mycenaean buildings generally use a post and lintel system, with wooden columns often tapering downwards. What was the origin of this tradition?) The girths of posts at Harenermolen suggest trees—most probably oaks—of the order of twenty to forty years old. They might have been grown specially in close proximity to one another, to make them straighter. Such trunks are not particularly large. Some large English henges incorporated trees much more than a century old.[2]

The heights of the posts are almost never known in any direct way. They were presumably not less than the height of a man. Small rings of relatively slender posts as at Harenermolen were usually let into the ground to a depth of only half a metre or so, but where the girths were massive, as at such English sites as Woodhenge, Mount Pleasant, and Arminghall, they could be much deeper. It must always be assumed that stability would have been lost had they been much taller than five or six times the length submerged, but this does

---

2   In practice, taper depends on the section of the trunk selected, and on the variety of tree. If the diameters of the posts (separated by distance d) at ground level are p and q, and these reduce to kp and kq at the height of the observer's eye (as shown in the previous figure), then the angle of correction in degrees will be about $28.65(1 - k)(p + q)/d$. Using two posts of 20 cm diameter separated by 10 m, with a factor of 0.8 for the taper (a good average for straight oaks), this comes to a little under a quarter of a degree. There are oaks and other trees with trunks tapered appreciably less than this, however.

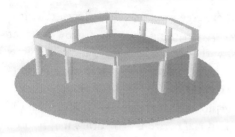

FIG. 116.   A schematic view of the Harener-molen barrow in its later phase, showing the mound extending beyond the limits of the corresponding post ring.

not argue for a minimum length. Reasons will be given later for certain working rules relating post girth to height and hole size.

In the case of the outer ring at Harenermolen, if the posts were used in a way to be explained shortly, they had to be higher than the enclosed mound, which at its highest point was approximately 1.7 m. Although not an impossible figure for the height of the eyes of a man in this region and period, it is not necessary to suppose that the distant horizon was viewed over the centre of the mound. Observation of the Sun or Moon could have been off-centre but still above a horizon created by the mound itself, in much the same way as at the long barrows. Those who have excavated such mounds have also often given reasons for believing that the rim of the mound extended outside the post circle (Fig. 116). The mound itself might therefore possibly have served as a sloping platform by which shorter people raised themselves to the right level. (There are comparable arrangements in many English observing ditches.) It is assumed that no observer stood very far from the nearby post. The Sun's and Moon's diameters are each about half a degree, and their discs could have been covered by a post of diameter 25 cm to anyone nearer than approximately 29 m.

In the following sections it will be shown from the alignments of the posts at Harenermolen that what was observed there was the first or last glint of light, whether of the Sun or of the Moon. Observations could have continued after sunrise or moonrise. Using the posts of the outer ring, the observer could have stood just inside the (outer) ditch. The image of the first or last glint of the Sun or Moon would then have been bounded on two sides by posts, one far and one near, and below by the artificial horizon that was the mound. The lintels above would then have completed a 'window', and have shielded the eye from the Sun and the glow of the sky—the brightness of which should not be underestimated.

Harenermolen: Alignments in Both Rings

The Harenermolen site is at present only about 4 m above sea level, and the surrounding terrain varies between a little below sea level and 3 m above it.

(Sea level in the early and middle Bronze Age was appreciably lower than it is now.) Forest cover was not significant, assuming that the barrow was not enclosed by trees. Occasional alders, with reeds, bog myrtle, and sedge grass predominated in the plain, while on the Hondsrug itself there was an assortment of willow, ash, alder, lime, birch, and oak. This list is in rough order of altitude—if that is the right word for slopes that are scarcely higher than the trees. One of the great advantages of artificial horizons is that they may be used to cut out the irregularities of the real horizon, especially of any tree line. If the alignments as estimated at Harenermolen are close to the truth, however, there cannot have been trees very close at hand, or at least, there must have been swathes cut through any forest close at hand. Given clearings of a few hundred metres in the right directions, the horizon would have been admirably suited to observation, weather permitting, and would not have changed much over long periods of time. Refraction apart, in no direction would the difference between the horizontal and the actual horizon have been more than about half a minute of arc—one of the inestimable advantages of prehistoric life in the Netherlands.

Broadly speaking, two traditions have been followed by those making claims for astronomical alignments in the planning of monuments. The first is to decide in advance on what one hopes to find, and then draw attention only to what conforms with that ideal. Another approach is to investigate all those directions that a monument seems to define, and the inherent plausibility of each. This second method is often rounded off with a quite misleading use of statistics. The strength of the conclusion is not necessarily greater, the greater the number of plausible alignments found in proportion to the total number of possibilities set by the posts.[3]

Here the procedure to be followed will be to cut out unlikely directions, ignoring for instance the alignments of pairs of posts too close to have been of much use. If one could be sure of the positions of posts within their holes, an accuracy of measurement better than a tenth of a degree would be possible, taking the survey at its face value. Taper is a slight problem, as already

---

3 Imagine, for instance, that a society fosters a cult of observing the Sun once a year, at the winter solstice, and that there is a custom of arranging four posts in a rectangle so that the lines of sight defined by the diagonals are directed to the rising and setting midwinter Sun. Not one of the four posts is redundant, and yet out of twenty-four potential (trapped) lines of sight only two will be used and meaningful. (There could be four that seemed to point to the equinoxes.) The post circles examined here are of course much more complicated than a simple rectangle, and the proportion of 'hits' might often be much smaller still. The size of this parameter is generally a very poor indicator of astronomical use.

explained. Changing it from 0.8 to 0.7, for instance, would produce a change of about 0.03°. There are such complications to consider as verticality of the posts and slight irregularities of the true horizon, but all told the Harenermolen situation is as favourable as one is ever likely to find for a timber ring.

With one exception, the alignments that seem plausible fall neatly into two groups, one of azimuths between about 40.8° and 44.4°, the other in the range 51.4° to 58.5°. In the outer circle, sixteen pairs of posts might serve our purposes, each with two alternative trapped lines of sight, and two directions for each of them. A surprisingly high proportion of the sixty-four directions survives, and two different observing methods seem to be indicated, namely (1) letting the Sun pass beyond the far post, while (2) allowing the Moon only to close up to the far post. If these rules were indeed adopted, the reasons should be obvious. First, the Moon does not by its brightness give much advance warning of its rising, and when it sets it is not as easy to keep its last gleam in view as with the Sun. It is also reasonably easy enough to look on its disc, and there is not the same need to keep it hidden behind the distant post in its first and last minutes of visibility.

Circles of post holes for astronomically significant directions, such as the directions of the rising or setting Sun at equinox or solstice, present a familiar problem—that of many post holes, not very regularly placed, from which it is possible to obtain some thousands of different angles by laying off lines tangential to suitably spaced pairs of them. The number of directions fixed by fifty-one posts of assorted girth is 51x50, multiplied by 4, the number of ways one may draw tangents to them. The result is not halved, since both directions along the lines joining pairs of posts must be examined. One would multiply by 6, rather than 4, if considering also lines through the centres of posts, but there is no obvious observing technique for these additional cases, except by looking over short posts. One multiplies only by 2, however, if viewing was invariably of the Sun or Moon trapped *between* sighting posts.

The posts of the earlier, inner, ring at Harenermolen seem to have a fair degree of symmetry around the east–west line, and the same is more obvious in the case of the outer ring—although the north and south side of the line are by no means perfect mirror images. That this is a fairly typical finding is itself a strong reason for believing the posts to have been placed with respect to the heavens. The human skeleton associated with the earlier ring also has an approximate east–west orientation.

The outer ring makes the best starting point, since its relative simplicity (eleven posts, 11x10x2 directions, many of them unusable as sighting lines) makes an analysis of all the orientations embodied in it relatively straightfor-

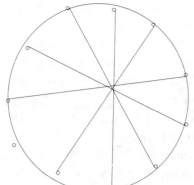

FIG. 117.   The eleven posts of the later ring at Harenermolen, showing the poor approximation to a circle but the rather good radial alignments. Note the residual post at the lower left. The lines drawn are not astronomical alignments.

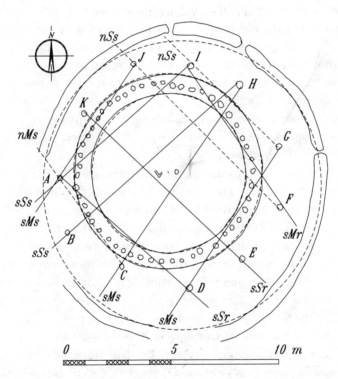

FIG. 118.   Eight potential alignments for the outer ring of posts at Harenermolen (continuous lines), with three somewhat less plausible ones (broken lines). Viewing is from the posts where the lines start. Notation: *sS* and *nS* are the Sun at winter and summer solstice, respectively, the first letter denoting either southernmost or northernmost. The final letter, *r* or *s*, denotes rising or setting. Similarly, *sM* and *nM* refer to the Moon at its southern and northern major standstills, the additional letter again denoting rising or setting. The three large broken circles should give an idea of the high accuracy of the first (inner) ditch, and of the low accuracy of the laying out of the outer, which was of course impeded by the pre-existing mound within it. See also Figure 119.

ward. Note that in a ring of posts that is small in relation to the girth of the posts themselves, it is impossible to take a line of sight joining nearby posts, for the view will be blocked by posts between them. In the Harenermolen case this cuts down the number of directions by about two fifths, and there is a similar effect even in the much larger Wessex treehenges. Out of a total of eight highly plausible alignments in the outer ring, four are on the Sun at the winter solstice and four on the Moon at its maximum southerly declination (Fig. 118). There are at least three other possibilities, two to the setting Sun at summer solstice, and one to the Moon at its northern maximum, but these are somewhat less plausible. No attempt is made here to investigate alignments on stars. This is not so much a question of the limited number of degrees of freedom (as just explained), but of suitability. The design of these monuments, with their forests of uprights, is not at all well fitted to the observation of the stars.[4]

What of the earlier (inner) ring? The replacement of its posts, as at many similar sites, speaks for the preservation of a tradition. It seems reasonable to suppose that if the outer ring (Lanting's Period 3) was used astronomically, then so was the other, especially in view of the evidence to be presented shortly for comparable activity at an earlier period in Britain. The argument will soon

---

4 It would be easy to claim too much for multiple alignments. Despite the large number of physically possible lines of sight, the designer's freedom was very much reduced by the fact that when a post was set up for one phenomenon, the number of possibilities of using it for another (by design rather than chance) was limited by how many post-spaces were still unfilled. This limitation can best be illustrated by giving one possible sequence for setting up the posts. There are of course others, some of them equivalent to this in their end result, and others not. (The abbreviations used are those of the figure, where they are explained.) First set up A at a suitable distance from the centre of the old barrow. Draw a reasonable circle for the rest. Fix D so that AD is to sSr (midwinter rising Sun). Fix I so that IA is to sSs (midwinter setting). ID will be automatically more or less north–south. Fix F so that IF is to sMr (southern extreme of the rising Moon). Fix G so that GD is to sMs (southernmost Moon set). Fix J so that JA is to sMs. Place a stake at the point where lines AG and ID meet, and use it to position post E opposite J and K opposite F. Place H approximately north of E and then C opposite H, as judged by the same stake as before. An idea of the degree of accuracy achieved in the placing of posts on a circle and in radial alignment can be had from the previous figure. The conjectural sequence offered here does not include the less satisfactory alignments. Note that in the final stages of the construction, since one of the alignments is to the Sun and the other to the Moon, K and C will not now be near to a north–south line. The lack of symmetry in this and other respects in not a sign of carelessness on the part of the builders but of principles of design that are simply not immediately evident. Note also that there is no provision for an alignment on the rising or setting Sun at the equinoxes. There is little evidence for an early interest in the equinoctial Sun, here or elsewhere in northern Europe.

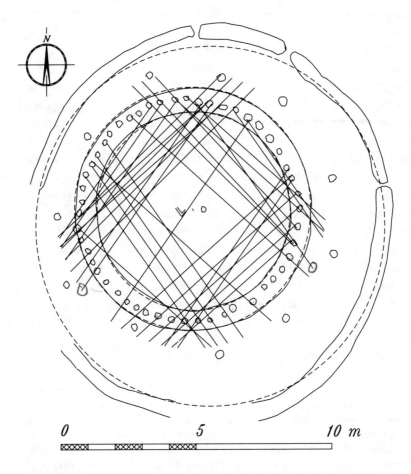

FIG. 119. Some of the numerous potential alignments for the earlier ring of posts at Harenermolen. Those closer to the east–west line are for the Sun, the others for the Moon at its major standstills, north or south. The plausibility of these alignments rests on indirect arguments and is weaker than in the simpler case (Period 3).

be supplemented by another, from post numbers. Lanting's Period 2 seems to be lacking in a ring of posts, but since he can associate no grave with that period, perhaps there was simply a refurbishing and elevation of the mound, with a continuing use of some sort of markers. The date Lanting assigned to Period 1 is in a range equivalent to 2100 BC to 2000 BC. If one considers theoretical alignments for 2000 BC and restricts attention to the ranges 40° to 46° and 51.5 to 55.5°, all major directions should be caught, if they are present, with a margin of at least 0.8° to spare. Thirty-four possibilities are marked on Fig. 119, all but seven of them looking south, as in the later and simpler ring.

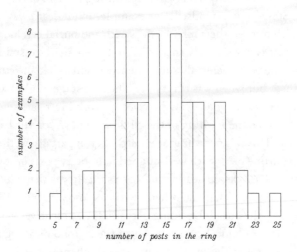

FIG. 120.   Number of posts in a sample of 73 timber circles of Glasbergen's type 3 excavated in the Drenthe area of the northern Netherlands. (A monumental thirty-poster at Sleen-Zweeloo is omitted from the graph.)

The role of the mound in observation presents us with a difficult problem. If the bounding horizon was set by the mound, then the very slight discrepancies between measured azimuths and those we might consider as in some sense 'ideal' can be accounted for by adjusting the height of the mound by only three or four centimetres at mid-mound (mid-secant). But this sort of argument is the thin end of the wedge, for with a little ingenuity lines of poor fit can be made acceptable. A line of sight that is acceptable in one direction (say for midwinter sunset) but not in the reverse direction (in this case for midsummer sunrise) might be made so by postulating an adjustment in the artificial horizon altitude set by the mound. It is not that this is unreasonable—it might have been done in various ways (notably by adjusting the floor level) just as at the long barrows—but that the argument is difficult to control. The fact that the posts fit the very low *natural* horizon so well suggests that the mound was a close match to it, for most adult observers.

This analysis of the earlier ring carries with it certain wider archaeological implications. Two circles were accurately drawn. The corpse was almost certainly buried after this was done. The east–west and north–south directions were probably found beforehand. The corpse's orientation need not have been very precise—how can such a thing be so?—but the central placing of the torso seems not to have been haphazard. The posts of that inner ring must have been carefully selected in advance, perhaps even dressed to size for use. Fifty-one

sizeable posts were certainly not set in place during the two or three days when the solsticial Sun was at a standstill, for example, and if death was natural, and not at that season, then their relationship with the burial ceremony becomes problematical. It is not unlikely that small rods were used to establish lines of sight and that the posts were only subsequently manhandled into the positions thus established, but when was this done? The first stage might have been the establishment of two or more key directions, involving relatively few posts, and the second stage the infilling of the circle with posts, on the basis of those already in place. This was not a unique enterprise, but part of a well-established tradition. An outline plan, with well-aligned temporary posts or stakes, might have been set up long before death. Another possibility is that a few key posts were long in place, and that the others, with the mound, were added in the months following the burial. Deciding between the alternatives would require more detailed archaeological evidence, but if the astronomical argument is to be accepted, then unless the ritual was an exceedingly protracted affair, lasting many months, the burial was not the first event in the complete ritual sequence.

Numbers of Posts

The argument as presented up to this point needs qualification. It is natural enough to suppose that when certain directions seem to have been favoured frequently in a single given monument this is a sign of a deliberate act. Suppose, however, that for some special reason a person were to point due east with one rung of a ladder. It would not be legitimate for a second person to conclude from the fact that all the other rungs do the same that statistics prove the orientation of all rungs to have been deliberate. The two cases are not quite equivalent, however, and their differences are important.

To judge any such case one must come to a decision about likely *intentions* and their likely consequences. The most probable of all human intentions in setting up a circular ring of posts is to mark off a space, whether for practical or spiritual purposes, with an enclosing fence. Aesthetic as well as practical considerations will usually then decree evenly spaced posts. But is there anything to be said about the *incidental* properties of such a circular fence? Consider any one of a set of fifty-one such posts, and suppose for the time being that the posts are points on a circle. Radiating from the post, lines of sight might be drawn to the others—say apart from the nearest ten, which in real life will be hard to sight. A simple piece of geometry tells us that the rays drawn will be spaced at equal angles—in fact in this case there will be thirty spaced at $3.53°$. Suppose now that we move round the circle and on to the next

post, and chart its own allocation of thirty rays. To do this is to do nothing
more than pick up the first diagram, and rotate it through twice that angle of
3.53°. Continuing in this way until the entire circle has been covered, at the
end of the exercise it will obviously be possible to group the directions into
thirty sets of fifty-one distinct azimuths, spread uniformly round the compass,
at 7.06° intervals. In a search for solar alignments in the last section of this
chapter, stretches of six degrees were considered, one in each of the four
quadrants. If one were to repeat the exercise now, clearly it would be possible
to find two clusters of identical alignments spaced at 3.53° within any such
stretch. Such a clustering of alignments (directions) is a direct consequence of
the equal spacing of posts: a clustering of near-identical directions will result
from any near-uniform spacing. Since the posts will in reality have a finite size,
the spacing of the thirty rays of each set will not be quite uniform, but there
will be near-replication of directions, even so.

This result takes some of the wind out of the sails not only of our analysis
of the ring from Period 3, but of the earlier argument for significance in the
alignments of Period 1. It does not nullify the argument—the second person
might have been right, in the example above, if the object was no ladder but
a set of ritually arranged spokes duly pinned together. The automatic clustering
of alignments in the rings likewise loses much of its sting where posts that are
by no means evenly placed seem nevertheless to have been deliberately and
symmetrically arranged to preserve directions. But it warns against a particular
type of statistical argument. It is far safer to rest the argument for solar or lunar
alignments on the observation that similar patterns of orientation are found at
many places, with symmetry of a sort around an east–west line (especially
obvious at Harenermolen in Period 3) that makes good astronomical sense. The
eleven posts will not work in the way suggested above unless a proportion of
them have this symmetry. The smaller the numbers of posts, the smaller the
chances of hitting a reasonably symmetrical arrangement. There are scores of
post circles that work well by virtue of this kind of symmetry, and this is the
statistic that matters most.

As explained, clusters of directions emerge naturally with any regular
monument, but for them to be useful for sighting the rising and setting Sun
or Moon they still have to satisfy very stringent conditions. The number of
posts chosen has to be such that it throws up at least one acceptable angle.
(Some of the possibilities will be considered shortly.) But what if more is
demanded than a single meaningful direction? Even near-symmetry with the
east–west line will not then be enough. If *two* clusters of directions are to be
found useful, the number of posts has to be extremely well chosen. Two

examples will be considered, each of them relating to a pair of significant directions. The first is for the Sun alone, but at midsummer and midwinter. The second is for the Sun at midwinter and the Moon at its maximum southern risings and settings. To illustrate the broad principle of optimal post numbers, the Harenermolen latitude is taken (53° 09' 05"), with a level horizon all round, for a period around 2000 BC. To simplify matters, regularly spaced circles are assumed throughout.

Midwinter and Midsummer Sun

The angle between solar extremes was approximately 3.07° (the difference between 44.12° looking one way and 41.05° looking the other). A circle with around fifty-eight posts would have given this rather closely, depending on relative post- and ring-diameters. A fifty-one-post circle would not have served without some irregularity in the spacing.

Midwinter Sun with Southernmost Moon

The corresponding angle is now 13.22° (the difference between 41.05° and 54.37°, looking now in the same general direction). A circle with thirteen or fourteen posts would have served well. An eleven-poster would have entailed irregular spacing, although at more northerly latitudes (over 56° N) it could have been exactly what was needed with uniform spacing.

Of course there is no claim being made here that any 'calculation' was or could have been done, except through trial and error, using the general principle arrived at intuitively that some numbers worked better than others. Even so, in time, some of the simple angle-properties of circle and triangle would inevitably have been grasped. Numbers in the fifties would have been found good for reversible solar alignments, and numbers in the low 'teens for southern extremes of Sun and Moon. In the same empirical way it would have been found that numbers in the high 'teens worked for the northern Sun and Moon. Multiples of these numbers would have worked more or less as well, so that, for instance, if thirteen posts were needed for a perfect southern Sun–Moon arrangement, so would fifty-two. The Harenermolen fifty-one should therefore not be looked upon as a poor approximation to a solar fifty-eight, but as a number highly suited to the midwinter Sun and southernmost Moon—as was indeed found by measurement to be so.

If these general principles apply to barrows elsewhere, then one may expect to find certain numbers of posts favoured above the rest. This is in fact the case. There are some differences between the northern and southern Netherlands, and because of the difference in latitude it is perhaps misleading to lump them

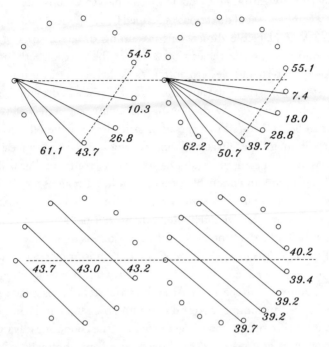

FIG. 121.   Directions set by rings of eleven and seventeen posts. The upper figures show complete sets of alignments radiating from a single post; the lower figures show how a single direction is repeatedly found across the ring.

all together. Doing so, however, it emerges that among Glasbergen's type 3, eleven-posters are the most common, with over twenty examples out of a total of about ninety. These numbers are steadily changing, as more are excavated. Separating out the northern examples (Drenthe and adjacent Friesland and Groningen), a count of seventy-three instances made by H. T. Waterbolk is summarized in Fig. 120. Of these, forty have even numbers of posts and thirty-three have odd. All numbers of posts between ten and twenty are reasonably well represented, but eleven, fourteen and sixteen are most common, with eight examples each. In the south, seventeen and eighteen are also common. Glasbergen's type 4 yields only two examples, but they could be treated as eleven-posters if it is to be assumed that their (presumed) arches defined the key directions. They are of great interest, since a similar ring ('henge') of comparable dimensions, also with eleven pairs of posts lying within a ditch, has been found at Goldington in Bedfordshire.

Is this seeming affection for certain numbers, for example the number eleven, purely fortuitous, or is it perhaps adherence to an architectural tradition

having nothing whatsoever to do with the heavens? It is not difficult to calculate a complete set of directions as defined by any perfect circle of perfectly spaced posts of plausible dimensions, assuming different sorts of symmetry—for example a post at the east, or a post at the west, or both, or posts to either side of eastern and western entrances. Whether the azimuths so determined match with actual solar and lunar possibilities will depend on altitudes and geographical latitude. With very slight skewing, the perfect eleven-poster turns out to be well suited to a spread of latitudes over the Netherlands and southern Britain, for the Sun at midwinter or midsummer, but not easily both, and the Moon at northern or southern extreme, but not both. That the eleven-poster occurs in reasonable proportions in all regions would be easily explained by its adaptability over a wide area. It is by no means alone in this, however. Ten posts offer even more flexibility—but not an 'open' eastern part of the ring. It is all a question of what phenomenon is to be viewed, and from where. Thus a fourteen-poster is good for the midsummer Sun and northernmost Moon in north and south of the country. A seventeen-poster is good for the midwinter Sun in the north. An eighteen-poster likewise; and this works well also for the midsummer Sun and southernmost Moon in the south. There seem to be signs of mild regional preferences in the count of excavated rings, but the numbers are too small to support any hard argument. Since local tradition is likely to have been very important, and because the rings as they were erected were simply not regularly spaced, it would in any case be foolish to try to reduce the subject to an exact art. One can, however, say that if their builders did have astronomical purposes in mind, they chose their numbers well. Conversely, if the overall argument is to be accepted, then post numbers offer us a potential clue as to which phenomena were favoured; but in the end only a careful analysis of individual cases can tell us what could have been observed.

To help clarify the points being made here, Fig. 121 (upper half) illustrates a pair of idealized rings, one of eleven and one of seventeen, and on each a set of sight lines is added, radiating from the western post. On both there is one extra line added from the many left undrawn, to illustrate a potential lunar direction. In both cases there are lines in the neighbourhood of 40°, easily made to coincide with risings and settings of the Sun in midsummer or midwinter by judicious skewing of the ring as a whole. The lunar lines are in the neighbourhood of 55°.

There is one last small but important piece of evidence from the Low Countries to be mentioned, before these general principles are applied to the Wessex

scene. As explained, angles that were not quite right could easily have been adjusted by trial and error, by moving a post or by cutting its width down to size. The apparent habit of planing posts has already been mentioned. A beautiful example was found by Van Giffen near Goirle in the province of Brabant (Tumulus II, Rechte Heide). This thirty-four-poster had a well-defined burial chamber lying in the line of midsummer sunrise and midwinter sunset, the slightly different directions of which were accurately defined with the help of two posts of *perfectly square section*, one for each. They were set in opposite quadrants, not diametrically opposite each other, but so that each could have served as a foresight to a normal cylindrical post as backsight. Their faces were not by any means directed towards the centre of the ring.[5]

Since in this Goirle example there are two alignments for events separated by half a year, the conclusion once again is that the plan of the monument was laid down either well before or after the death of the person buried within it. To suppose that death coincided with one of the solstices at all monuments where the solstices are indicated is to make an assumption about human mortality that is either odd or sinister. Human beings have no strong tendency to die naturally at the solstices. If death came regularly when a solstitial alignment was set up, then it was not a natural death.

The Earliest Stonehenge Structures

Among the least obvious of the many structures at Stonehenge are the surrounding ditch and the bank inside it, but less obvious still is the ring of fifty-six Aubrey holes, pits now filled with soil, their places now marked by discs of white chalk. More than half of them have been excavated, and the rest have been located by probing and also by soundings with a hammer. Depressions of some sort were first noticed in the seventeenth century by the antiquary John Aubrey, and on the basis of his remarks the holes were discovered or rediscovered—opinions differ as to whether they are what Aubrey found—in the 1920s by William Hawley, on the prompting of Robert Newall.

---

5   There seem also to be lunar directions implicit in the ring. Two other mounds on the same site (numbered IV and VI) contain central graves seemingly aligned on the maximum northern rising of the Moon, while mound V has its central grave aligned on midsummer sunset. Mound IV, a thirteen-poster, contains a second burial made at the time of the first, but this—perhaps of a wife—was in a trunk coffin lying in a perfect north–south line (midway between the northwest and southwest posts). Mound VI has a perfect north–south burial at its eastern periphery. There are other deliberate orientations of the burials in this region. Opinions differ, however, as to whether the grave from mound II, with the square-sectioned posts, is from the earliest period of the barrow.

The Stonehenge monument had been given to the nation by Mr (later Sir) Cecil Chubb in 1918. The Office of Works decided to examine the condition of its new inheritance, and the Society of Antiquaries obtained permission to excavate it. William Gowland had done good work on the site at the beginning of the century, but was now too old for the job. Lt-Colonel Hawley, his intended assistant, was chosen in his place, to be assisted in turn by Robert Newall, a local archaeologist. Funds were in short supply, and Hawley spent long periods alone, living in a hut on the site. Work began in November 1919 and was finally abandoned in 1926, by which time roughly half the site had been stripped, sieved, and sorted. William Hawley has been rather harshly treated by posterity for his lack of imagination. His much cited expression of intent, 'to collect facts without indulging in any theory concerning them', is almost always quoted out of context: it was in response to a technical astronomical question posed by Admiral Somerville, by which he was not surprisingly baffled. He was certainly not above speculation. His excavation methods were not refined, and his recording techniques are often irritatingly vague, but in these respects he was certainly no worse than most of his contemporaries.

The Entrance Post Holes

Hawley discovered many features of Stonehenge that were previously unknown, including the numerous post holes near the northeast entrance to the site (where the Avenue joins it), and signs of a central circular timber structure, now completely undetectable from ground level. (See Fig. 123 for an overall view of the post positions.) The entrance post holes found in 1922 were about forty in number. Covering the area of the break in the ditch (the 'causeway') and now assumed to date from the same period (within a century and a half of 3180 BC), they give the impression of defining a grid of some sort, although they are not very evenly spaced. It is hard to know how much the apparent unevenness is due to Hawley's planning technique. His plan of the holes lost something more when transcribed for printing, and the best published version is that transcribed by Alexander Thom, which is the basis for our Fig. 122.

There seems to have been no systematic recording of hole diameters and depths, but judging by the plan some posts, much heavier than the rest, seem to follow a line (L on the figure) close to north. This line seems to mirror the line of a corridor of posts to be discussed in the following section, and it is conceivable that both were towards the very bright but only fleetingly visible Rigel Centauri—in the present case to its rising. (A tentative date of 2700 ± 100 BC seems not unreasonable, but of course this is strictly hypothetical.) On this

assumption the heavier posts will have been earlier than the rest, and presumably somehow related to a central timber henge

Inset in the figure is a half-scale drawing showing superimposed on it the grid added by Thom. How dependent we are on our preconceived ideas in such matters may be judged from the very different, rectangular, grid added to the main figure. Thom's arrangement shows six circular arcs centred on the monument, and twelve radial lines. The functioning of this arrangement, which he interpreted very tentatively as a lunar device, will be explained in broad outline at a later stage. The alternative grid began from a dozen lines

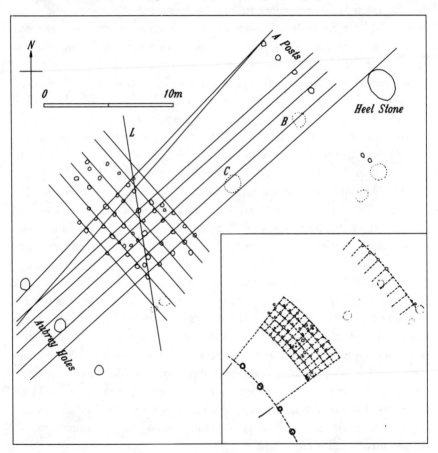

FIG. 122.   The causeway post holes at Stonehenge with our nominal grid of two sets of mostly parallel lines superimposed. Those passing by the Heel Stone are appropriate to the setting (or possibly rising) Sun at winter (or summer) solstice. The inset figure shows, at half the previous scale, A. Thom's superimposed grid of circular arcs and radial lines. For the context of these plans, see Fig. 123. The line L picks out heavier posts that are conceivably older than the rest and directed to the rising of Rigel Centauri.

placed purely by eye along what seemed to be the most plausible alignments. Since five of them were found to be virtually parallel, and since one of the five, grazing the Heel Stone, was found to be at an angle that—as will be shown later—is well suited to observation of the setting midwinter Sun, those five have been redrawn as exactly parallel. If the figure shows anything, it is that there is no compelling *internal* reason to have the grid a circular one.

There might of course be external reasons, as Thom thought, based on much later practice elsewhere. In 1972 C. A. Newham had attempted to explain these post holes in terms of a programme of lunar observation. His idea was an extension of the conventional interpretation of the monument as a whole—almost certainly mistaken—that midsummer sunrise was observed over the Heel Stone from the centre of the monument. He thought that the extremes of northern moonrise as observed from that centre were observed over a long period—he said over six cycles of the lunar fluctuation, 112 years. All his observation lines pass from the centre of the monument, in a range extending roughly from the extreme northern rising of the Moon to the midsummer rising of the Sun in the neighbourhood of the Heel Stone. His account is unacceptable for various reasons, not least because the post holes do not cluster as they should at the northern end of the range.

For Newham the entrance posts were *foresights*. To appreciate the motivation of Thom's much more sophisticated account it is necessary to consider the complexities of the Moon's motion, if only in qualitative terms. In the present book, absolute extremes of the Moon's risings and settings are often introduced without any reference to how they were established in the first instance. One way of explaining how it was done is to assume that observations were made over very long periods, even of centuries. Why it is necessary to wait so long, and why the case differs so radically from that of the Sun, is that—to express the case in modern terms—there is a short-period ripple on the long-period graph of varying lunar declination against time (see Appendix 2). Observations were made when the Moon was on the horizon. The Moon's declination is changing even in the course of the day, so that moonrise or moonset would not in general have occurred at the precise moment when declination was at a maximum. There are more serious complications, though, caused by the 'ripple' mentioned here.

Consider first the arrangement Thom found in mountainous regions where lunar extremes are believed to have been observed from stone monuments where there was some very distant (and unique) foresight, such as a mountain top. In this case it is the *backsight*, near which the observer stood, that is changed from day to day by anyone marking out the Moon's behaviour. For the sake of

argument, it will be supposed that interest is focused on the Moon's extreme northern rising. A row of slender posts (let us call them rods) marking the observer's positions day after day will obviously be spaced at distances that will depend on the distance of the distant foresight. The last rod position will only by a stroke of the greatest good fortune mark a true lunar extreme. Each month there will be another chance to check it, and each month the last rod will fall to the left or right of the previous one. Now the last of the 'last rods' will seem rather special to anyone performing this exercise. Suppose that a larger post is used to mark its position. At first people might have thought that they had found the absolute lunar extreme, but a mere six months later they would have found that a post placed at the 'last of the last rods' was in quite a different position from the earlier post. It might have been better or worse for those engaged in a search for the Moon's extreme—that of its northern rising, for example.

The posts so placed would themselves have become a focus of interest, if this activity ever took place as described. They too would have had a steady drift back and forth, such that it would have taken 18.6 years or so for the extreme post position to reveal itself. And to be even more precise, even that would not have marked the extreme of which the Moon is theoretically capable, and which we usually assume when comparing an alignment with a 'lunar extreme'. Again the reason is simply that the key observation is never quite at the peak of the curve of oscillating declination, whether we are talking of short-term or long-term oscillations. The discrepancy from the absolute theoretical maximum now might still be as much as a fifth of a degree, corresponding very roughly to two fifths of a degree in the azimuth of the rising Moon. This is a subtle point that might well have been missed by most communities looking for the extreme. However, there can be no doubt that the character of the rippling fluctuations as marked by post positions in the long term (that is, over the 18.6-year cycle), would quite certainly have been found, if the Moon's risings and settings were marked at all over a long period at a single place.

Now there are obviously quite separate psychological and scientific aspects of the case. Two long-term (18.6-year) extremes would have differed by a subtle amount. How would the discrepancy have been explained? After such a period of time, might the difference not have been put down to error? Assuming that the aim was to incorporate the extreme direction into a monument, how long could its builders have afforded to wait? A mature person would not generally have lived to see more than one full cycle. Was there a reservoir of knowledge in the community covering a much longer period? If so, might it not have encouraged the working out of rules allowing theoretical extremes to be

calculated from observed extremes? One such rule might have been worked out for the positions of the 'rods' at a six-monthly maximum, allowing the 'post' to be ideally placed somewhat beyond the observed limit. Another type of rule might have been used for the absolute extreme in the 18.6-year cycle, the position of the ideal post being now placed slightly beyond the limit of the last of the actual posts.

The idea of such rules might all sound far-fetched, but Thom made out a case for both types of extrapolation having been carried out with the help of various types of grid at stone monuments. While he based his argument on a mathematical analysis of the situation, he showed how relatively simple rules of geometrical proportion might have been devised from long experience. The question is, could the Stonehenge grid have been used in the way he believed was the case at some of the vast stone rows and sectors in Caithness and Brittany? While he did not go into fine detail at Stonehenge, he thought it likely. As mentioned earlier, the post spacing would have been mathematically related to the distance of the foresight, which can thus be calculated. This fact led him to a potential foresight, an admittedly inconspicuous stone a little over a mile away, at the northeast corner of the Fargo plantation.

Thom's claim as regards Stonehenge is not convincing, however. (It certainly runs counter to the claim being made here, that alignments internal to Stonehenge are all that are needed to explain its astronomical function; but this has still to be justified.) The grid of posts is much earlier in date than the grids of stones he found elsewhere with the claimed function. The idea that the posts were set out on circular arcs is one that can only be justified in terms of later practice, if at all. Sighting to the northeast does not seem to fall in with later practice at the site, notwithstanding the general consensus, and the proposed foresight is a very poor one. As seen in Fig. 122, well over half the posts in the space between the ditch-ends can be placed on parallels with a simple solar orientation. Of course the resulting sight lines are not highly accurate, but the fact that they do not satisfy us does not mean that they did not satisfy those who were responsible for them.

Geometrically speaking, the posts seem to relate better to the timber monument than to the stones, and the apparent absence in their holes of bluestone or sarsen fragments supports this idea. In ignorance of the plan of the timber monument at the *centre* of the Stonehenge area it is impossible to develop a more plausible theory, but the 'solar' parallels of the main figure could all have found a clear corridor through such a monument, for use by observers looking towards the southwest. For want of a better plan, alignments involving the nine posts to the northwest of the group can today be drawn in

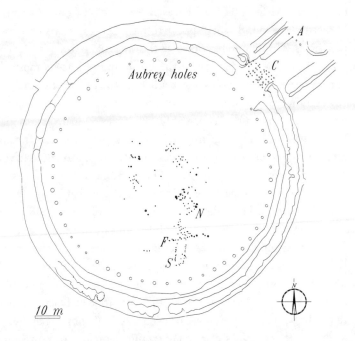

FIG. 123.   The Aubrey circle at Stonehenge, surrounding the numerous post holes that must have formed one, and possibly several, timber circles. Leading up from the south William Hawley found holes indicating an oblique corridor (*S*) with a façade (*F*) at its end. He found what he took to be another at *N*.   Timber post holes already discussed were at *A* (the *A*-post holes) and *C* (the entrance causeway post holes).

ways proving almost anything, and have not been taken seriously into account. The slanting lines radiating from the northern *A*-post on the figure, and again looking to the southwest, could easily be explained in terms of viewing over the timber monument at higher altitude. The lines drawn transversely to the first set could again easily be explained in terms of solar risings (winter solstice) or settings (summer solstice). This is not a solution carrying great conviction, but it has at least as much merit as the lunar theories. (This is not to say that lunar extremes were never a focus of attention at even the earliest Stonehenge—on the contrary.) Not the least of its merits is the way it links up with the placing of the Heel Stone. Whether it was erected before or after the timber posts and ring(s), that extremely important stone is unlikely to have been set up after their total disappearance.

The Timber Henge

The timber henge at the centre of the monument, parts of which were found by William Hawley, is of great interest since it seems to antedate all the stone

circles on the site. Although Hawley was able to excavate only sections of the central structure, he found what appear to have been sections of a complete ring of post holes. This would have been of the order of 30 m across. Its position is about 2 m from the inside faces of the great ring of sarsens most obvious today, but there are other holes almost adjacent to the sarsens, and it seems reasonably certain that the stones were placed over the top of many of the post holes, which are thus lost irredeemably. There were many signs of posts elsewhere on the site, posts that might have been part of other rings or that might have comprised only a few small arcs. While later excavations have added post holes to the known total, the overall pattern of construction is still very unclear. Gaps in timber rings are not uncommon, and that a ring can always be unfinished will soon be evident from the stones of the Q- and R-rings at Stonehenge itself. Nevertheless, it is unduly cynical, in the absence of fragmented arcs of posts on other sites, to suppose that the post system was never completed. One may still reasonably hope for more evidence from future excavation as to the original number of concentric rings of timber posts. There were perhaps fewer than in the southern phase 2 circle at Durrington Walls, but there might well have been three or even more full rings at Stonehenge.

Hawley also found traces of a fairly straight corridor of post holes that seems to have led up to the central structure from a gap in the surrounding bank, at its southern extremity. There were only two breaks in the ditch in its earliest period, one on the south side and one at the northeast. The timber corridor did not extend as far as the southern gap in the bank—if indeed the bank existed when the corridor was built—but Hawley described the ground between corridor and entrance as flinty and hard as though it had been much walked over.

The southern corridor had been 'blocked' at its southern end by three or four posts, in a way found frequently in the Dartmoor rows and in monuments elsewhere in Britain and the Low Countries. To speak of 'blocking' might give an exaggerated idea of what was involved. There was ample room for a person to have entered—although it must be said that words like 'corridor', 'entrance' and 'approach' are no less loaded with meanings for which there is not the slightest positive evidence.

The post holes in the central area of Stonehenge as known at present (Fig. 123) are likely to give a distorted impression of the original situation twice over. They tend to take on the shapes of restricted areas that have already been excavated; and those areas tend to be in the vicinity of the stones, where the post holes have been destroyed by later activity. Near sarsens 8 and 9 Hawley found some of the largest of them, but they were only about half a metre deep.

(The original surface level is virtually unknown, and Hawley's levels are not easy to interpret.) He decided that five of the holes had held a line of posts forming a screen or façade similar to that across the southern corridor (on his interpretation). He later found shallow furrows in the chalk south of his new façade, with post holes along them, and he wrote of a 'passageway' there as though it might have resembled the southern corridor of posts. For structural reasons he thought it to have been roofed—the posts were seated to only a shallow depth. It is difficult to know what to make of these additional finds. Since the furrows were found to have cut through Y- holes (for which see the following chapter) they are almost certainly later than even the stone monuments. This is a useful reminder that in seeking potentially early post circles on the basis of Fig. 123, we should certainly not be tempted to treat all post holes as equal.

British archaeologists with more fantasy than Hawley have shown a predilection for imagining roofs completely spanning such rings of posts as these at Stonehenge, even invoking an analogy with the practice of North American Indians. If any analogy is in order, it is one with the lintelled stone structures destined to be set up on the same site. This claim will be amply corroborated by analyses of further henge-type monuments in the following chapter.

The possibility that the timber henge had a sepulchral purpose cannot now be discussed, except in terms of practice elsewhere. On the whole it seems

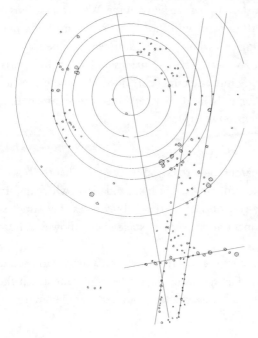

FIG. 124. Some of the very many speculative construction lines that it is possible to superimpose on the Stonehenge post holes. Note how the eastern side of the southern corridor seems to have been on a line (potentially to Rigel Centauri's setting in the south) that is tangential to what might have been the outermost complete ring of posts. The outermost of the circles drawn here takes in chiefly Hawley's supposed northern façade. The line through the centre is at right angles to his southern façade and might have been consciously placed athwart Rigel Centauri's rising.

unlikely, unless some sort of dedication burial or sacrifice was indulged in. In 1926, Hawley discovered a burial near the much-disturbed centre of Stonehenge, but it is of unknown period. The skeleton was laid in a northwest to southeast line.

There is bound to be a strong element of speculation in any geometrical analysis of the very incomplete plan of the post holes currently known, but there are one or two points worth making. We may draw innumerable circles that take in three or more of the holes. Some of the most plausible have the property of centring on points near the centres of the later stone circles. It will be noticed that the eastern post row of the southern corridor, if continued, would have been *tangential* to one of them, so adhering to a principle derived in Chapter 6.

From Hawley's plans it seems possible that the line in question, indeed the corridor as a whole, could have been consciously directed to the setting of Rigel Centauri as seen over natural ground at its extinction angle. On this tentative assumption, the year might have been within a century or so of 2660 BC. Another line has been added to the same figure in the direction of the rising Rigel Centauri, and it will be noticed that it is at right angles to the so-called façade. We recall the similar line, if that is not illusory, of the heavier posts between the ditch terminals at the northeast entrance. As suggested earlier, one of the finest of all timber corridors approaching a post ring, that at Zeijen in Drenthe, was perhaps also aligned on a star, in that case the setting Capella. There is an example of a corridor of posts at Durrington Walls that seems to align on the rising of Vega. Alignments will shortly be found involving lines of sight grazing the timber ring as a whole, and reminiscent of others already described in connection with Avebury. These solutions are not entirely satisfactory, since they entail viewing into and out of corridors. The whole question would repay broader study, for it is hard to accept that the symmetries at Stonehenge, for example, are entirely fortuitous

The Aubrey Holes

The gap in the southernmost part of the ditch strongly suggests that the central rings of posts were in use at the same time as the bank and ditch, which in turn seem to have been related to a ring of posts in the Aubrey holes. The simplest argument for a unified monument at the earliest stage comes, however, from considerations of geometry.

The Aubrey holes are laid out close to a true circle, on a much larger scale than the central ring or rings. The radius of the circle on or near which the centres of the Aubrey holes fall was found by Alexander Thom to be

141.80±0.08 ft (43.22 m). Hunters of metrical units—and Thom favoured a circumference of 131 'megalithic rods' of 2.5 MY or 6.802 ft—should not take such a dimension without questioning it, for it is possible that either the outer or the inner edge of the pits, rather than their centres, was what determined their position. An alternative explanation of the dimensions of the circle will be offered in Chapter 11. (There is no doubt, however, that Thom's units were in use at Stonehenge, as will be shown repeatedly.)

The Aubrey holes have not been completely excavated. They are conventionally numbered clockwise from that nearest to the Heel Stone at the northeast entrance. It was Newall who excavated the first twenty-one of them; thirty-two out of fifty-six had been excavated by the end of the 1920s; and then two more (numbered 31 and 32) were very carefully examined at Easter 1950, by Atkinson, Piggott and Stone. Atkinson and Faith and Lance Vatcher located the outlines of other holes, by laborious prodding, in 1973.

Charcoal from hole 32 provided one of the first important archaeological radiocarbon calibrations done by the pioneer Willard Libby, who found on the basis of it 1848±275 BC—a date that would now be relabelled 'bc' and can be set at a calendar equivalent of 2350±350 BC (see Appendix 1). This date is not significant as an indicator of the history of the holes. It has since been supplemented by other radiocarbon dates, and there are likely to be many more when this largely unexplored feature is more minutely examined. More than a dozen antler or bone dates associated with the primary ditch are now available, and overlooking their spread of uncertainties—and occasional uncertainties about the original location of the finds that are being dated—the dates seem to hover around the thirtieth century BC, which is likely to be much nearer the period of the Aubrey holes.

There are reasons for suspecting that the Aubrey holes once held posts which were to be used for observation, in the manner already explained for post circles generally, in conjunction with the surrounding bank. The bank would have served as artificial horizon. This idea of posts is not now generally held. Aubrey himself, in his notes for the survey he was making for King Charles II, described five depressions he noticed as cavities from which *stones* had been taken. (It is on the strength of this observation that the holes are named after him.) At first Hawley too thought that the holes had held stones (bluestones, he thought), but after the discovery of Woodhenge he opted for the idea that they had held posts. The notion is now out of favour on the grounds that there is no trace of the posts' remains. Hawley, however, claimed that the holes often had their inner edges crushed—which is a 'trace' of sorts—while R. H. Cunnington, writing in 1935, favoured posts on the grounds that the holes

were round in section, with steep sides and flat bottoms, and that there was a funnel shape to their filling. Richard Atkinson rejected the idea of posts, and called attention to potential parallels with the ritual use of pits in Greek religious life. Pits have often been found near Neolithic burials, even under long barrows, so this is not inherently implausible, nor is there any reason why the same pits should not have had different functions at different periods of history. Post holes would presumably have been emptied of any surviving posts when the stone structures commenced building. Fragments of bluestone and sarsen were found in the upper regions of the infill of the Aubrey holes, so that whatever they were, they evidently antedated the stone circles. Many of them contained cremated burials, but this says nothing of their original purpose, for in most instances the human remains were clearly deposited after the holes had been filled (or refilled). They seem to have had chalk rubble shovelled back into them, but this could have been taken from the bank, if its useful days were over. The rubble need not—as has been claimed—have been chalk from the holes themselves that was replaced soon after the hole was first opened.

The geometrical arrangement of the Aubrey holes, bank and ditch have given rise to various exaggerated assessments, oddly enough among the ranks of those generally hostile to the idea of a potential astronomical use. The holes are not laid down with machine-like regularity. With their steep sides and flat bottoms, the average of their maximum diameters is 1.09 m, the average of their minimum diameters is 1.03 m, and the average of their depths is 0.88 m. (The standard deviations are 0.25, 0.18 and 0.14 m respectively.) Assuming that the holes originally held posts, and using our later Durrington rules, on the basis of minimum diameters the heights of the posts above ground might have been 3.43 m (4.14 MY), and on the basis of depths 2.2 m (2.65 MY). Even the second estimate might be too high. It is the more reliable of the two, the large girths being perhaps a consequence of the need to carry heavy lintels (average length 4.85 m). The spacing of the holes is fairly regular, but less perfect than their placement on a circle. (The standard deviation in the positioning is about 43 cm in the first case and 17 cm in the second, but the whole question of spacing will require further comment.) The high quality of the circle has often been thought to show that there was a clear central area, but this is a poor argument. A rope (or chain of linked rods) could have been pulled taut at different angles through the gaps in a central structure, and difficult sectors filled in by approximation, if not by one of several conceivable geometrical procedures that might have been known. The diameter (judged by hole centres) was not small—as quoted earlier, Thom put it at 86.44 m.

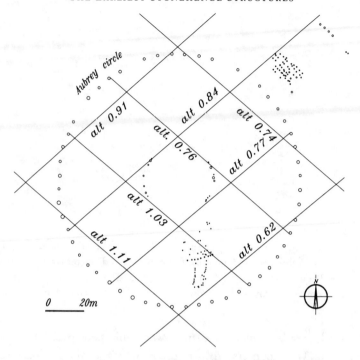

FIG. 125. Conjectured values of the altitudes set by the original bank at Stonehenge, looking towards the midwinter or midsummer setting Sun.

Why are some of the holes oval in shape? After inserting large posts in their holes, for instance to build what in England is called a Dutch barn, farmers from at least the Middle Ages onwards have followed the custom of putting a second post—or a split post—in the hole as a wedge. This makes for oval holes, and might conceivably explain some of the oval Aubrey hole sections.

The Size of Bank and Ditch

The diameters for the bank and ditch are still often quoted from W. F. M. Petrie, who has already been introduced for his enthusiastic and careful measurements of chalk figures (his practice of 'inductive metrology'). Correcting a minor inconsistency in his working, these are his diameters: to the inside edge of the bank:, 91.3 m; to the outside edge of the ditch, 114.2 m; and to the neutral ground between the two, 102.7 m. The bank was probably once highly regular. As Hawley found, the ditch was certainly not, although it was probably intended to be so in certain respects. Its method of construction can be inferred from Petrie's work. Having scribed two bounding circles in the turf, the digging of the ditch would have begun with the removal of turf, which was

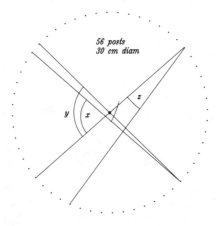

FIG. 126.   Selected lines of sight across an idealized post circle of the sort assumed to have stood in the Aubrey holes. A nominal figure of 30 cm diameter is used for the posts in this figure. The angles marked are discussed in the text. The lines shown are at the correct angles but are not necessarily in their most useful positions, for which Fig. 127 should be consulted.

largely piled outside it, making a small *outer* bank, perhaps 2.5 m wide and 0.75 m high. (This 'counterscarp'—to use Hawley's word for it—can still be easily appreciated in the sector from north to northwest, but it is highly probable that it originally surrounded the entire monument. Could it perhaps once have been the only bank, and represent a part of the very earliest earthwork on the site?) The ditch itself, 6 or 7 m across, was dug as a series of pits each a few metres across, with steep sides and flat bottoms, but of varying depths. These pits were eventually extended until they joined up, but if perfection in the form of the whole was intended, it was not achieved before the work was brought to a close.

Atkinson estimated a bank height of 6 feet and a width of 20, based on the quantity of excavated chalk. Petrie's ambitious measurements imply close on 19 feet (5.8 m) as the bank width, with 18.75 feet (5.7 m), as that of the ditch. Chalk does not settle stably, without something to bind it, at angles of much more than 33°, and 30° has already surfaced a number of times as an angle much favoured in Neolithic times. Now a height of 2 MY (5.44 ft, 1.66 m) above ground level, together with an angle of 30° for the slope of the bank's sides, gives a width of 18.84 ft or 5.75 m, almost exactly Petrie's figure. Petrie, who had his own ideas about a standard of length, had he known of Thom's Megalithic Yard might have pointed out that the inner diameter of the bank on his account was very close to 110 MY. The height (2 MY) fits very well with our very rough estimate of post heights (2.65 MY, but this might be too high).

Finally, it should be noticed that the estimated height and width of the quite separate *outer* bank at Stonehenge, following Atkinson's figures for it, imply an average slope of 31°.

Why Fifty-six Aubrey Holes?

The height of 2 MY suggested here for the larger bank is such that many adult observers could have just comfortably looked over it, had they stood on level ground. Smaller individuals could have walked up the lower slope, but this seems unlikely. All could have observed exactly the same events over the artificial horizon set by the far bank, if it was level and covered the distant natural horizon. For a line of sight across the monument to have been limited in the most precise way, one would expect observers to have been required to stand outside it, and presumably outside the ditch too, since access would then have been no problem. This immediately prompts us to see the lesser bank as a viewing slope, by virtue of which any person down to a height of say 0.9 m (3 ft) could have looked over both near and far banks. One of the immediate consequences of such an arrangement is that the precise height of the bank is of no great importance in an assessment of the altitude it sets, as long as it was reasonably constant above the general level of the ground. In all strictness, there is no need to suppose that the line of sight touched both banks—as long as the eye was reasonably close in level to the main bank's ridge (say 1.66 m, or 5 ft 5 ins)—since the distant bank-horizon was of the order of 80 m away.

At the long barrows and elsewhere, ditches were often used as observation points. The Stonehenge ditch was in places over 2 m deep, but in others only 1.35 m. Even observations made over the outer bank (looking outwards) at low altitudes would have been impossible. The innumerable alternatives will not be investigated here. There are so many signs of post holes and stone holes in the ditch, however, that one may be reasonably certain that some sort of sighting activity took place from it or over it. Perhaps one day, when ditches are taken seriously, we shall learn more. In Chapter 11 we shall examine just one place in the ditch, near the entrance at the northeast. From the side of a stone on the edge of the ditch there, observation over the great stone monument was almost certainly made. In other words, at least parts of the ditch continued to be used after much of it had been allowed to fill.

The altitude of the artificial horizon set by the principal (inner) bank obviously depends on the direction of observation, but what is not generally recognized is that the Stonehenge monument is on a very unusual site: roughly speaking, the contours across it all run in a north–south direction.

There has been much wear and tear of the inner area, especially in recent centuries, and the chalk level has apparently been lowered by the acidity of the rain over the intervening five millennia—although probably not as much as some have suggested—but there is no doubt that this trend in the contours has always been there. To give an idea of the state of affairs at the inner edge of the bank: its most northerly and most southerly points are equal in height to within a few centimetres. Assuming that the bank was of constant height above ground level, one can deduce approximately the altitudes set by it. They would have been slightly higher than the distant natural horizon. Estimates of the altitudes set by ground levels in the way explained are marked on Fig. 125 for eight specimen directions (four to midsummer setting and four to midwinter setting).

Posts in the Aubrey holes would have been admirably suited to the observation of the setting of the midwinter and midsummer Sun, and of the setting Moon at its southern and possibly northern extremes. The choice of fifty-six posts was almost certainly deliberate, and could not easily have been bettered for simple solar and lunar observance. To show this, in the way shown in connection with Harenermolen, two parameters must first be approximately established, one the angle of swing between the directions of midsummer and midwinter setting, the other the angle between, say, midwinter setting and the southern lunar setting. It is more convenient to work with those than with absolute directions, since they can be derived from the posts of an idealized ring (in Fig. 126 the first would be x or y and the second z) and then the whole figure can be turned until the three directions are simultaneously correct.

The angle of swing to be expected between the lines of observation of summer setting and winter setting, granted that the upper limb of the Sun was observed—as explained previously for Harenermolen—would have been in the neighbourhood of 81°. The angle between the southern Sun and Moon (z) is more sensitive to changing altitude, but is likely to have been within 0.1° of 12.5°.[6]

---

6   The precise figures depend on a number of factors. Taking lines across the middle of the site around nominal dates of 3000 BC, 2700 BC, and 2400 BC, with natural horizons gives 81.6°, 81.5° and 81.4°. Assuming an artificial horizon setting an altitude of 1.2° all round, the figures become respectively 81.0°, 80.9° and 80.8°. (This is meant not as a likely option, but only to give an idea of the range of possibilities.) Assuming a constant altitude all round, the figure changes little for a change of altitude. Thus for 1.2° all round in 2700 BC it was more strictly 80.92°, and for 0.6° all round it was 80.90°, hardly different. The value of z for the natural horizon was 12.4° for all three dates. An artificial horizon of 1.2° all round at the same three dates gives 12.7°, and one of 0.6° all round gives 12.4°, and 0.8° gives 12.5°.

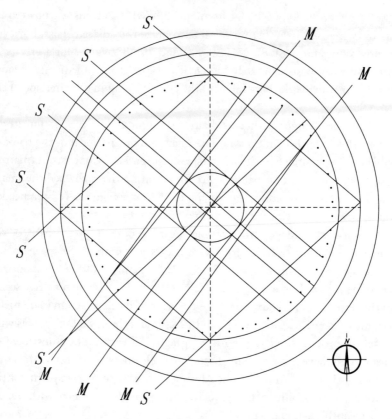

FIG. 127. An idealized Aubrey circle of fifty-six posts (here shown as of 40 cm diameter), drawn in a way that is both close to the actual circle and makes use of the angles discussed in connection with the previous figure. Note that some of the alignments on that figure are here shown only as parallels. Very many more lines could have been added, but those selected (terminating in *S* for the solar lines and *M* for the lunar) are of especial interest. Note that many of them are tangential to the circle representing the timber circle that once stood at the centre of the area. Note also that many post holes found near the northeast entrance all lie between the pair of *M*-lines drawn there.

The calculation of what is to be expected with a particular number of posts must take into account the girths of the posts themselves in relation to the size of the circle. On the face of things, the Aubrey posts were of various sizes, but it is not inconceivable that some of the holes were enlarged after they ceased to be used as post holes. From the dimensions of the holes and the assumption that heavy lintels were supported by the posts, it seems likely that they were of an average diameter not far removed from 30 or 40 cm. Consider the latter figure. With fifty-five, fifty-six, or fifty-seven posts the values for y (taking a crossing of sight lines at the true centre) set by an ideally regular ring are all

in the neighbourhood of 85°, far from our ideal 81°; and this is true even for posts of twice the girth. Taking the line to graze the adjacent post, however, the three values for x are 82.35°, 80.89°, and 79.48°. Values for a greater or lesser number of posts can easily be calculated, but it is immediately obvious that fifty-six provide the best value for the annual swing in the direction of the setting Sun.

This value changes with post diameter, ranging from 80.62° for 20 cm posts to 81.42° for 80 cm posts. If one knew the precise form of the bank, it would even be possible to estimate the size of the posts on this basis. As matters stand, 40 cm seems a reasonable figure. It would not have covered the image of the Sun or Moon—a minimum diameter of 75 cm would have been needed to do so—but it will emerge that this was not an urgent matter.

A completely independent argument can be offered on the basis of the parameter z. With fifty-five, fifty-six, or fifty-seven posts of 40 cm diameter, the values of z (see Fig. 126) are 12.55°, 12.32°, and 12.09°. Since a horizon close to the natural horizon requires z to be close to 12.5°, here fifty-five seems slightly better than fifty-six; but if the posts are reduced to 30 cm in diameter the figures become 12.69°, 12.45°, and 12.23°, and the advantage now is with fifty-six. Even with the larger posts, in practice, a very slight adjustment in position could have put right any discrepancy. Needless to say, even forgetting the other options with fifty-six, the advantages over fifty-five are plain, for the latter offers no possibility of being quartered to provide symmetry with respect to north, south, east, and west.

There is yet another possibility. Accepting now that the ideal number of posts is fifty-six, reducing the angle z so that it spans three rather than four intervals brings the angle to about 9.1°, depending on post size. For 30 cm the figure is 9.24°, for 40 cm it is 9.14°. These are close to the difference (8.8° in 2700 BC over the natural horizon) between the northern extreme of the Moon's setting and the direction of midsummer sunset, but even closer to the difference between the direction of the northern lunar extreme (rising or setting) and the reversed direction of the midwinter Sun (setting or rising). The figures are now 9.12° and 9.63° under the same conditions. Without listing the many possibilities, this means that the northern *lunar* extreme can also be easily worked into the overall scheme. This point is an important one, for it explains why fifty-six posts are used, and not merely fourteen or twenty-eight: with fifty-six one may take three-quarters of the angle z, and so introduce additional phenomena. The number fifty-six is clearly a very special one, astronomically and geometrically speaking, but its special properties would of course have been found by a long process of trial and error.

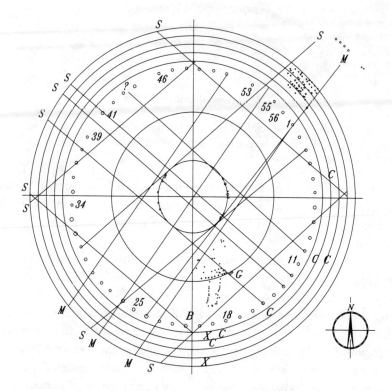

FIG. 128.   Plan of the positions of the actual Aubrey holes, on which most of the
sight-lines shown on the idealized figure (Fig. 127) fit almost perfectly, despite some
distortions in the Aubrey circle. The outer rings are idealized representations of the bank
(inner ring) and ditch (outer ring), each divided down the middle to mark mid-ditch and
mid-bank.

Ditch, Bank, Treehenge and Aubrey Holes

So much for attaining perfect azimuths for solar and lunar phenomena by dint
of choosing fifty-six posts. Before the actual lie of the Aubrey holes is examined,
an idealized plan is drawn, on which sight-lines are added to a geometrically
perfect set of fifty-six posts (Fig. 127). The post sizes are drawn as 40 cm
diameter, which is probably too great. (Had they been tall posts, the Durrington rule would have suggested 22 cm.) The size makes relatively little
difference to some very surprising properties that the ring is found to possess.

First, at least four of the ideal sight lines are tangential to a circle which
seems to take in some of the post holes found by Hawley in the central area. It

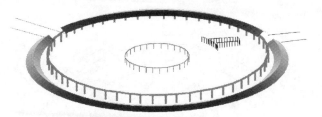

Fig. 129.   An idealized view of the ring of posts in the Aubrey holes, to which have been added only one of the timber rings conjectured to have been at the centre of the area, and the southern corridor.

is as though this inner post circle was being treated as a colossal post in itself. The idea was encountered previously in connection with Avebury, and it will be encountered again, most notably in the case of the ring of sarsens here at Stonehenge.

Second, another set of four key sight lines—those solar lines framing all the others drawn in the figure—intersect almost perfectly on the inner edge of the bank (north and south intersections) and the outer edge (near east and west). Petrie's measurements for the bank diameters are accepted here, equivalent to 91.30 m and 102.74 m. It will be recalled how neatly they fell in with the assumption of a bank of slope exactly 30° and height of exactly 2MY.

These precise measurements are not worth discussing further: the pattern suggested by the idealization must in the end be tested against archaeological surveys. When the test is performed, a highly satisfying arrangement results. This is shown in Fig. 128, based on Fig. 123, to which are added idealized rings for the bank and ditch. The fact that the ditch is represented as perfectly circular is not meant to imply that it was ever anything of the sort—but that it was fairly certainly *planned* to be so.

Key sight lines meet, as before, on the inner edge of the bank. The other two intersections come near to mid-ditch. Note how the post holes at the northeast entrance, where the ditch was partly refilled and much of it never dug, are mostly in the idealized ditch area, and that they follow the curve of the ditch—in fact one row lies close to the line drawn through the middle of the ditch. That these things were carefully worked out by the original architects is confirmed by another fact: the arc of posts near the corridor of posts (near *G* on the figure) is almost exactly midway to the outermost rim of the planned ditch.

There was very probably observation of the setting southernmost Moon and of the midwinter Sun through the middle of the central timber circle, as on the ideal plan, but the damage at the entrance makes this uncertain. There

was evidently observation of the midsummer Sun from the southeast quadrant, and it was precisely in this quadrant that most of the cremations discovered in and adjacent to the Aubrey holes were found—from a later period. Here almost every hole had its cremation, while the letter C in the figure marks where cremations were found in the bank (and CC where they were especially numerous). To some extent this depends on the extent of the excavation, but at least we can say that each of the four sight lines directed to the setting midsummer Sun has bank-cremations at its southeastern end. One of them (from hole 15 to 38) passes over or near to a grave found by Hawley (at G), and bank-cremations are certainly numerous near Aubrey hole 15. This temple-skimming line was presumably of much importance. Ten or more chalk objects of various sorts (balls, perforated objects, and a piece with zigzag scratchings) were found in holes 24 and 25 and the adjacent bank. It will be noticed that there are solar and lunar lines around in that neighbourhood, but there is no strict correlation between line and object.

The bank as considered up to this point is one of constant height as measured above a more or less flat but inclined site (Fig. 129). Another possibility is that the bank was truly level, just as the top of the later ring of sarsen stones was level. In the case of the bank, this would imply that it was about 2 m higher in relation to the ground at the eastern side than at the western. Such an arrangement, with its implications for the doubling of the bank's width, cannot be reconciled with the present remains, and does not merit any further comment.

The alignments listed here are by no means complete, but once a line of sight has been found it becomes a trivial matter to find near-parallels with much the same properties. What the ideal figure seems to lack are alignments on the Moon's extreme northern setting, but in the actual monument there is some slight distortion that seems to have been aimed at them (post pairs 9/47, 10/46, 13/43, 17/39, and 18/38), and another instance will be added later. The average azimuth is about 49.4°, corresponding to an altitude of about 0.6° for 2700 BC. The important point is that lunar settings could have been observed north and south, and that—as will appear from later Stonehenge history—the same directions were marked out by the so-called 'station stones' and by other devices. Some of the Aubrey alignments can also be related to the trilithons, the largest of the stones, which are in some ways their progeny.

There is another reason for not dismissing these lunar alignments as illusory. The standard deviation in the actual positions of the Aubrey holes (a statistical measure of how closely the Aubrey posts came to being at a constant spacing) is about 40 cm, which in a circle whose circumference is 271.5 m is

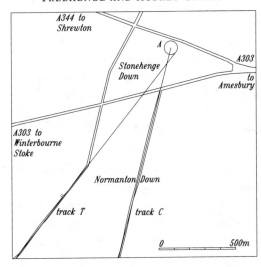

FIG. 130.   Tracks across Normanton Down. If continued, one of them (track T) would have been a tangent to the Aubrey circle (A) and the other (track C) would have passed through the centre. The rich barrow cemetery on Normanton Down stretches roughly across those words on this map.

surprisingly low. Equal spacings would have been marked out in the first instance, and dummy posts moved around until the final design on the landscape was achieved. The large posts would then have been erected. They might later have been trimmed to new positions by enlarging the post holes. (This offers another potential reason for their often oval forms.) In making a statistical survey of the Aubrey holes it is easy to lose sight of the fact that 'errors' in placing the holes are not random. There are slight shifts of phase near the entrance (55, 56, 1) and opposite (27, 28, 29), but more important still is the fact that holes 11 to 16 are closer than the average spacing. This is the range of lunar markers to one side of the site, and it falls squarely in the middle of one side of the rectangle formed by the station stones.

The timber henge, about which we know so little, seems to have been somehow related to the Aubrey circle, and more will be said of this relationship in Chapter 11.

The Aubrey Holes and Normanton Down Tracks

In the last section, lines of sight were mentioned that fell across the Aubrey ring and that were tangential to a ring of timber posts from what was the same or just possibly a slightly earlier period. In due course it will be shown that a similar principle was applied to the ring of Stonehenge sarsens. The Aubrey

circle has what is possibly a related property, in connection with perhaps two tracks across Normanton Down, to the south of Stonehenge. (It ought to be said in advance, however, that no very firm conclusion will be reached.)

Apart from another cutting right across them, and the main road to Winterbourne Stoke (A303) which does likewise, the two tracks in question are the only ones of note on the down to the south (Fig. 130). They were almost certainly straighter in the past than they are now, but even now long sections of them are good enough for it to be claimed that one of them passes through the centre of Stonehenge and the other is tangential to the Aubrey ring. It is not possible to say precisely which of the several Stonehenge centres the line passes through, but if these alignments are not illusory then the Aubrey circle is presumably indicated twice over.

These geometrical properties of tangent and centre beg to be considered as astronomical alignments. Their estimated average azimuths, taking their end points into account, are 14.9° (to centre) and 39.5° (tangent), both east of north. For them to be considered as lines of sight, it is necessary to settle the position of an observer, and from much of each track Stonehenge is invisible. The site comes into view at the top of the gentle rise on which the Normanton Down barrow cemetery was placed. (Most of the barrows there were from a much later period, but some are early, and the western end of a long barrow, Wilsford 30, is on the tangential track.) That rise was only marginally higher than Stonehenge itself—say at most 5 m higher. From it, the far horizon would have been at an approximate altitude of 0.2° over the centre or 0.1° along the tangent to the Aubrey ring.

The line tangential to the Aubrey ring (track T in the figure), at the altitude mentioned, is accurately aligned on the extreme northern rising of the Moon, with the upper limb on the horizon, for the period around 2700 BC. Uncertainties in the direction of the track make it unsafe to use this for dating either ring or track precisely. The derived date is nevertheless in keeping with what might have been expected. As explained previously, it is as though the entire circle was regarded as the remote sighting post; but how the line was actually established or used, it is difficult to say. The reverse line, to the Moon's extreme southern setting, would have been much easier to explain away, but it is a full degree out of true. Perhaps our line touches the Aubrey ring only by chance. If so, it is a strange chance that makes it fit our old 'rule of tangent and centre' and agree so closely with the Moon's extreme of rising at approximately the right period for the construction of the ring.

The line through the centre (track C in the figure) is more puzzling still. It is not precisely towards the rising of any bright star at the same period of

prehistory. The first really satisfactory solution looking north would have been for Arcturus, in the thirteenth century BC. This implies that it is not linked to the Aubrey ring, and so presumably neither is it linked to any lunar sight-line along the other track. It could be related to the period of round barrow building on the down. Reversing the line might be thought to suggest the setting of Rigel Centauri around 2880 BC, but once again, it is difficult to offer a method of use. All told, the two tracks leave us with more questions than answers, and had it not been for their familiar geometrical properties they would not have been worth mentioning.

Post Numbers as a Guide to Events

The case of the Aubrey circle showed that modest adjustments in post position can shift the focus of attention from one phenomenon to another. Nevertheless, there are close relationships between the number of posts in a circle and the phenomena for which the circle is likely to have been used, as the following general treatment of this question will show. The underlying principle will be illustrated with simple examples, assuming the latitude of Stonehenge and a horizon of height 0.6° all round. The period makes little difference, and the quoted figures are broadly representative of all of the third millennium BC, although they are quoted for around 2700 BC.

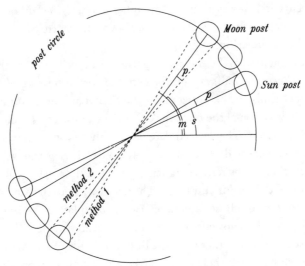

FIG. 131.   Posts for solar and lunar observation across the centre of a post circle. The azimuth of the Sun is s (here shown north of east). Two ways of observing the Moon are considered, and its azimuth (m) is represented by the appropriate one of the two angles marked.

Midsummer sunset was then at azimuth 40.67° (s) and the northern extreme of the setting Moon was at 49.38° (m), both north of west. The corresponding angles for rising are the same, for the same horizon altitude, in the northeast quadrant. The aim is to discover what limitations such solar and lunar figures as these would have placed on the design of a perfect circle of posts. It will be assumed that key lines of sight pass through the centre, or are parallel to such lines. (It has already been found that this is not strictly true in all cases at the Aubrey circle, and a fuller treatment would need to take that into account.) It is assumed too that the technique of observing the Sun is unambiguous: its disc is bright enough for the glint not to be missed as it sets just on the far side of the post. Since in later structures at Stonehenge the Moon will prove to have been observed in two different ways, marked as method 1 and method 2 on Fig. 131, both are considered here. For reasons that will soon be apparent, with a large number of posts—say more than thirty—the Sun- and Moon-posts had to be separated by at least one other post.

It should be obvious from the figure that in the simpler case, where method 1 is used for the Moon, the posts are separated by half of ($m - s$), or in the example cited, half of 8.71°. The angular separation of posts has to fit exactly N times into the circle, where N is the number of posts. Here N turns out to be 82.66, so that rounding to 82 should give good results for observing the Sun and Moon in a single coherent post circle. If there were no intervening post one might settle for forty-two posts, an even number.

Using method 2 for the Moon, the angular separation of the Sun and Moon post centres is ($m - s + 2p$) and adjacent posts are half this distance apart, where p is the angle subtended by the post radius at the centre of the Aubrey ring. With method 2, and posts of 40 cm diameter, $2p$ is 0.53°, the post separation is then 4.62°, and therefore the number of posts, after rounding, is seventy-eight (or thirty-nine if there is no spacing post).

So much for events in the two northern quadrants. Nothing has yet emerged approximating to a solution with fifty-six posts. Continuing along the same lines, alignments to the midwinter Sun and the extreme southern setting of the Moon can be introduced (40.24° and 52.64° respectively), and by the time all possibilities have been considered, there will be sixteen alternatives, including those already given. Those without spacing posts range from twenty-six to forty-two posts. To abbreviate the other cases: extremes of northern rising or setting of the Moon will be denoted by nM, and similarly sM is the southern Moon, and nS and sS are the northern (summer) and southern (winter) Sun. Then on method 1 the nearest even numbers of posts

are: 82 (*nM*, *nS*), 60 (*sM*, *nS*), 78 (*nM*, *sS*), and 58 (*sM*, *sS*). With method 2, the corresponding numbers are 78, 58, 74, and 56.

These numbers are all for 40 cm posts in a circle of the size of the Aubrey circle. To give an idea of changes with post size: doubling the girth of the posts changes the last set of four numbers to 74, 56, 70, and 54.

By scanning a complete list of such numbers, derived for a particular site (with approximately correct latitudes and altitudes), it should be possible to make a reasonable guess as to the phenomena observed there, simply from a count of the posts. Of course this cannot be more than an initial conjecture, to be more firmly established with the help of a detailed plan, but it is a conjecture that can be made even without reference to compass directions. There is here of course a tacit assumption that the circle is indeed astronomical, and that from one fundamentally correct alignment the rest will follow. There is no guarantee of the astronomical assumption, but judging by those circles examined, it does seem to be generally acceptable.

Applying this crude method to the Aubrey circle, for example, we should say that the number 56 immediately points to observation of the midwinter Sun and the southernmost Moon (*SM*, *SS*), the latter by method 2, with the midsummer Sun (ideally fifty-eight posts) a near possibility. These were the principal alignments found above from a more specific treatment. As for the number 58, it is an odd fact that had we been forced to reconstruct the circle on the basis of holes 11 to 16, the region between the 'stations', we should have settled for fifty-eight posts in all. This might be merely accidental, but it serves as a reminder that those responsible for the Aubrey ring did not perform any abstruse calculation. They would have found their alignments to the phenomena that most concerned their own ritual purposes, and after long periods of trial and error they could have added intervening posts. In time it would have been appreciated that the resulting rings could be refined, for example by using artificial rather than natural horizons. Geometry and astronomy thus went hand in hand in the service of religion. The first rings were presumably rudimentary, but very soon the numbers of posts would have grown to something of the order of those derived here. As centuries went by, smaller communities must have realized that by (roughly) quartering the number of posts they could do almost as much as at the great religious centres. The earliest barrow rings of many closely spaced posts—like the fifty-one at Harenermolen—were no doubt directly modelled on the great religious timber monuments of the time, of which the later post rings of eleven, fourteen, seventeen, and similar small numbers, were merely pale reflections. The following chapter will be concerned with some of the nobler ancestors.

THE GREAT TREEHENGES

Stonehenge's Timber Ancestry

T HE main purpose of Chapter 7 was to establish certain fundamental
principles governing the use of lintelled rings of posts, and their analysis.
Moving back in time to apply those principles, the most natural order to follow
is decided by the available evidence, and is still not a simple chronological one.
In respect of azimuths, the best information is from Woodhenge; in the matter
of post dimensions the best information comes from Durrington Walls; and
finally Mount Pleasant provides an invaluable clue as to the techniques and
purposes of lintelling. This seems the most logical order to follow, but it is
exactly the reverse of the historical order, and to keep that in view a brief survey
of changes in henge fashions will be offered first.

Considered from the point of view of their simple components, it was
natural enough that long barrows, with their surrounding ditches, and other
enclosures with ditched straight sides, many or all of them astronomically
aligned, should have given way in the end to enclosures surrounded by circular
banks and ditches. A long barrow could form more than one artificial horizon,
but not a great number. A circular bank, on the other hand, was a potentially
universal artificial horizon. It offered scope for allowing any direction whatsoever to be marked off in conjunction with it. By adding a ring of posts, many
or all of the key turning points of the rising and setting of the Sun and Moon
could be taken into account, and sets of simultaneous sightings along parallel
chords of the circle were also possible. The transition to this new style of
observation had begun to take place by the early part of the third millennium,
if our analysis of the Aubrey circle was correct and the radiocarbon dating of
the ditch is roughly correct (within a century and a half of 3180 BC on the basis
of a piece of antler found in it). One at least of the wooden post circles on the
central area of the Stonehenge site was essential to the correct functioning of
the ditch and Aubrey circle, so it was probably erected not far in time from
3180 BC.

Wooden structures gradually began to replace earthen, but astronomical observances continued to make use of ditches. Earth and wood must have long enjoyed a respected place in religious ritual, and no doubt there was a hierarchy of respect for different varieties of tree. In Britain, most of the charcoal specimens found in the post holes are oak, which was probably the wood used for all the main constructional work.

The first *stone* rings at Stonehenge (the apparently incomplete double ring of bluestones in the Q- and R-holes, to be described in a chapters 10 and 11) are very difficult to date, but were perhaps erected within a century or so of 2600 BC. Before and after then, southern Britain saw a number of large multiple rings, such as that at Mount Pleasant (at some time around the twenty-sixth century) and the first timber henges at nearby Durrington Walls (perhaps later, but only slightly so). Both of these are roughly similar, and resemble Woodhenge (perhaps of the twenty-third century), except that Woodhenge had an oval plan. They functioned in much more sophisticated astronomical ways than the later and simpler rings of Harenermolen type—but the existence of ovals in the Low Countries should not be overlooked. Broad principles were much the same in large and small timber circles, where solar and lunar observation was concerned. In some instances, observations could be made from key points in a ditch. Banks or mounds supplied the horizon. Lintels were so arranged as to eliminate glare, and so successfully was this done that the resulting structures could from certain places seem to be almost solid, even though in reality they were no more than skeletons.

The large henges did not have central mounds, and were not primarily burial places. It seems to have been from about the time of Woodhenge that henge architecture was being borrowed to enhance round barrows, places of burial. The first phase of the Harenermolen barrow dates only from the twenty-first century, but by this time the same broad style had been in use in the Low Countries and in Britain for perhaps three centuries. It is beyond all doubt that there was some sort of interaction between Britain and the continent of Europe in this matter. If barrow rings had been the only sign of henge activity on the continent, one might have argued—on the grounds of a natural evolution from large circle to small—that the dissemination of ideas was from Britain. The discovery at Quenstedt, however, of a monument that seems to have embodied some of the properties of both Mount Pleasant (with corridors crossing the rings) and Woodhenge (rings in oval form) shows that this conclusion might eventually need to be modified. Quenstedt is on the eastern edge of the Harz mountains, about 50 km northwest of Halle. This is not exactly near to Wessex—it is only slightly north of the latitude of London, but

about 800 km to the east. If the quoted dates of the Quenstedt henge are correct—they are in the region of 3000 BC—then it antedates the known large concentric timber ring-henges of Britain. Arminghall in Norfolk, the last example to be considered in the present chapter, was of much the same age as Quenstedt, but it was to a substantially different design.

Woodhenge

In relating the Aubrey circle at Stonehenge to the bank and the central structure, physical heights entered into the argument, since they helped to set the altitude of viewing, and hence the azimuths of the lines of sight to significant risings and settings. It will often prove possible to argue for the height of a structure on the basis of one line of sight—having made an initial conjecture as to what it was directed towards—and then verify it, if we are fortunate, from a different line of sight, where the altitude is set by the same structure in the same way. An important case in point is Woodhenge.

The discovery of the Woodhenge site, with its six nested oval rings of post holes, gave it a special place in archaeological history, but it fully deserves this place on its own merits. When the site was excavated in the period 1926–8 by Maud Cunnington and her husband B. H. Cunnington, they made a survey for which measurements were taken by their nephew, Lt-Col. R. H. Cunnington of the Royal Engineers. Alexander Thom later surveyed the concrete markers that they had caused to be placed over the excavated post holes. Both surveys are used here for the summary sketch of Fig. 132, where the ditch-system—omitted by Thom—is also indicated. The information now available on the post holes is less than perfect. The diameters of the circles on Thom's plan represent the sizes not of them but of the concrete markers, which were based on estimates made by the Cunningtons, who were guided to some extent by the dimensions of the bottoms of the holes. Those dimensions might have been misleading. It is not unlikely that the bottoms of the posts were artificially tapered—both at Woodhenge and at Durrington Walls they were charred, which would have helped to protect them against rot but would also have made them easier to seat in their holes. As for average post diameters, information from nearby Durrington Walls lends credence to the idea that the concrete markers are close to the original post diameters; and so consistent is the following reconstruction that it is hard to believe that the post sizes suggested are much in error.

The approximate average (top) diameters and depths of the post holes in the various rings in *inches* are, as given by the Cunningtons, 32/40 (*F*, the

innermost ring), 30/40 (*E*), 29/34 (*D*), 59/68 (*C*), 38/46 (*B*), 37/24 (*A*). These figures are interesting, for they show a fair degree of constancy in their ratios, which are between 0.75 and 0.86, with the exception of the outer ring (*A*, 1.54). It seems probable that ring *A* contained appreciably heavier posts in relation to their height than the others, while *C* contained the largest and most massive posts. Those in *B* were obviously also fairly large. It will soon be possible to say much more about these sizes and proportions.

Following the excavations at Durrington Walls, Geoffrey Wainwright and John Evans in 1967 carried out more excavations at Woodhenge, its southern neighbour, in the hope of clarifying the relationship of the two sites. They excavated a section across the bank and ditch in the southeast sector and found on the flat base of the ditch a pile of ten antler picks, one of which yielded a radiocarbon date equivalent to the range 2270±130 BC (1867±74 bc; some animal bone gave 1805±54 bc). The period fits well with the style of pottery found (grooved ware, like much from Durrington Walls), and 2270 BC is not an unreasonable mean date for the construction of Woodhenge. There are some who hedge their bets and keep open the possibility that the wooden henge monument was built at a different period from the ditch system, but against this there is an inclined platform of chalk in the ditch that we believe was designed quite deliberately for those who observed the Sun and Moon through or over the monument. The platform is about 30 m southeast of the centre of the monument, in the Woodhenge ditch section investigated by Wainwright and Evans, but it apparently continues beyond. (In some places the ditch is shallow enough for a platform to have been unnecessary.) Its highest point is about 1.25 m below the chalk surface of the monument, and its lowest point 1.6 m, so that it would have comfortably accommodated any adult member of the community.

Thom argued for oval rings of a particular geometrical design, each made of four arcs of circles, with perimeters that were multiples of 20 MY. His simple geometrical construction for the ovals is omitted from Fig. 132, to avoid obscuring the proposed astronomical alignments, which differ from his. He suggested that since each ring has a perimeter very close to three times its longer axis (its 'diameter'), the ovals might represent an attempt to find a geometrical figure for which, as it were, pi = 3. It has to be said that in the absence of his construction lines to guide the eye, the plan of Woodhenge does not look like the embodiment of a set of precise geometrical forms, but Thom's analysis is safe enough, as long as it is recognized that, for the architects of Woodhenge, astronomical properties were almost certainly important enough to override geometrical, in cases of conflict.

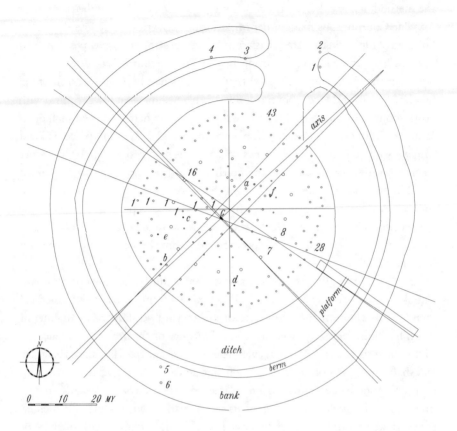

FIG. 132. The ditches and six nested oval post circles at Woodhenge (not perfectly to scale). At *G* a child's grave was discovered, with the skull cleft.

The Cunningtons were the first to propose—very hesitantly, in view of a sceptical archaeological environment—that the axis of the monument was directed to midsummer sunrise. They took this to be a line 39.5° north of east. Thom later found that the axis of his *geometrical* construction pointed to 40.8° north of east. Both assumed midsummer sunrise to be the focus of attention, and both gave the altitude of the corresponding natural horizon as 0.5°. Thom quoted a date of 1800 BC. When our 2270 BC is used for the calculation, however, the azimuth for sunrise at the summer solstice is found to agree with the azimuth of the axis in Thom's construction to an accuracy of one hundredth

of a degree. This concerns only an *axis of symmetry*, and has nothing to do with the method, if any, whereby the monument was used to observe the rising Sun.

The Cunningtons made other important discoveries. They found that the holes in ring C were fitted with ramps, suggesting massive posts hauled upright from the outside; and from the slope of the ramps and certain impact marks in the chalk they estimated that the posts had been 30 feet or more in height (9.1 m), or 24 feet above ground (7.3 m). A somewhat lower figure (with posts about 5.8 m in overall length) will be accepted here, but even such posts as these (in ring C), of oak, would have been around 1.7 cu. m. (60 cu. ft.) and so have weighed around 1.8 tonnes (taking green oak to weigh 1070 kg per cu. m). Oddly enough it will emerge that the lintels on ring C were almost equal in length to the posts, and the widths probably also matched—assuming rough similarity to the Stonehenge lintels. Ring C was perhaps the first to be erected, followed by F, E, D, A (where there were also ramps), and B. The Cunningtons' numbering for the posts started from the westernmost, working in an anticlockwise direction.

At G on the figure, in the innermost area, a child's grave was discovered. The skull was cleft—so much so that Benjamin Cunnington, himself a medical man, at first thought that they were dealing with two skulls. The manner of death has been regularly cited since the discovery of the grave as evidence for a human sacrificial rite. There is every reason to accept the idea, since the grave was shallow and was on the axis of the henge and at right angles to it, in a place that will shortly be shown to be related in other ways to the alignments inherent in the structure. The grave is today marked with a pile of cemented flints. It was thought to have belonged to a child, perhaps a girl, of three or four years old. The skull was sent to the Royal College of Surgeons for examination in 1934, but it was lost in a fire during the Second World War. There have been emperors less exposed to history.

Unlike the arrangement at Stonehenge, the bank was *outside* the ditch, but repeated ploughing has removed all hope of estimating its original dimensions except on the strength of the volume of chalk taken from the ditch. It was very probably of about the same height and form as that at Stonehenge, but less complete. The ditch was large, originally a little over 2 m deep for much of its length, and of the order of 5 m across. It was interrupted by a single wide entrance, to the north-northeast.

The site is fairly level, and in view of the alignment already noted it seems that if the bank was used as an artificial horizon then, however it was used, it did not mask the true horizon by more than a small fraction of a degree. Not only did the natural horizon in the direction of midsummer sunrise (first glint

of the Sun) fit the axis of geometrical symmetry of the monument around 2270 BC, as explained, but the natural horizon in the direction of midwinter sunset at the same period fits the placement of certain key posts. This alignment of posts (about 39.6° south of west) was perhaps the one appropriate to the monument's *use*. Perhaps these directions relating to the natural horizon are relics of the earliest phase of activity on the site.

Woodhenge: the Supernumerary Posts

The posts in question form a rather narrowly restricted corridor of light. They include posts at *a* and *b* (Fig. 132), that clearly did not belong to the rings as such. It might be supposed that the observer could have stood anywhere along the line, and if the last glint of the setting midwinter Sun down the middle of the corridor was all that mattered, then this is so. But what if there was a desire to trap the Sun perfectly between the pair of posts (*B5* and *b*) that ultimately limited the light? The fact that the Sun is about half a degree in angular size would have obliged the observer to stand behind posts *a* and *E12*, that is, near the other extra post on the main axis. The light from the setting Sun would have stood directly over the child's grave. To see the last glint, standing nearly in the same line but further back, brings one close to post *B21*, and in the hole for this post a chalk axe was found. There was another in *A16*, and there were chalk cups in *C7* and *C9*, all holes that held posts involved in important alignments. William Hawley found a chalk axe near the tallest Stonehenge sarsen stone, and it can hardly now be doubted that these objects were somehow related to solar or lunar ritual.

In Chapter 3 it was suggested that the Woodhenge *site*—not necessarily the monument—was in line with the nearby Cuckoo stone and the northern side of the Stonehenge Cursus. As it happens, Aldebaran would have been seen setting over the stone from Woodhenge around 2400 BC, but this fact might be of no importance. The line in question can be reconsidered in the light of the arrangement of *posts* at Woodhenge. Having found a crude use for the supernumerary posts *a* and *b*—there is a more precise use of *a* to come—one naturally looks for a similar function for the posts *d*, *e*, *f*, and *c*. Note that the ray through *c* and the centre of the monument passes over the Cuckoo Stone.

These extra posts, that clearly do not belong to the rings, were marked by the Cunningtons with concrete markers of a reddish tint that can still be made out today. The rays they delimited may be expected to have passed over the central area. So numerous are the posts on the site that by joining these special posts to others we can prove almost anything; but the fact remains that

alignments with other posts—not necessarily meaningful astronomically—invariably follow if each of the extra posts is joined by a line through the centre of the grave.

Some of them were probably posts for blacking out a part of the background sky, in a way to be explained. If not, and if they form a coherent group—which is by no means certain—then it is just conceivable that they were used to mark the directions of sunset at intervals of seventeen or eighteen days. They can be used to cover five such periods before and after the winter solstice, although there is a missing entry (around day thirty-six, before and after solstice). Since also half the year cannot be catered for by the Woodhenge 'special post' alignments, in the absence of similar results from other sites it is best to suspend judgement. There are two rings of eighteen posts (D and E), but this fact should be concealed from advocates of prehistoric eclipse calculation.

Woodhenge: the Third Dimension

There is no royal road to the correct analysis of such a monument as Woodhenge, but it has some very general properties that should not be allowed to pass unnoticed.

Even those who reject the geometrical constructions that can be placed on it will be obliged to agree that its axis of symmetry, as settled by the statistics of post positions, coincides with summer solstice sunrise in the century to which the radiocarbon dating points. Accepting that some of the posts were meant for solar observation, surely the highest and grandest of them would have been involved. If their height was important to their function, and if they were used to create artificial horizons as posts were used at Harenermolen and elsewhere, then we can expect the altitudes set by them to have been of between two and seven degrees. This follows from estimates of their probable sizes, and limitations on where an observer is likely to have stood.

There is another argument that converges on this. It is assumed that the same techniques were used at Woodhenge as elsewhere, that is, of trapping a ray of light from the Sun between two posts, one near and one far, at its extreme of rising or setting. There are two likely solsticial lines involving the massive ring C, one joining the appropriate edges of posts C3 and C11, the other joining C16 and C7. They cross at the centre of the grave. At first sight, astronomical considerations seem to indicate risings and the upper limb of the Sun. If the first line is directed to the rising Sun at the summer solstice (the angle of azimuth, close to 35.0° from the east–west line, does not permit it to be for midwinter setting), and the second to rising at the winter solstice (azimuth

46.4°; midsummer setting is impossible), then it can be shown that in 2270 BC the post positions require the lines of sight to be at an altitude of about 3.93°.

The really important point here is that both lines, despite their substantially different azimuths, require virtually identical altitudes (close to a gradient of 1 in 16).

This figure is crucial. There are problems of post girths and taper to be taken into account, but they do not matter much to this exploratory argument, since they affect both calculations in much the same way. What one must do next is juggle with the arrangement of the lintels to create a convincing artificial horizon that fits with what is known of post-hole sizes, especially depths, and the derived altitude. As explained, the ditch is a plausible viewing point, and it is well suited to both of these basic lines.

From this point onwards the assumption is made that a working rule was followed relating post-hole depth to post height. This seems plausible, in view of the relatively slight variation in the ratios of critical measurements of the post holes in a single ring, both here and at nearby Durrington Walls. Much will be made to rest on the ratio to be derived, namely of 2.5 for the exposed to the buried depth. It fits the Woodhenge and Durrington monuments extremely well. The argument need not be given in full here, and it cannot be claimed that there is a unique solution to the problem, but one of the strengths of the final arrangement, illustrated in Figs. 133 and 134, is that it springs a number of surprises on us that seem to be independently confirmed. There is in it a degree of idealization. The ground is supposed level—in fact it was found to be quite accurately level. The dimensions of the most important posts are rounded to the nearest 0.5 MY. This step is not critical, but there are signs of the use of this unit in the neighbourhood, and it makes good sense of Woodhenge. Certain key distances on Thom's plan of the monument, when correctly identified, also seem to be based on the same unit.

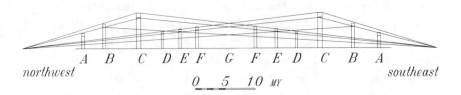

FIG. 133.   A vertical section through the northwest to southeast axis at Woodhenge, with posts (C16 to C7) and lintels of sizes required to produce usable lines of sight.

FIG. 134.   A general view of Woodhenge in its original state. The ditches surrounding the oval post rings are not shown.

Fig. 133 is somewhat stylized. It is appropriate to one section only (posts *C16* to *C7*), and shows the lintels correctly placed for post heights (in MY) of 2, 3.5, 5, 2.4, 2.75, 3 (rings *A* to *F* respectively). There are no posts adjacent to the section in question in rings *B* (left and right), *D* (left), and *F* (left). Left represents northwest and right southeast. Some of the rays drawn clip the edges of the lintels. It would have been easy enough to trim them, here as in reality, but they have been left in their idealized forms to show how extremely accurately the whole scheme fits together. Even as drawn, the trimming of lintels required is rarely more than 5 cm.

The procedure followed is to begin with the rule of 2.5 applied to the average post hole depths as measured by the Cunningtons. Heights are thus derived, and are subsequently rounded up or down. The ratios of heights (the rounded values) to depths (as quoted by the Cunningtons) are: 2.70, 2.48, 2.40, 2.31, 2.23, 2.44 (rings *A* to *F*). The most important ring will turn out later to be ring *B*, and its 2.48 is striking for its proximity to our 2.5. The figure of 2.7 (for *A*) could easily be adjusted to exactly 2.5, and doing so would bring other advantages. (With lower *A*-posts and higher lintels it would have been possible to black out the sky on the natural horizon. On the other hand, this might have been done by the bank in the far background to the view from the ditch.) In view of the care which went into the design of this monument it is hard to believe that the lintels were anything other than rectangular in section, as were the stone lintels at Stonehenge. In all cases it is assumed—although rarely is this essential—that the lintels are as high as the diameters of the posts on which they sit. The diameters are not by any means perfectly known, and one must rely heavily on the Cunningtons' judgement. At Durrington Walls there are more secure data that reinforce the rule of 2.5.

The scheme is far from being entirely idealized. The basic facts on which it is founded are the positions of the posts on the plan of the monument, and the consequent positions of straight lintels between them. Since trees usually have some natural curvature in the trunk, this might have been adapted to the curvature of the rings—bearing in mind that the stone lintels at Stonehenge

are curved. A curve in the lintels would allow us to stay within acceptable limits, but on the whole reduces the exactness of fit rather than improves it. In the three-dimensional reconstruction of Woodhenge shown in Fig. 134 the lintels are therefore assumed straight.

One consequence of the arrangement, entailed by the rule of 2.5, is that the posts of ring *C* are of lengths 7 MY, more or less identical to the lengths of their lintels—about which no conjecture is necessary, for we can measure them from the plan. This makes for a very pleasing type of uniformity in the scheme.

It could be imagined that lintels were omitted altogether, but this would be to sacrifice a principle suggested strongly by the derived scheme: the inner rings were used to create artificial horizons comparable to, but far more intricate than, those created by mounds of earth. The difference is that at Woodhenge there was only a skeleton 'mound', so that rays could be made to penetrate it and so set alternative altitudes. If this was the intention then the design is of considerable sophistication, as will be best appreciated once additional rays set by the skeleton monument are listed.

The following table is included to underscore the inner consistency of the scheme derived, a scheme that is intimately bound up with the sizes of the posts. All data are in MY (0.829 m). An asterisk indicates reliance on the Cunningtons' mean values.

Ring	A	B	C	D	E	F
Post height showing (*H*)	2.0	3.5	5.0	2.4	2.75	3.0
Post diameter (*D*)	0.5	0.5	0.75	0.33	0.4	0.5
Hole top diameter (*d*)*	1.13	1.16	1.81	0.89	0.92	0.98
Hole depth (*h*)*	0.74	1.41	2.08	1.04	1.23	1.23
Lintel thickness (*L*)	0.5	0.5	0.75	0.33	0.4	0.5
H/D	4.0	7.0	6.7	7.3	6.9	6.0
H/h	2.7	2.5	2.4	2.3	2.2	2.4
d/D	2.3	2.3	2.4	2.7	2.3	2.0
H/d	1.8	3.0	2.8	2.7	3.0	3.0
h/D	1.5	2.8	2.8	3.2	3.0	2.5

The first of the five rows at the foot of the table (that for *H/D*) might be seen as an indication of taste—the geometrical proportions of the visible column—whereas the last five quotients have more to do with mechanics. The wooden posts were anchored in the ground to much the same relative depths

as the stones in stone circles, although there the trimming of the stone was much harder, so that the variation in H/h is greater. Even so, at Stonehenge most stones fall in a range in H/h from 1.7 to 3.5, and the average is probably not far removed from the figure of 2.4 (2.33 if the idiosyncratic ring A is taken into the reckoning).

Although strictly unprovable, there were probably three simple rules, or recommendations, in operation: the hole depth was to be two and a half times the post diameter; the length of post above ground two and a half times the post depth; and for all but the narrowest and the widest posts, a hole was to be dug of diameter two-thirds of the hole depth. These rules are summarized in Fig. 135. (The second could be rendered 'a yard deep for every rod high'. The third is not obvious from the Cunningtons' figures, but will be derived from those for Durrington Walls, and is certainly compatible with the former.)

Woodhenge: the Integration of Sun and Moon

Important—inasmuch as it underlines the consistency of the scheme—is the fact that the very same post heights are ideal for other crucial rays crossing the monument from all four quadrants. Expressed otherwise: having deduced the heights using one ray, say midsummer sunrise, it is found that they reproduce perfectly the quite different angles of the others. (This has been done for one extra ray already, namely midwinter sunrise.) In a sense, this is the very reason for the oval shape of the plan of the monument. As set by the posts, the angle to the midsummer Sun is higher when it is observed setting than when observed rising, and therefore the distance for a given drop in height has to be

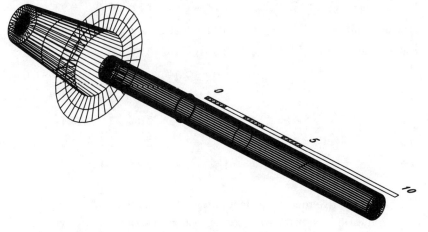

FIG. 135.   The conjectural rule governing the proportions of an ideal post. The units are arbitrary.

less. Admittedly this could have been corrected by varying the observer's position in the ditch, but it is now obvious that a decision was made at Woodhenge to compress the rings into an oval form.

It might be thought that the last argument is more circular than oval. After all, those who designed the monument were not obliged to give the line to the southeast quite the direction it has. Why not shift it by a degree or two to bring down the viewing altitude to that of the other ray, and so make a circular monument possible?

There was one very obvious reason for not doing so. Those responsible had evidently already settled on the axis of the monument using the natural horizon to midsummer sunrise. They now wanted a line to midwinter sunrise to be at right angles to that line. The only way of arranging this was with a high-altitude line. It does not matter to the argument which particular line this was—in fact since it is unlikely that the first development of oval monuments took place at Woodhenge, one should expect only to be able to illustrate the general technique here, and not an actual evolution. The general principle holds good, that wherever posts were arranged to give a high elevation, then using those same posts in the same general way to make the crucial rays cross at right angles they would have had to be further away from the observer in the northeast quadrant than the southeast.

How can one be sure that there was a deep concern with right angles if one cannot produce an exact case? The winter sunrise line $C16/C7$ (Fig. 132) is a little under three degrees from being perpendicular to the 'natural' axis. Is this acceptably close to a right angle? Perhaps not. The same line ($C16/C7$), however, is almost perfectly at right angles to a line joining $F3$ to the supernumary post a. Perhaps this line has something to do with the setting up of the monument. It is easy to choose a post length for a to force a fit, and it will not be done here; but note that post a is just half way between $A40$ and $F3$, posts in the same line. If an adult were to stand not in the ditch but to the side of post a, midwinter sunset could be made to appear under lintel B in the line described, with the 1 in 16 gradient yet again.

There are other potential solar alignments, but they offer minor difficulties and the point need not be laboured further. Far more interesting is the way in which the Moon enters the picture.

There are two alignments on lunar standstills that pass through the centre of the monument, one for the Moon at its most northerly setting and one at its most southerly. (Some dubious lunar minima are rejected.) The second of these is fixed by the northwest faces of $C12$ and $A12$ and perhaps by one of the posts outside the monument in the bank to the north (marked 1 on Fig. 132). This

is not particularly remarkable, in its relation to the overall structure, and might be illusory. The other is clearly not so.

The northernmost setting of the Moon was to be seen in the reverse direction of the line *C16/C8* that yielded the midwinter Sun's rising. It is a remarkable fact that the altitude at which the solar event was to be seen was precisely the same as that for the lunar event in the reverse direction. The gradient of both, in other words, was 1 in 16. It must be assumed that this curious property, which is highly specific to the latitude of place, had been discovered before the monument was designed, and that the monument was built to incorporate it.

The plane containing the lines in question was very nearly at right angles to another potential pair of solar lines (midwinter sunset as seen conventionally from the northeast ditch, at altitudes 3.45° and 3.6°; lines fixed by *C11/C4* and *C12/C3*). This in itself is remarkable enough.

The line (*C16/C7*) to the northern standstill passes the post *C7* that was found to have at its base a chalk axe and a chalk rectangle with depression. The same post was used for the Sun, so it is not certain that these objects are symbolic of the Moon. One common reading of such symbols is that they were related to a fertility ritual. Similar items were found at the base of post *C9*. This, with *C14*, might possibly also have aligned on the northern lunar maximum setting. If the chalk artefacts were concerned with lunar ritual, then the rule followed in all three cases mentioned seems to have been that they were to be placed at the foot of the nearest grand column along the lunar line.

Durrington Walls: the Constant Horizon

The excavation and reports on the timber structures at Durrington Walls, immediately to the north of Woodhenge, were done to an unusually high standard, but it is unfortunate that segments of both circles—the parts not destined to be covered by the new road—were left unexplored. The fact adds an extra dimension of conjecture to the three dimensions necessary in any reliable reconstruction, but it does not affect one remarkable property of the enclosure, which seems to have escaped previous notice.

The enclosure is vast and very roughly circular in plan, about 490 m by 468 m in all, on a southeast slope forming a shallow dry gully. There are two entrances through the surrounding bank and ditch, one in the northwest sector and one the southeast (Fig. 136). The river Avon is only 80 m or so to the southeast of the latter. (Henges are often close to water, but Durrington Walls is unusual in leading so directly to the river.) Much of the bank creating the

enclosure has been ploughed down over the centuries, but it was about 30 m wide, and parts of it are still 2.5 m above the ditch. This ditch was a massive one—5.5 m deep, in places more than three times as wide at the top, and with a flat bottom approaching 7 m.

Why the site is remarkable is obvious neither from the terrain as it is found today nor from a map of its contours. It is that after the construction of the ditch and bank, an observer standing where the southeast entrance to the southern monument was eventually to be built, and surveying the greater part of the bank, would have been presented with a horizon at a virtually constant altitude. More specifically, this property would have held good from a bearing of about 210° (from north) to somewhat beyond the bearing of the northern monument (that is, roughly north), a circuit that takes in about seven-tenths of the bank. This of course does not apply to the dip in the horizon at the western entrance. Even today, with the wear and tear of millennia, especially in the relevant western sector which has been much damaged in the present

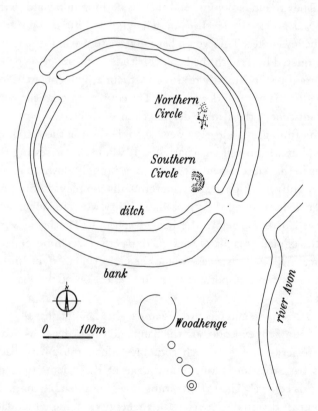

FIG. 136.   The orientation of ditch, bank and river in relation to the timber rings at Durrington Walls and Woodhenge.

century, it can be said that were the view not blocked by the new road, it would be possible to choose a viewpoint such that the mean altitude over this stretch would never stray by more than a tenth of a degree from its average value (which is around four or five degrees, depending on the height of the eye).

This noteworthy property depends heavily on the position from which the bank is surveyed. To an observer even as close as the centre of the future monument, a mere 15 m away, the altitude of the bank would have been appreciably less constant, no matter what the height of the eye above the ground. Present horizon altitudes have been slightly diminished by the erosion of the bank's ridge, and also by the rise in floor level at the point of observation, at present about 84.4 m above the Ordnance Datum at the entrance. If constancy of altitude was the aim, viewing from between 86.6 m (284 ft; with altitude averaging $4.21°$ over the constant sector) and 87.2 m (286 ft; $4.07°$) provides the most acceptable results; but then the observer's eye should be 2 m or more above the present ground level. This is probably an acceptable situation. The ground is sloping, and there is nothing untoward in the idea of a site that was artificially levelled, by removing soil higher on the slope and banking the lower area. This would have given a figure in the neighbourhood of the two quoted here, with the bank's altitude in the range $4°$ to $4.3°$. This is an important result, since there are at least four alignments to be found that require an altitude of the order of $4.1°$. (The equivalent gradient is 1 in 15.5, and is reminiscent of the 1 in 16 derived from Woodhenge.)

Viewing from ground level somewhat to the west of the monument gives fair results, but with much less constancy. It would be interesting to learn of any ditches to that side, allowing the eye to be brought down to ground level.

The dry gully in which the Durrington Walls complex was built must have been recognized as having this arena-like quality when its upper slopes were first surveyed, that is, before the bank was built. The bank, with all its irregularities of plan, was plainly designed to perfect an almost perfect natural arena. Here, once again, is a case where the perfection of sight lines crossing the horizon was more important than the perfection of the plan view of a monument.

Richard Atkinson and Geoffrey Wainwright thought that 900,000 man-hours of labour were expended on the bank and ditch alone. As Wainwright wrote, 'A society capable of such corporate efforts must have had a more prosperous base than our scanty knowledge of their domestic settlements would have us believe'. Their efforts imply too a considerable commitment to the religion that diverted so much of their energy from more mundane tasks.

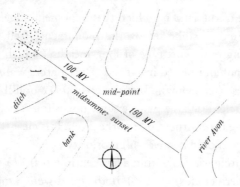

FIG. 137.   One of the long measures that might have been in round numbers of MY at Durrington Walls.

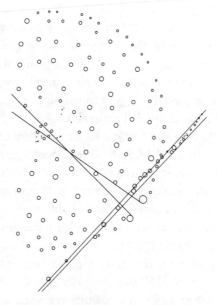

FIG. 138.   Durrington Walls, Phase 2 of the southern circle, showing the southeast façade, with 'bar'.

Durrington Walls: the Circles

The southern timber circle was the larger of the two, and has its centre rather precisely on the line joining the midpoints of the entrances to the enclosure. In fact the distance from the centre of the southern circle to the midpoint of the southern entrance is—allowing for slight uncertainty about the precise midpoint—100 MY. Continuing the line for another 100 MY brings one almost exactly to the river (Fig. 137), at a sharp bend. Viewed from this point on the

river, the altitude of the land on which the monument stands is identical to that of the key line of sight set by the monument itself, that is, to the midsummer setting Sun. This type of long measure, which will be recalled from Avebury, is not an isolated instance at Durrington Walls, for the line to midsummer sunrise (see below), if continued 400 MY uphill from the centre of the southern circle, reaches a point exactly opposite the end of the straight section terminating the southern part of the ditch. It is clear that in any future excavation this line should be given high priority.

The smaller circle was (to within a few centimetres) 175 MY to the north of the larger southern circle (Fig. 136). Both circles were completely renewed and redesigned at an early stage in their history, and the separate phases of the two monuments (with calendar dates BC as derived from radiocarbon sources) are apparently as follows:

Southern, Phase 1 (2320±170 BC): five roughly concentric rings of posts, ranging from 2.3 m to 30 m in diameter, with what was possibly an entrance to the southeast. The outermost 'circle' (*A*) has long arcs with no posts at all. Almost tangential to it there was a line of posts forming what might be seen as a façade. The second innermost (*Q*) had only four posts at any one time. Replacements bring its final number up to eight.

Southern, Phase 2 (2440±140 BC): a larger structure of six rings, nearly concentric, between 5.6 m and 38.5 m diameter. See Figs. 138 and 139 . The outer has two large post holes, seemingly marking an entrance—and certainly aligned on the rays of the setting midsummer Sun. Quantities of flint, pot, and animal bones were found in a burnt area (on chalk blocks outside this 'entrance') and also in a large cavity that the excavators called a 'midden', on the northeast edge of the monument (2850±150 BC).

Northern, Phase 1: of this little has survived, and it might be illusory.

Northern, Phase 2 (2350±150 BC): three circles, if one counts as a circle a central set of four large posts set in a quadrilateral with side about 5 m (see Fig. 140). The circles were approached by a corridor of posts and there was some sort of façade of smaller posts across the south side (about a third of the way up the figure) and reminiscent of that at the southern monument. In this case it was curved. In all cases of linear rows of posts on this site it is tempting to see the principles of tangent and centre at work.

Remains of a Neolithic settlement were found beneath the southern bank, dating from around the thirty-fourth century BC. A large hollow oval (12 by 6.7 m by at most 0.6 m deep) cut into the slope of the valley to the northeast of the centre of the southern monument was found to contain animal bones,

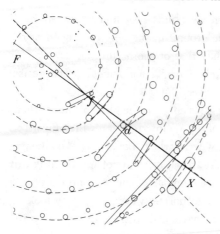

FIG. 139. A detail of the preceding figure, with some construction lines added. Note that the phase 1 structure near—but by no means at—the geometrical centre seems to be related to the two fundamental lines of sight marked as grazing the posts at X.

FIG. 140. Durrington Walls. Post holes at the northern circle (top third of the figure) and the approaching corridor.

bone pins, antler picks, pottery, arrowheads and stone tools. The most one can say about its position is that it was very probably associated with religious rituals of winter sunset, which could have been observed looking across either the monument or whatever preceded it, from a point between it and the monument. A radiocarbon date (2320±125 BC) suggests activity as late as 2600 BC, but there is every reason to suspect religious activity in this particular place from the previous millennium, and certainly well before the time of the timber henges. No doubt this oval repository for offerings continued in use at least until the end of the southern Phase 2 building. An extensive area of burning occurred on a platform outside the southeast entrance to the southern Phase 2 building, and around the platform were scattered flints, shards and animal bones. Similar things are well documented in connection with chambered tombs, while the deliberate breaking of pottery, the depositing of flints, and offering of meat is all known from and around stone circles and under round barrows.

It is virtually certain that the southern circle was used in solar ritual. Its geometrical centre was in the line joining the midpoints of the two entrances not only to its own entrances but to the entire Durrington Walls enclosure, and this line is the line of the Sun's midsummer setting

around the time the enclosure and henge were built. Its wider significance will soon be clear. The natural slope of the ground in the neighbourhood of the southern monument is slightly less than that of the natural horizon in this direction, and the azimuth in question (close to 35°, one cannot be very precise) is acceptable for that horizon around the year 2400 BC.

Following the principles of the previous chapter, the plans of the southern and northern rings as published by Geoffrey Wainwright (on which Figs. 138 and 139 are based) are examined to see whether they, like nearby Woodhenge, were somehow aligned on the Sun. There are various ways of approaching this problem, bearing in mind that little more than half of the area of the southern monument has been excavated. One would normally have begun by looking for well-spaced vertical posts that might have limited the alignments on the Sun at the solstices. This is out of the question, since vital posts are still unexcavated, and one can only estimate their probable positions. It is not unreasonable, however, to conjecture that key rays were made to pass over the centre of the monument. A ray perfectly central to the entrance cannot do so, since it is blocked by a post in ring D. There is, however, one line that we can draw of solar type (that is, passing beyond the far post in azimuth of rising or setting) that corresponds to an altitude of the Sun's upper limb of 4.1°. This, it will be recalled, is within the probable range of constant altitude of the bank enclosing the 'arena'. The bank's altitude is not critical, since the alignment is on the rising winter Sun in the southeasterly (downhill) direction. (Its azimuth is 47.2° south of east.)

There is a second line, using the other post at the southeast entrance. It misses, to be sure, the centre of the monument, but it does pass through a corridor created by posts known to us, and had it aligned perfectly on the Sun's midsummer setting at azimuth 34.8°, this would also have required an altitude of 4.1°. The (uphill) direction in question passes through the gap in the enclosure, which must have filled with soil to some extent in the long period since it was built, but the fact could not have made much difference to the altitude set by the landscape, and 4.1° is not an unreasonable figure.

There is yet a third alignment passing through the centre, almost along the line of the first ray, using the *same* entrance post, but now using its other face as a lunar-type marker. It is aligned on the northernmost setting of the Moon (azimuth 44.9° north of west) for the very same altitude.

The data for the azimuths cannot be known precisely, but at Durrington Walls, although something has been lost through ignorance of the positions of certain posts, we do at least have the advantage of decayed wood (the 'post-

pipe') in the cores of most of the post holes, and the azimuths of the lines mentioned are probably accurate to much better than half a degree. An error of half a degree in azimuth would affect the altitude we deduce by only 0.4°. And since the derived altitudes for the directions of the three different alignments are the same, confidence in them is raised accordingly.

Even this initial survey of the Durrington Walls plans has thrown up one thing that the monument has in common with Woodhenge: it seems that both monuments had a central or near-central focus. (Here it was assumed as a premiss, but the premiss did yield coherent results.) At Woodhenge it was the grave, while here it seems as though the centre of the circles was important for one of the principal sight lines mentioned, while all of them seem to have passed through a set of six central posts that the excavators associated with Phase 1. These six posts seem to be symmetrically arranged around the midwinter sunset/midsummer sunrise line, and there are stake holes in the neighbourhood that might have been concerned with setting up this structure (Figs. 138 and 139). By our rough rule of post-hole depths, the six posts were somewhere between 60 cm and 1.5 m tall—they were probably of different heights, and perhaps each had a significance, if not a sanctity, of its own. The enclosed area was presumably the most sacred of all, and in it there were traces of a hearth between the largest posts.

For Woodhenge, the conjecture was made that the monument embodied a gradient of 1 in 16. Here at Durrington Walls it emerges once again, or something very close to it. There is another common element, however, and one that is more important still: the two monuments seem to have used similar conventions as to the relative dimensions of posts and post holes generally.

Durrington Walls: the Dimensions of the Posts

At Durrington Walls, as at Woodhenge, it is possible to see that while there were no absolutely rigid rules in use, there were some rough working rules in operation. The meticulous survey makes an objective comparison of post-hole depths (h) and average post hole diameters (d) relatively simple. To these dimensions, post diameters (D) can be added, if the post pipe is an accurate guide to them. Some post pipes were such well-formed cylinders that they must be reasonably accurate. On the basis of the data recorded, the following initial conclusions are drawn:

(1) There is no strong preference for any particular value of the ratio of hole to post diameters (d/D), but there is a weak tendency to settle for a ratio around

2.5. The average over the 141 posts for which pipe and post hole diameters and hole depths are known is 2.66.

(2) For smaller posts, the ratios of hole depth to diameter (h/D), tends to cluster weakly around 4. For bigger posts the ratio can be higher, but for the largest of all, a ratio near 4 is again typical, and it is quite probable that 4 was accepted as a working norm, even if it was not zealously adhered to.

(3) The ratio of buried post to post diameter (h/d, where d is taken to be an average over the known pipe) can be large in the case of small posts, no doubt reflecting the difficulty of digging a narrow hole with antler picks. The bulk of the posts (113 out of 141 assessed) have h/d between 1 and 4 and an average of 1.5. Of these there are 90 that avoid the extreme ratios, and their average is 1.49. It seems probable that 1.5 was a working ideal.

In all this, the question of greatest interest remains unanswered. What were the rules for *post heights*, which were chiefly responsible for giving a monument its outward form?

The way to an answer has been shown for Woodhenge. At Durrington there is the altitude of 4.1° which will be shown to have been set by the posts and lintels of the southern monument in its second phase. From the ground plan it is found, exactly as at Woodhenge, that the sight lines in question often passed the edges of the lintels, as far as can be judged, at intervals (in plan) that were integral numbers of Megalithic Yards. It could be said that the *circles* were deliberately spaced in this way, and it is hard to quarrel with that way of expressing the matter, except that the horizontal distances between lintels were of prior importance, for it was they that determined the angle of the artificial horizon. Fig. 139 shows how the lintels of a particularly important set were placed in relation to the circles and two key lines of sight. To each azimuth, for a particular solar or lunar phenomenon, there is an acceptable altitude. A whole range of plausible values for the ratio H/h will therefore be considered, and rounded values of the post heights (in MY) will be sought, such that by their lintels they set that required altitude.

Before this is done, it is as well to be aware of the danger of seeking Thom's Megalithic Yard only as a unit of measure of circles (diameter, circumference) or of other geometrical shapes. From there it is a short step to applying standard statistical methods and assuming a normal distribution in what will then be seen as the errors of the builders. If a post was moved deliberately out of the circle in order to achieve a better astronomical fit, then the method will be vitiated, since the ultimate intentions will have been misjudged. To take another example: suppose that the aim was to achieve a standard gradient, say

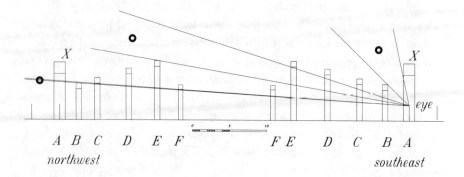

A   B   C   D   E   F   F   E   D   C   B   A
northwest   *southeast*

FIG. 141.   Potential sight lines at Durrington Walls (southern circles). The observer is imagined to stand in the middle of the heavy posts at entrance X (Fig. 139). The black rings mark regions of the sky not blocked out by lintels. The only astronomically useful lines of sight are those at the lowest angle (around 4° in altitude). The thin pencil of lines as drawn here goes from 3.95° to 4.14°.

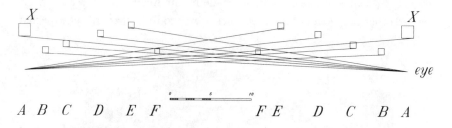

A   B   C   D   E   F   F   E   D   C   B   A

FIG. 142.   All potential sight lines from the same position as in the previous figure, whether or not they are capable of avoiding the uprights. Only the lintels are shown here. Those to the unexcavated northwest are positioned only on the basis of symmetry.

1 in 15 or 1 in 16, through the use of standard units of length. Where the artificial horizon is set by the midpoint of a lintel's length, if the latter is straight then the critical point on it cannot be expected to fall on the desired circle. If the pair of posts carrying the lintel are found to be off the supposedly 'ideal' circle, this may mean no more than that the *lintel* was being brought into some preconceived ideal position. (There are examples flanking post *d* on Fig. 139.) A statistical analysis of *post* positions alone cannot then be regarded as a guide to the planned centre or radius of the basic circle, or to any particular unit of measurement. It is a paradox that posts or stones that seem at first sight to have been inexpertly placed are on closer examination often found to have been placed with exceptional care. Even at Durrington Walls, where an incomplete excavation means that considerations of symmetry are needed, it is not necessary to force the evidence to find edges of lintels that are, to the nearest

0.1 MY, at such integral positions as 10, 15, 17, 30, 32, 36, 44, and 48 MY. This should encourage the idea that the spacing followed the unit named, although this is not assumed at the outset. Post positions, and the lintels that would have corresponded to them, are taken strictly from the excavators' plans.

Passing from ring A (together with the entrance posts marked X) to ring F, the average depths of the holes in each of the six rings—overlooking posts that are plainly unusual, such as those at the southeast entrance—turn out to be these: 0.43, (2.43 for the two entrance posts), 1.66, 1.93, 2.42, 2.86, 1.56, all for future convenience quoted now in MY. Using these averages, a whole series of possible rules relating height to hole depth is next considered—assuming that the rule was to take a factor of 2, 2.5, 3, 3.5 and so on, up to 10. Even without rounding, a factor in the region of 2.5 is found to work best astronomically. (Some reference to the landscape is necessary: there is no point in a line of sight that is blocked by the bank, for instance.) When in addition the post lengths are rounded to multiples of 0.25 MY, not only does the resulting scheme fit the constant-altitude requirement almost perfectly, but certain other properties of the monument come to light that are not expected.

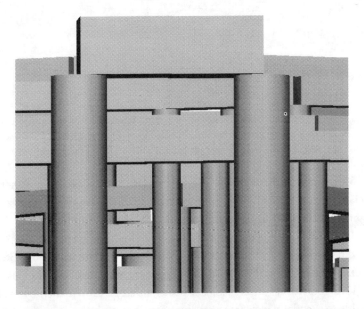

FIG. 143. The view through the southern Durrington Walls monument to a person approaching the left post of the southern entrance to it. Note how few are the 'windows' through which the sky may be seen; and how some could be eliminated by a slight sideways shift of the eye. The lowest would have actually been blocked by the earthen bank beyond. The impression of impenetrability is paradoxical, in view of what in reality was an open skeletal structure.

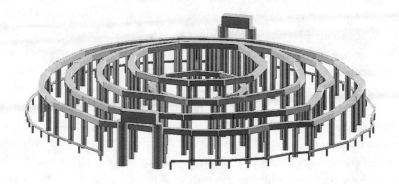

FIG. 144. A reconstruction of the southern Durrington Walls monument on the basis of post heights derived earlier. Posts to the far (northwest) side are placed from considerations of symmetry. Lintels over the entrances would presumably have covered flanking posts fully.

The search is for sets of at least three lintel edges more or less in line, to delimit rays, or at least two edges plus the eye of the observer. Here are the results of rounding:

unrounded	1.08	(6.08)	4.15	4.83	6.05	7.15	3.90
rounded	1	(6)	4	4.75	6	7	4

The rounding of lengths, as they are adopted here, means an adjustment on average of only about 8 cm, the width of the palm of the hand. Some of the posts were a hundred times this in length. This is a very satisfactory finding, but more satisfactory still is the exactness of the alignment of the lintel edges that limit key rays, something best appreciated from Figs. 141 and 142. It is the fact that they provide precisely the altitude of 4.1° needed for the semi-natural solar and lunar alignments within the 'arena' that makes the derived *post* heights so plausible.

Working to quarters of Megalithic Yards (tenths of a Megalithic Rod, about 21 cm) is to some extent justified by a property of the diameters of the post pipes in the central corridor in rings B, C, D, and E, all of them close to 0.75 MY, even though those rings comprised posts that were on average narrower than this. All key lintels are assumed to have been of this same width, and—for want of better information—of this same height. This is in many ways not a critical matter, but it will help to give the monument one of its most important properties.

The short posts of ring A seem to have been even shorter than those at Woodhenge, and yet there seems to have been no ditch close at hand for their use, as at Mount Pleasant and Woodhenge. The assumption of short A-posts gives rise to another problem of analysis. Were lintels accurately level, as are the stone lintels at Stonehenge? It seems likely that this was so with the exception of the outermost fence, which was perhaps only for keeping animals out. (Its posts, only 1 MY tall, might not have come above ground level at the northwest side. The chalk surface is not as steep as the present surface soil, however, and it might have been dug out to make it more level. Only when the excavation is completed will the answer be known.) At all events, the posts of the outer ring do not at present seem vital to the astronomical functioning of the monument. The following analysis is based primarily not on sight lines fixed by them but on a viewing height of 2 MY, as before. There were only two human bones found at Durrington Walls. One of them, a tibia belonging to an adult male, allowed R. Powers to estimate his height at 174 cm (5 ft 8.5 ins). Such a man's eye level would thus have thus been at about 1.65 m, or 1.99 MY.

The overall appearance of the southern monument is shown in Fig. 144, while the apparently solid wall facing a person approaching the southeast entrance (like that at the northwest) is shown in Fig. 143. Seen as a whole, say by moonlight, the monument would have had the appearance of a very solid mound. To someone standing along a central line, the altitude it would have set to anyone observing a star over the top of the lintels on rings B, C, D, E (all taken to be equally thick) and grazing them all would have been 15.17°. The star's azimuth would have been 40.0° if it followed the line through the middle of the entrance and the centre of the ring, and would have entailed a declination for the star of about 36.34°, perfect for Deneb around 2300 BC. This date is not reliable, however, for reasons explained earlier of Deneb.

Durrington Walls: the Southern 'Façade'

Assuming that it is of the same age, a line of at least twenty posts, and possibly several stakes, would have confronted anyone approaching the southern monument from the southeast gap in the bank (Fig. 136). Wainwright considered this line to have belonged to Phase 1. Post holes in it to the left of the entrance were scanty, but this was explained as due to the erosion of the chalk bedrock by occasional stream water. Was this some sort of façade to the Phase 1 structure? Wainwright himself thought it plain that the arrangement was 'intended to shield the sacred areas from the secular or the profane and may

even have marked the boundary beyond which only the selected few could tread'. Whether or not that was so, another explanation is more immediate.

In allocating the numerous post holes to structures in either of the two phases at the southern monument, it was natural to treat any hole that seemed to have been cut into, when a second hole was dug, as belonging to Phase 1. Now the line of posts is not perfectly straight, but it makes good sense if interpreted either as an alignment to assist in building the monument of Phase 2, or as an integral part of it, before the outermost ring was added. The direction is that of midwinter sunset, as seen over the bank.

The main reason for associating some of the posts with Phase 2 is that it is more or less tangential to circle *B* at the entrance to the monument, and that where it touches that circle it passes through the centres of its two largest posts (numbered 45 and 46 in Wainwright's plan). Alignments tangential to circles elsewhere have already been noted in plenty—on Dartmoor, at Avebury, and in the central timber circle at Stonehenge, for example. There is a good example at Arbor Low, where the main henge monument is connected by a small bank and ditch running tangentially from the main bank, and there are others both at Durrington Walls and at Mount Pleasant.

It is even possible that there are in the Durrington Walls 'façade' signs of two different periods of activity along slightly different alignments, one connected with the Phase 1 monument. The small deviations from a perfectly straight line could even have been the consequence of the posts' having been inserted during several successive winters, or on successive days around a single solstice, or both, in which case this line of posts takes on a special interest of its own. At the very least it suggests that we should look at comparable lines of posts elsewhere, as potential intermediaries in monument building, drawing boards on the landscape. If it is not to be understood in this way then the only obvious alternative is to suppose that—as so often elsewhere—the monument as a whole was treated as one of the two 'posts' limiting a view of the setting midwinter Sun.

Durrington Walls: the Four-Posters and Post Rows

The northern monument, perhaps in Phase 1 and certainly in Phase 2, and the southern in Phase 1, all had one striking property in common. They all had, within their rings of relatively small posts, four massive posts set in an irregular quadrilateral. One might imagine that these posts determined rather crudely either solar or lunar extremes of rising or setting, but with or without introducing lintels there is no firm evidence that this was their purpose. What

seems far more likely is that there was at least one alignment on a star—and possibly more than one. If they have been left until last, that is only because the necessary data are harder to come by.

There are lines of post holes leading up to the northern monument that are suggestive of a double avenue or corridor, crossed by another 'façade', but in truth no two lines are parallel (Fig. 140). There are at least three lines:

(1) One is almost in the meridian, passes through the centre of the northern circle, and is tangential to the southern.

(2) Another line passes through the centre of the southern circle and is more or less tangential to the four-poster circle in the northern. Continuing in this line (azimuth 8.8° east of north) brings us to one of six post holes on the northern bank.

(3) A third line of posts passes through the centre of the northern circle (azimuth 10.9° east of north) and is tangential to the circle (E) of the tallest posts in the southern.

It is hard to believe that these symmetries are accidental. If some star or other was the object of these alignments, then Vega was almost certainly involved. Line (3) passed precisely through the gap that was created by the north–south pair of posts, seeming to imply that the same technique of 'trapped rays' was used as with the Sun and Moon. This is hard to understand, in view of the difficulty of seeing the star and the posts simultaneously, and it seems more likely that some or all of these alignments were operative before the northern monument was built. The reason for saying this is that they traverse ground that is at a very constant gradient, except near the southern monument. In the case of (3), for instance, the average gradient for the flat section is 4.47°, but the line of that ground, projected back to the middle of the southern monument would meet the eye of our standard observer quite precisely. From there, Vega would have been seen rising along this line around the year 2440 BC. If line (1) was also for Vega, then it would have been correct somewhere around two centuries earlier. In setting, Vega would then just have touched the ground before immediately rising again—exactly the behaviour found at West Kennet and elsewhere. Line (3) seems to belong to Vega's rising in the neighbourhood of 2300 BC. (If the general idea is accepted, then the uncertainties in these dates are due mainly to depredations suffered by the bank in the crucial stretch, which was damaged, for example, by the building of the old A345 road.)

Wainwright showed that the posts in the bank predated it, albeit by a very small margin. No doubt the bank was being constructed at more or less the same time as the first monuments, that is, before the alignment through the

line of the massive posts just mentioned. The line of posts does not in itself indicate the Sun, Moon, or any bright star. It seems far more likely that they constituted a series of foresights for observations of Vega. How they and the small posts of the 'avenue' would have entered practically into the alignments it is impossible to say, but there is no reason why they should not have been picked out from a distance with the help of small fires or lamps.

It is interesting to note that observing across the quartet of massive posts in these same monuments, that is, using the other pairs, the star Aldebaran would have been seen rising across the northern monument for a century or so around 2500 BC and setting across the southern, again ideally several decades earlier. In the case of Aldebaran, risings and settings were widely separated in time of day, and if observed in this way would have been observed at two different seasons. Until the rest of the site has been explored, these potential alignments involve a much greater element of speculation than those for Vega, with their compelling geometrical symmetries.

Mount Pleasant

Although Woodhenge and the Sanctuary near Kennet and Avebury were the sites of buildings similar to those at Durrington Walls, neither was enclosed by earthworks on the same scale. Since it was suspected that enclosures at Marden, in the Vale of Pewsey, and Mount Pleasant, near Dorchester (Dorset), were once also comparable, excavations of both were undertaken in 1969 and 1970–1 respectively. All three enclosing earthworks were found to be associated with pottery in the Grooved Ware style, having stylistic traits in common, and all three yielded radiocarbon dates placing them within a century or two of 2500 BC.

Mount Pleasant is a very modest hill lying across a ridge to the east of Dorchester (Dorset). The enclosure there surrounded its summit, although far more obvious today is the copse of trees growing on Conquer Barrow to the west. The earthworks have been flattened by centuries—even millennia—of ploughing, but the bank is still detectible to the naked eye. G. J. Wainwright again directed the excavation and found, in addition to the earlier earthwork, a large and unexpected foundation trench. This gave evidence of a timber palisade that had been built to surround the hilltop around 2000 BC (1700 bc), at the same time as the circular timber building on the site had been supplemented or replaced by a stone cove at its centre, related no doubt to various stones away from the centre. This later phase was associated with shards of pottery in Beaker styles.

It was estimated that a veritable forest of 1600 oak posts had been used in the palisade. The casts of the post butts had been preserved in the puddled chalk in which they had been set, and it seems that each post averaged around 40 cm in diameter. Applying a 'rule of two-and-a-half', their depths suggest that some of them might have stood as high as 7.5 m above ground. They followed the natural contours of the ground where possible, and so would have presented a level line. They had been closely packed, about two to every metre of trench. This once truly massive structure must have required the best trees from perhaps 4 sq km or more of oak forest, and was presumably for defensive purposes. When it was eventually dismantled, some of the posts were withdrawn and some were burned in situ, but some had already rotted.

The site as such was shown to have continued in use for well over a thousand years. The stone cove was destroyed in the first millennium BC, after which the hill was given over to arable cultivation.

There were four entrances to the Mount Pleasant enclosure, as at Avebury. Only that at the southwest has so far been thoroughly excavated. Prompted by the arrangement at Durrington Walls, one should consider the possibility of a line of sight from that southwest entrance towards the elevated monument within the enclosure (Fig. 145). The ditch is here a complex one, with a self-contained compartment to the left side of the enclosure entrance. Standing at the midpoint of the causeway an observer would have seen the first glint of the rising midsummer Sun to the left side of the timber monument on the ridge. In other words, the line of sight would have been tangential to its outermost ring, with the Sun just appearing to the left of it. This is the arrangement seen on several previous occasions, whereby the timber monument as a whole acts as a composite sighting post. It is impossible to say precisely where along the line the Mount Pleasant observer would have stood, but if just within the ditch then the tangent ray could have been precisely 100 MY, the same unit as at Durrington Walls. The distances from the centre of the Mount Pleasant monument to the other ditches at the entrances look suspiciously like round numbers of MY (perhaps 200 to the north as well as to the southeast, and 250 to the east), but until more excavation is done it will not be possible to decide whether there is any particular feature to associate with the potential viewpoints.

The enclosure lies between two rivers, the South Winterbourne nearly a kilometre to the south—not close at hand, as at Durrington—and the river Frome only about 200 m to the north of the enclosure's northern entrance. This entrance was almost due north of the centre of the timber monument and of the single entrance causeway through the ditch that immediately surrounds it

(Fig. 145). The Iron Age palisade also had an entrance in precisely the same line. It is inconceivable that this line from the river to the monument was lacking in great significance, whether as a line of sight on the heavens or as a processional way, or both. Since the timber henge was somewhat to the south of the ridge, and not at its summit, and since its posts—as will be shown later—were rather short, it would not have been seen by anyone approaching from the river Frome before the ridge was crossed. Had there been any tall enough post, by day it would have been seen against the sky and would have marked the meridian and hence midday; but there seems to have been none. By night there was no striking stellar occurrence over the monument unless we turn back to the twenty-ninth century, when the bright star alpha Crucis would have been seen very briefly appearing directly above it. This is

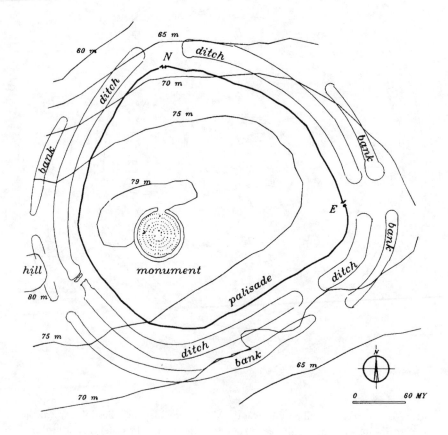

FIG. 145.   A general plan of the Mount Pleasant enclosure, with henge monument, palisade, ditch and bank.

appreciably earlier than the first radio-carbon dates, which are in the neighbourhood of 2500 BC (1961±89 bc, 2038±84 bc for the primary structure and
2122±73 bc for a pre-enclosure settlement).

Part of the ring-ditch surrounding the henge monument had long been
known from aerial photographs, but was formerly assumed to be the remains
of a barrow. The excavation revealed post holes, many of them eroded through
ploughing. They possessed one very unusual property, for two corridors
through them divided the rings into quadrants (Fig. 146). The north–south
corridor was a few degrees from the meridian, and was probably consciously

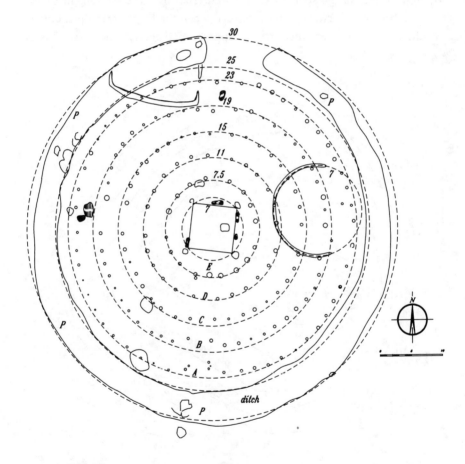

FIG. 146.   The ditches and post holes at the Mount Pleasant henge. Possible construction
lines are drawn, with their radii marked on them (in MY, like the scale). The shaded areas
are stone positions. Those at the centre, like the four post holes there, appear to flank a
square of side 7 MY.

aligned on the rising of the star Vega, making for another affinity with Durrington Walls.

The circular area within the ditch was about 43 m across, and in it there had been five rings of posts. Wainwright concluded that the rings had diameters ranging from 12.5 to 38 m, and that not all quadrants had been struck off from the same centres. Circles with diameters in round numbers of MY are superimposed on Fig. 146—not to imply that they exactly represent their architects' intentions, but to show that there is a rough logic to a scheme in which the circles increase from a diameter of 15 (circle E) to 46 (circle A) in steps of 7, 8, 8, and 8 MY. (Radii, not diameters, are marked on the figure.) The later stone cove had a side of about 7 MY, measured internally, and four post holes lie at the corners of the square, suggesting that its properties were never forgotten. The circular arc of the small internal ditch also had a radius of 7 MY.

The main ditch had been from 2.6 to 4.6 m wide, fitting closely with circles of diameters 25 and 30 MY. It had an average depth of 1.65 m from the modern ground surface. The range in depths was from 1.36 to 2.0 m, figures that are important, since they show that observations could have been made by a person standing at certain places in the ditch, even granting that surface erosion has taken place since. The external bank had more or less disappeared by the time the excavation was begun, but was outside the ditch, and if it was not unduly spread out it must have been near to the 2 MY in height that has here been suggested as a common norm. The ditch was very thoroughly excavated, and Wainwright's drawings of nineteen of the ditch sections include no fewer than three clear cases of viewing platforms of the Woodhenge type, at such levels that the observer's eye could have been level with the ground. They are where they should have been expected, namely at the northeast, southwest, and northwest. There are what could be seen as two others at the south side, one adjacent to a pit in the ditch bottom somewhat west of south, and the other about the same distance east of south. They are indicated by the letter P on Figs. 146 and 150.

Mount Pleasant: Alignments on Stars

The excavation showed that some of the posts had been replaced during the life of the monument. Using Wainwright's data, the average post-hole depths, commencing from the outer ring, are: 26, 30, 29, 34, 36 cm. His averages for the post-hole diameters are 43, 45, 44, 48, 53 cm, but these show erosion, and virtually nothing definite can be said of post diameters. If any rules for post

sizes were followed at Mount Pleasant, they might have been different from those derived from Woodhenge and Durrington Walls, but even accepting an appreciably larger ratio than 2.5 for post height as a multiple of hole depth, it is clear that the Mount Pleasant posts were much shorter than their Wiltshire counterparts. Had the surface not been eroded in any way, multiplying the hole depths by 2.5 would have made them only about half as tall as a man. Even if they were indeed mostly shorter than a man, so that this forest of posts could only have been traversed in comfort through its corridors, this does not mean that they had no other purpose. Their form and direction will lead to quite another explanation.

Ploughing has reduced many of the post holes to the point of disappearing, a fact that must influence any conclusions as to the overall heights of the posts, but it does not much affect the *gradients* deduced if the loss of surface is uniform. Whatever figure is taken as the average for the loss of the surface chalk, multiplying it by 2.5 leads to a length that has to be added to the posts of *all* rings equally. It will be suggested that somewhat less than 30 cm of the surface has been eroded overall.

Guided by practice at the other monuments, it seems from the hole diameters that the post diameters ranged from 17 cm (ring *A*) to 21 cm (ring *E*). Here is another sign that the posts were altogether smaller than those in the two Wiltshire monuments.

Why were the corridors not due north and south, east and west? A whole range of sight lines would have been possible with the posts in place, say from about 3° to as much as 11° east of north. All of them could have been used, but all of them point to the rising of Vega at plausible—but of course various—dates. Despite these possibilities, the corridors are set out in a manner that was plainly systematic, as the construction lines superimposed on Fig. 150 clearly show. If some of the posts in ring *A* are overlooked, the bounding posts in the north–south corridor are in reasonably straight lines, but splayed in different ways along the two axes. One wonders whether the idea was to set the lines at right angles in pairs, so as to segregate posts in quadrants, for this effect is achieved to within a degree or two. (Absolutely precise positions for the posts within their holes are unknown, so it is not possible to be more specific.) It will be seen that one of the corresponding eastern lines was tangential to the later internal circular ditch. These properties were not accidental. If the corridors were aligned on stars, viewing was presumably along the axes of the corridors, in which case the operative angles of azimuth were 7.6° east of north (or west of south) and 6.5° south of east (or north of west). This arrangement is unusual, even so.

The altitudes of the various horizons are far from certain, but for low altitudes Vega is the only bright star that rose or set on the north–south line during the period at issue. But how would it have been viewed? The northward natural slope must have been close to 2.2°, which would correspond to too late a date, but it would be easy to imagine an artificial horizon set by lintels, for example, across the isolated 'blocking post' in ring E, or even by the post itself. Viewing might then have been by someone standing on the step in the southern ditch bottom looking centrally over that artificial horizon. If this is correct, then the altitude set by the horizon to yield the right date for the monument would have been about 3.6°. Needless to say, this is a very weak argument. Two stones placed in the corridor at a later stage might have been used in the same way within a century of 2100 BC, either way—in agreement with a radiocarbon date assigned to the stone phase of the monument, but again a far from an exact figure. At all events, it seems very probable that the northern alignments were important, since the line running north–south remained important into the Iron Age. Apart from the fact that a northern palisade entrance was retained, there was a flanged bronze axe found at the end of the northern ditch that might have had a ritual purpose.

Looking across the monument through the other corridor, that is, at an azimuth of about 6.5° south of east, the star Aldebaran might have been seen rising when the monument was built. The viewing position is less important since the hill slopes away downwards, making the extinction angle for the star the critical altitude. The derived declination (−2.78°) is right for 2420 BC. The pits close to the ditch at both ends of this alignment were found to contain sarsen flakes. They might simply have been connected with the dressing of stones for the cove, but it has often been suspected from finds elsewhere that stone chippings had some sort of ritual function, and the potential Aldebaran sighting is consistent with this idea.

Mount Pleasant: the Glare of the Sky

Whether or not these alignments on stars were intended, there can be little doubt that the monument was meant to be used to observe the seasonal extremes in the Sun's rising and setting. The contours of the hill almost tell us as much, for the contours lie, loosely speaking, along and at right angles to those directions—in a way reminiscent of Stonehenge. This would have made the entire affair considerably easier to design, since it was level along one axis and had its greatest slope along the other.

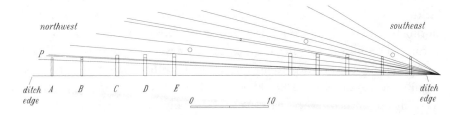

northwest   *southeast*

P

ditch   A   B   C   D   E   ditch
edge   0   10   edge

FIG. 147.   The profile of the northwest to southeast section at the Mount Pleasant timber
henge.

To settle the solar alignments more precisely one must first decide on the
form of the monument. The close similarity of post-hole depths means that
the rounding of post sizes to any large unit is out of the question. There is a
definite gradient in their sizes, but it is very slight. There are many possible
approaches to the problem, but starting from the factor of 2.5, post sizes can
be estimated provisionally, to consider what properties they suggest. Some of
the holes have been damaged excessively. Others are small by virtue of the fact
that they were not for the main posts in the rings. Ignoring these lower
extremes, the following 'shortest post heights' are found for rings A to E: 0.9,
0.92, 1.07, 1.12, 1.21, all in MY. These must all be increased by a factor of two
and a half times the loss of surface chalk, but it is instructive to begin by
pretending that no surface has been lost at all.

Such posts, all appreciably shorter than a normal man of the time, produce
a result that is extremely difficult to interpret intelligently. Neither using the
ditch nor the bank would an observer have been naturally placed to have looked
along the lines of sight set by the timbers of the monument—these lines come

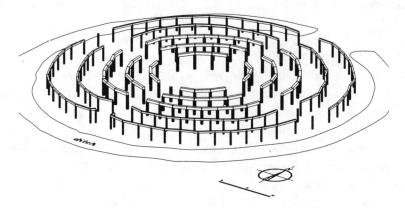

FIG. 148.   A general view of the main timber post circles at Mount Pleasant.

FIG. 149.   The blocking effect of the posts and lintels as presented to an observer in the northeast ditch looking in the general direction of midwinter sunset. The sky is here shown as white. The shading of the posts is merely to allow different rings of posts to be identified, near and far, and has no bearing on their actual illumination. It will be seen that the only sizeable gap is through the middle, and this could have been easily closed by increasing the thickness of the lintels. The small slits between some other lintels could likewise have been easily opened up for use. The holes through the lower part of the henge would have been blocked by the background.

down in all the wrong places. Considering what an observer would have seen from the ditch, however, one can see at once that the view possesses an important property, even though something is seriously wrong. Exactly as at Woodhenge and Durrington, the lintels are stacked up in such a way as to present an apparent 'wall' that might have cut out the glare of the sky, with potential slits as windows for the first or last glint of the Sun. But the wall in question is quite pointless, for it would have been backed—on this first account—by almost any bank, even one of modest height. The posts are simply not high enough to raise the wall to the sky. By how much must they be raised, to achieve the same effect as found elsewhere? Raising them so that the lowest lintels barely conceal a background bank that is 2 MY in height, they serve to define rays that converge on very reasonable viewing positions in the ditch. This finding is achieved by assuming that 36 cm of depth (or less) has been lost to the post holes, on average, by erosion of the ground.

Despite the strong element of conjecture in all this, the two very satisfying consequences of the basic assumption—a wall of lintels and good viewing positions—are joined by a set of highly plausible astronomical alignments.

The suggested heights of the posts lead to the profile of Fig. 147 in which lines of sight are depicted as before. The overall appearance of the monument in three dimensions as shown in Fig. 149 should give an idea of the seeming wall of timber blocking the view to the sky, as presented to an observer in the northeast ditch and looking towards the southwest.

The middle posts (2.3 MY or 1.91 m; ring E) are somewhat more than the height of a man, but the shortest (2 MY or 1.66 m; ring A) are at eye height, so that observation could also have been made by a person standing at ground level near to them, and looking up and over the slope of the nearer set of five

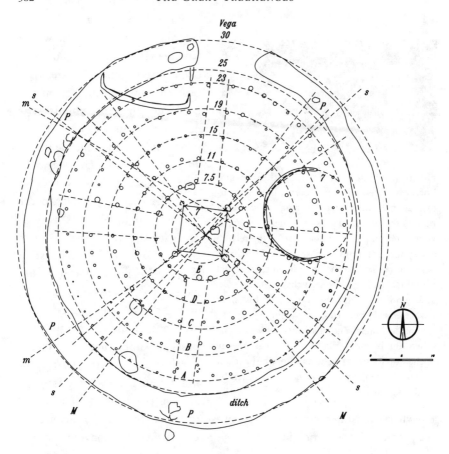

FIG. 150. Potential sight lines at the Mount Pleasant henge. Note how the posts closest to the small circular ditch to the east appear to have once followed that circle, and so might represent an early phase in the history of the monument.

lintels. Whether viewing was actually done in this way is doubtful, however, since the angles produced for uphill viewing are less than the slope of the hill.

It is not easy to decide conclusively between the various alternative ways of using the lintels. The following, all from the ditch, are methods of viewing that merit close attention:

(1) Over the far bank (horizon) and under the far A-lintels. Gradient about 1 in 28 (2.27°), marginally greater than that of the hill.

(2) Over the far lintel B and under the far lintel C. Gradient about 3 in 68 (2.81°).

(3) Over the far lintel E. There would be no upper edge to the 'window'. Gradient about 1 in 14 (4.54°).

(4) Over the near lintel *D* and under the near lintel *C*. Gradient 3 in 20 (9.49°).

The second of these is supported by what follows. It also explains why the *B*-posts are a trifle shorter than one expects from the slope of the 'roof' as a whole.

In deciding how the vertical posts fix the alignments in azimuth, there is a superfluity of near possibilities, but surprisingly few of them turn out to be truly acceptable, even with such a wide choice of gradients as presented here. Many pass well wide of the centre, and others fail to fit into a consistent pattern. There are eight alignments that have a strong claim on our attention, and six of them pass through an area no bigger than a human hand at the centre of the monument. All of them trap lines of sight between the posts of ring *C*, near and far (Fig. 150). Those marked with an *s* are for the Sun, at midwinter and midsummer, and the pair with an *M* for the Moon, at its maximum southern rising and setting. There can be little doubt that ring *C* is the crucial ring, for a variety of other reasons. It has extra posts inserted at places where they are needed for purposes of alignments on the Sun (see the southwest and northwest quadrants). And of course if the *B*-lintels are to fix the horizon, the last ring that can be used for the verticals of the windows is ring *C*.

Yet more interesting is the fact that ring *C* defines lines of sight that are off-centre as far as the main monument is concerned, but that are tangential to the circular inner trench. These lines, marked with an *m* in the figure, seem likely to have been set out for minor southern standstills of the Moon. If so, they are our earliest clear example. The circular trench, strongly reminiscent of those that surround the Heel Stone and two of the station stones at Stonehenge, seems to underscore their function. Posts nearby actually fit better to the line of the trench than to the circles in which they were eventually incorporated, suggesting an earlier structure. Note that the small extra post in the northwest quadrant of the *C*-ring also corresponds to a potential minor lunar standstill.

The main argument in favour of the alignments adopted in Fig. 150 is simply that they correspond to altitudes that fit extremely well with the three-dimensional reconstruction offered earlier. One should not expect high accuracy from a single ray, but an *average* of the altitudes calculated for a perfect fit with the eight separate azimuths can be found. Accepting a nominal date of 2500 BC, all eight calculated altitudes lie between 2.55° and 3.05°, with average 2.75°. This fits surprisingly well with the second option (2.81°) listed above. The numerical value is close and it offers support for the idea that the *C*-posts are to be taken together with the *B*-lintels. The consistency of the

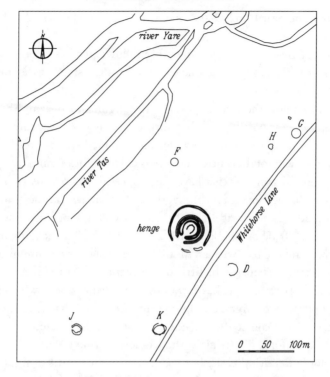

FIG. 151. The Arminghall henge and its immediate neighbourhood. Ring-ditches (mostly round barrows) are marked with letters. Various tracks and modern buildings are unmarked, as is the railway line that runs alongside the river Tas at this point. The main part of the city of Norwich lies to the north and west of the rivers.

overall scheme is an argument in its favour: no doubt other interpretations may be devised, but it is hard to believe that they would be very different and yet produce a more coherent whole. The number of occasions on which the claimed lines of sight pass over certain of the pits is a very striking aspect of this coherence. It is unlikely that these pits were dug after the removal of the posts.

The effect of such a design, when used at dawn or at dusk, would have been exciting, not only because it marked the turning of the Sun's or Moon's motion, with a brilliant gleam of light piercing a dark wall, but because any objects or persons in the central area would have been picked out against the dark backdrop by a higher level of illumination from overhead.

The Henge at Arminghall

The discovery from the air of a timber henge in the parish of Arminghall, Norfolk, produced perhaps the most venerable known example of this broad

class of monument in Britain, for charcoal from it was later to produce radiocarbon dates placing it most probably at the very beginning of the third millennium BC in calendar years. Part of its interest stems from the horseshoe pattern in the groundplan of its posts, reminiscent of the arrangement of the colossal trilithons at Stonehenge. It achieves its purpose with a pair of ditches, a bank, and single set of posts, eight in all. Simple as it might appear to be, it was in some ways much more ingenious than the post circles, for by placing the bank between concentric ditches it made two quite different artificial horizons possible.

The Arminghall site is on the outskirts of the city of Norwich—it is only 3 km south of the cathedral. The patterns of concentric rings of darker grass

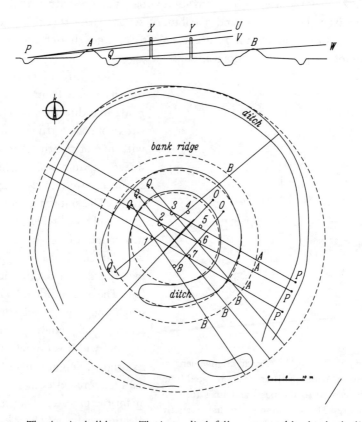

FIG. 152.   The Arminghall henge. The inner ditch follows reasonably closely the lines of the two broken circles marked, one of them 30 MY in diameter, the other 45 MY. The outer ditch is less regular, but surely for good reason. The broken circle of 100 MY diameter drawn near it, and concentric with the others, is for reference purposes only, and does not imply an imperfect ditch line. Ditch sections in the line 3/6 are shown at the top of the figure, but the posts, bank, and sight lines there are nominal, and intended only for reference.

seen from the air by G. S. M. Insall in June 1929 followed close on his discovery of Woodhenge and the excavations there, so that its character was correctly predicted before its excavation was undertaken by Grahame Clark in 1935. The site is on a low gravel shoulder at the edge of the flood plain of the river Tas, south of its junction with the river Yare (Fig. 151). It had survived by the merest good fortune: plans to put a railway across it had been abandoned long before, but an electricity substation was being built nearby, and even after the discovery of the henge was announced, the site was graced by an electricity pylon. While this provided a vantage point for photography, it cannot have added to the accuracy of bearings taken only by a magnetic compass. The area still has traces of many ditched round barrows. There are more than a dozen within 2 km of the site, one of them approximately in line with the axis of the henge. Even the river Tas and a tributary stream share this same general direction. Just as at Mount Pleasant and Stonehenge, the terrain was well chosen for the properties of its contours.

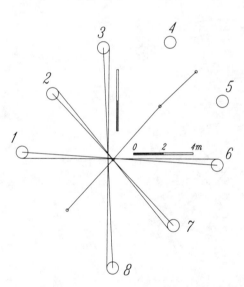

FIG. 153. The highly regular arrangement of the posts at Arminghall can be appreciated from lines tangential to the posts and lines through their centres. The two 4m scales are drawn strictly south-north and west-east, for comparison with adjacent lines. The small circles are drawn to mark the points midway between posts of pairs 4/5, 3/6, 2/7, and 1/8. The axis they define is to midwinter sunset over open ground through the entrance.

Most information about depths came from a cutting made in a direction which by a stroke of good fortune coincided with one of the three principal directions from which solar observations were fairly certainly made. The outermost and less regular of the ditches (Fig. 152) was found to be about 3.7 m wide at the lip, and approximately 1.2 m below the old surface. The bank inside it had been so thoroughly spread through centuries of ploughing that its original width is unknown, and its original height cannot be reliably estimated even from the quantities of material taken from the ditches. It could have been as much as 3 m high, taking into account the yield of both ditches. The inner ditch was approximately 2.1 m below the old sur-

face, which had up to 30 cm of topsoil over the gravel and sand into which the post holes were dug. The floor of the ditch yielded much charcoal, and shards of pottery. As Clark observed, the floor of the central monument was remarkably level, and no shards of pottery or any other cultural debris were found in the central area. There were no traces of a grave.

Charcoal from the base of post hole 7 produced long afterwards a radiocarbon date equivalent to 3100 ± 300 BC (2490 ± 150 bc). Assuming old timbers (because they were so massive), the monument probably stems from the thirtieth or perhaps twenty-ninth century.

The post holes were large, and only two (3 and 7, on the figure) were excavated thoroughly. All had sizeable ramps cut down into them, around 4.5 m long, to assist in the erection of the massive posts. All ramps were to the south-southeast, which Clark took to be the direction from which the timber was brought. The post holes had been sunk approximately 2.2 m into the

FIG. 154.   The most probable arrangement of posts and lintels at the Arminghall henge, in relation to the ditches. The overall height as drawn here is 5.8 m, more than three times human height. It is possible that lintels were only put on four pairs of uprights, but this is unlikely since stability would then have been lacking.

gravel, and the post-pipes remained clearly distinguishable. Clark concluded that the diameters of the timber in the two holes excavated had been about 90 cm and 75 cm. Their bases had been charred, possibly as a protection against rot, or merely because fire had been used in felling them, and the timber had been stripped of bark before its erection. There were burnt flints found in the two post holes investigated. One would not expect any rule relating post diameter to hole diameter to apply here, since ramps were used to simplify erection. Assuming a ratio of post height to hole depth of two and a half—as derived in different circumstances, admittedly—the exposed lengths of these massive posts would have been 5.5 m and 5.7 m respectively, which is even greater than the height to the tops of the lintels of the outer ring of sarsen stones at Stonehenge. The posts will later be shown to have stood in all probability 5.8 m above ground.

Posts of this size (nearly 8 m, including the buried sections) would today be hard to find in English oak forests, where the boles of trees of reasonable girth are rarely straight for more than 5 or 6 m. Clark was able to cite evidence, however, that the remains of prehistoric oak boles of 18 m and even 21 m had been found in the Cambridgeshire fens.

His plan of the monument can be supplemented by evidence from aerial photographs, but still it is not clear where the outer ditch ends. There is no reason to think that it was anything other than an open horseshoe. There is slight uncertainty about the precise positions of the posts—an important consideration with a relatively small monument. In a very obvious sense, the monument as a whole is aligned on the setting midwinter Sun, that is, following the axis of the horseshoe over the low natural ground of the river valley at 41.0° south of west. There is every reason for thinking that this line was accurately determined, and its position can be found regardless of the method of observing the phenomenon, for one of the properties of the posts is that pairing them off across the horseshoe and taking points midway between their centres, a very passable straight line results (see Figs. 152 and 153). If the side posts were used for observation, and estimating post diameters as before, then posts 6 and 8 give an almost identical result. The observer would perhaps have stood in the inner ditch.

That the monument is astronomically aligned seems clear from another very simple consideration: there are trapped sight lines lying approximately in the meridian (5/6, 4/7, 3/8). Clark spoke of irregularities in the post positions, but in fact the monument was very laudably regular, although not in obvious ways. It should be plain from Fig. 153 that the trapped lines of sight 1/6 and 3/8 are in the cardinal directions (see the scales placed adjacent to them for

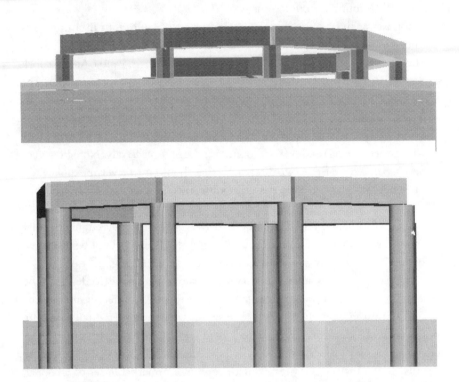

FIG. 155.   The different characters of the views from the two ditches, looking over the
bank at Arminghall. The upper figure is from the outer bank, the lower from the inner
bank. The reconstruction offered here for the windows through the posts and lintels can
be modified by changing their dimensions or bank height and position.

comparison). They and the trapped sight line 2/7, and the (only slightly
crooked) axial line, all pass through an area no bigger than the human hand.

There are other potential alignments looking across the axis of the horseshoe, but now the enigmatic bank must have played a part in setting the
altitudes. The observer must have stood in one of the ditches, for the bank to
have functioned as an artificial horizon; but in which? If in the inner ditch, the
angle would have been relatively small—say 3 or 4°—while if in the outer
ditch the nearness of the bank might have pushed the angle up to more than
10° with ease; but then it would have gone over the lintels entirely, unless the
posts were very tall indeed. The two essentially different arrangements are
shown at the top of Fig. 152, where sight line W from the inner ditch is the

lowest, and V is an acceptable option from the outer ditch (but the bank at A is drawn too high). Line U manages only to make use of the near post (X), however. This problem, of a sight line that seems to demand especially high posts, will be found a troublesome one.

A closer analysis of potential sightings is best begun from measurements of the azimuths. The most reliable are those drawn between posts 2 and 6 (estimated at 25.4° north of west, or its reverse), and posts 3 and 6 (48.8° south of east, or its reverse). The first may be described as a 'Q-type' observation, the second as 'P-type'. It is hard to see how they could be in the reverse directions. They are almost certainly not for the Moon. Assuming that the upper limb of the Sun is on the bank horizons, the ideal altitudes would have been 11.3° (midsummer setting) and 3.9° (midwinter rising) respectively. Note how very widely separated are these two directions, that should intuitively be the reverse of one another. The reason is the great difference in altitudes set by the two different arrangements.

There are other potential alignments of Q-type and P-type, roughly parallel to the two mentioned. They are marked on Fig. 152, but will not be discussed in detail. The Q-line skirting posts 1/4 will be mentioned again later.

The bank is an unknown quantity, but if the two stated altitudes are to be accepted then it becomes possible to determine its physical height unambiguously. Assuming it to have been concentric with the inner ditch, even its position can be derived. Accurate results are not to be expected, but it is an odd fact that with the figures quoted above the bank height comes to almost exactly 3 MY. In fact the site seems to contain a remarkable set of triangles illustrating the mentality of those who built the henge. The two altitudes deduced are close to gradients of 1 in 5 (which is encountered so often elsewhere) and 1 in 15 (close to values from Durrington Walls and Woodhenge), so yet again, it seems, one of the prerequisites of monument design was an adherence to standard gradients. The distance in the 3/6 line from the observer (at midpoint of the inner ditch) to the bank is 45 MY. The distance (in the 2/6 line) from the observer in the outer ditch to the nearby bank limiting the view from there is 15 MY. From the bank to post number 6 is 20 MY and from there to post number 2 another 15 MY. The lintel of post 6 must therefore (with a sight line of gradient 1 in 5 passing under it) be 7 MY (5.8 m) from the ground. This implies a tall but not implausible post, and is the basis for the reconstruction offered in Fig. 154.

There is here a difficulty to be faced. If the last sight line (type P) also passed under the lintel on post 2, this would need to have been 10 MY (8.3 m) from the ground. An unlikely figure? If the observer's eye-level was higher than

the ground, these figures would need to be adjusted upwards, and no simple adjustment of standing position will remove the difficulty easily. There are four clear alternatives open to us: to say that the entire network of angles and measurements is an illusion; to suppose that the place at which the observer stood was marked in some other way, perhaps with another post; to accept that the posts really were 10 MY tall; or that there was some sort of superstructure on top of the lintels. The second option balances caution with modesty.

The irregularities of the ditches call for comment. The outer ditch might have been added at a relatively late stage, when there was less than total freedom to choose the viewing position. Had the ditch not been pulled in appreciably, away from a true circle, the alignments and proportions found earlier would simply not have materialized. That the inner ditch seems to swell outwards to the southwest can almost certainly be explained in terms of an alignment towards midsummer sunrise, using posts 1 and 4. The azimuth is 39.0° north of east, which would have meant an altitude of 2.3° for the first glint of the midsummer Sun. Once more the altitude is close to a simple gradient—here 1 in 25 (2.29°). For an observation of type Q this seems quite inappropriate until it is realized that the likely ditch position (the lowest point Q on Fig. 152) is now further from the bank (B) than before. As drawn, it is exactly 50 MY, which would require there to be only 2 MY between the levels of the bank top and the observer's eye, as opposed to the 3 MY previously. Again by a fortunate chance Graham Clark excavated this region of the southwest ditch, and from his section—not quite in the ideal spot—it is clear that the observer would have stood at a depth of approximately 1 MY below the level surface, with eye at 1 MY above the surface. This is in perfect agreement with the idea of a midsummer alignment.

But the true axis of the henge was to midwinter sunset.

Treehenge and Barrow

From Arminghall it becomes clear that henge monuments as a class, with their unquestionable astronomical orientations, long antedated the Beaker period to which they were once assigned. In truth they are not a simple class at all—which is to say that, in terms of their modes of use, differences between what are commonly described as henges are far greater than differences between them and monuments often seen as quite distinct from them. Arminghall, for instance, might be seen as having affinities with the scaling posts of long barrows, even though one was for the Sun and the other generally the stars. Woodhenge had more in common with the Harenermolen tomb than with

either—which is not to say that they should be classified together, for there was more to these things than their orientation on the heavens. O. G. S. Crawford wrote in *Wessex from the Air*, in 1928, that 'whether Avebury may be a big disc-barrow or disc-barrows be little Aveburys one cannot say'. Actually one can say, but in many different ways, and subtler categories are called for than are currently in use.

Before radiocarbon evidence, it was an open question as to whether circular henges generally might have been derived from fenced barrows comparable with that at Harenermolen. Finds of pottery were eventually seen to point to Neolithic dates for some of the latter, and the radiocarbon evidence finally settled the question. That massive post circles without evidence of primary burial preceded fenced round barrows, and also those with only an earthen mound and ditch, should not be taken to imply that the one was ancestor to the other. They share certain qualities, but churches are not ancestors to cinemas merely because both have roofs. In accumulating evidence for a continuum of practice, attention must be paid to monuments across the old divides. What are the earliest datable indications of post circles around barrows? A good example is the barrow Amesbury G71 in Wiltshire, with its three post circles, and a radiocarbon date equivalent to 2550 ± 150 BC, a date that makes it roughly contemporaneous with monuments labelled 'Phase 1' at Durrington Walls. This still leaves a large gap between then and the period of Quenstedt and Arminghall.

If the vast circular henges were in some ways ancestral to round barrows, does this mean that the henges were chiefly an accessory to rituals of death? Judging by the Woodhenge child-sacrifice it seems likely that death loomed large in their use, so that the symbolism of the setting midwinter Sun, the Sun at its very lowest point, seems apposite. The henges are mostly near groups of barrows, round and long—all of them surely expressing a common religious purpose. That the behaviour of the Sun and Moon was observed across them does not mean that they had no other function; but that they might have had other functions does not mean that the two can be treated separately. When Grahame Clark wrote on Arminghall, he speculated that the British henges were sacred places with banks built so that an audience might climb up them to observe the ritual being conducted within. If very precise solar observation was carried out in the way explained here, then it can be said quite categorically that the banks would have been too precious, not to say too sacred, to have been trampled by a crowd of onlookers. It is not improbable that they were scoured and dressed in height as a seasonal duty, and that the same attention was given to the ditches—but they are still the poor relations of archaeology.

9

STONEHENGE ASTRONOMY—
A HISTORICAL PROLOGUE

First Reports

M OST of the elements needed for an understanding of the astronomical aspects of Stonehenge have now been set out. They differ so greatly from those used in the past that a digression is in order, to explain briefly what others have said on this score.

The earliest of reports that can be reasonably construed as a reference to Stonehenge, and one of the most often quoted, connects it with worship of the Sun. The writer was the historian Diodorus Siculus, who died some time after 21 BC. He compiled a history of the world, leading from the most ancient times to Caesar's Gallic War (54 BC). The following excerpt, from Book 5 of Diodorus' *History*, mentions neither Britain nor Stonehenge directly, but it is conceivable that they were the ultimate source of inspiration for his garbled account:

> Among writers who have occupied themselves with the mythology of the Ancients, Hecataeus and some others tell us that over against 'the land of the Celts' there exists in the Ocean an island not smaller than Sicily, and that this, situated under the constellation of the Bear, is inhabited by the Hyperboreans, so called because they live beyond the point from which the north wind blows.... The following legend is told of it: Leto [*mother of Apollo and daughter of Zeus*] was born on this island, and for this reason the inhabitants honour Apollo more than any other deity.... A sacred enclosure is dedicated to him in the island, as well as a magnificent round temple adorned with many rich offerings. There is a city there sacred to this god.

Diodorus goes on to describe the custom of playing on stringed instruments and singing to the god; and then to explain how the Moon appears near at hand when seen from the island, so that its prominences were visible to the human eye. (There are some who want to make this a statement to the effect that the Moon clings to the horizon, and then Callanish becomes a favourite

solution.) The god visits the island every nineteen years, the period called by the Greeks 'the year of Meton'. When this happens, there is dancing and zither-playing from the vernal equinox to the (heliacal) rising of the Pleiades. (For more on the subject of heliacal risings, see Appendix 4.)

In northern latitudes, where twilight lasts so much longer than in the Mediterranean, people did not fall so naturally into the practice of dividing the year by the first visibility of stars, but the Pleiades reference is what might be expected of a Mediterranean writer. Diodorus' source, Hecateus of Abdera, lived in the fourth century BC. His work is lost, but the association of Apollo with the Hyperboreans, a legendary race of worshippers of that god, is a conventional one. Since some scholars make the Hyperboreans a people who traded in amber with the Greeks, the story of the island might even have been inspired by reports of Zealand (Sjælland, Denmark). Denmark was not a Celtic region, but mention of Celts need not have belonged to the ultimate source, since the Greeks used the name 'Celt' indiscriminately for barbarians occupying northwest and central Europe—not an unreasonable thing to do, since the Celts were united more by culture than by tribe or race. Many of the cultural styles of the Celts had a Bronze Age ancestry, but their dramatic expansion into the Mediterranean area and the fringes of Europe took place only in the sixth and fifth centuries BC. Diodorus was a Sicilian, writing in Greek, and in referring to Apollo and the figure of 19—the number of years in the calendar cycle that we (mistakenly) call the Metonic cycle—it is clear that his sources were thoroughly contaminated both with Greek conceptions and knowledge that had been made possible after Roman conquest. The very idea of designating the Hyperboreans in terms of the winds is quintessentially Greek. As for Roman awareness of them, Julius Caesar has it in his *On the Gallic War* that the Druids debated and taught 'concerning the stars and their motion, the size of the world, the nature of things, and the strength and potency of the immortal gods'. Such a very general reputation must have been widely known, but it is clear that Diodorus knew nothing at all specific about the calendar practices of his Hyperboreans.

Some latter-day writers have seen in Diodorus' account a sign that he knew of important astronomical discoveries made at Stonehenge, in relation to the motions of the Sun and Moon. This is nonsense. It has even been used to support the thesis that Stonehenge was an eclipse predictor. The Celts and their Druid priesthood had nothing whatsoever to do with the building of it, and the most that can be said of their related practices is that they seem to have continued the old traditions of surrounding tombs with ditches and post circles. (A good example has been found at Frilford in Oxfordshire.) The 19-year cycle, which

brings the revolutions of the Moon back into step with those of the Sun, was a Babylonian discovery of about 500 BC, which passed from them to the Greeks. When Diodorus was writing, Stonehenge was older than are the works of Diodorus today. Even if he knew of older writers, who in turn knew of the existence of a British concern with the movements of the Sun and Moon, nothing whatsoever is added by that figure of 19. A great deal is known about Babylonian astronomy, a science that was extremely sophisticated long before the 19-year cycle was discovered, and yet even there, calendar techniques (of adding extra days to the month to keep it in step with the year) were relatively crude before the discovery of the cycle.

In short, to the extent that Diodorus hints in general terms at the serious practice of astronomy in the north, he was right; but even then he might have been right only by accident, since there was an ancient Delphic tradition that Apollo, the Sun-god, spent the winter months with the Hyperboreans—an astronomically odd thing to suppose. At least we can say that Diodorus had heard some report of a striking circular northern temple; and since there was then no better example in existence than Stonehenge, one may cautiously treat his as the first potential reference to that monument, albeit very oblique.

Stonehenge was mentioned by name in the medieval chronicles of Henry of Huntingdon (1130) and Geoffrey of Monmouth (1136). Geoffrey tells a long story of the building of Stonehenge by Aurelius Ambrosius, king of the Britons, directed by Merlin, magician and prophet. It was to commemorate the nobles treacherously slain by Hengist the Saxon. The stones were brought, according to this story, over the sea from Ireland, through the magical mediation of Merlin. Since one modern view of events is that the stones were transported by land and sea from geologically identifiable regions in Pembrokeshire in Wales, there are modern writers who are tempted to speak of folk memory at work in the Merlin story. Another view, and one that is gaining credence, is that the magic was glacial, and that the time of transportation was the last Ice Age.

There are medieval illustrations of the Stonehenge monument to go with the chronicles, although the illustrators did not always appreciate the point they were meant to be illustrating. Henry of Huntingdon's prose was not altogether clear: his description of the stones could be translated as 'doorways raised over doorways'. A Dutch manuscript (now in the British Library) written between 1573 and 1575, and giving a 'short account of English history collected from the best chroniclers', includes the first broadly satisfactory illustration of the monument, a pen and wash drawing. The signature 'L. D. H.' has been assigned to one Lucas de Heere. The sketch is useful in one

important respect: it shows the grand trilithon as having already fallen. (Sir Richard Colt Hoare's statement that it fell in 1620 was often quoted in the past.)

Excavation of sorts took place on the site in the sixteenth century, if an engraving in the antiquary William Camden's *Britannia* (1575) is to be trusted. In 1620, Stonehenge was studied in an exact fashion for the first time. The king, James I, was staying with the Earl of Pembroke at Wilton House nearby. Marvelling at the monument, he asked his architect Inigo Jones—the most distinguished of the time—to investigate the history of Stonehenge. Jones died in 1652, but his executor John Webb (the husband of his niece) found some 'undigested notes' on the subject and at the request of other scholars published what became a highly influential work, *The Most Notable Antiquity of Great Britain, vulgarly called Stoneheng, on Salisbury Plain* in 1655. Stonehenge was now made out to be a temple of the Tuscan order of architecture, built by the Romans between the time of Agricola and Constantine the Great, and dedicated to the god Coelus. It is worth mentioning that the book referred to the discovery of the skulls of cattle—an aspect of ancient ritual often verified since at related sites.

Eight years later, Walter Charleton—after corresponding with the great Danish antiquary Ole Worm—responded with a book (*Chorea Gigantum*, 1663) claiming that Stonehenge had been built by the Danes, as a royal court and a place for the election of kings. He set its period as the beginning of the reign of King Alfred. Webb replied to the criticisms (*A Vindication of Stoneheng Restored*, 1663), and the three works were issued together in 1725, with a valuable if slanted biography of Jones. Charleton had been much influenced by the work of Worm, who had published drawings and descriptions of Danish megalithic monuments in 1643 and 1651. Led on by similar analogies, this time with chambered tombs in Schleswig, the German traveller Georg Keysler in 1720 claimed Stonehenge for the Saxons. What was inevitably lacking throughout, however, was a set of even remotely acceptable chronological criteria.

It was in the 1660s that the antiquarian and diarist John Aubrey turned his thoughts from Avebury to Stonehenge, and made some useful sketches of this and other early monuments. His materials for a book, *Monumenta Britannica*, remained largely unpublished until John Fowles and Rodney Legg saw them into print in 1980. It has to be said that some of Aubrey's plans were heavily influenced by those of Inigo Jones, and to that extent are of only secondary value. His discovery of the ring of holes, the 'Aubrey holes' inside the bank, has already been introduced. He reported on the digging that had

been going on since the king had first shown interest, and the wonder is that anything of archaeological value remained for later archaeologists to investigate. In a passage written in 1665, Aubrey has a beautifully short way with those of his contemporaries who held to theories of the Roman or Danish origin of these monuments:

> The Romans had no Dominion in Ireland, or in Scotland (at least not far): therefore these Temples are not to be supposed to be built by them: nor had the Danes Dominion in Wales: and therefore we cannot presume the two last mentioned Temples to have been Workes of them. But all these Monuments are of the same fashion, and antique rudeness; wherfore I conclude, that they were Works erected by the Britons: and were Temples of the Druids.

He had decided that they were open temples because he thought that they could not be interpreted as defensive or domestic, or as primarily sepulchral. His awareness of the Druids came ultimately, of course, from Latin and Greek authors. Presumably there were others who had thought the same, since Inigo Jones had gone to some lengths to show that the Ancient British and their Druid rulers could not have been responsible. Jones had conceded that the Druids were skilled in astronomy, but noted that they were not renowned for their knowledge of architecture, for did they not worship in groves of trees? The plans published under the name of Inigo Jones can be seen as an extreme example of a rigid geometrical interpretation of a less than perfect monument.

A few excerpts from the work that Aubrey never managed to bring to a publishable state were printed by others, and a transcript of the original was seen by the young antiquary William Stukeley in 1717. He had been attracted to the monument by David Loggan's engravings of it. More than twenty years later Stukeley published his own book on Stonehenge, and another on Avebury, in which excellent field work was combined with fantastical theories of Druidical involvement that set the seal on an interpretation that has coloured the popular conception of the monument ever since.

Stonehenge and the First Calculators

Stukeley's motivation was largely theological—indeed he took holy orders in 1729. His aim was to promote the knowledge and practice of the ancient religion, conceived as having been in the spirit of Christianity, or at least of that faith as manifested in England. Despite this strange ambition, he was the first writer to make out a good case for astronomical alignments at Stonehenge—this in his *Stonehenge, a Temple restor'd to the British Druids* (1740). The book was followed in 1743 with *Abury, a Temple of the British Druids, with Some*

Others, Described. He could not avoid being carried along by the fashions of his time, which in his case—he had begun as a Lincolnshire doctor—inclined to the scientific. Finding that the nearby Cursus and the Avenue were laid out in interesting astronomical directions, he decided that they had been set out with the help of the magnetic compass, whose properties he surmised had been known to the Phoenicians. The Cursus, as we know, lies more or less east–west. The error, to one who thought the intention to have been to set it *exactly* along that axis, was about 5°. This, said Stukeley, was because of the declination of the magnetic needle, which did not give true north. In his day, new churches were often set in an east–west direction with the help of a magnetic compass—a custom that goes back at least as far as 1516, when an Augsburg mason, Lorenz Lacher, gave instructions on how to implement it. It explains many a small 'error' in the siting of churches, but it also no doubt explains Stukeley's belief.

Stukeley concluded from what he knew of the rate of change in the declination of the compass that the temple was built in 460 BC, not long after Cambyses' invasion of Egypt. This must surely count as the very first application of natural science to the dating of any prehistoric remains. He decided that fleeing Egyptian priests had come westwards to Britain, and had introduced their learning, arts and religion to the natives, in particular to the Druids. (The Druids had supposedly been in England since the time of Abraham, shortly after Noah's Flood. They were of Abraham's faith, and were brought by the Phoenicians.) This gave the impetus to the building programme, and perhaps, he thought, the immigrant community gave a hand with the work. As for the Cursus, he said of it that it was the 'finest piece of ground that can be imagined for the purpose of a horse-race', so arranged that 'a British charioteer may have a good opportunity of shewing that dexterity spoken of by Caesar: but the exquisite softness of the turf prevents any great damage by a fall'.

On the Stonehenge monument, Stukeley simply remarked that its principal line, coinciding with that of the Avenue to the northeast, was 'where abouts the Sun rises, when the days are longest'. For him this seems to have been enough. His older contemporary, the great astronomer Edmond Halley, also showed an interest in the monument, both in the microscopic character of the sarsen stone and in the problem of orientation. He, however, considered it to have been set up with reference to the quarters of the heavens (northeast, southeast, and so on), and rejected the idea of its having pointed precisely to the Sun's rising on the longest day.

Others followed with their own scientific arguments. John Wood, the architect of much of the finest work in Bath, actually laid out the Circus and Gay Street in that town, the latter on the analogy of the sarsen circle and the

Avenue. He was for long the most accurate surveyor of the site and published an extraordinarily detailed plan with his measurements of the stones (dated 1740) in his *Choir Gaure, Vulgarly called Stonehenge, on Salisbury Plain, Described, Restored, and Explained* (Oxford, 1747). Measurement was then in fashion, but only as an instrument of astonishment. Wood tells of a carpenter—one 'Gaffer Hunt'—who lived in a smoky hut on the site, and who kept measuring rods for visitors, to whom he acted as a guide. Hunt's hut was by what is now numbered stone 60 of the fallen northern trilithon, and he cut a cellar under the adjacent prostrate stone 59. His visitors were interested only in the *dimensions* of the stones, and in Hunt's memory 'no regular survey had been taken of Stonehenge'.

Wood judged the monument to have been a lunar temple—as in the case of Stukeley's Avebury. He believed that the Moon's movement was indicated by the thirty piers and architraves in the large outer circle, and by the twenty-nine in the circle of (outer) bluestones. The lunar month is of course more or less 29.5 days long. Modern opinion is that the number of bluestones in the circle might originally have been in the neighbourhood of sixty. How Wood juggled with the numbers of stones to obtain a calendar need not be explained, beyond noting that he claimed to have found the nineteen of the Metonic cycle in counting the *inner* bluestones. As already mentioned, others have grasped at simple calendrical ideas in relation to the Aubrey holes, many of them in the twentieth century. It is a path that has the unfortunate property of leading from anywhere to anywhere.

Symbolism on a Grand Scale

There have been three main types of astronomical analysis offered for Stonehenge in recent centuries. There is that which involved counting stones and reducing whole numbers to astronomically meaningful quantities, usually having to do with the calendar. This has been found appealing: it does, after all, seem to offer an easy road to precision. Those who practise it are inclined to assume that the counting of stones is a straightforward matter, an assumption that the history of Stonehenge proves to be false. A second sort of analysis aims to uncover symbolic, often mystical, geometrical forms. And a third considers orientation and related ways of functioning. With the exceptions noted, this is more or less the order in which Stonehenge caught the imagination of those who were prepared to follow in the footsteps of Diodorus.

In 1771 it was orreries—models of the planetary system—that were all the rage, so that it is not surprising to find John Smith writing a book with

the title *Choir Gaur, the Grand Orrery of the Ancient Druids, commonly called Stonehenge*. Take the five central trilithons, together with two of what he conceived to have been bluestone archways, and you have symbols of the Sun, the Moon, and the five planets then known. The Sun was symbolized by the great central trilithon. The plan was elliptical, oval—symbolizing the serpent's egg, the *ovum mundi* of the Ancients, the 'egg of the world'. This owed something to Stukeley's fondness for discovering serpentine forms on the landscape. For Smith, the thirty pillars of the outer ring, multiplied by the twelve signs (of the zodiac) make 360, the days of the ancient year. The inner circle was the lunar month. The harvest moon and the hunter's moon came into his account, which was embellished with a great deal of second-rate astronomical knowledge and mystical geometry involving the latitude of Stonehenge. There were echoes of all this, nevertheless, in the far more influential writings of the Welsh orientalist Thomas Maurice.

Maurice thought he perceived in the open plan of Stonehenge a similarity to Persian practice. By adding the original number of stones and lintels in the outer circle and reaching the number sixty, Maurice thought that he had found yet another sign of Asiatic astronomy. Charles Vallancey—an Irish antiquary who served as an engineer, later a general, in the British army—seized on Maurice's suggestions. Vallancey was a man committed to proving the likeness of the Irish, Egyptian, Persian and Hindustani languages. We are now in the last decade of the eighteenth century, and again in the midst of a new and powerful intellectual fashion. In France, Jean-Sylvain Bailly was making great discoveries as to the nature of early Indian astronomy, so it is not surprising to find a local archaeologist Henry Wansey asking in 1796 whether a learned Brahmin, contemplating the ruins, might not 'comprehend more of its design than we do'. There at least was a fashion that could lead nowhere. Wansey was convinced that Druids responsible for Stonehenge had been able to calculate eclipses, but that since their methods were unknown, we could no longer explain the theoretical uses of the monument.

The idea of an orrery symbolism was raised to still greater heights with a book by Edward Duke in 1846, *Druidical Temples of the County of Wiltshire*. Duke accompanied Sir Richard Colt Hoare on various Wiltshire excavations, many of them on Duke's land, and he kept the finds in a museum at his home, Lake House. Duke's suggestion was that 'our ingenious ancestors' made the Wiltshire Downs the site of a grand orrery or planetarium, with planetary temples arranged along a line running north and south, sixteen miles in length. The centre of the system—corresponding of course to the Earth—was set at Silbury Hill. The temples were four of stone and three of earth, and of these Stonehenge

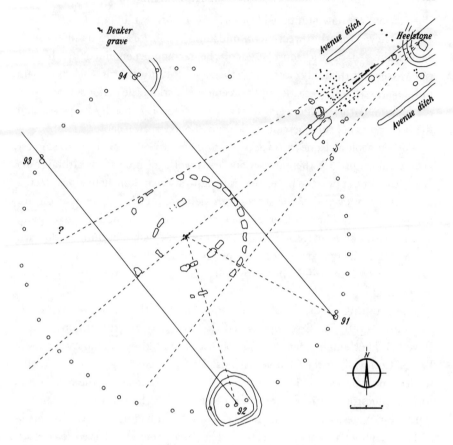

FIG. 156.   The station stones and the Heel Stone at Stonehenge.

corresponded to the Sun. Not surprisingly, Duke found numerous links with the astronomy of ancient Egypt. His claim that Stonehenge was from the same general period as the Egyptian pyramids was rather closer to the truth than the alternatives being offered at the time by professional archaeologists, but his reasoning was so weak as not to merit dissection. Of the Heel Stone he writes that it 'was a gnomon for the purpose of observing the rising of the Sun on the auspicious morn of the summer solstice'. He was probably the first to look for alignments off the central axis. Superimposed on the ring of Aubrey holes there were once the four station stones, two of them are now missing. (Those two were surrounded by what have been misleadingly called 'barrows', banks of earth surrounding areas about 11 m across, with no central mounds, but shallow trenches to the inside. William Hawley later found that these structures and their trenches had a floor with a mixture of yellow clay and chalk.

The stations are now numbered from 91 to 94, as shown in Fig. 156.) Edward Duke believed that the directions of midsummer sunrise and midwinter sunset were indicated by the short sides of the rectangle contained by the stations—they are certainly close. More than a century afterwards, C. A. Newham thought that the longer sides of the rectangle marked the major standstills of the Moon. Neither of these claims is as clear-cut as is generally supposed, and the finer points of the question will be postponed until Chapter 11.

When geology came into vogue, in mid century, writers began to suggest geological origins for the barrows and earthworks of prehistory, although no one at the time appears to have gone as far as to say that Stonehenge was erected by a glacier, or even that the stones were delivered to the site by that means. But when, and by whom, was it set up? Geology was largely in thrall to religion, on the matter of dating. One might suppose that this has nothing to do with the case, but the true period of Stonehenge comes uncomfortably close to the various dates then being offered by religious writers for the creation of the world itself.

Discounting Geoffrey of Monmouth, it was the geologist W. Boyd Dawkins (1880) who first appreciated the great distance the bluestones had travelled. He thought that they had been transported by human means from Wales, Cornwall, or the Channel Islands. Their place of origin was eventually settled, more or less, by H. H. Thomas in 1923. He matched the three main sorts of bluestone with outcrops of igneous rock in the Preseli Mountains of southwest Wales. He thought that Salisbury Plain had never been glaciated, and his views were generally accepted. The debate therefore turned to the sort of society that could have organized such a remarkable feat of transport—the distance is of the order of 240 km. And as though to prove that even professional archaeologists are not immune to the Zeitgeist, three years after the end of the first World War Flinders Petrie was to be heard asking whether the stones might not have been a form of war indemnity exacted from Welsh tribes.

The first serious doubts to be cast on the general thesis of human transportation followed the discovery in 1923, by one of his descendents, of a letter from William Cunnington, to the effect that a sizeable bluestone had been found in a nearby long barrow (Bole's Barrow). The long barrow was plainly some centuries older than the bluestone structures at Stonehenge. Doubts continued to be expressed from time to time, and after a study of the problem begun in 1985, a group of four geologists—Olwen Williams-Thorpe, Richard Thorpe, Graham Jenkins and John Watson—presented strong evidence that the mechanism for moving the bluestones to Salisbury Plain was an ice sheet, probably of the Anglian glaciation, rather than a series of a sea- and river-going

rafts. If so, perhaps the ice deposited the stones in moderately close proximity to each other and to the site, but even in this case, their dressing to size and shape, and their assembly alongside the even more impressive sarsens, would have been a feat presenting difficult enough questions of organization.

The debate refuses to die. In 1994, David Bowen presented evidence that the bluestones were first exposed to the air only 14,000 years ago, long after the time of the last ice sheets that might have brought them down to Wiltshire. The evidence is based on the accumulation of the isotope chlorine-36 in a sample of bluestone (one provided by Salisbury Museum) since it was first exposed to cosmic radiation. If it is accepted that the rocks were first exposed to the air as long ago as this, then human transport becomes once again the only plausible explanation for their subsequent transportation.

As for the culture responsible for Stonehenge, the nineteenth century saw a slow shift in views. The Belgae were then often mentioned alongside Celts and Gauls, so that if anything, the estimated date of the monument was getting later—worse rather than better. Outrageous conjectures continued to be made. W. S. Blacket, a writer on American archaeology, decided that Stonehenge was built by Apalachian Indians. In other respects a seemingly rational Victorian, he was able to call on Plato for evidence. In the prestigious Hibbert Lectures for 1886, John Rhys told his audience that they could do no better than follow Geoffrey of Monmouth. The temple, he said, was 'the work of Merlin Emrys, commanded by another Emrys, which I interpret to mean that the temple belonged to the Celtic Zeus, whose later legendary self we have in Merlin'. Such opinions are a reminder that astronomers have never had a monopoly of Stonehenge lunacy.

The Coming of the Theodolite

It is today a commonplace of popular belief that, as seen from the centre of Stonehenge, the Sun rises directly over the Heel Stone on the longest day of the year. This is not, and never has been, exactly true. The place of midsummer rising moves slowly eastwards with the years and the centuries, as a result of the precession of the equinoxes, the slow drift of the points in which the Sun's path (ecliptic) crosses the celestial equator. The astronomical knowledge needed to project backwards in time and decide when and where the Sun rose in the past was available long before the seventeenth century, although the necessary data were poor until the nineteenth century, and likewise the handling of precision instruments. (Actually Stukeley was using a theodolite for his fieldwork in the early eighteenth century, but his azimuths are poor,

perhaps because he set his instrument with a magnetic compass incorporated into it.) Although the change is a very slow one, this offers a method of dating any monument, granted that a line of sight to the extreme of the Sun's rising or setting is guaranteed. Archaeologists were slow to apply this method of dating, which is more difficult, of course, than the application of calendar computation to numbers of stones.

Henry Wansey (1796) refers to an application of the technique by 'Mr Waltire, who wrote, and delivered lectures, on Stonehenge' and who 'endeavoured to demonstrate that it has been immerged in the sea twelve miles deep; and that it was erected, judging by the precession of the equinox, at least seventeen thousand years ago'. Perhaps the first to derive a respectable answer from the method was a now forgotten nineteenth-century Yorkshire archaeologist, Godfrey Higgins. He was deeply committed to the history of religion, and was anything but conventional. (Christ, he believed, was a member of a monastic order of Pythagorean Essenes.) Higgins' best-known work, *The Celtic Druids* (1829), contains a passage in which he calculates the age of Stonehenge on the basis of the precession of the equinoxes. His method is flawed, but it is interesting to note that he was led to a date around 4000 BC, scarcely later than the date then most favoured for the creation of the world—but on the right side of it, unlike Waltire's.

After John Wood, W. M. Flinders Petrie was the first to make a really competent survey of the site, which he published in *Stonehenge: Plans, Descriptions and Theories* (1880). He had his critics, some of whom were happier with books bearing titles like *Archaeology with Spade and Terrier*, but for many years his was the standard survey. His theories as to ancient units of length will be recalled, and his claimed accuracy of measurement both at Stonehenge and Wilmington. From his careful survey of Stonehenge he decided that it was built at four different epochs. The ditch and bank came first, he thought, followed by the Avenue. Third came the main structure, that is, the circle of sarsen stones, the sarsen trilithons, and the four stations. Last of all, he thought, came the bluestone circle, the circle lying between the outer sarsens and the horseshoe of trilithons. Although he was badly out in his dating, his error would have been less but for an astronomical mistake in evaluating the changing obliquity of the ecliptic. He came to the conclusion that the date of the alignment on the midsummer Sun was in the range 730±200 years AD.

Petrie was probably the first to notice that the stations, arranged more or less symmetrically with respect to the main axis of the monument, lie on diagonals that cross at about 45° (45°±06', he said). He drew the conclusion that the circle had been designed so as to be divided into sixteenths (sectors of

22.5°), starting from the axis. Sir Norman Lockyer later seized on that idea, which he thought indicated a division of the *year* into sixteen, thus linking the monument with traditional Celtic festivals. Lockyer thought that sunset on May Day (the Celtic festival of Beltane) would have been seen over one of the stations from the centre of the monument, and an early November sunset (Samain, Hallowmas) over another. His arguments were weak, but the general idea of a sixteen-part year, with the parts not necessarily equal, has been developed by others. It has something to recommend it, at least for later monuments.

Lockyer's application of Petrie's method of dating made more noise than any other attempt has done, before or since. Few have had the privilege of causing so much archaeological indignation, and it is difficult to decide who was more mistaken, Lockyer or his critics. He was an extraordinary individual, with enormous energy and much scientific talent. Although he began as a civil servant, without a university education, he made several important astrophysical discoveries. He was largely responsible for the collection that became the Science Museum, and was director of the Solar Physics Observatory at South Kensington, London. He founded the leading scientific journal *Nature*, and edited it for half a century, no less. In 1894 he published his first venture into the dating of ancient structures by astronomical means, *The Dawn of Astronomy*, a book he wrote after visits to Greece and Egypt. An article of 1901, applying the same methods to Stonehenge, grew into a book, *Stonehenge and Other British Monuments Astronomically Considered* (1909, enlarging on another book of 1906). By this time he had taken many of the Breton monuments under his wing, and much else besides.

Lockyer's first tactical mistake was to construct in his imagination a romantic image of a prehistoric astronomer-priesthood, an image entirely without historical foundation. This added colour to his account—and to the faces of his critics—but can be stripped away from his main contentions easily enough. These were that there is a close connection between the structure of the 'temple' and the direction of the earthen Avenue to the northeast; that in the temple's present state of disrepair, the direction of the Avenue was the more reliable datum; that Stonehenge was a solar temple and that 'the greatest function took place at sunrise on the longest day of the year'. It remained to establish the azimuth of the line of the Avenue, for the mean value of which he settled on 49° 35' 51" from north. To this he applied the best available data on the changing obliquity of the ecliptic. Actually he weakened his position, when looking for an alignment on a distant object, for he settled on the fortified Iron Age encampment at Sidbury, 12 km distant and at an azimuth of 49° 34'

18". Even worse, in the eyes of his sternest critics, was the fact that he sighted on an Ordnance Survey benchmark there. With a natural horizon altitude of about 35' 30", this gave him a date of 1680 BC. He recovered some of his lost equilibrium in the end, when he admitted that he might be in error by two centuries either way, on account of uncertainty in the line of observation.

This essentially straightforward argument greatly irritated the archaeologists of the time—although the meticulous excavator of Stonehenge in 1901, William Gowland, accepted Lockyer's dating—and the sins of the fathers have been visited on the children of both partners to the dispute. Lockyer's free-ranging imagination was partly to blame, but also his instinct for propagating his ideas vigorously. (Among other institutions, he founded the British Science Guild to bring science to the populace at large.) Later techniques of dating have made his estimate far more acceptable than the archaeologists' alternatives mooted at that time, although this is of course not a valid defence of him. The opposition was able to fall back on no alternative absolute technique for dating. Some chose to object to his notion of a solar temple, preferring to think of Stonehenge as a sepulchre. Others thought it belonged to the Bronze Age, but judged his date to be incompatible with that period. Some pointed out that the builders of Stonehenge did not have theodolites—a bizarre objection. Some challenged the reality of the axis. They tended to be the most caustic and offensive, but their instincts were perhaps the soundest of all, for he gave no satisfying account of how the axis might have been related to actual observations of the rising Sun. Years afterwards, E. Herbert Stone tried to put an end to the acrimony, in what was for a time the best available descriptive survey of the monument and its surroundings, *The Stones of Stonehenge* (1924); but in vain. Scapegoats have come and gone since then, but seasonal Lockyer-sacrifice remains for some inexplicable reason a part of Wessex culture.

There have been numerous other excavators and interpreters of the monument. Herbert Stone revised Lockyer's calculation in the light of newer astronomical data, and found 1840 BC as the most probable date. It has already been explained how Richard Atkinson found a better figure for the line of the Avenue, but that in the last analysis high precision in these matters is immaterial if one cannot justify a method of observation and a precise horizon. This is the nub of any argument from alignments. Thus a true weakness in Lockyer's position was in his confident extension of the line of the Avenue to the axis of the ring of sarsens. They are not coincident, and in any case on archaeological grounds are now judged not to be from the same period.

In the chapters that follow, mention will occasionally be made of more recent attempts to identify alternative alignments. In 1966—following two earlier papers in the journal *Nature*—Gerald Hawkins caught the imagination of the public with a best-selling book in which a number of solar and lunar extremes were canvassed, not to mention an interpretation of the Aubrey holes as a counting device designed to operate a sophisticated calendar of the Sun and Moon that would have allowed eclipse prediction. He was followed by Fred Hoyle, who found another way of computing eclipses using the Aubrey holes. All interpretations of Stonehenge as an eclipse computer are based on the idea that the counters (whether Aubrey holes or stones) were for keeping track of cycles of eclipses that had somehow been previously appreciated. Neither Hawkins nor Hoyle had any serious regard for what was known of the history of the computational techniques that would have been required. There is no historical evidence whatsoever for this approach to eclipse calculation. From a single location only about half of all eclipses could have been observed, and no explanation was offered of how any simple theory of eclipse cycles could ever have been developed in the first place. What called down thunderbolts from the archaeologists, however—and in particular from Richard Atkinson—were the uninformed archaeological assumptions being made. When Jacquetta Hawkes joined in the attack, she ruined a number of small but telling points by her strange assumption that we have 'the right to expect close agreement between the astronomers themselves on the inevitability of their interpretations'. This was as naïve as if it had been said about professional archaeologists. It was in fact said about two men who happened to be professional astronomers but who were on this occasion trying to reconstruct prehistory.

Alexander Thom, a year after Hawkins' book, published the results of his own painstaking study, that had been long in the making, of 500 prehistoric stone monuments. While he scarcely mentioned Stonehenge, he did add a wry note that the scales of metres and feet on the Ministry of Works survey of it differed by one part in eighty. Others were less restrained. Where Hoyle's account had effectively meant that the Stonehenge people were keeping track of the *nodes* of the Moon's orbit (places on the ecliptic in the neighbourhood of which eclipses take place), as though that was not difficult enough, A. D. Beach decided that what was being tracked in prehistoric times was the direction of the lunar *apogee* (the furthest point from the Earth on the Moon's orbit). The idea was that—in ways unexplained—the relation between this cycle and the cycle of abnormal tides of the sea had been discovered, and that Stonehenge

would thus have been capable of facilitating 'cultural communication across the North Sea and English Channel'. The outstanding problem of cultural communication, however, was of that between astronomers and archaeologists. Hawkins' book spawned many other works, usually of a more elementary and summary character, but almost invariably they continued to commit the worst of Lockyer's mistakes. And the greatest mistake of all has been to suppose that the Sun was meant to be chiefly observed from the monument's centre.

STONEHENGE—AN INVENTORY

When this area had been extended . . . an extraordinary state of things was revealed. The ground was honeycombed with post-holes and craters of all sorts, sizes, and depths, many of them having been cut into one another in successive periods of digging and suggesting a series of changes. The long-continued burrowing of rabbits had increased the general confusion, making the difficulty of distinguishing the outlines of the holes far greater. I frankly confess that I have no explanation to offer in elucidation of this tangle, and I doubt if anybody will ever be able to explain it satisfactorily.

William Hawley, *The Antiquaries Journal* 6 (1926), p. 8.

S TONEHENGE is in a sense a single monument that was under construction and modification for two thousand years, and Hawley's uncharacteristic despair is a measure of the fact. Many of its elements—such as the rings of wooden posts at its centre and any that might have been in the Aubrey holes—were of course at length removed by those who developed it further. Other elements, such as the Aubrey holes themselves, simply passed out of sight and out of mind. The activities that went on around the site must have changed considerably over those two millennia. At first its surroundings were open grazed grassland, but by the time the great stones were being erected, farming had acquired a strong arable component. Cereal production, with the efficient storage of grain, would have meant that its builders could spend more time on their task, and might in turn have given rise to the establishment of a specialist group devoted to little else. There is no consensus as to the order in which it was built. The following bare inventory is not meant to be strictly chronological. It will eventually be shown that at every phase in the monument's long history certain aspects of its design were aligned on one or another solar or lunar extreme of rising or setting, although in the earliest phases attention was very probably given to certain stars.

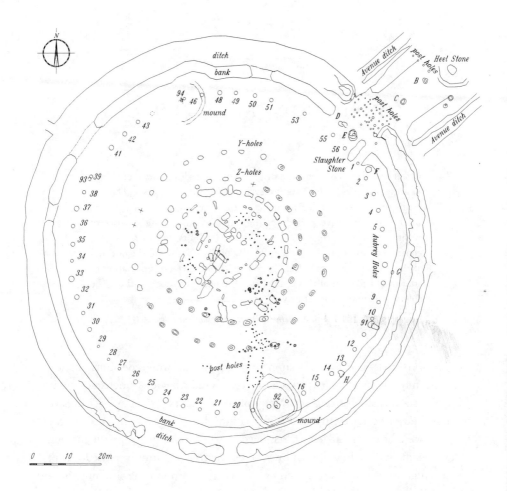

FIG. 157.   Some of the main elements in successive phases of Stonehenge's history. (The plan combines the work of several people, in particular W. M. F. Petrie, W. Hawley, A., A. S., and Alex S. Thom, and R. J. C. Atkinson.) The Y- and Z-holes and most of the post holes represented here are not normally visible. (The same applies to the Q-R system, which is not shown on this figure.) The irregular interior of the excavated parts of the ditch is only roughly indicated here, and its outline, like that of the bank, is rather arbitrary. Details of the inner area are shown in several later figures. The (incomplete) ring of large stones there and the horseshoe of stones within it are the sarsen stones, the most conspicuous of all. The many post holes in the inner regions can usually be judged by their very small size. They are very incompletely known, but are apparently related to the corridor of post holes on the south side.

Banks and Ditch

These were described in Chapter 7, where reasons were given for thinking that regularity of the main (inner) bank was of supreme importance. While one of the main functions of the ditch was to provide material for the banks, parts of the ditch were undoubtedly used as places from which to make critical observations of the Sun and Moon, and perhaps of the stars too, in the earliest phase. The outer bank (or counterscarp, to use Hawley's name for it) was a relatively slight one. The ditch between the banks is now almost completely silted up, but was originally from 1.4 m to 2.3 m below the present surface, and was never complete or very regular, either in width or depth. It was apparently deepest near the northeast entrance. Hawley gave the equivalent of 1.68 m as the average depth below ground level, a figure with which I can obviously have no quarrel—since it is just 2 cm more than the 2 MY eye level being assumed throughout—although his method of averaging is open to discussion. The principal (inner) bank seems to have been fairly accurately circular and (if the earlier argument is acceptable) of height close to 1.66 m (2 MY) and width about 4.75 m (5.75 MY). The only likely entrances through the system are the obvious one at the northeast (about 10.7 m wide) and a narrower and less certain example at the very south.

The main elements of the monument discussed here are indicated in Figs. 161 and 157, the former a detail of the inner area only. The token outline of the bank should certainly not be used to judge its original form, but even its original form no doubt fell short of its designers' intentions.

It has been noted that antlers from the ditch bottom were probably from the thirtieth century BC (allowing for the usual uncertainties); and that the post holes in the entrance causeway, which cover the part that spans the ditch section, could have belonged to the earliest phase of the earthwork and timber monument.

Timber Posts and Rings. Post Holes A

Hawley found numerous post holes among the stones in the area within the Aubrey ring in his excavations in the 1920s. Many of them within the sarsen ring appear to have formed one or more circles, possibly in an arrangement resembling the southern monument at Durrington Walls. In Chapter 7, ways of involving some of the posts in solar and lunar observation were briefly considered. Some of the post holes discovered in the central area but outside the sarsen ring suggest a corridor, entered after crossing the causeway over the southern ditch and passing through the gap in the bank there. The corridor

approaches the middle of the area, but obliquely rather than radially. Attention has already been drawn in Chapter 7 to analogies between it and certain linear structures that approached stone and timber rings elsewhere, along tangents and through centres—following in a tradition discussed in Chapter 6. This southern corridor could well have looked south to the setting of Rigel Centauri over the natural horizon, at the extinction angle. One cannot press the point, when the evidence is so circumstantial, but much the same line is to be found in another timber setting on the site. The numerous post holes on the main causeway, discovered by Hawley and excavated by him in 1922, were discussed in Chapter 7, with suggestions as to their possible use. (Hawley thought at first that they were stone holes.) Some of these too, substantially larger than the average, seem to follow a line to the rising of Rigel Centauri at much the same period of history as in the other case. It is hard to establish a reasonable range of error with what are fairly irregular holes, but very tentatively, accepting the stellar alignments, we should put the dates at within a century or so of 2660 and 2700 BC respectively. If the heavier entrance posts were of a different period from those around them then they were presumably the earlier set.

A row of four post holes found by Hawley near the Heel Stone lies across the general line of the entrance passage. There might have been as many as seven or even eight of these so-called A-posts there originally, one hole (at the

FIG. 158. Some of the excavated dumb-bell-shaped cavities with stone holes (shaded) that Richard Atkinson called the Q- and R-holes. (Based on his published plan, with later additions. Hawley's plan, with some common elements, is at a slightly different orientation.) These holes held bluestones. The surrounding stones are added to the figure in order to place it, and not because they were necessarily in position at the same time.

southeast) having been removed when the Heel Stone was encircled by its ditch, and two (at the northwest) having been submerged by the later Avenue bank. A hole found near the road in M. W. Pitts's 1980 excavation might conceivably make up an eighth.

The Aubrey Holes

These fifty-six holes, set in a circle of approximate radius 43.2 m, were discussed at length in Chapter 7, where it was suggested that the holes held posts of rather more than 2 MY height above ground level. In other words, they probably cleared the bank, leaving a small gap for the Sun to be seen above the bank but below lintels carried on the posts, so reducing glare. An alternative arrangement would have been for posts in the Aubrey holes to have carried lintels that themselves provided the artificial horizon, so supplementing the bank, which might have had that function at an earlier stage; but in this case the astronomical alignments found earlier would need to have been set by something other than the Aubrey posts.

If, as suggested here, the Aubrey holes were meant for short but hefty posts, then the presence of charcoals in the pits (one sample of which indicates a calendar date in the twenty-fourth century BC) is no real guide to their age, since there would have come a time when they had to be systematically emptied. It seems far more likely that they belong to the period of the ditch and one or both banks, or not more than a century or two after. The fact that some holes are relatively large might indicate more massive posts than the average, or might even have to do with the difficulty of removing their contents when the timber phase was past.

Bluestones in the Q- and R-Holes

In an excavation carried out in 1954, Richard Atkinson found a circular array of short radial dumbbell-shaped trenches, within the main sarsen circle (Fig. 158). Most of them contained two holes, packed with chalk, that had at one time been sockets for bluestones (the stones chiefly of Welsh dolerite, mentioned in Chapter 9). The holes of the outer ring were identified first, and named the 'Q-holes', on the strength of John Aubrey's affection for the Latin phrase *quaere quot*, 'ask how many'. The holes of the inner ring thus became the 'R-holes'. The two concentric circles, *if complete*, would each have had 38 stones. Their diameters were given as 74 and 86 ft (22.6 and 26.2 m). An instance of overlapping by a stone hole of the main sarsen ring implied that the Q- and

R-rings were earlier; added to which it is clear that at least some of the bluestones were reused for the surviving bluestone circle and horseshoe (see below).

There was an entrance corridor through the *Q*- and *R*-rings, with paired bluestones in addition to the two pairs of the rings themselves, and this entrance was more or less on the line of the main axis of the later monument. In fact in 1926 William Hawley had found parts of the trenches holding the entrance stones, and also two holes from each trench. It was noted at the time that this entrance had been in the line of midsummer sunrise; but of course, in the absence of a precise bearing, it can also be said to have been more or less in line with midwinter sunset—which without much doubt was its intended direction.

The 1954 excavations were resumed in 1956 and 1958. It was then discovered that the *Q*- and *R*-rings had never been completed. At least a quarter of the circle was lacking (southwest to northwest) and even within the remainder there were some dubious areas. It was conceived that something dramatic had happened, to cause a change of plan before this phase of building was complete. There was a double row of five stones, forming the northeast entrance. Judging by the preparation of the ground there were plans to supplement the pairs to either side of these ten, giving each pair a third stone, but if so, those plans were thwarted. The holes were seemingly never filled. The question as to the need for these extra stones will be considered in Chapter 11.

Bluestones were brought to the site, or perhaps existing stones were modified on the site, long after the earthwork phase, for bluestone chips occur not at the bottom of the ditch but only about halfway down the silt. An antler abandoned at the bottom of one of the *R*-holes gave a radiocarbon date equivalent to 2000±125 BC, but the date has since been rejected, and the sequence of the main Stonehenge features as derived from the overlaying of stone holes implies a date well over five centuries earlier.

Stone 97 and the Heel Stone (96) and Its Ditch

The elongated sarsen stone numbered 96, adjacent to the present main road (see Fig. 159), which cuts across the Avenue there, is much better known as the Heel Stone.[1] It is now inclined at about 24° to the vertical, in a plane

---

1 It was Flinders Petrie who devised the now generally accepted system of numbering the main stones. John Wood had used a somewhat similar system earlier. Various supplementary sequences have been added since Petrie's time to number the excavated fragments and locations, especially below ground.

approximately 43° west of south. The stone, if
straightened, would stand about 5.0 m above the
present turf level, and 105.6 m above the Ordnance Datum. It is buried to a depth of about 1.2
m. Surrounding the stone is a circular ditch of
approximate diameter 10.4 m, and 1.2 to 1.5 m
deep. Part of this ditch is overlaid by the southeastern bank of the present Avenue, showing that
to be a later construction. The Avenue was made
wide enough for its banks and ditches to avoid
the Heel Stone and its ditch.

FIG. 102.   The Heel Stone,
near the present road. See also
Plate 26.

As has been pointed out by almost everyone who has ever tried to prove
that the rising midsummer Sun was observed over the Heel Stone by an
observer standing at the centre of Stonehenge, it has never done so precisely,
and will not do so until the early fourth millennium AD. The illusion that it
does so is nevertheless what most visitors to the monument have in common.
The American writer Ralph Waldo Emerson, in his book *English Traits*, tells
of how on a visit in 1856 he engaged a local antiquary, Mr Brown, who called
this simply 'the astronomical stone' and the Slaughter Stone 'the sacrificial
stone'. He gave his visitor the impression that to see the midsummer sunrise
effect over the former it was necessary to stand on the latter.

The name 'Heel Stone' (or 'Hele Stone') has been transferred by some quirk
of history from stone 14, which John Aubrey described as bearing the imprint
of a man's foot. The foot was at some stage turned into a 'friar's heel'. Some
writers have adopted the spelling 'hele' in an affectation of medievalism, while
others have mistaken it for a word related to the Greek word for 'Sun'. For some
strange reason, no one yet appears to have suggested that the name comes from
the most obvious property of the stone, namely that it is heeling over.

It is often said that the Heel Stone is 'unworked', but it is impossible to
believe that this is entirely true. It shows no obvious signs of tooling, but its
width (the distance between its two potential viewing edges looking towards
the monument, measured at ground level) is just 3.00 MY, and it holds this
width more or less to eye-level. Now the distance between the two edges of
the stones at the entrance to the sarsen ring, numbers 1 and 30, is exactly half
this width—to within a hundredth part of 1 MY. The entrance is roughly
halfway between the Heel Stone and the far (southwest) bank, and the ideal
spot from which the Heel Stone would have seemed to be perfectly framed by
the sarsens, to an observer looking northeast, is on the very ridge of the bank,
between Aubrey holes 28 and 29. The grand trilithon would have partly

concealed this view, making it unlikely that the Heel Stone was ever seen so framed, but the spacing of the six extra stones at the entrance to the *Q-R* system were at more or less the same spacing as the later sarsens, and it seems not improbable that the Heel Stone was already in place when that system was erected. The property mentioned is certainly of a piece with an extensive and sophisticated pattern of proportional triangles in three dimensions that uses the Megalithic Yard as a measure, and the Heel Stone is one of the keys to that pattern.

One of the most gratifying of recent discoveries was that of a stone hole, now numbered 97, close to the Heel Stone. It was found during salvage excavations carried out by Michael Pitts and others in 1979, on the verges of the road running past the Heel Stone. Stone 97 might have been a forerunner of the Heel Stone. It is unlikely to have been a partner to it. The question of their relationship is a difficult but important one, and will be raised again in the next chapter.

At the bottom of the hole for stone 97 there were two post holes, each about 25 cm across, and some grooves, perhaps from the decay of timbers used in lifting out the stone, or possibly for drainage. There was also a gully running from the Heel Stone ditch, perhaps part of a provision for drainage of the ditch generally.

Of all items of information in the report of this last excavation, one of the most valuable concerns the level of the floor of the Heel Stone ditch, 98.95 m above the Ordnance Datum. (Hawley spoke only of the ditch's depth as 4 ft, or sometimes 5 ft.) Why this is so important will be explained in Chapter 11.

The Avenue

The earthwork known as the 'Avenue' has already been considered at some length (Chapter 6). Whatever its astronomical orientation, it is hard to believe that the monument was not approached along it, although when it is interpreted as a processional way it is as well to shun all images of more familiar religious rituals. It will be recalled that the Stonehenge Avenue was about 12.2 m wide and flanked by a low bank and a shallow ditch to either side of it (see Fig. 160), and that it falls away to the northeast, down to the dry valley bottom. Curving eastwards, then southeastwards, it headed for the river Avon.

FIG. 160.   A typical section of the Stonehenge Avenue in its present condition .

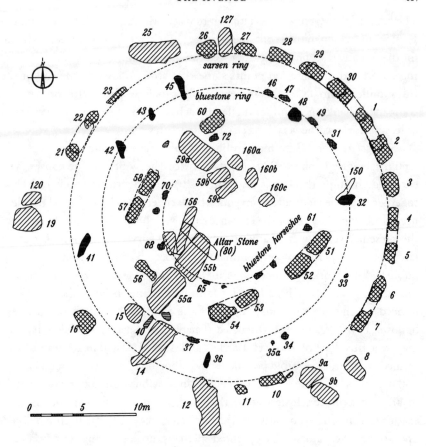

FIG. 161.   The central Stonehenge area, showing the stones in their present state. (The plan is based chiefly on a survey by A., A. S. and Alex S. Thom.) Diagonal hatching indicates sarsen stone, while horizontal hatching represents bluestone; double hatching is used for stones still standing, single hatching for fallen stones. The (broken) Altar Stone, the final (upright) position of which is not certain, is now partly covered by the fallen and shattered upright 55 from the largest trilithon, and by its lintel (numbered 156). The stones of the large trilithons are numbered 51 to 60, with lintels numbered a hundred higher. The main ring of sarsens originally had thirty stones. These are numbered starting from the main axis and working clockwise. There was a ring of bluestones outside the horseshoe of trilithons and a horseshoe of bluestones within that of trilithons. Nine lintels are in place, three of them in trilithons. They are shown by broken lines. Stone 14 fell inwards in 1750. The fall of trilithon 57–58 happened on 3 January 1797; it is now re-erected. The central trilithon had fallen by 1574 or so, when stones 12, 13, and 14 were still standing. Stone 22 and its lintel fell on 31 December 1900. The following year the leaning stone 56 was set upright, and after the First World War further stones (1, 6, 7, and 30) were made stable. Stone 23 fell in a gale in 1963. It has been re-erected. The three circular reference arcs are of radius 7, 14 and 18 MY precisely. Important omissions from the plan are the Q- and R-holes, which would have had to be superimposed on the bluestone ring (see Fig.158.).

The bank of the Avenue as it is known to us cut through the ditch around the Heel Stone, which in turn contained chips of bluestone. The most secure dating for the Avenue rests on radiocarbon assessments of fragments from the surviving banks and ditches, and points somewhat ambiguously to the end of the third millennium BC. It seems extremely probable that, with or without comparable banking, a similar final approach to the Stonehenge site was taken at least as early as the very first circular structures on it.

The separation of the median lines of the ditches averaged over the first straight length is about 22.9 m, over twice the width of the causewayed entrance through the banks and ditch surrounding the monument. This, together with the fact that the Avenue's bank covers post holes A, and the clear need to change the gap for the entrance causeway through the earthwork when the present Avenue was created, imply that the surviving version of it came later than the period of predominantly timber structures. When Stukeley published his work on Stonehenge in 1740, Roger Gale—who had assisted him there—wrote to chide him for failing to mention holes that they had noticed on the Avenue banks. Some of the implications of these 'manifest hollows' have already been discussed (Chapter 6). Surveys of resistivity and magnetic flux done by A. D. H. Bartlett and A. E. U. David in 1979 and 1980 seemed to indicate possible post holes and stone holes at various points along 240 m or so of the route of the Avenue. The indications were not precise enough to allow a firm conclusion as to the existence of any former avenue, but exacavation might eventually provide a clearer answer. It has been remarked upon by its excavators—disappointed, perhaps, at not having found datable material—that the Avenue was surprisingly free from debris. This is precisely what we should expect of a cursus-like monument.

Stones B *and* C, *and the Hollow*

William Hawley found two empty stone holes (B and C) on the central line of the Avenue, between the Heel Stone and at its upper end. (He later thought that they might have been created by tree roots, but its position seems to belie this re-interpretation.) It has occasionally been suggested that stones were moved to B and C from positions D and E, their 'central' positions supposedly linking them firmly with the relatively late Avenue. This is unlikely. It is not a sound inference if the stones were involved in setting lines of sight that are central, since a stone with that purpose stands of necessity to one side of the line it helps to define. To decide correctly whether either stone hole, B or C, is in this sense central requires us first to identify a meaningful alignment. Both

stone holes could conceivably have been related to the Q-R system, but the fundamental relationship of at least one of them (B) with the sarsen monument cannot be doubted, as will be explained in the next chapter. For the time being, one or two negative statements are in order. The median line of the Avenue might have grazed one of the stones in holes B or C, but it certainly did not graze both, for the line of centres of the two holes is not at all close to being parallel to that median line. When Richard Atkinson's survey of the Avenue was discussed in Chapter 6, mention was made of his surprise that its median line did not pass through any of the main centres of Stonehenge circles. Extending this type of geometrical approach to the problem of the affinities of the stones, taking only a plan view, does not seem likely to be very profitable.

In 1923, south of the Heel Stone, Hawley found a hollow covering an area of about 1.8 by 3 m (6 by 10 ft), filled with large quantities of sarsen chips (3760 fragments), and also sarsen sand. This was under the Avenue bank, so proving that before the Avenue earthwork, sarsens were being worked on the site—unless some strange ritual with sarsen flakes and sand was being acted out there. Hawley sometimes described this hollow as a stone hole, but if so, its function must have related to what was on site before the Avenue was built. Was a stone that was worked in the hole itself the source of the debris? If a stone ever stood in this hollow, it might be tentatively related to timber posts that stood in the neighbourhood of the Y-holes in the southeast quarter. If the hollow was merely a workshop, then it might have been used for the trilithons, for they were probably erected at much the same time as the present Avenue. This second idea might be hard to accept, if we are to believe that the axis of the Stonehenge site was assigned any sort of sanctity, unless the act of working the stones was itself given sacred status.

The Sarsen Trilithons

The most familiar of all the elements of Stonehenge are the outer ring of sarsen (sandstone) uprights and the still larger sarsen trilithons inside it. The term 'trilithon' was William Stukeley's (from the Greek words for 'three' and 'stone'), and simply designated an isolated pair of uprights capped by a single lintel. The great Stonehenge trilithons were originally five in number (ten upright stones and five lintels), and most of the stones remain on the site, with eight uprights and three lintels in position. They were set in a horseshoe into which one looks as one faces southwest (say from the Heel Stone). The uprights were all of more or less the same cross-section, but they were graded in height, the grand trilithon at the 'toe' of the horseshoe being highest. (It is surprising that

this fact alone did not persuade previous writers that the main direction for viewing was from the northeast, and not towards the northeast.) The sections of a typical stone reduce *from* say 2.3 m by 1.2 m at the bottom to 2.0 m by 0.9 m at the top, their outer faces being dressed to the curve of the horseshoe. Giving them this property must have consumed considerable time and energy, but the principle was extended to the lintels too. The lintels are themselves massive, those at the sides having been on average about 4.88 m in length, 1.22 m in width (increasing to 1.37 m on the upper surface), and 1.07 m in height. The weight of such a stone is of the order of 16 tonnes. As for their overall heights (with lintels): facing southwest, the nearest pair of trilithons (stones 51–52 and 59–60) would have reached to a little over 6 m, the next pair (53–54 and 57–58) to about 6.6 m, and the central trilithon (55–56) to 7.9 m, all above present ground levels. It will later be necessary to specify the heights in a different way, from a fundamental level to be defined in due course.

It will be suggested that the trilithons represent a slightly earlier phase than the enclosing ring of sarsens with which they are astronomically and geometrically associated, in various intricate ways, and the question will be raised as to whether they were conceived as an independent monument.

The Ring of Sarsens

The familiar sarsen uprights stand in a now incomplete ring, surmounted by what was once a continuous circle of curved sarsen lintels. The ring was once nearly 32 m across (outer diameter) and contained thirty uprights, of which seventeen still stand, eight survive in whole or part on the ground, and five are entirely missing. The uprights were tooled so as to make them, as far as possible, rectangular in section. On average they are 2.14 m wide and reach to about 4.1 m above ground level. The last measurement is likely to be misleading, since the ground level changes by half a metre across the ring, and one of the most remarkable of all the properties of the monument is the excellent degree of levelling of the *top surface* of the ring of lintels, which was held to within 17 cm—under seven inches—across the ring. One stone at least seems to have been dressed in position, to bring it down to the right level.

Although the uprights differ much in thickness, the average is 1.14 m. The best face—that most carefully dressed—is usually to the inside, but one should not make too much of this fact, for there are some key outer faces on which much care was lavished—on stones 1, 30, 16, for example—and this was for good astronomical reason. Including the buried part, which varied much from one to another, most of the sarsens in the ring were between

approximately 4 and 4.3 m above ground level (the difference compensating for the slope of the ground). The weight of each was of the order of 26 tonnes.

The length of the average lintel along its outer edge is about 3.3 m. The surviving lintels are approximately 1 m wide and 0.8 m in height. (Most of these measurements are based on Petrie's and Stone's.) They are held secure on the uprights by tenons on the undersides of the lintels, fitting into rounded mortises on top of the uprights, which are slightly dished for a good fit. Tongue-and-groove joints are used at the ends of the lintels, to fit one to the next. Such joints are often said to be more appropriate to woodworking. While that is no doubt where they originated, paviours still use both sorts of joint.

The mechanics of raising such stones and capping them with lintels is not a subject for this book, but it must be said that in the past too much attention has been paid to the use of ropes, and too little to what can be achieved using levered rollers, stacked logs (or split planks), and rocking devices. Here again, however, the old familiar problem has to be faced: our ability to invent a method, or to borrow it from the pyramid builders of Egypt, is no guarantee that it was used in Wessex in the third millennium.

All sarsen uprights and lintels were dressed to shape using heavy stone mauls, held in the hand without any haft. A heavy maul can be used to split off substantial pieces, and was not merely for fine dressing. Used mauls have often been found on the site, for example as packing material for the large uprights.

A cursory glance at the plan of the monument as a whole seems to show a substantial shift in direction (say 4° at a first rough estimate) as between the earthworks phase and that of the sarsens; but this shift had taken place earlier, judging by the Q-R axis, which is much the same as that of the sarsens. The change was brought about as the result of a shift in astronomical technique.

Stone Holes D, E, and the Ditch Stone

In the northeast entrance, just inside the ditch and in line with the bank, are two stone holes (labelled D and E) that are often regarded as having held pillars amounting to a formal entrance to the monument. This raises a number of questions that are far from trivial, since as far as their function was concerned, the stones originally standing inside and outside the northeast causeway across the ditch can be shown to have been among the most important. The evidence for what stood in the various holes—which include B and C—is a tangle of misunderstandings, and some of its history must be accounted for at the outset.

Two pairs of pillars are shown still standing, in the Inigo Jones plan. (The circumstances of the publication of this by Webb were given in Chapter 9, p. 396.) The larger pair is placed just outside the ditch, but this idea does not tally with what is known of the stone holes there. In what purport to be Jones' words,

> The great stones, which made the entrances from the outside of the trench, are seven feet broad, three feet thick, and twenty high.

> The parallel stones, on the inside of the trench, are four feet broad and three feet thick; but they lie so broken, and ruined by time, that their proportion in height cannot be distinguished, much less exactly measured.

This highly specific information cannot be spirited away without an argument, but it is suspect in several ways. In 1666, in a manuscript plan now in the Bodleian Library in Oxford, John Aubrey drew the inner pair at a plausible spacing, and also what might be regarded as one stone of the outer pair—not distant enough from the others to be stone *C* (see below). One might imagine that one of Jones's 'broken and ruined' stones had finally bitten the dust, except that they were the inner stones, whereas it is an *outer* stone that has gone. This fact, and the fact that Jones's 'outer' pair agree in size with the Slaughter Stone that is today (prostrate) on the inside, make it at least probable that somewhere along the line the Jones text simply interchanged inner and outer stones. If he did no more than this, his evidence would be extremely valuable, for it would be that the Slaughter Stone was then standing, together with a partner of like dimensions. One's confidence is shaken, though, when the text speaks of three separate entrances at each of which the same pattern is reproduced, with 'on the outside of the trench aforesaid [the ditch], two huge stones gatewise; parallel whereunto, on the inside, two others of less proportion'. This is simply unsupportable, and Webb drew Stonehenge with only one entrance—but still with the four entrance stones.

Aubrey's plan was done with that of Jones in mind—indeed probably in hand—but he was intent on checking off the parts and dimensions in person. A more reliable witness, he marked three stones at the northeast, although the question of their character cannot be answered from his sketch. The whole question is put in further doubt, though, by prints based on drawings of Stonehenge done by the artist David Loggan at an unknown date. (Even the date of Loggan's death is not precisely known, but is thought to have been the last year of the seventeenth century.) The more distant Heel Stone is clear enough in them, but there is no sign of any stones whatsoever in the region of *D* and *E*. Stukeley later (1743) dismissed the entire Jones quartet, and thought that they had come from a recollection of the Slaughter Stone and the two surviving station stones. (When Stukeley refers to two small stones 'within the

vallum' he means the station stones.) Another possibility is that the now missing station stones (92 and 94) were brought, perhaps much degraded, with other sarsen fragments from the site, to mark an entrance for the carts and carriages of visitors, and that they neither had nor needed stone holes. Stukeley was no doubt right about the Slaughter Stone: its dimensions were some-how—by misremembering, or by ill-understood notes—transferred to two of the 'gateway' pillars. The entire Jones–Aubrey evidence dissolves into virtually nothing, and in particular fails to warrant the claim that the Slaughter Stone was standing in the seventeenth century.

In his book *Stonehenge*, Richard Atkinson surmised that the stones D and E were sarsen, and 'to judge from the size of the holes were similar to stone 93, though possibly taller'. Stone 93 is one of the two surviving station stones, near the Aubrey ring to the west, and is a reshaped stump standing less than 1.2 m above ground level. The fallen station stone (91) is approximately 3 m in overall length. Elsewhere in the book, however, Atkinson writes that it is

> almost certain that the Slaughter Stone is the survivor of a pair of upright pillars which formed a gateway to the monument. The other pillar seems to have stood in a large adjacent stone-hole (E) which may already have served to support a stone in an earlier phase of construction.

Hole E would certainly have been well fitted to hold the Slaughter Stone, or a stone like it, so this is a likelier account. (Even the larger station stone (91) is less than half the size of the Slaughter Stone.) The conjecture is still not completely convincing, however.

It is reasonably certain that D held nothing so grand. Hawley, who found it, put its dimensions as (the equivalent of) 1.52 by 1.45 m, and its depth as 1.07 m 'below the ground level of the passage', which was much disturbed. The height of the stone above ground was therefore probably of the order of 2.5 m—say three-fifths of the height of the Slaughter Stone.

There seems to be nothing to recommend the idea, mentioned above, that stones in holes D and E were early and were later moved to positions B and C. They were all of them, nevertheless, in extremely well chosen positions, as will be shown in the following chapter.

In 1922 Hawley began to excavate the ditch just south of the main causeway, near to the present position of the Slaughter Stone. This first segment was interesting for several reasons. It was of such a depth that an adult's eye would have been near ground level; there was a hole for a sizeable stone that had been set at the inner edge of the ditch; and the ditch gave evidence of much human—very probably religious—activity there. There were signs of fires on the ditch bottom, which Hawley pointed out was very unusual, and many

bones, described as bison, and including a horn core and tooth. The position of this stone, like the others mentioned here, is intimately related to the sarsen monument and trilithons taken together.

The Station Stones (91–94)

As already mentioned, often associated with the stones at the entrance, although some distance away, are the station stones (91 and 93, with empty holes 92 and 94; see Fig. 157). They lie approximately on the ring of Aubrey holes, but not precisely on the place of any hole. Their exact positions were finally settled only in 1978, by Atkinson. There are shallow circular banks and ditches enclosing level ground, the so-called 'barrows', surrounding holes 92 and 94. The other pair does not appear to have had them. The stones probably all stood above ground rather more than the height of a man (say 3 MY).

The station stones, while seemingly insignificant, carry much information. They will later be shown to have continued a tradition relating to the Aubrey circle, and to have been intimately connected with the plan of the sarsens.

The Altar Stone (80)

The Altar Stone (80) is the largest of the stones not native to the region—it is about 4.9 m long (uncertain because of breakage) and averages 1.02 m wide, and 0.53 m thick. It seems to owe its fanciful name to the posthumous publication of the papers of Inigo Jones: '... whether it might be an *Altar* or no,' the text goes, 'I leave to the judgment of others'. It is of a greenish sandstone, with flecks of mica in it that make it glisten, especially when newly split. There is no other stone of the same micaceous character on the site, although small fragments have been found, presumably from the dressing of this. It is now broken into two pieces and is partly covered by the broken upright (55b) of the largest (and central) trilithon, and its lintel (156). The stone has been identified as Cosheston Beds sandstone, ultimately from south Wales.

The present position of the Altar Stone does not link it with the *Q*- and *R*-holes, but since their double part-circle contained a large round pit where the axis of the monument crosses it at the southwest, just to the northwest of stone 15, Atkinson conjectured that either a large bluestone once stood there, or that the pit was meant for the Altar Stone. The second alternative seems likely, and reasons will be given in Chapter 11 for accepting it. Of course it did not fall from there to its present place—it would have had to cross the line

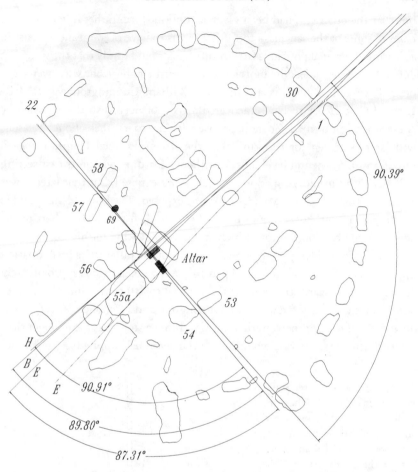

FIG. 162. The Altar Stone is conjectured to have stood as a pillar, at a crossing point for important lines of sight for which it acts as an artificial horizon. Other lines are likely to have skirted it. Two alternative positions of the stone are drawn and other variants are conceivable. For further discussion see Chapter 11. Lines from the Heel Stone (*H*), and the stones in holes *E* and *B* are shown here (see the key at lower left), all of them to the setting midwinter Sun—in some cases to the side of the Altar Stone (with a low horizon) and in others over it, twenty minutes or so earlier. The lines crossing these, more or less at right angles to them, are to midwinter sunrise, the first glint of which is seen through gaps in the side trilithons and over the Altar Stone, as well as over the bluestone 69.

of the trilithons to do so—but was moved deliberately and with a purpose that we shall also be able to explain.

During restoration work in 1958 it was established that the northwestern end of the Altar Stone had originally been trimmed at right angles to its length,

but that the other end had been given an oblique form rather like that of the bases of some of the sarsens, a form that seems to have been meant to assist in adjusting their final positions (Atkinson). This would imply that the stone was once a *pillar*, and indeed its function—as an artificial horizon twice over—can be well explained on this assumption. William Cunnington was said by Richard Colt Hoare to have uncovered a six-foot deep disturbance near the Altar Stone, but he made no more precise reference to its whereabouts. Reasons will later be given for thinking that the stone's exposed length above an important fundamental level (our 'Stonehenge Datum') was in its first setting 4.25 MY (3.52 m), leaving approximately 4 MY exposed, but that later it was erected so that only 3.75 MY (3.11 m) was exposed. The buried length added to the present turf cover would have fallen less than two inches short of the depth quoted by Cunnington, which is support of a kind for his story.

The suggested length for the exposed part of the pillar in its first situation implies that the ratio of the buried part to the exposed part was approximately 3.9 to 10, very nearly the same as the ratio (4 to 10) conjectured for timber posts, on the basis of data from Durrington and Woodhenge. Expressed differently: if the original length of the now broken stone was 6 cm longer than current estimates, the rule would have been rigorously applied. A conjecture

FIG. 163.   The Slaughter Stone, as seen from either side. The shape on the left is as the stone—now buried in a shallow trench—appears from above. The squarer end lies to the southwest and the straighter edge to the southeast. Notice how straight is that edge, and how deviation from the straight edge begins at or very near to what would have been ground level. X is the level at which the buried to the exposed lengths are as 4 to 10. Y is at the end of the straight edge, and is close to 5 MY from the mid-top of the stone, which is close to 8 MY in overall length.

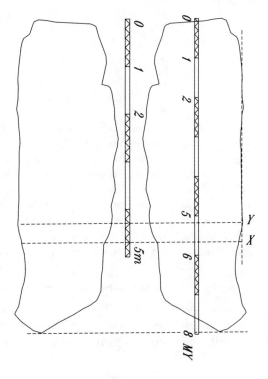

about the precise positions of the Altar Stone will be made in Chapter 11. What is proposed as the second position is illustrated here (Fig. 162). There might have been a third, as will be explained in due course.

The Slaughter Stone (95) and Holes D and E again

The large sarsen stone numbered 95, still generally known by the imaginative eighteenth-century name 'Slaughter Stone' (perhaps due to Edward King), now lies on the southeast side of the entrance causeway. It was at some stage extracted from its hole, and an extensive shallow pit was then prepared for it, so that it now lies more or less level with the turf. But from which hole did it come, and when? Many have assumed that it once stood where it now lies. After Hawley's work, others assigned it to E, as the nearer of the holes to its side. (Hawley, when he excavated E, thought it belonged there.) Opinion is divided as to whether it was moved or buried—or both—in recent centuries. Some believe that it was moved to make way for carts in historical times, but this theory takes little cognizance of the psychology of carters. Hawley put forward the hypothesis that the later Stonehenge builders buried it, having rejected it as unsuitable for their purposes. It will be shown that there is something to be said for this idea, which at first sight seems entirely improbable, in view of the unusually fine working of the stone.

As explained in connection with holes D and E, the idea must be dismissed that the Slaughter Stone has been standing at any period since the sixteenth century. William Cunnington dug around it in 1801, with Colt Hoare. He found that one end of the stone (the oblique end, now to the northeast) was rough and untooled, so this was plainly the buried end. (Buried under the stone by Cunnington himself was a bottle of port, found by the deserving Hawley more than a century later. 'The seal was intact but the cork was decayed and let out nearly all of the contents.') The sides and top of the stone, however, and perhaps its now exposed face, were tooled in a fluted manner. Such fluting, which is produced fairly naturally when a chisel is used on soft stone, might here have been something more deliberate—the idea was mooted earlier that such fluting might have been in imitation of the bark of an oak. Whether or not this is an illusion, there was certainly continuity in the techniques of observing the Sun and Moon, as between Stonehenge and the timber henges nearby.

The form of the faces of the Slaughter Stone is shown in Fig. 163. Its maximum overall length was 6.58 m and its maximum width 2.07 m. As far as can be judged, its thickness is about 0.79 m.

The former position of the Slaughter Stone has an indirect bearing on the standard astronomical claims made for Stonehenge. The stone used to be considered to belong to a hole beneath its present position. This idea has something to recommend it, since the main Stonehenge astronomical sighting line—as explained in the following chapter—passes from the Heel Stone edge and through the middle of the monument, and this line passes within half a metre of the northwest long edge of the Slaughter Stone. Hawley's findings, however, cast doubt on the existence of a suitable hole beneath it, since he found hole E to have been nearly 2 m deep, with impressions of irregularities that he thought might have matched those of the Slaughter Stone ('but I cannot state definitely if this is so'). Against this view there is a letter from Cunnington to a friend, showing that he believed he had located the Slaughter Stone's hole under it. He had, he said, 'dug around it and also into the excavation where it originally stood when erect'. He found antler pieces under it, evidence of digging in a prehistoric period, but whether to put it in its shallow grave or to dig its socket he did not speculate.

If the Slaughter Stone stood in a hole under its present position, its excavators have reported nothing by way of a hole of the requisite depth. There is another problem. As explained, the stone's northwest long edge is close to being in line with the most important solar axis of all, but this edge is not the stone's straight edge. It must surely have been turned over at the time it was buried, unless it partook in a different alignment.

Until such time as the stone is raised, the problem will remain unsolved, but at present all the evidence seems to point to Hawley's having been right, that the Slaughter Stone stood in hole E. (We see the rare speculative side of Hawley here. On the basis of his discovery of three lines of *post* holes in the northeast entrance, each of which he thought pointed to a stone in the D–E line as some sort of later replacement, he postulated a trio of stones, standing 'in line with the crest of the rampart', a sign of the site's use as a 'defensive dwelling'. The perspective was natural enough to a retired military man, but obviously went far beyond the evidence.) The artistic evidence is ambiguous, but we need not look far for three stones in the area in modern times. They could have been at D, E (the Slaughter Stone), and in the stone hole at the edge of the ditch nearby. What matters most to us is their original function and chronology. Just as the astronomical relationship of the Heel Stone to the main axis (the grazing lines of sight) tells us much about their chronological relationship, so it is with hole E, the sarsen ring and the Altar Stone. If the last of these had stood as an upright column strictly on the main axis in that sense, it would have blocked all but high-angle lines of sight. If it stood on a

perpendicular axis in the form of a line of sight through the slits in the trilithons 53–54 and 57–58, it would have created an excellent horizon for high-angle midwinter solar viewing once more, in fact towards sunrise now, as will be shown in the following chapter. It emerges that it is possible to hold the stone to this last line but move it into various positions that leave the main axis clear and yet at the same time create an artificial horizon for viewing across the sarsen ring along nearby lines.

The subject will be considered once more in Chapter 11, where it will be suggested that the stone in hole *E* was very probably meant to be just 60 MY distant from the Altar Stone. In this case, the Slaughter Stone, or whatever was standing in hole *E*, was intimately related to the Altar Stone. The transverse line of sight to the rising Sun at the same season was for an observer standing at stone 22 of the sarsen ring. As well as skimming the top of the Altar Stone, it skimmed the top of bluestone 69.

Another remarkable fact about the stone at *E* is that—as will also be shown in Chapter 11—an observer there is in a very special position as regards the compound monument of trilithons and sarsen ring, for in approaching them, it is on reaching that point that the grand trilithon is for the first time completely and precisely hidden by the ring.

It is very unlikely that the Slaughter Stone ever had a partner of comparable stature, although the lesser stone in *D* might have been ranked as a partner in some sense. It is hard to find any very convincing use for *D*. Since it is at the same distance as E, it has the property mentioned in the last paragraph. It could in principle have been used for the setting Moon at its southern extreme. The line of sight, like the others, would have entered through the central sarsens (30–1). It would have avoided the Altar Stone, and have passed through the gap between sarsens 14 and 13. The chief uncertainties are in the positions of the relevant stones, and the blocking effect of the bluestone horseshoe. At all events, the estimated low-altitude grazing ray would have done very well, at about 52.5° south of west.

That any or all of the Slaughter Stone and stones in *D* and *E* would have been regarded as a *gateway* by those who erected them—as many modern writers seem to assume—should certainly not be taken for granted, and is probably mistaken. They were the winter Sun's gateway. These stones were places from which events of a spiritual importance were observed, but that does not make them portals in the common sense. It should not even be taken for granted that stones ever actually stood in the various places at the same time. Only if they can be shown to function jointly can this be safely assumed.

Why was the Slaughter Stone buried, and when? Its burial cut into an Aubrey hole—not a very Neolithic thing to do. (It is unlikely that its hole cut into the bank, since early viewing from the ditch stone would have required a clear passage around this place.) If it was not buried after the sixteenth century of our own era, and was not simply pushed over from its original position but was moved from E, then it was very probably moved when Stonehenge was still in use. The reason for thinking this is that the stone was—albeit crudely—put with one edge in the main line to the winter solstice. Had there been available the expertise of the late Neolithic or Bronze Age, the stone would have been reused in some more striking capacity. Stonehenge might not have been in disrepair, but by the time of the stone's burial Stonehenge astronomy certainly was. If any single stone on the site is to be associated with the dreaded Druids, or be given the name of Slaughter Stone, this might as well be it.

The Extant Bluestone Circle

The bluestone ring, of about 23 m outside diameter, was a very indifferent circle. It lies between the sarsens of the main circle and the trilithons. More than thirty stones still survive in part, many of them only as fragments or stumps underground. Eleven are standing, five of them leaning, and opinions have differed greatly about the original total. John Wood (1740) opted for twenty-nine, while William Stukeley (1723), followed by many others, claimed forty. Atkinson, with the advantage of Hawley's excavations, estimated sixty, give or take a stone, and noted the irregularity of their spacings, shapes, heights, and sizes generally. He drew attention to the fact that only two of the bluestones were tooled: the slightly curved stones numbered 150 and 36, of about 2.4 m and 1.8 m in length respectively, had been in use as lintels in an earlier *tooled* bluestone structure, before they were reused as uprights in the present untooled bluestone circle.

The Bluestone Horseshoe

Inside the horseshoe of sarsen trilithons there are the remains of a horseshoe of very carefully tooled bluestone pillars, each of section roughly 60 by 60 cm. It is not unreasonable to speak of them as having been of graded heights, say from about 1.8 m at the ends of the horseshoe to perhaps 2.8 m at its 'toe' (where the now fallen stone 67 stood, 4 m long in all) above the present turf level. It might well have been the intention of the designers to have them ranged from 2.5 to 3.75 MY above a fundamental level, our Stonehenge Datum. The

importance of stone 69 in the horseshoe has already been indicated, as delimiting lines of sight over the Altar Stone. Stone 69 stood quite precisely 3.5 MY above that basic level.

Some of the bluestones in the horseshoe held lintels, but not necessarily in their present situations. Some show signs of rippled tooling. Two of them seem to form a matched pair (66 and 68), in that one is grooved along its length and the other (now a stump) was tongued, presumably along its length. This is usually taken to indicate that they once stood side by side, close together, but in an earlier arrangement they could equally well have had a large timber or stone plate (or series of balks) between them. One potential explanation will be offered later in connection with the Q-R system.

As Flinders Petrie showed, the horseshoe can be seen as a semicircle—almost precisely concentric with the sarsen circle—with short extensions from its ends. With occasional exceptions, as with the sarsens, the best face—which follows a circle very closely—is to the inside. Since the extensions contain only one good stone, virtually nothing precise can be said about them. Alexander Thom imposed on them an ingenious geometrical design, supposing the trilithons to have been set on an ellipse, which touched a circle (different from Petrie's), that accounted for only part of the horseshoe. Oddly enough, quoting the radius of Petrie's circle in Thom's Megalithic Yards, something Petrie could not of course do, it is 7.01 MY. An arc of 7 MY radius has been added to Fig. 161.

Another interpretation that has been offered of the horseshoe is that it is the surviving part of an *oval* setting. (Atkinson, in the last edition of his book *Stonehenge*, seems to suggest that there was an oval, but that it was rebuilt as a horseshoe, with different stone positions over that part of it.) The graded heights of the stones, and their similarity in this respect to the horseshoe of trilithons, might be thought to speak against all versions of the idea of an oval setting, but that would be to prejudge the issue. If further excavation should make it seem likely that there was once an oval, then its affinities with Woodhenge would obviously be worth investigating, for the two structures are probably not very different in age.

The History of the Dressed Bluestones

The horseshoe-shaped array of stones could be the source of the two dressed bluestones in the partly surviving bluestone circle. This might have been so, for example, if there was a change in plan over the use of lintels in the horseshoe after an initial period when they were in use. This might in turn have meant

a loss of dressed stones from the site, although material so hard-won would probably have been found another use in the monument. A more tangible problem is that of the numerous missing bluestones from the earlier Q-R system, of which the same might be said.

Atkinson at one juncture proposed the existence of another structure. He noted that there were (as he thought) eighty-two bluestones available from the Q-R system; that sixty would have been needed for the Y- and Z-rings (see below); and that we have exactly the difference, twenty-two, in the form of nineteen dressed stones in the existing horseshoe plus two dressed lintels in the extant ring, and the Altar Stone. This kind of argument cannot be reconciled with our belief that the number of stones in a ring depends on complex issues of visibility, and is not to be decided by such a simple consideration as the availability of stone. Of course, it is always possible that the people responsible for the Y- and Z-rings had lost the art of their precursors. Atkinson went on to conjecture that the missing sixty stones might have been used within the (largely unexplored) area inside the bluestone horseshoe or away from the site altogether. Three holes found in the right area by Hawley, and designated by him J, K, and L, led Atkinson to favour the first idea. Presumably he supposed that the entirely lost inner ring was stripped in preparation for a monument (in the Y- and Z-holes) that never materialized.

The Y- and Z-Holes

What are now taken to be the Aubrey holes were designated 'X' by Aubrey, so when Hawley and Newall in their 1923–4 excavations found two rings of pits (rings with outside diameters roughly 55 m and 41m) outside the main sarsen ring, they termed them the 'Y- and Z-holes'. Judging by their shape and spacing, the original plan was to have 30 stones in each ring. Twenty-four out of the assumed 60 holes have yet to be excavated, but most of them have been located by probing. The excavated holes had depths on average of 0.91 m for the Y-holes and 1.04 m for the Z-holes.

Atkinson pointed out that these rings were later than the sarsen ring, since hole Z7 cuts through the ramp for inserting sarsen stone 7; and that they never held stones, since their bases show no sign of compression. They seem to be unfinished, or at least Z8 was never dug, and he conjectured that some calamity struck the community, since the holes were found not to have been artificially filled in, but to have silted up naturally. A piece of antler from the bottom of Y 30 gave a radiocarbon date equivalent to 1540±120 BC and another from Z29 has yielded a date perhaps more than two centuries earlier.

It is conceivable that the stone holes were dug on the basis of pre-existing post holes. Even the sarsens might stand where once a circle of large timber posts stood. These are weak conjectures, but Hawley did find that $Z13$ had a previous post hole in it, going 23 cms (9 ins) below it; and $Z9$ and $Y16$ partially overlap post holes. Following the working rules for posts, we should expect them to have been very approximately 2.3 m (Y) and 2.6 m (Z) tall, based on hole depths.

The fact that the Y- and Z-holes match the stones in the sarsen ring, one for one, is a testimony to tradition, whether or not the analysis of that tradition given in Chapter 7 was correct. There is similar matching of numbers in the rings of posts at Mount Pleasant and Durrington. The geometrical form of the rings is interesting. Alexander Thom commented that they were obviously never intended to be on complete *circles*, but that they rather lie on *spirals*, and that the two are *similar*. These he tentatively reconstructed, each out of a pair of semicircles of different radius, meeting at one end. (He showed that the Z-holes fit moderately well to arcs of radius 22.5 and 23.75 MY and the Y-holes to arcs of radius 31.25 and 32.5 MY.) His construction is not very convincing. While the holes do seem to lie on crude spirals, the fit is a poor one. $Y1$. $Y8$ and $Y15$, as well as $Z17$, lie well off the proposed plan: for example, $Y1$ and $Y7$ are supposed to be on the same spiral arc, but their distances from the supposed arc-centre differ by no less than 2.6 MY (2.2 m).

The general problem of determining the intended shape of the rings is reminiscent of that at Avebury, where the outermost ring seems to have comprised a number of distinct circular arcs. Assuming that they were indeed seen as arcs of circles deviating from a master circle, it is not difficult to see why each was pulled in, and in the same way, on the southeast side. As will be explained later, this would have allowed its use as a marker of maximum southern *lunar* setting. The rings as a whole will be very tentatively related to the Aubrey ring—but this will prove to be a common property on the site, and is of no chronological help.

This completes our inventory of the main elements of known structures belonging to the classic period of Stonehenge's history. In round numbers, that period spanned a millennium and a half, beginning with the bank and ditch, a little before or after 3000 BC, and ending with the Z- and Y-holes. After this, from the later Bronze Age to the present, there followed a period of slow attrition, a period that seems set to continue into our own third millennium.

11

THE FIRST THREE STONEHENGES

I T is hardly feasible to present an argued case for astronomical activity at Stonehenge in chronological sequence. The most certain of data, by and large, are the most recent. The late has obliterated the early, and there are many gaps in what is known of the oldest constructions on the site—the treehenge, the bank, ditch and Aubrey holes. These have already been considered at some length, on the basis of practice elsewhere. In view of Hawley's discovery of post holes arranged in circular arcs more or less concentric with the later stone structures, it is beyond reasonable doubt—at least to those unafflicted with an urge to a spurious subtlety in defining terms—that there were timber henges on the Stonehenge site. As before, the word 'henge' is used here very broadly to indicate a monument that seems not to have been primarily a sepulchre, but that incorporated conspicuous stone or timber uprights with as many other parts (such as ditches and banks) as were needed to make it self-sufficient as a potential delimiter of astronomically significant directions. (This does not necessarily indicate the monument's *chief* original function; and such a definition will of course be unacceptable to all who deny that their henges have the stated property.) The great trilithons, taken together with some simple peripheral accessories, were a henge in this sense—give or take a few markers for observers' positions—whereas the bluestone horseshoe, being heavily dependent on other stones, is best treated as only *part* of a henge. The time is not ripe for the casting of better definitions, but there is a worthwhile distinction to be drawn between classical henges that were lintelled and those open henges like Avebury that never were. In drafting definitions, the most useful properties are likely to be those that have reference to the ways in which the henges functioned, but of course this involves a dangerous element of interpretation. The arrangement of the uprights (in circles, horseshoes, or whatever) is obviously more important than the counting of causeways, when it comes to settling celestial alignments. This is not to say that henges had no other use,

and those who expound the principles of other activities on these sites are welcome to add their own defining characters.

Stonehenge can be looked upon as a single evolving entity. This adds another dimension to our chronological difficulties. The position of a bluestone in the horseshoe, for instance, might be intimately related to stones in the sarsen ring and the great trilithons, but that fact in itself does not allow it to be placed before, after or with them in historical sequence. Even when new elements do not clearly enter into a network of relationships with pre-existing elements, continuity of design is usually plain enough. It seems that there were lintels at every stage, for example—they were doubtless present in the timber monument. Where to begin? To ensure an astronomical reading for any particular point of time, three components are essential: (1) the central group of stones or posts, lintelled or not, in relation to which the Sun or Moon was observed; (2) the stone or post—whether external, internal, or on the perimeter—from which the observation would have been made; and (3) the horizon, whether natural or artificial, that helped to determine the extreme directions of rising or setting. The first component of the three has always tended to attract most attention, but the others are no less important, and they present some of the most difficult of problems. This was hinted at in Chapter 10, in regard to the link between the Altar Stone (a horizon stone) and the Slaughter Stone (used for its viewing edge). It has been shown in a very limited way in relation to the old timber structures. The bank was capable of providing an artificial horizon for viewing across a system of Aubrey posts; and posts and stones to the northeast (including the Heel Stone) and elsewhere (station stones and nearby Aubrey posts) entered into schemes of lunar and solar observation. There was a strong indication that the corridor issuing from the central treehenge defined a *stellar* alignment, on Rigel Centauri. If this is so—and it is far from certain—then the question is raised as to whether we should treat the corridor as an approach to the inner area at all. How long solar and lunar lines of sight were mixed with stellar it is difficult to say, but the case of Avebury—where all were in evidence at a relatively late stage—should not be forgotten. In all of its stone phases, however, the main concern at Stonehenge seems to have been with the Sun and Moon alone.

Whether it remained so, far into the Bronze Age, is beyond the scope of this book, but on the subject of horizons it ought not to pass unnoticed that on the Stonehenge axis—that is, in the precise direction of the setting midwinter Sun—and standing at a distance of 250 MY (that is, 100 of Thom's megalithic rods) from the centre of Stonehenge, there is an oval disk barrow

(Amesbury 10). Perhaps something on its top once broke the horizon. The approximate direction of the axis of the oval goes without saying.

The Q-R Henge

It is impossible to look at the plans of the 'entrances' to the southern Durrington Walls monument and to the Q-R system at Stonehenge without entertaining the thought that they are related. There are many differences, of course. Facing the entrance at Durrington, where there seems to have been no corridor as perfect as that through the Q- and R-rings, was to look in the direction of the setting midsummer Sun. Here at Stonehenge one faces the direction of the setting midwinter Sun. In both cases there is a possibility—indeed at Stonehenge the only one that is widely canvassed—that it was the rising Sun that was actually observed, looking in the reverse direction. The double ring at Stonehenge, however, begs to be interpreted in the same way as multiple rings of timber elsewhere, that is, as having been planned to carry lintels at different heights, to cover the bright sky surrounding the Sun and possibly also define a horizon.

Whatever the ambition of its builders, it is extremely unlikely that there was ever a completed bluestone monument with such a plethora of lintels as at Durrington. The difficulties of working in stone were obviously much greater than with the old wooden monuments, and all the evidence points to the fact that only a minority of the columnar and slab-like bluestones were worked. The moderately regular shapes of the unworked stones seem to have occurred naturally, but worked bluestone lintels do survive—they were used as uprights in a later revision—and the care that went into them underscores the importance of precision in the preparation of lintels. But where were they all placed? This is an important question when deciding on the direction the observer was meant to face, towards the rising or setting Sun. It would help greatly if the physical arrangement at the southwest were better known. Consider a 'staircase' of five lintels at the northeast, above the entrance corridor: this would not have been used as a viewing frame by an observer near at hand, for it would not then have narrowed down the field of view sufficiently. The frame would have been used as such by someone standing at the causeway, in the neighbourhood of the Heel Stone, or in fact at any remote enough point to either side of the double ring. To decide the matter, precise lines of sight and altitude are called for.

Three alternatives may be suggested, given those general principles that have been found effective elsewhere.

C
A The Stones call'd Corfstones, 12 Tonn Weight
24 foot high, 7 broad, and 16 round
B The Stones call'd Coronetts, of 6 or 7 Tonns
C The place where Mens bones are dug up.

22. Stonehenge, as represented by a Dutch engraver for Edmund Gibson's expanded version of Camden's book *Britannia*. The engraver used a drawing by Walter Charleton but has allowed his imagination free rein, especially on the surrounding countryside. (*William Camden,* Britannia, *1695*)

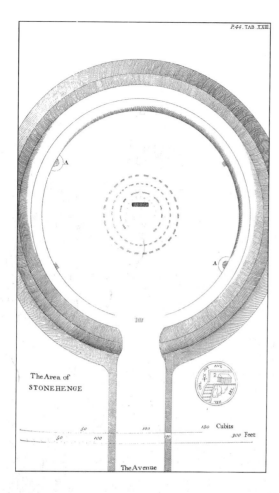

A

A'

The Area of
STONEHENGE

AVE

50   100   150 Cubits
50   100   300 Feet

The Avenue

23. *Left* William Stukeley's plan of Stonehenge, with some cautious conjecture. Note the station stones (AA and their opposites) and the Avenue. (*William Stukeley,* Stonehenge, *1740*)

24. *Below* An aerial view of Stonehenge in the snow, looking north east. The snow picks out depressions in the ground, especially the ditch and the Avenue beyond the main road. The Heel Stone stands out clearly against the road. Note the two station stones at the left and the right of the photograph. (*English Heritage Photographic Library*)

25. Stonehenge from the air, looking south west. The Heel Stone is prominent in the foreground. Note the prostrate Slaughter Stone beyond it, near the entrance through the ditch. (*English Heritage Photographic Library*)

26. The Heel Stone viewed from the southeast. (*English Heritage Photographic Library*)

27. The lower face of the fallen lintel (stone 156) from the grand trilithon, showing the large tenons on its underside. The meticulous dressing of the far upright (stone 56) that once helped to support it is rivalled by that much smaller erect cylindrical bluestone (no. 69) to the right. (*English Heritage Photographic Library*)

28. Looking towards the Heel Stone (left) more or less tangentially to the ring of sarsens at Stonehenge. The massive stones right of centre comprise trilithon 57–58 (with lintel 158). (*English Heritage Photographic Library*)

29. The tooling of the surface of one of the stones (16) at Stonehenge, perhaps intended to imitate the bark of an oak tree. (*English Heritage Photographic Library*)

The five bluestones that stood on the left of the 'entrance' corridor were fairly accurately in line with the corresponding edge of stone number 1 of the later sarsen circle. (See Fig. 161 of the previous chapter, and the general plan of Fig. 160. The stones at the other side of the corridor do not align with the corresponding sarsen edge.) As far as can be gathered from Richard Atkinson's published data, the axis of the corridor aligned on the northwest edge of stone B, and probably on that of stone C, and even conceivably the southern side of the southernmost A-post. The stones are judged on the basis of the holes in which they stood, so that there is an element of conjecture here, but over such long distances, accepting that the line skims B, the angle derived is relatively insensitive to error.

Later in the chapter it will emerge that there is a close connection between the geometry of the Q- and R-rings and stone B. It will also be shown that there is a no less compelling relationship between the position of B and the system of sarsens and trilithons. Stone B, in other words, is of great importance to us, since it provides a link between successive phases in the evolution of the Stonehenge complex of monuments.

The three cases worth considering are based on the idea that the far stones that decide the limiting ray are (1) in line with the left of the corridor, or (2) in line with the right of the corridor, or (3) determined by a stone that puts it between those limits. (Here 'left' and 'right' are to be understood from the point of view of a person looking towards the southwest.) Any of the three alternatives might be combined with the idea that there is another stone, delimiting the line at the far side of the ring. I think it very probable that there was such a stone, and that it was none other than the Altar Stone, in its first manifestation. This matter was raised in Chapter 10, where it was argued that the stone would probably have reached to a height of 4.25 MY above ground. It would have been the same amount above the eye of the observer at B; and as far as can be judged from the partial survey of the hole by Richard Atkinson—which was the occasion for his first suggesting that the Altar Stone was once here—its front edge was just 99 MY from the mid-point of stone B. (It is possible that a figure of 100 was in the thoughts of those concerned, but it will later be found that the distance of 66 MY between the mid-point of B and the front edge of the sarsen ring enters into a network of carefully planned proportions.)

If viewed from B, the limiting azimuths would have been about 41.6° and 40.3° for the first two cases respectively. If an intermediate ray was fixed by stone 56 of the grand trilithon, which might well have been in place, then we may take 40.5° as the azimuth, and this last intermediate line seems likely to

have been very close to the line to our Altar Stone (Fig. 166). The required corresponding horizon altitudes for the three cases for midwinter sunset (upper limb of the Sun, mid millennium) would then have been about 1.4°, 0.7°, and 0.8°.

It is impossible to say whether the main bank was at this time in good repair. Even an altitude of 1°, as seen from B, would have been quite feasible, bearing in mind the uncertainties. The second and third results are barely distinguishable on the basis of alignment alone, and both are quite plausible, since the natural horizon would have been approximately 0.6°.

In the second case, the resulting line of sight would have passed over the human burial found at the end of the Q-R corridor—but this is not in itself surprising, since the main viewing axis was preserved for more than a millennium. Hawley found that the grave held a disordered heap of bones as well as items from the Georgian period, that in turn hint at a rough and ready excavation then. A fragment of Beaker pottery probably signals a Beaker date.

It will be shown later that the grand trilithon was geometrically related to the Heel Stone in much the same way as the Q-R system was related to stone B. This does not of itself allow us to deny that stones in both places could have functioned with both monuments. On the contrary, it will soon be shown that they could..

When analysing timber monuments, we showed that lintels created highly effective artificial horizons. As a compromise between schemes (2) and (3),

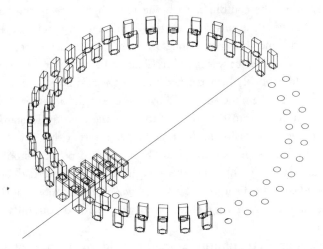

FIG. 164.   A stylized view of one possible arrangement of stones (and lintels at the entrance) in the Q- and R-rings, but without the suspected Altar Stone that probably filled much of the gap at the southwest end of the axis. The rings were never completed in the northeastern quadrant, and the stone holes to the south, if they exist, are still unexcavated.

FIG. 165.   The view through the entrance to the *Q-R* rings as drawn in the previous figure, from approximately the distance of the Aubrey circle.

suppose that the horizon was set at an altitude of roughly 0.75°. A line of sight at this angle for an observer at *B* would have been rather more than 1 MY above the floor of the *Q-R* corridor at its inner end, and might easily have been set by the upper edge of a lintel over the uprights at the inner end of the corridor. (This of course entails that it is not the sort of corridor through which one actually walks. It will be recalled that Hawley was surprised at the signs of very insubstantial posts in his southern corridor of post holes. Perhaps they held lintels.) To a person looking from the side of an upright where we suspect the Altar Stone to have been, that low lintel would not have cleared the horizon, but (still speaking approximately) a lintel 3 MY above the ground in the northeast *Q-R* corridor would have done so, and would have produced a sight line *at much the same altitude as that in the opposite direction*. Why this is an interesting arrangement will be explained in the following section.

There is an old bluestone lintel still surviving (stone number 150), slightly curved, and of about 2.9 MY in length. One cannot be certain that it came from the entrance—perhaps not, since its mortises are surprisingly close together (they are only 1.25 MY apart). Even so, 3 MY is roughly the length required of any lintel that spanned the paired posts of the entrance corridor, so this last dimension as a bluestone *pillar* height is not at all implausible. It is in keeping with stone-hole depths, and instances were found earlier of wooden posts and lintel lengths more or less matching. The lintel in question is not massive, and the gradient of the conjectured stacked array of lintels would need to have been shallow, for them to have served their assumed purpose of cutting out the glare of the sky around the solar image.

How would the lintels have been stacked? It need not be assumed that the gradient of the 'staircase' rose from the outside to the middle of the planned *Q*- and *R*-rings, as in the timber examples proposed and analysed earlier. The dumbbell-shaped trenches in which the stone holes were set were deepest to the outside, which seems to indicate that the lintels were highest to the outside. Such an arrangement is shown in Fig. 166. Lintels could have been used to obscure the background sky with the slope running in either direction. The general pattern of the *Q-R* system as it might have been when work on it was abandoned is given in Figs. 164 and 165.

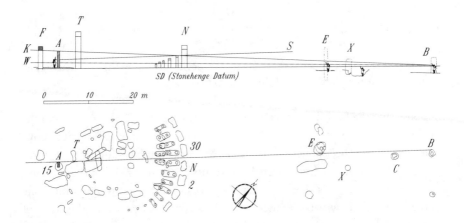

FIG. 166.   One possible arrangement of the Q-R lintels over the corridor at the northeast side of the incomplete double ring (see the plan below), together with what we take to be the first position of the Altar Stone (A). Some later additions to the monument are added to the figure: the grand trilithon (T), and the near and far sarsens (N and F) from the point of view of the observer at B, where all that now survives is a stone hole. An observer is shown at the Altar Stone. The highest of the corridor lintels sets a horizon to that observer equal in altitude to the horizon set by the lowest lintel, as seen from B. The alignments to the rising midsummer Sun (S) and the setting midwinter Sun (W) are for them on the same line, but in opposite directions. (See the plan. We have called them reversible alignments.) It is worth remarking on the fact that, on this interpretation, the highest corridor lintel would have exactly closed up the gap below the far sarsen lintel (see K), that is, on the later monument. It is not known whether the two ever existed simultaneously.

Reversible Alignments

An altitude in the neighbourhood of 0.7° is of interest in its own right, at Stonehenge latitude and epoch. A line of sight to the rising midsummer Sun is in a direction precisely the reverse of that to the setting midwinter Sun, in both cases, assuming the upper limb of the Sun to be on an artificial horizon with that altitude. If identical altitudes can be arranged for both directions, then a single pair of vertical stones might in principle be used to set the reversible azimuth. There would have been very good reason for wishing to achieve this arrangement: speaking quite generally, it offers economy of effort, and also a measure of symmetry in the design of a monument.

For the sake of brevity, this will be called a *reversible alignment*. Instances comparable with that just found for the Q-R system have already been encountered in timber monuments. Of course it is not the sight lines them-

selves that are perfectly reversible, but their plans, their directions on the ground.

Rather surprisingly, the altitude needed for reversible solar alignments does not change appreciably with time. At Stonehenge it can be taken as 0.71° over the entire period from 3000 BC to 1500 BC, if the position of the Sun's upper limb was what mattered (that is, first and last glint were being observed). The azimuth of the reversible alignment, however, did change appreciably over this period, namely from 40.50° to 40.21° (north of east and south of west).

What of the altitude thrown up by the two artificial horizons ascribed to the Q-R system of the last section? It could be held that they have no basis in fact, but they are not entirely conjectural, to the extent that accepting one of them more or less forces us to accept the other. The shared altitude is hardly more than that of the natural horizons to the southwest and northeast. This fact adds a little weight to the arguments for artificial horizons, whether formed by lintels, or banks, or both, inasmuch as the dimensions and placing of the archaeological remains plays a part in the argument and might perfectly well have yielded altitudes *below* the natural horizon.

The altitude of 0.71° required for a reversible alignment is equivalent to a gradient close to 1 in 80. (That gradient strictly corresponds to an angle of 0.716°.) Whether or not this is to be judged one of them, there are many simple ratios of whole numbers to be found at Stonehenge, in continuance of a longstanding Neolithic tradition.

The Levels of the Sarsen Trilithons and Circle

To most visitors, the sarsens *are* Stonehenge. Something of their sophistication will be seen merely by considering how their dimensions are related to the lie of the landscape. The available information is here much more reliable than in the case of the Q-R system, which no longer exists. One extremely important datum is that the monument was built rather accurately level. The current ground level is a poor guide to its original state, since it has been repeatedly modified over the centuries, but in any case it plays only a secondary role in the geometry of the structure. As soon as vertical distances are considered in relation to the ring of lintels on the main circle, it becomes clear that those distances were carefully worked out so as to to provide gradients in round numbers. This will not be so readily apparent if one uses modern units of measurement. All heights will be quoted in the form we assume they were originally conceived, in integral numbers of Megalithic Yards (0.829 m) above

the level called here the *Stonehenge Datum*. The architecture of the ring of sarsens appears to have embodied the following *ideal* as to stone sizes:

> The outer circle should have pillars 4.75 MY above the Stonehenge Datum, topped by lintels 1 MY in height, in both cases allowing for some latitude as long as the height of the top surface of the lintels is exactly 5.75 MY. (The ideal pillar was probably meant to taper, not necessarily regularly, from 2.5 MY at its base to 2.25 MY at its top.)

The Stonehenge Datum will be here taken as 102.27 m above the Ordnance Datum. This is a figure that could certainly be improved by a careful survey of the monument in three dimensions—something that has apparently never

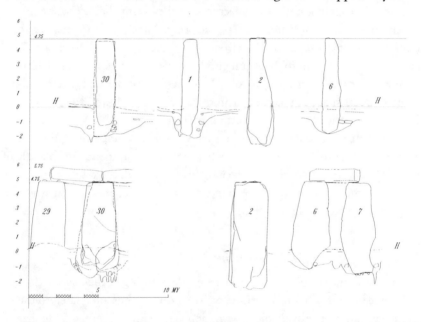

FIG. 167.   Various stones excavated by William Hawley, modified and assembled from his drawings. The upper row shows profiles with the inner surface of the ring to the left. In the lower row one is looking at the inner faces. Hawley's datum is the broken line marked *HH*, at the approximate level of the bronze peg at the monument's centre. Our Stonehenge Datum is the zero line, the units being Megalithic Yards. Stones 30, 1 and 6 (upper) and stone 30 (lower) are his outlines but are set upright on the present page (as broken lines when two versions are shown). The solid lines of 30 and 2 are based on his drawings of the restored stones (note the discrepancies in size). In each case, solid chalk begins at the lowest line, the line above is where coarse chalk rubble begins (a few packing stones are drawn), and the broken line was the line of turf in Hawley's day. Some of the stone holes show post holes below. His illustrations are not consistent in scale for the underground sections, and his scales have in three cases been adjusted for large errors, so that the above figure can be only approximate. It does, however, lend support to the claim that ideal critical heights above our Datum were 5 and 6 MY.

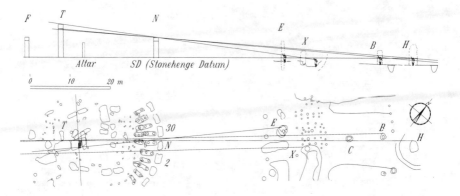

FIG. 168. Some of the limiting lines of sight under discussion, with stones shown in elevation (upper figure) that are not aligned in plan (for which see the lower figure, to which are added potential astronomical alignments that are not essential to the geometrical discussion). Key observation points are: H – Heel Stone; stones B and E (conventional notation for holes, but E is either the Slaughter Stone or a twin to it); X – the ditch stone at the terminal. For more detail of the elevations see Fig. 169.

been carefully done. Here it will be provisionally accepted and its consequences considered. That they hang together so well, and this in many unexpected ways, will be part of the justification of the suggested scheme—to which the monument does appear to approximate with fair accuracy, according to existing surveys. A rough visual impression of the situation may be had from drawings of five of the stones excavated—and in some cases set upright—by William Hawley (Fig. 167).

The central trilithon comprised stone 55, which when it fell at an unknown date broke into two pieces (see Fig. 162 of the previous chapter), and stone 56. The latter was already leaning inwards in the sixteenth century, and tilted further after the Duke of Buckingham's digging in 1620. It was set upright in 1901 under the direction of William Gowland. I suspect that he put it at most a hand's breadth deeper than it was originally meant to be. These uprights were very probably meant to be 8.25 MY above the Stonehenge Datum, capped by a lintel bringing the total height to 9.5 MY. Their lintel, once the loftiest of all, sat on very large tenons, of which that on stone 56 can still be seen, even from the road, at the highest point of the whole monument. The lintel has correspondingly large mortises on one face, but smaller cavities on the opposite face, as though a false start had been made. Another distinct possibility is that another stone was once seated on top of it.

The trilithons flanking the central one had uprights (numbered 53–54 to the left and 57–58 to the right) somewhat heavier than their loftier superior,

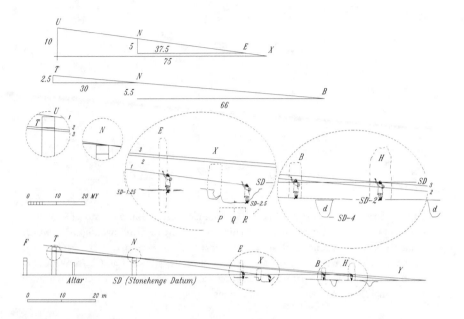

FIG. 169   This figure adds more detail to the last, where the notation for the stones is explained. SD is the Stonehenge Datum, the eye level of the observer at the Heel Stone (*H*). Levels below are given in the form 'SD − 4' (4 MY below SD). The Heel Stone ditch (*d*), at some late stage filled with rammed chalk, is of depth 2 MY and so might once have been used for observation, say at a planning stage. The rising terrain raises the eye of an observer moving forward from *H* to *B* by 0.25 MY. The observers in the main ditch (*X*) and at *E* can so position themselves that the lintel of the grand trilithon is just covered by the near edge of the sarsen lintel ring. Where precisely the former stood is open to three interpretations. If at *P*, a platform in the chalk would have been needed; if at *Q* (mid-ditch), one must assume a slight error in the levels drawn, but a 5 in 38 gradient would hold; if at *R,* the back of the ditch, the line of sight is virtually perfect and the gradient is 10 in 75. The observer at *E* is shown in the position giving an exact fit on the assumption of this last gradient, but in reality any nearby position behind the stone might have been used, or we might have placed the stone slightly away from its true place. The proportional triangles in the upper figure are an attempt to deduce the rationale of the geometrical arrangement (easily done for *B* and *H*, and rather less so for *E* and *X*). Three different types of line of sight are drawn in elevation (1, 2, 3), and a selection of potential alignments on the winter Sun are drawn in plan, as discussed at various points in the text.

but all of about the same width. They were conceivably meant to be 6.75 MY above the Stonehenge Datum with 1.25 MY added for the lintel. The uprights of the trilithons at the open end of the horseshoe were probably meant to be 6.25 MY, with lintels also of 1.25 MY.

The upper surfaces of the lintels at the three levels of trilithon were thus close to 9.75, 8.25, and 7.75 MY. It is important to realize that there were inevitably irregularities in the stones available for use that made it necessary for the builders to vary stone heights and lintel depths, but that the upper surfaces of the finished lintels and the lower surfaces of their middle parts, both of which could be used to define lines of site, seem to have conformed very closely with these ideals. The sixteen sarsen uprights still standing in the ring vary in total height within a range of about a quarter MY, but the lintels compensate for the slight inequalities so that, even in its present parlous state, the upper surface of the lintel ring varies over only about 0.1 MY (8 cm) of the ideal set out above. It should be needless to add that one may believe in the existence of a fundamental level, an ideal, without insisting that the ground was ever true to it right across the sarsen ring or beyond. This ideal was never the same as the ground level at the foot of every stone, but as it happens, it is close to the present ground level at stone 1.

Flinders Petrie thought that the upper surface of the ring of lintels had a definite tilt, running down from 4 inches above to 4 inches below the average level (about 10 cm above to 10 cm below, a gradient equivalent to 0.37°). If one could be sure that such a tilt was present in the building from the very beginning, and was not deliberate but arose from a levelling error, one might try to draw conclusions as to the technique used for levelling. His claim might seem to favour some sort of mason's level rather than, for instance, a water-filled clay or wooden trough. From the published evidence of heights, however, the variation does not seem to be as systematic as Petrie's suggestion requires it to be.[1]

The chief support for this metrical key to the plan of the sarsens comes from the possibility of extending it beyond the monument, in particular to stone 96, the Heel Stone. Set upright, this stone would have stood almost exactly 6 MY above the ground, with its top reaching to 4 MY above the Stonehenge Datum, so that its ground level was almost exactly 2 MY below that reference plane. Standing near its base, the early observer's eye would thus

---

1   Those who use Petrie's generally excellent measurements, which were made in 1877 and published in 1880, should beware his repeated reference to an Ordnance Benchmark on the Heel Stone. There is one there today, at 100.70 m above OD, that seems to differ from his by 2.12 feet.

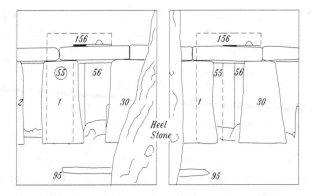

FIG. 170. The central stones as seen today from the left and right sides of the Heel Stone. Note the appreciable slopes of the sides of the stones 1 and 30, making a ground plan of the monument a very poor guide to critical lines of sight. The approximate positions of the fallen upright of the grand trilithon (55) and its lintel are marked with broken lines. (To the fore of its partner 56, are the fragments of 55 and other debris.) Stone 55 would have been completely hidden from the left, while from the right the straight edges of 55 and 56 would have been visible. The viewpoints shown here are not close enough to the edges of the Heel Stone to be treated as true viewing positions. The slit created by the two lintels is here emphasized (filled in black).

have been on the level of Stonehenge's fundamental ground plane. This arrangement looks almost as though it was a conscious extension of the old principle of observing from a ditch, where the eye is at ground level.

From the proportions between the stones on the axis of the monument, it becomes clear that their dimensions fit together in a way that is certainly not accidental. Consider the two sorts of function previously found for lintels in timber monuments, first as framing windows through which the Sun or Moon might be seen, and second as simple blocking devices to reduce glare. Astronomical purpose apart, consider then a line of sight passing *over* the sarsen ring and just managing to pass *under* the highest trilithon lintel (Figs. 169 and 168). It intersects the fundamental plane a few metres in front of *H*. An observer standing back from there—for instance at midpoint of the nearby Heel Stone *H*—will be able to see a very narrow slit between the lintels at *T* and *N*.

There was a ring of chalk created by digging a ditch round the Heel Stone (mid diameter and width approximately 10 and 3 MY respectively) and then ramming chalk rubble into it. The ring's remains survive inside the present Stonehenge boundary fence, but are not visible.

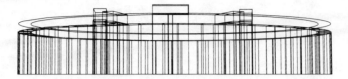

FIG. 171.   A skeletal view of the idealized dish-shaped figure created by the trilithon lintels over the drum of sarsens, as seen from the Heel Stone. The halo over the drum is the upper lintel surface

It is when we examine the gradients of the lines of sight singled out here (1, 2 and 3 in the figure) that the essential simplicity of the various arrangements becomes obvious, especially in regard to stone B. The observer can just see under the trilithon lintel, and by stepping back can open up the gap. The proportionality (as drawn in the upper part of the figure) might not seem particularly simple, with the occurrence of a length of 66 units, but it could have been spelled out very easily in many ways. In terms of rods (2.5 MY), for instance, it might have gone thus: one rod is to twelve rods as two rods to twenty-four, and as half a yard is to six yards (so making our sixty-six). It seems fitting that the case of stone B should be so simple, since we shall later find reason to relate it to the Q-R system.

In the cases of E and the observer by the ditch stone (X, on the figure), it is possible to find two or three quite plausible solutions, but the most appealing—which as it happens puts the observer at the *back* of the ditch—explains both positions in terms of a ten in seventy-five gradient. Again this could have been thought of in terms of rods of 2.5 MY (four is to thirty as two is to fifteen), making for a memorable formula. Similar triangles with integral sides for the placing of the Heel Stone are not so easily found. The calculation depends on the position of the lower surface of the trilithon lintel and the precise position of the observer (the horizontal distance to mid stone is 106 MY). On the assumptions made above, the gradient is 8 in 106, or 1 in 13.25. There are ways of simplifying this, but it seems best to await a decent survey before trying further to read the thoughts of the designer. (And how pleasant it would be to rip up the main road.)

Oddly enough, the two gradients discussed so far are in close agreement with the slope (to the vertical, now) of the faces of the trilithon lintels, which are wider at the top than the bottom. At a rough estimate, this slope amounts to 1 in 14. Although unable to appreciate the fact, an observer standing at B or the Heel Stone (but not at E or X, even without the obscuring sarsens) would therefore have been looking at the central trilithon lintel exactly at right angles

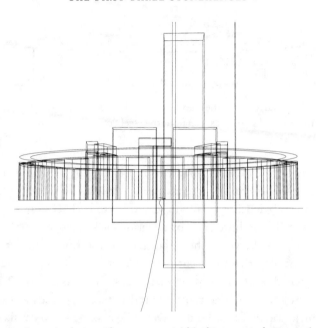

FIG. 172.   A schematized view of some potential blocking stones between the sarsens at Stonehenge and the observer at the right side of the Heel Stone (compare Fig. 171). To the near right is stone *B* ; beyond it is *C*, and then come stones of the size of the Slaughter Stone, one at its current position and the other in hole *E*. No assumption is made as to whether such stones were simultaneously present—they were almost certainly not. A relatively small shift in the position and size or shape of a stone can clearly make a great difference to what is seen beyond it. The line drawn along the ground is a main axis of the monument.

to its face. That simple fact suggests a remarkable degree of planning. With the meagre data available, the fit is slightly better at the Heel than at *B*.

The second arrangement described here is reasonably well appreciated, even today, by anyone looking from our 'standard height' (the 2 MY eye level of an observer around 1.70 m tall) from the roadside behind the Heel Stone. From the right side, the sugar-loaf form of the tenon (itself 33 cm tall) on the top of the surviving stone (56) of the great trilithon will then appear to stand on the lintel joining sarsen stones 1 and 30. The gradient of the line of sight is today, in the absence of the far lintel, difficult to measure, and in any case a slight incline of stone 56 makes a precise measurement meaningless. For future reference, the general appearance of the crucial central stones as seen from the left and right sides of the Heel Stone are shown in Fig. 170.

That stone *B* and the Heel Stone were both connected with the sarsen monument is apparent not only from the placing of the lintel on the central

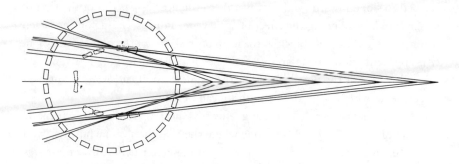

FIG. 173.   The blocking of lines of sight by the ring of thirty sarsen uprights, for various critical positions of the observer.

trilithon but from the lie of the two nearest trilithons. Uprights 51–52 carry a lintel still, and stand on the left of the observer. Stone 59 has fallen, leaving 60 alone—without lintel, of course. In plan, the outer faces of the trilithons' lintels were slightly curved, but the inner faces were flat. Now there can be no doubt that the planes of the inner faces of those trilithon lintels (the pair nearest the observer, one to the left and one to the right) passed very close to both B and the Heel Stone. They were almost certainly meant to be directed to one or the other. But to which? On the basis of the surviving lintel, there can be little doubt that the Heel Stone was the focus. Present appearances even suggest that it was the *centre* of the stone that was at the focus. At all events, an observer standing close to the Heel Stone would have seen only the near ends of the lintels, rising out of the outer ring of sarsen lintels. The other lintels would have been seen between them—that is, the middle pair—continuous with them, but lower. None of the lower edges of these four trilithon lintels would have been judged to be touching the upper surface of the outer ring—that is too much to ask—but even here one has the feeling that the proportions were carefully planned, since the ratio of the distances from the midpoint of the Heel Stone to the nearest edge of a trilithon lintel was precisely eight-sevenths the distance to the edge of the ring, in the same line.

What would have been seen in the unfilled spaces above the ring would have depended on the obscuring effect of any stones placed between the main monument and the observer—stones such as might have stood in holes B and C and E. Consider first the appearance in their absence.

The middle trilithons (53–54 and 57–58) seem to have been set up with an observer at the Heel Stone in mind, since their lintels would from there have

seemed to touch exactly the visible ends of the nearer lintels. They would have seemed to slope inwards and downwards to the near upper rim of the ring of sarsen lintels, producing the effect of, as it were, a dish standing on the sarsen drum, with in the dish a block in the form of the lintel of the highest trilithon. (An approximation to the arrangement seen is shown in Fig. 171.) We are reminded here of the possibility that the highest lintel carried an additional structure, of which, alas, almost nothing can be said.

As for the potential obscuring effect of nearer stones, the schematic diagram of Fig. 172 depicts a stone where the Slaughter Stone now lies and a stone of similar size and form in hole *E*. (I believe that in reality there was only the one stone, namely the Slaughter Stone, in hole *E*.) The figure also shows rectangular blocks representing whatever stood in holes *B* and *C*. The observer is taken to be standing to the right of the Heel Stone. Heights and shapes of stones are purely conventional, but ground levels are fairly accurately

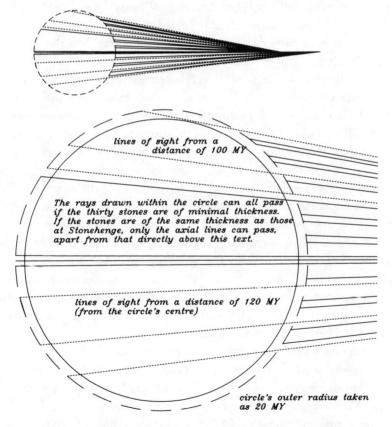

lines of sight from a distance of 100 MY

The rays drawn within the circle can all pass if the thirty stones are of minimal thickness. If the stones are of the same thickness as those at Stonehenge, only the axial lines can pass, apart from that directly above this text.

lines of sight from a distance of 120 MY (from the circle's centre)

circle's outer radius taken as 20 MY

FIG. 174.   The relatively ineffectual blocking of sight lines by a ring of thinner stones. The lower figure is a detail of that above it.

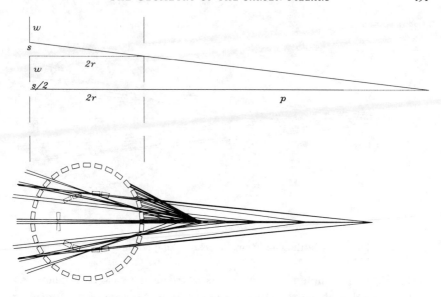

FIG. 175.   An approximate solution to the problem of placing the observer so as to
guarantee the blocking of unwanted sight lines. The situation is reduced to similar triangles
(upper figure), only those gaps flanking the centre being taken into account.

represented. As explained, the eye is at the ground level of the monument, the
Stonehenge Datum.

The left half of the view would have been obscured by the Heel Stone for
an observer standing back from it; but there is no reason to speak as though
observers were restricted to an absolutely fixed viewing position. The alignments to be derived later will suggest that the observer could have changed
position. Marker-ditches, such as that round the Heel Stone, might have been
meant to guide the observer and ensure a constant distance from the viewing
edge of the stone. (Those who make this assumption, however, ought to be
prepared to reconcile it with some of the distances in round numbers of MY to
be introduced below.)   The ditches might equally well have marked off a
restricted or sacred area.

The Geometry of the Sarsen Pillars

Astronomical motives apart, the various arrangements described here speak for
a strong sense of architectural harmony. They are reminiscent of, but improve
upon, the architectural schemes inherent in the timber monuments examined,
and in the vanished and never to be completed Q-R system. It has now been
shown that one of the most important of all geometrical aspects of Stonehenge

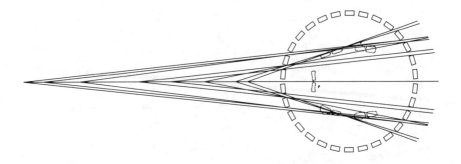

FIG. 176.   Lines of sight through the monument looking northeast.

is that there are simple proportionalities in triangles in a vertical plane. An ability to work with carefully planned similar triangles was used to achieve an even more surprising result than those of the last section. It has already been shown how, in such timber monuments as those at Woodhenge and Mount Pleasant, and in the corridor through the Q-R-circles, lintels could have been stacked to cut out the glare of the sky without an enormously heavy superstructure. The Stonehenge circle of sarsens—which of course had no comparable system of multiple lintels—quite certainly achieved much the same result with its upright stones, and it did so in a remarkably economical way. The principle is very easily understood from Fig. 173, in which the plan of the thirty sarsen bases is drawn, albeit in an idealized manner that makes no allowance for the irregularities of the stones. Selected lines of sight are drawn for observers standing at various critical points along the northeast axis: they are the limiting cases of lines that are free to pass through the sarsen ring. Most sight lines are prevented from doing so by the nearer uprights—that is, the field of view is occupied mostly by them—while others are stopped by the uprights on the far side of the circle. What is of interest is the general problem of what happens when the observer's proximity to the centre is varied.

The geometry of the monument is taken to be such that the inner faces of the stones—the better-finished faces—are exactly 2.5 MY across, and the gaps on the inner side 1.25 MY. (This application of an *ideal* implies an inner radius of 17.905 MY, which compares well with 17.91 MY deduced from Petrie's and Thom's linear measurements.) The tapering of the stones is ignored. An accurate assessment of intentions is difficult, in view of the fact that of the sixteen uprights presently standing only four are to the west of the north–south

axis, and two of them have been re-erected. Only three of the sixteen have never been disturbed, but even those three fit the hypothetical geometry well.

Ignoring first of all the trilithons, which are added to the figures as broken lines, it will be seen that—apart from the axial lines, only one of which is drawn—very few lines of sight can pass right through the monument. To a great extent this is due to the thickness of the sarsen uprights. If the stones had been only of token thickness, many more lines of sight would have passed through, but in practice the sides of the stones block them. It is surely not by accident that those that would otherwise have passed through are blocked by the trilithons. Those drawn at the smallest angle to the axis are for an observer at the middle of the packed-chalk ring round the Heel Stone. They are blocked by the nearest faces of the uprights of the horseshoe of trilithons. The stones of the horseshoe more or less continue to have that effect as the observer approaches the monument. Eventually (at about 58.6 MY from the centre) it is the middle pair of trilithons that takes over the task of blocking the problematical sight lines. At a distance of around 49.6 MY from the centre, which is almost exactly on the Aubrey circle, there is a narrow pencil of lines that can pass.

In other words, one important function of the trilithons was to block the few residual rays that might otherwise have passed through the sarsen ring. They do so well, and broadly speaking one can say that to an observer anywhere along the line of the axis of the monument, from the Heel Stone to the entrance (say level with the Slaughter Stone), when the Sun was low in the southwest, the monument was seen only as a dark mass, pierced by the light of Sun or sky through a single central (axial) slit.

This raises the question of the possibility of a processional ritual. The question is one that can be answered without reference to the finer points of the monument's structure, as long as one considers observations of the Sun at low angles over a fixed barrier, say the southwest bank.

At the winter solstice at the third or second millennium, the Sun sank at around $0.116°$ per minute of time. Viewed from the Heel Stone by a standing upright observer, the (angle of) altitude of the bank, whatever its condition, would have been greater than when it was viewed from the Aubrey ring, and from there it would have been higher than when viewed from, say, the entrance to the sarsen ring. Could the observer have walked in such a way as to keep the last glint of the Sun precisely in view? In fact this would have been quite straightforward: almost precisely a minute of time would have been needed to walk the first stage, about 37 m, demanding a very leisurely pace. To keep the setting Sun in view while walking from the Aubrey circle to the entrance to

the sarsen ring, about 30 m, the observer would have had even longer—more than two and a half minutes. Such processions would therefore have been quite feasible, although whether they were practised in reality one can only conjecture.

The Geometry of Obscuration

The gaps that it would have been most important to block in any such monument were those flanking the central slit. The problem of blocking them must have been long in the thoughts of the henge-builders. It seems highly probable that it was eventually solved—before the sarsen circle was built—by a consideration of simple geometrical proportionalities. In Fig. 175, which is not to scale and concentrates only on sarsen uprights in the central strip of the more general illustration in Fig. 173, the problem is simplified by reducing it

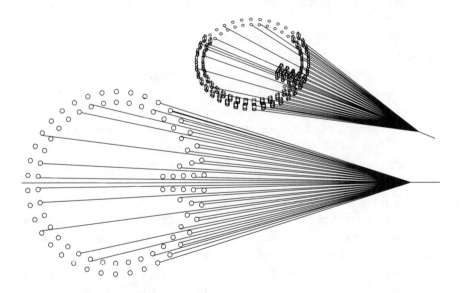

FIG. 177.   A typical pattern of gaps open to view through the Q-R system, here as seen by a person at the Aubrey ring. The upper figure is a perspective view. (We are reminded that the rings were never completed, and might have been less complete than shown, at the south.) The lower is a plan view at a larger scale, showing at what point of the line of sight a stone in this heavily idealized scheme (with cylindrical stones) stands in the way. The sight lines drawn (for an observer at the Aubrey circle) would all be tangents to the stylized stones on the *far* side of the ring, if they passed through the first rings. These lines mark the potential limits of visibility. *All* are eventually blocked, apart from lines through the entrance corridor and (not shown) to either side of it. Note how the stones at the south (bottom left corner of the figure) and west are a relative luxury.

to one of straight lines. The width of the stones (whose thickness is here entirely ignored) is w, and the space between them is s. The distance from one side of the 'circle' to the other is $2r$. The observer is at distance p from the nearer stones of the monument. The situation shown is one in which the first gaps to the side of the axial window, on the far side of the circle, are exactly blocked by the near stones. By simple proportion, s is to $2r$ as $(w + s/2)$ is to p. Of course in spelling out such a proportionality, other distances than p might have been taken, with other triangles, although they would have yielded essentially the same result—an accurate enough result for the small angles in the present case.

There are good reasons—based on practice in the vertical plane—for thinking that the architects of Stonehenge were skilled in handling such proportional triangles. One does not have to believe that they did more than experiment with physically modelled triangles, and so effectively realized that the ratio of w to s was of importance for the blocking of sight lines. Consider the dimensions of the monument: taking values of w and s appropriate to the inner faces of the sarsen ring, their ratio could hardly have been simpler: it was 2 to 1. As a multiple of the radius r, p then had a Stonehenge value of 5. (In general terms it can be expressed $2(w/s) + 1$, although in doing so one obscures the intuitively simple result, which could have been grasped by merely manipulating small rods.) The distance of the critical position for the observer from the inner faces of the stones by the entrance (those numbered 30 and 1) was therefore 89.5 MY (that is, $5r$). One is brought to a point about 11 m behind the Heel Stone, a point now under the main road at its northeast side. (As it happens, it is close to the place at which 'ray 1' to the eye of our observer at stone B comes down to ground level.) This is the limiting case, nearer than which a dark outline of the monument was guaranteed, at least up to the Aubrey circle or thereabouts.

In the initial placing of the Heel Stone, ground levels would have been of prime importance, with the blocking effect a secondary consideration. The relative dimensions of the stones, the gaps between them and the circle radius could easily have been chosen to match a Heel Stone *already in position*. The approximate centre of the older circles could still have been accepted without difficulty for the newly tailored sarsen ring.

All this is to presuppose that viewing was to the southwest. What of observation in the opposite direction, that is, looking towards midsummer sunrise? Fig. 176 shows the sight lines equivalent to those already discussed, and there is no doubt that the trilithons are again reasonably effective from certain distant places of observation. The critical points, however, do not for the most part relate to any obvious artefacts corresponding to the Heel Stone

and others to the northeast. There are also one or two extra lines of sight that seem to threaten to pass through the ring, although that question is today difficult to settle, since the crucial upright of the most northerly trilithon (stone 59) now lies on the ground. From nearer places at the southwest, such as the Aubrey circle and bank, the very first gaps to right and left of the central slit are left wide open. All told, there is no good reason to take the midsummer lines as seriously as those for midwinter.

The Blocking of Rays through the Q- and R-Circles

In the case of the Q- and R-sectors, no precise measurements are available for the sizes of the stones, but since thirty-eight stones and the same number of spaces were apparently *intended* to fit into a space of (outermost) radius about 15 MY, the width of one stone and one space was very close to 2.5 MY. In the light of the plan of the stone holes, it is not improbable that the ambition was to make the stones 1 MY wide and the spaces 1.5 MY. Applying the argument from simple proportionality to the outer ring, this would mean placing the observer at or nearer than 50 MY from the centre. The formula derived in the last section yields precisely 50 MY, and this figure needs to be modified only very slightly (to 50.46 MY) when we take the blocking effect of the inner ring into account.

How seriously should the precision of this statement be taken? In view of the irregularities of the rings of stone, as judged from their holes, one might be inclined to dismiss it as risible, in view of the uncertainties of the excavations. Whatever the irregularities of workmanship, however, if it seems probable that there was a formal ideal towards which the builders were working, then the proposal made here must be taken seriously. The reason is that it brings us almost precisely to the Aubrey circle, and so supplements and strengthens a conjecture made on the basis of astronomical arguments, at the beginning of the present chapter.

As far as is known, the Q-R system—and of course the two rings were part of a single system, as the dumbbell trenches prove—comprised only outer and inner sectors and supplementary stones at the entrance. It probably had no interior blocking stones comparable with the trilithons. On the other hand, it did not need help of that sort. The only really problematical gaps for an observer standing at the Aubrey circle are those flanking the entrance. These would have been largely but not entirely stopped by the simple device of one extra stone to each side—the third and innermost stones of the triples. The extra stones

in the entrance corridor seem to serve no comparable blocking function, which should strengthen a belief in their having served rather to carry lintels.

The general form of the stones was of course not cylindrical but roughly rectangular, although they were far less regular than the sarsens. The corners of the stones would have helped in the blocking of rays, but it is of interest to note that those corners would have been almost superfluous: given a perfect plan, all sight lines are blocked by or before the furthest stone in the line of sight, apart from those through and to either side of the entrance corridor. Were the gaps flanking the entrance really left largely unstopped? There are various potential blocking stones (for instance in the bluestone horseshoe), but it seems safer to assume that too much has been lost from the inner area at this early stage for it ever to be possible to say how any further blocking was effected.

Once its rationale is appreciated, the overall plan of the Q-R system is capable of throwing much light on what at first sight is a very different hypothesis being put forward here, namely that many prehistoric monuments were lintelled for the purpose of cutting down the glare of the horizon. What the architects did now was stagger vertical pillars—considered as pairs, or as triples—in exactly the way we believe horizontal lintels had been customarily staggered. Both had been done simultaneously elsewhere in timber—for example at nearby Durrington Walls, as in Fig. 147 above—and it was clearly from timber monuments that the idea came. Lintelling with stone was much more difficult than with posts, however, so that the technique of obscuration with verticals alone must have been greatly appreciated.

We can almost imagine that we are reading the thoughts of the designers of the Q-R system, when we consider the dumbbell-shaped trenches in which these doubles and triples of stones were placed. Had vast slabs of stone been available and open to manipulation, perhaps they would have been used instead of the bluestones, yielding something resembling a giant paddle wheel. On the other hand, the clear intellectual merit in achieving the required blocking effect in an economical way must have been appreciated too.

Unlike the much taller sarsens, the Q-R bluestones would not have broken the horizon by a very great margin, except for an observer fairly close to them. Their heights are not known precisely, but on average they are not likely to have been much taller than a man. Can it be that their function was more complex than that of eliminating glare from the sky, and that they themselves were meant to provide an artificial horizon as a replacement for the old bank? To provide an extensive horizon, one of the rings at least would have needed to carry a ring of lintels. This idea is not favoured by the assumption that most of the stones of these rings were incorporated into the inner bluestone struc-

tures. From what is known of them, bluestone lintels do not seem to have been numerous.

It remains to consider the supposed incompleteness of the Q-R structure. (For a reminder as to its supposed extent, see the upper half of Fig. 177.) Archaeologists have usually assumed that it was intended to be a complete ring, but as far as its blocking function was concerned, only half of the system—whether to the southwest or the northeast matters little—was greatly needed. This can be appreciated from the figure, from which it will be seen that relatively little work was done by the far rings. This very fact offers important support for an astronomical interpretation: the erection of the stones appears to have stopped not just anywhere in the sequence, but at the beginning of a quadrant marked out by astronomically significant directions. That the bluestones were meant to cut out glare or to act as an artificial horizon when looking across the monument to the southwest, in anticipation of the setting of the Sun and with the Sun still above the horizon, is surely supported by the fact that the stones screened the sky more densely to the side on which the Sun was to be seen . Once again, it seems, the archaeological evidence speaks against the idea of the ritual viewing of midsummer sunrise.

Sarsen Ring and Midwinter Sun

Important geometrical properties have now been found that relate the architecture of the central monument to various critical points, and in particular to the place of stone hole B and the Heel Stone. Because one monument was superimposed on another, there is inevitably some confusion as to the sequence of events. The two pillars kept their significance for the simple reason that the older and newer stone circles followed similar principles, but on the whole, stone B seems to have been more closely tied up with the earlier Q-R system. The motive for it all can only have been that the setting midwinter Sun was to be seen by an observer standing at such points as these—in fact at the right-hand side of the appropriate stone, looking southwest—and looking through an aperture in the middle of the monument. This is the most fundamental alignment of all at Stonehenge, and while it reached to a higher state of perfection in the sarsen monument, it is as well to remember that just as the far sighting-edge on stone 56 was one of the most perfect upright edges at Stonehenge, so, if we are not mistaken, was its counterpart in the Q-R henge also very finely finished.

The principles of their use have been demonstrated here repeatedly: some part of the Sun at its midwinter extreme just manages to appear to the left of

the far upright (56, and beyond it the re-erected sarsen 16, in the later case), while its image is trapped in a slit created with the help of the nearby Heel. Such a claim must be justified, of course, not only by tradition but by the appropriateness of the angles involved. Only with the sarsens can they be reasonably well determined. The azimuth between the edges of the Heel (at eye-level) and stone 56 (near ground-level) is 39.81° south of west, on the basis of rectangular coordinates taken from the survey of the central strip done in 1923 by E. H. Stone. (It is high time that this was re-done, after a thorough investigation of the form of the fallen and broken stone 55 and its hole.) But by what was the horizon created?

A decision on this point is reached in two stages. From radiocarbon dating and arguments as to the sequence of building activity on the site, it seems that the parts of the monument under discussion were not many centuries removed from 2500 BC. For this period, the azimuth in question corresponds to a setting midwinter Sun (last glint of the upper limb) at an altitude of approximately 0.4°. This cannot have been set by the upper levels of the monument, which were much too high, and is unlikely to have been set by the far bank, if this was in its original condition. (This could conceivably have set a horizon as high as 0.9°.) The altitude, however, is close to that of the natural horizon in this direction, without trees. Of course it is far more likely to have been additionally set by a stone in the central area of the monument. It is a strange fact that if the Altar Stone were to have been placed at the very centre of the monument across the main axis, lying on one of its largest faces, it would have created a horizon of about 0.38° as judged from the Heel Stone, more or less exactly what is called for. One should not, of course, rely heavily on measurements that were not taken with such a calculation in mind, but it is hard to forbear mentioning that the thickness of the Altar Stone usually quoted (1 ft 9 in) would make the gradient of the line of sight almost exactly 1 in 150. Trimming for the inevitable but slow changes in the Sun's behaviour would have been easy, either by raising the stone or by moving it closer.

In summary: The last glint of the upper limb of the setting midwinter Sun, that is, at solstice, was observed to the left of stone 56 of the grand trilithon, setting over an artificial horizon barely masking the natural horizon. The observer stood just behind and to the right of the Heel Stone (then erect, although the fact is of little consequence), and used its (northwest) edge to delimit the line of sight. This axial line is one of those shown in the lower part of Fig. 179. This repeats what had already been done in the Q-R henge, where perhaps the Altar Stone (in its first position) played the same role as stone 56, or rather its now fallen partner 55.

Altar Stone and Midwinter Sun

It was explained briefly in Chapter 10 how the Altar Stone might at some stage have stood in yet a third position—our second and more tentative proposal being that it was once prostrate—so as to have acted as an artificial horizon to an observer standing neither by B nor by the Heel, but by whatever was then in stone hole E. Referring to Figs. 181 and 165, it will be seen that the line of sight that just passes under the far lintel of the sarsen ring could also have grazed the top of the Altar Stone if this had been about 4 MY above the level of the Stonehenge Datum. How precise was the fit depended on its position of course. It must be assumed that it stood in a hole under the fragments of the fallen stone 55 of the grand trilithon, having been pushed forward by that enormous stone. The very special position of the stone, together with a height of 4 MY, makes it look suspiciously like that which stood 4.25 MY above ground in the most important position in Q-R henge. An even stronger argument is that the horizon altitude it would have set for the setting midwinter Sun fits well with the azimuths set by the limiting sarsens and by the stone at E. The argument will need to be spelled out, since much hangs on the conclusion as regards the geometrical skills of the architects of Stonehenge.

The azimuth depends on various assumptions, and even on the survey chosen, but was almost certainly between 43.1° and 46.0° south of west. This would have corresponded to the last glint of the setting midwinter Sun for an altitude of between approximately 2.1° and 3.7°. Either figure could have been set by the Altar Stone, given a suitable observation point. The uncertainties in the data reflect our ignorance of the precise position of stone 55 and of the Altar Stone itself, and uncertainty as to what was standing at the time. William Gowland excavated in the neighbourhood of the former in 1902, but his account is unclear, except in his description of the shallow seating of the stone that allowed its collapse. It is a broad stone, and would have blocked the view over the Altar Stone that seems inherently the more probable of the two options —namely on the assumption that the hole for the latter will prove to be under the middle of fragment 55b. Where it stood to set the horizon determined the Sun's altitude and so the height of the stone above ground. And so conversely: a height of 4.25 MY, for example, would mean that the centre of its hole was under the edge of 55b, rather than the middle.

That the question need not be left here will be evident as soon as we examine it first from a purely geometrical point of view—fitting lines of sight under and over stones, and so forth—and then with reference to another completely different astronomical alignment using the Altar Stone.

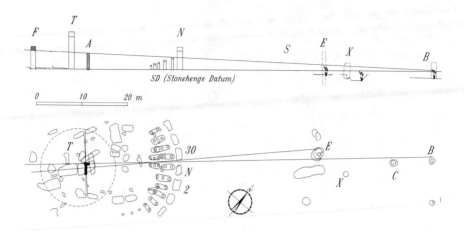

FIG. 178.   The line of sight of an observer by stone E (which probably held the Slaughter Stone) to midwinter sunset. The upper figure is in idealized form, following our previous conventions. The lower half of the figure has a plan view of the surviving stones, to which are added alternative positions for the upright Altar Stone. (They will be clearer on a detail of the present drawing in Fig. 179.) The alternative selected here is that in which the Altar Stone (of 4 MY above SD) presents its narrowest face to E. The line of sight to E would have passed over the Altar Stone at a gradient of 3 in 60. A transverse line of sight over the Altar Stone is shown in Fig. 180, and the two together fix the stone's original position.

The eye of the observer at E, judging by ground levels, was 1 MY above the Stonehenge Datum (SD). The ground under 55b seems to be just about 0.25 MY over SD. A line of sight from E over an Altar Stone 4.25 MY above the *ground* cannot pass the far lintel in our ideal scheme, but 3.75 MY above the ground is not only acceptable, it gives a geometrically perfect fit, a slit of zero size, so to speak, that could have been opened up by the observer's moving backwards somewhat. The gradient set would have been one in twenty, since the distance of the near edge of the Altar Stone from E (as seems probable from considerations still to come) was 60 MY, and the top of the stone was 3 MY above the eye. (These data are noted on Fig. 181.) The altitude of 2.86° requires an azimuth to the last glint of the midwinter Sun of about 44.4° south of west. This is a line that can be accommodated by the stones, as far as can be judged, but perhaps only if the Altar Stone presents its narrowest profile to the observer at E. Three cases are drawn in Figs. 181 and 179, and it will be seen how

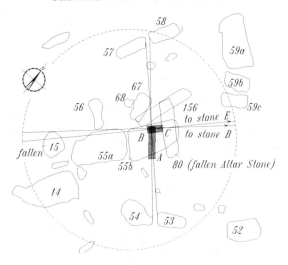

FIG. 179.   A detail of the previous figure. By placing the Altar Stone with narrow face towards E, space is left for the important line of sight to B, and the transverse line of sight through the side trilithons (see Fig. 180) is also well defined.

limited is the movement allowable to the stone if it is not to interfere with what must have been important lines of sight, to the Heel Stone and to B.

As to the functioning of the new arrangement, the Sun would have been seen through the small window above the Altar Stone rather more than 20 minutes before its final midwinter setting, as seen from the Heel Stone through the main aperture, or from B, as marked on these figures.

The support promised for the arrangement described comes from the fact that the Altar Stone is perfectly fitted to act at the same season as an artificial horizon for a valuable transverse sight line to the rising Sun, limited by the side trilithons 53–54 and 57–58. The observer would have had to stand behind, and look through, the gap between sarsens 21 and 22. One of the inner edges of those sarsens would have been used, but which? The edge of stone 22 is perfectly in line with the edges of 58 and 54, which is a good reason for preferring that pair. Another reason is that it yields such an excellent fit to the astronomical facts.

The distance to the near edge of the Altar top in this preferred solution was just 17.5 MY, and the difference of levels between the top of the stone and the observer's eye was 1.75 MY, making for a gradient of 1 in 10 and an altitude for the upper limb of the rising midwinter Sun of 5.71°. Such precise statements are made possible by a very remarkable bluestone, number 69 in the bluestone horseshoe. Standing just inside the horseshoe of large sarsen trilithons (see Fig. 180), the stone is notable for its shape and its position. In

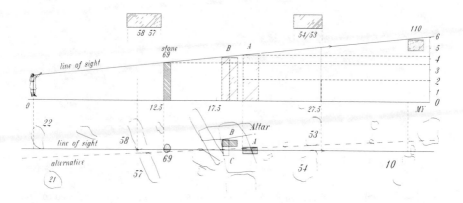

FIG. 180. A line of sight to midwinter sunrise, limited (in plan, see the lower half of the figure) by the trilithons 58–57 and 54–53. The line grazes the top of bluestone 69 (in the horseshoe) and the Altar Stone (A) at a gradient of exactly 1 in 10. Distances are marked in the upper part of the figure in MY. The broken line in the lower figure offers an alternative line of sight, that would have required a very slightly higher gradient. Both lines are well defined by an Altar Stone broad side on to them, notably that in the favoured position C. Options B (height 4 MY, like C) and A (height 4.25 MY, both above SD) are shown in the upper figure, where C can be taken as the left half of B.

shape it is a smooth pillar of finely worked spotted dolerite with an exceedingly flat and almost level top. This upper surface has what looks like a fine lip round the edge, as though it might have been meant to have something rest on it. Its position is no less memorable: its near edge is just 2.5 MY from what would have had to be the sighting edge of the trilithon stone 58 in this case; and its present height above the Stonehenge Datum is within 2 cm of 3.50 MY. But where was the observer and where was the Altar Stone? The range of options is surprisingly limited, as will be appreciated from Fig. 180. The lintel sets an upper limit to the altitude. By varying the position of the stone, one can vary its permitted height, but of course it must not be allowed to interfere with the views from the northeast, down the main axis towards midwinter sunset. Working within these constraints gives a very narrow range of possibilities, and an Altar Stone of 4 MY above SD (3.75 MY above ground) is virtually forced upon us. The gradient of the resulting line of sight turns out to be precisely 1 in 10 (5.71°). The observer with eye at 2 MY would have stood exactly 12.5 MY from the near edge of stone 69, and 17.5 MY from the Altar Stone. Some idea of the way in which the line of sight threaded through the stones at the observer's end of its path—in relation to their present status—may be had from Fig. 182.

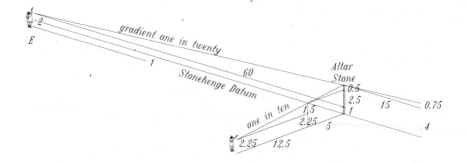

F<small>IG.</small> 181. The lines of sight of Fig. 180 in a perspective view, showing the need to find two astronomically acceptable arrangements simultaneously, for a single Altar Stone. Heights are in MY. The longer sight line passes *under* the far lintel (here at the right). An additional constraint, set by the sarsen lintel *over* which the nearer observer looks to midwinter sunrise, is not shown.

That the stones set these integral distances—and the sarsens and trilithons add yet others, as shown in the figure—is surprising, but it is no more than a geometrical property. It is outshone by the astronomical properties of the line of sight so defined. As far as can be judged from modern measurements, the azimuth set by the edges of sarsen 22 and trilithon upright 58 (see the lower part of the figure) would have been 49.9° south of east, which corresponds almost perfectly (within 0.1°) with the ideal azimuth for extreme midwinter sunrise at the stated altitude, around 2500 BC. There is little point in trying to refine a figure of this sort, much less derive a date from it. Its strength lies in the fact that it accommodates two quite different alignments simultaneously. Not only are they different, but they are close to being at right angles. (For the various angles between the transverse lines and the axial lines, see Fig.179.)

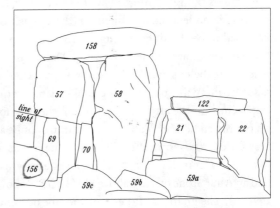

F<small>IG.</small> 182. The transverse line of sight, for midwinter sunrise, in relation to the stones nearest the (hidden) observer—shown in their existing state. The Altar Stone would have been off the picture, to the left, on the assumption that it stood upright.

There is a weak alternative to the preferred solution that takes a sight line grazing the other edges of the trilithons (see the broken line in the lower part of Fig. 180). The change in azimuth means a change in altitude, that is, in the gradient set by stone 69 and the Altar Stone. The gradient must be in the neighbourhood of 1 in 12.9, the observer must stand further back, and the Altar Stone is 4.1 MY above the Stonehenge Datum. The line would not have cleared the lintel, but would have crossed stone 69 only at its edge, and it would not have grazed either of the sarsens 21 or 22. For these reasons the arrangement cannot be taken seriously, even though it might seem to fit more closely with the rule inferred earlier for a simple pair of sighting stones. It is perhaps also worth mentioning that the preferred line of sight, if continued, grazes a post hole that Hawley found when he excavated Z-hole 9, which cut through it. The post hole might be a vestige of the trilithon erection procedure.

As yet, no mention has been made of lunar alignments. It will be recalled that over natural ground at Stonehenge the angle between solar and lunar extremes is very close to a right angle, and it might be wondered whether a reverse line of sight through the gap between the trilithons could have supplied a northern lunar extreme, fitting such a pattern. In view of the steep gradient (1 in 10) to midwinter sunrise, it comes as a surprise to find that reversing that line, in its direction over the *natural* horizon, gives almost precisely the direction to the Moon's northern extreme of setting in the northwest (altitude 0.3°). How it could have been arranged for this to thread through all the stones, however, is not clear, in view of the blocking effect of stone 69 and the Altar.

Perhaps it was the gap through the other pair of trilithons that fixed a nearly parallel line of sight with this lunar property, or perhaps the lunar lines were operative through both pairs of trilithons at some stage before bluestone pillars were introduced into the inner region of the monument. It is just conceivable that both pairs could have set solar lines only—the azimuths are closely similar, although there is some doubt as to whether or not the sight line through the other pair of trilithons (51–52 and 59–60) would have managed to skirt the sarsen stone 7 or would have been blocked by it. The sight lines would have been at only slightly different altitudes, corresponding to the slightly different azimuths fixed by the gaps in the trilithons.

Geometers, Engineers and Astronomers

The pair of alignments crossing the Altar Stone has important implications for the intellectual processes involved in building Stonehenge, and they should not pass unnoticed. This is not the first example of a pair of significant

directions engineered at right angles, but it is hard to conceive of a clearer instance of the quite brilliant way in which data over which man has no control (solar risings and settings) were made to conform to a pattern of strict geometrical perfection. Gradients of 1 in 10 to sunrise and 1 in 20 to sunset, contrived to be at right angles to one another, cannot have come easily. Gradients must have had the same objectivity for the architects of Stonehenge as angles have for us, but one can only conjecture as to the thought processes by which they were manipulated. With the help of scratched diagrams, no doubt, these people must at the very least have been able to formulate statements of the kind 'a rise of one for a distance of ten on the level is equivalent to a rise of three-quarters for a distance of seven and a half on the level, for the same line of sight'. What is more, our Neolithic geometrical astronomers were clearly dealing in *triangles*, and not simply in 'ups' and 'ons'. The proof is at those sites where the hypotenuse is 'drawn', for instance up the ridge of such a long barrow as Wayland's Smithy, or in the plan of the same. That theirs was not an arithmetically trivial activity may be judged from Fig. 181. It involved *large* integral numbers and *fractional* distances—assuming that the Megalithic Yard, and not the quarter-yard—was the operative unit. The frequent occurrence of multiples and submultiples of ten strongly hints at a system of counting on a scale of ten, or possibly twenty—but not of twelve, for example.

In this context are to be found the germ of a theory of proportional triangles and an arithmetic of geometrical proportions, better known from the work of Pythagoras, Thales, and other early Greek philosopher-geometers from the sixth century BC onwards. It is of course difficult to say whether their predecessors had anything equivalent to the Greek conception of geometrical proposition (theorem) and proof, but the type of statement cited above has the makings of a theorem, whatever its actual justification. When historians sing the praises of the early Greek geometers, they often single out the theory of proportion for especial attention, describing it as a characteristically Greek invention. The reason is not far to seek: it played an important role in arithmetic, geometry, music, astronomy (planetary theory and gnomonics), theories of the elements, even medicine. It might be taking matters too far to see the origins of Western science in Neolithic monuments, but it would be as great a mistake to suppose that the Greek achievement was without precedents. The conventional story, even as told by the later Greeks, is that Egypt was the source of their geometry. If this is true, it can only be a part of the truth.

What of 'astronomical' practice—in this case settling the precise day of the Sun's extreme risings and settings? In round numbers, the azimuth at

Stonehenge changes by a little less than a hundredth part of a degree, as between the day of the solstice and the day before (or after). Over an interval of two days, the change is about three-hundredths of a degree. This certainly could not have been judged in a small ring (without a distant marker), and it is doubtful whether it could have been appreciated at Stonehenge: it is equivalent to about 4 cm shift in the position of either of the defining edges of the long (axial) Stonehenge alignment. Over a period of three days from the solstice, the change is nearly seven-hundredths of a degree in total, and the shift of place on the monument is nearly 10 cm, which might have been detectable. To quote precise figures, however, would be to conceal an important fact: the shift depends in part on atmospheric conditions, which can vary substantially from day to day.

An assumption commonly made in this context is that a simple modern approach to the problem would have been taken. This is far from obvious. The simplest modern technique for observing the approximate extreme of a slowly changing quantity—in fact it goes at least as far back as classical antiquity—is to observe what happens on either side of the extreme, and halve the time interval for equal effects, to find when the extreme was reached. Thus the Sun might be observed several days before and several days after the solstice, and the time of the solstice be taken as the day halfway between given pairs of equal

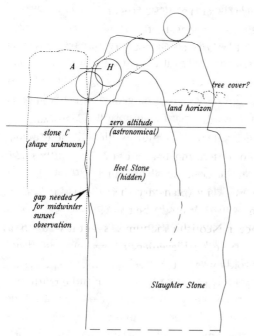

FIG. 183. The approximate path of the rising midsummer Sun in relation to the Heel Stone (hidden), the Slaughter Stone, and stone C, assuming an imaginary viewpoint at the southeast edge of stone 16. In reality the stones of the trilithon and sarsen ring would have hidden this view almost entirely, but something like it could have been had from the general area in front of the grand trilithon stone 56. It is conceivable that stone 97, the predecessor of the Heel Stone (slightly beyond and to the left of the latter) was used in some such way for the observation of the Sun at summer solstice.

solar positions. This presupposes a great deal about the *purpose* of the observations, which in the case of the procedure explained has to do with settling a date with a view to developing a scientific theory. It would not have satisfied those who wished to say simply '*Today* the Sun is at its lowest in the sky...' It is just conceivable that the averaging procedure might have been followed in the planning of a great monument such as Stonehenge—'Three days ago the Sun was at its lowest, so keep note of the mark we made of its direction of setting at that time...'

When the monument was in regular use, it would presumably have been as a religious instrument that allowed an appropriate announcement to be made on the critical day. But by whom? By the common people, without astronomers guiding them? Would the architects of Stonehenge, having gone to such pains to plan this extraordinary series of monuments, not have kept permanent control over its use? The necessary knowledge had by this time become very sophisticated, and it is hard to believe that it was shared by the populace as a whole. For some reason, the notion of a scientific priesthood is today anathema. Perhaps that is only because we have lived so long without one.

The Sarsen Ring and Midsummer?

It is natural to ask again whether the very different, and traditional, way of interpreting Stonehenge has anything to recommend it. Those who have assumed that the observer's position was *within* the monument have found that the only way to achieve a reasonably narrow fit is to suppose that the midpoint of the Sun's disc appears in the neighbourhood of the peak of the Heel Stone. Those who are prepared to quote figures for this arrangement usually do so for a time some centuries after 2000 BC. A typical assumption is that observers stood at the geometrical centre of the sarsens. Tacit in all this is the positioning of the eye at that place—merely switching eyes without shifting position would have been enough to move the Heel Stone through a sixth of the solar diameter relative to the Sun's image. How precision in positioning the eye was achieved is not explained, nor is it usual to enter into the problem of former standing levels. But can nothing be salvaged from this type of explanation? Could an observer not have looked *across* the monument—using the grand trilithon, for example—from the southwest?

There are relatively few acceptable places to stand, since the ground rises to the southwest, and gradually brings the apparent position of the peak of the Heel down to the natural horizon. An observer standing in some suitable position behind stone 16, using the same edge of trilithon stone 56 as before,

now to limit the left-hand side of the field of view, could have looked along the reverse direction (reverse in plan along the ground) of the ray from the edge of the Heel Stone that was directed to midwinter sunset. To such an observer, only a slit to the Heel Stone edge would have been open to view. Nevertheless this place will be taken as a point with reference to which the general situation can be discussed.

Consider an imaginary horizon set at precisely the level of the *top* of the Heel Stone, before it leaned forward. Since the Heel Stone tapers, this is to talk about a line in space, not marked by any stone now standing. The altitude of this horizon, for a person with eye 2 MY above the level of the Stonehenge Datum, would have been 1.00°. This, together with the reversed azimuth mentioned, would have been more or less the level of the upper limb of the rising midsummer Sun, depending on the epoch. (In 2000 BC it would have been so to within a hundredth of a degree.) In other words, the top of the Heel is at the level (but not the azimuth) of a perfect horizon for an exact reversal (in plan) of the ray to midwinter sunset. For the time being, this is no more than a curious coincidence; but is there no other stone that might have delimited the midsummer ray here defined?

The Slaughter Stone is the most obvious candidate. Its nearly flat top and its one excellent straight edge were far superior to the edges of the Heel Stone. It is occasionally represented as having been erected and removed by the time the Q- and R-rings were erected, but this is unlikely—even its tooling and the perfection of its form cast doubt on that idea (see Fig. 166). At its widest, it was 2.5 MY across. The middle of its top surface—like that of the Heel Stone—was 4 MY above the Stonehenge Datum and 5 MY above ground level at the stone.

If the Slaughter Stone stood in hole E, then it is entirely irrelevant to the present discussion of midsummer sunrise. For the sake of argument, suppose it to have been moved from there late in the history of the sarsen monument, and erected in a hole that is at present hidden underneath it. Assuming that it is no accident that the line of sight from the Heel to stone 56 skimmed the inner (northwest) edge of the Slaughter Stone, it might possibly have provided some sort of artificial horizon in front of the Heel Stone. The face the Slaughter Stone would then have presented to the monument would have been approximately 40 MY from the midpoint of the Heel Stone's viewing edge, and any observer on the line of sight under discussion would not have been able to see the Heel Stone at all. It is hard to understand why so much energy has been spent in the past in discussing the appearance of the rising midsummer Sun

over the Heel, by people who assume that the Slaughter Stone stood where it now lies.

Putting the obscuring effects of the stones well and truly on one side for a moment, the path of the rising midsummer Sun would have been as drawn approximately in Fig. 183. A stone of very generous proportions in hole C has been added to show its relationship to the others. What is notable is that the upper limb of the Sun would have been in the direction of the Heel Stone's tip (azimuth 38.92°) when it reached an altitude of around 1.49°, the estimated altitude of the top of the Slaughter Stone. This takes us well clear of the natural horizon—which is now tree-covered, and might then have been so too.

Unfortunately this will not do: the scene as described is hidden. The situation with 'viewpoint' at stone 16 is no longer a simple two-stone affair, in which the view can be opened up temporarily by merely moving the head to one side. If an artificial horizon is to be scraped up out of the Slaughter Stone, it will be necessary to move the observer forward of stone 56 of the grand trilithon. What would have been seen from there is not very different from what has already been described. Indeed it is only marginally better than the traditional—and entirely inaccurate—picture of the Sun rising over the Heel Stone pure and simple. It can be seen only in a wide frame, namely the gap between sarsens 30 and 1. It seems to offer no possibility of alignment on the edges of uprights near at hand. If this crude midsummer sighting was ever added to the Stonehenge repertoire, it seems likely that it was at a late period, when Neolithic values had given way to a baser currency. And of course if the Slaughter Stone was never placed as supposed, then the old problems associated with demonstrating an interest in midsummer sunrise remain unresolved.

The Sarsen Ring and the Moon

In Chapter 7, attention was drawn to certain potential solar and lunar lines of sight tangential to a central ring of timber posts. Some of these lay across the Aubrey ring, and another was the line of a track on Normanton Down, which seemed as though it might have been directed to the extreme northern rising Moon. Were there no comparable lines touching the sarsen ring?

One such potential line of sight requires an observer to stand behind the limiting edge of the Heel Stone. The principle of trapping sight lines between remote uprights is the same as before, except that the line in question is of a sort we might have expected with a solar line, the setting point being to the left of the far stone. Looking roughly southwest (at azimuth about 51.2° south of west, in fact) the sight line in the present case would have grazed the

monument at sarsen upright stone 7. There are now trees on the horizon, but without them the natural horizon in this direction would have been close to 0.13°. Around the year 2500 BC the ideal azimuth for the southernmost setting of the Moon at this altitude was about 51.46° south of west. In view of the uncertainties of measurement, the discrepancy, of about a quarter of a degree, or half the Moon's disc, is not excessive. It was reducing in time at the rate of roughly a quarter of a degree per millennium, but there is no point in our trying to derive a date from all this.

The line in question twice crossed the line of the bank. At the near point this was no problem, for it passed through the entrance gap. If a stone ever stood in hole F just inside the bank by that entrance, it might even have helped to fix the ray, but this is not essential. (Current opinion seems to be that holes F, G, and H never held stones, but are tree-holes.) The crossing of the line of sight over the far point of the bank, however, presents a slight problem. If the bank was still at what we earlier assumed to be its *original* height, the far natural horizon (1200 m from the Heel Stone) would not have been visible at all. In fact to see it, the bank would have had to be at almost exactly its *present* height. The higher the bank, the worse the agreement with the Moon's extreme of setting for the given historical period.

As time passed, if this particular type of observation continued to be made, the horizon used would have needed to be raised. It was indeed raised—assuming, as before, no trees beyond—when a round barrow on the distant ridge was put on precisely this line. Whether or not this act was seen as a corrective for a growing error, it is quite possible that the barrow's position was planned to be on this important line.

Looking to the other (north) side of the sarsen monument as a whole from the same place, the lines of sight tangential to the sarsen ring from the Heel Stone were in no obvious alignment with the setting Sun, or with the Moon at its southern extreme or minor standstill. Over natural ground the latter was over 32° south of west, but the direction set by the monument was less than 29° south of west, no matter which side of the Heel is taken. (Sarsen stone 24 is needed to give an accurate figure, but is missing, and the direction is based on stone 23, a relatively thin slab.) One line passes, oddly enough, over a long barrow on Normanton Down, which could have been sited long before with Rigel's setting in view, as seen from some point of the Stonehenge site, but this is a very insecure conclusion.

Despite all these ambiguities, it seems almost certain that the monument was meant to align on the minor southern lunar standstill, and this in a very different way from those described so far. The general appearance from the Heel

Stone of the highest lintel of all, that of the grand trilithon, has already been discussed (and see Figs. 169 and 170). Standing at the side of the Heel Stone, an observer would have seen a fine slit between that lintel and the lintels of the sarsen ring. It is a simple matter to calculate the size of the slit, on the basis of our previous assumptions about stone sizes, but it would be very pleasant if at the same time we could say why the Heel Stone was placed where it is, from a geometrical point of view. It suggests no very obvious set of similar triangles, such as those found from the positions of *B* and *E*, for example. The best approach seems to be to ask what the slit would be if the observer were to have stood opposite the centre of the Heel Stone, to the side of it of course. The answer is almost exactly, but not quite, 0.25 MY. On the assumption that that was meant to be an *exact* figure, we ask where the observer was meant to stand to get it. The answer is: at a distance of 106.67 MY from the back of the grand trilithon. This looks very unpromising, until it is realized that the triangles concerned have a perfect 3 in 40 gradient (2.25 in 30 and 8 in 106.67). A far greater problem is that of finding consistency in the surveys available of the stones, to check for what can in principle be rather accurately measured. I suspect that E. H. Stone's is the most reliable, and from it deduce that the observer, on this account, would have stood just 0.35 MY (29 cm) behind the back of the Heel Stone. This is an extraordinary geometrical result, that has little to do with astronomy; and it raises immediately the question of the status of stone hole 97, first properly identified by Michael Pitts in 1979, when it was realized that the hole was older than the Heel Stone ditch (which in turn was older than the Avenue bank). The centre of the hole fits almost perfectly with the distance deduced from a 3 in 40 gradient; but of course the Heel Stone fits so well that both options should be left open.

What then of the potential astronomical arguments? Beginning with the Heel Stone, if an observation of what was previously supposed to be standard lunar type was made, then the observer would have stood to the left of it, and we inquire into the arrangement where the upper limb of the Moon was just able to pass into the slit, to the right of stone 55. (Using what has been called here the point of furthest reach makes little difference, and will be ignored in this simple account.) Where precisely did the fallen stone 55 stand? This problem has already been raised. It will be tentatively assumed that its distance from stone 56 was 1.25 MY, just about a metre. The distance used to be put at about 0.56 m, but E. H. Stone's estimate was between 3 and 3.5 ft (say 0.9 and 1.07 m), and ours is 3.4 ft (1.04 m). Even an error of a foot shifts the azimuth by only a fifth of a degree.

There is some uncertainty about the epoch, and there are other small imponderables, but the azimuth set by 55 for an observer to the right of the Heel Stone was 38.89° south of west, and for an approximate date of 2500 BC. An observer immediately behind the left edge of the Heel and using the standard technique of lunar observation would have seen the last glint of the setting Moon at its minor southern standstill (on the left of the slit). This would have been at an altitude of 4.59°, which is to be compared with the altitude of 4.29° we deduce from our theoretical gradient of 3 in 40. To give an idea of the way different factors influence the situation: taking an observer on the right side of the Heel, using the other end of the slit, the required altitude would have been nearly a degree higher, appreciably too high. As for the effect of time, a change of 1000 years could have been accommodated by displacing the eye through about a foot (30 cm).

Stone 97, about 4 m from the Heel, could not have produced the same result with the same lintels, but this is where we must return to the case of the Sun, for the right hand side of 97, taken in conjunction with the old familiar edge of stone 56 of the grand trilithon, would have yielded an azimuth of 40.69° south of west, which it may be recalled is an acceptable low-level alignment to the setting midwinter Sun. This figure, an estimate based on the careful excavation of stone hole 97, is so remarkably close to the line from the inner (left-hand) edge of sarsen stone 30 (namely 40.74°), that one may suppose them to have been the same line. The conclusion to be drawn from all this is that stone 97 set a solar line for low altitude (0.89°), but that it became redundant when the Heel Stone was set up with a double function, for observing two extremes, one of the Sun and one of the Moon. The Heel Stone was a remarkable compromise, but it did not have quite such a geometrically perfect position as its predecessor: if our basic hypothesis about stone sizes is correct, however, it was only misplaced by eight or nine parts in a thousand.

Now the azimuths for the lunar standstills do not differ greatly from those for low level solar observations. Could the lines not perhaps serve *both* purposes, working with different horizons but looking at precisely the same azimuth? Can we not find an altitude of the right amount (5.64° would be needed) to produce a lunar line to correspond to the solar line of sight from stone 97 to stone 56? Or an altitude of 5.46° to do the same between the Heel Stone and stone 55?

It will be obvious that this cannot be straightforward, since the angles in question are rather greater than 1 in 10, which the monument is not tall enough to create for an ordinary standing observer at either of the two stones, the Heel or 97. In fact solutions to both problems can be found, but in different ways.

In the case of 97, one simply approaches the monument to a place from which the right altitude is indeed set. That place turns out to be the stone hole E. It will be found that the right hand side of 97 is in line with the left of hole E and the left of trilithon stone 56 (speaking from the point of view of a person looking southwest). Since two of the three stones are no longer in place, one should not insist on this point, but there is little doubt that it would have been a feasible alignment (40.69° south of west, looking under both lintels at or near the altitude of 5.64°). If this is a correct interpretation of the thinking of those who wished to elaborate on their use of stone 97, then it tells us something of the sequence of the placing of stones, with E following 97, but perhaps coming before the Heel Stone.

The other solution is perhaps more interesting. Rather than approach the monument, they had the option of simply lowering the eye. They did so by precisely 2 MY, as can be stated with some confidence in view of the meticulous excavation of the Heel Stone ditch, by Michael Pitts in 1979. The ditch floor in the eastern section he illustrated was evidently just 4.04 MY under SD, and in the western a few centimetres higher. Unfortunately, the crucial part of the ditch is still under the main road, but it was no doubt at much the same level. Estimating the position of the observer at the northeast of the ditch, and looking along the right-hand face of the Heel Stone, the altitude set by the near lip of the ring of sarsen lintels was—using our ideal data—just 7.75 MY in 82.5 MY, or 5.36°. What was required was 5.46°. This is a far better result than one has any right to expect, and it is based on an accurately surveyed azimuth, and two levels, one of which is a plausible extrapolation from a recent survey, the other resting on the coherence of our entire account of the sarsens.

Before leaving this ditch alignment, it is natural to ask whether it embodies any simple proportionality. Whether it was worked out consciously or not, it is hard to say, but the gradient quoted is exactly 3 in 32.

In summary, the grand trilithon was so designed as to allow for two key observations from the Heel Stone, one of the setting midwinter Sun at its base, the other of the setting Moon at minor southern standstill at its top. Stone 97 allowed the former, and set an azimuth that allowed the latter from the stone E, to the front of it. In addition, the Heel Stone ditch enabled an observation of the same lunar phenomenon at high altitude. And since the Moon's behaviour at this time might not be intuitively obvious, perhaps it is worth adding a brief description of what would have been seen before and after the minor standstill. As the Moon set, its last glint within the slit would have gradually shifted, day by day, from the right-hand end to the left, and it would then have reversed. At other times, it would not have reversed, and would have gone on

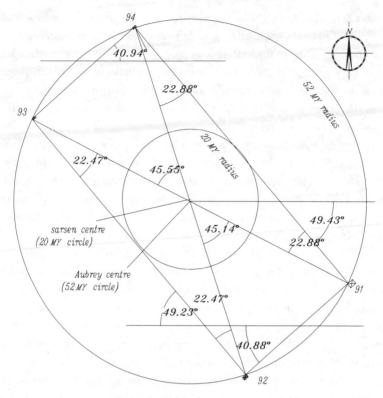

FIG. 184.   The station stones rectangle.

setting further and further to the south. If this second type of behaviour was regarded as 'normal', then a minor standstill has a touch of the miraculous about it, and perhaps this was a reason for paying so much attention to it.

The Moon and the Stone Stations

There are at least two further lines of sight towards lunar extremes associated with the sarsen circle. These involve the four station stones close to the Aubrey ring, about which so much has been written in recent years. They have been mentioned on several previous occasions here, and are shown on Fig. 156, as well as in Fig. 184. Colt Hoare detected the rectangular arrangement, at two opposite corners of which unhewn stones were to be found, now numbered 91 (a 2.7 m stone, fallen even then) and 93 (a 1.2m stone, evidently reshaped and presumably previously larger). At the other corners of his rectangle there were, he said, 'two small tumuli ditched round, so as to resemble excavations'. Those mounds (sometimes called 'barrows'), are now numbered 92 (southern) and 94

(northern). It was Hawley who found that there had formerly been stones at the centres of both. In enclosure 94, Colt Hoare found a cremation burial, but in 92 nothing. The ground at all four stations is in fact more or less level, although the ground at 91 seems to have been a little *below* the surrounding ground. William Stukeley, John Wood, and John Smith, all writing in the eighteenth century, saw all four places as depressions—perhaps partly an illusion based on expectations.

Hawley estimated the stone in 92 to have been of much the same size as the surviving 91. Since the Aubrey circle was disturbed by the ditching round 92 and 94, they clearly belong to a later date than that circle. An argument offered by R. S. Newall in his little guide to the monument (1953), purporting to show that they must be earlier than the sarsen monument, cannot be accepted. It is based on the common view that since the lines joining 91 to 93 and 92 to 94 cross at 45°, therefore they must have been within sight of one another. The argument goes that this could not have been the case had the monument stood in the way. It is a weak argument: even had the Stonehenge geometers not known enough to construct the rectangle without plotting diagonals, the stations could have been set up at more or less the same time as the sarsen circle, that is, as part of the same project. It will be shown that they are intimately connected with the sarsen circle, but this probably in continuation of an older practice. Much of the mystery of the supposed 45° intersection will be removed when their function is explained. As for the earlier tradition, it will be set out all the more plausibly if we can first account for what survives—or survives at least in part.

It is not necessary to review all the astronomical ideas of Edward Duke, already mentioned in Chapter 9. He emphasized *solar* alignments. He saw in the side 92–91 an alignment on midsummer sunrise, and in 94–93 another alignment on midwinter sunset. In a rough and ready way this claim is unexceptionable, since both lines are more or less parallel to the main axis of Stonehenge; but more precision is called for. If the stone has not been modified, the top of 91 would have been close to the level of the horizon, as seen by an observer standing at 92. One can be more precise than this, however.

Note that Duke chose viewing points within the enclosures. The fact that the Heel Stone is surrounded by a ditch is a reason for taking his assumption seriously.

First to the geometry of the stations. There are some properties of the stations that should not really astonish us. Since the natural horizons at the site are such as to make any solar alignments of the sort envisaged by Duke virtually parallel, and since the four stations are more or less on a circle, it is inevitable

that a very close approximation to a rectangle will result, given that one pair of opposite points is on a diameter. This is a simple geometrical truth, which need not in all strictness have been appreciated for the rectangle to have been so created. And if a diameter could not be established by a direct line of sight across the middle? Quite simply, if one angle at the circumference was made a right angle, it would have stood on a diameter, so that the parallelism of one pair of opposite sides (guaranteed, say, by aligning both on midwinter sunset over the same horizon) would have guaranteed that a complete rectangle resulted, with both diagonals passing through the centre. (Of course in practice we can only speak of lines within small fractions of a degree of parallelism, etc.)

What all this certainly does *not* guarantee, however, is that the diagonals will cross at 45°. Flinders Petrie (1880) claimed to have measured 45°±6', but he was obliged to make a number of conjectures that do not chime with the stated precision in the end result. Richard Atkinson, after the 1978 investigation of hole 94, and taking estimates of stone centres, found 45° 11' 4.

To ensure that 45° resulted, if indeed this was ever the aim, a very simple procedure might have been followed: each of the shorter sides of the rectangle needed to be a chord of just an eighth part of the defining circle. It will later be shown that such a geometrical construction had already been used at the time of marking out the Aubrey circle, which had its own 'stations'.

It was apparently C. A. Newham who first saw that the longer sides of the station stones rectangle were directed towards lunar extremes. Several others followed him, but all were apparently concerned to find *distant* markers, that might have been used to raise the accuracy of the supposed observations. Newham believed that enormous posts placed in post holes excavated in what is now the car park—holes now marked with white paint on the tarmac—served as distant markers. Alexander Thom went further in supposing that a mound at the northeast was a solar (midsummer) marker. Both foresights have since been shown to be illusory: as Aubrey Burl has pointed out, wood in the postholes had radiocarbon dates four or five millennia older than the sarsen monument; and Newham's mound proved to be modern. Thom suggested other distant foresights, or rather places where foresights might have been: Gibbet Knoll at over 14 km, Figsbury ring at over 10 km, and Hanging Langford Camp at over 12 km. They are implausible in themselves, and superfluous, since the monument contained the only foresights that were ever needed.

There have been some who have dismissed the idea of lunar alignments, with the argument that since—as an accident of latitude—the lunar alignments are more or less at right angles to the solar alignments, they would have

been created even by people who did not realize what they had done. Others have hinted that the 45° at the centre might have come about unintentionally, since a division of the (Aubrey) circle into eight would have been a natural one. It is hard to believe that those responsible for the Stonehenge architecture were so ignorant of the symmetries it embodied. This seems doubly improbable, in view of the lunar alignments from the Heel Stone. It is never easy to prove or disprove intent, but if, with the sceptics, one is to accept that a single pair of sides of the rectangle was set up with intent, that is surely unlikely to have been the pair of *shorter* sides. Why should the 'accidental' sides have been the sides of greater length? It is in any case wrong to speak of the stations rectangle as though it was exact, just as it is wrong to say that the solar and lunar lines are perfectly at right angles. It is the fact that there are slight but measurable differences between the alignments and the directions in a perfect rectangle, together with the fact that the alignments meet the astronomical requirements of the place, that should persuade us that they were once fitted to solar and lunar tasks. But the strongest argument against this type of scepticism is that the idea behind the 'lunar sides' of the rectangle, once it is properly understood, looks like a natural extension of the idea behind the lunar line from the Heel Stone—and yet this is not at right angles to the supposed 'solar axis', accidentally or otherwise.

What, then, was the source of the idea behind the stations rectangle? Something approximating to the Aubrey circle seems to have been the starting point of operations. Since there is nothing else conspicious in its neighbourhood, it is tempting to say that the Aubrey circle was clearly involved, but much caution is needed here. It is possible that what had begun life as a circle of 52.13 MY radius—a number to be explained shortly—had brought to the attention of the sarsen builders the fact that the number 52 had itself interesting properties. It is evident from the example of Woodhenge and Durrington that it was well known that lines at right angles to the solar axis could serve as lines of lunar extremes. The precise directions having been set, the pair of stones 91 and 92 might have been erected at opposite sides of the available area within the bank. But precisely where? If the 'stations circle' had a radius of 52 MY, the construction might have made use of a right-angled triangle of sides 20, 48, and 52 MY, as William Dibble has suggested. The diameter of the sarsen ring might then have been determined as a consequence of this construction, as a circle trapped within the two parallels.

What reasons are there for wondering whether the radius of the 'stations circle' was meant to be 52 MY precisely? More than a century ago, Flinders Petrie made an estimate of it that—using Thom's unit—can be written as 51.95 MY. According to Atkinson's 1978 data for the coordinates of centres, reduced again for convenience to Thom's unit, the two diagonals were (91 to 93) 104.55 MY and (92 to 94) 104.83 MY, making for a mean radius of 52.35 MY. Of course, if the interpretation being offered now is correct, the ideal circle would have been slightly different from both figures, since it would have passed through parts of the stones other than their centres. A less direct piece of evidence as to the 52 MY measurement stems from Dibble's conjecture (1976), that the rectangle contained by the station stones splits into what are very nearly two Pythagorean right-angled triangles with sides 5, 12 and 13. This would have given an angle of 22.62° in place of 22.5° at the centre of the rectangle. Atkinson's figure for the measured angle is 22.59°, which seems to favour the idea, although again it has to be remembered that he worked to centres.

Those who like the argument for a triangle with sides in the ratios 5:12:13 are under no obligation to accept that the sides were intended to be 20, 48, and 52 in Megalithic Yards. On the other hand, those who believe that the Megalithic Yard was in use at Stonehenge may feel that there is support to be had from the way it seems to bring into harmony two different sorts of evidence—from measurement and from a geometry of whole numbers. And those who resist the idea should think twice before accepting a 5:12:13 triangle in the first place, lest it force the dreaded standard upon them.

It is never going to be possible to put the Pythagorean triangle hypothesis to a direct test, in the absence of two stones and four precise positions, but a knowledge of their former centres allows considerable progress. They are marked on Fig. 184 by rectangular boxes that approximate to the stone sizes, based on what little evidence survives. There is no solution to the problem that does not rest on a bevy of presuppositions. Those made here involve the idea that sighting was done from the sides of stones in the usual way (they were all very probably slightly taller than a man). The assumptions need to be supplemented with others as to stone widths. Numerous plausible alternative arrangements have been considered, and the best fit found—that shown in the figure—has significant corners of the four supposed stones on, or very near to, a circle of exactly 52 MY, drawn with its centre at the centre of the Aubrey circle. (Simply for reference, a 20 MY circle is drawn in the figure with centre at that of the sarsen circle.)[2]

Footnote overleaf

The sides of the resulting rectangle are such that, around the year 2000 BC, the shorter sides would have aligned exactly on the upper limb of the rising midsummer Sun for altitudes 0.39° (north side) or 0.42° (south side); or on the setting midwinter Sun for altitudes 1.05° (north) or 1.02° (south). The present ground levels are not those of the past, but the height differentials will be much the same, since the ground is fairly flat; and the altitudes in the neighbourhood of 1° are what are to be expected if the old bank horizon was not too degraded. In the midsummer direction the altitudes are only about a tenth of a degree on the low side for the natural horizon—not an unsatisfactory result, bearing in mind the uncertain evidence.

Which of the alignments along the shorter sides is to be preferred? It is possible that both were significant only as tokens, symbols of a certain cosmic situation that had been represented in the same way for centuries. What probably mattered more were the alignments over the longer sides of the rectangle. They raise the question yet again of the use of the monument as a grand 'post', but confining ourselves to the station stones rectangle as such, and disregarding the large sarsen ring, the question arises: In which direction would the Moon have been observed? The southern maximum lunar rising would not have been the focus of attention, assuming the data given earlier, but the upper limb of the setting Moon at its northern extreme could have been observed over a horizon of 0.60° (western side) or 0.52° (eastern side), at approximately the same period as before. These altitudes are greater than that of the natural horizon, without trees, and even slightly higher than a 2 MY bank would have created, but there is more to be said on this question, and on the sizes of stones on which the estimates depend.

When the ring of sarsens is considered, as limiting the view of the setting Moon at its extreme position on the horizon, the alignments derived are—if they are not illusory—more reliable than those between the conjectured station stones themselves. The edges of stones 16 (to the southwest) and 30 (to the northeast) are accurately known, and have not changed appreciably since they were erected. They are to be supplemented with the weaker information gleaned

---

2   The placing of stone 94 is the least satisfactory. Stones 92 and 93 could have been used in what is taken to be a standard way with the Moon. Stones 91 and 94 might have been used for the Moon with the other convention—the use of the solid drum created by the ring of sarsens as 'post' would have been enough to change priorities here. Numerical values of the estimated angles, quoted to 0.01° on the figure, simply reflect the ideals embodied in the figure itself. The angles at the centre and vertices are close to anticipated values. (Note that the lines through the centre are not straight.)

earlier in this section—thus halving the uncertainty, but not removing it entirely.

An observer standing just behind the stone (92) in the 'south barrow', and using the northeast edge of 92 as backsight, might have sighted the upper limb of the Moon, setting at its northern extreme. The ray would have been limited by the monument at an azimuth of 50.18°, if the same size of stone is assumed as previously (1.5 MY at viewing height). Widening the stone to 2.5 MY makes the azimuth 49.62°. An observer looking in the same general direction from stone 91, with the stone on his right and the monument on his left, might have seen the same phenomenon of northern maximum lunar setting. The azimuth set by the monument, on the same assumptions as before, would have been 49.63°.

These are very satisfactory results. The higher azimuth (for a narrow stone) required 0.2°, which is impossibly low and may be rejected at once. The horizon altitude in the northern direction was about 0.33°, assuming no trees on the horizon. (With this natural horizon one should expect an azimuth of 49.83°.) Around 2000 BC, the azimuth of 49.62° required a horizon at 0.43° altitude, and one might be inclined to leave matters here, with the thought that such a small discrepancy is easily explained in terms of trees, or changes in ground level, or poor estimates of stone sizes. It turns out, however, that the height of an intervening bank that can explain the higher horizon is almost exactly 2 MY above local ground, and this suggests that the bank in this direction had been kept to its (presumed) old height.

It surely also tells us something about the size of the missing stone 92: it was large, like 91, and it was unlike 93 and 94, which were in a sense no more than tokens. Perhaps, like stone 91, stone 92 was pear-shaped, with its stone hole smaller than its maximum width. Alternatively, they might have been 'male and female'—to use the interpretation of the paired forms at Wayland's Smithy and Avebury. What is also striking about the arrangement here explained is that on this calculation the lines of sight, when extended beyond the circle of sarsens, passed within 10 cm—a hand's breadth—of the edges of stones 93 and 94 as previously deduced. (The ray cuts 10 cm into the postulated rectangle for stone 94, and misses 93 by about the same amount.)

This is a strong argument for the observation of the Moon at Stonehenge, and it is strengthened by other considerations. The most compelling argument will come from the trilithons, but one suspects that some future study of the pattern of cremation and burial might add support—as, for example, in the case of a Beaker burial outside the ditch but along the line passing 94.

The Trilithons

When viewed from the Heel Stone, the monument has been found to present two lunar alignments, one passing the lower left edge of the drum and one central. There was also the possibility of viewing from the ditch, as explained earlier in this chapter. Viewed from two of the stone stations (91, 92), at least, the monument produced alignments on the northern maximum of the setting Moon. Before asking whether there were others, it will be useful to draw attention to certain additional architectural symmetries.

For an observer standing at ground level, the trilithons and sarsens together would have blocked out the sky over the horizon rather thoroughly from all four points, leaving in all cases the lintel of the nearest trilithon and the grand central trilithon showing above the rim.

For the sake of brevity it will be convenient to label the trilithons in a new way, namely as $T1$ (nearest to station 91), $T2$ (nearest 92), $T3$ (nearest 93), $T4$ (nearest 94), and $T0$ (the grand trilithon in the middle). Note that the line from the gap in $T2$ to station 92, and that from the gap in $T3$ to station 93, are virtually at right angles to the inner faces of the stones and to the lintels they carry. There is no corresponding rule with the other trilithons. It has already been explained, however, that their faces more or less line up with the Heel Stone, and might have been meant to do so perfectly.

It is a somewhat surprising fact that the spacing of the trilithons gives an appearance of careful planning in relation to the *Aubrey* circle. Taking the line joining the gap in $T1$ to that in $T4$, and the parallel line between the gaps in $T2$ and $T3$, it goes without saying that the symmetry of the horseshoe in relation to the axis of the monument means that they will be more or less parallel to the lines for lunar maxima between the stations, since they are at right angles to the solar axis. It seems unlikely that they were lunar lines of sight in the finished monument, since by that time they were probably completely blocked. There is only the merest possibility of the lines having passed to the sides of blocking pillars. If not blocked, they would have functioned well with the natural horizon for northern lunar maximum at setting, seen from near Aubrey holes 13 and 15.

It is impossible to put a very precise figure on the spacing of those important lines, but it was certainly 10.0 MY to within a tenth of this unit, and might have been much closer to that figure if stone 58, when it was re-erected in modern times, was not put in quite its original position. Note that although the gaps in the trilithons are substantial fractions of 1 MY, the slantwise placing of the stones nevertheless limits the lines in question to within a few centimetres. Moreover, it seems that the Aubrey centre (and not

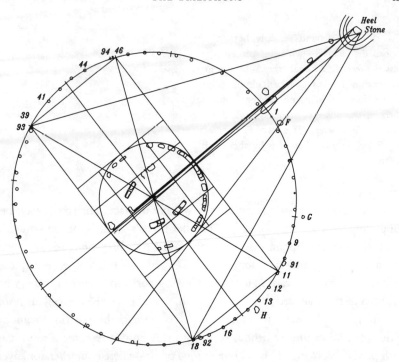

FIG. 185. The repeating unit of 10 MY in the squares that appear to frame (weakly) the sarsen ring and trilithons, and that yet seem to relate more strongly to the Aubrey circle and station stones. The grid of squares at the centre as drawn here has sixteen cells each of side 10 MY.

the sarsen centre) is mid-way between the lines in question. Perhaps also significant is the fact that if we complete the 10 MY square, the two vertices near *T2* and *T3* seem to fall close to the 7 MY circle of the inner bluestones horseshoe. This beautifully symmetrical arrangement is summarized in Figs. 185 and 186, where *A* is the Aubrey centre. Fig. 186 also illustrates a property of the trilithons that seems to hint at their relationship with the centre of the Aubrey ring—the position of which might have been preserved with a marker of some sort.

There are not many clear-cut possibilities for solar or lunar alignment in the finished monument (that is, of trilithons and sarsen ring taken together) when viewed from its side. There are reasons, none the less, for suspecting that the trilithons had an identity of their own before the sarsens were ever erected around them. These were touched upon at the end of the last section, where it was pointed out that the slits in four of the trilithons, assuming that originally there were no pillars (bluestones, Altar Stone) within them, would have created two alignments on the setting Moon at its northern maximum. These would

FIG. 186.   One and possibly both of the
central diagonals shown here seems to have
passed precisely through the Aubrey centre.
One of those lines as it happens almost aligned
on the rising midwinter Sun over the natural
horizon, the observer standing near Aubrey
hole 41. The re-erected stones of T3 (stones 57
and 58) strictly disallow this by about half a
degree.

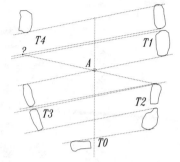

have been usable, only if the sarsen ring was not in place. They could have been
supplemented by a very appealing parallel lunar sight line of the same kind
(northern extreme moonset) for an observer at Aubrey hole 16, this being
limited by the grand trilithon, viewed sideways. While one cannot quote a
precise azimuth, for want of a precise viewing position, a post in Aubrey hole
41, used in the standard way for the Moon, would have given excellent results
over the natural horizon. What is more, this is a remarkable position for another
reason: the other four trilithons seen from this point presented a solid mass,
with perfect blocking. This is not a unique point—there is another, for anyone
looking southeast and standing by Aubrey hole 40, for example—but it is
easily verified from a plan of the monument that the trilithons seem almost to
have been placed with this property in mind.

   Does this sort of property show that there was once a time when the
trilithon monument stood without thought for a future sarsen ring around it?
It is instructive to consider arguments for and against that idea. The massive
Arminghall horseshoe of posts that so resembles the sarsen trilithons had no
surrounding circle of massive posts. The sarsen ring could not have been built
in its entirety before the stones of the horseshoe of trilithons were brought into
the central area. On the other hand, one can easily see why the idea of
independence at Stonehenge is not normally considered, even for purposes of
dismissal. There were after all (timber and stone) rings at Stonehenge before
the great horseshoe of sarsens. It is usually supposed that when the Stonehenge
people built the horseshoe they had to begin by dismantling the half-completed
bluestones. (These are likely to have remained on or near the site, to be brought
back to the central area for the bluestone ring and horseshoe.) The trilithons
and sarsen ring are of the same material, and both are of dimensions that seem
to fit together in an astronomically and geometrically meaningful way. It is
therefore natural to suppose that both were planned together and erected close
in time—say over two or three decades.

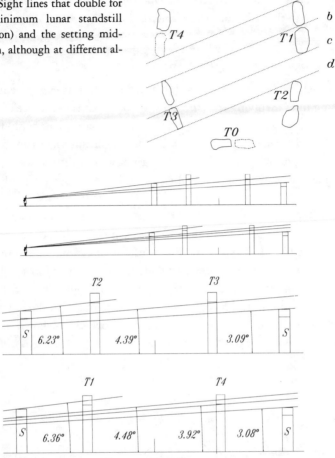

FIG. 187. Sight lines that double for northern minimum lunar standstill (setting Moon) and the setting midsummer Sun, although at different altitudes.

FIG. 188. The relation between sight lines grazing the lintels on the trilithons, for an observer at the distance of the Aubrey circle. The two cases shown are for an observer on the southeast side (the upper at Aubrey hole 15 and the lower at hole 13) looking through slits in two trilithons. The angles set for other directions will be roughly similar to those marked on the right. Observers looking across the monument from the northeast will have had almost perfectly symmetrical views. Note how in each case the two highest sight lines (ignoring the short lines, which are for future reference) are blocked by the lintels of the sarsen ring, while the two lower have free passage and have the additional advantage that they are fixed in direction (azimuth) by the trilithon uprights. Whether they can pass the *uprights* of the sarsen ring is another question.

In support of this second argument are the many architectural and astronomical symmetries—it should hardly be necessary to review them here—that can only be understood when the horseshoe and ring are taken together. But even this is not conclusive, for there is nothing inherently strange about the

addition of new symmetries (those involving the sarsen ring) to old ones (those belonging to the trilithons in isolation).

The Trilithons—an Independent Monument?

In very general terms it can be said that there are two types of potentially useful sighting lines involving the trilithons, as seen from the distance of the Aubrey ring. One sort would have been usable with the natural (or bank) horizon and the other with relatively high altitudes. Before considering them, consider four different types of sight line, threading through the lintels, when an observer stands at the distance of the Aubrey ring, in the general area of the station stones.

The lintels on the near trilithons would have been wholly or almost wholly visible above the top of the lintels of the sarsen ring, while those on the far side would have been hidden by the lintels of the ring—except where parts were visible underneath those lintels. This situation, illustrated in a general way in Fig. 188, complements what was found for the appearance of the trilithon lintels as seen from the Heel Stone. The figure in question shows the four sorts of sight line through the lintels—when not blocked. As shown in the figure, all of the lines are for observers at the southeast side, one set passing centrally

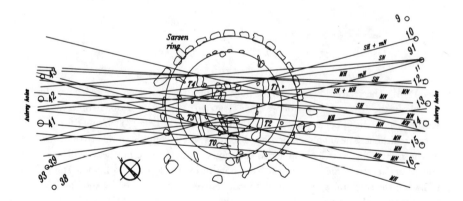

FIG. 189. Various potential sight lines for observers standing at various places on the Aubrey circle, of which eleven use the trilithon monument alone—that is, assuming that the sarsen ring is not in place. The type of event is indicated by the letters S, M, or m (midsummer Sun, major lunar standstill, minor lunar standstill) and the horizon is indicated by the addition of N or H (natural or high). The four sight lines for high altitude are all created with the help of the sarsen ring, in the way explained in the text.

through the trilithons *T1* and *T4*, the other for *T2* and *T3*. Sight lines for observers on the northwest side of the Aubrey ring were virtually mirror images of those drawn. None of those drawn here is of particular value, but some variants on them certainly were, as will be shown in this section.

In the category of lines over the lower horizon there are four sight lines with azimuths close to 30° north of west or south of east, shown in outline in Fig. 187, where they are denoted by letters *a* to *d*. At least two, and perhaps all of them, would in this case have been for the northern minimum lunar standstill (setting Moon), with azimuths averaging at 29.8° north of west, and altitudes averaging at 0.55°. These lines are remarkable—whether by chance or not it is difficult to say—since they would have doubled as lines to the last glint of the setting midsummer Sun if this was over some artificial horizon at altitude around 6.8°. Moreover, altitudes of this order were set by the sarsen ring in two different ways: by the outer edge of the top of the ring of lintels, as seen by an observer at the distance of the Aubrey circle (at Aubrey hole 10, near station 91, would have been ideal), or by the inner edge of the lintels ring, as seen by an observer standing near the appropriate sarsen of the ring on the opposite side. The character of the first alternative is illustrated by the two short sight lines of Fig. 188.

There are many possibilities. Rather than give a long catalogue of them, the most probable lines of all types are drawn, solar and lunar, where the observer stood to the southeast, are shown on Fig. 189. Eleven of the lines marked make no use of the sarsen ring, which is needed, however, for all high altitude lines.

Fig. 190 should give a rough idea of the possible use of the combined monument as a means of producing windows for both solar and lunar extremes. The figure shows a stylized view from Aubrey hole 12. While far from realistic,

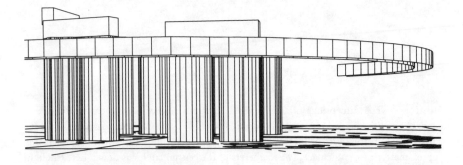

FIG. 190.   This stylized view from Aubrey hole 12 should give a rough idea of the creation of windows and the blocking effect of the various central stones.

it illustrates how a slight sideways movement could close off all but the slit in the far trilithon (*T3*). The same figure shows, too, an important window, limited above and to the sides by the near trilithon (*T1*) and below by the top of the lintel on *T4*. This in fact provides another high-altitude alignment, now on the setting Moon at its northern maximum. There is of course uncertainty as to the observer's position. If Aubrey hole 12 was in use, then we should get an excellent fit with an altitude of 6.2° and an azimuth of 39.4°, for the Moon's upper limb. Its importance seems to be underlined by the fact that the ray

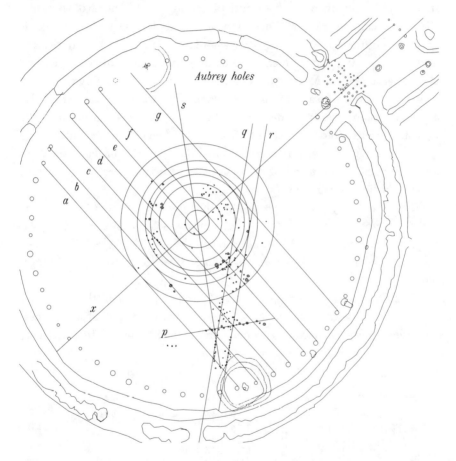

FIG. 191.   The dimensions of conjectured circles of timber posts seem to indicate a connection with the Aubrey ring, as indicated here by a series of potential lines of sight. These make up the series of lunar lines *a–g* and the solar line *x* (to which the others are approximately perpendicular). The diameters of the central circles as drawn here (though highly speculative) are approximately, in terms of Thom's megalithic rods of 2.5 MY: 3, 6, 9, 12, 13, 15, 20. The lines *p*, *q* and *r* of the southern corridor and façade were introduced in Chapter 7. The line *x* touches stone hole 97 (not shown) at its upper end.

would then be more or less square to the near trilithon (*T1*). This last characteristic of the monument seems to be duplicated with a sight line from Aubrey 11, which was again virtually square to trilithon *T3*, and well fitted to a northern minor lunar standstill over the natural horizon.

It is surprising to discover relatively few hints of an interest in risings. The exception is the possibility of seeing midwinter sunrise in the way explained in the last section.

What is particularly striking in all this is the apparently strong correlation between those places from which the absolute extremes of the Moon's setting were to be seen over the natural horizon (Aubrey 12 to 16) and the area where Hawley discovered a high concentration of cremated burials. He found them in the filling of Aubrey holes and just under the turf, on the bank and within it. There was an especially heavy concentration of such cremations near holes 14 and 15. Others were found near 10, and a few others between 16 and the southern gap in the bank. Atkinson associated these with the first phase of the monument, and even though this does not seem likely, it has to be said that a series of places from which the extremes of the Moon's setting could have been observed with respect to one central monument might easily have been usable with respect to any other monument on this site, at least assuming it covered a comparable area.

There are reasons for thinking that the post holes found by Hawley and others in the central and southern areas were themselves at an earlier period related to the pattern of Aubrey holes (see Fig. 191). These reasons have to do with the way in which circles drawn through the central posts—admittedly in a highly speculative way—sit naturally between lines of sight across the Aubrey circle. When the stations were put into position, whenever precisely that was, the Aubrey circle was still in mind, judging by its use for cremations. It is not surprising, therefore, that the timber rings should appear to have been related to the Aubrey posts in much the same way as the central stones were destined to be related to the stations.

To return to the system of trilithons: in trying to decide whether it was conceived as an entity independent of the sarsens, it might be asked whether many of the trilithon alignments found above would have been blocked by the sarsen uprights. If it is agreed that they were once astronomically meaningful and were subsequently blocked, then here is an argument for independence. The fact that many of these are now missing makes it impossible to be absolutely sure, but it is possible that not a single one of our sight lines was so blocked; and for the record, none seems to have been blocked either by the stones of the *Q-R* system (as far as it is known) or the bluestone horseshoe. Some

do head directly for uprights of all three structures, but these are the high altitude lines, and are all capable of clearing the uprights in question. There is in the end no good reason to say that the trilithons were erected without any thought to a future ring, although neither can it be said that they and the sarsen ring formed parts of a single grand scheme. At the risk of labouring a point, all the evidence pointing to a unified plan—the fact that both elements use round numbers of MY, the fact that the trilithon lintels would have seemed to sit on top of those of the ring—can be explained in terms of a harmonious adaptation to a pre-existing structure.

But did the trilithons precede the (fragmentary) Q-R system? If not, and there was a phase when all stood simultaneously, then how were the trilithon stones manoeuvred into position? After Atkinson's first announcements of his findings of the dumbbell settings, some argued that the stones of the Q-R ring were in position first but were moved away for a time whilst the trilithon horseshoe was erected. There is a geometrical argument against this, as will be explained in the following section, but since the Q-R system seems never to have formed a complete ring, there is no case to answer. There is one strong argument, in fact, for the Q-R stones in the neighbourhood of the grand trilithon having been in position during the erection of one of its uprights, stone 56, namely that its ramp makes an uncomfortable sideways approach from the northwest. This must surely count as the most extraordinary of all Stonehenge engineering feats, with the possible exception of the raising of the lintels on the trilithons.

It would not be surprising if the remains of closer timber parallels to the Stonehenge trilithons were to be found, nearer in time and place than the much earlier example at Arminghall. There are small and unimpressive open rings of stone in Scotland that might be described as horseshoes, or open ovals. In a composite monument at Lugg, County Dublin, there are traces of very numerous postholes, but two pairs of massive holes there have been taken as evidence for the use of trixylons. As for the horseshoe shape, it is shared, roughly speaking, by the 400 or so Irish 'wedge tombs'. The typical entrance (the opening in the horseshoe) is higher and wider than the rest, and in the great majority of cases faces the setting midwinter Sun. The Irish 'court tombs', of which well over 300 are known, most in the north of the island, resemble the horseshoe less closely, but tend to face in the same direction. The horn-shaped forecourts of Neolithic barrows offer another rough parallel, and so do Breton cromlechs. As always, the ultimate test of cultural descent is not shape but use; and here the resemblances between Stonehenge and the rest seem very remote indeed, and are probably best forgotten.

The Geometrical Design

It is one thing to derive numerous geometrical—at root astronomical—constructions, but quite another to guarantee that they are consistent, or can be fitted into a plausible design sequence. Suppose, for example, that the Heel Stone was present with or even before the trilithons, but that the centre of the sarsen circle was to be placed on or very close to the line to midwinter sunset, already built into the grand trilithon or some precursor to it. (The argument might be better applied to the stone that stood in hole 97, but the more tangible Heel Stone will serve for the sake of discussion.) The direction from the Heel to the Moon, at its southern extreme of setting over the existing (artificial) horizon, was something over which there was no control, except by adjusting the level of the effective horizon. Suppose then that the radius of a projected sarsen ring were to have been settled by ensuring that the Moon at that southern extreme was just able to pass beyond the complete drum of sarsens. A certain degree of shuffling of the sarsen centre would have been possible, and given a little leeway, it could have been discovered that a sarsen circle with outer circumference 120 MY was possible (diameter 38.2 MY).

This potential historical sequence fits the artefacts in question moderately well, but the same general type of geometrical construction fits other elements of Stonehenge—there are so many of them—and there is no guarantee that another starting point would not explain the sarsen ring better. As it happens, taking the missing stone 97 as an alternative to the Heel Stone produces much better results for the Moon's southern extreme over the natural horizon, seen along a ray grazing the drum of sarsen uprights. But one might take a completely different approach. One might, for example, imagine that a stations rectangle was added to a supposedly pre-existing Aubrey circle, which it divided into eight (or sixteen) parts—starting from a suitable starting point decided by astronomical alignments in the way already explained. The directions of the longer sides that emerge will be right for the Moon, and will give the 45° at the centre of the rectangle, as explained earlier. The sarsen circle might then be imagined as having been designed to sit snugly between those lunar lines of sight, and so be really determined by the size of the Aubrey circle. While it will be approximately the same, there is no guarantee that such a hypothetical sarsen ring will be of the exactly same size as before. Consistency cannot be guaranteed so easily. It has already been pointed out that the station stones functioned in a way that produced a somewhat less than rectangular arrangement. They were in any case not quite on the circumference of the Aubrey circle—a first concession to inexactness, if a combination of the suggested constructions was being aimed at. Speaking generally, therefore,

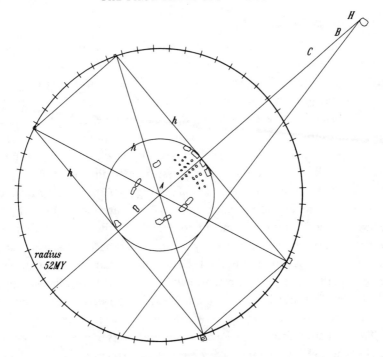

FIG. 192.   The construction as described in the text, *exactly* applied to a circle of radius 52 MY and then superimposed as closely as possible on the Stonehenge situation, with a stations rectangle included in the construction.

what might seem at first to have been slight imperfections in the architectural arrangement were perhaps really no more than consequences of the impossibility of perfectly satisfying all criteria simultaneously.

The important point here is that in offering a possible design history, such over-determined situations must be treated with great care. There are some who are prepared to explain their occurrence in terms of fortunate coincidence, if not of mystic pentangles, the Star of David, the Lost Atlantis, or the like. Fortunate coincidences are unfortunately very difficult to dismiss. Here, for instance, the two explanations above do nearly converge, so that it might be claimed that, after many years of experiment, it was simply found that the two geometrical constructions yielded more or less the same result, and that there is no more to be said about the matter. It could be said that the sarsen ring seems not to have been a perfect circle, but a very slightly elongated figure—an ellipse, perhaps. Another tactic would be to say that the Heel Stone (or 97) was positioned *after* the sarsen ring, and was so placed that the line of sight from it to the Moon at its southern extreme of setting would just skim the monument. This idea does have the merit of avoiding the idea of chance

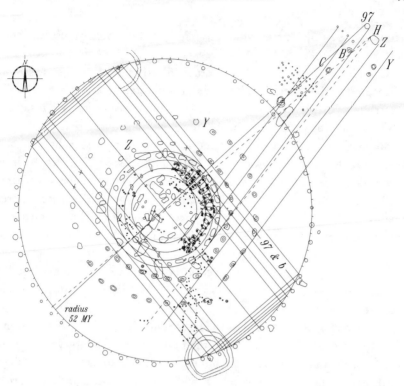

FIG. 193.   The stations rectangle construction of the previous figure, to which various similar constructions have been added for reference. Where the stone stations construction of the previous figure relates the Heel Stone to the sarsen ring, this figure shows that it may also be related simultaneously to stones 97 and *B* (which both seem to share in an alignment to the southern extreme of the setting Moon). Taking the *left* side of the latter stones is necessary, but this is a practice we believe was normal with lunar observations. Following the same principle with the Heel Stone, holes of the *Z*-ring seem to be picked out by the lunar line (for which reason the observer's position at the Heel is marked as *Z*). Something sharing an edge with the recumbent Slaughter Stone might have served a similar purpose for the *Q-R* system. One of the *A*-posts at the entrance would have served for them too, just as another produces a lunar line with the trilithons 51–52; but these are both probably accidental. The stone that once stood at the edge of the main ditch (near the Slaughter Stone and ditch terminal) might have been similarly related to a timber monument, but the lines are not drawn.   There is no backsight serving for the *Y*-ring, but it will be noticed that there are holes along a lunar line of sight that would have lain very roughly along it. The above diagram draws attention to another property of stone 97: a line from its right-hand observing edge drawn through the centre of the sarsen circle passes through the most distant Aubrey Hole. The Heel Stone does not share this property (see the broken line). The other broken line drawn here is the lunar line from the Heel, which is less perfect than that from 97.

coincidence. But a better way is to stress the failure of the station stones to sit exactly on the Aubrey circle, which on archaeological grounds must have come first.

Consider again the procedure postulated earlier, relating the Heel Stone (or stone 97) to the sarsen ring. It begins with an external observer (near a stone or post), in a position allowing a solar alignment, as seen over a circle's centre (close to, if not identical with, the Aubrey circle), and a ring that serves to set an alignment on at least one extreme lunar position as seen by the same observer. It then ends with a possible extension to a stations rectangle. If we try to scale the resulting geometrical figure up or down in its entirety (that of Fig. 192), and then try to match the geometrical figure with earlier material remains, we do find a number of broadly acceptable lines to the lunar extreme that fit rather well with various stones (or rather holes that held stones) at the northeast. These are summarized in the caption to Fig. 193. It seems quite likely that the geometrical construction at issue might have been earlier applied to the periphery of the Q-R system; and there is a strong suspicion, not illustrated, that it was, earlier still, applied to a timber circle. Stones B and 97 fit the sarsen ring better than does the Heel Stone. Strangely enough, it seems as though an edge of the latter (Z in the figure) might have played a part in the arrangement of Z-holes although they were fairly certainly dug at a much later date. Alexander Thom saw both Y- and Z-rings as spirals. If they are, they are certainly lacking in geometrical elegance.

For the record, if the shorter sides of the various stations rectangles (chords of the Aubrey circle, perhaps) stood on arcs equal to 5, 6, 7, and 8 parts of a circle of 52 parts radius, the circle being divided into 56 equal parts, then the diameters of the four central circles (equal in length to those four chords) would have been approximately 28.79, 34.35, 39.80, and 45.12 parts respectively. Of course making these data correspond with reality depends on a decision as to what measurement was basic. An Aubrey circle of 52.13 MY internal radius—a figure based on A. Thom's measurement of 86.44 m—would have had a 40 MY core for the span of seven holes, for example, in other words, for the sarsen ring.

Such geometrical relationships as these, that seem to hint, however weakly, at real relationships between the better known elements of Stonehenge, unfortunately reveal very little that was not already suspected. Stones B and C are gone, but when did they go? The stations rectangle associated with stones in holes B and 97 (see the rectangle singled out on Fig. 193) fits better with the Aubrey holes than do the stone stations, and this is in keeping with their having been on the scene longer. Stones B and 97 were quite certainly related

geometrically to the trilithons and the sarsen ring, as we have seen, but so was the Heel Stone. It is the Heel Stone that seems to fit best with the station stones. Like them it is surrounded by a ditch. This all seems to point tentatively to their having been set up at much the same time, and after B and 97.

This is not to retract the claim that the Heel and the sarsens were closely related, but to emphasize that geometrical relations could have been established after the main monument was erected, given ingenuity enough. How deceptive geometrical symmetries can be may be illustrated by another example. To a close approximation—but one that of course depends on the precise points selected on them—the Heel Stone is one Aubrey-circle diameter distant from the grand trilithon. It is admittedly hard to see any significance in this, unless it is in the following approximate truth: whatever was seen from the Heel Stone, by someone looking in the direction of midwinter sunset over an artificial horizon set by a lintelled post-structure at the nearer part of the Aubrey circle, would have corresponded to what was seen over the far side of the circle by someone standing by the grand trilithon and looking in the same direction.

If we knew nothing of stone 97, we might be tempted to make much of all this. Have we perhaps selected the wrong stone? It is as well that those with an axe to grind use other surveys than their own. The circle diameter (following A. Thom) is 86.44 m. The distance from the midpoint (viewing edge) of the Heel Stone at ground level to the inside face of stone 56 (following E. H. Stone's survey) is 86.49 m—in other words, it differs from the first by less than six parts in ten thousand. But taking the back face adds another 0.94 m, and then we have an almost perfect fit with the centre of stone 97, which we have already had reason to suspect preceded the Heel Stone.

One way or another, this seems deliberate. A circle like the Aubrey circle does not carry its diameter imprinted on it. If the agreement is more than mere coincidence, can it be that there was a permanent marker of some sort at the Aubrey centre? That would at least explain how it comes about that so many lines of sight, ostensibly set up over a very long period of time, pass so near to that centre. On the other hand, no marker peg is needed to store information of the kind extracted here, such as that one stone is placed by a 1 in 10 gradient, another by a gradient of 1 in 20, a third by 3 in 32, and so forth. With that information, the sarsens and trilithons themselves are all the markers that were needed.

Such geometrical properties as the construction relating an external observer, a circle, a ring, and a stations rectangle, represent the achievements of people

constrained primarily by astronomical events, that is, by directions towards what appeared over the horizon. They were able to draw their diagrams on the terrain, but over the nature of the terrain they had little control, except in the matter of choosing it. Careful choice was of the first importance, for quite apart from geographical latitude, the third dimension of the figures described on the landscape had an important bearing on their very size. How this was so will be explained. As for latitude, it was this that created the near right angle between lunar and solar rays, something of which there had been an awareness for many centuries in this broad region, when the Stonehenge site was first chosen. They knew how the horizon affects such angles, and they had learned how to trim the azimuths by creating new horizon altitudes. In short, they were deeply aware of the importance of levels. We now know how observers at stone 97 and at the Heel stood with eye on the level of the Stonehenge Datum, which for the sake of discussion can be spoken of as the level of the centre of the monument. The distance from the Heel (or any earlier equivalent observation points) to the centre of the basic geometrical diagram (that of Fig. 192) was therefore determined by the gradient of the terrain in that direction, the direction of the midwinter setting Sun, through the height of the observer's eye. This is only one of many geometrical properties in the vertical plane that have here been unearthed.

(Only a small adjustment would have been likely here, by tampering with ground levels, although there is a sense in which the fundamental plane, the Stonehenge Datum, could have been defined irrespective of true ground level at the centre.)

Other distances would then have followed from this automatically. From the basic centre, a perpendicular to the Moon-line would have fixed the radius of the central ring of stones or posts it was to graze. From this point on, the argument could take different directions. One might suppose a stations rectangle to have followed—fully determined in size and direction by the central ring and Sun and Moon directions, if it was to have a 45° angle between diagonals. If the outer circle, say the Aubrey circle, was already in place—determined, perhaps, by some previous construction of a similar sort—then the new stations rectangle would not have fitted it perfectly. This sort of compromise is very probably true to Stonehenge history. Geometrical ideals are being constrained, in other words, by the heavens, by the terrain, and by previous artefacts and traditions. The art of finding compromise solutions under these circumstances was not pure geometry—it was a very much more difficult art, but one that was brought to a high degree of perfection, none the less.

In summary, the tentative conclusions that follow are that while stone 97 and perhaps the Heel could have had earlier functions (with the trilithons, for instance), yet the stations and the sarsen ring were designed to fit with one or the other; that the Aubrey circle had its own station posts and inner ring at an earlier date, and was perhaps intended to function with the outer ring of the *Q-R* system in the same way. The planned ring in question was to be taken in conjunction with what stood in hole *B*, although *B* could easily have been found a use at the sarsen stage. (We have no idea about the respect in which these outliers were held, but their function makes it likely that they were highly respected, and so might have been allowed to help determine such things as sarsen heights.) Earlier still there was a timber circle, perhaps related in the same way with what stood in hole *C*. In those earlier phases, the design would have been much the same as later designs. One might be inclined to add that the dimensions of the earlier structures must have been less perfectly adapted to the terrain than those of the Heel-sarsen phase, remaining to our day, but this is an unsafe conclusion. Nothing is known about any earlier monument level, that is, the 'Stonehenge Datum' of the time. Getting the right levels was an art in which the Neolithic people had been well versed since the time of the long barrows. It is probably not too fanciful to say that successive adjustments to monument levels are among the most significant of all pieces of information lost to Stonehenge history.

Finally, it is worth reiterating just how extraordinarily important was the terrain in determining the dimensions of Stonehenge as a whole. The scale of the sarsen ring, for example, and many of the harmonies of scale of the monument in its most magnificent phase, were in large part decided by the site, in the way explained. Complex astronomical reasons meant that some adjustment was necessary—the sarsens had to be pushed back a little from the central position, for instance—but the basic dimensions of the circles belonged to the *site*, in the loose sense indicated. They were related to it through the height of the conventional human eye. To have found a site that allowed in this way for multiples of 10, 5, and 2½ MY was surely more than an accident. In a sense, these measures occurred naturally, as a property of human anatomy; but only after a long search would such a 'natural' site have been found. Stonehenge is to be added to a list of sites outstanding for its contours, a list that includes, for example, Durrington Walls, Wilmington, and the Uffington White Horse. Stonehenge and Durrington had more subtle metrical properties than those evident at the sites of the chalk figures, and what stood there was, even in that respect, higher on an intellectual scale.

A Chronological Summary

It has now been shown how successive phases of Stonehenge could have been used, mainly in relation to the Sun and Moon. While a few of the conclusions reached have a bearing on the relative age of various structures on the site, they introduce little new evidence as to date, in fact much less than did the analysis of star alignments from other sites. Pulling together the chronological evidence, however, the sequence presented long ago by Richard Atkinson seems to need some rearrangement. The revised radiocarbon dates from the second edition of his book *Stonehenge* (1979) have since been again revised slightly, and more specimens have been dated. His suggested division into periods is consequently in need of modification, but since it has become a standard of reference—heavily overladen with subdivisions by his successors—it may be taken as a starting point.

Atkinson's *Period I* took in the construction of the bank, ditch and Aubrey holes, and also the erection of the Heel Stone, stones *D* and *E*, the timber structure at *A* and even the inception and use of the cremation cemetery in the Aubrey holes and the station stones, assumed to be at the end of the period. This is an exceedingly long period, of the order of a thousand years: three antler pieces from the enclosure ditch are now dated at 3180 ± 155 BC, 3160 ± 155 BC, and 2790 ± 220 BC, while the cremation in Aubrey hole 32 is put at 2325 ± 395 BC. (These corrected figures are from M. W. Pitts' work of 1982.) It seems advisable to subdivide this period, and to get rid of the idea that the cremation is of much significance for the use of the site as a whole. The station stones too should be moved to a later date, together with the sarsen ring—to which they are intimately related. What remains of Atkinson's Period 1 might be taken to cover roughly the very end of the fourth millennium and perhaps three or four centuries of the third.

No definite argument for refusing to have the Heel Stone in this period has been found, apart from the fact that it seems to duplicate the function of stone 97 and add others of its own. One might claim that the Heel Stone had a vital function in combination with some or other central monument. It could have been associated with a timber monument—for example, with a timber ring near to the later sarsens ring, through the geometrical construction offered in the previous section—although the mixture of materials might make this seem unlikely. But whatever claims of this kind are admitted should surely be transferred to stone 97. On the whole, it seems wise to remove the Heel Stone from the earliest period.

Stones *D* and *E* should probably be removed from Period I, for reasons explained. Of what is left, the ditch, Aubrey holes and timber monument at

the centre of the area very probably functioned together, possibly with some stellar alignments but certainly with solar purposes too, and the phenomena of chief concern were the southernmost setting of the Sun, that is, at the winter solstice, and the southernmost setting of the Moon.

The placing of stone 97 very probably followed what amounted to a previously established tradition of lunar and solar observation, whatever the function of the causeway post holes and their relationship to the old timber structure, but whether this should be counted as part of the old order or as part of the new cannot be firmly settled. (An alternative interpretation of the causeway holes might be that they were to set the construction lines of later stone structures; but their spacing does not easily fit with the idea.)

Atkinson's *Period II* begins with the widening of the entrance causeway and transfer of stones in holes *D* and *E* to holes *B* and *C*. The movement of those stones has already been rejected here. *C* has here been found a potential use at the earlier timber stage, and *B* possibly at the later stage of erecting the *Q-R* system and certainly in the sarsen phase. This Period II, Atkinson said, included the digging and filling of the Heel Stone ditch, the construction of the first part of the Avenue, and the erection of the unfinished double circle of bluestones in the *Q*- and *R*-holes. Like Period I, this includes many different types of activity, and the time range is again a long one, at least three or four centuries. Again the Heel Stone presents problems of relative dating. Antler from the Heel Stone ditch yielded dates reducing to 2200±155 BC, which is later than many dates assignable to events in Atkinson's Period III. Putting the problem aside yet again, we can at least be sure that the *Q-R* system is correctly placed soon after the timber period. We have already given a tentative argument for putting the trilithons somewhat before the sarsen ring; and one of the sarsen stone holes cut through the hole of one of the *Q*-stones.

Atkinson's *Period IIIa* ('2000 BC') takes in the transport of the sarsens from near Marlborough, the dismantling of the double bluestone circle (*Q-R*) and the erection of trilithons, sarsen circle, Slaughter Stone and companion. It has been suggested here that the station stones belong to the sarsen ring, and probably to the same period. (They could always have been added later, of course, but still would be intrinsically bound up with the sarsens.) As for the Slaughter Stone, it was linked geometrically with the trilithons and the Altar Stone, and that it had a partner in the sense of a stone of comparable stature is much to be doubted. The Slaughter Stone and Altar Stone should be moved into the earlier (trilithon) part of this period, very probably with stone 97, and even the Heel Stone, which is in a position so intimately bound up with the trilithons. The later date of the antler in the ditch around the Heel Stone can

be explained in terms of the late addition of a ditch to a pre-existing stone. This would fit very well with the idea of the discovery of a third alignment using the Heel Stone. The discovery of a second, the lunar alignment, would have been cause enough for the earlier move from 97.

Atkinson's *Period IIIb* begins with the tooling and erection of stones of the dressed bluestone setting, and ends with the digging and abandonment of the Y- and Z-holes. Antler from Y- hole 30 is now dated at 1535 ± 130 BC. His *Period IIIc* is that of the dismantling of the dressed bluestones and their re-erection in their present circle and horseshoe. This he set at $1550-1100$ BC, the second date coming only from an estimate of the time of the extension of the Avenue from Stonehenge Bottom to West Amesbury. This occurred in his *Period IV*, for which there are two dates: 1315 ± 245 BC (antler from the ditch at West Amesbury) and 1000 ± 125 BC (antler and bone, Amesbury terminal).

It is all too easy to become sidetracked by radiocarbon dates when attempting a final periodization. They are essential, of course, but those currently available refuse to hang together well when calibrated, as we have been doing, with relatively narrow calendar time ranges and lower confidence levels, rather than say with time ranges of four or five centuries and high confidence levels (see Appendix 1 for the distinction). To take an example relating to the trilithons: an antler piece found in the erection ramp for the upright 56 of the grand trilithon is dated to 2135 ± 220 BC, following the alternative we have preferred throughout, and yet two other specimens of antler from trilithon stones 53 (or 54) and 57, dated more recently, suggest dates of 2520 ± 60 and 2380 ± 80 BC respectively. There is barely any overlap between two of the dates; two just touch at 2460 BC; and two are well separated, with no overlap. Had we possessed only the first specimen, and had we used only the central date, we should have been nearly four centuries away from the date similarly—and of course naïvely—obtained from the second. One may play endless games with weighted averages, but perhaps 'around the twenty-fourth or twenty-fifth century' is as near as we should come to dating the trilithons. To balance the evidence for absolute dating would require a book in itself, but at least a broad picture that has now emerged can be set down, albeit dogmatically.

The ditch and banks were dug perhaps a little before or a little after the turn of the millennium, 3000 BC. The Aubrey holes were more or less contemporaneous, and were from the first meant to hold posts. Central timber structures followed, perhaps soon after. Stone C was of potential use with them. This pre-stone phase probably takes us up to a century or so on either side of 2600 BC. It might or might not have included the timbers at the northeast. If

not, then they were used for setting up the stones, perhaps those of the Q-R system.

The Q-R system displaced the central timber rings. (A late date from antler out of one of the R- holes is irrelevant.) They were used with stone B and might have been in use for a century or so. They were eminently usable, even though the rings were not full circles. Dissatisfaction with them was no doubt what led to their early rearrangement, but in the meantime work on the next phase was beginning.

The trilithons (with stone E and stone 97, and only later the Heel Stone) followed, say within a century of 2500 BC. The placing of 97 and the Heel Stone (which are surely the same stone in different manifestations) related the level of the observer's eye to the centre of the timber circles, but the precision with which the stone(s) in the two places fit with the trilithons makes it unsafe to insist on moving it/them into an earlier period. The possibility certainly cannot be ruled out, since there might have been older timber equivalents to the trilithons and the sarsens, and in more or less the same place, so that all signs of them were obliterated. It is this possibility that makes it unwise to judge the age of the outlying stones on the basis of their geometrical relationships with the central stones.

The sarsens came very shortly after the trilithons, all probably having been planned together—but again not necessarily so. The station stones belonged with the sarsens, and are not likely to have been added long afterwards. The Heel Stone perhaps acquired its ditch at the same time, since two stations seem to have such similar ditches to the Heel's. The Avenue in more or less its presently detectible form might have overlapped all of these activities in time. The widening of the entrance causeway by filling in the eastern end of the ditch might have predated the Avenue, however, in view of what has been said about the two possible functions of the posts at the northeast entrance (that is, their use with the timber henge or for planning the stone henges). This, the period of most intense activity at Stonehenge, was probably over by the twenty-third century.

The bluestone circle followed fairly shortly afterwards, and the bluestone horseshoe a century or two after that, but still inside the third millennium. The poor relations of Stonehenge, the Z- holes and the Y- holes, came last, being a century or two on either side of 1900 and 1700 BC respectively.

The widespread adoption of Atkinson's periodization has been due to the fact that his has been—with good reason—the most influential work of the twentieth century on Stonehenge, but his chronological scheme is not one that

will lend itself to endless adaptation, and the time is surely ripe to drop his I–II–III division. A division into periods is in any case only of interest to the extent that it groups together activities that were planned in unison or shared in a conscious tradition. In deciding what this is, we are most liable to be confused by elements that continued in use through more than one period, that is, in conjunction with more than one central monument. In this respect, the most problematical item of all is stone 97, the role of which we believe was taken over by the Heel Stone. That mournful lump of stone symbolizes in so many ways the glory of Stonehenge.

LOZENGE AND CALENDAR

The Lozenge Motif

THE diamond-shape or lozenge is a symbol commonly found, from Ireland to Persia and beyond. It occurs naturally in latticework, such as basketwork, or crisscross floor and wall decoration, and for this reason much caution is needed in interpreting it, and in deciding whether individual cases were self-consciously symbolic, or even self-consciously lozenge-shaped. Is the trelliswork motif on Irish monuments—for instance at Newgrange—to be seen as a set of lozenges, or does it occur by an accident of geometry? What was in the mind of the person responsible? Simple lozenges are common on pottery from an early period. In the oldest Balkan forms (from the seventh to the fifth millennium) there are lozenge-shapes with what are plainly human associations, for they are very often found on the female form, frequently on the belly, and thus suggesting a fertility symbol. The lozenge occasionally alternates with spirals or zigzags, seen by some interpreters as phallic snakes, shells, or water. A piece of bone (a horse mandible) found in Kendrick's Cave, Llandudno, and dating from about 8000 BC, was covered with a zigzag decoration. Clay plaques of around 5000 BC from eastern Serbia mix nested lozenges with spirals—the two supreme geometrical Neolithic symbols. (One example is drawn in Fig. 194.) One could multiply occurrences almost endlessly, but to what purpose? Just as today many different meanings are regularly read into the shape, it might be that, in the past too, the lozenge was many things to many people. In some of its contexts it seems to have had a connection with the Sun or Moon, but even if some of its meanings were in a broad sense astronomical, others were certainly not, and the earliest were almost certainly not.

The genesis of even the simplest of symbols is often complicated. Suppose, for example, that a religious architect were to have marked out two parallel lines towards the rising midwinter Sun and then to draw across them two parallel lines (with the same spacing) towards the setting midwinter Sun. A

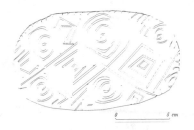

0   5 cm

FIG. 194. Clay plaque with characteristic spirals and lozenges, from an
early fifth-millennium settlement at
Vrsač, Serbia. This is well over a thousand years older than the Newgrange
example of Fig. 195, in which precisely
the same motifs are associated.

lozenge-shape would result, its angles depending on geographical latitude and local horizon. With the Moon, another lozenge would be produced, of a different
shape. Suppose now that from an earlier
time there was a certain cluster of ideas in
which the lozenge already had some sort
of symbolic role—an evolving cluster,
perhaps, but quite possibly one that first
had sexual meaning. If cosmic religions
were giving rise to experiment with
alignments towards the risings and settings of the stars, Sun, and Moon, then the
new 'astronomical' symbol might very
easily have been made to relate to that
older cluster of ideas. Such an association
might have served to reinforce old associations, and so take on a life of its own.

Earlier occurrences of the symbol need not have been overtly astronomical,
and even if the context was later transformed into a symbolism of alignments,
an ordinary person, asked about symbolic meanings, might well have answered
in terms of the older symbolism—the Moon, fertility, or whatever it happened
to be.

Just possibly hinting at a 'lozenge of alignments' are the strings of lozenges

on the edging of lintel stones in the
chambered tomb at Newgrange in
Ireland, dating from the fourth
millennium. It is true that cutting
across the edge of a slab of stone,
crisscross patterns emerge very
naturally. (The system of Roman
numerals is sometimes said to have
occurred in this way.) However, it
seems probable that the *placing* of
the relevant Newgrange stones was
significant. There is one with what
could be described as a string of
butterflies (|X|X|X|) at the en-
trance and over the roof box, at the
southeast—towards midwinter

FIG. 195. Spiral and lozenge ornament on
one of the Newgrange kerbstones. The stone
is almost diametrically opposite the long entrance corridor, and about 28° west of north
from the mound's centre.

sunrise. There is another (<><><><>) on the lintel at the other end of the same passage, but now as viewed from inside the chamber. Two single lozenges are placed symmetrically, one above and one below a pair of complementary (S-form) spirals. There are also two strings of them on corbels in the northeast and southwest recesses of the central chamber. One of the best of the ornamented kerbstones has a lozenge pattern below a spiral motif (See Fig. 195), and there are yet more examples of both, elsewhere at this remarkable tomb. Since Newgrange has given evidence of precise astronomical orientations, these associations are not hard to countenance. But they are not proven.

It is possible that the link was not an immediately astronomical one, but funereal. The lozenge became a common decorative device, and was often found in a repeating pattern around vases. In the European Bronze Age, for instance on bell beakers, these seem very often to have had funereal associations. The later the period, the more frequent the motif seems to become. In Greece, especially after a resurgence of grave cults in the eighth century BC, the shape seems to have been placed on most grave ceramics; but it had been used without break in the preceding centuries. It appears in isolation on tombstones. Gold leaf in the form of an eyed or bordered lozenge was often placed in the mouths of the dead: perhaps it was this custom that led to the tradition of placing a coin in the mouth ('Charon's obol') as payment to the ferryman.

Without wishing to claim that there was any direct link with northern Europe, one ought not to overlook the many Middle Eastern seal cylinders that show the lozenge in various forms. The lozenges are never held or touched by human figures portrayed on the seals in such a way as to make them seem to be material objects. They are never superimposed on anything else. They occur in all periods from at least 3000 BC onwards, and in all the main cultural centres of western Asia. Their orientation on the seal seems to be unimportant, and merely a matter of available space. Out of a random sample of thirty-three seal impressions with the lozenge on them, I find that only seven fail to show the Moon or a cross, and four of those seven include a bull, which one might be inclined to consider as the Moon's proxy. There is not a single case without some sort of clear celestial indication. In every case but one (and that has the cross for the Moon), there is at least one figure indicating a constellation, and usually there are several.

The fine detail in all this is not important: what matters is that in the Middle East the lozenges go with constellations but are not themselves constellations. They might therefore represent either the Sun or the Moon, or one of the planets, or a property of any of these, such as a phase of the Moon or an extreme of rising or setting. There is reason for thinking that at least in

Britain too the lozenge shape had a celestial meaning, and in fact became associated with specific astronomical alignments. There is some evidence for this idea deriving from a barrow near to Stonehenge.

Bush Barrow

Bush Barrow is in the so-called Normanton cemetery, a group of Early Bronze Age barrows near Stonehenge. This is the perhaps the finest group in the country, and it is one that has yielded some of the richest finds from the period. Its two dozen or so members lie in a line roughly northwest to southeast across Normanton Down, about a kilometre south of the great monument. Bush Barrow (Wilsford G5) is one of the most conspicuous of the group, an exceptionally large bowl barrow, nearly 49 m across. It was drawn by William Stukeley, who gave it its name and waxed lyrical about the sweet-smelling flowers on it. The country people, he said, called it 'the green barrow'. His illustration of a 'Prospect from Bushbarrow' (1776) shows Stonehenge in the distance. He dug the barrow but found nothing, and it was left to William Cunnington to locate its extraordinary contents in September 1808. With his friend Sir Richard Colt Hoare he too had earlier failed to find anything.

Cunnington's labourers, digging in from the top, discovered the skeleton of a tall, well-built man, by whose hand was a much-corroded bronze dagger. Two more fine daggers were there, one of copper, one of bronze. The hilt of one of them had formerly been inlaid with hundreds of very tiny gold pins in a zigzag pattern—this being one of several cultural links with comparable burials in Brittany. The hilt was shattered in the act of excavation, and the pins dispersed before they were properly appreciated and examined. There was a mace-head of a fossil-laden stone from Devon, that had been on a wooden rod, seemingly decorated with zigzag rings of bone that were found nearby; a flat bronze axe on which were traces of a textile, perhaps the clothing of the deceased; and a leather plate of some sort, perhaps headwear. There was also a bronze spearhead. The most impressive of all their finds, however, were three pieces of goldwork of the finest workmanship.

One of these was a lozenge-shaped plate, incised with an intricate pattern of straight lines. This, about the size of a hand (18 cm in length), was found on the breastbone, as though it had been placed on—even worn on—the chest of the buried man. It had been fixed to a thin piece of wood. There was also a tiny lozenge with a more basic incised pattern. The third item of gold is usually described as a belt hook: it lay by the man's right arm. These spectacular finds were first housed in the so-called 'Moss House' in Cunnington's garden; later

they were added to Colt Hoare's collection at Stourhead; and from there they were moved to the Museum of the Wiltshire Archaeological and Natural History Society at Devizes, to be finally bought for the museum in 1883. In 1922 the Society, concerned with security, placed the Bush Barrow goldwork on indefinite loan at the British Museum, and put electrotype facsimiles on exhibition at Devizes. In 1985, in preparation for an Edinburgh loan exhibition, the large lozenge was cleaned and irreversibly modified in shape. Colin Shell and Paul Robinson have shown that the resulting domed profile cannot possibly have been its original shape. This, and other gold pieces from Devizes, are now back in the museum there.

The high status of the interred man was indicated not only by the richness of the burial but by the unusual construction of the barrow itself, which was based on blocks of chalk. It was presumably originally left as a smooth white dome, and must have taken on a splendid appearance when seen on the horizon from Stonehenge. The barrow dates from within a century or so of 1900 BC, that is, at the end of the most significant period of activity at Stonehenge. That the man, prince or priest, had some connection with the monument, which was still being actively transformed, is highly probable, considering the splendour of his burial. The lozenge-shaped plate might support the idea that this was so.

The Bush Barrow Lozenge Was Not a Calendar

The precise form of the lozenge is important to the tentative argument to follow, which is that the object might have symbolized Stonehenge, or the sort of astronomical activity that took place there. It carries a geometrical figure, far more intricate than is apparent at first sight (see Plate 12). It was meant to be flat, and ruled with lines that were straight. Those who doubt its sophistication should try to reproduce it, with pen and ruler, from first principles. Those principles must of course first be detected. One plausible construction will be given in the following section, but first certain previous analyses will need to be considered and rejected.

The gold is a thin foil, between one and two tenths of a millimetre thick—say between five and ten thicknesses of domestic aluminium foil. It was bedded on a thin layer of beeswax or resin on the lozenge-shaped wooden plate, and wrapped over its edge. If the edges of the gold were never perfectly straight, this would only have been because slightly curved edges were produced when the wooden plate was smoothed. The lines marked on the gold were undoubtedly what really mattered to its maker, and they were originally

as good and straight as an ordinary modern draughtsmen would produce using a ruler and pen. Such lines as these would have been easily marked, without undue pressure, using a pointed tool, probably of bone or antler.

In recent years there have been at least two alternative explanations of the incised pattern, one numerological, the other calendrical. In 1979 Keith Critchlow measured the lesser angle and decided that it was within half a degree of 80°, from which he deduced that it pointed to a mystical use of number symbolism, in this case indicating the number *nine* (since 80° is two-ninths of a circle). The smaller Bush Barrow lozenge has a lesser angle, but it was close enough to 60° for Critchlow to claim that here the number *six* was indicated. (The latter is such a small object that it seems unfair to make it carry such a heavy burden of proof.) Now there is a very fine gold lozenge from another rich 'princely' English barrow, comparable in size with the slightly larger example from Bush Barrow. This, the Clandon (Dorset) Barrow lozenge, is now in the Dorset County Museum. Critchlow decided that it contains an angle of 102.75°, or nearly two-*sevenths* of a circle (102.86°). There was a certain sleight of hand involved in switching from the smaller angle in the lozenge in one case to the larger in the others, simply in order to get *two*-sevenths, *two*-sixths, and *two*-ninths; and no indication was given as to how these highly sophisticated geometrical constructions were actually performed. In the unlikely event that they were, then the ingenuity of Archimedes was forestalled. The angles are in any case very difficult to establish in the case of the Clandon Barrow lozenge, which has been badly crumpled in the course of its long history.

An interpretation of the Bush Barrow plate of a completely different sort was offered by A. S. Thom, J. M. D. Ker (posthumously), and T. R. Burrows, in a paper published in *Antiquity* in 1988. I had mentioned to John Ker in 1977 that the sharp angle of the lozenge is very close indeed to the amplitude of the Sun's horizon position at Stonehenge latitude. Whether this is meaningful is a difficult question to answer. The three authors finally went much further, however, and decided that the object was 'carefully fashioned for use at Stonehenge by an engineer-surveyor-astronomer-priest, as an *aide mémoire* for a calendar'. Fragments of wood that the excavators had thought were remains of a shield were now described as the remains of an alidade (a sighting rule) and wooden drawing board or plane table. In some passages they seem to suggest that the object was merely a repository for angular data, but in other places that it was actually used for solar and lunar sightings, with the alidade (an arm supposedly fitted with mica or smoked-glass vanes for solar use) laid through certain points (such as as *P* and *Q* of Fig. 196 of the next section).

Various points of the zigzag are then supposed to have served as indicators of the rising and setting positions of the Sun at appropriate seasons.

This seems intrinsically unlikely, for two sorts of reason, mechanical and cultural. There is no sign of pivoting, or of abrasion that would have ensued had an alidade been moved over the plate regularly. (The tiny holes in the sharp angles of the outer lozenge are highly unlikely pivots, for they are small, unused, and not well placed.)

As for the calendar idea, it extended the ideas of the late Alexander Thom on the use of a 16-'month' calendar in Britain in the early second millennium. This required that there were alignments directed not only towards lunar and solsticial events, but towards those other places on the horizon where the Sun rises and sets. The days of the two solstices and those of the two equinoxes divide the year into four parts. The year will be divided into eight parts if one adds to them four other days, halfway through the seasons: these correspond more or less to traditional May Day (Beltane), Lammas, Martinmas, and Candlemas. If the eight days of year-division were truly indicated by any megalithic monument, then one might choose to argue for its use as an outline calendar.

It does not seem to be widely known, but there was an Old Norse and Icelandic method of dividing the horizon into eight sectors and relating the time of year to the place of sunset. The tradition even survived into our own century, but it was codified as long ago as the twelfth century, when Stjornu-Oddi drew up tables to make the farmers' method more exact. Another Scandinavian custom of halving, that long survived in Iceland, was related to a calendar fixed by the solstices. The year was divided into two halves, called *misseri*, and the people reckoned not in years, but in half-years. From the beginning of summer to midsummer they counted weeks of summer passed; they next counted weeks of summer still to come; and then similarly for winter. Martin P. Nilsson, an authority on such matters, thought that this was pre-Christian in origin. It was certainly crude by comparison with the system Alexander Thom believed to have operated in the Bronze Age. He thought that even a sixteen-part year was indicated by the alignments he had collected. His arguments here, as in the simple solstitial cases, were based on statistical counts (histograms) of those alignments he thought independently obvious—such as might have been suggested by a large menhir and a very conspicuous mountain peak in its neighbourhood. He thought he could derive a calendar that broke up the year into eleven intervals of 23 days, four of 22 days, and one of 24 days; or alternatively, into thirty-two divisions of 11 or 12 days.

The eightfold division, at least, seems not implausible; and for the sake of argument we might admit sixteen divisions. The idea put forward by Archie Thom and collaborators in connection with the Bush Barrow lozenge did little justice to it, however. Their reconstruction did not allow for the incorporation of all of these 'months'—3, 5, 11, and 13 were missing from the scheme, and in four cases half-months had to be introduced. Despite this fact, they drew conclusions about the maker's having used an intercalary day similar to our 29 February. It is a modern prejudice to suppose that those who divided the year into parts—say into sixteen—necessarily related those parts to counts of days. The idea might not be wrong, but it is not something that should be taken for granted, especially when such a subtle claim is to be made dependent on it.

It is worth drawing a parallel here with a Middle Eastern culture that has much to do with the distant ancestry of our present calendars. The priests of the lawgiver Hammurabi early in the second millennium not only unified the gods of the old city-states into one great pantheon, they also established an ingenious calendar based on the joint movements of the Sun and Moon. For this they very probably used 'directional' observations, but the exactness they needed to establish a calendar, in the long run, was an exactness in counting and in working out schemes for cycles of day-numbers. Beyond that they needed only one or two good solstice observations, so as to know from what day the count was to be made. This made the type of 'monumental astronomy' associated with earlier (and also later) northern peoples more or less superfluous. In summary, astronomy as a part of human and religious experience was at first a qualitative subject; it became codified in stone and in a series of rules; but it did not progress rapidly until it went further and derived arithmetical rules, for which a script was highly desirable although not absolutely necessary. The literate cultures of the Middle East and Mediterranean region won out in the end because of the inordinate advantages of writing over chiselling.

Finally, if the calendar-solution thus seems to be contrived, the extraction of lunar lines from the Bush Barrow lozenge by the three joint authors was even more so. No line was as accurate as should have been expected had the figure been originally drawn, as claimed, to an accuracy of better than a tenth of a degree: the errors in azimuth, on the lunar assumption, were of the order of magnitude of the Moon's diameter, five times as great. To obtain the lunar azimuths, lines joining various other vertices were held to be significant—but they were lines provided only by the modern interpreters, and are not to be found on the plate at all. If such a procedure is to be allowed, the number of possible permutations is enormous.

The Lozenge as Geometrical Construct

At first sight the Bush Barrow lozenge is symmetrical, but it is sufficiently well drawn for us to take a slight asymmetry seriously. According to measurements made by T. R. Burrows on the rhombus along the inside of the zigzag , one angle is markedly less than the other (80.25° as against 80.89°), while the vertices would have defined diagonals (not drawn on the plate) at right angles to within about a hundredth of a degree. The diagonals of any perfect rhombus (a parallelogram with equal sides) will of course be perpendicular, but the same is also true of the kite-shaped figure that this was perhaps meant to be. For the time being it will be assumed that the shape was meant to be symmetrical.

In trying to assess the sequence followed when the figure was incised, one must look for lines that could have been drawn independently of others, and for lines that seem to be interdependent (for instance, lines that are in exact ratios). If there are lines of a standard unit of length, there is a good chance that they are independent of others, unless created as proportionals.

The chances of finding a standard unit of length might be thought slight, since Thom, Ker and Burrows looked in vain for Alexander Thom's notorious 'megalithic inch' (one fortieth part of a Megalithic Yard). It is true that they gave numerous measurements equal to five of these units, but they were chosen between such odd points that they could not conceivably have been used for the construction.

There are, however, distinct traces of submultiples of 1 MY. There are nine compartments to the central rhombus, each itself a rhombus, and each has a side almost exactly one hundredth part of Thom's Megalithic Yard. Furthermore, the shorter sides of the 36 right-angled triangles in the zigzag all approximate even more closely to exactly two such units. There seems to be good reason for believing that either the smaller unit, or its double, was in use in the Stonehenge region in the early second millennium. By analogy with the centimetre, this *hundredth of a Megalithic Yard* will be abbreviated HMY. For consistency with Thom's work it will be supposed equal to 8.29 mm. Just as Thom defined a megalithic rod as 2½ MY—a unit found repeatedly in monument design—so it will be noticed that two and a half of the new unit equal Thom's megalithic inch. The two small units need not be taken as mutually exclusive.

If the dimensions of the triangles in the zigzag were based on some definite unit, then regardless of the order of drawing, at some stage or other the following problem had to be solved: Given a unit of length, construct a rhombus with sides equal to four times the hypotenuse of a right-angled triangle having the shorter sides equal to two units. Expressed in this way the

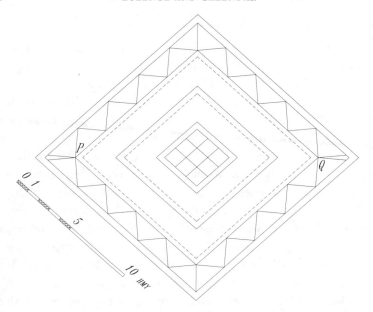

Fig. 196.   Selected lines on the Bush Barrow lozenge. Only those that can be exactly
reconstructed (as a symmetrical figure, as explained in the text) are shown as continuous
lines. The broken lines helping to outline the middle bands are taken from the actual plate.
The lesser angles of the rhombus are here taken as 40.2°.

construction is not a difficult one, but the fact that it was carried through in
a highly accurate way tells us that the constructor was far more than a 'maker
of decorative objects' as usually understood. It was no doubt realized that the
length required was that of the diagonal of a square of side 8 HMY. The truth
of this has nothing to do with the shape of the basic rhombus.

The nine-compartment central rhombus offers no problems, other than
those of accurate work on a small scale. The next problem is that of understanding the four-line banded frames. It seems very probable that the central
frame was added first, of such a width that the resulting figure was exactly one
third of the outer rhombus constructed thus far (the inner edge of the zigzag).
The outermost frame was probably then added to make a figure on four times
the scale of the innermost frame. The *outer* edge of the simple middle frame
was almost exactly mid-way between the *outer* edges of the frames to either side
of it, and can be added to the lines of the exact construction (the unbroken lines
of the figure).

If this reading of the figure is correct, everything mentioned so far is fully
determined. The banding of the two remaining frames can be explained in
different geometrical ways. It is possible that they were simply meant to have

the same width as the innermost. Whatever the method of placing them, the remainder of this remarkable figure must be taken as one of the earliest proofs on a small scale of a deep concern with geometrical proportionality. It offers retrospective support for our claim that the same concern, on a monumental scale, is in evidence from a period much more than a millennium earlier.

Nothing has been said here as to the reason for taking a basic shape with angles close to 80° and 100°. There is no obvious geometrical reason for this, or simple geometrical construction (such as one based on a 'Pythagorean' triangle with integral sides) that would explain it. The explanation offered below is an astronomical one.

Finally, it should be noticed that the construction offered in this section, based as it is on the idea that absolute lengths were used for the zigzag , strictly speaking excludes the possibility of a non-symmetrical kite-shaped figure.

The Lozenge as Symbol

An astronomical reading of the Bush Barrow lozenge is not difficult to find—which is why it is so hard to decide on its truth. Ornament is frequently geometrical. Is it not enough to say that the clever use of triangles here might have been no more than a *jeu d'esprit* ? If so, at least it should be allowed to dispel some of the frequently expressed scepticism about Bronze Age geometrical skills; but the high degree of accuracy in the scheme surely calls for a deeper purpose than that of merely gratifying the eye. In a study by Joan Taylor published in 1980 she suggested that the same craftsman was responsible for both the Clandon and Bush Barrow plates. Their principal angles differ by anything up to three degrees. Such a small angular difference would have been of little consequence for a purely decorative ornament, but the implications for any astronomical explanation might be more serious, if the same explanation is expected to work for both, and the two are from the same workshop. The Clandon plate is badly buckled, but damage apart, there is at first sight nothing on it resembling the accurate geometrical constructions of the Bush Barrow plate. When the inside measurement of the innermost 'frame' is taken, however, it turns out to be 4 HMY, strongly suggesting that the two do indeed have something in common, if only a unit of length.

On the assumption that the purpose of the best incised lozenge-shaped plates was to represent in some way key directions to the extremes of sunrise (or sunset), what can be said about their angles? Do they not depend on the altitude of view, as well as on geographical place? It is a surprising fact that if a constant horizon altitude is assumed all round, then the value of that altitude

makes relatively little difference to the amplitude of swing as between extremes of rising and setting. At Stonehenge, for instance, around 1900 BC, the amplitudes for the solar extremes remain within a tenth of a degree of 80.6° for any altitude below 2°. Even with an artificial horizon of altitude 3.2°, the amplitude is only 81°. (The relevant natural horizon is for all of the relevant arcs below 0.5°.) Similarly for the Moon, the amplitude varies little with altitude, assumed constant all round.

From photographs, the two (acute) angles on the Clandon plate average at about 75° and 79°, in place of the reported 80.25° and 80.89° for the two Bush Barrow angles. The obtuse angles are also unsymmetrical, say 102° and 104°. It is not difficult to fit the lesser angles of the Clandon Barrow plate to the Sun's swing over an artificially (or naturally) constant horizon in the latitudes of Normandy and Brittany, around the epoch 1900 BC. Archaeologists have made much of the cultural affinities of these plates with work from Brittany, but it is not necessary to press the point, for there is another clear possibility, namely that the Moon's behaviour is involved. The amplitude of the Moon's horizon positions would have fitted well for southern English latitudes. This raises the whole question of the Moon in relation to the much finer Bush Barrow plate, which provides more reliable evidence.

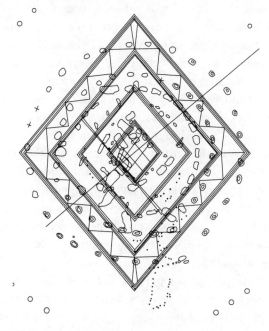

FIG. 197. The Bush Barrow lozenge superimposed in one of numerous possible ways on a plan of the Stonehenge monument. It is not claimed here that this correctly represents the maker's intentions.

Since the main Stonehenge axis is solar, it has so far been assumed here that the plate was meant to lie with its long axis in an east–west direction, or very nearly so, so that the sides then indicated solar extremes. Since at Stonehenge the lunar extremes are more or less at right angles to the solar, it is a simple fact that turning the plate through 90° will make the sides indicate the lunar extremes. In other words, the lozenge could well have had a dual solar and lunar character. There are in fact two possibilities that need to be distinguished, one relating the plate to the Stonehenge monuments, the other relating it to the wider landscape. One of many ways of fitting the lines on the plate to the monuments is shown in Fig. 197. The scheme is included, not because it is thought to represent the

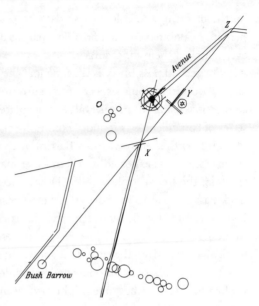

FIG. 198.   The line of sight to the northern extreme of the rising Moon, as seen from Bush Barrow, exactly as it would have been set by the angle of the Bush Barrow lozenge. The line passes over potentially significant points X and Z, the last being the point at which the Avenue turns off eastwards to the river. The line still has far to go before it crosses the natural horizon to the northeast. The lower circles mark the positions of selected barrows of the Normanton Down group.

plate's original purpose, but to satisfy the curiosity of those who want to examine its potential as an overlay to the site, a map of sorts. Scaling one band to fit the sarsen ring, the innermost seems to fall on a lunar line through the trilithons. There are various other points of fit, but it has to be said that there are many possible scalings, and it is hard to see how such questions could ever be decided.

When it comes to assessing the accuracy of the angles embodied in the overall shape of the plate, it seems to fit best with lunar maxima (especially northern). The larger angles in the rhombus fit well with the altitudes set by the Stonehenge terrain, assuming an epoch around 1900 BC. Two of the fundamental sides require altitudes of 0.43° and 0.45° for the date chosen, just about right for the rising Moon at its northern maximum; and the other sides require altitudes of 0.3° and 0.33°, close to the natural horizon at maximum

northern setting. And lest these data be passed over too quickly, it should perhaps be pointed out that no older analysis of the Stonehenge monument has ever matched them for accuracy.

The second possibility is that the lozenge belonged to Bush Barrow itself, and related it to some aspect of its surroundings. In attempting to find a connection, using the precise value of the plate's 'lunar' angle, a very surprising series of coincidences is found. Looking from (or perhaps it was the intention to look *over*) the centre of Bush Barrow at an angle of 49.9° north of east, an angle close to the expected northern lunar maximum for the right period and altitude, the line of sight would (1) have been approximately parallel to the track passing near to the barrow, (2) have passed over the junction (X in Fig. 198) of the road with the track that aligns on the centre of Stonehenge, (3) would have passed through the very northwest corner of the Avenue, where it turns off eastwards to the river. Not shown on the figure is the Greater Cursus, which has an isolated stone on its northern side, and the line would have passed so close to this that the stone might have been meant as a marker for it. There is no suggestion that these various points were visible one from another—the old horizon is now ruined by military buildings and there is nothing to be found now in that area—but it does seem not implausible that Bush Barrow had a lunar significance, and the lozenge too.

When found, the position of the Bush Barrow skeleton was with head to the south (an unusual arrangement) and the lozenge was found with its acute angles north and south, which could be seen as the correct 'lunar' orientation.

How convincing is all this? The argument might be thought to stand at the top of a very slippery slope, for there are other gold lozenges extant, most of them with smaller angles. One, with an angle of 70°, might be claimed for latitude 46° if solar, or latitude 54° if lunar. A dual function is out of the question. And what of the little 60° Bush Barrow lozenge? There is little point in listing others, for there are at least two possible explanations for them that can preserve an astronomical reading. One is that the smaller lozenges were merely tokens, imitating finer and more carefully drafted specimens that were well known for their astronomical purpose. The master copies might even have been drafted on stone. The other saving explanation might be that the lozenge as symbol was much older than any of these plates, and that the Bush Barrow plate was simply embellishing an older symbolism in a highly sophisticated and astronomical way. In this case there is no suggestion that the smaller and simpler lozenges were imitative of their much finer and larger counterparts, but that at least they all shared in an older meaning.

In the dual astronomical explanation offered here, no place has been found for the zigzags round the edge of the Bush Barrow lozenge. If the two-unit lines themselves represent directions—which is not a particularly compelling idea—then they will be about 5.8° to either side of true north, south, east and west, no matter whether the plate is held in 'lunar' or 'solar' orientation. This might lead on to thoughts of star alignments, and of such directions as that of the southern corridor leading to the timber monument (see the lower edge of Fig. 197), or the late extension to the Stonehenge Avenue. Once again, however, there is no way of putting such speculation to the test.

This is not to say that it is wrong. There are many other prehistoric linear symbols—crossed lines, zigzags and rhombs—that very probably point to a cult of alignments. Similarities between the passage-grave 'art' of late Neolithic Britain and the Boyne passage-graves of Ireland have long been appreciated, and the latter certainly have solar alignments built into them. The geometrical designs scratched on the walls of the houses at Skara Brae and on pottery found there, are closely paralleled, for instance, by the kerbstone motifs at Newgrange. The same motifs are also found on some Rinyo–Clacton pottery. They are found on two small and crudely incised square chalk plaques that were found in a pit near Stonehenge Bottom, when the road was being widened in the 1960s. One of those plaques is edged with a three-line zigzag and has similar chevrons as well as lozenges within. The other looks like nothing so much as the plan of a complex building, but it too has some skewed lines, and two lozenge shapes on the reverse.

One of the finest examples of chalk carving from prehistoric times has incised designs that seem to share in whatever tradition it was that the lozenge shape expressed. The Folkton drums, now in the British Museum, are among the most problematical of artefacts. Three carved chalk cylinders, they were found in 1890 by William Greenwell on the site of a small Bell-Beaker round barrow at Folkton, in the East Riding of Yorkshire. They were found not with the main burial but accompanying the skeleton of a child—one at the head and the others at the hips—just inside the outer ditch. The body of the child was laid north–south, with the head to the north, and to someone standing by it, the bearing of the centre of the mound was ten or a dozen degrees north of west. The cylinders measure roughly between 10 and 15 cm in diameter, and between 8 and 12 cm high. Their geometrical marking—to which stylized eyes and nose were

FIG. 199. The domed top of the largest of the Folkton drums. See also Plate 15.

added in the manner of megalithic art—could easily be found a broad interpretation along the lines provided here for the simple lozenges, but like almost all decoration in this style it is not carefully and exactly ruled. The very portability of the drums, not to mention the eyes they bear, make one wonder whether they were originally used as movable markers for an observer's position. Zigzag   decoration is associated with single or double 'eyes' on numerous portable plates and cylinders from Spain and Portugal, many looking as though they too might have been used as portable markers for ritual observing positions. (See Plates 12 and 17.) They were often allocated one to each body, in passage graves, but that they do not belong only there is suggested by the strong resemblance many of them have to the much larger static upright human figures found in the same regions.

The top of the largest Folkton cylinder—like the others it is a domed top—has a series of concentric circles at the centre of a four-pointed star-like figure. This could be interpreted as a symbol of the key directions of solar or lunar extremes in relation to the central barrow (the circles); but once again, since the decoration is so inexact, there is no possible way of confirming this idea.

The same is true of the many other lozenge and chevron shapes found on Neolithic and Bronze Age artefacts. Indeed, a pottery vessel from Folkton has a fine lozenge-creating crisscross of lines over its entire base, and surely nobody would dream of relating this directly to a solar or lunar ritual. The fact remains that like the cross of Christianity or the crescent of Islam, the lozenge and chevron could easily have been taken over from an older symbolism and given a precise meaning, before being eventually repeated again and again without much thought for it.

RITUAL AND BELIEF

Tokens of Religion

ONE of the strongest arguments for the idea that the heavens occupied a central place in Neolithic and Bronze Age religion is the very scale of the architectural enterprises into which astronomical alignments were incorporated. This is not only a question of architectural scale, but of the attention given to geometrical and astronomical detail in the planning. Those responsible for these things must have been highly honoured members of society, if only by virtue of their ability to pronounce on the patterns of return of Sun and Moon to their extreme positions. Once the principle is accepted that key astronomical events could be accurately foreseen in this sense, then it seems probable—by a very broad analogy with almost every early literate culture known—that the events entered into religious explanations. The danger here is that in analysing neat geometrical forms by exact scientific methods there is a strong temptation to 'intellectualize' the associated religious life. To take an example from the Middle East: had nothing more than the highly mathematical astronomy of the Babylonians been available to explain the history of Babylonian astrology, a completely false picture would have emerged, for it is known that astronomical prediction followed there in the wake of prediction based on the inspection of animal livers and other omens. There is very little firm evidence of divinatory techniques from Neolithic Europe, but it would be nonsense to suppose that the highly rational 'astronomical' framework discussed in this book was not blended with other networks of explanation that would now generally pass for superstition.

It can hardly be doubted that the motivation of those responsible for Stonehenge was of an essentially religious character. To explain Stonehenge entirely in terms of religion, however, would be only to escape from astronomical enthusiasm by embracing its religious counterpart. Religions are in large part systems of belief that take account of unseen powers in the universe, powers that can be *understood* up to a point and that might hopefully be *controlled* in

the interests of human individuals. Understanding precedes control—or rather imagined understanding precedes imagined control. Astronomical understanding was important, but it can only have been a part of a larger system. What people of different cultures believed about the fortunes of the dead, for example, was far more basic to human feelings and fears than their beliefs as to the risings and settings of stars, Sun and Moon, however closely related were these different provinces of the mind. Except by attempting to draw parallels with the human psyche in general, it is virtually impossible to decide such questions, although there are a few indicators of what seem to have been significant changes in outlook—as, for instance, the change in burial rite, from inhumation of the body to cremation. (This particular change happened on a large scale in Britain chiefly after our period—say around 1300 BC, with the introduction of urnfield burial.) Religion has its explanations, but in a sense they are on the reverse side of the coin from those of the sciences, and deal with a realm where ordinary cause and effect do not operate. Religion advances by appeals to the emotions—of guilt and terror, for example, rather than reason. If a house repeatedly collapses, the religious reaction is not to re-examine the architectural principles by which it was built but to ask whether an offence has not been committed against the gods, or perhaps against deceased ancestors. By and large, the rules by which the gods are believed to operate will be human rules, the rules of one's ancestors or one's neighbours or one's enemies. When the gods are celestial objects, however, sooner or later it will be found that they are more predictable than are creatures of emotion. And in such ways as this, religion may nourish astronomical science, and in doing so need not lose its ascendancy. The stars have often been judged divine by those who could offer highly mathematical accounts of their behaviour.

Ritual is as close as most archaeologists are prepared to go, in their approach to prehistoric religion. Ritual is the visible action—the setting up of a pillar, the deliberate breaking of a pot, or whatever—as distinct from the belief that gave rise to it. Any stylized, formal, repetitive action may be described as ritual. In general it is judged to be religious only when we ourselves do not deem the ritual likely to produce the required results by empirical and scientific means. (This does not mean that we cannot share the belief.) Even that is a weak definition, for it leaves us with the problem of distinguishing between magic and religion. The two are not difficult to separate, or at least to define differently, especially when the rites can be observed at close quarters. What is crucial is the associated belief. Even the notion of magic is not a simple one. At one extreme, natural magic involves little more than causing human astonishment by means approximating to those of the natural sciences. (The

name 'magic lantern' preserves this meaning.) At the other extreme, spiritual and demonic magic has much in common with the practices of religion. While its practitioners may act outwardly as though they are dealing in natural causes, by invoking the *supernatural* their behaviour is more characteristic of the religious. If an activity involves offerings of goods, or sacrifices, or prayers, or anything of the sort that points to an act of propitiation, an act of buying off supernatural beings in the way one can buy off human beings, then it will generally be described as religious. Sufficient though that kind of behaviour may be to qualify it as religious, it is not a *necessary* part of religious activity. Belief in a supernatural existence, on the other hand, is surely a necessary part of religious belief, whether or not it involves any attempt at propitiation. What exists outside of nature need not be thought to possess a human character, although, historically speaking, the chances are great that it will be assigned human attributes.

To decide on whether a people held to such beliefs we are ultimately dependent on personal testimony. In mute prehistory, it is hard to see how the question can be judged at all, except by drawing shaky analogies with cultures that are reasonably well known. To take an example of such an analogy: a great deal is known from later history about cults of a mother goddess. Any trace in prehistory of a rite of fertility or birth will therefore seem to point, however cryptically, to religious belief. At the base of one of the shafts at Grimes Graves (a flint mine of the Windmill Hill culture) there was found a pedestal of chalk blocks on which was an obese female chalk figurine with a chalk phallus beside it. This is usually accepted as evidence for magic or religious ritual. Those who are convinced that it involved a mother goddess in some way will claim that it crossed the divide between magic and religion. There are relatively few instances of Neolithic finds as suggestive as this, however.

Analogy has often been used to argue for a belief in the possibility of *controlling* supernatural powers. Unusual deposits of animal bones—sometimes described as evidence for a 'bull cult'—and of human bones, occasionally with the removal of parts such as the jaw bone, are often linked with religious belief. So too is the absence of occupation debris on a site, since it seems to suggest respect or awe for the gods. The charring of bones in some of the Cotswold–Severn tombs has been seen as a sign of the lighting of ritual fires. In the Bronze Age and after, there are signs of deliberate ritual deposit of goods in water. Tacit in all of these claims to have found signs of religious ritual is an awareness of the fact that in later cultures there was a religious meaning in comparable activities (rituals of dismemberment, water, fire, and so on).

Votive deposits generally, the careful display of them, and the ritual breakage of deposits, all point in the same direction. (A 'votive deposit' is an offering to the gods made as one takes a vow or expresses a desire or a wish. Here again, in using the phrase archaeologists are tacitly accepting an analogy with practices known from historical times, without the slightest direct evidence from prehistory that vows were taken or wishes expressed. But in view of the human weakness for wishing wells, only the strongest of sceptics will resist this particular analogy.) Signs of human sacrifice also seem to point to propitiation of the gods, especially when it was the sacrifice of children. A sacrificed adult male might have been an enemy or a criminal. Some examples are discussed later in this chapter. The argument from sacrifice to propitiation is almost as difficult as that from henge execution to sacrifice. Much later, for example, the Celts are to be found using sacrifice for quite different purposes, as a means of divination, by observing the death throes of the victim. Perhaps they thought that the victim was beginning to see 'the other side'. At least this seems to point to beliefs of a religious character. The slight evidence for the tying of sacrificial victims to poles at the bottom of deep shafts has also been thought to indicate a belief in gods, in this case of the underworld; but this practice was also a much later development, outside our period.

There are few signs of any astronomical involvement in any of these classic symptoms of early religious activity, but the mere fact of monuments concerned with death having been repeatedly related to the stars, Sun or Moon is surely an indicator of religious belief, if not of belief in the divinities of the heavenly bodies in question. (It is conceivable that the stars were regarded not as gods but as ancestors.) If so, then—ignoring its evolution—such a religion was extraordinarily long-lived, far outstripping in duration the world's leading religions of the present time. But how far is this inference to religious belief justified? Once again, there is a possible approach through what is known from later history, taking the religious associations of a particular artefact known from historical times—preferably with textual support—and trying to trace its lineage as plausibly and continuously as possible, back into prehistory. Two or three variants of the approach will be sketched in what follows. The method calls for numerous caveats, the most important of which will be explained in connection with the first approach, which is linguistic, and traces common elements in Indo-European languages stretching from Asia to the west of Ireland.

The problem in this case is one of historical discontinuity. What are the dates of the great westward migrations that brought the largely male-oriented Indo-European society to Europe and Britain? Putting aside professional

disagreement over its place of origin—was it the Balkan–Carpathian area, or somewhere nearer to Iran?—and even over the very notion of a proto-Indo-European language, expert opinions on the chronology have varied in recent decades to an extraordinary degree, in fact by as much as three millennia. The archaeological material discussed in our earliest chapters, the period of the long barrows, dates from a culture that was agricultural, probably fairly peaceful, and fairly static. Inasmuch as deities were revered that were human in form, judging by sculpted and ceramic remains, they were at that period very probably predominantly female. It has been shown here that the relevant cultures in Britain were greatly concerned with the stars. According to the best modern opinion, the westward-moving Indo-European cultures that overlaid it, and that had certainly arrived in Britain by the second millennium, were probably making inroads into the older Wessex traditions early in the third millennium, or even earlier. Now what is taken to be the religion of the great age of Stonehenge will depend entirely on where the dividing line is placed. What seems highly probable is that the great divide occurred within a century or two of 3000 BC, at much the same time as attention was turning from the stars to the Sun and Moon. If this is so, linguistic sleuthing will be of very dubious value for understanding the long-barrow religion, and even afterwards will have to deal with a complicated medley of what might well have been two very different religious outlooks.

One of the oldest and simplest of the scholarly findings of the linguistic approach still has much to recommend it. It is that the names for the gods were very slow in developing into personal names—Zeus, Jupiter, and so on. The first such names were themselves apparently derived from phenomena, from simple objects or powers—sky, dawn, Sun, Moon, fire, wind, water, and so on. The many European words for god that are related to the Latin *deus*, for example, are said to come from an Indo-European root-form meaning simply 'bright sky'. No doubt these powers developed personalities in the course of time, but they do seem to have remained rather abstract entities in cultures that are known through their literatures, for example the Greek. And lest it be thought that the barbarians to the north were somehow less capable of abstraction, it is as well to remember that Brennus, the Celtic king of the Gauls, laughed at the Greek use of human images of stone and wood at Delphi. That, at least, is what Diodorus Siculus tells us, and he presumably had no Celtic axe to grind.

Sky-religions have proved to be readily accepted by people at many different stages of religious evolution. They can be found grafted on to crude animism, to polytheism, or monotheism. They are perfectly compatible with a belief in earth-divinities, and indeed many early religions have a triple layer

of divinities—the gods above, of, and beneath the earth. Broadly speaking, however, it is the gods of the sky and the celestial regions that have tended to become the supreme deities. Greek writers, for example, long before the great influx of eastern cosmic religions, started unquestioningly with the heavenly bodies—made of fire, which like earth, water and air was an inherently divine element—before moving on to tell of deified men and women. There is a strong element of 'divinity above' even in such highly abstract monotheistic religions as Judaism and Christianity. Prehistoric northern religions were almost certainly not monotheistic, but by at least the time of the long barrows of the fourth millennium, the heavens had very probably already become the most important seat of supernatural power. Again, the reason for this claim is the great scale and complexity of the monuments that were accorded cosmic properties.

Signs of a Priesthood?

Religions have a social dimension that one would imagine ought to be easier to detect than systems of belief. If rituals involving other than celestial divinities—rituals such as sacrifice, the invocation of the gods for assistance, thanksgiving, and so forth—are held to have left their mark, can the astronomical evidence offer nothing comparable? The firmest evidence concerns those places *from which* ritual observations would have been made—in the Neolithic period especially from ditches, at Stonehenge from the Heel Stone, and so forth—and those places *over which* the heavenly body was seen. It has here been shown, for example, that there was a fundamental difference between the kind of observations made across long barrows and those made from the Heel Stone looking across Stonehenge. The latter—primarily of Sun and Moon—could not have been competently made by more that one person at once. The former—chiefly of stars—might have been made by several people simultaneously. Does this imply a trend towards the institution of a specialised priesthood? There is no need to suppose that priestly duties would have been seen as a loss to the community: from a strictly economic point of view the building of Stonehenge was on the debit side of the balance sheet. In any case, there have been specialized 'priestly' duties that could be combined with other occupations in many—perhaps most—early societies. There have been societies with priestly hierarchies, reaching down from the ruler to the humblest water carrier. It is hard to believe that those with expertise in celestial geometry were not held high in general esteem, but that is not to say that they headed a priestly hierarchy, even supposing that there was ever any such thing.

As another inference relating to potential ritual: several situations have here been described that would have lent themselves to an astronomically meaningful *procession* of people. Since observation from the terminal points of such a procession are enough to explain away the main alignments involved, the idea of a procession must remain an open question, but on balance the act of procession does seem likely. The idea of leaving individuals scattered statically across downland or moorland, waiting for something to happen, is one without the element of drama that religious ritual prizes so highly.

There are other and more ambitious approaches to the social question of a priesthood. Euan Mackie has argued for a priestly elite as a class of experts, 'a lay aristocracy', responsible for the building of megalithic monuments. The essence of his argument begins from the observation that there were people who did great things, there were people who were richly buried, and there were people who had fine dwellings and for whom fine objects were made. In this last category he notes the superior qualities of Grooved Ware pottery and he sees it as having been a Wessex product meant for the members of his theocracy, its pottery decorated with religious symbols (zigzags, spirals, etc.). He holds that they would have constituted a natural ruling group, and that the archaeological evidence is consistent with its having come from Iberia to Britain. Settling among the recently established Neolithic farmers, he imagines this religious caste to have achieved dominance and to have kept apart in death as in life—the passage graves being their 'temple tombs'.

This spirited string of hypotheses stands up reasonably well to the archaeological evidence, but its weakness is that there are so few tests by which the most interesting parts of it can risk refutation. It stands up only as a not unlikely story. It does not fit well with an earlier period, when multiple burials were in vogue, and when—on our account—observation was potentially democratic, even though burial practice then went together with many sorts of expertise and great enterprise.

The Objects of Worship

The involvement of stars, Sun, or Moon in any ritual does not of itself necessarily imply worship of *them* in any direct and obvious sense. The ways in which selected bright stars were related to the overall design of long barrows strongly suggests a link between the stars and the dead, perhaps the spirits of the dead in some sense. If this is so, then it might have been *the dead* to whom worship was primarily directed, rather than to some celestial god or divine principle.

Bearing in mind the strange pattern of behaviour of the stars as seen over long barrows at West Kennet and elsewhere, it is conceivable that the stars were seen, if not as the souls of the dead themselves, then as genial visitors to the dead, possibly famous ancestors. Perhaps they were thought to carry the soul of the dead upwards. This is of course highly speculative, and does not fit easily with later northern mythologies—although that is no great obstacle, for if there was indeed a great divide between the cultural groups of the star-period and Sun-period as proposed, the idea would have belonged to the remoter side of the divide. If ancestor worship was involved, then the stellified ancestors were probably regarded as very ancient, since some long barrows seem never to have contained burials and still to have been the focus of star worship. The chalk figures, the cursus terminals, as well as the hill enclosures and those 'blind' long barrows, were without any clear connection with the dead. It has been shown in earlier chapters how some of them, at least, might have evolved naturally out of long barrow customs, and for this reason one would expect them to have been related to the world of the dead in some way.

As for the stars, the way in which highly specific stars were selected, and the fact that different stars were chosen in different areas—as between Cranborne Chase and the Stonehenge region, for instance—would be consistent with a regard for the stars as gods, or as totems, or as ancestors. It is of course conceivable that over many centuries they gradually changed their status—say, beginning as ancestors and ending as gods. It is not necessary to suppose that all people were regarded as fated similarly after death; but my guess would be that in this regard the period of the long barrows offered a better chance to common humanity. As it happens there is a virtual absence in many western pre-Christian legends (whether transmitted in pagan or through Christian literatures) of a heaven above us to which souls go after death—with or without the idea of religious retribution meted out in that heaven. But again, the religion of the long barrows is very far removed from what is known of northern religions from literary sources.

Was there any distinction drawn between human body and human spirit? In the absence of texts, the question seems to be unanswerable. Were the stars surrogates for the souls of the dead? It is commonly supposed that as long as burial was of the complete body in a tomb—and the tomb resembled a home, but one that was presumably regarded as everlasting—the next life was considered a continuation of the present life. If a spirit was conceived as existing separately from the body, then it might have been associated with a substitute body, such as a statue, but—so the story goes—one would in such cases expect the afterlife to have been seen as earthbound. It is often suggested that only

when such a belief in a duality of body and soul had truly taken hold could cremation replace inhumation: the destruction of the body by fire would then have been seen as freeing the spirit and sending it to the sky. There are so many exceptions to this simple division that it cannot exclude the idea of 'star-spirits' in the earlier period. Egypt, for example, is a classic case of a tomb-culture in which the body was preserved, and yet it developed many traditions of an afterlife of the spirit in celestial regions.

Beyond the possibility of some sort of belief in star-spirits, there must have been a complex of religious attitudes forever beyond our reach. One might imagine that the notion of death, at least, is simple enough—until one recalls Plutarch's remarks about the idea that a second death follows the first. (After the first, by his account, the virtuous ascend only to the Moon; thereafter they may pass on to a perfectly happy divine life.) It is not suggested that this idea has any direct relevance whatsoever to Neolithic belief, only that if such a theologically complex belief ever occurred, it is hard to see how we could ever be in a position to reconstruct it. The situation would have been little different had we been privileged enough to observe mute astronomical ritual actually taking place.

As with the stars, so with the Sun, it is difficult to decide whether this was itself the object of worship. While Stonehenge can now be seen to have belonged to the period of concern for the Sun and Moon, rather than the 'astral' period, and while the massive monuments on the site were all in some sense 'temples of the Sun and Moon', it is not at all improbable that they were the scene of a religion that knew many other gods. While the Celtic religion must have been very different from that of late Neolithic Wessex in many respects, it is as well to remember that the names of around three hundred Celtic gods are currently accepted by scholars, on the basis of a whole variety of Romano-Celtic inscriptions. This is not to trivialize the Sun and Moon, but how can we know that they were truly primary objects of worship?

Mesopotamian attitudes to the heavens might be invoked, if only as a reminder of the need to keep an open mind on this point. The religious priority of Anu, Enlil, and Ea shows that even where ritual solar and lunar observations were made, this does not necessarily imply that gods of the Sun and Moon had religious priority. Anu, the sky, was seemingly originally given pride of place: his attributes included royalty, and so provided a justification for the idea of kingship at a later date. Enlil, 'Lord Wind', was his son, and in time took over many of Anu's roles in mythology. Ea was typically lord of the underworld ocean. None of the three, in other words, was identifiable with a celestial object.

Even in matters of divination in Mesopotamia, signs in the sky were on a par with signs from animals and plants on earth.

In the Greek world of Homer's poetry the Sun was called on to witness oaths and asked to influence events, but so too were the gods of rivers and winds, of heaven and of earth. Pre-Hellenic Greece provides us with an excellent example of a society that set male and female sky-potencies—namely the Titans and Titanesses—in some sense over each of the Sun, Moon, and planets. Of these Hyperion and his sister Theia were sometimes represented as parents of the Sun; Atlas fathered the Pleiades; Phoebe was sometimes seen as commanding the Moon; Oceanus, son of Earth and Sky, was the river encircling the world out of which stars and planets rose, and into which they set; Tethys was his sister and consort; and so on. Eventually the resulting fourteen were reduced to seven. The Titans, to continue with the example, were king-gods who controlled not only the heavens but also the weather. It is quite possible that before the Sun, Moon, and stars took on their now familiar classical personalities, they had for millennia occupied a spiritual place on a par with other natural phenomena, whether of the rarity of thunder and lightning or of the commonplace nature of rain, running water, stones and trees. This animism has survived, in some societies, into historic times—for example among the natives of North America.

Worship of the heavens may obviously, therefore, be practised without necessarily predominating; but once again, it would seem perverse were we to play down unduly the role of the Sun and Moon at Stonehenge. Of course they might have played second fiddle to water, stones and trees, but it would be wrong to suppose that the patterns of religious evolution of Greece and Mesopotamia are necessarily universal. The colossal Stonehenge monument to the Sun and Moon is after all without known parallel in early Mesopotamia or Greece.

Might it perhaps be a mistake to focus on the Sun as an *individual*? Might it not have been the *light* of the Sun that mattered? We recall that the Sun's light was in some cases made to illuminate chambered tombs through their entrances at certain times in the year—as at Gavr'inis in Brittany and Newgrange in Ireland—or to fall between wooden posts and across the dead in their burial mounds, as at the site of the two long barrows at Giants' Hills, Skendleby, Lincolnshire. For an example from early historical times: Homer's *Odyssey* (ed. T. W. Allen, xv.403–4) describes the island Syros as the place of the turnings of the Sun, and an early commentator explains that there was a cave there by means of which the turnings of the Sun were shown. This is presumably a reference to the sort of thing in evidence at Newgrange and other

chamber tombs, where a particular spot inside the tomb was illuminated by the Sun's rays only at a certain time of year. In fact the word translated here as 'cave' (*spelaion*) could also refer to a grotto, where gods were worshipped. Was the trapping of light above the Altar Stone not evidence for some sort of ritual of illumination at Stonehenge? All things considered, however, it is perhaps rather perverse to try to disengage the Sun as an object from the illumination it provides, and it seems most probable that the latter was seen as significant only because the former was an object of adoration. And of course parallel remarks might be made about the Moon.

The signs left to us of even the 'celestial' gods remain highly ambiguous. It has been shown how the architects of Stonehenge, and of other monuments before and after it, arranged for the rays of the Sun and Moon to fall on their ceremonies in different but determinate ways. There were differences as between rising and setting, and as between the different seasons, and these were reflected in the ways in which the rays were made to cross at certain key places. These differences underline the need to ask whether the Sun and Moon might not have been assigned different identities in their different aspects—rather as Venus has in historical times been spoken of as both the morning star and the evening star.

The point may be illustrated by reference to the Sun-cults of the age of the pyramids in Egypt, cults that were inconsistent in many respects. When eventually the priests of Heliopolis reduced the mixture to some sort of order, they drew a distinction between Khepri, the Sun rising in the morning, and Ra-Atum, the Sun setting in the evening. Something similar was done in the Rgveda of Hindu mythology. The Sun (Surya) was there made an object of worship in its three distinct places—at rising, at culminating (when it reaches its southernmost and highest point in the sky in its daily motion), and at setting. The Sabians of Harran (a Syrian sect probably no older than the ninth century of our era) prayed at those same three times. But whether the Sun had a dual or triple personality in the Neolithic or Bronze Age is, and seems likely to remain, a question beyond hope of a solution. Archaeology provides numerous instances of alignment on extremes of rising and of setting, but not on those events as they occur every day, and it is hard to see how it could.

A tripartite personality seems rather unlikely, in the absence of a clear line in the meridian. In any case, how would one decide whether an alignment on the southernmost point of the horizon indicated a meridian sighting of the Sun, the Moon or a star? That this cannot be easily decided is evident from Greek practices in historical times. Greek priests are said to have sacrificed while facing north, with their sinister left hand to the west, but only because

the west was what it was, the place of death and the setting Sun. The north–south line in this case is only *accidentally* related to the Sun's culmination. If such alignments are not always what they seem, then this is likely to be even truer of the religious practices inferred from them.

Very precise alignments on the extremes of the rising or setting Sun, however, are not to be brushed aside so easily, and Stonehenge gives all the appearances of having been, first and foremost, a temple to the setting midwinter Sun. There is more at stake here than the interpretation of the Sun as an object. Should setting not be equated with death? This is widely attested throughout history and across the entire world, and the orientation of burials is frequently decided accordingly. (Thus, to take a living tradition, the reasons behind which are known: the East African Nuer, according to E. E. Evans-Pritchard, believe that death follows the setting Sun while the east is the side of life. The corpse is never allowed to face north or south, and those taking part in the mortuary ceremony at a later time in the year sit facing the setting Sun as they offer up an ox to liberate the soul of the deceased.) But with what beliefs was midwinter setting connected in Neolithic Wessex? Was it a question of marvelling at the fact that the Sun dies then, only to be reborn? Was it a question of imploring the Sun to turn around, and stop going ever more 'winterwards'? (The Hopi of North America are said to have done just this.) Or of giving thanks for the fact that it had done so? Was there worship of some sort of year-god, as in Mesopotamia and ancient Greece, regarded as dying and being reborn at appropriate seasons? If so, was the year-god in any way linked with the institution of kingship? While there are many rough parallels with known societies, there are no longer any close analogies of relevant pedigree well fitted to help decide these questions.

Myth, Explanation and Logic

It is now second nature to us to discuss the world in terms of cause and effect. Aristotle, whose analysis of those twin notions long remained definitive, reminded his readers that they were neither simple nor without alternatives. Writing in the fourth century BC, he distinguished between those who described the world in terms of myth and the supernatural, and those who attempted to account for it by natural causes. This last group he described, perhaps surprisingly to us, as 'theologians'. Were there any such theologian-physicists in Stonehenge society, concerned to explain celestial events in a reasonably non-human and ordered way, either as caused by other events or as their causes? It seems very probable that there were, since people whose religious architecture demonstrably embodied arithmetical as well as geomet-

rical proportionalities are likely to have had the necessary mentality. In short, they would have wanted to fit their world into an orderly pattern, with or without invoking the supernatural.

No doubt human and physical categories were thoroughly mixed in their explanations, just as in the oldest literary cultures known to us. There is no sharp division between primitive myth and primitive science. (Animistic explanations do not now generally pass as acceptable science, but that is largely because Aristotle surreptitiously ruled them out of order by not including them under his list of four types of cause.) One of the main purposes of myth is to achieve a certain purpose. Myths are not usually seen as fictions, parables, or allegories by those who tell them. They are considered as in some sense true, but even so, their meanings are usually held to be somehow 'below the surface'. There are myths that are spoken aloud or chanted in ritual acts, as though they were simply narratives for general enlightenment, but even they are usually seen as a means of bringing something about—for example, the well-being of the community or its ruler. (The Greek word *muthos* was used of the spoken part of enacted ritual.) It was not necessary that change be brought about. Historical myths, for instance as recited in ritual by the Jews at their seasonal festivals, could be designed to help bring about a continuation of the existing situation—and in this case confirm a covenant between God (Yahweh) and Israel. Other myths might be to bring about something desired in the future, for instance at the end of the world (eschatological myths). All of these types have authority, usually obtained from tradition—or from an author who takes no credit for the myth, and who might even assign it to revelation. They are frequently transformed from time to time, and this often in association with some sort of social shift—since they are often intended to justify a social or political situation. All are important in their own way, but to dwell on their external aspects is to miss the point that myths usually have an explanatory function. Some of the earliest of known myths, from Sumeria, are of this type—for example a myth explaining how the mattock was invented by Enlil. The many myths concerning the world's creation are grander in content but similar in character.

Myths often contain abstract impersonations of rivers and trees, the sea and earth and sky, fire and earthquake—their behaviour being explained in terms that every person can comprehend. There are myths of transformation—whether of humans into elemental spirits, supermen, animals, or whatever can achieve things that men cannot normally achieve—and myths of creation. The origins of mankind, of animals, of mountains, of the universe itself, even of the gods, are commonplace. While from the Neolithic period in

Europe this is all beyond our reach, the geometrical and astronomical links between ritual sites and nearby springs and rivers—for instance at Durrington Walls and the Sanctuary, and the final destination of the Stonehenge Avenue—make it very probable that water was an important ingredient in religious explanation there. Libations of water were used in many ancient religions. Early Greek philosophers took water to be a fundamental element (Thales made it the most fundamental) and made great play with the opposed principles of wet and dry. Other parallels might have been drawn with *fire*, except that its ritual uses are so various, and in the case of cremation so necessary. There are several instances where traces of central fires have been found at timber and stone circles, and a good case is to be made out for fire as a means of aligning distant long barrows in threes. Putting a finer point on the interpretation of such things, however, is a question beyond our reach.

What is surprising in any count of the myths known to history is how very many have to do with periodic natural change and the seasons—such as the alternation of day and night, winter and summer, and phases of the Moon. What is of primary human interest may admittedly be the cycle of plant and animal growth, reproduction and fertility, and finally death, but the *correlation* of these things with the cycles of the Sun, Moon and stars is almost universal. Those who try to dismiss all modern astronomical analyses of prehistoric monuments as a misdirection of energy from some modern scientific Zeitgeist must come to terms with this fact of history. Not that it is a very surprising fact, for whether we like it or not we are all subject to these cycles.

Myths may of course explain many other things than the physical world—for instance tribal custom or religious behaviour or belief. Some have seen myths as invented to explain ritual practices, although this seems to be putting the cart before the horse. Some—at least as early as the Greek philosopher Euhemerus (fourth century BC)—have explained myths in terms of history. What is told of the gods is then supposedly an echo of the deeds of great men and women from the past. Max Müller, late in the nineteenth century, tried to interpret whole swathes of Greek myth as solar myth in disguise, not always very plausibly. His efforts made a welcome change from other interpretations, but they threw no real light on prehistoric belief. What is clear, even without his analysis, is that stories were told of the stars and of the Sun and Moon, just as they were of gods and heroes generally, and that the Sun and Moon often entered together into the same network of myth. That they almost certainly did so in Neolithic times becomes clear from the several cases found in which solar and lunar alignments are found in a single structure, and found there often in combination, for instance at right angles or as opposed lines.

This, alas, must be thought a very trite conclusion, but in interpreting the symbolisms of preliterate cultures one has to be satisfied with small returns. Without certain presuppositions, however—such as that of a certain logicality on the part of the people studied—it is impossible even to begin, and this raises an important question of method. A whole generation of historians of 'primitive' thought long ago decided that this particular presupposition was unacceptable. They were influenced especially by a series of works from the pen of L. Lévy-Bruhl (1910, 1922, 1927). His absurd argument, which is still being echoed in some quarters, maintains that primitive people invariably explain natural phenomena in terms of mystical and generally unseen powers, and that their mentality is 'prelogical', and even innocent of the law of contradiction. (This is the law that is traditionally stated 'X is Y and X is not Y cannot both be true'. It is now often given as 'Not both P and not P ', where P is some proposition.) Even invoking the supernatural to explain away a difficult point requires the acceptance of the gods acting in accordance with this rule, if not with some constant rule of behaviour. (It is a god's privilege to behave arbitrarily.) But to claim, as we are doing, that the principles of solar and lunar behaviour have been understood in even a limited way requires much more besides. If this book shows any one thing it is that even a preliterate society can reason in a highly logical way.

It is a very strange idea that because persons believe in unseen powers they are thereby illogical. It is true that the presuppositions made by those who create a myth might for various reasons be unacceptable to us, but even then there is likely to be a perfectly acceptable logic in its working out. One of the most pointed properties of many of the oldest known philosophical and cosmological texts is their recourse to 'pairs of opposites' in which to phrase explanations. One group of followers of Pythagoras, for example, listed ten pairs of opposite principles: *limited* and *unlimited, odd* and *even, one* and *many, right* and *left, male* and *female, stationary* and *moving, straight* and *curved, light* and *darkness, good* and *evil, square* and *oblong.* Other Greek philosophers made use of others, such as *hot* and *cold*, and *wet* and *dry*; and they were used in all the classic physical and medical theories of the Greeks. (The propositions that are made using such pairs of notions are strictly not always contradictories, but are often 'contraries'. From the fact that one of two contraries is false, the truth of the other need not follow. For example, the fact that Stonehenge is not square does not imply that it is oblong.) Now it would be hard to conceive of a surer material sign of similar ways of thinking in a preliterate society than the existence of deliberately contrasted artefacts. There is one very obvious example in Wessex prehistory, that is, the pairing of types of upright stone, as found in

the Avebury monument and avenues, at Wayland's Smithy, and elsewhere. Their shapes have led many to suppose that they were seen as male and female, but that is really a secondary consideration. They might easily have signified right and left, old and young, dark and light, or any one of a hundred other things; but what matters most is that they seem to point to a process that fits the description 'logical' in the sense used by narrow academic commentators. It is admittedly a very narrow sense and does not begin to do justice to the Neolithic situation, but it answers the Lévy-Bruhl argument in its own terms. It might have been more to the point to argue that an architect whose monuments do not fall down shows a grasp of logic at least as good as that of an anthropologist whose theories do. As for other examples of 'opposites', one can only speculate, but for historical reasons, not to say psychological, one can be reasonably certain that day and night were a crucial pair. Sun and Moon also beg to be included on our prehistoric list—and some of the demonstrated overall architectural properties of the monuments mentioned earlier, as well as the Avebury stones, seem to support such a contrast.

Solar Symbols

The idea of a solar wheel fairly certainly goes back to the second millennium BC, and by its associations it can take us back to much earlier symbolisms still. While it might be thought an exaggeration to describe it as having to do with 'causes', it would certainly have helped to *explain* the Sun's behaviour, and this at first sight without any hint of animism. However, it is known that a horse was in some cases added to the explanation of the solar movement, and the new animistic dimension turns the explanation well and truly into the realm of myth. Granting that some such mythological explanation prevailed, while it tells us nothing about any corresponding religious belief, might provide a small fragment from religion's symbolic shell, although even this cannot be taken for granted. (The Greeks, for instance, had much solar mythology, and in many regions of Greece the Sun was saluted with reverence without there being a corresponding cult of the Sun. There was at least nothing of the profound sort to be found, for instance, on the islands of Crete and Rhodes.)

What then of the origins of the myth of the solar wheel, and what can it tell us of Neolithic belief? The evidence for the myth itself lies in discs of gold, and in circles and spirals associated with them. In attempting to bring northern prehistory to life, archaeologists who blanch at the thought of treating even a single monumental alignment as astronomically meaningful will often be happy to read the Sun into almost anything that is circular and gold. Gold has

been the metal of the Sun in historic times. Grave goods in the Stonehenge region from around 2000 BC include button-like discs of beaten gold with a central cross, resembling a four-spoked wheel. The same general design is found in Minoan Crete, in Brittany, in Ireland—for example on gold discs from Ballina, County Mayo—and even more frequently in the Iberian peninsula. It is not hard to imagine that after the invention of wheeled transport the Sun was believed to be carried across the sky by it. Certainly in historical times the Sun's chariot has been a common theme of art and poetry. (Phaeton, in Greek myth the son of Helios, the Sun-god, whose chariot he so recklessly drove, here enters history as the first joyrider.) But firmer evidence than this is needed.

Two amber discs have been found in women's graves from the Stonehenge region: set in wide gold rings, chased with concentric circles, they too have been regarded as Sun symbols. 'It is these discs rather than the unique temple itself [Stonehenge]', wrote Jacquetta Hawkes in her book *Man and the Sun*, 'which most clearly link the cult of the Sun God in Britain with that of the adjacent parts of the continent'. She had in mind the bronze and gold Sun-chariot found in a Danish bog at Trundholm, now dated around 1650 BC. Six four-spoked wheels carry a frame and a horse that is represented as drawing it. On the frame of the chariot is a disc, covered in circles and spirals, a disc that was gilded on one side and bronze on the other. For this reason it is now often interpreted as representing the Sun by day and by night, according to the side considered. The whole is harnessed to the model horse, which has a neatly braided mane and tail. Hawkes noted that the symbols on the disc are occasionally found on Danish bronze razors, which sometimes show an image of a boat, often carrying what appears to be a Sun, amidships. She concluded that shaving in Bronze Age Denmark might have been a ritual act. Sun-carrying boats in Østfold (Norway) and Bohuslän (in Sweden, across the Skagerrak from Danish Sjælland), strongly resemble the Danish examples, except that there depictions of them are cut into slabs of rock.

The Trundholm horse was not unique, for there was a similar find in 1895 at Hälsingborg in Sweden, but this has since unfortunately been lost.

The wheel was certainly destined to become a powerful solar symbol. It was so in Europe by the time of the Celts and it reached its apotheosis in the popular cult of the Greek Apollo, who around the fifth century BC became identified with the older Sun-god Helios. The fact that the inhabitants of the island of Rhodes had long sustained a vigorous cult of Helios has led some to see Sun-worship as mainly of Middle Eastern origin, but the chariot association suggests that there were influences from a northern direction too. There are later echoes of the solar horse in Viking mythology, two millennia after the

Trundholm chariot. The Icelander Snorri Sturluson (1179–1241) summarizes passages from earlier sources in his *Gylfaginning*: Hrímfaxi is the horse of night, Skínfaxi the horse of day, with shining mane, drawing daylight across the sky. The idea is extended to the Moon's vehicle, which is steered by Máni (Moon). In Greek and Lithuanian mythology the morning and evening stars, Venus twice over, are made into the horses drawing the Moon. It is this persistence of the image that makes it seem right to read the Trundholm chariot, with its decoration of spirals, as a solar symbol—although that does not exactly solve the problem of how it was used—and to go then further back in time and interpret the innumerable Neolithic spirals and circles of earlier northern cultures as solar symbols. Whether horse or boat was used to carry the Sun was obviously a question of culture, and one can only speculate as to the means—if any—whereby the Stonehenge Sun was believed to be transported.

The argument, in summary, begins from the premise that the numerous spirals and circles of Neolithic Britain and Ireland, going back in a more or less continuous sequence to the middle of the fourth millennium at least, are solar and religious. That they are religious is strongly suggested by their occurrence in Neolithic tombs in places as far afield as Portugal and the Orkneys. Ireland is particularly rich in the symbolism, and there it is plainly associated in some cases with solar alignments. This all reinforces the belief that the Sun itself was an object of religious attention throughout the corresponding period, certainly early in the third millennium if not even earlier. It leaves us in little doubt that Stonehenge and other sites where the alignments are found *without* any (surviving) symbolism or proven role as sepulchres, are likewise of a religious character. It is conceivable that they had other purposes, such as a calendar function or a part in the retailing of myth, but none of these possibilities seems as certain as the simple truth that the Sun played an important role in religious observance there. Of course there are those who will say that this has always been obvious. But on what evidence? On the rising of the midsummer Sun over the Heel stone?

High Places

Alexander Thom's work on later monuments, often set in a mountainous landscape, showed their designers to have made use of distant prominences. While not proving Thom's ideas, the account by Martin P. Nilsson of how the solstices were found by early nineteenth-century Norwegian farmers fits it very well. A farmer would have a stone bedded in the earth, from which the Sun's extremes of rising and setting would be observed with reference to selected

mountain peaks. The architects of the Wessex monuments did not find themselves in a similar terrain, but they did set their monuments as meaningful silhouettes against the sky, whether by putting them on inclined ground, or by artificially lowering the eye in relation to them. While it might be hard to understand how such an abstract entity as the sky could ever have been seriously considered a deity, in a 'logic of opposites' it would have been contrasted with earth, an almost universal deity; and as something like 'starry heaven' the sky has been objective enough for people to speak of its falling down—some still do so—and it has been revered in many cultures, often in association with cults of high places. Such cults really do no more than extend the principles seen at work in our Neolithic 'cults of the horizon'.

As in the case of the solar wheel, so with 'high places' it is possible to find links with later and better known history. From Mesopotamia there are the Akkadian seals from the late third millennium showing the Sun-god Shamash rising between mountaintops, and there is more than a suspicion that ziggurats were among many other things surrogate mountains. High places have often been associated with tree cults and temples. From at least as early as 2000 BC, the inhabitants of Minoan Crete placed sanctuaries on mountain peaks. One such sanctuary is on Mount Júktas, due south of the palace at Knossos, and is reputed to be the place of burial of the Cretan Zeus. Seen from the palace, the peak has almost the classic 30° gradient of such places as Silbury. Two altars at its south end both face east. A peak sanctuary depicted on a rhyton (a vessel used for pouring libations, item 2764 in Herakleion Museum, and deriving from the mid second millennium BC) is shown trapped between goats' horns, and below it there is a rectangular window completely filled with a pattern of *spirals*, suggesting a solar association. The later Greeks, as Homer makes clear, showed a concern with cairns visible from the sea. They also often aligned their tombs towards the key points of the Sun's rising and setting. It is of course only by the accident of Greek literary influence, that of all cults of high places those of Mount Olympus are among the best known. There are many comparable examples from the literatures of Rome, the Jews, Mesopotamia and Persia. The seafaring Scandinavian peoples, as recently as a thousand years ago, worshipped cairns by which they navigated, and also grave mounds: this is known from reports of the difficulties experienced by the early Christian missionaries when they tried to eradicate such practices. Beowulf, hero of the great Anglo-Saxon epic of that name, asked to be buried in a mound on a headland that would serve as a guide to sailors, a request that hints at the survival of a link between burial custom and navigational tradition in northern lands.

It is impossible to say whether the cairns and distant hill-tops on which so many late Neolithic and Bronze Age monuments were aligned were themselves a focus of worship, as in the case of their distant relatives, but one of our findings seems to point to some such conclusion. The alignments of long barrows in threes and fours, and the cursus idea generally, all suggest that attention was paid to distant places on the far horizon, places at which the dead were often buried. By reason of this burial association, the custom was plainly implicated in a system of religious belief; and since the lines joining the barrows were to the risings and settings of bright stars, the stars must have entered into that system—a conclusion that merely supplements what has already been found by an analysis of stellar observances at individual long barrows.

Is there any conclusion to be drawn as regards attitudes to the long barrows themselves? The 'high places' of the Mediterranean and Middle East are today often romantically described as 'junctures of heaven and earth'. In fact some Babylonian sanctuaries actually bore that name, prosaic though it might seem by comparison with others, such as 'Mountain of the House', 'Mountain of Storms', or 'House of the Mountain of all Lands'. Middle Eastern attitudes seem likely to be more accurate pointers to the original meaning of barrows on the landscape than our own sterile way of regarding them, like other 'foresights' and 'backsights', as nothing more than neutral markers of risings and settings. They were surely far more, for they did nothing less than link our world with another. The Gilgamesh epic speaks of the mountain Mashu on which is the gate through which the Sun appears on rising. (It is often depicted on cylinder seals.) A Mesopotamian passage reminiscent of this, but from a much later text—possibly of the eighth century BC, but with earlier components—occurs in a series of incantations against witches. Written in the Akkadian language and known by the name *Maqlû*, the work speaks of a city called Zabban—whether real or imaginary is not certain—in which there are two gates. Through one of them the rising of the Sun was seen, and through the other its setting. It seems probable that the time of year of the ceremonies directed against witches, living and dead, was the autumnal equinox. Part of the purpose of the incantations was to annihilate the ghosts of dead witches to prevent their return to the netherworld. By implication, the ghosts share with the Sun a common entrance to this world, and a common exit. An incantation is not a myth—it has no narrative framework—but it does presuppose something of the sort, and it is hard to escape the feeling that northern myth shared with that of the Middle East, and many other places too, the principle that where the Sun set was the entrance to the netherworld, a land of the dead. Of course this does not mean that all cultures shared the northern Neolithic obsession

with accurately establishing precise horizon directions. This might have been only a northern foible, while in the Middle East more attention might have been paid to visibility problems (heliacal risings, and so forth). There are still enormous gaps in what is known of both cultures in these respects.

In the course of Middle-Eastern history, the solar, lunar and planetary gods became associated with *particular* high places, but perhaps regardless of strict alignment on any particular phenomenon. Again, the last point has been little studied. Each stratum of a Babylonian ziggurat is said to have had a different planetary association, and such 'high places' were the location for many non-celestial gods, apparently for the simple reason that again they provided access to destinations of the dead. They were even said to support the heavens, as did Atlas in Greek mythology—a favourite theme in Hellenistic art and ornament. There is an interesting sequence of events here, for in Greece in pre-Hellenic times the heavens were thought to be held up by a number of pillars (perhaps only four, the number accepted by the Egyptians) around the rim of the world, and within the ring of Ocean. Atlas, at first only guardian of the pillars, then took over their function (see Homer, *Odyssey*, i.53). His name might have been taken from that of Arcadian mountains that were thought to serve the same purpose, but other mountains were later given his name. Hesiod in his *Theogony* varies the account slightly. He relates how Atlas holds up the sky while standing in the Underworld. It is hard to say how strongly localized were these traditions, but their very existence shows how difficult it is to interpret what are ostensibly very simple archaeological findings. How many would be prepared to argue that a pole found at the bottom of a shaft could have been put in that odd situation to hold up the sky? Or even, more plausibly, that four posts in the middle of a round barrow, or perhaps even a complete timber henge, might have been conceived to do the same? Of one thing we may be sure: to enter the mind of pre-classical antiquity it is necessary to shed all ideas of spheres, astronomical and divine, and to concentrate rather on earth, sky, the boundary between them, and the places to which that boundary gives access.

Sun, Moon and Sacrifice

Sacrifice, the forfeiting of something of value in order to establish some sort of relationship with the realm of the sacred, takes many forms and has been given many different justifications. One common attitude is that of communion, of contact with the gods or perhaps with the recently deceased, through sharing for instance a common meal. In this there may also be the idea of drawing on

the strength of the sacred to whom sacrifice is made. Many Neolithic monuments have deposits of animal bones in key places, as though ritual meals had been held there. How they were regarded is of course unknown. It is conceivable, but perhaps improbable, that communion in this case was with the community rather than with some supernatural realm. In many known historical (or contemporary) instances, sacrifice is a sign of a desire to avert evil from a supernatural quarter. In some societies, for instance among Australian tribes, offerings could be made to anything seen as dangerous, for example rocks or animals. Gratitude resulting in freewill offerings is hardly different in character from these things; there is simply a different time scheme being followed in the payment. Still there is the idea that supernatural beings have human appetites and human wants. Unfortunately for the chosen victim, it is all too often supposed that the highest want of the gods is a human rather than an animal sacrifice. This is often the case where the lives of others or all individuals in a community are in danger, in which case the victim is seen as a substitute.

The fact that many literatures have references to sacrifices taking place at sunrise hardly proves an astronomical connection, let alone a connection with the turning points of the solar year, but there is a loose association of sacrifice with the solstices in northern lands, even though persuasive evidence for it is mostly slender and late. The summer solstice seems a plausible time, if a guarantee of a good harvest is called for. Greek legends point to the practice of the Phrygians in making human sacrifice at reaping time, and there is evidence too from other parts of the eastern Mediterranean. Germanic tribes, on the other hand, devoted the feast of Yule to the dead, and introduced agricultural symbols into it (such as a sheaf of the previous harvest, in the form of a man or woman or some animal) in such a way as to make one wonder whether they point to ancient customs of sacrifice. In the last analysis this evidence must count for very little, and yet it does seem to be distantly connected with customs associated with the Beltane fires of Scotland and Ireland and the bonfires of other Celtic countries.

These customs seem to point weakly to a connection with a precisely regulated calendar, even though most reports come only from the last three or four centuries. The mock deaths associated with the fires, the various ways in which people have been doomed to die, say within a year, and even the rumoured practice of despatching the aged, are interesting inasmuch as they are related to very specific times of the year. The Scots in historical times seem to have favoured the beginning of May, halfway between the spring equinox and the summer solstice; and also Hallowe'en, half way between autumn equinox and winter solstice. In Brittany, bonfires have more often been at the

winter solstice itself, but again the idea of mock deaths is known. There are reports that as late as the last century at Scottish sites the people formed rings of ashes, with stones round the circumference representing local persons involved in the ceremonies. It is of course possible that this idea is a modern misreading of Bronze Age rings of stones that had no such function originally. On the other hand there is no reason why any astronomical role they might have had need have ruled out such a representative function, even from the foundation of the rings. When the traveller and historian Pausanias of Lydia (flourished c. 150 AD) visited Greece, he found stones called by the names of deities. At Pharae he found thirty such squared stones, each with the name of a god on it. Perhaps they functioned as altars. He mentions that in former times all the Greeks had worshipped unwrought stones rather than images. Before we attach much weight to Pausanias, however, we should remind ourselves that he is nearer to us in time than he was to the architects of Stonehenge.

Ibn Fadlan, a tenth-century Arab traveller in northern lands, is nearer to us still, but he offers a curious link between European human sacrifice and the use of timber uprights. He tells of a sacrifice he saw among the Swedish settlers on the Russian Volga in c. 922. A slave-girl was strangled by an old woman called the Angel of Death and her helpers, before the girl's body was burned beside that of her master. Ibn Fadlan adds that these people worshipped upright wooden stakes encircling a larger central post with its top carved like a face, before which their sacrifices were made. (Oddly enough, the sacred stone of the Arabs themselves, the nusb, was sometimes hewn in the form of the deity.) There are crude faces carved on some of the prehistoric standing stones in Brittany, Spain and elsewhere, and these in turn are often involved in networks of astronomical alignments, but there is no known reason to connect them with human sacrifice.

Human sacrifice, unassociated with any particular calendar, has been imagined in many a Neolithic or Bronze Age situation. Some of the Irish cist graves, with a pair of burials, have occasionally been interpreted as indicating one natural and one unnatural death, the second to provide a companion in the afterlife. There are relatively few strongly argued cases of Neolithic sacrifice, but one of the best, that of a man whose skeleton was found together with four arrowheads near the centre of a timber circle at Sarn-y-bryn-caled in Wales, seems to hint at a practice on which the Greek writer Strabo reported, albeit more than three millennia afterwards. He tells that Iron Age Celtic peoples often shot their victims to death with arrows before impaling them in places of worship. There were also four arrowheads of high quality lodged in the ribcage of a skeleton found in the Stonehenge ditch, the man having seemingly

been shot from behind. The context no less than the manner of death seem to speak for sacrifice. Strategically placed skeletons at important sites always give rise to the question of foundation sacrifice. A malnourished woman was buried in the ditch at the north entrance to Marden henge, for example, and when the timber rings at the Sanctuary were replaced by stone circles, an adolescent was evidently buried by one of the stones. This looks like a sign of a foundation sacrifice, as does the burial of a deformed woman by the south entrance to Avebury. (Deposits at key places on the Avenue leading up to it have been considered at length, but no one seems to have seen them as sacrificial.)

The clearest example of relevance here is of course that of the child at Woodhenge, binding together lunar alignments and solar. This again prompts one to ask whether sacrificial rites in the Neolithic and Bronze Age were at astronomically propitious times, and in this case the probabilities seem to come down on the side of that idea. Some of the cremations at Stonehenge, although they are late, have also been shown here to have had lunar associations. There is some slight supporting evidence from an Iron Age date: a body found at Lindow (Cheshire) is reminiscent of others found in Danish bogs, that is, garotted, stabbed, and thrown into a bog; and it was of a man who had eaten mistletoe. In recent centuries this plant has been collected on Midsummer Eve—of course a solar festival—for magical purposes. It is impossible to say how far back in time the practice goes—perhaps not very far, but in any case the mistletoe association is not likely to have begun with the Sun, unless it was shared by Sun and Moon. The reason for suspecting this is that in the Celtic religion, according to Pliny's *Natural History*, mistletoe on the oak was cut with a golden sickle on the sixth day of the Moon. He says nothing of the season of the year, but the hint of precision, aiming perhaps at the eve of the Moon's first quarter, might indicate a time when the Moon reaches to its point furthest north on the horizon. This occurs at first quarter near the spring equinox. (For more information on this astronomical point see Appendix 2, section 8.) The custom Pliny is describing is likely to have had a much more ancient origin, as the remains of Lindow Man show, but how ancient it is impossible to say.

Whatever the truth of the matter, Pliny's story is that the druids, in white robes, cut down the mistletoe on the appointed day and caught it in a white cloth. The berries of the mistletoe are of course a watery white, and were probably on this account associated with the Moon. The plant was nevertheless also parasitic on the oak, so here there is an association with life and spirit. (In later Gaelic, mistletoe was 'the spirit of the oak'.) Added to these connotations is the fact that—according to Pliny, in the same passage—two white bulls were then sacrificed, and prayers for prosperity were offered up to a god. 'They

believe that mistletoe, taken in drink, grants fecundity to barren animals, and is an antidote to poisons'. This testimony is late, in comparison with the Stonehenge structures, and yet about a dozen balls of white chalk or sandstone have been found there (mostly in the ditches), as they have at other Neolithic monuments (more than twice as many have been found at Windmill Hill, for instance, and others at Durrington Walls), and in much earlier passage graves throughout Britain and Brittany.

The Cult of the Ox

There is an obvious and plausible connection between the chalk balls, the white Moon, and that ubiquitous symbol of fertility, the testicles of the bull. Two of the Stonehenge balls were found (separately) lying near the cores of ox horns. Fertility is the complement of death; fertility and the Moon go together in many ways, and the Moon and oxen likewise. There can be no serious doubt about these associations and their long-standing character. There is pottery from the Balkans from a time before the Wessex long barrows that leaves little doubt about a firm association of three symbols: the cross, the bull's horns, and the lunar crescent. This is an invaluable piece of evidence. It might even offer a context for the Bush Barrow and Clandon lozenges, for there are several much earlier Balkan examples of a design strongly resembling what is found on the latter. But still it tells us nothing of a deeper religious meaning, or even whether there was such a meaning. Through Roman sources we know of the pre-Roman use in Gaul of the Moon as a symbol of death, but still, late as it is, it tells us little. Early Greek literature points back to many rituals of fertility and death involving oxen in Iron Age Europe. (And as for fertility, was Europa herself not carried off by Zeus disguised as a bull?) Even in the presence of written texts there is much disagreement as to the purpose of this complex of ritual—fertility, death, Moon and the heavens generally, and oxen. A good example concerns the annual sacrifice of a bull at Athens, after which its hide was stuffed with straw and it was set up, yoked to a plough. (This is reminiscent of a whole class of so-called 'hide burials' in which cattle heads and hooves are found. They are known from many parts of Neolithic Europe, not least from the Fussell's Lodge long barrow.) In his classic *Golden Bough* (ii.294), J. G. Frazer interpreted this sacrifice as representing, or promoting, the resurrection of the slain corn-spirit at the end of threshing, but many other readings have since been given. It has been said, for example, that what mattered most was the sacrifice of a divine animal, which, when eaten sacramentally, was believed to strengthen the tie of kinship with the divine. If agreement is out of the

question when texts are available, what hope is there when all that is left are archaeological fragments from a period two or three millennia earlier?

As in the case of astronomical alignments, so with the remains of oxen, it is the context in which they are found that points most clearly to some sort of religious association. Bones of domestic cattle have been found in the great majority of long barrows. Those found in the burial chambers at West Kennet had seemingly been treated as the human bones had been, rather than as the remains of food offerings. Excavators have often said the same of bones from other long barrows. As long ago as 1869, J. Thurnham made the point that the bones of oxen in unchambered Wiltshire tombs were usually found near to the human remains, but above them, the skull and feet of oxen being most often encountered. In the ditches at Windmill Hill, there were the complete skeletons of goats and sheep, but with oxen it was almost invariably the skulls that were found. At the nearby Beckhampton long barrow, where it will be recalled no human burial was found, there were nevertheless ox skulls. The same was true of the Thickthorn Down long barrow and the Stonehenge Greater Cursus long barrow—to name two others with cursus connections discussed earlier here. It has long been suspected that human bones found in long barrows give evidence that they were moved from place to place, presumably as objects of veneration, and there is some evidence that cattle skulls might have received the same treatment. S. Davis and S. Payne have recently described a barrow with a very large number of such skulls piled up within it, and they have argued that the deposits were made at an appreciable interval after the deaths of the beasts. It is therefore especially interesting to learn that an ox skull and ox mandibles found on the level of the floor of the Stonehenge ditch have such early radiocarbon dates that they are likely to have been preserved for generations, even centuries, before they were deposited.

Such fragments of information might not in themselves point to a lunar connection—the placing of cattle remains in relation to astronomical alignments might one day establish a link—but it leaves little doubt as to the existence of some sort of cattle cult of extraordinary tenacity. Something of the sort was in evidence at the Uffington 'White Horse', the chalk figure of a bull, if we are to be believed. It is in evidence in an Amesbury Bronze Age barrow in which the skeletons of two children were found, placed symmetrically over the skull of a cow. The Uffington alignments were stellar, but a potential link between the Moon and the stellar constellation of the bull has already been explained, and all our evidence is that by the time of the high Stonehenge period the Moon had assumed a greater religious importance. But as to deeper religious meanings, they are entirely beyond recall.

The extraordinary persistence of the simple device of placing skulls on buildings can be illustrated even in the modern world. The practice of putting antlers on a forest house gable, or a horse's skull on a farm building might seem innocent enough convention, but they were often regarded in the past as charms, and on that account the church preached against them. The same is true of ox skulls, which were so important to the ancient Greeks that they were turned into a standard feature of stone ornament. They survive to this day in neo-classical architecture. (The English technical term is *bucrane*, or *bucranium*, from the Greek for 'ox skull'.)

Putting aside such relatively recent developments, do all the scattered Neolithic findings point to a fertility ritual? Was it really a chalk phallus that Richard Atkinson found, near stone 57, and that can no longer be found—rather as in some sub-plot from *Anglo-Saxon Attitudes* ? Was the Moon regarded as itself divine? Or as a destination for the dead, as in parts of India? Should we be trying to detect Neolithic echoes in Pliny's account of the white bulls? Or trying to read meaning into the mistletoe sacrifice of Lindow Man? To do any of these things is to risk a similar fate to his.

Prejudice and Principle

There is an obvious fallacy in viewing prehistoric astronomy through a haze generated by literate cultures whose achievements just happen to be better known. It is easy enough to bear the danger in mind when considering the testimony of Pliny, Diodorus, and Ibn Fadlan, for example, but less easy to clear our minds of the presuppositions instilled by the Christianization of our culture, or perhaps one should say by age-old Mediterranean influences. How much are we allowing ourselves to be deluded by classical astronomical language? Or by the Christian calendar, which is certainly entangled in the Beltane traditions mentioned earlier in this chapter—even if they do have pre-Christian elements? Or by the known practices of monumental orientation in Egypt, the Christian world, and Islam? Some of the last-mentioned practices are put on record in Appendix 6, at the end of this book. Many of them would not have been easily transferred to northern latitudes, but there are some who write as though northern and southern worlds are part of a seamless web. Others are prepared to look even further afield. There was a habit, developed in some anthropological quarters in the 1920s for instance, of drawing parallels between the megalith builders of Europe and Polynesia. While interpretations that sweep across half the world are no longer in fashion for the Neolithic

period, there are lesser claims that can be just as insidious, in particular where northern traditions are accepted as echoes from prehistory.

The interpretation of pillars, whether of stone or timber, will illustrate the point. Pillars in one form or another are of course commonplace. While in a religious context some made alignments possible, there was also the isolated pillar, with what seems often to have been an entirely different purpose. The Phoenicians, for example, a Semitic people who with their principal colony Carthage carried their customs right across the Mediterranean world, worshipped such cosmic gods as Ashtart (the Greek Astarte, corresponding to the planet Venus), and various gods associated with the Moon. These and others they gave human form, but divinity in a more abstract sense they represented by a lofty cone, a grand version of pillars found in the religious rituals of countries further east. A similar transformation occurred in Egypt, where the small cone became the monumental obelisk. Once we are on this tack it is hard to know where to stop, unless restrained by two conditions, of relevance and continuity.

It is obvious that not all prehistoric pillars were objects with cosmic associations, but there is an intriguing cluster of northern ideas around the cult of a 'world tree'—of reverence for carved posts, for the king-post supporting a house, and so forth. A post could stand symbolically for the tree, whose roots went down to the underworld, the land of the dead. Pillar worship is the object of a historical reference by Rudolf of Fulda (about AD 860). He tells of a pillar worshipped by the Saxons at Eresburg that had been destroyed two generations earlier (in 772) by Charlemagne. It was 'a trunk of wood of no small size, raised up high in the open air, [called] Irminsul in the language of their nation, the pillar of the universe, supporting as it were all things'. How much he was influenced by Latin learning is hard to decide—one cannot be sure how widely read he was. The number of potential misunderstandings is legion, since the cosmic image he mentions is found among the ancient Greeks and Romans, not to mention the inhabitants of India. There are, for example, many references in classical literature—obviously not all known to him—to the most famous of all sacred stones in Greece, the stone at Delphi, which some said was the exact centre of the Earth, 'the navel of the world'. This reminds us again of the role of Atlas. It seems probable that the people of Stonehenge would have shared a belief in the need for some sort of support for the sky.

If the Christian church frowned on the reverence shown towards pillars, this was often because of phallic associations. Clement of Alexandria was one of many to inveigh against this symbolism. Writing in the second century AD, he chaffs the heathen for setting up 'pillars of shamelessness'. The literature of

phallic imagery, like the phenomenon itself, is measureless. Many prehistoric menhirs on the Celtic fringe of Europe were Christianized in one way or another—by the carving of characters or crosses on them—or turned into commemorative stones, to save them from phallic interpretations. Those who went in for this sort of thing were about as effective in acting as guardians of public morality as was the English Lord Chamberlain at the height of his powers. When women in Brittany ceased 'sliding' along consecrated menhirs to help them conceive children it is hard to say, but as late as 1923, country-women visiting St Paul's Cathedral in London were clasping the pillars there to achieve the same effect. And that was certainly not in the mind of the architect.

This might all seem to be very remote from Stonehenge, but the tempta-tion to forge a historical link is great, especially through the medium of northern history. The contamination of sources can then become a serious problem. It is plain enough when we come to the writings of Widukind, a late-tenth-century writer on the Saxons, when he also tells of their worship of Irminsul. After a bloody night battle the Saxons set up their eagle standard at the eastern gate, with an altar to victory. Widukind tells of how they worship their holy things in the manner of their forefathers: by the name of Mars, by a replica of columns imitating Hercules, and 'by the place of the Sun, called by the Greeks Apollo'. Widukind then even goes on to argue from a spurious similarity of the Greek name Hermes to Hirmin (Irminsul) that the Saxons had Greek origins. (Later generations tried to reverse the equation.) Misled though he might have been by his ambition to prove a point, the fact remains that it was the *place* of the Sun that was said to matter. This is a far cry from the silent archaeological remains of three millennia earlier, but it does hint, however faintly, at a continuing tradition. The horizon was paramount.

Some modern anthropologists are not afraid of running risks comparable to Widukind's, finding as they do similar cosmic images among modern cultures as far afield as the Kwakiutl of British Columbia and the Nad'a of Flores Island in Indonesia. The Plains Indians of North America, for their annual sun dance ceremonies at the summer solstice, began by sacrificing a tree, the trunk of which then became the central pole of a medicine lodge from which the Sun was observed as it rose over some notable point on the horizon. Such parallels are not hard to find, but to find them juxtaposed to discussions of prehistoric monuments, without any attempt to defend continuity of tradition, is to be reminded of supposed native American parallels with thatched roofs over Woodhenge, the Sanctuary, and even Stonehenge.

There is nothing new in the idea that historical (especially textual) evidence can be misinterpreted. What is surprising is that so many fragments do seem to fall into place in the reconstruction of prehistory. The tent-like mortuary houses still in use in rural districts in Friesland in Glasbergen's experience seem likely to have at least five millennia of history behind them. Superficially, at least, one might say the same for the farmhouses of the northern Netherlands. Such remarks make some people uneasy, whereas they seem prepared to accept calendar customs without question when they are demonstrably younger. Perhaps it is that calendars seem to be more intimately bound up with the laws of nature. The 'calendar' that mattered most in Neolithic times had at least two crucial dates, those of the solstices. A primitive historical example of this from Iceland was given in the last chapter. Another, from an anonymous thirteenth-century Icelandic narrative of tenth-century events, *Gísla Saga Súrssonar* (The Saga of Gísli the Outlaw) tells of Thorgrímr, a priest of Freyr. He is said to have 'intended to hold a festival at the beginning of winter, to greet the winter, and sacrifice to Freyr'. He was later murdered by Gísli and laid in his grave mound, whereupon it was later noticed that the snow never settled on the southwest side of the mound, and the ground never froze there. 'People supposed that he was so esteemed by Freyr for the offerings he had made to him, that the god did not wish it to freeze between them.' This all speaks plainly enough of a festival of the setting midwinter Sun. Moreover, to show that the tradition of a Sun-wheel had never been forgotten: the Sun in *Skírnismál*, a poem probably Norwegian and as old as the late ninth century, is there called the 'elf-wheel', the 'demon-wheel'.

Such stories are simple enough, even trivial, but in human terms they are infinitely more complex than the astronomical phenomena that gave rise to them. The Neolithic and Bronze Age timbers and stones that are distantly related to such stories must clearly have spawned many others that can never be known to us. There are severe limits to the number of occasions on which it is reasonable to try to extrapolate from history to prehistory, in the way we have tentatively tried to do with the solar wheel, the spiral motif, the calendar of sacrifice, and cults of high places, for example. This is not to say that the archaeological remains are of lesser value. On the contrary, they embody the geometrical forms that were dressed in different ways in successive ages. Those forms were created in answer to a religious experience, but they are at the very source of modern science. In the sixth century BC, the renowned Greek poet and writer Xenophanes warned against making the gods in our own image:

> Yes, and if oxen and horses or lions had hands, and could draw with their hands, and produce works of art as men do, horses would draw the forms of the gods like horses, and oxen would make them look like oxen, and all would make the gods' bodies in the image of their own.

It would not be unjust to satirize modern astronomer-archaeologists in a similar way, but there is one difference: the evidence is overwhelming that early religion was intimately bound up with the stars, Sun, Moon, and the heavens in general. The true sceptic is not the person who returns endlessly to that basic question, but one who holds speculation in check when examining the finer details of a developed argument. Being prepared to revise such arguments constantly, even drastically, is not the same as surrendering to zealots who refuse to listen to any argument. Like the ox, the horse, or the lion, the astronomer might in the end prove to be right.

Radiocarbon Dating

Radiocarbon dating of archaeological samples of organic materials depends on the radioactive properties of an isotope of carbon that all such materials contain. The nucleus of radiocarbon (carbon 14, an isotope of normal carbon 12) is unstable, and when an atom of it decays to nitrogen 14, it emits an electron. The emission of electrons from a sample of material containing carbon 14 atoms can be detected using suitable equipment in the laboratory, and the relative proportions of carbon 14 to carbon 12 calculated. Whilst all living material contains carbon, an extremely small proportion of it is radiocarbon (roughly one atom in a million million). When the living thing dies, and ceases to take in carbon from its environment, the proportion gradually falls, due to the radioactive decay. This is a very slow process: rather less than half of the carbon 14 atoms in an antler used for digging the Stonehenge ditch have changed to nitrogen 14 in the interval between then and now. Measures of radiocarbon proportions can thus be used to give an estimate of the interval since the death of whatever it was that the sample came from, but there will be various reasons for uncertainty in the result.

Radiocarbon dates are always qualified with an indication of their statistical accuracy. For example, a radiocarbon date of 2180±105 bc, for a specimen of antler from the bottom of the Stonehenge ditch is usually understood as implying that there is a 68.3 per cent chance that the date of the object lies between 2285 and 2075 bc. (This is a statistical uncertainty known as one standard deviation. Other ranges of uncertainty are sometimes used, but then they are stated explicitly. A growing tendency is to opt for *two* standard deviations, or 95.4 per cent confidence.) The reason for the unfamiliar lower case of the letters 'bc' is that the first calibrations of the rate of decay, made in the 1950s and 1960s, were found to be in error. This was suspected, for example, from reasonably well-dated Egyptian materials. Rather than attempt to revise at regular intervals all old dating in calendar terms, a distinction is made between calendar dates (quoted as BC) and radiocarbon dates produced in the old way (bc), and the precise correlation of the two is under constant review. (The very long-lived tree, the Californian Bristlecone Pine, has been of greatest value in this revision.) Radiocarbon dates as given in these pages have been corrected, following the recommendations of the special 'Calibration

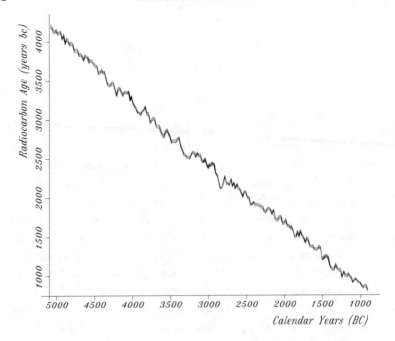

FIG. 200.   A correlation of radiocarbon and calendar dates for four millennia before 1000 BC.

Issue' of the journal *Radiocarbon*, 28, no. 2B (1986), under the editorship of Minze Stuiver and Renee S. Kra.

The triple graph drawn above (showing extremes of uncertainty, and the mean) will allow for approximate conversions. Note how a single radiocarbon date, including the example just cited, may correspond to a number of different (but all potentially correct) calendar dates, with a spread of perhaps two or three centuries. This has nothing to do with the uncertainty alluded to above, but is a consequence of the fact that the proportions of radiocarbon in the atmosphere have not always been what they are now, nor have they been constant. In converting the radiocarbon date in the example, one would have to take as limiting dates (1) the earliest calendar date corresponding to 2285 bc, and (2) the latest date corresponding to 2075 bc. The results are around 2880 BC and 2545 BC. What began as a range of 210 years in uncertainty has ended, therefore, as a range of 335 years.

In all strictness it may occasionally be necessary to split a range of probable dates into two ranges, separated by an interval where the true date is unlikely to have fallen. Many writers quote calendar dates 'before the present' (BP), by which they usually mean 'before 1950.0'. How long this odd custom will continue is a matter of great uncertainty.

The Astronomical Framework

Azimuths of Rising and Setting

To search for acceptable astronomical alignments in any structure—disregarding the question of whether or not they were deliberately placed there—it is first necessary to establish a relationship between (a) the azimuth (i.e. direction of a point on the horizon, measured round the horizon typically from north) of the rising or setting of the object, whether a star or a specified part of the solar or lunar disc; and (b) the altitude of the horizon at the appropriate point. The latitude of place and the semidiameter of the disc will enter into the relationship, as will the date, since the apparent places of the stars and paths of the Sun and Moon all change with time. There are changes in (c) the obliquity of the ecliptic, (d) the inclination of the Moon's orbit to the ecliptic, and (e) the positions of the lunar nodes, that is, the points of intersection of the ecliptic and the lunar orbit. The nodes complete one revolution of the celestial sphere in approximately 18.6 years. Other material factors are (f) the refraction of light in the Earth's atmosphere, and (g) parallax.

The first part of the appendix deals with some of these basic matters. The last part adds some refinements to the theory of lunar standstills, in principle necessary if one is to avoid the risk of calculating azimuths with a potential error of more than a lunar diameter.

Parallax

While they are observed from the Earth's surface, the positions of the Sun and Moon are usually initially calculated with reference to planes through the Earth's centre. For our purposes, the Sun is so distant that no significant error is introduced in ignoring the difference. The Moon is so near, in relation to the diameter of the Earth, that parallax affects the observed altitudes appreciably. If the Earth were a perfect sphere, the adjustment would be simple, but in fact the oblateness of the Earth also introduces a small complication. Suppose the observer's distance from the Earth's centre is r and the geocentric distance of the Moon is R (see Fig. 201, in which N is the pole, O the observer, C the centre and P and Q points on the equator of the Earth). Z' is the geocentric zenith and Z is the zenith defined by the local horizon. It is assumed, for the

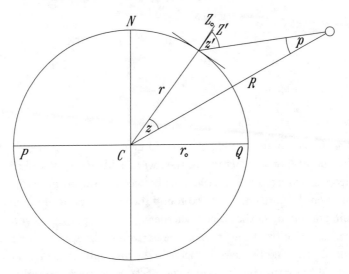

FIG. 201.   The geocentric parallax of the Moon.

time being, that there is no refraction. The zenith distance (z') of the Moon's centre then differs from its geocentric value (z) by an amount (its parallax, p) given by:

$$R \sin p = r \sin z'. \tag{1}$$

Here $p = z' - z$. Expressed in terms of altitudes (complements of the zenith distances), $p = a - a'$.

If the Earth were a sphere, Z and Z' would coincide, but in reality the angle ZOZ' ($= g$) varies with the distance of O from the equator, that is, with the observer's geographical latitude (ϕ). With or without this oblateness factor, p still depends on ϕ, in a way conventionally expressed in terms of the horizontal parallax. This is simply the value of p (say p') when z' is a right angle:

$$\sin p' = r/R. \tag{2}$$

In the special case where O is on the equator and R is the mean orbital distance (R_0),

$$\sin p_0 = r_0/R_0 .$$

Here p_0 is called the mean equatorial horizontal parallax, an astronomical quantity with a value of about 57' 03" (0.95075°). Fluctuations in the lunar distance give rise to fluctuations about this mean parallax of about 4'.

Parallax is conventionally split into component constants as follows:

$$\sin p = (r/r_0)(R_0/R) \sin p_0 \sin z', \tag{3}$$

where p_0 is as quoted, r/r_0 is expressible in terms of the Earth's eccentricity (e) by the equation

$$(r/r_0)^2 = [1 - e^2(2 - e^2) \sin^2 \phi]/[1 - e^2 \sin^2 \phi] \tag{4}$$

and R/R_0 is known from the orbital motion of the Moon. By definition, of course, R_0/R is unity in the average case. In a working formula for the average situation, one may take a series expansion in powers of e, ignore higher powers than the second, and take 0.08199 as the value of e. In the average situation, (3) and (4) then give

$$\sin p = (0.016594 - 0.0000554 \sin^2 \phi) \sin z', \tag{5}$$

so that p takes approximately the value on the right hand side of the equation, in radians, or in degrees

$$(0.95079 - 0.00317 \sin^2 \phi) \sin z'. \tag{6}$$

Atmospheric Refraction

This is a complex phenomenon: the refractive index of the atmosphere varies with height, since it is dependent on temperature, pressure, the water vapour content of the air, and other minor factors. Light passing from a celestial object to the observer follows a curved path that is conveniently divided into two parts, one produced beyond the limiting horizon (astronomical refraction) and one nearer than it (terrestrial refraction). The theory governing the latter is needed in particular when calculating the apparent altitude of points of the horizon from their distances and heights—as taken, for instance, from Ordnance Survey maps. This component of the total refraction is subject to large and erratic fluctuations, but the astronomical component is also not immune from them. Although there are various empirical laws available (in analytical form), it is usually easier and more reliable to work from empirically derived tables of astronomical refraction. The general pattern of a light ray as it approaches the observer is a downward curve as it enters successively denser layers of air. Measured from the horizontal, the angle of the ray from a point object, say from a star, as it travels through space is less than the angle at which it is seen by the observer. The former ('true') altitude, that can be used in the standard trigonometrical formulae of the celestial sphere, is found from most tables in a rather tedious way—after entering the table with the apparent altitude and subtracting the correction supplied by the table. A more useful form for a simple table of refraction is one that correlates true and apparent altitudes directly.

The Celestial Sphere

In deriving relations between observed and calculated angles, the usual conventions of spherical astronomy are followed here. All celestial bodies (stars, Sun, Moon, etc.) are treated as though they are on a single spherical surface—an

acceptable convention if one is concerned only with *directions* centred on the Earth. It is traditional to think in terms of arcs of great circles on the sphere (cut by planes passing through the centre), and to speak of them as 'distances', but not forgetting that they are representative of the angles they subtend at the centre. The centre is taken to coincide with the Earth's centre, or with the observer if distances are very great. In Fig. 202, N and S are the north and south celestial poles, directly above the terrestrial; Z is the observer's zenith (ignoring the subtleties discussed earlier in connection with parallax); N', E', S', W' are north, east, south, and west points of the horizon. The altitude of the pole (NN') is equal to the observer's geographical latitude (ϕ). Here again the oblateness of the Earth may usually be ignored.

There are several systems of celestial coordinates, some local to the observer (as with altitude and azimuth) and others more general. The celestial equator is one plane of reference, and the vernal point (where the Sun crosses the celestial equator at the spring equinox) an important coordinate origin. Declination (denoted by δ) is the angular distance from the equator (see XX' in Fig. 202, and compare with geographical latitude), usually counted positive to the north. The geocentric zenith distance of X is ZX, and the third side of the spherical triangle ZNX is completed with ZN, the complement of ϕ. Continuing the arc ZX to meet the horizon in Y, the astronomical altitude of X above the horizon is XY (denoted by a). The azimuth ($N'Y$) specifies the direction of X (or Y) with respect to the north–south line. Any other point of origin (e.g. E') may be taken in place of N', and there is much to be said for reckoning azimuths north and south of the line $E'W'$. For the time being, the azimuth (A) is taken as the angle NZX.

There are several fundamental trigonometrical formulae for spherical triangles, used below without proof. (For further detail see any standard treatise, such as W. M. Smart, *Text-Book on Spherical Astronomy*, Cambridge, 4th edn, 1944.) The declination of X is related to true zenith distance and azimuth by the equation:

$$\sin \delta = \sin \phi \sin a + \cos \phi \sin z \cos A, \qquad (7)$$

or, in terms of the true altitude of X above the horizon,

$$\sin \delta = \sin \phi \sin a + \cos \phi \cos a \cos A. \qquad (8)$$

The Earth rotates on its axis, but one may as easily regard the entire star sphere as turning with the daily rotation about N and S. If X is not too close to N or S (in fact if it has a declination between ($90° - \phi$) and $-(90° - \phi)$) it will rise somewhere on the eastern horizon and set on the western. (Only the case of observers in the northern hemisphere is considered here. X may be an object invisible for other reasons than proximity to the poles—for instance

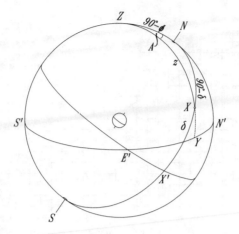

FIG. 202.   Celestial coordinate systems.

because its light is lost in that of the risen Sun.) The visible and invisible daily paths of the Sun and Moon will vary from day to day. How they do so will be considered next.

With a star, its places of rising and setting will go more or less unchanged throughout the year, and indeed for long periods of time. The altitudes at which the stars are seen to rise and set over a low horizon depend on their brightness, as explained in Chapter 2. For this reason it is not possible to give a simple relationship between star declinations and azimuths of rising and setting, even for a single geographical latitude. The graph of Fig. 203, however, shows the relationship between azimuth and declination in a specimen case.

Motions of the Sun and Moon

Fig. 202 illustrates the movement of the entire sphere of stars with respect to the observer's horizon. The Sun and Moon move with the annual and monthly motions on that sphere of stars, and so have a compound motion. In Fig. 204, the heavy line represents the annual path of the Sun (the 'ecliptic', a great circle) on the star sphere. When the Sun is at its closest to N, daylight is greatest (summer solstice); when nearest to S, shortest (winter solstice). When the Sun crosses the equator, in spring and autumn, day and night are equal. These simple statements need qualification: there is the problem of twilight, for instance, and also the question of local variations in the lengths of daylight as a result of irregular horizon altitudes. Speaking generally, though, the rising and setting positions of the Sun oscillate between northern and southern limits in azimuth, corresponding to maximum and minimum declination (ε, the

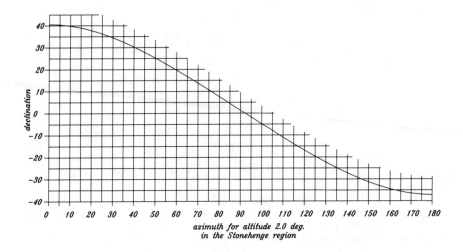

FIG. 203.   The relationship between azimuth and declination for a star at altitude 2.0°
(the approximate extinction angle of Aldebaran, for example) at the latitude of Stonehenge.

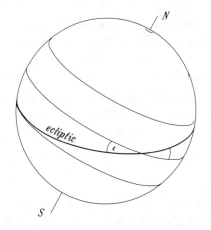

FIG. 204.   The ecliptic, the path of the Sun on
the celestial sphere.

angle known as the obliquity of the ecliptic, now about 23.5°). At Stonehenge, for instance, the Sun rises in the approximate azimuth range of 40° north to 40° south of the east–west line. The four special points of the Sun's path with which this volume is mostly concerned are the extreme positions (declinations $+\varepsilon$ and $-\varepsilon$, the solstices) and mean positions (declination zero, the equinoctial points).

Although the angle at which the ecliptic is inclined to the equator is today approximately 23.5°, it varies slowly with time according to a rule with the approximate form

$$\varepsilon = 23°\,27'\,08.29'' - 47.080''\,T - 0.0059''\,T^2 + 0.00186''\,T^3. \qquad (9)$$

Here T is the number of centuries elapsed from AD 1900.0. For 2000 BC, for instance, $T = -39$ (overlooking the trifling single year that in principle upsets our reckoning between accurate dates AD and BC). The change in the obliquity of about two-thirds of a minute of arc per century may seem unimportant, but over many centuries it has a marked effect on rising and setting positions. It

is substantially less important, however, than horizon altitude and refraction.
The following table lists some obliquities (in degrees and decimal parts) from
3500 BC to 1100 BC:

3500	3000	2500	2000	1500	1000
24.072	24.028	23.981	23.929	23.875	23.818

The extremes of the solar declination are simply ε and $-\varepsilon$ for the epoch in
question. With the Moon, matters are complicated in several ways. The Moon's
orbital plane is inclined to the ecliptic at about $5.2°$ (i, on Fig. 206). The Moon
travels round its orbit from a node and back (N_1 to N_2 to N_1) in 27.212 days.
This is not quite the 27.322 days it takes to return to a given point on the star
sphere, since the nodes are themselves moving slowly backwards, traversing
the ecliptic completely, as already stated, in about 18.6 years. Both types of
month differ materially, of course, from the common month (synodic month,

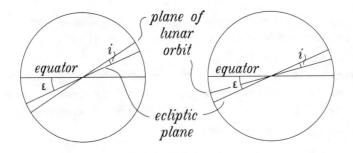

FIG. 205.   The maximum and minimum declinations of the Moon.

29.531 days) reckoned from new moon to new moon, for that is dependent on
the Sun, which has its own motion.

It should be intuitively obvious that the declination of the Moon, its
angular distance from the equator, is capable of reaching an absolute maximum
when the nodes N_1 and N_2 coincide with the equinoctial points of the ecliptic.
With that configuration, the Moon is in principle capable of reaching to a
declination of $(\varepsilon + i)$—see the left hand side of Fig. 205. After another
half-revolution of the nodes the situation will be as on the right side of the
figure, and for the time being the Moon will be unable to reach to a declination
more than $(\varepsilon - i)$ above or below the equator. The variation in the lunar
declination over one cycle of the nodes has the pattern shown in Fig. 207.
Although it is easy enough to write down a reasonably accurate set of equations
for the fluctuation, and derive from them the fluctuation in azimuth of rising
and setting, again we are here chiefly interested only in the four extremes of

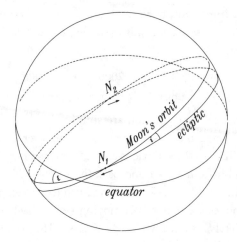

FIG. 206.   The path of the Moon on the celestial sphere, in relation to the ecliptic. They intersect in the lunar nodes, N_1 and N_2.

declination, at which the Moon's risings and settings are at what A. Thom called lunar standstills—'major' when the declination is $\pm(\varepsilon + i)$, and 'minor' when $\pm(\varepsilon - i)$.

In the account offered thus far, no notice has been taken of a certain periodic fluctuation in the inclination of the Moon's orbit. A more precise account will be found below. It should not be ignored if azimuths accurate to more than a quarter of a degree or so are required.

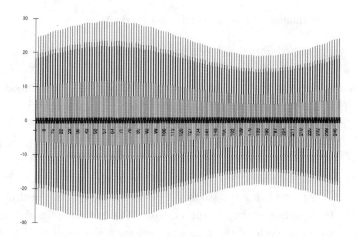

FIG. 207.   The variation in lunar declination over one cycle of the nodes (approximately 18.6 years). The Moiré pattern is merely a consequence of the method of reproducing the (continuous) graph.

Computation

We now have materials enough to enter into two different sorts of computational procedure, direct and inverse. The direct takes us from known declinations, geographical latitude, and horizon altitude (or rather horizon profile, since it will usually be irregular), to the azimuths of rising and setting. The inverse procedure is that which leads to a declination, say for a star or centre of the Sun or Moon, from the known azimuth of rising or setting of a particular point of the object. (Thus one might be led from the discovery that a series of alignments all give declinations in the neighbourhood of 29° to the conclusion that they were deliberately chosen for the Moon's major standstill, that is, where the declination is $(\varepsilon + i)$.) The equations first derived for the direct method will be more or less immediately applicable to the inverse procedure.

Suppose that the declination, which will generally be taken to have one of the six key values $\pm\varepsilon$, $\pm(\varepsilon + i)$, $\pm(\varepsilon - i)$, is astronomically accurate, and that an accurate value is known for the semidiameter of the Sun or Moon, if needed. The solar and lunar images will be distorted (flattened) by refraction, and if the semidiameter is added or subtracted for any reason at the 'terrestrial' end of the calculation, this should be taken into account. Needless to say, altitude and declination in equation (8) must correspond: it is wrong to take one in a form modified by refraction and the other not.

An acceptable solution can be found by working with the centre of the body, and using equation (8) to relate them to the azimuth of the centre. This is also that of the upper and lower limbs, assuming that azimuth is not affected by refraction or parallax. The geometrical ('astronomical', 'true') altitudes of the upper and lower limbs are simply $(a \pm s)$, values which are related to the observed horizon altitude by the refraction function (that embodied in refraction tables). This may be written in general:

$$x = f(x') \tag{10}$$

where the 'true' (but non-geocentric) altitude is on the left, and x' is the observed angle. In the case under consideration, writing the observed horizon altitude as a',

$$(a \pm s) = f(a'). \tag{11}$$

In the case of the Sun, equation (8) may then be written

$$\sin \delta = \sin \phi \sin(f(a') \mp s) + \cos \phi \cos (f(a') \mp s) \cos A. \tag{12}$$

The upper sign is appropriate to observations of the upper limb, and a' is the observed horizon altitude, but δ is the true declination of the centre of the Sun, and one is able to substitute at once any of the key values of the declination.

In the case of the Moon, the true non-geocentric altitude (say a'') is what is refracted, giving

$$a'' = a \pm s - p = f(a'). \qquad (13)$$

(Here p is subtractive since altitudes are complements of zenith distances. See under equation (1).) The parallax here is a function of the non-geocentric true altitude (see equations (5) and (6)). Writing the function as $p(a'')$,

$$a \pm s - p(a'') = f(a'),$$

or, more usefully,

$$a \pm s - p(f(a')) = f(a'). \qquad (14)$$

The value of a taken from (14) may then be substituted in (8). It is important that parallax be reckoned on the basis of $f(a')$ rather than a', especially when horizon altitudes are high. At $10°$, ignoring the effect would be equivalent to making an error of more than ten per cent in the semidiameter.

In the case of what I called the 'method of furthest reach', the calculation is much simplified. Equation (8) is now applied not to the declination of the centre but to that of the observed point of the Sun or Moon. This is easily done, since the instantaneous direction of motion of the body as it meets the horizon is at right angles to the arc of declination (the great circle through the poles). Denoting the adjusted declination by δ', therefore, and that of the centre by δ,

$$\delta' = \delta \pm s,$$

where the upper sign covers

    (a) northernmost standstills (Sun and Moon);

    (b) minor southern standstills (Moon);

and the lower sign applies to

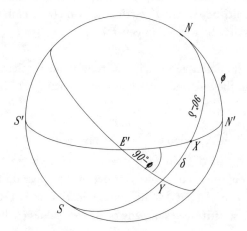

FIG. 208.   The angle of rising or setting of the Sun or Moon.

(c) southernmost standstills (Sun and Moon);

(d) minor northern standstills (Moon).

Equation (8), applied to the point of furthest reach, then becomes, for the Sun,

$$\sin(\delta \pm s) = \sin \phi \sin (f(a')) + \cos \phi \cos (f(a')) \cos A. \tag{15}$$

Here a' is the observed horizon altitude. In the case of the Moon (cf. equation (14)) the term $f(a')$ is to be replaced by

$$f(a') + p(f(a')).$$

This is all that is needed to relate the observed azimuths of furthest reach (A) to the observed altitudes (a') and the known declinations of centre.

The same equations ((12) and (15), or versions of them modified for the case of the Moon, as explained) also permit work in the inverse direction, that is, from a known azimuth and altitude to a declination of centre.

Angle of Rising or Setting

It is occasionally useful to know the angle (θ) between the horizon and the arc described by the body of the Sun or Moon as it rises or sets. The angle is affected somewhat by refraction, but in an approximate calculation this may be ignored. If one suspects that the Sun was observed setting, for instance, by seeming to run down a distant mountain ridge, a first approximation to θ may be found quickly, and if the case seems interesting enough, a careful plot can then be made on the basis of altitudes and azimuths worked out along the lines already explained. A knowledge of the true angle is in any case of use if one wishes to calculate the true declinations of different parts of the solar or lunar discs.

At zero altitude, θ is the complement of NXN' in Fig. 208. By the sine rule for spherical triangles, applied to triangle $NN'X$,

$$\cos \theta = \sin \phi \sec \delta. \tag{16}$$

At non-zero altitudes the derived angle will differ from this, but the approximation is reasonable at altitudes of a few degrees.

Fluctuations in the Lunar Inclination

The mean value of the inclination of the Moon's orbit to the ecliptic is 5° 08′ 42″, and this does not change appreciably over the few thousands of years that concern us, although the actual value of the inclination fluctuates with an amplitude of about 0° 09′ around the mean. The value of the adjustment depends on the ecliptic longitudes of the Sun and Moon, L_s and L_m respectively, and may be taken as given in minutes of arc by the expression

$$8.65 \cos 2L_s - 0.70 \cos 2(L_m - L_s) + 0.65 \cos 2L_m.$$

(This version of the expression follows L. V. Morrison's correction to the version introduced into the literature by A. and A. S. Thom, who followed a slip in J. M. A. Danby's standard *Fundamentals of Celestial Mechanics* (1962). See L. V. Morrison, 'On the analysis of megalithic lunar sight-lines in Scotland', *Archaeoastronomy*, no. 2 (1980), pp. 64–77.) If the expression is positive, increasing the value of i, the Moon will rise and set further to the north during a major standstill; and there are similar changes to be taken into account for all standstills of the rising and setting Moon. The extreme values of these changes are easily calculated, but much interest attaches to the circumstances under which the changes occur. It will be seen that the maximum value of the inclination ($5° 17.4'$) is when the Sun is on the equator, that is, at the equinoxes, and when the Moon is at first quarter or last quarter. When the Sun is at the solstices, the inclination of the Moon's orbit may be as little as $4° 58.7'$, again with the Moon at first or last quarter.

In Fig. 209, the extreme values of the Moon's declination are shown (that is, combining obliquity and inclination), over a typical series of lunations in the neighbourhood of that which gives a major northern and a major southern standstill. For the sake of clarity, only the extremes of the declination graph are represented, but the overall (triply) sinusoidal pattern of declination for a longer period should already have been noticed in Fig. 207, where the very slight ripple in the outline represents the perturbation now under discussion. The current figure is simply a detail of the extremes at the widest part of the bulge of the earlier figure. Qualitatively speaking, Fig. 209 gives the horizon positions of the rising or setting Moon: the higher the peak of the curve in the upper half of the figure, the further to the north does the Moon rise and set; the lower the trough in the lower half, the further to the south. The precise relation between azimuths and declinations is the subject of the earlier sections of this appendix.

The new moon is strictly unobservable, lost as it is in the glare of the Sun. Although the Moon becomes visible within a day or two of new moon, the general insignificance of corresponding declinations (and thus azimuths) when it does so is noteworthy (see the points marked 6, 21, 23, 25, 34, 36). Although semitic peoples have attached great religious importance to the first observation of the lunar crescent after the new moon, they have taken no particular notice, as far as can be seen, of lunar standstills.

The quarters give more or less the true extremes. At first quarter (the disc is shown blackened on the left half) the Moon has passed the Sun in ecliptic longitude by about 90°, so the Sun is high in the sky when the Moon rises, but has set long before the Moon sets. Only under very special atmospheric

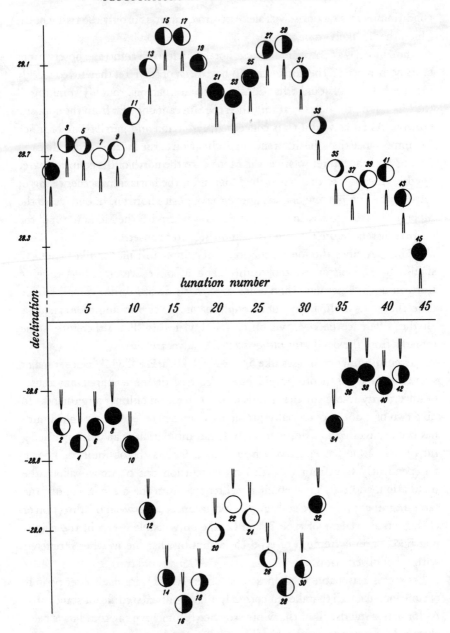

FIG. 209. Extreme values on the graph of the Moon's declination for a typical series of lunations around major northern and southern standstills. The period covered is about 45 months. The lunations are numbered consecutively and the approximate phase of the Moon is shown for each (new moon, first quarter, full moon, third quarter, or whatever).

conditions is this moonrise visible. At third quarter, it is only the rising of the Moon that is likely to be visible.

Full moon is a conspicuous event, notable in its own right, and observations of its occurrence on the horizon could have been observed if they fitted readily into the scheme of standstills. Consider the alternatives: roughly speaking, if the Moon is on the horizon at full, then the Sun cannot be far from the opposite horizon. As far as visibility is concerned, refraction and parallax are of much less importance than the difference in declination of the Sun and Moon. In cases 7 and 37, at the winter solstice, the Moon is to the north of the ecliptic degree opposite the Sun, so that when the Moon is on the horizon, whether rising or setting, the Sun is a few degrees above the opposite horizon. In both cases the Moon is difficult to see. In cases like 22, however, with the Moon south of the ecliptic, it sets before the Sun rises, and rises after sunset.

This describes the ideal situation, but winter full moons like 7 and 37 should not be dismissed too readily. The Moon moves rapidly—roughly thirteen degrees per day—and a day on either side of full moon makes little difference to its declination, but through change in ecliptic longitude can make all the difference between visibility and invisibility. First, therefore, some remarks from the devil's (or rather sceptic's) advocate.

Even alignments to cases like 5, 9, 35, 39, 20, and 24, while neither major standstills nor full moons, might have been recorded. There are many causes of uncertainty in the smaller details of interpretation of lunar alignments. To take two of a dozen potentially problematic instances: even after an azimuth has been converted to a declination, only a combination of an obliquity and a lunar inclination has effectively been found. Unless the obliquity is known independently (say from the year) no conclusion can be drawn about the inclination, and thus none about its difference from the mean. Secondly, the same alignment might be ambiguous, for instance, as between the direction of (1) an actual extreme of type 7, and (2) the only visible Moon in the neighbourhood of an extremum of type 15 (assuming that the weather interfered with other observations).

It seems reasonable to suppose that observations were made over periods of time long enough to stake out correctly alignments to significant standstills. As for major standstills at the winter solstice full moon, they could have been observed wherever an artificial horizon was created high enough to ensure that the Sun had well and truly set by the time the Moon rose. It might have been twilight still, but the Moon would have been visible, given the right atmospheric conditions.

Which types of lunar alignment are then most likely to have been favoured? For reasons that have now been explained, the following three cases seem most probable:

1. Northern lunar setting at first quarter, being more or less the ideal major standstill. Occurring near spring equinox (see case 15). Inclination (i) is increased over its mean value by 8.7' (but other factors reduce this figure, as will be seen). In this context it is intriguing to recall Pliny's reference to the culling of mistletoe by the druids on the sixth day of the moon.

2. Southern lunar rising at third quarter, being true major standstill. Two weeks later than the above, near the spring equinox (see case 16). Inclination as above, but declination now negative (south of equator).

3. Southern lunar rising or setting at summer full moon. The inclination at this type of major standstill is then a minimum (10.0' below the mean, but see below), but the assumption is that the brightness and general character of full moon makes it an attractive proposition.

The example of Stonehenge, however, recommends a fourth case:

4. Northern lunar rising or setting at winter full moon. The inclination is that under case 3. Given a regular horizon such will occur with the Sun above the horizon, but sunset may be guaranteed either by an artificial horizon or an unusually high lunar horizon.

These suggestions do not preclude alternatives (such as phases near full moon, or cases where the best that can be found over a short period is for a nondescript phase), but the cases listed here do seem inherently more probable than the rest.

There remains the problem of how the perturbation affects minor standstills. From similar arguments to those given already, first-quarter spring settings and third-quarter autumn risings seem intrinsically likely to have attracted attention (as being near the absolute limit), as do summer full moons (on account of their appearance and brightness). Adjustments to the inclination are exactly as in the corresponding cases for major standstills, and the corrections in azimuth are of the same order of magnitude.

Other Theoretical Adjustments

Several adjustments of lesser importance are desirable, when considering the extremes of lunar declination. In general, the Sun, Moon, and lunar nodes will not reach their own extremes (the 'ideal' positions, simple multiples of 90° in longitude) at precisely the same times. The theoretical maximum declination will need to be modified, although unless the precise date is known, the *average*

error is as much as can be calculated, and this might not correspond well with the series of observations made when the monument was being set up. It is reasonable to add 0.3' at major standstills and subtract the same at minor standstills, to allow for the nodal displacement. The same qualification has to be made in regard to the Moon's rising or setting. In this case the average adjustment is about 3.9' at major and 2.5' at minor standstills. Yet again, a small periodic uncertainty (of the order of 0.15') is introduced because of the dependence of the obliquity on the position of the lunar nodes. For a fuller treatment of these matters, see the study by L. V. Morrison mentioned earlier.

In summary, these additional adjustments entail replacing our +8.7' and −10.0' by +4.1' and −13.8' respectively, at the major standstills considered. At the corresponding minor standstills, the effective additions to the inclination are +10.5' and −7.4' respectively.

What difference does it make, whether the mean inclination or an adjusted value is taken? Broadly speaking, at Stonehenge it might make a difference in azimuth of the order of a complete Moon-width. Measuring azimuths from the east–west axis, and taking as norm the upper limb of the Moon on the natural horizon around Stonehenge at 2000 BC, typical values based on approximate values for the natural horizon are as follows:

1. Mean 48.95° north of west, corrected 49.10°.
2. Mean 53.74° south of east, corrected 53.91°.
3. Means 53.74° south of east (corrected 53.20°) and
   53.54° south of west (corrected 53.01°).
4. Means 48.28° north of east (corrected 47.79°) and
   48.95° north of west (corrected 48.47°).

The categories are the four discussed earlier. Somewhat similar discrepancies are found for minor standstills.

Finally, therefore, these additional qualifications to the first broad survey must be taken into account whenever a lunar alignment is being claimed, corresponding to as poor an accuracy as half a degree in the azimuth. And even then, small uncertainties will remain, as explained.

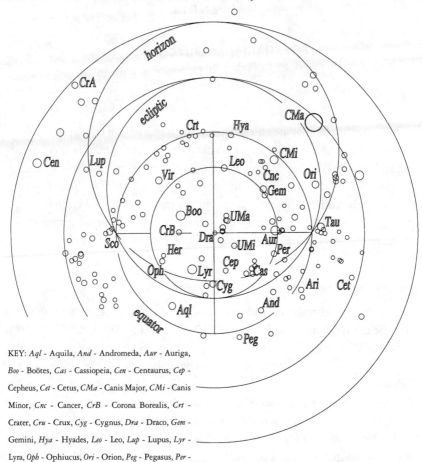

KEY: *Aql* - Aquila, *And* - Andromeda, *Aur* - Auriga, *Boo* - Boötes, *Cas* - Cassiopeia, *Cen* - Centaurus, *Cep* - Cepheus, *Cet* - Cetus, *CMa* - Canis Major, *CMi* - Canis Minor, *Cnc* - Cancer, *CrB* - Corona Borealis, *Crt* - Crater, *Cru* - Crux, *Cyg* - Cygnus, *Dra* - Draco, *Gem* - Gemini, *Hya* - Hyades, *Leo* - Leo, *Lup* - Lupus, *Lyr* - Lyra, *Oph* - Ophiucus, *Ori* - Orion, *Peg* - Pegasus, *Per* - Perseus, *Sco* - Scorpio, *Tau* - Taurus, *Tri* - Triangulus, *UMa* - Ursa Major, *UMi* - Ursa Minor, *Vir* - Virgo

FIG. 210. A star map for the latitude of Stonehenge for 3000 BC, including stars brighter than magnitude 4.5. Compare this with the map at the end of Chapter 1, used chiefly to introduce the names of the brightest stars. As on that map, the outermost circle encloses all bright stars that could in principle have been seen. On the present figure, abbreviations for constellation names are added, adjacent in each case to the star in the constellation designated *alpha,* usually the brightest. The magnitudes of the stars are indicated by the sizes of the circles representing them and the precise positions of the stars in 3000 BC are the centres of the circles. The Sun's path (ecliptic) is added to the present figure, touching the Tropics of Cancer and Capricorn. The northern point of the horizon is at the bottom, and east is to the left. As before, and as on a star globe, the constellations as drawn are the reverse of the shapes as seen in the sky. There are some advantages in this traditional arrangement (which was usual on medieval astrolabes, for example). The stars move with the daily rotation in a clockwise sense around the north pole, the centre of the cross and broken circles. Placing one foot of a pair of dividers at that centre and the other at the star of interest, by rotating the dividers one will know whether the star can rise or set at Stonehenge, and where approximately on the horizon circle it does so.

Tables of Directions

The following brief tables are chiefly meant to give an idea of how geographical latitude, horizon altitude, and epoch affect the azimuths of solar and lunar rising and setting. The upper limb of the Sun or Moon is considered in all cases. In the case of the Moon, no attempt is made to account for the subtleties discussed at the end of Appendix 2. Azimuths are invariably given in degrees north (+) or south (−) of the east/west line, since the (near-)symmetries as between rising and setting are then immediately obvious.

Extreme Solar Risings and Settings at Various Epochs

Azimuths for Stonehenge, latitude 51°10'42", assuming an approximate profile for the natural horizon as follows: NE: 0.60° E: 0.65° SE: 0.70° SW: 0.60° W: 0.45° NW: 0.30°.

Data begin from epoch 4000 BC when the obliquity of the ecliptic was 24°06'43".

(R – Rising   S – Setting   amp – amplitude)

Year	Obliqu.	R smr	R equ	R wntr	R amp	S wntr	S equ	S smr	S amp
−4000	24°06'43"	40.88	0.09	−40.64	81.52	−40.45	0.38	41.47	81.92
−3500	24°04'20"	40.81	0.09	−40.56	81.37	−40.38	0.38	41.39	81.76
−3000	24°01'42"	40.72	0.09	−40.48	81.20	−40.29	0.38	41.30	81.59
−2500	23°58'50"	40.63	0.09	−40.39	81.02	−40.20	0.38	41.21	81.41
−2000	23°55'45"	40.53	0.09	−40.29	80.82	−40.10	0.38	41.11	81.21
−1500	23°52'29"	40.43	0.09	−40.19	80.61	−40.00	0.38	41.01	81.00
−1000	23°49'03"	40.32	0.09	−40.08	80.39	−39.89	0.38	40.90	80.79

Extremes of Lunar Risings and Settings

Natural horizon profile as before, Stonehenge latitude, azimuths commencing 4000 BC.

N – north   S – south

	Eastern horizon				Western horizon		
Year	Max N	Min N	Min S	Max S	Max N	Min N	Min S	Max S
−4000	49.62	30.04	−32.61	−53.14	50.30	30.55	−32.44	−52.90

N – north   S – south

	Eastern horizon				Western horizon			
Year	Max N	Min N	Min S	Max S	Max N	Min N	Min S	Max S
−3500	49.54	29.97	−32.54	−53.05	50.21	30.48	−32.37	−52.80
−3000	49.45	29.90	−32.46	−52.94	50.12	30.40	−32.29	−52.70
−2500	49.34	29.81	−32.37	−52.83	50.01	30.32	−32.20	−52.59
−2000	49.23	29.73	−32.28	−52.71	49.90	30.23	−32.11	−52.48
−1500	49.12	29.63	−32.18	−52.59	49.79	30.13	−32.01	−52.35
−1000	49.00	29.53	−32.08	−52.46	49.66	30.03	−31.91	−52.22

Azimuths of Solar Risings and Settings— Varying Latitudes

In all cases a horizon of zero altitude is assumed. The upper limb of the Sun on the horizon.

Data for Stonehenge latitude, epoch 2000 BC, obliquity 23°55′45″.

R – Rising   S – Setting   amp – amplitude

Lat.	R smr	R equ	R wntr	R amp	S wntr	S equ	S smr	S amp
45	36.05	0.85	−33.98	70.03	123.98	0.85	36.05	−87.93
48	38.51	0.94	−36.14	74.65	126.14	0.94	38.51	−87.63
51	41.52	1.05	−38.78	80.30	128.78	1.05	41.52	−87.26
54	45.27	1.17	−42.05	87.32	132.05	1.17	45.27	−86.78
57	50.14	1.30	−46.22	96.36	136.22	1.30	50.14	−86.09
60	56.81	1.47	−51.79	108.60	141.79	1.47	56.81	−84.97

Azimuths of Lunar Risings and Settings— Varying Latitudes

In all cases a horizon of zero altitude is assumed. The upper limb of the Moon on the horizon.

Data for Stonehenge latitude, epoch 2000 BC, obliquity 23°55′45″.

(N – north   S – south)

	Eastern horizon				Western horizon			
Lat.	Max N	Min N	Min S	Max S	Max N	Min N	Min S	Max S
45	43.26	26.97	−27.21	−43.56	43.26	26.97	−27.21	−43.56
48	46.40	28.63	−28.90	−46.75	46.40	28.63	−28.90	−46.75
51	50.34	30.62	−30.93	−50.76	50.34	30.62	−30.93	−50.76
54	55.50	33.04	−33.40	−56.03	55.50	33.04	−33.40	−56.03
57	62.79	36.04	−36.45	−63.52	62.79	36.04	−36.45	−63.52
60	75.61	39.85	−40.34	−77.20	75.61	39.85	−40.34	−77.20

Azimuths of Solar Risings and Settings— Varying Altitudes

Data for epoch 2000 BC when the obliquity was 23°55'45". On the horizon:
Upper limb of the Sun.

(R – Rising S – Setting amp – amplitude)

Alt.	R smr	R equ	R wntr	R amp	S wntr	S equ	S smr	S amp
0.0	41.72	1.05	−38.96	80.67	−38.96	1.05	41.72	80.67
0.2	41.31	0.75	−39.34	80.65	−39.34	0.75	41.31	80.65
0.4	40.92	0.45	−39.72	80.64	−39.72	0.45	40.92	80.64
0.6	40.53	0.16	−40.10	80.63	−40.10	0.16	40.53	80.63
0.8	40.16	−0.12	−40.48	80.63	−40.48	−0.12	40.16	80.63
1.0	39.79	−0.40	−40.85	80.64	−40.85	−0.40	39.79	80.64
1.2	39.43	−0.68	−41.22	80.65	−41.22	−0.68	39.43	80.65
1.4	39.07	−0.96	−41.59	80.66	−41.59	−0.96	39.07	80.66
1.6	38.72	−1.23	−41.96	80.69	−41.96	−1.23	38.72	80.69
1.8	38.38	−1.50	−42.33	80.71	−42.33	−1.50	38.38	80.71
2.0	38.04	−1.78	−42.70	80.74	−42.70	−1.78	38.04	80.74

Azimuths of Lunar Risings and Settings—Varying Altitudes

Stonehenge latitude. Upper limb of the Moon on the horizon. Data for epoch
2000 BC, when the obliquity was 23°55'45".

Alt.	Eastern horizon				Western horizon			
	Max N	Min N	Min S	Max S	Max N	Min N	Min S	Max S
0.0	50.61	30.75	−31.06	−51.03	50.61	30.75	−31.06	−51.03
0.2	50.14	30.40	−31.42	−51.51	50.14	30.40	−31.42	−51.51
0.4	49.68	30.06	−31.77	−52.00	49.68	30.06	−31.77	−52.00
0.6	49.23	29.73	−32.11	−52.48	49.23	29.73	−32.11	−52.48
0.8	48.80	29.40	−32.45	−52.95	48.80	29.40	−32.45	−52.95
1.0	48.38	29.08	−32.79	−53.43	48.38	29.08	−32.79	−53.43
1.2	47.97	28.76	−33.12	−53.90	47.97	28.76	−33.12	−53.90
1.4	47.57	28.45	−33.46	−54.39	47.57	28.45	−33.46	−54.39
1.6	47.17	28.14	−33.79	−54.87	47.17	28.14	−33.79	−54.87
1.8	46.78	27.84	−34.12	−55.35	46.78	27.84	−34.12	−55.35
2.0	46.40	27.54	−34.46	−55.85	46.40	27.54	−34.46	−55.85

Heliacal Rising and Setting

There are other means of identifying the seasons of the year than by alignments to sunrise at the solstices. One of them that is historically very important, but that cannot leave any (unscripted) archaeological record, is by the observation of what are known as 'heliacal' risings and settings. An explanation of the method is added here since it lends itself to very basic and simple procedures that probably originated in the period before the written word.

To specify the beginning and ending of the seasons with reference to the coincidence of the Sun with a star or constellation or zodiacal sign ('the Sun enters Taurus on such and such a date', 'spring begins when the Sun enters the sign of Aries', and so on) requires a certain degree of astronomical sophistication, for the signs are not visible as clearly defined objects, and the stars and the Sun are not visible together. A more intuitive method was to identify a point in the year in terms of the rising of a star or group of stars just before sunrise, or the setting of the same just after sunset. These are the so-called heliacal risings and settings. Another convention was to record the last visible risings at evening twilight, or the first visible settings at dawn. These go under the names of acronychal risings and cosmical settings.

To present the system somewhat differently: the order of the twelve signs of the zodiac as we know them (they take their names from the constellations in their ancient positions) is Aries, Taurus, Gemini, Cancer, Leo . . . and so on. In the course of a year, the Sun moves round the zodiac in this order, so that when it is in Taurus, say, the stars in Aries will be visible above the eastern horizon at the end of the night, but most of the stars in Taurus will not then be visible. As the Sun leaves Taurus for Gemini, the stars in Aries will appear an hour or two sooner, and the stars in Taurus will become visible at the end of night. Matters will continue in this way through the year.

The MUL·APIN text, a Mesopotamian tablet that reveals astronomical practices in that part of the world between roughly 1300 and 1000 BC, provides an early historical example. According to this, the star cluster we know as the Pleiades in the constellation of Taurus is first visible on the first day of zodiacal month number 2, and the Bull's muzzle (Aldebaran and the Hyades) is first visible on the twentieth day of the same month. An example of the Greek use

of the same ideas is to be found in Hesiod's poem *Works and Days*, dating from the end of the eighth century BC:

> When the Pleiads, Atlas' daughters, start to rise,
> Begin your harvest; plough when they go down.
> For forty days and nights they hide themselves,
> And as the year rolls round, appear again
> When you begin to sharpen sickle-blades . . .
>
> (lines 383–7; translated by D. Wender)

Long after Hesiod, the Greek astronomer Euctemon (Athens, fifth century BC) listed precise dates, as the MUL·APIN text had done. He need not have known of the older list, and in fact his dates were appreciably different, since the stars had moved their positions in the sky by several degrees in the meantime due to precession. After Euctemon, other Greek astronomers followed suit, for example Eudoxus (around 370 BC) and Callippus (around 340 BC). They constructed public calendars known as *parapegmata* which correlated weather predictions with the risings and settings of stars. As time went on, the astronomical content of this genre of literature dwindled, and writers allowed their meteorological imaginations full rein.

There is no reason why specifying a time of year in terms of first and last visibilities of stars should not be combined with that of calendar-reckoning by the Sun's changing positions on the horizon at rising and setting—and indeed Hesiod seems to do just that. At his most sophisticated, he speaks of the season when the Sun spends 'less time with the Greeks and more with dark-skinned men'—an allusion to the period following the Autumn equinox, when (as we should express it) the Sun passes from north of the celestial equator to south. He says that when sixty days of winter have gone by after the solstice, then Arcturus blazes forth in the twilight. This is a heliacal rising but includes reference to a solstice as well. Hesiod later refers to a solstice alone, telling us that the time to sail is fifty days from the summer solstice.

Modern commentators often seem to imply that the 'modern' way of calendar reference—with respect to solstice and equinox, defined in terms of the circles of the celestial sphere, the equator, and the ecliptic—is the natural successor to the labelling of the seasons in terms of the first and last risings and settings of named stars. It is not even approximately known when people first got a feeling for this latter sort of 'astronomically' defined calendar—which in a sense is an inessential byway of astronomical science—but it is likely to have come in some form at a very early date. This much can be said simply because, from an interest in the *places* of the rising and setting of stars at a very early date, it seems almost inevitable that when those stars were observed over long

periods, it would very soon have been noticed that they were not to be seen during certain periods of the year. The two different traditions would therefore have gone naturally hand in hand, the one—the more exact—a tradition of marking places on the horizon where rising and setting took place, and the other a tradition of correlating different sorts of seasonal weather with first and last sightings.

The observation of the risings and settings of the *Sun* at the extremes it attains at the solstices offers a completely different approach to the keeping of a calendar, and the two should not be confused—although they might have been interrelated. The idea that is mooted by many modern writers is that the precise days of the solstices (or days as near as possible) are found by observing the directions of risings and settings, and the year is then divided into quarters, eighths, or even sixteenths with reference to these fundamental reference days. The greatest difficulty in carrying out this programme arises because there is very little daily change in the Sun's direction, around the time of either solstice. The easiest way round the difficulty of dating the solstices would have been to take the day midway between two dates on which a specific direction somewhat short of the extreme is attained.

It is only possible to conjecture that such procedures were followed. The fact that ours is a solar calendar does not mean that all primitive calendars must have been likewise. To operate this system one has to have a fairly good idea of the number of days in the year. And lest it be thought an obvious system, let it be noted that Babylonian and Indian calendars in the second and first millennia BC measured out the Sun's movement round the sky using star-markers that had been paced out, so to speak, by the Moon's monthly motions. Once again, the placing of the Moon with respect to the Pleiades had a key role, and was used to decide whether extra days should be inserted into the calendar. (Compare our own leap-year rules.)

Heliacal risings and settings are something that ordinary people can observe much more casually than even the horizon-places of rising and setting of Sun, Moon, or stars. It might be that the one was a homely matter, a rough and ready affair, and the other more a question of ritual observance. The weather would have introduced uncertainties, affecting the cutoff in the visibility of especially faint stars near the horizon. The long-term effect of precession would have been such as to make custom—and poetry embodying custom—eventually out of date; and the 'homely' traditions would not have travelled well over great differences of geographical latitude, whereas the more exact alternative methods would have done so.

The Rising and Setting of Venus

Venus is by far the brightest of the planets, and since various early cultures have left written evidence that the movements of Venus were carefully observed in a general way, it is reasonable to consider the possibility of prehistoric alignments on the planet—for which there is no explicit historical evidence. As already explained in Chapter 2, the fluctuations in the horizon positions of Venus's rising and setting are in character rather similar to the Moon's. Venus goes once round the Sun in about 225 days. As seen from the Earth, the planet stays in the vicinity of the Sun, sometimes leading and sometimes following, and shuttles around the zodiac on average once in a year. It passes the line joining us to the Sun every 584 days (its 'synodic period'). In eight years it will have shuttled around the Sun (as seen from the Earth) almost exactly five times, and it is by this happy chance that once Venus' motions over a period of eight years have been accounted for, they will be found repeating themselves over the next eight years; and so on for long periods of time. (In fact five average synodic periods are just 2.4 days less than eight calendar years.)

The orbit of Venus is inclined at 3.39° to the plane of the Earth–Sun system, and its ecliptic latitude typically fluctuates a degree or two north or south, with occasional surges to seven or eight degrees. The planet's declination (measured from the celestial equator) is the crucial parameter, however, for risings and settings. It oscillates between extremes which are not constant. Some of the turning points in declination are quite modest, and attention may be reasonably confined to those that are greater than 25° or less than −25°. Taking a typical eight-year cycle from the beginning of the thirty-sixth century BC, there were then six extremes in each category, the greatest reaching to 25.87° and the least to −25.98°. Anyone who was focusing on Venus's extreme positions, and doing the job with care, might have found the horizon positions corresponding to these declinations, since both were in principle observable. In both cases, Venus was an evening star, to be seen at setting.

A less careful observer of extremes might have settled for horizon positions corresponding to some sort of average declination, this depending on what was visible. In the eight-year period, the three extremes with Venus as a morning star were barely usable, but there were three good southern settings and three good northern settings in the period, with the Sun far enough away from the

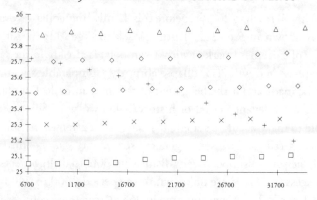

FIG. 211. Maximum declinations of the planet Venus in excess of 25° during the thirty-sixth century BC. The maxima are grouped into families, distinguished by six different symbols. The lower axis shows the time in days from an arbitrary origin.

planet to allow it to be easily seen. Three in eight years of each sort might have been enough to hold the attention of anyone with an ambition to mark the alignment.

The period of eight years more or less characterizes the longer term. If the maximum declinations lying beyond the 25° limits are plotted over a period of about 77 years (and the minima follow a similar pattern), the result will be a series of points shown in general character on the graph in Fig. 211. The graphs themselves are not drawn, to avoid confusion, but it might be noticed that all these events *repeat at eight-year intervals*, as we might have expected. The maxima, in other words, may be grouped in families, and we may follow the life history, as it were, of any particular family. Notice how the members of five of the six families are gradually rising, over the period drawn here. The top line has not yet reached 26°, by the end of the period, but in due course

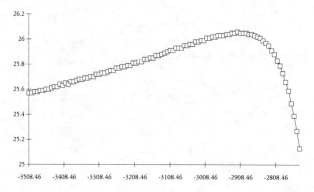

FIG. 212. Maximum declinations of Venus in a single family of maxima (see the previous figure) over a long period of time. The lower axis is in years BC.

(2916 BC) it will reach to 26.06°, before this 'family line' collapses dramatically, in the way shown in Fig. 212. Turning back to Fig. 211, the single falling family line of extremes (marked with + symbols) is already in the same sort of declining phase and will also collapse abruptly. Comparable statements to all these can be made about the behaviour of the minimum declinations.

Unless the relevant period of history is known with fair precision, it is impossible to make accurate statements about the extreme positions of Venus' risings and settings, but some general statements can be made that are reasonably helpful in supporting or dismissing potential alignments. Declinations in excess of 26.12° are unknown in the period 3600 to 2400 BC. (High values, such as the 26.74° encountered in 965 BC, can be discounted for present purposes.) A good working value for the period 3600 to 2000 BC would be 25.9°±0.2°. At the geographical position of Stonehenge, for example, those figures correspond to azimuths of orientation within half a degree of 44° north of west and 44.5° south of west. Alignments on risings cannot be ruled out, but they seem much less probable than alignments on settings.

Alignment in Later Religions

There are numerous instances of astronomically directed worship in other societies. There is remarkably little archaeological or literary evidence for the early observation of the equinoctial Sun—which produces a roughly east–west line. When a civilization for one reason or another chooses east (or west) as a favoured direction for reasons connected with the Sun, it seems to do so rather imprecisely. A close study of the Minoan civilization will probably show that a fairly accurate equinoctial alignment was known there—at Knossos, for instance—and probably under Egyptian influence. It has long been recognized that the sides of many of the Egyptian pyramids are fairly accurately east–west and north–south. An ancient goddess, Seshat, the 'Mistress of Builders', had a hand in this. She had many duties connected with festivals and the calendar, but is also often shown involved in the foundation ritual of temples. She occurs in a relief showing the foundation ceremony for the temple of Seti I at Abydos, that took place around 1300 BC. Seshat is made to use these words to the king:

> The hammer in my hand was of gold when I hammered in the wedge, and it was you who held the chord. Your hand held the spade when the corners [of the temple] were fixed in keeping with the four pillars of heaven.

In a relief at the Sun temple of the king Niuserre at Abu Gurab, that might be twelve or thirteen centuries earlier, there is a similar illustration of what seems to be exactly the same ceremony, which was therefore not at all new, and it was destined to have a long history. Seshat was eventually often depicted with a pole on her head carrying a seven-rayed star. More than a thousand years after Abydos, at the founding of temples at Edfu and Dendera, the language used was not very different, except that now there was mention of aligning the building on the rising of a particular star that was supposed to rise due east. The direction of the star was acting as proxy for that of the Sun's equinoctial rising—and not a very good proxy, as it happened. The star is here commonly supposed to be that in the middle of the handle of the Plough, then represented by a bull's thigh—a constellation distinct from our Taurus.

The astronomical orientation of buildings need not necessarily mean a religious use, although the line dividing the religious from the secular is often hard to draw. Even in the twentieth century German peasants are said to have

aligned their farms on the Sun, with the help of a priest for the offering of prayers and the sprinkling of holy water, wherever possible. The idea of a sacred mountain is commonplace in Mediterranean as well as Eastern mythology, and mountain, temple, and royal residence are frequently found linked. The Babylonian king Gudea built his temple, and Sennacherib the city of Nineveh, according to plans based on ancient astronomical principles. The notion of the temple universe was also applied—but perhaps as an extension of its application to grander buildings—to ordinary dwellings. From ancient times to the present in India, an astronomer might be called on to assist the mason in the placing of the first stone of a house. Whole cities in China and Japan were planned on similar principles. The Egyptian hieroglyph consisting of a cross (x) within a circle, when used non-phonetically (that is, alone as an ideograph), denoted a town or city, perhaps indicating an idea of preferred directions.

That not all architectural alignments on the heavens are religious in character is illustrated again by the Greek medical writer Hippocrates, who reports the alignment of the streets of towns to avoid disease-carrying winds. There is no evident religious connection here, but there is an astronomical one, for according to Greek legend the winds were the sons of Eos, the dawn, and Astraeus, the starry sky. A network of simple ideas can be extremely intricate. Aristotle, in his book *Meteorologica*, said that there were some who had argued that the solstices, like the winds, were actually caused by air—a conclusion that could easily be drawn in a country where the summer solstice was followed by strong winds. While these examples are unlikely to be of much relevance to northern Europe before the second millennium, it is as well to remember them as a check on using the glib phrase 'observations of the solstices', as though it were a simple notion.

The logic of the orientation of churches and temples is not always obvious. The Christian habit of worship by an indoor congregation looking towards the altar, the latter at the end of a church lying either to the east or at least to the eastern half of the horizon, results in the door of smaller churches being at the west (or western part). In ancient Greek religions, however, where the temple was entered only by a select few, the ordinary people remaining in the court outside to witness the sacrifice, the entrance front and the altar before it are most important, and tend to be at the eastern end. The private individual usually (but not always) sacrificed with back to the temple and facing east. Statues of gods before house doors or temple doors were called *daimones antelioi*, 'deities facing the Sun'.

The Greek tragic poet and dramatist Euripides (fifth century BC) wrote

his play *Ion* as a theatrical myth to give seniority to Ion's supposed descendants, the Ionian Greeks over the rival Dorians and Achaeans. Ion was there made out to be the son of Apollo, by Creusa, wife of Xuthus. Apollo carried the baby off to Delphi, where Ion became a temple servant. At one point in the play (lines 1132–7) he set up a large sacred tent and planned its orientation meticulously, so that it would face neither the midday Sun nor the Sun's dying rays. On its roof were embroidered images of the Sun, Moon, and certain stars. This is just about as close as one can get in any European literary source to the astronomical practice of orientation of sacred buildings. One should not of course suppose that the priesthood would have found the description correct in its detail.

Early Christianity too connected its worship with that of the Sun. Tertullian (*c.* AD 160–240), himself a convert to Christianity, tells us that some regarded the Christians to be Sun-worshippers because they prayed towards the east. There were many later justifications for this custom, such as that it was the direction of Paradise, but yet again it serves to remind us that the attitude of the individual is what usually decides the arrangement of a building. The part played by the Sun in theological argument should not be overlooked. During Christianity's first two or three centuries there were various opinions as to the date of Christ's birth, but the most authoritative made it coincide with spring. The history of the God-Redeemer was repeatedly presented as parallelled by the life of the Sun. For some reason that is not clear, attention was then shifted to the winter solstice. At first, January 6 was favoured, although sometimes this was said to be the day of Christ's baptism. Almost as soon, December 25 was being used in the Western Church by some groups. The Church was anxious to draw the attention of its members away from the old pagan feast days, and the December date did this very well, for it coincided with the 'birthday of the invincible Sun' of Mithraism, and the end of the Roman Saturnalia (December 24). This need not have been the main reason for the shift, but it was a persuasive one. The March equinox became identified with the day of conception, and the winter solstice with the day of Christ's birth. This might seem a strange choice of time for a birth, but on reflection it makes good sense. It is the idea of the 'invincible Sun', the Sun that after the winter solstice is returning in strength, the days growing longer and the light showing its power for victory over darkness.

In view of this solar symbolism at the very heart of Christian doctrine, it is not surprising that the architects of Christian basilicas and cathedrals adopted much of the cosmic symbolism of religions of the Sun. Astronomers were employed in the planning and dedication of very many of them. In the

English-speaking world there is a common belief, based on hearsay rather than experience, that most Christian churches lie in an east–west direction, with the altar and principal window in the east. William Wordsworth is obviously not as well known as he might be: his poem on the building 'in an antique age' of Rydal chapel, Westmorland, tells of how the masons waited until sunrise on the day of the patron saint, St Oswald (5 August), before placing the altar in its direction. This was a common practice, judging by results. Even less familiar is the story of the Puritans' attempts to eradicate such practices, so that Sir Walter Mildmay was in 1584 persuaded to build the chapel of Emmanuel College, Cambridge, in a north–south direction. The smouldering embers of the controversy took flame again in the mid eighteenth century, but the Scottish Freemasons managed to keep the old traditions alive. Their instructions as to the conduct of a night of prayer, followed by the sighting of the line to the rising Sun with the help of poles, would have delighted the builders of a small provincial Bronze Age circle in everything but accuracy.

Most of the earliest Christian churches were certainly directed to the east in some way. The Christian Church of the Holy Sepulchre in Jerusalem is circular, but it was built with the cardinal points in mind: it had two entrances to the east, there were niches outside for altars on the north, south, and west, and the sepulchre itself lies east–west and faces east. All of this must reflect the customs of an earlier Sun-worship. But even straightforwardly rectangular churches do not always have an east–west orientation. Many face towards sunrise at one or other solstice. In Italy, and southern Europe generally, numerous different conventions are followed. Many churches throughout Europe seem to have been directed, like Wordsworth's Rydal chapel, towards sunrise on the day of the patron saint of the place.

In a Christmas sermon in the year 500, pope Leo I criticized his flock for saluting the rising Sun, and in so doing turning their backs on the basilica of St Peter's. They might possibly have picked up the habit from worshippers of Mithras, perhaps from eastern troops in the service of the Roman armies. Tacitus had long before related how Vespasian's army at the second battle of Bedriacum (AD 69) hailed the rising Sun 'in the style of the Syrians'. At much the same time the pro-Roman Jewish (Pharisee) historian Josephus was describing the Essenes, a pre-Christian order of Jewish monks. They are, he said, ascetic, brotherly, and morally earnest, who never speak a word about profane affairs before sunrise, but 'offer up some ancestral prayers as though begging the Sun to rise'. This was not Sun worship, but it points back in time to such on the part of their ancestors. Indeed, more than five hundred years earlier the prophet Ezekiel had told of God's displeasure at the behaviour of about

twenty-five men who were standing between the porch and the altar of the temple, and were worshipping the Sun in the east with their backs towards the temple. It goes without saying that in neither this case nor that of Pope Leo's flock would it have been possible to insult the place of worship in the way suggested had its builders not first given it a solar orientation.

Cities, buildings, and even fields were similarly orientated in classical antiquity. There is a vast medieval legacy of the same building practices, just as there is a legacy of songs of praise to the Sun and Moon—but seen, of course, as tokens of God's creation, rather than as the objects of worship in their own right. Perhaps the best known is a hymn to the Creator by St Francis of Assisi. And to this day, Christians in parts of northern Greece bow to the rising Sun, and cross themselves. Seven centuries before Christ, Hesiod had given a rule of prayer and offering at sunrise and sunset. As Plato reports in his *Apology*, at the trial of Socrates the philosopher noted that a belief in the godhead of the Sun and Moon was the common creed of all men.

It would be hard to find more persistence in the custom of religious alignment than in Islam, a faith six centuries younger than Christianity, but of course having many common roots. Islamic tradition requires certain acts, such as prayer, burial of the dead, the recitation of the Koran, the call to prayer, and the ritual slaughter of animals for eating, to be performed in a special direction known as the kibla. The Prophet Muhammad is said to have offered a threefold definition of the kibla. Outside the sacred precincts of Mecca, that is, in the world at large, the devout Muslim must face those precincts—and many complicated astronomical schemes, not to mention a great many crude folk-traditions, are used to settle on the way of doing so. Within the sacred precincts, but outside the sacred Mosque that surrounds the Ka'ba, the kibla is the direction of the Mosque. Within the Mosque, the Ka'ba sets the direction. This is a modest building, erected in the sixth century of the Christian era, and it replaces an older building that was destroyed by fire. It incorporates the so-called Black Stone, meteoritic in origin, which Muhammad claimed to have a connection with Abraham. He said the same of the Ka'ba itself. The Ka'ba has a rectangular plan, with sides in the approximate ratio of 8 to 7. Its long axis points about 60° south of east. It is a simple matter to confirm by calculation an early tradition that this axis was aligned on the rising of the southerly star Canopus, the second brightest star in the sky. The direction fits well with an epoch not far removed from the beginning of the Christian era. Tradition also has it that the directions at right angles to this were towards summer sunrise and winter sunset, and both are reasonably close to the truth, even though alignments with the Moon—not mentioned in Islamic

lore—seem to fit better with reality. So sure were the Muslims at Córdoba of the direction of the Mecca sanctuary that they built their own Grand Mosque facing a direction at right-angles to summer sunrise. This introduces multiple errors into what was, even so, a clear intention, and one that is known to have been adopted in mosques elsewhere: it was to make the edifice parallel to the Ka'ba, and to face winter sunrise.

BIBLIOGRAPHY

The following highly selective bibliography includes mostly works that can be read without extensive archaeological or astronomical knowledge. As for the latter, Appendix 2 above gives an introduction to the relevant parts of spherical astronomy, together with a few appropriate references to other literature. For a general history of astronomy, a subject with roots anchored in prehistory, see my *Fontana History of Astronomy and Cosmology* (London, 1994), or (for greater detail) the several volumes of the *General History of Astronomy* currently being issued by Cambridge University Press under the general editorship of M. A. Hoskin. General surveys of archaeology are so numerous that it might be thought invidious to mention only two, but both are the products of several authors and are well illustrated. *Past Worlds: The Times Atlas of Archaeology* (London, 1989 and later editions), appeared under the general editorship of Christopher Scarre; and *The Oxford Illustrated Prehistory of Europe*, was edited by Barry Cunliffe (Oxford, 1994). Together they will serve as a reminder of how narrow, in terms of human history, is the theme of the present book.

CHAPTER 1

For a concise and well-annotated survey of general patterns in the spread of early farming cultures see H. T. Waterbolk, 'Food Production in Prehistoric Europe', *Science*, 162 (1968), pp. 1093–1102. A valuable collection of articles in *Palaeohistoria*, 6 and 7 (1959), edited by H. T. Waterbolk and P. J. R. Modderman, deals with the Bandkeramik culture. (The dating in all this material is in need of some adjustment in the light of later revisions in radiocarbon dating.)

CHAPTER 2

P. Ashbee, *The Earthen Long Barrow in Britain* (London, 1970), covers Britain in some detail (note especially details of his Fussell's Lodge excavation) while R. Joussaume, *Dolmens for the Dead* (London, 1988, translated from the French original of 1985), is a general survey of chamber-tombs throughout the world. M. S. Midgley, *The Origin and Function of the Earthen Long Barrows of Northern Europe* (BAR International Series 259, Oxford, 1985), also has important comparative material. The Newgrange 'roof box' is discussed in many places. See, for example, J. Patrick, 'Midwinter sunrise at Newgrange', *Nature*, 249

(1974), pp. 517–9. For this important tomb generally: M. J. O'Kelly, *Newgrange* (London, 1982), and for a survey of claims made as to its 'scientific' character Andrew B. Powell, 'Newgrange – Science or Symbolism', *Proceedings of the Prehistoric Society*, 60 (1994), pp. 85–96.

Specific studies used in this chapter include: R. J. C. Atkinson, 'Wayland's Smithy', *Antiquity*, 39 (1965), pp. 126–33, which must be supplemented by A. Whittle et al., 'Wayland's Smithy Oxfordshire: Exacavations at the Neolithic Tomb in 1962–63 by R. J. C. Atkinson and S. Piggott', *Proceedings of the Prehistoric Society*, 57 (1991) pp. 61–101; L. V. Grinsell, 'The Lambourn Chambered Long Barrow', *The Berkshire Archaeological Journal*, 40 (1936), pp. 58–63, and J. J. Wymer et al., 'Excavations of the Lambourn Long Barrow, 1964', *The Berkshire Archaeological Journal*, 62 (1965–6), pp. 1–21; S. Piggott, The West Kennet Long Barrow Excavations, 1955–6 (London, 1962). For an interpretation of primary and secondary uses at West Kennet, with bibliography, see Julian Thomas and Alasdair Whittle, 'Anatomy of a tomb—West Kennet revisited', *Oxford Journal of Archaeology*, 5 (1986), pp. 129–56. For the Avebury area, see: M. E. Cunnington, 'The "Sanctuary" on Overton Hill near Avebury', *Wiltshire Archaeological and Natural Historical Magazine*, 45 (1931), pp. 300–35; A. Burl, *Prehistoric Avebury* (London, 1979). Paul Ashbee, I. F. Smith and J. G. Evans, 'Excavation of Three Long Barrows near Avebury, Wiltshire', *Proceedings of the Prehistoric Society*, 45 (1979), pp. 207–300, is the fundamental study of Horslip, South Street, and Beckhampton Road. Excavations of the two Lincolnshire barrows are described in: C. W. Phillips et al., 'The Excavation of the Giants' Hills Long Barrow, Skendleby, Lincolnshire', *Archaeologia*, 85 (1936), pp. 37–106; and J. G. Evans, D. D. A. Simpson, et al., 'Giants' Hills 2 Long Barrow, Skendleby, Lincolnshire', *Archaeologia*, 109 (1991), pp. 1–45. The Grendon barrow is described briefly in A. Gibson, 'A Neolithic Enclosure at Grendon, Northants,' *Antiquity*, 59 (1985), pp. 213–9. The important excavation report on Hazleton North, with many cautionary remarks on earlier assessments of similar long cairns, is in Alan Saville, *Hazleton North. The Excavation of a Neolithic Long Cairn of the Cotswold–Severn Group* (London: English Heritage, 1990). The Burn Ground (Hampnett) excavations are reported in W. F. Grimes, *Excavations on Defence Sites, 1939–1945*. Vol. 1: Mainly Neolithic—Bronze Age (London, HMSO, 1960).

For a general account of British prehistory, see J. V. S. Megaw, *Introduction to British Prehistory* (Leicester, 1979). For others, focused on Stonehenge, see C. Burgess, *The Age of Stonehenge* (London, 1980) and A. Burl, *The Stonehenge People* (London, 1987). On the earliest periods see also D. Collins et al., *Background*

to Archaeology: Britain in its European Setting, revised edition (Cambridge, 1973).

Wider surveys include C. Renfrew, *Before Civilization* (London and New York, 1973); J. Murray, *The First European Agriculture* (Edinburgh, 1970). D. L. Clarke, *Beaker Pottery of Great Britain and Ireland* (Cambridge, 1970) considers pottery as a cultural indicator. D. and R. Whitehouse, *Archaeological Atlas of the World* (London, 1975), has synopses, maps, and bibliography for the entire period, and is useful for site-names outside Britain.

R. H. Allen, *Star Names, Their Lore and Meaning* (New York, 1963; first edition 1899) is now somewhat dated, and gives bibliographical leads that are not easy to follow, but it is a mine of historical and mythological star lore. B. E. Schaefer, 'Atmospheric Extinction Effects on Stellar Alignments', *Archeoastronomy*, 10 (1986), pp. 32–42 is an important study of the lowest angles at which stars are visible.

The main works of Alexander Thom are: *Megalithic Sites in Britain*, Oxford, 1967; *Megalithic Lunar Observatories* (Oxford, 1971); and (with his son A. S. Thom) *Megalithic Remains in Britain and Brittany* (Oxford, 1978). A full listing of his writings will be found in C. L. N. Ruggles (ed.), *Records in Stone. Papers in Memory of Alexander Thom* (Cambridge, 1988). Stjornu-Oddi's table is discussed by B. M. Olsen and E. Briem in K. Kalunds, *Afmaelisrit* (Copenhagen, 1914).

CHAPTER 3

For a recent account of the context of the Dorset Cursus, with useful bibliography, see John C. Barrett, Richard Bradley and Martin Green, *Landscape, Monuments and Society. The Prehistory of Cranborne Chase* (Cambridge, 1991). Earlier works are R. J. C. Atkinson, 'The Dorset Cursus', *Antiquity*, 29 (1955), pp. 4–9; A. E. Penny and J. E. Wood, 'The Dorset Cursus Complex: a Neolithic Astronomical Observatory?', *Archaeological Journal*, 130 (1973), pp. 44–76; and also J. E. Wood, *Sun, Moon and Standing Stones* (Oxford, 1978), pp. 82–4 and 101–3. Important information on the context will be found in H. C. Bowen, *The Archaeology of the Bokerley Dyke* (London, HMSO, 1990).

On the Stonehenge Cursus: J. F. S. Stone, 'The Stonehenge Cursus and its Affinities', *Archaeological Journal*, 104 (1947), pp. 7–19; P. M. Christie, 'The Stonehenge Cursus', *Wiltshire Archaeological and Natural History Magazine*, 58 (1963), pp. 370–82; J. Richards, and others, *The Stonehenge Environs Project*. English Heritage Archaeological Report no. 16 (Historic Buildings and Monuments Commission for England, London, 1990). A more popular account of the last is J. Richards, *The English Heritage Book of Stonehenge* (Batsford, London,

1991). For some aerial photographs of 1920, see also Royal Commission on Historical Monuments (England), *Stonehenge and its Environs, Monuments and Land Use* (Edinburgh, 1979). On the Lesser Cursus see especially the last two of these.

The Coombe Bissett Down parallelogram is well shown in Plate XX of O. G. S. Crawford and Alexander Keiller, *Wessex from the Air* (Oxford, 1928). Keiller's excavations at Windmill Hill are published in I. F. Smith, *Windmill Hill and Avebury. Excavations by Alexander Keiller, 1925–1939* (Oxford, 1965).

On the Dorchester excavations: R. J. C. Atkinson, C. M. Piggott, N. K. Sanders, *Exacavations at Dorchester, Oxon.* (Ashmolean Museum, Oxford, 1951); and R. Chambers (summary report), *Proceedings of the Prehistoric Society*, 49 (1983), pp. 393–4. A. F. Harding and G. E. Lee, *Henge Monuments and Related Sites of Great Britain* (BAR (British Series) 175, Oxford, 1987), is an invaluable work with aerial photographs and further references to the rings and cursus mentioned in this section. For the solitary Essex example of a cursus, but including useful bibliography and references to many others, see John D. Hedges and David G. Buckley, *Springfield Cursus and the Cursus Problem* (Essex County Council, Occasional Paper No. 1, 1981). Alex Gibson (with contributions by eight other writers), 'Excavations at the Sarn-y-bryn-caled cursus complex, Welshpool, Powys, and the timber circles of Great Britain and Ireland', *Proceedings of the Prehistoric Society*, 60 (1994), pp. 143–223, includes a useful survey of radiocarbon dates for cursus monuments (pp. 179–80). Whilst it was too late to be taken into account here, this article shows a strong tendency for cursus dates to fall into the fourth millennium BC. Our 'tangent and centre' principle is well illustrated at least twice at Sarn-y-bryn-caled.

CHAPTER 4

Although neither recent nor profound, Morris Marples, *White Horses and Other Hill Figures* (London, 1949), provides much circumstantial information on all the chalk figures discussed here. For carefully plotted outlines of the figures as they were in his time: Sir Flinders Petrie, *The Hill Figures of England* (Royal Anthropological Institute, Occasional Papers, no. 7, London, 1926). L. V. Grinsell, *White Horse Hill* (London, 1939) deals with Uffington. On the Wilmington Long Man: E. W. Holden, 'Some Notes on the Long Man of Wilmington', *Sussex Archaeological Collection*, 109 (1971), pp. 37–54; Rodney Castleden, *The Wilmington Giant* (Wellingborough, Northants, 1983). On Whiteleaf and the barrows there: Sir Lindsay Scott, V. G. Childe and Isobel Smith, 'Excavations of a Neolithic Barrow on Whiteleaf Hill', *Proceedings of the*

Prehistoric Society, 20 (1954), pp. 212–30. On the Cerne Giant: S. Piggott, 'The Name of the Giant of Cerne', *Antiquity*, 6 (1938), pp. 214–6; *RCHM, Dorset*, vol. i (1952), p. 82; L. V. Grinsell, 'The Cerne Abbas Giant: 1764–1980', *Antiquity*, 54 (1980), pp. 29–33.

CHAPTER 6

Published since this was written, there is now a general account of rows and avenues, with a valuable bibliography and listing of sites: Aubrey Burl, *From Carnac to Callanish: The Prehistoric Stone Rows and Avenues of Britain, Ireland and Brittany* (New Haven and London, Yale University Press, 1993).

The classic description of the Dartmoor archaeological scene in general is R. H. Worth, *Dartmoor* (Plymouth, 1953). See also C. J. Davidson and R. A. G. Seabrook, 'Stone Rings on SE Dartmoor', *Proceedings of the Devon Archaeological Society*, 31 (1973), pp. 22–44; and A. Fleming, *The Dartmoor Reaves* (London, 1988). For a useful survey of recent work on Dartmoor and elsewhere, with lists of sites, see D. D. Emmett, 'Stone Rows: The Traditional View Reconsidered', in V. Maxfield (ed.), *Prehistoric Dartmoor in its Context, Devon Archaeological Society, Proceedings*, 37 (1980), pp. 94–114.

There is an abundant literature on Avebury. There are good general plans in I. F. Smith, *Windmill Hill and Avebury* (Oxford, 1965, see above). For the Avenue: A. Keiller and Stuart Piggott, 'The Recent Excavations at Avebury', *Antiquity*, 10 (1936), 417–27, with plan of the northern part. There is a more accurate (but less complete) plan in A. Thom and A. S. Thom, 'Avebury (2) The West Kennet Avenue', *Journal of the History of Astronomy*, 7 (1976), pp. 193–7. Part (1) of the double article is in the same volume, pp. 183–92, and has plans of the enclosure itself. For John Aubrey's account and drawings of the Avebury monuments, see his *Monumenta Britannica, or A Miscellany of British Antiquities* , ed. by John Fowles, annotations by Rodney Legg (Milborne Port, 1980; or second edition, Boston and Toronto, 1981). For a good survey of the antiquarian evidence, with a reassessment of it in the light of modern archaeology and especially useful for Stukeley's role, see P. J. Ucko, M. Hunter, A. J. Clark and A. David, *Avebury Reconsidered: From the 1660s to the 1990s* (London, 1991). For a more general survey, well illustrated with photographs, see A. Burl, *Prehistoric Avebury* (Yale University Press, 1979). N. Lockyer wrote on the Avebury avenues in his *Stonehenge and other British Stone Monuments Astronomically Considered* (London, 1909), as well as in subsequent notes in *Nature* (the journal he founded). E. H. Goddard answered him in 'Avebury: Orientation of the Avenues', *Wiltshire Archaeological and Natural History Magazine*, 35 (1907–8), pp. 515–7.

For a summary (by M. Ponting) of much work on the Callanish sites and a corrective (R. Curtis) to earlier surveys of the main site as discussed above, see again C. L. N. Ruggles (ed.), *Records in Stone* (Cambridge, 1988), pp. 423–41.

CHAPTER 7

The wooden roadway in Somerset, and some of the wooden objects associated with it, are described in J. M. Coles, F. A. Hibbert, and B. J. Orme, 'Prehistoric roads and tracks in Somerset, England: 3. The Sweet track', *Proceedings of the Prehistoric Society*, 39 (1973), pp. 256–93. The sophisticated jointing of lintels and base boards found at Bargeroosterveld is described in H. T. Waterbolk and W. van Zeist, 'A Bronze Age sanctuary in the raised bog at Bargeroosterveld (Dr.)', *Helinium*, 1 (1961), pp. 5–19. R. Meiggs, *Trees and Timber in the Ancient and Mediterranean World* (Oxford, 1982), considers the use of timber in a much later Greek context but is generally instructive.

For works on excavations of the great henges at Mount Pleasant, Durrington Walls and Woodhenge, see the bibliography to the following chapter. Although there is now a need to revise all the dating in S. J. de Laet, *The Low Countries* (London & New York, 1958), the book gives a good idea of cultural patterns, often going far beyond the promise of its title. W. Glasbergen's important monograph was published in two parts, 'Barrow Excavations in the Eight Beatitudes', *Palaeohistoria*, 2 (1954), pp. 1–134 and 3 (1955), pp. 1–204. Compare Sir Cyril Fox, *Life and Death in the Bronze Age* (London, 1959). The main modern source on Harenermolen is: J. L. Lanting, 'De grafheuvel van Harenermolen: een nieuwe bewerking van oude gegevens', *Groningse Volksalmanak. Historisch Jaarboek voor Groningen* (Groningen, 1978–1979), pp. 181–207 (in Dutch, with references to the original literature).

The series of articles reporting William Hawley's excavations are under the general title 'Exacavations at Stonehenge', in *Antiquaries Journal*, 1 (1921), pp. 19–41; 2 (1922), pp. 36–52; 3 (1923), pp. 13–20; 4 (1924), pp. 30–9; 5 (1925), pp. 39–50; 6 (1926), pp. 1–16; 8 (1928), pp. 149–76. A concise survey of Stonehenge and surroundings will be found in the work listed earlier: Royal Commission on Historical Monuments (England), *Stonehenge and its Environs, Monuments and Land Use* (Edinburgh, 1979). For further Stonehenge bibliography, see the chapters below. R. H. Cunnington's remarks on the idea that there were posts in the Aubrey holes are in his *Stonehenge and its Date* (London, 1935). C. A. Newham's views on the causeway post holes are in his pamphlet *The Astronomical Significance of Stonehenge* (Leeds, 1972). The work of Alexander Thom referred to in this chapter is his *Megalithic Lunar Observatories* (Oxford,

1971), Chapters 9 and 10, to be supplemented by Alexander Thom, Archibald Stevenson Thom and Alexander Strang Thom, 'Stonehenge', *Journal for the History of Astronomy*, 5 (1974), pp. 71–90. Douglas C. Heggie, *Megalithic Science* (London, 1981), provides an introduction to many of Thom's ideas and an assessment of their plausibility. For Fred Hoyle's eclipse theory of the Aubrey holes, see the bibliography to Chapter 9 below.

CHAPTER 8

The Cunningtons' work at Woodhenge, together with four circles and an earthwork enclosure to the south of Woodhenge, is described in M. E. Cunnington, *Woodhenge* (Devizes, 1929). There is a short chapter on the excavation at Woodhenge by Wainwright and Evans in the work on Mount Pleasant listed below (1979).

G. J. Wainwright, *The Henge Monuments: Ceremony and Society in Prehistoric Britain*, London, 1989, gives a summary of, and full reference to, the author's original reports, in particular to these three items, the first published with I. H. Longworth: *Durrington Walls: Excavations 1966–68* (Society of Antiquaries, London, 1971); 'The Excavation of a Later Neolithic Enclosure at Marden, Wiltshire', *Antiquaries Journal*, 51 (1971), pp. 177–239; and *Mount Pleasant, Dorset: Excavations 1970–1971* (Society of Antiquaries, London, 1979).

An account of the Quenstedt monument in English is H. Behrens, 'The First "Woodhenge" in Middle Europe', *Antiquity*, 55 (1981), pp. 172–8. For the Arminghall henge: G. Clark, 'The Timber Monument at Arminghall and its Affinities', *Proceedings of the Prehistoric Society*, 1 (1936), pp. 1–51. A useful and comprehensive listing of timber circles in Britain and Ireland is the work by Alex Gibson and others listed at the end of the bibliography to Chapter 3 (but many of the astronomical asides in the article are unreliable).

CHAPTER 9

On the station stones, see: C. A. Newham, *The Enigma of Stonehenge* (Leeds, 1964), and *Supplement to the Enigma of Stonehenge* (Leeds, 1970); A. R. Thatcher, 'The Station Stones of Stonehenge', *Antiquity*, 49 (1975), pp. 144–6; R. J. C. Atkinson, 'The Stonehenge Stations', *Journal for the History of Astronomy*, 7 (1976), pp. 142–4.

In addition to the books referred to in the text (by William Camden, William Stukeley, John Wood, John Smith, Edward Duke, Godfrey Higgins, W. M. Flinders Petrie, Norman Lockyer, E. Herbert Stone) see: R. J. C. Atkinson, 'William Stukeley and the Stonehenge Sunrise', *Archaeoastronomy*, 8 (1985), pp.61–2; J. Easton, *Conjectures on that Mysterious Monument of Ancient*

Art, Stonehenge on Salisbury Plain (London, 1815, a useful collection of extracts from earlier writers, beginning with Geoffrey of Monmouth); Edgar Barclay, *Stonehenge and its Earth-Works* (London, 1895); Admiral Boyle T. Somerville, 'Orientation in Prehistoric Monuments in the British Isles', *Archaeologia*, 73 (1924) p. 193; Gerald Hawkins, 'Stonehenge decoded', *Nature*, 200 (1963), pp. 306–8; Gerald Hawkins, *Stonehenge Decoded* (London, 1966); F. Hoyle, 'Stonehenge: an eclipse predictor', *Nature*, 211 (1966), pp. 454–6 and 'Speculations on Stonehenge', *Antiquity*, 40 (1966), pp. 272–6. A more accessible and developed account is in his book *On Stonehenge* (London, 1977), pp. 43–90. This gave rise to a number of other studies, including the variant by A. D. Beach, in 'Stonehenge I and lunar dynamics', *Nature*, 265 (1977), pp. 17–21. For R. J. C. Atkinson's critique, see his 'Moonshine on Stonehenge', *Antiquity*, 40 (1966) p. 212–6 and 'Hoyle on Stonehenge: some comments', *Antiquity*, 41 (1967) pp. 92–5. There followed Jacquetta Hawkes, 'God in the Machine', *Antiquity*, 41 (1967), p. 174. See also Stuart Piggott, *The Druids* (London, 1968); John Michell, *A Little History of Astro-Archaeology* (London, 1989); John Michell, *Megalithomania* (London, 1982); and C. Chippindale, *Stonehenge Complete* (London, 1983). For the survey by A. Thom and others see the bibliography to Chapter 10.

CHAPTER 10

A fundamental work that has appeared since this book was written is Rosamund M. J. Cleal, K. E. Walker, and R. Montague, *Stonehenge in its Landscape: Twentieth-century Excavations* (English Heritage Archaeological Report no. 10, London, 1995). It includes important contributions by fourteen other writers, together with accounts of the chief excavations of the twentieth century (W. Gowland, W. Hawley, S. Piggott, R. J. Atkinson, J. F. Stone), including invaluable redrawn plans, summary records, and full *fin de siècle* attention to the landscape. The volume includes a full list of radiocarbon dates and a long but selective bibliography. It becomes at once the most important single source of its kind—and one that will instil a sense of terror in all who try to frame archaeological definitions ('Phase 2 Stonehenge is hard to class as a henge').

In addition to the references at the end of the previous chapter, see, for antiquarian interest, a useful bibliography of works on Stonehenge published before 1902: W. J. Harrison, 'Bibliography of Stonehenge and Avebury', *Wiltshire Archaeological Magazine*, 32 (1902), pp. 1–169. Especially important was Richard Colt Hoare, *Ancient History of North and South Wiltshire*, 2 vols (London 1812–1821). The first volume concerns only South Wiltshire and includes plans and elevations of Stonehenge. For further information on their

work see W. Long, *Stonehenge and its Barrows* (Devizes, 1876). Still useful for its linear measurements is W. M. F. Petrie, *Stonehenge* (London, 1880). For the survey by A. Thom, A. S. Thom and Alex S. Thom, see 'Stonehenge', *Journal of the History of Astronomy*, 5 (1974), pp. 71–90.

William Gowland's brief excavations are reported in his 'Recent Excavations at Stonehenge', *Archaeologia*, 57 (1902), pp. 37–105. The series of papers of 1923–1928 in which the most extensive modern excavations were published by W. Hawley is listed in the bibliography to Chapter 7. An analysis from the same period, with some useful engineering insights, is to be found in E. H. Stone, *The Stones of Stonehenge* (London, 1924).

The most easily accessible general description of the monument, and the most influential of recent times, is R. J. C. Atkinson, *Stonehenge* (London, 1956, revised 1979 but never rewritten, as he planned). This remains a fundamental source for disentangling the various periods of building. See also his 'The Stonehenge Bluestones', *Antiquity*, 48 (1974), pp. 62–3; (with J. G. Evans) 'Recent Excavations at Stonehenge', *Antiquity*, 52 (1978), pp. 235–6; 'Some New Measurements on Stonehenge', *Nature*, 275 (1978), pp. 50–2. The last paper was discussed in W. E. Dibble, 'A possible Pythagorean triangle at Stonehenge', *Journal of the History of Astronomy*, 7 (1976) pp. 141–2, to which Atkinson's reply is appended ('The Stonehenge Stations', pp. 142–4). For the excavations near the Heel Stone: M. W. Pitts and others, 'On the Road to Stonehenge: Report on Investigations beside the A344 in 1968, 1979 and 1980', *Proceedings of the Prehistoric Society*, 48 (1982), pp. 75–132.

Influential works from the last half century include: S. Piggott, 'Stonehenge Reviewed', in W. F. Grimes (ed.), *Aspects of Archaeology in Britain and Beyond* (London, 1951), pp. 274–92; 'Recent Work at Stonehenge', *Antiquity*, 28 (1954), pp. 221–4; 'Stonehenge Restored', *Antiquity*, 33 (1959), pp. 50–51; G. Smith, 'Excavation of the Stonehenge Avenue at West Amesbury, Wiltshire', *Wiltshire Archaeological Magazine*, 68 (1973), pp. 42–56; J. Richards and others, *The Stonehenge Environs Project*, 1990 (see the Bibliography to Chapter 3, above, and the reference there to his book *Stonehenge*, deriving from it).

On the geological and petrological aspects of the stones at Stonehenge, see R. S. Thorpe and others, 'The Geological Sources and Transport of the Bluestones of Stonehenge, Wiltshire, UK', *Proceedings of the Prehistoric Society*, 57 part 2 (1991), pp. 103–57 and its bibliography.

CHAPTER 11

See the bibliography to Chapters 9 and 10. The corrected radiocarbon dates of the last section are taken from M. W. Pitts and others, 'On the Road to

Stonehenge: Report on Investigations beside the A344 in 1968, 1979 and 1980', *Proceedings of the Prehistoric Society*, 48 (1982), pp. 75–132, referred to above.

CHAPTER 12

Numerous examples of lozenge shapes from the pre-Indo-European culture of southeast Europe, many with clear sexual connotations, are illustrated in Marija Gimbutas, *The Goddesses and Gods of Old Europe, 6500–3500 BC* (London, 1982, substantially revised from a 1974 edition). C. A. Shell and Paul Robinson, 'The recent reconstruction of the Bush Barrow lozenge plate', *Antiquity*, 62 (1988) 248–60 discusses the plate and the vexed question of its original form. Keith Critchlow gives a numerological account of the Bush Barrow and Clandon plates in his *Time Stands Still. New Light on Megalithic Science* (London, 1979). For calendrical and metrological ideas on the former plate see A. S. Thom, J. M. D. Ker (posthumously), and T. R. Burrows, 'The Bush Barrow gold lozenge: is it a solar and lunar calendar for Stonehenge?', *Antiquity*, 62 (1988) pp. 492–502. For a general context, see Joan J. Taylor, *Bronze Age Goldwork of the British Isles* (Cambridge, 1980). The discovery of the Folkton drums was described in W. Greenwell, 'Recent researches in barrows [etc.]', *Archaeologia*, 52 (1890), pp. 1–72. For the King Barrow Wood plaques see F. de M. Vatcher, 'Two incised chalk plaques near Stonehenge Bottom', *Antiquity*, 43 (1969), pp. 310–11. The subtitle to an important study by M. P. Nilsson omits to mention that it contains also much useful information on star lore: *Primitive Time Reckoning. A Study in the Origins and First Development of the Art of Counting Time among the Primitive and Early Culture Peoples* (Lund, London and elsewhere, 1920).

CHAPTER 13

An encyclopaedic source on religious matters generally, published under Mircea Eliade's editorship, is *Encyclopedia of Religion* (New York, 1987). Useful for its general survey of burial styles and ritual over a wide cultural area (from the Atlantic to the Indus valley and beyond) is E. O. James, *Prehistoric Religion* (London, 1957), although most of his examples of religious belief are not prehistoric. For the somewhat distantly relevant Nuer, see E. E. Evans-Pritchard, *Nuer Religion* (Oxford, 1956). Euan Mackie's ideas on a Neolithic theocracy are put forward in his book *The Megalith Builders* (London, 1977).

For his often overenthusiastic but classic treatment of solar myths, see F. Max Müller, *Lectures on the Science of Language* (6th ed., London, 1871); compare Jacquetta Hawkes' popular *Man and the Sun* (London, 1962); and B. Gelling

and H. R. E. Davidson, *The Chariot of the Sun* (New York, 1969), for its illustrations. An old series of articles still valuable for Lithuanian Sun myths is W. Mannhardt, 'Die lettischen Sonnenmythen', *Zeitschrift für Ethnologie*, 7 (1875), pp. 73–104, 209–44, 280–330. Kr. Barons (1835–1923) was the original compiler and publisher of 182,000 Latvian folk song texts, one of the largest bodies of oral literature in the world, with much on cosmic myth. A modern work leading into this corpus is V. Vikis-Freibergs (ed.), *Linguistics and Poetics of Latvian Folk Songs* (Kingston and Montreal, 1989). For the Scandinavian world see J. R. J. North, *Pagan Words and Christian Meanings* (Amsterdam and Atlanta, 1991), and *Heathen Gods in Old English Literature* (Cambridge, forthcoming), especially Chapter 9, on sky gods. For Nordic calendars see Martin P. Nilsson, *Primitive Time Reckoning* (Lund and elsewhere, 1920), already mentioned in connection with Chapter 12. On pre-Hellenic cosmic belief, and for later misunderstandings about the role of Atlas, see Erik Wiken, *Die Kunde der Hellenen* (Lund, 1937, in German)

Influential studies of myth in general—but the tip of a vast iceberg—include G. S. Kirk, *Myth, its Meaning and Functions in Ancient and Other Cultures* (London and Berkeley, 1970), and E. R. Leach, *The Structural Study of Myth and Totemism* (London, 1967). A typical work by L. Lévy-Bruhl is his *La Mentalité primitive* (Paris, 1922), translated by L. A. Clare as *Primitive Mentality* (London, 1923). Theories in which things are classified under opposite heads or reduced to pairs of opposite principles are considered under the heading 'Polarity' in G. E. R. Lloyd, *Polarity and Analogy: Two Types of Argumentation in early Greek Thought* (Cambridge, 1966).

For the child sacrifice at Woodhenge, see M. Cunnington, *Woodhenge* (Devizes, 1929), and for the Lindow victim, I. M. Stead, J. D. Bourke and D. Brothwell (eds), *Lindow Man: The Body in the Bog* (London, 1986). On the Celts, Stuart Piggott, *The Druids* (London, 1968), and Miranda Green, *The Gods of the Celts* (Gloucester, England, and Totowa, N. J., 1986), are both well illustrated. Ibn Fadlan's account of human sacrifice can be found in A. Zeki Validi Togan, *Ibn Fadlans Reisebericht* (Leipzig, 1939). The Saxon references to Irminsul can be pursued through Clive Tolley, 'Oswald's Tree', in T. Hofstra, L. A. R. J. Houwen and A. A. MacDonald (eds.), *Pagans and Christians* (Groningen, 1995), pp. 149–73. Perhaps the most remarkable collection of cattle skulls yet found in a British tomb is described in S. Davis and S. Payne, 'A Barrow Full of Cattle Skulls', *Antiquity*, 67 (1993), pp. 12-22.

APPENDIX 6

On Mesopotamian civilizations see A. L. Oppenheim, *Ancient Mesopotamia, Portrait of a Dead Civilization* (Chicago, 1964). D. Nielsen, *Die altarabische Mondreligion* (Strasbourg, 1904), was an influential study of Moon religions in the Middle East. There is a vast literature on Egyptian solar myth and corresponding architectural alignment. As an example of the first, A. Piankoff, *The Shrines of Tut-Ankh-Amon* (Bollingen Series 49, vol. 1, New York, 1955), discusses the dead king's solar voyage. As for the second, A. N. Lockyer, *The Dawn of Astronomy* (London, 1894, reprinted Cambridge, Mass., 1964) was a pioneering work that needs to be read with caution. G. S. Hawkins has sections on Karnak alignments in a chapter of F. R. Hodson (ed.), *The Place of Astronomy in the Ancient World* (London, 1974). The most important general study of the Karnak temples is P. Barguet, *Le Temple d'Amon-Rê à Karnak* (Cairo, 1962). See also G. A. Wainwright, *The Sky-Religion in Egypt* (Cambridge, 1938). A valuable compendium of source material, with commentary, is Marshall Clagett, *Ancient Egyptian Science* (2 vols (continuing), American Philosophical Society, Philadelphia, 1989–).

Not always astronomically reliable, but a classic study of orientation in historical times, especially of churches, is H. Nissen, *Orientation: Studien zur Geschichte der Religion*, in 3 parts, Berlin, 1906–10. A concise source of information on Islamic practices is D. A. King, section 4 of the article 'Makka', in *The Encyclopedia of Islam*, vol. 6, Leiden, 1989, pp. 180–7.

INDEX